Hollywood's Silent Closet

A Novel By

Darwin Porter

Rave Reviews for Hollywood's Silent Closet

A vivid tale of lust, greed, ambition, fame, failure, and death in early Hollywood. Porter paints pictures that are luscious, lush, and langorously decadent.
John Bleeker

There's never been a juicy read like this one about Hollywood's lavender and very gay past.
Time Out for Books

A stunning chronicle from the boudoirs of yesterday. Sex, murder, scandal, and love-making too hot for the screen—it's all here.
X-TRA!

There will be rioting in the streets of Hollywood because of this book. Whole sections of the city will go up in flames. One hot read! Suppress it at all costs.
Inferno

This is high-testosterone Hollywood at its most compulsively readable. The 60s didn't invent sex. The stars of the Silent Screen did.
Cruiser

A ricocheting tale of the famous legends of yesterday who ravished women on screen and men off-screen. A hum-dinger.
Outrage

The Myra Breckinridge *of the Silent-Screen era. Wild and woolly nights in pre-code Hollywood.*
What's New in Fiction

Dramatic...provocative...a bombshell...brilliant...compelling... As improbable as any soap opera. But so was the life of Durango Jones.
Gab

Heeeere's Durango Jones. What a man!
James Stafford

Darwin Porter does everything but stick our fingers in a light socket to give us a sexual buzz.
Fab Magazine

Porter's newest book will have the stars of the Silent Screen—from Valentino to Barrymore—spinning in their graves.
Lothian

It brims with the detail and gay decadence of a once-golden era.
Stanford Bylines

Sink your teeth into scandal. We get not snarky innuendoes but stark facts. Darwin Porter names names and doesn't spare the guilty.
Angles

Take off your rose-colored glasses and wander back into Hollywood's fabled but foibled past.
Siegessaule

From the first Tarzan to the handsomest movie star in Hollywood, our hero (Durango Jones) had them all. Even Valentino.
La Movida

A bona-fide hero who seduced and devoured Hollywood hunks across the 20th century. If they were worth messing up your mouth with, Durango was there to get them.
La Noche

Who slept with Mary Pickford's three husbands, her two brothers-in-law, and even her brother? Durango Jones, that's who!
La Trova Roma

Durango Jones was every gay man's dream. He made more Hollywood stars happy than did anyone else of his generation.
Between the Covers

The story of the smiling, golden-haired, blue-eyed hunk turned sexual predator.
Queer Biz

A vivid portrait of the decadent, homosexual, and gossipy world of pre-talkie Hollywood. All the sins weren't depicted on the screen. Neary impossible to put down. The first book of its kind.
Kathryn Cobb

A young beauty of a man with charm and charisma, Durango Jones blazed a trail through the male bedrooms of Hollywood—and lived a long time to tell about it.
Esther Phillips

Scathing scandals and tasty tidbits from the Valentino era. The novel even provides measurements for these old-time screen favorites who mesmerized the world.
George S. Mills

This novel goes where no book on Hollywood has gone before. A gigantic <u>chef d'oeuvre.</u>
Joan Blourer

UNZIPPED! It's like unbuttoning the flies and reaching inside to fondle the goodies of such stars as Valentino, Clark Gable, John Gilbert, Charlie Chaplin, Wallace Reid (handsomest man in Hollywood); Francis X. Bushman (best hung matinee idol of his era); John Barrymore, Norman Kerry (the Errol Flynn of his day), and Elmo Lincoln (filmdom's first Tarzan).
G-Scene

Lotte Lee's films may have turned to dust, but Darwin Porter's affectionate memoir of this Silent Screen vamp (a.k.a. Durango Jones) rescues from obscurity filmdom's first male siren).
Books Today

An indispensable book for all lovers of Hollywood's gay scandals. From horse-hung Charlie Chaplin to pretty Wallace Reid, here's the gay lowdown.
Advance Reviews

This is the story of Durango Jones, scandalous exhibitionist of a golden age, a lost boy-man, a male nymphomaniac.
Nat og Dag

Durango Jones thrilled millions—all of them in bed.
Munich Found

He was called the Queen of Hollywood, a golden boy from the wheatfields of Kansas.
Hinnerk

No wonder the movies were silent back then. The stars were doing something else with their mouths!
Sortie

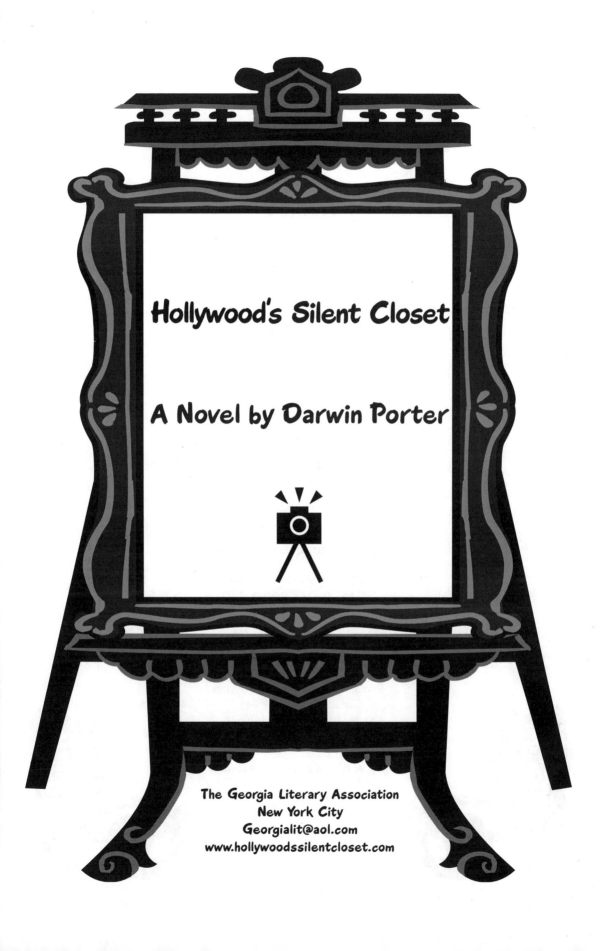

Hollywood's Silent Closet

A Novel by Darwin Porter

The Georgia Literary Association
New York City
Georgialit@aol.com
www.hollywoodssilentcloset.com

Also by Darwin Porter

BUTTERFLIES IN HEAT
MARIKA
VENUS
RAZZLE-DAZZLE
BLOOD MOON
MIDNIGHT IN SAVANNAH

*****

Hollywood's Silent Closet
Copyright 2001 by Porter & Prince Corporation

ALL RIGHTS RESERVED
First edition published in the U.S. in April 2001
ISBN 0-9668030-2-7

Publication made possible by a grant from
The Georgia Literary Association

Contact us at georgialit@aol.com
or at P.O. Box 140544
Staten Island, NY 10314-0544

Photos courtesy of Photofest, New York City
Cover design by Russell Maynor

Memoria

This novel commemorates the men and women who created motion pictures. A lusty crew, they included some of the most startling talents of their age, some of whom arrived in Hollywood after stints as junk dealers, nude models, and staff members at bordellos—both male and female. Many of them became legends around the world, or, as Charlie Chaplin put it, "I'm known in countries that have never even heard of Jesus Christ."

This book also commemorates my loving memory of Stanley Mills Haggart, my long-time partner. He was once an actor in silent pictures and knew many of Hollywood's biggest names, including Mary Pickford, Douglas Fairbanks Sr., Charles Chaplin, Gary Cooper, and Greta Garbo. He later became a "leg man" for Hedda Hopper, the controversial gossip columnist.

Many of the stories in this book were drawn from Mr. Haggart's personal experiences. Over the years, he introduced me to many of the former greats of the Silent Screen—or what was left of them. Some of them died embittered, sometimes succumbing to drug addiction or alcoholism long before their eventual deaths. Others were living quiet, uneventful lives, often modestly, even though all of them had once known great wealth and enormous prestige.

To those who survived the Silent-Screen era and went on to live deep into the 20th century, I am profoundly grateful for the stories they told. Most of them recounted these tales with the provision that they would never be printed during their lifetimes.

Hundreds of people, including stage hands, costume fitters, and makeup artists, contributed anecdotes, and the author is especially grateful to the following:

Pola Negri (that exotic Polish beauty who spent most of her life denying who she was); **Gloria Swanson** (a bitch, of course, but what a fascinating one); **Mae Murray** (who always ran up big bills for me to pay, but was brilliant in re-creating the subtleties of a long-ago era); **Richard Barthelmess** (a husband to many women and a wife to many men); **Ramon Novarro** (who knew much more than he should have); **Francis X. Bushman** (who was willing to let you take a look if you thought he was exaggerating its size); **Marion Davies** (a bright, intelligent woman, not at all like the character she inspired in *Citizen Kane*); **Douglas Fairbanks, Jr.** (who knew more about early Hollywood than Louella Parsons herself); **Antonio Moreno** (who was still bitter for having lived most of his life "as a lie"); **Buddy Rogers** (who knew how to keep secrets until he no longer cared); **Theda Bara** (in memory of that long ago and soggy afternoon when I was too young to drink but did anyway); **Rod La Roque** (who was willing to dispense information provided my bikini came off); **Natacha Rambova** (who wanted to rewrite the story of her life, turning it entirely into fiction); **Norman Kerry** (who admitted that all those rumors were true when he no longer had a reputation to protect); **William Boyd** (who gave his last interview in 1968 but threatened to sue if anything was published during his lifetime); **Alice Terry** (for her wonderful and at times painful memories of Valentino and Ramon Novarro); **Laura La Plante** (for those wild nights in California); **Blanche Sweet** (who no longer felt any need to keep the secrets of other stars); **Leatrice Joy** (who knew the best but also the worst things about John Gilbert); **Lillian Gish** (ever the discreet one during her recitation of stories about D.W. Griffith and countless others); **Hedda Hopper** (who grew increasingly indiscreet as she aged); **Dorothy Gish** (for the good times we had in Rapallo—and the startling revelations she made); **William Haines** (who knew everything about everybody); **Mary Astor** (who paid a terrible price for keeping a diary); **Clara Kimball Young** (who knew what it was to be screwed by the studio system); **Loretta Young** (who was grateful for that young man we arranged for her in Hollywood); **Florence Vidor** (for that lovely and information-filled visit to Pacific Palisades); **Lila Lee** (for the endless dinners in Key West, and for those Hollywood Babylon-style tales); **Reginald Denny** (for his hospitality in Richmond, England, and his stories about John Barrymore); **Tom Moore** (who spoke of his famous marriages and his infamous brothers, Owen and Matt, both movie stars in their own right); **Tallulah Bankhead** ("We'll all be dead soon enough, dahling, so who gives a fuck what they say about us then?"), **"Broncho Billy" Anderson** ("There may be longer dicks in Hollywood, but none as thick as mine."); and **Dolores del Rio** (who shared her Newport Beach home and her many memories with us, especially those that concerned Ramon Novarro).

The author also owes a debt to Mr. Haggart's former friends, comrades, and co-workers in the film industry, including Barbara LaMarr, Rudolph Valentino, Wallace Reid, Olive Thomas, Jack Pickford, Tom Ince, William Desmond Taylor, Mabel Normand, Clarine Seymour, John Barrymore, Bobby Harron, Tom Mix, Nita Naldi, Richard Dix, Sessue Hayakawa, Mary Miles Minter, Thomas Meighan, Pearl White, Mae Marsh, Charles Ray, Fatty Arbuckle, Nazimova, Erich von Stroheim, Samuel Goldwyn, Theodore Kosloff, D.W. Griffith, and Renée Adorée.

To all of these people (may they rest in peace), and many others not mentioned here, I am grateful.

For Danforth Prince

Foreword

My name is Durango Jones.

I began life as a failure. My mother, Maria Jane, wanted me to be born at the stroke of midnight on January 1, 1901, the dawn of the 20th century. She had timed it so that I would be the first American baby to pop out of the womb in the new century.

She virtually willed me out of her womb at the stroke of midnight. But my head was too big and I got stuck. I didn't enter the world until five minutes after midnight. The century had already begun without me, and babies born elsewhere grabbed the much-disputed and dubious title of first American child of the 20th century.

Although I failed and disappointed my mother at birth, I did not fail at everything. In time I became one of the most notorious figures of the 20th century. Until 1970 my scandals were mentioned only in whispers. But in the past three decades I appear in virtually all Hollywood memoirs and endless tabloids. Nearly ninety percent of what has been written about me is a God damn lie, although I have never officially denied anything. Let the jackals yell.

It is not true that I had an affair with Humphrey Bogart, Frank Sinatra, and Ronald Reagan. It is true that I had affairs with virtually everybody else, except Fred Astaire. To me, even on the darkest night, Astaire was not a sex symbol. The sexual charms of Mickey Rooney and John Wayne also eluded me. I was more attracted to the likes of John Barrymore, Wallace Reid, and yes, Charlie Chaplin.

A recent story that Tom Cruise, Matt Damon, and Brad Pitt got their start at a male bordello owned by me is also false, even though I am not unfamiliar with male whorehouses, both as a patron and an employee.

I am rushing through these final memoirs before the party to end a century, one I am giving on December 31, 2000, the beginning of the real millennium and not that fake one the world had back on December 31, 1999.

Age has diminished my recall a bit, and I am to be forgiven if I get Douglas Fairbanks' dick confused in my mind with that of John Gilbert. But what I am about to tell you is the absolute truth, as improbable as it may sound.

The only person I ever fell in love with was Rodolfo Valentino, although he was much more interested in lesbians than me. Nonetheless, I had my admirers. It's embarrassing to admit this—certainly immodest—but in my day I was hailed as the most beautiful boy of the century. I was Thomas Mann's Tadzio in *Death in Venice.* My blond hair and blue eyes for at least half a century could be found buried in the crotches of some of the world's most celebrated actors, everybody from John Barrymore to Ramon Novarro.

Until I was dethroned by Nancy Davis (Reagan) in 1948, I was known as the fellatio queen of Hollywood. The first movie star cock I ever sucked was that of a very young Buddy Rogers who went on to become the third husband of Mary Pickford installed as Hollywood royalty at Pickfair. The last cock I ever sucked was that of Cal Culver after he'd caught my fancy starring in one of the most famous gay porno flicks of all time, *Boys in the Sand.* In between there were so many others, so very many others.

Don't get the wrong idea. I didn't spend all my life with a dick in my mouth. In between such bouts, I had three careers.

I was an unsuccessful actor for decades. For a very brief time in 1919, I appeared on the screen as a beautiful woman in one of the most notorious films ever made. For twenty years in the Forties and Fifties, I was a gossip columnist, ranked just behind those two monstrous bitches, Hedda Hopper and Lolly Parsons of the weak kidneys. The last decades of my life I've been the head of one of the most successful artists' representatives in Hollywood.

I still remember some of our biggest clients, especially Barbra Streisand and Harrison Ford. But some of our newer clients are unfamiliar to me, although I occasionally read their contracts through my failing eyesight. I'm talking Ricky Martin, Meg Ryan, and Kevin Bacon, whoever in the fuck they are. I grew up in an era when stars had names you could remember: Bette Davis, Joan Crawford, Tallulah Bankhead, Mae West, Gloria Swanson, and Charlie Chaplin.

Now before I expire I want to record what happened to me in the 20th century. I am well aware these memoirs will make me sound shallow. But what the hell. I'll be dead soon anyway, and a lot worse has been said about me than shallow. A lot worse.

It's true that my gang was often more concerned with who was going to play Scarlett O'Hara than what Hitler was doing in Europe. But that was the way we were. For some of us, the only way we knew a war was on was that suddenly we California gay boys had one hundred service men to entertain every evening instead of the usual ten. As I said, shallow is the word.

It's amazing how you can live a hundred years devoted to trivia. But I can't reinvent what happened but tell it like it was. What a glorious century it was. If only I could go back and relive those moments, which is ridiculous. I can't. The next best thing is trying to recapture them in my memoirs.

Regrettably, the agency has sent over this secretary who looks like the Bitch of Buchenwald and seems to disapprove of every word I dictate to her. Because she's so uptight and so disapproving of my life story, I'll throw in even more salacious details than I had intended, and even dictate a few extra dozen episodes that discretion told me to take with me to my grave.

Chapter One

What was the first clue that I was going to become the most notorious faggot of the 20th century? It was a minor one. When I was but a boy, I slipped out of our house in Lawrence, Kansas. Four blocks away I made a private deal with the owner of a grocery store. The window of his 1870 store was filled with dusty cans, sagging packages, half-opened cardboard cartons, and faded paper banners advertising brands of groceries.

Behind the counter, the store's owner, Mr. Gregg, agreed with a twinkle to let me decorate his window. I went off and returned grinning with a jelly glass rescued from Maria Jane's pantry. In it I'd placed a short-stemmed rose. In the front corner of the grocery window, where everybody could appreciate it, I set the flower.

A rose in the window somehow became the symbol of my life.

Back at the house I told Maria Jane that I wanted to be an interior decorator when I grew up. Mother and I lived in a stone house built by Swedish settlers in the late 19th century. It was solid and simple, its thick stone walls giving us a feeling of security after my father, a doctor, had died of a stroke, leaving us with almost no money.

The house had been abandoned and we were able to purchase it for two-hundred and fifty dollars, which was about all the money we had. The windows had long ago been broken by neighborhood boys. In the kitchen was a rusty pump. As there was no electricity, we used kerosene lamps. At the edge of the property was a ramshackle outside toilet, a half moon carved on its door.

Maria Jane suggested I take loose flat stones to make a walkway leading from the dirt road to our front door. "You are an artist," she said. "You can fit these stones together to make a beautiful design." I did just that and planted blue iris on each side.

From the cistern, we fished out three dead rats, then purified the water with bundles of charcoal lowered on a clothes line. In window boxes we built, we planted purple and cerise petunias. Butterflies would come here to suck the nectar from the flowers. At the front door I planted violets.

Maria Jane always gave me a nickel for the collection box at Sunday school—three cents for the church, two for the missionaries. Not much of a church-goer, I skipped services and headed for what was called "the palace of sin," the Patee Theatre on Massachusetts Street. I anchored in a front row to watch Pearl White in *The Perils of Pauline.*

At a rinky-dink piano, Mrs. Patee sat under the screen, playing familiar old tunes. During the action her music accented the rescue of the heroine or the downfall of the villain.

Nothing was as exciting to me as the movies. In a world of darkness, I wanted to join the actors on the silver screen. Their problems had more reality for me than life in the real world. In the movies you knew that Pauline was good, pure, and right. The villain was always mean and wore black. There were no gray areas.

Outside the Patee, things weren't as clear cut. Schoolmates teased me that I was too pretty to be a boy. I had blond curly hair, blue eyes, golden skin, and a cherry-red mouth.

One handsome cowboy, who was known only as "Frank," had come to Kansas for the summer. Apparently, he'd come with some relatives from Montana seeking to sell some inherited land way outside of town in a place no one had heard of. Growing bored with the isolation, Frank often drove into town in a beaten-up old Model T. I wanted to drive just like he did, and was anxious for someone to teach me.

I met Frank several times hanging out in front of the Patee Theater, as if he wasn't sure if he wanted to go in. He was the sexiest young man I'd ever met. Later I found out he was a year younger than me. He wasn't beautiful like me but had a rugged handsomeness that made me swoon.

Lithe and lanky, he could easily play a sagebrush hero if he wanted to go into the movies. All this gangling, taciturn, and rather shy young man would need was a pair of tight fitting pants, an old shirt and vest, and a black string tie to hide his Adam's apple. When he saw me, he would purse his lips and drawl in the slow-paced voice of a rugged frontiersman, "How you doing today, Durango? Now that's a name I like. Durango. I hate being called Frank."

"Maybe you'll change it one day."

He looked at me as if the idea had never occurred to him. "Maybe I will," he said reflectively.

One day Frank invited me to go riding with him off deep into the woods somewhere. Never had I wanted to accept an invitation more in my whole life than I did Frank's. But one part of me held back. I was afraid. I felt some forbidden pleasure awaited me in the woods, but I was too scared to go.

Besides, Frank had a bad reputation. Many girls wanted to date him because he was good looking. It was even rumored that he'd fathered two babies. The teenage pregnant mothers had left town. I wasn't really sure what Frank was going to do to me once he got me deep into the woods. In panic I fled from him as he called me to come back.

I must have run for a mile that day, finally falling down in a meadow in total exhaustion. It was then that I felt my erection. All I could think about for days was what Frank looked like without his clothes on. He was one well-built boy.

Instead of running off with Frank, I went to the movies every chance I got. There I found that extra dimension of glamour missing in my own life. Even with all my flowers, I could do little to brighten the bleak landscape of Kansas. It was just too vast. The people moved slowly and talked slowly and ate too much. But in the movies the action was always fast paced. I'd walk home, imitating the jumpy movement of the screen actors.

As I grew older I decided to give up my ambition as an interior decorator. I wanted to become a movie star. If I were indeed as beautiful as people said, I could surely break into the movies on looks alone.

When Maria Jane introduced me to strangers, the first comment they always made was on my beauty. Back then girls—not men—were called beautiful. I always felt embarrassed by my physicality, especially when my body began to grow and fill out. I avoided football and rough games like that. But I was somewhat of a natural athlete and a good swimmer. I'd hike and run for miles, then go home in the late afternoon and stand in front of my full-length mirror and study my body in great detail.

Already six feet tall, I was filling out and putting on some weight and a bit of a muscle. Nothing like a weight lifter. More of a natural swimmer's build. I couldn't help but notice that my penis was growing as rapidly as the rest of my body. I didn't know how long it would fully grow when I became an adult, but it was well on its way.

I had seen only three boys nude before when we'd gone swimming. I had so much more between my legs than they did. The boys seemed to resent my presence with them. On the one hand they wanted to call me a pretty little sissy boy, but when they saw that I was more developed sexually than they were, they felt threatened and never invited me to go swimming with them again.

Through white criss-cross organdy curtains, I could look out from my bedroom window onto the adjoining woods, crowned by an old stone windmill on the top of a hill. Its wooden arms lay sadly in disarray. I often wished I could repair it. Its lower level was all secret and damp like the Patee Theatre. Sometimes I'd crawl in it. Boys from the town would secretly take girls there for some exciting, mysterious reason.

Frank kept pursuing me and invited me to the gristmill. But I kept refusing him. He grabbed my arm. "All the girls like what I've got," he told me. "They call me the pussy stretcher. You want it too. You're just afraid."

I broke from him and ran away again. The image of his nude body was always with me, especially late at night.

One day when swinging from the limb of a tree near the windmill, my groin exploded as I reached the upper branches. The explosion came with the thought of Frank kissing me. If I were the prettiest boy in Kansas, Frank was the handsomest, but so much more rugged and masculine than me. Somehow I was electrically connected to the tree, the air, and everything around me. I tried to imagine what Frank was going to do to me, but I wasn't sure exactly what that would be.

No one at school had told me anything about sex. The subject came up only with Frank. One day he invited me to go with him to the abandoned windmill that afternoon. This time instead of running from him, I confronted him. "What do you want with me? All the girls are after you. You can have anybody you want."

"That's true, but none of the girls is as pretty as you. Besides, I want to try something different. You're the prettiest thing I've ever laid eyes on."

"If I do go to the windmill with you, would you give up all those girls and spend all your time with me?"

"Hell, yes. I don't want those bitches. I want you. That cherry-red mouth of yours is going to waste."

Even though I was tempted to say yes, I decided to hold off for at least one more day. "Let me think about it. I've never been with anybody before."

"That's what I want. A real virgin boy.

Someone I can train to satisfy me. I'm tired of girls. They're too easy. No girl will do what I want done to me."

"I'll meet you tomorrow at the windmill at four o'clock," I promised, then ran from Frank as fast as I could. I'd made the commitment and knew if I didn't show up at that windmill, Frank might beat me severely.

Too nervous and frightened to think about Frank and tomorrow afternoon, I sneaked off to the Patee Theatre. A western was supposed to be shown, but the film hadn't arrived yet. The feature from the day before was run instead.

Onto the screen came the most mysterious and fascinating woman I'd ever seen. She was billed as Theda Bara, and the name of the film was *The Serpent.*

Theda Bara, or so it was said, was foreign, and this repelled and fascinated me at the same time, because I'd been told that foreign usually meant bad. In Theda Bara I discovered what our rector was always preaching about—true evil as reflected in the face of this vampire, called the "wickedest woman in the world." Theda promised all sorts of exotic delights. She could carry me off to places I'd never seen where actions would take place I could only dream about.

Mrs. Patee said Theda Bara was called a "vamp," and I much preferred that to vampire. Vampire sounded too much like a blood-sucking monster. Mrs. Patee claimed that Theda Bara was the name of an anagram meaning "Arab Death" and that she was born in the Sahara to a French artiste and his Egyptian concubine and possessed supernatural powers. To me, Theda Bara took her place with the great sirens of history—Cleopatra, Salome, Camille, Du Barry, and Pompadour.

Leaving the theater, with images of Theda Bara in my head, I imagined myself a vamp willing to face up to the exotic thrills that sexy Frank would present to me tomorrow afternoon.

*****

My date with destiny had arrived, both eagerly anticipated and dreaded at the same time. At exactly four o'clock, I spotted Frank walking up the hill like a cowpoke toward the windmill. When he saw me, he pulled off his shirt in the hot Kansas sun, revealing a perfectly developed and well-muscled body. The sunshine bathed him in a golden light, and he was the single most exciting male I'd ever seen in my life.

"Good, you're here," he said, coming up to me and pushing me inside the cool dampness of the windmill. "You're shaking," he said, putting his hand on my shoulders.

"I'm nervous."

"It's okay," he said reassuringly. "When it's over, you'll feel good. Completely relaxed." He slowly undid the buttons of my shirt and let it fall to the ground. He ran his hand over my chest, tweaking my nipples. "I've never felt a bitch with skin as smooth as yours."

I was still trembling as he unbuckled my pants. At first I thought he was going to play with my cock but instead he reached for my buttocks, squeezing them and then taking his index finger and gently encircling my hole, causing erotic thrills to go through my body.

"I learned to do this when I lived in England," he said. "All the schoolboys over there do it."

That was the first time I'd ever heard him mention England. Up to now, I thought he'd never been out of Montana. Frank was one mysterious young man.

Before I knew what was happening, he pulled me to him and kissed me, his tongue probing deep inside my mouth. Until that moment I didn't know that anybody stuck a tongue inside another person's mouth. When I didn't seem to know what to do with this invasion, he pulled back slightly, then whispered huskily, "You suck it, little darling."

That was all the command I needed. I sucked on that tongue like it was the tastiest lollipop I'd ever had in my mouth. To this day I still remember the taste of Frank's tongue. It was the most delicious flavor I'd ever had. My dream of heaven would be to spend it sucking on that long and thick red tongue.

But in time Frank had his fill of that. He took my hand and guided it to his erection which seemed to have a beginning but no end. "Unbutton my pants. Take it out."

I fumbled with his buttons and finally freed his hooded cock. It was gloriously long and thick. "Skin it back."

I eagerly did as told, revealing a large red knob. With one hand he pressed against the back of my head, lowering me to the ground where this magnificent prick stared at me in the face. The aroma of it was intoxicating. "Swallow as much of it as you can." He guided it between my cherry-red lips.

Then the most amazing thing happened. Years later I learned that I should have gagged and been clumsy and inept, even using teeth on the shaft which was a no-no. But the moment Frank's prick entered my mouth, I sucked it in greedily, devouring it. As it penetrated my throat, I realized that I had found my true vocation in life. I might go on and become a movie star like Theda Bara but my main goal was to suck cock. I

was born to the job.

The moans and precum emerging from Frank were all the encouragement I needed. I licked, sucked, kissed, and nibbled like the most powerful suction pump of all time. Frank grabbed the back of my head and held onto me as if I might desert him at the crucial moment. That was hardly my intention.

"I'm gonna shoot, kid," he said. Even though I wasn't entirely sure what he was going to shoot, I welcomed the hot cream that exploded from him as the tastiest nectar I've ever had in my mouth. I swallowed every drop and kept sucking as if begging for more.

Finally, he had to push me away for a little rest. "I've got to let up a bit," he said, stroking my head. "Lick my balls until I'm ready to go again." Until presented with his low hangers, I had never contemplated the joy of ball licking. Even though I infinitely preferred the rod, I licked tenderly and erotically, feeling his sac was far more delicate than the big, hard rod and required only the tenderest of tonguing. "That's it, kid," he said, lying back on the ground to enjoy this latest pleasure. "I never got anyone to suck my cock before," he said. "All the girls refused me and said I was too big. I knew when the time came, it was going to be good. But it's the best sex I've ever had. You are a natural. You were born to suck a man's dick."

A half hour must have gone by before he pushed my head away. He pulled me up to him and kissed me long, hard, and passionately, letting me suck more of that delectable tongue.

Pushing himself up, he lowered his body over me as he raised my legs in the air. At first I thought he was going to suck my cock. But he had another plan. In a sudden move, his mouth and tongue attacked my anus, causing me to gasp in pleasure. I'd never known such a thrilling sensation in my life. I developed an instant erection and felt I was near exploding.

After a few minutes of that, he raised himself up and before I knew what was happening, he inserted his long rod deep within my gut. I screamed in pain as he fell on me, muffling my outcry with his mouth. "My first virgin boy pussy," he said, taking his mouth off me when I'd quieted down. For the first few minutes it felt like a knife cutting into my gut until I got used to the invasion. "God, you're tight," he said. "It's even better than your mouth and your mouth is from heaven."

When he was fully inside me, I went wild, bucking and meeting his every thrust. I wrapped my arms around him and planted tender little kisses on his neck. Not only was I a natural born cocksucker, I was destined to be fucked by men. The feel of his unrelenting pumping into me had the unexpected effect of causing me to explode into my own orgasm. It was a violent eruption but he never stopped pumping even when I was crying out and gasping for breath.

He let out a loud yell himself and exploded within me, spurt after spurt filling me until I didn't think I could hold it. He collapsed onto me, his head nuzzling my neck which he licked and bit rather hard. I welcomed the attack. I didn't want him to pull out, ever, and he took his time, staying in me at least another half an hour before he finally withdrew. I clenched down and held him inside me for as long as I could. When he pulled out, I felt a great loss and wanted him to invade me again and stay there forever.

Standing over me, he reached for his trousers, stepping into them and buttoning himself up. He looked down at me and smiled.

"Be here at four o'clock tomorrow afternoon," he ordered. He flashed another smile, showing the most perfect set of white teeth I'd ever seen. "Until then, little darling."

*****

When I wasn't at the Patee Theatre, and when I wasn't satisfying the insatiable libido of Frank, I would often go and visit Martha and Henry Ingalls. They never seemed to do any work, and spent all summer sitting out in rockers on their front porch. They were ever ready for a chat.

Apparently, the high point of their lives—a tale told endlessly—was their friendship with "the Harris boys." Willie Harris, the lesser known brother, was a real-estate agent located in Lawrence. But it was his brother, Frank Harris, who fascinated me more.

Frank Harris was one of the greatest editors of his day, as head of the London *Evening News,* the *Saturday Review*, and in the United States, *Pearson's*. He gave breaks to writers such as H.G. Wells and Joseph Conrad. As a drama critic for the *Saturday Review*, he helped launch the theatrical career of George Bernard Shaw.

Martha and Henry talked of how Frank had taken an active part during the celebrated trial of Oscar Wilde on charges of homosexuality and how he'd written a superb biography of Wilde. If that association with Wilde wasn't scandalous enough, Frank had secretly written *My Life and Loves*, which was touted as the most honest autobiography ever. Martha and Henry knew that the autobiography would never be published in America, because it detailed Frank's sexual exploits.

"I remember Willie so well," Martha said. "I first met him in 1871. He had a goatee black as midnight. He stood just a little under six feet tall. I think that's why Frank was always jealous of him. Frank was only five feet three."

"That's not true," Henry corrected her. "He was five feet seven if he was an inch."

She stopped rocking and glared at him. "How do you know how tall is five feet seven? You're only five feet four. I've towered over you since the day I met you. My mama said I should never have married a man as short as you."

Henry shut up, as Martha continued, "Frank was always chasing after the ladies. One time he took up with a married woman who lived on Massachusetts Street. She must have been a common slut to cheat on her husband. I think women who cheat on their husbands should be shot."

"Frank always judged a woman by the shape of her ankles," Henry said. "If she didn't have pretty ankles, Frank wasn't interested. Same way with me."

"How dare you say that," Martha challenged him. "You know my ankles are always swollen. You're just saying that to get my goat."

"It broke my heart," Henry said, "when a good man like Frank got involved defending that pervert at his trial, Oscar Wilde."

"Who was Oscar Wilde?" I asked.

"Wilde was that awful pervert that the law got," Henry said. "They found out he was having sex with young men and paying them for it."

This news came as a complete shock to me. I knew that prostitutes charged men for sex but I'd never heard that boys charged men for sex. It gave me something to think about—not that I planned to charge Frank. I was in love with him, and he could have it

for free.

"Henry," Martha said sternly, "you shouldn't be filling Durango's head with stuff like that."

"What's a pervert?" I asked.

"It's a man who has unnatural sex with animals," Henry said.

I swallowed hard. So horrified was I, I felt my stomach rumble.

"Remember that every man has a lot of good in him and a lot of bad," Martha lectured me. "You have to remember the good."

"I will, m'am," I said, before excusing myself. There was a lot to think about, mainly to learn more about this Frank Harris. I too wanted to write a memoir of my life and loves one day. But first things first. I had to live a life worth writing about. In my own *Life & Loves*, I'd document only my major affairs, knowing I wouldn't have time for the fleeting encounters. Unlike Frank, I wouldn't pursue women. I'd go only for men, and there were plenty of them strutting around.

One night Maria Jane took me to Mrs. Polly's Boarding House for dinner. Her white-framed home stood at the end of Main Street. A veranda ran along the front and around to the side. A lot of people were sitting out in rockers.

No sooner had we arrived than a bell clanged. Everybody got up from the porch, heading through the front screen door. The guests filed into the big dining room set for two dozen places.

The table was all in white with lots of cut-glass bowls of pickles, apple butter, and big pitchers of fresh milk. Beside Maria Jane, I listened as Mrs. Polly said grace. Then she and her sister, Miss Bell, brought in huge platters of food through a swinging door that led to the kitchen.

The biggest platter was pounded round

steak, though it was followed by a mountain of fried chicken. Then came creamy bowls of mashed potatoes, with globs of melting butter in their centers. Steaming corn on the cob was next. I could hardly lift the platters passed around. It was like Thanksgiving.

In a good mood, I begged Maria Jane to let me go to the movies.

"You're filling your mind too much with that junk at the Patee," she said. "Movies can put a lot of false ideas into the head of a boy. You should sit around and listen to the grown-ups talk. You'll learn something that way."

Out on the porch that night, everybody found his or her favorite rocker. While Theda Bara appeared on the Patee screen as *The Eternal Sappho*, I watched the fireflies. The main point of the conversation was predictions about the weather tomorrow.

I felt liberated from this porch crowd of weather soothsayers when I fled the following afternoon into the arms of my sweetie, Frank. As I got to know Frank more intimately, it became clear to me why he could find no girl in Kansas at that time to do what he wanted sexually. Frank had some kinky ideas about sex. He liked to have his entire body washed with my cherry-red lips and sweet tongue, especially his armpits and his ass. At first eating his ass was repulsive to me but in time it became one of the sweetest memories of my youth.

When you love a guy, or so I was to learn, you're prepared to do a lot to please him. Even when Frank had three beers and demanded to piss in my mouth, I gave in. Although repulsive at first, I imagined I was drinking beer and in time the act no longer revolted me. The way I figured it, you did what your man wanted even if the idea at first turned you off.

After my session with Frank, I slipped off to the Patee. He didn't like movies and never went with me. The lure of Theda Bara in *Cleopatra* was too powerful. In the film I'd never seen so much of a woman's breasts exposed before. The sight did not thrill me. I much preferred the hard and golden chest of Frank with his beautiful nipples which he liked me to suck on endlessly.

As I was leaving the theater, Mrs. Patee stopped me. "I just received a call from Maria Jane. She said I was not to let you into my theater to see any more Theda Bara films."

Crushed and devastated, I made my way home, there to discover Maria Jane waiting at the front door. "I didn't know a bad picture meant so much to you."

"How do you know it's bad?" I protested. "You haven't seen it."

"It's all in the papers," she said. "The Better Films Committee has come out against it." Maria Jane wrung her hands in despair. "I'll pray for you."

That night we entertained the Voorhis family. They told us they were going to California. "Everything's easy out there," their son, Jerry, said. "You can pick oranges right off the trees. There's work for everybody. You can get to meet movie stars."

I wanted to go right away but Maria Jane held back. "It's too much for me to consider," she said.

Charles Voorhis was president of the bank, and Jerry was planning to go to Yale to study social science. Maria Jane predicted that Jerry was either going to become a minister or a statesman. In time, Maria Jane turned out to be right. Jerry became a political footnote to history. In 1946 Richard M. Nixon made his maiden appearance in politics by defeating the incumbent congressman, Jerry Voorhis, in a nasty campaign.

The next afternoon, after I had committed some unspeakable acts on Frank, I begged him to run off to California with me. His refusal frightened me, as he had a far and distant look in his eyes I'd never seen before.

The next morning I understood a lot more. Word spread across Lawrence that the good-looking cowpoke had gone back West with his family. The land they'd inherited had been sold to a young couple who'd moved here from Ohio. Several old-timers claimed the young couple paid too much for the spread, but I didn't give a damn about that.

How could Frank leave me without even saying good-bye? I was madly in love with him. He loved me too or at least that's what he claimed every night when he wanted me to do those unspeakable things to him that no girl would do.

I felt the way a bride must feel when deserted at the altar. There was no reason to live. I was eager to experience life but thought of suicide since I knew I'd never get over Frank. There would never be another man for me but Frank. Of that, I was certain.

That night my world came to an end. The two most important things in my life—Frank and Theda Bara—were gone. I had nothing left to live for and planned to flee at once to California by myself.

I'd already decided how to support myself, realizing there must be a lot of men like Oscar Wilde around today who would actually pay good money to go to bed with a beautiful boy, especially one as experienced as I was. I'd learned my sexual lessons well from Frank before his abrupt departure. He'd even taught me to drive a car.

My sagging spirits soared somewhat when Maria Jane informed me that beginning tomorrow night I'd be sharing my room with a new boarder. His name was Buddy Rogers.

*****

With a grim face, Maria Jane read the morning figures of a flu epidemic killing thousands upon thousands. That and the toll of American casualties on European battlefronts made for long, dreary afternoons when adults met to talk.

We'd been asked to accommodate a young man from Olathe, Kansas, who wanted to stay away from the infected area, and we readily agreed as we were always short of money.

When Mr. and Mrs. Rogers arrived with their son, Buddy, whom they called Charles, I was captivated. Nowhere in this part of Kansas did such a beautiful boy exist except for me, of course. Three or four years younger than me, Buddy already stood six feet tall, slim with jetblack hair and golden brown eyes that had a certain sparkle in them. His parents quickly introduced themselves as Bert and Maude and said they lived on a farm. Bert was a newspaperman and later a probate judge in Johnson County.

Maude and Bert went off to talk to Maria Jane, who was a bit aghast to find out they were Christian Science devotees, a religion of which she disapproved, although she remained respectful of their faith. In public, at least, Maria Jane, always had impeccable manners.

I carried Buddy's suitcase and led the way upstairs to the hot cramped room we'd be sharing. Up close to him, I thought he was growing more beautiful every minute.

He spotted the three-quarter wooden bed we'd be sharing but made no comment.

"How's life in Olathe?" I asked.

"Pretty dull, pretty quiet," he said. "Olathe is Indian for beautiful but there's nothing beautiful there."

"I'm sure that's true now that you've left town."

His face turned red at my brazen remark, and he looked slightly puzzled as if he might have misunderstood.

"The girls in Olathe must be in mourning now that you're gone," I said. "You are very good looking."

"I'd say you've got me beat by a country mile," he said, turning his back to me and taking off his hot jacket followed by his shirt. I didn't turn to look away but stared at his trim, muscled, but not overly developed body. Eager for the night to come, I could hardly wait for Buddy to take off his trousers. I wanted to see all that this beautiful boy had to show—and more.

As the day wore on, I found Buddy polite and quietly charming, although I suspected he was a bit aloof and self-contained, as if inhabiting his own universe. He was an introvert and rather undemonstrative like most of the rest of the people in Kansas.

Later Bert and Maude gave Buddy and me money to go to the Patee Theatre to see Mary Pickford's latest movie, *Poor Little Rich Girl*. Maria Jane didn't object to my seeing Mary Pickford movies. Buddy told me that Miss Pickford was his favorite movie star. I told him I liked Mary's films but infinitely preferred Theda Bara.

"Theda Bara's a witch," he said with a bit of anger in his voice. "Miss Pickford is so sweet and nice, with pretty yellow curls."

After seeing Mary emote, we walked home together, taking the slow and meandering route. I wanted to be alone with Buddy as much as possible and didn't even want to share this magnificent boy with Maria Jane.

"Do you want to be in the movies?" I asked him. "With your good looks, I think you'd be a natural."

"Not at all," he said. "I want to make a living from my music. But I know how to act. I did Booth Tarkington's *Clarence* in school."

Even now, as I recall this lovely boy, it seems ironic that he had so little desire to be an actor. Over the years to come, I avidly followed his career as he portrayed college boys, salesmen, lawyers, and pilots, becoming celebrated as "America's boy friend," as his future wife, Mary Pickford, was to be known as "America's sweetheart." I remember seeing Buddy in *Wings* eight times in 1927, and was thrilled that it was the first film to win an Academy Award, even though Paramount paid Buddy only sixty-five dollars a week to play the young airman with Clara Bow, Gary Cooper, and Richard Arlen.

His films never impressed the critics, but in the years to come he would keep churning them out: *Dance Band, Golden Hoofs, Abie's Irish Rose, Fascinating Youth,* and *Mexican Spitfire's Baby.*

This unassuming boy would one day, with Miss Pickford at his side, preside over a legendary home, Pickfair, on a mountaintop overlooking Los Angeles. Miss Pickford and Buddy Rogers became Hollywood royalty.

As he walked with me through Lawrence, Buddy's future was unknown to him at the time and probably even unimagined. Looking back, it seems amazing that a decade later after we watched Mary Pickford on the screen that Buddy would be cast opposite her in the 1927 *My Best Girl.*

Twenty years before Mary Pickford was to sample Buddy's inches when she married him in 1937, I got there first. Let the world know that I was the first person ever to seduce that cute Buddy Rogers.

It didn't happen the first night or even the second. But as we lay in bed on the third night in our underwear, one of the hottest nights ever recorded in Kansas, the talk turned to girls. The subject didn't interest me at all but I felt it might get an arousal out of Buddy who seemed committed to the heterosexual lifestyle.

At some point in our erotic dialogue, I told him, "I bet you'd like to have Mary Pickford's cupid red mouth wrapped around your cock, riding up and down until she sucks all the juice out of you."

Buddy didn't say anything at first but I heard a little moan escape from his throat. Slipping out of my underwear, I began to masturbate. Being the true all American boy that he was, Buddy too peeled off his underwear and started to masturbate along with me. But I had no intention of letting that cream of his go to waste. When he was completely caught up in the throes of passion, and had gone too far to protest, I lowered myself over him and slipped his dick into my mouth where I sucked as if he were some life force.

At first he tried to push me off him but I had him. He was close to erupting. Instead of pushing me, he grabbed my head as he held me down onto his magnificent dick and shot his first load into a human mouth. The cream I tasted was the sweetest I was to know for the rest of my life, and I've practically had everybody. All the men had a different flavor but no one ever tasted sugar laced like Buddy.

In the days and weeks ahead we never mentioned our nightly bouts in bed but they continued. In fact I was onto Buddy every night. He never kissed me. Once I begged him to reciprocate my sucking but he never did. After finishing him off, I would keep his cum in my mouth while I masturbated, swallowing it only when I reached my own orgasm.

We had long ago abandoned sleeping in our underwear. Every night I lived for the unveiling. Before I would turn off the kerosene lamp, Buddy would take off all his clothes in front of me so I could appreciate his beautiful body and that lovely dick between his legs.

On Saturday nights, and sometimes on Fridays, I would leave the house with Buddy and go with him to his guest appearances with a little jazz band. For Friday shows, he would get ten dollars which was a lot of money back then. However, his fee was raised to twelve dollars for the big Saturday show.

The first night I went with him he played the drums. But he told me he could play the saxophone just as well. Both Maria Jane and I knew he could play the trombone! We heard it almost daily at our home.

Although I was considered the prettiest boy in Lawrence, girls always seemed to avoid me. When word spread that Buddy was staying at our house, many girls in Lawrence made up excuses to come and visit us. In spite of the latter day label of "America's boy friend," he dated no girls while he was in Lawrence.

Buddy stayed with us for three months, and I cried when Bert and Maude came to take him back to Olathe. By then I had fallen in love with him and had virtually forgotten about Frank.

Upstairs, as he was packing his suitcase, he came over to me. I didn't think he wanted any more sex. Knowing that he would be leaving in the morning, I had attacked him three times the night before, fearing I would probably never get to taste such sweet cream again.

He stood in front of me. "Thanks," he said. He pulled me to him and gave me a long, lingering kiss. Decades later, I can still recall the sweetness of his beautiful mouth. I didn't get tongue as with Frank, but I got one of the world's most succulent mouths, cherry-red like my own lips.

After he had departed in a car with Bert and Maude, we promised to write but perhaps knew we never would. It was time to move on. I had to begin the search tomorrow for another boy friend.

When he'd gone, I cried for two hours and told Maria Jane I didn't want supper as I was feeling sick.

The next morning as I was cleaning up the room I had shared with Buddy, I had reason to question Buddy's devotion to Mary Pickford as his favorite movie star. In the bottom of the drawer where he'd kept his clothing, I discovered a picture of my own favorite, Theda Bara.

*****

One day all of Lawrence was excited, as people ran about hysterically. "The war is over," our neighbor shouted up the hill at me. "There's going to be a big parade."

Not wanting to miss out on that, I rushed back to our house and began to devise a costume for myself. On the front pages of the *Journal*, I'd seen pictures of the German dictator with a long mustache and a spiked helmet. Out of an old football helmet, I decided to make a headdress like the Kaiser.

The helmet was hard to make, especially the big spike on top. But I finished in time to join the festivities on Massachusetts Street. Breathlessly I arrived, taking a place right in front of a flag carried by the American Legion.

"Get out of here, you Hun," the leader shouted. He took the pole of the American flag and punched me in the kidneys. In disgrace I sat on the curb, trying to conceal my helmet as I watched the parade pass me by.

More rejections were on the way, but not until after I'd visited the Jackson home on the other side of Windmill Hill. Mr. Jackson had short hair and two gold teeth which he showed often because he smiled a lot. Mrs. Jackson was tall and bosomy, and liked me a lot.

They lived in a tall wooden house with steep front steps. After the supper dishes were done, Mr. Jackson would get out a large aluminum kettle with a tight-fitting lid. With a long spoon he'd add bacon grease, then some salt, and finally some white popcorn. Jiggling the kettle, he'd wait and so would we for the explosion inside. After popping, he'd put the kettle in the center of the kitchen table where we would help ourselves.

The next day I had a brilliant idea. I went to Mrs. Patee and suggested to her that she could make a lot of money by opening a popcorn concession in the theater lobby. "I'd like to run it," I said. "I'll split the profits fifty-fifty. I'll even furnish the popcorn."

"I don't want people spilling popcorn all over my theater," she said. "Popcorn in a cinema. You sure have some ridiculous ideas."

I became very angry at this latest rejection and called Mrs. Patee a rotten skunk. "Mr. Durango Jones, why don't you take your business elsewhere in the future?"

"But you're the only movie theater in town."

"I know," she said smugly.

"Just you wait and see. When I grow up, I'm going to become Theda Bara's leading man."

Mrs. Patee burst into hysterical laughter, her snaggled teeth showing. "That's the craziest idea I ever heard of in my life. You and the vamp."

"You'll live to eat your words," I said, still angry.

"By the time you become a man, the vamp will be old enough to be your grandma."

Turning from the sight of her, I'd never considered that. Would Theda Bara ever grow old? The concept was hard to take. Once captured on film, a person remained forever young. *Didn't they?*

Later that night I walked by the Patee from which I was barred. The lights were out. I whispered good-bye to the theater, wondering how many people in the future would occupy my seat. I wanted to break into the theater and seal off my seat. It seemed wrong to have others sitting where I'd spent all those happy hours alone with Theda Bara.

Back home with Maria Jane, I learned that beginning tomorrow morning we'd have a new boarder.

Shortly before noon Margaret Barker moved in with eight stage trunks. Maria Jane had to give Margaret her bedroom, and had to retreat to a tiny little alcove in back of the kitchen. We desperately needed the money.

Margaret, as she insisted on being called, made two pronouncements—one, that she was the third richest woman in Jacksonville, Florida, and, two, that she'd been a stage star in Chicago.

Her wisping curlicues of red-blonde hair tumbled into her eyes as if by design. Her figure was what was called "pleasingly plump." All her conversation was animated with the most amazing facial gestures. At one moment she'd be very sad and demure, a long-suffering American sweetheart who rivaled anything Mary Pickford could do on the screen. Within minutes she'd switch to a mean, calculating look that was more daringly provocative than Theda Bara.

She was always bubbling over with some new story or some exciting past adventure. Her eyes were sad although her face, especially her lips, was always brightly painted. She wore a great deal of jewelry which she claimed was real, although Maria Jane warned me, "Don't believe everything you hear." Margaret claimed that some of her jewelry was collected from admirers on two continents, including "a crowned head of Europe."

One day she summoned me to her bedroom which was heavily scented in rose water. "I can't pay the rent," she abruptly confessed. "You've got to speak to Maria Jane and put in a good word for me."

I was stunned. Up to then I'd been telling my friends what a rich woman she was.

"Please," she said before bursting into tears. As I reached to comfort her, she grabbed me and locked me in a tight embrace, giving me a wet kiss and rubbing her tear-streaked nose into my neck. Frightened, I pulled away.

"Don't be afraid," she said soothingly. "If you do a favor for little ol' Maggie, little ol' Maggie might do a favor for you." She reached for the buttons of my trousers. "Like help you with junior there."

I didn't know that women ever propositioned men, much less boys. Fearful that Maria Jane would find me in Margaret's room, I rushed upstairs and into my savings, carefully concealed in a sock in my closet. I gave Maria Jane Margaret's rent for one week, and she accepted the money without question.

After that Margaret became increasingly friendly. She kept telling me, "You haven't claimed your reward."

One day as I was passing by her room, she opened her door and invited me in. I was too embarrassed not to accept. On her dressing table, she had a photograph of a man surrounded by a bevy of single pictures of women. "Who's that?" I asked.

"That's Maurice Barrymore."

I had heard of him, and Maria Jane had once seen him on the stage. He was the father of John Barrymore, one of my favorite actors. I'd seen him at the Patee in *Raffles* and *On the Quiet.*

Maurice Barrymore would be called a hunk today. The amateur boxing champion of England, he became celebrated for having "swagger," and taught American actors how to swagger. This fabled debaucher, poet, playwright, and actor, was a *jeune premier* whose picture women wore in their lockets.

"Maurice was madly in love with me," Margaret said, "before I deserted him for an Italian count." Around Mr. Barrymore's picture, she had pasted photographs of other women she identified as Madame Modjeska, Olga Nethersole, and Lillie Langtry, the latter also the mistress of Edward VII. Margaret had drawn mustaches and beards on these ladies. "All of them were former mistresses of Maurice," she said. "But they never captured his heart the way I did."

A knock on the door, and Maria Jane stood there, looking stern and firm. "Son," she commanded, "I think you'd better return to your room. Mrs. Barker, I don't think you should entertain my boy any more in your room alone."

Head hung low, I sheepishly filed past Maria Jane and was too ashamed to even look Margaret in the eye.

The next week I was worried because Margaret's rent was fast approaching again, and I didn't have any more money to support her like Maurice Barrymore did.

However, I found I had nothing to fear. Margaret had met Phil Holywell, who had rented a room in a nearby house, and he had invited her to go with him to Colorado where he claimed he was going to try his hand at ranching. Maria Jane was shocked and outraged that the two of them were going off together without benefit of marriage.

At the rail station to see them off, I was frankly a little jealous of Phil. Margaret handed me a letter she'd written to John Barrymore. "I know John very well," she said, "if you know what I mean." She winked at me. "Like father, like son. He owes me a favor or two. If you go to California, and he's there making a movie, present him with this letter. He'll remember me well, and I'm sure after reading my letter he'll help you break into the movies."

I thanked her profusely as she gave me a big juicy kiss, replanting a lot of her lipstick onto me. I never washed it off until dinner when Maria Jane's fried chicken removed the final traces.

*****

Maria Jane and I were excited when a letter arrived from Bridgetta Clark, who used to be our next door neighbor in Kansas. She had gone to Hollywood, and was all bubbly with her good fortune there. Her biggest break was to come in 1921 when she played Donna Louisa Desnoyers, the mother of Julio, a role immortalized by Rudolph Valentino in *The Four Horsemen of the Apocalypse*. Long before she was cast in the part, she had become friends with Rodolfo as he was then known.

Rodolfo, she said, didn't want to be an actor but had hoped to join the British Royal Air Force, which was then recruiting in the San Francisco area. He was rejected because of poor vision in his left eye.

"Not all people are bad out here," Bridgetta wrote. "Rodolfo is from southern Italy. He dances the tango and is devoted to his mother whom he calls a Madonna. Isn't that nice? Only he fears she is disappointed in him. She wants Rodolfo to come home and be a farmer."

Bridgetta urged both of us to come out at once. "At heart, Jane, you are an actress," she wrote. "I always remember those DAR concerts, the hoop skirts, and all that lovely music you played on your Steinway. Bring Durango too. He is so good looking—he will surely become a movie star in a few years, maybe even sooner."

As visions of stardom danced in my head, I wrote Bridgetta first thing the next morning and begged her for a quick response. When her answer came, it was addressed only to me, and I slipped upstairs to read the latest news from Hollywood in secret.

Bridgetta claimed that Rodolfo was staying at the Alexandria Hotel at Fifth and Spring in Los Angeles. He was being supported by a very handsome actor, Norman Kerry, of Rochester, New York. She claimed that Rodolfo was anxious to move out of the hotel and into a small apartment or cottage. Fearing his meager wages weren't enough, he was eager to share his living quarters with someone who'd pay half the expenses. She said she had spoken to Rodolfo about me, and he'd agreed to live with me, but I'd have to be there within three weeks because Norman Kerry would no longer be supporting him after that time, and Rodolfo couldn't afford to stay at the Alexandria if he had to pay his own expenses.

Maria Jane had already written Bridgetta that she had no intention of coming to Hollywood. With a trembling hand, I wrote Bridgetta that I wanted to be the roommate of Rodolfo. He sounded like an exciting and dashing man. I'd never had a foreigner before, and Rodolfo seemed the opposite of the all-American Buddy Rogers. Maybe I could become Rodolfo's Theda Bara and seduce him.

Not knowing where I would get the money, I agreed to share half the expenses with Rodolfo wherever we found a place to live. I assured Bridgetta that I would be arriving on her doorstep within the month. Not letting Maria Jane know what I was doing, I secretly mailed the letter.

The next day began as one of the happiest of my life before turning into tragedy. My popcorn-loving friends, the Jacksons, came by and asked Maria Jane if I could drive them to the next town to see a vaudeville show. Mr. Jackson had an eye irritation and was afraid to drive. Fortunately, Frank had taught me to drive his battered old vehicle before leaving town, and I was eager to get on the road. Maria Jane reluctantly agreed.

The team we were going to see were "Buck and Bubbles," who in time became a legendary comedy-dance duo. Bubbles was to play "Sportin' Life" in the original 1935 production of *Porgy and Bess*, and Buck's final performance was with Judy Garland at the Palace Theater in 1967.

Until Buck and Bubbles, no blacks had

appeared in white theaters in the Middle West. At first the Jacksons and I didn't know that the two performers were black, because they appeared in black face. That was to make the audience think they were white.

Later, as we met Bubbles backstage, he told us about his life with the carnival. Buck was shorter, with a warm, friendly smile and a firm handshake. His real name, he said, was Ford Lee Washington. His baggy, plaid suit was big enough for two men his size.

"That's a funny costume," I said.

"That costume," he said, looking forlornly at me, "is all the suit I got."

It was late when we got home. Our house was all lit up by kerosene lamps and neighbors were in the front yard. I braked the car and rushed to the yard where Mrs. Patee was the first to greet me. She was very sympathetic toward me and seemingly had forgotten that I'd called her a rotten skunk.

"Maria Jane passed on suddenly this afternoon," she said. "She was tending her flowers in the front garden. One of the neighbors passed by and saw her body keeled over."

I burst into tears and ran toward the house, but in the living room some other neighbors told me that Maria Jane's body had been taken to the funeral parlor.

The next day passed as in a nightmare. I cried on and off, yet didn't have the great sense of personal loss I might have had if Maria Jane had loved me more. She was an American puritan and, I felt, secretly disapproved of me. If she knew more of my involvements with Frank or Buddy, she might have kicked me out of the house.

She'd never kissed me or held me in her arms. She hadn't loved my father either but seemingly endured him. As I got dressed in my only suit to attend her funeral, I felt lonely and abandoned in the world but eager to get on with my life. I had planned to leave Maria Jane anyway and to send her big money from all the huge bundle I would make in Hollywood.

The funeral was a disaster, and at one point I vomited. Maria Jane's body had been laid out in our little living room for the neighbors to come and inspect her remains. These same neighbors brought large bowls of potato salad, fried chicken, and other platters of food. Flies buzzed back and forth from Maria Jane's face to the food. The neighbors shooed the flies away and helped themselves to the bounty. I told them I wasn't hungry.

Some men out in the back yard were drinking white lightning. "Let's get on with the burying," the pastor of Maria Jane's church said. The neighbors filed out of the house and headed for the cemetery. Maria Jane's body was placed in a hearse. I was invited to go along, but decided to drive the Jackson car instead. I don't even remember the actual burial, as I fainted at the grave site and was taken inside the church where I was given a drink of cold well water and placed on one of the wooden church pews until I recovered.

Back at our house, I was startled to discover Mrs. Patee. She abruptly informed me that she had decided to sell her theater and retire. She'd learned that a large cinema was going to be built on Massachusetts Street and she didn't feel she could compete. She'd also found out to her horror that the new theater people were planning to sell bags of freshly popped corn in the lobby. "You knew the future," she told me. "I should have listened to you." Then she offered me one-thousand dollars in cash for our house, and I cemented the deal that night. She said she had to move in right away, and she'd give me an extra three-hundred dollars for our furnishings because she felt Maria Jane had fixed up the house "real beautiful." I told her I'd be gone by ten the next morning.

Saying good-bye to Kansas forever, the recently orphaned me boarded the Sante Fe Chief the following day. It was the thrill of my life. I didn't want to go to sleep for fear I'd miss something. The states west of Kansas excited me, even though I saw nothing at times but a coyote.

I'd sneak back to the little smoking compartment in the caboose. Men gathered here to smoke cigars and pipes and tell tales of high adventure. One man claimed he'd killed an Indian, another spoke of the exciting Gold Rush days in Alaska. The smoke was suffocating, but I liked sitting around hearing stories from men who had led exciting lives, knowing that soon I too would be leading a life of thrills and adventure.

Even better than the caboose were the stops at a Harvey House. Our arrival would be met with a young girl in uniform out front clanging a big dinner bell. Descending from the steps, I could smell the wafting aromas of the big dining room. The long tables were set up in advance, with enormous stiff white napkins standing like bouquets of white roses in each glass. The Harvey girls who waited on us were pretty in their fancy blue dresses and their starched white aprons, their smiling faces greeting us under blue bonnet hats. They'd pass heavy platters filled with pork chops and sizzling steaks.

After leaving Harvey House, the train rolled along, past tall mountains and cactus-studded deserts. I knew I'd soon be in California.

I had three immediate goals in this order:

(1) To become the biggest male movie star of all time.
(2) To enjoy my first Italian lover with my seduction of Rodolfo Valentino.
(3) To bed the matinee idol, John Barrymore, who looked like he had a great physique.

An old man seated next to me turned and said, "It's a golden land out there, boy. I made a million dollars in San Francisco and lost every cent of it in the earthquake." He leaned closer and whispered in my ear, as I drew back from the stench of his breath which smelled of whiskey and tobacco. "A pretty little boy like you who looks prettier than any girl could get into a lot of trouble out in Hollywood. There are men in Hollywood who will want to do a lot of dirty things to you. Saying no won't be enough. They'll force you to do what they want."

After a polite few minutes, I moved away from this man with his yellowing beard, even though I felt his eyes on me wherever I went on the Sante Fe.

As I listened to the sound of the train on the tracks, the old man's words seemed to echo in my ears. But I wasn't afraid. Regardless of what happened to me, I knew that in addition to becoming a movie star, I'd be collecting juicy tales for my memoirs which I would write decades from now.

Chapter Two

I came, I saw, I came, I conquered.

No sooner than I had departed from the Sante Fe, I knew at once that Hollywood was my kind of town. Before I had gotten to Bridgetta's, I had been propositioned twice—once by a young porter, and again by a taxi driver.

A friendly young couple from Missouri, my dining companions on the train, had asked me why I was going West. I told them I was under contract to Adolf Zukor. A bit of an exaggeration but I knew that my white lie would soon be self-fulfilling.

My body had filled out and I was rather muscled, and that thing between my legs had probably reached its full dimensions, and it was of an impressive length and thickness. In the past few years, my face had become more masculine but still retained its pretty boy look. One passenger on the Sante Fe had guessed my age at fourteen. I was told that the younger you looked in Hollywood, the better.

Once reunited with Bridgetta, I learned sadly that her early optimism about Hollywood was more tempered. Because of the influenza epidemic, many movie theaters had been shut down by health officials. Some of the minor studios had closed entirely and others operated at only minor capacity. But with the end of the war, there was more activity and more jobs available. Big salaries were being offered again, and movie stars were spending freely, at least those who had jobs. Bridgetta was currently unemployed.

Nonetheless, Bridgetta had gone ahead and rented a lovely Tudor-like cottage for us in back of an older property in the Hollywood Hills. When she informed me the rent was one-hundred dollars a month, I was flabbergasted. I'd never heard of such rents before. In Kansas you could have room and board for five dollars a week. She said it was a lovely cottage in a neighborhood filled with movie stars, including Francis X. Bushman, the fabled matinee idol.

As she drove me to the cottage I would be sharing with Rodolfo, Bridgetta told me I'd need a car in Hollywood. "Otherwise, it's impossible to get around from studio to studio," she said. "The place is too spread out."

The prospect of owning a car was thrilling to me, especially when I learned I would have to take only eighty-five dollars from my savings to purchase one from her neighbor, who was a salesman. "He's got to sell it because his firm has transferred him back to New York," Bridgetta said. "I'll have him drive it over tomorrow."

After kissing Bridgetta good-bye and thanking her for her hospitality, I retreated inside our Tudor cottage, the one I would share with Rodolfo, hoping it would become our love nest. Regrettably, the actor had a job out of town, and I wouldn't get to see him until three days later.

Inside the living room I discovered five framed photographs of Rodolfo. It was love at first sight. Exotically foreign with slick black hair and a chiseled profile, Rodolfo was a man I could fall in love with overnight.

In our shared bedroom closet, I discovered his clothes which surprised me. He had a collection of bright, colorful shirts and ties. Maybe they wore such garb in Italy, but no man in America decked himself out like this. Rodolfo must be not only dashing but daring. I searched through a chest of drawers to discover his undergarments. To my horror, but also to my delight, I found out he wore silk underwear in cherry red, turquoise, lemon yellow, and shocking pink. Pink underwear on a man. Up to then, I thought underwear came in only two colors— white or red flannel long johns. I could hardly contain myself at the thrill of meeting this Romeo who I knew would sweep me off my feet.

At a knock on the door, I eagerly rushed through the living room to open it. Instead of this Italian dream boat, I met Elizabeth Hutchinson, the epileptic daughter of a doctor. Her father owned the cottage we were renting and she lived in the main house up front with its panoramic view of Los Angeles.

"I need constant watching," she said, "as I might have a fit at any moment." She carried a spoon with her which someone could use to stick in her mouth if she had a fit. That way, she'd be kept from biting her tongue.

She'd met Rodolfo and I was eager for news of him but she was more interested in finding someone to take her to Angelus Temple at Echo Park to hear the woman evangelist, Aimee Semple McPherson. Elizabeth faithfully listened to all of Sister Aimee's broadcasts. I'd heard Sister Aimee on the radio and had found her voice raucous, shouting about salvation, the need for repentance, and the blood of the lamb. The air waves had seemed to tremble with her God almighty voice. Then she'd switch to a low, husky tone and croon sweet songs.

Reluctantly I agreed to drive Elizabeth to the temple in her father's car. This was not my dream of a first night in Hollywood. I had visions of being invited to glamorous parties filled with movie stars, perhaps Gloria Swanson or— and this I could only dream—Theda Bara.

I told Elizabeth of my interest in getting a movie contract. She assured me that with my good looks and charm, it would just be a matter of time. She informed me that Francis X. Bushman and his co-star, Beverly Bayne, lived right across the street from us. "They were secretly married until word leaked out. Both of them fear that news of their marriage, and of Bushman leaving his wife and children, will destroy their careers."

Elizabeth also told me that Adela Rogers St. Johns, the famous newspaperwoman, lived right next door to us. "She knows all the big stars, and they come to visit her. With Bushman across the street and Adela next door, you'll think you're at a movie premiere with all the stars coming and going in their fancy cars. Only yesterday I saw Wallace Reid when he came to visit Adela."

My heart skipped a beat. If there was one man in the world who could make me forget about Rodolfo, it was Wallace Reid.

Then at the height of his fame, Wallace Reid was called "the handsomest man in Hollywood." He played clean-cut young American men— all virtue, no vice. Strapping and handsome, he exuded post-war optimism. I still could recall him in the role of Jeff, the fighting blacksmith, in *The Birth of a Nation.* There were also a couple of scenes in *Intolerance.* Not only could Reid act, but he had a fine physique to go with that handsome face.

After promising Elizabeth I would drive her to the temple, I headed for the shower. Even though fascinated by Rodolfo and the upcoming prospect of sharing the double bed with him in back, I also dreamed of Wallace Reid.

After all, Wallace Reid was called "the King of Paramount." If I got to meet him, I might not only seduce him but he might get me my big break in movies.

I'd just arrived in Hollywood, and already my list of men to seduce was growing daily: Rodolfo Valentino, John Barrymore, and now Wallace Reid.

*****

Although my first night in Hollywood did not go as envisioned, I learned that even religious revivals in California were filled with first-rate entertainment. On the way to Sister Aimee's temple, Elizabeth kept telling me that she just knew that if the evangelist would lay her hands on her, she would be healed forever. This quiet, gawky but sweet girl seemed to be a true believer.

We arrived at Sister Aimee's circular temple which she'd built by selling little bags of cement for five dollars apiece. Like a movie house, a large marquee in front advertised the sermon of the day.

Inside, a vast balcony had ramps on either side, connecting with the front stages. Elizabeth and I held hands tightly in excitement, awaiting the appearance of Sister Aimee, which came an hour later.

Her robe was white, her flowing cape blue. We loved her chestnut hair piled casually on her head and the two dozen American beauty roses she held. Descending to center stage, she sat on her throne, as a tabernacle choir sang music composed by Sister Aimee herself.

It was baptismal night. Later in the evening, Sister Aimee called on those who wanted to be saved to come forward. Against a woodsy backdrop, she stood in a large pool in the center of the stage surrounded by fake rocks and ferns. Attendants brought "sinners" to her.

As the attendants flopped them backward into the water, Sister Aimee placed her hands on their foreheads and blessed them before lifting her arms upward to heaven.

Elizabeth and I were so thrilled with Sister Aimee's act we decided to go back the next night. She was every bit as exciting as Pola Negri or Gloria Swanson—perhaps not Theda Bara.

The following night the marquee outside promised that Sister Aimee would tell the story of *My Life*. We could hardly wait for her entrance.

The lights darkened, then went on again to spotlight Sister Aimee swinging from a big tree in front of what was supposedly a large Canadian farmhouse where she was born. The evangelist wore a red and white checked gingham dress and a matching bonnet. Swinging back and forth, she carried a milk pail dangling from her left arm.

Rising from the swing, she took her pail over to a real cow standing on stage beside the fake house. After milking the cow, she brought the pail to the edge of the stage. Dipping out the milk, she invited disciples to come forward and drink it.

For her finale that evening, she appeared as the star of her own operetta, *Naughty Marietta*. Her entrance from the back of the stage was under arched garlands of roses held up by her choir. In a crinoline hoop skirt, with shoulders revealed, Sister Aimee whirled and curtsied, singing love ballads to Jesus in a style that must have inspired Jeanette MacDonald in her thirties movie career.

At the end Sister Aimee came to the edge of the stage, crooning her own song, *Only a Rose for You*. In her hands she held a rose. As she softly sang, she took off the petals one at a time, kissing each one before distributing them to her followers who came forward one at a time. After that, she pleaded with her audience for money to carry out her work. "I don't want to hear the rude jangle of silver," she shouted. "Only the rustle of paper."

I was embarrassed, as I had only a quarter in my pocket. A clothes line came our way. Elizabeth pinned on a five-dollar bill. Followers were attaching one-dollar bills to the clothes pins.

When she'd pleaded for money, Sister Aimee called out to all those who were sick and crippled to come to her altar to be healed. That was the moment for which Elizabeth had waited for so long. She asked me to accompany her.

At the altar, a white-haired, stout woman who looked like a stern nurse in a mental hospital came to Elizabeth and whispered, "Where's your card?"

"What card?" Elizabeth asked.

"The one from the 500 Room," the woman said sharply. "You have to have a card before Sister Aimee can cure you."

We were directed to the 500 Room, an ugly commercial building adjoining the temple. At first I wasn't allowed to enter until I explained that I had to be with Elizabeth at all times because of her medical condition.

The room was managed by Ma Kennedy, Sister Aimee's mother. Unlike her daughter, Ma Kennedy lacked any glamour whatsoever. She was skeleton thin with a wrinkly neck and obvious false teeth that didn't fit well. Through glasses enclosed in metal spectacles, she glared at us, studying the papers Elizabeth had been asked to fill out and scratching her kinky white hair under a thin net.

At first she tried to sell us lifetime subscriptions to a news magazine published by the temple. We declined which brought a hostile stare of such venom from Ma Kennedy that we felt we were going to be ejected from the 500 Room.

When Ma Kennedy learned that Elizabeth was the daughter of a doctor, she tried to get her to sign papers pledging vast sums of money to Sister Aimee. She even wanted Elizabeth to sign over her eventual inheritance from her father. Instead of that, Elizabeth presented Ma Kennedy with a check for one-hundred dollars which her father had given her. Reluctantly, when Ma Kennedy seemed to think she would get no more money out of Elizabeth, the stern old woman handed her a "healing card."

At the altar, card in hand, Elizabeth stood in line with me beside dozens of other sick or disabled people hoping for a miracle cure.

At long last it came time for Elizabeth's cure. Ma Kennedy had filled out a paper about Elizabeth which one of the attendants had brought to Sister Aimee. Over a loudspeaker and on radio, Sister Aimee proclaimed, "Here is this dear, young woman, Elizabeth Hutchinson, the daughter of one of the greatest physicians of California. But his medicine has failed her, and she has turned to me." Then Sister Aimee read off a list of the "diseases" which Ma Kennedy had diagnosed for Elizabeth along with the in-house doctor. To my horror and amazement, I noticed the fact that Elizabeth was an epileptic was missing from the list. Elizabeth had none of the so-called diseases on Ma Kennedy's paper which apparently had been prepared by the temple's doctor.

Calling Elizabeth forward, Sister Aimee laid one hand on the young woman and raised her other hand to the ceiling. Within minutes following Sister Aimee's silent prayer, she proclaimed Elizabeth cured of all the diseases read on that card.

The music swelled. Radiant, Elizabeth rose from a kneeling position, stood up, took my hand, and smiled. She whispered to me that she was certain she'd been healed.

At the end of the services, as we left the temple, Elizabeth stopped in the temple store to purchase sentimental photographs of Sister Aimee, records of her songs, and a book. "I don't know why you like Theda Bara so much," she said. "To me, Sister Aimee is the real goddess, not some fake movie star who's just pretending to be someone she isn't. Sister Aimee doesn't pretend. She is the real thing."

On the way home, only two blocks from Elizabeth's house, she had an epileptic seizure. I braked the car and reached for the spoon, inserting it into her mouth. Her entire body was shaking and I feared at first she was going to die. Fortunately, a police car came by at this time and two young officers spotted our distress. Seeing Elizabeth's violent condition, they rushed her to the hospital where I called Dr. Hutchison to come for his daughter.

Two hours later, when I told Elizabeth and her doctor father good night, I drove back to the Tudor cottage. This would be my one and only session with religious revivals in California.

As I brought the car to a stop out back, I was stunned to see lights on in our cottage. In my excitement, I practically stumbled as I crossed the lawn to the front door.

Could it be? Could Rodolfo have returned a day earlier from his dance job?

*****

I'd always been taught that foreigners were the personification of evil, and proof of that was staring back at me as I entered our living room. Sitting on the sofa was one of the handsomest Latin men I'd ever seen, wearing a pair of tight-fitting black pants with a revealing crotch and a butterscotch yellow silk shirt that was unbuttoned to reveal a smooth, hairless chest.

Upon seeing me, he rose from the sofa and extended his hand. "You must be Durango. I'm Rodolfo Alfonzo Raffaelo Pierre Filbert Guglielmi di Valentina d'Antoguolla. But you can call me Rodolfo."

"Bridgetta has told me so much about you," I gushed. "I'm so excited living in Hollywood and so grateful you agreed to share the cottage with me to cut down on expenses."

He smiled enigmatically. "Perhaps we can do more together than cut down on expenses."

I smiled back, not really certain of what he

he meant. I hope it was what I thought he meant.

As we walked through our cottage together, I had time to evaluate the enchanting look of this sexy man. He moved through the cottage like a sensuous panther on the prowl. With his patent-leather hair, he had graceful manners. Every movement of his was precise. He was damned beautiful.

He'd made some spaghetti for us, and it was the best I've ever had. He'd even bought a bottle of wine to drink with our meal, and I enjoyed it although afraid to drink too much since I usually downed dinner with two glasses of milk.

Over pasta he talked a lot about himself, beginning with his days at a farmhouse in the south of Italy in a little town called Castellaneta. He spoke of its whitewashed stone walls and how the Mediterranean sun poured in to light the portraits of madonnas and the crucifixes in every room.

His papa, Giovanni Guglielmi, was a small farmer and veterinary doctor who'd died when Rodolfo was eleven. His mother was the daughter of a Parisian doctor, Pierre Filibert Barbin, and she was left to rear three children, including a brother, Alberto, and a sister Maria. Another sister, Beatrice, had died at an early age.

As Rodolfo talked, I could hardly hear his words, and could not remember all those impossible names. It was his photogenic eyes I remember the best. They were electrifying. When he turned them on you, you felt on fire.

His face saddened when he spoke of his arrival in New York as an immigrant. "I was penniless. Lonely. Sometimes I lived in cheap rooming houses with tramps. Sometimes I didn't even have the money for that and slept on a bench in Central Park. When I was desperate for food, I would go to this bar where I met older men. Some of these men would give me a dollar if I let them put their mouth on me."

This revelation came as a complete shock to me, even though I'd heard that the pervert, Oscar Wilde, had purchased young boys. I never thought I'd actually be meeting a young man who had sold his body. The idea of selling my own body had kept occurring to me on the Sante Fe Chief as it headed west.

"Believe it or not, one of my jobs was picking insects off rose leaves in Central Park," Rodolfo confessed. "In time I turned to dancing. I was a natural born dancer. In New York I danced with women who called me a gigolo. But I made a living. Once I was hired by a night club. They paid me fifty dollars a week. I danced all night and slept all day. I never got a chance to see the sun. Coming from the sunny south of Italy, seeing the sun is very important to me."

When the time came for Rodolfo to focus on me, I almost trembled at my lack of autobiography compared to his which seemed so exotic to me. I told him of my dull upbringing in Kansas and how I'd been initiated into sex by Frank and later how I had seduced Buddy Rogers. Even though Rodolfo said he had no great desire to be an actor, I confessed that becoming a movie star was my overriding ambition.

"You will be a matinee idol," he said. "With your good looks, you are a natural. But I am too foreign looking. The only parts for me in Hollywood are villains."

"You don't look like a villain to me," I said. "I think if you get an important role, you'd make women swoon at the sight of you. American women are ready to embrace the foreign. Look at Theda Bara. How foreign can you get?"

"I know, I know," he said a bit impatiently. "But when it comes to leading men, Hollywood seems to like the all-American, wholesome, corn-fed boy from the Middle West. A young man much like yourself."

"That's true. But tastes are changing."

"I hope you're right." Back in the living room he took off his shirt so I could better admire his torso. He invited me to kneel at his feet, and take off his shoes. "You can massage my feet if you want to. Many men like to do that. My feet are always tired from dancing."

Until Rodolfo, I had never thought of feet as an object of sexual desire. But I was learning fast. When he commanded me to suck his toes, I was at first appalled until I actually tasted those toes. After the first five minutes of sucking, I became addicted to them. A new sexual pleasure for me.

Lying back on the sofa to enjoy my toe-sucking, he told me, "In a few minutes I'm going to take you into our back bedroom and fuck you all night. But you must promise me one thing."

"What's that?" I asked, momentarily stopping my toe-sucking and eager to promise almost anything to get deflowered by this Latin lover.

"You must promise not to fall in love with me while I'm fucking you," he said. "Too many men fall in love with me when I fuck them, and I am not ready for love in my life right now."

"It's all right," I assured him. "I promise not to fall in love with you, but that is hardly going to take away my pleasure of getting fucked by you."

"It's agreed. I say this because I'm about to end a relationship with Norman Kerry who's been supporting me at the Alexandria Hotel. Do you know anything juicy about him?"

"Quite a lot," I said, and meant it. When Bridgetta had first mentioned Norman Kerry to me, I didn't know who he was. For some reason Mrs. Patee had never played any of his films at her theater. But on the Sante Fe Chief coming west, I had read about him in a movie magazine.

Kerry was a dashing, handsome actor, the Errol Flynn of the silent screen. He was starring in a movie called *Soldiers of Fortune*. His first appearance was in *Manhattan Madness*, a very minor role in a film that had starred Douglas Fairbanks. In time Kerry appeared with Mary Pickford herself, along with Alice Brady and Constance Talmadge. Back in Hollywood again, after serving in the army in World War I, he was aggressively pursuing Rodolfo.

"I've got to stay friendly with Norman," Rodolfo said. "He got me a job as an extra in a film called *Alimony*. It paid only five dollars a day, but I needed the work."

Later, before going to bed, Rodolfo asked me what I was going to do for a living in Los Angeles. I informed him that I had a small savings from the sale of a homestead in Kansas, and, if need be, I could fall back on that if the going got rough.

He seemed relieved to hear that. He smiled seductively at me before taking me into the bedroom. "When times get tough, I'll take you with me to the Los Angeles Athletic Club. Once there I will show you how to make a living with me. At least it will pay the rent."

The statement shocked me and I wanted to pursue the subject. How in the world could Rodolfo and I make a living by going to the athletic club, other than working as attendants? But something in his eyes told me that this wasn't the time to pursue that subject.

In the bedroom he slowly began to remove my clothes. "Your body is beautiful," he whispered into my neck as he gently licked that neck. "A golden boy."

I was trembling at his touch, and reached to run my fingers through his hair.

He backed away. "Don't touch my hair," he ordered. "I like to keep it perfectly groomed even when I'm fucking someone."

As he unbuttoned my trousers, I reached for him, slipping my fingers inside his fly to find a penis of width and depth. It totally fulfilled my expectations of what he'd be like down there. I was anxious to taste him. But first when my trousers had fallen from me, and he'd removed my underwear, he drew me to him and gave me a long, passionate kiss, inserting his tongue, which I eagerly sucked as with Frank.

I had lied to him. Although he'd made me promise not to fall in love with him if he seduced me, I was already hopelessly in love with him after the first kiss.

*****

The next morning dawned bright and sunny just as Rodolfo liked his days. The night before—the most blissful of my life—had led me to discover every inch of my lover's body, every delectable morsel. The new light of day brought a final revelation, a thin white scar on his right cheek. Later I was to learn he'd nicked himself while shaving at the age of five. He'd wanted to become a man like his father but, of course, was far too young to grow a beard.

When Rodolfo had penetrated me last night, it was as if he'd never withdrawn all evening. Neither of us got much sleep. I'd feel him growing hard within me for yet another time when I thought he'd be completely satisfied and exhausted. He would ride me again as I'd screamed out of pleasure and pain, not knowing where one ended and the other began.

Rodolfo awoke with smiles and passionate kisses, demanding that we shower together. After I had soaped and washed him clean, I kissed his body in the most intimate areas before preparing a breakfast of coffee, orange juice, and pastries. Rodolfo didn't eat bacon and eggs like the midwesterners I grew up with.

The new day found him bubbling over with excitement and anticipation. Before their breakup, Norman Kerry had introduced him to a producer, Emmett Flynn, who wanted to test Rodolfo for the role of an Italian count in the provocatively titled film, *The Married Virgin*. If Rodolfo got the role, his salary would be fifty dollars a week, and he desperately needed the money.

Before departing to go to a studio, Rodolfo left some vague instructions about how I was to hang out at the Hollywood Hotel where he just knew some producer would notice my "incredible good looks, blond hair, and blue eyes." At the end of the day, or so he predicted, I would be cast as the lead in a film. Even I thought that this time-table was a bit hasty.

As I was doing the breakfast dishes, there came a loud pounding on the front door. At once I thought it was the salesman come to deliver the new car I'd purchased for eighty-five dollars. I didn't understand why he wanted to pound the door in.

Opening the fragile door, I confronted not the salesman but a fearsome man who looked like an American version of Erich von Stroheim. He said his name was Frank Stevens and that he was a detective from New York sent to track down "Rudy di Valentina."

He spoke in such a harsh, loud voice I feared he'd wake up the neighborhood, not only Francis X. Bushman and Adela Rogers St. Johns, but perhaps Elizabeth too. With her, Stevens might even bring on another epileptic fit.

Taking a lesson from Maria Jane, I invited Stevens inside our living room and offered coffee which he accepted, demanding that it be served black with no sugar.

Over coffee Stevens became extremely confidential, almost as if he were willing to make a deal. He told me that Rodolfo was in serious trouble in New York and might be deported. Having just fallen in love with Rodolfo only hours before, I went into a state of panic. The mere thought of taking Rodolfo from my bed and sending him back to Italy was more than my tender young heart could fathom. Already I'd lost two lovers, both Frank and Buddy, and I wasn't about to lose my third if I could prevent it.

Stevens carried a briefcase which he opened and showed me some reports and tabloid scandal sheets. I read them avidly only to discover that Rodolfo had fled New York after Mae Murray had posted a thousand-dollar bail to secure his release from jail.

Miss Murray, of course, would later become the queen of MGM and would be forever linked to the Erich von Stroheim film, *The Merry Widow*. I recognized the name of this actress and dancer, although Mrs. Patee never showed any of her films. I was immediately jealous, suspecting that Miss Murray and Rodolfo might be lovers. Why else would she post a thousand-dollar bail in New York for him?"

The story of Rodolfo's troubles in New York were so complicated and convoluted that I never understood them thoroughly at the time, much less decades later in my tell-all memoir.

Before I'd read the lurid headlines, I had assumed that Rodolfo must have been involved with women during his café-dancing gigolo days in New York. Now the evidence was overwhelming.

The tabloids revealed that the police had raided the home of a Mrs. Georgia Thym and had arrested her as a blackmailer. At the time she was drawing blackmail money from three state politicians and a prominent banker who'd been caught in bed with a twelve-year-old boy. Finding Rodolfo in the house with Mrs. Thym, the police had arrested him too, sending him to jail for four days. Out in California, Mae Murray had learned of Rodolfo's plight and had wired a thousand dollars for his bail.

Rodolfo, or so the story said, had met Mrs. Thym at a dance hall and had gone home with her that very evening. The arrest of Mrs. Thym when Rodolfo was at her house appeared to be a set-up. Rodolfo had made a powerful enemy in Jack de Saulles, a rich and socially prominent New Yorker. Rodolfo had been involved romantically with Mrs. Bianca de

Saulles, described as "an ivory figurine from South America."

This South-of-the-Border beauty had apparently married de Saulles for his money. When Bianca had learned that her husband preferred other women to her, she, too, started stepping out. This led to the dancing arms of Rodolfo, who, the story said, had fallen madly in love with her.

Jack de Saulles had learned of his wife's dalliance with Rodolfo and had planned to divorce her. To lower any settlement Bianca might demand, he wanted to link her sexually to Rodolfo. He felt he would have an even better case if Rodolfo had ever gone to jail. It was believed that Jack de Saulles tipped off the police to Mrs. Thym, since he was having Rodolfo trailed by private detectives. By going home with Mrs. Thym, who was known to purchase men's bodies, Rodolfo had fallen into the trap set by de Saulles.

The story grew so complicated at this point that I felt Rodolfo and I should turn it into a movie script.

Before the courts had heard the de Saulles divorce case, which also involved the custody of a child, Bianca shot and killed her husband in July of 1916. Rodolfo became intimately involved in the murder case and its lurid tabloid headlines.

In the divorce papers being drawn up, Bianca named Joan Sawyer as correspondent. Joan was a well-known dancer at the time and had hired Rodolfo to appear with her in vaudeville and at the Woodmansten Inn. Rodolfo was supposed to be called as a witness to confirm the affair between Jack de Saulles and Joan Sawyer. De Saulles also planned to name Rodolfo as his wife's lover and dancing gigolo to make the divorce proceedings all the messier. All that ended with the fatal gun shot fired by Bianca.

Fleeing New York at once, Rodolfo joined a touring musical group, *The Masked Model*, and was paid seventy-five dollars a week. The troupe headed west where Rodolfo ended up broke and stranded in San Francisco. That's when Norman Kerry had lured him to Hollywood. To pay his train fare to Los Angeles, Rodolfo had joined the Al Jolson touring company since Norman Kerry had sent him no

funds. But Kerry had met him at the train station in Los Angeles and had lent Rodolfo money as he'd installed him at the Alexandria Hotel.

After I'd read the reports, Stevens glared at me. "I traced your Latin lover boy to the Alexandria where his boyfriend, Norman Kerry, was paying his bills every week. But your boy skipped out suddenly when he learned I was on his trail. I don't know what story he told you."

Not knowing what to do, I was flabbergasted when Stevens demanded that I "produce" Rodolfo at once. Without being invited, Stevens jumped up and headed for the back bedroom. "Is this where you two sex perverts went at it last night?"

I demanded that he leave our bedroom and return to the living room. Stevens told me that unless Rodolfo and I could come up with five-thousand dollars, he'd be arrested and taken back to New York for questioning in the de Saulles murder—and no doubt would be deported.

Before getting up to leave, Stevens told me that unless I had the money when he came by tomorrow morning, it was "curtains" for my lover. He said if we could raise the cash, all records about Rodolfo would "disappear" from the New York Police Department files and "my spic" could go on to become a film star or whatever he wanted to be, without any more interference from the New York police. Stevens claimed he could guarantee us that.

When he'd gone, I felt hopeless and helpless, wanting to talk to Rodolfo but not really knowing where he was. At first I was tempted to call Bridgetta but didn't think she knew anything about all this lurid tabloid fodder about Rodolfo. It would be wrong to involve her, I decided. All I could come up with after my recent expenses coming to the coast and acquiring this cottage and a car was one-thousand dollars, a long way short of Stevens's demands. I knew Rodolfo didn't have any money.

Puzzled and confused, I wandered out into the sunny patio to water the flowers like Maria Jane used to do—in fact, a task she was performing when she'd keeled over dead in the front yard. This morning I felt like Maria Jane must have in her final hour. It was amazing how I could be so happy one minute and so devastated the next after only a knock on the door.

My spirit was buoyed momentarily by the delivery of my car. It was an Essex. I was anxious to test it on the road but I wanted Rodolfo to be with me when I drove it for the first time.

After the salesman left and I had taken an old towel and polished the green car to brightness, I went inside the house to wait for the return of Rodolfo so that I could tell him of the threat from Stevens. Once reunited with Rodolfo, we could plan an escape, perhaps even a return to Kansas where I could introduce Rodolfo to the Middle West. No one would think of looking for Rodolfo on the vast plains of Kansas, and that way he wouldn't be deported back to Italy. Perhaps I could get a job at the new movie theater in Lawrence, managing the popcorn concession although I suspected I couldn't support both Rodolfo and me on that meager salary.

Another knock came on the door to our cottage. It was certainly a busy morning. This knock wasn't as violent as the pounding by Stevens, but it was a steady rapping, demanding entry.

When I opened the door, I came face to handsome face with the dashing swashbuckler of the silent screen himself, Norman Kerry.

Without being invited in, Kerry stormed into our living room. "Where is he?" he shouted at me. "I know he's hiding in here somewhere." He turned and stalked toward our bedroom in the rear.

*****

"Listen, you lovesick little fool," Norman Kerry said, seated across from me in the living room Rodolfo and I shared. "You must have just arrived in town. It's time I taught you a lesson."

"I just got here," I said, "I'm from Kansas and proud of it."

"As if coming from Kansas was any great achievement," he said with a sneer. "I'm from Rochester and so what?"

"Rodolfo on his own agreed to come and live with me," I said. "If he didn't want to stay with you at the Alexandria, that's between the two of you. You've got to let him go. He's in love with me now. He's mine."

"What an asshole you are," Kerry said. "Rodolfo belongs to no one except himself. Like Mae Murray, he's self-enchanted. Do you think he's yours because he fucked you last night?"

"Call it what you want, but I think we have an understanding. I think he loves me."

He sat back on the sofa and without asking lit a cigarette after he rolled it himself. "Rodolfo never knows from day to day whether he's going to be a man or a woman. Sometimes he's the man with me, and I like that a lot. But sometimes he begs me to paint his face like that of an actress before the camera. Then he wants to be raped by me."

"I don't believe that," I said a little too defensively. "He's all man. You're just saying these awful things because you're jealous and want him back."

"Bullshit!" Kerry said, blowing smoke out so aggressively that Bette Davis must have learned and used the technique in those films she made in the forties. "Surely, even a little piece of cornsilk like you from Kansas knows what bullshit is."

"Yeah, we know bullshit in Kansas, and that's just what I'm getting from you." I stood up, defying him. "Get out! You weren't invited here in the first place. I'll tell Rodolfo you called."

"Why bother?" Kerry asked, getting up. "He'll probably be back at the Alexandria Hotel tonight begging me to fuck him. Or at least begging me to give him money. You see, he's a gigolo going with both men and women. Did you inherit money or something? Rodolfo doesn't fuck unless there's money involved."

"I have no money."

"You're not going to get any in this town either," Kerry threatened. "I know the heads of all the studios. The word will get out. You'll not work a day in this town when I blacklist you. What's your name anyway?"

"Frank Stevens," I said. The name of the New York detective was the first I could think of.

"Frank Stevens," Kerry said. "I'll remember that. You'll never see your name up in lights. I'm big in this town. Norman Kerry's name is plastered around the world. My pictures are shown even in Asia. Wherever I go people recognize me. Both men and women are attracted to me. I get fan letters from hundreds of women. Young men send me their pictures and want to spend the night with me. They want to be my boy." He looked provocatively at me. "Boys very much like yourself. I must admit, however, I've never received an offer or a photograph from a boy as pretty as you."

"If I weren't so mad at you I'd be flattered that you think I'm good-looking." I was trembling all over. "Mr. Kerry, I'm sure you're a very nice man. After some things I've learned today, I'm also sure that what you said about Rodolfo is probably true."

He crushed out his cigarette and turned to me. "Exactly what did you learn?"

"I don't know if I should tell you, but I feel I must tell someone and get help," I said, sitting back down. Without being asked, Kerry also sat down opposite me. "I don't know where Rodolfo is, and I fear he may be in serious trouble. Even face deportation."

A panic came across Kerry's face, and in that instance I could tell that he had some genuine feeling for Rodolfo. Far from being jealous, I felt a sympathy and understanding for the actor. After what Stevens had told me, I had slowly come to realize that Rodolfo belonged to the world if he became a big-time movie star. Both men and women would be lined up seeking his sexual favors.

In time and probably sooner than later I'd be tossed aside. I feared I might be junked even sooner than Kerry. The handsome actor could help Rodolfo's career. What could I do? When my money ran out, I'd have no way to support myself and might have to go back to Kansas. Even back in Kansas, I had no place to go— no job—and I'd even sold our modest little house to Mrs. Patee.

Kerry had waited patiently for me to tell him what trouble Rodolfo was in, and after a long hesitation I blurted out the whole interview with Frank Stevens. I even told him that my name wasn't Frank Stevens but Durango Jones. I figured if Durango Jones got blacklisted, I could always change my name. I'd learned that everybody in Hollywood seemed to change their names any way, especially Rodolfo who had the most ridiculously long name in the history

of the world.

"I'm well aware of Rodolfo's troubles in New York," Kerry said. "Both Mae Murray and I know all about them. In fact, Mae is considering casting Rodolfo as her leading man in her next picture. If he does well, she might also cast him as the leading man in the second picture she's got lined up."

"That's exciting news," I said. "The idea of Rodolfo becoming a movie star thrills me, even though I know it means I'll lose him."

"You might not lose him," Kerry said. "If he likes you and views you as something other than a sexual conquest for the evening, Rodolfo can be very loyal."

"I'm glad to hear that," I said weakly, as I was thoroughly confused. I felt I was supposed to hate Kerry but as the morning wore on I found myself drawn to him more and more. He was very handsome.

Kerry settled back, rolling himself another cigarette. He seemed like he planned to stay around for a while. Surely he didn't plan to wait until Rodolfo returned.

"I know for a fact that those police records about Rodolfo have already disappeared from the files in New York," Kerry said. "I have a powerful connection in the mayor's office. As proof of my devotion to Rodolfo, I personally saw that everything was cleaned up on the East Coast and that he was ready to go west without any more interference from the police. Mae had known him back east, and I'm from New York. It's all handled back there."

"Did you know Rodolfo in New York too?"

"That's how I met him. I might as well tell you the truth. Because I'm a motion picture star, I can't go out cruising on the streets looking for beautiful boys to seduce. When I'm in New York, I use this contact. He sends boys to the hotel rooms of men. One night he sent over Rodolfo who hardly spoke a word of English at the time. After a night with him, I was smitten and we've been friends ever since."

"Then if what you say is true, this Frank Stevens is just impersonating a detective. He's a blackmailer."

"If you're going to get involved in Hollywood, you'll learn that half the people out here live and get jobs because they've got something on somebody else. It's how the town functions."

"That's a little alarming," I said. "I could get into big trouble myself, considering my interests."

He smiled at me. I could almost detect a twinkle in his eye. "You can call me Norman."

"Thanks, Norman."

"You don't have anything to worry about," he said. "Unless you become a big star. That's when they start coming out of the woodwork. Everybody you didn't want to know or everybody you had rather forget. It's happened to me."

"I'm sorry to hear that," I said. "What are we going to do about Frank Stevens?"

"I'm glad you said we. It makes me feel like part of the family. I want to be included in what's going on between Rodolfo and you. Don't worry about Stevens. I'll see that the crook is taken care of. When he comes around for his blackmail payment, he'll encounter a member of the Los Angeles Police Department. Before the day is over, he'll be in jail."

As he told me his plan, I feared I was intruding too much too soon in Rodolfo's life. Here I was making commitments and arrangements about the most personal details of his life, and I had known him only for one night.

"You don't have to worry," Norman said. It had quickly become "Norman" and not "Kerry." "Rodolfo and I have shared many times. Since I'm going to become part of your family, I'll let you in on one of my sexual secrets. You'll find out soon enough any way. Rodolfo and I have our own private moments, especially that male-female thing. He's always the female. I'm always the male. Dressing up as a female isn't part of this actor's repertoire. What we really like to do is get a pretty boy like yourself. Rodolfo will then fuck the boy. My favorite thing is swooping down where Rodolfo has been and cleaning out the boy. Licking up all that sweet cream." He looked at me both sternly and seductively. "Does that repulse you?"

"No," I said, suddenly shaking all over. I was getting an instant erection which I felt I could not conceal from Norman.

"I then descend on the boy while Rodolfo sucks my anus," Norman said. "It's great sex. Then we both take turns licking and sucking the boy until he climaxes."

I was breathing heavily. At first I'd been horrified by seeing Norman Kerry at the door. Now I wanted him to stay forever. Visions of Rodolfo and him attacking me flashed through my head as my erection grew bigger.

"We're going to do that to you," Norman said. "Maybe tonight. You want it, don't you?"

"Yes, I do." I looked down at my erection which was being carefully evaluated by Norman.

"Your dreams are going to come true," he said. "You're going to have the two handsomest men in Hollywood assaulting you. The rules are different out here. Back in Kansas I'm sure you had to date someone endlessly before he or she put out. In this town we sometimes don't even wait an hour before we're humping. That's what I love about Hollywood. I like to meet, kiss, then fuck, sooner than later. It's called instant gratification, and this is my kind of town."

"It's what I want to do," I said. "I never really knew this about myself but I think I'm a kind of whore. Repulsive men I run from. But when a man is attractive, especially as handsome as you are, I feel that man could ask me to do anything and I'd do it. Does that mean I have no morals at all?"

"It means your hormones are working overtime," he said. "You'll fit into this town. Thank God you didn't bring your Middle Western morality with you."

"Please stay the day and wait for Rodolfo's return," I said, almost pleading.

"I can't do that," he said. He looked at his pocket watch. "I've got to be at a studio in about two hours. I brought my car and it takes only twenty minutes to drive there so I have some time. There was no room in your driveway. I parked in the driveway of Francis X. Bushman. I've been to many parties at his house. Unfortunately I've blocked him in. He might decide to go out at any time. God knows what he'll do to my car if he finds me blocking him in."

"Don't worry," I said. "I'll go over there and leave a note telling him where you are. He can come and knock on our door if he wants you to move your car."

"That would be just fine," Norman said. "Usually I can find parking space on this street but Adela must be having one of her big lunches." He frowned. "She didn't invite me."

After writing the note, I excused myself to go across the street to the home of Francis X. Bushman, whose films I'd seen, admiring him for his virility. He was the most masculine man in films with the possible exception of Elmo Lincoln, who played Tarzan.

Norman got up and stood before me at the door. "You want me to kiss you just like Rodolfo does, don't you? Tongue and all."

"Please, Mr. Kerry." I had meant to say yes.

"That's Norman to you." He took me in his strong arms and I melted into them, giving myself over completely to him, even being so daring as to reach between his legs to feel the hard flesh waiting to be satisfied.

"When you come back," he whispered in my ear, "I'm going to be in the back bedroom. The same bedroom you shared with Rodolfo last night." He looked deeply into my eyes, and I could hear the rapid beating of my heart. "You know what I'm going to do to you, don't you?"

"I know," I said, reaching for him again so I could taste his lips. The smell of tobacco on his mouth made him more erotic somehow.

"I don't think I've ever met a pretty boy who so obviously wants it as much as you do." He smiled and kissed me again, licking my lips and even my nose before rising to plant a kiss on each eyelid. "Your excitement is going to make it doubly thrilling for me." With his left hand he reached behind me, cupping each cheek of my ass. "This is going to get the pounding of its young life."

Barely able to conceal my mounting excitement, I raced across the street and planted the note on Norman's car which was blocking the Bushman driveway. Hoping I wouldn't run into anybody, I hurried back across the street, noticing the cars parked everywhere and hearing the laughter emerging from the house of Adela Rogers St. Johns. I imagined she had invited all the bigtime stars to her luncheon. Normally I'd be out there spying through the bushes. But right now I had my own rendezvous with my own movie star, and I knew he was ready and raring for me.

As I reached the living room, I locked the front door and headed for the bedroom in the rear. So eager was I for another deflowering, I began to rip off my shirt even before I entered the room.

There, completely naked in the center of the bed, Norman was waiting. I couldn't look him in the face. My eyes were glued to his throbbing erection which I was eager to taste. On unsteady feet I moved toward it, knowing I would never release it until I had thoroughly drained him.

*****

By the time Francis X. Bushman came pounding on the door to my cottage, and by the time Norman Kerry had long ago missed his appointment, I had fallen madly in love again. Perhaps later in the afternoon I'd be in love with Rodolfo too, but as I rushed to the door thoughts of Norman buzzed through my brain like wildfire. He'd taken me where no man had ever gone before.

At the door I confronted Francis X. Bushman, the first major matinee idol of the screen. With his chiseled chin, aquiline profile, and muscular tapered torso, he was an American version of a Greek god. This heroic specimen was "the Gibson man," named after artist Charles Dana Gibson. He was America's first male pin-up, and I was so in awe of him I couldn't speak.

"Where's that old sod, Kerry?" he asked. "He's blocking my driveway."

"He'll be here in a minute," I promised, inviting him to come in.

Bushman stepped into the living room, perhaps suspicious of what he might encounter.

Bushman's initials, F.X.B., were the most famous in America, along with that of his wife, Beverly Bayne, or B.B. He'd just ended a seven-year reign as King Romeo from 1912 to 1918 and had made more than six million tax-free dollars.

At this point Norman emerged from the back bedroom, adjusting his gray suit. "Francis," he said, walking toward Bushman and extending his hand. "Good to see you again. It's been awhile."

Bushman looked first at me, then at Norman. "I thought your heart belonged to that

Valentino boy. Now I see you've taken up with a blond."

"It's like ice-cream flavors," Norman said. "You can like chocolate." He looked at me and ran his fingers through my blond hair. "But you can also sample the delights of vanilla."

As Norman and Bushman sat at my little wrought-iron garden table in the front yard, I was instructed to go and move Norman's car onto the street now that Adela's luncheon guests had departed. Across the street to my astonishment, I spotted a lavender-colored Rolls-Royce. In Kansas all cars were black, and I thought my Essex was daring painted green.

Back in my front yard, Bushman thanked me and offered me a lavender-colored cigarette from a package he was already sharing with Norman.

"I've got to be going," Norman said, reaching over and kissing me on the mouth in front of Bushman, who didn't glance away but studied us as closely as if he were looking at a movie screen.

"Good-bye, Norman," I said, fearing I sounded like a schoolgirl with a crush in front of these worldly sophisticates.

"Thanks," Norman said, kissing me again. "Tell Rodolfo I'll be by to pick up you young boys at eight o'clock tonight. I'm taking you to your first Hollywood party. You'll meet all the big stars."

"He's already with me," Bushman said. "Why does he want to meet any more stars? They call me the handsomest man in Hollywood."

"In case you haven't heard, F.X.B., Wallace Reid has captured that title from you," Norman said.

Norman turned and left, walking up the driveway. Although he kissed me, I had expected more in the way of a farewell. Norman was treating our love affair very casually, but I guess that was the way it was done in Hollywood. I'd have to learn the rituals.

After he'd gone, Bushman invited me to sit with him in the bright sunlight, and he offered me one of his lavender-colored cigarettes. I hadn't smoked much, except with Frank, and I took it cautiously, wanting to appear suave like Norman.

Still a little tongue-tied around Bushman, I

need not have worried. No one in Hollywood was interested in learning who you were. People always talked about themselves, and that was fine with me because I was eager to learn anything about one of the greatest stars of all time, adored by millions around the world. I had seen his *Romeo and Juliet* in 1915, and Bushman was definitely the most muscular Romeo of all time. In many ways he had a profile like that of John Barrymore.

"Norman said you need a job, and I am to offer you one."

"What would that be, Mr. Bushman?"

"Call me Francis," he said.

"I suppose you need me to answer your fan mail," I said. "I hear you already have sixteen secretaries who do nothing but answer requests. Probably that photograph of you the studio distributes. Forgive me, sir, but you look almost nude."

"I am almost nude," he said, "in the briefest of loincloths. The whole world—both women and men—apparently want to see me nude, and that is fine with me. You see." He leaned over and blew smoke in my face but not in an offensive way. Believe it or not back then, blowing smoke toward someone was considered part of the mating ritual. "I am an exhibitionist."

"I don't really know what that is," I said, completely dumbfounded.

"An exhibitionist is a man who likes to take off his clothes in front of other people," he confessed. He reached down to adjust his ample crotch. "For the publicity photographs, I have to wear the loincloth. But, for the private collectors among my fans." He raised an eyebrow and blew more smoke my way. "I am the perfect specimen of a man, and I'm proud of my shape. I'm also known for having the largest penis in Hollywood. It's gargantuan. It's more than Beverly can take. She can only take the first eight or nine inches, leaving all those other inches out in the cold and unsatisfied."

"That sounds like one very, very large penis."

"Men exaggerate about the size of their penis, but when I take you across the street to my studio, I'll show it to you. You'll see that I don't have to fantasize. It's the real thing."

"I would love to see your studio," I said.

"I'm in Hollywood trying to break into the movies. I hope I'm successful like you."

"Before you become an actor you need to be many things, like myself. I was a professional bicyclist, later an acrobat. I drove a meat wagon delivering bloody carcasses from store to store. In all, I had forty-two different jobs until I discovered that I was in great demand both as a photographer's model and a sculptor's model. There are nude photographs of me all over New York and California, and many, many pieces of sculpture. Believe you me, I have a greater body than Michelangelo's *David*. Also the sculptors I posed for depicted my genitals realistically, not like the tasteful little weenie Michelangelo put on *David*. I look more like Hercules."

As the afternoon progressed, Francis seemed a bit lonely as Beverly was in San Francisco and he wanted someone to talk to. I had thought that bigtime movie stars had endless appointments during the day. If Francis had been planning to go somewhere in his lavender-colored Rolls-Royce, he seemed to have forgotten about it.

His eyes were a bit sad as he revealed to me a scandal that had brought him low. Amazingly, I had not read about it in the Kansas papers. Apparently, the local newspaper editor in Lawrence didn't figure it was news fit to print.

Francis's marriage to Beverly Bayne had been kept secret because the studio feared that audiences would lose interest in them since they were no longer "attainable."

But the tabloids learned that before Bayne, Francis had not only been married, but was the father of five children. His contract with Metro forbade him to disclose this fact which came out in the divorce proceedings. Lurid accounts claimed that the super-idol of the screen was also a wife-beater and that he also beat his children. Francis had denied these rumors, and told me too they weren't true, but across the country theaters refused to show any more Bushman/Bayne films. After being hailed as the best known name and face in the world, Francis X. Bushman at an early age found himself retired, although with his millions still intact.

Across the street, Francis showed me his house, including a boudoir in lavender just like his Rolls-Royce and his cigarettes. He let me look at all the publicity beefcake photographs of himself and five statues of himself in the nude. His genitalia was as pronounced as he claimed it was, at least in the sculptures.

Back in his private library he revealed photographs of himself with a frontal view. "Mr. Bushman...I mean Francis," I stammered. "I didn't know men had cocks that big."

"Only a few on God's earth, I'm exceptional. You'll probably seduce many men in your day but I could just bet that you'll always remember Francis X. Bushman for having the biggest penis ever."

"I'm sure that's true," I said. "It's very impressive. But I don't exactly know what kind of work I can do for you."

"You know how to drive, of course," Francis said. "Remember I told you I used to drive a meat wagon. I need your help in a modern-day equivalent of driving a meat wagon."

"That I don't understand at all."

He laughed. "I need you to make certain deliveries for me. Delivering the Francis X. Bushman meat, so to speak. You can use my Rolls-Royce. Certain rich collectors in the Los Angeles area want nude photographs of me and reproductions of my sculpture." He pointed over to a series of plaster nudes of himself which ranged in size from four to eight feet.

"I could do that."

"The job pays a hundred dollars a day, but the work is not steady. It's only on occasion I'll need your services."

"That's incredible. I never heard of a delivery boy making a hundred-dollars a day."

Francis smiled. "But, don't you agree, these are exceptional deliveries?" He smiled again. "Let's call them special deliveries."

"I'd love to have a job like that."

An enigmatic look crossed Francis's face. "There's another job I would like you to perform for me."

I had been in Hollywood long enough to know what that meant. Eagerly I moved toward him but, to my surprise, he pushed me away. "No, no, not that. I'm not Norman Kerry." He got up suddenly and went over to a cabinet and removed a long object like a penis. "Have you ever seen a dildo?" he asked, handing it to me.

"Never." I fondled the object, finding it very erotic.

"Some of my biggest fans want me to mold a dildo from my body, and being the true exhibitionist I am I have agreed. Both men and women throughout the world will want a dildo modeled from the actual penis of the great Francis X. Bushman. Years from now when my films have turned to dust, future generations will still talk of the Francis X. Bushman dildo and will insert it in their anuses or up their vaginas."

The idea was so astonishing and revolutionary to me that at first I didn't know how to react. As a conversational partner, little cornsilk me was clearly outmatched by this towering figure of the screen who in real life appeared even more formidable. "But what sort of job could I do to help you with your dildo? You mean, distribute reproductions of it?"

"That too." He looked over at me the way I'd seen him emote in *A Romance of the Dells*. "When the artist comes to pose me for my dildo, I want you to be in the studio with me. Your job will be to see that I am kept erect at all times. It's important that the world see Francis X. Bushman extended to his fullest glory, and not an inch less. For the job, I will pay you the sum of one-thousand dollars."

*****

For the party Norman took Rodolfo and me to the Garden of Alla (later changed to the Garden of Allah). Little could I have imagined at the time that this mansion was going to become my home during most of the decades I spent trying to become a movie star.

The then Garden of "Alla" was the home of Alla Nazimova, one of the most exotic women who ever blazed across the silent screen. At the time I was taken to her mansion, Nazimova's position in the silents was far greater than that of Greta Garbo in the Thirties. I had seen the films of Nazimova at the Patee Theater in Lawrence and thought this Russian actress was a goddess, although not quite as alluring as the vamp, Theda Bara.

Norman told us that Nazimova had paid sixty-five thousand dollars for this California Spanish house at 8080 Sunset Boulevard. She'd remodeled it and built a swimming pool in the shape of the Black Sea. The area in which she'd moved was still undeveloped and the end of the line for the Big Red Cars trolley line from the heart of Los Angeles.

Even though it seems impossible to imagine today, this section of Hollywood was viewed as country back then. The road that led to Laurel Canyon was still dirt with its citrus and avocado orchards. Farmhouses stood to the east, growing beans and other vegetables. There were orange groves and cedar trees along with palms.

After Norman had assured Rodolfo that Frank Stevens would be dealt with tomorrow morning, Rodolfo's good spirits returned as he'd won the part in *The Married Virgin*. He felt stardom was at hand.

Norman rushed off to find Nazimova, leaving Rodolfo and me alone in her garden, which the actress had planted with masses of semitropicals such as poinsettia, hibiscus, mimosa, loquat, bamboo, ferns, and birds of paradise. It was a true Garden of Alla, with exotic birds of prey darting about.

Rodolfo grabbed me by the arm. "Norman has penetrated you, hasn't he?"

"He's probably told you," I said. "I won't lie. We've had sex together."

Instead of being jealous, Rodolfo smiled. "I'm glad. I never really was going to leave Norman. He's good for my career. I was planning to sneak off and see him privately for sex and not tell you. Now that he's fucked you, the three of us can have sex together. That's what Norman likes anyway." He kissed me passionately on the lips. "But let's not talk of that right now. I don't have sex on my mind. I want to see the name of Rudolph Valentino splashed across the world just like Norman Kerry. I do not want scandal in my life like Francis X. Bushman. Scandal can ruin a career."

I had already told Rodolfo about my involvement with Francis X. Bushman that day, and he demanded to know every detail. He was vastly intrigued. I want some day to have a dildo made of my own penis. It may not be as big as Bushman's, but it will be bigger than most people can take. In my life I won't be able to get around to fuck all the people who want me to fuck them. With the dildo, I can do it by proxy. You must promise not to tell Norman. He would be very jealous."

"Is someone using my name in vain?" Norman asked, appearing out of the shadows. "Nazimova will see us now." He led us to a vast tiled living room which rested under a beamed ceiling. The sofas and armchairs were upholstered in purple velvet. I had decided that all big stars liked either lavender or purple. The room evoked my vision of a European baronial mansion with its massive fireplace, grand piano, and gilded candelabra.

In the hallway stood Alla Nazimova dressed in a gown of peacock feathers. I had read much about this actress, including the fact she'd been born on June 4, 1876 at Yalta in the Crimea. Her command of English was limited, but her 1906 appearance on the stage as *Hedda* electrified audiences. She stood before us feline and pantherlike. When she spoke, her Russian accent was marked but her enunciation good.

Even though Norman had told us that she was a lesbian, preferring the company of the most beautiful young girls in Hollywood, she could also relate seductively to men. She gave Norman a wet kiss on the lips before turning to meet Rodolfo who would later become such a major figure in her life.

As we stood in this baronial parlor, it was inconceivable to me at the time that Rodolfo and Nazimova would grace the screens of the world when they would later star together in *Camille*.

Finally, Nazimova turned her attention to me, if only briefly. She extended her hand and it took me an awkward moment before I realized I should curtsy and kiss her hand. In Kansas Maria Jane had taught me little about handkissing. I was a bit disappointed I got only a hand from Nazimova. When she'd met Rodolfo for the first time, she'd kissed him on the lips— and a very wet kiss it was. When Nazimova kissed she apparently believed it should be an exchange of saliva among friends.

She looked me over carefully before turning her eagle eye to Rodolfo. She seemed to be comparing us. "Nazimova has a great instinct for sensing talent in the theater. A greater instinct than anybody in Hollywood."

I'd already realized, even before meeting Francis X. Bushman, that stars were not modest in talking about their beauty or their talents.

"I think Rodolfo is on the verge of great stardom," she pronounced with such authority that you believed it was true. "He could not have been a star until now. The Twenties are rapidly approaching. Hollywood will completely change in the Twenties." She looked over at Norman with a slight contempt. "Your World War I good looks will still be around. But Hollywood in the Twenties, I predict, will embrace the foreign and exotic look in both men and women. Rodolfo and I will no doubt become the biggest stars of the Twenties."

"Thank you," Rodolfo said, almost gushing. "I needed to hear that. I'm about to star in a big picture."

Nazimova never gave her attention to any one person for very long. Even though predicting major stardom for Rodolfo, she cut him off as if signaling she didn't want to hear about his big picture. She focused on me again, however, briefly.

"When Norman told me your name was Durango Jones," she said, "I found that amusing. I thought I'd be meeting a star of Western pictures. But you're not like your name at all. Not rugged and handsome as I presumed you would be. You are instead the prettiest boy I have ever met. But it will spell your doom in motion pictures. You need to find some other type of work. Perhaps you could become a great agent. Managing the careers of others."

Those were the last words I wanted to hear from a grand movie star. But perhaps Nazimova was right. How could she possibly have known that I'd become the most successful agent in Hollywood history for the last fifty years of my life, managing some of the greatest names in show business long after I'd abandoned my pursuit of stardom.

At the time I protested Nazimova's pronouncement about my future career—that is, as much as one dared protest in her presence. She delivered her pronouncements like God issuing the Ten Commandments. "I thought good looks could get you into pictures."

"Handsome men can get into pictures," Nazimova said. She turned again with a slight contempt and cast a sharp eye at Norman.

"Sometimes a handsome face is all an actor has to offer the camera. A handsome face can take an actor far even if he has no talent." She turned once more to me. "But in your case you are not only handsome, you are stunningly beautiful. No leading lady of the screen would want to appear opposite you. You are prettier than any leading lady in Hollywood."

Our cozy quartet ended at that moment, as the door opened and at least two dozen guests filed into the living room, commanding Nazimova's attention. Norman was busy greeting old friends he hadn't seen in a long time. Taking Rodolfo under her control, almost like a manager, Nazimova personally introduced my boy friend to the cream of Hollywood society.

Like an abandoned bride at the altar, I was left alone, not knowing anyone and too shy to go up and introduce myself.

The evening was not a total disaster for me, far from it. At a light tap on my shoulder, I turned to stare into the famous face of my alltime idol.

Theda Bara stood before me. "Be a sweetheart, darling, and tell the waiter to bring me a whiskey. Tell him not to be stingy and no ice. Whiskey should never be served with ice."

"Miss Bara," I stammered. "I....."

"I know, I know," she said a bit impatiently. "You're awed out of your damn skin to meet The Vamp herself. Off camera I am a real woman who needs her whistle wet."

As I signaled the waiter to bring Miss Bara a whiskey, I was surprised that she'd used such an American expression as "whistle wet." Somehow that didn't seem appropriate for the Goddess of the Nile.

Whiskey in hand, Miss Bara turned her serious attention to me. "And who might you be other than the most beautiful man I have ever seen in all my born days, and in Hollywood I've had my pick of the beauties."

"I'm Durango Jones."

"Surely not," she said in amusement. "That's a made-up name. No one is named Durango Jones just as no one is named Theda Bara."

"Your name is not Theda Bara?"

"Would you believe Theodosia Goodman?"

I was crestfallen. Surely the star of Fox's *A Fool There Was*, directed by Frank Powell and based on Rudyard Kipling's "The Vampire," could not be named Theodosia Goodman. That

made her sound like the daughter of a Greek dry goods salesman.

"I've seen all your movies at the Patee Theater in Lawrence, Kansas. That is, before my mother, Maria Jane, forbade me to see them. She thinks you are the most evil woman of all time and that your films would corrupt innocent me."

"Your mother is right," she said. "There is nothing I like better than corrupting innocent youth. If it's all right with Nazimova, I can arrange to use her bedroom for an hour or two." In one gulp she downed the generous glass of whiskey the waiter had presented. "I want you to take me upstairs and fuck hell out of me. I bet that's been your dream all your young life. To fuck The Vamp herself. Amazing, isn't it? You've probably just landed in Hollywood. For all I know this is your first Hollywood party. And right away you get to fuck The Vamp." She laughed slightly, touching my arm. "Not that that is a big distinction. You wouldn't be the first handsome young man in Hollywood who has fucked The Vamp." She moved closer to my ear, whispering in it before injecting a flick of a tongue. It was so delicate I imagined that it was the kiss of a serpent's tongue. "If there's one thing I have a passion for, other than whiskey, it is handsome young men."

I was breathing so heavily I'd become nervous, even shaking a bit in her presence. Although my dream had been to become her leading man, it was merely a fantasy. I never expected to be faced with the reality of the situation. In the actual presence of Theda Bara, I wanted to run and hide. I saw no way out except to tell her the truth. Maria Jane had always told me that when confronted with such a situation as I was now facing, only the truth would do. "Miss Bara," I said, slightly stammering, "you said you liked handsome young men. That is something we share in common. I too make love to handsome young men."

At my revelation, the woman known as "the reddest rose in hell" leaned over and kissed me on the lips, an act Nazimova had reserved for Rodolfo and Norman, but not for blond me. "In that case, let's be sisters," she said, linking her arm with mine and heading for the bar. "You might have loved me as The Vamp, but those films are killing me. Believe it or not, I am a serious artist, or at least I was before fans such as yourself started believing what they saw on the screen. Even in interviews I have been forced to live the role of The Vamp."

"After telling you my secret, you can be yourself with me," I said, not really meaning it. Theda was still The Vamp, even though I liked the off-screen woman far more than the fearsome female creature on the screen at the Patee. Theda on screen frightened the hell out of me, but in real life I found her strangely comforting. At least she had rescued me from the loneliness of this party where my two boy friends had deserted me to pursue their own interests or careers with no regard for me.

At the bar sipping another whiskey, Theda said, "A man named Goldfarp made up all those lies about my being born just around the corner from the Sphinx. I've never been to Egypt. My whole background was middle-class Jewish. Ohio, no less. But my real origin didn't sell newspapers or make me a big star of the screen."

"But you must have cooperated in the illusion," I said hesitantly.

"Not really," she said. "I thought the wild stories spread about me were so ridiculous no one would believe me. But I didn't know at the time that people want to believe illusions more than they want the truth. That explains the whole success of films."

"I had no reason not to believe all the stories about you," I said. "All my life I'd heard about evil. Well, evil is a hard thing for a boy to understand. But when it's wrapped up and packaged as you are on the screen, it's something to see and understand more clearly."

"That is so very true. But the films destroy artistic expression. Films record only the hysterical, the intense, the fever point, at least my vamp films. They have nothing to do with real life."

"I don't know why that has to be," I said. "Films can be about real people and situations."

She paused for a moment. "Perhaps so but nobody would want to see them. People are surrounded by mundane events. They don't go to the films to see everyday occurrences. Whenever I make a film that deviates from my vamp image, the public stays away in droves. My fans don't want to see me as a sweet, or-

dinary gal like Mary Pickford. They want to see me seducing a man to his death, bringing about his ruin, destroying his family. Shit like that."

"I understand your feelings, but you virtually rescued me from the dullness of growing up in Kansas," I said. "You taught me to fantasize. You let me escape from the dreariness of my life. You taught me to dream. You, in fact, led me to Hollywood."

"Thank you and I appreciate that. But for me Theda Bara has made me a virtual recluse. I am even forbidden to attend a public Turkish bath, and I adore them. I had to have one built for myself. If I make appearances on the street, I have to be heavily veiled. Not like myself in real life at all. The vampire image dictates my life." She reached out and gently touched my hand. "Of all my films, which was your favorite?"

"*Cleopatra.* When I saw you in that film, I actually believed you were the modern reincarnation of the ancient Egyptian queen."

"I believed it myself," she said, sighing and seeming to contradict everything she'd said up to now. "A lot of time, energy, and money went into that film. The Sphinx rose in Ventura County. The waterfront of Alexandria was built in Los Angeles. The battle at sea was staged at Balboa Beach. I virtually lived in the Metropolitan Museum with its curator, trying to get inspiration for my costumes." She smiled. "I told the press: 'I breathe Cleopatra. I sleep Cleopatra. I am Cleopatra.'"

Having been taught hand-kissing from Nazimova, I bent over and kissed Theda's hand. "I never thought I'd ever get to meet the Serpent of the Nile," I said facetiously.

"You're a nice young man," she said. "Come by some day for tea. I'll give you my address and phone number. Since we share an interest in handsome young men, perhaps you and I can work out a deal. We might end up sharing our young men. You find a particularly well-endowed one who's great in bed, and you set me up. I can do the same for you."

Of all the invitations I had expected to receive in my life, an invitation to tea from the sex goddess known as "Arab Death" was the last thing I could possibly have conjured up. And the invitation to share handsome young men with Theda Bara was beyond my wildest dreams, even those I conjured up to masturbate by.

"Speaking of well-endowed men," Theda said, "here comes the king of them all."

I turned around at the bar to stare into the face of Elmo Lincoln, the screen's first Tarzan. I'd seen him in D.W. Griffith's *The Birth of the Nation* in which he'd played several roles. One was that of White Arm Joe, the owner of the dingy gin mill broken up by the handsome Wallace Reid. In *Intolerance* I'd seen him as the towering muscular warrior, Belshazzar's "Mighty Man of Valor," battling the barbaric hordes of Cyrus the Persian. It was as Tarzan that I best remembered him, clad in a leopard skin that covered most of his chest. In spite of the physique photographs of Francis X. Bushman, the bare chest of a man was considered even more objectionable and scandalous than female nudity in those days. Elmo Lincoln showed a lot in that film. I'd stolen a movie still of him from the Patee Theater and had taken it home and hidden it under my mattress where I had often retrieved it to use as an aid in masturbation. Now, to my surprise, I was sandwiched between the two fantasies of my Lawrence boyhood: Theda Bar and Elmo Lincoln.

Elmo took my hand and smiled deeply into my eyes as Theda introduced us. "When I'm with Theda," he said, "she claims I am the most well-endowed man in Hollywood. But I hear at other parties she makes the same claim for Francis X. Bushman."

"It's a Mexican stand-off," Theda said. "I've been to bed with both of these pussy stretchers. I think it's a tie."

"It's not a tie, bitch," Elmo said, although he softened the word "bitch" and it wasn't as hostile as it might have sounded, as there seemed to exist a genuine affection between the two. "From what I've heard, I've got Bushman beat by an inch."

"I couldn't judge," Theda said. "When those final inches from both Francis and you went into me, I was seeing stars at that point. No men before or since have equaled the two of you. You can't use me as a judge."

"Isn't that an amazing coincidence?" I asked. "Only today I agreed to go to work for Francis X. Bushman."

"You did?" Elmo's face seemed lit by a burning fire. He took me firmly by the arm as he excused himself from the presence of Theda Bara, promising we'd be back soon.

"You and I need to go to the men's room," Elmo said. "Nazimova has installed a set of six urinals side by side because her parties are so well attended by heavy drinkers." He led me into the empty men's room and directed me over to the fifth and sixth urinals at the far end of the toilet.

As I stood beside him looking down, he unbuttoned his pants and pulled out the longest, thickest penis I'd ever seen except in the photographs of Francis X. Bushman. He reached over and took my right hand, placing it on his rapidly expanding cock. "Play with me. Skin it back. I want you to get it fully hard."

Trembling all over, I ran my fingers across the thickness of it and pulled back the foreskin to reveal a huge purplish head. As I masturbated him, his penis swelled to its fullest length. I didn't have a ruler but I could swear that it was more than a foot long.

"If you're going to work for Bushman, you'll surely get to see his dick fully extended," Elmo predicted. "Take a good look at mine. When you see what Bushman has, get in touch with me. I'll give you my phone number. I want you to meet with me and tell me the absolute God's truth, something that the Bara bitch won't do. I want to know if Francis X. Bushman has more than a foot of thick dick like I do."

"I promise, I promise," I said with growing excitement. The thrill of playing with so many of Tarzan's inches enthralled me. I was sweating profusely.

All the excitement wasn't confined to me. Elmo was obviously responding to my skilled hand. Suddenly he exploded into the urinal. He reached down and rescued some of the thick cream, rubbing it against my devouring lips where I eagerly licked his fingers clean.

At this very moment, Wallace Reid chose to walk into the urinal. "Hi, Elmo," he called out. "I haven't seen you since we made *Intolerance* together. Griffith is crazy, isn't he?"

"Reid," Elmo said. "Nice to see you. This here boy is named Durango Jones—that's his real name."

Wallace Reid came and stood next to me at the urinal. With my dick hanging out hard from the excitement of having played with Tarzan, I didn't know what to do. Considering the unusual circumstances of meeting the handsomest male star in Hollywood, I felt it inappropriate to shake his hand, especially considering where my hands had so recently been.

At the urinal, Wallace reached into his trousers and unbuttoned them, pulling out his cock. It was almost like an unveiling for me. I hesitated a long moment but I couldn't keep my eyes away from that view for long. When Wallace shook it a few times for my benefit, making it grow larger, I stared down at it. What I saw was the world's most beautiful cock. In all my days, I had never seen a penis of such loveliness with a real silky look to it.

"It's only half the size of Elmo's," Wallace said. "But at least a woman can get fucked by it, and a pretty boy like you can enjoy sucking it. You can fit my dick into your mouth. Elmo would choke you."

Embarrassed, I stopped staring and buttoned up, going over to the sink to wash up and prepare myself for a return to the party after this long sojourn in the men's room.

After urinating, Wallace came over to me and stood by me at the sink, as he washed his hands. Elmo had left the men's room without washing his hands.

"I hope you don't become a picture star," Wallace said.

"Why?" I asked. Here was the second movie star of the evening suggesting that he didn't think I should be in films.

"If you break into the movies, I will no longer be known as the handsomest man in films," Wallace said.

"That's very flattering," I said, staring at his beauty as reflected in the washroom mirror. "You know I live in the cottage next door to Adela Rogers St. Johns. I understand that you come there often to visit her."

"In fact my roadster will be there tomorrow at noon," he said. "After I have lunch with Adela, I would like to drop in to see you. Will you be home? You know Dr. Hutchinson, don't you?"

"I will indeed," I said with mounting excitement. "If you're coming to see me, I will defi-nitely be there. And Dr. Hutchison is my landlord. I am friends with his daughter, Elizabeth.'"

"There is a great big favor I want to ask of you," he said.

"Anything for you. Anything at all."

He kissed me tenderly on the lips, a kiss that made my entire mouth sting with pleasure. He took one look at himself in the mirror to make sure he was properly groomed. At the door, he paused. "Until tomorrow."

Barely able to control my giddiness, I too checked my appearance in the mirror and, feeling reassured, went out the door only to encounter Rodolfo a few feet away near potted ferns. He was standing with a young woman.

"Durango," he called out to me. "Come over here." I did as he said, wondering who this young woman was. She didn't look like any movie star I had ever seen.

"Durango's my roommate, the one I have been telling you about," he said to the attractive young lady. "Meet Jean Acker. I have know her only thirty minutes and in that little time I have proposed marriage to her. She has accepted. Jean is going to become my bride."

Chapter Three

To this day I have never understood why Rodolfo proposed marriage to Jean Acker after just meeting her. In the few hours he'd spent with me, sharing his hopes and dreams, marriage had never been spoken of. Just as I planned never to get married, I mistakenly assumed that Rodolfo would never marry either.

My involvement with Norman and my learning some of the lurid details of Rodolfo's past life as a gigolo had convinced me that my initial dream of enjoying a romantic life with Rodolfo in a vine-covered cottage was never meant to be. Just as I had decided that Rodolfo belonged to the world, I had made the same decision for myself. My new slogan in Hollywood was going to be, "So many men, so little time."

Even though involved with Rodolfo in the imbroglio with Jean Acker, I was still making plans for tomorrow which I hoped centered on the seduction of the handsomest man in Hollywood, that divine Wallace Reid with the world's most beautiful dick.

Rodolfo's plan to marry Jean Acker caused me astonishment but it did not break my cheating heart. After driving us from the party back to our cottage, Norman was furious. None of his previous screen performances had ever generated such emotion. On the way back I was eagerly expecting a sexual encounter with the three of us as erotically outlined in a scenario already presented to me by Norman. The prospect of what was about to happen had given me an instant erection.

Norman had learned of Rodolfo's proposal of marriage to Jean Acker from an enraged Nazimova who had called Norman upstairs to her library for the lecture of his life. Apparently Nazimova held Norman totally responsible for Rodolfo's outrageous proposition.

While in the library, Norman had learned that Jean Acker was Nazimova's "love of my life." Norman had also learned quite a bit about Miss Acker as Nazimova was very articulate in defending her turf. Then twenty-six years old, Jean Acker was part Cherokee and had been a dancer in vaudeville and a two-bit actress appearing not on Broadway but in various roadshow productions. Under her Louise Brooks haircut, she had a pretty face but hardly remarkable by the Hollywood standards of the day.

Even at the party where all the women were flamboyantly dressed, especially Nazimova in her peacock feathers, Jean Acker had appeared in a severely tailored suit and looked very mannish. She was not living with Nazimova at the Garden of Alla but had been installed at the Hollywood Hotel the way Norman Kerry had booked Rodolfo at the Alexandria.

Using her great clout at Metro, Nazimova had convinced studio bosses to put Jean under contract at two-hundred dollars a week, a goodly sum back in those days, although I could make more as a delivery boy for Francis X. Bushman. Norman had learned that even though Metro had signed Nazimova's protégée, they didn't know what to do with her, finding her "too ordinary looking."

Before casting her in a film, Metro had released some early publicity photographs of her showing her barefoot in shorts and a striped blouse but I felt she looked matronly, even though only in her mid-twenties. Both Norman and I couldn't understand Rodolfo's attraction to her.

Rodolfo offered no help in our enlightenment. "You two are all American," Rodolfo said. "You don't understand the romantic impulses of the Latin lover. We are ruled by our emotions. It is this dynamic quality that will make me a great star. On the screen women will never know from moment to moment what I will do to them. I might grab them and lift them onto my brilliant white stallion and carry them away with me in the desert where I will repeatedly rape them as their fingers dig into my back. At first they will resist me but before the end of the rape a woman will be begging me to repeat the rape. My greatest dream in life will be to portray an Indian Chief with all the virginal maidens lined up at the door to my teepee where I will deflower them one by one before turning them over to my braves to rape."

Norman and I had a completely different reaction to Rodolfo's fiery outburst of his ambition. I agreed with Nazimova's assessment of him and could easily see how the audiences of the rapidly approaching Twenties might fall for such a dashing, romantic hero with his exotic good looks. Norman Kerry, in contrast, was so decent and handsome that he could play a minister if need be. No one would ever believe Rodolfo as a preacher.

"You are crazy," Norman shouted at Rodolfo. "I've always known it but overlooked it. If you go through with this marriage, you and I are through. As of tonight, my financial support of you is over."

"I don't need you to support me," Rodolfo said. To my shock, he slapped Norman's face but he did not strike back. He rubbed his face instead and looked amazed that Rodolfo would hit him. Instinctively and perhaps stupidly I moved between them, thinking that might prevent Norman from hitting Rodolfo.

"That's it!" Norman said. "I can have anyone in Hollywood I want. I don't need to get mixed up with your sick little girl boys."

Norman's words rained down like fireballs on me. Surely he didn't mean to include me. "What about me?" I demanded to know. Before he'd climaxed inside me, Norman had told me he was madly in love with me and wanted to spend the rest of his life devoted to only one pursuit—the penetration of my beautiful rosebud which he had spent more than an hour sucking and licking before invading with his sturdy shaft.

"Durango," he said with a wry amusement, as he rubbed his face from Rodolfo's stinging slap. "If that's your real name. No one is named Durango. I find you a great kid. A wonderful guy. One of the prettiest boys I've ever fucked. Blond and beautiful. You're great sex. You'd do anything in bed to please your man, and I like that. Your dick is fantastic and so are your silky balls. And you must know what I think of your rosebud. Nonetheless you're still a type in Hollywood. It's filled with beautiful blond boys, and I want to get around to enjoy as many of them as I can while I'm still in my prime. The only reason I was going to continue to have sex with you was because Rodolfo would be there." He looked forlornly at Rodolfo. "I like to fuck little blond boys on one-night stands. But when it comes to falling in love, only the foreign, the exotic, the mysterious will do for me." He looked again at Rodolfo who turned and walked toward the bedroom, pulling off his shirt.

"This is not the end," Norman said to me. "Who knows? You may become a big-time movie star too. I just know Rodolfo will. He'll probably become the biggest male star of all time. For all you know, I might even end up playing your father in a film to be shot in 1928. That's how it works in Hollywood."

"Please don't go," I pleaded with him, taking him by the arm. "I need you. Rodolfo needs you. You're a star."

"You and Rodolfo don't need me any more," he said. "Believe me, both of you can find greater sponsors in Hollywood than me. Bigger names. I predict that."

"I wish you'd stay," I said. "You might help me bring Rodolfo to his senses."

"No one can bring Rodolfo Valentino to his senses," Norman predicted. He pulled me to him. "Give me a kiss. You have the most succulent cherry-red lips in Hollywood. Some time when I have need of your services, I might give you a call." He kissed me long, hard, and passionately before releasing me and heading out the door.

Rushing to the back bedroom, I discovered Rodolfo entirely nude selecting a wardrobe for himself, this time apparently as an apache dancer. He turned to me. "I want you to dress up like a cowboy in your denim and a flannel shirt. Wear that pair of boots you brought from Kansas."

"Why are we getting dressed?" I asked, completely confused by his actions.

"We have a job tonight," Rodolfo said. "I told the client about you. He definitely wants the both of us."

Still not at all sure what was about to happen to us, I did as Rodolfo commanded and tried to make myself up like a Western cowboy. "I want to talk about your proposal of marriage to Jean Acker, the lesbian."

"That is my business," he said, coming up and standing before me. He took my hand and placed it on his dick. "If you want to continue to get penetrated by what I've got between my legs, you'll shut up. You'll do as I say. Sometimes I'll be with you, and sometimes I'll be gone for days. We must have total freedom in our relationship. No one owns anybody else. When I'm gone, you'll be free to do as you wish. I know that there are many men in Hollywood you're eager to sample. Some I will sample with you. Others I prefer to devour on my own. You must understand that. Total freedom between us."

"Okay, I guess," I said with great hesitancy. I truly understood nothing. "I don't really know how your marriage to Jean Acker figures in all this. Why would any man want to marry a lesbian?"

"I will never reveal that to you, my little pet golden boy," he said enigmatically, kissing me lightly on the lips before going over to try on a leather pouch that encased his genitals seductively. He tossed a similar pair to me. "Try these on. Our client will want to see us in matching pouches."

"Who is this client you keep talking about?"

"One of the biggest names in motion pictures. A really big movie star."

"What will we have to do?"

"Not much," Rodolfo said. "I've been to his mansion many times. His tastes in sex are very simple. You will not have to be penetrated."

"I wish you'd tell me who it is."

"I like to keep you guessing until you actually meet him," he said. "I bet you've seen all his pictures. He also pays more than any other male client in Hollywood. Now that I can't depend on Norman for money, I have to see that you and I make some very good money. Film work is so unreliable."

"How much money will he pay us?"

"One-thousand dollars for the night."

I was astounded, as I'd heard that many boys who hired themselves out to men got only ten dollars, maybe twenty at the most. "That's a lot of money."

"It's especially a lot since you'll get to meet a big star who might cast you in one of his films. He also doesn't ask a lot."

With me dressed as a cowboy from the Middle West and Rodolfo as an apache dancer, we headed up the driveway where a long, purple-colored limousine waited to take us to some mysterious mansion. The moment I spotted the limousine, I knew our client must be a big star. Apparently, all the big stars in Hollywood had purple cars.

*****

It was only after we'd gone five blocks that I noticed that our chauffeur was Japanese. He was clad in a purple uniform. By now I had come to expect that color everywhere. In Kansas nothing had ever been purple, not even the curtains at the Patee Theater which were scarlet.

At the corner of Yucca and Argyle, the limousine pulled into a Spanish-style mansion with an overlay of Oriental fixtures. As the chauffeur directed Rodolfo and me to the front door—painted in gold—a liveried footman dressed like a fantasy in an Oriental nights film opened the door for us.

I was very nervous as we were ushered inside the door which evoked the entrance to a temple. Once the door was shut, a Japanese houseboy appeared, dressed only in a loincloth. He dropped to the floor in a bow so low his forehead touched the pink marble surface. Rising up, he said, "I am here to serve you, masters." He ushered us into a private library behind a large living room that looked like a Japanese garden.

"Who lives here?" I whispered to Rodolfo, who didn't answer me but smiled enigmatically. We were asked to be seated on upholstery covered in purple and red silk, the finest and most elegant I'd ever seen. Although I didn't know who our host was, I could certainly assume he was not only rich but had a fondness for objects Japanese.

Rodolfo maintained his amused silence as I took in the glory of the room with its rare art and objects of treasure. The houseboy returned with hot wine for us to drink. Until that night, I never realized that wine could be served hot. The drink relaxed me, and I stopped shaking.

Within minutes after drinking the wine, the houseboy opened the door to usher in our host, who was clad in a gold silk robe. I recognized him at once. He was Sessue Hayakawa, a towering star of the silent screen. When he'd appeared opposite Fannie Ward in the 1915 *The Cheat*, directed by Cecil B. De Mille, I had been enthralled. Mrs. Patee had shown the film twice that day, and I had stayed for both screenings.

Playing the villain, Hayakawa had shocked audiences of his day when he'd ripped Ward's dress off her shoulders and branded her exposed flesh with a hot iron. One woman sitting near me in Mrs. Patee's theater had screamed. Although his portrayal of such a "heavy" had shocked audiences, it curiously enough had made Hayakawa some sort of pre-Valentino sex symbol. Of course, today's audiences would not know Hayakawa were it not for one "comeback" film, *The Bridge on the River Kwai*.

After all, foreign men were supposed to do brutal acts like branding women. Audiences expected the Prussianesque Erich von Stroheim to skewer babies on his bayonet, crap like that. No clean-cut American actor like Norman Kerry could get away with such savagery, however.

"Mr. Hayakawa," I stammered, "I'm so happy to meet you. I've seen all your films."

Rodolfo didn't say anything but shot me a glance of reprimand. Turning to Hayakawa, he said, "We are here to serve you, master." Dropping to his knees, he bowed low, his forehead touching the floor. Taking my cue from Rodolfo, I too bowed low before the Japanese actor.

"Get up, my beautiful young boys," Hayakawa said. "Both of you will serve me well tonight." He walked over and kissed Rodolfo on the lips before turning to me. "I have tasted every inch of your beautiful Latin lover's body. It is descended from the Gods." He smiled seductively at me. "As for you, my blond beauty, I have a great hunger to eat every inch of you." It sounded very cannibalistic to me. "Your lips are as red as the cherries that grow in Japan in the summer." He reached over and kissed my lips, licking them with his skilled snakelike tongue.

All mention of sex disappeared as the houseboy returned with more hot wine and some Japanese delicacies for us to sample. Hayakawa smiled benignly as we ate but didn't enjoy any of the refreshments himself. He asked no questions about us at all but spoke of the movie business, especially his own role in it.

I was quickly learning that Hollywood actors spoke only of themselves, and you didn't need to tell them anything about yourself, which was just as well since they led such glamorous lives and had so much to talk about. In contrast I was just beginning to live the experiences that would one day fill the pages of my memoirs.

"I wanted to be in the Japanese Navy and I studied that as a career," Hayakawa said. "But I abandoned that dream and decided I wanted to be a Shakespearean actor instead. But Thomas H. Ince had other plans for me. That producer decided I was going to be the reigning star of the silent screen, and so it has come to be."

Although a big star, Hayakawa wasn't exactly the reigning star of the silent screen. But who was I—a paid call boy—to challenge this great star? Surprisingly and in spite of his Oriental appearance, Hayakawa also appeared in decidedly American roles, playing an American Indian, for example, in *Last of the Line*. Wisely Ince had made sure there were no close-ups of Hayakawa in case American audiences would doubt his role as an Indian.

Rodolfo had also told me of his dream to play an American Indian in films. I found it surprising that this Latin lover from Italy and this Oriental potentate from Japan wanted to appear as American Indians. I certainly didn't. I wanted to be a glamorous male movie star smartly dressed in black tie.

Tears welled in Hayakawa's eyes as he spoke of Tsuri Aoki, the lovely Japanese film star who was also a stellar light on the silent screen. "She is so beautiful. I want to spend the rest of my days locked in her arms, making mad, passionate love. I dream of her day and night. She is my fantasy come true."

Again I hardly felt it was my place to challenge these assertions by Hayakawa. Perhaps he did love Tsuri Aoki but that didn't stop him from calling two handsome young men for God knows what forbidden pleasure he had in mind.

We were soon to learn what those forbidden pleasures were, as Hayakawa's face changed, growing stern like a military commander, perhaps something he'd learned when studying for a naval career. He ordered us to a large bedroom in the rear where incense burned. It was draped in lavish silks and dimly lit. The atmosphere was forbidding, romantic, and intoxicating.

Once the houseboy had left us, Hayakawa told Rodolfo to take off all his clothes. "As the Americans say, I want you naked as a jaybird for this workout." Slowly and seductively, like a stripper, Rodolfo removed all his clothing except for the leather pouch. "Leave that on for the moment," Hayakawa said. "I will personally remove that." He turned to me. "Now my blond lovely. You are even more beautiful than Tsuri Aoki, and she is the world's loveliest creature. You, too, take off your clothing but very slowly. I want to enjoy every inch of that body of yours as it is unveiled."

Again taking a cue from Rodolfo, I too stripped for Hayakawa's eyes as he studied me intently, almost like Ince directing one of his films. When I was totally nude except for the leather pouch, he told me he would remove that personally.

Hayakawa commanded us to lie down on a large bed side by side. The feel of the mauve-colored satin sheets thrilled me—that and being shoulder to shoulder with Rodolfo.

Hayakawa didn't do a thing for me. He stood over us and dropped his robe. He was completely nude underneath it. Although I am sure that there are men with smaller penises in the world, I had up to that time never seen one as minuscule as that which was attached to Hayakawa. His small cock seemed buried in a mass of black pubic hair, and his testicles might more appropriately belong to a nine-year-old boy. He was certainly no Francis X. Bushman or Elmo Lincoln. I silently prayed that I would not be called upon to arouse that little sleeping dragon.

Hayakawa bowed over Rodolfo and slowly removed his leather pouch. When he'd pulled it completely from him, he planted tiny kisses on Rodolfo's penis and testicles. Moving over to me, he sighed as he removed my leather pouch. Stripping me completely nude, he said, "It's as big and beautiful as Rodolfo promised me." He fell on my cock, planting the same type of little kisses that he'd bestowed on Rodolfo.

Reaching under a satin pillow, Hayakawa removed a long feather which he proceeded to use on both my genitals and those of Rodolfo's. Within minutes he had produced two of the most impressive erections. Hayakawa pulled back my foreskin, spat on my cock, and descended on it to suck voraciously like a vulture devouring road kill. His skilled lips were like a suction pump. I moaned in ecstasy before he deserted me to perform the same act on Rodolfo who cried out in pleasure.

I did not know then and I can't remember how long this continued. Hayakawa would bring me to the point of eruption before taking his mouth from me and attacking Rodolfo. Finally, when I could take this no more, I grabbed his head and held him down firmly on me, exploding in his mouth. He slurped and slurped until I had long been drained and wanted him to get off me. Suddenly, Rodolfo's cock was at my lips. I opened my mouth and devoured him, sucking him as Hayakawa had sucked me. But at his moment of explosion, Rodolfo withdrew from me and violently penetrated Hayakawa's throat, depositing his sweet cream there.

If I thought this was going to be the end of the evening, I was wrong. Hayakawa took us into a Japanese bath off his bedroom where he bathed and oiled our bodies, exploring every inch of our flesh until he seemed to tire of that after about two hours.

It was already four o'clock in the morning when a nude Hayakawa rose up and stood over us. "I do not mean to be disrespectful," he said. "Both of you provided me with great entertainment, and I want to book both of you every Saturday night until you become big-time movie stars like me and can order your own call boys to perform." He smiled down at us. "In spite of your allure, the big entertainment of the evening is about to begin."

Putting on a red silk robe this time, Hayakawa disappeared as the houseboy came in carrying a royal blue silk robe for Rodolfo and a cerise-colored silk robe for me, a color that seemed to match the shade of my lips.

After putting on the robes, the houseboy directed us down a long hallway filled with Japanese prints and into a dark chamber where only a spotlight was turned on to illuminate a slab of granite.

Trembling, I sensed some sadistic torture was about to take place. "I've had it," I whispered to Rodolfo. "I'm out of here."

"No, you little fool," Rodolfo said. "I've been through this shit before. All you have to do is watch."

The door opened and a large Japanese man clad in a loincloth came into the room carrying a hot branding iron. In a far corner of the room he placed the weapon in an iron pot which I thought was for illumination but was actually fire.

The man was very fat and looked like a Japanese wrestler. Two other rather thin Japanese men came into the room escorting a young boy who appeared to be Mexican and about fourteen years of age. He was completely nude and shaking in fright. The strong men placed the boy on the slab of granite and then proceeded to bind both his hands and feet with rope. Seemingly aware of what was about to happen, the boy was crying softly. I wanted to intervene to rescue him. "The boy permits it," Rodolfo whispered in my ear. "He's being highly paid."

At the sound of a clashing cymbal, Hayakawa entered the room and came and stood before us, dropping his robe. He was completely nude. With his left hand he reached to fondle my genitals, and with his right hand he did the same for Rodolfo.

At a signal from Hayakawa, the Japanese wrestler in the corner removed the branding iron from the fire pot and headed across the room. Sensing his approach, the young Mexican cried out even before the iron burned into his right buttock. The smell in the room was of burning flesh, and the boy let out a piercing scream of such anguish that I shuddered, imagining myself in his place.

At the moment of impact, Hayakawa erupted in orgasm, having risen to his full length of three and a half inches. His hands hadn't left our genitals, but he had exploded in orgasm upon seeing the boy branded.

Putting on his robe again, Hayakawa quickly left the room trailed by Rodolfo. I too followed them, although I hoped that the fun and games of the evening were over.

An hour later after we'd dressed and been given ten one-hundred bills by the houseboy, we were ushered into the main living room. Dawn was breaking across the pink Hollywood sky.

"You both have pleased me greatly, and I am very delighted with you," Hayakawa said. "I might use both of you in one of my pictures. That is, before you become the star of your own films."

"We'd like that," Rodolfo said, bowing low before Hayakawa.

"We would indeed," I said, echoing Rodolfo and also bowing low.

"I must be off," Hayakawa said. "I'm going to meet Tsuri Aoki. She is waiting for me. I will penetrate her vaginal walls. She accepts me even though it hurts her. When my mighty tool enters her, I make her bleed. Even though she screams in pain, she knows she must accept my massive invasion." With that pronouncement, he was gone.

I turned to look at a bemused Rodolfo who said nothing. By silent agreement, we both let Hayakawa have his fantasies. After all, he was a star of silent pictures, and what were they but fantasies?

In the years to come, as I pounded some of the finest butts in Hollywood, I encountered

Hayakawa's brand on some of them, including those of three young men who went on in time to become legends of the silent screens of the Twenties.

*****

The next morning Rodolfo didn't speak of our previous evening, but kissed me good-bye as he departed for a wardrobe fitting. He said it would be "very late" tonight when he returned to our cottage. He might not be back, in fact, until tomorrow morning.

I might have been disappointed were it not for the fact that I was expecting Wallace Reid after his luncheon with Adela Rogers St. Johns. If knowing Wallace Reid depended on my being friends with my landlord, Dr. Hutchison, I was determined to solidify that friendship.

Without being invited, I knocked on the door of Elizabeth Hutchison in the front house. A matronly attendant answered and asked me in. I hadn't called on Elizabeth since her epileptic attack following our visit to Sister Aimee's temple, although I had spoken to her several times on the phone.

Appearing well and fit, Elizabeth was enjoying the morning sun on her enclosed porch. She introduced me to a friend of hers, a red-haired beauty named Adrianne Hodges, who looked like an early version of Arlene Dahl.

After the three of us had enjoyed morning tea, Elizabeth excused herself to take some medicine, promising to return soon.

Adrianne took my arm and led me to the Hutchison garage where she showed me the limousine she'd arrived in. Her father, a banker, was a friend of Dr. Hutchison. The limousine had been specially designed for Adrianne by General Motors. I was stunned when I saw it, as it far excelled the limousines of Hayakawa and Francis X. Bushman.

Adrianne's vehicle was like a simulated stagecoach, all black and yellow, with an open place in front for the driver. The upholstery was in leopard skin, a motif also evoked by the uniform of her chauffeur. I thought Adrianne must be very rich, and I envied her, although I knew fame and fortune were but around the corner

for me too.

Adrianne wrapped a mink coat around her shoulders which she retrieved from the rear seat and walked with me in the garden. The morning was hardly chilly enough for fur and I was in shirt sleeves but she wore the fur anyway. She was also loaded down with enough sparkling jewelry to attend a coronation ball. In the garden she told me her father was very wealthy, and was doing much to help her promote her career. He'd bought her a mansion in Beverly Hills and a bungalow in Santa Monica where she could entertain directors.

After Adrianne had left in her "stagecoach," I stayed on and had another cup of tea with Elizabeth. This time she invited me into her library which was filled with pictures of Wallace Reid. From the library a large picture window overlooked the driveway of Adela Rogers St. Johns. "Whenever Adela tells me that Wallace Reid is coming to visit, I sit here for hours waiting for him to drive up so I can get a glimpse of him. Adela wants to introduce me but I'm too shy."

At first I was tempted to inform her of my upcoming meeting with Wallace Reid, but I held back until I learned more about Wallace's interest in wanting to meet Dr. Hutchison. There was something rather suspicious about the whole thing.

"In my condition I know no man will ever marry me," Elizabeth said. "I must fantasize. I live for the movies, and Wallace Reid is the handsomest man in the world. The woman he loves will certainly have been blessed by the Gods."

After assuring Elizabeth that I was certain she'd find a husband one day who would love her for the special person she was, I went wandering through the neighborhood. The Rolls-Royce of Francis X. Bushman was gone from his driveway, and I had not received a call from him yet. I suspected he didn't have a job for me at all, but I sure hoped he did.

Since arriving in Hollywood, I had done virtually no exploring at all. I was eager at least to walk through the neighborhood where we lived. Later, after my rendezvous with Wallace Reid, I planned to drive to the Hollywood Hotel. Rodolfo urged me every day to go there, although, to my surprise, he never seemed to patronize the place, preferring the Alexandria instead.

I had waited by the phone all morning thinking Norman Kerry might call to apologize for his barging out in anger the previous evening, but he didn't. Perhaps later in the day Rodolfo and I would hear from him.

I stopped in for some bacon and eggs at Hollywood and Gower. Outside the window I spotted an ancient crone with a hunchback. My waitress, who confessed that she was from Texas and had come to Hollywood to be an actress, told me the old woman stood there forlornly every day. "We call her Stella Dallas," the waitress said.

Stella Dallas fascinated me. She wore an extremely wide and droopy straw picture hat with a long, frayed ribbon resting on her golden yellow hair which was badly dyed. Dozens of beads hung from her mauve print dress. On nearly every finger was a ring, and her wrists were weighed down with clanking bracelets.

Stella's lean face with its hollow cheeks was bone white with flour. Fuschia pink rouge brilliantly spotted the hollows of those cheeks. Her makeup was applied to make bee-stung lips, although Mae Murray practically claimed exclusive rights to that mouth.

I couldn't figure out what Stella Dallas was up to. Surely picking up a man, any man, was a remote possibility.

She seemed to stare into space, as if looking into a window to the past. I knew that some time in her life she'd had a greater day. Perhaps before the turn of the century, she'd been a famous beauty or a celebrated mistress of someone important. It was unlikely she'd ever been a movie star, even in the early days of film, since they didn't have movie stars that far back.

A good-looking young man asked if he could join my table. He looked like a virile hero of the movies. He projected a masculine strength that was vaguely familiar. Even though I didn't recognize him at first, I knew him at once from his screen roles when he introduced himself as Richard Barthelmess. Discovered by D.W. Griffith, he seemed to be appearing in every film in town—*The Hope Chest, The Girl Who Stayed Home, Three Men and a Girl, Peppy Polly, I'll Get Him Yet,* and *Scarlet Days.*

"I haven't seen you in here before," he said.

"I'm new in Hollywood. Durango Jones is the name."

"You're very beautiful," he told me. "Almost too beautiful to be a man. But no one is named Durango Jones."

"You are very handsome yourself," I said.

"Not as much so as Wallace Reid."

Although on the tip of my tongue, I let discretion rule. I almost confided in him that I had a rendezvous with Wallace Reid later in the day. As a town, Hollywood was getting smaller.

I found Barthelmess intriguing. He immediately gave me permission to call him "Richard." One of the first rumors I had heard since arriving in town was that Richard got his start in life by posing for dirty French postcards which were now considered collectors' items. In some respects, that exhibitionism reminded me of Francis X. Bushman.

"Your career certainly seems to be taking off," I said. "And you don't look yellow to me at all."

Richard burst into laughter. He knew at once that I was referring to the role of "The Yellow Man" he played in Griffith's *Broken Blossoms.*

"I think Lillian Gish and I were a little too sensitive in that film," he said, lifting his coffee to his perfect lips. "People expected a spectacle from Griffith and got a fragile and sensitive film instead. The public just didn't get it."

"I enjoyed it immensely," I said. Actually I didn't like the picture at all. "I cried when you killed yourself in the film."

"I'm glad somebody appreciated it. Actually Griffith must not be too disappointed in my yellow man performance. There's talk he's buying *Way Down East* and plans to cast me as an honest farm boy opposite—guess who?—Miss Lillian Gish again."

"Good luck."

"Are you an actor?" he asked.

"Trying to be."

"Perhaps I'll help you get started. I'm becoming more powerful in this town every day." With that pronouncement, he reached over as his hand dug into my thigh.

"If you want that hand to travel, it is perfectly welcome to do so," I said. I'd become a total whore after only a short time in Hollywood.

"That's an invitation I'm going to accept."

I settled back in the seat and opened my legs giving Richard free access.

"They grow them big wherever you come from," he said. He lowered his voice. "I'm glad you're letting me feel you up. I can only get excited by a man with a big cock. Many with average size dicks do nothing for me. How about you?"

"I'm versatile. I take all sizes."

"That's good to hear," he said, "because I'm not really huge. I'm not small either. More average in size."

"Fine with me."

He smiled at me. "I think we should team up. Give it a try. I like what I feel. It's getting harder and thicker by the second."

"You'd better stop," I said. "I won't be able to stand up."

As the waitress approached, he removed his hand from my crotch and stared out the window at Stella Dallas. "She is always there guarding the corner as if it were her private turf. Sometimes I stand and watch her walk into the shadows of Hollywood Boulevard."

"I wonder where she goes at night."

"No one knows," he said. "All that we know is that we'll see her standing silently in the sun in the exact same spot the very next day."

"I'm sorry we can't spend time together today," I said. "I'd really like to get to know you."

He looked over at me and licked his lips. "I want to taste you."

"I'm handing out samples. I'd be honored to go to bed with Richard Barthelmess."

"With your looks and that big thing between your legs, you'll probably be a bigger star than I am." He wrote down a number on a piece of paper.

"Please call me when you're lonely. Although I suspect a pretty boy like you is always fully booked. In case you aren't, I'd like to spend a night with you. Maybe several nights. If you go to bed with me, you can later tell all your friends that you seduced D.W. Griffith's greatest male star." He blew me a slight kiss but disguised it a bit in case anybody was looking.

After he'd gone, I carefully folded his telephone number in my wallet. Perhaps Richard Barthelmess would replace Norman Kerry in my life. He'd certainly not replace Rodolfo, however.

Still with plenty of time on my hands before meeting Wallace Reid, I inquired from the waitress about a plaster castle across the street. "Some mysterious gentleman lives there," she said. "We call him the baron."

Crossing the street, I stood in awe of the castle with its turrets and winding steps. The interior was enclosed behind a thick, iron-studded door that was ajar. From that door emerged the baron with a walking stick, apparently out for a constitutional. He was partially bald with a glistening scalp which he attempted to cover with long strands of overly dyed black hair. Dangling from his neck was a black cord holding a monocle. In full makeup, he had a chalk-white, powdered face and blackened eyebrows. He was attired in a formal black frock coat and gray pin-striped trousers. With his silver-tipped cane, he headed down the street, leaving the door to his castle partially opened.

When he was out of sight, I decided to look inside, figuring I could make up some excuse if caught. Once behind the facade, I was startled to discover there was no furniture or decoration of any kind, only the dusty imprints of coats-of-arms which had been removed from the walls.

I climbed a winding staircase that led to what appeared to be a doorway. Reaching the top, I discovered the door was fake like a stage prop. Downstairs again, I tried all the doors, discovering that they too were dummies. Only one was real, and it led to a tiny little rat's nest, with a leaking toilet, an army-type cot, and a little table in the corner with a hotplate.

The baron's "castle on the Rhine" was just a fake movie prop.

I figured I'd sampled enough of Hollywood life for one morning, and was eager to get back to our cottage where I'd bathe and dress up as appealingly as I knew how for my meeting with Wallace Reid.

Even as I hurried home, I couldn't believe that the handsomest actor in pictures was coming to see me. What could he possibly want?

*****

After sampling the fried chicken of Adela Rogers St. Johns, Wallace Reid appeared on my doorstep and knocked gently. Ready and raring to go for more than an hour, I had been waiting for him in the living room. I'd even borrowed one of Rodolfo's cerise-colored silk shirts which I hoped matched the shade of my lips, knowing how men were attracted to my mouth. I'd brushed my blond hair until it was lustrous.

Ushering Wallace into our living room, I was in awe of Hollywood's handsomest man, a giant figure standing six foot three. Too bad he never lived to play F. Scott Fitzgerald's Gatsby. He would have been perfect for the part, absolutely convincing as a Princeton man.

Long before Rodolfo was to bring the brooding sex symbol to the silent screen, Wallace appeared in total contrast—a naïve and kindly appealing all-American matinee idol. No woman would want Rodolfo for a son— only a lover, but many older women would want to adopt Wallace Reid as their very own. Younger women would surely have other ideas for this Greek god.

Only that morning I had read in a magazine that Wallace Reid "was the kind of man who fills his wife's boudoir with red roses."

Although innocent love was his specialty, I hoped my encounter with the great Wallace Reid would not be another Mary Pickford movie, more a Theda Bara film.

Wallace was hailed for his million-dollar blue eyes, and those very eyes that were gracing the screens of the world were looking at me, a curious mixture of piercing but languorous.

"Good to see you, Durango," he said. "I've been thinking about our getting together today ever since I met you."

"I'm really honored to have you here." I took the hand of this modest and unassuming pin-up boy, and he held mine for a long time, continuing to look into my eyes. At that point, I had fallen hopelessly in love with America's first male flapper. A magazine had said it all: "Wallace Reid is jazzing the jug business by day and hugging the jazz business by night," whatever in the hell that meant.

As we sat on the sofa talking casually, past images of him flashed through my mind, as I conjured up Wallace on the screen in roles that ranged from a barbarian in a helmet to a race-car driver.

"I never intended to be an actor," he confessed. "Actually I dreamed of a career in cinematography. My daddy, Hal, was both an actor and writer, one of the early birds in the film industry. He introduced me around various sets when I was just a teenager."

"I bet you were spectacular even then."

He raised an eyebrow provocatively just as he did in the movies. "Perhaps you're right. I found that a lot of producers in Hollywood like teenage boys. I got many offers." He raised the other eyebrow. "Both on and off the screen."

I laughed and spontaneously reached and touched his hand. He held it for a long moment before releasing it. He wanted coffee and followed me to the kitchen as I made it. "Jesse Lasky spotted me one day in a G-string playing an Indian."

"I'd like to see you in a G-string," I said.

"Or without one," he said, looking bemused. "Or without one."

"Jesse liked what he saw because he offered me a contract with Famous Players," Wallace said.

Later when I was to meet Jesse Lasky himself at the Hollywood Hotel, he confided that Wallace was the "most charming, personable, and handsome young man I've ever known." He'd smiled enigmatically. "And the most cooperative."

Back on the sofa as we sat drinking coffee, a frown crossed Wallace's perfect brow. "Lasky is working me too hard, a film a month. I'm like a frozen custard machine turning out the goodies. There is no time to rest, no time for myself. He says by 1921 I'll be the top male star in films. But, to get there, I have to do one racing car picture after another."

"I'm sure you'll get there," I predicted. "You're practically there already. But you do look a bit tired. Perhaps you'd join me in the back bedroom. I'm great at giving massages. It might relax you, and you can sleep this afternoon. Catch up on your rest."

He took my hand and raised it to his lips. "You know I want to go back there with you. But there are strings attached." His face grew severe. Up to then, I had never known that Wallace Reid could look so stern. "Before the massage, before the bed, there is one thing you must agree to do for me."

I looked dreamily into his eyes. "For you, anything. I mean that."

"Good." He pressed his hand against his head. "I've got these awful migraines. They are killing me. The headaches started when I had a freak accident on the set of this damn car-racing movie. I was hit in the head by a prop and my head was gashed open. It required eleven stitches." He bent over and parted his chestnut hair, revealing a deep scar. "Fortunately, my face wasn't gashed and my hair covers the scar. A doctor prescribed morphine to stop my pain." He sighed and pulled me close to him, so close I could smell his sweet breath. "I've been on morphine ever since. I got hooked on it."

I settled back in shock as I took in this strapping figure of a man. More than any other male star Wallace seemed to exude post-war optimism. Here was one of the biggest names in Hollywood—right up there with Douglas Fairbanks, Charlie Chaplin, and Mary Pickford—admitting to me that he was a drug addict. If word of this got out, it would make headlines around the world.

He searched my face and I think at that moment he knew I would keep his secret.

"Last night you told me you knew Dr. Hutchison. If you asked him and told him it was for me, he would give me my weekly supply of morphine."

"Are you sure?" I asked. "Maybe he'd say no. It might not seem right to him."

"You've not been in Hollywood for long. Doctors here will more or less do what a star asks of them. I don't want to approach Dr. Hutchison myself, just in case he might turn me down. It would be too compromising." He looked searchingly at me. "But you could do it for me."

"I can try," I said. "I'll explain how it would bring relief to your headaches so you could get on with all your fine work on the screen."

"Yeah, play that up." He finished the rest of his coffee and slammed down the cup. "Of course, I'd pay generously for the morphine." He paused. "Very generous. And I would also do something else. Adela has told me that the

doctor has an invalid daughter. I understand that I'm her favorite movie star. She collects pictures of me. Tell the good doctor that I would come by every week to call on his daughter. I think her name is Elizabeth."

"That would thrill her beyond belief," I said. "I just know it. The doctor will be very pleased."

Wallace took my hand again and squeezed it hard. "You'll do it? I mean, right this afternoon?"

"Right after I leave you, I'll go and call on Elizabeth. She'll know how I can get in touch with the doctor. I'll pretend I need a physical examination. I'll go to the doctor's office. He's a very respected doctor, and I just know he wouldn't do this for anybody. But for you. For Wallace Reid."

"You're putting yourself out for me, and I appreciate that. You'll soon see just how much I appreciate it."

I smiled at him. "You don't have to unless you want to."

"You want it, don't you?" He leaned closer to me, gently nibbling my ear.

"Ever since last night at Nazimova's urinal, I've been thinking of nothing else."

"It's a pretty one I've got, right?"

"The world's most beautiful along with the world's handsomest face."

"You flatter me. Unless you saw me as that Indian in the G-string, you don't know the rest of my body."

"I've not seen every single inch of it, but I want to."

"And I want to share it with you too—in fact, I think I'd enjoy that. All the producers and directors who have had me have been ugly. You're young and beautiful. With you, it'll be different. With those other men, I just lay back in bed until they'd had their fill of me. Then I get up, put on my clothes, and go home."

"But with me..." I was eager to hear more.

"With you, we could begin by kissing. Your mouth is cherry red. I make no promises after that." He reached for me, pulling me only an inch from his mouth. "Let me begin by kissing you and let's take it from there. I might go where I've never gone before with another man."

I melted into his arms.

FADE OUT

While memories of the divine Wallace Reid danced in my head, I felt glorious in the late afternoon. I had just been fucked by the world's most beautiful cock, and Wallace had virtually signed a guarantee that he'd never fucked a boy before. His homosexual experiences, or so he had claimed, had been confined to lying back on a bed and being the recipient of fellatio.

I got him that way, too, but oh so much more. He assured me that our love in the afternoon session would be but the beginning of many blissful fucks. He said I was much tighter than the women he'd known, and fucking me provided far more pleasure for him than entering the loose cavity of a woman. Whether he was telling the truth or not, I didn't care. I just loved hearing him say it.

Dr. Hutchison couldn't have been more charming and understanding. He credited me with saving the life of Elizabeth, and said he would do any favor—within reason—for me. He would be honored to prescribe morphine for Wallace Reid if that would keep him from constant pain, and he was doubly honored that Wallace would call on his daughter once a week. "That would give her a reason to live," he'd told me in his office. "I might as well tell you. Elizabeth has attempted suicide two times before. I fear the third try might be fatal."

The doctor said that the morphine would be delivered to my cottage every Saturday, and that I could then turn it over to Wallace. Elizabeth would prepare a lunch for us at noon every week. "For professional reasons," the doctor said, "I prefer to keep my distance. But I send my respects to Mr. Reid. Tell him how much I admire the clean-cut all-American men he plays on the screen. Tell him he should make more racing-car pictures."

After promising I'd deliver his message to Wallace, I left the doctor's office with one goal in mind. I was going to visit the already legendary Hollywood Hotel. Rodolfo had been asking my impressions of it, and I'd kept postponing going there. What I didn't want to tell Rodolfo was that I was a bit shy.

Now that I was a confidante of such big stars as Elmo Lincoln, Francis X. Bushman, Norman Kerry, Nazimova, and Theda Bara, I felt I could more easily name-drop if I encountered any other big-time stars at the hotel.

Arriving at the hotel at the corner of Hollywood Boulevard and Highland, I selected a rocker on the front veranda to watch the parade of stars come and go. A rambling wooden structure with a wide front porch, the hotel had only a few shrubs to screen it from the boulevard.

Built as a resort at the beginning of the century, it was surrounded by orange groves and fields of golden grain. At first there were only two bathrooms for the occupants of its thirty bedrooms. As film luminaries started to check in and demand private bathrooms, more bedrooms and bathrooms were gradually added. After all, you couldn't rent a room without a bath to stars who were known for spending hours at a time in their bathrooms.

Thursday nights, I was soon to learn, the rugs were rolled back, and you could dance to "Alexander's Ragtime Band." One Hollywood magazine claimed that the hotel was the "Sodom and Gomorrah" of the West, and I was eager to find out if that were true.

I had inquired at the desk if John Barrymore were in residence, as I had my letter of introduction from Margaret which I planned to present to him. The attendant told me that "Jack" was due in just a few weeks, as he was performing on the stage in New York but was coming West. I was very excited at the prospect of meeting John Barrymore.

In eager anticipation, I had to wait two long hours before I spotted my first movie star. With three large trunks carried by bellboys, Blanche Sweet arrived to check into the hotel.

Memories of the Patee Theater in Lawrence, Kansas came back to me. Blanche Sweet was the star of the first film I'd ever seen in 1911. It was *The Lonedale Operator.* Even today the film is known for introducing D.W. Griffith's revolutionary cutting techniques. As a courageous telegraph operator, Blanche fought off payroll bandits until the law came to her rescue. She was windblown and pleasantly plump, and I had found her robust allure more appealing than the more ethereal visions of Dorothy and Lillian Gish. Lovely, winsome, or even helpless creatures belonged on the screen. There would also be roles for the Mae Marsh types of the world. But it was good to see a husky, cornfed girl on the screen too.

As I stood looking at Miss Sweet, visions of her 1916 appearance in *The Ragamuffin* danced before my eyes. It was directed by William DeMille, the brother of Cecil. In person, Miss Sweet was just as alluring and beguiling as she was on the screen.

As I stood gazing in awe at her, I found it daunting to think that she might have reached the peak of her career between 1910 and 1914. That would make her virtually the first film star. She seemed to speak directly to the audience through the camera.

Throwing caution to the winds, I came close to her. The manager had just told her that her suite was still being readied after it had been vacated by Carl Laemmle, the big cheese at Universal Pictures. The manager apologized profusely and invited her to sit down on a red sofa while he ordered her some afternoon tea. Seating myself near her, I too ordered tea as it seemed the fashionable thing to do.

When tea was served, I kept glancing at Miss Sweet, and she boldly returned my attention, smiling only once. It wasn't a demure Lillian Gish smile but a genuine smile like I'd known back in Kansas.

Unable to be silent any more, I blurted out. "I'm honored to see you in person, Miss Sweet. I live next door to Adela Rogers St. Johns, and she told me if I ever met up with you, that I was to deliver her regards. I'm Durango Jones."

"No one is named Durango Jones," she said. "But my real name is Blanche Sweet. Sweet. Like sugar. You can't make that up. All my family is named Sweet. But, let me assure you, I'm the only sweet one in the brood."

"That you are," I stammered. "I've seen all your pictures."

"That's nice," she said. "How is Adela?"

I didn't want to tell the truth—that I was yet to meet Adela. "She's fine. Only today she entertained Wallace Reid for lunch."

"Dear Wallace," Miss Sweet said.

I didn't want to tell her how well I knew Wallace, far better than I knew Adela Rogers

St. Johns. But I had read stories that Adela had written about Blanche Sweet. Adela had found that Miss Sweet had "a personality so stimulating, so intriguing, so full of interesting vibration, that she'd certainly never, never bore you."

Miss Sweet looked me over carefully. "Did anyone ever tell you that you're the most beautiful boy who ever landed in Hollywood? Don't let Wallace Reid get a glimpse of you. Right now he may think he's the handsomest man in Hollywood but you've got him beat. I didn't know God made men as beautiful as you. In fact, you're so God damn beautiful you're almost indecent."

"Thank you, Miss Sweet."

"You can call me Blanche."

"Blanche."

"It looks like you've got a great body to go with that face of yours. I'd sure like to see more of that body. Perhaps you'll come upstairs with me." She turned and looked in disdain at the front desk. "If that fucking suite of mine ever becomes available."

Shocked and a bit nervous, I didn't know how to proceed with the conversation. I was surprised that female movie stars said "fucking" in hotel lobbies. My ears couldn't quite believe that Blanche Sweet was inviting me upstairs for sex. But then hadn't Theda Bara done the same thing? In Hollywood, if a woman wanted a man, she didn't seem shy about asking. I admired the spirit of that. But there was no way I could deflower Blanche Sweet. Wallace Reid perhaps. Rodolfo Valentino. But not Blanche Sweet.

In desperation, I blurted out. "I'm flattered by the offer, but I already have a steady girl."

"Who's the whore who got there before me?" Blanche demanded to know.

"Theda Bara."

"That rotten vamp bitch."

At that point, the manager arrived informing Blanche that her suite was ready. Without turning to look at me or even say good-bye, Blanche, along with her trunks, headed upstairs.

Sitting forlornly in the lobby of the Hollywood Hotel, I regretted that I wasn't a bisexual like Rodolfo or Norman Kerry. If I were, I could have seduced two of the biggest stars in films, Wallace Reid and Blanche Sweet, all in one day.

In the adjoining restaurant, dinner was announced. I decided to stay on at the hotel for a little longer because I just knew that Rodolfo would not be returning home for the evening. I'd be lucky if I got to see him tomorrow. It didn't take a great imagination to figure out where he was. No doubt in bed with Jean Acker.

I was jealous and furious even though I had no right to be. If Rodolfo were seducing Acker, what was I doing? Waiting home mending his socks? Hardly. I was lying in bed getting a violent pounding from Wallace Reid who at his climax fell on me and bit my neck savagely. He'd assured me it was the tightest fuck of his life and the greatest orgasm, and I believed him. I knew he'd be back for more. Not only my ass, but those deliveries of morphine from the office of Dr. Hutchison.

The dining room was filling up quickly. It was a big, rambling restaurant opening onto the rear gardens. The names of its famous guests were inscribed in gold in the ceiling. Costing fifty cents each, meals were served family style, and you dined lavishly.

One of the thrills of dining here was that you never knew what producer or star you might be seated next to. Dorothy Gish, perhaps, a frequent visitor. Certainly D.W. Griffith who was known to hang out here. Even the great Mabel Normand, "as beautiful as a spring morning," as Mack Sennett described her. Gloria Swanson was a frequent visitor, or so I had been told.

Anticipating sharing my table with one of these stars, I looked up at the approach of my dinner companion. "Mind if I join you?" he asked.

It was Charlie Chaplin!

*****

With basic instinct, I knew not to tell Charlie Chaplin that I'd seen all his films. The entire world had seen his films, and he didn't need to hear it from me. I was completely astounded to find that the most important film star on earth didn't have a retinue of bodyguards and studio chiefs following him around salivating.

Later I learned from a bellhop that Charlie was hungry and had wanted dinner while waiting for the arrival of a very young girl which he claimed he wanted to audition in an upstairs bedroom. The dining room was completely democratic, and bigtime stars sat and gossiped freely with anybody in Hollywood who had an extra fifty cents to pay for dinner.

Being the star he was, Chaplin immediately took the lead in conversation. Stars, I had found, are rarely interested in anybody other than the face staring back at them in the mirror or the image projected upon the silver screen.

"This whole place is a dream," he said, looking around the room at the hungry diners. "It was built on a dream and it has become a dream factory. One day all the beauty that is here will be swept away."

"It's still here," I said. "I live in a cottage that has exotic foliage. My friend, Elizabeth, explained it all to me. Seven different varieties of lupine. The blue is my favorite. Red berries on pepper trees. Mariposa tulips. Even yellow pansies."

"You sound like a botanist," Chaplin said. "Tell me you're a botanist and don't want to be a movie star."

"I'm no actor," I said, not daring to confide my real ambition. "I haven't decided what I want to do yet. I'm still young. I'm still trying to make up my mind."

"With your good looks, I'm sure you'll try for a movie career," Chaplin said. "The movies were the last thing the developer of this place wanted."

"What do you mean?"

"Back in 1883 a real-estate developer, Horace Henderson Wilcox, owned all this land. It was a ranch eight miles northwest of Los Angeles. He wanted to subdivide the land and create a utopia here. A place where Methodism reigned. He was dead set against alcohol. Anybody who drank liquor was barred from Hollywood. Can you imagine? The way Wilcox saw it, this was to be a real Christian community dedicated to family values."

"It's just as well Horace can't see it now," I said.

With a twinkle in his eye, Chaplin tested his breaded steak and smiled at me. "You're right.

It's just as well." After sampling some mashed potatoes, he looked at me as if seeing me for the first time. "What is your name?"

"Durango Jones."

That twinkle came in his eye again. "No one is named Durango Jones. I won't bother to introduce myself. The whole world knows who I am. I'm famous in some parts of the world that have never heard of Jesus Christ. I've become so famous that it's getting harder and harder for me to lead a private life."

"You must be pursued by fans wherever you go."

"That's true," Chaplin said. "They give me no peace. I dislike the press intensely. What I give the world is on the screen. I don't feel I owe the world the most intimate details of my private life."

"Look what details about the divorce of Francis X. Bushman did for his career," I said, quoting from a magazine I'd read in the lobby of the Hollywood Hotel. "It has practically ruined his career. I work for Francis, you know."

"As a matter of fact, I didn't know." He looked at me with renewed interest. "Exactly what do you do for him?"

"A chauffeur."

"That's most interesting," he said. He seemed to be studying me closely. Was he embarrassed to be dining with a lowly chauffeur?

"I know Francis well. But we were never friends. He and I both worked for the Essanay Company. I remember my first day there. A Miss Louella Parsons was head of the scenario department. I was very rude to her when she gave me a script. I told her that I write my own scenarios. Later I was trying to find a pretty young girl to cast as the lead in my first picture for them. They sent me a woman who had no reaction at all. No emotion. I turned her down. That young girl was Gloria Swanson. She later told me she deliberately was bad that day because she didn't want to get cast in a slapstick comedy with me."

On looking back, my first conversation with Chaplin seemed ironic. By 1950 screens around the world were showing Gloria Swanson in *Sunset Boulevard,* and one of the most memorable scenes in the film is Swanson doing Chaplin, slapstick comedy at its finest.

"Francis is such an exhibitionist," Chaplin said. "He's always at the athletic club walking around in the nude showing off what he's got. I'm told that Elmo Lincoln has something even bigger. What a lot of people don't know is that I'm third in the Hollywood race after Elmo and Francis. I might be called 'The Little Fellow' but most of my growth went into my dick. A lot of the young women I bed complain a lot but that doesn't stop me from plunging ahead."

I was mildly shocked at the turn in the conversation. Sex was the last thing I associated with the screen image of Charlie Chaplin. He was hardly Wallace Reid, much less Rodolfo, not even Norman Kerry.

"So, you're a driver?" Chaplin asked.

"A good one," I said. Another lie. I could drive but I was hardly experienced in heavy traffic. In New York I felt I would pile up the car after only fifteen minutes behind the wheel. But in Hollywood with its wide open spaces, I didn't have much trouble.

"I have a good driver, but he stepped on a rusty nail," Chaplin said. "His foot is badly infected. The doctor said it will be about three weeks before it heals."

"That's too bad. Are you looking for a driver? Francis doesn't employ me very much—just part-time"

"I do need a driver in the afternoon," Chaplin said. "I'm at the studio the rest of the time." He leaned over and whispered confidentially to me. "Are you very discreet? Can you keep a secret?"

"Yes, sir."

"Good." He leaned back. "I can trust my regular driver, and I was going to wait until he'd recovered before I resumed this special activity of mine. But I can't wait any more. We must listen to our hormones, don't you agree?"

"I certainly listen to mine, at least since arriving in Hollywood."

"If you drive for me, you must tell no one where we go and what I do." He looked sternly at me, almost threateningly. It was a look I'd never seen in his films.

"I promise you."

"I want you to drive me five days a week—just Monday through Friday. I'll give you one-thousand dollars a week."

I was shocked, as I read that Chaplin was

extremely tight with money. That seemed like an awful lot of money. "I'll take the job," I said, hopefully not too eager. I couldn't imagine where Chaplin wanted to be driven for that kind of money. With Francis and Chaplin paying drivers a fortune, I thought I should seriously consider abandoning my job as a movie hopeful and pursuing the career of a chauffeur instead.

A bellhop came and whispered something in Chaplin's ear. The actor looked at me sternly for one more time, as if undecided if he could trust me or not. Finally, his facial muscles relaxed, and he wrote something down on a little notepad he carried in his pocket. "I want you to meet me at this address tomorrow afternoon at two-thirty."

I looked at the address, not knowing where it was but determined to find out and show up on time.

Chaplin turned and walked away, heading for his urgent rendezvous in one of the upstairs bedrooms.

Finishing my lunch in peace, I even ordered two extra desserts, because at this point in my life I never gained unwanted pounds, but seemed to burn up all the calories I consumed.

Back at the house, Rodolfo was nowhere in sight and he hadn't called either. But at ten o'clock a call came in from Francis X. Bushman. He wanted me to make some deliveries for him at nine the following morning. I readily agreed, figuring I could make the deliveries and still have time to drive Chaplin too. Of course, I avoided telling Francis that I would also be driving Chaplin for the next three weeks.

Deciding finally that Rodolfo was not going to show up all night, I brushed my teeth and was heading for bed as the phone rang again. Thinking it was Rodolfo, I ran so fast to answer the urgent ringing that I almost tripped.

It was not Rodolfo but Theda Bara. She sounded distraught. "Bad things are happening to The Vamp," she said. "The studio is not treating me right. I need you to come to my house at six o'clock tomorrow evening. A photographer is coming to take a very important picture of me. I need you to pose in the background. You must find a gold loincloth for yourself. I have the other props. Will you do this for your favorite film star?"

"Of course, Miss Bar...I mean Theda. I'll be there loincloth and all."

"This photograph is vital. I have so many things to deal with. I may have personified evil on the screen, but the real evil is behind the screen. Please, Durango, be there. Help me."

"I will, I will," I promised.

After hanging up, I felt I'd had a memorable day. Wallace Reid, Francis X. Bushman, Theda Bara, Charlie Chaplin, and an offer from Blanche Sweet. It seemed the only people I hadn't encountered were Mary Pickford and Douglas Fairbanks. Even John Barrymore loomed on the horizon.

None of these screen legends warmed my bed that night. There was only one person I wanted in bed with me, and he was missing.

His name was Rodolfo Valentino.

*****

Leaving the cottage in time to report to work for Francis, I still had not heard from Rodolfo, although I hoped he would show up later in the day. I didn't know how to get in touch with him. When I was at the Hollywood Hotel, I'd secretly anticipated that I might run into Jean Acker or Rodolfo there, as I'd understood that Nazimova paid for a weekly room at the hotel for Acker. But no such luck. After tipping the bellhop, I'd learned that Acker still had her room at the hotel, but she'd not been there for three or four nights.

Across the street, I encountered two Mexican boys who were supposed to help me with the deliveries of Francis's merchandise. It was my hope that these young boys would escape the branding iron of Sessue Hayakawa.

Francis was still asleep in his lavender-colored boudoir. I learned that Beverly Bayne had returned unexpectedly from San Francisco and that the dildo modeling session with the artist had been postponed. I was to drive the lavender-colored Rolls Royce. The limousine was already famous in Hollywood, as Francis had a spotlight in the vehicle that illuminated his famous profile when he drove after dark.

We had eight addresses to deliver the Bushman goodies to. Most of these deliveries were "art" photographs of Francis, and these were to go to the homes of "bachelors" who were great fans of Francis and eagerly collected photographs of him. The Mexicans also fitted three nude statues of Francis into the limousine, each carefully wrapped in blankets for delivery. Fortunately, one of the Mexicans had actually been born in Los Angeles and knew virtually every street in both Hollywood and the larger city. With him as a guide, I used my driving around as a sightseeing adventure.

We rarely knew the occupants of the houses we were delivering to that morning, with two rare exceptions when the owners made themselves known to us. I realized before noon that the collectors of Francis's memorabilia fell into two categories—the "bachelors" who viewed Francis as an erotic sex symbol and who wanted his pictures—perhaps for aids in masturbation, which I of all people could understand.

There seemed another type of collector, too, and these were women. Hollywood back then was a village, and word had spread quickly about what Francis was up to. Some actresses wanted a nude statue of Francis in their gardens just as a conversational piece at parties. It would be today's equivalent of Tom Cruise sending around realistic nude statues of himself for which he'd posed. There was definitely a market for this type of merchandise, even though I felt a little embarrassed peddling it.

At the home of Gloria Swanson, we actually met the recipient of Francis's tallest statue. "Don't think I'm buying this statue because I have some romantic fantasy about Bushman," she said, emerging into her garden dressed as if attending a formal dance even though it still wasn't noon. She was in full makeup. "I'm having a party tonight, and I want to be the first to unveil the nude statue of Bushman. Before that, I had a statue of Michelangelo's *David* in the Garden which I had removed. I understand that *David* can't compete with Bushman."

"I'm very pleased to meet you, Miss Swanson," I said. Even at that young age, Swanson seemed an imperial bitch.

She studied me carefully. "You look good enough to be in pictures," she said. "Perhaps I'll cast you as a leading man in one of my pictures. I'm going to become the biggest star at Paramount."

I liked a woman with confidence. "I'm Durango Jones," I said, extending my hand which she ignored.

"No, darling," she said, "no one is named Durango Jones. We'll have to change that." She eyed the Mexicans as they began to unwrap the Bushman nude. "You really do need to get into some other kind of business." She raised a finger to me. "Naughty, naughty, delivering nudes of Bushman. What would your mother say? Surely you can find some more respectable profession."

Standing before the statue as the blanket fell to the ground, Swanson said. "My oh my, what a wonderful day." She turned to me and flashed a smile that looked like sugar-coated chiclets of gum. "I could have had the real thing," she said, rather brazenly I thought.

"What do you mean, Miss Swanson? This is the real thing. Actually posed for by Mr. Bushman in his studio."

"No, no, my child."

I noticed that Swanson was calling me a child. She and I must be the same age.

"When I worked for Essanay, Bushman was the great god of the studio. It was just a short time ago that he was the biggest star in pictures. Now he can't find work." She looked at the statue admiringly. "Unless he wants to go back to being a sculptor's model. One day he emerged from his dressing room wearing his trademark, a monstrous violet amethyst ring. He'd been fitted for tights that day. The studio buzzed with the rumor that wardrobe had to make a special device to conceal his ample endowment in those tights. Otherwise, the picture might be judged obscene. Without saying a word, Bushman sat down in an empty chair next to me. No sooner seated than his hand reached out and clamped down on my right knee. He had great authority. Like he owned that knee and would soon own me. He might have been the biggest star in Hollywood, but he got the biggest slap of his life. Without saying a word, he got up and retreated—and that was that. The beginning and end of the Swanson and Bushman love affair."

I smiled demurely, feeling outclassed in the presence of Swanson and fearing I looked like a day laborer.

She stared once more at the statue. "Tell Bushman when you see him that I think the statue is a bit much. Surely the sculptor must have added extra inches to the endowment. I've seen men in the nude before. No man looks like that." She waved her hand at me. "Now be off with you. I've got to put the final touches to my makeup before a studio photographer arrives."

"It's been an honor meeting you, Miss Swanson."

She turned her back to me and headed toward her house.

If Gloria Swanson was a surprise, the next delivery shocked me even more. It was to the home of Elmo Lincoln. This time Elmo rushed out to greet me, remembering me from our session in the urinal at Nazimova's Garden of Alla.

"Durango," he said," I can't wait to see the Bushman statue. You brought me photographs too."

"Everything is here, Mr. Lincoln."

He smiled at me. "You can call me Tarzan, and thanks for the hand-job. You're really good. I'll call you some night when I can't find a woman willing or even able to accommodate me."

He ordered the statue of Bushman placed in the center of his garden. "Now I can see for myself," he said, eagerly awaiting the unveiling. The Mexicans untied the ropes and dropped the blanket. Elmo stared at the statue with an incredulous look. His face turned red with anger. "He's faked it."

"But you can judge from the photographs," I said. I handed him an envelope encased in lavender paper. He looked at only one photograph before tossing the whole packet on the ground and stomping on it. "I'll be back in a minute."

I retrieved the photographs from the ground, planning to save them for what would become in time the largest collection of male movie star nudes in the world. Bushman was my first until I stopped collecting after obtaining a nude of Tom Cruise in 1994.

Elmo came back into the patio with a hammer. With his strong muscles, it took him no time at all to castrate Bushman. "I'll leave the statue of Bushman here for the world to see," he vowed. "All my friends can see Bushman's statue at my parties." He stood back and examined his chiseling more carefully, almost like a proud sculptor. "Now Bushman is a perfect concave." He turned to look at me. "Come into the house and get your money. It was worth it. You can take those God damn photographs. I don't want them in my house."

Elmo promised to call me for "emergency" services should he need me. But he never did.

I called him once or twice but never got through to him even though I left urgent messages.

I was to see him only one more time before he died in the early 1950s. Quite by accident when working as a gossip columnist I encountered him doing a small bit part in a Charles Starrett western for Columbia. Although he knew of me as a columnist, he either didn't remember our first and long-ago meeting at Nazimova's or chose not to.

*****

Arriving at the address Chaplin had given me, and right on time, I was directed to the back parking lot where a large black limousine was shown to me. "Can you drive this?" the grip said. He looked like Wallace Beery.

"Sure, no problem," I said.

"Then get behind the wheel and wait for The Little Fellow." He turned and left.

Chaplin appeared ten minutes later dressed in a black suit and white shirt and tie. He hardly looked like The Little Tramp, but he was immediately recognizable, even without his familiar costume as the clown.

I'd been told that cinematically Chaplin could do no wrong, but, as I was soon to learn, that pertained only to his life on screen. I'd grown up watching the actor who was now getting into the back of his limousine. I'd seen the unutterably crude and vulgar Keystones made under Mack Sennett's baton. It was hectic buffoonery. I'd seen him in the first feature length comedy, *Tillie's Punctured Romance* with Mabel Normand and Marie Dressler. My favorite—even to this day—is *A Dog's Life*. Off-screen, The Little Tramp was an entirely different character.

When I asked him where he wanted to go, he said, "Any schoolyard. The first one you see where little girls can be found on the playground."

I was startled but drove on, heading for a large school ground that I'd passed only that morning when delivering the Bushman trophies. There had been rumors that Chaplin was a chicken hawk—the younger the better—but I didn't know whether the stories were true or not. Unless he was going to the playground for a game of ball, I suspected this gossip was deadly accurate. I said nothing, not really knowing what to say. I feared I was moving through my early days in Hollywood with my mouth wide open in astonishment, letting others do all the emoting.

"I have a sympathy for young girls," Chaplin said from the back seat, adjusting a flower in his lapel. "Youth should be a pleasant time of growing up without care. But for some of these girls, life is very rough. It was for me. My youth was strictly from Dickens. Hand to mouth. My father was a vaudevillian. He died when I was young. My mother was a music hall soubrette until she lost her voice. In time she lost her mind as well."

"I'm sorry to hear that, Mr. Chaplin," I said, regretting how weak my response was but I didn't know what to say to him. We were nearing a school ground where at least thirty young girls, who looked about fourteen to sixteen years old, were playing.

"Park the car near the corner over there," Chaplin commanded.

I did as instructed, and no sooner had the limousine come to a halt than he bounded out of the car heading toward the playground and the little girls. He came to a stop a few feet from them and launched into his familiar routine as The Little Fellow. In moments he had the girls clustering around him and screaming with laughter.

I felt a little guilty for having my initial suspicions. It appeared that Chaplin liked performing so much he entertained school kids when not before the cameras.

Chaplin must have performed for thirty minutes before a school bell rang. The performance was over, and the girls scattered in all directions, heading home. That is, except one. Chap-

lain detained a young girl who looked about fourteen. She had the most expressive eyes I'd ever seen. Framed by dusky lashes, they were mysterious somehow. Even as she looked at me, her eyes seemed to change colors, going from a sea green to a black purple. Her nose and mouth were perfectly chiseled, and she had long, dark, wavy hair down to her shoulders. Her skin was alabaster. In all my life—before or since—I had never seen such a beautiful girl. She was almost too beautiful.

I jumped out and opened the door for them. "This is Durango," Chaplin said, introducing me which he really didn't have to do.

"What a funny name," she said, smiling at me before turning all her attention to Chaplin. The Little Tramp seemed to mesmerize her.

"What is your name, little girl?" he asked.

"I'm Reatha Watson," she said, "and I'm so happy to meet you. All my friends tell me I should be playing the Mary Pickford parts. Don't you think she's getting a little old to be playing a young girl and that Hollywood needs a new fresh face?"

Hearing her speak, I wondered how innocent and sweet this brazen little creature was.

"You're right," Chaplin said. "Mary Pickford's getting long in the tooth, but don't tell the bitch I said that. Get in the car."

Once they were seated in the rear, I asked Chaplin where he wanted me to drive them.

"Just drive around," he commanded with such authority he frightened me. "Stick to the back streets where there's no traffic. We don't want to be disturbed, do we Reatha?"

"No, Mr. Chaplin," she said. "I came with you because I want you to get me a screen test. I want to break into the movies."

"I think you'd be perfect," he said. "I just might put you in my next film. There's a role for a little girl like you. But you've got to convince me you can act even before I take you to the studio."

"I can act," she protested, a little too harshly for my tastes. "Just try me."

"Sampling you is just what I had in mind," Chaplin said. "In fact, before I take you to the studio, I might audition you right here in the car. You wouldn't object to that, now would you?"

"I'd be really pleased to show you what I

can do."

Not daring to look at what was going on in the back seat, I kept my eyes glued to the road, trying to find streets devoid of traffic or pedestrians. I knew in Kansas Chaplin could be put in jail for stunts like this, but I assumed the laws in California might be different since Hollywood seemed more liberal about such dalliances.

"In the film you've got to kiss me on the lips, just like Theda Bara kisses a man," Chaplin instructed her. "Can you do that?"

"I think so," she said. I could hear the reluctance in the young girl's voice. "I've never kissed a man before."

No longer able to control my temptation, I glanced back to see Chaplin plant seven to eight tender kisses on Reatha's lips which were as cherry red as my own mouth. These seemed pleasant enough for her, and she didn't object.

"In the new film we've got to go a little bit more for the movie audiences of today," Chaplin said. "When I kiss you again I want you to open your mouth. I'm going to stick my tongue in your mouth, and I want you to suck on it like it's a piece of rock candy."

"I could never do that," she protested. "It's nasty."

"Durango," Chaplin called up to me. "Stop the God damn car. Our friend wants out. She can't take direction. In films a good actress has to do as the director says. I'm kicking you out of this car and you'll never work a day in films in Hollywood. I'll see to that. I'll have you blacklisted at all the studios."

She burst into tears. "Please, please," she said. "I can take direction. I was just a little afraid at first."

"Do you think Pearl White likes getting tied up on railroad tracks?" Chaplin asked.

"I never thought of it that way."

"Movie stars have to do a lot of things they don't like," Chaplin said. "It's not all glamorous clothes, fabulous furs, tons of jewelry, and big limousines—not to mention mansions and so much money you have to carry it to the bank in a wheelbarrow."

"Could I have all those things just like Mary Pickford?" she asked, her tears drying up.

"Yes, yes," Chaplin said, growing impatient. "Now open your damn mouth and suck my tongue."

Without any more protests, she did as Chaplin instructed. As I continued to drive, I felt peace had returned to the back seat. Judging from the little moans of pleasure from Chaplin and later from Reatha, I sensed the aspirant actress was learning to take direction very well. Although I couldn't hear his exact words, Chaplin whispered directions in her ear.

Raising up, Chaplin said, "I'm going to take it out and I want you to suck on it like you sucked my tongue."

"Please..." was all she said in a pleading voice, although she didn't push Chaplin away.

Again, not able to resist the temptation, I looked back in my rear-view mirror as a rather thick penis emerged from Chaplin's pants. It was uncut and nearly ten inches long. Chaplin hadn't exaggerated. The big penis looked like it belonged on a much larger man like Francis X. Bushman or Elmo Lincoln. Since Chaplin was so little, the penis appeared grotesque.

The next thirty minutes were horror for the little girl, although Chaplin perversely seemed to enjoy his assault on her. Only after promising her both a screen test and a hundred dollars did Chaplin succeed in getting his penis into her mouth. Predictably she gagged. But The Little Fellow with the big dick was persistent. It was obvious to me he'd performed this sexual routine with little girls many times before. As his penis entered her mouth, Chaplin penetrated virgin territory. If he'd asked me, I could have brought Chaplin to a spectacular climax, but he didn't go that route, it was clear, and seemed definitely heterosexual.

Before Chaplin finally reached his climax, Reatha had vomited twice. Conveniently someone had stashed towels in thc back to mop up liquid evidence of any indiscretion. As Chaplin climaxed, he let out a jungle yell, somewhat out of character for The Little Tramp, more in the spirit of Tarzan.

Reatha was crying as Chaplin demanded that she drink up all his cream and swallow it. "Imagine it's sweet, creamy milk," he instructed her.

After Chaplin had buttoned up, he told me to take the girl back to the playground. I did as requested and returned to the scene of the crime. On the way back, Chaplin thrilled her with visions of her future glory and all the films she'd be starring in in the years ahead.

"After appearing with me in one or two films, you'll get thousands of fan letters," Chaplin predicted. "In your third film we won't need me as the star to draw audiences. Your name will be so big you can carry a film by yourself."

The little girl giggled, seemingly having gotten over her vomiting and distaste.

"Will you meet me here tomorrow afternoon at the same time?" Chaplin asked, handing over the hundred dollars to her. By that point, I was glancing frequently into my rear-view mirror.

"Okay, I guess," she said a bit reluctantly.

"You do want that screen test, don't you?" Chaplin asked.

"Oh, please, Mr. Chaplin, I really do."

"Tomorrow afternoon we might carry this audition a little more than we did today," Chaplin said. "Tomorrow you might make five-hundred dollars if you cooperate."

"I'll be waiting," she promised. "Five-hundred dollars? It's a dream."

"Also, I noticed two or three other little girls on the playground," Chaplin said. "I'll point them out to you tomorrow. They are not half as pretty as you, but we are always looking for talent to appear in minor roles. It's obvious you are star material. But even a star like you is going to need supporting players."

"You tell me who they are," she agreed, "and I'll speak to them. What young girl wouldn't want to meet the great Charlie Chaplin?"

Releasing her on the now empty playground, Chaplin told her good-bye and asked her never to tell her parents what had happened. I thought that sound advice. After driving off, I asked him where he wanted to be taken next, feeling Reatha in her amateurish way had at least satisfied his libido for the moment.

"Take me home. I want to rest."

On the way there, Chaplin dozed off but woke up suddenly as if emerging from a deep trance. "How would you like to make one-thousand dollars tomorrow night? You're very pretty, you know, and you can pull it off."

At first I didn't know what he was suggesting. Was this a proposition? Did Chaplin also go for pretty boys? "You're paying me very well as it is," I said, totally avoiding the point of his question.

"That's not what I mean. The driving is one thing. What I'm offering is an acting assignment."

I was thrilled. So this is how one broke into the movies. Charlie Chaplin himself had discovered me.

"I want you to dress up as a woman and play a practical joke on a friend of mine," he said. "Not really a friend. Someone I want to get even with. Will you do it? You might have to go pretty far."

"For one-thousand dollars, I would make a most convincing woman."

After dropping Chaplin off, and being told I could keep the limousine for three weeks, I headed back to the cottage. On the way there, I stopped off at a costume shop that had just opened. It seemed that everybody in Hollywood needed a costume these days. I was looking for a gold loincloth for my session with Theda Bara later in the evening.

After securing just what I wanted—loincloths were all the rage in Biblical epics—I headed back to the cottage wondering if Rodolfo had returned.

Even though it wouldn't be in front of a camera, at least I could write in my memoirs that my first acting assignment in Hollywood was in the role of a woman while directed by Charlie Chaplin himself.

*****

With a gold loincloth tucked into a pocket of my trousers, I arrived at Theda Bara's home in Chaplin's borrowed Locomobile. After a knock at the door, it was thrown open by a skinny black maid who said, "You must be Durango Jones." Instead of a magnolia voice, she spoke with a pronounced British accent. I know all black maids in films are supposed to be fat like Mammy as portrayed by Hattie McDaniel in *Gone With the Wind*, but this one was bony and thin, almost a figure like Katharine Hepburn had in her 1932 *A Bill of Divorcement* opposite John Barrymore.

In the kitchen and to my astonishment I encountered an ordinary looking Ohio housewife, Theodosia Goodman. Could this be the same woman who as Theda Bara had brought such exotic mystery into my life at the Patee Theater in Lawrence with her portrayal of The Vamp in such roles as *Carmen, The Serpent, The Eternal Sappho, Cleopatra,* and *Salome*?

"Durango," she said, placing a large wooden spoon on a counter. She'd been checking a simmering pot of corned beef and cabbage, whose strong odor permeated the house. "Thank you for coming on such short notice."

"Theda," I said, kissing her on the cheek. "I hardly recognized you."

"When I found out we weren't going to be lovers but friends instead," she said, "I decided I would let you see me as I really am—not always Theda Bara but sometimes Theodosia Goodman."

"Thanks for being so natural with me," I said. "I'm honored."

"Get him a drink," Theda called to her maid, who turned out to be a woman named Sarah Pinheiro from Trinidad. "If I remember he likes whiskey on the rocks."

I wasn't sure that was what I liked but from that night on, I always ordered whiskey on the rocks—decade after long decade. In fact, I'm having such a drink right now at the millennium as I dictate these recollections to the disapproving Bitch of Buchenwald who I suspect wishes she could be making a lamp out of my withered old skin instead of learning the most lurid details of my notorious past.

Forgive an old man for wandering from the subject—and back to Theda.

In the garden as Theda and I sat having our whiskey, a forlorn look came into her eyes, and her round face turned sad. She took my hand and looked deeply into my eyes, "The Vamp is dead!"

I withdrew slightly at this pronouncement, not believing my ears. Vamps are eternal. They live forever. How could The Vamp be dead? "What in hell are you talking about?" I asked with more force in my voice than I usually employed with the legends of the silent screen. "Half a million people a day see your films."

"I know," she said. "I've come a long way since I was paid twenty-five dollars a week in a tacky road show. But, I'll let you in on a secret. Hollywood likes to build you up—make you a big star—let you climb to the top." She

looked at me with those large wide eyes that had thrilled audiences in *Heart and Soul* when she was denounced as a "sex bitch" and "love pirate." "Then they destroy you."

"My God," I said as Sarah came back into the patio with new drinks for both of us. I needed the second whiskey to get up my courage to pose in that loincloth which was the second best thing to appearing totally nude. "In the last year or so you've been in more films than ever. I've seen them all: *Under the Yoke, The Forbidden Path, When a Woman Sins...*"

Theda interrupted my recitation as a bitter frown crossed her brow. "Mae Tinee called that one 'as punk as most of the photoplays in which I have been so unfortunate as to witness Miss Bara.'"

"Forget that bitch!" I said, again rather forcefully. The liquor was making me more strident than ever. "Let me go on—*The She Devil, The Light, The Message of the Lillies, La Belle Russe, Siren's Song, When Men Desire, A Woman There Was, Lure of Ambition.*"

You left out *Kathleen Mavourneen.*"

"Maybe I did that deliberately," I said. "I know you went against type in that one. It wasn't your biggest picture—we both know that."

"There was none of The Vamp in *Kathleen,*" she said, "and I loved the picture for that very reason. I'm even giving serious thought to marrying the director of that picture, Charles Brabin. He's an Englishman. How did you find me in *Kathleen?*"

"I thought you looked lovely," I said. It was a lie. I hated the picture. Theda had gold curls like a bad imitation of Mary Pickford framing the legendary Vamp's chalk-lined eyes. Instead of the shimmering, seductive gowns associated with The Vamp, Kathleen wore tattered cotton dresses.

"I was the sweet little colleen of rhyme and innocence," Theda said, still seeming to resent the public's refusal to accept her in a Mary Pickford role.

"I thought things were going great between you and Fox," I said, downing a hefty swig of my second Scotch of the evening. "I know you're getting tired of The Vamp parts—or, as you so colorfully put it the other day in a magazine article—'The word vampire has become a stench in my cinematographic nostrils.'"

"I've begged Fox to give me different parts, to let me broaden my range and cut out all that Vamp shit. I must tell you the truth. My three-year contract with Fox is over. Early in 1918 they were paying me $1,500 a week, although I deserved far more. Finally, after I raised holy hell, they upped it to $4,000 a week. I know that sounds like a lot of money, but that cunt, Mary Pickford, is hauling in one million a year."

"Your pictures are wonderful," I said. "You should be right up there with Mary Pickford in earning power."

"Listen to this," she said, downing the rest of her drink and screaming for Sarah to bring a new one.

I dared not caution her to go easy on the booze, fearing she'd be drunk by the time the photographer got here for what I'd learned would be a publicity still.

"When it came time for contract renewals, I asked for $5,000 a week," she said.

"Sounds fair to me," I said, sitting back and enjoying the first early breeze of the evening in the rose-scented garden.

"I fear I've overplayed my hand," Theda said. "At contract renewal time, I told them the God damn Vamp parts had worn threadbare, and I was through with that characterization. They even had me vamping as sweet little Juliet opposite Romeo. My nerves are shattered. I just can't go on as a Vamp, and Fox knows that. I told them that in words not altogether ladylike."

"What was their reaction?" I asked.

"The reaction, God damn it, is that Fox isn't going to renew my contract. The idea of a Theda Bara appearing on screen as a real person is ridiculous to those money-grubbing bastards. My agent is talking to Paramount without much luck. He's even approached some filmmakers in Europe about casting me. When you can't get work in Hollywood, you head for Europe. One or two studios, including one in London, has expressed some interest, but only in more Vamp pictures."

"My God, I can't believe that," I said. "I thought the decline in a career came after long years of dismal failure—not overnight."

"It looks like my film career is coming to an end just as fast as it was launched," she said. "With nothing else to do, I'm returning to New York and my first love, the theater. I'm going to do a Broadway play, *The Blue Flame.*"

"That sounds great!"

"Florence Reed, Norma Talmadge, Mae Murray, they will all take the train to New York for my opening at the Schubert, if for no other reason than to see me make a fool of myself. After all, my first film was *A Fool There Was.*"

Theda's shocking revelations about her sudden decline as a film actress were interrupted by the appearance in the patio of Rod St. Just, the photographer escorted by Sarah bringing renewed drinks for everybody, including Theda who was already appearing rather high-spirited in spite of the dismal news she'd just broken to me.

Rod was a rather handsome young man dressed entirely in white from his hat to his shoes. He looked like a 1919 version of the 1956 movie star, Tab Hunter, if there is anybody on earth who stills remembers darling Tab. The only concession to color Rod made was that he wore red socks, a shocking combination for the time, later picked up by the 1940s movie star, Van Johnson.

After kissing Theda on both cheeks, a first sighting for me, he held out his hand to me. He did it in such a grand manner I didn't know if I were to shake his hand or kiss it.

"And this divine boy must be the fabulous Durango Jones," he said.

"Pleased to meet you," I said awkwardly.

"Word is quickly spreading through Hollywood that the world's most beautiful blond boy from the Middle West has arrived," Rod said, taking his whiskey from Sarah. "I understand that you've jerked off Elmo Lincoln at Nazimova's Garden of Alla, that you've sucked off Wallace Reid, been a pimp for Charlie Chaplin, and are being regularly fucked by that divine new Latin lover in town, Rodolfo Valentino." He appraised me for a long time, lingering at my crotch which to my total embarrassment began to rise in my pants under his scrutiny.

I was also embarrassed for other reasons, mainly at Rod talking this way in front of my goddess, Theda. Also, it was my first exposure to what a small town Hollywood was.

Gossip seemed to spread faster here than in Lawrence, Kansas. The only dalliance he hadn't heard about was Norman Kerry.

In spite of his presumption, I liked Rod immediately, little knowing at the time how important he was to become in my life.

In the years to come, and through Rod's death, I was to acquire the world's largest collection of male nudes of film stars, many at their prime and with full erections. It hadn't taken Rod long to learn after arriving in Hollywood that actors like to show off their most prized possession, even if they didn't have that much to reveal. If they had a lot to expose, they were even more eager to drop their trousers. (More about that later, dear reader.)

"Theda, get dressed, for God's sake," Rod scolded her. "You look like a butcher's wife in the Chicago meat district."

In the boudoir Sarah directed us to, Rod ordered me to strip completely naked. At first I was uncomfortable peeling off everything, even my underwear, in front of him, but he quickly put me at ease.

No one had ever praised my assets as flatteringly as Rod did, including the size of my penis. "I've got to take many pictures of that whopper," he said, bowing down in front of my throbbing hard-on. "But I can't put a loincloth over that until I deflate it a bit."

Without my knowing what was happening, Rod had fallen on his knees in front of me and swallowed me in one gulp, and I'm large, all the way to my pubic hair. He treated me to the world's most expert blow-job. He might be a great photographer, but was also a skilled artist of fellatio. Up to now I thought I was a winner in that race, but Rod clearly had me beat.

After swallowing every bit of my cream, and begging for more, he finally let me go after we'd given Theda time to make herself up as The Vamp once more. The backers of her Broadway play didn't want her in Mary Pickford curls and tattered cotton dresses, but as "the wickedest woman on earth."

Rod rejected the gold loincloth I had picked up at the costume shop, preferring one he'd brought himself. After he fitted it on me, I stared at myself in the mirror. I might as well have been nude. I looked so sexy in it that I turned myself on. Of this there was no doubt: I could definitely fill out a pouch, especially in the wake of Rod's blow-job. He was better than any suction pump.

In spite of her recent protestations, Theda was the ultimate professional, and cooperated with Rod. When Sarah showed us into the dressing room off the star's boudoir, Theda was The Vamp once more. In an unearthly pink-red light, her face was brilliantly illuminated to show off her exotic beauty. Her jet-black hair fell about her chalky white face in tangled coils. From deep pools, her eyes captured the baleful, brooding light. In stark contrast to the whiteness of her face, her mouth was aflame in scarlet. "Am I wicked and seductive enough for you?" she asked Rod. Seeing me, she let out a wolf whistle.

Rod liked Theda's make-up and revealing Cleopatra gown, with jeweled "cobras" covering her breasts. He pronounced her look "brutal and fiendish." "You are half serpent, half woman," he said before ordering me to stand behind her. Sarah presented me with a six-foot tall peacock fan. My job for the evening was to fan this vampire from hell.

In time, the photograph that Rod took of Theda and me that night has been reproduced around the world. *La Giaconda* is still reproduced more times than our picture, but we must be in second place in the race.

It was only after I was getting dressed, having fended off Rod's second attempt to give me one of those all-powerful blow-jobs, that he informed me we had a date with destiny tomorrow morning. It was Rod who was going to mold the dildo from the gargantuan and erect penis of Francis X. Bushman, and I was to be there at ten o'clock in the morning "to assist," whatever that meant.

*****

Back at the cottage after a wicked day, there was still no sign of Rodolfo. I fixed myself a ham sandwich which I consumed with a glass of milk and headed for bed. It must have been two o'clock in the morning when I heard the persistent ringing of the telephone. Eagerly I jumped out of bed nude and rushed to the living room to answer it, expecting Rodolfo.

It was the voice of a woman. She identified herself as Jean Acker. "Rodolfo has told me everything about you," she said. But it wasn't really an accusation. "Do not think I am jealous. I not only understand such love between men, I encourage it, at least in Rodolfo's case."

"I'm glad we have your permission," I said. "Is Rodolfo okay?"

"He is fine. Both of us are at the Hollywood Hotel. I want you to come here at once. Rodolfo wants you to drive him back to your cottage. He hasn't slept in days and is very weak. You must come at once."

"What's your room number?" I asked.

"Never mind," she said. "I do not allow men in my room. I'll meet you in the lobby."

"I'll leave as soon as I get dressed," I said before hanging up and rushing to get into my clothes.

On the way to the Hollywood Hotel, I found myself crying and driving at the same time. The emotional outburst came upon me suddenly. Lana Turner must have copied this scene from me when she filmed *The Bad and the Beautiful* in 1953.

At the hotel I found Jean Acker sitting in the same spot where Blanche Sweet had perched. She certainly wasn't Blanche Sweet and didn't even look like a movie star. I was amazed that Metro had placed this little Cherokee squaw under contract.

"Sit down beside me," she commanded, no doubt using Nazimova as her role model for authority.

"Are you still planning to marry Rodolfo?" I asked, praying her answer would be no.

"More about that later," she said rather grandly. "Rodolfo will be down soon. But I am here to pour out my heart to you on an entirely different matter. I have no one to confide in, and Rodolfo says I can trust you. That I can unburden my heart to you because you're from the Middle West, and Midwesterners are very understanding people."

"Exactly what is threatening you?" I asked, not really wanting to hear her problems. All I wanted to know was news of Rodolfo.

"Nazimova threatens me," Acker went on. "Every Sunday afternoon she gathers the most beautiful young women in Hollywood around her pool. All of them have gorgeous figures—far better than mine. The Garden of Alla is called the '8080 Club' after its address on Sunset Boulevard."

"Being from the Middle West I'm not getting it. If you're marrying Rodolfo, I assume you're leaving Nazimova."

"No one leaves Nazimova until Nazimova is ready for them to leave. She claims she loves me but at these all-girl parties she disappears into her bedroom with one, two, or even three of the most beautiful. She does not invite me to join them."

"From what I know of Nazimova, you could hardly expect her to be faithful."

"That she isn't. Sometimes women arrive from Europe, and Nazimova speaks to them in French so I can't understand what they are saying. Sometimes as she is talking to these women, they turn and look at me and laugh. Nazimova is obviously telling them bad stories about me and making me out to be a fool."

"Then walk out the door," I said. "You don't have to put up with treatment like that."

She took my hand which I only reluctantly offered. "Nazimova is my sponsor. Without her, I would have no contract with Metro. Without her, I could not become a big-time movie star. Rodolfo is in the same situation with Norman Kerry. Without Kerry, Rodolfo can't work in pictures." She sighed and looked at me through tear-streaked eyes which I didn't know if they were real or fake. "We are love slaves purchased on the auction block."

"I think marriage is out of the question then," I said, feeling relieved. "You can't marry anybody until you've settled this thing with Nazimova."

"I'm in love with Nazimova," she said. "I love her madly. No matter what she does to me, no matter how she humiliates me, I will always come back for more punishment."

"That's sick."

"It's not sick. It's the way of love. The way of the human heart."

"None of these romantic complications make sense to me."

"Nazimova is not only my lover, she introduces me to the most important people in Hollywood. She throws more than all-girl parties. She stages some of the biggest parties and dinners in Hollywood, like the one where I met you. Mae Murray shows up. Even Constance and Norma Talmadge. Certainly Dagmar Godowsky. Sometimes producers come to Nazimova's parties. The Mdvani brothers also come. They claim to be Georgian princes. Sometimes we dress up in beautiful costumes. Only last week Nazimova invited her guests to dress up like the era of Louis XV at the Court of Versailles. Dagmar came as Madame du Barry. Naturally, Nazimova insisted on being Marie Antoinette."

"I don't know this Nazimova, having met her only briefly," I said. "But she seemed to me like she was the star of a script she was writing herself."

"That is so perceptive. She moves through your life like a full orange moon. She lights your way and controls your moods. But when that moon goes behind a cloud, you are lost and cannot find your way."

"That may be true, but at least she got you a contract with Metro. Both Rodolfo and I want movie contracts too."

"I may have the contract," she said, her face falling in disappointment. "But Metro has no work for me now that they have signed me. One producer told me I'm not beautiful enough. Nazimova isn't beautiful either, but she's a big star. Theda Bara isn't really beautiful."

"You're lovely enough," I said, "but I must confess I'm jealous of you. I wish Rodolfo could belong solely to me. But I know him well enough to realize that will never happen."

"Rodolfo and I have been together since he left your cottage."

"That much I know."

"It is not what you think. There was no sex. Rodolfo learned that his mother died, and he turned to me, a woman, for comfort."

I was startled to hear that news. How I wish he'd turned to me for comfort in his grief and not the little Cherokee. Forgetting the dead mother for a moment, I abruptly asked, "Why did you agree to marry Rodolfo so suddenly?"

"Because I love him."

"How could you love him? He proposed marriage the first second he met you. Besides, I thought you loved only women. You still have Nazimova."

"You don't understand," she said. "I love women for sex. But for a spiritual joining of two souls, I must turn to a man. Not for sex. For sex, my future husband will have to look elsewhere."

"Frankly, I'm a little suspicious of your claim that you love Rodolfo. Didn't you meet and talk with Theda Bara just the other night about Rodolfo?"

Her face expressed a mild shock. "I vaguely recall Miss Bara. I might have met her."

"I have just come from Theda Bara's house," I said. "Before leaving she told me she'd had a brief conversation with you and Nazimova. Rodolfo had already proposed marriage to you, and he'd excused himself to go to the men's room. Theda said it was then you told her that you found Rodolfo to be a professional lounge lizard. Nazimova dismissed him as 'just a gigolo.' That doesn't sound like love to me. Aren't you really marrying Rodolfo just to get your revenge on Nazimova for cheating on you with all those beautiful women?"

"That's a lie. A lie." She burst into tears. "You don't understand. Once Nazimova loves you, she feels she owns you. I have to get away from her."

"But you seem deeply in love with Nazimova. I don't think you really want to escape from her."

"One part of me wants to be at her side forever. But there is another side of me. Perhaps it is my Cherokee blood. But I long to be free."

"If you want freedom, marriage is hardly the answer."

"For me it is. I feel that in time I can escape Nazimova's clutches by being Rodolfo's wife. He is going to become a bigger star than Nazimova. As the wife of the biggest male star of all time, I will no longer need Nazimova."

"All the wrong reasons to get married."

"Perhaps in the Middle West," she said, a bit contemptuously. "But in Hollywood people marry for all sorts of reasons."

Our conversation was suddenly interrupted by the appearance of Rodolfo walking down the stairs to greet us in the early morning.

I felt I should say something to him about the loss of his mother, but he hardly seemed to be griefing at all. In fact, he had a romantic glow to him.

"My bride to be," Rodolfo said, smiling and winking at me as he bent over to kiss Acker on her cheek.

She withdrew from his touch. "The smell of Norman Kerry's semen is still on your body. I'm closing my door to you tonight."

"So be it," he said, turning to look deeply into my eyes. "Is your door open to me tonight, my little lamb?"

"By all means," I said, reaching out and gently touching his arm. "It is our door and it's always open to you."

"You are in love with Rodolfo yourself," Acker said, rising in anger from the sofa.

I looked first at her, then at Rodolfo, and back at Acker again. "Of course I am. I'm also proud of it." I was defiant.

"Good night, gentlemen," she said, before heading up the stairs.

Rodolfo watched forlornly as she disappeared. When he turned to me, he said, "I was not with Jean. I was in another part of the hotel where Norman Kerry made love to me."

"But you guys had a fight," I said in protest, not wanting to hear he was alone with Norman.

"Norman and I are always having fights," he said. "We fight. We make up. We fight." He smiled. "That is what lovers do. Now let's go home."

On the way out the door, I turned to him. "I still can't understand why you're marrying Jean Acker. After a bit of a talk with her, I understand it even less. That is one confused Indian."

Rodolfo seemed dismissive of my question. "Jean knows a lot of important people. She can help my career."

"Is that a good reason to marry her?"

He did not answer but stood flaring his nostrils as he breathed in the early morning air.

Ushering Rodolfo into the front seat of Chaplin's borrowed Locomobile, I started the car and turned on the lights.

"Norman has satisfied my libido for tonight," he said. "So be duly warned not to expect too much from me. You can bathe me and I'll go to bed with you. But that's it for tonight. Of course, you can lick my body. Perhaps when morning comes, and it's a beautiful day like in the Mediterranean, and I've had a good night's sleep, I will rape you savagely."

"Why can't you just make love to me?" I asked, trying to steer the car through bleary eyes.

He grabbed my wrist and held it in a tight grip, digging his fingernails into me and causing pain.

Finally, he released his hold. "It is important that I not only rape you, but make you bleed. Norman fucked me tonight and made me bleed. It caused him great sexual excitement. If I can make you bleed in the morning, I too can experience what Norman felt."

"I don't know about this..."

He interrupted me. "Don't worry about it, my pet. After your Rodolfo makes you bleed, and after I've satisfied myself inside you, I will lick your wound clean. My tongue can be a very soothing instrument."

When I started to protest, he put his finger to my mouth. "Tonight you don't have to speak. Like the movies, pictures should be silent, and I want to admire you as in a photograph with no words. We will return now to our love nest."

With that dubious commitment, and with fear and dread of the morning, I steered the car into the hills and an uncertain future.

Chapter Four

Alone in the shower as Rodolfo slept, I still couldn't believe what had happened to me. Like the innocent cornfed boy of Kansas, I had allowed Rodolfo to tie me up to our brass bed in a spread-eagle position.

That's what Norman Kerry had done to him, and Rodolfo awoke at six o'clock eager to repeat his experience at the Hollywood Hotel—only with the roles reversed. Stark naked and my face down in the pillow, I'd been the helpless victim of Rodolfo's assault.

Before that morning, I'd never heard of fantasies of dominance and submission, master and slave. Back in Lawrence, we didn't speak of such things, although in retrospect I had been indoctrinated into this S&M world to some degree by Frank, my original deflowerer.

Once tied up, Rodolfo's mouth had descended on me with savagery, as he bit into my neck and seemingly took hunks out of my tender back. Things had gotten out of hand—and fast. Using only saliva for lubrication, Rodolfo had entered me like a rape, with no love, only force and violence. I'd screamed out at his initial penetration, and it had gotten worse from there. He'd moved into me and attacked at angles designed to cause pain and not pleasure. If he'd wanted me to bleed, I felt he was succeeding. Rodolfo had hammered his cock into me, and I didn't feel I could withstand the attack much longer without fainting. He'd fucked like a wild bull, constantly biting into my neck.

I'd twisted my body as if to escape him,

but I was completely tied up as he'd hammered long and hard in me. His cock had never felt wider and longer. At one point his penis felt three feet long. I thought it would come out through my mouth.

His body was drenched in a passionate heat I'd never known in him before. Every inch of him had seemed to be convulsing as I'd gritted my teeth and waited for the inevitable. He'd ground into me like a powertool as his eruption exploded. I'd clamped my eyes shut and had been softly moaning. But he'd slammed into me so hard as he'd exploded that I'd cried out. With his right hand, he'd pressed my face deeper into the soft pillow to muffle my cries. A dizzying heat had overcome me, and I'd been left gasping for breath.

Pulling out of me abruptly, Rodolfo had cleaned himself on the sheet and had fallen into the next pillow, forgetting his promise that he'd apply his soothing tongue to my wound. "The best ever," he'd said. "The very best." Those were his last words before he'd closed his eyes and had fallen into a deep sleep after untying me. He'd been snoring lightly as I'd slipped from the bed and into the bathroom where I'd discovered that I was bleeding.

An hour later, it was a battered boy who'd arrived at the home of Francis X. Bushman where I was directed to a studio in the rear. There I encountered Rod St. Just dressed all in white except for those red socks and surrounded by a complicated array of trays, pails, spatulas, and bags of chalky white plaster. Rod sensed that something had happened to me, and needing to confide in someone, I told him of my recent attack by Rodolfo. It was the beginning of dozens upon dozens of stories of sexual exploits that Rod and I would share over the years.

Rod's reaction had not been at all like I thought. "That sounds hot!" he said. "You're a lucky girl. I wish he'd done that to me."

"But he made me bleed. It hurt like hell."

Rod smiled at me and kissed me on the lips. "And you loved it, bitch, and will be there tonight begging for more."

As I was soon to learn, Rod viewed any sex, especially rape, as a divine gift sent directly from the gods.

But discussions about the condition of my rectum were soon diverted onto more immediate and pressing needs. It was time for the casting, in plaster, of the sexual organ of Hollywood's most famous stud.

There was tremendous sexual energy in the air when Francis X. Bushman came into the studio. He was dressed only in a long silk robe, and I suspected, as I'm sure Rod did, that he was completely nude underneath the garment.

"You ladies are in for a treat," he said to us, smiling seductively. "Both of you like to service real men, I know. I'd never be this intimate with men who slept with women."

"Darling," Rod said, "I not only sleep with men, I can't stand to get ten feet near a woman. I will sign that in blood if need be."

"And, Durango, I know your tastes already," Francis said to me.

"If you're anything like that statue and those photographs, both Rod and I are in for a treat," I said, shocked at my own frankness.

"That you are," Francis said, untying his robe and letting it cascade to the floor of the studio. He was entirely nude. Seeing a picture of the endowment of Francis X. Bushman or even viewing a lifelike statue was one thing. The real thing in the flesh was an awesome sight. Whereas most men dream of possessing eight and a half inches, Francis had that while still in a flaccid state. His penis was not only long but thick, and his balls were massive low hangers.

Francis X. Bushman stood as living proof that God did not create all men equal. To my secret mind, I suspected that if Francis attacked me like Rodolfo had, I would have to be rushed to the emergency clinic at the hospital. I couldn't imagine how Beverly could take such a massive tool night after night. Francis must have stretched her out so that she'd been too loose for all other men.

His entire body was in perfect contrast to that horse dick. His thighs were massive and solid, and his muscular chest was beefy and fully developed. No wonder he liked to show off his body. Not only that, he had what many considered the handsomest face in Hollywood, more rugged and classical than the more pretty boy look of Wallace Reid.

After giving us plenty of time to admire his physique and that powerful cock, Francis walked into the back room and lay down on a soft mattress as Rod prepared to cast the mold.

"This is where you come in," Rod told me. "Are you ready for Durango?" he asked Francis.

"Ready, willing, and able," Francis said. "In fact, I need servicing real bad. Since she got back from San Francisco, Beverly has been holding out on me. After casting the mold, I'll need Durango to hang around a bit to relieve me."

With awkwardness and shyness I moved toward Francis. He was not only a big-time movie star but my boss.

"Only a human mouth can make me fully hard," Francis told me, reaching for me and taking my head and forcing it down between his legs. For a moment, I thought his flaccid cock was too big to fit between my lips. The prospect of it getting larger and larger terrified me. Putting my fist around it, I realized fully just how big it was.

I licked the soft, fleshy area just beneath the glans, as Francis started to grow like the world's most fearsome fuckpole.

It was all I could do to get the head of this hard hunk of salami into my mouth, but I tried valiantly. Doing my best to keep from gagging, I descended inch by inch. Inhaling deeply, I forced myself under control. Francis was growing by the second, as I pushed forward. Slowly, very slowly, this monster was going deeper and deeper. I feared it would soon invade my throat, and I tried to back away but Francis held me firmly in place. I knew then I was there for the duration.

He allowed me to retreat a little, but soon pressed down on my head again, urging me to take more of him. Just as I thought I was going to smother, he yanked my head from his penis and called out to Rod. "Come at once. The great Francis X. Bushman is ready to be cast and immortalized."

Rod was clearly an expert. This was not his first dildo cast. He set about at once to take an impression of what would in time become the world's most famous dildo, now valued at thousands upon thousands of dollars for anyone who still has one. I view the one I was given later that week as one of my most prized possessions.

When he'd finished, Francis called for me again. "Durango," he said with force and authority. Posing for the dildo had obviously stimulated his libido, as it would for any exhibitionist like Francis. "You and I have some unfinished business," he said to me. Looking over at Rod, he said "Why don't you leave us alone now?"

Rod shrugged his shoulders and headed for the adjoining room, looking with undisguised jealousy at me. "Lucky girl," he said to me with a sneer before reluctantly leaving the room. He obviously had wanted to stay and watch, or even volunteer his services in my place.

Francis ran his fingers through my blond hair. He felt my throat muscles, massaging with his fingers as if preparing me for the invasion that was to come.

"This morning I'm going to go where no man has ever gone before or will ever go again," he said.

Francis X. Bushman turned out to be a prophet!

*****

Returning home to recover from the assault from Francis X. Bushman, I planned to gargle for an hour to relieve the soreness in my throat. I wasn't exactly sure what to do to bring relief to my sore ass, following the attack that morning from Rodolfo. By eleven o'clock I was still sore at both ends.

After my bath and thinking I had time to recover, I received a call from an assistant to Chaplin. He informed me that the star wasn't at the studio but at his private home entertaining "two world famous guests," and I was to go there at once. After putting down the phone, I eagerly searched my wardrobe to see what outfit would make me look stunning to meet these important people, whoever they were. I'd recently invested my savings in a new wardrobe, as Rodolfo said I looked like a farmer.

As I drove to Chaplin's home, I was prepared to encounter virtually anyone. The most influential people in the world, including politicians, stars and European royalty, always requested "an audience" with Chaplin whenever they visited Hollywood. If not Chaplin, then definitely Douglas Fairbanks or Mary Pickford. Chaplin, Pickford, and Fairbanks were the closest we came to having royalty of our own.

Suddenly I realized I was thinking of Hollywood as my town and not Lawrence, Kansas any more. As each day of my new life unfolded, I was leaving Kansas, its cornfields, and front porch rockers far behind. Even the Patee Theater was becoming a distant, nostalgic memory. I didn't need to remember Theda Bara on the screen. I could now call her and go over to see her.

At Chaplin's house a servant told me to go over to the garage where Chaplin's Locomobile, purchased for four-thousand dollars, was being serviced. In the garage I encountered Chaplin's full-time chauffeur, walking with a crutch because of his injured foot.

The chauffeur, Toraichi Kono, was obviously Japanese born—I later learned he was from Hiroshima—and he spoke English with a virtually impenetrable accent, evocative of "the Jap villains" as portrayed in World War II movies.

"If you think you're going to become Charlie's full-time driver, you are very, very wrong," Kono said. "The job belongs to me."

"Don't worry," I assured him. "I'm just doing this until some big-time producer discovers me and signs me to a long-term contract."

"You are a little fool, as star struck as everybody else in Hollywood." After that pronouncement, he showed me some fine points about the car which he felt I should know. He also told me he'd studied engineering and wanted to have a career in aviation. "Now look at me. A God damn chauffeur for an imbecile."

"I don't understand," I said, completely astonished. Surely he wasn't calling the great Charlie Chaplin an imbecile.

"You heard me," Kono said. "I am descended from great and honorable forebearers in Japan. Charlie is nothing but Cockney trash. From the slums. He has become rich and can afford to hire me as a chauffeur only because he fools the general public. They are imbeciles too. Only imbeciles would go see one of Charlie's films. They are for morons. I don't go to movies. I stay home with my beautiful Japanese sweetheart. I read the classics to her."

"Did you come to Hollywood to be an aviator or did you secretly want to be a movie star like Sessue Hayakawa? I mean no one thought a person from Japan could become an American movie star until Hayakawa proved them wrong." Kono unbuckled his trousers, dropped them, and pulled down his underwear, revealing a brand mark on his ass. "When I was much younger, I encountered the great Sessue Hayakawa. He's a sex pervert. A sadist. Stay away from him or he'll brand you too." Kono was pulling up his trousers just as Chaplin's manservant entered the garage. He looked at me suspiciously as if I had just given Kono a blow-job.

The servant instructed me to go up to Chaplin's sun roof and tell "his most honored and honorable guest" that Chaplin's limousine was ready to drive him home. The manservant appeared typically American but he too spoke with just a hint of a Japanese accent. Perhaps he'd worked too long in the company of Kono.

Heading for the sun roof I expected to encounter almost anyone, having read about all the distinguished world figures who came to Hollywood to call on Chaplin. For one moment, I suspected that it might be the King of England. If it were, I wouldn't be surprised even though I didn't know how to greet a bona-fide king.

On the roof, I encountered not the king of England but the king of Hollywood. And was I ever disappointed.

Douglas Fairbanks lay nude on a chaise longue sunning himself. At first I was so startled to encounter the great star that I didn't know

what to say. Seeing him nude made it doubly difficult for me.

I would like to record in my memoirs how I seduced Douglas Fairbanks on that fateful day, but, alas, such was not the case.

At the time Douglas Fairbanks was the most dashing, romantic figure of the era, an early version of Errol Flynn but he held no attraction for me.

Of course, I was immediately drawn to his penis. He was no Charlie Chaplin. His dick in its flaccid state was only average in size, but it curved remarkably to the left. Up to then, I'd never seen such a marked curvature in a man's penis. It astonished me. I thought all cocks grew straight out from a man's body, like my own or that of Rodolfo or Norman Kerry, certainly Wallace Reid.

After having checked out the Fairbanks genitalia, I concentrated more fully on the rest of him. In the films Fairbanks appeared at least seven feet tall. In real life he was no taller than Chaplin himself, and The Little Fellow was just that except for what he carried around between his legs.

Fairbanks already had a dark, olive-colored skin, but he liked to darken himself to a deep tobacco color by constant sunbaths in the nude. One Hollywood writer had said, "Douglas Fairbanks would make a dandy golf bag."

Even though he might be small in stature and had that unfortunate curvature in his dick, Fairbanks looked like the superb athlete that he was. His young body was finely chiseled, and it was obvious that he worked out a lot, perhaps in an athletic club. I'd read that he could perform handstands on chair arms.

Up to now I'd seen Fairbanks emote only on the screen. Even though I'd viewed every inch of him, at least his frontal view, he still hadn't opened his eyes and still hadn't spoken. I'd heard somewhere that you never spoke to royalty unless specifically addressed.

It might be hard for future generations to imagine the fame back then of Charlie Chaplin, Douglas Fairbanks, and Mary Pickford. The word "superstar" hadn't been coined, but they were the very first and last of the superstars. No star ever since has equaled them in fame. Today you can encounter a dozen or so movie stars at any party you attend. I can't even remember their names unless they're Elizabeth Taylor. In my view, she's the only real big star left.

But back then the holy trio of Chaplin, Pickford, and Fairbanks dominated the screens and fantasies of the world. No one was more globally recognized and adored than the tiny-mustached, splayfooted, baggy-trousered clown, the girl with the pinafore and golden curls, and the creature before me—Douglas Fairbanks himself whose very name evoked improbable dreams of high romance and the invincibility of right over wrong—in essence, the man who could achieve the impossible dream.

Suddenly, this world legend opened his eyes, squinting them to protect them from the burning California sun, now at its most powerful midday force. "Hi, I'm Douglas," he said. "You must be Durango Jones. Where did you come up with that moniker?"

Before I could say anything, Fairbanks rose from the chaise longue, jumped down on the floor of the sun roof, and on all fours came toward me, nipping at the leg of my trousers with a very authentic dog bark.

"Now, now, you mean dog," I managed to say. "I want to pet you, but don't bite me." My soothing voice seemed to take the bite out of this ferocious attack dog, and he stood up on his legs and went over to a cabinet which he opened. He reached in and pulled out his underwear before putting on his suit.

Years later I learned that Fairbanks at major dinner parties at Pickfair liked to crawl under the table and attack his famous guests, perhaps a duke, a prince, or a president, even a society matron from back east. Once under the table Fairbanks would bark at his guests, while biting into their legs.

Back on the sun roof, I found his behavior less shocking than I might have. Having already met several Hollywood stars, I figured that a barking, biting dog was less shocking than some of the scenes I'd encountered, including the recently concluded one with Francis X. Bushman.

Fully dressed, the dog incident behind us, Fairbanks got into the front seat with me and directed me to a studio where he claimed he had to "pick up a little sweetheart."

On the way there, he turned out to be likable and charming, a very down-to-earth guy, all smiles and wit. He moved closer in the seat to me as if he were putting a move on me. Since I wasn't interested, I didn't know how to respond. Refusing Douglas Fairbanks a sexual favor was unthinkable. I braced myself for the inevitable.

"Are you a homosexual?" he asked.

Not willing to conceal my true nature, I said, "I am indeed. I've just arrived in Hollywood, and many people in this town already know of my sexual interests."

Fairbanks lowered his voice. "Would you ever consider doing a few sexual favors for me?" he asked. He withdrew suddenly. "I hope I'm not insulting you."

"You're not. It depends on what you want done. Do you want to sodomize me or have me go down on you?"

"No, no," he said, laughing. "Not for me. I sleep only with women. But I entertain some of the most important guests in the world. Most of them request that I fix them up with a beautiful showgirl when they come to Hollywood. But sometimes I know they want a beautiful boy instead."

"I see," I said. "You'd like me to entertain some of your guests who have special interests."

"Exactly."

I thought about it for a moment, and said, "I'd be honored."

"Of course, there will be a lot of money in it for you. Who knows? You might end up a princess in some remote Balkan country." He laughed at his own prediction.

"I'll give you my phone number, and you can call me any time, Mr. Fairbanks."

"Since we know each other so intimately," he said, "I'll let you call me Doug."

"Okay, Doug." As he directed me on my way, I said, "In case I haven't told you already, I am honored to meet you. You're my favorite actor on the screen. But don't tell Mr. Chaplin that."

"I won't," he promised, smiling again. "As you know now, the great Douglas Fairbanks has nothing to hide from you."

He laughed again at his own wit, before steering me toward the back entrance to a studio where a guard came over and recognized him. "She'll be out in a minute, Mr. Fairbanks," he said. "I'll tell her you're here."

"You can do one more favor for me," Doug said when the guard left.

"What's that?"

"Where do you live?" he asked.

"In a little cottage next to Adela Rogers St. Johns," I said. "It's across from the home of Francis X. Bushman."

"I know the area well," he said. "I've been to parties in the neighborhood. Is anybody at home at your cottage right now?

"No one."

"Fine," he said. "The place I was going to take my girl is occupied right now with an out-of-town guest. As you know, I'm in a messy divorce and I must see my little girl secretly for the moment. Do you mind letting us use your cottage for an hour or two? There's a hundred dollars in it for you."

"It's a modest place," I said.

"We'll bring the romance to it."

"You are most welcome. Be my guest. There's no charge."

"That sounds great!"

A security guard opened the rear door of the studio and escorted what looked like a young girl in golden curls to the door of Chaplin's limousine. He opened the door and the girl jumped into the car. By then Doug had stationed himself in the back seat.

Ignoring me, she fell into his arms and began kissing and fondling him passionately. In those days stars regarded chauffeurs and house servants as sub-species and felt any activity could be performed in front of them.

It was only when she pulled back from kissing Doug's face, that I saw that the young girl was actually Mary Pickford!

Doug signaled me to drive toward my cottage.

Behind the wheel I was nervous as I steered the two most famous people on earth, other than Chaplin, to my little cottage where Mary, no doubt, would be enthralled at Doug's promising curvature.

*****

I had not a clue as to what Rodolfo was up to today, and I was damn certain he didn't know what I was doing. At that moment, I was brewing coffee to offer to the most famous couple in the world after they'd made love in the same bed where only hours before Rodolfo had savagely raped me. I was still sore. I just hoped that Mary wouldn't be sore after getting stabbed by that Fairbanks curvature. From the sounds coming from my bedroom, I suspected Mary was enjoying the assault.

After the little girl with the golden curls quit screaming out her passion, the cottage grew strangely silent. In about an hour I heard them taking showers in our bathroom. Fortunately I had gone to the laundry yesterday, and had also changed the sheets following Rodolfo's assault.

Her golden curls covered with a turban, Mary came into the room first. "Thanks for the hospitality." She wasn't like a little girl at all but a mature woman of the world. "Doug assures me you're very discreet."

"That I am," I said, offering her coffee. It seemed inappropriate to tell her how much I'd enjoyed all her films. Actually, I hadn't enjoyed them at all that much, as I preferred far more seductive women on the screen, including my beloved Theodosia Goodman when she wasn't cooking all that smelly corn beef and cabbage.

At first I didn't know what to say to Mary Pickford, and she seemed embarrassed to meet me under these circumstances. "In the bedroom, Doug told me you're temporarily driving for Charlie. If that's the case, then I know you must be discreet. What went on here was mild compared to what Charlie is up to. For the life of me, I can't believe he doesn't get arrested or at least hauled into court. You promise me you'll look after the dear man, won't you, and keep him out of trouble?"

"I'll do my best," I said as I looked into her winsome, expressive face that was usually hidden in curls. She seemed very practical, sensitive, and sensible and totally lacking in the imperial qualities already displayed by a very young Gloria Swanson.

At this point and totally nude, Doug, still wet from the shower, came into our living room. Mary took a towel from her lap that she'd been holding and wiped drops of water off his back.

Doug accepted the coffee from me but seemed unaware of my presence, unlike Mary who had been most cordial. "I forgot to tell you what happened to me in the steam bath yesterday with Lionel Barrymore," Doug said, concentrating solely on the woman he'd just seduced.

Mary turned to me and smiled as if trying to include me in the conversation. "Doug just loves his steam baths."

"At first I was in the steam bath with three other guys, including Lionel," Doug said. "All of us were buck naked except Lionel who'd modestly retained a big Turkish towel to wrap around his body. When the other two guys left, Lionel sat still for a minute, then he jumped up and headed for me, reaching and grabbing my cock. He practically fell on me trying to suck it into his mouth before I got away."

"Oh, Doug," Mary said, seeming to dismiss the story. She had far more sophistication and poise about the incident than I might have suspected.

She turned to me again as if to include me in the conversation once more. "I've known about Lionel for years. I once made a film with him. It was called *Friends*, and it also starred Henry B. Walthall."

"I remember it well," I said. "I saw it at the Patee Theater in Lawrence, Kansas. Up to that time, I had never seen a close-up of a star before. Were you the genius who developed it?"

She smiled. "I invented the close-up. Lillian Gish makes the same claim, but don't you believe her."

"I had never seen Mr. Barrymore in a film before," I said. Doug looked slightly bored at the way the conversation had turned.

"He was never in a film before," Mary said, "and he hated his look on the screen. 'Am I that fat?' Lionel asked. At first I ignored his question but he forced an answer out of me, and I told him the truth. That he was too fat. He promised to give up beer at once. Actually the studio heads at Biograph didn't like the close-up at all. Their reasoning was that they were paying me good money, and for their dough they wanted to see all of me, including my feet."

That brought a laugh from Doug, who, noting the time, jumped up and headed for our bedroom to get back into his suit. After dropping Mary and Doug off a half hour later, and promising them the use of my cottage again, I headed back to Chaplin's home. Once there, I encountered the Japanese chauffeur, Kono, who, to my amazement, presented me with a large bottle of iodine.

"What in hell am I supposed to do with this?" I asked. "Somebody got a cut finger?"

"You'll find out later," Kono said mysteriously. "Things are likely to go a bit far today, and Charlie will want you to paint him."

"Paint him with iodine?" I asked, completely bewildered. "I don't understand."

"You will later," he assured me, "should the need arise." He went back into a bathroom off the garage and returned with some cotton swabs. "You may need this to apply the iodine." With that instruction, he turned and hobbled off. The manservant came out of the house and told me that Chaplin was running late. I was to get behind the wheel and start the car for a speedy getaway once Chaplin came out of the building. The servant made it sound as if he were participating in a bank robbery for a film.

In fifteen minutes Charlie emerged through his back porch and practically ran to his limousine getting into the back seat. "We'd better hurry," he said. "I have a very important guest. He's taken up all my time. I'll want you to entertain him later."

I'd already entertained one of his important guests, Douglas Fairbanks, and I wondered who this second guest was. Chaplin was always surrounded by famous people.

"Did Mary and Doug go at it again?" he asked with a mildly prurient look on his face.

"Indeed they did," I said, "in the privacy of my cottage."

"Thank you for being discreet," Chaplin said. "Here you are today driving around the three most famous people on earth. You'll forgive us our harmless indiscretions, won't you?"

"I see nothing," I said, "hear nothing."

"That's the way it should be," he said. He settled back into his seat. "I've been thinking about Reatha all day. She is marvelous. So graceful, so dainty, so beautiful. I think I've fallen madly in love with her."

"Don't you think she's a little young?" I asked, fearing I had overstepped my bounds the moment the question came from my lips.

"Don't be a fool," he said. "I've been in love with girls of twelve. Even ten. Reatha is a bit old for me but still highly desirable."

"Do you really plan to make her a movie star?"

"Hell, no! I tell all the young beauties who get underneath me that line. After I've fallen madly in love with them, I never want to see them again. With rare exceptions, I have no interest in a young girl after I've deflowered her. I love the virginal slimness of a young girl, especially their as yet undeveloped arms and legs. I love to kiss and suck their breasts before they've blossomed into cows. I love to caress and fondle them and stick my tongue into their sweet mouths. I also like to stick something bigger than my tongue in them." .

"Don't you hurt them?" I asked. "Especially if they're virgins, which they usually are."

"Hearing them squeal with pain as the monstrous Chaplin cock slides into them is sweeter to my ears than any Mozart concerto."

After that pronouncement, the rest of the ride was in silence. Arriving at the playground, I feared I might get fired as all the young girls had gone home for the day. I'd driven Chaplin to the grounds too late.

Suddenly, from behind the bushes the stunningly beautiful Reatha emerged, dressed in virginal white. I started to get out of the car but Chaplin opened the door in the rear and virtually pulled the girl inside.

"Thank you, my little lovely, for waiting so patiently for me," he said. "I'm sorry I'm running late today."

"I'd wait for hours and hours for you, Mr. Chaplin, even in the rain," Reatha said, getting into the car. "You're my favorite film star."

"Then come and give your favorite a very wet and deep kiss," he said.

"With tongue?" she asked rather innocently.

"With tongue."

Not looking into the rear-view mirror, I drove for about thirty minutes, hearing only mild noises of love from the back seat.

Chaplin reared up, showing his famous face to me. "I think Reatha and I are going a bit far today. It's risky driving around in the car. That cottage of yours sounds intriguing. Would you take us there?"

"You're welcome to be my guest." For the second time today I headed back to my cottage. The two most famous people on earth had fucked there already. Why not the third most famous person on earth? Or was Chaplin third? Although I had not taken a poll, I felt Chaplin was more famous than Doug and Mary, certainly more famous than the king of England or the president of the United States. Only Cleopatra had them beat, and she was dead.

Back at the cottage again, I apologized to Chaplin for the unmade bed. He didn't seem to mind at all. He whispered in my ear, "Actually I'd like to fuck Reatha on the same bed where Doug penetrated that darling Mary."

Back in the living room, I headed for the kitchen as Reatha walked with a certain trepidation toward the back bedroom.

In the kitchen I washed the coffee pot and put on a fresh brew. When I would eventually tell Rodolfo of my day's experience, he would surely think me mad.

Later in my life I would forget entire decades. But this day which I am dictating to the Bitch of Buchenwald has always stood out as one of the most memorable in my life, and why wouldn't it? It did, after all, have an all-star cast. At the time I was making the coffee, I thought the drama of the day was about to end. But there were further surprises for me, adventures that would last far into the night.

"Durango," Chaplin shouted. "Get your ass back here."

Hurrying to the bedroom, I discovered a completely nude Reatha. She covered her breasts with her hands upon seeing me enter, leaving her vagina exposed. She had very little hair around her opening. Lying beside her, Chaplin had a full erection, which was throbbing in the air with all its uncut inches waiting to be serviced.

"Do you have that iodine on you?" he asked.

"Yes, sir," I said a bit awkwardly, considering the circumstances. Nothing I had learned in Lawrence, Kansas, had prepared me for a moment like this.

"Then swab my God damn cock with the iodine," he commanded. "I don't want to take my hands off Reatha. I've got her aroused, and I can't stop to break the mood."

Reaching for the iodine, I bent over the bed

and gently swabbed the mighty cock of the not-so-little fellow until I'd painted it bright red. When I'd finished, he ordered me from the room.

Back in the front, I heard a piercing scream from Reatha, then silence. I prayed he hadn't killed her. Would I be an accessory to the murder?

About an hour later, after many loud sounds coming from the bathroom, Reatha emerged from the back. Tears were in her dreamy, expressive eyes. She held up five one-hundred dollar bills to me. "He gave me this," she said. "He's going to make me a star, but I hurt. Real bad."

Still sore in my throat from the assault by Francis X. Bushman, and still raw in the rear from my darling Rodolfo's rape, I could sympathize with this very young virgin who obviously was a virgin no more. "Did the iodine burn?" I asked.

"I don't know what burned," she said. "Everything hurt. It didn't feel good at all. Charlie said your painting him with iodine will keep him from getting blood poisoning."

We were interrupted at the sudden appearance of a fully dressed Chaplin who was beaming and bright faced. "It's getting late," he said. "I've got an important guest waiting for me back home, and I can't leave him alone any more."

On the way back to the playground to drop off Reatha, I heard her ask him. "What about that screen test? Will I get cast in your next movie?"

"My next movie doesn't have a part for a girl as young and sweet as you," he said. "But the movie I'm about to make will have a major starring part for you."

Reatha looked as if she didn't believe him. As Chaplin opened the door for her she asked him, "How can I get in touch with you? I'm not always on this playground."

Chaplin's face flashed anger which he quickly masked. "I noticed you have a phone," he said to me. "Give her your phone number."

Reaching into the glove compartment, I wrote down my phone number and address. I smiled at this incredibly beautiful girl as I handed her my number. Somehow I felt a bond with her, as both she and I were being used as pawns by all these great stars. She took the

number from me and with the world's most stunning eyes smiled at me again, bending over and giving me a kiss on the cheek. She stood back on the sidewalk and looked dejected.

"Don't worry, my dear, dear girl," Chaplin said. "Durango handles all my auditions. He'll put you at the top of the list."

"I'll call you real soon, Durango," she promised.

As I drove away, I knew that girl would indeed call me. In that one moment as I gave her my phone number, I felt she might become an important friend of mine. I needed more than sexual conquests. I needed friends too. Was Theda Bara my friend? Possibly. How about Rod St. Just? He and I definitely had the makings of a friendship.

As I drove away, I looked back at the girl in white on the sidewalk. Chaplin had taken a kind of innocence from her, and I felt sorry she'd lost it so soon. As she faded from view, I had no idea at that moment that the girl we were leaving behind in just a short time would become one of the legends of the silent screen, a career that burst into full bloom almost overnight and with no help at all from Chaplin.

Back at Chaplin's home, he jumped out of the car, seemingly having forgotten all about Reatha. "You've got to meet my important guest," Chaplin said to me, ushering me into his living room. "He wants you to take him somewhere later this afternoon for a private dance concert."

In the living room, an exotic young man bounced up from an overly padded sofa and rushed into Chaplin's arms, kissing him succulently right on the lips. "I'm so glad you're back. I've been so happy here enjoying the home of one of the world's greatest talents. Your comedy is *balletique*. You are a dancer!"

Escaping ever so gently from the homosexual embrace, Chaplin turned to me. "Durango Jones, meet the legend himself, Vaslaw Nijinsky."

*****

Even in Kansas, Maria Jane and I had read

about the legends and exploits of the great Nijinsky, including his fabled leap across almost the whole of the St. Petersburg's Mariinsky stage in the Blue Bird *pas de deux.*

In the flesh Nijinsky wasn't quite the romantic hero or *danseur noble* I'd expected. His legs were too short for a ballet dancer, and he was somewhat stocky, with overly developed calves and thighs. Anna Pavlova had once dismissed him as Diaghilev's pet, a reference to their homosexual union, but even she had to admit Nijinsky was unsurpassed in *L'Aprés-midi d'un Faune.*

Nijinsky came up to me and planted a wet, sloppy kiss on my lips, just as he had with Chaplin. I was later to learn that this was how he greeted most people to whom he was introduced.

"Charlie tells me you are the beauty who will drive me to my concert," he said. "I am honored to ride in the same automobile with you."

"The honor is all mine," I said. "I will view you as a treasure trove directly descended from Mount Olympus." In my short time in Hollywood, I had become rather florid and purple in speech.

As I turned around, Chaplin had disappeared. I felt the Tramp was relieved to get out of our presence, and he also seemed pleased to turn the entertainment of Nijinksy over to me. It was my suspicion that Chaplin and Nijinsky would never be friends.

The manservant of Chaplin appeared out of nowhere and told the dancer that he had packed all the items he'd need for his performance and was placing the suitcase in the back seat of the limousine. Nijinsky seemed to hear that but was of the ilk who ignored servants, although that didn't explain why he was showing such attention to me, a mere driver. I later learned that Nijinsky ignored servants who were ugly. If beautiful, he paid excessive attention to them, including his endless wet kissing.

Even as we talked, he kissed me a few more times, each one wetter than the other. I feared I was drying up all his saliva. I noticed that Chaplin had discreetly wiped the dancer's saliva from his face, but I felt for me to do that might be insulting. I could only pray that the air would dry the slobber off my face before Nijinsky refreshed the supply.

He held my hand as if we were lovers. "I have a great secret to confess to you."

"You can trust me to be discreet. Chaplin does."

"There is no need to keep my secret," he said. "After tonight, I will never dance again."

An alarm came over me. "What's the matter? Is something wrong? Your health?"

"I'm in perfect health," he said, anger flashing across his face. "Do not be insulting."

"Forgive me," I said. "I don't understand."

"For that insult I demand you feel every inch of my body, including my legs. Feel everything and then retract your words."

I stood awkwardly in front of him, not knowing how to proceed. He took my hands and placed them on his chest. "Now feel me," he commanded in a voice ringing with authority.

I gingerly proceeded to feel his chest. "Feel harder," he shouted. "Only then can you determine how healthy I am and eat your vile words."

By the time I reached his stomach muscles I was sweating, thinking I would skip over the genital area and proceed to feel his sturdy legs. Looking up at Nijinsky, I saw him eying me with a fierce determination. "That too," he barked at me.

Closing my eyes, I braced myself for the challenge. Nothing Maria Jane had ever taught me in Lawrence, Kansas had prepared me for this moment. Here I was in the living room of the world's most famous person, Charlie Chaplin, about to feel one basket of goodies belonging to the world's greatest dancer, Nijinsky.

The dancer was wearing a pair of thin white pants. Gently I massaged his penis and balls, before moving on to his legs. "No, return there," he shouted to me. "Only when you have massaged it to its full glory, can you determine what a healthy male specimen I am."

There on the floor and on my knees, I massaged Nijinsky to a full and impressive erection, and it was easy to determine why Diaghilev had been so enthralled with this dancer.

Apparently I had massaged him enough. He pushed my hands down to his calves, and I felt every inch of his famous dancing legs ending with his feet. My job done, I stood up and faced him in time to receive another wet, sloppy kiss.

"You are the greatest male figure I have ever encountered," I said, lying to him. After all, I had devoured Francis X. Bushman, and no one had a physique quite like that. No one.

"Good, we will be friends," Nijinsky said, heading out the door. He turned to look at me like I'd been an unruly pupil and he the stern teacher. "But no more insults to Nijinsky."

In the Locomobile, Nijinsky got in the front seat with me. I was still in awe of driving what Jean Cocteau had called a "victorious attack of rose perfume." Even Proust had found Nijinsky "submerged in erotic twilight."

To me, this androgynous dancing creature had a thoroughly mysterious sex appeal. I sensed that all the more after feeling his basket of goodies which I was eager to sample in spite of my sore throat and ass. As I have already confessed, I was becoming a bit of a whore, following in the example of my beloved Rodolfo.

After giving me an address, Nijinsky settled into the seat and looked straight ahead at the road but with vacant eyes. It was then that I learned about the second part of his nature. When nothing caught his interest or excited him, Nijinsky retreated behind the stone face of Buster Keaton.

That face could be strikingly unprepossessing. On stage, or so I had been told, he had the grace of a butterfly. When not wanting to have his space disturbed, he could retreat behind a wooden manner with mechanical gestures.

At one point, seeing a grove of orange trees, he ordered me to stop the car. That indifferent mask had been replaced with an almost child-like face eager to open the presents Santa Claus had brought him for Christmas.

Leaping from the car as if on the Mariinsky stage again performing the Blue Bird *pas de deux*, Nijinsky ran into the grove. He executed a series of *rivoltades* but didn't land in the ordinary fashion. He shifted in the air and began yet another set. I couldn't believe my eyes as I got to see Nijinsky dance and only for my benefit. The body with its short, rounded muscles, which I had so recently felt, wasn't the handsomest figure in the world except when he danced.

Once Nijinsky danced, all bodily imperfections disappeared. He was capable of performing unparalleled feats. It was like acrobatic dancing. I was hardly a dance critic, and had only seen visiting ballet troupes perform in Kansas, but Nijinsky seemed to prolong his step sequence more extravagantly than any dancer I'd ever heard of or seen since. He brought a sense of fantasy to every classical gesture, carrying dance to an unforeseen dimension, performing a *grande pirouette* in rhapsody. Even though there was no music in the orange grove, I heard the swelling volume of an orchestra.

Nijinsky spun around and stood on the tip of his toes. Suddenly, he ended the performance with no graceful conclusion. He just stopped dancing. With the same grace he'd displayed in his dance, he gathered up some oranges in the grove, then raced toward the car.

"We are going to be late," he said, dropping the oranges on the floor of the limousine. "I love California. You can live off the fruit of the land."

Back into the seat again, he assumed his indifferent mask for another ten minutes. Jerking up in the front seat, a look of undeniable pain came across his face. "I miss my Romola so very much," he said in a mournful voice. "She is my one true love. Without her I am nothing. She is my life. My soul."

With that pronouncement about his wife, he retreated back into the comfort of Chaplin's upholstered car and said no more until we reached our destination.

I was quickly learning. These great artists usually spoke of such towering love for their spouses either before or after a homosexual dalliance.

If I may jump ahead in my story, I actually met Romola Nijinsky later on in my life. By then I was a nationally syndicated entertainment writer. It was in Paris and in the dressing room of Mikhail Baryshnikov. The way Nijinsky had described Romola on that long-ago day in California had led me to expect a Russian princess of glacial beauty and exquisite grace. What greeted me was a fat, dumpy woman who had somewhat the appeal of the squaw of Nikita Khrushchev.

In a frumpy dress, Mrs. Nijinsky wore a tacky, moth-eaten mink stole. Even with the passage of time and its inevitable decay, Ramola at her peak could never have been the ravishing beauty I'd imagined. She was no Reatha Watson.

As I pulled the car into the driveway of a grand mansion, Nijinsky reached out and took my hand. "As I told you, this will be my last performance. It should be recorded on camera. It will be a special performance. For connoisseurs only. Some of the greatest Nijinsky fans from all over the world have journeyed all the way to Hollywood to watch my final dance. It will be very special. You will enjoy it."

In the rear of the mansion, Nijinsky greeted both of his queenly hosts with wet, sloppy kisses. The hosts virtually ignored me, even when introduced, and concentrated all their attention on the dancer. One of the hosts looked like a 1919 version of Liberace, and the other was a pre-Clifton Webb clone. It soon became obvious they were paying a lot of money for Nijinsky's final dance.

I was to learn that one-hundred "bachelors" had been invited to this performance which was to be held in a gilded ballroom of the mansion under massive chandeliers imported from St. Petersburg. A special stage had been built just for Nijinsky, and two of Hollywood's best lighting experts had been hired for the occasion, as had a full orchestra assembled by the Clifton Webb clone. He was, so I learned from a servant, the money behind the queenly team who were Nijinsky's sponsors. Apparently, there was some oil fortune from Texas lurking in some bank vault somewhere.

I never found out what Nijinsky was paid that night, only that it was an "ungodly sum" in the view of one servant. Another servant, a stout female cook, pronounced it a "king's ransom." She confided to me that the Webb clone paid her eight dollars a week.

After helping Nijinsky prepare himself for his performance, I was told I could see the show backstage, as all the chairs in the ballroom were taken. The dance concert would be in two acts. For the first act, Nijinsky had selected a pair of the sheerest white tights I'd ever seen. It clearly outlined his genitalia. He might as well have been nude. He was to appear with his torso exposed.

As the lights dimmed and the spotlights were turned on, Nijinsky was highlighted on the stage. When the all-male audience saw his tights, a murmur arose. Nijinsky began to dance. There is good dancing, and there is even great dancing, and there is the dancing of Nijinsky. In later years I would see and write about dance performances by world class artists such as Erik Bruhn, Baryshnikov, and of course, Rudolf Nureyev. But nothing I have seen since ever equaled the pure magic and majesty of Nijinsky's final public performance, although it wasn't exactly that public.

Nijinsky in private life might be a tormented genius, but on stage he was the master of flamboyant virtuosity. No one before or since ever matched his *ballon* or his ability to sustain a jump in the air. He was performing a scene from *Le Spectre de la Rose*, a technical *tour de force* in which Nijinsky literally went from man to rose.

I'd felt Nijinsky's ankles, and this dance called for the greatest of rare ankle muscle endurance. Not only that, but he had to have the ability to take off cleanly and seemingly effortlessly after his muscles had been strained to almost inhuman endurance. He did so beautifully. In later years Baryshnikov would attempt to follow in Nijinsky's footsteps, but Baryshnikov was badly miscast in the role and could not meet the challenge. The younger dancer claimed he found it "impossible to get through the role."

Encountering a sweating, panting Nijinsky backstage in his dressing room, he reached for my arm, his fingers digging in. "For my farewell to the world of dance, I must do something special. Something I had not planned on until tonight. All my life my penis and my testicles have been confined in a pouch. I know I have an appreciative audience out there. They want to see all of me without benefit of clothing. For the first time in my life I want to appear on stage totally nude. As I dance, I want my cock and balls to dance with me, moving gracefully with my body movements." He stood before me. "Peel off my tights and free my beautiful genitals for all the world to inspect and enjoy."

In front of his sweaty body, I peeled down the tights, exposing him. He fluffed himself as if to enjoy this new found freedom. "Get me a robe," he said. "I don't want anyone to know what I'm going to do until the second act begins. At my command, you remove the robe from my beautiful body which has inspired lust in certain men around the world."

If there are any men still alive who were there that night, the nude performance of Nijinsky must be indelibly etched in their brains. I have seen grand performances in my day—in theater, films, and in the ballet world—but nothing lingers longer and more vividly than Nijinsky's adieu. Amazingly, Nijinsky seemed to will his genitalia to move with the perfect harmony of his well-trained body. The all-male audience was thrilled. After the initial loud murmur, they settled into spellbound awe at what they were watching.

I cried at the end of Nijinsky's farewell adagio. It was filled with tragic intensity. He was a dream-maker on stage. His unique fluidity made the strain on his legs invisible. His nudity wasn't a striptease but seemed to flow lovingly from his body. It was a *tour de force*. As the curtain came down, there was endless clapping along with calls for Nijinsky to come out and take a bow.

Nijinsky instead called for his robe and demanded that I follow him to the dressing room. Once inside he locked the door and ignored the rapping on it, even though it was clearly the hosts calling for him to come out and take a bow.

His body was covered with sweat. Dropping the robe, he demanded that I remove all my clothes. A bit nervous, I obeyed him. Fully nude, I stood before him for inspection. "No, no, you little fool," he said. "I am not interested in the front part—only the back part. Turn around."

As I turned around, he grabbed each of my buttocks. "Perfect," he said. "They are fully rounded globes, and the skin is smooth. They are worthy of Nijinsky's prick." He pointed to a sofa at the far end of the dressing room. "Over there."

I did as told. Once at the sofa, I knew exactly how to lie down. I turned my face into the cushion of the sofa, leaving my back and buttocks exposed for the inevitable Nijinsky assault.

"After the dance, Nijinsky gets all pent up and must have relief," he said.

Moving toward the sofa, I looked up only to encounter an erect penis emerging from sandy brown pubic hair. He reached below to fondle his testicles. Without any preliminary moves, Nijinsky moved over me and plunged all the way into my ass, without benefit of lubrication or anything else. I muffled my scream into the pillow until I got accustomed to his attack.

Nijinsky's artistry and grace were left entirely for the stage. As a rapist, he was brutal and demanding, everything strictly for his own pleasure. I was left with the feeling that I could have been anybody—a mere hole to offer him relief. He moved fast and mechanically, intent only on his own approaching orgasm which I welcomed when it came. He pulled out of me at once even while still spewing.

I had never been fucked like that until decades later when I was a columnist and visited Nureyev in Paris. Even though way past my prime at the time, Nureyev had thrown me a mercy fuck. It was the same fuck as Nijinsky had given me oh so long ago. It was as if Nureyev had been taught to fuck by Nijinsky—all demanding, all brutal, a rapid entry, a constant hammering, an eruption, and then a sudden withdrawal.

As far as dancers go, my only regret was that I never got Baryshnikov or Erik Bruhn to fuck me, so I have no basis of comparisons with them and Nijinsky or Nureyev.

Nijinsky wasn't talking fantasy that night. He kept his word. Even though he was to live until 1950, he never danced again.

In all honesty, it was not apparent to me that on the night I met him, Nijinsky was already moving toward madness. Between that night of his adieu to the dance and his eventual death, he would be confined to various asylums.

*****

Two days later, during which I nursed my very sore ass and my slightly less sore throat back to some semblance of normality, Chaplin instructed me to meet him, with his car, at the Hollywood Hotel. The staff there told me that Chaplin had to leave the hotel for about an hour, but that he would return soon, and that I was to wait for him in his suite. Someone ushered me upstairs and opened the suite's door for me.

Thinking I was alone in the suite, I began to inspect five different satin gowns that were spread across a double bed. I fully expected Chaplin to dress me in one of these gowns, but for what purpose?

"Darling," came a distinctive voice from a young woman standing at the bathroom door. "Do you like to dress up like a woman too? I've always found it delightfully amusing."

Whirling around, I discovered a remarkably beautiful young woman with a slight Southern accent. "And who might you be?" she asked.

"I'm Durango Jones."

"Someday when I get to know you better, you'll tell me your real name. I'm Miss Tallulah Bankhead of Alabama."

"Pleased to meet you."

"Not as pleased as Chaplin was," she said. "He just fucked me before rushing off. He's got the reddest dick in Hollywood. It's so red it's like he's painted it."

"I know," I said, smug in my intimate knowledge of how Chaplin's dick got painted.

"He's got a big one, though," she said. "Of course, your darling Tallu hasn't fucked Francis X. Bushman yet. I hear Beverly Bayne has a vagina the size of the Grand Canyon."

"He's pretty huge," I said. I was quickly becoming a first-hand observer of Hollywood dicks. "I work for him."

"You must have one sore ass," she said.

"I do, but not from Bushman."

"How delightful. I've fucked my way around Hollywood in the first few days I've been here. I'm sure you have too. We've probably had the same pricks in us."

"Are you an actress?"

"Darling, I'm a fucking movie star. You haven't heard of Tallulah Bankhead, the movie star?"

"Forgive me, but I just got into town. I'm from Lawrence, Kansas. We didn't get all the movies at the Patee Theater."

"Then I'll forgive you," Tallulah said. "I made

When Men Betray back east. It was as trifling as it was silent. I got two-hundred dollars for appearing as the star. Samuel Goldfish hired me to appear opposite Tom Moore in *Thirty-a-Week* which is about all I got from that stinker."

"You mean Samuel Goldwyn?"

"Yeah, but I call him Goldfish. That's his real name. Tom Moore was the cutest actor I'd seen in films, but he refused to fuck me. I like to fuck all my leading men, not that I've had that many roles."

"There are a lot of handsome leading men out here," I said.

"I know, but I don't think most of them know how to handle a hot mama like me. In the fuck department, my one major ambition is to bed the divine John Barrymore himself."

I was startled. That was an ambition we shared, but I wasn't going to reveal that to Tallulah. It would be a secret contest to see who got to sample Mr. Barrymore's wares first.

"Are you out here trying to get a movie contract?" I asked.

"You don't have to be a genius to figure that one out," she said. "I've been trying to bait Goldfish but that slippery bastard isn't biting. You see, my first two films did not immediately ignite world excitement, and I'm heading back to New York and the stage. I'm even considering going to London to try my luck."

"That sounds very exciting," I said.

"Perhaps." A frown crossed her face. "It also signifies failure. I obviously didn't fuck the right people out here on the coast. Frankly, my darling, I wanted to be a God damn movie star. But Mary Pickford I ain't. I couldn't even seduce her brother-in-law, that darling but unobtainable Tom Moore."

"I bet you'll go over big on the stage," I predicted. "You score big hits in London and New York, and you'll have Hollywood shouting for your return."

Before she could answer, Chaplin burst into the suite. "Good, you're here," he said to me. Smiling, he turned to Tallulah, "I hope you enjoyed it as much as I did."

"Of course, I did," she said before bursting into laughter. "You know how to hammer a big dick into my virginal Alabama pussy."

"Come now, Tallulah," Chaplin said. "You

lost your virginity at the age of four to some Confederate soldier."

"How did you find that out?" she asked before bursting into laughter again. Apparently, she told jokes to herself which she found highly funny.

Chaplin looked to me. "I hope you're ready to play our game. Tallulah has generously agreed to help me dress you as a woman if you're willing to go through with the deal. There's good pay in it for you."

"You cute boys have it made," Tallulah said to me. "I understand Charlie here is paying you more money than I got for my entire two-film movie career."

"You should have dressed up as a man," I said.

"That gives me an idea," she said. "I think in London I'll play the role of a man now and then." She kissed Chaplin on the cheek. "Charlie, let me begin with you. I hear there's a Francis X. Bushman dildo being distributed around Hollywood. Would you volunteer to let me try it out on you?"

"I don't go that route," Chaplin said. "Perhaps Durango." He winked at me.

"Believe you me, I know a lot about the Francis X. Bushman dildo," I said. "It's to be admired, fondled, and placed on your mantle for all to see. It's not to be inserted in any orifices."

"Too bad," she said. "Perhaps before leaving Hollywood I'll find a volunteer who'll let me play the role of a man."

"Try Nazimova," I said. "I bet she'd like that. I can take you to the Garden of Alla."

"That's a great idea," she said, turning to Chaplin. "Don't you agree?"

"Lesbians hold little interest for me," Chaplin said, inspecting the gowns on the bed.

"I think I'll sample women before leaving Hollywood," she said. "Fucking the men out here sure didn't advance my career." She turned and flashed a look of contempt at Chaplin who ignored her.

"I'll try to set something up for you," I said.

"Down to work, girls," Chaplin said with the commanding authority of a director. "We've got to turn Durango here into the most ravishing woman in Hollywood." He stood back, evaluating my figure. "Pull off all your clothes.

Tallulah has happily volunteered to make your dick disappear.

"Disappear?" I didn't like the sound of that.

"How big is your dick, darling?" she asked.

"Nine inches," I said proudly, knowing horse-hung Chaplin wouldn't necessarily be impressed with that.

"No, no, darling, how big is it soft?" she asked.

"About three and a half inches," I said. "I've never really measured it soft."

"From a female impersonator in the east, Tallulah has learned the art of making a man's dick disappear," Chaplin said. "I want nothing showing when we put silk panties on you."

Embarrassed, I began to disrobe in front of this wicked pair, not able to imagine what fate awaited me.

Chaplin was no stranger to female impersonation. At the Patee Theater in 1915, I had seen his campy performance in *A Woman*. In the film, Chaplin interferes with two lechers in the park, both trying to accost a lovely young girl. Chaplin himself picks up Edna, another young girl who succumbs to his facile charm and invites him to her house to have a meal with her mother.

Later Edna's father shows up with a companion. It turns out to be the same two lechers Chaplin had confronted in the park. They start to tussle with Chaplin, but he flees upstairs. Once in Edna's bedroom, he shaves off his mustache and dresses up as a woman. Downstairs the lechers accept him as such, and begin to flirt with him. With fluttery gestures Chaplin drives the men to the point of sexual lust. The release of the film caused massive protest throughout America but the only banning of the movie came in Sweden where censors refused to allow the film's release. That ban wasn't lifted until 1931.

Tallulah made me promise not to reveal how she made my penis disappear—well, practically disappear. I will honor that long-ago commitment and not tell it now. Tallulah always claimed she'd learned the technique from Mae West who lived among and worked with a number of female impersonators—in fact, was accused of being a female impersonator herself. Even some of Mae's biggest fans claimed she was a man masquerading as a woman. The only person I ever knew who went to bed with Mae West was an actor named Brad Dean. Years later I asked him for a definite report from the battlefield of Mae's bed. "Tell me, is Mae West a man or a woman?" I asked.

"Hell," Brad said, giving me a quick kiss on the lips. "I was too polite to ask."

But I'm wandering off, the curse of senility. Back to dress-up time as a woman, my first introduction to drag.

With two experts working me over, I was turned into a spectacular woman. Men might have thought me beautiful as a man, but I was even more stunning as a woman. Directed by a genius like Charlie Chaplin, I experienced the miracle of sexual transformation. Both Chaplin and Tallulah thought I looked enough like a woman to pass for one even on camera.

"Mary Pickford's getting a little old to be the little girl," Chaplin said. "Maybe we've found a replacement."

Tallulah stood back checking out the results of her work and appearing almost jealous at how fabulous I looked in my beige gown that was so delicate it appeared to be lingerie.

"Before we meet our famous guest of the evening, I want you to go with Tallulah down to the bar," Chaplin said. "She'll give you some tips about how you can seduce our friend without his finding out you're a man."

"I'll need them," I said. "I mean, we can carry this seduction just so far before this big shot finds out I'm a man."

"Don't worry your pretty head about it," Tallulah said, taking me by the arm. "You look so terrific as a woman that I would readily agree to lick your pussy if I met you at a party."

"I've got to go now," Chaplin said. "I hope it goes smoothly. Tomorrow I want you to give me every detail. Every delicious detail. I'll be dining out on this story for months."

At the bar a very young but very experienced Tallulah went into vivid detail about how I was to keep this famous guest from feeling both my crotch and my breasts. "Just watch his hands while he's kissing you. When he's carried away and about ready for a sexual assault, get down on your knees in front of him, unzip his trousers, and give him a fabulous blowjob. That always distracts them."

"Hot damn!" I said. "I hope I can pull this

off."

The bar was a bit crowded tonight, and I recognized several stars, including Blanche Sweet who had tried to seduce me. She'd never know me in my fetching gown. Tallulah had given me a few pointers about how to carry a handbag.

Sitting by himself in a far corner of the bar, I spotted Rodolfo. At first I was tempted to go over to him but decided against it, considering how I was dressed. I suspected he was waiting for Jean Acker who apparently wouldn't let him go upstairs to her bedroom, even though they were engaged and about to be married.

It wasn't long before the eagle eye of Tallulah herself spotted Rodolfo. She nudged me. "See that darling man sitting over there seemingly burying his sorrows in a glass of whiskey. He must be Latin."

"I hadn't noticed him," I said.

"Darling, I've just decided he is going to be my lay of the evening."

Even though I tried desperately to dissuade her, I encountered that fierce Bankhead determination. She wanted Rodolfo for the night, and she was going to have him. "Excuse me, honey, but your Alabama mammy is working the bar." She adjusted her breasts.

"But where am I supposed to go?" I asked, trying to disguise the raging jealousy I felt as Tallulah was heading out to devour my man.

"Oh, yes, silly me, I forgot all about your own upcoming dalliance," she said. "You're to knock on the door of suite ten exactly at ten o'clock." She kissed me on the lips. "And, good luck, darling. I'm in room fourteen of this fleabag. Call me in the morning. Or I'll call you. I want to see some of the action going on at Nazimova's. Even back east, we've heard tales or is that T-A-I-L-S?"

And with that, Tallulah was gone, heading toward Rodolfo's table. I looked at the clock on the wall. I still had thirty minutes before encountering this mysterious but famous guest in suite ten. Since I had the time, I ordered another whiskey from the waiter and watched as Tallulah launched into her preliminary overtures leading to the seduction of Rodolfo.

Within twenty minutes Rodolfo was leaving the bar with Tallulah, presumably heading up to her room. Apparently, he hadn't been waiting for Jean Acker but was seeking a little action at the bar.

He could have been home with me. I felt betrayed and frustrated until I faced the reality that I, too, wasn't exactly waiting at home, darning his socks, and listening for the sounds of his tango-dancing footsteps at the door. This same thought had occurred to me several times before.

"Just a gigolo," I whispered to myself before deciding to head to the ladies room and check my makeup for one final time.

Perhaps it was the intoxication of the whiskey but staring back at me in the mirror in the women's toilet was the world's most beautiful woman—not Reatha Watson, but a runner-up.

Whoever it was in suite ten would soon fall under my exotic and erotic spell. After all, I hadn't seen all those Theda Bara movies for nothing.

My knees were shaking as I knocked gently on the door to suite ten. I sucked in the air, inflating my *faux* breasts.

The door was opened by Samuel Goldwyn himself.

*****

Although at that moment I looked like the most luscious broad who had ever descended on Hollywood, the producer staring back at me was hardly Buddy Rogers, much less Wallace Reid. Up to now I'd dated only handsome devils.

My heart sank when I first encountered Goldwyn, not knowing at the time how important he'd become in my life. He looked like a haberdasher from First Avenue in New York. In a blue business suit, with a white shirt and thin tie that had food stains on it, he was hardly the immaculately groomed Rodolfo Valentino. Actually his wrinkled trousers looked two inches too short, and he wore white socks with black shoes, just like they did in Kansas.

Before inviting me in, he stepped back to appraise my towering figure. "You are the prettiest gal in Hollywood, and what is your name and where do you come from?"

"My, oh, my," I said. "So many questions and I haven't even been invited in."

"Sorry about that," he said, stepping back and gesturing for me to enter. "Come into my evil web and meet a foxy fox."

"Mr. Goldwyn, spiders live in webs, foxes in holes."

"I'm a movie producer—not a veterinarian. Come on in and let me get you a drink. Whiskey for the lady?"

"That's fine," I said to his back as he headed to the bar. "Now to your appraisal and your questions. Thank you for complimenting my beauty—that is, if I have any."

"You've got it, baby," Goldwyn said. "Does Poland have cabbage, you've got beauty."

Not really getting the comparison to my beauty and Polish cabbage, I went on, "My name's Lotte Lee." Both Tallulah and Chaplin had agreed on that fetching name for me which, in their view, already sounded like a star of the silent screen. "And I'm from Kansas."

"Kansas—now that's a great state," he said, handing me a drink. "I bet your family owned oil wells."

"We have more corn in Kansas than oil wells, Mr. Goldwyn."

"You can call me Sam." He rubbed my right cheek. "Smooth as a baby's ass. Tallulah and Charlie told me all about you," he said, inviting me to join him on the sofa.

"Exactly what did those two tell you?" I asked, fearing his answer.

"The bitch Tallulah said you are one man-crazy broad. Can't get enough. You're said to give the best blow-jobs in California."

There was absolute silence on my part as he stared at me waiting for an answer. "I can believe Tallulah said that about me. She goes a bit far."

"Over the top with her," he said. "Or is it bottoms up? When I fucked her this afternoon, she asked me which of her three holes did I want to stick it into."

I was breathing a bit heavily and more than a little nervous.

"You didn't answer the question," he said. "Is it true? About giving the best head?"

"I've been known to bow low into a man's lap from time to time," I said, perhaps a little too defensively. "But only if he's good to me."

"I can't find many women out here who will

give head," he said. "Wives absolutely refuse, at least after we marry them. Charlie says he finds that a problem too. But with that big dick of his, I can see why a gal wouldn't give him head."

After finishing my whiskey, he offered me another one. "It's last call," he said. "I don't want you too drunk for the fun and games later in the evening. Tallulah got shit-faced before I fucked her. I don't like to fuck drunken broads."

"I've never been drunk in my life," I said. "One drink or two—and that's it for me."

"Don't think I'm generous with whiskey," he said. "I'm economical. My studio is having a few financial problems. Those Will Rogers pictures couldn't save it. When my guests leave, I take any spare whiskey they left in their glasses and pour it back into the bottle. I save a lot of money that way."

Repulsed, I said, "Let's forget that second drink."

"I'll pour one for myself." Back on the sofa, he settled in comfortably, placing his hand on my knee. "Tell me about yourself. Do you want to be an actress? What a stupid question. Every good-looking broad out here wants to be an actress."

"It wasn't hard to figure that one out," I said. "I want to be a movie star. Tallulah does too."

"You can forget Tallulah. She doesn't have the right spark for films. She's too obvious. Too vulgar. Thinks too much of herself. Now take Mabel Normand. That's a real star."

"She's one of my favorites."

"Mine too. She drives men wild, especially Mack Sennett and me. One man tried to kill himself over Mabel by drowning himself in a toilet bowl. I've fallen for Mabel in a real big way. That bitch, Blanche Sweet, told everybody that I'm a 'stark-raving, crazed, insane, lunatic madman' over Mabel." He smiled enigmatically at me. "Maybe I am. That's why Charlie and Tallulah fixed you up with me tonight. Your job: make me forget about Mabel. At least for one evening."

"That's a big job," I said to him, rubbing his cheek as he'd rubbed mine. "If Mabel were the moth to your flame, I'll be a beautiful butterfly draining you of your nectar."

"Don't give me a hard-on too soon," he said.

"Not until we've talked a bit." He settled back on the sofa. "I've not only fucked up with the Will Rogers films. But I've hired the wrong bitches as stars."

"Who do you mean?" I asked, genuinely curious for whatever movie gossip I could pick up.

"Geraldine Farrar, that fucking diva, and Pauline Frederick, would-be diva."

"I've not seen much of them."

"Nor has the rest of America," he said, sinking back with a despondent look on his face. "Their pictures have bombed, and they were to become my two biggest stars. Local assholes are calling my studio the old ladies' home."

"There's a certain irony in hiring Farrar as a silent screen star," I said. "I mean, after all, she's noted for her incredible operatic voice. I don't think silent movies would do her justice."

"Tell me about it. I am guaranteeing the broad $125,000 a year," he said. He downed the rest of his whiskey as a bitterness came across his face. "That Frederick bitch had no class at all. Her movies also don't make money, and she's going to hold me to our contract. I'll have to make a few more movies with the slut, and I'm sure the public will stay away in wheelbarrows. No one wants to see Pauline Frederick up there on the screen. The public wants new, fresh faces." He rubbed my cheek again. "Gals like you."

"That's very flattering."

"I mean it," he said, as his hand began a slow ascent up my gown. "I'm thinking of offering you a three-year contract at two-hundred a week. How does that grab you in the ass?"

"It does nothing for my ass," I said, "but it sure causes a tingle in my honeypot."

Goldwyn burst into a wild laughter that sounded a bit like a maniac in an asylum. "I think you'd make a great vamp."

"That I don't understand," I said, blocking his hand as it was about to enter the danger zone. "Everyone's saying that Theda Bara is finished vamping. The Vamp craze is over."

"Bullshit!" he said, sitting up as a certain anger flared. "It may be over for Theda, but fads that powerful don't die overnight. A dead horse isn't dead until you drained the last milk out of it."

I sighed, no longer attempting to correct Goldwyn. If he thought horses gave milk, so be it.

"The way I figure it, I could make about five or six vampire movies—not the heavy crap that Theda did, but in a lighter vamp. You'd be perfect as a new styled vamp of the Twenties. We're talking about shorter hair, thinner waistlines, more modern dresses. But you'll still drive men to death, madness, and destruction, the way Mabel has driven me."

"Could I do all that on screen?" I asked, sounding coquettish like Scarlett O'Hara years before the character was created.

"I can't wait to shoot a close-up of you," he said. "Your face is incredibly beautiful. Those lips of yours are cherry red like a Christmas tree. Too bad movies aren't shot in color."

"Colored pictures? That sounds unreal."

"It's an unreal business." He stuck out his tongue like a snake. "You've heard a lot about me?" he asked, seemingly to change the subject abruptly. "Tell me some of the things you've heard."

"I don't think I can repeat very much of what I've heard."

"Come on," he urged, "do it for Sammy. Your boy Sammy."

"Only yesterday I read in a magazine that Adolph Zukor called you a 'Jersey cow that gives the finest milk. But before you can take the bucket away, he has kicked it over.'"

At first he didn't say anything, and I feared I'd gone too far, probably having been around Tallulah too long.

Shrugging off Zukor's comment, he pulled me close to him on the sofa, inserting his tongue in my mouth. Not having a lot of options, I sucked on it as if it belonged to Rodolfo.

He backed away to lick my face, trying to insert his tongue up my nostrils. He reached for my hand, pressing it into his crotch. I didn't feel much but what I did feel was getting hard.

"I could be like a father to you, guiding your career."

At that moment the only guiding he was doing was getting me to unbutton the trousers to that wrinkled suit.

"Tallulah said even though you give the greatest head in Hollywood, you don't like to get plugged that much."

"Tallulah got it right," I said, nibbling softly at his ear. "You can find plenty of dames out here to fuck. But no one will do for you what I can do."

"Your services will be in big demand," he said, "especially when I spread the word among the leading men of Hollywood. Only the other day that up-and-coming actor John Gilbert told me he was looking for a hot bitch to suck him off."

I reached in and pulled out Goldwyn's four-inch stiff dick. As I stared at it, I was completely bewildered. "There's no cap to your dick."

"You stupid bitch! Haven't you ever seen a circumcised Jewish dick before?"

"I never knew God made men like that."

"God had nothing to do with it," he said. "Some fucking rabbi took too much of my precious foreskin away. I just know it cuts down on the sensation—clipping off your skin like that."

Cap or not, I started sucking on Goldwyn's prick as if it was my last supper. I'd had bigger and better cocks in my short life, and God only knows I'd devour thousands more in my prime, but on that long ago night I was determined to give this movie producer the thrill of his life.

As he lay gasping from my expert blow-job, he kept muttering plans for my career. As all four inches were in my mouth, he announced that my first film would be entitled *Vampira*.

I'd arrived. At last I was on the dawn of becoming the queen of the silver screen as Lotte Lee. I would have preferred to see the name of Durango Jones on marquees. Perhaps God would be good to me. Maybe I'd have a double career—reigning as the king of the screen as Durango Jones while also presiding on my throne as Lotte Lee.

My mouth became a suction pump, as I mimicked some of the fast action of Rod St. Just. Even though I had Goldwyn squirming on the sofa and proclaiming it was his "best ever," my mind was elsewhere, certainly not on his sawed-off little prick.

The big female stars of the screen flashed through my cock-sucking mind:

Mary Pickford, Blanche Sweet, Geraldine Farrar, Pauline Frederick, Mabel Normand,

Theda Bara, Gloria Swanson, Constance and Norma Talmadge, Mae Marsh, Mae Murray, Mary Garden, Pearl White, Alla Nazimova.

Move over, bitches. Make way for the biggest star of them all. Lotte Lee has hit town.

At that glorious thought, Samuel Goldwyn exploded in my mouth. Tiny dick or not, he was a cum factory. Never before or since have I tasted so much cream in one fiery blast.

*****

Beginning the morning following the Goldwyn blow-job, the events in my life speeded up like a silent screen film run at fast speed. Even now I am not sure if I'm getting the proper events in sequence, as one experience—often tragic, forever erotic, and sometimes glamorously thrilling beyond belief—unfolded into another without transition.

It was a glorious, heady time, and Hollywood was just discovering itself. We still had boycotts, often from church groups, but the dreaded Production Code with that sickening little pervert, Will H. Hays in charge, was a long way in our future.

Back then, we were free to put our favorite pastimes on the screen, including "lustful kissing" (of which Rodolfo would become the expert), suggestive dancing, "white slavery," racial mingling, "sex perversion" (of which I would star), excessive violence, illegal drugs, nudity, vulgarity, profanity, and that old favorite, adultery. It was a scintillating era, and I was determined to participate in it to the fullest, either as Durango Jones, all-American he-man, or Lotte Lee, the new vamp of the silent screen. I shuttered at what my friend Theda would think of my screen portrait as a vamp.

Upon awakening in a lonely bed—where was Rodolfo?—I was actually aware that I'd been had. Goldfish probably told every little star-struck bitch he seduced that he'd send over a movie contract in the morning. Weren't all male stars, directors, and producers doing that with the hopefuls who arrived daily on the Sante Fe Chief from the great bread basket of the Middle West?

Getting out of bed, I showered and pre-pared myself for a day as Durango Jones, not knowing at this point when I'd summon back sultry Lotte Lee.

The first call came in from Tallulah, and I quickly informed her of what had happened. She promised she'd keep my secret in case Goldwyn were really serious about offering that contract. "You must give a better blow-job than I throw a fuck," Tallulah said. "I think I made my first mistake with Goldfish when he penetrated me. I asked him, 'Are you in yet, darling?' Naughty, naughty Tallu. The sound you hear, darling, is me slapping myself on the wrist."

Promising to keep my promise, I told Tallulah that I'd heard Nazimova was giving a big party that night, and I'd figure out a way to get us invited. At the party, she would get to meet Nazimova. When I put down the phone, I didn't exactly know how to get invited to Nazimova's bash, but before the end of the day I would surely think of something.

As if an answer to my prayer, Wallace Reid called. He sounded a bit nervous and agitated, informing me that his supply of morphine was running low, and he might not have enough to last until Saturday.

Reluctantly I promised that I would contact Dr. Hutchison and see if he would increase the supply.

"That's great," Wallace said. "We could meet tonight. In fact, I'm going to a party at Nazimova's. She said I could bring a friend or two. Wanta come with me?"

"A party at Nazimova's?" I asked in all innocence. "That sounds wonderful. After all, that's where we first met and began our affair."

"I wouldn't exactly call what we have an affair," Wallace said, a bit too defensively for my taste. "I'd say we get together for a weekly rendezvous where I can explore a side of my nature I usually keep hidden."

"That's a bit wordy to describe what we have, but I'll go for it just as long as I'm allowed to peel every stitch of clothing off you and do what I want with your nude body."

"When I'm with you, I'm all yours, but don't fall in love with me and the world's most beautiful dick," he said. "I will only hurt you. But remember that when we're together in public, you're going to be presented just as a fan, and to some limited degree, a buddy. But for the record, officially speaking, I'm only interested in women. And not just my wife."

"Your wife?" I was astonished. "I didn't know you were married."

"In fact, my wife, Dorothy Davenport, may be at the party tonight. You'll get to meet her."

"Then I have an idea. Let's go as a double date. I know this beautiful young actress—she's made two films. She's Tallulah Bankhead from Alabama."

"I think I've heard of her," he said. "She made a film with Tom Moore. In fact, I saw Tom Moore the other day. He'll be at the party with his brothers, Owen and Matt."

"Owen Moore? Does that mean that his wife, Mary Pickford, will be there too?"

"Owen doesn't go out with Mary any more," Wallace said. "We might have to drive him home. He's drunk all the time. He knows he's losing Mary to Doug Fairbanks."

"I see," I said, pretending I knew nothing of the Pickford/Fairbanks romance.

"Your Tallulah sounds fine, unless she's terrified of meeting Nazimova."

"It's Nazimova who should be afraid of Tallulah."

"That aggressive, huh?"

"You'll love her," I said. "She's charmingly refreshing. Not at all like the typical empty-headed starlet you meet out here."

"Let's make it a foursome," he said. "Since I'm a little unsteady behind the wheel, why don't you come by for Dorothy and me at eight-thirty tonight?" He gave me his address which I rapidly scribbled down.

Before ringing off, it was obvious he wanted to ask me another favor—not just the morphine. "You've got to understand. When I'm with you, I'm with you. But when I'm not with you, I want to be with women—and not just Dorothy. In addition to taking dope, I cheat on my wife."

"How can I help you?"

"I don't want to make you jealous," he said, a bit reluctant to come clean with what he was getting at. "But I've fallen in love with a very glamorous woman—so far, from a distance, but I want you to be the go-between for us. Tell her of my intentions and let us take it from there. See what she'll say. I can arrange for you to meet her."

"Who is this lucky gal? I need to know who my competition is. Probably some *femme fatale*."

"Gloria Swanson."

There was a long pause on my part. "I see." I felt crestfallen.

"I want you to deliver a note to Miss Swanson at her studio," he said. "I'll make arrangements for you to go to her dressing room."

"Whatever you want, Wally," I said with no enthusiasm at all. "But I must warn you, I think Miss Swanson is rather booked up these days with that ugly little Herbert K. Somborn."

"Durango, you sweet boy, we're not in the Middle West any more. Married or not, women in this town play the field. An invitation to seduction by Wallace Reid is hardly turned down by any one."

"Certainly not by me."

"Good," he said. "We'll meet behind a potted palm tonight at Nazimova's. Better yet, the urinals. You'll give me the morphine, and I'll give you my note to Swanson and tell you how to deliver it to her. Your path to Swanson will have already been cleared by me. I know the production manager of the picture she's working on. He owes me a big favor. All I have to do is let him reach inside my trousers and play with my balls. That's it. If I let him do that, he'll do anything for me."

"Until tonight, Wally." I put down the phone, feeling a bit dejected.

Contract or not from Goldwyn, I still had my temporary jobs for Francis X. Bushman and for Chaplin. At a loud knock on the door, I rushed to see who it was. The most unexpected people arrived on the doorstep of the cottage I shared with Rodolfo, and I was eager for this new surprise, as I'd been lonely this morning waiting to make the deliveries for Francis.

It was a messenger from Samuel Goldwyn, my beloved Goldfish of the previous evening. After tipping the messenger a quarter, I retreated into the living room to read the note. It was from Goldwyn himself, thanking me for last night. He said he was eager to begin filming *Vampira* in two weeks, and wanted me to go to the studio of Rod St. Just tomorrow morning at ten for publicity stills. Later that same day I had to meet with his publicity department. Goldwyn was eager to announce the film, *Vampira*, with me in the starring role, and he wanted to get press coverage for me as his new star.

Even though thrilled beyond belief, I wished the contract had been for Durango Jones and not Lotte Lee. But a contract was a contract, I decided, and was hysterically amused that Rod St. Just was the photographer assigned for the publicity stills. Rod would see through my disguise in a minute, and know at once that I was Durango Jones. I also knew he'd keep my secret—in fact, might be the one person in Hollywood who would help me pull off the disguise. As for Chaplin, I would confront him this afternoon and remind him that I was keeping his secrets and wanted a reciprocal agreement. Earlier he had planned to have a joke on Goldwyn whom Chaplin suspected to be homophobic. He was going to spread the word across town that Goldwyn had been tricked into going to bed with a man thinking it was a woman. But after my little session with Chaplin, I just knew that he'd never tell the world the true identity of Lotte Lee. Chaplin had too much to loose if he did, not that I was a blackmailer.

Right there and then, I decided that the only people who would be privy to my secret would be Rod St. Just, Tallulah Bankhead, and Charlie Chaplin.

I'd even thought about how to handle the amazing resemblance between Lotte Lee and Durango Jones. I would announce that Lotte was my sister. Obviously we'd never be seen at the same function together, and we'd certainly not make the same film together. Or would we? Had films progressed to the point where it would be possible to fake a double role for me with Lotte Lee starring opposite her handsome leading man, Durango Jones. If such a thing were possible, and in Hollywood, everything appeared possible, it would certainly need a very understanding and cooperative director. I'd put that idea on the back burner.

The telephone rang again. It was from an assistant to Samuel Goldwyn. I was told to give "Miss Lee" a message from Goldwyn himself. He wanted me to register at the Hollywood Hotel where he could "see me from time to time," but he also wanted a central address where I could be reached. The reception staff at the hotel would take important messages from me; otherwise, Goldwyn might be calling the phone in the cottage for days at a time, not knowing when he'd catch me in, as I hardly maintained a regular schedule.

The idea thrilled me. At two-hundred dollars a week, I could certainly afford a room at the hotel. I also knew that if a resident, I could monitor the activities of Rodolfo and Jean Acker better.

It was with a sad heart that I walked across the lawn and knocked on the back door of Elizabeth Hutchison. Her attendant ushered me into Elizabeth's sun porch where she was sitting covered in a blanket even though the day was warm.

"Wallace is dying to meet you this Saturday," I said. "I thought I might prepare a picnic for us and go up in the Hollywood Hills."

"That would thrill me," she said. "Every day I can't think of anything else but meeting him." She looked at me with great sensitivity and understanding, as if reading my thoughts. She was a very intuitive person. "You didn't really come here to tell me this. It's something else, isn't it?"

I decided to blurt it out. "Wallace needs more morphine, even before Saturday. He's in great pain. He needs it today. I just don't have what it takes to call Dr. Hutchison and ask him to increase the order."

For a long time Elizabeth didn't say anything, but kept looking into her lap, as the shadows caused by the morning sunlight danced on her face. She raised up, "Come by at six o'clock. My father's coming over. He'll bring the morphine."

"Thank you so much for doing this." I was embarrassed to look her in the eye. It was obvious that we both knew we were doing something we shouldn't, and even contributing to Wally's self-destruction.

Elizabeth raised up her face to me, almost forcing me to look deeply into her eyes. "Our friendship with Mr. Reid will require that we pay a price."

"It does," I said, agreeing. "I find there is a price tag attached to everything out here in Hollywood."

For the rest of our visit, we talked not of Wallace but of my career as Durango Jones which didn't exist at the moment, except as a temporary chauffeur. She asked about Rodolfo, and I informed her that he'd be marrying soon.

"Does that mean he'll be leaving the cottage?" she asked.

"I'm not sure," I said. "Rodolfo is a man of great mystery."

"You're in love with him, aren't you?"

"There's no need to deny it. I am in love with him. But it certainly won't be a traditional relationship."

"So few relationships out here are."

Seeing what time it was, I kissed Elizabeth good-bye and headed across the street to make the morning deliveries for Francis. A servant of his told me that "Mr. Bushman and Miss Bayne were still sleeping" as they'd attended a party last night.

The Bushman trophies must be really selling as I had seven deliveries, including photographs, statues, and the now famous dildo, to various homes. I gathered that most of the Bushman trophies were to go to old queens but the final delivery intrigued me. It was to the home of Fatty Arbuckle. I'd been watching Roscoe or "Fatty" Arbuckle at the Patee Theater ever since he was discovered by Mack Sennett in 1913 while working as a plumber's helper. I'd seen this 300-pound butterball as he'd appeared in farce after farce, all custard pies and pratfalls, mayhem and mud.

Graduating from the Keystone Kops, Fatty moved into the two-reel comedies, appearing opposite Chaplin in *The Rounders*, Buster Keaton in *The Butcher Boy,* and even Mabel Normand in *Fatty's Flirtations.*

In 1917 he'd signed with Paramount, having moved from a three-dollar-a-day paycheck in 1913 for Sennett to five-thousand a week when Paramount welcomed him with a big sign proclaiming "The Prince of Whales."

What did Fatso want with twelve dildoes of Francis X. Bushman? Fatty appeared in person to accept the dildoes. Freshly emerging from a Turkish bath, he wore a large towel draped around his corpulent body. A servant of his showed me into a California room that opened off his bedroom wing.

"Has Bushman tried out his dildo on you?" was the first question Arbuckle asked.

"Not yet," I replied, "and I hope he never

does. I wouldn't be walking if he had."

"That big, huh?" Arbuckle said. "That's why I ordered it. I'm quite small myself."

"Be careful if you plan to use it on yourself," I said.

"Don't be a fool," he said, anger flashing. "I'm not going to use the fucking dildo on myself. This jovial jackanapes of the screen likes party girls, the younger the better. I love my liquor and my ladies."

"Then why the dildo if you don't mind my asking."

"I've always dreamed of having a big dick like Bushman," he said with surprisingly candor. "Since nature didn't reward me with such, I intend to push the Bushman dildo up into the cunts I go to bed with. Bushman will be my proxy fucker so to speak. I'll hear their screams as the Bushman dildo penetrates them, and I'll get hard hearing those screams. Usually, I'm impotent. I'll imagine that it's me, Roscoe himself, entering the women. Their cries will be music to my ears."

"Whatever turns you on," I said.

He looked over at me. "How long have you been in the sex industry?"

"I'm not really in the sex industry," I said. "I'm just making deliveries for Mr. Bushman."

"I don't know where you came from, but I bet your mother never expected her son would end up delivering dildoes."

"She's passed on now. If she weren't dead, news of what I'm doing would surely kill her."

"What's your name?" he asked.

"Durango Jones."

"No one is named Durango Jones. Whatever your real name is, I might have a deal for you. Are you into men?"

"I'm a proud homosexual male."

"Why don't you leave your phone number and address?" he asked. "I have these real wild parties. I've never done this to a boy before. Give me one of those dildoes to inspect."

I reached into the box and produced a replica of Francis X. Bushman at his proudest extension.

"That is some monster meat," he said. "It's about eight times what I've got. How would this deal interest you. What about coming to one of my infamous parties? Put on a little show for us. Many of my guests like boys as much as they do girls. Let me slip the dildo up you. Slowly, of course."

"I don't know."

"There's a thousand dollars in it and that's just from me alone. Some of the other men will contribute. For all I know, you might walk off that evening with anywhere from ten to fifteen thousand dollars."

"That's an awful lot of money," I said. "But I'd like to think it over."

"What you mean is, you'd like to go home, lubricate the dildo real well, and try it out on yourself for a few times before agreeing to my offer."

"You've got that right. If I agree to it, and for that amount of money, I'm likely to agree to anything, I want a lot of rehearsal."

"I'd call it stretching exercises," he said.

"Something like that."

He seemed to like me and invited me to breakfast. Over breakfast, he told me about his early days in films when he'd shared a dressing room with Chaplin and Mack Swain. "That Chaplin's got a dick on him," he said. "Wish I was hung like that. Only trouble is, he smells all the time. He really needs to take a bath."

That was not my impression of Chaplin. I gathered that he'd learned to bathe more frequently after his days of working with Arbuckle..

"Chaplin once borrowed my baggy trousers for one of his great comic scenes in a film," he said. "And he wore the old shoes of Chester Conklin. It was a great routine. I was there the first day Chaplin appeared wearing the costume that would make him famous, even the little mustache. Actually the mustache wasn't real at all. It was a rectangle of black crepe glued under his nose. He even twirled a walking stick that day. The Little Tramp was born."

As fascinated as I was by Fatty Arbuckle, I knew I had to leave to meet Chaplin himself. Obviously I'd chosen not to tell him that I too knew Chaplin, especially considering the circumstances in which I knew the great comedian.

At the door to his mansion, Arbuckle stood in the foyer, and I sensed he wanted me to linger a bit longer. He seemed reluctant to say what he was about to. "You're a very good-looking man," he said. "Hell, let's be truthful.

You're so fucking good looking you look like a beautiful woman. I've never had a young boy before, and I'm finding women too loose for me. Norman Kerry told me that a boy's ass is so much tighter, and the sensation is far greater for men who have small dicks."

"I don't know about that," I said, backing away.

"Don't be afraid," he said. "Before I push the dildo into you, I might consider fucking you myself. I'd obviously have to fuck you first, because once I insert Bushman's dick into you, you'll be ruined for all other normal men." Before letting me go, he kissed me on the lips. "Did anyone ever tell you your lips are the color of luscious, voluptuous, and very ripe cherries?"

"No, Mr. Arbuckle, you're the first."

With that I was gone, getting behind the wheel of Bushman's limousine, along with the Mexican assistants. I was glad the deliveries were over for the day. I still had to face Chaplin and drive his Locomobile. What surprise would good ol' Charlie have in store for me today?

*****

When I arrived at Chaplin's, The Little Fellow wasn't ready. I learned that he had a sudden inspiration and had to get some ideas committed to paper. Considering where he might want me to drive him, I didn't mind the wait, fearing that if Chaplin picked up more school girls like Reatha Watson we'd both be arrested.

The chauffeur, Toraichi Kono, hobbled out of the back cubicle at the garage. He seemed charged with the authority of overseeing the comings and goings around the Chaplin house. Although he still resented me, he was more relaxed in my presence, no longer fearing for his job.

"Charlie seems to be using you as a pawn for whatever little game delights him at the moment," the chauffeur said as a greeting to me.

"You might say that."

"I hope Nijinsky didn't give you a sore ass."

"That's my problem," I said rather evasively, not wanting to take Kono into my confidence.

"Charlie's in that special mood today," Kono

said. "There will be more fun and games, but, I must warn you, with a very different twist."

I looked puzzled. "You speak with all the mysteries of the Orient," I said. "Who are you trying to be? Sessue Hayakawa?"

"Don't ever mention that pervert to me again. I'd like to take his fucking branding iron and stick it up his ass."

"Whatever Chaplin has in mind, I'm ready, willing, and able. If I could handle Nijinsky, I think I could handle any of his other guests. Dare you tell me who Chaplin might be entertaining today?"

"There is no one today," Kono said. "But I will... How do you Americans put it? Spill the beans? Tomorrow he wants you to drive him to visit Marion Davies and William Randolph Hearst."

"My God!" The prospect of meeting the mighty press baron and a star of the magnitude and beauty of Marion Davies thrilled me. I was enthralled by her when she'd appeared in *Cecilia of the Pink Roses*. In a way, I dreaded the prospect of losing my temporary job as Chaplin's chauffeur because I felt that through the actor I could get to meet everybody important, perhaps even the president of the United States one day and most definitely the king of England.

I not only had Chaplin to introduce me to the famous people of our day, but there was that tantalizing offer from Doug Fairbanks. Would he call me one night and arrange a sexual liaison with someone very important who desired a handsome young blond boy? Thank God I'd left Kansas and didn't plan to return. When you're young, hung, and beautiful, Hollywood was the place to be, especially considering my sexual proclivities. I no longer had to masturbate to a photograph of Francis X. Bushman or Elmo Lincoln. That Beverly Bayne seemed to keep Francis under tight wraps, and Elmo promised to call only when he couldn't get a woman. Apparently, he was having no trouble at all finding a woman, as he hadn't called. But I hardly needed those mammoth cocks to satisfy me.

"Often at the Hearst parties," Kono said, "there will be lots of people. Usually movie stars but other important people as well. Tomorrow will be very intimate—just the four of you. Your job will be to keep Hearst amused which will give Charlie some time to slip away with Marion."

"You mean they are an item?"

"An item? What kind of stupid word is that? Is that some modern hipster talk?"

"Forgive me. I meant to ask is Chaplin having an affair with Marion Davies? I should think that would be very risky. I hear Hearst is insanely jealous of Marion."

"That's where you come in," Kono said. "Your job will be to see that Hearst doesn't suspect anything."

I shuddered at the responsibility. How could I, a lowly chauffeur from the Middle West, keep the great William Randolph Hearst distracted, while Chaplin sneaked away to fuck Hearst's mistress?

"Today you are going to see a side of Charlie you have never seen before," Kono said, "unless you saw *A Woman*. "Most of the time Charlie is essentially normal. But he has his off-moments."

I wondered if picking up virginal school girls in playyards was normal, but Kono seemed to think so.

"Most of the time he does things that men do. He attends prizefights at Doyle's Sports Palace out in Vernon. He likes to go to baseball games. Sometimes he hangs out with the players at Barney Oldfield's Saloon."

"Exactly what are you trying to say?"

"I am not trying to say, I am saying that Charlie is not normal today. He's an artist, and he knows that an artist must be both male and female."

"I understand that. There has always been a certain androgyny in his performances. Chaplin has always been a character of a sexually indeterminate stage." That wasn't my own point of view, but I'd read it somewhere in a magazine and decided it was the thing to say.

"You understand that perfectly," Kono said. "It's because of that androgyny that Charlie enjoys such a large following among homosexual men. Hart Crane even sent a poem dedicated to Charlie. It was called *Chaplinesque*. Frankly, I think Hart Crane wants to fuck Charlie. He'll probably show up on our doorstep one day."

As Kono went on lecturing me, I began to

feel there was something decidedly unmasculine about the character of The Tramp. At the Patee Theater I had seen Chaplin films that contained explicit references to homosexuality, even though my more innocent self didn't recognize them as such at the time. I remembered the film, *Behind the Screen*, in which Eric Campbell spies on Charlie kissing Edna who is disguised as a man. Campbell assumes that Chaplin is kissing a man. Often when faced with a bully such as in the film, *Pay Day*, Chaplin becomes coquettish and begins flirting with the macho beast.

"Homosexuals sympathize with Chaplin because they too have been marginalized by society," Kono said, as I remembered that he fancied himself an intellectual and Chaplin the vaudeville buffoon. "Chaplin demonstrates the moral superiority of the isolated and alienated individual in society."

That Kono was viewing Chaplin's films as artistic statements seemed in contradiction to earlier pronouncements that the films were aimed at idiot audiences.

At that point Chaplin came skipping down the lane apparently imitating Mary Pickford more than the Tramp. Although dressed in men's wear, he had a woman's shawl draped across his shoulders and carried a rose in his left hand. He came up to me and raised the rose to my chin, tickling me with it.

"You darling man," he said, assuming an effeminate voice. He turned and smiled at Kono before looking deeply into my eyes. His own eyes had a flirtatious twinkle about them, and his look evoked his appearance in *A Woman*. "I wonder if I'll be safe with this brute of a man from the cornfields of Kansas. A woman such as myself may not be safe with a big, handsome brute with the name of Durango Jones."

"You'll be fine with me, Mr. Chaplin," I said, feeling embarrassed. We were certainly carrying androgyny a bit far. Only yesterday he was dressing me up as a woman, the fabulously beautiful Lotte Lee. Today he seemed to want me to be Francis X. Bushman.

He reached and felt the muscle of my right arm. "When you get me out on the road at some secluded spot, I know you could overpower me. After all, I'm only a helpless woman. Men like you have always used brute strength to make a woman do your bidding, regardless how ghastly the sexual request."

With that as a farewell, we bid adieu to Kono and headed for a private party south of Los Angeles at a cafe called Levy's. The host had booked the entire cafe for the private party, and I was eagerly looking forward to attending.

Once there, I was disappointed when Chaplin didn't invite me to go inside. Apparently chauffeurs were meant to wait outside in the limousine until Chaplin left the party. He stayed for two hours. At one point I heard screaming laughter and got out of the car to look inside. Chaplin was entertaining the guests with his impersonation of Theda Bara in *Salome*.

At a hillside near Laguna Beach, Chaplin ordered me to park the car near a belvedere overlooking the Pacific Ocean. Oceans were still new to me at the time, and I found the sunset awesome. There were streaks of lavender in the sky, my favorite color. It was then that I had to confess to Chaplin that he must not tell of the charade with Samuel Goldwyn, the producer. Goldfish, as I informed Chaplin, had not only fallen for my disguise, but planned to sign me on as an actress in *Vampira*, starring me as Lotte Lee, in spite of my height.

Far from spoiling his joke on Goldwyn, Chaplin was mesmerized by what I was telling him. It was as if he himself wanted to pull off a charade like that. "It's amazing. Just amazing." He kept repeating that over and over again. "You did look like a woman. As a man, you are very handsome, perhaps too beautiful. I think you were meant to be a woman."

"I'm all man," I said, a bit too defensively.

"That you are and before this night ends we will put your manhood to the test." With that enigmatic statement, Chaplin got back in his car and directed me to a private rendezvous eight miles away. "I keep this little cottage we are going to for very special dalliances. Now that I'm the keeper of your Lotte Lee secret, I can take you into my confidence and tell you one of my secrets. It is a secret so fearsome that it would drive the Tramp from the screen. I have rarely revealed it to anyone. But since I have blackmail on you and could ruin what might be a promising career for you, I can let you in on my deepest secret."

"I'm eager to learn."

"In time, my pet. The Little Fellow before the night is over will make himself known to you."

At a rather bleak and sparsely furnished cottage deep from nowhere, Chaplin ushered me in and told me to make myself comfortable. He'd worked up quite a sweat during the Salome impersonations and wanted to take a shower as well as "dress up a bit."

In his small living room, I poured myself a glass of whiskey without asking permission. A maid came in and asked me if I wanted some ice. I told her I was fine. She looked vaguely familiar. Perhaps I'd seen her as a character actress in some film at the Patee.

Chaplin called me into the bathroom and asked me to hand him a towel. "Has my maid offered you a drink?"

"Some ice," I said.

"People on Hollywood Boulevard call her Stella Dallas," he said. "She dresses up and goes there every day, thinking in vain some producer will discover her. She's a bit touched in the head—just like my mother. But she was once a big vaudeville star in London. I've worked on the same programs with her." He winced as if dismissing a painful memory. "Now you naughty man, I've got to get dressed." He told me to go into his back bedroom and remove all my clothing.

Doing as I was told, I headed for the bedroom. At least I'd found out who Stella Dallas was. I'd have to share the secret with the new man in my life: Richard Barthelmess.

What I didn't know was what Chaplin had in store for me. In front of a large dressing mirror, I removed my clothing piece by piece as if I were a stripper.

Standing fully nude in front of the mirror, I was proud of my body although surprised at how boyish it remained. I was nineteen years old but looked hardly fifteen. Only my cock and balls were fully developed. The rest of me looked as if I were only on the road to manhood and hadn't arrived yet. Perhaps that was why Chaplin was interested in me. He liked them young, and I—at least in my view at that moment—was the youngest kid ever to arrive in wicked Hollywood.

At a sudden noise from the dressing room, I turned around to stare into a remarkably beautiful Chaplin disguised as a woman and standing in the doorway. He wore a lot of makeup. It was an amazing disguise. As he entered the room, he moved and acted exactly like a woman. It wasn't an impersonation the way he'd done on the screen. Brilliant actor that he was, he had transformed himself into a female.

He looked me over carefully and it was obvious he approved of what he saw. He lay on the bed, a delicate hand fluttering in the air.

"I want you to attack me savagely," he said. "Rip all my clothing from my body." He raised his voice as it took on a command like that of a director. "RAPE ME."

*****

Back in my cottage, as I dressed for Nazimova's party, I still couldn't believe what had transpired only hours ago. I'd fucked Charlie Chaplin and had done so brutally upon his command. Even in the middle of the rape, I'd understood that it wasn't Chaplin I was seducing, but a part of the Little Fellow that he rarely revealed to the world. It wasn't so much homosexual rape but the attack of a young man upon a woman.

Once penetrated, Chaplin had amazingly reverted to being a woman except for that big dick of his which had gotten in the way. When I'd achieved a fast and rather forceful penetration, Chaplin had erupted. He would do so again about thirty minutes later when I'd achieved my own explosive climax.

He'd met every thrust of mine begging for more. It was as if he'd wanted to be completely possessed and dominated by a male figure. The more commanding I'd become, the more submissive he'd become. He might be the most famous person in the world, but all his glory and power disappeared under a savage sex attack. He'd become every young girl who'd been carried away from civilization to the camp of the barbarians. His face had assumed a mask of pure ecstasy. As he'd felt me nearing my climax, he'd started to whimper, the sounds of his voice coming out like little cries of protest.

"I don't want it to end," he'd whispered in my ear before nibbling on it gently. "It's the best ever. Only one man—and that was back in England—has made a woman out of me. The others could never do that."

Even after I'd climaxed in him, he'd held on to me, not wanting me to withdraw. He'd licked my neck and kissed my lips, demanding my tongue which he'd sucked voraciously.

We'd both been running late for other appointments, but Chaplin had wanted us to linger in the afterglow of our passion. Although Chaplin back then was never an object of sexual allure for me, I had to admit to myself that it was one of the most satisfying sexual experiences of my life. He'd made me feel more of a man than I'd ever felt in my life, and I'd obviously allowed the woman in him to escape and fulfill her passion.

"I can't always be a man," he said, as he'd gotten dressed. "It's important that I bed a woman too. An artist has many needs, and I'm an artist. Perhaps the world's greatest. I must have all sides of myself fulfilled." He came toward me as I was slipping into my trousers. "Tell me that you understand that." His eyes had pleaded with me.

"I'm not an artist like you," I'd told him. "There are many things I don't understand." I reached for him and pulled him into my arms, kissing him passionately and inserting my tongue. "All I know is that you brought me to a point of excitement I've never known before." I kissed him again. "I can't wait until we do that again."

"Then it doesn't disgust you?" he said, his eyes almost innocent like. "You're not revolted by me? Before, some men have been disgusted with me after they had their way with me."

I'd pulled him closer and had tongued his ear. "Do I look like a man who's disgusted?"

At the door Chaplin took my arm. "Before we go," he'd said, "I have a simple request. May I kneel before you and kiss the head of it? Worship the object that has given me such profound pleasure."

"I'm always there for you."

He'd kneeled in front of me and had unbuttoned my trousers, taking out my penis and wet-kissing the head of it. "For me," he'd said, standing up again and wiping his mouth, "It's the most beautiful object in the world. I'll dream about it tonight." He smiled at me. "And tomorrow night and every night after that, too."

On the way back to Hollywood in his Locomobile, he'd informed me that I was no longer his driver. He'd said that he would find another driver until Kono's foot healed. "You are now my boyfriend. I'll leave instructions with the staff that you are to be admitted to my home at any time of the day or night. Tomorrow I will have a room prepared for you. It will always be there for you. You can lock yourself away from the world there." He'd smiled at me and took my right hand, kissing it before sucking each of my fingers. "But I'll have the key."

*****

On the way to pick up Mr. and Mrs. Wallace Reid, Tallulah did all the talking. Not knowing she would ignite a jealous rage in me, the talk was devoted to her night with Rodolfo. "That Valentino gave me a divine fuck. Probably the best I've ever had—that is, until I meet up with John Barrymore. Valentino is hung twice as big as Goldfish, but a couple of inches short of Chaplin. Unlike Chaplin, Valentino's dick isn't bright red but a nutty brown, a very impressive Italian salami."

Tallulah didn't need to tell me what Valentino's cock looked like, as I knew every inch of it. She was thrilled to be going to Nazimova's star-studded party, and thanked me repeatedly for the invitation.

At that long-ago point in her life, Tallulah was very much like the actress Katharine Hepburn would play in *Morning Glory* in 1933. Crazed with theatrical ambition, she was without guile. She talked too much and seemed desperate to entertain even or especially if she had to say and do something outrageous to attract attention.

At the Reid house, Wallace was waiting in the foyer. Before I could even get out of the car, Tallulah had bounded out the door and was practically devouring Wallace. "You're the handsomest man in Hollywood," she said, "although I haven't seen as much of you as I'd like."

"Just say the word," he said. "What you don't get to see on the screen you can observe first-hand."

At that point Dorothy Reid, his wife, came into the foyer wearing a gown that made her look years older. Even before we were introduced, this housewife-like woman with sad eyes and a hangdog expression, took an instant dislike to Tallulah and me. It was obvious.

Wallace ushered Tallulah into the back seat, and she practically pulled him in with her, and launched into a heated dialogue. Somewhat reluctantly Dorothy got into the front seat with me. "I suppose you're one of those star-struck children of America who comes out here thinking you're going to be a big-time movie star." She said that even before the car had reached the end of the driveway.

"I'm an actor," I said rather coldly wondering what was evoking hysterical laughter from Tallulah in the rear.

Dorothy looked sternly at me. She held my gaze so completely that I almost ran off the road before I took my eyes off her.

"I call Wally's friends Bohemians," she said.

The word was unfamiliar to me at the time. "What do you mean by that, if I might ask?"

"You know what I mean," she said with a certain undisguised contempt. "They are Hollywood Hell Raisers. When they're not making some silly picture, they devote their lives to drugs, alcohol, and debauchery. Wally has turned our home into a cheap roadhouse. His Bohemian friends have taken over our lives. They hang out all the time, drinking and partying. And, I'm sure this is no surprise to you, they take dope—and lots of it."

With Wally's latest supply of morphine concealed in the glove compartment, I made no comment about this last remark.

Wally directed me to a home five blocks away. He told me he had agreed to pick up two actresses because their transportation arrangement for the evening had fallen through. The way he nonchalantly called them actresses made me think they were movie hopefuls like myself. That is, like myself as Durango Jones. Hardly like myself as Lotte Lee, the new Hollywood Vamp.

As Wallace went to the front door to pick up the actresses, Dorothy availed herself of the opportunity to get into the rear seat with Tallulah, positioning herself so that she would sit between her husband and the Alabama belle. Instead of hysterical laughter, there was only stony silence coming from the back compartment until Wallace arrived with the two women. He ushered them into the front seat with me.

To my amazement, I turned to stare into the faces of Dorothy and Lillian Gish. "This is Durango Jones. Meet the Gish sisters."

"No one is named Durango," Dorothy kidded me.

"Let him call himself what he wants," Lillian said. "His name is probably Horace Seymour Sourpickle, and he had to change it for marquee magic. You're an actor, of course."

"That I am," I said, starting the car when I saw that Wally was safely in the back seat.

"We can just assume that any pretty man we meet out here is an actor," Dorothy Reid said. "They all want to be Wallace Reid."

"Too bad you're blond and too handsome," Lillian said. "Dorothy--my sister, Dorothy, that is--is looking for an unknown to appear with her in her new film."

"It's called *Out of Luck*," Dorothy Gish said. "The male star will be paid one-hundred a week. But I need a dark Latin type."

"I know the perfect actor for you if I'm not suitable for the role," I said. "He's Rodolfo Valentino and he's a sensation. He's going to become a big box office draw of the Twenties. Who knows? You might be known one day for discovering him."

"No, dear heart," Lillian said. "We'll be known as the two greatest actresses of the screen—not a talent agent." She looked over at Dorothy Gish. "At least I'll be known as the great tragedienne of the screen. Dorothy, of course, plays lighter parts."

Thoughts of Rodolfo evaporated fast as the Gish sisters seemed to launch themselves into a festering sibling rivalry. As the sisters had their minor argument, I could hardly hear their words. I was too enthralled to be transporting the Gish sisters to a Hollywood party. Dorothy and Lillian Gish didn't have the fame of Mary Pickford or Chaplin, but they were among the most celebrated people on earth.

I'd loved Dorothy in the rollicking western *Nugget Nell*. Dorothy specialized in light comedy, whereas the ethereal, somewhat unreal Lillian was given the heavy dramatic parts. Lillian was a fragile beauty, her face reflecting an astonishing sensitivity. There was a birdlike fragility to her suggesting that she was not of this world. How I'd loved her in *Hearts of the World* as she wandered through the war-torn battlefield clutching her bridal veil, and in the rural romance, *True Heart Susie.*

At the end of the Gish sisters' argument, I was able to nail Dorothy down for a commitment to meet Rodolfo to test him for the part. She didn't seem a woman to make idle commitments, so I assumed she'd keep her agreement.

After the argument, the Gish sisters seemed to make up quickly. Lillian reached over and kissed Dorothy six—or was it seven times—on the lips. They were birdlike kisses—no heavy tongue action although there was a sensuality to the kissing.

"Don't be shocked," Dorothy said. "We are only lesbians for the week."

"Maybe for a month," Lillian admonished her. "Nazimova has convinced us to give lesbian love a chance, and, as artists, we feel we should do that if only to broaden our experience of the human condition."

"Men can be brutal anyway," Dorothy said.

I said nothing as I was appalled. Dorothy and Lillian Gish as lesbian lovers? The idea was unthinkable. However, the more I thought about it, the more believable and possible it became.

"Actually Lillian has had more experience with lesbian love than I have," Dorothy confided.

For the first time I smelled liquor on her breath. Were the adorable Gish sisters secret alcoholics?

"Lillian first tasted the pleasure of female love with Mildred Harris," Dorothy said.

"Don't tell him that," Lillian cautioned. "Chaplin is furious at me. *Still.*"

I'd first seen a picture of Mildred Harris in 1914 in a *Photoplay* I'd read in the dentist's office in Lawrence, Kansas. Like Mary Pickford, Mildred was a perfect child in front of the camera, with a head of natural flaxen

curls and large expressive blue eyes. In films she was always getting mistreated or kidnapped by villains. As Dorothy in the *Wizard of Oz* series, she'd made me weep.

"It was either Mildred or D.W. Griffith who was pursuing me during *Birth of the Nation,*" Lillian said. "I was only seventeen at the time."

"D.W. was also after Mae Marsh," Dorothy said.

"But I was the one Griffith wanted to marry, and I thought briefly about it," Lillian said. "That is, until Mildred came along offering me a more tender passion."

Although I'd heard that Mildred had tricked Chaplin into marrying her because she'd claimed she was pregnant, that had proven to be a false alarm. At the time, Mildred might have been as young as thirteen, and Chaplin could be cited for statutory rape. I'd never met Mildred and I suspected she was no longer living with Chaplin or else he wouldn't have offered me a room at his house.

When we arrived at Nazimova's Garden of Alla, the Gish sisters bounded out of the car and headed for the party. Wallace grimly accompanied his wife Dorothy inside, and I was left to escort Tallulah.

"Darling," she said, taking my arm and giving me a wet kiss, "last night I had Valentino in the wake of Goldfish and Chaplin. Tonight it's going to be either Nazimova or..." She kissed me again. "Or else I'm going to *cum* between the Gish sisters." She burst into hysterical laughter just as Nazimova approached us in the foyer to greet us.

*****

As Tallulah and I stood in the foyer waiting for our hostess to greet us, I felt some strange bond with her. She'd fucked two of my boy friends, Rodolfo and Charlie (it was no longer Chaplin). With her, it had been a one-night stand. With me, the link would last for years. Not only that, but it was a race between Tallu and me to see who would be the first to bed John Barrymore.

Nazimova appeared dressed as Salome. Without waiting for an introduction, Tallulah rushed to greet her. "I didn't know this was to be a costume party," Tallulah said to the actress. "If I had known, I would have come as Peter Pan with my dick hanging out."

Nazimova was a woman who took herself and her screen work with deadly seriousness. She looked aghast, not knowing what to make of this young upstart with the basso and bourbon voice.

"I am Alla Nazimova," she said. "Not that I need an introduction. I am known on all the continents of the world."

"I'm Tallulah Bankhead, and I'll become one of the great names of this century as well. There will come a day when my mail will be addressed 'She, New York' and I'll get it."

"I certainly like a woman with your confidence, regardless of how ill founded it might be," Nazimova said before turning to look at me. Her face was sad. "Mr. Durango Jones, Jean Acker is here. She's waiting in the library to see you with some news."

Before I could say or do anything, Nazimova had graciously glided me into the darkened library lit only by a candle. There I turned to face Jean Acker who looked like a little woman who might have led a wagon train west.

"It's over between us," she said upon seeing me. "I have told Rodolfo that I will never marry him. He is yours now."

Moving toward her, I saw that she'd been crying. "It's best this way," I said. "Rodolfo is not at a stage in his life where he should be marrying anybody. In maybe a few short months, everything will change for him. Only tonight Dorothy Gish has decided to cast him as the lead opposite her in her new film."

Acker looked astonished. It was as if she had to say something to top my story. "Rodolfo is not the only one who is going to be a star. Metro has cast me as the lead in a new movie."

Assuming it would not be a lesbian movie, I asked, "Who will be your male star?"

"Fatty Arbuckle."

Concealing my astonishment, I realized once again what a small and incestuous world Hollywood was. I had already kissed Arbuckle on the lips before Acker got her chance at him. But what was either of us doing with Fatty Arbuckle, when Wallace Reid, Norman Kerry, and Richard Barthelmess waited in the wings

for us? I deliberately left Charlie off that list. In the future when I was alone with Charlie, I had agreed to think of him only as a woman.

Acker and I sat alone in the library for four or five minutes, occasionally exchanging meaningless words with each other but holding hands as we digested the impact of her break from Rodolfo.

"Where is our man?" I asked.

She looked at me but didn't answer.

"If he's back at our cottage, I'll excuse myself from the party and go to him at once. He needs comfort now, I'm sure."

"Perhaps," she said. "But I don't think he's rushing to your arms. He left the Hollywood Hotel with Norman Kerry. They've booked a room together at the Alexandria."

"Oh, I see," I said, dropping her hand.

Acker rose and looked somewhat disdainfully at me. "I am returning to the party. I will stand at the side of Nazimova. She is my true love. The thing with Rodolfo never happened. It is history."

When she was gone, I checked my looks in the mirror and headed back to the party. I was furious at Rodolfo for not coming to me but wandering off with Norman instead. Somehow before the night was over, I planned to get my revenge.

In Nazimova's courtyard, I encountered a frantic Wallace Reid who had been looking everywhere for me. Fortunately, he was no longer with that bitch wife of his, the ugly Dorothy. "Thank God you're here," he said. "I couldn't find you anywhere." He grabbed my arm with such force I was shocked. "Have you got it?"

"Yeah," I said. "Don't worry. Christ, you're frantic."

"Let's go to the men's room." In the toilet, the urinals were deserted. In a stall, I gave him another supply of morphine which I had obtained from Elizabeth Hutchison who was eagerly awaiting our Saturday get-together.

After examining it, he stuffed it in his pocket. He looked at me and smiled and seemed less manic than before. "You've earned this." With that pronouncement, he pulled me close to him and kissed me passionately, inserting his tongue which I eagerly sucked. Although I didn't find this the most romantic rendezvous point, I was kissing the man called the handsomest in Hollywood and what queen would turn down Wallace Reid?

When he'd seemed to tire of my lips, he unbuttoned his pants and pulled out an erect cock, still the world's most beautiful. "You'd better go for it now while it's still stiff. Later on in the evening I'll be too far gone to be of much use to you."

In any condition, Wally was a feast for all seasons. Although he had a rather ripe scent, my lips and tongue enjoyed my prize. He was letting me explore his most secret parts, and I thrilled at the taste of this beautiful man. He let out a moan and his knees buckled as I attacked him with fury, wanting to savor every texture and smell. It was obvious that he was rapidly approaching a powerful orgasm, and I wanted this moment to last far longer.

I pulled off a bit and began licking up and down his shaft instead. But he wanted immediate relief. He grabbed each side of my head and held it firmly while he entered me again, pumping furiously as he almost guaranteed an immediate climax. He thrust himself as deep into my throat as he could before exploding with a fury that caused him to yell out. I fastened onto him until I had drained the last drop and still refused to release him. He literally had to force my head off him. He pulled me up so that I was facing him squarely in the toilet stall. He kissed me again with fury, biting my lip slightly and tasting his own semen. "Good boy." With that, he released me.

Adjusting our clothes, I left the booth first to be followed immediately by Wally. Just as we did that, we were discovered by a man entering the urinal. I recognized him at once. It was Jack Pickford, brother of Mary Pickford.

I'd first seen Jack Pickford at the Patee Theater in Lawrence co-starring in the 1915 successful picture, *A Girl of Yesterday*, which featured his sister Mary. Jack had never been my favorite movie star, and he was not at the top of my list of men to seduce in Hollywood. I felt he had a movie career only because of the power and prestige of Mary.

At the moment of our meeting, I didn't know the status of Jack's career. I'd heard rumors that Adolph Zukor had once put him under contract for five-hundred dollars a week, but that the contract had been arbitrarily and unilaterally canceled. I'd also heard that Goldwyn had signed both Jack Pickford and "Bobby" Harron, the handsome juvenile in many of Griffith's landmark films.

If I had ever planned to be introduced to a movie star, this was not the occasion I would have chosen. But since Wally didn't seem embarrassed, I didn't feel I had to suffer humiliation either.

Jack shook my hand and seemed perfectly at ease with the situation as if it were an everyday occurrence to him to see two men emerging from a lone toilet stall.

"Good to meet you," he said to me. "Durango Jones, is it? What a name."

"I'm honored, Mr. Pickford, to make your acquaintance," I said.

"Good to see you, Wally."

"Hi, Jack," Wally said. "This is the boy I was telling you about." He kissed me on the cheek. "Thanks for the good time in more ways than one. I'll see you later at the party."

With more than awkwardness, I stood looking at Jack and he at me, as if not knowing what to do next. "I was not aware that Wally had even mentioned me to you." At first I thought Wally might be trying to get me a role in one of Jack's pictures.

"It's okay," he said. "I know everything. Your secret's safe with me." He walked toward the urinal and looked over his shoulder at me, as if beckoning me to follow.

Not really certain of the protocol in such situations, I went and stood by him at the urinal. "Go on," he urged. "Unbutton me and take it out for your viewing pleasure."

With a nervous hand, I unbuttoned the fly of Jack Pickford and reached in and pulled out a not unimpressive penis. Once I'd removed it, he ordered me to skin it back so that he could urinate. "I always like to piss with the head skinned back," he said. "It's cleaner that way."

Deep into his piss, he said, "I'll give you five-hundred dollars. I want you to meet me as soon as you can buy heroin with it." Finishing his piss, he shook his cock several times as it increased in girth. "Your reward will be this baby all the way down your throat."

"Heroin..." I started to protest.

He pulled me close and kissed me long and hard. "A good time is waiting for you, I've written down my number." He reached into his pocket and pulled out a piece of paper and some money. "You get that heroin and you've got me. I want the same deal with you Wally has."

I wasn't exactly sure if I even wanted Jack and was completely uncertain I could obtain heroin. I certainly wasn't going to go to Dr. Hutchison for any more drugs than he was already supplying.

"I'll see what I can do," I said. After all, I was meeting Rod St. Just tomorrow, and if there were any heroin for sale in Hollywood, he would know where to find it. I just knew that somehow.

After finishing his kiss, Jack took me by the arm. "I want you to meet my little sugar baby."

Moments later I was standing in the presence of the beautiful Olive Thomas, the former sprightly Ziegfeld Follies' queen and now Selznick Pictures star. This brunette showgirl by the age of sixteen had been the darling of the *Vanity Fair* café society crowd in New York. She'd shocked the world when news leaked out that she'd posed nude for Alberto Vargas, the young Peruvian artist, who had pronounced her "the most beautiful woman in the world." I'd seen her at the Patee Theater in such light comedies as *Prudence on Broadway, Betty Takes a Hand,* and *The Follies Girl.*

At that moment in time it could not have been known to me that I was dealing with two people who would one day be the showcase figures in two of the biggest scandals ever to hit Hollywood: Olive Thomas and Wallace Reid.

Back then, I exchanged meaningless conversation with Miss Thomas, having only recently kissed her boy friend. I found it strange meeting wives or girl friends of men I planned to seduce or was seducing. With Tallulah, it had been all right. If anything I related to Tallu as if she were a man. But I felt embarrassed in the presence of Olive Thomas.

When Jack headed over to the bar for drinks, she turned to me and dropped the little girl mannequin pose. "I'm not as innocent as I look. I know what Jack is up to."

"You mean drugs?"

"Of course, the drugs. She had a funny look on her face when she stared at me. "If not the drugs, then what?"

"The drugs. You don't approve, I gather."

"If he doesn't stop, he'll kill himself. Wally too. Do you know him?"

"We've met," I said enigmatically.

"Don't let these guys get you hooked. You'll be sorry you did."

As Jack headed back from the bar with drinks for us, I observed carefully this idol of the screen. He had a certain male charm but I wouldn't have gone out on a snowy night for a rendezvous with him. Ironically, he was called "The Ideal American Boy," a reputation he'd earned by appearing in such films as *Seventeen.* Olive became known as the "Ideal American Girl" after her appearance in *The Tomboy.*

"I can't complain too much about what Jack does," Olive whispered to me.

"Why not?"

"He lets me have my indulgences too," she said. "Not the drugs so much. I like to get fucked by gangsters while he watches."

With that shocker, Jack was suddenly upon us, dispensing drinks.

Right in front of Olive he said to me, "you get me my stuff and you'll get a chance to experience first-hand what drives this bitch crazy." He fondled his crotch.

Only that morning, I'd seen a magazine article naming Olive Thomas and Jack Pickford America's "Ideal Couple."

*****

Long before the party was in full swing, both Tallulah and Nazimova had agreed their romance was not to be. Nazimova liked artistic, submissive young women she could dominate. Tallulah would be the one to strap on the dildo. The Gish sisters, Wallace Reid, Jack Pickford, Olive Thomas, and most definitely Norma and Constance Talmadge did not inspire Tallulah either.

Over a drink with me at the bar, she devised a plan to enliven the party. "These are the same old faces we've seen far too much of on the screen. Hollywood is eager to look at a new face, and right now you're it."

"What do you mean?" I'm in demand no-where—not even as an extra."

"Darling, what I mean is the town's buzzing with news that Goldfish has discovered a hot new female star, Lotte Lee. The publicity department hasn't even gone to work on you yet, and already the word is out. Small town, isn't it?"

"About every fifteen minutes I start to shake all over," I said. "I fear I can't pull this one off. I'm no woman—I'm a man. The camera will be too revealing."

"Perhaps not," she said. "You fooled Goldfish." She slammed down her drink. "Your mama has an idea. I'll borrow one of Nazimova's dressing rooms. There are a lot of gowns here. I'll dress you and make you up as Lotte Lee. If you can fool this crowd of jealous hawks, you can fool the movie-going public."

"That's a point," I said. "But I don't know." Taking my hesitation for acceptance, Tallulah barged away to get permission from Nazimova to use one of her dressing rooms. Later she told me that Nazimova had assumed she'd wanted to slip away with a trick for the evening.

Gathering up five gowns, we retreated to one of the back bedrooms with an adjoining dressing room. Nazimova always kept her bathroom mirrors heavily lit as in a stage mirror, which made it easier for Tallulah to apply my make-up.

Putting falsies on me, she chose a rather tasteful champagne-colored gown with long high heels. Surveying her handiwork, I was impressed. With my flame-red mouth, even I could believe I was a woman.

Filled with Tallulah's confidence, I entered the party on her arm, only to confront Nazimova.

"Who are you?" the imperial actress demanded, surveying me from head to toe.

"The gate-crasher of the evening," I said. "I'm Lotte Lee. I told Tallulah I shouldn't come here without an invitation."

"Darling, you'll love her," Tallulah said. "She gives great head."

Ignoring Tallulah, Nazimova seemed en-tranced with me. "You're the new woman Goldfish is signing. I hear he's planning to make you the new screen vamp."

"Something like that."

"You should be a sensation," Nazimova said. "You're very beautiful, if a bit tall." Right before my eyes, Nazimova seemed to be falling in love with me.

"I fear I'll be but a mere flash in the pan," I said. "A cheap commercial exploitation—not a great *artiste* of the screen like you."

"I want to get to know you better," Nazimova said. "Perhaps you could call me this week and we could arrange a private rendez-vous here at the Garden of Alla. I would be enchanted."

Tallulah had long ago grown bored with our flirtation and was seen talking in front of a nearby potted palm with a very handsome young actor, Tom Moore, with whom she'd just made a picture.

Suddenly, a very jealous Jean Acker appeared at Nazimova's side. "You have other guests," Acker told Nazimova in a voice with barely concealed hostility. Acker studied my face closely. "Don't I know you? You resemble someone I know. Surely we've met before."

"I'm the sister of Durango Jones," I lied.

"Yes," Nazimova said as if discovering who murdered someone in a play. "I thought your face familiar too. Your brother is here tonight. He came with Tallulah and Wallace Reid."

"I know," I said. "We are actually twins." I think Maria Jane had told me that it was possible to give birth to twins, one a boy, another a girl.

"The resemblance is amazing," Nazimova said. She kissed me on the cheek. "I'll see you later, dear heart."

Acker only stared back at me before wandering off arm and arm with Nazimova to greet a bevy of eight newly arrived female guests, each lovelier than the other.

Seeing that I was freed from the clutches of Nazimova, Tallulah called me over to meet that gorgeous hunk of manhood, Tom Moore.

Tom Moore, as everybody knew, was one of the famous Moore brothers, all screen actors. It was an era of famous brothers, Lionel and John, George and Raoul Walsh, and Dustin and William Farnum. Matt was in pictures but

Owen was far more famous than any of them—not because of his screen roles but because he was the husband of the most famous woman in the world, Mary Pickford.

I wasn't the only one in Hollywood who knew the shaky status of that marriage.

Tom Moore smiled at me and seemed enchanted. Since all the Irish Moore brothers were known to be womanizers, I felt I would never have a chance to get in his trousers as Durango Jones. From what I'd heard, the Moore brothers, unlike Norman Kerry and Rodolfo, didn't go that route.

"I've already heard about you," Tom said. "But you're far more beautiful than I heard."

"Lotte's a great cocksucker," Tallulah said.

Tom flushed red with embarrassment, and so did I. Only Tallulah could say such a thing and get away with it.

"I chased after him during the whole time we were shooting that horrible picture," Tallulah said. "But I got nothing. I did manage to cop a feel during one of our love scenes. Believe me, Lotte, there's quite a package there. Go for it."

I smiled at the young actor. "Ignore Tallulah. She gets carried away."

"Since you two have met, I'm out of here," Tallulah said. "I've still got one night in Hollywood, so I'm looking for fresh meat." Before leaving me, she said, "I ran into Goldfish at the Hollywood Hotel. Your suite is ready. He's filled it with red roses waiting for the arrival of Lotte Lee."

When Tallulah was gone, Tom moved closer to me. It was a thrilling experience. I suddenly realized that as Lotte Lee, an entire world of gorgeous men was mine. As Durango, only some men were available to me. Now the possibilities were endless.

"I bet you're going to be the biggest female star in pictures," Tom said. "Perhaps you'll use me in one of your pictures. My pictures aren't doing too well. Nothing like that God damn Fairbanks shithead. He's after Mary, you know?"

"I didn't know," I lied. I certainly wasn't going to reveal to Tom Moore that I had driven his sister-in-law to my cottage to fuck Fairbanks.

"I love my mother, although she's pretty crude," he said. "She's told Owen to take Mary for every cent she's worth—and she's worth a lot." He leaned closer to me. "Goldfish has talked about you all over town. I hear you have a specialty." His lips lightly brushed my ear.

I assumed that was a reference to my talent as a fellatio artist. Since I planned to seduce this hunk, I decided to set the stage for my sexual offer. "That's right. The only way I like it. A man either understands that in the beginning, or else no dice."

"That's great with me," he said, his face lighting up. "I can get all the pussy I want in this town. But I hear what you do to a man isn't easy to find."

"I think you want to date me," I said, touching his left arm. He instinctively made a muscle for me. I liked what I felt.

"Why don't you let me take you back to the Hollywood Hotel tonight?" he asked. "A pretty gal like you could get in a lot of trouble wandering around Hollywood all by her gorgeous self."

"That would thrill me, although I don't want to make Tallulah jealous."

"There's nothing between Tallulah and me," he said. "She's too aggressive for me. I like a more demure woman. Besides, you're far prettier than Tallulah. I'm a real ladies' man. I go for real women. Tallulah talks and acts like a drunken sailor."

"In that case, I'll take the gentleman up on his offer. And such a handsome gentleman you are."

"Yep," he said immodestly. "I'm considered the handsomest of the Moore brothers."

"Owen and Matt are handsome too," I said. "At least to judge by their pictures."

"You don't have to judge just by their pictures," he said.

I raised a provocative eyebrow. "What on earth do you mean?"

"We like to share," Tom said. "When I find something good, I like to pass her name on to my brothers so they can sample it too."

"What a delightful treat that would be for me," I said. "All three Moore brothers."

"When you've had us all," he said, "I want you to tell me who is the best."

"It's a promise."

We were interrupted by the appearance of

a strikingly handsome man. I immediately recognized him as the rising young star, John Gilbert.

"In a town of beautiful women," he said, "there has to be one who shines greater than all the rest. Even if she towers over me."

"You flatter me, Mr. Gilbert," I said. "I'm Lotte Lee."

"Goldfish has spread the word that you're going to be the biggest thing in pictures," Gilbert said. "I can't wait until we co-star together. Just wait until we do love scenes together."

"Move on, Johnny boy," Tom said. "I saw her first."

Gilbert looked with a slight contempt at Tom. "Who wants a drunken Irish boy when they can have the epitome of a dashing, daring romantic film star?"

"Now, I won't take that shit," Tom said, growing belligerent.

I took Gilbert's hand. "I'm sure we'll work together." In way of parting, I whispered in his ear, "I have a suite at the Hollywood Hotel."

Pulling me away from John with his catch of the evening, Tom took me by my arm and guided me across the courtyard toward the pool and the exit. We paused only briefly.

Tallulah had taken off all her clothes and was doing cartwheels around the edge of the pool.

Chapter Five

It was a historic moment. Not only was I installed in a suite at the Hollywood Hotel by Samuel Goldwyn, but I'd spent my first night as Lotte Lee in the arms of one of the best-looking movie stars in Hollywood, Tom Moore. The prize that had eluded Tallulah now belonged to me. That Tom was also the brother-in-law of Mary Pickford only added to his allure.

He'd brought a bottle of whiskey to the suite with him, and could that man ever hold his liquor. In spite of the drink, he'd still managed to climax three times before the rooster crowed. I'd wanted the word to get out: my tits and that thing between my legs belonged only to my daddy—I didn't say Goldwyn but the implication was clear. I wanted Lotte Lee to be known in Hollywood for her lips and tongue, and after a night with me I'm sure Tom would only enhance my reputation, especially as he'd promised to arrange dates with his brothers, Owen and Matt. I knew in Owen's case that Mary Pickford wasn't keeping him busy at night.

In the years before he'd succumbed to drink, Tom Moore was a beautiful man with a sculpted body like a statue. When fully erect, he measured six and a half inches and was thicker than most pricks. Of course, he was no Elmo Lincoln or Francis X. Bushman, but he was adequately equipped to show a woman like me a good time. He had a sweet taste to him I'll always remember. A dear, gentle man, he'd stripped completely nude in front of me, and slowly, very slowly, I had proceeded to

discover every inch of his fine body with my lips and tongue. He'd kept moaning softly as I'd tasted every part of him, occasionally saying that, "No woman has ever done this for me." When my tongue had entered his rosebud, he'd screamed out in pure ecstasy. No tongue had every gone there before and he'd loved it.

At five o'clock Tom had fallen into a deep sleep, and I'd gone to the bathroom to check my makeup, which I had done frequently throughout the night. I'd left Tom a note, promising to get in touch with him soon, and had driven back to the cottage. I had to face the photography and surprise of Rod St. Just, and I feared I might not be looking my best after a night in the strong arms of Tom Moore.

At the cottage I saw Rodolfo's car in the driveway, and I was thrilled. He was back with me. The planned marriage with Jean Acker was off. Tiptoeing into the living room, I feared he'd spot me as Lotte Lee. From the sounds of light snoring, I knew he was asleep in our much-used bed in the rear.

I quickly slipped into the bathroom and transformed myself from Lotte Lee into Durango Jones. Totally nude and having only three hours before my photography session with Rod, I went into the bed and into Rodolfo's arms. He was my one true love. I was faithful to him in my fashion, in spite of my whoring around. After all, Rodolfo had my heart; the others, only my body.

He awakened about thirty minutes later and his eyes opened wide, the way they'd do in all his famous movies of the Twenties, and he reached for me, crushing me into him. "Thank God you're here. It was awful when I got back and you were gone."

"I'll always be here for you," I said, kissing him frantically, my tongue flicking out to taste his sweetness. At least it was sweet to me. He always had a slight garlic flavor to his breath because of the meal he'd consumed the night before. But I found it aromatic.

"It's over between Jean and me," he whispered in my ear. "You've got me forever."

I melted into his arms even though I knew his promise to be with me was something to say in the heat of a morning's passion, as the first rays of sunshine came into our bedroom.

He made breakfast that morning—Rodolfo was a good cook—and we caught up on all the news, never mentioning Acker again. As a minor piece of news, I informed him that my sister, whose screen name would be Lotte Lee, had arrived in Hollywood and was going to be signed to a contract with Samuel Goldwyn.

"When can I meet her?" he asked.

"Never!" I said. "She looks like a pretty version of me. Once you meet her, I'll be dropped."

"No way," he promised. "Sisters I don't do. Sisters are to be respected. I am, after all, an Italian gentleman."

The big news I saved for last. "I've met Dorothy Gish. I'm setting up a meeting between the two of you. She's going to consider you as the male lead opposite her in her next picture."

He raised his eyebrows in a look of total astonishment. Rushing to me, he lifted me off the floor and whirled me around. No news could have pleased him more. Back on the floor again, I was kissed repeatedly by him. I'd never seen such gusto.

"My one big chance," he shouted. "And you did it for me. When I'm a big star, I'll be so grateful to you. Forever grateful."

About forty-five minutes later, when a call came in from the studio where Dorothy Gish was working, Rodolfo knew I was not fantasizing. "Miss Gish," or so I was told, would see Rodolfo at the studio at noon today. I had wanted to accompany him but had other commitments that I couldn't tell him about. He was disappointed that I could not go with him, but decided finally that it was better that he meet Miss Gish alone.

Since we still had time, he invited me to go with him into the Hollywood Hills for a long walk in a breeze-swept day. Far from fantasizing about his upcoming stardom, he wanted to talk nostalgically of his days growing up as a boy in southern Italy. At times he could be very pensive, a quiet, contemplative man.

He spoke lovingly of his mother, Beatrice, that slight French woman who was devoutly religious but also compassionate. He told me how she'd fallen madly in love with his father, a captain in the Italian Cavalry. He made the sun-drenched town, Castellaneta, where he grew up to be some fantasy place, filled with loving people and overflowing with Mediterranean bounty.

Their home, with its spacious rooms and sunny courtyard, with servants' quarters in the rear, seemed idyllic, and I longed for him to take me there one day.

He told of his first love, Teodolinda, a little ten-year-old girl from the village. He claimed he'd adored her, and she'd occupied all his daydreams. But one day he became upset with her and knocked her down in a ditch. "Even today I don't know why I turned on her like that. A strong emotion came over me. I have very mixed feelings about women."

He told of his father's death. No longer a dashing cavalry officer, he had dissipated into a sickly skeleton of a man. "His last words to me were, 'Stand by your mama and honor her always and defend your country against all its enemies.' After saying that, he died in my arms. And now mama. She's gone too. I am but an orphan hoping you'll adopt me."

When Rodolfo spoke of his life, every story was always sad. He told of how unfit he was for the discipline of a military school where he was sent. Instead of regulations, he read books filled with adventure and romance.

"Didn't you want to be a dashing cavalry officer like your father?"

"Not really. I was eventually expelled."

"What did you do? I don't know if I want to hear this."

"The school officials hated me. They knew how eager I was to see King Vittorio Emmanuele and his Queen when they announced a visit to our little town. Even in those days I liked to dress up. But they locked my uniforms up and told me not to attend the ceremonies. I broke out and found a uniform far too big for me. There were no horses around so I found this ancient donkey who had known better days. I pretended the poor broken down creature was my white charger, and that I was a knight in shining armor. Me and that donkey stole the show. I got more attention than the king himself. I also got kicked out of the academy."

Even as we talked intimately, and even as I told him of my days of growing up on the plains of Kansas, I knew that Rodolfo and I would never be completely honest with each other.

What was I leaving out? First, he didn't know that I was Lotte Lee and that my picture within a few days would be splashed across the pages of the nation's major newspapers, heralding me as Samuel Goldwyn's hot new female star.

Rodolfo didn't know of my involvements with other stars, and I especially did not want him to know what had gone on between Charlie and me. In retrospect, I felt he might handle all this information as he wasn't possessive of me. But if I told him what was really going on in my life, he might feel an obligation to tell me what he was up to, especially during his long disappearances.

I felt he wanted to keep his mystique, and that was all right by me providing that I could still be a figure in his life. With Jean Acker now gone from his life and safely back in the arms of Nazimova, I wondered who would replace her. It might not be a woman. It might be another man. Then I got an idea. Perhaps Lotte Lee herself would make a play for Rodolfo. If he wanted a woman he might end up with Lotte instead.

The day was moving in fast on us. Both of us had an appointment with destiny. Rod St. Just had a difficult assignment of photographing me as the world's most beautiful woman, Rodolfo had to convince Dorothy Gish that the two of them as a team could light up the silent screen.

"If I become a star," he said, "I will owe it all to you."

"You will have made yourself a star," I assured him.

Totally unaware of my own upcoming stardom as Lotte Lee, Rodolfo seemed to feel that I was somehow being left behind. "When I'm a big star, I'll make the breaks for you—just as you are doing for me today."

"We'll both get there," I said. "We'll just take different roads."

"But promise me one thing, when we both become the biggest stars in Hollywood, we'll still be there for each other," he said.

"I will always love you. To the very end."

*****

When I arrived at the studio of Rod St. Just, he was expecting an appearance by Lotte Lee. Instead he got me. "Durango," he said, a look of surprise flashing across his face, "what in hell are you doing here?"

"I've come to be photographed," I said, barging in.

"That's great," he said. "I'll get some good shots of you. But right now Goldfish has hired me to photograph Lotte Lee. It's his new discovery. All the studs in Hollywood are talking about the great head she gives. Tom Moore was seen leaving her suite at the Hollywood Hotel this morning. And he was drained dry."

Once the door was safely shut, I turned to Rod and placed a hand on my hip, imitating an effeminate male. "What you see is what you get."

"What in hell is that supposed to mean?"

"Lotte Lee and Durango Jones are one and the same."

A tough veteran of the boudoirs and back alleys of Hollywood like Rod didn't need long to recover from shock. Somehow the whole development made sense to him, especially when he learned that Chaplin and Tallulah Bankhead had made me up as a joke on Goldwyn who had fallen for it.

"Now, listen girl," Rod said. "If you're going to be Lotte Lee, you can fool most people but not someone with the hawkeye of the world's greatest still photographer—Rod St. Just."

In minutes Rod was on the phone calling

two make-up people, a hair stylist for my wigs, a facial expert, and a "body makeover person," the latter, a profession with which I was unfamiliar.

Years later in 1950 when I saw Gloria Swanson as Norma Desmond in *Sunset Boulevard* prepare for her imagined comeback in pictures, I relived what I went through that morning. If I thought the Lotte Lee created by Tallulah and Charlie was spectacular, I had not reckoned on the stunning achievement of Rod and his boys. They made me so beautiful that I would have fallen for Lotte Lee myself had I been a young man who went that route. After all, if I had been heterosexual I could have screwed Blanche Sweet.

Over a ham sandwich for lunch, Rod and I relaxed privately in the dressing room. "You know, it's been done before," he said.

"I thought I'd be the first," I said, looking mildly disappointed.

"Did you ever see any of the pictures of Julian Eltinge?"

"They didn't show *The Countess Charming* at the Patee Theater in Lawrence, Kansas," I said. "But I've heard of him. *Her. It.*"

"I know Julian very well. Like you, Julian is very handsome as a man. But as a lady, stunning. In fact, he's making a movie now, and I might get a small part in it for your boy Rodolfo if he wants it."

"Opposite Julian Eltinge? Could I trust that bitch with Rodolfo? Please set it up for him. Right now he's meeting Dorothy Gish to see if he can get a role opposite her."

"Why not both Eltinge and Gish? They make pictures so fast he could do both roles. It would take only a week."

"Go for it."

"Fine," Rod said. "I'll set it up."

"That is, if Chaplin won't be jealous."

"Don't be coy with me, bitch. Spill the beans."

"First, have you ever seen Julian perform?" Rod asked.

"Never."

"I first saw her in New York—in fact, the Eltinge Theater on Broadway is named for her. She is, after all, the most famous female impersonator in America. She was terrific in that Jerome Kern musical, *Cousin Lucy*. After she'd gone to Hollywood and filmed *The Widow's Mite* and *The Clever Mrs. Carfax*, she spotted Chaplin standing alone on a street corner. I don't know what the most famous man in the world was doing hanging out on a lonely Hollywood street corner late at night, but Julian swears it is true."

I smiled enigmatically, anxious to tell Rod of my latest adventure with Charlie but only after he'd finished dishing the dirt on the comedian and Julian.

"Eltinge introduced himself to Chaplin and invited him into the bar for a drink," Rod said. "Chaplin had already appeared in drag in two Keystone pictures and one at Essanay, so he was eager to talk to Julian. Chaplin had seen each of Eltinge's films."

"I want to see them too," I said.

"I can get Goldfish's studio to arrange it. Anyway, Chaplin was staying at the Stowell Hotel. But somehow Eltinge got him to move in with him at the Los Angeles Athletic Club. Those two must have been a sight at the club!"

"Do you think they were lovers?" I asked.

"What do you think? They slept in a double bed together. Of course, they were. I'll let you in on one of Hollywood's best kept secrets. Only a few people know it. Mary Pickford among them. Chaplin is known as a molester of little girls, but he's got a secret vice too. He likes to dress up on occasions like a woman and get fucked by a man."

"My dear, guess who his latest boy is?"

Rod looked like I'd thrown a Keystone pie in his face. "You're sitting there, you gorgeous hussy, telling me that you're Lotte Lee, the new Goldfish pussy, plus Chaplin's new boyfriend. Not to mention a few sidelines—like being the lover of Wallace Reid and Rodolfo Valentino. You're such a whore but the fastest rising one in Hollywood."

"I'm going to take over Tinsel Town, baby cheeks. You wait and see. For all you know, I might become the next Mrs. Charlie Chaplin should he decide to marry Lotte Lee. It would be a spectacular ceremony. Charlie and I might have a double wedding with Douglas Fairbanks and Mary Pickford."

"Have you had him too?" Rod asked. "Slam it on me. After all your revelations today, I'm ready for anything."

"I haven't but who knows what surprises lie in store for me in my future?"

"Before you pursue Fairbanks too aggressively, I must warn you. His dick has an unfortunate curvature. Mary seems to like it, but for you...I don't know."

"I've already seen it on Charlie's sun terrace."

"Is there anyone left in Hollywood you haven't gotten your hooks in?"

"Richard Barthelmess. But I've met him. He came on to me real strong. And then there's John Barrymore. I'm still waiting for him to show up."

"I don't know Barrymore but I know Richie very well. He's gay as a goose. Before he became a star, he posed for some hot nudes for me. And before coming to Hollywood, he posed for dirty French postcards. They're still sold along the Left Bank in Paris, although I don't think many buyers know they're getting full frontals of the great Richard Barthelmess. Stick around, my pet, after the gang has gone, and I'll show you photographs of Richie boy. That way, you'll know if it's worth your while pursuing that one. Some are fully erect."

"Sounds like fun."

Two hours later when my first photographic session with Rod had ended, and he felt he'd obtained stunningly beautiful pictures of Lotte Lee, the crew dispersed and I did get to gaze upon the pictures of Richard Barthelmess in all his glory. Indeed, I planned to call him as soon as I could fit him into my rapidly growing agenda.

Seated comfortably in Rod's studio, I realized he'd just become my best friend in Hollywood. We had seemed to get the sexual thing over between us, and could now relate to each other as sisters. With him, I didn't have to be the masculine cowboy Durango Jones or even the beautiful Lotte Lee if I didn't want to. With Rod, it didn't matter who or what you were.

He had news about the script of *Vampira* that was being prepared for me. "Goldfish won't really know what it's about, but it's being written by one of my sisters. She plans to make it the first homosexual film ever made, although only homosexuals will know that."

"That requires some explaining," I said, growing a bit uneasy.

"It's about this rich woman who is a vamp, real sex-crazed. She takes it upon herself to find the five most perfect male specimens in the world and plans to offer each of them a contract for fifty-thousand dollars a year if they will go with her on her yacht sailing the Seven Seas. Presumably at the end of that year, she will pay them off and search for five new replacements."

"So far, I really go for this part."

"The film will show more male nudity than has ever been seen on the screen before."

"Could I suggest Francis X. Bushman for one of the star roles?" I asked.

"I think that's a marvelous idea if Goldfish will go for it. Francis isn't exactly overworked these days. Come to think of it, Richard Barthelmess would be great as one of the men. After all, he's shown it all in front of the camera before."

"I've got three more hot men to go. I'm one lucky woman."

"There's a fantastic discovery being considered for one of the roles. William Boyd."

"Never heard of him."

"You will. I hear he's going to become a big star."

"Any news on the other two?" I asked, eagerly awaiting his response.

"All the male roles are star parts. They're going for Thomas Meighan."

"I loved him in *The Mysterious Miss Terry* with Billie Burke. I saw it at the Patee Theater in Lawrence, Kansas. And I've just seen him in *The Miracle Man* with Lon Chaney."

"Maybe you'll get to see a lot more of him. Since you're sitting down, I'll tell you who is up for your fifth lover?"

"I'm all ears."

"Tom Moore, my darling."

"Been there already."

Later, Rod filled me in on news of my director William Desmond Taylor. Rumors were flying that he was the lover of both Mabel Normand and Mary Miles Minter, the latter a rival of Mary Pickford. "I've even heard that he's fucking Mary's mother, Charlotte Shelby," Rod said.

I already knew that Taylor was quite a

Lothario.

"Darling," Rod said, "I'll arrange a meeting between Taylor and you. We often go to Fruitfly. It's a queer meeting den of guys and gals like us. The men can be as effeminate as they want and the women as masculine. In fact, many of the women dress in kimonos. They wheel around drugs—opium, morphine, and marijuana—in tea carts."

This reminded me of the five-hundred dollars I carried belonging to Jack Pickford. "What about heroin?" I asked Rod, explaining the request I'd received from Jack.

"Heroin isn't hauled out by the tea cart, but bring the money," Rod said. "I'll introduce you at the club to someone who can get it for you— or rather Jack. So, he's your next conquest?"

"I guess. But to tell the truth Lotte Lee is only going after him because he's Mary Pickford's brother."

"Doesn't his being voted 'The Ideal American Boy' have something to do with it?"

"That too. What self-respecting homosexual male wouldn't want to seduce America's ideal American boy?"

The phone rang. Rod got up to answer it. "It's for you," he said. "The party wants to speak to Lotte Lee."

"Hi," came the voice from the other end. "It was a bit difficult to track you down. But as you'll find out I'm one persistent man."

"Who is this?" I demanded to know.

"This is John Gilbert. Jack to you. I'm calling to set up a date."

*****

That afternoon, as Durango Jones, I was ushered toward Gloria Swanson's dressing room, carrying a personal and confidential letter from Wallace Reid. Apparently, my entrance into the studio had been cleared by the highest authority. I decided to end my career as a messenger boy. That included delivering the Bushman dildos as well. As Lotte Lee I had more important deals to discuss with Francis than his physique photographs with their full frontals. My Lotte wanted to star opposite him in *Vampira*. I'd do this final messenger boy favor for Wally—and that was that. You'd think that supplying him with morphine from Dr. Hutchison was homage enough.

Confronted with Miss Swanson, she stared at me intently in that witch/bitch way she had even then as a young woman. "Oh, yes, we've met," she said. "You're in the sex industry working for Bushman. Now I see you're also working for Reid."

"Miss Swanson, I have an important letter for you from Mr. Reid," I said.

"Put it on my dressing table over there," she commanded. "Normally, I would refuse to accept such a letter. But the head of the studio demanded that I take time out to see you. Since I'm going to be asking for a lot of money soon, I decided to obey like a meek Mary Pickford."

"Mr. Reid was hoping you'd read the letter in my presence and let me know your answer."

She looked disdainfully at the letter. "I'll give you my answer now and you can carry it back to Reid." She picked up the letter and ripped it to shreds, tossing it on the floor. She went over to a desk in the corner. "Reid even sent his valet by one day to ask for my signed autograph." She reached for a stack of pictures. "That I will grant him. I send out photographs of myself to the lowest, dirtiest pig farmer in Iowa. Why not Reid?" She seemed to slash— not write—her name across a very glamorized portrait of herself. She handed it to me. "Leave my dressing room at once before I call a security guard and claim you attempted to rape me."

I headed toward the door at once. But she called me back. "I think I do have a message for Reid. Tell him I deplore addicts. He can take his morphine and shove it where the sun don't shine." She slammed the door behind me.

Mission accomplished even if failed, I was grateful to be out of the overwhelming presence of Gloria Swanson.

Driving home as fast as I could without getting arrested, I was anxious to meet with Rodolfo and learn if he'd been cast in the picture with Dorothy Gish. He was already waiting in the living room when I got home. His wide eyes looked despondent.

"You didn't get the picture," I said, rushing over to him.

"I'm in the film, but I got the part of the villain. There's very little money involved. The good news is that the film will be directed by D.W. Griffith. Perhaps he'll see what I can do and cast me in more romantic parts."

"I'm sure he will. You just need to be given a chance." Noticing a suitcase in the corner, I said, "Are you going on a trip?"

"Only for a day or two. Just to think things over. I'm still suffering from the death of my mama. I want to get away and be by myself some place where I can walk alone by the sea like I used to in Italy."

"Would you care to tell me where you're going?" I asked tentatively.

"I prefer no one to know," he said. "I want to be alone." In that, he echoed Garbo long before anyone had ever heard of her. He kissed me long, hard, and passionately.

Hoping to detain him, I said, "There's more news on the casting front. A friend of mine, the photographer, Rod St. Just, thinks he can get you a role opposite Julian Eltinge."

He looked puzzled for a moment. "Oh, my God, now I'll have to make love on screen to a female impersonator." With that, he was out the door. In moments, I heard his car spinning gravel in the driveway.

Alone and dejected, I called Charlie's house to learn how much time I had before we were scheduled to meet William Randolph Hearst and Marion Davies. Instead of the butler, I got the Japanese chauffeur, Kono, on the phone. "Charlie's out for the evening." He giggled to himself. "He said tell you that in case you called, Miss Davies is not feeling well today. The rendezvous has been canceled until tomorrow or the next day."

"Am I needed there?" I asked, thinking I had a lot better offers for the upcoming night than sitting around waiting for Charlie to return.

"Your bedroom is ready and waiting—but no Charlie in it." Kono giggled again.

"That's very nice," I said, "but I have an audition to go to."

"I know what kind of auditions you have," Kono said. He giggled again. "Until I get well, Charlie has hired a new chauffeur. You've been promoted to the boudoir, no longer a driver." He hung up the phone before he could giggle again.

Rodolfo had cooked a meal for himself before departing on his mysterious journey and

had left the kitchen in a sloppy mess. He believed in dirtying pans—not washing them. After cleaning up the kitchen, and clad only in a pair of denim pants without my shirt, I headed for the far corner of the back yard to empty the garbage.

It was on that occasion that I confronted my neighbor, Adela Rogers St. Johns, who was also carrying out her garbage to the same bin.

"Miss St. Johns," I said, "forgive the way I'm dressed but I've been wanting to come over and introduce myself. I'm Durango Jones, your next door neighbor."

She looked me over carefully. "No one who has a body like yours needs to keep it covered. As for the name of Durango Jones, you're going to have to come up with a better moniker than that in this town. Durango is too unbelievable and Jones too common."

"I love your news reporting."

"In that case, come over and have tea."

"The way I'm dressed?"

"Especially the way you're dressed," she said, taking my hand. "I'm serving tea to the prettiest gal in the world. I'm sure she'd like to meet the handsomest man. The two of you are too beautiful to be real."

It was on the terrace that I renewed my acquaintance with Reatha Watson. The memory of the way Charlie had seduced and abandoned her on the school grounds still struck a discord in my heart. Pleased but also puzzled, I came up to her and kissed her on the lips. "Reatha, what are you doing here?"

"I meant to call you, but as Adela can tell you, I've been in a bit of trouble." She looked vague.

"I didn't know you two knew each other," Adela said as she poured tea for us. "I guess you've read about what happened to Reatha?"

Actually, I hadn't. My life had speeded up so fast that I hadn't seen a newspaper in days.

Adela was shocked at that. Anyone who didn't read newspapers was like a rock fallen from a strange universe to her.

In the next few minutes the headlines about Reatha were spread before me. It seemed that Reatha had gotten into a car with her step-sister and her boyfriend, plus another man. Both girls had disappeared which had launched a search by the Los Angeles police when they were reported missing. The step-sister eventually returned home, and Reatha had been found wandering on the outskirts of Los Angeles. Shaken and looking bewildered, she'd refused to tell what had happened to her during the mysterious abduction.

In juvenile court, Adela had befriended Reatha who appeared frightened by the notoriety of having her picture splashed across the pages. The judge had told Reatha that she was "too young and beautiful to be wandering in the city alone." He'd ordered that she go back to join her folks in the country.

Even now, Reatha still refused to tell Adela or me what had happened to her when she'd been abducted. The whole case brought back memories of my first encounter with Reatha on the schoolground and her getting into the car with Charlie. But both of us chose not to tell Adela of yet another scandal.

When Adela returned to the house to answer an urgently ringing phone, I had time to be alone with Reatha. "I'm doing what the judge says," she said. "I'm going back home. But I feel like I'm not a girl any more. I know that in age alone I'm just a child. But there's a real woman inside me—not a girl."

"In time, all the things a woman does you can do," I said. "But you need to go back to school. I had the same feelings when I was your age. You've got time. Why don't you go back home and grow up, then return to Hollywood? I may be a big star then. I'll help you."

"Like Chaplin promised?" A look of the saddest disappointment came into her expressive eyes.

"Not like that," I said, taking her hand in mine and holding it gently.

She stopped to admire the white and gold butterflies fluttering among the flowers in Adela's garden. "You said I had time," she said. "Time is the one thing I don't have. Life is much too short."

"Yours will be long," I predicted.

"We'll see about that." There was a forlorn sound to her voice, like it was coming from some place far away that only she knew about.

"When I do return to Hollywood," she said, "it won't be as little innocent Reatha Watson getting abducted by men. I will return as the screen goddess Barbara LaMarr."

*****

On shaky legs, I made my first appearance as Lotte Lee in the bar of the Alexandria Hotel, one of Rodolfo's most cherished hangouts. During his lean days in Hollywood, he lived on the free ham sandwiches distributed here. The publicity stills taken by Rod St. Just had not been released to the press yet, so I felt I could go places without hordes of adoring fans mobbing me.

As I entered the mostly male bar as Lotte Lee, there was animation, the sound of drinking, talking, and laughter in the smoke-filled room. As I came into the bar, the noise died down slightly. The appearance of a beautiful woman always attracted attention. I later learned that women did not enter the bar unaccompanied unless they were there for one purpose. Frantically I looked around the room for John Gilbert but couldn't find him. Had he stood me up?

Before the first hot stud could move in on me, I was approached by a young waiter who looked vaguely familiar. He invited me to follow him to a dimly lit table in the far corner where he informed me that Mr. Gilbert would be joining me shortly.

"Don't I know you from some place?" I asked, as he graciously seated me and lit a candle.

He bowed slightly. "I am José Ramon Gil Samaniego," he said. "Please call me Ramon. It is an honor to meet such a grand lady like you. Mr. Gilbert told me you are going to become a big star for Samuel Goldwyn."

"He got that right," I said, giving the handsome waiter my order for a whiskey. The young man was strikingly handsome and looked Italian or perhaps Mexican.

I was startled to see John Gilbert walking toward my table escorted by, of all people, Sessue Hayakawa.

John bowed low and kissed my hand, introducing me to Hayawaka, not that we needed any introduction. I knew him well. Hayakawa knew me even better, at least my most intimate body parts.

A recognition came across Hayakawa's

face. "Forgive me," he said, sitting down opposite me as John joined me in my own booth, moving in close. "Surely we haven't met before. I would have remembered meeting such a beautiful lady."

"I think you know my brother, Durango Jones," I said.

There was a long, awkward pause. "As a matter of fact, I do," Hayakawa said. "The resemblance is stunning."

"We're twins."

"I see." Hayakawa appeared embarrassed, no doubt wondering what Durango had told me.

"I had no idea you two gentlemen knew each other," I said.

"We've made a picture together," John said.

"Forgive me for not seeing it," I said. "I saw every movie shown at the Patee Theater in Lawrence, Kansas, but I must have missed yours."

"It was called *The Man Beneath*," Hayakawa said, "and it co-starred Helen Jerome Eddy."

"Before that, I wasn't getting much work and, in fact, lived on the free ham sandwiches here," John said. "Since meeting Sessue my luck has turned."

I paused a moment, wondering how well Hayakawa knew John. Later in the evening when I would no doubt be licking John's ass, would I discover the mark of the branding iron of this Japanese star?

My attention turned to John. After all, I didn't have a date with Hayakawa until Saturday night when I'd be Durango Jones again. "I loved you in that First National film, *Heart o' the Hills*. I thought it was one of the best pictures Mary Pickford ever made."

"That dance we did in that movie where Mary tries to outdo me at a church social brought down the house," John said. "Later on, when it got such audience approval, the director, Sidney Franklin, said it was his idea, but he's a liar." A strange bitterness crossed John's face before he turned and smiled at me. "Please call me Jack. May I call you Lotte?"

"Sure you can."

We were interrupted by the appearance of Ramon, the waiter. The handsome young boy looked at Hayakawa with a certain awe but also a flicker of intimidation.

"My young pretty," Hayakawa said to the boy. "Is it still on for Saturday night?"

"Yes, sir," he said meekly.

Hayakawa turned to me before looking at the waiter. "Good," he said. "You'll get to meet Miss Lee's brother, Durango Jones. The two of you will be sensational together."

The dawn of recognition came. Now I knew who Ramon was. He was the young boy that Hayakawa had branded on the night of my visit with Rodolfo to his mansion. Without saying another word, Ramon placed our drinks before us and turned on his heels, heading back to the bar.

"I met that lovely creature," Hayakawa said, "when I was making a movie called *The Jaguar's Claw* in 1917. I got Ramon a job as an extra."

"So he wants to be an actor," I said. "Who doesn't? Perhaps I'll cast him in one of my films for Goldwyn."

"The whole town is buzzing about you," John said. "I hear your first film is called *Vampira*."

"I play a femme fatale," I said. "A woman who drives men crazy."

"That I can believe," he said, taking my hand and placing it to his tender lips where he gently kissed it. "The aroma of you is intoxicating."

"I really must go," Hayakawa said. "It's been an honor meeting such a lovely lady. Perhaps our paths will cross again."

"Perhaps they will," I said enigmatically, thinking of the Saturday night coming up.

When he'd gone, John moved even closer to me. "I'm glad he's gone. I'm polite to him and everything. But he's a real pansy. No young boy is safe with him. I hear he gets off by branding their naked asses."

"Surely not," I said.

Sitting next to him made it easier to forget Hayakawa. John kissed me several times on the lips. At one point he took my delicate hand and placed it between his legs. "It's all yours, baby. I've heard what those pretty red lips of yours can do to a man."

The package was impressive, although nothing in the same universe of Elmo Lincoln and Francis X. Bushman. But it was firm and fully packed, enough to enchant those dykes, Marlene Dietrich and Greta Garbo, in the

Thirties.

Ramon returned with more whiskey, and John kept drinking, so much so that I felt he might not be of much use to me later when I invited him up to my suite for the night.

The whiskey put him in a nostalgic mood. As we talked, I observed him closely. Although shockingly short—it was the era of short men and midgets like Gloria Swanson—he was extraordinarily handsome but also had irregular features. His was not a rugged face, and he looked slightly weak. He would later correct that by growing a mustache which improved his appearance considerably.

Both Rodolfo and John had an elegant physical grace to them, an aesthetic appeal that would turn them into the two greatest lovers of the silent screen, although John would never quite equal the great Valentino. Yet John had a magical presence to him with piercing dark eyes that when turned on you made you think you were the most special person on earth.

Regardless of what you said, he seemed to absorb it as if it were the Ten Commandments being read for the first time. His smile was dazzling, and he could both disarm and conquer. In other words, he was a heartthrob you couldn't say no to, especially if you were a helpless young lady about town like me who had known only one man in her life—the movie star, Tom Moore. Before the evening ended, I knew I'd bagged my second conquest as Lotte Lee—John Gilbert whose screen fame was growing by the day.

He was sexually magnetic, with a high-flying spirit that seemed to scream out his joy to be alive. "When we go to bed," he whispered in my ear, "and I know we will, don't fall in love with me. I have not only a roving eye, but a roving heart as well."

I liked a man with confidence. John Gilbert wouldn't be the only man who warned me not to fall in love with him before I'd even bedded him.

"I will try to restrain myself," I said, with just a cutting edge of sarcasm.

"Don't get me wrong," he said. "I need love but from many different sources. I was born unloved and unwanted. I think it has scarred me for life. My mother called herself Ida Adair and she was an actress, a tall, voluptuous figure with a sensuous face. She told me I was the product of a careless night, and she never wanted to get careless with a man ever again."

"I guess you interfered with her career," I said.

"I interfered with her life. I even had to iron my own shirts before I was six years old. What I hated most was when I had to dress up like a girl to play a part in one of Ida's plays. I made my stage debut when I was only two weeks old. Eddie Foy carried me out on stage. Whenever the script called for a child, I was it. I even played one of Nora's children in *A Doll's House.*"

"Sounds like an exciting life to me," I said. "I grew up in dull, cornpone Kansas where nothing ever happened."

"I never knew from week to week who my new daddy would be," he said. "Ida was constantly introducing me to a new daddy. I eventually came to call them daddy of the week."

At first when I'd met with John I was expecting only a sexual encounter. The more he talked, the more I came to like and respect him as a man. Was I falling in love with him? Perhaps. It turned out that Durango Jones was not the only person in the world who could fall in love after just an hour. Lotte Lee, his sister, was capable of the same.

When John spoke of his childhood, it was like something out of Dickens. Abandoned by his mother when he was six, he lived with a seamstress who had a daughter earning her living as a prostitute. In New York they shared a dingy flat on Amsterdam Avenue. "I slept on a mat in the corner of the room. The daughter told her johns to pretend I didn't exist. Night after night I was exposed to cruel, ugly scenes. Sometimes one of her clients would send me down to the corner saloon for a pail of beer. I was so tiny I couldn't see over the bar counter. They often didn't feed me. I remember some nights when I went looking for something to eat in garbage cans."

"All that is behind you now," I said. "You're going to become one of the biggest stars in Hollywood."

"Will we appear together on the screen?" he asked.

"We would burn up the screen," I predicted.

"Lotte Lee and John Gilbert."

"I love it," he said. "Only the billing is wrong. John Gilbert and Lotte Lee."

"Touché."

Two hours later in my suite at the Hollywood Hotel, I explained the ground rules to John. My breasts and honeypot were off limits. I told him they belonged to Goldwyn. My love-making consisted of tongue and lips.

"That's what I want," he said. "I get enough of the other wherever I go."

Totally nude on my bed, he got the tonguing of his young life. My eyes drank him in as he removed all his clothes, revealing a cock of meaty promise. His torso wasn't muscular but that of a young swimmer. He spread his legs apart for me in a defiant gesture revealing a substantial uncut penis that was thickening. His balls rested like two eggs in a fleshy sac.

Moistening my lips and breathing deeply, I descended on him, pulling his foreskin back to taste his cockhead. After a while I buried my face in his scrotum, losing myself deep in the folds of his flesh. The smell was muskier and riper here. I took each of his balls in my mouth and washed them tenderly as he squirmed and moaned.

In spite of the whiskey, his dick rose to its full magnificence, as I swallowed it whole until my nose was buried deep into his black pubic hairs. As I deep-throated him, it was clear that I was driving him into a frenzy. He was panting, moaning, almost begging me to stop. At that point in his life John Gilbert hadn't received many blow jobs before. He fucked my face with fierce, quick strokes. His body began to shudder as he screamed out, "I'm gonna shoot."

And that he did. Before dawn came, he climaxed two more times in my mouth. By then I had gone where no man or woman had gone before. I'd even licked greedily at his rosebud. He later assured me no one had ever done that before. I told him it was intoxicating. He made the same pronouncement as my tongue had nuzzled deep into each armpit.

At five o'clock, he'd informed me that I had discovered erogenous zones in his body that he didn't know existed. Once or twice he'd reached for my breasts but I always moved his hand away. "That's a no-no," I said.

I awoke with him cuddled in my arms. Today I had to meet with Goldwyn and sign my contract. I'd been assured that the script of *Vampira* was almost ready, and I was anxious to read what scenes I'd be called upon to play as Lotte Lee.

Taking one final look at John's naked cum-soaked torso, I dressed and left the room. At the reception desk, I asked for messages.

"A message from your studio, Miss Lee," the receptionist said. I read that one carefully. I was due there at eleven o'clock that morning, and I had to look my gorgeous best.

The other message was from Owen Moore. Apparently his brother, Tom, had told him the delights he could expect from Lotte Lee. Although I knew Owen and Mary Pickford wouldn't be married for long, I was eager to seduce the second brother, having heard rumors that he used to drive Mary wild. That was one call I planned to return.

On an impulse, I asked the receptionist if Jean Acker were in residence. I suspected that Rudy might not have gone away at all, but was actually upstairs in her room.

"You haven't heard?" the young man asked. "There was an item about it in the morning's paper. She married Rodolfo Valentino yesterday."

*****

Back in the cottage as I prepared myself to visit Goldwyn, I neither experienced hurt nor rejection from Rodolfo's ill-fated marriage to Jean Acker. He didn't belong to me, and I was hardly lonely the nights he was away.

For all my love and caring for Rodolfo, I knew in the hot light of a Hollywood day that my relationship with him would always be a sometimes thing—and maybe not even that.

At this very moment, I had no clue that I would ever see him again. I might have launched myself in Hollywood with Rodolfo, but that seemed like a long time ago. For better or for worse, I was involved with Charlie and Jack, with the prospect of Owen Moore beating down my door. And John Barrymore hadn't even arrived on the scene.

"Fuck Rodolfo," I told the gorgeous woman staring back at me in the mirror. "Fuck Jean Acker." I was Lotte Lee about to take over Hollywood as its newest and hottest female star. Move over, Theda Bara.

An hour later, as I was ushered into Goldwyn's studio, he jumped up to greet me, closing the door behind me and enfolding me in his arms for a wet, juicy kiss with plenty of tongue. He was no John Gilbert. Certainly no Rodolfo. As the great actress and vamp, Lotte Lee, I viewed our encounter as a screen test, and I passed admirably.

At his desk, Goldwyn unbuttoned his trousers and presented his tiny weenie to me which I devoured like a woman denied food for days. The dick might be small, but the cum erupted in buckets, and I swallowed every drop of it and pretended to want more. "You are one hot bitch," he finally said, gasping for breath. "Jewish girls won't do what you just did."

In a bathroom adjoining his office, I made emergency repairs before going in to sign my first movie contract. I knew it wouldn't be the last.

Goldwyn wanted me to sign up for three pictures, beginning with *Vampira,* at the impressive salary of two-hundred dollars a week. I was thrilled, thinking of the glamorous wardrobe I could buy just with my first week's salary.

After signing the contract, he handed me the script of *Vampira*. "It's a dirty picture, and I like clean pictures," he said. "Fun for the whole family. But I also need money. I'm hiring William Desmond Taylor to direct it. He's a dirty pervert. Goes to bed with both young boys and women, providing each of them is beautiful. Right now he's fucking my dear Mabel Normand. He's also banging Mary Miles Minter and any cute little boy ass he can pick up on the side."

"I'm anxious to read the script and meet with Mr. Taylor," I said.

"He's enough of a pervert to understand this picture," he said. "Frankly, it's too sick for me. I'm a normal man, not another William Desmond Taylor visiting all the queer meeting places in Los Angeles."

"My dream, Sam, is to make you proud of me. I want to be a star."

"You've got the looks for it," he said. "What a gal. The problem now is, can you act? Taylor's got his work cut out for him."

At the door I tasted more of the juicy tongue of Goldwyn before he finally released me. I'm sure that decades later Marilyn Monroe read of my exploits and realized that she could break into movies the same way I did—that is, down on your knees in front of some man who might give you a break. Marilyn and I both should have worn knee-pads.

Back at the Hollywood Hotel, I discovered that John Gilbert had departed for his own studio. But he'd left a note. "I warned you not to fall in love with me. What I should have done is warn myself not to fall in love with you. I count the hours until we are together again."

Having John Gilbert fall in love with me wasn't exactly on my time schedule. The hours in my life were rapidly filling up, and I wondered if I had time for all my suitors. I was, after all, leading a double life as Durango Jones and Lotte Lee. My calendar for the upcoming Saturday alone already included everybody from Wallace Reid to Sessue Hayakawa. What about Charlie Chaplin? Rodolfo? There was action on the sidelines too. Possibly Jack Pickford. Certainly Owen Moore. Exotica awaited in an expected call from Douglas Fairbanks. I just knew he'd line up a date for me with the king of England.

The phone rang. It was Owen Moore. "Tom has told me a lot about you," he said. "We Irish brothers believe in sharing. How about it?"

"I'd be honored to meet you, Mr. Moore," I said. "I just love your films."

"A fan, I see." He sounded a bit smug. "You'd better go and take a look at the morning papers. You're gonna be the big star. I can't believe how gorgeous you look in those pictures released by Goldfish's studio. Tom assures me you are even more beautiful in person."

"That you will have to see for yourself."

"Can I drop by your hotel at two o'clock tomorrow afternoon?" he asked. "I've got to see Mary later. Don't tell anybody but I'm divorcing the bitch, and I plan to take her for millions."

"Your secret is safe with me." After some

more idle chit-chat, I hung up, agreeing once again to the secret rendezvous. I had a lot more important things to do than seduce Owen Moore, but the prospect of knowing Owen Moore as David had known Bathsheba overwhelmed me. Judging from his movie roles, Owen wasn't as handsome as his brother, Tom, but Owen was still one good-looking man. In her younger days, Mary Pickford was always quoted in magazines raving about Owen's good looks.

On the phone again, I called Charlie's residence only to get Kono. "Where are you?" he shouted. "Charlie's upstairs and he's frantic. You've been scheduled to meet Hearst and his mistress at five o'clock today. They're out in Santa Monica."

"There's still time," I said. "Tell Charlie I'll be there right away." In a fast transformation, Lotte Lee became Durango Jones. As I headed for the door, I reminded myself to act like a man as I walked through the lobby of the Hollywood Hotel. The phone rang. I picked it up to hear the voice of Rod St. Just. "It's on for the evening," he said. "We're meeting William Desmond Taylor for drinks at nine o'clock, a little supper, and then we're off to a special club."

"I'll be by after seven thirty to pick you up," I said, hoping the get-together with Hearst and Marion Davies would be only for tea.

At Charlie's home, Kono was waiting and seemed impatient with me. I was wearing my best suit, a vision in dark blue with a white shirt and tie. I wanted to look respectable for Mr. Hearst in spite of my activities of the previous night, as I lay in my suite at the Hollywood Hotel in the arms of John Gilbert.

Kono told me to go upstairs where Charlie was getting ready. "You are now number one geisha." Instead of slugging Kono, I headed upstairs where Charlie was trying to put a knot in his tie and wearing a white shirt whose collar was too tight for him.

I went over to him at once and took him in my arms for a long, lingering kiss. "I've missed you, baby," I said.

"Not as much as I've missed you." He pointed to the newspapers lying on his bed. My picture as Lotte Lee was splashed across the pages. "Goldfish is going to make you a star—maybe even bigger than me." A frown crossed his face as he checked out his appearance in the mirror. "No, no, not that. No one will be as big as me. But you'll be a fabulous star. Only Tallulah and I will know your secret."

"William Desmond Taylor is going to direct my first picture," I said. "I'm meeting with him tonight."

"Watch his roving hands," Charlie said. "Goldfish could not have selected a more decadent director in all of Hollywood. I gather this won't be a clean family picture like one of my films."

"Hell, no, I'm a vampire."

After selecting another shirt for Charlie and giving him another tongue job down his throat, we headed for his Locomobile for the journey to call on William Randolph Hearst and his mistress, Marion Davies.

The couple was staying at a rambling beach house, and Charlie and I were ushered into a large hall filled with tapestries. Up to now, tapestries hadn't occupied much of my time. While waiting for the famous pair to come out and greet us, Charlie explained each of the tapestries to me. Kono might find him Cockney trash, but Charlie was learning fast. His hanging out with some of the more famous people in the world had broadened his knowledge and insight.

The ex-Follies girl, Marion Davies, was the first to come down and greet us. I knew the rumors about Charlie and her were true. They were having an affair apparently right in front of "W.R.," although I didn't know then if he were aware of it or not.

In a white dress with bee-stung red lips, blonde-haired Marion greeted us. Far from viewing her as a rival for Charlie's affection, I liked her at once.

She kissed me on the cheek. "Durango Jones," she said, "as if anybody could be named that." She gave Charlie a quick kiss on the lips and invited us into the spacious living room. "I'd offer you guys a drink but W.R. just ordered all booze removed from the house."

"We're fine," Charlie said.

"Are you still trying to louse up that poor girl, Mildred Harris?" Marion asked Charlie.

At that point Charlie had never mentioned his wife to me.

"Let's not get into that," Charlie said, anger flashing across his face.

"Mildred's no angel, but she ain't all that bad." She turned to me. "Mildred shouldn't have gotten messed up here with Charlie in the first place. A woman like me can handle Charlie, but not a kid like Mildred."

A house servant called Charlie to the phone, and Marion took my arm. Giggling, she led me across the living room to a small library adjoining. In the library she removed one large book and produced a flask. "Have some," she said. "It's gin."

I giggled along with her as she drank from the flask. After her third drink, she reached to caress my cheek. "A little advice from America's most famous mistress," she said. "We show gals get old, sugah, so get that ice or else no dice. Charlie's cheap, you know. You'll have a hard time prying that one loose with his dough. But let him know that you're not opposed to a few gratuities."

I was a bit astonished to find that Marion was relating to me as mistress-to-mistress and treating me in the confidential way she might with a woman. It was a first to me.

While waiting for Charlie to return, I told Marion that I was an agent for my sister, Lotte Lee.

"Lotte Lee, the blonde vamp!" Marion exclaimed, enjoying the first warm glow of the gin. "She's prettier than me. I've seen her pictures in the paper. I'm jealous. I don't dare to introduce her to W.R. He'd desert me for her for sure."

"Forgive me for asking you this," I said. "I know how presumptuous it is. But are you and Charlie serious? I mean, I've heard stories."

She burst into laughter the way she might when viewing a Chaplin film. "Charlie and I have this harmless flirtation. After all, I have to have some fun in my life. I'm young and living with a man thirty-four years my senior. He's gone from me a lot, and he has no intention of divorcing his Catholic wife. She was a chorus gal like me before she got all grand."

"Then there's nothing between Charlie and you?"

"In Charlie's case, I wouldn't call it nothing," she said. "He's got twice as much as W.R." She bent over and kissed me on the cheek again. "I'm sure you know that better than I do, sugah. All the men in Hollywood are afraid to get near me. They dare not risk the wrath of W.R. and his newspaper. One actor had a kissing scene with me, and he was so afraid of angering Hearst by a screen kiss that his knees were shaking. After he'd kissed me like a Presbyterian deacon, he went whoosh when the director called cut. W.R. has spies everywhere."

"But why isn't Charlie afraid of Mr. Hearst, too?"

"With Charlie, it's the danger that's part of the attraction. Besides, Charlie is too big a star for W.R. to harm. Those two guys also genuinely like each other."

Another servant appeared, informing us that Hearst would be right down in time for tea. I was nervous about meeting the press baron, but Marion assured me he was a nice guy. Before Charlie returned and before W.R. appeared on the scene, Marion patted my knee. "I'm awful lonely here some nights. When you've got no beau to take you out, give me a call and we'll get together for some girl-to-girl talk."

"I'd love that. I really would. And I'll bring us a pint."

"No pint for me, sugah," she said. "If you're showing up on my doorstep, make it a gallon."

Our little chit-chat ended abruptly at the sudden appearance of the fabled William Randolph Hearst himself.

"The best way to handle him," Marion whispered in my ear, "is to treat him like the President of the United States. That's his dream."

When Hearst spoke to me in a high-pitched, weak voice, I was startled. The voice didn't match the massive body. "Durango Jones, is it? We may have to change that name if I cast you opposite Marion in her next picture."

*****

Charlie still hadn't returned, and at one point

Marion excused herself. That left me alone with W.R. himself. I was practically trembling.

"Don't be afraid of me," he said, in his prissy, squeaky voice that didn't carry well. "I'm just a harmless pussy cat."

"That I doubt, Mr. Hearst."

"Tell me about yourself," he said. "I know you know everything about me already."

As tea was served and Charlie and Marion still hadn't come back, I sketched my life in very brief and broad details, especially leaving out data about my sordid affairs in Hollywood with Rodolfo, Norman Kerry, Wallace Reid, *et al.* I informed him that I was the agent for my sister, Lotte Lee, who had just been signed by Goldwyn.

"I saw your sister's picture in the paper," he said. "The resemblance to you is amazing. I have an eagle eye for such things."

"We're twins," I lied.

W.R. seemed to be appraising me as if viewing me under a magnifying glass. "I fear Miss Lee is serious competition for Marion. You don't come across beauty that often in life. After meeting Marion, I have never looked at another woman. But your Lotte Lee is one gal who could turn an old man's head." He sat up abruptly and slammed down his tea. "When can I meet her?"

"I don't know, Mr. Hearst, but I'm sure something could be set up soon. That is, if you'd really like to meet her."

"I command it," he said, "and I'm a man who is used to getting what he wants. I will confess my motive to you in advance. Your sister, as I've said, is one pretty gal. I think I'd like to make Marion jealous. She thinks I don't know she's having an affair with Chaplin. Any fool knows that. Louella Parsons is one of my spies. She tipped me off about Chaplin the first night he went out with Marion."

"I'm completely unaware of any sort of liaison," I said. "Chaplin belongs to me, and just to me. I'd put my foot down if he had a roving eye."

"You're a pretty boy but not a convincing liar," W.R. said. "I knew Chaplin had a homosexual streak in him, but he's also a ladies' man. He's not going to get my lady, though. I'll see to that."

"I'm sure he wouldn't cross you," I said.

"You could destroy his career in your newspapers."

"I could but I won't," W.R. said. "Although I've heard that Chaplin has Marxist tendencies. Do you know anything about that?"

"He never discusses politics with me."

W.R. clapped his hands like a prissy librarian. "You two are too busy making love, yeah?"

"Something like that."

"Forgive me for asking, but are you the man?"

"Yes, Mr. Hearst. Always the man."

"I thought so. I've seen Chaplin impersonate women at parties. He's just too good at it to be all man the way I am."

As Hearst studied me, I too evaluated him. He combined boyishness with shrewdness, kindness with ruthlessness. Although he possessed great power and wealth, he appeared very natural and pleasant, even though I feared he could turn on you at a moment's notice.

"I'm going to ask a big favor of you," W.R. said. "And I want you to know that William Randolph Hearst doesn't ask favors of anyone without compensation."

"I'd be honored to do a favor for you, and no money needs to be exchanged."

"For five-hundred dollars a week, I want you to give me a full report on Chaplin's activities, especially who he is bedding. Not you, of course, I'll just assume that. I don't have much to do with homosexuality so you can spare me the details of your love life with The Little Tramp."

"What you really want to know is, is Charlie going to bed with Miss Davies."

"You've got that right."

At that point Marion entered the room with Charlie. My boyfriend wasn't exactly buttoning up his trousers but both of them gave off the aura that they had just made love to each other.

Accepting tea from a servant, Charlie said, "Chief, you must let Marion play comedy. She's a natural comedienne, and I should know one when I see one. With her charm and appeal, she could have them lined up at the box office."

"I know what's best for Marion," W.R. said, flashing anger for the first time.

Perhaps she'd had too much to drink, but

the normally affable Marion became belligerent at this point, her eyes narrowing. She lay on an elaborate red velvet sofa à la Madame Récamier in her reclining style. Although radiantly beautiful and at the peak of her youth, Marion called out to Hearst in a voice that sounded like a fishwife screaming about the day's catch. "Hey, fatso!"

A look of controlled fury settled on Hearst's face. "I trust you're calling a servant and not referring to me."

She fastened her large blue eyes on him. "You, William Randolph Hearst, is who I'm calling. Ever hear of him?"

"What do you want?" he asked in that little high-pitched voice of his.

"Get me a drink," she shouted at him. "Make it champagne."

Although Marion obviously wanted a drink, she was also showing Charlie and me what great power she had over this potentate.

At first W.R. looked like he was going to sit firmly in his chair, not budging an inch. On second thought, he got up and hobbled over to the cabinet at the side of the room, returning with her champagne.

She accepted it disdainfully and turned her attention to Charlie. W.R. excused himself and invited me to accompany him outside, ostensibly to show me the swimming pool.

Once in the open, where breezes from the ocean stirred up the hot air, he turned to me. "I hope we've got a deal. Excuse Marion. She's normally very sweet and sensitive to me. But when Charlie's around, she grows belligerent."

"It's a deal. I'll let you know everything."

"I want you to introduce me to your sister," he said. "I'd like to take her to dinner, and I want to be photographed with her. I can certainly arrange that. Every paper will carry the picture. That photograph will bring Marion around. She doesn't want to lose me."

"I'll check with Lotte," I said. "I'm sure she'd be delighted to meet the great William Randolph Hearst."

Returning to join Charlie and Marion, I had no idea what I'd be telling W.R. to earn my five-hundred bucks a week. Marion's advice was already ringing in my ears. My glory days as Lotte Lee would surely end. Time alone would take care of that boyish/girlish look I

now possessed. I was almost a beardless youth, but how long would my role as Lotte Lee last? I predicted three years at the most. I had to make use of it.

Although freshly arrived in Hollywood, I was already making money—not the bushels Mary Pickford was hauling to the bank, but a lot of dough, nonetheless. I was going to save it and invest in real estate, in spite of the fact that the talk of the day was getting rich in stocks.

I didn't know how to make investments in the stock market, but I knew land and buildings—solid and safe. I'd have to ask Marion about that. After all, she'd landed one of the world's most powerful barons. There were rumors that W.R. was worth four-hundred million dollars, but it seemed impossible for any man to possess that much wealth. Maybe he had ten million, maybe more. It was difficult for me to conceive wealth beyond ten-million dollars.

The moment I entered the room, Marion jumped up and rushed toward me. "Has W.R. hired you to spy on me?"

"Nothing like that," I said. "I like you too much to tell secrets on you, if I knew any. I have a few secrets of my own."

She winked at me. "I know, sugah. Charlie has told me."

I looked over at Charlie who had a boyish, mischievous look on his face. "You told her. Only Tallulah and you were supposed to know."

"I did it for insurance purposes," Charlie said.

"What in hell does that mean?"

"Marion and I won't tell the world you're Lotte Lee, and you won't confirm to the Chief that we're having an affair."

"That sounds like a fair trade-off to me."

Marion came up to me and kissed me on the cheek. "Now that we've gotten that out of the way, we can be friends, sugah." The way she greeted me would decades later evoke that way Marilyn Monroe played her role in *Some Like It Hot*. In some eerie way, it was as if Monroe had transcended time in order to re-create Marion as she appeared on that faraway day in California.

As Charlie Chaplin, Marion Davies, and I sat on the sofa enjoying the breezes from the ocean, we were not adults playing deadly games. At least for a moment we were like children again, and in a way that was what we were. All of us had not at that point acquired the jaded sophistication of the years to come. We were old enough to have sex, but not old enough to be cynical about the complexities of human relationships.

On that day and for a long time to come, Charlie and Marion would become substitutes for the playmates I never had during my lonely childhood growing up in Kansas. Back then I had to hide myself from the world. Was I ever in the wrong place living in Kansas. As each day went by, Hollywood became more and more my kind of town.

Our frolicking on the sofa in the Santa Monica beach house appeared innocent enough, but before the night was over I suspected I'd descend into one of those opium dens in Los Angeles, accompanied by my new best friend, Rod St. Just, and my new director, the handsome, debonair, and dashing William Desmond Taylor.

As the sun set over the Pacific, it seemed like a dream world to me. Fame, fortune, and love waited for me around every corner. I had achieved what I thought was impossible back on the plains of Kansas—an enchanted life.

*****

Arriving back at Charlie's home, I encountered Mildred Harris in the living room. After one quick and disapproving glance at his wife, Charlie fled to his bedroom upstairs, locking the door behind him. Kono assured me he'd be there for the rest of the evening.

I had to transform myself into the ravishing Lotte Lee for my upcoming meeting with William Desmond Taylor, and I had no desire to entertain Mrs. Chaplin, of whom I was a bit jealous. She was hardly my favorite actress on the screen, and I viewed her as a very minor talent.

Hollywood historians have been unkind to Mildred Harris, and regrettably I must admit they are right. Although looking like a mere child, another Mary Pickford clone, there was a ruthless, self-indulgent aura about her. When she spoke, her voice was not that of a little girl

but a mature woman with a goal. "Are you Charlie's latest?" she asked.

"I'm Durango Jones, a very good friend of his."

"The Little Tramp has no friends," she said. "He's self-enchanted. I hear he's fucking Marion Davies now."

"Miss Davies and Charlie are friends—nothing else." I said that with all the conviction I could muster in front of this teenage girl from Wyoming who had been appearing in films since she was eight years old. She was always some father's loving daughter or some star's younger sister. Kono had found Mildred "the most beautiful girl in the world," although I would award that accolade to Reatha Watson, another one of Charlie's conquests.

Mildred appraised me rather cruelly I thought. "If you think you're getting money out of Charlie—forget it! He's the cheapest bastard walking the planet."

"I don't have an interest in Charlie's money," I said. "I'm not a gold-digger."

"Contrary to rumors, I'm not either. If you want gold, stay away from Charlie Chaplin. The rent on our first house was three-hundred a month. Charlie refused to pay more than two-hundred and fifty in rent. He made me pay the other fifty dollars from my salary. And he's one of the highest paid artists in the world."

"He's known great deprivation," I said. "It's made him appreciate the value of money."

"Before our baby boy died at birth, Charlie agreed to let me purchase some furniture for his room. When the furniture arrived, he seemed pleased with it. But later when the bill came in, he refused to pay for it. He made me pay for it."

"Would you excuse me?" I asked. "I've got to get ready for an appointment."

"Hell, no, you won't," she said, her face turning harsh, making her look far older. "You don't understand. When we were married, Charlie promised to give me fifty dollars a month for mother and me to cover our personal expenses. That promise went sour. He started giving me fifty dollars every two weeks, and then nothing at all."

"Miss Harris," I said, knowing she liked to be called Mrs. Chaplin, "Your battle with Charlie over money is no concern of mine."

"I bought all his socks and handkerchiefs—even his pajamas," she screeched.

"Excuse me," I said, heading for my room upstairs.

"He'll betray you too," she said, running after me. "He used to wait outside the studio for me to come out. He was madly in love with me. Then after the baby died, he started leaving the house, disappearing for weeks at a time. He turned cold."

I turned around to confront her. "It's over! Don't you know that? Charlie's not there for you any more."

"He'll kick you out and abandon you just like he did me," she said. "But I'm his wife. I can make him pay in court. You're a man. You can claim nothing. He'll use you and toss you aside like he did me."

Ignoring her words, I raced up the steps to my room where I had to prepare myself for William Desmond Taylor. Rod St. Just and I were going to meet first for drinks at the director's bungalow. It wasn't hard for me to blot out Mildred's words. My role with Charlie was different. First, I wasn't married to him and didn't plan to take his money. I hung around with Charlie not for the sex but for the adventure. Already I'd met William Randolph Hearst and Marion Davies. My association with Charlie was definitely paying off. I could expect a check for five-hundred a week as a "spy" for William Randolph Hearst. The newspaper baron had practically told me he wanted to take a second mistress—the great Lotte Lee herself, if for no other reason than to make Marion jealous.

As long as I could stay associated with Charlie in some capacity, I just knew in my heart that a life of romance and adventure waited for me. The sex wasn't bad either. Charlie was a skilled lover, a man who could bring me to spectacular climaxes, although Hollywood seemed filled with hot hunks who could do that.

In my bedroom before getting dressed I called Owen Moore. I hardly expected Mary Pickford to pick up the phone, as I knew they were no longer living together as man and wife. Owen came onto the phone at once, and I "destroyed" him with my Lotte Lee voice, turning him into another one of my helpless

Vampira victims.

Instead of meeting at the Hollywood Hotel, he suggested I drive out to his beach house at Santa Monica tomorrow afternoon, the one he shared with Jack Pickford. He said that Jack already knew my brother, Durango, and was eager to meet me too. I told Owen that I was not only looking forward to meeting him but being introduced to Jack Pickford himself, as I also adored his film roles. Jack, it seemed, wanted me to bring Durango with me, since Durango had "a little present" for him. I told Owen to inform Jack that I would bring the present, since Durango had another commitment. "What a lucky gal I am," I said. Owen Moore, husband of Mary Pickford, and Jack, brother of Mary Pickford. Not only that, but two of the handsomest actors ever to appear on the screen.

"You ain't seen nothing yet," Owen assured me, "Until you've seen Jack and me in action."

"I have ground rules," I said. "You must agree to my ground rules before I'll play."

"Don't worry baby," Owen said. "All the studs in Hollywood know your ground rules. If anything, it excites us guys all the more."

"That's fine with me." Before ringing off, I said, "Don't jerk off or anything tonight. Tell Jack to hold back too. I want a real full load from you guys tomorrow afternoon."

"Just talking to you has given me a big erection," Owen said. "If you're lucky, my brother Matt might come over after he finishes work at the studio."

"I've seen pictures of him too. Why not another one of Mary's brothers-in-law? If you're both as good as Tom, I'm in for a real treat."

"You are with me—and Jack too. Gals tell me I'm better than Matt or Tom. And I kept America's little sweetheart screaming for 'more of Moore' for years."

"Until tomorrow," I said scribbling down the address. Lotte Lee didn't need a chauffeur. Lotte Lee was a chauffeur, although I had to get over to Francis X. Bushman's and tell him no more deliveries. I'd appear at his home as Durango Jones, agent for Lotte Lee, and a man wanting Francis to star opposite his sister in *Vampira*. I just knew that Francis would go for the role as he'd get to expose more flesh than any man had ever done before on the screen.

On the way to the home of William Desmond Taylor, my upcoming director, Rod St. Just could not talk of *Vampira* or even me as Lotte Lee. He claimed that his mouth was still sticky from the hot cum of Antonio Moreno. Antonio, who would one day rival Rodolfo on the screen, was the closest male friend of Taylor's.

"He's a real Spaniard," Rod said. "Originally he wanted to be a matador, and could he ever fill out a suit of lights. I've taken some frontal nudes of him which I want to show you. I think you'll be delighted to sample that Spanish sausage."

"I can't wait."

"Antonio is a great friend of Tommy Meighan and Jack Pickford."

"I'll knock off Jack tomorrow, and, God willing, I'll get Meighan if he appears opposite me in *Vampira*."

"They will pale in comparison to Antonio Moreno," Rod predicted. "He's every bit as sexy as your Rodolfo. In fact, I suspect Antonio and Rodolfo in the years ahead will be racing neck to neck for the same roles."

"Good," I said. "I need a replacement for Rodolfo himself. I'm sure you've read of his marriage to Jean Acker."

"That lesbian," he said. "I give that marriage about forty-eight hours."

"I wish I knew where he was."

"What does it matter?" Rod asked. "Either as Durango Jones or Lotte Lee, you've got all the men in Hollywood. You don't need Rodolfo."

"But I think I love him."

"Honey child, you love anything in pants who's got a club swinging between his legs," he said. "You and I are just alike. Two Hollywood pussies on the make."

Rod drove recklessly, just as he lived. Several times I feared we would have an accident before reaching Taylor's house. But some guardian angel seemed to protect this wild thing called Rod St. Just.

"Before we call on Billy Taylor, give me all the low-down on Marion, Hearst, and Charlie," Rod said.

I granted him his request, filling him in on the juicy secrets. I had to confide in somebody.

As a reward for keeping him posted, Rod virtually promised he'd deliver that sexy, delectable, and succulent Antonio Moreno into my boudoir.

"Don't tell Taylor I've had his boy," Rod warned as we neared the director's residence. "He thinks he's got that chorizo just for himself. But Antonio likes variety. Taylor's handsome. But he's old. Antonio likes hot young male bodies."

*****

By the time we'd reached Taylor's bungalow complex, the director had already gone to Fruitfly, leaving us a note on his door that he'd meet us at the club.

En route to Fruitfly and behind the wheel of Charlie's Locomobile which he'd lent me, I was Lotte Lee taking charge of her life. In the seat beside me, Rod St. Just, photographer extraordinaire, filled me in on all the latest gossip. According to Rod, at least half—maybe more—of the male stars in Hollywood were homosexuals.

Based on my personal experience, that wasn't entirely true. John Gilbert, Owen Moore, and his brother Tom, were heterosexuals. Of course, John and Tom had already been made love to by a man, but they didn't know that. Owen was next in line for male seduction, and he wouldn't know that either.

Goldwyn was a bit anti-homosexual, and even he had been sleeping with a man. Namely me. For my health and the reputation of screen vamp Lotte Lee, I decided it would be best if none of these gentlemen ever found out I was the handsome and sexy cowboy, Durango Jones, from the wheatfields of Kansas.

The prospect of meeting my director, William Desmond Taylor, scared the pink panties off me. He'd be looking at me closely through a camera, and I feared I wouldn't make the grade as a woman, at least in his eyes. Fooling drunken men in hotel bedrooms was one thing. Tricking an astute director was quite another.

All the pictures of his that I'd seen, including

Tom Sawyer, The Varmint, The Soul of Youth, and *The Furnace* were remarkable for their reality.

Many rumors were rampant about what Taylor did before arriving in Hollywood. I'd heard that he'd been an Irish student, Kansas rancher, Klondike miner, construction engineer, a British soldier, and a London stage actor. When a member of his family discovered him on the stage in a small part, his father, a colonel of British troops, had him banished to a farm at Harper, Kansas. So Taylor, like me—or rather like Durango Jones—got to experience Kansas life firsthand.

In time he escaped like I did and played juveniles in such well-known plays as *Cleopatra* or *Fedora.* Taylor had made *The World Apart* with my darling Wallace Reid. He'd even directed both Jack and Mary Pickford, and was said to be in love with baby-faced Mary Miles Minter who, in spite of her childlike screen roles, was a slut, at least according to Rod.

At the members-only Fruitfly, an attendant who looked like a young Mexican boy led us down a long and dimly lit corridor that smelled of urine. We entered an outer foyer where Rod paid fifty dollars for the two of us. No club in America at that time charged such an outrageous cover, but the Fruitfly was special, according to Rod, and could get away with such larceny.

Ushered into the rear, I held my head high and my *faux* breasts erect as I was shown inside this night garden of a thousand forbidden pleasures. The room was so very dark that I could make out no one. It was lit by dim red and blue electric bulbs, mostly blue. The place was smoke filled. The smoke was like fog, in fact, but it didn't smell like tobacco. The aroma was strange to my nostrils, and was like what I'd imagine an opium den to be.

Even though I couldn't see, Rod, as if by some kind of human radar, told me some of the big names patronizing Fruitfly that night. They included Blanche Sweet, Mabel Normand, and Tom Ince, the director. Having already turned down Miss Sweet's invitation to go to bed, I didn't exactly want to run into her. But I was anxious to meet Mabel Normand. She was one of my all-time favorites.

Rumor had it that when William Desmond Taylor wasn't screwing Mary Miles Minter, he was bedding Mabel Normand—that is, when she wasn't getting plowed by either Mack Sennett or Samuel Goldwyn. Mabel and I had a lot in common: we were both the mistress of Samuel Goldwyn. If we ever got together, we could swap Goldfish stories.

Before the night was over, Rod promised to introduce me to Tom Ince. Based on having seen photographs of me, Ince, again according to Rod, wanted to direct my next picture after I'd finished shooting *Vampira.* Tom Ince was one of Hollywood's leading directors of dramatic films, and I was anxious to meet him. He was also very handsome, and in my view and based on his published photographs could have been a leading man in films himself.

Rod disappeared for a moment in the back and returned soon after to tell me that Taylor was still involved with Mabel Normand and would join us in a few moments. Some man he'd picked up in the back rooms stood behind Rod. He moved to the side and introduced me to Tom Ince himself.

"Even in this smoke-filled room," Ince said, "your beauty casts a radiant glow." He reached for my hand and bowed low as he kissed it.

"So flattering," I said in my Lotte Lee voice. "I cannot believe I'm being presented to the great Tom Ince himself. And, I might add, the most good-looking gentleman I've encountered so far in all of Hollywood."

"We obviously like what we see," Ince said, taking my hand and guiding me over to a bar. Rod excused himself. I had given him Jack Pickford's five-hundred dollars, and the photographer was off to secure the heroin.

On that far away evening in Los Angeles, as I stood at the bar drinking a whiskey with Tom Ince, I had not a clue that my involvement with him would propel me into one of the most sensational scandals in the history of motion pictures. Back then, if I recall properly, it was nothing but fun, excitement, and glamour.

Tom Ince was my kind of man, that Mr. Right you could settle down with in a rose-covered cottage. He was gorgeous, absolutely gorgeous, and so very masculine. Even his voice gave me a hard-on, although my genitals were artfully concealed thanks to Tallulah's advice as my wardrobe mistress.

Ince quickly became "Tom" as we chatted. Lotte Lee now had two Toms in her life, if Tom Moore could be called "in my life" after only one seduction. I was definitely left with the feeling he'd be back again to sample some more of Lotte Lee's special love-making technique.

Tom Ince was like men I'd seen and admired on the fields of Kansas as they worked with farm machinery or did construction work. Tom had wide eyes, a finely chiseled nose, and one of the most perfectly developed set of lips I'd ever seen on a man. I was anxious to taste them.

Giving in to my impulse and spurred on by whiskey with which I was still a bit unfamiliar, I leaned over and planted a kiss on Tom's beautiful mouth. In spite of his drinking and smoking, his mouth and even the manly aroma of his breath thrilled me. As I've said, he was my kind of man. Even though he was fully dressed in a suit and tie, I was anxious to see what he looked like when stripped naked.

"I suspect Rod has already told you," Tom said, "but I want to star you in my next picture. It's very dramatic and very sexy and calls for you to wear spectacular gowns. Goldfish definitely wants to do it."

"To be directed by Tom Ince would be one of the crowning achievements of my life," I said. "But how do you know I can act?"

"Baby, any woman who looks as good as you can be a star. I'll tell you how to act, how to play every scene. You just do as I direct you and you'll be sensational."

I moved closer and whispered in his ear. "I will do anything you tell me to do." And if he didn't get the point, I moved in even closer until my lips were touching his ear. "*Anything!*"

He was breathing heavily. "I don't know when a woman has excited me as much as you. I'm surrounded by beautiful women all week, and often they do nothing for me. But you're different. You're like no woman I've ever met."

He got that right. "I've met a lot of handsome men but you're like something I've been waiting for all my life."

"It doesn't matter to you if I'm married or anything like that, does it?"

"I don't ask men if they're married. It's of no concern to me. If a man shows me a good time, why should I care if he gets up in the middle of the night, puts his trousers back on, and goes home to the wife and kiddies?"

"I like that kind of talk. You're just the kind of liberated woman I've been looking for. I hate the clinging type."

"I cling plenty in bed," I said. "I don't let a man out of my bed until I've definitely satisfied him. Drained him of the last drop."

He bent over and kissed my lips gently. "Word has spread throughout Hollywood about the succulent lips of Lotte Lee. All the town's studs are anxious to have you work them over."

"I thought you'd never ask," I said.

"No one's looking in this smoky joint," he said. "Reach over and unbutton me and feel what's waiting for you. A big sausage. Let me know if you think you can handle it."

I thought if I could handle Elmo Lincoln and Francis X. Bushman, I could deal with any man that came after those two horsedicks. Slowly I unbuttoned Tom's trousers and reached inside. I find that most men exaggerate but not Tom. It was a big one. I reached down to weigh the balls. They were big too. Sometimes men have big dicks but tiny balls. Not Tom. Mother Nature had fully equipped him. "I'm so sorry I have another invitation tonight. I'm meeting William Desmond Taylor, my director. Otherwise, I think you and I should get together."

"Sooner than later," he said. "I have a great idea. I live in this huge Spanish-style mansion. It's in Benedict Canyon. I call it Días Doradas. I designed the place myself. Many of the big stars are coming Sunday for a huge party. If you'll join this charmed circle, I'll take you into my quarters and you'll get the surprise of your life."

"What do you mean?" I asked, intrigued out of my mind.

"You'll find out when you get there. Otherwise it would be no surprise."

At that point I spotted Rod emerging from the back rooms. "Mabel and William have said *adieu* for the evening. He wants you to come back."

Rod arrived at the right moment. Another rod—this one attached to Tom Ince—was hardening and thickening fast. Reluctantly I took my fingers off it, eager to see and sample more of it. "Until Sunday," I said, giving Tom a juicy kiss on his beautiful mouth.

He leaned over and whispered in my ear. "Tonight when I masturbate I'll imagine that it was your delicate fingers wrapped around me—not my own rough hands."

"You and I have a date with destiny," I predicted before rushing off to meet my second director of the night, William Desmond Taylor.

*****

Before being ushered into the august presence of William Desmond Taylor, my ever faithful companion, Rod St. Just, told me of his own delicious plans for the evening. Robert (Bobby) Harron, the handsome D.W. Griffith star, was in one of the back rooms and drunk, at least according to Rod. "He's mine for the grabbing," Rod said with total self-confidence. "I may have to give him some black coffee before he can get it up, but I've been dying to seduce this delectable morsel."

I envied Rod getting Bobby Harron while I had to appear as Lotte Lee with a man who could be Bobby's father. I'd always had a secret crush on Bobby. If I recall, even Maria Jane back in Kansas approved of him. He was handsome and wholesome looking, and not at all muscled like Francis X. Bushman. Even though appealing, he was quite ordinary, a type in Hollywood that became known as the boy next door.

Griffith had always cast him as the perfect young man of innocence, a hero who did the right thing and stood for family values. If only his audience knew he patronized the Fruitfly and was about to spend an evening with Rod St. Just. The first film that shot Bobby to stardom was Griffith's *Intolerance* when Bobby had played "The Boy" to perfection. Actually he'd begun playing leads back in 1911, and he'd scored another big hit in 1914 when Griffith cast him in *Judith of Bethulia*. Bobby was that innocent hero for an innocent time, always appearing in harmless stories. Just how innocent Bobby really was I planned to find out for

myself after Rod had had his fill. I knew Rod liked to try men out only once, as in my case, before either becoming friends with them or dropping them completely. "So many men, so little time," was his constantly repeated sexual motto.

After giving me the heroin, Rod disappeared for the rest of the evening, assuring me that I was to prepare for an evening of debauchery with William Desmond Taylor.

Unlike the flirtatious Tom Ince, Billy, as he soon became known to me, was a British gentleman of impeccable manners and charm. In his more mature way, he was quite handsome. His reputation as a ladies man had already preceded him.

As masculine looking women in kimonos paraded by, a waiter wheeled in a tea cart. At first I thought it was refreshments, but Billy told me it was a selection of recreational incentives that included opium, marijuana, and morphine. He preferred a marijuana cigarette and offered me one too which I reluctantly accepted.

"May I say you're the most beautiful woman in Hollywood," he told me.

"Even more beautiful than Mabel Normand and Mary Miles Minter?" I asked, having decided to become a little provocative. Perhaps it was the marijuana which I found immensely soothing and liberating.

"Mary and Mabel aren't real beauties," he said. "They're great sex. In your case, you're a great beauty and—I'm only guessing—great sex too. Forgive me for being so bold. But you appear to be a liberated woman of the world. We are, after all, in an opium den where men can speak their minds freely."

I reached for his hand and gently kissed it. "I'm really afraid. Since you're my director for *Vampira*, I have a confession to make. I'm worried I can't act. I think Goldfish got a bit carried away when he offered me that contract."

"My little darling," he said, moving closer and whispering in my ear, "don't be afraid of the camera. And don't be afraid of me. I'll be there protecting you and your image through every scene."

"Thanks," I said, taking another draw on the marijuana cigarette. "I'll need all the help I can get."

As the night and the marijuana wore on, I felt a kind of cozy comfort with Billy. He was an erudite and sensitive man, and he made me feel like a real woman in the presence of his self-assured masculinity. For a liberated hour or two, I forgot I was the Kansas cowboy, Durango Jones, cornfed and hung.

"I've lived a rich and varied life," he said. "Since I'm called upon to reproduce real life in film, I draw upon my past experiences. A story can't be presented on the screen in a human, gripping manner unless the director has been in contact with the situation depicted."

"Surely your life can't have covered all the situations you're called upon to depict on the screen."

"In my life, I've seen it all," he said, smiling enigmatically, making me wonder just how experienced he really was. For all I knew, the men I'd been with, from Rodolfo to Wallace Reid, were mere boys. William Desmond Taylor was the first true man of the world I'd ever met.

"The job of the director demands the knowing of something about a great many people and things."

"I'm sure I know what you're talking about, but give me an example."

"For instance, I never thought that being marooned all one winter in the backwoods of Alaska would be one of the most valuable things that could have happened to me. It was a terrible period for me. I had only a train of sled dogs for company. But it was being with those dogs so constantly that gave me a love for animals. I learned how to handle them. They say I'm very successful when I use animals in my pictures. If that's so, it is entirely due to the six months alone with those dogs."

"I have found your pictures true," I said, not just flattering him, but really meaning it. "You seem to focus on the tantalizing detail that makes your films believable. You always go for the human quality, and when you do that you have achieved art. You are an artist, and I'm honored to work with you." At that grand pronouncement, Billy laid a firm hand on my leg which I did not remove.

"How would a man act if he were about to be killed by a crazy man——or in danger of death from any source?" he asked. "Once in the Klondike my cabin was entered by a man who calmly announced he was going to kill me. He quoted passages from the Bible as authority. I took the Bible from him and showed him where his quote to me was wrong—and he forgot all about killing me. But for a moment there I faced death. Some of the stars in my films face death, and I'm able to convey to them the emotions I felt back in the Klondike."

His hand traveled up my leg, and I feared I'd have to remove it gently before he made some unfortunate discoveries. Like I wasn't really Lotte Lee but her brother.

Deep into his second marijuana cigarette, he leaned back against a banquette. "A man must know many things in life to reproduce real situations on the screen. All the technical directors in the world won't help if a man who is directing the picture doesn't know life as it really is."

Again I blamed the marijuana but I felt in a strange confessional mood with this man. "I fear I'm not the liberated woman I'm supposed to play in *Vampira*. My character has supposedly seduced half the men in the world, and I've not had that many experiences. As a woman, I'm still a bit innocent."

He leaned over and kissed my ear, inserting his tongue. It felt so good I started to get hard, which was about the last thing I wanted Lotte Lee to do.

"I know, my sweet, but you're very fortunate in that you have William Desmond Taylor to take you into womanhood through every stage of the part. I will know what to tell you to do."

His hand was moving dangerously close to my honeypot. "I have a secret I must share with you," I said. "If you tell anybody, it could ruin my career even before it gets launched. But I fear if you don't remove your hand at once, you're going to make a major discovery."

"The moment you walked toward me, I knew your secret. You can fool those drunken cowboy studs in Hollywood, but you can't fool me." He whispered in my ear again. "I know you're a man. In spite of that, I'm going to turn you into one of the screen's most seductive vamps. Forget Theda Bara. She belongs to yesterday. Too obvious."

"You know," I said with a desperation creeping into my voice, "if I didn't fool you, I don't think I can fool the rest of America."

"You'd be surprised. As a director, I have a battle-trained eye. Just call me hawkeye. The American public will not appraise you with such severity."

"Knowing I'm a man, you still want to go on with me in the part?"

"Of course, I do, my dear," he said, licking my ear as his hand descended into my crotch where my hard-on was making the concealment of my genitals a bit painful.

He grabbed me and crushed me into his strong, muscled body, inserting his tongue in my mouth which I greedily sucked. After what seemed like five minutes, he broke away, only to lick my neck and place gentle bites along its curvature. Learning that I was a man didn't seem to have cooled his passion.

"I thought you were such a ladies man," I said. "Does part of your experience include sex with boys?"

"You've got that right. There are two things I adore more than all others on earth. A woman's vagina and a boy's ass, both of which I eat before fucking. I can't get enough of either, and I like them both equally. Don't you find that in ice cream, it's hard to determine if you like strawberry or peach better? Both are good."

"I don't agree. I like only men. The idea of being with a woman doesn't do a thing for me. I actually turned down Blanche Sweet."

"Don't let that worry your pretty head," he said. "We've all turned down Blanche Sweet."

Forgetting about Rod St. Just and Bobby Harron for the evening, I headed to Billy's bungalow, eagerly anticipating a wild night of sex with my new director.

Leaning back in the seat and obviously experiencing the afterglow of the marijuana, he said, "I want to make a request of you, and I hope you'll not be offended."

"Fire away," I said, trying to keep Charlie's Locomobile in the right lane.

"You know I want to spend the night fucking you."

"You can, you know," I replied.

"For that, I'm very grateful. But when I find a delectable specimen like you, I share him with my best friend. With your permission, I'd like to call my friend to come over. That is, after we've gotten you out of that Lotte Lee costume."

"Your best friend?" I was both puzzled and immensely intrigued at the same time. "Would I know him?"

"Yes, my pet. You'd be but one of millions of women around the world dreaming about taking the prick of Antonio Moreno."

I nearly ran the Locomobile off the road. Rod St. Just had already had him and had promised to fix me up. Little did Rod know that I'd get to Antonio before Rod could arrange that date. "I think Antonio Moreno is one of the sexiest men who's ever appeared on the screen."

"I do, too, my dear. I've been in love with him since the first day we met."

If truth be known, I was looking forward to seducing Antonio Moreno far more than I was in taking it up the ass from Billy.

Inside his bungalow, which seemed filled with books, I quickly did a striptease for him, ridding myself of my Lotte Lee drag and getting more comfortable. He made only one request—that I give him my pink panties as a souvenir. He went over and unlocked the closet filled with lacy undies. He'd tagged each pair of lingerie with the initials and date of conquest. One pale pink nightgown of a filmy silk was provocatively embroidered MMM. Was that a souvenir from that innocent little darling of the screen, Mary Miles Minter?

To this array of lingerie, including undies from Zelda Crosby and Mabel Norman, was added the panties of Lotte Lee. Before depositing my souvenir in his closet, he made a point of delicately kissing the crotch where I had stuffed my ample load before venturing out as *Vampira*.

Giving me a robe to cover my nudity, he placed a call to Antonio who assured him he'd be right over. Billy offered me a drink which I accepted. "I thought you were a beautiful woman but you're Hollywood's prettiest boy as well. Forget Wallace Reid. You're a stunner. But I don't even know your real name."

"It's Durango Jones."

"Okay, don't tell me then. I love it. Durango. Sounds Mexican. Unlike Antonio, you don't appear to have one drop of Spanish blood."

Waiting for Antonio to appear, Billy spoke

of the upcoming shooting schedule. Goldwyn wanted the picture finished in a few short weeks, and filming was to begin in just a few days.

At one point, Billy seemed tired of discussing the script and reached over and picked me up in his arms, carrying me to his bedroom in back. He pulled off my robe and gently placed me on his bed, where he proceeded to lick every inch of my body with one of the world's most skilled tongues.

Keeping his promise, he descended on my ass and began to suck and lick as if he'd discovered the world's tastiest pudding. He had me screaming with the sheer joy of it all. When he tired of that, he pressed my face against his soft pillow and shoved his cock, thick and deep into me. I arched my back to receive the penetration, as my mouth gaped wide. At first I gasped with the pain of it all. But he was too skilled a lover to hurt me for long, and in moments the hurt turned to exquisite pleasure. My young, lean body was being raped, and I was enjoying it too much to care.

We must have been at it for a full fifteen minutes when I vaguely sensed movement in the bedroom. Without dismounting, he flipped me over. He was still plugged into me, but I was now on top of him, my hard cock bobbing up in the air as he humped me with his back pressed against the mattress.

With my face no longer buried in the pillow, I looked up to see Antonio Moreno enter the room. Piece by piece, he was slowly removing all his clothing, and doing so tantalizingly like a striptease artist. Male strippers were rather rare in those days, and it was a treat for me, making me enjoy the plowing of Billy all the more.

When Antonio at last dropped his white underwear, I was treated to at least eight and a half inches of rock-hard Spanish dick, uncut and ready to go.

He moved toward me. Since the only hole left for him was my mouth, I expected to be feeling him soon at the back of my throat. But Antonio had other plans. He fell on me and swallowed my cock whole, letting it enter deep into his throat. He'd obviously done this before.

I don't think I've been happier in my life. My whimpers of pleasure virtually turned to screams of primal triumph. I wanted this

moment to last forever. I'd entered a state of total bliss as I felt Billy nearing his climax. Seeming to sense what was happening in the rear, Antonio sucked more voraciously than ever, as I too neared my climax which came with the brute force of an explosion. Antonio slurped down every bit of cream, as Billy emptied his load deep within my guts. I was left gasping for breath on the bed.

But not for long. Within what seemed like only a second, Billy had pulled out of me and Antonio had penetrated me while I lay flat on my back. I felt my earlier estimation had been wrong. Instead of eight and a half, his cock must have been nine and a half, maybe even more. It was thick and hot and seemed to widen as it pumped me.

He lay on top of me, looking deeply into my eyes with the most penetrating brown Spanish eyes I'd ever seen. As he fucked me in the most exquisite manner, hitting pleasure points not achieved by Billy, I looked real close into the face that had thrilled me in 1914 when he'd starred in Griffith's *Judith of Bethulia,* in which Bobby Harron had also appeared.

He stuck out his tongue to lick my face. When he descended on my lips, I was eager to taste it. But he held back before sticking his tongue in my mouth. "From this day forth," he said, "Antonio Moreno is your new husband." That tongue then penetrated my eager mouth, as Antonio pounded harder and harder, each delicious inch threatening to make me erupt again.

Withdrawing his tongue, he whispered in my ear, "I don't get out of the saddle until I've exploded three times."

On that long-ago night, Antonio Moreno, the screen's first Spanish stud, kept his promise, even if it did take three hours.

*****

It was all I could do to escape from the clutches of the divine Antonio Moreno, who wanted to spend "this and every night" with me. Antonio claimed he was my husband and was entitled to conjugal rights at any time of the day or night.

So intense had our love affair blossomed—right in front of the eyes of my director, William Desmond Taylor—that it was like a speeded-up silent film itself, the way all my life had gone in Hollywood.

Back on the plains of Kansas, I would never believe that I'd be fleeing from Antonio for the night. I definitely wanted to keep him in my life, and he was certainly husband material. But since arriving in Hollywood, my calendar had become full, so loaded in fact it was hard to fit a hot Spanish matador into my constantly burgeoning schedule.

Before Antonio departed, there were endless kisses, deliciously wet. Billy insisted that he be included, and forced us to suck on his tongue repeatedly between our own extended bouts of kissing. Since he was such a good friend of Antonio's, the actor obliged, even though I knew he wanted to be sucking my mouth instead. And since Billy was my upcoming director, I extended all casting couch privileges to him that were his due.

Freed of Antonio with promises to have a rendezvous "before the rooster crowed," I watched as he departed. Billy then let me go into his bathroom where I quickly became Lotte Lee again and, after another thousand kisses and endless groping, I was freed of him too. But not for long. We both understood that.

Before departing, the director told me he could well understand Antonio's passion for me, and he would permit that to a certain extent, but only if I satisfied that part of him that called for male love.

Agreeing to all his terms, I told him how excited I was he'd been selected—of all the directors in Hollywood—to guide me through my first picture. "My first picture could make or break me," I told him, stating the obvious. "Goldfish could drop me in a moment if I fail."

"With me as your director, you'll not fail," he assured me, and it was what I desperately needed to hear.

Back at the Hollywood Hotel, there was an urgent message from Kono, Chaplin's chauffeur. It seemed that Charlie had disappeared, and he wondered if he might be with me. I had heard that Charlie often "disappeared," so I didn't immediately panic.

Even more surprises awaited me. A second message was from the great Mabel Normand herself. Her handwritten note was brief.

"My dear Miss Lee," the note went. "It's about time we got together for a come-to-Jesus meeting. Whores arrive in Hollywood daily, and I'm used to them. But both Goldfish and William Desmond Taylor! That's a bit much for me to take. You'll agree to meet with me or else I'll tear out every bleached hair in your hussy head. Love and kisses, Mabel Normand." She'd left a phone number.

As Lotte Lee, this was my first experience in dealing with a jealous "other woman," who just happened to be one of the most famous women on earth, a movie star whose name recognition was just under that of Charlie, Mary, and Doug. I'd deal with Mabel tomorrow, or even the next day if I could postpone it that long. If the actress started tearing at my hair, she might find out it was a blonde wig.

More messages awaited me. I was to meet Samuel Goldwyn in the morning. The script of *Vampira* was waiting for me. The prospect of having to act in a full-length film terrified me. Flowers arrived from Owen Moore, with a note telling me that he and Jack Pickford awaited me tomorrow afternoon at the house they'd rented in Santa Monica.

Flowers also arrived from John Gilbert with a note. "I'm in love with you, Lotte. Please reserve time in your life for your one true man. Kisses, and more kisses, my beautiful blonde lovely. Tonight my dreams will be of you." A bit sentimental but he was one of the handsomest and most desirable men in Hollywood.

It seemed that everybody was calling me except Elmo Lincoln.

At the door to my room, I noticed that it wasn't locked. Security, I decided, must not be very good at the Hollywood Hotel. Entering the darkened room, I shut the door behind me and locked it.

As I searched for the light, I was grabbed in the dark by a nude man. Before I could resist, he'd crushed me into his arms, his tongue darting between my cherry-red lips. Though coated with alcohol, I recognized the breath of that darling man after my own heart, Tom Moore, back for a repeat performance. He was raring and ready for action.

If he wasn't already erect, he soon was, especially when the fingers of Lotte Lee descended to feel his goodies. After a close inspection with my skilled and sensuous fingers, I decided to change my original estimate of Tom. Instead of giving him six and a half inches, I'd definitely label him seven and a half. Perhaps he was more inspired tonight than in our previous encounter—or less drunk.

He told me he had to leave soon as he had a very early call in the morning. The crew of his next picture was heading out very early for a desert location, so we'd have to make it quick. I tried to oblige and speed him on his way. But after his first eruption, he demanded a second. Before he could request a third pounding of my throat, I managed to glide him out the door gently, with promises to get together real soon.

As he was leaving, I spotted Jean Acker unlocking her door. The new bride had the room across from me. She looked at me with a somewhat puzzled face before going inside her room. Rodolfo wasn't anywhere to be seen.

Acker didn't seem to recognize Tom Moore, male movie star. After leaving my room, Tom wasn't looking his best but appeared rather worn out. Although extraordinarily handsome, I feared he wouldn't photograph in the morning as gorgeous as he usually did.

After a lovely bath, I put on a black nightgown and made my face up even though going to bed. I figured if any man tried to slip into my room again in the middle of the night, I wanted to be prepared and definitely look my best.

Through the paper-thin door, I heard a discreet rapping on Jean Acker's door across the hallway. The rapping was persistent even though it was late at night. "Please, Jean," the voice of a man said. "Let me in. I'm your husband. Jean, please. Open the door."

Could that be Rodolfo trying to get into his new bride's bedroom? Of course, it was Rodolfo. Who else was married to Jean Acker? He simply wouldn't leave, although it was obvious to me she wasn't going to let her new husband in.

When fifteen minutes had gone by, I took a daring step. Slowly I opened my door, but no more than a foot. The light was on in back of

me, and I was clearly visible to Rodolfo.

He turned and looked quizzically at me. "I'm sorry if I've disturbed you."

"You didn't really," I said. "But I fear you might be disturbing Miss Acker. She wants to be left alone for the night."

"It's our honeymoon," he protested.

"Why don't you come and spend your honeymoon night with me, a real woman?" I asked, growing bolder by the minute. I opened the door wider so he could see more of me.

He looked at my face closely. "Don't I know you?"

"I'm Lotte Lee, the twin sister of your friend, Durango Jones."

At that revelation, Rodolfo lost all interest in Jean Acker. "My God. Durango has told me of you. You've been signed by Goldfish. You're going to become a big star."

"I hope so," I said, stepping aside and letting this handsome hunk come into my suite. Jean Acker must really be a lesbian. No woman in her right mind would shut the door on Rodolfo Valentino, honeymoon or no honeymoon.

Over a drink Rodolfo seemed in a confessional mood. At first I'd wanted to ask him why he wasn't back at the cottage making love to Durango Jones. I suddenly remembered that I was Durango as well as Lotte Lee. Without my being aware of it, I was separating Durango and Lotte Lee. It seemed unfortunate that we had to share the same bodies. If not, I'd find it easier to live my life. This constant changing from man to woman was a bit of a drag.

"Has Durango told you about us?" Rodolfo asked, his eyes opening wide.

"Everything," I said coyly. "We share secrets."

"I see." He didn't seem embarrassed that I knew of his secret life.

"What do you think of my brother?" I asked him. "Are you in love with him?"

"From the very first, I loved him," he said. "But it is a love that belongs to a compartment of my life. I do not intend to live my life as a homosexual, even though I have little love for women."

"You were pounding on Jean Acker's door. You married her."

"I do not turn to women for sex but for some

spiritual reunion," he said. "A woman provides that for me. If I want raw sex, I can seduce your brother. He is the best sex I've ever had. But it's not enough for me. I need a woman's affirmation."

"Perhaps you should turn to me," I said. "I'm a woman."

"That you are—and the most beautiful one I've seen in Hollywood. Both you and Durango should appear on the screen. You as the beautiful female star, he as your equally beautiful male lead."

"I'll lay that idea on William Desmond Taylor. He's my director."

"I hear you're making a film called *Vampira*. I'm working too. Tomorrow I'll be directed by D.W. Griffith in a film with Dorothy Gish. It will probably be really big at the box office."

"I'm sure it will." I raised my glass to his in a toast. "Here's to us becoming the biggest female and the biggest male star in Hollywood."

Although in just a few short months, he was to be adored by millions, tonight Rodolfo appeared lonely and love starved. He obviously wanted something Durango couldn't give him or else he wouldn't be pounding on the door of Jean Acker. In time he would be called "The King of Sex" and "The Screen's Greatest Lover," but right now he couldn't get his new bride to open her bedroom door to him.

Instead of love talk, he wanted to tell me about himself, especially his early struggles. As Durango I'd already heard many of his tales but appeared eager to learn anew. "In New York I swept out a store," he said. "I earned twenty-five cents for doing that—maybe fifty cents if lucky. I slept on park benches in Central Park. Tonight I feel just as lonely and trapped as I did back then."

This man who was the perfection of male physical beauty seemed but a boy at heart, a boy who'd lost his mother and could find no substitute for her. His turning to dykes such as Jean Acker hardly struck me as the solution for his loneliness.

"I've done everything to survive since coming to this country," he said. "I've even been a prostitute. I still am in some ways. I continue to prostitute myself before Norman Kerry. How low can a man sink? A man like me of noble birth?"

He spoke of his frustration in finding work in Hollywood, and he didn't like the roles he might get. "A foreigner, especially a Latin, means a villain in Hollywood. The first time I went into a casting office, I encountered this old lecher. He ordered me into a backroom where he told me to take off all my clothes, even my underwear. He claimed the role called for a perfect physical specimen. After he'd kneeled before me and feasted off me, he told me I was the wrong type for the role. The wrong type! I could have killed him. I felt like a cheap whore. A whore who doesn't even get paid."

I said little to Rodolfo since he wanted to do all the talking. But my face showed him that I was truly interested in everything he had to reveal about himself.

"There is a possibility I might play a role opposite Nazimova," he said. "At least that's what Jean Acker is promising me. I know Nazimova calls me the gigolo. But only hours ago, Jean got mad at me and told me what Nazimova really thinks of me. Nazimova claims I'm far too swarthy for movies...and fat." He seemed outraged by the latter remark. "She also said my bushy black eyebrows were grotesque, the bitch."

"You don't look fat to me."

"I train at the Los Angeles Athletic Club. I keep my body in perfect shape. I'm not fat."

"Would you care to share that body with me?" I boldly asked. "Nazimova is only one woman. Wouldn't you like another woman's opinion?"

"Indeed I would," he said. He put down his drink and stood before me, as I took in his male beauty which I was seeing for the first time through the eyes of Lotte Lee. Slowly he began to strip in front of me, revealing a finely proportioned muscular body, of which I knew every inch, having put it to the tongue test.

His body was not the grotesque buildup associated with weightlifters. He stood about five feet eleven inches tall and weighed one-hundred and sixty-five pounds. His teeth were gleaming white, and his smile was warm and intoxicating. As he stripped down to his underwear, he revealed a body as chiseled as a Greek statue, all smooth skinned and dark complexioned. When he moved toward me, it was with grace and elegance. In time men around the world would imitate his panther-like movements.

At this moment, I was still seated, as he moved toward my chair, dropping his underwear. My face was staring at his lovely thick penis. Before my eyes, it extended to its full eight and a half inches.

"Take my cock and put it in your mouth and worship it and make me feel like a man again after what happened to me in front of that locked door across the hallway."

I gleefully obliged, reaching out for his buttocks and pulling him closer and closer to my cherry-red lips. He plunged in for the night. Tom Moore was but an appetizer, a distant memory.

*****

Slipping out of bed, I transformed myself into the fully made-up Lotte Lee before Rodolfo woke up. When he did hear me moving about the suite, he ordered me to come over and kiss him, even though he still had his garlic-laced morning breath. I gladly obliged.

I was delighted that after Rodolfo had taken a horse piss, he went immediately to the phone to call Durango at our cottage. Still nude and looking glorious, he slammed down the phone. "I've called Durango repeatedly and he's never there, the little bitch."

"He must not know about us," I said. "It would hurt him."

"Our little secret," he said before heading for the shower.

Since the suite contained an extra guest bedroom, I was going to have Durango Jones registered at the hotel. That way, he could receive messages, and I could come and go either as Durango Jones or Lotte Lee. For all I knew, Elmo Lincoln had called. Perhaps Douglas Fairbanks. Maybe even Richard Barthelmess. Durango was missing too many messages, and the staff at the hotel could take his calls.

When I heard Rodolfo singing in the shower, I quickly dialed the number of my new husband, Antonio Moreno. He invited me to breakfast.

"I've been dreaming about you all night," he said. "I have fallen in love for the first time in my life."

"And I too have been dreaming of you, my dear, dear husband," I said in my Durango Jones voice. He insisted on my coming over at once so he could make "mad, passionate love to me."

My calendar was loaded for the day, but I agreed to go anyway. Somehow I'd fit in a quick session with Antonio either before or after I called on Goldwyn to pick up the script for *Vampira* and to give him his anticipated blow-job.

Now that I'd met Antonio, I wanted him to play one of my leading men in *Vampira*. Tom Moore would be perfect for his role, and I'd always fantasized about Thomas Meighan ever since I'd seen him on the screen. He didn't have the beauty and youthful vigor of Wallace Reid, but he was one of the biggest stars of 1919.

Audiences back then, dominated by adults, liked mature leading men who were physically strong, handsome (not pretty), dependable, and neatly dressed. Meighan looked like a man who was definitely a top and could show a woman a good time or even a man if the actor went that route. With the Twenties looming before us, I just knew Thomas Meighan was going to become one of the decade's biggest stars.

Francis X. Bushman and Tom Moore were already intimately acquainted with me either as Durango or Lotte, and I eagerly anticipated my second meeting with Richard Barthelmess based on our brief encounter. The one actor I didn't know was William Boyd. I wondered if I sucked Goldwyn enough I could get him to drop William Boyd from the role and give it to my newly discovered Antonio Moreno?

I'm always shocked by the coincidence of life, particularly in Hollywood of those days. The town was so small you eventually ran into any and everybody. The phone rang and when I picked it up I heard a husky male voice identifying himself as William Boyd. Even though moments before I'd been thinking of dumping him as a leading man, as if I possessed such star power, he won me over after only a few minutes of conversation. I didn't know who William Boyd was before the call, but I felt I knew him real well after our brief talk. He'd already received a copy of the script of *Vampira*.

"I'm new to Hollywood," he said, "and I'm eager for our love scenes."

"Not as eager as I am," I said, even though I'd never even seen a photograph of him.

After arranging a date with him, I quickly got off the phone. Rodolfo was emerging from the shower with a fully erect penis which looked longer and thicker than it had last night. At the risk of spoiling my make-up, I fell on my knees before this Latin god. When men needed to be serviced, Lotte Lee was their gal.

Since Rodolfo had to be at the studio at six o'clock that morning, I agreed to drive him there but only after I'd placed a call to Kono. Charlie still hadn't come back from wherever he'd gone, and the chauffeur was clearly worried. "Charlie has a lot of enemies. Someone out here could have had him killed."

"I doubt that," I said, promising to check in later. After all, with our present arrangement, if the most famous man on earth wanted you, you had to make yourself available, regardless of your other commitments. In another separate and very private call, I had to check in with the Chief himself. If William Randolph Hearst wanted to meet the up-and-coming Lotte Lee, I'd better make her available to the newspaper czar.

Rodolfo begged me to go with him to the early morning set of *Out of Luck,* which starred Dorothy Gish. He promised to introduce me to the director of the film, D.W. Griffith. In those days, few starlets turned down an invitation to meet Hollywood's most famous director—in fact, the world's most famous director. Although at the moment I was committed to William Desmond Taylor, Lotte Lee could have her head turned around by the great Griffith himself.

Rodolfo carried through with his commitment. We arrived at the studio where chaos reigned. Indians—some dressed in full war regalia with battle paint—were on the warpath. It was obviously round-up time, as I noted cowboy after cowboy in broad-brimmed hats and spurs. Horses stood idly by, panting in the hot early morning sun of California. African natives with deadly looking spears

were preparing to launch an attack against a group of white explorers, no doubt consigning them to the stew pot later in the day.

In this ramshackle cluster of hastily erected studio buildings, it looked as if World War I were being refought. Both Italian and German soldiers, in full military uniform, mixed with Revolutionary War Yankee soldiers fighting in battle against the British. I spotted at least thirty Minutemen, about ten of whom I could have happily married. I'm such a whore.

The stars were on parade, some of the biggest names in Hollywood, arriving by limousine. In the early morning glow paraded Mae Murray, Rodolfo's friend. He rushed over to give her a quick kiss on the cheek and a promise to meet for lunch, although he did not introduce me to her. Were they having an affair? Gloria Swanson arrived, as did William Farnum, Henry B. Walthall, Earle Williams, all the big names.

As I swirled around, I found myself as Lotte Lee being introduced and shaking hands with the great D.W. Griffith himself. He thrust some papers into Rodolfo's hands and ordered him to read a hastily revised script. Rodolfo kissed me on the cheek, excused himself, and departed for the day.

"Pretty lady," Griffith said, finally focusing his attention on me. "I hear you're about ready to take over Hollywood. Goldfish is damn lucky to sign a good-looking dame like you. I wish I'd discovered you myself. I could certainly show you a better time as I've got at least three inches more than Goldfish—maybe more."

"You're quite a man," I said. "Everybody in Hollywood knows that."

"Too bad I didn't sign you before I decided to pull up stakes here."

"What do you mean?" I asked. "Leave Hollywood? For you, that's unthinkable."

"Hell, no. I don't know if you saw that cartoon the God damn Los Angeles paper printed of me," he said. "They're prying into my private affairs, and I don't like that one God damn bit. I'm heading back to New York to escape snoopy reporters."

"I've never been to New York but I understand reporters there are even more vicious."

He looked at me with a puzzled look, as if

he hadn't considered the possibility of that. "I've got my eye on an old mansion of fifty-two acres of grounds at Mamaroneck, New York. The wife of a millionaire who lived there went insane. They had built a *cell de luxe* for her. It's palatial with plush, silk hangings and iron bars at the window. At least I've found an appropriate place for my scenario department—an insane cell."

Griffith was easily distracted, and when an aide came up with some emergency, Griffith grabbed my arm and directed me to the stage door of Dorothy Gish. As Durango Jones, I'd already encountered both Lillian and Dorothy on the way to Nazimova's party. The director introduced me to Bobby Harron who was waiting outside Dorothy's door.

"The boy next door," he said to Bobby, "meet *Vampira*. Drop Dorothy Gish and go for this hot tamale. She'll make a man out of you." With a quick kiss on my cherry-red lips, Griffith was off without even an invitation for a date. For that, I could depend on William Boyd and, of course, my darling husband, Antonio Moreno.

Bobby Harron looked none the worse for wear after a hot night with my dear friend, Rod St. Just.

I was delighted to see him, and was thrilled that I was getting to meet some of Rod's favorites such as Antonio, even before Rod could introduce me. At the Patee Theater in Lawrence, I, as a mere child, sat through Bobby's *One Busy Hour* in 1909, *Her Mother's Oath* in 1913, and *The Rebellion of Kitty Belle* in 1914. Who could forget him in *The Birth of a Nation?*

Bobby was a sweet, personable young man. It was hard to imagine that only the night before he was at Fruitfly before disappearing for a night of debauchery enjoying the talented but petulant mouth of Rod St. Just. As we chatted, I was surprised to find that Bobby was from New York. He didn't fit into my stereotype of what a New Yorker was like. If anything, I thought Bobby would be from Virginia. Moving north, Iowa at best.

I figured him to be twenty-seven—or somewhere in that valley—but he still retained the look of a cute juvenile. In spite of all the films he'd made, he was not a star. He was a young man who appeared in films but didn't

have any real following the way Wallace Reid did.

Nonetheless, he was cute and sexy in a wholesome way, the kind of boy I might have ended up with if I'd met him at a church social in Kansas and hadn't got mixed up with the handsome, lanky cowpoke, the potentially dangerous Frank.

Right in the middle of my talk with Bobby, the dressing room door opened and out walked Lillian Gish. I had met her as Durango Jones but not as Lotte Lee. She ignored Bobby, in fact, cast a look of disdain at him as only she could do. She reached out to shake my hand. "I'm Lillian Gish, and I know you must be Lotte Lee. I recognized you from your photograph in the newspaper."

"I'm honored to meet you, Miss Gish," I said, wondering if she'd been in Dorothy's dressing room, licking her sister's pussy.

"I've heard that Richard Barthelmess is going to be one of your leading men," she said. "He is simply divine, the most beautiful face of any man who ever went before the camera."

"I understand he's set to appear opposite you in *Broken Blossoms*," I said. "D.W. Griffith himself, as director."

"I wish D.W. had offered me the role," Bobby said.

Finally, Lillian paid him some attention. "You're not right for the part." She quickly shifted her focus on me. "Dorothy sees the same magic in this handsome young swain, Mr. Barthelmess, that I do. Dorothy will soon be making films under her own production banner, and it's Dick Barthelmess who she is going to put under personal contract."

At that pronouncement, the hurt and rejection on Bobby's face were painfully apparent. Even though he'd just spent the night with Rod St. Just, was he smitten with Dorothy herself? He certainly didn't care much for Lillian. That was obvious.

Lillian was summoned away. She took my hand and gave me a little birdlike peck on the cheek. "You are divinely beautiful, but a bit tall. When I saw your face, I felt I'd seen it before. I study faces and know them well. Didn't we meet some time before?"

"You know my twin brother, Durango Jones," I said hesitantly.

"Durango Jones. Of course, Wallace Reid introduced us. As a brother and sister, you two are Hollywood lovelies." With that, the towering star of the silents, and the film's best single actress, disappeared. As I watched her go, I realized she had more talent than Gloria Swanson, Theda Bara, and Mabel Normand, and certainly Blanche Sweet, even if all that actress talent could be repackaged into one woman.

I shuddered to think that she might attend the showing of my upcoming film and judge my acting as Lotte Lee in *Vampira*. The Goldwyn movie didn't seem to be her kind of film, even though it hadn't been shot yet. I felt more at ease after deciding Lillian had better things to do than attend a screening of *Vampira*.

With Lillian gone, I devoured the boy next door. Bobby had been with Griffith since he was but a boy. He'd been a prop boy, an extra, and finally a leading man in a long list of Griffith's finest pictures, from the old Biograph days to *Hearts of the World* in 1918.

"What film are you making now?" I asked Bobby, who waited patiently at Dorothy's door for her to come out.

"It's a busy time," he said. "I'm shooting *True Heart Susie,* and I've just finished *The Girl Who Stayed at Home.* I'm scheduled to shoot *The Mother and the Law*, and, after that, *The Greatest Question.*"

"I'm just booked to do *Vampira*," I said. "It may mean the end of my career."

"I'm sure you'll do well," he said. "Probably become a bigger name than me. With all the films I've made, stardom has eluded me."

"You're a big name," I assured him. "America loves you." At this point, not knowing when Dorothy would appear and not at all confident that Rod St. Just would introduce me to this succulent morsel, I grew bold. "I think you're not only very handsome but very charming. I've always dreamed of making love to a man just like you. In fact, after seeing one of your films, I went home and..." Here I deliberately hesitated, a brief pause not lost on Bobby.

His first look was one of disbelief. "I don't usually have that effect on women."

"You do on this woman." I smiled seductively as I imagined *Vampira* would right before she was about to enjoy a tasty treat.

"I'm flattered—in fact, I'm so flattered I'm starting to get an erection," he said.

"Why not call me some time at the Hollywood Hotel and let me handle it for you. I'm just as good as Rod St. Just."

"You are?" He looked startled. "Rod is supposed to be better than anyone. Until I met you, I felt I had to turn to men for that kind of pleasure."

"Not at all," I assured him. "Lotte Lee is even better." It seemed strange speaking of myself in the third person, but I felt that Lotte was a different person from me and had her own identity. When I was Lotte, I didn't feel like Durango Jones any more.

As if on cue, Dorothy opened the door of her dressing room and emerged in full stage makeup, wearing a white billowy Victorian frock. "Good morning, Bobby," she said.

"Will you meet me for lunch?" he asked.

"All right but no hand-holding," Dorothy said.

"I promise." He kissed Dorothy on the cheek and also planted one on my cheek. I wanted to reach out and grab him and stick my tongue down his throat, but resisted the impulse in front of Dorothy. As if remembering something, he said, "Oh, I forgot. Dorothy Gish, Lotte Lee." He turned and left.

Dorothy looked deeply into my eyes. "I'd swear we've met before."

"You know my agent and twin brother, Durango Jones," I said.

"Oh, yes, delightful boy. I must speak to Durango again about Rodolfo Valentino."

"I understand you were instrumental in getting him the part," I said. "I know Durango mentioned Rodolfo to you, and apparently Mr. Griffith himself went along with the idea."

"That's true." She paused, a frown crossing her face. "From what I'd heard from your brother, I thought Valentino was suitable for the role of the leading man. But after meeting him, D.W. cast him as the villain and gave the leading man role to Elmer Clifton."

"I'm sorry to hear that. I think Rodolfo would make a great leading man."

"In that case," she said, a bit disdainfully, "perhaps you'll cast him as your leading man. Believe me, I know talent when I see it. The

American public would never accept Valentino as a leading man who gets the girl at the end of the reel. A screen lover, he's not. But he'd make the perfect villain, and we need plenty of those in movies too."

A maid came out of her dressing room and handed her a message. After a quick glance, Dorothy crumbled the paper in her delicate hands. "I'll not pay it," she virtually shouted.

"Pay what?" I asked.

"My dental bill. I had only two tiny cavities filled, and what do you think the dentist charged me—$350 for less than an hour's work. Unlike Mary Pickford, I don't get paid an exorbitant salary. All the world believes motion-picture stars wear sable on Monday, mink on Tuesday, and ermine on Wednesday. We're made to suffer financially not only from dentists, but doctors, lawyers, and milliners—all the way down the line.

"Right now I'm living fairly modestly," I said, "but I'm sure I'll soon find out what you're talking about."

Except for Mary Pickford, actresses work hard for their money. If you work for D.W., you toil especially hard. But what does it get him? I mean what good does it do anyone to kill themselves working, because the worms will get you in the end."

A ghoulish thought, but I didn't say anything. "It was such a pleasure meeting your sister this morning."

"I'll never be the great artist that Lillian is. I have another ambition entirely. I want to keep a red cow that gives a quart of milk at twenty cents a day, and I want to have some nice white chickens that lay dollar-a-dozen eggs."

When Dorothy excused herself, I encountered the mother of the two famous sisters, the wise and practical Mary Gish who apparently had been helping Dorothy make up her face.

Emerging from the dressing room, Mary Gish was kind and ingratiating, welcoming me to Hollywood. "I insist that both Dorothy and Lillian save a part of their salary every week. When girls grow old, their earning capacity grows less. Girls seldom think this can happen. They believe their salary is a fixed income for life. Heed my words, young lady. Save now or suffer later."

At first I wanted to dismiss Mary Gish's advice, but after telling her good-bye, I reconsidered. Perhaps it was my good fortune and fate to meet up with the mother of the Gish duo. Mary Gish started me to thinking. Up to now, I'd concentrated only on getting into men's trousers. Perhaps in the future I could get into the pockets of those trousers as well.

I'd better start buying up some California real estate while it was still affordable. Hollywood seemed to be growing overnight, as more and more studios opened. A tall building in downtown Los Angeles might one day sell for one-million dollars, although I found that thought highly unlikely.

Right now Lotte Lee was dashing to breakfast with her handsome new "husband," Antonio Moreno, before rushing into the arms—or at least the trousers—of my producer, Samuel Goldwyn himself.

Both of these upcoming rendezvous moments were worthwhile—sexually intoxicating in the case of Antonio and career enhancing in the case of Goldwyn. But I needed loftier challenges.

One occurred to me, although I'd had this thought before. Why not become the second Mrs. Charlie Chaplin after he divorced Mildred Harris? Being married to the world's most famous man was some achievement even if he were stingy with money.

As his wife, Lotte Lee, I could be a glamorous addition on his arm as we made public appearances together. And as Durango Jones, I could become his stud for the evening. Even if our marriage would be merely the mock, the ceremony only pretend, I still wanted to go through with it.

In me, Charlie could find both the woman he desired and the man he thrilled to, all rolled into one gorgeous package—namely Durango Jones a.k.a. Lotte Lee.

Chapter Six

Back at the cottage I shared with Rodolfo— that is, when the great lover was at home—I became Durango Jones again, as I rapidly prepared for breakfast with my new husband, Antonio Moreno. On the way there, I was eager to read the script of *Vampira* and knew I had to make my visit with Antonio brief. His home was fairly modest, as he wasn't pulling in the big bucks of Mary Pickford or Charlie.

He greeted me at the door in a pair of knit underwear, showing a prominent bulge. Pulling me inside, he crushed me against his finely honed physique, letting me taste his delicious long tongue.

The smell of baked goods was in the air, and I was hungry, knowing I couldn't live exclusively on a diet of semen.

In the kitchen he poured coffee and let me sample his fresh rolls. "Where did you learn to bake like this?" I asked.

"As a boy in Algeciras, Spain," he said, "I worked late at night and in the early morning carrying loaves of new bread and rolls to the stores and various markets. I worked nine hours each night and was paid one peseta, which was a lot of money for me in those days. But I was too dog-tired to pay attention at school the next day."

After sampling two rolls with lots of creamy butter, I told him of my adventure that morning at the studio. Of course, I didn't tell him I'd been at the studio with Rodolfo and as Lotte Lee. I could spare him such details. "I even met D.W. Griffith," I said proudly.

"D.W. helped me so much," he said. "When I first met him, he hired me as an extra. I worked hard, lived frugally, and had little or no pleasure. One day D.W. called me to him and told me he'd decided to make me a regular member of his stock company at a salary of forty dollars a week."

"You were on your way."

"It was like a dream. I played in pictures with Mary Pickford, Blanche Sweet, the Gish sisters, Bobby Harron, and Lionel Barrymore. Lionel fell madly in love with me, but he was too fat. I didn't have any romantic interest in him at all."

"Who would? But John Barrymore—that's a different story."

He smacked his lips before sampling more of his own coffee. "Yes, I'd open my ass to John Barrymore any day." A frown crossed his face. "That is, I would have before I met you. Now all my rich cream belongs to you."

"It doesn't have to," I said, fearing I was wandering into a commitment. After all, I was still in love with Rodolfo.

"There is one problem in our marriage," he said, "and I hate it."

"What's the matter, my sweet baby?" I asked.

"It's Billy."

I knew at once he meant William Desmond Taylor. "What's wrong?"

"I spoke to him only this morning," Antonio said. "He's delighted that I've found you, even though he still thinks of me as his boy."

"Is he jealous?" I asked timidly, not wanting to infuriate my new director who could destroy me in my debut role as *Vampira* if he turned against me.

"He's not really jealous—in fact, he's delighted. He said with you aboard, he could double his pleasure."

"You mean, have us both?"

"Exactly. He wants a great deal of our love-making to be as a threesome. He even wants to watch us make love, especially when he's become sexually exhausted by Mary Miles Minter or Mabel Normand. He's even fucking Charlotte Shelby, Mary's mother. The goat is insatiable."

"What are we going to do?"

"Give in to his wishes at first," he said. "Perhaps Billy will tire of us and find some other boy. There are other problems. Like all Hollywood stars, I'll have a wife as part of my baggage too, so I'll have to be with her most of the time."

"I understand that," I said. "I don't really want to know too much, if anything about the wives of men I'm involved with. I like to pretend they're only in the background—in fact, don't even exist."

"I know, my pet. But when I'm fucking her, I'll fantasize about fucking you. That way, I can guarantee a hard-on. Otherwise, I find it difficult maintaining an erection while fucking a woman."

"The prospect of such an act is more ghastly than I can consider."

To cap our breakfast, he insisted I drink a glass of Spanish brandy with him. Since he was a film star, I knew a great deal about his life but he knew nothing of mine. Over the brandy I told him of growing up in Kansas with my twin sister, Lotte. William Desmond Taylor had already told Antonio that my sister was going to star in *Vampira,* and that I'd make my living as her agent.

What Antonio didn't know, and what William didn't want to tell him, was that Durango Jones and Lotte Lee were one and the same. I had already divided my life and my friends into two categories—those who would know me as Durango Jones and those who would know me as Lotte Lee. So far, only four people knew that Durango and Lotte were the same—Marion Davies, Charlie, Tallulah, and William Desmond Taylor. Suddenly I realized there was a fifth, Rod St. Just. But Rod knew everybody's secrets. My dear photographer friend knew gossip even before it happened, or so it seemed.

"My best friend is Rod St. Just," I said.

Antonio looked surprised, then smiled with a kind of wry amusement. "There's nothing between Rod and me if that's what you're thinking. He's cute and I let him give me a couple of blow-jobs—that's about it. Rod rarely blows a guy more than once. Twice at the most."

"He's had me too."

"He likes to photograph guys' cocks. He took pictures of me, some with full hard-ons. But I wouldn't let him photograph my face. No one will know whose dick it is, but I hope they'll be impressed."

With that pronouncement, he stood up, the bulge in his underwear growing more prominent by the moment. He reached for my hand. I got up as he led me into his bedroom where he removed every stitch of my clothing before taking off his knit underwear to display a full and impressive erection. He ordered me to lie down on the bed. By this time my own erection matched his.

He placed his legs above my head, descending slowly over me, as he moved toward my own penis, which he delectably captured in his mouth. A fantastic sixty-nine began, and as he fed inch after inch into me I felt I was falling in love again.

It was at that very moment I felt I had to call Jack Gilbert. Why, when sucking Antonio and getting blown in return, should I be thinking of one of Lotte Lee's conquests? Let Lotte fend for herself.

In the meantime, I had this darling Spanish matador to deal with. I sucked him voraciously, and when we both exploded at the same time I knew I'd have to excuse myself soon to become Lotte Lee again if I were going to meet Samuel Goldwyn. I could hardly show up at Goldwyn's studio as Durango Jones.

With endless juicy kisses and fresh cum in my mouth, I dressed and headed out the door, racing back to the cottage to emerge again as Lotte Lee. Before heading out for my appointment with Goldwyn, I called Kono to find out if Charlie had returned from his mysterious disappearance. Still, no word. Kono claimed if he didn't hear from Charlie soon, he would call the police. Fearing headlines, I warned him not to. Kono reluctantly agreed to do nothing.

Earlier I'd called Rod and he'd told me that Julian Eltinge was eager to meet both Rodolfo and me. There was still a possibility that both Rodolfo and I could appear in the same film with the female impersonator, since one role called for a cornfed type like me, the other a villainous Spaniard, a role that would go to Rodolfo who wasn't very interested in playing villains but needed the money. I told Rod that Rodolfo and I would meet with Eltinge at any time.

Before ringing off, I got a little bitchy and said to Rod, "I've just bagged myself a new husband."

"As if I didn't know," Rod said. "William Desmond Taylor—that was obvious from the beginning."

"For once you're a little off," I said. "At last there's some gossip that Rod St. Just doesn't know."

"Who in hell is it then?" he said. "Tell me and I'll practically deliver Bobby Harron to you on a plate with his head chopped off."

"The one, the only Antonio Moreno." Before Rod had a chance to say another word, I put down the phone.

After a final call to the studio, I was told to drive to Goldwyn's home instead of his office. That surprised me but I headed there anyway. If he had a wife, and I wasn't even sure he was married, she must be in New York or somewhere.

On the way to see my producer, I felt a certain pride that Durango Jones might break into the movies too. An exciting prospect loomed before me. What if Lotte Lee and Durango Jones both became screen stars? I nearly drove Charlie's Locomobile off the road just thinking about such a delicious possibility.

*****

When I, as Lotte Lee, arrived at Sam Goldwyn's house, a young Chinese man directed me into a large living room where my producer seemed to be presiding over a morning coffee. He rushed to greet me, giving me a fatherly peck on the cheek and a kiss on my lovely hand. "Lotte, so glad to see you. You've arrived just in time to meet the world's greatest authors."

"I'm honored," I said, feeling slightly overdressed in this demure crowd. I scanned the faces, seeking Gertrude Stein, et al, but instead encountered Rex Beach, Gertrude Atherton, Elmer Rice, Mary Roberts Rinehart, and Maurice Maeterlinck. I was introduced to each of them, discovering to my surprise that Maeterlinck, the Nobel Prize-winning Belgian poet and author of the hit play, *The Blue Bird,* spoke not one word of English other than "hello."

Although the names of these writers are largely forgotten today, the assemblage was the equivalent of bringing John Grisham, Danielle Steele, Mary Higgins Clark, Tom Clancy, and Gore Vidal together—all in one room.

It seemed that Goldwyn was deep into his new experiment, hiring what he called "Eminent Authors" to write scenarios for him. At that time no serious writer viewed films as a worthy undertaking, often denouncing them as superficial and filled with stereotypical characters, recycled badly from plays or novels.

Although Goldwyn was a borderline illiterate, he presided with great authority over this gathering of the literati.

I spoke briefly with Rex Beach, who had a devoted following, thanks to novels that included *Masked Women, Jungle Gold,* and *The Spoilers.* He promised to write something for me. Of all the writers present, Beach seemed to understand Goldwyn perfectly. Both possessed a lack of artistic discrimination. Beach had written the character of "Laughing Bill Hyde," an awkward, painfully shy, and whimsical cowpoke with a Western drawl. It was ideal for the Ziegfeld Follies and perfect for Will Rogers, whom Goldwyn had signed to a two-year contract, although I'd understood that Rogers's success on the stage did not carry over into silent pictures.

"There's nothing but plagiarism out here," Beach assured me, switching from coffee to a morning whiskey. "After shooting a tale I wrote about Alaska, one shithead filmed the same God-damn story in the Deep South. Instead of my Eskimos, he turned the characters into mulattoes. And he didn't alter the plot one bit."

Goldwyn told me later that he was getting all these famous authors for anywhere from $150 to $300 a week. "All except one," Goldwyn said to me, pointing over at Maeterlinck. "I was out of my mind. He demanded one-hundred thousand a year, and for some reason I gave in to him. He's a real dumbbell, too. He'd never heard of all these other famous writers." According to Goldwyn, the highest paid writer was also "the most fucked-up."

"Have you filmed anything of his?" I asked.

"Hell no! The first piece of shit he gave me was the story of some boy in blue feathers. The plot, which had to be translated from the French, involved a feather bed. The feather bed was the villain of the piece. He also turned in a so-called love story about a married heroine. If we'd filmed that, we could show it only at smokers."

Later, in the toilet that was adjacent to my dressing room, I encountered the well-known scriptwriter Mary Roberts Rinehart, an academic-looking woman who seemed like she was in the wrong place at the wrong time. "Hollywood is a crazy place," she told me, "filled with pretensions and show-offs. When I first came here, Goldfish summoned me to his studio, and sent a blimp to pick me up, telling me it was safer than a taxicab. Can you imagine? I refused to ride in it, so instead, he sent an open taxi filled with half the flowers in California."

The exploits of Mrs. Rinehart were well documented in Sunday supplements. She'd nursed the wounded in Mexico during the Pershing campaign, trekked across wildernesses on horseback, and had driven ambulances. In effect, she was sort of an early female version of Ernest Hemingway.

"Since I came to Hollywood, I've written absolutely nothing," she said. "All I've done is pose for publicity shots. They seem to think I'm a starlet like Mae Marsh or Mae Murray, and believe me, I don't have the attributes."

"You look lovely," I said.

"So do you." She studied my face closely. "A beautiful, tall woman with just a touch of masculinity. Only a touch. Are you a lesbian?"

"No, I literally devour men."

"You certainly tower over most of them," she said. Skeptically, she stared at her face in the mirror. "I didn't look like this at all until I got to Hollywood. This make-up Goldwyn's boys forced on me makes me look jaundiced. They've raised my eyebrows so I look perpetually surprised. Outside of Hollywood, I have a rather prominent mouth, but here, the make-up moguls have transformed it into a demure-looking rosebud that I don't think suits me at all. But as long as I'm under contract to Goldwyn, I guess I'll keep playing the game. Good luck, sweetie. You at least have a lot more physical attributes than I ever did." Smiling, she turned her back to me and ordered another drink.

One by one I chatted briefly with all the writers in the stable, including Gertrude Atherton, the California novelist who told me she was the great-grandniece of Benjamin Franklin. Back in Kansas I had read one of her romantic novels. I talked to Gouverneur Morris, the great-grandson of one of America's founding fathers. He wrote action dramas but seemed very disappointed with his progress in motion pictures. "We are the slaves to illiterates," he said, looking with disdain over at Goldwyn.

Arriving late was Rupert Hughes, a novelist and short-story writer. Of all the male writers, he was the only one who seemed to take a sexual interest in me, the glamorous and seductive Lotte Lee. I never took him up on his offer, and perhaps I'm sorry now I didn't. Rupert's brother established a multi-million-dollar tool company that would one day be inherited by Rupert's nephew, Howard Hughes.

With the exception of Rex Beach and Rupert, all the other writers were terribly disappointed by their entrance into films. Rupert, however, was delighted. His soapy mother-love melodrama, *The Old Nest*, had earned nearly a million dollars for Goldwyn.

Standing near Goldwyn in the garden, we heard a large automobile coming up the drive at high speed. When it came to a screeching halt, it turned out to be a Hispano-Suiza filled with people. "You're about to meet Frank Joseph Godsol, the son of a bitch putting up the money for *Vampira*," Goldwyn said. "I can't stand the asshole."

"I'm terrified of meeting him," I said. "His reputation has preceded him." Actually what I couldn't confide to Goldwyn was the harsh appraisal I feared from Godsol. He was known as a connoisseur of the most beautiful showgirls in California and New York. I feared I wouldn't measure up.

Barging into the garden, Godsol was trailed by a retinue of staff, including a maid, a secretary, a beautiful but slightly vulgar actress, and what turned out to be his valet. He and Goldwyn disappeared into a corner of the garden and seemed to be having a heated argument about money.

Godsol was darkly handsome and a very tall figure, with the physique of an Olympic swimmer. He smoked a large cigar, the smoke of which he blew into Goldwyn's face. Both pockets of his trousers were literally bulging with dollar bills.

He was a famous Raffles-like character in Hollywood of those days. Since 1912 he'd wheeled and dealed for the Shubert organization at home and abroad. He was said to own several theaters in Europe and had committed all sorts of swindles in his day, most notably when he'd promised the French army dozens of healthy horses but had hauled over spavined mules instead. Tecla pearls were purchased by some of the grandest necks in Europe and America until they were discovered to be artificial.

At last Godsol came over to meet me, telling me I could call him "Joe." Good looking, athletic, and suave, Joe was clearly the sexiest man at this gathering. "So you're the pussy who's going to star in *Vampira.*" He stood back to appraise my figure. "She's quite a looker, Goldfish. One tall mama."

I held out my hand to him but he ignored it. "I don't shake women's hands," he said. "I either stick my tongue down their throat and demand they suck it or else I pump ten inches of stiff hard dick into them."

The blonde he'd brought along giggled. "It's true," she said in a voice that sounded like it was trained in Brooklyn.

Goldwyn turned and walked away in disgust. It was all too clear he hated Godsol but was forced to deal with him for business reasons.

"For *Vampira*," Joe said, "we're not going to limit that fag, William Desmond Taylor. The sky's the limit as far as budget is concerned. I've made a deal with the Du Ponts of Delaware to finance Goldfish. In the last four years that company has earned one-billion big ones. Munitions and gunpowder—that's the kind of business to be in when there's a war on."

"I hope you'll be proud of the picture," I said, feeling that Godsol was literally undressing me with his eyes.

"Proud, shit! I want it to make money. To do that, play it down and dirty. You can get down and dirty, can't you, baby?"

"I've been known to."

The blonde Brooklyn whore giggled again until Godsol ordered her back in the car.

After she'd left, Godsol said, "I fucked the bitch last night. But in the light of day, she bores me. After I leave Goldfish's place here, I'm ordering my driver to head out toward the desert where it's real hot. When I find a really remote place, I'm going to dump the bitch after I rip her dress off. Maybe the rattlesnakes will get her. That's how I handle the women in my life." He smiled at me. "But not you, baby. You I would treat like a queen."

This vulgar bastard had incredible sex appeal. I despised the man but was literally drawn to him as well. He signaled his secretary who hurried over with a script. At long last the shooting script of *Vampira* was in my hands.

"Read it, learn your part, and look as sexy as hell before the cameras," he told me. "From now on, what Joe tells you goes. Goldfish might think he's running this studio, but Frank Joseph Godsol is the big cheese."

"Thanks for the script," I said. "I'm dying to read it."

"I'm dying to fuck that pretty mouth of yours," he said. "All the studs in Hollywood claim you give the best head."

"Any time you want it, Joe."

He moved closer to me. "Think you can handle it? It's the biggest dick in Hollywood."

Having encountered Elmo Lincoln and Francis X. Bushman, I doubted Godsol's claim.

"I can handle anything you've got, stud." With that, I turned and walked away from him, knowing he was checking out my figure.

Coming back into the living room, I encountered Goldwyn again. "Honey," he whispered to me, "I know you want my juice this morning, but I'm too drained. Mabel Normand's upstairs. She demanded that I fuck her all night. Would tomorrow be okay? I'll give you a nice big load then."

"It's okay, Sammy," I said. "I'm disappointed. But it's certainly worth waiting for." He gave me a big wet kiss before ushering me upstairs toward his library where he said he wanted me to read the script for *Vampira*.

As I told him good-bye, I headed down the corridor passing Goldwyn's master bedroom. The French doors were wide open. Glancing inside, I spotted a nude woman sprawled across the bed. She seemed to be waking up. Sitting up sleepily, she glared at me. "Get the hell in here, bitch," she shouted at me. "We've got to talk."

It was only then I recognized the source of that voice.

It was Mabel Normand herself.

*****

"Do you know what a big star I am?" Mabel Normand demanded of me, as she staggered drunk or drugged but definitely nude from the bed. She looked awful, not the breath of springtime she'd been in her early films. Her eyes were in deep shadow as if artificially blackened by the makeup kit of Theda Bara. "The one-film wonder." She looked at me with disdain.

"I don't expect to have a glorious career like you, Miss Normand," I said with appropriate modesty. "I'm hardly the queen of comedy and I'm sure Miss Bara will laugh at my attempts at vamping."

"This vamp shit ended in 1918," Mabel said. "It's over, baby. Why don't you pack your bags and head back to the farm where you came from? Show your pussy to some love-starved, shit-kicking farmboy and forget about the films.

That's my advice to you, bitch."

"Thank you," I said firmly, "but I'm staying here and making *Vampira*. I may be laughed off the screen, but I will have tried."

"Don't give me that purer than thou shit," she said, staring at her sotted face in the mirror. "Who in the hell do you think you are? Mary Pickford? You're Goldfish's latest whore. He's getting tired of me. Had a hard time getting it up for me last night."

"Sammy and I are merely friends," I said, an obvious lie and she knew it. "We have a professional relationship—nothing more."

"Don't bullshit me, you twobit whore." She fluffed her tits which at her young age had begun to droop a bit. "My name is Mabel Ethelreid Normand. You can call me Ethelreid." She didn't disguise the sarcasm in her voice. "I was educated in a convent. You can't make this up. My parents were in vaudeville."

"I've seen many of your films, and I admire you very much."

"A fan, huh? My fans are disappointing. My career is on the backburner. I've recently made a film so bad it can't be released. They say I've become unreliable. That I'm addicted to cocaine." She glared at me and shouted. "Do you think I'm a drug addict?"

"Harmless encounters with recreational substances don't make one an addict," I said, as a memory of my darling Wallace Reid flashed before my eyes.

"You're more sensible than I thought. The first time I laid eyes on you, I figured you for another dumb Hollywood slut. A tall one at that. But you've managed to ingratiate yourself with William Desmond Taylor *and* Samuel Goldwyn. I hear your agent—that is, your brother—is fucking both Charlie Chaplin and Antonio Moreno. God knows who else. John Barrymore will surely be next."

"I have only a professional relationship with your friend, Mr. Desmond."

"Like hell! You probably sucked him off last night and let him fuck you, among other acts of depravity. Antonio is strictly a homosexual so at least you'll be safe with him, but your brother had better keep his trousers on around that one."

Wrapping herself in a large and fluffy towel, Mabel headed for Goldwyn's sun terrace, frowning in the bright light, which made her look far older than her years. Years of drugs and constant partying were beginning to leave hideous telltale clues in her face, which I suspected makeup could no longer conceal.

As I watched her get her bearings in the glaring day, I realized that the movies had come of age. Many of the fresh faced and shining lights of the teens were in great decline after the war. There was talk of actors becoming has-beens, an expression I'd never heard before.

The careers of Fairbanks, Pickford, and Chaplin were still strong, but many stars were fading, most notably Theda Bara and Francis X. Bushman.

Mabel Normand could now be added to that list, along with dear, sweet Bobby Harron. Tomorrow belonged to the up and coming, certainly Gloria Swanson, hopefully Rodolfo, and maybe even Reatha Watson if she could return to Hollywood as the more grownup Barbara LaMarr.

I didn't know how Durango Jones and Lotte Lee fitted into that hierarchy. We belonged to the Twenties too, after which we'd probably become forgotten footnotes, if that.

"Goldfish is giving me $3,500 a week, a phenomenal salary," Mabel said, turning to me as if challenging me. "It ain't Mary Pickford's type of money but it ain't peanuts either. How much are you getting?"

"We haven't worked out the details yet," I said, another lie.

"He'll probably start you out at $150 a week," she said. "You're no female Chaplin like me, and I'm not sure how your vamping will play out at the box office."

"My challenge will be to bring something new and fresh to the screen," I said. "Forget *Salome* and *Cleopatra*. Make the vamp a modern woman for the Twenties."

"You just go and do that, sugartit," she said with disdain. "And good luck to you."

"I'll need luck and plenty of it."

She sat down and seemed to plop there like a dead fish. "I don't know why I'm jealous of you. After all, we won't be competing for the same parts. You can have Goldfish. Last night was the last sexual bout I plan to have with that daddy. Those mighty four inches are all yours if you want them."

I said nothing, not wanting to arouse any more fury in her.

She appeared on the verge of tears. "My world is starting to fall in on me. Not just little golf balls from the sky but great big bowling balls slamming down on my head." Like an imperial goddess, she waved her hand to me. "Go in that bedroom and get me my black dress. Except for the moments I'm in front of the camera, I wear only black."

Returning to the messed-up bedroom, I spotted her black dress lying on the floor. I picked it up and brought it out on the terrace to give to her. She yanked it from me, pulled the towel from her naked body, and slipped on the dress without bothering with undergarments. "I'm getting outta here."

"It's been an honor meeting you, Miss Normand," I said.

She walked over and stared deeply into my eyes. "If you think you're going to have Billy Taylor all to yourself, you're sadly mistaken. That bitch, Mary Miles Minter, is hot for him. Even her mother, Charlotte Shelby, is getting fucked by our friend Taylor. If you want to become the latest in his stable, the line forms on the left and right."

"I have no romantic interest in him at all," I said, which was the truth.

"If you and I ever go out on the town, sugar," she said, "just make sure you've got a flask on your hip. Don't carry a dainty flask. Carry a big silver one. Keep the hooch flowing I always say, don't you?"

"Yeah, sure."

"Let me give you some final advice," she said. "If you want to get laid, I can introduce you to some finer and hotter studs in Hollywood than Samuel Goldwyn and William Desmond Taylor."

She headed for the exit at the edge of the terrace. As if forgetting something, she turned and looked me over carefully. "By chance, are you a lesbian?"

"I go strictly for men," I said.

"Is that true? Nazimova told me that I should have a lesbian affair. I thought if you were a lesbian, we might get together some time and lick pussies—whatever lesbians do."

"Count me out on that."

"Too bad," she said, casting an angry frown

up at the midday sun before disappearing down the steps and into her uncertain future.

*****

With the script of *Vampira*—still unread—in the seat beside me, I headed for Santa Monica and the beach house of Owen Moore and Jack Pickford. I also carried the heroin which Rod St. Just had acquired for me at Fruitfly.

Goldwyn had told me that he wanted to talk to me after I'd read the script. He also assured me that he'd be sexually "up and running" for our next rendezvous. After a lot of juicy kisses in his kitchen, I told him good-bye, but only after I'd had to suck on his tongue for a long time with my cherry-red lips.

I recognized the address of the Moore/Pickford beach house and pulled into the driveway.

I didn't know what to expect, but in the soaring heat of the Santa Monica sun, I was shown into a large living room overlooking the ocean by a houseboy. He disappeared quickly, leaving me to introduce myself to Owen Moore, the erstwhile husband of Mary Pickford, although I suspected he wouldn't be the sweetheart of America's own sweetheart for very long.

It didn't really shock me, but in those pre-airconditioned days, Owen Moore was entirely nude sitting on a chaise longue before open doors where the breeze from the ocean came in to cool him. His was a natural body with average sized genitals, although he had a handsome face—not quite the beauty his brother, Tom, was, but a good-looking guy you wouldn't turn down if encountered late at night in a gay bar when your prospects for the evening were running out.

"Lotte," he said, not bothering to get up, "Forgive the way I'm dressed but Jack Pickford and I like to be casual out here. You can take off your clothes if you wish."

"Owen," I said, "I'm far too modest for that."

"You'd look great in the nude," he said. "You look like you've got nothing to be shy about."

"Only Goldfish gets to see the whole thing. I'll turn and leave if you don't want to play by my rules."

"Stick around," he said. "Your rules are fine with me. Tom has told me everything. I hear you're great at your specialty. Not just great. The best in Hollywood."

"I try to live up to my billing." He offered me a drink which I had to pour myself. It was obvious that he'd had quite a few, even though the day was young.

Over drinks, he preferred—as all actors do—to talk about his career instead of my own. His feelings for Mary seemed a contradiction. He didn't really want her any more, although it was clear he desired her money. "Mary confronted me one night," he said. "Me or the bottle, was her challenge. I chose the bottle."

He'd appeared in only one film that year, *The Crimson Gardenia*. He'd made no films in 1918. Yet in 1910 he'd starred in an astonishing twenty films. "I fear if Mary goes from my life, directors won't cast me in anything," he said.

As a prophet, Owen was no crystal ball gazer. He was to work throughout most of the 1920s, making his last film, *A Star is Born*, in 1937, two years before his death of a heart attack in Beverly Hills.

"Your talent will transcend your marriage to Mary," I assured him, not really believing my own words.

"Perhaps it will," he said reflectively. "That is, if I don't show up drunk on the set and get fired."

In the next two hours I became Owen's bartender. Could that actor from County Meath, Ireland drink? At one point he became nostalgic, telling me when he'd first fallen in love with Mary. "It was very romantic. Griffith had packed us off to the Orange Mountains west of New York. We were put up in a small summer hotel. The place was beautiful—on a lake with an old canal. Green pastures surrounding stone farmhouses."

"I never knew how you two guys met," I said, sipping my own drink and wondering how I'd ever reconnect with Rodolfo as Durango Jones.

"All of the crew would have dinner, and

Mary and I would go for an early evening stroll by the river. Sometimes we'd take a little boat out on the lake and look for the evening star. For music, we were entertained by singing frogs. Fireflies were our only illumination as I held her in my arms. Where did love go?"

As if remembering the times they'd made love together, I watched as Owen's penis grew to a sturdy six inches, very similar in size and thickness to that of his brother, Tom, although Tom had him beat by an inch at least.

Fearing this might be my only chance to make love to the dick of Mary Pickford's husband, I descended at once on Owen. Even though drunk, he loved it. The feel of Lotte Lee's warm lips on him had him rising to the occasion. He pumped his cock back and forth in my mouth, as if wanting to reach my throat, but it just wouldn't go that far, and that seemed to frustrate him.

His streaks increased in tempo, as my hands traveled up and down his body, feeling every crevice. The sounds coming from my slurping seemed to whet his sexual appetite all the more. His balls formed a tight pouch close to his body.

Since he'd been drinking, he held out for a long time. But as his eruption neared, he threw his arms back on the chaise longue and called out, "Mary, Mary, Mary, this is so good. So good."

He rammed that cock into my mouth as deep as it would go and exploded. There was a wonderful moment as his cock pulsed and then released. The sweetness of the load—probably scented with Irish whiskey—completed the magic of it all for me. When I'd first seen him, I didn't think I really wanted him. But with my belly full of him, I felt a genuine affection.

"That was so terrific, baby," he said. "I really needed and wanted that. You're going to be my baby, aren't you?"

"Of course," I said, wondering how many men I could be a baby to. "You're not jealous of Tom, are you?"

"Not at all. Tom and I share. But tell me one thing."

"You don't have to ask. I know what you want to know. Don't tell Tom, but you're much better." I felt that was a harmless lie.

"I just knew it," he said, sitting up and requesting another drink from me as his cock deflated. "Of course, I won't know the full results of my competition with my brothers until you've had Matt. He's coming over right after he gets off from work."

"I can't wait," I said.

Instead of Matt, I got a vision of Jack Pickford, just as nude as Owen, descending the stairs. Obviously his wife, the film star, Olive Thomas, wasn't in the Santa Monica house today. For Lotte there was a certain thrill enjoying the male contingent of two of America's most famous marriages—that of Owen Moore and Mary Pickford and of Olive Thomas and Jack Pickford.

Even though nude, Jack extended his hand as if we were meeting at a formal dinner party. "Lotte Lee, what a good-looking dame you are. Really tall. I was expecting Durango but Owen said you'd deliver the goodies instead."

"Durango couldn't make it," I said. "He's my agent and he has an appointment to talk contracts with Goldwyn."

"I hope you fare better with him than I did," he said. "He's tight with money." He looked down at his genitals. "I hope you don't mind meeting me without my clothes."

"Not at all."

"I bet if Durango were here, he'd love it," he said.

"I'm sure he'd be impressed."

He took the heroin from me and seemed to weigh it in his hand before placing it on the bar. "Tell your brother I owe him one," he said to me, fondling his genitals. "He can have this any time he wants it."

"A real treat for him."

Sexually satisfied and more than a bit drunk, Owen had drifted off into a stupor, giving me time alone to seduce an already nude Jack Pickford. Jack's looks could be taken either of two ways—he was "cute," or else he looked a bit like the dreaded Will H. Hays, who would terrorize film directors for years, demanding that even the most harmless scenes be cut from pictures if they were, in his view, salacious.

On that long-ago afternoon, I preferred to see the cute side of Jack. His drinking and womanizing were legendary, even though he was married to Olive Thomas. Back in the days when few men pumped up their muscles, Jack had a natural build. He obviously didn't go to the gym, and he drank too much, but he wasn't in the least bit fat. Like Owen, he had an average-size dick, with a generous hood over his penis.

After returning from the bar, he pulled me into his arms and kissed me long, hard, and passionately, inserting his tongue, which I greedily sucked. As I fondled his balls, I felt his erection rising, zooming up to a full six and a half inches, a half inch more than Owen himself.

"Thanks for the white stuff," he said, releasing my mouth for a fast breath of air before he put his hands on my shoulders and lowered me to my knees to worship "my bird," as he called it.

No sooner had I completely swallowed him than he exploded in my mouth. Pulling out, he said, "I did it again. Let me stick it in any hole and I shoot right away. Olive complains about that all the time. But she's got her gangster boyfriends. Besides, she likes huge cocks. I don't know why it is, but many gangsters have really big dicks. I've seen her get fucked by enough of them to know."

If I'd been a gossip columnist—a later profession of mine—I would have been thrilled to learn these private details about America's "Ideal Couple." After he'd disappeared into a bathroom with the bag of heroin, I adjusted my makeup in the mirror and headed for the living room where I found the coolest spot.

When he came back, Jack had modestly placed a towel around his waist. "That was good. Both you and Durango are welcome to enjoy me at any time day or night."

"Thanks for such unlimited access." As an actress, I could disguise the sarcasm in my voice.

The dope loosened Jack's tongue, although it was rather loose before the heroin. "I always knew I'd be a star," he said reflectively. "When Mary and I got to Hollywood in 1910, it was just a drab hick town. Mostly retired farmers from the Middle West who set the moral tone of the place. I paid $5.50 a week for a dingy room near the Biograph studio on the corner of Washington Street and Grand Avenue."

"Was that Biograph's first venture out here?"

"The very first. Believe it or not, I was Mary's double in several pictures. I'd ride horseback for her or else take a fall for her. Dressing in drag was never a problem for me. Owen has done the same for her."

"I love your films," I said. Actually I didn't.

"I could have done better in pictures if I hadn't started to drink so much. I was just a skinny kid when I got here. After work, the men on the crew would dare me to have some whiskey, and then they'd make fun of me as I reeled around." He opened the towel to reveal his deflated cock. He ran his hands through his pubic hair. "See this lush bush?"

"I can hardly miss it," I said, leaning back on the sofa and allowing my *faux* breasts to protrude.

"I had already reached puberty but my hairs took a long time growing. One time four guys on the crew invited me to a local bordello. I was still a kid and very shy. To put it bluntly, I just had no hair crowning my bird. One of the guys was an actor. He took a fake mustache out of his stage kit and gave me a decent-looking set of pubic hair. That night I was the star of the whorehouse. The girls loved it. I've been chasing dames ever since."

"You started early," I said. "Why not make a hobby of it?"

"I did just that. Before my fifteenth birthday, I knew all there was to know about women and whiskey, not necessarily in that order. Before Mary and I went back home to mama, we'd saved up $1,200. That was a hell of a lot of money. When we got back home and showed it to mama, she thought it was stage money. All of us got drunk that night. Mama really likes the bottle."

"Even Mary? I didn't know she drank."

"She could drink us all under the table. But she's a secret drinker. We can't have America's Sweetheart drinking in public, now can we?" At this point he got up and gave me a wet kiss on the lips, reached for his towel, and headed for his bedroom. "I'm going to have more of this good stuff you brought. Tonight I'm joining Mary and maybe Doug for dinner at the Alexandria Hotel. Wanna be my date?"

"That would be nice," I said. "I've always wanted to meet them." I didn't let Jack know that Durango Jones had already met this famous pair.

"Good, then it's a date."

I was mildly surprised that the break-up of Mary's marriage didn't seem to affect the friendship of Jack and Owen.

"Will Olive Thomas be at the dinner?"

"Hell no!" he said. "She's out fucking Joe Godsol tonight."

I settled back on the sofa again in mild surprise. If Olive liked gangsters with big dicks, the backer of my film, *Vampira*, obviously fit the bill. I felt it was but a matter of time before Lotte Lee herself would be tasting the cream of "Joe." I could well afford to wait as I had other agendas for the evening. Having decided I'd never get to see Rodolfo again, I called Antonio since he'd wanted to meet me later tonight. With all I had going on, I decided this was not the night to phone John Gilbert.

I didn't know if I should go with Jack Pickford or not, as I'd promised Kono to track down Charlie Chaplin. Not knowing where to even look for Charlie, I called Kono to learn that Charlie still had not shown up. I told Kono not to worry, that Charlie was in secret discussions with Mary Pickford and Doug Fairbanks about launching their own studios. "It's all very hush-hush," I assured Kono. "If you go to the police and expose Charlie's secret negotiations, he'll fire you."

That seemed to satisfy Kono, at least for the moment. Before hanging up, he told me that William Randolph Hearst had called. He wanted to speak to Durango—namely me— personally. I promised to return his call as soon as possible. After all, I have to do something to earn my five-hundred dollars a week.

As thoughts of the upcoming night raced through my brain, I heard a car pull into the driveway. I got up from the sofa and looked out the window. Even though he'd worked all day, Matt Moore hopped out of the car with all the vigor of a teenage boy. Though not as cute as his brother, Tom, he was one good-looking guy. All the Moore brothers were dolls.

Barging into the living room, he confronted me. "You're Lotte Lee," he said in lieu of an introduction. "Tom has told me everything."

"I bet he didn't tell you one thing," I said, imagining how Theda Bara would handle this situation.

He looked at me with a knowing smirk.

"What might that be?"

"Did he tell you that of all the Moore brothers, I want to take the pants off Matt Moore most of all?"

"Hot damn!" he yelled, moving toward me.

*****

Matt Moore was the youngest Moore brother I'd seduced and in many ways the sweetest. The sexiest was still Tom, but Matt was the most appealing. Even though he must have been at least thirty years old when I'd seduced him, he reminded me of a nineteen-year-old.

His cock was very similar to that of Tom and Owen, a sturdy six inches at least, maybe more, and uncut like his brothers. I'd seen several of his unmemorable films that very year, including *A Regular Girl, The Glorious Lady, Getting Mary Married,* and *The Bondage of Barbara.* In fact, I recalled seeing films of his such as *The Doctor's Testimony* back in 1914 at the Patee Theater in Lawrence.

Matt was certainly the gentlest of the Moore brothers and seemed amazed that I could swallow all six inches of him. Apparently, the women he'd tried to get to go down on him before me had balked at swallowing him whole. Little did he know he was dealing with Lotte Lee or else her brother Durango Jones who'd swallowed Francis X. Bushman.

Matt was merely a party favor for me, but I'd sucked him voraciously, and had been rewarded with an eruption that was almost as good as Tom's. Matt had wanted to give me juicy kisses after I'd blown him so I figured he was giving himself a blow-job by proxy, although I'd never be so undiplomatic to point out something like that.

Being a true Moore, Matt retired to the bar after his climax for some Irish whiskey, which he claimed was better than any brew made in Scotland.

On the stairs Jack Pickford gave me a kiss and, after a knowing look over at Matt, a wink, claiming he had to meet his wife, the lovely Olive Thomas, before having the rendezvous at the Alexandria Hotel with Mary and Doug. He spoke of them so casually that for a moment I forgot they were among the top three most famous people on earth. Since I'd known them—at least as Durango Jones—in rather intimate circumstances, I wasn't afraid of having dinner with them in my identity as Lotte Lee, future Goldwyn vamp.

Jack gave me another kiss after agreeing that I'd get to the hotel on my own steam by eight o'clock. He warned, "Mary keeps people waiting. She doesn't like to be kept waiting herself." I promised him I'd be on time.

Before heading out the door, Jack told me that he'd sampled the heroin. "Good stuff. You're a woman after my own heart. Keep me supplied with that and I'll keep you supplied with this." He reached down and cupped his crotch.

I smiled indulgently. Who did he think he was dealing with? I was Lotte Lee. Either as Durango Jones or Lotte herself, I had the hottest studs in Hollywood.

Back at the bar, I gave Matt a lot of my tongue which he willingly sucked, and he gave me even more. Even better than going down on him, I liked kissing the Irishman. He was a great kisser. Tom was better in the stud department, but Matt was better with the tongue. Owen, although still a very attractive man, was my least favorite because he possessed the most disagreeable personality. I felt he had the capacity to be a very mean drunk, and wouldn't be surprised if Mary had had her share of beatings.

Knowing I had at least two hours before dinner, I decided to call Antonio, my husband. He'd wanted me to come over right away. But since I couldn't change back into my Durango Jones clothing and then become Lotte Lee in such short notice, I put him off until later, claiming I had to see Goldwyn about the script. That seemed to satisfy him, although he told me that William Desmond Taylor wanted us both to come to his house as soon as it could be arranged for a three-way. "Later, later," I said, putting down the phone.

Having drained all the men in the household and wanting to keep all my lovers on the string, I dialed John Gilbert, my beloved "Jack." He seemed as drunk as Owen Moore when I called him, but we agreed to meet at The Blue Moon,

a notorious cafe halfway between Hollywood and Santa Monica. John assured me that the management was very discreet and had very, very dark booths in back.

I quickly drained Matt's mouth dry, and told him I'd be back soon to dress for dinner. I'd brought a change of outfits, and I needed a full dressing room to prepare myself as Lotte before my dinner with Doug and Mary.

Unlike our first meeting at the Alexandria Hotel, John Gilbert was waiting for me when I arrived at The Blue Moon, looking like the ravishing beauty I pretended to be, Lotte Lee herself. He seemed very glad to see me, and I thought he looked good enough to eat.

"You've already become a big star, too busy to see the man who loves you passionately," he said.

"I'll never get that busy," I said, kissing him wetly on the lips, hoping I didn't taste of Matt Moore, Owen Moore, and Jack Pickford. John Gilbert was the male equivalent of a female sex symbol. In front of me, he seemed so real and tangible while at the same time was as remote as that dashing matinee idol appearing on screens around the world even as we kissed.

He directed me to a back room where we slid into a booth. Not wanting to be disturbed by a waiter, he offered me some of his own whiskey, which I gladly shared, if for no other reason than to cleanse my breath of my recent encounters. If John detected the smell or taste of other men on me, he gave no clue.

He kissed my hand gently, the way he'd done with Mary Pickford in *The Heart o' the Hills*. Handsome and charismatic, he had me laughing at the latest gossip and regretting that I couldn't spend the entire evening with him. At that moment I was sorry I'd accepted Jack Pickford's invitation.

John Gilbert's exciting news of the day wasn't that he was getting a new movie role, but that he'd been accepted for membership in the Los Angeles Athletic Club. "I mean, it's got everything," he said, his eyes lighting up. "The club dining room is unbelievable. The biggest names in Hollywood dine there. Even that Latin lover, Antonio Moreno."

At the mention of that name, I downed some more whiskey.

"I've dined with Richard Barthelmess who's going to be one of your lovers in *Vampira.*"

The mention of Richard's name struck a strange chord in me. I'd been setting up his seduction as Durango Jones, not as Lotte Lee. With some of these men, I didn't know whether to be Lotte or Durango.

"Just the other night I dined with Marshall Neilan," John said.

I already knew that Neilan was the highest paid director in Hollywood, even though he was only in his twenties.

"I've dined with James Kirkwood, too, even Raymond Griffith," John said.

I was impressed, knowing that these were some of the richest and most successful men in Hollywood of that time.

All that talk of money and power seemed to have the effect of an aphrodisiac on John. He reached for my hand and placed it on his rapidly rising erection.

"Where can we go?" I asked.

"Right here," he said, his breathing heavy. "I'll cover your head with a tablecloth."

Knowing I wasn't the first woman who'd ever crawled beneath a table for a man, nor the last, I got down on my knees and unbuttoned the fly of his trousers. John was ready for action, having risen to his full and impressive length.

Like her brother, Durango, Lotte Lee was an expert at servicing men this way. Before long I had John, drunk or not, moaning for more and feeding me every fat inch he had. That's not all he fed me. He erupted violently, as his body seemed to go into convulsions. It was one hell of a climax and I stayed on him until I knew I'd swallowed every last drop and still some.

With many good-bye kisses and promises to meet sooner than later, I was off, driving back to the Pickford/Moore house, with my mind on both Charlie and Rodolfo, as I didn't know where either of them was.

Back at the house, Matt had passed out drunk on the sofa, and Owen was nowhere to be seen. Carrying my Lotte gown, along with some accessories, I disappeared into what apparently was the bedroom of Olive Thomas. It was the salon of a real actress who spent a lot of time before dressing room mirrors

applying makeup. When I'd finished putting the final touches on Lotte Lee, I checked my figure in a full-length mirror, deciding that I, if straight, might go for Lotte too.

So far, the evening was going too perfectly. Upon going back to the living room, I encountered a half-dressed Owen Moore. He was heading out the door, and he had a gun.

"Owen, come back," I screamed after him.

"Fuck that," he said angrily. "Tonight's the night I'm going to kill that climbing bastard."

That reference wasn't hard to figure out. He obviously meant Douglas Fairbanks. "Come back, don't do it."

"Where are they?" he demanded to know. "I know they're dining with Jack tonight, but he wouldn't tell me where."

When he'd waited a long time glaring at me, and I didn't come up with an answer, he said, "I'll find them on my own. Fuck you!"

I ran after him, but he pushed me away. "They're at the Hollywood Hotel," I shouted after him.

He turned around as if suspicious of me. "Before morning, headlines around the world will be screaming about the death of Douglas Fairbanks." Drunkenly Owen staggered toward his car and started it, spinning gravel as he headed for the main highway.

Jumping into Charlie's Locomobile, I headed for the Alexandria Hotel to warn Douglas. I figured that by the time Owen got to the Hollywood Hotel and didn't find Douglas, he might head for the Alexandria. That would give me time to get there and warn Douglas so he could escape.

At the Alexandria Hotel, I encountered Ramon, the handsome waiter branded by Sessue Hayakawa. Ramon smiled knowingly at me and led me over to the Pickford/Fairbanks table. The room was quite dark, and I spotted Jack Pickford heading toward the table too, apparently on a return from the men's room.

Jack quickly introduced me to Douglas and Mary. Mary told me that they already knew my brother, Durango. At least she wasn't pretending that that afternoon in my cottage with her beloved Douglas and his crooked dick never happened.

Even before Douglas could compliment my

beauty, I interrupted him, telling him of Owen and the gun headed for the Hollywood Hotel.

"Doug," Mary said, taking his hand. "You've got to get out of town. A drunken Irishman like Owen might do anything."

At first Douglas looked stunned, searching Mary's face, my face, and even Jack's, but not saying anything. Only weeks ago, a rumor had spread through the theatrical district in New York that Owen Moore had killed Douglas Fairbanks. It almost made the newspapers before the rumor was disproved.

"Hell," Douglas said. "I bet Owen is too drunk to shoot straight."

Nonetheless, with sufficient urging from Mary, he agreed to take the train to New York.

"A scandal now could ruin us all," Mary warned him. "Our careers. Everything we've worked so hard for."

"You know Owen when he's had one too many," Jack said. That remained his only contribution for the evening.

"It's best," Mary said, kissing Douglas before turning to me. "If Durango still has that cottage, could Doug stay there until the morning train leaves?"

"Of course," I said, delighted to have Douglas Fairbanks alone for the evening, even if his dick were crooked. He was still Douglas Fairbanks, "the most popular man in the world."

"Durango's out of town," I said. "I'm looking after the cottage for him."

"It'll be a perfect hideout," Mary assured Douglas. She looked skeptically at me, wondering no doubt if her future husband would be safe hiding out with Lotte Lee. Apparently, Lotte's reputation had already preceded me all over town. Little could Mary have known that I had seduced both her husband, her brother-in-law, and her brother only this afternoon.

In moments we were gone, but not until Douglas had held Mary in his arms, kissing her passionately as if this farewell were going to be forever.

In Charlie's Locomobile, Douglas seemed to have second thoughts and appeared on the verge of urging me to take him back to the Alexandria. "I'm all derring-do and flamboyant swordmanship," he said. "I'm a swimmer, rider, roper, tennis player, boxer, and gymnast. Owen Moore is a drunk. I have nothing to fear from

him."

"What about a bullet?" I asked.

The rest of the ride was in silence, although I wondered if Rodolfo had returned. How could I, Lotte, explain showing up at the cottage with the boy friend of America's sweetheart?

*****

As Durango Jones, I'd entertained Douglas Fairbanks in my cottage before. Back then, his chief interest centered on Mary Pickford. Tonight Lotte Lee had this dashing but short man all to herself. Total honesty forces me to confess, even at this late date, that my interest in him would have been minor if he were an insurance salesman or a shoe clerk. I'd no doubt pass him by as I pursued such big game as Wallace Reid, Rodolfo Valentino, or John Gilbert.

Since Doug had hearts fluttering all over the world, I took a closer look at him. As I offered him a drink, I noted his dazzling white teeth with his jaunty smile. He was certainly filled with an electrifying energy. In a day when both men and women guarded themselves from the rays of the sun, he was totally bronzed. From past experience, I knew he had no tan lines but was brown all over.

"Mary and I don't want scandal," he said. "Even our dating each other could ruin our careers. If Owen takes a shot at me, it's all over for all of us."

"Maybe he'll settle down if you're out of town for a few days," I said.

"Owen will always be a hopeless drunk," he said. "He's a fucking lunatic. He'll never be under control. I don't know what Mary saw in him in the first place."

"The Moore boys have a certain charm," I said, "when they're not drunk. Owen seems to have the worst disposition of all of them."

"Tell me about it." Doug asked if he could use my phone, and I readily agreed. He finally got through to a friend, Allan Dwan, in Chicago, asking Dwan to meet him in Salina, Kansas, and ride back with him to New York, although Dwan would have to return to Chicago alone. Doug had an idea for a film scenario, and he needed Dwan's cooperation. Apparently, Dwan agreed to this unconventional and backtracking invitation.

Seating himself across from me, as I offered a fresh drink, Doug said, "I'm d'Artagnan and he doesn't run from anybody. I'm fearless."

"Just this one time," I said. "No one will think you a coward. You're doing it for Mary's sake."

"Yes, for Mary." He sipped his drink and settled back on the sofa. "As a boy, my favorite novel was Alexandre Dumas' *Three Musketeers*. My head is filled with dreams of d'Artagnan. I will bring him to the screen. I'll be so graceful I'll float through the air just like Nijinsky." A frown crossed his face.

"What's the matter?"

"I just thought of something. It could all be over for me soon. It could be the end of my career. What if Owen sues Mary for divorce, naming me as correspondent? It might be the end for both of us. The public won't accept behavior like that from us."

"Personally I think Mary could buy Owen off," I said. "I think he wants money more than Mary."

"Beth wanted money more than me, too."

"Money is the solution," I said.

"Enough for marital troubles," he said. "What about you? You're about to become a big star, but do you have anybody to love you at night? Except for Goldfish, of course."

"I'm not in love with Sammy if that's what you mean," I said, a little too defensively.

"I know you're not," he said. "Who could be? Goldfish and I share one thing in common, however."

"What's that?"

"We're both Jewish."

I looked surprised. Back then, it always came as a bit of a surprise to meet someone Jewish, especially if you came from Kansas. Being a Jew was regarded as something exotic. "Does Mary know that?"

"She does indeed. But so far her mother doesn't know. And Mary's mother runs her life."

"I'm sure she'll accept that. You are, after all, viewed as the world's most desirable man."

He leaned forward and gently touched my hand. "Desirable enough to make you forget Goldfish for one memorable night?"

"If that's a proposition, I'm flattered," I said. "But the honeypot belongs only to Goldfish."

"All the guys in town are talking about your specialty," he said. "Tonight I want to sample that more than I want the other. Most guys do. If I want to fuck somebody, I'll fuck Mary or any number of show business hopefuls who think I'll give them a big break. Mary and I haven't been alone together for days. I need some relief before getting on that train tomorrow for New York. How about it?"

"The least a gal can do for the great Douglas Fairbanks," I said as he moved closer to me, taking me in his arms and sliding his tongue down my throat which I sucked as hungrily as if he'd been Rodolfo himself.

Breaking away after what seemed like ten minutes, he said, "Why don't I take a shower? Get all nice and fresh for you. Maybe then you'll agree to go around the world on me. I'd love that. Mary won't do that. She'll kiss and let me fuck her. But America's little sweetheart doesn't believe in blow-jobs, asshole eating, ball sucking, armpit slurping. All those good things, including toe-sucking. But I hear you've mastered these arts perfectly."

I stood up to get him fresh towels. I looked down at him in my most seductive *Vampira* method. "You've heard it right," I finally said.

As Doug sang in the shower, I heard the phone ringing. It could be anybody, perhaps Elmo Lincoln wanting to ram that big thing down my throat. Picking up the receiver, I heard the voice I'd been waiting for. It was Rodolfo. "Durango," he said. "I've been desperately trying to reach you."

"Where are you?"

"I'm with Norman Kerry," he said.

"What about your wife?" I asked, deliberately not concealing my jealousy.

"Things aren't going too well in that department," he said. "She's left Los Angeles. She's making a movie with Fatty Arbuckle. No competition for me there."

"That's wonderful. How's Norman?"

"He's great," he said. "He wants the three of us to get together. He's going to get me a part in his next film. I think I'll play his brother."

"You don't look like brothers."

"Maybe they'll rewrite the script. Make me

a half-brother or something. There's a role in it for you too."

"Do you mean that?" I asked. Although Lotte Lee was slated for stardom, Durango had received no film offers. I was thrilled.

"I also talked to my friend, Rod St. Just," I said. "That offer with Julian Eltinge is still on. If we work it right, we both can work with him."

"Making love with a female impersonator will not advance my screen career," he said.

"Does that mean you won't take the role?"

"I'll do it," he said. "I've done worse. Once when I was really desperate in New York, I even took it up the ass, and you know I'm a top. Except maybe sometimes."

"I don't know that from anything that's happened recently."

"It's all there for you, baby," he said, "I know you love it. I want to meet you tomorrow. We're going to make up for any time we've been away from each other."

"I need you, darling," I said. "Please come back to me. Your Durango loves you."

"I love you too," he said. "Very much in spite of Norman and Jean."

I thought it pointless to bring up my sister, Lotte Lee, at a time like this, much less Tallulah.

"Things are really starting to happen for me," he said. "I think Mae is also going to use me in one or two of her pictures. For old time's sake."

"That's wonderful," I said, just a little bit jealous at his getting all these offers of work. Of course, I knew he meant his old friend, Mae Murray, and not Mae Marsh.

Impulsively I pretended my career as Durango was moving ahead. "I've got my Mae too."

"What do you mean?" he asked abruptly as if challenged.

"I'm getting a part in the next Mae Marsh film. My sister, Lotte, is getting me a job arranged through Goldfish. I'm also becoming Lotte's agent, so things are looking up for both of us."

"I see," Rodolfo said. He didn't seem happy at my good fortune.

I'd lied about the Mae Marsh connection but I knew that Goldwyn employed her. After a hot blow-job, I could get my dear little Sammy to give Durango at least a minor part.

"I can see it now," Rodolfo said. "I'll be co-starring with Mae Murray in something and you'll open the same week co-starring with Mae Marsh."

"Something like that," I said as I heard the shower stop running. Douglas had obviously washed every crevice clean and would soon be ready for my tongue job. "I love you, darling," I whispered into the phone with Rodolfo.

"I'll be at the cottage around seven in the morning," he promised before ringing off with a loud kiss on the other end of the phone.

I heard Doug calling for me from the bedroom. Crooked cock or not, he was going to have one of the most memorable nights of his life. After all, he was the king of Hollywood, and temporarily Lotte Lee was going to be his queen. Licking my luscious cherry-red lips, redundantly painted a vivid scarlet, I headed to the backroom to sample the delights of this swashbuckling cavalier hero.

"D'Artagnan, here I come," I whispered under my breath, knowing what a sword-swallower I was.

*****

After one night with Douglas Fairbanks, I had fallen madly in love with him as Lotte Lee. I don't think I would have had the same fascination with him if I'd been Durango Jones. Douglas was strictly a man to be consumed by ladies. That curvature of his prick I'd noticed when I'd first seen him nude seemed hardly a problem once I got it in my mouth. If anything, it seemed to straighten out in my throat. There were men in Hollywood better hung than Doug, although he could guarantee at least seven and a half inches, in about the same range as Mary Pickford's brother-in-law, Tom Moore, and definitely an inch or so more than Mary's present husband, Owen Moore.

It'd been a beautiful night. Doug had given me such pleasure from his bronzed body.

As he'd moved toward me on the bed, I was still clothed. "You know the ground rules?" I'd said.

"Those ground rules are fine with me," he'd said. "Just show me a good time. I need it."

That was a request I'd been only too eager to fulfill.

He'd eased himself onto his back on the bed I sometimes shared with Rodolfo, assuming—quite accurately—that I'd do all the work. I'd cuddled close to him, kissing his neck and cheeks before tonguing him. I'd moved my lips over his face, and at one point our lips had met. He'd inserted his tongue in my mouth, and had found a devouring suction pump waiting to give him the pleasure he'd wanted. Tongue had met tongue, and the kissing had seemed to last forever.

As I'd kissed him, I had reached below to find him in his full glory. As my fingers fondled and searched his body in a journey of discovery, I knew he'd been needing relief. My tongue and lips had traveled lower on his body, tasting his nipples and enjoying the silken smoothness of his youthful stomach.

I'd found myself licking the endearing skin around his pubic hair. I'd reached below and grasped the curve of his buttocks. With his great athletic ability, he'd raised himself up and had given me complete access to his rosebud. I'd descended like a blood-sucking vampire, and he'd screamed into the night. I'd suspected that no one had ever gone there before. He'd lifted his hips to grant me more access, but I'd penetrated as far as I could go. I could almost feel his flesh prickling in tender excitement.

"Have me!" he'd shouted at me. "If there's a God in heaven, take me now." He'd been pleading. Arching his back desperately, he'd demanded relief as I'd descended on his prick, taking it down in one succulent gulp. The throbbing of his prick had been the most intense I'd ever known. His pleasure appeared to be so great that he'd been in actual pain seeking his relief. Such intensity could not hold for long, and within three minutes he'd exploded violently in my throat. His moans broke the stillness of the room, and he'd held my head onto him until long after he'd been satisfied. "I just can't let you go."

And he'd kept his promise. I'd fallen asleep with his deflated prick in my mouth. Whenever I'd awaken in the night, I'd tasted more of him, although he's seemed to sleep peacefully for the rest of the night. I'd wondered if he'd slept so well in the arms of Mary Pickford.

Before Doug had awakened, I'd slipped into the bathroom and emerged as Durango Jones after my hot shower. As Durango, I went into the kitchen and made the morning coffee before going back to the bedroom to wake him up to catch his early train.

"Durango," he said, sitting up abruptly as if awakened from a bad dream. "Where's Lotte?"

She had an early morning call," I said, "and told me to drive you down to the station."

He looked a bit surprised. "That's great. Thanks a million." Bounding out of bed stark naked, he turned to me and said, "We'll keep all this a secret, right?"

"My lips are sealed," I said, heading back to the kitchen. "I left clean towels for you, and there's a freshly brewed pot of coffee."

On the way to the station, Doug had promised me a part in his next picture. "It won't be a big part, but it'll get you on the screen," he'd said. "It's the least I can do for you."

Usually I would take no notice of such promises, but Doug seemed like a genuinely nice guy who meant what he said. And he did, after all, owe me a favor or two. Although I didn't expect my stardom to equal that of Lotte Lee, there appeared to be some hope that Durango would get on the screen after all. That reminded me of the ridiculous lie I'd told Rodolfo about appearing on the screen with Mae Marsh. I'd have to press that case with Goldwyn, especially when I had him in a good mood.

Before going back to the cottage, I stopped first at Antonio's house to find him fully nude and still asleep on top of his bed. In the night he'd kicked the sheets off. I had let myself in quietly, since Antonio, my "husband," had given me the key. He didn't have to go to the studio that day, or so he'd told me when I'd called last night.

The mysterious disappearance of Charlie had to be handled later in the day, but first I had to do my duty with Antonio, and such a pleasant job it was. As he lay sleeping, I descended on him, giving him a delicious wake-up call by a vigorous sucking. Within moments, he'd opened his eyes and comprehended what I was doing. Seeing it was me, he cried out, "Take all of me. I'm hot this morning, baby."

As always, he lived up to his billing. Nearly

two hours had gone by before Antonio let me out of bed. He did have to go to the bathroom for an emergency piss, but he was soon back and raring for action, demanding that I allow him to penetrate me. "Give me every inch," I commanded," and he'd done just that.

Over breakfast, Antonio shared some of his hopes and dreams with me. Even though he was my husband, I didn't really know him. "I used to work for the Gas and Light Company," he said, "all the while dreaming of a career on the stage. No one thought of movies in those days. Maude Adams was appearing back in Northampton where I lived. For Charles Frohman's company, they were rehearsing for *The Little Minister*. I'd always admired Maude Adams, and I was determined to make my debut with her. Believe it or not, the manager glared at me with one of those hard, cigar-in-the-mouth scrutinies and gave me a small part in the play. That night I went home and slept with the gods."

"With me, it was always films," I said. "I don't think I even thought of the stage for one moment."

"Times are different now. I stayed with the Frohman company through their next productions, *The Sister of Jose* and *Peter Pan*. By 1910 my theatrical engagements were over, and I returned to Europe."

"Did you go back to the stage?"

"I did when I got back from Europe filled with fresh zeal. I even did a repertoire of Shakespeare's plays. In summer I appeared in stock before heading for Broadway. Through an actress friend, Helen Ware, I obtained a part as a young Spanish count in *Two Women*. After Broadway we toured the country with that one. An old Englishman, Walter Edwin, told me my future was in motion pictures. I took his advice and headed west, applying for a movie job at Rex Studio. I made five dollars a day. I met D.W. Griffith who eventually made me a regular member of his stock company."

"That's when I heard of you," I said.

He leaned over and kissed me on the mouth, "And that's how it's going to happen for you too. You'll be a bigger star than I ever could be."

"You're too modest," I said. "Frankly, I think you're going to become the hottest stud in pictures."

"Maybe you'll never be an actor," he said.

A frown crossed my face. I didn't like hearing that. "And why not?"

"What if you become so successful as Lotte Lee's agent that you won't have time for films?"

"I never thought of that."

"Speaking of Lotte Lee, I have a big favor to ask of you," he said. "Believe it or not, two of my best friends are Jack Pickford and Tommy Meighan."

"Hollywood is a small world," I said. "I know Jack very well, and Tommy Meighan, of course, is slated to be one of Lotte's lovers in *Vampira*. What's the favor?"

"I'm a Spaniard, and as a Spaniard it's important that I appear to be very macho," he said. "Jack and Tommy don't know I'm a homosexual, and they always invite me out when I've got to take a woman. Do you think Lotte could be talked into being my date for the evening?"

"I'll check with her," I said. "I think Lotte would love to date Antonio Moreno. The publicity photographs would be sensational. Antonio and Lotte as a couple would get us both great press."

He leaned over to me, sticking out his tongue to taste my cherry-red lips. "One question. Is Lotte as beautiful as her brother, Durango Jones?"

"Even more so," I said, getting up with the intention of rushing out the door, even though he begged me to stay for more naughties in bed. But I just couldn't. I expected Rodolfo at the cottage this morning, and I had to memorize that damn scenario of *Vampira*.

As I was leaving, Antonio called me back for one more passionate kiss. He also informed me that we had to go see William Desmond Taylor. The director, it seemed, wanted to watch us make love to each other, but for his own pleasure, he wanted to direct!

*****

Arriving back at the cottage as Durango Jones, fresh from the arms of the man who one day would become an arch Valentino rival, I spotted Rodolfo's automobile in the driveway. At long last he'd returned. As I got out my key, I noted the front door slightly ajar, so I rushed in. There I confronted a nude Rodolfo on the sofa. He seemed to have emerged fresh from the shower.

At first neither of us spoke, as our eyes devoured each other. There was a magnetism between us that hadn't abated. I thought we were going to rape one another before even speaking. He rose from the sofa as I rushed toward him, losing myself in his athletic arms. Not tasting of its usual garlic, his breath was sweet and pure, the taste of his tongue so delectable I still remember the exact flavor and texture, even after the passage of decades.

There were no words spoken between us as he gently removed all of my clothing, my erection meeting his. He lowered me to the sofa. "We must not talk now," he whispered in my ear before kissing it and nibbling on it. "Only the words of love."

I moaned as I felt his dick about to enter me. "I do not want you to prepare for me," he said. "I want it natural."

My whole body quivered as he approached my ass. He did not hesitate for long. I tried to relax as he pushed into me, entering deep rather quickly, making my entire brain feel as if it were exploding. The heat of his body overpowered me and I became blurry.

The pain in my ass was intense. It felt like a hot sword cutting me apart. I yelled and cried out, but his lips covered mine, muffling my screams. Showing no sign of withdrawal, he attacked with hard, deep thrusts. I felt his full, thick balls bouncing against me, as the pain disappeared to be replaced by exquisite pleasure.

He rode me for ten—or was it fifteen?— minutes before one final fuckthrust that filled me completely with his cream. As he shot like volcanic lava, I responded in turn, shooting my load high and far, splattering my chest. He descended with his mouth, slurping up as much of my cum as he could. I was out of my mind with a delirious kind of joy. He collapsed on me, as I felt so exhausted I feared I would never walk again. He did not pull out of me, but licked my neck in the afterglow. "What a fool I am to be away from you for one minute," he said.

Within the hour he was back in the shower, this time with me. Afterward in the kitchen, he made a pot of coffee, not bothering to dress. I knew how much he liked to show off his finely sculptured body. It was like a perfect statue really, not one flaw on his whole torso.

"Why do you leave me?" I asked. "We're so good together. We could surely satisfy each other. There would be no need for others. No Norman Kerry. No Jean Acker."

"You don't understand, you little lovesick fool. I am not going to settle down and lead my life as a homosexual in this rose-covered cottage with a beautiful blond boy. I must experience a full life. That means lots of different experiences with lots of different people."

"By people I assume you mean women too."

"That too. I am not a homosexual. It's true I don't like sex with women that much. I prefer men. But I cannot eliminate women from my life. They are important to me even if they don't sexually fulfill me. Sometimes I like to lie with a woman with my head on her breasts. If she demands penetration, I can usually oblige but it is the maternal loving and the cuddling I really want."

His remarks made me a little bitter, and I became bitchy, a quality I detested in myself. "How do you find married life?"

He flashed his Italian anger at me, his eyes opening wide just as they would when he would one day co-star with Gloria Swanson in that bomb, *Beyond the Rocks*. "It's not a real marriage. It was an impulsive thing."

"I'm sure it's not a real marriage," I said, remembering the night I caught him knocking on Acker's door at the Hollywood Hotel. I was determined never to mention that night he'd spent with Lotte Lee—that is, not unless he brought it up.

"Jean refuses to see me," he said. "She's left town and is on location making a film with Fatty Arbuckle. I've written her a letter and I want you to drive out to her film site and give it to her."

"Why should I do that?"

He looked at me with an incredible intensity I had never seen in his eyes before. "Because you love me. Because I said for you to do it. Because you'd die a slow death if I cut you off from my love-making." With that pronouncement, he turned and headed for the bedroom. "I haven't slept in a long time. I'm very sleepy. When I wake up in a few hours, I want you to come into the bedroom. With our tongues we will explore every crevice of each other's bodies."

As I dressed, I heard the gentle snores of Rodolfo from the back bedroom. Instead of joining him, I had other missions to accomplish, namely a call to Francis X. Bushman. Although I still technically worked for him, I hadn't even called him in a long time. When I rang him up, he picked up the phone himself. "Durango," he said, "I've been calling the cottage frantically. I thought you'd died."

"I'm sorry I haven't checked in," I said apologetically. "As you know I've become my sister's agent. That has kept me very busy."

"Goldwyn has sent me the script of *Vampira,*" he said. "I love it. I thought I'd never get another film offer in this town. When can I meet Lotte Lee?".

"Soon," I promised. "Soon."

"That would be terrific," he said. "I'm dying to start shooting. I need a comeback picture."

"You'll be great in the part," I said. "It calls for a muscular Greek god. Like you."

"You flatter me," he said, "but you speak the truth at the same time."

"I'll make all the arrangements and will call you back to set up a convenient time for you."

"Perhaps Lotte will come to my home," he said.

"That could be arranged," I promised.

"I'll make sure Beverly has gone shopping or something. When I meet your sister, I prefer us to be alone."

"I understand."

Before ringing off, he said, "There is one more problem. Now that you're the bigtime agent for a bigtime star, I will still need a boy to make the deliveries."

"I'll arrange for my replacement."

"That would be very good," he said. He hesitated a long moment as if he had something difficult to tell me. "As you know, I'm quite a man with the ladies. But you're a great guy, and you've done me a lot of favors. I understand you—or at least your sister— helped me get this part in my comeback film."

"What are you saying?"

"I think we should get together—just the two of us. In strict privacy. For all your many kindnesses, you deserve a reward once in a while. Besides, you're the only person, male or female, in Hollywood who can swallow the whole thing. Talk to you real soon." With that, he put down the receiver.

Next, as Lotte Lee, I called Goldwyn to learn he was busy all afternoon. He apologized that we couldn't get together. "I know you need it, baby. But your Sammy has other rounds to make."

"With Mabel Normand?" I asked, pretending to be jealous.

"Not Mabel this time," he said. "Mae Marsh. She wants to pitch a film scenario to me."

"All right," I said. "I'll let you get away with it this one time, but you've got to make me a promise."

"Anything for you, my sweet baby with those cherry-red lips."

"If you shoot the film with Marsh, you've got to get a part in it for my brother, Durango Jones."

"That's easy to arrange," he said. "No problem at all. I thought you were going to ask something big like a raise."

"Oh, that," I said. "You pay me well."

"Good. That faggot, Taylor, is ready to shoot *Vampira.* I want you on the set early Thursday morning looking terrific."

"I will never have looked better," I promised him.

He sighed. "All the women are after Sammy. Not just Mae Marsh and Mabel, but Jane Cowl, Mary Garden, Maxine Elliott, Madge Kennedy. All the big names."

"You can add Lotte Lee to that roster," I said, hoping to flatter him and relieved I didn't have to face those randy four inches today.

Catching up on my phone calls, I called the Chief, W.R. Hearst himself, only to be told he was in an important meeting. His secretary said he'd been expecting my call and it was urgent that I drive out to the Santa Monica house by four o'clock that afternoon. I promised her faithfully I'd be there. After all, I had to do something to earn my five-hundred bucks a week, a hell of a lot more money than I was making as Lotte Lee for Goldwyn.

The next call was to Kono, and I dreaded it. When I finally got him on the phone, he appeared hysterical. "It's Charlie! You've got to come at once."

"I'll drive over right away," I said. "What's the matter?"

"I don't know. But a big scandal is coming. A big scandal. Charlie thinks his career is ruined. He's locked himself in his room threatening to kill himself. I'll call the police, right?"

"Hell, no! Don't do anything like that. There *could* be a big scandal." I scribbled a note for Rodolfo in case he woke up early. Fleeing the cottage, I steered the Locomobile toward Charlie's home and to whatever horror awaited me there.

*****

Arriving in Charlie's Locomobile at his home, I was confronted with a distraught Kono. "Charlie may have already killed himself. Maybe you're too late."

"Do you think he'll let me in?" I asked.

"He said it was very important that you come to his bedroom. Big, big trouble. I don't know what."

After several loud knocks on his bedroom door, Charlie demanded to know who I was.

It's Durango," I shouted through the thick door. "Let me in."

After a long moment, Charlie with great hesitation opened the door into the darkened room where black velvet curtains had been pulled to blot out the bright light of the California sunshine.

I took him in my arms as I had before. There was no passion now. I was one male friend offering comfort to another. He seemed smaller than I'd ever seen him before, drawing himself up in a bundle to be cuddled and protected by stronger arms. As I held him close, I felt his entire body quivering.

"You've got to tell me what's gone wrong?" I demanded, releasing him slightly.

At the very first sign of my pulling back, he clung to me even tighter. I felt his tears. In the dim light I couldn't make out his face but I just knew he'd been crying for hours.

He still didn't say anything but clung to me for what seemed like five minutes. Having found the comfort he sought, he slowly broke away from my arms and went over and sat in a far corner of the room at a small table where he sometimes had his morning coffee.

"It's all over for me now," he said. "My career, my hopes, my dreams—everything. I'm ruined. The public will no longer accept me when the scandal breaks."

"What God damn scandal?" I said, raising my voice. "You've got to tell me what happened so I'll know how to help you. Or else get help for you."

He reached out for me, grabbing my left arm as I came closer to him. His grip was so strong it hurt.

"I had a private meeting with Mary and Doug," he said. "We're planning big independent deals for the future. Everything was going splendidly. Before leaving the studio, Mary introduced me to a very young Mexican girl who had come north to break into films. Both Mary and Doug were really giving her the cold shoulder, but were stunned by her beauty. They said they have no roles for her, even though commenting how incredibly lovely she looked. If anything, I think Mary was a bit jealous."

"For God's sake, what happened?"

"Mary sort of brushed the girl off on me," he said. "More to get rid of her than for any other reason. I swear, she was as beautiful as Reatha Watson."

Memories of Reatha floated through my mind, and I knew what Charlie had done with this new young Mexican girl. My fear now was that he'd killed her.

"I ran away with this girl. Her name is Dolores. I took her to our secret place. Stella Dallas looked after us. Dolores was a virgin and bled a lot at first. But I had to have her. I made her do a lot of things to me, things I shouldn't have forced her to do."

"Such as?"

"I fucked her up the ass and muffled her screams while I did it." He reached for my arm again, gripping it as if demanding forgiveness. "There was more bleeding. Severe bleeding this time. She screamed for me to pull out but I got carried away. I couldn't stop. You must understand that."

"Where is the girl now?"

"She's still with Stella who's tending to her wounds."

"Maybe she'll be okay—a little sore, but okay."

"She's not going to die," he said. "She's too healthy for that. This Mexican spitfire is smart. She's demanding money. A lot of money. If I don't pay up, she's going to the press. She claims she'll tell them everything. I'll be ruined."

"You won't be ruined if you pay up," I said. "How much does she want?"

"I don't know. You're the only person I can trust. I want you to go there at once. Stella will let you in. You've got to talk to the girl. See what kind of demands she has. For all I know, she's from peasant stock. Maybe she doesn't know anything about money. Start off by offering her five-hundred dollars."

"Sounds a bit low to me."

Even in the darkness, I could see Charlie flashing anger at me. "Do you think I'm made of money? Now get your ass over there and negotiate a settlement."

Charlie wasn't very lovable to me at this point, but I took him in my arms and kissed him and told him I adored him. As I left the room, I heard him sobbing from the bed and, in spite of what he'd done, I felt sorry for him. Of course, I knew my sympathy should be for the young girl.

And it was, especially after I arrived at Charlie's hidden cottage. There I confronted Stella Dallas. Without her garish Hollywood Boulevard makeup, she looked like an old harridan often seen cleaning men's urinals.

Dispensing with any preliminary greeting, she ushered me at once into Charlie's bedroom. There in the soft glow of candlelight, a young girl lay on the bed. Even though her face had a deathly pallor, she looked like a stunning Hispanic beauty. Other than Reatha Watson, Dolores was the most beautiful young girl I'd ever seen. She looked to be no more than fifteen.

"She's lost a lot of blood," Stella said. "I think something is seriously wrong. Maybe internal bleeding."

At the sound of voices, Dolores opened her eyes. "The bastard," she said in heavily accented English. "I wish him dead. He'll pay for this."

I bent over her and felt her brow. She was feverish. "We will meet your demands," I promised. "You must never tell anyone."

"My lips will be sealed only if they're paid to be sealed," she said in a dry, wispy voice spoken as if on death's door.

I'll get a doctor," I said. "I'll say you were raped. We don't know by whom. Maybe several guys. We found you wandering alone down by the beach. You were bleeding heavily."

"Get me a doctor," she said, her voice growing fainter. "And money. I need a lot of gringo money for my silence. We call it the Yankee dollar." At that pronouncement, she seemed to fade away.

Checking her breathing, I asked Stella to stand by her bed while I went and called Dr. Hutchison. He was the only doctor I knew, and I also felt he'd be very discreet. After getting him on the phone, I told him my concocted story, and he promised to come at once when I gave him directions.

In less than an hour, Dr. Hutchison had driven to the cottage where he rushed into the bedroom. After the fainting spell, Dolores still hadn't come to. The doctor ripped off her dress and examined her vaginal region. "I think she's ruptured somewhere," he said. "She's got to get to a hospital. She might die."

The doctor and I carried her body to his car. He claimed he'd personally drive her to the nearest hospital and get her admitted. I told him I'd follow in my car.

"We don't have much time," Dr. Hutchison said. He paused only briefly at his car door. "Whose cottage is this?"

"It belongs to my mother," I said, motioning to an anxious Stella who stood in the doorway.

"Sorry I didn't get to talk to her," he said. He patted me on the head. "Tell her she's got a fine son."

While waiting at the hospital, I called Rodolfo waking him up. I claimed I had to meet with Goldwyn about the *Vampira* scenario and couldn't keep our late afternoon love-making fest, even though I desired it so much.

"It's okay," he said. "Mae Murray's got me

a dancing job at this after-hours club in West Los Angeles. "I won't be back in the cottage until about four this morning."

"I'll be there," I promised.

"I've written the letter to Jean," he said. "It's on the kitchen table. I didn't seal it. You can read it before delivering it to her the first of the week. You must promise to do this for me."

"Of course, if it's what you want."

"It's what I want." His voice had a fierce determination in it.

"I'll do it," I said, figuring I could at least renew my acquaintance with Fatty Arbuckle.

At that point Dr. Hutchison came down the corridor, telling me that Dolores may have to undergo surgery. He agreed to stay at the hospital for part of the night until he was assured she was well.

I gave him details about how I could be reached at the Hollywood Hotel and left a note for Dolores, promising I'd be at her bedside as soon as she was allowed visitors. With nervous anticipation, I hoped she wouldn't speak to anybody after regaining consciousness until I'd had a chance to negotiate with her.

After profusely thanking Dr. Hutchison, he said, "Give my regards to Mr. Reid. Tell him I hope my prescriptions for his pain are working."

"Beautifully," I said before thanking him again and eagerly shaking his hand once more. After that, I retreated to the cafeteria where I placed a call to Kono.

"Charlie let me in his room," he said. "He has this special powder he takes with milk when he can't sleep. Sometimes he can't sleep for days at a time. But this special powder." .

"Yeah, yeah," I said interrupting him. "Let me speak to him."

"No can do." After he's had this special powder, he won't be awake until morning."

"Tell him the problem is being handled," I said. "I'll see him in the morning." With that, I hung up and headed for the Locomobile.

Durango Jones, that cornfed teenage cutie from the fields of Kansas, had an appointment with the great William Randolph Hearst himself.

*****

It was hard for a boy of nineteen not to be intimidated by a baron like William Randolph Hearst. He had wealth beyond most kingdoms but appeared kindly, genuine, and natural with me. I'd heard stories, though, of his ruthlessness and shrewdness. Yet he also, at least in a social meeting, possessed a certain boyishness, especially with that high-pitched voice of his. A visit to him was like calling upon a king. There was a rumor back then that he "owned most of Mexico," or at least held deeds to vast tracts of land there.

Instead of offering me an alcoholic drink, he sent one of his staff members to fetch me a glass of cold milk. He obviously knew I must have grown up in Kansas.

Settling back on his terrace, away from the burning rays of the sun, he talked in a slow, relaxed manner. The tone was even confidential. "Everyone thinks I'm faithful to Marion, but that's not always the case." He had a certain twinkle in his eye. "I have a roving eye, the same eye that attracted me to showgirls in the first place. Once a man has that roving eye, he doesn't get rid of it easily. Even in my old age."

"You don't look old at all," I said, trying to flatter him. Actually he did look old. "You appear to have more vim and vigor than men half your age."

That remark seemed to impress him. He ordered a servant to put on some music. As he got up, I detected a charming gaucheness to him. To my utter surprise he began to dance a wild charleston that years from now would have rivaled that of Joan Crawford in *Our Dancing Daughters*.

He invited me to join him and I tried to keep up. Maria Jane didn't raise no dancer but I did my best, although I was hardly as skilled as he was. It was total madness. Here was I, Durango Jones, dancing the charleston with William Randolph Hearst on a late afternoon on a terrace in Santa Monica that overlooked the Pacific Ocean.

When the record died, W.R. collapsed into his chair, and I joined him, seemingly just as exhausted as he was.

"I'm also a wild tap-dancer," he said between breaths. "Do you want me to demonstrate my tap-dancing talents?"

"Better not," I said, sipping the cold milk a

servant had brought me.

As we talked more, I felt a terrible loneliness in the Chief, although I couldn't imagine why he'd be lonely. He could summon anybody to wherever he was, even presidents of the United States.

"I miss Marion," he said. "She's supposed to be in Florida with her sisters but I've not been able to get in touch with any of them."

"I hope nothing's wrong."

W.R. leaned over toward me. No more Mr. Nice Guy, his face flashed anger and his eyes narrowed. I was a bit afraid.

"There's plenty wrong," he said. "Where's Chaplin? I'm paying you five-hundred dollars a week and I want information. He's in Florida with Marion, or somewhere with Marion, isn't he?"

I gently placed the glass of milk on the table. It was showtime. I had to earn my five-hundred right then and there. "Charlie disappeared for days."

"I knew it." W.R. almost rose from his chair but leaned back, as if deciding it wasn't a good idea.

"Charlie's back at his home now," I said, "and he hasn't been with Marion. I don't know where she is but she wasn't with Charlie."

He leaned over toward me. "Where was Charlie?"

"My lips are supposed to be sealed, and I know you'll treat what I'm about to tell you in the strictest of confidence."

"You know I'll do that," he said. "Everything I know doesn't end up in my newspapers."

Very slowly, and not in possession of a lot of information, I related to W.R. the incident involving the mysterious "Delores," including her hospitalization.

"I can check on that," he said as a way of warning. "I can send Louella over there."

"I know that," I said. "What I'm telling is the absolute truth. Charlie could have killed her."

"I don't know why I like The Little Tramp so much," W.R. said. "He is, after all, a disgusting pervert. Some day he's going to get into big trouble. Maybe end up in jail."

"I worry about that all the time," I said. "How do you think it makes me feel? I'm very jealous. His running off with all these women is like a knife stabbing into my heart. You're jealous of Marion. I'm jealous of Charlie."

A look of total surprise came over his face. "Can men be jealous of each other the way a man and a woman can? I didn't think that possible."

"A man and a man can do almost anything a man and a woman can do except have children."

"You are certainly teaching me some of the finer points of homosexuality, although I don't know what I plan to do with all this information."

"Store it up," I said. "It might come in handy some time."

Later as the sun started to set, W.R. showed me some recent art acquisitions, including a painting by Sir Joshua Reynolds. He moved closer to me in the corridor, whispering in my ear. "Don't tell anybody but some of the pieces within my fabled collections are fakes. So far, no one has ever figured out the truth, and I've had art experts to dinner here."

"Your dinner parties are fabulous, or so I've heard," I said. "I read about them all the time."

"The time has come for you to stop reading about them and start attending."

"Do you mean that?"

"It's my house," he said. "Marion is famous for her dinner parties. As soon as she returns, I want you to have a standing invitation to attend any of our soirees. That invitation also goes for your sister, Lotte Lee. You'll meet everybody from foreign potentates to polo players, from movie stars to chorus boys. Marion has very eclectic tastes."

"I'd be thrilled," I said.

"You don't even have to call. Just show up on any night you desire—or every night—and join in the festivities."

"I don't know what to say."

"Say nothing—just show up."

He took me outside to enjoy the first ocean breezes of the evening. The sky was still bathed in a pinkish glow. "I'm building a castle north of here. I'm going to have my own zoo. There will be tigers, apes, birds, reptiles, lions, bears, even orangutans. I plan to stock it with ewes, elks, and buffaloes, certainly a lot of deer roaming about."

"That sounds fabulous. I can't wait to visit."

Back in the library W.R. cut down on the

milk train and actually requested a drink for us of the alcoholic type. That surprised me because I'd understood that he disapproved of drinking. At least he disapproved of Marion's drinking.

"It's the excess I dislike," he said. "I understand why a man might like a drink of wine every now and then. You can't live on milk alone. You note I said man. I definitely don't think a woman should drink. Women can't hold their liquor. There is no more disgusting sight in all the world than a drunk woman."

That was one point of view I didn't plan to challenge. Who was I to voice a different opinion around one of America's most fabled and informed editorial writers?

"If it's still possible, and if she isn't booked for the evening, I want to invite your sister, Miss Lee, to have dinner with me at eight o'clock tonight at the Alexandria Hotel."

"She'd be delighted. I'll go and call her right now. She has a suite at the Hollywood Hotel."

"Fine," he said, getting up. "I'll have a limousine pick her up say, around 8 o'clock, and take her over to the Alexandria. I always get the best table there."

As I headed for the library to make a call to nowhere, W.R. beckoned me to return. "I hope you don't mind. But I'm calling Louella. I'll get her to have Miss Lee and me photographed there. When it happens I'll make a big fuss and pretend to be angry. But I can assure you that our picture will be published in a few hundred newspapers tomorrow."

"Marion will be very jealous."

"Serves her right," he said, before heading out. "You're a good boy, Durango. But you've got to see me tap-dance next time." With that promise, he just faded from the terrace into that big house of his.

I had to get to the Hollywood Hotel, where I'd quickly transform myself into the devastating female vampire, Lotte Lee.

*****

Picked up right on time in a limousine sent by W.R., I checked my appearance one final time to reassure myself that I had lost all vestige of Durango Jones and had indeed become the enchanting, full-breasted Lotte Lee, a precursor to Marilyn Monroe. Surely Marilyn got her walk and that sexy voice from me. But how could she? *Vampira* had turned to dust before she started going to movies. Someone must have told her.

Before entering the dining room where I was told W.R. was waiting for me, I called a waiter aside. He had a serious case of acne and looked very effeminate. "You're Lotte Lee," he said. "Could I have an autograph?"

I autographed his menu, almost signing Durango before I came to my senses. "Could I request Ramon as the waiter tonight for Mr. Hearst's table?"

The waiter smiled smugly. "That gal is out on the town tonight. Her night off."

"I see," I said.

"Guess who that one is dating? She was picked up by none other than Antonio Moreno himself. The heartthrob and my all-time screen favorite."

"I see," I said again. Watching the waiter leave, I was both jealous and freed of any guilt. So my "husband" was dating Ramon, the handsome Hispanic waiter. My jealousy quickly turned to relief. Up to now I thought I had to rush about Los Angeles and Hollywood hysterically servicing all my beaus. Now I realized I could take my time.

Those beaus, including Rodolfo, weren't exactly languishing in their homes, waiting for me to come by. When I wasn't in their arms or in their beds—or both—they were fully occupied. Of that I was certain. Not only Rodolfo and Antonio, but John Gilbert, the Moore brothers, and most definitely Wallace Reid who did not conceal his many affairs, like Charlie himself. Thinking of Charlie, I remembered that poor girl Dolores and how I had to end the evening with W.R. in time to get to the hospital first thing in the morning.

At the table I spotted W.R. talking to Louis B. Mayer who was standing. The Chief rose to greet me and introduce me to Mayer who appraised my figure lasciviously.

"So, I get to meet Lotte Lee herself," Mayer said. "That scumbag, Goldfish, has really scored a knock-out punch with you. Up to now, I thought he hired only old ladies like Geraldine

Farrar and Pauline Frederick."

"I'm just a little teenage girl trying to make her way in wicked Los Angeles," I said, sounding like Marilyn Monroe on that yacht with Tony Curtis in *Some Like It Hot.*

"This town is filled with wolves," Mayer warned me.

"And you're looking at the biggest one of them all," W.R. said, before sitting down and gently brushing Mayer aside. "We'll talk about that deal some other time, L.B."

Mayer helped me into my seat, his hand running up my back caressingly. "When you've had it with Goldfish, I think I could make a deal with you. I could get you better roles and bigger distribution than Goldfish."

"That's very kind of you but right now I have a contract to fulfill, and being from Kansas I take contracts very seriously."

"Glad to hear that," Mayer said. "If you do, and I'm sure it's true, you'll be the only gal in Hollywood who does."

After both of us told Mayer good-bye, I turned all my blue-eyed attention to the Chief himself. He might be ruthless to some men in the newsroom, but with me he was a kind and gentle soul, almost intimidated and boyishly awkward at being in the presence of such a magnetic streak of sex like Lotte herself.

"I can't tell you how thrilled I am at meeting the great William Randolph Hearst himself," I said. "When Durango called me, I couldn't believe it. A big man like you wanting to see a little gal like me. A teenager, no less."

W.R. smiled at me and moved a bit closer in his seat toward me, or did I imagine that? "You're so worldly and everything," I said. "You've read all the books, I'm sure, and have so much knowledge about who runs the world. You know most of the world leaders, I'm sure. Back in Kansas, instead of reading, all I could do was run from the boys ever since I was twelve." I looked modestly down at my breasts. "You see, I started to fill out a bit even back then."

W.R. seemed to be breathing heavily. It took little formal education to tell he was a bit smitten with Lotte Lee.

Over dinner he talked of his dreams which seemed to be to acquire art, to become president of the United States, and to make Marion a movie star, bigger than Mary Pickford.

Suddenly, he turned to me and asked, "Do you turn somersaults?"

Taken aback, I didn't know what to say at first or why he was asking. "Once or twice as a kid. I was never very good at them."

"Marion does great somersaults. She says it peps her up before she goes on camera."

It was then I understood the talk. It wasn't really about somersaults. It was about Marion, whom he obviously missed. He didn't want to be dating other women but felt he had to pay Marion back for her involvement with Charlie and perhaps others. I knew nothing of her extramarital affairs. As I thought that to myself, I realized "extramarital" wasn't the exact word. Marion wasn't married to Hearst. Therefore, any affairs she had on the side could hardly be called extramarital. I guess "cheating" on W.R. would have to suffice.

Over dinner we grew more relaxed with each other, the conversation becoming less strained. W.R. placed his hand on my knee every now and then but it went no further. I, naturally, made no protest but let him have his feel.

At one point he complimented me profusely on my feminine beauty before launching into a nostalgic remembrance of the way things used to be in Hollywood just a few years back. "Until recently movie studios were armed camps," W.R. said. "When tough cowpokes weren't before the cameras, they often doubled as guards. They carried loaded six-guns and Winchesters."

"I don't understand," I said.

"A lot had to do with the patents war. Edison's Motion Picture Patents Company tried to collect a fee from everyone making movies. Thugs were hired to sabotage films. Often they'd start fires. These thugs even shot at producers and directors. At one point Cecil B. DeMille carried a sidearm for protection."

"That sounds like the wild and woolly west," I said. "Glad to see that things have become more civilized."

Over dessert W.R. informed me that Louella Parsons might join us. "Louella works for the *Telegraph,* but does private jobs for me. I've asked her to stop by our table if you don't mind. I want an item to appear about us. Also, when we leave the restaurant a photographer is going to take our picture."

"My God," I said, "I've got to check my makeup."

"Don't worry," he said. "The photographer is the best in the business. He'll make you look good. His name is Rod St. Just."

That caused a slight gasp from me but I said nothing.

As if on cue Louella paraded into the dining room, waving at W.R. and me. She headed directly for our table where W.R. introduced us. After telling me how wonderful I looked, she sat down and launched into an attack on California, claiming New York was her kind of town and she didn't know why anyone would want to live in Los Angeles. "It's still just a cowtown as far as I'm concerned," she said.

The talk turned to motion picture gossip writing, still a relatively new field, and "Lolly" defended it almost with violence. "We wouldn't know anything about Anthony and Cleopatra or Louis XVI and Madame Du Barry if historians hadn't gossiped about them."

I'm sure she meant Louis XV, not his descendant who faced the guillotine, and I'm certain Hearst caught her error but he said nothing. Throughout the rest of her gossipy life, historical facts and figures didn't matter to this woman who in time would become a monster but was still young enough on the night I met her to pass merely as overly aggressive.

"I want to interview you," she said to me. "I want to know all about your life. Especially the men in your life. I've heard stories."

"Please understand," I said, a little too defensively. "Mr. Hearst and I are just friends."

"Will Marion take it that way," she asked "when she reads my column?"

"I'm sure she will," I said. "My brother Durango Jones—he's my agent—is very friendly with Marion. They're great pals."

"Why don't you and Durango have dinner with me?" Lolly asked. "I could do a double interview."

"I'm not sure that's possible," I said. "But I'll try to arrange something."

I thought Lolly would never leave, and instinctively sensed in her a potential enemy. How right I was. In the decades ahead, we'd

become bitter rivals as gossip columnists. After paying the check, W.R. graciously escorted me toward the door where Rod St. Just waited. We pretended we didn't know each other. He snapped our picture several times, although W.R. staged a meek protest at the invasion of our privacy.

I was ushered into the back seat of W.R.'s limousine. On the way back to my hotel, he took my hand, holding it firmly. "Do you mind if I kiss you?" he whispered in my ear.

"It would thrill me."

He took me in his corpulent arms and planted a wet kiss on my lips but gave me no tongue action like John Gilbert.

"Forgive me for asking this," he said, "but I've heard stories."

I looked him directly in the eye. "Those stories are true."

"No one has ever done that to me before," he said. "It never came up with my first wife. I once asked Marion but she said it was disgusting."

"I'd be honored," I said, falling to my knees in the back of the limousine and ever so slowly unbuttoning his trousers. Before the last button had been unfastened by me, out popped five uncut inches of ruddy dick. Skinning him back, I plunged down on Mr. Hearst who moaned so loudly I felt he was having a heart attack. He obviously liked this kind of sex. The way I figured it, a man who was worth four-hundred million dollars should have every request satisfied.

In spite of his age, he was fast on the draw and had filled my mouth with newspaper baron cum before we arrived back at the Hollywood Hotel.

"It was a wonderful evening," he said with a smug look on his face.

"I enjoyed it too," I said. I leaned in close to him, kissing his ear. "Anytime you want a repeat performance, call me."

"I will," he promised. "Tell your wonderful brother, Durango, that a check will be waiting for him every week at the Hollywood Hotel until he changes his address."

"He'll be delighted to hear that."

"I'll see you at the next party Marion and I have," he said, before wishing me good night.

Rushing into the lobby, I found several

messages awaiting me, one from Samuel Goldwyn and another from Charlie himself, even another missile from Mabel Normand. Grabbing up my messages, I headed up the stairs. Before Rodolfo returned at four o'clock, I planned to pay a surprise visit on my "husband," Antonio Moreno. Perhaps I'd catch him in the act with Ramon.

At first I didn't think I'd be jealous upon leaning of Antonio's involvement with Ramon. But as the evening wore on, I couldn't think of much else. The concierge at the desk handed me a bouquet of violets. "These are from John Gilbert," he whispered to me. "He gave me a large tip and asked me to let him into your suite. I hope you don't mind." He winked at me. "After all, he is John Gilbert, and I don't know any lady in Hollywood who would turn him down."

"It's fine," I said. "No one turns down John Gilbert."

As I headed up the steps, I decided Antonio and Ramon would have to wait for later in the evening. With a load of cum from W.R. himself resting in my stomach, I checked my makeup before rushing upstairs into the arms of one of Hollywood's alltime heartthrobs.

In the light from my bedroom lamp, John Gilbert lay completely naked playing with his cock. Under his black curly hair, he smiled at me, inviting me over for a deep kiss. Sticking out my tongue, I descended on him, searching for his lips under his slightly crooked nose and black close-set eyes. He took me in his arms with a very strong grip and for the first time I noticed how big his ears were.

"I've been hearing talk about you, Jackie," I said. "The talk is that you're running after every gal in Hollywood."

"There's plenty of talk about me. How do you like this one—that I'm a third-rate actor produced by a second-rate pair of vaudevillians."

"That's pretty good," I said, smiling at him and kissing him again.

"How do you like this one? They say I like teenage girls and I arrange drinking and sex orgies."

"You've never invited me," I said as provocatively as I could, wondering if those rumors were true.

"Chaplin isn't the only one who likes teen-age gals."

"I'm a teen-age gal," I said.

"I know, baby, and your Jackie has such a nice surprise for you." He guided my hand to his hard-on. "Your Jackie has been getting plenty of ass lately. But what your Jackie hasn't had lately is a good around-the-world from his favorite gal."

As my tongue traveled his body, he moaned softly. I could feel the life within him. He seemed bursting with a desire to live and to play the romantic both on and off the screen. Although he was supposed to have had vast experience with countless women, his body had the freshness of a young boy.

After he'd exploded in my mouth, he jumped up and lit a cigarette before pouring himself a drink at the bar. He was filled with amusing plans for us. He was going to teach me how to play tennis, to drink the best champagne, to learn to tango and rhumba. Suddenly, he turned to me. "Was that the best semen you've ever tasted?"

"The very best," I said lying, thinking Tom Moore's was much sweeter.

"I knew it! I just knew it!" He seemed gleeful. "I've already become a legend in Hollywood for my sexual powers."

I wasn't exactly certain what the sweetness of his semen had to do with his sexual powers. To me, they seemed like two different assets.

He bent over and kissed me on the same cherry-red lips that had so recently tasted his genitalia. He was gone into the bathroom for a good fifteen minutes, emerging again fully dressed in a suit and tie. "I want to go to the clubs with you tonight. My car's parked outside."

"I just can't," I said. "I have to be at the studio first thing in the morning. A gal needs her beauty sleep."

At the door, he blew me a kiss. "That leaves Jack Gilbert wandering alone in a Hollywood night."

"If I know Jack Gilbert, I'm sure he'll find company very, very soon."

"That I will, my chéri," he said. He opened the door but shut it suddenly. "I'll have several wives in my life, but I have a proposition for you. When I see you again, I'm going to ask you to marry me. It will mean great publicity for both of us and will advance our careers incredibly." With that pronouncement, he was gone.

As I lay on my bed, the taste of John still in my mouth, a certain disillusionment came over me. As much as I enjoyed his body, I also didn't really care if I ever saw him again. He was a very shallow man, and in the years to come I couldn't understand what Garbo and Dietrich saw in this actor beyond his surface charm. I certainly didn't plan to become Mrs. John Gilbert. Getting together for a blow-job was one thing, but sustaining an identity as a woman within a marriage required quite a different talent.

Since only a part of me had been sexually satisfied, I was still very horny. The lusty Durango Jones side of me cried out for relief. Hurrying to the bathroom, I transformed myself into the Kansas cowpoke before heading downstairs and out into the night for an unexpected rendezvous with Antonio Moreno and that divine little Hispanic waiter, Ramon.

Chapter Seven

Since Antonio had given me the key to his home, I figured I wouldn't telephone and warn him of my impending arrival.

At Antonio's home, I very gently turned the key, letting myself into the darkened living room. As I expected, I heard sounds of passion coming from my husband's bedroom. Having experienced everything Antonio had to offer, I knew that Ramon was in for a good time. A night with Antonio would get Ramon loosened up for the fun and games tomorrow night at the home of Sessue Hayakawa.

Waiting to join in the action myself, I pulled off all my clothes in the living room before heading for the origins of the moaning. A dim light glowed in a far corner, casting an amber glow across the bedroom. At least I was learning what Antonio did on the nights he wasn't in my arms.

Ramon was on his side, enjoying a deep penetration from Antonio. Back then Ramon evoked what I would later remember as a combination of a Hispanic Luke Skywalker and a teenage Christopher Reeves. Even though I knew he was far from innocent, Ramon had a fresh-faced look to him that almost beckoned a man to top him. His complexion was silky smooth, and he had bright brown eyes, with a shock of glistening black hair falling over his right brow as he took the fierce pounding from Antonio. Ramon's cute little dimples cried out to be licked, and you wanted to brush those perfect white teeth with your tongue.

Jerking suddenly when he became aware of my presence, Antonio seemed hardly surprised to see me. It was almost as if he were anticipating my entrance into his bedroom. Ramon at first seemed to be in a state of panic at spotting a stranger enter the room, but Antonio assured him it was all right before resuming his very determined pounding of his perfect Mexican butt.

Ever the gay opportunist, I moved in on the other side of Ramon, rubbing my fingers across his soft, hairless skin. Lowering my head to his crotch, I let my tongue flick against the thick thrum of extra skin at the tip of his cock. I'm sure this cock had never entered a vagina. When I found the entry, I wormed myself inside, my tongue sliding inside the super-soft skin of a hot, throbbing cock that measured just under eight inches. I'm never wrong about these things. His hands reached out to clamp me in place but nothing could pry me off him now. Once I tasted him, I became wild, plunging deeper and deeper until I was burrowing my nose in his pubic hairs.

It was the most delightful cocktail ever made, even better than my beloved Rodolfo. His cock felt warm, safe, and snug in my mouth. With me attacking his front, and Antonio following up with the rear guard, Ramon had obviously entered a celestial paradise. He slammed his cock as far as it would go into my throat. His moans came from the depths of his soul, as he kept crying out for "Jesus" in Spanish. With a piercing scream, he exploded inside me, as I drank every drop down my gullet, demanding more.

Having experienced it myself, I could well imagine what Antonio's pulsing, quivering cockhead felt as it hammered into the velvety channel of this perfect boy. Antonio's hands caught huge fistfuls of Ramon's lovely black hair. Right before he exploded, Antonio became a ferocious lion, seemingly wanting to attack his victim and cause a bit of pain before erupting.

As I pulled off Ramon, leaving him a mass of liver, and Antonio yanked out abruptly, both men collapsed on the bed. I raised myself up, towering over them. "The night's not over yet," I said. "It won't be over until Durango has been completely satisfied."

A deep, British-accented voice was heard behind me. "Satisfaction guaranteed."

I whirled around to see William Desmond Taylor entering the room. Apparently, he too had a key. As he looked down at three young and beautiful men, he slowly began to undress in front of us.

Billy lived up to his promise. He'd taken turns pounding me and giving me blow-jobs. The passion was so intense that both Antonio and Ramon recovered quickly, joining in the fun. I was the object of all the sexual attention, and I felt I'd entered heaven. From lips to dicks, I tasted everybody, and all of these men got their fill of me but only for that evening. I knew each of them—together or singly—would be back for more when they'd recovered. After kissing each of them good-bye with promises to be with them soon, I was off into the night.

I decided to drive back to the cottage I shared with Rodolfo. Maybe he'd be back from his dancing gig if indeed that was what he was up to. Shortly before four o'clock, Rodolfo arrived, sweaty and exhausted from a night's work. He took me in his arms and gave me long, passionate kisses, telling me there might be others in his life, but none as important as me.

At that inappropriate moment, he read me the letter he'd written to his wife, Jean Acker, and practically got me to sign a commitment in blood that I'd deliver it to the set where she was making a film with Fatty Arbuckle.

"My Dear Jean,
I am at a complete loss to understand your
conduct toward me, as I cannot receive any
satisfactory explanation through
telephoning or seeing you. Since I cannot
force my presence upon you, I guess I'd
better give it up. I am always ready to furnish
you a home and all its comforts to the best
of my moderate means and ability, as well
as all the love and care of a husband for his
dear little wife. Please, dear Jean, darling,
come to your senses and give me an
opportunity to prove my sincere love and
eternal devotion to you. Your unhappy
loving husband,

Rodolfo"

When I came into the bedroom, Rodolfo had fallen asleep. His face was drawn as he snored lightly. In a way I thought it was just as well that he didn't expect a full night of passion from me. I was exhausted. He'd mentioned something about having a commitment to go horseback riding in the Hollywood Hills with somebody. He didn't say with whom. Later that morning I was to meet Wallace Reid and go on a picnic in those same Hollywood Hills with the star and Elizabeth Hutchison, along with Wally's weekly supply of morphine.

But, first, I had other things to do. Leaving the cottage, I positioned myself behind the wheel of the Locomobile and drove to Charlie's home. No servant was stirring. All was quiet. Softly I let myself in and climbed the stairs, pulling off all my clothes in the bathroom, letting myself into Charlie's bedroom. He was asleep but awoke when I came into the room.

"No sex," he said softly. "I just want you to hold me in your arms and tell me you love me in spite of everything."

"I love you," I said to him before he drifted back to sleep. I had hardly closed my eyes before I, too, fell almost into a coma.

When I woke up, it was mid-morning, and Charlie was in his library working on a film scenario.

I dreaded the morning, as I had to face the young Mexican beauty, Dolores, and learn of her blackmail demands.

*****

A bribe of twenty dollars to a nurse got me into Dolores's room before visiting hours. A minor operation—or so I was told—had been successful, and she was out of harm's way. Feeling more compassion for the young Mexican teenager than for Charlie, I decided on the spot not to let Charlie know that, even though I was his messenger and negotiator. Charlie could afford the money, and he should definitely pay up for the harm he'd caused. It served him right, or so I thought, for causing pain and suffering to this teenager. Besides, I was just a little bit jealous. Why was Charlie turning to this Mexican girl when he had me?

In the patient's hospital room, I was once again overcome by her beauty. Her appearance, even after surgery, evoked the stunning face of Reatha Watson. She was sitting up in bed, sipping some liquid through a straw.

"It's very good for Mr. Chaplin that you kept your promised appointment," she said.

"I told you that we were preparing to meet your demands, and I meant it."

"What is your name?" she asked.

"Durango Jones."

"That's amazing," she said, her eyes lighting up. "My family lived in Durango, Mexico, until Pancho Villa's rebels chased us out in 1909. I was only five years old."

"What's your name?"

"My full name is Lolita Dolores Martinez Asunsolo y Lopez Megrete."

"What an enchanting name," I said. "A bit long for a marquee if you want to become an actress."

"I can always shorten it, and how did you know I plan to become an actress?"

"You're very beautiful, and what beautiful girl doesn't want to become a screen actress?"

"Perhaps you're right." She sipped slowly from her straw, as if evaluating me. "Chaplin promised me a part in one of his movies. That's why I went with him in the first place. But he's such a liar. He had no intention of getting me a job."

"You've learned a valuable lesson. Never trust a man in the film industry."

"When I come back to Hollywood, and I will return to this town in spite of my first experience here, I'll heed that lesson. Most Americans distrust Mexicans. They view us as inferior. We're a past foe, a race apart. If we have dark skin, we must always play villains in movies. But I have porcelain skin. I can play many roles—a French woman, a Polynesian."

"I bet you'll be a big star one day."

She stiffened, sitting up archly in bed. "Let's cut this pleasant little conversation and get down to some serious negotiations. I am no Mexican peasant girl that Chaplin can buy off for a hundred dollars. My father was once a bank president. I know the value of money, especially American money. I am an aristocrat. When I was fourteen, I was presented at the Spanish court."

"How much money do you want?"

"Twenty-thousand dollars," she said. "That's not a lot to ask. The question comes down to this. Does Chaplin want to retain his career or give me twenty-thousand dollars? The choice is his."

"You'll go to the press?"

"I certainly will. Just as soon as I'm out of this hospital. I'll look great before the cameras. Perhaps launch my screen career prematurely."

I studied her face intently, finding a fierce determination there. "Make it twenty-five thousand, and we've got a deal."

Her eyes brightened, and she flashed the most wondrous smile at me. "You mean that? You really mean that? Unlike Chaplin, you're not lying?"

"The money will be delivered here today at three o'clock," I promised, without knowing if I could convince Charlie to pay up.

"With that much money, I can return to Mexico. I'll study acting there. I'll go to charm schools. I'll learn about grooming, glamour. When I return to Hollywood, I'll be a sensation."

"Good morning," I said. "I have to go and arrange for this money for you. Someone from Chaplin's bank will make the delivery."

"I want the gringo dollars in cash—no check."

"In cash," I said. At the door I stood with awkwardness and hesitation. I was very inexperienced in dealing with a blackmailer. "I'm sure you'll provide me with plenty of golden hours on the screen one day."

"You can count on it."

Shutting her door behind me, I hurried down the corridor practically bumping into Ramon. We were both shocked to see each other after the orgy of last night.

"What are you doing here?" I asked. "I hope you didn't get injured last night."

"I'm fine," he said. "But I got a call from my cousin. She's had an operation. I'm here to see her."

"Is her name Dolores?" I asked.

"Yes, how did you know?"

"I heard one of the nurses mention her," I said reaching gently for his arm. "Take care."

"We have a rendezvous tonight with Mr. Hayakawa."

"We certainly do," I said, wondering if I should keep that appointment or not.

"I hear someone very important is going to be there. A king or something."

"A king? We're to perform for royalty?"

"Something like that." He gave me a brief hug. "I'll see you later tonight. Right now I've got to see my cousin to see if she's okay." With that, he rushed away from me, heading down the corridor to the room where Dolores lay recovering from her surgery.

My negotiations with Dolores over with, I had some serious talking to do with Charlie, plus various other appointments throughout the day and night. Durango Jones (a.k.a. Lotte Lee) was one busy man/woman.

It would be years before I encountered Dolores again. By then, she was a film star and had shortened her name to Dolores Del Rio.

*****

In his tempestuous, headline-haunted life, Charlie faced many scandals. But he didn't have to face the latest scandal with Dolores if he'd agree to pay the twenty-five thousand dollars. The way he'd ranted and raved when I'd informed him of the amount of the blackmail made me think he equated twenty-five thousand with one-million dollars. He simply refused to pay even though it could mean the end of his career. There was something about this talented man who came from a poverty-ridden childhood that made it virtually impossible for

him to part with his hard-earned money.

At one point he'd barged from the bedroom, refusing to discuss money with me, even though as Charlie's negotiator I'd made a firm promise to Dolores to see that the money was delivered to her. I had no doubt that she'd go to the press with her sordid tale of sexual perversion if Charlie didn't pay up.

Later, as I sat on Charlie's patio having a drink, I didn't know what to do. I kept thinking how different Charlie was from his screen portrait. On screens around the world, including India and China, he was The Little Fellow. An underdog. Always mute, the Tramp was immortal in his shabby derby, worn-out shoes, and baggy clothes. With his brush mustache, he was a small man who carried himself with a jaunty walk, aided by his elegant bamboo walking stick. Somehow that kindness would eventually triumph over the meanness of the world.

The liquor blurred my mind but gave me time to come up with a solution. Since I didn't know what to do or say to Charlie at this point, my solution was to call W.R. himself. He already knew the story of what had happened to Dolores. Surely one of the world's most important men who dealt with millions of dollars a day would know how to handle a twenty-five thousand dollar blackmail. I got up from the patio and went into Charlie's library where I called the Chief. In a minute or so, one of his assistants had summoned him to the phone.

I told him of the blackmail demand and that Charlie refused to come up with the money.

"Well, well," he said. "This calls for some drastic action. In some cases like this, I have started to use Louella Parsons. She doesn't work for me officially—not yet at least, although one day she will—but I've found her very effective in cases like this."

"How could she help?"

"Believe it or not, one of the most gossipy women in this century can be very discreet when she's getting paid to shut her lip. I'm calling her, telling her the whole story, and sending her over to Charlie."

"Charlie will kill me."

"He won't know you're behind it. Louella can tell Charlie that if this little matter isn't hushed up, it'll be in her column the next day. I think that will make Charlie part with his money. What a tight-wad."

"What if he won't come through?"

"He will. Charlie's a cheapskate but not a stupid man. This little self-educated Cockney peasant will come around. Give me the name of the hospital. I will personally send the money over to this Dolores. I'll force Charlie to pay me back. Not in cash. I have another idea. I'll buy a twenty-five thousand dollar necklace for Marion and send the bill over to Charlie. He'll pay...or else."

"What does, 'or else,' mean?"

"Don't worry about that. Charlie will know what 'or else' means."

"Thank you for helping me."

"It's okay. The least I can do for you after arranging that rendezvous with your charming sister. By the way, have you spoken to her this morning?"

"She called me first thing," I said. "She's smitten with you. She thinks you're the greatest."

"I think she's very special too, and I want to see her again."

"She was hoping you'd say that. She adores you."

He chuckled to himself, as if he were mighty proud of his accomplishment in dating Lotte Lee. "Louella's on her way." With that prediction, he put down the receiver.

Within the hour, the ever dependable Louella arrived to do the dirty work. On this hot day, she was wearing the type of hat later made famous by her arch rival, Hedda Hopper.

I introduced myself to her as Durango Jones. She found my name amusing, suggesting I might have to change it if I wanted to be a serious actor. "Sounds too much like a rodeo star. Make mine a triple," she called over to me at Charlie's bar. "I need it in this heat."

Over drinks she spoke not of Charlie or the mysterious Dolores, but told me how enchanted she was to meet Lotte Lee. She asked me to set up an interview with my sister as soon as possible.

Louella was a world-class drinker. By the time her third triple had been downed, she had me laughing at the indiscreet gossip that flowed from her lips. "How well do you know Lotte's new director, William Desmond Taylor?" she asked, leaning toward me and breathing her drunken breath on me.

At first I feared that Louella was on to some scandal that involved Lotte Lee and Billy. "I don't know him very well," I said. "I just met him one time. We discussed *Vampira*, and he told me how eager he was to work with Lotte."

"Let me tell you where I was this morning," Louella said. "All Hollywood knows that William Taylor is screwing both Mabel Normand and Mary Miles Minter—and that's just for openers. I just came from an interview with Mary Miles Minter and her mother, Charlotte Shelby."

"Sounds like fun," I said.

"Anything but," Louella said, demanding another drink. "Don't be so stingy with the Scotch, honey. Charlie can afford it." Over another drink, she told me that Charlotte invited her over to "meet my golden child," who was one of that coterie of perennial ingénues being groomed as a second Mary Pickford. "I was told to bring my daughter, Harriet, to play with Mary."

"How did it go?" I asked.

"A disaster. Minter was a fully grown woman, and a lusty one I hear. Charlotte had dressed her up like a nine-year-old kid. She was all golden curls like Mary Pickford herself. Peroxided, I might add. Her little girl voice was completely fake. I'm sure she has a deep bitch-in-heat voice when she screams for Taylor to fuck her. She carried on with Harriet about dolls but my daughter hated it and couldn't wait for us to get the hell out."

"That's embarrassing."

"Children know," Louella said. "As soon as we'd left the apartment, Harriet said, 'Mary Miles Minter is no young girl. She's just pretending. She's fully grown. Don't take me there ever again.'"

Deep into her fourth drink, I confronted the fabled Louella that I was to encounter so frequently in the years ahead. She appeared daffy but on the trail of a story she could be as fierce as a bloodhound. "Tell Chaplin if he wants to continue to work in pictures, get his Cockney ass down those steps." She squinted her eyes as she leaned toward me. "And be quick about it."

*****

It'd been a strange night, the first hours spent comforting Charlie, who was completely unaware of the role I'd played in getting him to meet the demands made by Dolores. After a call to the hospital to learn that W.R. had delivered the money, I bid an *hasta la vista* to Dolores. She claimed she was returning to Mexico in a few days—a lot richer she could have added but didn't. It is almost inconceivable to imagine how much twenty-five thousand American dollars meant in Mexico at that time.

When Louella confronted Charlie that she knew all about the Dolores scandal and was prepared to reveal it to the readers of the *Telegraph*—and she could have added, the world—Charlie was quick to agree to put up the money. In this case he would stand good for the purchase of the twenty-five thousand dollar necklace for Marion Davies.

Again, Charlie didn't want sex that night but sought comfort in my arms. After Kono had delivered the special sleeping powder—whatever it was—Charlie soon passed out, and I was free for the rest of the evening.

That meant I could flee back to the cottage where, fortunately for me, Rodolfo was waiting. What he wasn't getting from his new wife, Jean Acker, he got from me. In fact, after that night with Rodolfo, if Jean Acker had appeared and had been willing to open her vagina to him, she wouldn't have aroused him. I was certain of that.

Awakening with a bounce and raring to face a new day, Rodolfo fixed breakfast and told me he was off to the stables for an early morning ride with a "friend." Since he didn't want to reveal the identity of this mysterious person, I didn't inquire further. After all, I didn't tell him that Wallace Reid was due to arrive at the cottage in just one hour so it was just as well that he was clearing out unless he wanted a three-way.

When Wally arrived, he didn't go directly to the cottage but stopped first at the home of Adela Rogers St. Johns where he called me to come over and join them for coffee. I hadn't seen Adela since our meeting with Reatha Watson.

On that long-ago morning, she regaled Wally and me with the claim that John Gilbert had proposed marriage to her. "He claims I'll have to wait one year until he sows more of his wild oats because he wants his marriage to me to be faithful."

"How unusual for a Hollywood husband," Wally said, grinning and cracking that famous screen smile of his.

I was very jealous on learning this bit of news but artfully concealed it. "Are you going to accept his offer?" I asked.

She turned to me and smiled. "Of course, I'll consider it. After all, Jack is the second handsomest man in Hollywood." She raised her coffee cup and looked over at beautiful Wally as if to acknowledge that he still held the title of most good-looking. "But there's a problem here."

"Do tell," I said, leaning forward and hoping to get as much information as I could.

"My deepest fear is that Jack will use up all his passion with other women and come home to me only when he wants someone to mother him." She frowned and her face indicated that she wanted to dismiss any further discussion of Jack.

I suspected she wanted to be Mrs. John Gilbert desperately but with her newspaperwoman's cunning, she knew the marriage would be a disaster from the first night.

"When can you arrange an interview with that gorgeous sister of yours?" Adela asked. "I called Goldfish and he said you could set it up, perhaps at his office or home. How about it?"

"I'll get on it right away," I promised. "After all, *Vampira* and Lotte herself need all the publicity they can get."

Wally smiled that adorable smile of his and finished the last of his coffee before asking me, "When do I get to meet her too?"

Before I could answer, Adela intervened. "Now stop it, Wally. You're already married to that wonderful Dorothy. You don't need to meet any more vamps than you already have."

"If Wally wants to meet Lotte, I think they should," I said, although I softened my voice so as not to offend Adela. "Only the other night she was telling me that Wallace Reid was the one star in Hollywood she wanted for her next picture."

"Hot damn!" he said, getting up, stretching his well-muscled arms, and telling Adela he had to leave. Both of us kissed her good-bye on the cheek and thanked her for the coffee before disappearing past the garbage cans to the cottage next door.

The door to the cottage was open. I remembered leaving it unlocked but not open. In those days—believe it or not—people in Los Angeles often didn't lock their doors, especially if they were merely going next door to have coffee with a neighbor.

Once out of hearing distance of Adela, he turned to me and grabbed my arm, rather desperately I thought. "Have you got it?"

"Elizabeth dropped it off this morning," I said. "I hid it in the kitchen."

"There's where I'm heading before any bedroom action," he said, trailing me into the kitchen. I paused only briefly as if sensing someone was in the house. I definitely felt a stranger had been here. Perhaps Elizabeth had come by checking to see when Wally and I would be ready for a picnic she'd planned in the Hollywood Hills. I had called her earlier that morning and told her we'd be there at ten o'clock. Inspired by Rodolfo, I planned to go to the same stables and rent horses for Wally and Elizabeth. Who could know? Perhaps we'd accidentally meet up with Rodolfo and his mysterious friend while riding in the same Hollywood Hills.

When Wally emerged from the bathroom, presumably after sampling some of the morphine, he was fully nude and what a glorious sight. I'd seen a lot more dicks since I'd last gone to bed with him, and the one hanging between his legs was still the prettiest of them all. Decades from now, after sampling one-million more cocks around the world, I'd still award Wally's prick with the coveted prize of most beautiful. There was just something about it. We'd have to bring back Michelangelo from his grave to sculpt a penis as pretty as the one attached to Wally.

I was eager to taste it, as I too was fully nude lying on the bed I shared with Rodolfo. Right now I wasn't thinking of Rodolfo but of Wally, and my own dick had risen to its full

glory. The sight of my nude body brought a lustful look to Wally's eye, and a sudden rising in his lower regions. By the time he descended on me, he was fully aroused. I tasted his sweet lips as I brushed his teeth with my tongue.

Wallace Reid was one of the world's great kissers, and that tongue and lip action must have lasted a good twenty minutes before he positioned himself for a delectable sixty-nine. A sixty-nine wasn't something I usually indulged in with my other lovers, but it was my favorite sex with Wally, something I looked forward to every week.

But this morning was different. After a few minutes of exquisite pleasure for me, he raised himself up and pulled me off him. He looked deeply into my eyes when his face was only an inch from mine. "I want you to fuck me."

Such an invitation was a dream to my ears. Durango Jones didn't get an offer to fuck many of his conquests, and I was only too eager to accept.

Even though I tried to be careful, I hurt him at first until he got used to it. I think the morphine eased the pain. At no point did he want me to stop, urging me to penetrate deeper and deeper. I don't know how long I was in him but he begged me to fuck him harder.

Thanks to all my early morning love-making with Rodolfo, and a nineteen-year-old's endurance, I knew I'd fully satisfied Wally before I headed inevitably for my own final satisfaction—an eruption deep within his body. The moment my release came, Wally exploded all over my belly as I descended with my cherry-red lips to taste his burgundy-colored mouth.

We lay like that for a long, lingering moment until I became concerned that we'd be late for our picnic date with Elizabeth. As we both got up, we heard a noise from under the bed. Peering down, I spotted a young woman. I reached in and pulled her out. She was hysterical.

When the woman rose to her feet, she stared at the nude Wally who soon retreated to the safety of the bathroom without saying a word to her. I reached for a sheet to cover my nudity.

The young woman was stunningly beautiful, in the class of Reatha Watson and Dolores. I don't think I had ever seen anything as exquisite as her. Bronze hair and great violet eyes topped the body of a seductive wood nymph. She was irresistibly lovely. If I desired women, I would have fallen madly in love with her myself.

"I guess I should be grateful to you," she said between sobs.

"What are you doing here?"

"For a year I've been following Wally everywhere, hoping to have an affair with him. I followed him to this cottage. But I've learned something today that has broken my heart. Wallace Reid is no man. He's a she-male." She headed for the living room, but stopped abruptly to look back, her beautiful features darkened with hatred and contempt. "You two are the most disgusting creatures I've ever known."

Locking the front door behind her, I retreated to the shower with Wally where we took turns soaping each other. He seemed to have little concern at this invasion of his privacy.

Over coffee Wally told me he knew who the young woman was. "The price you pay for stardom," he said. Her father was a five-star general in the U.S. Army, and her mother was one of the most noted hostesses in Washington. According to what he had learned, the young girl had run away from a fashionable boarding school and sold her jewelry to come west and pursue Wally. "She sent me a key to her apartment," he said. "She gave my valet a diamond ring worth thousands of dollars to admit her to my dressing room. Once there she tried everything in her power to get me to seduce her."

"She's very beautiful," I said. "Why didn't you? You are, after all, quite a man with the ladies."

"I thought she'd fall in love with me," he said. "Inevitably I'd have to leave her. I really feared if I got involved with her and then grew bored with her and dumped her, she'd kill herself. It was just an instinct."

"Without meaning to, you apparently have gotten rid of her for good. But aren't you worried she'll go to the press?"

"Newspapers don't print shit like that," he said. He rose to his feet to get dressed. "I'm ready to meet Elizabeth and go on that horseback ride you offered."

On this unsettling morning, I rented three horses for us at the stables after I bribed the stable boy to tell me the trail Rodolfo had taken. The boy had just arrived in Hollywood and hadn't seen but one movie in his life, so all he could reveal about Rodolfo's riding companion was, "She is female." I prayed it wouldn't be Jean Acker.

Around Wally, Elizabeth was completely tongue-tied and in awe of this famous screen star. She'd wanted desperately to meet him, but once in his presence could only gape at his male beauty. The pictures and even the films that still survive of Wally don't do him justice. In person he was a stunningly handsome man, filled with charm and grace. When he looked at you, his eyes seemed to drink you in, making you think that every word uttered by you was of monumental importance.

We came to a rest after but an hour's ride. Wally found a lovely green spot for our picnic. Since we didn't want to eat right away, we sat on a hill overlooking the sea. He told Elizabeth that he, too, had wanted to go into medicine, among other professions he'd thought about had he not become a film star. "I felt I had a natural bent for medicine," he said. "One time when our troupe was on location in the High Sierras, I set four broken fingers for one of the prop boys. I did a pretty good job of it, I must say myself. Later, when we returned to civilization, a Los Angeles surgeon examined the boy's hand and said I did a real professional job."

Since Wally knew Elizabeth and I were both aware of his use of morphine, he told us of the incidents that led up to his addiction to the drug. In the winter of 1913 he gave chase to a runaway horse on a Los Angeles boulevard. He said he was in a wild gallop when his own horse lost its footing on the pavement and fell. "He carried me with him and my left leg was pinned beneath my mount. I suffered a severe sprain of my left ankle and couldn't wear a shoe for several days. What I didn't know was that this injury would continue to bother me for the rest of my life."

After the good-tasting picnic Elizabeth had prepared for us, Wally told us of yet another injury he'd sustained only this year. "I was with an acting troupe in northern California. A train caboose jumped the tracks on a trestle bridge near Arctas and turned over. I ended up with a three-inch scalp wound which required six stitches to close. I was given morphine to ease the pain from the injury."

"There's no sign of the injury on your face," I said.

"The surgeons did a great job," he said, asking for another one of Elizabeth's deviled eggs.

That picture shot in northern California was a jinx," Wally said.

"I saw it three times," Elizabeth said, suddenly finding her voice. "*The Valley of the Giants,* and you appeared in it with Grace Darmond."

"She was the ingénue," he said. "A scene in the script called for us to ride down an incline in a logging car. While filming that scene, an iron block swung toward me and Grace. I just knew it would hit her. I threw myself directly in front of her. The iron block struck me in the head. I was very badly injured. The doctor up there prescribed morphine for my pain. I still suffer the most God awful migraines from that injury."

After eating all that food, both Elizabeth and Wally were sleepy and wanted to doze a bit in the sun. She had brought blankets which she lovingly spread out for Wally. I figured it might be wise to give them some time alone so I told them I'd be following a trail up in the hills for an hour or so and would join them later.

Fifteen minutes later I spotted two riderless horses. If I'd followed the trail like the stable boy said, this could only be Rodolfo and his mystery friend. Lured by their voices I came to a rocky plateau perched over a cliff. Their horses had been tied up on a grassy knoll, but human voices were coming from under an outcropping of land that provided a cozy nest overlooking the sea. I could stand right over Rodolfo and his friend without being detected, yet hear every world. I wasn't proud of myself for spying on him, but I was so curious—and so jealous—I did it anyway.

At the sound of a distinctive woman's voice, I knew immediately who Rodolfo's riding companion was.

It was Gloria Swanson.

In 1980 Ms. Swanson wrote her autobiography, *Swanson on Swanson.* In that book of lies and distortions, she claimed that she and Rodolfo were just good friends who related to each other in a professional way. That would be true if the profession was the world's oldest. The wicked bitch lied. Gloria and Rodolfo were lovers.

Up to now I had no idea that Rodolfo knew Swanson as intimately as he did. This was the first glimpse I'd had of his private life when he wasn't with me, other than his pounding on the door of his new bride and his picking up Tallulah in the hotel bar.

After she'd turned down the beautiful Wallace Reid, and had been known to reject Francis X. Bushman, I'd gotten the impression that the actress didn't like handsome men. She'd been married before to the ugly, big-nosed Wallace Beery. Frumpy Herbert K. Somborn was her second husband, and he looked like a Presbyterian deacon.

"Herbert works to distribute Clara Kimball Young Productions," I overheard Swanson telling Rodolfo. "She's looking for a handsome young man to appear opposite her in her latest film, *The Eyes of Youth.* I think I can get you the part. We've been invited for dinner at her house. I'm sure I can get her to extend the invitation to you."

"I'd be thrilled," he said. "I've always wanted to meet her, but she's not half the actress you are."

"Thanks, dear heart. You can bring your wife."

"That's hardly possible," he said. "She won't even speak to me."

"What's the horror's name?" Swanson asked. "Jean Acker, I think. A little nothing working in a nothing film with Fatty Arbuckle. Why don't you drop her? Pretend you never married her?"

"I'm very confused about the whole mess. At times I think I want her but at other times I want to run away from this sham of a marriage. I'm going to make one last try. I've written her a letter, and I have this friend, Durango Jones, who's going to deliver the letter to her."

"Durango Jones. That's a name I know. I met him once or twice through dreadful circumstances."

"I had no idea," he said. "He's the new agent for Lotte Lee. They're brother and sister."

"I've been hearing a lot about that one,"

Swanson said. "The talk is she's the whore of Goldfish. I'm also told that if any hunk in town unbuttons his fly, she'll fall down on her knees. The bitch must wear padded stockings."

"Those are just rumors," he said, defending Lotte's honor. "You know the filth spread in this town about everybody."

"I guess you're right," she said. "I shouldn't judge her hastily. I'm the victim of unfounded rumors too." There was a long pause. "If you know Miss Lee, I'll ask her to come with you to Clara's house for dinner. I'd like to meet her."

"That's a great idea," he said. "It would also distract Herbert. Throw him off the track, as you Americans say. If I show up with Lotte, he won't suspect that you and I are having an affair."

"Perfect. Throughout the evening you should pretend you're in love with Lotte. It won't make Clara jealous. You don't have to be a gigolo to get a part in her film. Clara's already tied up romantically."

"That's a relief to know."

"Oh, dear heart," Swanson said. There was a long pause. I assumed Rodolfo was kissing her. After a few minutes, her voice could be heard again. "I don't know why I married Herbert. There is no passion between us, the way there is between you and me. The forty-year-old bachelor I married is a good kisser, but there is no magic in bed."

"Maybe you were impressed with his position," he said. "He is, after all, the president of Equity Pictures."

"Perhaps," she said. "At least my marriage to Herbert is more understandable than your marriage to Jean Acker. A lesbian! Why would any red-blooded man want to marry a lesbian?"

"I can't answer that," he said. "I'm attracted to lesbians. Not as bed partners. I have you for that. But in some bonding of souls."

"That's rubbish," Swanson said in her dismissive way. "I think Acker is only toying with you. After all, she is Nazimova's girl. She probably is using you to make Nazimova jealous."

"I've thought that might be true," he said. "But since I did this crazy thing in marrying her, I've got to go through with it. It could destroy my career. I want to be a screen lover. But

what if the world learns that my new bride locked me out on our wedding night? No man— or woman for that matter—would pity me. They would hold me in contempt for not knocking down that door, barging in, and demanding my conjugal rights. If the true story got out, I'd be laughed at as a hilarious freak."

"I wouldn't lock you out if you married me."

"Are you serious?" he asked, his voice rising. "You would marry me after you divorce Herbert?"

"Yes, yes, dear heart. I want to be the second Mrs. Rodolfo Valentino. I'm ready to give marriage a final try."

"I can't believe that this is happening to me. A poor, struggling immigrant from Italy. Married to the great Gloria Swanson. It sounds like a dream."

"Dreams come true," she said. "At least in Hollywood."

Frankly—and this I was to learn more as the years went by—actors such as Swanson and Valentino often got carried away with the sound of their own voices. This pair was practically writing a scenario for a future script. They were speaking of one day appearing on the silver screen together as co-stars. I wasn't certain if after this day passed each would even remember talk of marriage. Besides, Rodolfo already had a wife, and as time would tell, getting rid of her would be no easy task.

When their voices died down, I could hear only a stray sound or two. I knew they were removing their clothing, and that Rodolfo planned to make love to the little midget.

As I walked back through a ravine to mount my horse, I felt that someone else was nearby spying on the lovers. I pretended to ride away but tied up my horse when I rounded a bend and slipped back on foot.

Concealing myself behind a tree, I spotted a man dressed in black standing in the very same spot where I'd recently spied on Swanson and Rodolfo. Other than voyeuristic pleasure, I wondered why he too was spying on the lovebirds. A blackmailer perhaps.

He seemed relatively harmless, and I was overdue at the picnic with Elizabeth and Wally. Upon leaving I made a noise when I stepped on a broken twig. The spy in black turned around, and I got a good look at his face, but I don't think he spotted me. He turned back to the ravine and to his eavesdropping on Swanson and Rodolfo.

It was only when I'd mounted my horse again and headed back to Wally and Elizabeth that I remembered where I'd seen that face before. It was none other than the German baron who lived in that fake castle across from the cafe where I often went.

As I rode back to my picnic site, I was deeply troubled. What possible motive could the baron have for spying on Gloria Swanson and Rodolfo Valentino?

*****

Later that night I found myself stripped nude with Ramon Samaniegos, whom I already knew intimately so there was no shock or embarrassment when Sessue Hayakawa escorted us to his private salon and ordered us to disrobe.

Drinks and marijuana were provided for us, and we were told to partake freely so that "you will be relaxed." Sharing a marijuana cigarette with Ramon, I asked about his cousin, Dolores.

"She's fine," he said. "She wouldn't tell me what happened to her, but she blackmailed some very important man into giving her a great fortune."

Choosing not to reveal to Ramon my own involvement in this blackmail, I kept quiet. For a long time we said nothing, just enjoying the effect of the drug. I felt totally comfortable being nude with this beautiful young Mexican man, and I wished I could spend the evening alone with him without Sessue overseeing the action. The Japanese actor told us that we'd be entertaining a very important guest.

The marijuana put Ramon at ease, and he talked of his childhood in Mexico. "Your name really surprised me," he said. "Durango. That's the town where Dolores and I came from in Mexico. I was the second son of a rich dentist." He said that rather grandly. "The Samaniegos family actually came from Greece centuries ago. Eventually we migrated to Spain and in time sailed to Mexico with the great Cortez and his conquistadors."

I thought that assertion a bit fanciful but said nothing. It was obvious that Ramon, in spite of his present circumstances, was filled with great pride.

"I was forced out of Mexico by Pancho Villa's henchmen," he said. "We made it across the border and stayed for a while with relatives in El Paso. But I decided to pursue my dream as an actor and came up to Los Angeles."

Wearing only a loincloth, a beefy Japanese masseur entered the room, ordering Ramon to a marble platform in the far corner. Ramon did as he was instructed and was told to lie down on his back. He reclined with his cock at a 45° angle.

As the masseur bent over Ramon, he reached for some special oils on the shelf. Very gingerly he applied the oil to Ramon's body, rubbing it deep into his skin. Every inch of his body, even his face, was covered in these oils. Only his cock and balls were spared.

Ramon was told to turn over so that the oils could be applied to his buttocks and back. From the shelf the masseur removed a small bottle whose liquid was applied to Ramon's rosebud. That gave me a preview of what we could expect later in the evening. The brand of Sessue was clearly visible on Ramon's butt.

After Ramon was oiled, the masseur ordered me to come and lie on the same platform while Ramon rested in the corner. At first I expected the marble to be cold but was surprised to find the block warm. The platform must have been heated from somewhere below. I too lay on my back to receive the scented oil treatment.

When the masseur had finished, he didn't tell me to turn over on my stomach. He merely grabbed me and flipped me over like a pancake. I too received that special ointment for my rosebud. With my eyes closed, I felt manly hands all over my body, spreading the fragrant oil. The masseur seemed to reach pressure points in my body that caused me to relax so much I felt myself falling asleep.

After the oiling, we were given red silk robes to wear and then directed into the same room where Rodolfo and I had watched in horror as Ramon was branded. After a few minutes Sessue came into the room and asked us to drop our robes.

The Japanese actor then kissed each of our mouths, inserting his tongue, before falling down on his knees to plant tiny little birdlike kisses on each of our genitals. Straightening up, he told us we were to entertain one of the most important guests he'd ever invited to visit him in Hollywood.

He revealed to us that Prince Prajadhipok himself would soon be entering the room for us to "amuse him." The name meant nothing to me, and I'm sure Ramon was equally dumbfounded. It turned out that Prajadhipok was the brother of King Vajiravudh of Siam.

When the little prince entered the room, I was startled by how ugly he was. Decades later I was enthralled by Yul Brunner in *The King and I*. Instead of the dashing and handsome Yul, with his eight-inch uncut cock, I got this little midget.

We had been instructed to bow low before Prajadhipok, our noses touching the floor. Instead of feeling subservient, I treated the whole episode as a joke—and so did Ramon. Sessue ordered Ramon and I to perform a hot sixty-nine on a luxurious silk-covered palette in the center of the floor.

Both Ramon and I rose to the occasion and were enjoying our own show so much we temporarily forgot about Prajadhipok and Sessue. A few minutes later we became aware of the actor and his royal friend who were disrobing. Easing up from Ramon's cock, I looked up to see Prajadhipok fully erect moving toward me to enter me. Sessue had elected to bestow his honors upon Ramon.

When I said fully erect, I guess I meant it. Prajadhipok's penis extended no more than two and a half inches from his body. When soft, it must have virtually disappeared into a large mass of pubic hair. He grabbed my neck and forced me down on Ramon again, as he maneuvered himself on his side and without formality penetrated me.

As he proceeded to hump me, it was the worst fuck of my life. Sessue, whose dick was only slightly larger than that of Prajadhipok, sodomized Ramon. Because Prajadhipok's cock was so small, it was like he was constantly jabbing at my rosebud. It was like getting entered time and time again without any real penetration. His jabbing motions were painful, and I prayed that he would climax soon. God heard my prayers.

Soon cum from the royal house of Siam was spewing out, and Prajadhipok withdrew, giving me some relief although my ass was still painfully sore. A minute later, Sessue rewarded Ramon with his seed.

Prajadhipok, still nude, his little cock deflated, stood over Ramon and me and leaned over and whispered something to Sessue. Sessue smiled and rang a bell, signaling for the same masseur who'd oiled us.

Sessue bent over Ramon and me and whispered, "His Royal Highness wants to drink from both of you. But in his country it is against tradition for a royal prince to work to bring one to climax. Therefore my masseur will do it."

The masseur cracked his fingers before descending on Ramon. He took hold of Ramon's young balls with his oily left hand, and with his right grasped Ramon's cock, bringing it to a full erection. Perhaps he knew some mysterious sex secret of the Orient but in moments he had Ramon fully erect and moaning. Ramon suddenly cried out, spewing his cum. Like a hungry warrior, Prajadhipok then descended on Ramon, pushing the masseur away and licking and tasting every drop Ramon had spewed out.

As Ramon lay on the pallet gasping for breath, the masseur descended on me, repeating the same action. When I erupted, Prajadhipok also descended on me as if I were his last supper. After his taste treat, the prince rose, smacking his lips.

Putting on their robes, Sessue disappeared into another part of the house for some opium smoking with Prajadhipok.

The masseur allowed Ramon and me to put back on our robes. We were directed into a hot steam room where two tiny little Japanese boys, each nude, took off our robes and asked us to get into a pink marble tub together. Surrounding the tub were various fragrances and scented oils.

Each of the young men soaped our bodies, massaging our shoulders and even washing our hair. They were both experts. A bath from them was like ecstasy as the hot steaming water lulled us into a peaceful trance, induced no doubt by the rich scent of the oils.

My young man even massaged my tits, touching each one separately with a feathery technique I'd never known before. Herbs were placed in the bath water, and I closed my eyes, as did Ramon, enjoying the sensual pleasure of the greatest bath each of us had ever had.

My young man gave my head a long and deep massage, making me relax totally in the foggy room. Afterward, pure cleansing spring water was poured over our bodies. As we left the tub, the young men bowed before us, rubbing our bodies dry with large but soft towels. When they'd finished drying us, each attendant knelt before us, skinning back our cockheads and planting tiny kisses there. The masseur brought our street clothes, paid us for the night's services, and then directed us to the door where Sessue's purple limousine waited for us.

In the back seat we giggled like girls, ditching our dates for the night. Neither one of us had ever heard of Prajadhipok.

Years later in 1925, we learned a lot more about this royal prince when he became King Rama VII, replacing his elder brother. Prajadhipok, as Rama VII, became the last absolute monarch of Siam until various revolutions forced him to abdicate on March 2, 1935, after which time he continued to live in England until he died at the age of 48 on May 30, 1941. Neither Ramon nor I ever saw him again, which was just as well as far as I was concerned. One fuck from Prajadhipok was enough to last me a lifetime.

Ramon asked to be taken back to the Alexandria Hotel where he had a small room on the top floor. "I'd like to invite you to my room for the night," he said, "because I really like getting fucked by you. But I'm a bit of a whore and I have a fantastic date for tonight."

"Someone you met at the hotel?"

"That's right. My dream man is always at the hotel. He's an actor like me and very exotic. I love Antonio Moreno and I think he's really hot. But this one is even hotter."

A strange sensation came over me. "Is your dreamboat Italian, by any chance?"

Ramon's eyes sparkled as he stared at me in back of the limousine. "As a matter of fact, he is. I'm surprised you knew that. His name is Rodolfo Valentino, and I can't wait to strip him down for action."

*****

Back at the cottage, I waited for Rodolfo to come home from his night with Ramon. Rodolfo stumbled in at three o'clock. After a day spent fucking both Gloria Swanson and Ramon, I didn't think he'd have anything left for me but he did.

He was in a loving mood, and I accepted him in my arms, trying to blot out the other lovers he'd known that day. When he told me he wanted to spend all day sleeping, I left him snoring in bed and headed for Antonio Moreno's house.

Instead of getting him alone in bed, Antonio called William Desmond Taylor for a Sunday morning three-way. Once both men had been satisfied and were sleeping it off, I left a note that I had to see Goldwyn. Actually I had a more intriguing rendezvous in mind.

I drove to the Hollywood Hotel and some thirty minutes later I was applying my final makeup as Lotte Lee when the phone rang. It was Tom Ince whom I hadn't seen since meeting him at Fruitfly. He told me that his Saturday afternoon surprise party was on, and that John Gilbert wanted to drop by to pick me up if I didn't mind.

"I'd be delighted," I told Tom. "Jack and I are old friends."

John arrived at my hotel suite within the hour. Since we were late for Tom's party, he unbuttoned his fly and pulled out his cock. "I need relief real bad," he said. "Sorry we don't have time for kissing and all that good stuff." Since he was hardening rapidly, I fell on my knees before him. After ten minutes of getting worked over by my suction pump mouth, he exploded in my throat. Following a quick check of my makeup and some emergency repairs, we were off to Ince's party.

"Have you ever been to one of Ince's parties, or heard of them?" John asked from behind the wheel of his car.

"I know nothing of them."

"You're going to be in for a few shockers

today. This afternoon is devoted to cowboys."

Beginning in 1915 John had first appeared on the screen as an extra in films for Ince-Triangle pictures, so he and Ince were old buddies. To my surprise I learned that some of these films had both starred and been directed by William S. Hart. These included *Hell's Hinges* and *The Apostle of Vengeance.*

On the way to Ince's home, John told me how he got his start at "Inceville," which he said was like a fantasy of moviemaking on eighteen-thousand acres along the shore above Santa Monica. "I felt I'd stumbled into a dream, with Babylonian temples, a Scottish manor house, battlefields, even a Japanese fishing village. Sets of every imaginable description greeted me. At the pier Ince had a whole navy—Chinese junks, gondolas, sailboats, ratty old schooners, pirate ships, an Arab dhow—you name it."

"I'm really excited by the prospect of working with this guy one day," I said. "I hear he's terrific. He seems to be doing for films what Henry Ford is doing for the automobile."

Ince lived in the sprawling Spanish-style hacienda, Días Doradas, in Benedict Canyon. It was in this showplace that he invited the top male stars in Hollywood, along with the women, most often starlets, to entertain them.

Tom Ince greeted me like a long lost girlfriend. Right in front of John, he took me in his arms and gave me a lingering kiss, tongue and all. John didn't seem to mind turning me over to Ince. In moments John had headed to the swimming pool where he was to emerge later in a form-fitting bathing suit with a top. A cheap trashy blonde starlet had caught this roving Romeo's eye, and I knew I needn't bother with him for the rest of the day.

Ince offered me a drink, which he commanded his bartender to serve me. He told me he'd join me later for "fun and games," but right now he had to match up his guests with each other. For some unknown reason, he took me to a far corner of the living room where he left me alone with William S. Hart, the king of the cowboys.

Of all the men in Hollywood I'd dreamed of meeting, William S. Hart was the last on my list. One of the original screen cowboys, the most western of all western stars, was actually born in Newburg, New York, in 1870. That would make him nearly 50 years old, a bit long in the tooth for me even though he was still turning out movies, his most recent being *Poppy Girl's Husband, Money Corral, Wagon Tracks,* and *John Petticoats.*

"Two-Gun Bill," as he was called, was a storybook hero to most of the kids of America, even though he sometimes played a villain. Although his westerns reflected a Victorian moralizing, W.S. Hart had a lusty side to him. We had hardly begun our chat when he placed a firm western grip on my knee which was clad in silk stockings. Perhaps my reputation had preceded me.

Although I didn't know it on that long-ago afternoon, I was meeting another screen legend like Theda Bara whose career was winding down. In just a short time Hart's career would be over—not just because of his age but because of bad publicity surrounding a dismissed paternity suit. Before that happened, William S. Hart was the last man I expected to see driven from the screen by a sex scandal.

A flamboyantly dressed cowboy moved toward us, hoping to join us, but Hart motioned for him to leave us alone. "I can't stand that asshole," he said. "That's Tom Mix. If a cowboy dressed like he did in the Old West, we'd strip off his clothes, sodomize him, and kick him out of our camp."

Contrary to Hart's opinion, I found Tom Mix rather dashing and very handsome. Little did I know at the time that Tom Mix was about to dethrone Hart as the major western cowboy of the silver screen.

I studied Hart's face closely as he talked to me, having seen it so many times on the screen, where he often appeared in horse operas as an evangelical type of westerner—sometimes even as a priest.

"It's funny I ended up as a cowboy even though I grew up with Indians and trail herders when I went west," he said. "Did you know that I spent twenty years on the Broadway stage as a Shakespearean actor?"

"I would love to have seen you on the stage," I said, not really meaning lit.

His grip on my knee tightened. "You didn't come here to talk about acting, did you?"

I leaned over and kissed him lightly on the

cheek. "If you must know the truth, Mr. Hart, I came here to see just how virile all these screen cowboys really are."

He leaned in closer to me. "Ever the fine director, Tom Ince directed you to the right man. That is, if you like your men rugged. He also told me about your specialty. No woman has ever done that to me before."

"Could I be the first?"

It was evident that this cowboy was getting excited. "Can we go upstairs together?" he asked politely. "Tom told me you really like to do it."

I stuck out my tongue provocatively, tracing it around my cherry-red lips. "Ready for action, Mr. Hart?"

In one of the upstairs bedrooms, this screen hero appeared nervous as hell and obviously self-conscious. "What should I do?" he asked.

"Strip down," I said. As he pulled off his clothes in front of me, I took in his well-built figure although he had the beginning of a paunch. His body was hairless, except for a patch in the middle of his chest. When he'd peeled down to all but his shorts, he looked helplessly at me, asking, "What now?"

"Let me," I said, moving toward him. I ran my hands down his back to the waistband of his shorts. I kissed him on the neck before peeling his underwear down. As he kissed me, I firmly gripped his buns. He gave me no tongue as was the case with most of my men.

After he stepped out of his shorts, I ordered him to lie down on the soft bed. He looked so vulnerable lying there with his dick growing hard. When I saw it rise to its full length of five and a half inches, I knew I could show him a good time without stretching my jaw muscles.

I ran my fingers over his stomach and thighs, momentarily skirting his excited cock. Each time my hand moved toward it, his dick jerked in anticipation as if it were ready to cum.

My fingers wandered to his nut sac where two very average sized orbs greeted me. He moaned as I squeezed them. Enough for such foreplay. I descended at once on his cock, plunging all the way down on it until my nose was buried in his pubic hair. Since he wasn't very big, this wasn't hard to do. He tried to drive his cock in even deeper than he was, but there was no meat left to work with.

I applied my most powerful suction to him. He cried out like a cowboy at round-up and exploded with a violence within my mouth.

Talk about fast on the draw. He must have spent no more than a minute in my mouth. Once he erupted, his cock deflated at once, and I knew there would be no second bout.

In his post-orgasm state, he appeared deeply embarrassed at what we'd done and reached to cover his nakedness with a sheet.

I excused myself, heading for the bathroom. After reapplying my makeup, I came out and wandered back downstairs, only to learn from Tom Ince that William S. Hart had left the party.

I was never to see him again, except on the screen.

*****

Tom Ince wanted me to circulate and meet some legendary screen cowboys, but so far I wasn't faring well. William S. Hart was not my kind of cowpoke. As I sat talking on the sofa in the Ince living room to "Broncho Billy" Anderson, I felt he wasn't going to be my dreamboat either.

Even more than Hart, Broncho Billy was the father of the movie cowboy, the first western star I'd ever seen on the screen. I was surprised when he told me he got his start posing nude for photographers. A nude Broncho Billy wasn't what I'd seen on the screen at the Patee Theater in Lawrence, as the cowboy enthralled audiences with such films as *Patricia of the Plains, A Western Woman's Way, Shanghaied, Naked Hands,* and *The Red Riding Hood of the Hills.* Most films included Broncho Billy in the title, including *Broncho Billy's Greaser Deputy.*

The Arkansas-born Billy was in his mid-thirties when I first met him, considerably younger than William S. Hart. He said he'd retired from films in 1916 when he went to New York and purchased the Longacre Theatre where he produced plays. "Most of them bombed," he told me. "So I'm back in Hollywood producing a series of shorts with Stan Laurel. Things aren't going well now that I'm back."

Decades later I remembered sitting in the audience at the Academy Awards when it was announced that Broncho Billy was getting an honorary Oscar for his contribution to motion pictures. The year was 1957, and I was delighted to note that in 1965 he came out of retirement for a cameo role in the *Bounty Killer.*

Back on that long ago afternoon at Ince's party, Broncho Billy, a very short man, wore a suit and tie and looked as if he had just returned from church. He was ruggedly handsome with piercing eyes and a bad haircut, but he was far from pretty.

"I got my first job in *The Great Train Robbery* in 1903," he said, "as a bit player. I had told the director I was an expert horseman. Up to then all I'd done was pose as a cowboy for a magazine cover. When I mounted the horse from the wrong side and was thrown off, I was reduced to playing two or three bit parts, including that of a tenderfoot dancer."

This big and beefy man reached over and took my hand as we talked. I realized that Ince had already told some of his guests about me, and he was giving me a chance to audition some of America's leading western hero movie stars.

"I made hundreds of one- and two-reel Broncho Billy westerns," he said, "even though I never mastered how to ride a horse." He leaned over and looked at me with his sharp, steely eyes, then he planted a little kiss on my cheek. "I like you," he whispered before resuming telling me about his early days in Broncho Billy westerns.

"I used Marguerite Clayton as my leading lady in *Shootin' Mad* and other films," he said. "But if Miss Lotte Lee had been around, I'd have used a pretty miss like you."

"Thank you, kind sir," I said, batting my eyelashes. "Frankly, I knew I couldn't compete with William S. Hart," he said. He took over my fans. Now Tom Mix is about ready to do the same thing for Hart."

I knew Broncho Billy had something on his mind other than long-forgotten western films in which he'd starred.

"Tom Ince told me about you," he said in a soft husky voice, "and I'm eager to try your specialty. I don't get much action like that. Once or twice before—that's it."

"Care to tell me about it?" I asked. "It'll make me more horny than I am."

"I'll tell you if you promise not to get disgusted," he said.

"Who am I to judge after some of the things I've done?"

"You seem like a fairly sophisticated and liberal type of gal. I guess it's okay to tell you. I've had that done to me, not from a woman but a man. We had this extra working on one of my films back in 1913. He couldn't ride a horse any more than I could. One real sissy. One night the cowboys were gathered together drinking, and we decided to play strip poker. The sissy joined us. He proposed whoever lost the game had to go down on the rest of us. We reluctantly agreed to play, although no cowpoke there planned to suck any dick. We were just toying with the sissy. Hot damn! In less than an hour he'd lost every hand—no doubt deliberately—and was naked as a jaybird. He was ready to carry through on his promise. Some guys got up and went outside for a smoke, but I remained in the cabin with about five others. We turned out the lights, and this sissy sucked us all off. None of us had had a gal for a long time, and we welcomed the relief."

"I hope I'll be good as that sissy," I said.

"You'll be better, I'm sure. 'Cause you're a gal, and gals know more about how to satisfy a man than any guy could."

"I'm not sure I agree with that. But instead of arguing, let's wander upstairs to one of Tom's bedrooms."

Once I got him in the sack, Billy Broncho would only unbutton his shirt and unbutton his trousers, which he slipped down to his knees. Staring at me was a four-inch cock hard as a rock. It might not be the longest dick I'd ever seen, but it was the thickest. It was so thick, in fact, I didn't think I could get my mouth around it. But I finally managed after some wrenching effort on my part. Talk about a jawbreaker.

He let out a half-moan, half-cry as I finally swallowed the last inch. His strong cowboy hands gripped my ears, pulling me down further onto him. Going down on Broncho Billy was just like trying to swallow a quart jar. It didn't take him long to reach his peak. In a flash he crammed all he had into my mouth, violently forcing my head down as he spurted his honey-sweet cum. That of William S. Hart had a slightly bitter taste to it but Billy's cream was ambrosia.

"Thank you very much," he said rather formally, getting up and heading for the bathroom. "Don't tell anybody about this," he said, pausing at the door to the bathroom. "My fans might find sex like this—even with a woman—perverted, and I should set a good moral tone for them."

"My lips are sealed," I said to his disappearing back, wondering if my jaws hadn't been dislocated.

Back in the living room, Tom Ince had lined up another introduction for me, yet another cowboy to whom I could offer my services. Despite a disappointing encounter with William S. Hart, and a slightly less than thrilling rendezvous with Broncho Billy Anderson, I knew at once I'd hit the jackpot, as a flamboyantly attired and extremely handsome cowboy stood before me.

"Miss Lotte Lee," Tom Ince said, "meet Mr. Tom Mix."

*****

Tom Mix, the man standing before me, had brought real showmanship to sagebrush operas, unlike the stark realism of William S. Hart. Mix was a rugged adventurer, or so I'd been told, and unlike Broncho Billy, Mix could really ride a horse as he'd been a rodeo performer before breaking into the movies.

He was a real hell-for-leather action kind of guy in spite of his wardrobe—a lavender-colored cowboy outfit with a towering twenty-gallon hat and tall white boots. He was the original rhinestone cowboy, the type you'd expect to arrive at your door honking the horn of a low-slung automobile with Texas longhorns mounted on the front fenders.

A diamond-studded belt buckle held up his trousers, and he wore diamond-studded spurs. I had no doubt the diamonds were real—not rhinestones. The initials, TM, seemed engraved on his wardrobe wherever room allowed.

The cowboy hero of many a "fistic fracas," this breezy, cheerful, larger-than-life character stole my heart, at least for the moment. This strapping son of a lumberman stood six feet tall. He was all flash and dash, both in real life and in his slam-bang adventures.

Noting that William S. Hart had shooed him away earlier when he'd tried to approach us, Mix said, "Hart's an asshole."

I settled back comfortably on Tom Ince's sofa, which was turning into a casting couch, no doubt having served that purpose many times before I got here.

"I'm gonna make westerns for today's market," Mix said. "Not like Hart. He's old-fashioned. People are tired of his dusty western scenes. I plan to bring modern touches to the west in the movies I'm gonna make in the twenties. Why not auto-racing in a western movie? I'll even use airplanes. Anything to put speed into films. I want to do everything with flair and dash."

Mesmerized by his good looks and masculine charm, I said, in my most provocative manner, "Sorry to hear that. I like a man who takes his time."

He smiled and leaned over, giving me a quick kiss on the mouth. "Tom Ince has already told me of your specialty. I can hold back until you're completely satisfied, then I'll deliver the load of a lifetime into that pretty mouth of yours."

As we sat on that sofa and talked, as a prelude to sex, I learned a lot about Tom Mix that afternoon other than the length of his dick. He was born in Du Bois, Pennsylvania, not the far west. But the little town of Du Bois was very rural in those days, so Mix learned such stunts as bareback riding, even how to stand up on a galloping horse.

"I joined the army but went AWOL," he said. "My own life's been interesting enough, but studio biographers are hard at work reinventing my life story. In the releases coming out, I was born outside El Paso in a log cabin where my mama used to shoot at angry mountain lions who came around to bother us. I was with the Rough Riders at the battle of Cristabel. I was a scout and courier for General Chaffee and saw hand-to-hand fighting. I was wounded but recovered in time to go to China for the Boxer Rebellion. I was in charge of a rapid-firing gun during the siege of Peking. Next came the Boer War...and on and on and on."

"Sometimes out here in Hollywood I don't know what's real and what's made up," I said. "But that's the movie business. I love it."

Mix reached into his wallet and pulled out some pictures. I didn't know what to expect. His wife? Did he have a wife? Children perhaps? Instead he showed me several recent photographs of his beloved horse, Tony, the most famous in the movies.

After I'd finished looking at the pictures, Mix leaned over and kissed me again. This time I felt the flicker of his tongue. "You know what?" he whispered into my ear. "I share one thing in common with Tony."

"What's that?" I asked as if I didn't know.

"Let's go to one of the bedrooms upstairs," he said. "I want to show it to you and see if a pretty gal like you can handle it. Most gals I meet run when I drop my trousers."

In the bedroom upstairs, where I'd so recently seduced William S. Hart and Broncho Billy, I showed Tom Mix that Lotte Lee was not one to run when faced with a big cowboy dick that was thick and measured nearly nine inches. After all the little stuff I'd had in my mouth earlier, the king of the cowboys gave me a challenge but one I could easily handle.

We'd begun by kissing, and Mix kissed as well as he rode horses. Of course, I gave him a few pointers, for which his future wives and endless girlfriends should be grateful.

When I descended on that thick meat, it plunged down my throat until my nose was buried in his pubic hairs. My cherry-red lips and tongue tasted, licked and sucked to my heart's content, as my skilled fingers caressed his big balls. I sucked furiously, my lips working back and forth along his dick. He groaned with utter pleasure as I slavered on his erection. His groans became more and more and more insistent. My head was bobbing furiously as I was determined to give sensual pleasure to every inch.

I could tell Mix was nearing his peak. He spread his legs far apart to give me greater access, and his huge cock swelled to an even bigger size. He lurched his hips upward and drove his entire length as deeply as he could down my throat. I welcomed the savage pounding from the massive girth in my constricted throat. With a loud cry, he erupted into my wildly sucking mouth. His entire body shuddered. His cum came in wave after wave.

I was reluctant to let my prize go, but eventually I pulled off. He took his firm hands and wrapped them around my neck. "Not so fast, beautiful woman. No one gets off Tom Mix's dick until this cowboy is totally satisfied." I felt his thick meat hardening in my mouth once more.

*****

When Tom Ince introduced me to Blanche Sweet, I was still getting my throat muscles readjusted after the pounding by Tom Mix. In the case of Blanche, I knew he didn't have seduction on the menu. As Durango Jones, I had already turned down an invitation to bed Blanche at the Hollywood Hotel.

"You look familiar to me," she said when I presented myself as Lotte Lee. "Haven't we met before?"

"A first for me," I said, "and I'm honored. You are my favorite actress on the screen." I lied. Actually I never cared for her films that much.

"You're blonde—that's good," she said, "but I resent the competition. I got my first job in moving pictures at thirteen because they needed blondes."

In the light of the afternoon, her hair became a dull spun gold with a glint of sunshine in it. Her eyes were ultramarine as she spoke of her "pretty little home where the sparrows entertain me and the moon comes out blood red." She was dressed all in black with a black silk pleated skirt, black stockings, and black patent leather pumps.

"Everyone claims I'm as old as the hills," she said. "But I'm young. No chicken, but young. They think I'm old because I got my start at such an early age. I appeared on the stage when I was only a year and a half old. It was a melodrama called *Blue Jeans*, and they trotted me out. The male star kissed my baby foot. I became an actress 'toot sweet,' so to speak." She turned to me like a district attorney. "Have you seen *A Woman of Pleasure?*"

"Not yet," I said. "I'm sorry. How could I

have missed it? I see all your pictures."

She downed her drink and burst into hysterical laughter. "You haven't seen it, because it hasn't been released yet."

"That's a good reason."

She stood up and walked over to the open window overlooking the pool. "See Jack Gilbert down there," she said, looking back at me. "Come over here."

I went and stood by her side at the window.

"That looks like a promising mound in his swimsuit," she said. "What do you think?" .

"A nice package, I would say," sounding uninterested and a bit noncommittal.

"I hear he fucks like a rabbit," she said.

"I wouldn't know." That was a truthful statement. After all, he'd never fucked me.

"He's promised to fuck me after his swim, and I'm real horny," she said. "From what I hear all over Hollywood, you like to take a man only in your mouth."

"To each her own."

"I'll make a deal with you. Since you and I are the two most beautiful gals here, I'll give you Tom Ince and I'll take Jack for myself."

"Fair enough," I said. "I'm eager to sample Tom. In fact, that's why I really came here but I had to work my way up to him." Just as I remembered my encounter with Tom Mix, I saw him come into the pool area, wearing a bathing suit. Up to now I'd been too busy looking at his mid-section but suddenly I noticed he had the ugliest knee caps in the industry. However, any man with a slab of meat like Tom Mix could be forgiven this one physical imperfection.

Since Blanche Sweet didn't know that Lotte Lee possessed a bigger cock than that of Jack Gilbert, she wandered out to the pool area where I saw her take a large beach towel and head for John as he emerged dripping wet.

In moments Tom Ince was at my side, with a whiskey in hand for me. "Sorry I've been neglecting a pretty miss like you all afternoon but I've been busy seeing to the needs of my guests." He chuckled privately as if telling a joke to himself. "Let's go sit on my upper terrace where we can be alone."

Upstairs we could see all the action by the pool. Tom Mix was talking intimately to the trashy blonde starlet who John Gilbert had

initially paid some attention to, and John himself was kissing Blanche under sheltering palms at the far side of the pool. About twenty others, an almost equal mix of men and women, mingled around the pool. William S. Hart was long gone, and Broncho Billy was nowhere to be seen.

Tom Ince had had a bit to drink and was in a fun-loving mood. He was a fabulous story-teller and had me immensely intrigued. Between stories he would reach over and give me his succulent tongue to suck.

"I really meant it when I said I want to direct your next picture." He looked longingly into my eyes. "When I started out, I wanted to be an actor too, but I soon realized I'd do a lot better behind a camera than in front of one. So I went from being an actor to becoming a director. I was surprised that I was offered a job directing westerns. But I grabbed the chance. I even hired that stone-faced Shakespearean actor named William S. Hart and made him the biggest western star of all time."

I looked down at the pool where Tom Mix was passionately kissing the trashy blonde starlet. Apparently, those blow-jobs I gave him hadn't diminished his libido. "Hart's got major competition," I said. "That Tom Mix is one hot man."

"You're right," Ince said. "Old Billy Hart is just that—old. Film-goers like hot young western stars, and I think Mix is going to be one to take over in the saddle."

When the bartender arrived with more drinks, we both eagerly accepted. I was feeling lightheaded and imagined—at least for that afternoon—that I was in love with Tom Ince.

As we drank, Ince spoke of his early days in pictures working for Carl Laemmle, the German immigrant who was an early pioneer producer. "Laemmle had set up the Independent Motion Picture Company with a bootleg camera. Since Edison's boys were hiring private dicks to check on the use of its cameras, and those boys were known to break heads as well as cameras, Laemmle reasoned that we'd be safe shooting in Cuba. He'd lured Mary Pickford away at a fantastic salary of $175 a week."

"That's still a lot of money," I said. "Goldfish

is offering me $200 a week."

"You'll get more if *Vampira* wows them at the box office."

"We sailed from New York to Havana in a small chartered vessel over rough seas. Mary was aboard with her mother, Charlotte, her brother Jack, and her sister, Lottie. Owen Moore was also aboard. I was to direct."

"Sounds like a real family affair."

"Actually Owen was married to Mary but couldn't get her away from Charlotte long enough to fuck her. When he finally did get her alone and her bloomers down, Charlotte burst into the cabin and caught them in the act. Charlotte blew her stack. She demanded that I make the captain turn back to New York. But I refused, and we sailed on to Havana."

"Mary hadn't told her family that she was married to Owen?" I asked.

"No, they found out on the boat. Charlotte cried for three days and nights. Jack stood by the railing with his little dog. He too cried most of the way to Havana. Lottie wouldn't even speak to Mary."

"I guess they thought they owned Mary. She was their meal ticket, and they didn't want to let her go."

"Something like that. Even though Charlotte learned Mary was married to Owen, big mama wouldn't let them sleep together. When that Irish drunk, Owen, got to Havana he went on a three-day spree of rum, rumba, and Cuban gals."

"So Owen started cheating at the very beginning of the marriage?" I asked.

"Don't all Hollywood husbands?" He leaned over to give me more tongue to suck. "What happened down in Havana would make a zany film in itself. Our living quarters were fit only for diseased rats. We got sick eating the food. It seemed our Cuban chef discovered some cold cream kept in the refrigerator and mistook it for lard. As for me, I pretended I had more experience than I did. Actually I'd lied and had never directed a film before. Mary's hair kept coming uncurled in the humid heat, and she complained that she was the only white girl there, calling the locals 'natives.' She claimed they were all staring at her and she was afraid that she might get abducted and raped."

"Mary without her curls," I said. "Hard to imagine."

"That was only the half of it. Our equipment was defective. Something went wrong. Mary's hair photographed dark when the film was printed. She bickered constantly and complained every minute on the minute. The cameraman had had a bit to drink and called her a bitch. At that point, Owen stepped in and attacked the cameraman, breaking his nose and knocking him down. Owen jumped on him and broke three ribs."

"You should have captured that on film."

"You're right. It would have been better than anything else in the flicker. The Cuban police came to arrest Owen but Charlotte had dressed him in drag. Owen, like Jack Pickford, has often appeared in drag, doing tough stunts for Mary which are shot at a distance. By some ruse, Charlotte got both Owen and Mary on a vessel bound for New York." Suddenly, at the far end of the pool, someone caught Tom's eyes.

I watched as John rose from a chaise longue. The bulge in his bathing suit had become more prominent. He took Blanche Sweet's hand and led her up the garden steps to a bedroom suite on the second floor.

Just as John had reached for Blanche's hand, Tom too held mine, leading me upstairs and then down a secret gallery which opened at the press of a button. At first I thought he was taking me to his private boudoir. But I was shocked to discover that along the way concealed peepholes opened to reveal a panoramic view of each bed.

"This is how I get my rocks off," he said. I have seen first hand the boudoir action of the most famous couples in Hollywood."

He invited me to look into a peephole. There I saw John Gilbert as clear as day removing all his clothing, a body not unfamiliar to me. Miss Sweet also took off all her garments. By the time he descended on her, he was fully erect. Apparently, my blow-job hadn't satisfied his libido either. He lay on top of Blanche, inserting his cock in her as his lips descended to cover her mouth.

At this point Tom gently pulled me back. He took my hand and placed it on his very impressive erection. "Please," he said, "suck me off while I watch Blanche and Jack go at it."

*****

Back at the Hollywood Hotel, I transformed myself into Durango Jones again, as I hoped to spend the night with either Antonio, my husband, or Rodolfo. But, first, I had to call Rod St. Just to tell him of my most recent adventures.

In the past few hours, I'd made it with the up-and-coming star, Ramon Samaniegos, the Prince of Siam, Sessue Hayakawa, Rodolfo, John Gilbert, Antonio Moreno, William Desmond Taylor, William S. Hart, Broncho Billy Anderson, and Tom Mix, and, my most recent host, heavy-hung Tom Ince himself.

At the end of my recitation, Rod pronounced me a "star-fucker." Thus, a new word was added to the American vocabulary as my reputation spread throughout Hollywood.

Either as Durango Jones or Lotte Lee, I was determined to go after the biggest and the bravest.

Chapter Eight

During a call to the Chief, he informed me that Marion had returned to Santa Monica with her sisters, Ethel and Reine. "She was in Florida after all, a state she hates."

"She wasn't with Charlie," I assured W.R. "Believe me, The Little Tramp has enough trouble right now without thinking of Marion. Any time you need some dirty work done, Louella is the gal to do it."

"I know that," he said. "I think I'll need her services in the future." He paused only momentarily. "And yours, of course. By the way Marion is furious. She's so jealous of Lotte Lee she can't stand it. She's been going around the house breaking objects—thank god, nothing priceless."

I smiled, knowing that Marion must be only pretending to be jealous because Charlie had already let her in on the secret—that Lotte Lee was actually Durango Jones.

W.R. made me promise to come out to Santa Monica this week for one of their parties. "And bring Lotte with you. I'm anxious to see her again."

"At least one of us will be there," I assured him.

When I arrived at Charlie's house, Kono looked frantic. "Charlie said for you to come upstairs to his library just as soon as you get here."

"Is he okay?"

"Okay is not the word. All night he's been threatening to kill himself. Where in the hell were you? You should have been here helping me, helping Charlie."

Brushing past Kono, I rushed upstairs and into Charlie's library where he was waiting for me. I took him in my arms, kissing him long and passionately. He welcomed my presence, warmth, and manly comfort.

What greeted me was a terribly shattered man. He'd had all night to realize how close he'd come to the brink, how easily his career would have exploded if news of his involvement with underage Dolores had leaked to the press. "I hate that cunt, Louella Parsons. I will hate her until the day I die, the dirty bitch."

"You're the most famous man in the world," I told him as if he didn't already know that. "I think a lot of people in Hollywood hate you."

"Louis B. Mayer, for openers," he said, "and a cast of thousands."

"You've got to be careful—real careful," I cautioned. "The hound dogs are chasing the fox."

He grabbed hold of me and kissed me again. "I won't let them. I'm smarter than these American assholes out here. They hate my guts. Some of them call me the Cockney tramp."

"You're a wonderful man," I said, "and the world's most talented artist."

In his library he sat on the sofa holding my hand. "When I was only sixteen and appearing in vaudeville on the London stage, I turned to whores," he said. "There were no questions asked. Nothing. When I climaxed, I got out of my bed, sterilized myself, and left the room after paying the fee. It was as simple as that. It is only when I get involved with these money-grubbing bitches that I run into trouble. All of them want my money."

"They're so young. It's so dangerous. Any one of them could ruin you. You've got so much to lose. I wish you'd settle down with me and forget all the others."

"You don't understand," he said, squeezing my hand the hardest he ever had. "I'm not a homosexual. Far from it. I sexually desire women. Very young girls actually. I'm like a satyr."

"But our love-making is terrific with each other," I said. "I find it very satisfying."

"I do too but I need it only at certain times," he said. "I want to be free the rest of the time to pursue other interests. Our relationship can't go on if you don't understand that."

I bent over and kissed him on the mouth, the most sensual kiss I knew how to give him. "I do understand. I just want you to know I'm here for you if you need me."

Impulsively he got up from the sofa and walked toward the door. "Come with me. I've got a surprise for you."

As he held out his hand to me, I joined him, and we walked arm and arm down the steps in front of Kono's disapproving eyes and entered the courtyard leading to the garage. To my astonishment, I saw a motor-propelled "stagecoach" sitting in the driveway, the same one I'd inspected at the home of Elizabeth Hutchison when she'd introduced me to her aspirant actress friend, Adrianne Hodges. Designed by General Motors, the limousine was painted a canary yellow, and it seemed to glow brighter than the California sunshine.

"It's all yours," Charlie said with pride. "You deserve it for saving my career."

I was like a kid at a very bountiful Christmas, as I knew Charlie was stingy with money. Anxious to try out the car, I invited him for a ride into Orange County. He gladly accepted.

Once on the road, he told me that Adrianne's father had been arrested on a charge of embezzlement. He'd stolen tons of money to promote his daughter's film career. She had to surrender her houses, the limousine, the jewelry, and the furs, and was now running a very modest little bungalow court motel in West Los Angeles.

After we'd stopped for lunch at a café, Charlie wanted to be taken to his secret hideaway where Stella Dallas made us coffee before disappearing into the cottage out back. Although I was anxious to talk to her and learn of Charlie's life when they'd appeared together on the London stage in vaudeville, she was the discreet servant who observed all but said little. It was obvious that around Charlie's hideaway she was demure and mousy, reserving her flamboyant attire and dazzling personality for her appearance on Hollywood Boulevard where she believed that some producer or director would rediscover her so she could make a spectacular comeback.

Over coffee Charlie astounded me with what would in time become the most generous offer of his entire life. For rescuing his career and "for all the other countless things you'll do for me in the future to save my skin," he offered me a contract for life in which either he or his estate would guarantee me one-thousand dollars a week for the rest of my life.

I eagerly accepted the offer because it meant financial independence for me, allowing me to pursue an artistic life and various careers, knowing I would have money to live on for the rest of my life, since I was firmly convinced that Charlie would die a multi-millionaire.

Even though I had the promise of five-hundred dollars a week from Hearst and the prospect of Lotte Lee one day drawing a star's salary, these were dubious pursuits as far as my future was concerned. The great courtesan herself, Marion Davies, was right: I'd better get that money or jewelry while I was still young and pretty.

By mid-afternoon I'd devised a scheme which even now, as I dictate to the Bitch of Buchenwald, I'm reluctant to reveal. All of us do one crazy, stupid thing in life, maybe a lot of stupid things. Without any reason or rationale, I asked Charlie to marry me while I was dressed as Lotte Lee.

"You're crazy," he said. "First, I'm married to that bitch, Mildred Harris. Second, you're a man and I'm a man and I don't know any country where same-sex marriages are recognized. The idea is lunacy."

"I took Charlie in my arms and kissed him long and hard, tonguing his neck and unbuttoning his shirt to taste his tits. I finally got his trousers unbuttoned, and then proceeded to plunge down on his huge cock, giving him the blow-job of his life. After about ten minutes of intense sucking, he exploded in my mouth. As I raised up off his cock, his cum still dripping from my mouth, the sight of that excited him. He grabbed me and pulled me up to him, licking and sucking his own cum from my lips. That was perhaps the ultimate act of narcissism.

After he'd had his fill of me, he got up from the sofa and said he was going to the back bedroom to rest. "I'll marry you. It won't mean a thing but I'll go through with this silly play-acting."

"It would mean a lot to me," I said to his disappearing back.

Faster than a horny male jackrabbit about to mount his girlfriend, I was on the phone talking to Rod St. Just, outlining my crazy scheme. If anybody could get a discreet preacher to marry Charlie and me, it was Rod. He could arrange for virtually anything, as the decades to come would prove.

Like Charlie, he called me a lunatic but agreed to cooperate. Rod seemed to understand that I wanted to marry the most famous man in the world for my own satisfaction, even though I couldn't announce that wedding to the newspapers and even though in the eyes of the state the marriage would have no validity. At least Lotte Lee could call herself "Mrs. Charlie Chaplin," a title that would be known to only the smallest coterie of people, including Stella Dallas, Rod, and perhaps the minister.

Rod knew a retired minister who had been a friend of his grandfather. He claimed he could pick him up and deliver him to Charlie's hideaway but the pastor would expect at least a hundred dollars, which was more money than he'd ever seen at one time in his life, or so Rod assured me.

"Can we trust him?" I asked. "If this story broke in the press, there would be not only ridicule but trouble."

"This old coot doesn't even know who Chaplin is," Rod said. "I'm sure of that. "All his life he's preached against sex outside of marriage, divorce, gambling, alcohol, and—get

this—movies. He thinks anyone who attends the flickers is going straight to hell."

"He's our man. Get the fucker over here while I transform myself into the seductive Lotte Lee."

"That's my gal."

Not having the right clothes and not having time to drive back to the Hollywood Hotel, I went to the cottage in back and knocked on Stella's door.

"Come on in, honey," she said in a slightly clipped British accent.

Once inside the small cottage, I told her my ridiculous fantasy to marry Charlie and pleaded for her discretion and her help in transforming me into Lotte Lee.

"All of us—even me—have our dreams, and if your fantasy is to become Mrs. Charlie Chaplin, in spirit if not deed, then I'll help make you up, ducky," she said. "I've got some beautiful old clothes that will fit. My figure has become far too robust for these gowns but I still save them, thinking one day I'll lose this suet and fit into them."

As I stripped in front of her, right down to my BVDs, she found a beaded dress from 1905 that still looked stunning in spite of the years. "I once sang in this dress when our show was attended by the royals," she said. "The audience gave me a standing ovation."

"I bet you were terrific," I said and meant it.

"I've known Charlie since he was just a little boy," she said. She leaned over to me after I'd slipped on the gown. "In fact, it was I who introduced a virginal Charlie to the pleasures of sex with a woman."

I looked at her in astonishment.

"Even then he had a big one for such a kid, and he took to my pussy like it was a birthday cake and he hadn't had food in a year."

"I hope you don't mind my relationship with Charlie," I said. "I mean, I hope you don't find it disgusting."

"Not at all, my lovely little pearl," she said. "Growing up in the theater, I've been surrounded by homosexuals all my life. In fact, I think I was ten years old before I realized that men not only slept with each other, but with women too."

When Rod arrived with the minister, I felt

he was so decrepit that he was likely to expire during the wedding ceremony. As the beautiful Lotte Lee, I was kissed by Rod and introduced to the minister. Stella had bedecked herself in her most flamboyant attire and was heavily made up as she appeared as my bridesmaid.

After talking with Charlie in the back, Rod agreed to stand in as best man for him. It was with some reluctance that we got Charlie to agree to go into the living room. He appeared dressed in a black suit and without a mustache. In fact, The Little Tramp didn't look like Chaplin at all. It was amazing how he didn't look like himself when he wasn't playing The Little Fellow.

Assuming he could see at all, the minister gave no sign that he recognized this famous face. Deep into the wedding ceremony, I suddenly became aware that there was no wedding ring for the bride. As if by some inner radar, Rod sensed my growing concern and with a brief signal from his expressive face let me know he'd brought the ring. Where he got a ring on such short notice, I don't know. But Rod was a man who always came through in a crisis.

Throughout the ceremony, Charlie looked bored and anxious for this charade to be over with. It had never occurred to him that he would also be called upon to produce the ring. At the proper moment, Rod handed the ring to Charlie who examined it only briefly before putting it on my finger. He'd done this before with Mildred Harris so he knew the right finger. I found the ring dazzling—all glittering with diamonds and rubies. It must have cost a fortune.

Indeed it did. When Charlie got the bill for the ring two weeks later, it came to fifteen thousand dollars—again, a colossal amount of money back then. After ranting and raving for two weeks, he finally paid for my ring. I still have it today and have never had it appraised in eighty years. I'm sure my estate will enjoy hawking it to some larcenous jeweler.

When it was time to kiss the bride, Charlie came alive for the first time and gave me a long, deep kiss with tongue penetration. It wasn't the typical bridal kiss, but then this wasn't a typical marriage. At the end of the ceremony, the preacher did not offer his congratulations

but demanded his hundred dollars at once. Charlie claimed he'd arrived without any money, but I knew I had that much in Durango's wallet. I paid for the wedding with my own money.

Rod gave the bride a kiss and told me to call him first thing in the morning. Apparently, Goldwyn had been trying to reach me and had called Rod. We were due to go to Catalina Island where Gloria Swanson was filming *Why Change Your Wife?*

It was directed by Cecil B. DeMille and co-starred Thomas Meighan. William Boyd was an extra in the picture, but slated for stardom opposite me in the upcoming *Vampira*. Rod's assignment was to photograph me for publicity purposes with both Meighan and Boyd. Although Boyd had called me for a date, I had had my mouth so full lately I hadn't had time to get around to this stud horse.

I also hadn't had time to contact another one of my leading men, Richard Barthelmess, who had left such a devastating impression on the lesbian Gish sisters. I suddenly remembered that Barthelmess wanted me as the boy, Durango Jones, whereas I would have to relate to both Meighan and Boyd as Lotte Lee.

If this kept up, I feared I would have to write down a list of men to seduce either as Durango or Lotte. I felt I might get them mixed up. And then there were the men I could relate to both as Lotte Lee and Durango Jones, including Charlie and William Desmond Taylor.

My other husband, Antonio, and my other husband, Rodolfo, knew me only as Durango. This gender-bending was getting very confusing, and perhaps would become more so as Rodolfo and I appeared in that film with the world's leading female impersonator, Julian Eltinge.

After the ceremony, Stella discreetly disappeared back into her cottage, and I headed for the bedroom for my honeymoon night with Charlie. I didn't bother to check in with my husband, Antonio Moreno, or attempt to locate Rodolfo, wherever he was.

Right now I had conjugal duties to perform as Lotte Lee, the newlywed Mrs. Charlie Chaplin.

As I entered the room I confronted a nude Charlie lying in our bed, playing with his large cock. He looked up at me as I moved toward him.

"Get out of that God damn drag," he commanded. "Go into the bathroom and turn yourself back into Durango Jones. I don't want a woman. I need to get fucked all night by a real man."

*****

Rodolfo was emerging fresh from the shower in the early morning light as I, as Durango, came into the cottage. Both of us no longer asked where the other had been the night before. He tossed the towel at me. "You know you want to get your hands on my body, so finish drying me off."

A command like that was followed religiously by me as if Moses had just returned from the mountain with my marching orders.

An hour later with my belly full of Italian cum, I kissed Rodolfo good-bye. He said he was going to the beach that day with Mae Murray and "some friends" he'd met at the Alexandria Hotel. I wondered if one of those friends was Ramon Samaniego, but didn't dare ask.

I told him I was going with my sister to Catalina Island. Goldwyn had arranged for us to meet two of Lotte's leading men, Thomas Meighan and William Boyd.

He flashed anger as his jealousy flared. "Boyd I've never heard of, and I can't stand Meighan. Producers put American-type shits like him in films instead of going for the more exotic look. On the screen Meighan looks like a stern Victorian husband. Directors should be casting me. The world wants something new and different. They don't want to go to the movies to see the man who mows the lawn next door." With that, he stormed out of the house.

Fortunately, I had parked my stagecoach on another block overlooking the house of Francis X. Bushman, because I didn't have an alibi as to where I'd gotten such a lavish present. I knew Rodolfo would see it eventually, and I decided to claim that it was a present from Goldwyn to Lotte, who let me borrow it.

Brushing aside Rodolfo's anger for the moment, I drove to the home of my husband, Antonio Moreno. This time I didn't catch him in bed with Ramon. No doubt Ramon was heading for the beach at Venice.

The beautiful nude body of Antonio lay invitingly on the bed, waiting for me to devour him, which I proceeded to do at once without even saying good morning.

Later, Antonio made me some freshly brewed coffee and prepared one of his delicious Spanish tortillas as he attacked William Desmond Taylor.

"I thought he was your best friend," I said.

"He was until you came along."

"I'm not a best friend. I'm your boy friend. Your wife, really."

"I'm ready to move on from Billy boy," he said, placing the tortilla in front of me. "He's done me a lot of favors. He's pulled a lot of strings for me in this town, and I rewarded him with sex."

"You never loved him?" I asked. "I thought you two guys got on great."

"Hell, no. What I'm about to tell you is strictly between man and wife, but I was always his male whore. He did professional favors for me to advance my film career, and he's been terrific at that, and to return the favor I opened up my ass to him, my mouth, or plugged him if that's what he wanted. Any time he wasn't fucking a woman, he summoned me to his bed to perform. He's still doing that. Now you're included as his whore too."

"I don't see that I have any other choice," I said. "He's directing Lotte's first film. If I anger him, he'll take it out on Lotte. Her first film will be her last film."

"He's got us where he wants us," he said. "We have to do his bidding whether we want to or not. His next conquest will no doubt be your sister. Knowing Billy boy, he'll want a three-way with you and Lotte. For all I know, he'll call me to join in the orgy too."

I tried to soothe Antonio's nerves as best I could, but it was obvious that his resentment of William was growing more severe, festering every day. He told me he'd been called over to Taylor's bungalow last night where he'd encountered Mary Miles Minter. William had given them opium as a prelude to a three-way. He had demanded that Antonio fuck him as he fucked baby-faced Minter.

"I was allowed to go home at five o'clock this morning," he said. "I didn't want to get in the same bed with that Minter bitch. I hate her. She disgusts me. She pretends to be a little girl but she's a *puta*. You know what she did? After I'd climaxed in Bill's ass, and he'd erupted in her, she went down and cleaned out his ass with her tongue. And she's baby Mary, the so-called little girl rival of Mary Pickford."

Antonio told me that he was going to sleep all day, recovering from his ordeal of last night, and that at six o'clock that afternoon he was driving over to the house of his buddy, Jack Pickford, and that his wife, Olive Thomas, would be there too. He wrote out an address and asked me to join them there at six o'clock for drinks and dinner.

Kissing him good-bye at the door, I told him I'd be delighted. I tried to reassure him, rather unconvincingly, I felt, that the thing with Billy Taylor would finally resolve itself if we played along for the moment.

Antonio was dazzled by my "stagecoach" limousine and wanted to go for a morning ride, postponing his recuperative sleep, but I told him I was already late and had to drive at once to San Pedro where the boat ordered by Goldwyn waited to take Rod St. Just, Lotte, and me over to Catalina Island.

Back at the cottage, with little time to spare, I transformed myself into the always seductive Lotte Lee, the downfall of half the men in Hollywood, and drove to the boat where my stagecoach attracted everyone's attention, even Rod's when he wasn't lecturing me that I was late and had held up the departure for an hour.

"Theodore Kosloff's on board," he said. "He's one of the stars of the picture. You may have made him late for his appointment on the set. DeMille will be furious."

Ignoring Rod's whining, I bounded aboard the boat for Catalina, reassured that I looked like some golden girl in the bright, California sunshine. The name of Theodore Kosloff thrilled me, as it surely would any homosexual male living in California at the time. I'd fallen in love with his screen image when he'd appeared as an Aztec imperial warrior, Guatemoc, opposite Geraldine Farrar, who was awkwardly cast as Montezuma's daughter in the 1917

flicker, *The Woman God Forgot*. This Russian ballet dancer had also appeared on stage with Nijinsky whom I'd already seduced and had never seen again.

Although only five feet, seven inches tall, Kosloff was "all man," or so the rumor of the day had it. Extremely lithe, he was known for his perfect body, a man who bore some of the aura of Rudolf Nureyev, who would emerge in the decades to come. Energetic and full of expressive grace, Kosloff was lean and muscular, with high cheek bones filled with deep hollows.

I'd read that Theodore had opened a ballet school in Los Angeles. In homosexual circles, rumor was that many of the young men enrolled in the class did so not to learn ballet but to appreciate Theodore in his tights. I understood that the tights covered a massive load of goodies between his legs, and some people swooned when seeing Theodore dancing virtually naked in a ballet.

On deck, waiting to greet me, Theodore was even more a treat in person. He was wearing a pair of white shorts and had taken off his shirt to enjoy the morning sun. Upon seeing him, I didn't think he had been born of woman but had actually had his body carved by Michelangelo. Rod introduced us, and I extended my hand.

He bowed low and kissed it in the continental style before rising to look deeply into my eyes. "I would say that the most beautiful woman I've ever seen on earth is worth holding a boat for."

"You flatter me," I said, all but ignoring Rod who stood awkwardly nearby. He mumbled, "Three's a crowd," before moving rapidly across the boat where one of the handsome blond-haired crew members had attracted his eye.

Theodore put his arm around me, directing me to a remote corner of the boat. As we looked out at the fresh sea after the boat started on its journey, he remained close to me. We'd just met but it was like we were on a date.

He breathed in the sea air and his chest swelled, making him more enticing than he was when I first saw him, if that were possible. "I fell in love with California when I first set foot here," he said. "But I've had many a harrowing moment since. Making pictures is dangerous business. Just ask Cecil. He's my best friend."

"I've heard of the risks," I said. "Someone told me that Cecil used to carry a gun in case of trouble from the goons hired by Edison's men."

"That's true," Theodore said. "Cecil got me out of some bad jams too. There was this gang called Black Hand. After I'd been seen on the screen once or twice, I received a threatening letter from them, demanding that I leave ten-thousand dollars in one-hundred dollar bills in a leather suitcase near the railway tracks."

I looked astonished, fearing that some equivalent kind of extortion might happen to me once I became known on the screen as Lotte Lee. "Did you do it?"

"Not at first," he said. "Cecil hired some Pinkerton detectives. I was supposed to make the delivery myself—that was one of their demands—but at the last moment I lost my nerve. Then the gang threatened me again. That time I went through with it. Cecil put real money in the suitcase in case of trouble. He feared if they opened the suitcase and found fake money, they might abduct me or kill me."

"The price of stardom," I said.

"I stood by the tracks with the money," he said, "and the Black Hand boys showed up, grabbing the suitcase and checking to see if the money was real. At that point the Pinkerton boys appeared and gave chase. They even fired at the gangsters but they got away with the money. Fortunately, both Black Hand and Pinkerton forgot about me, and I fled to safety. I could have gotten killed."

"I looked deeply into his Russian eyes. "What a loss that would have been to the females of this world."

"When you see all of me ready for action, you'll know just how right you are."

"Then the rumors about you and those ballet tights are true."

"In my ballet tights, I merely give the pansies a preview of coming attractions. They see me soft. I'm more impressive when hard."

"I bet you are," I said as he found my mouth and clamped his over my cherry-red lips. I opened wide to receive his searching tongue—long, thick, and probing. With the grace of a ballet dancer, he steered me into a tiny utility cubicle on deck.

Before I knew what was happening, he reached under my dress, grabbing my ass. At first I tried to pull away but that was hopeless, considering the size of his muscled arms. I feared he would quickly find out I wasn't a woman.

He had another plan of action. His finger reached under my bloomers and lovingly circled my rosebud before he rammed it all the way inside me, causing me to gasp.

I cried out in pain at the startling insertion but he covered my mouth with his again. That finger had started to give me a thrill instead of hurt, and he further distracted me by inserting his tongue again, which he seemed to want to extend down my throat. I could feel his breath rasping in his own throat. I reached to feel his cock which extended long and thick in his shorts.

In moments he'd pulled away from me, raising my dress and ripping down my bloomers. "I like to take women from the rear," he announced. Without lubrication, he entered me, and I felt a stinging pain as if I'd been knifed. He humped hard and fast, a trick he no doubt learned from Nijinsky. Obviously Russian men did not believe in foreplay.

Within three minutes, I had grown accustomed to the invasion, as he settled in for a rough ride to the finish line. He was steadily groaning, as he plowed deep into my guts. I feared that some crew member might burst in on us at any minute, but Theodore had other things on his mind.

His arms clasped tightly around my body, and I felt I'd do anything he wanted. My hips worked in rhythm to his thrusts. With a satanic ferocity, he tore into me as his groans intensified. I could also hear the rapid beat of his heart, as his thrusts became harder and more violent. He would pull back, then slam into me again. He did this repeatedly, and my ass was kept in a state of almost constant convulsion. His big balls kept slamming up against my exposed flesh, and the sensation was driving me toward an orgasm of my own.

His moans turned into sobs of pleasure right before he produced a guttural cry, then erupted inside me, jet after scalding jet of thick white nectar. He seemed to be still spurting as he pulled out of me without warning, causing me to gasp at the sudden withdrawal and wanting his return.

Buttoning up his shorts he said, "Thank you, my lady. Let's do that again sometime. You really know how to show a man a good time."

After he'd departed, I pulled up my panties and headed for a toilet on the lower deck. Just as I entered the toilet, I spotted the handsome blond-haired crew member standing up and spewing a load into the powerful suction pump that was the mouth of Rod St. Just, who was on his knees.

Rod turned only briefly to see who it was. When he spotted Lotte Lee, he resumed his expert sucking. The sailor winked at me. "Don't worry, pretty gal. I'll be able to give you a load too before we reach Catalina."

*****

Filled with Norwegian sailor cum, Rod St. Just and I arrived on Catalina Island where Theodore quickly disappeared, as he was late to shoot a scene in which he was featured. I blew a kiss to Theodore with promises to "hook up" really soon. If anyone, man or woman, in Hollywood wanted to get fucked, Theodore was the man of the hour.

Rod went to round up William Boyd and Thomas Meighan and to set up an appointment for our publicity stills later in the day. He also told me that Gloria Swanson was at the location and he'd introduce me to her as Lotte Lee. As Durango, of course, Rod knew I had already met Swanson and was none too eager to have her evaluate me in my incarnation as an actress.

An assistant to DeMille came for me, and told me the great man himself would like to meet me. Excusing myself, I checked my makeup and dress in a portable dressing room before being ushered forth to meet DeMille.

I'd already met some of Hollywood's most famous directors, including Tom Ince, William Desmond Taylor, and D.W. Griffith. Either as Durango or Lotte, I'd made quite an impression on Ince and William, but I feared D.W. Griffith might not succumb to the charms of Lotte. The lesbian, Lillian Gish, or even Mae Marsh seemed more his type. He probably wouldn't know how to handle a hot-blooded gal like Lotte.

Rod had told me about DeMille's latest film, a social comedy, *Why Change Your Wife?*, starring Gloria Swanson, Theodore Kosloff, Bebe Daniels, and Thomas Meighan, with newcomer William Boyd playing an extra. The picture originally was to be directed by DeMille's brother, William.

DeMille had cast Meighan as a hapless male, with two ferocious felines clawing each other for his stud services. Those roles obviously belonged to Gloria Swanson and Bebe Daniels. The crew was still talking about Miss Swanson and Miss Daniels being filmed on the floor tearing at each other's hair. That was one cat fight I'd like to have seen. Certainly Lotte could never film a scene such as that. My blonde wig might fall off. I'd heard that DeMille's picture was somewhat autobiographical, as he too was caught between two jealous women, one of whom was his wife.

In the far corner of the set, I spotted DeMille directing Theodore in a scene. Although he had yet to make his epics—those extravaganzas like *The Sign of the Cross, The King of Kings*, and *The Ten Commandments*—he was even then one of the biggest names in Hollywood. Called both extraordinary and contradictory, he was considered stubborn, loyal to his friends, ruthless to his enemies, a brilliant film director but a perfectionist martinet. After years of struggling against adversity, he'd scored hits with his early silents such as *The Cheat, Joan the Woman*, and *Male and Female*.

Short and tyrannical looking, DeMille approached me dressed in jodphurs and tall black boots. Standing five feet, eleven inches, he looked like a man in his early thirties. An avid reader of movie magazines, I already knew a lot about DeMille. This dashing, fierce-spirited director was from sturdy Dutch stock. Unlike some directors and producers in Hollywood, DeMille was no immigrant. His family first came to America in 1658, settling in Massachusetts. Back when I met him, DeMille looked rather athletic with a well-shaped chest and muscled limbs. Although he was accused of making "sex films," as some alleged, he was also known to be devoted to the Bible, interpreting it literally.

Nervous as he approached me, I was less concerned at how he'd evaluate my figure, especially my *faux* breasts and hips, than I was at how he'd regard my feet. I was attired in high heels with open toes, a style of footwear that would gain more acceptance in the Forties with Joan Crawford than with me.

The buzz in Hollywood was that DeMille was a foot fetishist. He often told people that he fell in love with his wife, Constance, because he'd been enchanted by her feet when he first spotted her walking up a staircase. Part of an audition for DeMille involved one's footwear and having him fondle and kiss the feet of an actress to see if they were erotic. Gloria Swanson had obviously passed the foot test.

Before me, DeMille bowed low and kissed my hand as if he were from the continent like Rodolfo. After complimenting me on my looks, he launched some barbed insults at Goldwyn. "Goldfish got you first, I see," he said, "and what a lucky break for that skunk. As you may know, Jesse Lasky and I formed the Lasky film company in 1913 with that devil, Goldfish. The following year we produced a six-reeler, *The Squaw Man*, our first Hollywood film. We did okay with that one."

"It was a terrific picture," I said. "I've been hearing how you're developing Miss Swanson into a big star."

"My prediction is that she'll become the biggest star in Hollywood of the Twenties." He studied me closely. "That is, if you don't beat her out at the box office." He examined my figure closely, spending a lot of time concentrating on my feet, which I thought he found delectable, no doubt wanting to suck each toe individually.

He stood back from me. "I don't know if this bothers you or not," he said, "but you're the tallest actress in Hollywood. Compared to you, Swanson is a midget. Compared to anybody, Swanson is a midget. This is the era of short men in film. Chaplin. John Gilbert, you name them. You even tower over me. Your leading men will have to be photographed standing on a soap box."

I smiled, refusing to be intimidated about my height. As Durango Jones, I was proud of my six feet. "I guess my men will have to measure up, or else they won't cut it with me."

Understanding at once my innuendo, he burst into laughter. "Would you consider me as the director of your next film? It'd be a real challenge for me. You're such a different type from Swanson."

"To work for the great Cecil B. DeMille would be the thrill of a lifetime," I said. "I bet we could make a fantastic picture together."

"Instead of casting you in an epic, I'd like to feature you as a modern vamp. These modern social comedies and dramas I'm doing will be what the audience of tomorrow wants to see."

"I think you direct women beautifully. Not just Swanson, but Pickford as well."

"Don't mention the name of that Pickford bitch to me," he said. "I may be the only voice in America ranting against that money-grubbing cow, but I can't stand her."

"I'm sure there are others who agree with you," I said, trying not to show my cat's claws.

"Pickford absolutely refused to show her feet on camera," he said. "She even called me a sexual nut. I struggled through two films with that Canadian trash. The first picture we were to do together was *Other Men's Shoes*, but Pickford refused to appear in a film with that title. She said too many people knew of my interest in feet, and with shoes in the title, the picture would be ridiculed."

"Mary is a very determined young woman, or so I've heard," I told DeMille. "It must have been tough bending her to your will."

"Impossible," he said in disgust. "*Other Men's Shoes* became *The Romance of the Redwoods*, and we shot it in Northern California near Santa Cruz. It was a Gold Rush picture. Pickford objected to every shot of herself. She claimed I made her unglamorous. But I was praised by the critics for my scenes with her, including a scene of her praying and illuminated by a single gas lamp."

"I thought the lighting brilliant," I said. "I hope William Desmond Taylor can do the same for me."

"You'll be lucky if you survive *Vampira* with that pansy dope-addict." He leaned closer to me, looking down at my feet. "What you need is a real man directing a woman like you."

Under his breath, he whispered, "Theodore has told me what a good time he had with you on the boat coming over."

I pulled back, trying to maintain some ladylike demeanor.

"My second Pickford film, *The Little American*, involved the sinking of the *Lusitania*. Pickford was torn between an American and a German lover. I struggled through that one with her too, and she was constantly demanding more money every day. I mean, she was getting eighty-thousand dollars for eight weeks of work. Christ almighty! Geraldine Farrar was pulling in only twenty thousand for the same time frame."

"I loved your pictures with Farrar, especially those she made with Wallace Reid. He's my favorite. In this little theater in Lawrence, Kansas, I saw Farrar with Mr. Reid in *Maria Rosa* and *Carmen*. I loved *The Temptation* too. Her co-stars, Pedro deCordoba and Theodore Roberts, are wonderful, but nothing to compare to Wally Reid. I was delighted the following year when you cast Farrar opposite Mr. Reid again in *Joan the Woman*."

"I nearly lost Farrar on that epic," he said. "That's another God damn money-grubbing heifer. We had to hold up shooting for two weeks until she finished another film. After costing us all that money, with a crew sitting idle, she then demanded ten-thousand dollars for her 'lost time,' and she was the reason the shooting schedule was fucked up."

"I won't be as demanding," I said, "if you and I work together. Besides, Goldfish is paying me only two-hundred a week, so I'm cheap."

"But for how long?" he asked. "If *Vampira* goes over big at the box office, you'll be just like the other pussies. Demanding top dollar. You know people like Jesse or Adolph Zukor like to get some return on their money."

I leaned down slightly and kissed him succulently on the cheek. "You'll find me very cooperative, and I'd love to do some feet scenes."

He looked first at my feet and then into my eyes. "You mean that, don't you?"

An assistant approached with a question, which DeMille answered abruptly and rather aggressively, I thought. He turned to me again and resumed discussion of Farrar as if we'd never strayed onto the subject of feet, even though he kept looking down at the ground where I stood in my high heels.

"When we were shooting *Joan*," he said, "Farrar was hefty enough to wear a suit of armor, but horses scared the shit out of her. She practically fainted every time my crew had to force her on a mount. She not only had to ride but carry a massive broadsword and even a heavy-as-lead fleur-de-lis banner too. Finally, I had to get an expert horsewoman to do all the long shots of her, using Farrar for only the most intimate close-ups."

"I still remember that burning-at-the-stake scene," I said. "That was horribly realistic. I mean those looked like actual logs you were setting on fire. Barbecued Farrar."

"It almost came to that," he said. "We soaked her body from head to feet in this special solution. It was supposed to render her fireproof. The crew took cotton which they soaked in ammonia and stuffed it into her nostrils and mouth so she wouldn't be overcome by the smoke. But ammonia made her violently sick. In other shots, we placed her in tanks filled with oil. These were set on fire, but Farrar got only minor burns. The way she screamed and hollered you'd think we were a pack of cannibals cooking her for dinner."

"I remember the film well," I said. "That looked like a real woman at the stake going up in flames."

"It was a wooden figure," he revealed to me. "We could film only so far without actually burning Farrar alive. She demanded to see the final sacrifice. She stood on the set watching the figure go up in flames. The sight made her collapse. Two hefty guys on the crew had to drag her to her dressing room where she vomited."

An assistant called DeMille to the set. He turned for one final good-bye to me. "I'm perfectly serious about our doing a picture together," he said. "I'm very anxious to see how *Vampira* is going to turn out." He bowed low and kissed my hand.

Before he left, a young man, looking no more than eighteen, approached DeMille with a sketch. With a hawk eye, DeMille studied it carefully, initialed it, and handed it back to the artist. "You did good, son," he said, before turning to me.

"Miss Lotte Lee," he said, "meet Walt Disney. He did some advertising work for me on *Male and Female*, and he's brilliant. Try to get Goldfish to hire him for *Vampira*."

"I'm pleased to meet you, Miss Lee," he said. "I've seen photographs of you but you're even lovelier in person."

I thanked him and asked for his card. "If you're as good as Mr. DeMille said, I'll definitely recommend you. If I'm the star of *Vampira*, that picture will need all the advertising it can get."

He reached into his pocket and pulled out a card, giving it to me, then asked me to consider him again, before walking down to the pier.

The same assistant who'd summoned DeMille to the set where he was shooting a scene with Thomas Meighan came for me. "Miss Swanson has learned that you're on the set. She'd like to meet you. If you don't mind waiting over by the pier under that umbrella table, I'll be back for you in half an hour to take you to Miss Swanson's dressing room."

"I'd love to meet Miss Swanson," I said. "I'll be waiting. If you see Rod St. Just, I'd like to talk to him."

After the assistant left, I strolled over to the pier and sat down, not wanting to let the sun burn my lily-white skin only days before filming began on *Vampira*.

At the pier I noticed that Walt Disney had staked out a place to work on a new sketch by the boat that had carried us over from San Pedro. The blond sailor that Rod and I had so recently blown had stripped down to his BVDs and was soaking up some sun. His body was young and muscular, and it thrilled me to see more of his flesh. In the toilet I'd only gotten to see his cock and balls, not the rest of him.

I couldn't help but notice that Walt Disney too was taking in the sight of this bathing beauty. Obviously aware that he was being admired by a new fan, the sailor rose from a blanket on the deck and stretched his well-muscled arms in the late morning sun. He was a golden boy, a true Greek God.

Who could fail to notice the prominent bulge in his underwear? Apparently in spite of all that sucking from Rod and then myself, the young sailor still had a load to offer. After he'd done his stretching exercise in front of Walt, he signaled for the artist to come aboard.

Like a bitch in heat, Walt boarded the boat. After a few words exchanged between them, Walt disappeared with the sailor below deck.

When DeMille's assistant came to summon me to the dressing room of Swanson, neither Walt nor the sailor had come back on deck.

*****

"So you're Lotte Lee, the new Goldfish sensation," the midget said, as I towered over her after being shown into Swanson's dressing room.

I never knew what to say to demented, tempestuous stars, and I was seriously pissed off at her for fucking Rodolfo. But I assumed whatever ladylike grace I could and reached to shake her hand.

The clothes cow wore only a robe and had cold cream on her face to remove her screen makeup. *"Don't Change Your Husband* made me a star, and the sequel DeMille is directing is going to be even better," she modestly claimed after a few minutes.

I liked a woman with confidence. "I hope my *Vampira* does for me what *Don't Change Your Husband* did for you."

"Who knows?" She seemed dismissive. "Many young gals come to Hollywood, and a handful get cast into films, but only a handful of that handful actually make it as stars. As a star, you're going to tower over most of your leading men. God, Mary Pickford—not to mention myself—must come up to your navel. Instead of *Vampira*, why not call the film, *The Tall Girl?*"

Miss Swanson, there is no operation known to shorten me, and I don't plan to saw off my legs, so I'll make do with what I have," I said. "I have no objection to towering over men. When I want to kiss them, I'll just lift them up to my level."

"Touché." She suddenly dropped her robe revealing her complete nudity. She took my hand. At first I feared a lesbian adventure but she led me into an enclosed courtyard where the Catalina sun shone brightly. "Let's talk while I perform my morning healing ritual."

To my complete surprise, she stood on her head against the wall, spreading her legs and revealing to me her open and gaping vagina. "I've had a very bad vaginal infection," she said. "My doctor hasn't been able to cure it. I decided on my own treatment. I'm going to expose my vagina—its deepest crevices—to the bright sun every day. I just know that will cure me."

Trying not to look at the hole that had so obviously intrigued her first husband, Wallace Beery, I pretended to carry on a normal conversation in spite of the bizarre circumstances.

As I observed her, admittedly under the worse of scenarios, I realized she was actually rather ugly with an unattractive body, tits far from appealing, and a face that was not necessarily beautiful—more exotic, really. Her beauty was only an illusion created for the screen.

"Do you have any boy friends?" she asked me.

I hardly wanted to reveal that Rodolfo, whom she'd recently fucked, was my boy friend. "I am free at the moment."

"I happen to know that young new actor, Valentino, is going to call you for a date. Your brother, that amusing Durango Jones, can set it up, I'm sure. We're going to have dinner with Clara Kimball Young. We want you to come."

"That's marvelous," I said. "I've always admired her."

"Get one thing straight, and understand it now," she said with such fierce determination that she evoked her character of Norma Desmond confronting William Holden in *Sunset Boulevard*, a picture she'd make decades in the future, of course. "Valentino is my lover, and no one is to know that, especially my husband. I think Valentino is going to be big in pictures. Pretend to be his date but keep your hands off him."

"My brother has told me all about him," I said. "He's not my type at all. I go for the Wallace Reids or the John Gilberts of this world. I don't like men who look like Italian gangsters."

"Glad to hear that," she said. "That means

we can be friends."

There was a knock on the front of her dressing room. Her maid, Hattie, was out on an errand, so she asked me to answer the door, but only after I closed the curtains to the courtyard to protect her privacy. I could well understand why she wouldn't want to be photographed.

At the door a messenger delivered two dozen huge yellow chrysanthemums. After giving him a quarter tip, I shut the door and surreptitiously read the card. It was from Theodore Kosloff. "Thank you, dear lady, for last night. It was the most memorable of my life. Until we repeat it." So that bitch, in spite of a vagina infection, was not only fucking Valentino, she was fucking my most recent conquest, Theodore.

Back on the patio I resumed talking to the gaping hole. "Flowers," I said, "from an admirer."

"I'll read the card later," she said. "So many men send me flowers. Flowers last but such a short time. I much prefer diamonds. Diamonds are forever."

"I like jewelry, too," I said, showing off my ring.

From her upside down position, she said, "That looks like a wedding ring. Are you secretly married?"

"No," I said proudly. "It's from an admirer."

"That's a lot of admiration," she said. "That ring must have cost twenty-thousand dollars, at least."

"Much more," I said. "I regard it as a mere trinket."

"I can't believe it," she said. "I'm a star and I get flowers. You haven't even appeared in a picture yet, and already men are giving you jewelry that you can use to support yourself in your old age."

There was another knock on the door. "I'll get it." It was the same messenger bearing more flowers. He got another quarter. I checked this card too. It was in a different handwriting. "I'll remember yesterday afternoon for as long as I live," the note read. "I'm ready for a repeat performance." It was signed "Thomas." Could it be Thomas Meighan who was playing Gloria's husband in the film?

"More flowers," I said to her as I came

back onto the patio.

"Being a woman, I'm sure you read who the cards were from?"

"I confess. Theodore and Thomas."

"My two leading men in the film. Thomas, my husband, and Theodore, my lover."

"Two very handsome men," I said.

"Both are quite different," she said matter-of-factly. "Thomas is hung more or less like Valentino. In the eight-inch department. But that damn Russian has a cock that belongs on a horse. If he'd lived at the time of Catherine the Great, he could have been her favorite stud horse. Frankly, I don't like men who have cocks much longer than eight inches. What about you?"

"I take on all sizes," I said. "I've never found one too small. Nor too large for that matter."

"You don't want to get a reputation for handling men who are too big. You might be called the cow of Hollywood."

"Like yourself, I'm a very young woman, and I aim to take on all comers. Let's face it: there are more pretty men in Hollywood than anywhere else in America. Only after knowing hundreds of men will I be able to settle down with my final choice—no doubt in a rose-covered cottage."

"Dream on," she said bitterly. "We'll probably end up old and discarded. As bag ladies on the street."

"Not me," I said. "I'm going to secure my future right now when I'm young and pretty."

"And tall," she said.

"There was another knock on the door, and I agreed to answer it, expecting more flowers for Swanson. Getting another quarter ready, I threw open the door only to confront the devastatingly handsome Thomas Meighan himself.

*****

Thomas Meighan must have been all of thirty when I first met him, but he was my kind of man. He stood six feet tall—my height—which was a commanding presence in those days of short stars. He was the kind of leading man a blonde bombshell like me wants to have appear opposite her—rugged, strong-jawed, and good looking, with piercing blue eyes that could undress you, although in my case I hoped that wasn't possible because of that big piece of meat between my legs.

"I come to call on Gloria," he said, "and have the pleasant surprise of meeting the star of my next picture instead." He extended his hand. "You're Lotte Lee. I recognize you from your photographs. They hardly do you justice."

"Thomas Meighan," I said. "I'm delighted. The most dashing man on the screen today standing right before me and looking good enough to eat."

He winked at me—men winked in those days—and leaned over to give me a gentle kiss on the lips. Although gentle, the kiss sent tingles up my spine, and I wanted to explore more of this hunk. "I taste just as good as I look," he said.

Hearing our voices, Swanson called through the curtains. "Tell Tommy I can't meet him for lunch today. Darling, you entertain him."

"Will do," I called back to Swanson. Leaving her to the sun, I linked my arm with my handsome leading man's and walked toward the ocean to get to know this living doll much better. There was not one inch of him that I didn't want to sample with both tongue and lips. God, I was such a whore.

He looked just as delectable as he had that year when he'd starred opposite Swanson in DeMille's *Male and Female* which also featured Lila Lee and Theodore Roberts. Back at the Patee Theater in Lawrence, I had thrilled to the performances of Thomas, especially in his American debut in *The Fighting Hope*, made for Jesse Lasky and starring Laura Hope Crews, her first film too. Of course, Laura Hope Crews would go on to screen immortality as Aunt Pittypat in *Gone with the Wind*. How could I forget Meighan in such pictures as *The Trail of the Lonesome Pine* with Charlotte Walker; *M'Liss*, a Western drama starring Mary Pickford, and *The Forbidden City* with Norma Talmadge, the latter made only last year.

"I wish you luck on this film," I said. "You've had such a great year already. Not only *Male and Female*, but *The Miracle Man*. I should have played the Betty Compson part, however.

You managed to get audiences to notice you even with Lon Chaney in the film."

"He's a scene-stealer—that one," he said. "Don't you do a film with him. I must say, nobody, but nobody, in the audience—the men at least—would look at Chaney when they could gape at Lotte Lee."

"You flatter me," I said, reaching over and giving him a light brush kiss on the cheek. Back on that sunny Catalina day, it wasn't a question of if I would get to unbutton the fly of Thomas Meighan, but when.

"I can't wait until we do some of our love scenes together," he said. "I'm already jealous of all your other beaus in the film."

"Forget about them," I said. "Unless they change the scenario, you're the one who captures my heart in the final reel."

"Man, oh man, do I like that prospect," he said, directing me over to a deserted picnic area. At the side of a shack, concealed from any passers-by, he took me in his arms and covered my mouth with his. I opened my mouth for his invasion which came with the full force of an aerial bombardment. I sucked his tongue voraciously in a manner I was now accustomed to. If Lotte Lee was already known throughout Hollywood for the succulent head she gave, I was determined that she become equally famous as a great kisser.

Unlike so many men I already knew, Thomas was no homosexual. If his lovemaking with Lotte Lee was any indication, he was strictly a man for the ladies. Of course, one could never be absolutely certain. Thank God, he didn't know all the secrets of Lotte Lee unlike some others.

Once or twice he reached for my breasts, but I whispered that only Goldwyn got to play with those. Although I'd rejected his mammary exploration, that didn't prevent me from reaching between his legs.

He wore thin white pants and I got a good feel. It was a basket as fully promising as that of another Thomas, Thomas Ince. My expert fingers came up with a good five inches, and Meighan wasn't fully hard yet. I figured when I got him alone, I would discover at least a final three inches.

Our kissing was getting too hot and heavy, and not only was my makeup being spoiled, but I was getting much too hard myself. I broke away from him. "I don't know if you've heard what I like," I said as I kissed his lips, his nose, his chin, and his cheeks with my cherry-red lips. "But I need my mouth filled with cum, and I bet yours is the sweetest tasting in Hollywood." That got him to rise another inch.

"I know Rod St. Just is going to take pictures of us this afternoon," he said. "I think if we go to my dressing room now, and you get to know my body, we'll relate better before the camera."

"I think that is the most splendid idea," I said, walking arm and arm with him to his dressing room. "I hope I'm not taking you away from Gloria. I don't want her to become jealous."

"There's nothing between Gloria and me, really," he said. "No romance, no love, if that's what you mean. I fucked her when we made *Male and Female* together. I'm out here alone on Catalina Island, so I thought I'd feed her the pork again."

"How romantic."

"In spite of that card I sent, I don't care for Gloria all that much," he confessed. "She's not that great in bed." He leaned down. "I hate to say this but she's got a bad smell down there. I was going to eat her out but the odor turned me off. I fucked her instead."

I knew he must be referring to her vaginal infection but said nothing. I knew that many men fucked women even if they smelled bad.

Alone in his dressing room, with the door locked, I resumed kissing Thomas. It wasn't so much a kiss as a tongue suck. Helpless in his arms, I ran my hands over the smooth cloth of his white shirt, feeling the firm warmness of the body beneath the freshly starched crispness. Another hand ran up his strongly muscled back and down along his slender hips until I grasped his firm buttocks. At the same time I became aware of a mounting hardness.

Unbuttoning his shirt, I removed it from his body, and he voluntarily raised his arms, allowing me to take off his undershirt.

Soon he was feeling the hot, sweet fullness of my lips on his tits, and little moans came from his throat. I found his skin soft and warm, as I slid my tongue across his chest, steadily moving toward his navel. His black leather belt stood in my way, and I unbuckled it and unbuttoned his fly. His white trousers fell on the floor, and I was greeted with a pair of crisp white underwear which I unfastened and let drop to the floor too.

Thick, long, hard, and uncut, the Meighan penis was a delight for my eyes. He was a prize male with the sexual aura of a massive hunk with low hangers. I locked myself around him in a lustful embrace, ready to consume this desirable man.

I kissed everything I could, even his silky brown pubic hairs. I licked, bathed, and sucked over his midsection to his balls, not missing an inch of manflesh. Finally, it came time to reclaim my prize.

With my tongue flicking rapidly, I descended on him, slowly taking each thick inch at a time until his pubic hair tingled my nose. The saliva in my mouth became a gusher as I filled myself with him, opening my throat.

My ravenous mouth was like a hot, hungry predator. When I had him completely encased in my mouth and throat, my suction action began, bringing moans from his own throat as his whole body writhed in the pleasure I provided it. Several times I had to back away because I knew I was bringing him too close to climax, and this was one blow-job I wanted to last.

His whispered plea was deep and throaty. "Don't stop. Don't ever stop." Several times I brought him to the edge, pulling back at the last moment so I could continue to savor him. The Meighan cock was a true work of art, and I wanted to appreciate it fully. After all, devotees could stand before a work of art for hours, appreciating and admiring it.

Thomas's midsection was pale, almost like translucent ivory. The other parts of his body, including his chest and muscled legs were more of a nutty brown, showing he'd been exposed to the sun.

His was a body filled with life, love, and lust.

I hungered for a taste of him and decided I could no longer hold back. As I fondled his balls, his moans grew in intensity and I plunged deeper on him, sucking like he was the breath of life. I was truly having this man, especially enjoying his full pouch and what it promised me. The base of his cock was feverishly hot, and I knew it wouldn't be long. He moaned softly and his cock jerked in my mouth. His cockhead was the color of a dusty rose, and I backed slightly off the base to enjoy the full eruption when it came. His cock grew thicker and then exploded. He filled my wet mouth with a radiance, and I was absolutely right in my prediction. There was a sweetness to him.

His life-blood seemed to flow into my hungry mouth. His body jerked and jumped, feeding me more of his cum. He cried out as he shot his final load into me. I wanted this moment to last forever but it invariably ended. I held him in my mouth as long as possible before he pulled out. My cherry-red lips kissed the head and its shaft. I was closed-mouth but gentle, knowing how tender he must be. He too seemed to want the sensation-filled experience to last as long as humanly possible.

A loud rap on the door signaled the end of our dreamy sequence. Getting dressed, he told me DeMille wanted him to shoot a love scene with Gloria Swanson that afternoon.

*****

Rod and I ate lunch together waiting for Cecil DeMille to release Thomas Meighan from his shooting schedule. Although at this point in time I was just getting to know Rod, I could tell he had some sort of surprise for me. That photographer always liked to play "pay back." Just as I had startled him in announcing that Antonio Moreno, one of his former tricks, was my husband, Rod, I just knew instinctively, had a little surprise in store for me.

Rod wandered off after lunch and left me alone under a shade tree. There I met a demure and soft-spoken woman by the name of Laura Maynard.

"You must be Lotte Lee," she said, shyly introducing herself. "My husband is slated to star with you in *Vampira*."

I deliberately did not want to meet wives, especially of men I'd seduced, and I wasn't at all sure who Laura was married to. I knew she wasn't Beverly Bayne, the wife of Francis X. Bushman, whom I'd seen so many times on the screen.

"Forgive me," I said, "but I'm new in Hollywood. I read the film magazines but I don't recognize your face. Of the five male stars who'll appear with me in *Vampira*, which one are you married to?"

"William Boyd," she said.

"My God," I said. "I'm delighted to meet you. Of course, all the other four actors are known to me because of their films. But I have never even seen a picture of William Boyd."

"*Why Change Your Wife?* is his first film," she said. "DeMille discovered Bill, and thinks he'll go far in Hollywood. He's appearing only as an extra in this picture. *Vampira* will be his first starring role, and we are so hopeful."

"I'm very anxious to meet him," I said.

"He's tall and platinum blond and very, very handsome."

"I can't wait," I said, suddenly realizing how inappropriate that sounded. As I've pointed out, I'm not good at dealing with wives.

"That brings up an embarrassing point," she said. "You are a very beautiful woman. A bit tall but so is Bill. I'm very jealous of Bill. I'm afraid when he meets you, he'll fall in love with you and dump me. Compared to you, I'm a bit mousy."

"Please, please," I said, brushing aside her concerns. "I have my own boy friend, and I'm very much in love."

"That is such a relief for me to hear," she said. "Every day that goes by, I think I'm going to lose Bill to another woman. Or another man for that matter."

My eyebrows raised slightly at that last remark. "He goes both ways?"

"He's a heterosexual, but he's also a hell-raiser. A bit of a sex maniac really. Although he prefers to go to bed with women, if a beautiful female isn't readily available, he'll let a man service him. I know I shouldn't be telling you this, but Bill takes sex wherever he can find it. It's put a terrific strain on our marriage."

"I can see that it would," I said. "I'm sorry. But never fear, if he comes on to me, I'll reject him. With kindness, naturally."

"Right now he's staked out Gloria Swanson," Laura said. "I know that Miss Swanson has already seduced Thomas Meighan. I fear Bill is next on her list."

"For your sake, I hope not." I sat back in my chair, enjoying the rest of my cold lemonade. "Can you tell me something about your husband before I meet him? After all, we're going to be starring in the same film."

"Let me see," she said, settling back. "He's twenty-four years old. He was born in Ohio and was one of five children, all boys. He ran away from home when he was only seventeen, and supported himself by odd jobs. He's never told me what some of those jobs were. Only that they required 'more brawn than brains.' He was some sort of model, I think. I don't know what kind."

"Perhaps a sculptor's model," I said. "A lot of actors start out that way, even Francis X. Bushman."

"I didn't know that. Bill refuses to talk about his past. He always says something flippant like, 'If you have a broad chest, blond chair, a big cock, and are devastatingly handsome, you can always find work 'cause a pretty boy doesn't have to go hungry.'"

"That's provocative."

"I know he used to entertain at what he called private parties. I've never been to parties like that, so I don't know what kind of amusement goes on there."

A young man arrived with a message from Rod. Both William Boyd and Thomas Meighan, freed from their duties for the day, were now ready to pose for the publicity photographs to promote *Vampira* even before filming began. I told Laura good-bye, as she departed on an early boat back to the mainland.

The first shots were just between Thomas and myself. Since we already knew each other intimately, we got along fabulously. Back then several scenes were inserted into films where the woman star was depicted biting into the arm of the male star. *Male and Female* with both Thomas and Swanson contained such a scene. Rod suggested we duplicate it. I pretended to bite into Thomas's arm as Rod took our pictures. After we'd finished, Thomas turned to me and said, "It tastes better with salt and pepper."

I whispered into his ear, "You taste best natural. No condiments needed."

After a wrap-up with Thomas, he kissed me good-bye but not before telling me that he'd spoken with his best buddy, Antonio Moreno, who he'd learned had been invited to a party that night at the home of Jack Pickford and Olive Thomas. Thomas asked me to go with him to the party. To my utter surprise, I realized that it was the same gathering to which Antonio had invited me as Durango Jones. I didn't see how it was possible to accept one invitation as Lotte from Thomas and the same invitation from Antonio as Durango. "I'd love to go," I said, kissing Thomas good-bye and promising to meet up with him later.

I decided I'd call Antonio and tell him that I, Durango, was held up at Catalina Island discussing a future film with Cecil B. DeMille, but that my sister would arrive at the party with Thomas Meighan and that Lotte was "dying to meet" him.

From the pier I could see Rod coming onto the shut-down set with another one of my co-stars from the film. It could only be William Boyd. Although he'd called me for a date, I had never gotten back to him to accept. As Durango Jones or Lotte Lee, I'd been too busy entertaining too many tricks.

In the reddish light of the fading Catalina sun on that long-ago day, I thought that a true golden boy was moving toward me. His hair was so blond it was almost gray. Back then, the young man was Melville's Billy Budd and all the other dazzling hunks that ever came west to California to break into pictures.

It was only when he got close to me that I realized we'd met before, but not formally. The last time I'd seen this stud, I was down on my knees on the boat that carried us from San Pedro. He was filling my mouth with cum.

"Miss Lotte Lee, meet your future co-star, William Boyd," Rod said, taking obvious delight in my shock and surprise.

"I feel we already know each other well enough for me to give you a kiss on those cherry-red lips of yours," William said, carrying out his promise.

He tasted delectable, and his breath smelled like fresh dew. "I don't know what to say," I said. "Tell me there is no need for me to be embarrassed."

He leaned over to me and kissed both sides of my cheek. "What happened back on the boat, when you thought I was a member of the crew, was a mere preview. I don't care how many men you already have in your life, the name of William Boyd has just been added to that list."

And so the cowboy hero who would one day be known to millions of kids as Hopalong Cassidy rode into my life.

*****

Since William's wife had already gone back to the mainland, and Rod had finished with the publicity photographs, I still had two hours left before sailing away with Thomas Meighan for the Pickford/Thomas dinner.

When my new beau, William, invited me for a drive around Catalina Island, I accepted. It wasn't much of a decision. Even before we'd finished the shoot with Rod, I was madly infatuated with this dashing new actor, knowing that what I'd sampled with him was merely a preview of coming attractions.

As we traveled around the island, I could hardly take in the scenery, as I was enthralled by the rugged looks of this handsome man.

In the bright sunlight, I decided that his hair wasn't blond, but gray, a silvery gray and prematurely so at the age of twenty-four.

We stopped for a cold drink at a little cantina that looked like a shack you might find somewhere along the Mexican border. I was anxious to learn as much about William as I could. His father had been a day laborer after the family moved to Tulsa, Oklahoma, but died while William was still in his early teens. His mother died soon after.

"I decided to run away," he said. "I had my other four brothers but each of us had to fend for ourselves. There's a lot that can happen to a kid on the road." A bitter frown crossed his brow, and I knew he was reliving some horror that happened to him—no doubt at the age of fifteen.

"I did regular jobs as I grew older—grocery clerk, surveyor, oil-field worker," he said. "So many people who picked me up told me how handsome I was."

"You are very good looking, and not typically so," I said. "There's something unique about you."

"I'll take that for a compliment," he said, reaching over and taking my hand which he turned over to kiss the inner palm. "All my former bedmates kept telling me I should head for Hollywood, and they finally turned my head. I hitched a ride here, several rides here. I sure sang for my supper a lot of times before making it to California, but here I am."

"Lucky for me," I said.

"I'll take that as a compliment too, pretty lady," he said. "You're as tall as I am, but one hell of a good-looking woman." He leaned back, downing his beer. "I picked up some fancy clothes from the owner of a men's store. Of course, I had to sleep with him but he gave me the clothes for free. I looked real spiffy. Enough so that I caught DeMille's eye. He gave me this job, and claims there may be even bigger roles for me after I finish shooting *Vampira* with you."

"For you and me, *Vampira* could make or break us," I said. "All the other actors in the film are stars. You and I are the unknowns. I'm a bit nervous."

"I want to do a lot of rehearsing of our love scenes in private before we face the cameras."

"I'd like that," I said. "Hell, what am I saying? I'd love it!"

Leaving the cantina, William drove to a little inn by the water. "We've got time," he said, taking me in his arms and kissing me. "I've got to have you."

After I'd sucked his tongue long enough to satisfy him, I said, "I would think there wouldn't be much left. Rod St. Just, Lotte Lee, and that kid, Walt Disney—all in one day."

He reached for my hand and placed it between his legs where I felt an enormous hard-on. "I've got to get this big thing taken care of. For me, blow-jobs aren't enough. I like to fuck, and I want to fuck you."

In panic, I broke from him. "You're one hot stud, but I don't let men fuck me. My honeypot belongs only to Samuel Goldwyn. I give blow-jobs and that's that."

He reached for me and pulled me close to him again. For the first time in my life, I really wanted to be a woman and get fucked by this handsome stud. He put his mouth to my ear and inserted his tongue, causing me to squirm in passion.

"If there's anything I like better than a hot pussy, it is teenage boy ass," he said.

Startled, I broke away from him. "How did you know?"

"An instinct. Some little telltale clue even though I don't know what it was." He pulled me to him again and kissed me deeply.

In a tiny little bedroom on the upper floor of this seedy inn, where rooms were rented by the hour, he removed all my clothing, then took off every stitch of his own. He was stunningly beautiful, like a sculptor's model, with a well-defined chest, narrow waist, and long, tapering legs. His body was covered in parts with a light dusting of blond hair. His cock was already rock hard, as was mine as he descended on me.

Usually I was the one who devoured a man's body, especially if I were the clothed Lotte Lee. But this time William did for me what I did for such men as John Gilbert.

The touch of his hands and lips along my body was electric, causing tingling sensations throughout my body. I trembled at his ministrations. He began stroking the length of my cock and moved closer as I jumped and swelled under his touch. His breath was coming heavily as he grasped my cock and plunged down on it. He swallowed all of me, and I knew this wasn't his first time. His mouth was wet and moist, as he continued to go down on me with a fierce suctioning action. I ran my fingers through his hair and traced patterns across his broad shoulders as he gave me an exquisite pleasure. His lips worked back and forth as I groaned in utter ecstasy. His tongue was like velvet, his lips a torturing ring of flesh.

Not wanting to bring me to climax at that moment, he pulled off abruptly. I gasped at the withdrawal of such pleasure, perhaps like a newborn plunged into a cruel world.

As he'd attacked my cock, he lifted me up, squeezing my buttocks before plunging his tongue into my rosebud, causing me to squeal with delight. His tongue had such force it was like getting fucked.

A burning desire kept me at fever pitch, as William moved his large cock deep into me, inserting it slowly so I could get used to the massive invasion. When I felt his balls slam against me, I cried out, reaching up and pulling him down so I could suck his tongue.

With wild, aggressive strokes, he attacked me, turning my insides into a boiling pit. I felt an increase in the size of William's cock inside me, the intensified exertion of his driving lunges, and I knew he was soon ready to shoot a load in me.

The increased pressure on my prostate brought me to the brink of orgasm. As the first scalding spurt from him entered my body, I cried out as I exploded too. I had completely abandoned myself to the joys that this tall Viking God could provide for me. I had totally surrendered myself to him, and even though appearing as Durango I felt more like a woman than I had at any time of my life. There was no sign of separating. He didn't seem to want to pull out of me any more than I wanted him to leave. He could stay forever, or so I felt at that very moment.

About the last thing I needed in my life was to fall in love. But that was exactly what had happened to me. I wanted to be with William Boyd every waking moment of the night and day, and, yes, even in sleep. I felt he'd invaded the deepest recesses of my body, and each plunge of one of his powerful drives had made me love him more.

When we finally separated, I knew I might reclaim my senses. But in this derelict bedroom that had known countless clandestine lovers, I was filled with such an overwhelming desire for this man I stunned even myself.

The next hour or two passed as in a dream. Even when I returned to my identity as Lotte Lee to make the boat crossing back to San Pedro with Rod and Thomas Meighan, I could only think of my time in that fleabag with William. In spite of the tawdry room, it was like a golden palace to me, the bed spread with red roses of love.

The sea air and Thomas behind me seemed to erase William from my mind, as I spotted Antonio Moreno waiting for us on the shore.

As Durango Jones, Antonio called himself my husband. But he'd never met Lotte Lee.

*****

With Antonio Moreno as the driver, and me in the middle, and with Thomas Meighan on my right, we headed for the house of America's loving couple, Jack Pickford and Olive Thomas. I'd already met Olive Thomas as Durango Jones, and Jack I knew rather intimately as both Durango and Lotte Lee. It was all very confusing.

Although Samuel Goldwyn didn't seem to mind, and some of my "short" lovers such as John Gilbert were not unduly concerned, Antonio was a bit taken back by my height. Read that he was surprised at Lotte's height. I've always had this theory that Hispanic men like to tower over their girl friends or wives.

He kept complimenting my beauty and seemed amazed at how closely I resembled "your brother, Durango." All the way to the Pickford/Thomas house, he kept commenting on the amazing resemblance. "You not only are as tall as Durango, but you have his same build and bone structure," Antonio said.

"There are some parts of us that are different, however," I warned him, as he burst into laughter.

This seemed also to amuse Thomas who leaned over and gave me a kiss. Perhaps it was meant to be a kiss on the cheek but I wanted his tender red lips. I turned my head to get the full enjoyment of this handsome man. Although I was madly in love with William Boyd, I would be a fool not to be turned on by Thomas Meighan, the "male" in the Swanson film, *Male and Female*. As for Antonio, I did not plan to pursue him as Lotte Lee. Seducing him as Durango Jones was quite sufficient.

The decor of the Pickford house seemed to consist of stills from their various films, including lots of pictures of Jack's sister, Mary. There were even pictures of Owen Moore, but none of Douglas Fairbanks, with whom I was also in love. Maybe, I wasn't exactly sure about loving that one.

Vivacious and terribly pretty, Olive Thomas greeted me at the door. The former "Raving Beauty of the Follies" complained that she'd recently recovered from an ulcerated tooth, but was back in good health again. She remembered meeting "your brother" at the party at Nazimova's, and commented on how tall I was. "As tall as your brother," she said. "Your resemblance to him is amazing."

She led me over to the bar and offered me a drink. I noted that Thomas and Antonio were already deep into their drinks. This was the first time I'd seen Antonio in a situation of male-bonding. Up to now, I'd known him only in homosexual circles. But he moved with macho grace into the heterosexual world of one of his best friends, Thomas himself.

"If it turns out I'm just a flivver star in pictures, I can always be a carpenter," Olive said.

Startled, I asked her what that meant. "You know how to use a hammer and nails?"

"Hell, honey, I've built movie sets for directors."

Under her curl-festooned head, she looked much too delicate to be a carpenter.

Jack came down the stairs and welcomed me to his second home. Unlike his appearance at his beach house at Santa Monica, he was fully dressed tonight, even wearing a jacket and tie. He kissed me on the mouth right in front of Olive but seemed more anxious to join his buddies, Antonio and Thomas, than he was in talking to me.

Olive led me out onto her terrace overlooking the water, and we settled in for a long girl-to-girl talk. I had no idea what she knew of my involvement with her husband, and she didn't seem to care.

"I cannot believe I'm a Hollywood star married to a Hollywood star," she said after her second drink. "The brother of Mary Pickford, no less. It's all a dream come true. My girlhood was so depressing—in fact, I didn't really have a girlhood. I grew up in a smoky Pennsylvania industrial landscape. Grime, labor, and sweat—life was unbearable. My marriage was so unhappy I fled to New York and lived for a while at my cousin's house in Harlem. I was desperate for work and found it behind a basement counter in Horne's Department Store. I'm still an expert about gingham."

"I had no idea you were married before," I said.

"Jack is my second husband. The first piece of shit I married was Bernard Krug Thomas of Pittsburgh. What a loser. He's now a timekeeper in a local steel mill."

The menfolk decided to play a game of poker and weren't much interested in how Olive and I entertained ourselves. I spoke of my upcoming role in *Vampira*, and she wished me luck. Without any particular reason, I told her that my brother, Durango, was not only my agent but wanted a screen career for himself. "So far, not much is happening for my brother," I said. "But Durango may get a bit part in a film with Julian Eltinge."

"Julian's one of my best friends," she said. "Let me call him up."

"Well, it's not set yet," I said.

"We can drive up to see him. He lives just up the hill."

"I'd rather him meet Durango instead." Actually what I couldn't confide in Olive was that I feared meeting the world's most famous female impersonator while I was dressed as Lotte Lee.

Jumping up, Olive went to her phone and dialed Julian. She returned gleefully. "He'd like us to drive up for a drink tonight. He'd love to meet you. He knows all about *Vampira*, and wants to use your brother in his new film. You and a young actor named Valentino from Italy."

Reluctantly I agreed to go along for the ride. Jack, Antonio, and Thomas took little note of our leaving.

"I'm anxious to try out my new roadster," Olive said, directing me to the garage. "It's a sixteen-valve Bugati painted a canary yellow."

Impressed as I was with her car, I felt it didn't even compare for style and drama with my own canary yellow "stagecoach" Charlie had purchased for me.

"When it comes to cars," the slightly drunk Olive claimed, "Jack and I are doomed. Only last week a car driven by Jack hit a little boy. Jack had been drinking. The kid was badly hurt and the family may sue. When it rains, it pours. Two days ago driving back from the dentist my coupe hit a nine-year-old boy and seriously injured him. That's why I had to go out and buy this new roadster."

"Is that accident going to lead to a law suit?"

"Of course, honey," she said. "Movie stars are always sued."

Behind the wheel of her roadster, Olive

seemed a reckless driver. At one point I offered to drive for her. After all, I'd been a chauffeur, if only briefly. It was a steep climb up the mountain, and she was going too fast to make the curves. At one point she veered dangerously off the road but got back on track again. Spinning around a curve, she missed her turn and went crashing into a stone wall. The alternative would have been going off a cliff!

We were severely jolted but I felt I'd received no injury. "Are you okay?" I asked her.

She slumped over the wheel but then bolted up. "I'm fine. A little shook up."

A resident from a house that was built over the slope of the hill called out to us as we both got out of the car to survey the damage. Apparently, he'd been sitting out on his front porch with his wife. "You gals ok?" he called down to us.

"We're fine," Olive yelled back up to him. "But my roadster took it pretty bad. Mind if we use your phone?"

In the house of a citrus grower, we were offered freshly brewed coffee by his meek wife. Olive placed a call to Jack to come and get us. I knew Jack had been drinking heavily and wondered if he were able to make it up the hill himself without having another accident. Olive gave the citrus grower a hundred dollars and asked him to arrange to have her roadster towed to a garage in Los Angeles tomorrow. She gave him an address which she knew from heart. Apparently, Jack and she were known at the repair garage.

In twenty minutes a car arrived for us containing two of the handsomest young men I'd ever seen in my life.

As it turned out, these two dreamboats, Jimmie and Willie Duffy, were Olive's brothers. Jimmie looked about twenty-five, the other no more than eighteen, maybe even younger. Olive anchored in the back seat with her baby brother, and I sat up front with the strapping older brother who looked good enough to eat.

His hair as black as Olive's, the older brother had high cheekbones and a massive brow and jaw. Every now and then he turned his Marine-hardened body to stare seductively at me with his large brown eyes. In addition to a lot of

solid muscle, he had soft, youthful skin and a slightly goofy smile, a look I would see decades later on the screen in the image of Jimmy Stewart.

The former Marine might look like a Greek god but had very limited ambitions, or so he said. His desire was to set up an electrical shop in New York with Olive's help.

Back at the house, Antonio, Thomas, and Jack inquired only briefly about our well-being before returning to their poker game. Apparently car accidents weren't big news at the Pickford/Thomas household. To my surprise, Owen Moore came out of the kitchen. Naturally, he had a fresh drink in hand. Seeing who it was, he kissed me on the lips but seemed more interested in a poker game tonight than in me.

I wasn't lonely, however, as I found Olive's brother, Jimmie, waiting for me on the terrace. I wanted to yank down his trousers and pluck off his shorts, but I had to make preliminary conversation instead.

"You're one beautiful woman," he said. "As tall as me."

"Thanks for the compliment," I said. "You're one beautiful man. It looks to me like you've got a great body under those clothes. Of course, I can't be sure until I've inspected every inch of it with my tongue."

He looked startled. Apparently where he came from, women did not make their intentions so bluntly known.

"Lady, if that's an invitation, I'll show you all I've got and then some," he promised.

"It's the 'then some' that really interests me."

I moved so close to him he could only accept it as an invitation to take me in his arms and give me a U.S. Marine kiss. In minutes we were in a bedroom upstairs where he disrobed for me. I wasn't disappointed. He had four and a half inches soft, and I expected much more to rise out of him when I started my expert tonguing of his rock-hard body.

He seated himself in one of his sister's chairs as I kneeled before his wide-spread legs to lap and suck those wrinkled sperm-pods of his. His muscled thighs were aromatic with flavor as I licked every inch of them. Instinctively he sensed where I wanted to go next, as he raised his legs and took his fingers to pry open his rosebud for a deep penetration by my tongue.

My fingers traced patterns across his broad, hairless chest before I descended onto the prize of the evening, a towering pole of manmeat.

As I took every inch of him, I felt I was devouring the enormous genitalia of a phallic icon discovered in the ruins of Pompeii. I was dizzy-headed at his male aroma and taste as he felt my warm lips and flicking tongue. The way he was moaning it was almost more than he could bear. As I savored him, he was thrusting his cock into my throat. It was rock hard but silky in texture. He was brushing my tonsils.

We must have carried on this way for fifteen or more minutes. But I knew he wanted relief. He growled at me, "Suck me dry!" It was a command I instantly obeyed, and his first shot came with such a sudden force I felt my head would be blasted off.

His eruption had gone clear down my throat, and I eased up at once so that I could better taste and savor his load. I gulped all he had and stayed glued to his cock until it stopped spewing. Even so, I was still reluctant to release it from my lips. Finally, he reached down and removed his cock himself as I gave him tender little kisses and licks as he pulled away.

As he got dressed and headed for the door after thanking me profusely, he said, "I don't know how long I'm going to be in Los Angeles, but if you need a rock-hard Marine for a boy friend while I'm here, you've got one. In the meantime, and if you don't mind, I'm going to send up my teenage brother for some of this good stuff you're offering."

He kept his promise. It was a long night of drinks, drugs, and sex. I not only devoured the brother, who had everything his older brother did, minus only one inch, but in time both Thomas Meighan and Owen Moore, on separate occasions, wandered upstairs for a little lips-and-tongue action.

Only Antonio remained downstairs. In spite of his macho stance, he chose not to have Lotte Lee get into his trousers. What did I care? As Durango Jones, I could have him any time I wanted.

*****

My life had become chaos, and I loved it. My double identity as Durango Jones and Lotte Lee added to the heady blend of sexual excitement and thrills.

There I was sweeping a splintering wooden floor with an aging broom in Lawrence, Kansas one day, and in weeks I had propelled myself into the forefront of Hollywood. I'd become a movie star even though I hadn't appeared before the cameras yet.

Not only that, but I was Mrs. Charlie Chaplin, married to the most famous man in the world. My husband was Antonio Moreno, and my lover was Rodolfo Valentino who I suspected was on the verge of major stardom. And, of course, there were the boy friends on the side, notably John Gilbert and now the divine gray-haired wonder, William Boyd, one of the sexiest men I'd ever known in my brief life.

As I drove to the set where Jean Acker was making a film, *The Roundup*, with Fatty Arbuckle, I couldn't believe that I'd actually agreed to deliver Rodolfo's note to his erstwhile wife.

Journeying to Lone Pine, I arrived at the set where Fatty was shooting for the day. None of the day's work called for an appearance by Acker who was secluded in her room at the Lone Pine Motel, or so I was told. I never saw *The Roundup* when it was released, and it probably has turned to dust. As time would tell, the film certainly didn't advance the career of Acker, and within months Fatty himself was headed for ruin.

A cameraman working on *The Roundup* pointed me to the room where Acker was lodging when I told him I had an urgent message from her husband in Hollywood. After a lot of pounding, she finally came to the door clad only in a ratty bathrobe. I couldn't understand why Metro had cast her in this film, much less why Rodolfo had married her. When I explained my business, she invited me in rather reluctantly.

I handed the note to Acker, and she read it with a kind of bored contempt on her face. "I think I'll save his letter," she said. "If he becomes the big star he thinks he is going to be, it might be worth something one day."

"That's one way of looking at it," I said with obvious disgust. I was so jealous of this bitch I wanted to strangle her.

"Do you know that Valentino has been badgering me to let him come here?" she asked. "I've wired him that the motel has room only for members of the film company."

A large unmade double bed confronted me, so I knew that wasn't true.

At that moment an attractive woman emerged from the bathroom, wearing only a towel around her full-breasted body.

"Durango Jones, meet Grace Darmond," Acker said.

In an inappropriate setting, I greeted Miss Darmond, a minor actress who would achieve nominal stardom in a few low-budget films during the early Twenties. Wally Reid had already told me stories of his physical dangers and hazards when he'd made a film with her. Of such films as *Handle with Care*, critics— the kinder ones—found Darmond "pleasant if not talented." Most reviewers had nothing to say of her charms. These charms, however, evidently worked to capture Acker from Rodolfo.

"It would be most kind of you," Darmond said, "not to let Nazimova know I'm here."

"That's right," Acker said. "Nazimova tried to make me jealous by having an affair with Grace, and she tried to make Grace jealous by having an affair with me. But it has backfired for her. I met Grace and fell in love."

"I'm also in love with Jean."

"Does that mean it's completely over between you and Rodolfo?" I asked.

"It was never on between the two of us," Acker said. "He's all yours if you want him. Frankly, I think his breath smells of garlic all the time." She leaned over and gave Darmond a kiss on the lips. "Grace's breath always smells like the flowers of spring."

As I headed for the door, Grace Darmond called after me. "Don't make trouble for me with Nazimova."

"If you do, you'll regret it," Acker threatened. "I could get your boy friend into a lot of trouble and ruin his career even before it begins."

"I will tell no one of Miss Darmond's presence here," I promised, a commitment I meant to keep. With that good-bye, I left the room, shutting the door loudly behind me. I couldn't stand to be in the presence of Acker.

On the way back to the car, I saw a big fat woman with a huge red bow in her hair coming toward me, heading for the Lone Pine Motel where I'd just left. "Durango Jones, we meet again," a man's voice said. It was only then I realized the big fat woman was really Fatty himself dressed in drag for a scene in the film he was shooting.

"You look mighty fetching this morning," I said. "If I liked women that way, I'd go for you myself."

"Been doing those stretching exercises?" he asked. "Gonna take me up on my offer of letting me stuff the Bushman dildo up your butt? Top dollar for such party entertainment."

"I've given your offer a lot of consideration," I said, "but I must turn it down. I do know of someone who might be interested." My immediate thought was of Ramon.

"Good," he said, taking me by my arm and leading me into his suite. "I've got the best lodgings at the motel. But why not? I'm the fucking star."

In his two-room suite, a masseur was waiting. Fatty asked me to help him out of his drag. Even though hideously fat, he seemed completely at ease with his body. He had a certain grace of movement not found in a lot of overweight men. Standing before me, he dropped his baggy underwear, revealing a very tiny penis and small balls.

As a masseur pounded his corpulent body, Fatty was in a nostalgic mood, speaking of his horrible childhood. The son of the cook at the motel, a 280-pound wonder at thirteen, had reminded Fatty of his own childhood. To my surprise, I found out he was from Kansas like myself and that his middle name was "Conkling." He'd weighed 14 pounds at birth. His father, thinking Fatty illegitimate, used to beat him a lot. The family moved to Santa Ana in 1888, and his mother died a year later.

"I was only twelve but my dad ran away soon after mama died," he said, "and I had to survive by doing odd jobs at a hotel in San Jose. One time I was singing in the kitchen, and caught the attention of a woman hired to sing professionally at the hotel. She took me to a neighborhood theater the next night where I won amateur night. Not long after I met this showman, David Grauman, and he launched me as a singer and dancer in vaudeville."

"I didn't know a lot of these things about you," I said, especially your being from Kansas and everything."

"You think I tell the film magazines this shit," he said. "I tell them what they want to hear, and they print what they want to. In 1904 I joined the Pantages theater circuit and toured the West Coast. Yes, sir, indeed, 1906 found me right in San Francisco at the time of the earthquake. I thought I was going to be killed but lived to help clean up the debris. We were forced at gunpoint to haul off the shit."

He rolled over on his back, as the masseur continued his pounding. "I made my first film in 1909. It was a Selig production called *Ben's Kid*, and I was so embarrassed I didn't want anyone to know I was in it. I also got married that year to a real good woman, Minta Durfee, a singer. But we're separated now."

"From then on," I said, "the world knows your biography. You're the best that Keystone had. I'd never seen anyone get hit with a pie until I saw you in *A Noise from the Deep*."

"Hell, I not only got hit with pies," he said, "I learned to throw them. I was the only actor at Keystone who could throw two pies at the same time in different directions."

"Nothing has ever topped your Fatty & Mabel series," I said. "You guys must have earned a lot of money for Sennett."

"We were doing fine until Mabel caught her man, Mack, in a dressing room with another woman. She stalked out of the studio."

"That's one piece of ass I bet Sennett regrets having."

"It was rough after I left Sennett. I went through a lot of pain. I developed a carbuncle on my leg, and it nearly had to be amputated. I lost eighty pounds and became addicted to morphine. But I recovered in time to make *The Butcher Boy* in 1917."

"Let's face it," I said. "Charlie Chaplin is semi-retired. The comedy crown has been passed on to you."

"This year has been my greatest," he said. "Adolph Zukor has offered me a contract for a million dollars a year."

That made me think of the paltry sum of two-hundred a week I was drawing from Goldwyn.

"In the last eighteen months, I've starred in nine feature films," Fatty said proudly.

Over lunch Fatty packed away a loaf of bread, a pound of meat loaf, three cans of pork and beans, and six helpings of mashed potatoes topped with creamy butter.

He invited me to attend a party that night he was hosting at a nearby lodge. "I'm coming as a big baby in diapers," he said. "I'm going to ask favorite guests of mine to take off my diapers and spank me. For a really special guest who I hand-pick, I'm going to dirty my diapers and get the lucky party to change them." He looked provocatively at me. "If you stay for the party, you might be that lucky party that Fatty will make potty for."

That invitation sent me fleeing into the afternoon with promises to Fatty to get together soon. I also promised to introduce him to Ramon who I knew from experience appeared at private parties for much-needed cash, and Fatty promised a lot of money for the Bushman dildo bash.

As soon as I arrived back in Los Angeles, I called Ramon at his small apartment. I told him of my encounter with Fatty and how he wanted a performer to put on a show with the Bushman dildo.

"Just how big is that dildo?" Ramon said. "I can take on Valentino and Antonio Moreno, and they're big guys."

"Darling, you haven't seen anything yet, until you've seen the Bushman dildo. He's the biggest of the biggest, with the possible exception of Elmo Lincoln."

Ramon invited me over for a little session before he went to work that night at the Alexandria Hotel. I agreed to go and found him at his apartment where he answered the door in the nude and demanded to be fucked at once.

Later as he sat with me having a drink I discussed the delivery job for Francis X. Bushman, and Ramon said he'd be really interested in taking it. "Sounds like I could make a lot of money and meet some of the real big names in Hollywood."

After I called Francis, I learned that Beverly

Bayne would not be back until much later in the evening. The actor seemed eager to meet Ramon and me. He also wanted to talk more about *Vampira* since I was Lotte's agent. Before ringing off, he said, "I'll expect you boys soon. Meeting Ramon is okay, but the one gal I want to be introduced to is your sister, Miss Lotte Lee herself."

Putting down the phone, I wondered what the heavy hung Francis X. Bushman was planning to do with my poor Lotte.

A quick call to the Hollywood Hotel revealed that Rodolfo had called once, William Boyd three times, Antonio twice, and Mabel Norman once.

Through a message from Kono I learned that Charlie also wanted to see me—after all, I was his wife. It looked like a busy time for both Lotte Lee and Durango Jones. Marion Davies had called inviting Charlie and me to Santa Monica for a party. Obviously she'd returned from Florida.

William Desmond Taylor, my director, wanted to meet privately with me. We were about to begin shooting *Vampira*. Both John Gilbert and Thomas Meighan had called, and both Louella and Adela Rogers St. John wanted interviews.

My boss, Samuel Goldwyn, had called with a double message. He remembered my request to find work for Durango in the new Mae Marsh film, and told me to tell my brother to show up on the set at eight o'clock in the morning. He also wanted Lotte to come by his offices as soon as possible. He claimed he had something for her. I just assumed that meant a mouth of his cum.

Richard Barthelmess had also called. That call confused me. Although I'd met him as Durango Jones and we'd more or less promised a sexual encounter, he might also be calling because he wanted to meet Lotte Lee. He was, after all, slated to be one of her leading men in *Vampira*.

A most intriguing call had come in from Rod St. Just. He wanted us to go out tomorrow evening on a double date. He'd called Bobby Harron whom I'd already met as Lotte, and Bobby said he'd like to meet me too. That is, he'd like to meet Durango Jones. I was having an identity crisis.

Rod said he'd just taken some very "hot" photographs of a dashing new hunk in town, Richard Dix, who was going to be his date for the evening. Rod informed me that I had enough men already, and that Dix was his discovery and I was to keep my hands to myself, not to mention lips and tongue. "Of course, I won't make you promise that," Rod said.

The name of Richard Dix was unfamiliar to me. How could I have known back then that he was slated to become one of the most legendary names of the silver screen?

*****

When I first took Ramon to the house of Francis X. Bushman, I was not the sexual sophisticate I thought I was. I knew about standard fucking and sucking, but I was not fine-tuned in the art of kinky sex. Hollywood was nothing but kinky sex, as I was to learn—often painfully—in the decades ahead.

Certainly the first time Rodolfo and I encountered Ramon getting branded by Sessue Hayakawa should have provided a clue. After all Ramon was not tied up and forcefully branded by Sessue. He came into the room voluntarily and allowed himself to be tortured in this way—all for a fee. When I suggested Ramon for the dildo performance that Fatty Arbuckle wanted, I must have sensed that there was a side of Ramon's nature that wanted to be punished.

While fucking him, I discovered that he kept repeating, "Hurt me, hurt me." Whereas I viewed sex for pleasure, Ramon seemed to seek out suffering and pain. The more he screamed that I was hurting him, the more intense his passion became, exploding into a violent orgasm.

Francis seemed intrigued with Ramon, much more so that he'd been with me, in fact, and I was a little jealous. Francis X. Bushman was hardly my dream man, even though rather dashing and handsome. Coming home at night to sit on his flagpole was hardly my fantasy.

Francis greeted us in a purple robe. As he talked to us, he deliberately let the robe come open, revealing that he was completely nude. I'd seen Francis's massive equipment before and knew it rather intimately, but Ramon appeared fascinated, even mesmerized. It was obvious he'd never seen a man like Francis before. It was an awesome sight, and Ramon couldn't keep his eyes off the Bushman genitalia.

Francis seemed amused and even a bit excited at Ramon's intense interest. Although they were talking about the deliveries of the Bushman trophies, including the now famous dildo he'd modeled for, it was clear to me that Francis had other plans for Ramon. Francis was the greatest exhibitionist in Hollywood, and in Ramon he'd found the perfect viewer. It appeared to be an ideal match.

Nothing proved better what a small town Hollywood was than the meeting of Ramon with Francis X. Bushman, the heavily built former sculptor's model. His physique seemed especially powerful in comparison to Ramon's. In time the world would see these two men cast opposite each other in one of the most famous silent screen films of all time, *Ben-Hur*. In the film, they became antagonists but on that long-ago day they were practically love-birds. If the world turned away from Bushman and boycotted him and his films after his secret marriage to Beverly Bayne was revealed, I wondered what those same fans would think of the way he was eying Ramon.

All the ingredients were there. Francis had a physique he wanted others to worship. Men or women. It didn't make much difference to Francis. He pleased all comers. Ramon worshipped powerfully built men like Rodolfo or Antonio. In sex, Ramon admitted he liked to play "the role of the woman."

I was so mesmerized by the sexual chemistry going on between Francis and Ramon that I had hardly heard their conversation. "The name, Samaniego, will not do," Francis said. "It's too long for a marquee, and a lot of the American public will not know how to pronounce it. You must change it."

"But it's my family name, and I'm proud of it," Ramon said. "The Samaniego family is one of the most aristocratic in Mexico."

"That's fine for Mexico, but if you want to be a movie star you must come up with a shorter name and something more romantic."

"How about Ramon Aragon?" I said. "That sounds majestic."

Neither men seemed to like that name. "A province of Spain," Francis said. "Not bad. But perhaps something more lyrical is needed. A neighboring province. Navarre."

"Novarro," Ramon shouted, almost gleefully, suddenly abandoning his objection to getting rid of his family name. "*Ramon Novarro.* I like that."

"I love it," I said. "It sounds great."

"And so from now, you'll be called Ramon Novarro," Francis said.

After changing Ramon's name, Francis invited us into his little library off to the side of his studio. A day bed rested there. When he dropped his purple robe, both Ramon and I knew what we were destined for. Francis generously offered me the "warm-up," which meant I was allowed to plunge down on his massive cock while Ramon was presented with his low-hanging balls. With all that sucking and licking going on, I knew it was but a prelude to what was going to expire.

In less than fifteen minutes, Ramon was lying on the day bed with his legs up in the air. "I'm sorry, my little pet, but I refuse lubrication," Francis said. "To get off, I have to experience the thrill of a natural penetration."

"Yes, yes," was all Ramon had to say. It was now apparent to all that Ramon wanted the penetration to hurt him.

And hurt him it did. Even though Ramon screamed in pain, he wouldn't let Francis pull out. Ramon's cries seemed to inspire Francis to greater and greater pounding of the young boy's butt.

What was I doing all this time, other than being a fascinated voyeur? Francis had demanded that I descend on his rosebud for an attack of my own. Lips, that is. No one penetrated Francis X. Bushman. He was definitely the fucker, never the fuckee.

My slurping of that rosebud goaded Francis into more powerful thrusts. We must have carried on for another fifteen to twenty minutes before Ramon shouted that he was "climaxing." He actually used that word instead of something more graphic.

That seemed to be the signal for Francis to explode into the young Mexican. I stayed glued to my post until Francis was gasping for breath, and I was certain that he'd completely unloaded. I was the first to pull off, and Francis remained in Ramon for a long time, as if debating whether to attack him for a second go-round. But apparently he decided that was too much for both him and Ramon to endure.

As he slowly pulled the largest penis in Hollywood from the tight, tight confines of Ramon's ass, Francis ordered me to come and give him a wet, sloppy kiss. Since Francis certainly knew where my mouth had been, I could only consider this command an act of narcissism. He wanted to taste that part of himself he couldn't reach. With the size of his dick, I knew he could auto-fellate himself, but right now I had some serious kissing to do. While Ramon, filled with FXB cum, lay beneath us, I kissed and tongued Francis.

When he rose from the day bed, his massive meat towering above us, he was still at half mast. He looked first at me, then at Ramon. "I have fucked many times. I used to fuck the sculptors who I modeled for, and, as you young men have heard, I'm known in Hollywood as quite a man with the ladies. For obvious reasons." He looked down at his genitalia, then gazed once again at me before focusing lovingly on Ramon. "But in all my years of experience, that was the single most intense orgasm I've ever known."

*****

As Durango Jones on the set of my first film, I inquired as to the name of the flicker in which I'd be appearing. "It's a Mae Marsh vehicle sponsored by Goldfish," a grip said. "It's got no title yet. But from what I've seen of what's been shot so far, Goldfish had better release it without a name. Safer that way."

With that enigmatic statement ringing in my ear, I reported for makeup where my own natural cherry-red lips were painted a vivid and vulgar scarlet. After that I went to wardrobe where a prissy-looking queen dressed me as a butler in a black outfit at least two sizes too big for me. The queen managed to make the trousers half fit by pinning them up in back, getting in the customary grope as he did so.

An assistant told me that I was to report to Mae Marsh's private dressing room in fifteen minutes. I learned from the queen that this was never done except if one were a co-star. Extras didn't get to visit the dressing rooms of stars, but, in my case, a note had come in from Goldwyn himself. At least I was being treated with extraordinary courtesy.

Fortunately, I'd known several stars intimately or else I would have been intimidated at meeting the great Mae Marsh. Only one actress in silents equaled her and that was Lillian Gish. Like her major competitor, Lillian, Mae Marsh had been a Biograph star, working for D.W. Griffith. The world still remembers her for her roles in *The Birth of a Nation* and *Intolerance*. Her frail, wispy look had decorated countless other films as well, and she was a far better actress than Mary Pickford. Mae Marsh's face was beautifully expressive, mirroring whatever emotion the director called for. Mary Pickford should not have agreed to appear with Mae in *Lena and the Geese*, as Mae stole the picture. Mae could play any role—a Stone Age maiden in *Man's Genesis*, or a phone operator who rescues society matron Claire McDowell from bandit Harry Carey in *The Telephone Girl and the Lady*.

In many films she co-starred with my date for that night, Bobby Harron. I recall seeing both of them in *The Wharf Rat* at the Patee Theater in Lawrence.

Unlike her imperial highness, Gloria Swanson, I found Mae Marsh warm and cordial as we chatted over coffee. Perhaps she thought I was closer to Goldwyn than I really was, although as Lotte Lee I got rather intimate. "I'm adrift," she confided. "I should never have left D.W. I loved that man. A truly great director. But my career has come to a standstill since I signed with Goldfish. He doesn't know what to do with me. This picture, I fear, is going to advance no one's career, especially yours."

"You're still one of the top names at the box office," I said.

With that expressive face, she looked soulfully at me. "Yes, but for how long? My fans won't go on seeing me in crap like I'm making these days. Eventually they'll stop coming to my films. All my parts now seem maudlin and cloying."

"You've always been better than your material. Of course, you were in the Griffith blockbusters, but you made so many lesser films that were a true delight. Like *Hoodoo Ann*."

"You're very kind," she said, checking her makeup in her dressing room mirror. "I need some good parts like Pickford is getting." She slammed down her lipstick. "God, I'm jealous of that bitch, and she's getting Doug Fairbanks too as if that handsome Owen Moore isn't enough."

"He drinks a bit."

She looked at me with arched eyebrows. "Doesn't everyone?" She resumed making up her face. "It was because of Pickford that I had to change my name. My actual name is Mary too but I had to change it to Mae. In my first appearance on the screen, I even wore one of Pickford's discarded old costumes. Bobby Harron, that dear boy, taught me how to make up my face, and D.W. fell for me in a big way. I was another one of those fatherless girls he could play big daddy to."

"You're not only my favorite star," I said, telling a lie, "but you were my mother's favorite too. Maria Jane didn't go to films a lot but she would go to see a Mae Marsh flicker. Mother felt most films, especially ones starring Theda Bara, were immoral."

"I hope I never did anything tasteless on the screen to offend Maria Jane. I did appear in one film that both Mary Pickford and Blanche Sweet turned down because they had to show too much skin. Or, as Little Miss Mary put it, 'I refuse to indulge in a public display of my nether limbs.' What bullshit!"

"I remember it," I said. It was another D.W. special called *Man's Genesis*. You were cast as Lilywhite and Bobby Harron played Weakhands, inventing the stone ax right before our eyes."

"Pickford was furious and mad with jealousy when she saw the final version," Mae said. "The bitch claimed that if a little girl fresh from a department store—meaning me—could give a performance as good or better than stars like her, then she thought she'd better return to the theater where years of study protected an actor against the encroachment of amateurs."

"It must be so very difficult for you always getting compared to Mary Pickford."

"If not Mary Pickford, then Lillian Gish," she said. "One critic wrote, 'Mae Marsh is our dream not of heavenly beauty, like Lillian Gish, but of earthly beauty.' God knows what they'll write about your sister. I hear you're both the brother and agent for Lotte Lee, Goldfish's latest and hottest discovery."

"That's right. Lotte will offer no competition to you. Different types."

"That's a relief to hear." She checked my body up and down, beginning at the toes. "I'm assuming you're here because you want to be an actor yourself."

"You got that right."

"I'm surprised Goldfish is backing *Vampira*," she said. "I thought this vamp shit was all over. When Theda Bara gets back from appearing in that play in New York, I hear she's all washed up."

"Perhaps Lotte will bring back the vamp or else give it a modern interpretation."

Mae looked skeptically at me. "I'm not so sure. I also hear your sister is the tallest actress in Hollywood."

"Men will just have to measure up to her, I guess."

Called to the set, I found that all I had to do was come in through a door, carrying a silver tray on which rested a calling card from a gentleman. I handed the card to Mae, who was appearing as the lady of the house sitting on a sofa. Without looking up at me, she took the card from the tray and dismissed me. The camera moved in for a close-up as her face turned into a mask of horror. Apparently, the name of her gentleman caller had sent alarm through her body.

My work was done for the day. Two months later I learned that my part had been cut. The director decided that I was "so beautiful" that I stole the scene from Mae. He said I photographed so spectacularly that I distracted from the plot. The scene was reshot with an ugly butler.

When I complained about this, I was told that I'd be perfect for the role of a butler so devastatingly handsome that the lady of the house falls in love with me and cheats on her husband. No such part existed at the moment.

After returning to the Hollywood Hotel, I

dressed myself up as Lotte Lee and paid a visit to the offices of randy Samuel Goldwyn who was very anxious to get me down on my knees in his private little dressing room to the side of his office. He promised me he'd show up tomorrow on the set of *Vampira* for the first day of shooting.

Having already caught up with my mandatory visits to Antonio, Rodolfo, and Charlie, I was free for a few hours—that is, until I received a message from William Desmond Taylor to come to his bungalow for some script changes he wanted to discuss with me. When I got there, I found that William did have some very good script changes in mind. He also wanted me to get out of my Lotte Lee drag and become Durango Jones. Once that was done, I got fucked in the ass before he let me go.

After a shower, I left William's bungalow in time to encounter his neighbor, Edna Purviance, the beautiful, natural, and charming female lead in so many of Charlie's films. She was cutting some roses for her bungalow and invited me in, since she seemed to know all about me.

I knew she was a former mistress of Charlie's and was perhaps still having an affair with him, although I'd understood that the passion had cooled off considerably after his marriage to Mildred Harris. What Edna knew of my own involvement with Charlie was not for me to know.

Although she invited me in for tea, she poured me a brandy instead. I noticed that her own brandy was three times the size of my own. I looked around her living room when she got up to answer a ringing phone, noting that most of the decorations consisted of film stills from movies in which she'd appeared with Charlie, along with silver loving cups, Chinese prints, and an assortment of musical instruments.

After her phone call, Edna seemed to disappear for five minutes. When she came back into the living room, she wore a Japanese silk kimono of sunkist-yellow and emerald green. From a chair opposite me, she removed some pink chiffon fluffy-ruffles and sat down. She curled herself up cross-legged. A little pink pajama leg peeked from beneath the kimono. Her large, forget-me-not eyes gazed questioningly at me, as if she found me

fascinating. Her preposterously long, dark lashes swept young cheeks as white and smooth as marble. She had the look of a white angora kitten.

Edna eyed me rather skeptically. "If I have any advice for you as a young man starting out in Hollywood, it is to keep your slim figure." She pursed her lips. "Charlie likes waif-like creatures, and I fear he's growing a bit tired of me."

"You two light up the screen," I said.

"Thank you, but it's a struggle for me to keep down to my one-hundred and twenty-three pounds. I like things like ice-cream sodas and strawberry shortcake, so I have to exercise. Charlie wouldn't let me work with him if I get overplump."

"You have a perfect figure," I said. "I also like the way you keep your blonde hair naturally straight. Thank God you're one actress in Hollywood who doesn't go in for Mary Pickford's curls." Her soft hair was the color of sunflowers in moonlight.

I became aware that she was evaluating me in such a way that she instinctively seemed to know I'd been sleeping with Charlie. "Charlie is always running away with other little creatures far younger than my years. I know I'm still young but perhaps a little too long in the tooth for him." She looked at me with a stern and penetrating set of eyes. I'd never seen that look from her on the screen.

Getting up, she moved toward me, taking my hand. "Let's tiptoe into the bedroom," she whispered in my ear.

Panic-stricken at the idea of seduction, I backed away.

She caught my hesitation at once. "No, dear boy, it's not what you think. I want you to see something. But be very quiet. We don't want to disturb the baby."

She slowly opened the door to the bedroom and invited me to look in. There on her bed lay Charlie himself, completely nude and sucking his thumb in sleep. He was curled in a fetal position, and I couldn't help but note that his cock had recently been coated with iodine.

As if I'd witnessed enough, Edna took my hand again and invited me to return to her living room. She gently shut the door to her bedroom, leaving Charlie to his slumber.

*****

Although I'd never met her before, Edna Purviance was a name as familiar to me as my own mother's, Maria Jane. She'd starred with Charlie in pictures that had elevated him to the front rank among movie stars. Edna had replaced Mabel Normand as Charlie's leading lady from the Sennett era.

Although not a great actress, and certainly no Mabel, Edna staked her allure on the fact she didn't appear to have any pretensions at all. She was a natural before the camera.

Born in the gold-mining Nevada town of Lovelock, Edna was only twenty-three when I first met her, although she'd been in films for years, having made her first flicker, *A Night Out*, for Essanay in 1915. Cross-eyed Ben Turpin was in that one. Edna and Charlie were a real team effort in *The Immigrant* in 1917, and by then they were also a pair when the cameras shut down for the day.

In his autobiography, written decades later, Charlie claimed that he and Edna were "inseparable." Of course, like everything else in Charlie's memoirs, that was an exaggeration. The only person that Charlie was inseparable from was himself.

From working in a family boarding house in Nevada to holding down a secretary's job in San Francisco, beautiful Edna had caught Charlie's roving eye when he'd gone to San Francisco with—of all people!—Broncho Billy Anderson, to search for possible leading ladies for their new stock company. Having recently devoured Broncho Billy at Tom Ince's party, I could hardly imagine him out on the town with Charlie. But, from reports, the two men had "inspected" every chorus girl in San Francisco. Their requirements for a leading lady had been tough. She must be a sexy nymphet, but also a mature woman, both zany and eccentric, and also "tranquil." Tranquil?

When Charlie first heard of Edna, he learned that she sometimes walked a duck on a leash. "She's the one," he cried out. "I've got to have her in my next film."

At a dinner party on the first day of shooting for *A Night Out*, Charlie boasted he could hypnotize anybody in just sixty seconds. Edna was skeptical, and Charlie bet her ten dollars he could put her to sleep. Edna accepted the bet. But Charlie feared he couldn't succeed so he whispered to her to fake it.

She did, making two or three staggering steps before falling into a swoon in his arms. Edna had generously relinquished her triumph for the sake of a good joke, winning Charlie's esteem and affection. It also convinced him Edna had a sense of humor.

To Edna's affectionate note the following morning, Charlie had written back: "My own darling Edna. It wasn't just my heart throbbing when I received your sweet letter. Your style of love tends to make me crazy over you."

In her living room, Edna settled back comfortably with her drink, although she kept glancing at the door as if expecting someone. "It will be just a matter of time," she said, "before Charlie moves me out of my dressing room and replaces me with a sixteen-year-old." She looked toward her bedroom door where Charlie lay sleeping. "In Charlie's case, it might even be a twelve-year-old."

"You're very lovely," I said and meant it. "I'm sure you'll endure for many years to come."

"I'm not so sure," she said, downing the rest of her drink and heading for the liquor cabinet to pour herself another. "As you've no doubt noticed, I like to have a drink or two. Charlie, as you also know, disapproves of alcohol, especially when consumed during working hours. He says it's unprofessional and therefore intolerable. I always show up with a slightly pinker face on the set and walk just a bit unsteadily. 'Watch yourself,' he chides me. 'The camera reveals all. You can't hide drunkenness from the camera's eye.' He's right, of course, but then addictions aren't easily broken."

I said nothing at this point, and was rather shocked to learn she was an alcoholic. Why I should be shocked at anything I encountered in Hollywood at this point seemed absurd. By now, I should be prepared for anything. Having seen Sessue Hayakawa brand Ramon, plus several other sights, led me to expect the unexpected.

Edna and I were interrupted by the sound of a car braking in her driveway. "If you're expecting company, I'll leave," I said, starting to get up.

With the grace of a swan, she moved her hand to signal me to remain seated. "It's another one of my beaus. He's one of the biggest stars in Hollywood. If you're star-struck, like everybody else in America, you'll want to meet him. He's very handsome."

As a matter of fact, I did want to meet this dashing beau. I never turned down a chance to meet a star, even Fatty Arbuckle. In my view, a star was a star, and not all men could look like Wallace Reid or John Gilbert, or even the Moore brothers, especially tasty Tom.

Whoever this beau was, Edna didn't have to let him in. He had his own key. Looking up, I was astonished to see the strikingly beautiful Thomas Meighan come into the living room. Waving slightly to acknowledge me, he bent over and gave Edna a wet kiss on the lips. Lucky Edna, I thought. Unknown to Thomas, I as Lotte Lee knew just how delectable his lips were, and I certainly had become familiar with that thick sausage in his trousers. The mere thought of what he had hanging made my mouth water.

After introductions, Thomas settled on the sofa opposite me while Edna brought him a drink. "I've met your sister," he said, "and I'm enchanted by her."

"She was certainly thrilled by you," I said, "and is eager to work with you on *Vampira*."

"As you probably know, my work with DeMille on Catalina Island will be over soon, and I'm ready and raring to shoot this new film," he said. "Hot damn! It's going to be controversial."

"That it will be," I said, reaching over to touch his leg, before forgetting who I was. I had to remember I was Durango Jones, not Lotte Lee.

A stern look crossed Edna's beautiful face. "Please warn your sister, Miss Lee," she said.

"About what?" I asked.

"Although Charlie seemingly belongs to the world," she said, "Thomas is my beau. Your sister must keep her hands off him. Or, from what I hear about her, her lips. I've already called Gloria Swanson this morning and warned her to stay away from you." This time she spoke directly to Thomas. "I've heard rumors."

He looked angry and slammed down his glass. "You what? You called Gloria? I told you never to do that. You've embarrassed the hell out of me."

"It's true, isn't it?" she asked. "You've had a fling with that bitch, Swanson?"

"Like hell I have," he said defensively, even though I knew it was true. "I can't stand her. I work with her—and that's that."

Hoping to moderate this conflict, I interrupted. "I've been on the set. Believe me, there's nothing going on between Swanson and Thomas here. Lotte visited Swanson in her dressing room. She's got a very serious vaginal infection and is having treatment. That's one pussy that's not on active duty, if you'll forgive the expression."

"You're telling the truth, aren't you?" Edna asked, not really expecting an answer.

Thomas turned to me, a grave frown crossing his brow. "A vaginal infection. It's not syphilis, is it?"

"Nothing serious like that," I said.

Edna got up and said she would make us some sandwiches and tea. When she was out of hearing distance, the actor turned to me, "I really like your sister. Do you think it's okay for me to call her at the Hollywood Hotel for a date? Edna doesn't have to know."

I leaned over to him as close as I dared. "My sister shares everything with me. She's told me everything."

He seemed intrigued, his face lighting up in expectation. "Tell me, won't you?" he asked. "I mean, what does Lotte really think of me?"

"You really want to know," I asked. "I mean, can I speak frankly?"

"Tell me everything she told you."

"Okay," I said. "You asked for it. I leaned even closer to him. "She said you have the biggest dick she's ever encountered in her life. She claims your dick is not only long, but thick. She says your balls are big and terrific. Really succulent. She also said you gave her the sweetest load of cum she's ever tasted in her whole life. She's really hot to suck your cock again and again. She told me she can't get enough of a cock as big as yours. She compared you to a horse. Said you nearly choked her."

His face was a vision of pure delight. It was like the best news he'd ever received. "She told you all that? The very biggest ever?"

I couldn't help but notice a swelling in his tight white pants. The story of Lotte's opinion of his sexual prowess had obviously enchanted him. "I envy her," I said. "You see, I'm a homosexual. Sometimes Lotte and I share her men. She's the great cocksucker in the family. But I like to get fucked in the ass. Only a man big like you can satisfy me. Right this minute I want to take that dick of yours and suck it really hard, then have you plunge it up my ass for the ride of your life." By now I saw that he was at half-mast. A little more talk like that, and I just knew he'd be fully hard.

"Listen," he said, leaning over to whisper in my ear. "I came here to fuck Edna but I have plugged a few cute boys in my day. I mean, I'm into women and all. But I'm not adverse to a cute boy, especially one like you who's so cute you look like a girl. I've let a few boys go down on me or let me plug their ass."

"Glad to hear that," I said, reaching over to fondle his genitals, causing him to reach a full erection. "Let's step into the hallway bathroom?"

"What if Edna comes back?" he asked, as my grip on his cock tightened.

"I'll come out first and distract her," I said. "Make a request to send her back to the kitchen. I'll tell her you had to get something from your car."

"Okay," he said, moving with me into the bathroom in the hallway. Once inside the cool, tiled room, I wasted no time, dropping to my knees and unbuttoning his trousers to free his big cock. It loomed up before my tongue and lips, seemingly bigger and tastier than the lollipop Lotte had enjoyed on Catalina Island. Could it be possible? Could Durango Jones produce a bigger erection in Thomas Meighan than Lotte Lee?

I gobbled him up, in spite of the length and thickness of him. In one lunge, I let him plunge deep into my lusting throat. He pushed forward, as I met his grinding hips. I pulled his trousers down farther so I could feel and fondle his round, hard buns. I sucked like a leech, my head swimming in ecstasy. I pulled off him but

he grabbed me and forced my head back down on his cock. I resisted mightily. Freeing myself, I pulled down my trousers and presented an easy target to him.

As he entered me without lubrication, the mixture of pleasure and pain was intoxicating. When he was fully inside me, his cock no longer hurt but thrilled me with electric charges of exquisite delight. I squeezed tightly around him as he began his ride. He was a rough fucker. I knew what Edna and Swanson must feel with this pussy stretcher inside them. Panting and sweating, he moved his cock like a piston, and the fuck seemed to last forever. Even so, it was over much too soon for me. He let out a throaty growl, as I felt the jerking throbs of his orgasm. What a glorious feeling.

I was the first to clean up and the first into the kitchen to help Edna with those tea and sandwiches. Fortunately, she'd received a call from the studio and had been delayed.

When Edna and I finally came into the living room, Thomas was sitting nonchalantly on the sofa, reading a screen magazine, ironically a review of his appearance with Swanson in *Male and Female* for DeMille.

Just as Edna was pouring tea, a fully dressed Charlie, in black suit and tie, emerged from the back bedroom and seemed astonished to see me talking with Edna. He was even more surprised to meet Thomas for the first time.

The tea with the four of us couldn't have been more awkward. Conversation—if you'd want to call it that—was strained until it was almost unbearable for everyone.

For me, my emotions were all confused. Here I was talking to the mistress of Charlie. She could hardly know that along with Mildred Harris I was also "Mrs. Charlie Chaplin." She also couldn't have known that Charlie didn't want me as Lotte Lee but as her brother, Durango Jones. Here I was also talking to Thomas Meighan who had known the mouth of Lotte and both the mouth and ass of me as Durango, even though he was also Edna's beau.

Here was Charlie talking to Thomas and not knowing that his "wife" —namely me—had sucked off the actor and that his boy friend, Durango, had been plugged by him. What Charlie did know was that Thomas and he were both sharing Edna's passion in the back bedroom. It was all a comedy of errors. If it weren't for the theme of homosexuality rampant in the story, it could have been a scenario for one of Charlie's scripts.

After good-byes, Charlie demanded that I drive him home. Once there he seemed furious and snapped at Kono as he barged into his living room.

Later, as I gave him a soothing bubble bath and a long massage, plus a great fucking, he felt totally relaxed, especially when I slipped him some sleeping powders. I wanted him deep in dreamland, perhaps plotting his next film, while I ran out into the night in my "stagecoach" to encounter that delectable little cutie, Bobby Harron, as well as Rod St. Just's mysterious date, Richard Dix.

If I knew Rod, his date would no doubt be a hunk and a half, and I'd have to maneuver to slip him my phone number at some point in the evening. That wasn't being disloyal to Rod who preferred messing up his mouth only once with each conquest.

My real thoughts for the night were on Bobby. Dorothy Gish might push him aside in favor of Richard Barthelmess, but her loss would be my gain. I'd not only have Bobby but would face Richard Barthelmess on the set tomorrow morning as the filming of *Vampira* was launched.

Richard had already met me as Durango but tomorrow he would be introduced to me as Lotte Lee as well. He'd already expressed his sexual interest in Durango. How would Lotte fare with the handsome actor?

That problem would be solved tomorrow. Right now I could just taste little Bobby Harron, and by the time I arrived at Rod's house my mouth was watering. Literally.

*****

Although I'd met Bobby Harron while I was impersonating Lotte Lee outside the dressing room of Dorothy Gish, I was introduced to him once again by Rod St. Just in the photographer's living room.

In the foyer, Rod had whispered to me that he'd taken some nudes of his new discovery,

Richard Dix, and while this athlete had his trousers off Rod wanted a little "session" alone with him in his back bedroom. Rod invited me to stay up front and have a drink with Bobby while he, Rod, sampled what he called "Dix's dick."

As Bobby and I sat on Rod's sofa talking casually, he told me of his meeting with my sister, Lotte. "Christ, she's as tall as you are and very good looking. I found her fascinating." He paused only slightly. "And seductive."

"I thought your heart belonged to Dorothy Gish," I said.

"Since you're Rod's close friend, and I know he's already told you about me, we can speak frankly, can't we?"

"By all means."

"I'm really confused. One day I think I'm one way, the next day I'm another. D.W. Griffith, whom I love, respect, and admire more than anybody else in the world, hates fruits, and I don't want to become one. He's always urging me to become more of a man and chase after women. It was D.W. who told me to pursue Dorothy, and I tried to get her interested in me. But she doesn't really care for me at all, and Lillian positively detests me."

"Forget Dorothy," I said. "Dump her and go on to your next conquest. Women find you very attractive. Lotte was drooling all over herself after meeting you."

"That was very flattering, and I found her most alluring," he said, "but, to tell the truth, I'm not man enough to satisfy a hot-blooded woman like that. She'd chew me up for dinner, and it would only be an appetizer for that *Vampira*."

"I see that Lotte's reputation has preceded her."

"Rod told me you were a homosexual so I can talk openly with you," he said. "I'm not a stud in bed like all the womanizers out here— Fairbanks, Chaplin, and Wallace Reid. I like tenderness in bed. Cuddling. Warm kisses, stuff like that. I'm not into this violent sex stuff. I hope you're more understanding of what I'm saying, but I'm more the delicate type in bed. I like to be taken. I don't like to do the aggressive stuff. I'm the passive type."

"You've found your man," I said, moving closer to him and taking his hand. "In bed I like to do all the work while my partner lies back and enjoys it. I also like to fuck cute boys. I'll be tender with you." It was a promise I had no intention of keeping. Tired of Lotte down on her knees, I wanted to fuck a pretty little boy like Bobby Harron with violence until he was screaming out for more. But I wasn't about to tell him that for fear I might scare him away when seduction that evening seemed inevitable.

"I would like that," Bobby said. "You're the cutest boy in Hollywood. I never thought of myself as attractive. I think I look like a Victorian schoolboy."

"That might be true," I said, "but please understand that many guys find Victorian schoolboys very attractive."

"You make me feel good, and I've been a little depressed lately," he said.

"Without knowing you, I could tell that." I felt a tenderness for this young man, so unlike the passion I experienced with Antonio or Rodolfo. I took him in my arms and kissed him warmly, inserting my tongue. His body just seemed to collapse into mine, inviting me to do whatever I would with him. Bobby Harron was a true bottom, and I planned to have a lot of fun with him before the cock crowed at dawn.

When we broke apart, he looked into my eyes. "Richard and Rod will be involved for quite a while in the back bedroom. After all, I know how demanding your friend Rod is. He never lets a man leave his bedroom until he's drained the last drop."

"What did you have in mind?" I asked, whispering in his ear.

He pulled away. "I want what you want, and we have all evening for that. But first I've asked someone to meet me in the Gaiety Bar down the street. I'm breaking off with someone, but I don't really want to break off. I'd like you to go with me. You might make my friend jealous and cause him to realize that I'm really desirable if I can attract a handsome person like you."

"I'll do my best to make him jealous," I promised, "only if I can reclaim my reward later."

"It's all there for you," he said, "even if you do have the impossible name of Durango. Frankly, I think it sounds sexy. At least it's a name people will remember."

What Bobby didn't reveal to me, and what I didn't discover until I got to the Gaiety, was that the lover he was having difficulties with was Charles Ray, one of the most famous stars of silent pictures. Fresh from the Tom Ince production of *Bill Henry*, Charles introduced himself to me, virtually ignoring Bobby.

Although Bobby gave interviews, such as one to Louella Parsons, claiming that Charles Ray was the greatest film actor of them all, Charles didn't seem too grateful for Bobby's flattery on the night I met him.

Charles specialized in playing lanky small-town boys with a fresh face resting under a battered straw hat and an open-neck shirt revealing a hairless chest. With a fishing rod slung over his shoulders as he headed down to the local river, he was what Tom Sawyer might have been like.

At the time of our introduction, Charles was at the peak of his career, just what the post-war audience wanted to see. He was the eternal "nice boy," the one girls married although they might secretly dream of being devoured by more exotic types like Antonio Moreno.

Frankly, I found Charles's screen image a whining milksop at times, although Maria Jane back in Kansas adored him. She never said so but I always suspected she wished I'd been a Charles Ray type instead of the dubious and highly suspicious Durango Jones of questionable morality.

Although Charles was always pushed around by villains in the early part of his films, he found his balls by the final reel, turning with a vengeance on his tormentors and winning the wholesome girl.

Charles would exist in his present roles during those so-called innocent years after the end of World War I and the beginning of the roaring jazz age of the Twenties. Charles Ray was the Pat Boone of his day, or so I thought until it became clear that he and his chief admirer, Bobby Harron, were homosexual lovers nearing the end of their affair.

At the Gaiety, Charles was not the country boy he portrayed on screen. He was a sexually sophisticated young man with much experience, as I came to realize, with both women and men. He'd pursued Bobby and had won the boy's heart, until Bobby had come to bore him.

When Bobby got up to go to the men's room, Charles confided in me that it was all over between Bobby and him. "Every man likes to be adored, and Bobby worships me like a fan even though he's a big movie star in his own right. But believe it or not I'm tired of being an object of veneration. I want a lusty hunk to make love to me with all the passion and fire I have in my soul. I just don't want to fuck someone who lies back in bed like a Victorian virgin. I want someone to fuck me back. Be aggressive the way I am in bed. Every time I go to bed with Bobby, I feel I'm deflowering Lillian or Dorothy Gish. I think as far as sex goes he uses the Gish sisters as his role models."

One never knows what a few drinks will do to fuel an evening. An hour later found me calling Rod to tell him that we'd meet Richard Dix and him later at the Fruitfly which was a club that really didn't get going until the early hours of the morning.

I'd only accepted Rod's invitation for such a late night because I'd received a call from William Desmond Taylor, who'd become "Billy" to me, telling me that I wouldn't be needed until the third day of shooting on *Vampira*. Some background shots were being filmed in Los Angeles before I made my appearance. That was good news to me; otherwise I wouldn't be out on any dates late at night. I wanted Lotte to get a good night's sleep before she faced the cameras as *Vampira*.

Later, after two marijuana cigarettes in Charles Ray's apartment, the disrobing began. I was the first to pull off my clothes, followed by Charles himself and a somewhat reluctant and shy Bobby. In bed I found that neither had fantastic bodies but were lean and fairly muscular for young men of that era. In the penis department, I towered over all of them, with Bobby weighing in at a respectable five inches and Charles beating him with at least seven inches. Charles also had a much thicker cock.

As we made love on that bed, it was supposed to be a three-way, but it really wasn't. I went down first on Bobby and then on Charles and kissed both men passionately. When it came time for major action, Charles avoided any outright sexual encounter with Bobby. As I pumped Bobby's tender ass, Charles vigorously plunged into me. It was a wonder Bobby wasn't crushed under the weight of it all.

As I plunged deeper into him, it was evident to me that I was going into a recess where no man had been before, certainly not Charles Ray who because of what nature gave him could only plow so far. It was those extra inches of mine that seemed to break through the Victorian schoolboy reserve, turning this up-to-now passive youth into a screaming bitch in heat, demanding harder and harder fucking on my part, as if I weren't already pounding him into a quivering mass of liver.

Charles rammed into me with all the force and sexual violence he could, and as I felt him nearing his climax, I sensed my own orgasm building. As Charles blasted into me, I cried out as I too erupted inside grateful Bobby who burst into tears as he spewed out his own seed, coating my chest. I bent over to kiss the crying boy as Charles bit into my neck in his final throes of passion.

Later, Charles and I were the first to clean up in his bathroom, followed by Bobby. With towels draped around our nudity, we heard Bobby singing in the shower. Apparently he was happy again to be reunited with Charles.

"That's the last mercy fuck I'm throwing Bobby," he confided in me as he offered me a Scotch. That came as a surprise to me. I was the one who'd fucked Bobby, not him. "Why don't you go on to the Fruitfly without us?" he said. I want to tell Bobby it's over between us. I don't want to see him any more."

"I think it's really going to break his heart," I said. "He's really in love with you."

"Don't you think hearts were meant to be broken?"

"Perhaps," I said. "I'm not going to get my heart broken in Hollywood. There are just too many men out here for me to stew too much over one."

"That's my philosophy exactly," he said. "I meet someone and get carried away with them. I think it's the one. But after not more than three months, I grow bored. I want someone prettier, someone with a better build, a bigger cock—you understand."

"I'm just like you, I fear," I said to him, as I raised my glass for a farewell toast. "I can be loyal too."

"Actually that someone prettier with a better build and a bigger cock is none other than Durango Jones," he said, trailing me to the door. "After tonight I want you to be Bobby's replacement."

"That's very flattering," I said. "An offer like that from a big-time movie star like you."

"I fucked you tonight but I want you to return and fuck me," he said. "We'll not need Bobby this time."

"I see," I said, standing at the door close to him.

His tongue out, he moved toward me, and I took him in my arms, kissing him passionately and sucking his tongue until I practically drained his mouth dry. "You throw a mean fuck," I said. "I would like to return the favor some night."

"I'd like you dropping in every night," he said, pulling me close to him for one final plunge into my mouth with his thick tongue.

"I'll think about it," I said enigmatically, kissing him lightly on his cheek before departing into the night. Whatever passion I'd had for Bobby Harron and Charles Ray had disappeared.

In my "stagecoach," I headed for the Fruitfly and an introduction to Rod's new discovery, Richard Dix.

*****

Rodolfo and I were now using the Hollywood Hotel as a message center. He'd called in earlier and told me he'd be back at the cottage at four o'clock in the morning. As always, there was never an explanation as to where he'd been. Since I wasn't much into revealing what I was up to, it was a perfect reciprocal arrangement.

That meant that I, as Durango Jones, had a few hours to spend at the Fruitfly. Forgetting about the problems facing poor Bobby Harron with his wandering lover—or former lover— country boy Charles Ray, I drove my "stagecoach" to the notorious club, wondering if I'd encounter Billy—that is, William Desmond Taylor—or Tom Ince there. Maybe—God forbid—Mabel Normand.

A head waiter showed me back to one of the "cabinets" in the rear where I was invited to enter the private domain of my dear friend, Rod St. Just, and his date for the evening, Richard Dix.

Rod jumped up to greet me with a kiss on the lips, but the six-foot dynamo of male flesh, Richard Dix, remained seated, as we were introduced.

He smiled at me and took my hand which he did not let go of even as I seated myself next to him. Richard Dix just had to be an actor. No man with that commanding presence and rugged good looks, with dark features, could be anybody else, at least back in those days.

When he looked into my eyes, I knew I wanted all 180 pounds of him. "Durango Jones, meet Richard Dix," Rod said.

"I think I'm in love," I said.

He leaned over and kissed me on the mouth with just a flicker of tongue. Richard turned to look at Rod and smiled before focusing on me again. "Rod here informs me that he likes to be with a guy only once, which leaves me free to shop around for someone else."

"While you've got that shopping cart, I'm ready to be plucked from the shelf," I said. The line sounded really corny, and I did not want him to take me for a buffoon.

"Rod has told me you're the brother and agent for Lotte Lee, and I'm really anxious to meet you," Richard said. "And Miss Lee, too. I want to break into films. Rod thought you might help me. I hear you're real close to Samuel Goldwyn."

"I like a man who gets down to business first so we can have fun and games later," I said.

"I'll let you two guys get to know each other," Rod said. "As I leave in search of fresh prey, I'll lock the door to the cabinet. There's plenty to drink here, and you won't be disturbed."

"Rod," Richard called to him, "I can't wait to see those pictures."

"I know they'll be terrific," Rod said. "Do you mind if I show them to Durango?"

"I'd be honored," Richard said. He looked over to me and flashed a football hero smile. "I'd be especially interested to know what Durango thinks of those close-ups of me fully hard."

"A totem pole—that's what he'll think," Rod said, blowing me a kiss as he left the cabinet. I heard the lock click.

Over a drink, Richard told me about himself, and I knew at once he was meant to be an actor. All actors I'd ever met, or most of them, immediately told you about themselves. He definitely wanted a role in Lotte's next picture, although I planned to try to get him a minor part in *Vampira*. He was that sexy and that good looking.

When I first met Richard, he was twenty-six years old, born in St. Paul, Minnesota, as "Ernest Carlton Brimmer." "I changed my name to Richard Dix," he said. "I thought it would look better on a marquee."

"Nearly everybody changes his name out here," I said.

"I like Durango Jones," he said. "What a great name to come up with."

"You won't believe me but it's my own name."

"Suit yourself," he said, settling back into the soft sofa. "I did the usual shit back in St. Paul," he said. "Acting in school plays. But mostly I liked to play both baseball and football. I got a job as a bank clerk but I spent my evenings training for the stage and finally got hooked up with a local stock company."

"How did you manage to make it to Hollywood?" I asked.

"Dad died, which meant I had to support my mama and my sister," he said. "I got a job as a leading man for the Morosco Stock Company and ended up here in Los Angeles. I really want to break into pictures."

"Have you got any work in film yet?" I asked.

"Actually I did," he said. "But it was two years ago. I played the butler in a little nothing picture called *One of Many*. I don't think that led to my discovery."

"Let's see what I can do for you," I said. "There are five male leads in Lotte's movie *Vampira*, but there are several minor parts for men. As a vamp, Lotte's character likes variety."

"Whatever you can do for me I'd really appreciate it," he said. He leaned over within spitting distance of me.

I could feel his magnetic presence, and he really thrilled me with his masculine aroma. "This doesn't have to be a casting couch," I said. "It's not one of those sing-for-your-supper deals." I looked deeply into his eyes. "That is, unless you're a homosexual and really want to fuck me."

He smiled and took my hand again. "Actually I'm a man for the ladies. Since working in the theater, I've learned that men control the jobs, and many of those men want to get into my trousers. I let them."

"You don't have to with me," I said. "I think you're very handsome and would have a great screen presence. But you don't have to put out."

"I want to," he said. "It's like this with me. It was a fantastic discovery I made. I could get stage jobs by dropping my trousers. It's hardly a sacrifice on my part. Getting a blow-job is a thrilling experience. I've had one or two gals do that for me but the men were better at it, especially Rod. He was the best."

"Wait until you sample me," I said. He reached for my hand and placed it between his legs where I felt an ample package getting harder.

"So, figure this," he said. "I get jobs by giving pleasure to men who in turn give pleasure to me. I really like to get sucked, and I never said no when presented with a tight asshole. I like to fuck some men's assholes better than I like to fuck a woman, especially if that asshole is real tight. It's a great thrill for me."

"I'm glad we clarified that."

"Rod gave me a great blow-job, but what I really need this evening is some serious fucking," he said. "I mean, I like to enter and stay there for a very long time."

He pulled me into his arms and moved his open mouth to me, and I welcomed the invading tongue. Richard Dix was one hell of a kisser.

On that long-ago night, Richard thrilled me as he would on the screen for years to come, appearing in westerns, baseball stories, mystery thrillers, programmers, and potboilers. Even now I can recall the taste of his sweet mouth just as much as I remember his masterful performance in *Cimarron*, winner of best picture of the year which also won for him a nomination as best actor in 1931.

It thrilled me to slip my hands along those broad shoulders and feel his straining muscles in his neck, which so enticed me that I licked every inch of his throat. That was one full-sized country ham hock in those trousers of his, and I was eager to eat it. I went to work on his belt buckle and the buttons of his fly. At last I had freed one of the most impressive dicks in Hollywood, a good eight and a half thick inches which made both Charles Ray and Bobby Harron, already established movie stars, look pathetic in comparison.

Moving himself from the sofa, he stood before me and did the most disarming but enticing act. He pulled off his boots and stripped off every piece of his clothing, until he was fully nude. As he removed his shirt, I practically swooned. This was one well-built actor.

He lowered himself over me and began removing all my clothing. With a little help from me, I soon was as nude as he was. I sensed he wanted to fuck me right away, but I had other ideas. "Before we get really serious here," I whispered in his ear as my fingers weighed his heavy balls, "I want to tongue every inch of that hunk-like body of yours."

"Hot fucking damn," he cried out. "Get to it, cowboy."

He tasted as good as he looked. By the time I'd explored every crevice and every inch of flesh, he was raring and ready for some deep probe of my body. He moaned loudly as he pile-drived into me bronco to buster. I fused together with this randy male animal from Minnesota as he rode me to dizzying heights.

As he fucked me, I played with his balls, anticipating what delights awaited me there. We were in perfect harmony. He flung me back on the sofa and began biting my neck in passion. Once he started to fuck, he became wild, no longer caring if he hurt or not. He'd gone beyond that, and I wanted him to, as I just had to experience the full passion and fury of my raging bull for the night.

After we'd rutted around for a good thirty minutes or more, he rewarded me with a long and powerful string of jism as if he hadn't cum in a month in spite of that blow-job from my buddy, Rod.

As he moved inside me, I came in a blissful orgasm that had me nearly fainting.

He eased his body down on mine. "I'll be fully recovered in an hour," he whispered in my ear, followed by his hot tongue. "Do you like balls?" he asked.

"More than life itself," I said.

"You've already felt them and know I have a big pair," he said. "If there's anything I like better than fucking itself, it's to get some guy to sniff, lick, suck, nuzzle, and play with my balls for half the night."

That night and for many years to come, I remained convinced as I lay under him taking a pounding that Richard chose an appropriate name when he called himself "Dix."

*****

After stroking the fires with Antonio and later Rodolfo, as Durango Jones, I put in a call to John Gilbert, pretending to be Lotte Lee, and arranged another date as soon as possible. He wished me luck on the opening shoot of *Vampira* and even offered to visit the set. I declined the invitation, figuring that with all those other men, not to mention my new love, William Boyd, I'd be busy enough without John. There were other invitations, so many other invitations. One of them was for a shindig hosted by "the Chief," W.R. Hearst himself. Kansas was never like this.

As Charlie and I made our way in the stagecoach to Santa Monica to call on William Randolph Hearst and Marion Davies, I knew the night belonged to us. The cream of Hollywood would be there, none bigger than Charlie Chaplin. He had no problem arriving at the party with a man since his reputation as a womanizer was well known in Hollywood. Besides, he figured, it was better to show up with a Hollywood agent like me than a woman, since he was still married to Mildred Harris.

The moment we entered the party, Charlie was set upon by dozens of admirers, often big stars themselves, and I was left to fend for myself until Marion Davies came to my rescue. She hustled me off into the library for a secret drink. She was like a giggly little girl and looked far younger than her years. "When I got back from Florida, I had a big fight with W.R. over Lotte Lee," she said with just a touch of conspiracy in her voice. "He doesn't know that I know you're Lotte. So I pretended to be jealous out of my mind."

"You are putting the poor man on," I said as a form of mild chastisement, softening the accusation with my winning smile.

"Wait a minute, sugar," she said, "he was putting me on by pretending to be dating Lotte." She downed a stiff drink. "Did he try anything? I mean, like put his hand on your knee, shit like that?"

"He was a perfect gentleman all evening," I said, lying. "In fact, he spent most of the night talking about you."

Into the library at this point barged Louella Parsons, so I knew our private conversation was at an end. In spite of Louella claiming that "Marion never looked lovelier" in her daily column, Marion seemed bored with the columnist and excused herself.

I found myself alone in the clutches of the gay illiterate herself. She made no reference to her role in blackmailing Charlie to pay off Dolores del Rio before she made serious trouble for him—and indeed, Louella went to her grave without revealing this scandal even when Dolores del Rio became a big Hollywood star herself in the 20s. "You darling boy," she said, "surely the handsomest in Hollywood. Wallace Reid and Francis X. Bushman have nothing on you. I've been hearing the most wonderful things about *Vampira*, and I desperately want you to set up a meeting with your sister." Louella was carrying her own drink, and I realized she'd had quite a few. "There must be some truth in all the rumors I've heard."

"Lies, all lies," I said.

"You're putting me on," she said. "Don't kid me. Louella doesn't like to be kidded or else she can get very nasty."

"I thought you didn't like California," I said, "but I hear you're spending more and more time here."

"I'm a New York glamour gal," she said,

"but the movies are shifting west and I think I'll have to come out here and become a cowgirl too."

"You'd be a wonderful addition to the Golden West."

Louella, through drunken but brutal eyes, stared me down. "Get me another drink." At the door to the library I signaled for one of the waiters to fill her drink order. When that was accomplished, she looked more at ease. Louella without her customary drink at a party could be a very frightening creature. "I've heard stories," she said, "plenty of stories."

"About whom?" I asked.

"About your sister," she said. "I hear she's having an affair with Owen Moore now that he's breaking up with Mary."

"Completely untrue," I said. "You can take it from me. Lotte confides everything in me. She can't make a move without me."

"Very well," she said skeptically. "I'll take your word for it. But I hear Lotte is also having affairs with Jack Gilbert, Thomas Meighan, and Tom Ince."

"She wouldn't have time to work all those men into her schedule. Trust me on this one."

"That's not all," Louella said. "I hear she's the mistress of Samuel Goldwyn. There's more. She's also shacked up with William Desmond Taylor. But then who isn't?"

"There aren't enough days in the week for her to get around to all these men," I said.

She looked unconvinced. "I'm not so sure. In spite of her height, I hear she's a regular *femme fatale*. I really want to meet her and ask her some of these questions directly."

"Lotte never discusses her private life," I said. "She's too much of a lady. Our mother was very Victorian and proper, a good church-going woman, and Lotte could never give an interview about her own love life."

"I want red meat, boy," Louella said.

"Okay," I said, "but it's not for publication."

"I'm not so sure I'll agree to that," she said. "My column is one greedy bitch demanding more and more revelations."

"I will tell you Lotte's real secret," I said. "She doesn't want it known. But she does have a beau. He's William S. Hart."

Louella wasn't as surprised by this revelation as I thought she'd be. "On other occasions I might think you were joking. But, as a matter of fact, Blanche Sweet told me she saw your sister and William S. Hart in a cozy situation at the home of Tom Ince."

"It's true," I said, "but Lotte would die if news got out."

"Lotte Lee, Hollywood's newest vamp, and that cowboy granddaddy, William S. Hart," she said. "It's the odd couple of the year, but stranger couplings have happened out here."

At this tense moment, W.R. himself came into the library. "Louella, Durango," he said in the kindly, courtly way he often had when someone wasn't angering him. "My co-conspirators." He motioned to an attendant to escort Louella out of the library. "I've arranged for you to have five minutes with Churchill," he said to her. "No more."

"Oh, W.R., you've made my day," she said. "I can't believe that little old me is actually going to get to interview Winston Churchill."

At the door, Louella stopped in her tracks as W.R. called back to her. "Don't ask him anything stupid." he said.

"Oh, W.R.," she said, staggering on her drunken way toward Churchill. "You're such a kidder."

When she'd gone, the Chief turned to me. It was my second inquisition of the evening from a newspaper hawk. We chatted pleasantly for a few minutes, with me giving him information about Charlie and various tidbits of inside gossip about Hollywood. After all, I had to earn my five-hundred dollars a week. But throughout our private little talk, I knew he was planning to ask me some sort of question. Finally, he focused rather soulful eyes on me and said, "I understand you're taking Marion to the movies Friday night."

Was this a trap to determine if I'd been truthful to him? Had Marion actually told him I was taking her to the movies, or was he just pretending that she'd said that to see if I would agree to anything to protect Marion?

I lifted my drink, fearing that W.R. would disapprove of my consumption of alcohol but it did give me a minute to think.

The Gods rushed to my aid that night. In the door where Louella had so recently departed barged Marion herself. Apparently, she'd been planning to tell me about this mysterious movie date when Louella interrupted us. Sensing my dilemma, she called out, "Are you getting permission from my loving man here to take me to the movies Friday night?"

"More or less," I said, turning to smile at W.R. "It's okay with you, isn't it?"

"I'll miss Marion," he said, "but she needs to get out occasionally with someone her own age." He headed for the door but turned back to look at Marion. "At least going to see a film with Durango is better than your sitting here getting stewed every night." He then glanced at me. "Given your proclivities, you are the only man in Hollywood I can trust to take Marion out. Certainly not Chaplin."

When the Chief had gone, Marion turned to me. "I meant to tell you all about it but then Louella staggered in. I need you to serve as my beard Friday night. Pick me up here like a regular date. I want you to take me to this private apartment. I'm having a hot affair."

"Obviously one different from Charlie this time," I said. "Who's the lucky guy?"

"I don't want to tell you until we get there," she said, "but this guy is hot, hot, hot. No lady has been truly fucked until she's had this stud. When you see him, I bet you'll fall for him too."

"I can't wait," I said.

She looked skeptically at me. "It might be unwise to take you to meet him, whether you're serving as my beard or not."

"What's the problem?"

"I don't know for sure," she said, "but I've heard rumors back in New York that my beau kept a little teenage boy at the Plaza. For all I know, once he sees you he might dump me."

I kissed her affectionately on the cheek. "Let's not fantasize," I cautioned. Taking her arm in mine, we headed back to the party.

The moment Marion got me back into the mainstream of the party, she quickly deserted me for other friends, but left me to talk to Florence Vidor.

Though hardly a household word today, the actress from Houston, Texas, was a towering presence on post World War I screens. Taking her name Vidor from her husband, King Vidor, she had starred in *A Tale of Two Cities* in 1917, and this is the picture I most remembered. Cast in upper-class or aristocratic parts in the main, this Vitagraph star had appeared in many

Sessue Hayakawa vehicles at Paramount. I wanted to ask her if Sessue had branded her but didn't dare.

She had a maturity and elegance to her, although still in her twenties, and she reminded me of a high-fashion model more than an actress. Having really nothing to say to Florence Vidor, I attempted small talk. She wasn't much help with the conversation. "I understand you've been under contract to Tom Ince," I said. "I met him recently."

"That's nice," she said, making it sound like a dismissal of me. "He more or less got us started. He employed my husband, King, at five dollars a day, but he was offered only two days of work a week. Generous man, that Ince, don't you think?"

It was all too apparent that the subject of Tom Ince was not the way to ingratiate myself with Miss Vidor. "I've recently seen you in *Poor Relations* and *The Other Half*," I said, trying to get the conversation going.

"I preferred *The Countess Charming*," she said. "Or *Till I Come Back to You*."

"Those were great too," I said, having seen neither of them.

"Young man," she said to me, a mask of hardness crossing her features. "King and I separated two years ago, although we are not officially divorced. I came to this party tonight because I'm in the market for a new husband. I suspect you are a homosexual, and therefore of no use to me. I do not understand homosexuality and have no more need to talk to you."

Stung by her insult, I watched as she walked away. Within moments she was dancing in the arms of a very handsome young man whom I would have preferred for myself.

Marion came to my rescue, taking my hand and leading me over to a corner of the room where Charlie stood talking to Winston Churchill. After introducing me, she retreated again. The resolutely wooden Churchill seemed bored with Charlie who was pontificating on the failures of the Conservative government and its "short-sighted" policies.

When Charlie was around people he felt were better educated and informed than he was, he took to the soap box as if to impress. Churchill seemed rather dismissive of Charlie.

"In England we'd have you beheaded for some of your ideas," he said to Charlie and sounded as if he meant it.

When Charlie lectured Churchill for another five minutes, the British statesman appeared boyishly disgruntled. He seemed relieved when Charlie excused himself to have his picture taken with W.R. and Marion.

That left me alone with the great man himself, who back then wasn't all that great or famous. "Your friend here is a real Bolshevik. His politics are going to get him into deep trouble in his lifetime. I tolerated all of Chaplin's Communist propaganda, but find him a total fool. I like his films, however. He's the finest star out here. By the way, I love the way you Americans call these second-class vaudeville acts and former chorus girls stars."

"Charlie has been a wonderful friend to me," I said. "But when he starts talking politics, I think of something else. We get along fine that way."

Churchill turned and looked at me with a bulldog stare so penetrating I think I'd rather be interrogated by W.R. "Exactly what do you do for Chaplin?"

"I'm just a friend," I said, not knowing how to respond.

He cleared his throat and, if I heard right, he passed a little fart. It was so tiny one could hardly detect it. Sensing my discomfort, he said, "American food doesn't agree with me." As if aware of my actual relationship with Charlie, he said something that sounded like, "Sodomites. The British navy would sink without them."

Had he actually said that or had I misunderstood him? Even now I'm not sure but that's what it sounded like.

"When Charlie wasn't lecturing me on a subject he knows nothing about, British politics, I gave him some advice about his films," Churchill said.

"And what was that?" I asked, really eager to find out.

"I told him he should play Napoleon," Churchill said.

"How did you know he's always wanted to portray Napoleon on the screen?"

"It was basic instinct," he said. "In my opinion, Chaplin's ego matches that of the little

French bastard. I've read volumes on Napoleon and have this splendid idea for a scene in the film. There are fantastic comedic possibilities in my idea. Chaplin could play Napoleon taking a bath. His brother, Jerome, comes running into the bathroom where Napoleon is splashing about. Jerome is attired in a fancy military uniform with gold braid and polished boots. He hopes to embarrass the dictator who was known for having a small penis. Napoleon is furious at getting his bath interrupted and rises from the soap and suds to order Jerome out of the bathroom. At this point the little dictator slips and falls back into the water, splashing Jerome's uniform." Churchill chuckled mightily at this scene spinning in his head, and seemed truly delighted at the idea.

I pretended to laugh but didn't find it all that funny, although I knew Charlie had enough talent to pull off such a scene. But, alas, he never made the film.

Churchill looked uncomfortable, and I asked him if anything were wrong.

"Young man," he said, "I need to see a man about a horse, an expression I've recently learned in America. I've had a lot to drink, and I want you to guide me across the floor into the toilet. I'm a bit pissed but need to take a piss."

Guiding Churchill through the party where he was greeted repeatedly, we finally arrived at the toilet where Marion had installed three urinals side by side, very similar to what Nazimova had done at the Garden of Alla. Taking advantage of the opportunity, I stood beside Churchill and took a piss with him. I finished at least one full minute before he did, but not before I spotted a long, thick cock hanging out of his trousers.

And, if I may jump ahead and interject a little World War II history to my narrative, I am happy to report that Pecker Checkers of the World have revealed that of all the war leaders, Churchill was clearly the winner in the penile department, measuring in at a lusty eight and a half inches when fully hard. Mussolini was runner-up at seven and a half inches. Roosevelt and Stalin tied, with each having barely six inches. Hitler lost the contest, measuring just under four and a half rather thin inches. The Nazi leader also lost in the ball sac department, as one of his testicles never descended at birth.

Chapter Nine

The first day of shooting on *Vampira* began with me on bended hosiery in front of Samuel Goldwyn in a side office. Decades from then, Marilyn Monroe more than anybody would have understood that an actress must do what an actress must do. Long before Nancy Reagan (then known as Davis) was proclaimed fellatio queen of Hollywood in the late 40s, Lotte Lee ruled Tinseltown with her succulent cherry-red lips and talented tongue. All the men proclaimed I was the best. Only my darling friend, Rod St. Just, gave me serious blow-job competition.

Before coming to the studio, I'd spent four hours alone with Rodolfo and had fitted Antonio in for at least an hour and a half that morning. Our director, Billy Taylor, unlike more temperamental directors, allowed visitors onto the set, and the front office informed me that John Gilbert would be showing up later in the day for a brief visit. I could well imagine what kind of encounter that would be. Goldwyn had arranged a sumptuous dressing room for me, even better than the one DeMille had secured for Swanson on Catalina Island.

I wasn't due on the set until an hour from now, and I was so nervous I wanted to bite my scarlet-coated fingernails. Up to now, no one had ever determined if I could act. My first visitor was Billy who explained the day's scenes with me very carefully and even affectionately. I was far from being in love with William Desmond Taylor, and seriously resented how he intruded himself into my love affair with

Antonio, but today I turned to him like a trusting father.

"I'd invite you to lunch but I'm seeing Mary Miles Minter and her mother, Charlotte Shelby," he said. "Tomorrow maybe. They'll be visiting the set several times. Perhaps you'd like to meet them."

"My first day on the set and I'll be a wallflower," I said, pouting my lips in the bee-stung way practically copyrighted by Mae Murray.

"You'll not be alone," he said. "I happen to know that Richard Barthelmess is going to invite you to lunch. He's got some friends dropping by the set at noon today to wish him well. Lillian and Dorothy Gish for openers. Also Alla Nazimova."

"What an impressive cast," I said. "Nazimova? Richard's not a beautiful gal. What does Nazimova want with him?"

"She's been a family friend for a long time," he said. "She's the one who got him interested in motion pictures. Three years ago they made a film together, an adaptation of her play, *War Brides,* for Lewis J. Selznick."

"That one must not have been shown in Lawrence, Kansas," I said. "I thought D. W. Griffith had him tightly wrapped. I was surprised Richard agreed to appear in *Vampira.* I mean after *Broken Blossoms* he can write his own ticket. And I hear he's set for Griffith's *Way Down East.*"

"Richard is a homosexual, and this is going

to be the first and perhaps greatest homosexual film ever made, except only the smartest people will know it's a pansy film. It'll be an inside thing. I so intrigued Richard with the project he couldn't turn it down. He found it too fascinating." He looked at me with a knowing smirk on his face. "Richard likes to get fucked, incidentally, if you want to try him out as Durango Jones. I fucked him myself only this morning, and he loved it. I don't think he'll be very attracted to you as Lotte Lee, but as Durango he'll go for you in a big way."

"Thanks for the inside tip," I said. "It might come in handy if I get horny later in the day."

Billy soon left but not until he'd arranged a three-way with Antonio and me later in the week. As I was being made up by a very talented artist booked by Rod St. Just, a call came in from Cecil B. DeMille inviting me to join him at his country estate, "Paradise," that weekend.

He said that Theodore Kosloff had been enchanted with me when he'd met me on the boat coming over to Catalina Island. I'd been more than enchanted with Kosloff. That was one ballet dancer after my own heart. DeMille told me that Kosloff would be there with Natacha Rambova, whoever in the hell she was. I figured I'd be able to entice Kosloff away from Miss Rambova for a few hot and heavy hours. I eagerly accepted DeMille's invitation. The director also assured me he wanted to discuss a script for my next picture. Of course, I'd have to clear that with Goldwyn, but I was mighty interested in the DeMille scenario. Who knows? If this vamp revival crap didn't work out, DeMille might make me into a second Gloria Swanson.

A messenger knocked on my dressing room door with a hand-written note from Richard Barthelmess. He'd like to meet me before we were both called to the set. I eagerly accepted.

Within five minutes, Richard showed up and he was just as handsome, even more so, than I remembered him when I'd met him at that cafe when I was my real self, Durango Jones. Around women, he was even more gracious and charming than he'd been with me as Durango. He was one classy guy, and as we talked, I was enthralled with him, wishing I'd been dressed as Durango and not as Lotte Lee.

He told me he was a close friend of my brother's--a bit of an exaggeration--and claimed he was disappointed that Durango was not on the set today.

"He'll be here after we wrap for the day at five," I said. "He told me he's dying to see you again."

"Then you know?" he asked a little nervously, uncertain of my response.

"Durango tells me everything, and he's really taken with you. My brother considers you one of the most handsome men in Hollywood."

"He does?" He looked surprised. "I'm flattered. There are a lot of good-looking guys in Hollywood besides me. Wallace Reid, for example."

Just as I was getting to know Richard, a rap on the door and a call summoned both of us to the set where Billy was waiting. The script called for a love scene. I was put off. Couldn't Billy have worked up to that? Did my first moment on film as Lotte Lee have to be making love to Richard Barthelmess?

Richard and I were ushered onto the set of *Vampira*, a robber baron mansion owned by the character I played, Leonora de la Mer, who called her opulently decorated manor Sacré-Coeur. As a director, Billy Taylor was exceedingly gracious and gentlemanly, almost courtly, unlike DeMille whom I understood often insulted actors. Billy used a director's vocabulary known mainly to himself. Used to working with the more direct and straightforward D. W. Griffith, it was obvious Richard was experiencing extreme difficulties in understanding Billy. In his direction to us, Billy told us we had to be "artistic but realistic," whatever that meant. "You must move in shades—numerous shades, that is—from the sublimely pathetic to the strikingly spectacular. It must be a picture to touch the heart but also one to arouse sexual desire in both men and women." Finally, he got down to talk both Richard and I could understand. Turning to Richard, Billy said, "You must be masculine, red-blooded, and an ideal lover who combines strength and character with fantastic sex appeal."

"In other words, look like you would deliver a good fuck," I told Richard, only to receive a reprimand from Billy. The director told me that

I was to undress Richard with my eyes the moment he walked on camera. Since I did that with most men, I found it an easy part to play.

From its initial presentation to me by Goldwyn, the script had been rewritten and simplified. I found the new version much easier to follow and to play my character of Leonora, a vamp who literally devoured handsome, well-built men, the more the merrier. From Richard Barthelmess to Francis X. Bushman, Leonora was to acquire a household staff of the most virile of men who would be hired for one role but expected to play another part—that of satisfying her insatiable libido.

Richard was to be my chauffeur. Ushered before me by a staff member, we exchanged pleasantries before I asked him to remove his jacket. He complied but asked why he had to take off his jacket. In his role of chauffeur, he anticipated wearing a jacket as he drove me around. I told him I wanted to see if he could fit into ten new chauffeur uniforms I'd ordered for my previous driver who had to leave town suddenly for reasons my character doesn't explain. A bit suspiciously, Richard removed his jacket. The scene proceeded with me asking him to take off his white shirt because the glare of white was hard on my eyes. I told him if I could see the upper part of his torso bared, I might better tell if he could wear the new clothes ordered.

As Billy directed me at one point, I was actually depicted using a tape measure to gauge the full width of Richard's shoulders. By today's standards, he would not be a buffed body from a gym in Chelsea in New York City. But back then his body was enticing to me. It was athletic and in perfect shape, and I couldn't wait until the late afternoon when my brother, Durango, would no doubt find every little hidden crevice in it with his voracious tongue. The scene proceeded with Richard and me lying on the sofa, as he kissed me deeply. Even though I knew Richard might not like women that much, I opened my mouth to him, demanding his tongue. He reluctantly obliged and I sucked like I wanted his life force. In the meantime, the camera trailed my hands in close-up as I ran my long-nailed fingers over his muscled back, digging in when his kissing aroused me

to a fever pitch.

Although it was my first time on the screen as Lotte Lee, Billy seemed pleased with our work and informed me there would be another scene or two to shoot this afternoon. Even though a major production, Billy had been given only three weeks to complete the entire film. How different from Elizabeth Taylor's *Cleopatra* decades later.

Billy had arranged for a lunch for all of us, and I was to join Richard and his friends, the Gish sisters as well as Nazimova.

Nazimova arrived first and after kissing Richard asked to be directed to my dressing room for a little toilet emergency. On the way there, she informed me that she was a "close friend of your divine brother, Durango." I knew that wasn't true but had no intention of challenging her.

While loudly using my toilet, Nazimova told me how she'd met Richard when as a struggling Russian Jewess she'd lived in a theatrical boarding house in New York run by his mother. "Richard's mother helped me through many a gray day. Sometimes she fed me when I had no money or forgave me when I couldn't pay the rent. When I started going places, I gave Richard a part in my first movie. He had just then graduated from a college in Connecticut."

Emerging from my toilet and pulling up her bloomers, Nazimova cornered me before meeting the Gish sisters. "Is your brother still with Valentino?"

I knew she was eager for news of Jean Acker. "They are still together but only occasionally. Each leads very separate lives."

"So I've been told," she said, searching my eyes with the intensity of W.R. himself. "Do you know everything?"

"Durango tells me everything about his life." I said. "I make no judgments."

Nazimova burst into laughter that sounded a bit hysterical. "From what I hear, you can't throw stones living in the glass house you live in. I've heard tales as tall as you are."

"They're all true," I said. "When it comes to men, I'm insatiable."

"Keep your hands off Richard," she warned. "You'll just embarrass him. Give him to Durango instead."

"You read my intentions exactly. My brother

will be here this afternoon. On the set this morning, Richard pulled off his shirt before my character of Leonora de la Mer. Perhaps this afternoon he'll unbutton his trousers for Durango."

"Durango has probably told you about Jean Acker—Valentino's so-called wife—and me." I nodded that he had. "It's all over between Acker and me," she said. "Acker isn't fucking Valentino but she's shacked up with this dyke, Grace Darmond."

"She didn't waste any time getting over you or Valentino."

My remark angered Nazimova but she recovered quickly. "There was nothing between Valentino and Acker. They have never gone to bed together. I hear Valentino is fucking Swanson, your brother Durango, and Norman Kerry, perhaps Mae Murray too."

"Who knows?"

"You do." Nazimova moved in closer to me with more intensity than the hawkeye of Louella Parsons herself.

"I don't understand. I'm not privy to the private life of Valentino," I said.

"Don't kid me, bitch. I had a spy at the Hollywood Hotel. That honeymoon night with Jean Acker interested me. I learned Acker wouldn't let Valentino into her room but the door opened wide across the hall and Lotte Lee was only too anxious to grab the Italian stallion."

"Your spies are very good," I said, startled that she knew that.

"Does your brother know you've been fucking Valentino?"

"No, and I don't want to make him jealous. Perhaps you'll keep that episode confidential."

"I will indeed but I found it highly amusing. Since I know something on you, I'll make a fair trade and give you some dirt on myself. I got over Acker real sudden like since I've got two of the hottest women in Hollywood sharing my bed. Mildred Harris for one."

That was one big surprise. Nazimova was having an affair with Charlie's wife. I found that a bit ironic, considering that I too was "Mrs. Charlie Chaplin." Nazimova and Mildred Harris were one secret almost too good to keep to myself. Charlie should know of this. It might give him some ammunition in his upcoming

divorce when he got rid of the first Mrs. Chaplin, leaving only me, Lotte Lee Chaplin, on the stage.

"Not only I am fucking Mildred, but I'm also in love with Natacha Rambova. I'm sure you've heard of her. She's divinely beautiful and very talented."

Actually I had heard of Natacha Rambova, but only this morning and from DeMille who had invited her along with Theodore Kosloff to his country estate, Paradise, for the weekend. Other than that, I knew nothing of her, assuming she was just another aspiring actress, of which hundreds were arriving daily by train in Los Angeles. "I can't say I know of Natacha Rambova. But what an exotic name."

Just as Nazimova was to explain who Natacha was, there was a knock on my door. Thinking it was a messenger summoning us to lunch, I opened it only to discover a clean-shaven John Gilbert looking divinely handsome.

He knew Nazimova, at least slightly, but seemed eager to get rid of her. He told her that the lunch was ready with the Gish sisters. Sensing what was about to happen, the sexually sophisticated Nazimova quickly excused herself and headed for table.

John shut the door behind me, locked it, and moved toward me with a gleam in his eyes. "Baby, baby," he said, "have I got a big surprise for you."

*****

Lunch with Richard, the Gish sisters, and Nazimova was light, gay, and uneventful. All the talk about D. W. Griffith seemed to bore Nazimova, but kept the other three enthralled.

"I want you working for me soon," Dorothy said to Richard. "But I must warn you, I'll be the boss."

"It will be a case of the Greek meeting the Greekess," Nazimova said. "A headstrong temperamental girl meeting an obstinate little Napoleon."

That remark took some time for everybody to digest, and a few moments passed while the guests pretended to be eating.

"Now, now," Lillian said in her birdlike,

cerebral way. "Dorothy and Dick will have their spats. After all, they are but two spoiled children. But in time both will come to their senses and do what is right for the picture."

"I feel so depressed most of the time," Dorothy said. "I guess I get temperamental."

"You feel depressed," Nazimova interjected, "because your comedies aren't as good as they should be."

"When Dorothy's moods are black, they are black," Richard said. "One day I came to her dressing room and found her looking at the want ads in the paper. She felt her film career was nearing its end. Dorothy told me that the only thing she could do was get a job as a cook where a family lived exclusively on prepared breakfast food."

"That's right," Dorothy piped in. "I could bring in the milk bottle every morning."

"I hear Griffith respects you," Nazimova said to Dorothy. "That there's nothing about show business you don't know. Let's face it: you were launched on the stage at the ripe age of two."

"D.W. and I were at sword's point a good deal of the time," Dorothy said. "But he always called me in for consultation when there came a rough place in the story that needed work."

"D.W. can always put Dorothy in a rage," Lillian said. "He loots from her comedy unit. Anything or any actor who takes his fancy. That goes from props to leading men. When he began *Broken Blossoms* he took Dick for the part of the Chinaman, leaving Dorothy without a leading man."

Feeling that I, Lotte Lee, the star of the picture whose set they were visiting, was being completely ignored, I tried to add something to the conversation. I turned to Lillian. "The scene in *Broken Blossoms* where you hid in the closet from your brutal and drunken father still stands out as the finest thing you ever did— one of the finest things any actress ever did."

Lillian beamed at me as if used to compliments, however misguided. "I have a peculiar habit of living all my parts," she said. "If, for instance, I'm playing the part of a French peasant girl, I live her life for weeks. I read nothing but books of French peasant life— keep away completely from my American friends—and even eat the food a French peasant girl would eat."

"I was amazed at how you were made up to look Chinese in *Broken Blossoms*," I said, turning to Richard. "Especially the slant eyes."

"That was accomplished by pasting a strip of adhesive tape from my temples, the other end being under my cap," he said. "I understand that W.S. Hart has heard about that now that he's getting old. He's going to use the same technique in his next picture. It's like an instant face-lift. The tape pins up the sagging cheeks."

"Dick went to Chinatown and studied the locals for days on end," Lillian said. "He learned to see without looking as the Chinese do. A Chinaman's glance never seems to travel out to meet anything as a white man's does. Dick even learned to shoot as Chinese highbinders do—without lifting the gun from the hip. I have never seen any other actor go after a part with such systematic effort as Dick." She glanced lovingly at her sister, making me think the lesbian experimentation between them was still on. "Except darling Lillian here."

A messenger came summoning Richard and me back to the set. After bending low to kiss both of the Gish sisters, I told Richard I would join him soon. Nazimova motioned that she wanted to see me in private.

Once we were out of hearing distance of everybody else, Nazimova whispered to me. "My dear friend, Dagmar Godowsky, and I would like to get together with you some night. Of course, Mildred and Natacha must not know."

I was startled. This was Lotte's first lesbian invitation. Dagmar Godowsky was a name familiar to me. The daughter of pianist Leopold Godowsky, Dagmar was breaking in as a minor film star, having appeared that very year in *Bonds of Honor* and *The Kids and the Cowboy*. She'd recently told the press that her life was an "express train going nowhere," but in time she'd make some interesting stops along the way. One as a Valentino leading lady on film and another as the mistress of Stravinsky.

"I'll think about it," I said, knowing that little midget, Nazimova, would be very disappointed if she went down on me. She'd discover more about Lotte Lee than she wanted to know.

Bending down to the earth, I kissed

Nazimova good-bye, having no desire to become one of her supporting players and certainly not a new addition to her stable of girl friends, not that I had the equipment for that.

That afternoon I felt that Richard and I made a hot screen team together. Billy Taylor claimed I added to Richard's sex appeal on screen, whereas Lillian Gish seemed to "desex" him. Richard liked that compliment. Later when Billy had ordered a break, Richard whispered to me, "When I'm before the camera with you, I feel my balls are clanking on the floor."

When Billy shut down filming for the day, he summoned me into his office asking me to give him a quick blow-job. "Watching you make love to Richard Barthelmess all day gave me a perpetual hard-on. This film is going to be terrific."

Just as I'd begun my first day on the set by falling on my knees before my producer Goldwyn, so I ended my day kneeling on the carpet in front of my director, Billy Taylor. I sucked him voraciously and kept him moaning with pleasure all the time. He could not have known that I didn't have my heart and soul in that blow-job.

After I'd drained him dry, I kissed him as if the cameras were rolling before disappearing into my dressing room alone where I was to transform myself into Durango Jones to await the appearance of Richard Barthelmess.

By the time Richard knocked on my door, all my identity as Lotte Lee had been erased and I was once again the sexy cowboy from Kansas, Durango Jones. Having kissed him for most of the day, I was eager to explore into deeper terrain.

"We meet again," Richard said as I opened the door. He looked around cautiously. "Is Lotte gone for the day?"

"She is indeed and she told me to tell you that you're terrific," I said. "She hopes you'll be cast in all her future films."

Locking the door to my dressing room, Richard took me in his arms. "I've been waiting for that call from you ever since I met you in that café."

As I felt his lips on mine, and as I sucked his tongue, he wasn't the same man I'd been kissing all afternoon. As he aroused me by kissing me as Durango, I could tell that

Richard's heart wasn't into kissing Lotte. Kissing Durango was his specialty. As much as I'd enjoyed his kissing on the set of *Vampira*, his kissing of me as a man was much more passionate and inspired. Before Billy's cameras, it was a duty kiss and for all I know it had revolted him. But with me holding him in my arms as a man, he attacked me, seeking sexual gratification. I planned to give him just that.

While we exchanged tongues, his hands traveled. "I can't believe how big that thing is," he whispered in my ear. "For me, a guy's got to be really big down there or else I'm just not interested. You measure up fantastically. What I always dream about but seldom get."

"Why don't we ease out of our clothes and really get to know each other," I suggested.

He did just that, removing all my clothes with compliments galore. He stood before me, stripping off his own clothing. He was a tempting morsel but far from heavy hung. Fully hard, he looked average, maybe a little less than average.

But I was sticking up long and thick in the air, and he fell on my cock, sucking all of it down his throat. Though hardly an expert like Lotte Lee, Richard was good and practically brought me to a roaring climax. When he sensed an eruption on the way, he backed off, leaving me completely unsatisfied. He had other plans for me that night.

Lifting me up, he exposed my rosebud. "I always like to rim my top," he pronounced before the assault of his talented tongue sent sheer delight through my entire body.

Finally when I could stand this no more, I pulled his head off me, tossed him back on the sofa with his legs up in the air, and penetrated him, delighted by his squeals of pain. "You want 'em big, baby," I said in my most masculine voice, "then be prepared to scream."

His moans of pain soon turned to pleasure, and I must have ridden him like a bronco a good twenty minutes before I was ready to explode. In the middle of my attack on him, he shot cum once, and I felt I was going to fuck another eruption of jism from him as I climaxed inside him myself.

I did just that. I had the beautiful hunk blasting off for a second time, as he dug his nails into my back and promised undying love to me.

After five deflated minutes inside him, I was ready to pull out. But again he had other plans for me. "No way, José," he said. "That was the best sex I've ever had in my life. No one has ever fucked me like that. You're not pulling out of me until I've had you a second time. At least. Ride em' cowboy," he called out.

"I'll do just that," I said as a perverted idea crossed my sex-crazed mind. As he fought my pulling out, I yanked out anyway and presented my rather juicy cock to his succulent lips. "Before I fuck you again, suck me really hard."

Obeying my command like a sex slave, he swallowed me whole, letting me explore a deep recess of his throat.

When I pushed his legs in the air and entered him for the second time, he was crying. Not just crying, but sobbing. At first I thought I should pull out until I saw that his face was a mask of passion and desire. I bent over and kissed him gently in contrast to the fierce fucking I was giving him.

"I'm so happy," he said, pulling me down on him again. "No man has ever made me this happy before. I'm crying because I know that nothing in my life will ever be this good again."

*****

Although up to now I'd seen Mae Murray only from a distance, I was at last given a chance to meet her personally, courtesy of Rodolfo. As the Teens drew to an end, Rodolfo appeared in a number of forgettable films, his work often lasting no more than a week and earning for him the less than princely sum of one-hundred dollars a week.

His role finished on *Out of Luck* with Dorothy Gish, Rodolfo had secured a part with Mae Murray, his friend from New York, in her starring vehicle, *The Big Little Person*, which evoked the era of handsome, gallant knights on white horses rescuing beautiful blonde damsels in distress. Late at night as we enjoyed pillow talk, Rodolfo often spoke of his boyhood dreams of chivalry and medieval

glory. He'd fantasized about being a jousting knight. To actually impersonate one on film enthralled him, and I was eager to see how the shooting had gone.

At the studio I encountered the young Walt Disney whom I'd met before as Lotte Lee on Catalina Island. As I introduced myself as Durango, I concealed my jealousy that he'd also enjoyed those divine inches, both long and thick, of William Boyd. He spoke about the work he was doing, sketching some of the designs for the picture. Little could I have known then that one day he'd do a lot more with princesses, knights, castles, and all that good stuff.

Actually this teenage boy was so charming that I forgave him for going down on William. He told me that Valentino had indeed gotten to wear a suit of armor and ride a white horse. "I designed the look myself." Walt said. "But the property department screwed up royally. They showed up with armor that would make Valentino look like a clown in a tin suit. It wasn't armor but a cheap imitation. When he saw it, Valentino refused to wear it."

"I'm surprised," I said. "He's my friend and I thought he'd be more compliant than that. I mean he's struggling for every break."   .

"Valentino stood his ground," Walt said. "He even went down the street to a prop house and rented a real suit of armor, paying for it with his own money. When he got back to the studio, the suit turned out to be much too large for him.

"Oh, shit," I said.

"That wasn't all." Walt continued. "We had to help Valentino into the suit and artfully cover the fact that the armor didn't fit. We had to help him onto his horse. The picture is supposed to be serious but getting on the horse, if filmed, would be funnier than anything in the film."   .

"At least he got through it, I hope."

"Just as he finally mounted and the camera was ready, the sun slipped behind a dark rain cloud," Walt said. "Shooting couldn't commence again until the sun came out and that wasn't for two hours. Valentino said that in that mass of metal he felt like he was boiling in the hottest Turkish bath in hell. He patiently waited and waited while wilting before the sun finally came out again. After all that, his appearance in that damn armor will last less than three minutes on the screen."

"That poor man will do anything to break into show business," I said.

"When Valentino got out of that iron strait jacket," Walt said, "he claimed he knew what the victims of an Inquisition torture chamber felt like." Walt pointed me to the sound stage where he said Mae Murray and Valentino were waiting.

As I started to leave, he said, "May I ask you something personal?"

"Sure, what's up?"

"You're a homosexual, aren't you?

"Takes one to know one," I said mockingly but cheerfully to him.

He smiled and winked. "I saw Valentino in the shower. He's got a big thick cock. I'd really like to go down on him if you could arrange it."

"He's every bit as good or even better than William Boyd," I said with a slight smirk on my face before heading toward the sound stage.

Shown to the sound stage where Mae and Rodolfo were said to be, I encountered one of the most stunning scenes I've ever seen on film or off. As the sun set in the west, blazes of red light poured through the windows of the large barnlike stage, which evoked a square dance hall in the Middle West.

Tango music was playing. On center stage Rodolfo in black leather boots, a suede hat, and a black gaucho outfit was dancing the tango with Mae Murray who wore a dress of sparkling white sequins and high-heeled shoes. It was a stunning tour de force, the greatest and hottest dance I've ever seen.

In just months from that afternoon, Rodolfo would go on to earn world acclaim for his famous tango dance with Beatrice Dominguez in *The Four Horsemen of the Apocalypse*.

Mae Murray, eventually known as the queen of Metro-Goldwyn-Mayer, is remembered today mainly for the famous Merry Widow waltz in which she dipped, swayed, and moved in beautiful rhythm with John Gilbert, his eyes never leaving hers. If the tango with Mae Murray and Rodolfo had been filmed, it is my belief it would have dwarfed the thrill of those other legendary screen dances. Alas, like so many moments of that era, it was never captured for immortality.

Almost as bad, their tango dance was never finished. A stagehand interrupted them, closing down the studio for the day. "This ain't no dance hall, lady," he said to Mae. "Let's haul ass out of here." In the years to come, Mae would have had him beheaded for his rudeness, but back at that point in her career she didn't have such box-office clout.

In her dressing room, Mae chatted with us, and I tried to appear delighted to meet her. Actually I was very jealous. I'd seen how Rodolfo had looked into her eyes as they danced. He always maintained, even to his dying day, as did Mae, that they were merely friends—never lovers. I doubted that very seriously, and I'm never wrong in matters of the heart. I saw what I saw.

Those were two lovers dancing on that sound stage, thinking they were not being observed, especially by one of the boy friends of the male dancer, Mr. Rodolfo Valentino.

There was always confusion about his name until he finally changed it to Rudolph Valentino. In *The Big Little Person* he was credited as Rudolpho De Valentina. In a previous film, *The Married Virgin*, he'd been billed as Rodolfo de Valentini.

Aside from her obvious beauty, it was easy to see why Rodolfo was attracted to Mae. She built him up whereas other women, such as Jean Acker, tore him down. Throughout her life, Nazimova had mixed feelings and emotions about Rodolfo. He was either dashing, romantic, and handsome, or else a maggot-eaten Italian sausage. There was sexual tension between Mae Murray and Rodolfo. The sex between them was there, but it was more than that too. Both actors genuinely liked each other. "You stand out in a crowd of extras," she told Rodolfo as they discussed the day's shooting. "You give off a glow like a powerful light bulb. Some people operate on forty-watt bulbs. You are definitely one-hundred and fifty. You light up the night. You and I both have star quality. Most performers, even some of the stars themselves, don't."

Rodolfo seemed to thrive on those words of praise. As for me, Mae gave me little confidence, as she noted my blond hair. "In my films," she said, "I'm the blond beauty. I don't need competition from a man who looks even prettier than I am." She reached over and ran her porcelain fingers across Rudy's scarred cheek. "I prefer my co-stars to have raven dark hair. I think the ebony of a man's hair contrasts perfectly with my blonde locks."

Later when Mae had dressed in her street clothes, if indeed a dress of pink sequins could be called that, we headed for the Ship's Café where all the stars used to gather for drinks and food, but mainly gossip and fun.

It seemed that everybody I knew was there. I was startled to encounter Dorothy Gish with Richard Barthelmess. I was still carrying around a belly of his cum. Olive Thomas was there with Jack Pickford, and we promised to get together real soon. Getting me alone in the men's room, Jack told me he wanted some more of that "delicious" cocaine, and like the fool I was, I agreed to get it for him. He could easily have gotten it for himself at the Fruitfly, but was afraid to drive through Los Angeles since he was always drunk and wrecking his vehicle and didn't want to be caught with heavy drugs on him too.

Gloria Swanson and her husband, H. K. Somborn, arrived, and we were introduced to her ugly little spouse. Swanson gave no clue that she was having an affair with Rodolfo, especially in front of Mae. Swanson confirmed that Rodolfo would take my sister, Lotte, to a dinner soon to be staged at the lavish home of Clara Kimball Young.

Wallace Reid appeared with his sullen wife, Dorothy, whom I despised, and two big movie stars showed up without men: Alice Joyce and Blanche Sweet. I suspected neither of them of being a lesbian, and just assumed they were shopping for a hot date for the night.

In spite of all the big names at the Ship Café that early evening, Alice Joyce was the one star I'd wanted to meet. Like me, the Vitagraph Girl, as she was called back in her heyday of the Teens, was born in Kansas. At the time I was introduced to her by Mae, Alice Joyce was just nearing the big-30. Even Maria Jane approved of Alice, as she was also known as "The Madonna of the Screen."

Having worked as a telephone operator at age 13 and a fashion model afterward, Alice achieved popularity as a charming, proper leading lady in many shorts. She was the eternal ingénue before switching to more mature parts such as playing the mother of Clara Bow in the wildly popular film, *Dancing Mothers*, in the years to come.

Just that very year, Alice was appearing in such films as *The Spark Divine, The Winchester Woman, The Vengeance of Durand, The Third Degree, The Cambric Mask, The Lion and the Mouse,* and *The Captain's Captain.*

These were all forgettable films but it was another role that Alice played that most intrigued me. She was the wife of my sometimes boy friend, Tom Moore. Alice didn't know it at the time but I was very familiar with those Irish inches that penetrated her.

Rumor had it that she and Tom Moore were on the verge of divorce, which came true just a few months later. That left Tom free to marry me, but he never did, the good-looking mother-fucker that he was. However, as I was to keep all my orifices plugged in the Twenties by other handsome leading men, I didn't miss him all that much.

"My husband is looking forward to appearing with your sister in *Vampira*," Alice said with a sophistication and disdain she never brought to one of her angelic movie portrayals. "I just hope he doesn't show up drunk on the set."

"He'll be great," I said with all the confidence I could muster.

In front of everybody, Alice confronted me. "Is it true that Tom is having an affair with Miss Lee?"

"Not at all," I said a little too defensively. "Lotte has been linked with half the men in this town. Frankly, I think it's Goldwyn's publicity men starting these ridiculous rumors. They're just trying to make Lotte into a real vamp to fan interest in the movie. My sister was raised in a convent." As I stared Alice down, I felt like a real insider, since the actress couldn't possibly know that I, Durango Jones, was Lotte Lee, the seducer of her wandering husband. Unlike Alice, I had had all the Moore brothers, including Matt and Owen.

Mae seemed to have little interest in the confrontation between Alice and myself. She turned to Blanche Sweet, and the Merry Widow's face showed her acute disappointment. "You really should not be smearing yourself with Pompeian Beauty Cream in advertisements," Mae lectured Blanche. "Stars cannot allow the public to think they can obtain beauty from a bottle of cream."

Blanche smiled deferentially at Mae and didn't challenge her attack, although it was apparent from the look on Blanche's expressive face that she'd go on advertising whatever in the hell she wanted to.

When Rodolfo and Mae wandered off, Blanche signaled me to remain behind for a moment. "That Murray cunt is a total air-head. What in hell are you doing hanging out with that bitch when Alice and I are waiting to show a good-looking boy a good time? Have you ever played sandwich? Alice and I will play the roles of sliced white bread enclosing you on either side, and you can be the meat stuck between us." I cannot recall what my response to that invitation was, but I managed to escape and head elsewhere.

Milton Sills and Doris Kenyon arrived, and all eyes turned when Marion Davies walked in accompanied not only by her ever dependable W.R. Hearst, but also D.W. Griffith. W.R. remembered Mae from his pre-Marion days in New York when he was chasing after showgirls, and he called her "Little Murray."

Griffith apparently had seen Mae many times at the nightclub, Sans Souci, in New York, and he chastised her for going over to Zukor. "You little so-and-so," he said, reprimanding her. "I discovered you. You should have come with me."

I seriously doubted if Mae Murray could have blended into a D.W. Griffith flicker. She was certainly no Lillian Gish, or even a Dorothy.

Mabel Normand showed up with William Desmond Taylor. Billy assured me that the first day's shoot with Lotte and Richard Barthelmess had gone terrifically. "She photographs like a doll." He spoke to me in front of Mabel as if he didn't know that I, Durango Jones, was actually Lotte Lee. Later he whispered in my ear, "I love you, boy, and take it from me you've got the tastiest sausage and the hottest rosebud in Hollywood."

Mabel Normand did little more than glare at me. She told me she'd called Lotte several times but her calls hadn't been returned. "It's about time Lotte and I went out on the town," Mabel said. "I've got a few bones to pick with her."

Mae intruded in our conversation to lecture Mabel on how tasteless it was to endorse Gossard's corsets. "A film star must keep herself pristine and inviolate before her fans," Mae said. "When you advertise corsets, you make yourself all too human."

Through blurry eyes, Mabel looked up at Mae and said, "Go fuck yourself!" That sent Mae scurrying off with Rodolfo to a distant table.

I joined them there, only to find Rodolfo in a sulky mood, as Mae tried to comfort him. Rodolfo looked at me as I came to table. "Griffith told me on the set of *Out of Luck* that I might one day become a star if I lost twenty-five pounds," Rodolfo said.

"Your body is perfect," Mae chimed in.

I figured the bitch knew every inch of it. "I agree," I said, hoping to reassure him. "You work out all the time. You're in great shape."

"Griffith has hired me tonight to appear as a prologue dancer with Carol Dempster at the premier of *The Greatest Thing in Life*." He smiled at Mae and then at me. "Mae has another engagement, and I'd like you to come with me."

Star-struck me gladly accepted, as I figured I'd at least have a chance to meet another member of Griffith's stable of stars, the controversial Carol Dempster herself.

"I think Griffith is very confused sexually." Mae said. "That's why he can't deal with a hot-blooded Latin like you."

"I know I scare him," Rodolfo said. "At heart he's a Victorian. He told me on the set that I was exotically sexual, but also boyish, and he just couldn't handle that in one package."

"Maybe to him you need to be either a Victorian boy like Bobby Harron or an exotic siren like Theda Bara," I said. "You're both and I think that makes you a very exciting screen presence."

"Thank you," he said. "Griffith claims I look too much like a foreign fellow to him. He said women won't accept a man as a romantic hero who looks like me. He sees me only as a villain."

"What about Sessue Hayakawa?" I asked. "He's incredibly exotic, and women swooned whenever he got out the branding iron."

"What about *Scarlet Days*?" Mae asked. "I thought he was considering casting you in that upcoming production with Clarine Seymour and Carol Dempster."

"He did consider it," Rodolfo said. "At least I think he did. At the last minute, he decided to give the role to Richard Barthelmess."

At that remark, the semen of Richard settled heavily in my stomach.

"It's so stupid of Griffith to give the role to Barthelmess," Rodolfo said. "He can't play the dashing bandit, Alvarez. They'll have to plaster down his hair and paste a fake mustache and goatee on him. He'll be ridiculous on the screen, whereas the role is perfect for me. I even look the part, and no one would have to plaster down my hair."

Time would prove Rodolfo perfectly correct in his assessment. Decades later Griffith confessed that he'd made a big mistake in casting the wrong actor, Richard Barthelmess, in the part instead of Valentino. "I could have made Valentino a star long before Rex Ingram did it for me," Griffith said.

"There is one bit I want you to see in *Out of Luck*," Rodolfo said, addressing both of us. "It's the best thing in the picture. It was Griffith's idea. I play a real cad. At one point I bite into one of my female victim's pearls to see if it's genuine."

"Don't be disappointed," Mae said, taking Rodolfo's hand and gently stroking it. "You may have lost *Scarlet Days*, but Bob Leonard and I have good news for you."

Bob Leonard was either Mae's live-in boy friend or husband. I was too polite to ask.

Rodolfo's eyes widened like they would do in the films he'd make in the early Twenties.

"You're going to appear opposite me in *The Delicious Little Devil*," Mae said.

I felt a little bit jealous that I, as Durango, was being excluded from all this role assignment, although I had my stardom as Lotte Lee to fall back on.

"What's it about?" Rodolfo asked. "Tell me about the part. Do I play a villain?"

"You'll play the role of Jimmie, a millionaire Irish contractor," Mae said.

He didn't look at all surprised. "Irish," he said, his face beaming. "I can play that."

"I'm to play a vivacious cabaret entertainer by the name of Gloria de Moin," Mae said. "I've had an affair with the Duke de Sauterne. Jimmie is shocked at seeing me dance in skin-colored tights with transparent draperies. The script even calls for me to be actually nude in a pool."

"The movie sounds terrific," I said, not really meaning that but hoping there might be a part in it for me as Durango.

Mae ignored me, casting her eyes entirely on Rodolfo. "As it turns out, I'm not a notorious Parisian with a past after all," she said. "I only impersonate this shady woman to advance my career and make myself more interesting to men. My character turns out to be a girl from the same slums where you, playing Jimmie, come from. Our daddies once worked on the same job site as bricklayers."

As the air was filled with talk of Rodolfo's future stardom and how much *The Delicious Little Devil* would do to advance the already skyrocketing career of Mae, it was suggested that I drive them for an early evening swim at the beach before Rodolfo had to make his dance debut with Carol Dempster.

On the way to the beach, I was somewhat disappointed that on the first evening of making my screen debut as Lotte Lee, I would be spending it with these self-enchanted stars who were interested only in their own careers.

Earlier that afternoon I'd received a call from William Boyd and had turned down a date with him to be with Rodolfo.

When I got to the beach house, I slipped off to call William for a midnight date, hoping he hadn't already committed himself to another hot number, male or female. Fortunately, I found him still at home listening to the radio. He gave me the address of the apartment where he was living and told me he'd expect me at midnight.

"I have to warn you," William said. "At midnight I'm likely to show up at the door with no clothes on."

"That will save me from having to undress you," I said in my Durango voice. Dreams of what awaited me in the arms of this dashing blond-haired Viking stud flashed through my brain. I really hadn't spent enough time devouring all that male flesh.

"Show up either as Lotte or Durango," William said. "I'm hot for either body. Or, if you wish, you both can do me. I'll let Lotte give me the world's greatest blow-job, followed by a wild ride deep into that delectable ass of Durango."

"A promise I'll hold you to," I said, dashing off to get a bathing suit before joining Mae and Rodolfo on the beach.

*****

In our bathing suits, Mae seemed to take more interest in me. "Your body is very different from that of Rodolfo's," she said, "It is that of a golden boy. Are you considering a film career for yourself, or do you plan to devote all your time to promoting your sister?"

"I'd like to be a star," I said. "Rodolfo and I share that dream."

"I told you you're not suited to my films because I don't use blond-haired men," she said. "But I can introduce you to some stars who might get you started in walk-on parts. Wallace Reid and I made a film together. It was called *To Have and to Hold*. Wally had just played a key role in *The Birth of a Nation*. Would you like me to introduce you to Wallace Reid? We had a brief affair and are still friends. He might get you a part in his next picture."

"I already know him," I said, not letting on how much I really knew Wally. "He's never really talked about getting work for me."

"Come to think of it," she said, "the reason's obvious. With you in one of his pictures, Wally would no longer be known as the handsomest man in Hollywood."

"I'll take that for a compliment." For a long time, neither of us said anything, as we looked at Rudy swimming in the darkening sea. Mae wore a red ruffled bathing suit that looked a bit silly on her. I, on the other hand, appeared in a white, form-fitting bathing suit that left little to the imagination. I believed when dressing for the beach in showing off my finest assets, a package of which I was proud to display,

something I had in common with Rodolfo. I noticed Mae repeatedly checking out my basket of goodies.

"I had a lot if misgivings about coming west," she said. "I did it to escape a wealthy broker named Jay O'Brien."

"I've heard of him," I said. "Isn't he called the Beau Brummel of Broadway? Pearl studs and all that."

"He is indeed, and I can still smell the lilac vegetal he wore. That scent has traveled across the coast to haunt me. He courted me with a passion and was insanely jealous. I was both attracted to him and repelled at the same time. I was making $175 a week as a Ziegfeld girl, but Adolph Zukor offered me $300 a week if I'd come out here and make films. He promised to give me $1,000 a week at the end of two years."

"That sounds like good money," I said. "Goldwyn is giving Lotte only two-hundred a week."

"My early directors didn't think much of my acting," she said. "In one scene I was supposed to look startled. Without my knowing it, a grip shot off a gun near my head. I looked startled all right. I wanted to kill them. All the directors thought I was daft when I demanded music to set the mood for my scenes."

"You were ahead of your time," I said. "I understand many actresses like Geraldine Farrar demand that today."

"Cecil B. DeMille directed me in *The Dream Girl*," she said. "As a dancer, I sometimes moved involuntarily in a light step. I felt it expressed my character. DeMille screamed at me for that. He told me he wasn't directing the Ziegfeld follics."

"I met DeMille only recently," I said. "He's shooting a film with Gloria Swanson. He said he wants to direct Lotte in her next film."

She looked horrified. "He's a sick nut in spite of the fact he virtually carries the Bible around with him. He's got a fetish about feet. He tried to devise every scene he could where my feet would be bare." She held up her dainty feet for my inspection. "I've got beautiful feet, as you can see, and DeMille practically drooled over them."

"There's talk you're going to become one of the biggest stars in films," I said.

"It's not talk, darling," she said, "but a virtual reality. Finally, I've adjusted to films and I'm glad I'm here. Later on, you'll meet my divine lover, Bob Leonard, a red-haired Irishman. He's going to direct my fifth movie, *The Plow Girl*."

"I'd like to meet him and, of course, can't wait to see the film." I didn't mean a word I said, but that was mandatory to say to stars at the time. Mae Murray was the last actress I'd cast in a film called *The Plow Girl*.

She smiled at me. "Bob and I are now free to live our lives. But Jay O'Brien showed up out here, threatening me with his jealousy. He even forced me to marry him. He took me to this preacher while one of his henchmen secretly pointed a gun at my head during the entire ceremony. Over dinner of squab and champagne at the Alexandria Hotel, I excused myself to go to the ladies' room. I managed to escape through a window in that toilet. Once outside, I hailed a taxi and went to the safety of the guarded studio. Zukor provided me with an armed guard, and he finally got O'Brien to go back to New York. The marriage was dissolved."

"That sounds as good as any movie script," I said. "Perhaps you'll get someone to write a scenario."

"Perhaps," she said enigmatically, her glance drifting to Rodolfo still swimming in the ever-darkening sea. "Rudy has had his own Jay O'Brien."

"I don't understand," I said.

"There was this wealthy German baron in New York who fell in love with Rudy when he was forced to hustle men for money to keep from starving. The baron let Rudy live with him and bought him expensive clothes, taking him out every night to luxurious restaurants. The baron fell hopelessly in love with Rudy, but something went wrong with the baron's finances. He lost everything and by then Rudy had fallen for another beauty, a woman."

A chill went through me. This talk of the baron seemed vaguely familiar.

' "The baron was so in love with Rudy that he followed him out here," she said. "The baron claims he once lived in a castle on the Rhine. To recapture his faded glory, he lives in a *faux* castle on Hollywood Boulevard. It's not a real castle—just a movie set."

The impact of that hit me. I'd seen the castle and spied on the baron. It must be the same baron I'd spotted in the hills that day spying on Swanson and Rodolfo making love. "This man sounds obsessive and dangerous."

"I think he is too, and I've warned Rudy repeatedly to be careful of him. At one point I even suggested that Rudy go to the police. But he just laughs at me, claiming that the baron is perfectly harmless."

"I'm not so sure," I said. A vague memory was aroused. Late one night after Rodolfo and I had made passionate love, I wandered alone in our little garden to enjoy the sweet smell of the roses. I didn't see anybody or hear any sound, but I was instinctively aware that someone was there. It was as if we were being spied upon.

Since no other house overlooked ours, Rodolfo and I often left a small lamp glowing as we made love. He liked to look at the expression on my face when he penetrated me. With no curtain pulled, someone could have come up right to the window and looked at us during the entire time we were making love. I shuddered at the prospect. Had the baron been outside that window, staring in at us just as he peeked on Swanson and Rudolfo that morning?

At that point Rodolfo emerged from the surf looking virtually nude. He'd yanked off his jersey top for more freedom, and wore only a form-fitting swimsuit that fitted his muscular body like a modern bikini does today. He was glistening in the late glow of twilight, and appeared to be some beautiful young Neptune emerging from the sea before the appreciative eyes of Mae Murray and me, two persons who had enjoyed every inch of that spectacular body.

D.W. Griffith was wrong about losing those pounds. In my educated view, the only thing Rodolfo needed to loose was an eruption of cum, and that's exactly what he released fifteen minutes later as I went down on him in one of the dressing salons.

Mae had invited us to her house for a quick drink before we left for the theater and Rodolfo's dance performance with Carol Dempster.

Bob Leonard came out to greet us, and he looked as if he'd been drinking heavily. After all, he was an Irishman, just like the Moore brothers—Tom, Matt, and Owen, listed in my order of sexual preference.

Leonard appeared jealous to see Rodolfo and Mae together, but offered him a drink nonetheless. I declined, staying outside in the garden when Mae introduced me to two cousins, Gretchen Young and Colleen Traxler, who were staying with her for three months. Mae said she was teaching the girls to dance.

Colleen disappeared inside the house too, leaving me alone with Gretchen, who appeared no more than seven years old, if that. She was sweet, sweeter, and the sweetest, too much so for my taste. An extremely graceful child, she had haunting violet eyes. Scrawny as a bird, she wanted to dance for me, and I watched as she moved with such elegance it evoked an image of a young and rail-thin Martha Graham decades hence.

"If you stick around," she said after her dance, "I'll make you some pink lemonade. It's my favorite. Later we can play Puss in Boots."

These offers were not tempting enough for me, as I had other prospects for the night, namely William Boyd. Nevertheless, the child intrigued me, and I did have a glass of pink lemonade with her as she related how her family had moved to Hollywood where her mother ran a boarding house.

"I got my first job in films at the age of four," she said. "I was an extra. I have sisters, too, all born in Salt Lake City like me. All of them are going to become film stars just like me. Their names are Sally Blane, Polly Ann Young, and Georgiana Young."

I didn't ask why Sally's name wasn't also Young. But in sister Sally's case, Gretchen turned out to be a prophet. Sally Blane did indeed become a famous actress.

"I'm learning everything I can from Miss Murray," Gretchen said. "Every single dance step. But I can't stand her bee-stung lips. I don't want to go through life looking like I've been stung by a bee."

The sugar in the pink lemonade seemed to go right to Gretchen's head. Manically, she revised her earlier goals, claiming she was not going to be "a mere actress in films, but the biggest star in Hollywood. My name will live in the history of film long after everybody has forgotten about Pickford and Chaplin."

"That's a very big ambition for such a little girl," I said, hoping to return to reality.

"I may be little now but one day I'll be the brightest star in the galaxy."

"Gretchen Young," I said, "that's a name I'll have to remember, not that I could ever forget you."

A panic crossed her face. "No, no, don't remember me as Gretchen. When I become a screen star, I'll be known as Loretta Young."

I wasn't to see Loretta's face again until 1921 when I was viewing *The Sheik*, starring one Rudolph Valentino. Still an extra, Loretta played an Arab girl.

*****

Hollywood was comparing D.W. Griffith's attempt to make a star out of Carol Dempster with W.R. Hearst's campaign to make a star out of Marion Davies. Because Dempster was such a controversial actress, I was anxious to meet her, perhaps to add a page or two to my memoirs of the stars, which I planned to write decades from now when I'd acquired a lot more experience and tales to tell.

After a dancing prologue with Rodolfo and Dempster, the movie curtains would rise on the latest Griffith epic, *The Greatest Thing in Life*, starring—who else?—Lillian Gish. The male leads intrigued me, ranging from heavy hung Elmo Lincoln, the Tarzan of my size-queen dreams, to sweet little Bobby Harron with his "parlor-sized" prick.

The film world at that time was completely incestuous, and slowly but steadily I was making my way around to all the big stars, creating an impression on some, having almost no impression on others, and luring some to my bed either as pretty boy Durango or as the seductive vamp, Lotte Lee. Rod St. Just's labeling of me as the world's first star-fucker grew more apt by the day.

Everyone's career seemed to overlap back in those days in filmdom. Rodolfo would be dancing with Carol Dempster, who'd trained with modern dancers Ruth St. Denis and Ted Shawn, and Miss Dempster was set to film *The Girl Who Stayed at Home*, with my own little darlings, Bobby Harron and Richard Barthelmess. Bobby and Richard had no love for each other and were becoming bitter rivals for the attention of both Dorothy Gish and D.W. Griffith.

Richard was working overtime, shooting parts of *Vampira* while simultaneously rehearsing for his role opposite Dempster. Both Bobby Harron and Carol Dempster were also set to appear as supporting players to Lillian Gish in *True Heart Susie*. That's not all. Bobby was also slated to appear opposite Lillian in *The Greatest Question*, although she seemed to hold him in contempt. We certainly turned out films in those days as quickly as one made popcorn.

Although Dempster was better known in Hollywood as the mistress of D.W. Griffith, the public viewed her as a star. Griffith had launched his mistress as an extra in his film, *Intolerance*, in 1916.

Relatively forgotten today, unlike such Griffith girls as Lillian and Dorothy Gish, or even Mae Marsh, Dempster had one of the most controversial careers of a leading screen actress. Griffith had become smitten with this dancer from Duluth, Minnesota, and had taken her under his wings, even proposing marriage to her which she'd turned down. As his protégée, Griffith hadn't trained her but had made the hopelessly inept Dempster, with her bump-tipped nose, an instant star.

Although viciously attacked by the critics of her day, Dempster had a certain screen presence but was definitely an acquired taste. Her appearance—that is, very skinny and somewhat gangly—and her kinetic energy seemed better suited for comedy than drama. Audiences back then wanted their leading ladies to look ravishing like Lotte Lee. Griffith may have thought Dempster gorgeous but she had less than perfect facial features. Griffith hired Hendrik Sartov, a close-up specialist, to photograph his mistress as sumptuously as possible in a secret soft-focus technique.

After Rodolfo conferred with Dempster and the stage manager, he went off to put on his dancing costume for the evening. Dempster invited me to her dressing room, ostensibly to talk about how my sister viewed Richard Barthelmess since both she and Lotte would be co-starring with him in two films at the same time.

In her dressing room, she spoke openly about her relationship with Griffith. "There's nothing to conceal from you," she said. "The whole town talks of nothing else. I think D.W. is using Richard as a threat to hang over Bobby's Harron's head. Now that Bobby is getting older, he fears D.W. will dump him in favor of Richard. Such a thought makes Bobby suicidal."

"I hope not," I said. "Bobby is a fine actor, and I think his career could still soar, at least through the Twenties."

"An optimistic prediction," Dempster said. "I think in spite of all the work he's getting, his career is winding down. Look at all the movies Theda Bara made last year, and now suddenly there's no more work for her in films."

"Bobby's still a big name," I said.

"That means nothing in Hollywood," she said. "Out here you're built up only to be torn down." She leaned over to me as she applied her make-up. "I don't know if you know this, but both Bobby and Richard are homosexuals. Perhaps they'll end up walking off into the sunset with each other."

"I didn't know that about them," I said. (*Liar, liar, pants on fire.*)

"D.W. is always lining up someone waiting in the wings to give his stars fright," she said. "He took some roles originally intended for Lillian and cast me. He even forced me to appear in a picture, *The Girl who Stayed at Home,* with Clarine Seymour. She's my main rival for D.W.'s affection."

"I saw the picture," I said. "You were terrific. So were Bobby Harron and Richard Barthelmess. I didn't think much of Miss Seymour playing Cutie Beautiful."

"Wasn't that an adorable name for D.W. to give her?" Dempster asked. She seemed genuinely angry and upset at her director, and I suspected their romantic involvement was nearing its end.

"D.W. is even considering writing a film scenario about my feuds with Lillian," Dempster said. "To star both Lillian and myself. He plans to call it, *Once and Future Favorite*, with me playing the current favorite, of course. That director's manipulativeness is near-Jovian."

I answered the door to her dressing room and encountered a messenger who said she was due on stage with Rodolfo in ten minutes.

"I feel so insecure tonight I don't think I can face a live audience," she said. She picked up a newspaper and tossed it on the floor. "The press is trying to destroy me. In this very paper alone, some bag of pig shit wrote I was rather plain in appearance and usually inept as an actress. I'm always being compared unfavorably with Lillian Gish, especially in her close-ups. Fuck, Lillian Gish invented the close-up. Only yesterday a reviewer wrote that I was too sugary and kittenish, a pale imitation of Lillian Gish."

I wished her luck as she headed for the stage. Once there, I encountered Rodolfo and gripped his hand before taking my seat out front to watch the show.

Dempster may not have been a great actress, but she was a marvelous dancer, as was Rodolfo attired in tight black pants with a white ruffled shirt. He looked handsome and dashing with his hair slicked back. His olive-colored skin was in perfect contrast to the porcelain features of Dempster, which were set off even more so by the red silk dress she wore.

It is a bit sad that all copies of *The Greatest Thing in Life* have turned to dust. If the film I witnessed that night had survived, it might have changed the false impression that Griffith was a racist, fostered by his making of the Klan friendly *The Birth of a Nation*.

In *The Greatest Thing in Life*, Bobby Harron appeared as a southern gentleman named Edward Livingston who patronized— in both senses of the word—a French-born cigarette counter salesgirl as played by Lillian Gish appearing as the character of Jeannette Peret.

What made the film memorable and what shocked the audience of that time was a scene toward the end of the flicker. Livingston becomes an American soldier in World War I and is wounded in battle but rescued by a black soldier. In trying to save Livingston, the black soldier himself is wounded, and the two men tumble into a shell hole together.

Feeling his life slipping away, the black soldier calls out for his Mammy, asking her to kiss him. Cradling the young soldier in his arms, Bobby Harron pretends to be his Mammy and bestows a kiss upon the wounded man. The audience did not hiss or boo, but gasps could be heard through the auditorium. The screen was years away from depicting a white woman kissing a black man, but on that long-ago night Griffith broke through the smooch barrier, except it was a white man kissing a black man.

After the show, Rodolfo piled into my "stagecoach" and we headed for the Alexandria Hotel for some champagne and supper. Ramon was our waiter. When I returned from the men's room, I spotted Ramon whispering something to Rodolfo, and I knew those two love-birds were plotting one of their secret trysts.

To make it easier for them, I told Rodolfo that Lotte wasn't feeling well, and I needed to go to the Hollywood Hotel to comfort her.

Rodolfo seemed a bit relieved that he didn't have to make excuses to get rid of me for the rest of the night, and I soon departed after giving Ramon a quick kiss in the foyer when no one was looking. After all, I had my own relationship with Ramon to maintain.

Before the cock crowed, I planned to meet with William Boyd. When I'd exhausted that blond stud and could drain no more juice from him, I was heading for my early morning call on Antonio Moreno. Surely after William I'd no longer be famished for blonds. Only a thick Spanish sausage would do as the dawn broke across the Los Angeles skyline.

Although I felt I should be getting my beauty sleep, my libido was working overtime. Tomorrow I wasn't needed on the set except for one shot, and that was with both Tom Moore and Francis X. Bushman. Durango already knew Francis, of course, but Francis had never met Lotte. Tom Moore and Lotte knew each other intimately. I knew Tom's plumbing a lot better than he knew Lotte's.

Within the hour, those thick, deep inches of my Viking god, William Boyd, were turning me into a love-sick school girl. Once inside me as Durango, William's cock seemed to expand in girth and length, as he lunged wildly before releasing a scalding load of manjuice in me, automatically triggering my own orgasm.

His kneading, striking hands worked my body, and he didn't want to pull out, or so it seemed. There was no sign of separating. In only moments, he expanded again, his cock never softening nor his pace flagging, as he plunged into me again and rode me for a much longer time. It seemed like a full thirty minutes before he rewarded me with another extravagant offering of sperm.

After pulling out, he lay exhausted on my bed, gasping for breath. But I still wasn't satisfied. I was hungry for America's future Hopalong Cassidy. I wanted to taste every crevice of his magnificent body, and I did just that, launching my savory feast with the little toe of his left foot. It was one big foot to work over, as was his right one. It seemed the night would be over before I'd worked my lips and tongue all the way to his neck, ears, and throat before plunging down on his mouth to suck his tongue.

Durango had become *Vampira*.

*****

It had all been arranged by Durango. In the "stagecoach," I as Lotte Lee would pick up Francis X. Bushman, driving him to the studio and allowing my new co-star to get acquainted with me on the way there. Durango was very well acquainted with Francis, especially his anatomy. From what I knew of Francis, Lotte could expect a heavy come-on in the back seat of the limousine, with a chauffeur hired by Goldwyn.

At least I no longer had to chauffeur Charlie around, but was installed in his guest bedroom, and at least I no longer had to make deliveries of the famous Francis X. Bushman dildo or his equally exciting nude statue.

My chauffeur parked next to Francis's lavender-colored limousine, one of the longest cars in America, and a manservant ushered me into the Bushman/Bayne living room where the handsome matinee idol awaited me. Still not dressed for the studio, he was attired in a lavender-colored robe and smoked tobacco wrapped in lavender-colored paper with a long lavender-colored cigarette holder. On his hand rested a gigantic amethyst ring.

Francis was charming and solicitous of me as Lotte, and just seemed to assume that he'd be bedding me sometime during the course of the shooting schedule of *Vampira*. He spoke of the bitter disappointment of his fans deserting him in droves when they learned he was married and the father of five children. "Every woman in America felt I had betrayed her," he said. "As long as they felt I wasn't married, I was still available in their eyes."

"I think it became too much for them when you divorced your wife and married Beverly Bayne," I said. "Audiences have started to change a bit now, but you were appealing to a real Victorian crowd in most of your films."

"I plan to modernize myself in my role in *Vampira*," he said. "I play a bit of a cad but a sexy and romantic one. I'm told that's what women audiences today are demanding. The Victorian husband as provider, they already have at home. I think women today are seeking a dashing, romantic hero who'll sweep them off their feet."

Since we had time for coffee, Francis told me of his early days growing up in Maryland. "My first press releases said Norfolk, Virginia," he said, "but that was to discourage reporters from tracking me down and finding out about my wife and children. I was one of twelve children. My mother gave us names like Mary Magdalen or, another sister, Bernadette Soubirous. I was actually an altar boy, and I attended a school which prepared young boys for the Christian Brotherhood."

Saying nothing, and sipping my coffee, I realized something must have gone astray with his ambition.

"I've always been proud of my physique," he said, letting his robe slip open a bit to expose his manly chest. "I did body-building exercises promoted by Bernarr Macfadden. Macfadden changed my whole thinking about sex. According to Macfadden, sexual allure is God-given and God-made. What do you think?"

I think God made us very sexual creatures," I said, "and we'd be going against him if we didn't give in to all our urges."

"A woman after my own heart." The robe came open a little more, revealing all of his chest and the beginning of his thick pubic hair. I already knew what swung heavily below that mass of pubic hair.

"Boxing, wrestling, long-distance running, weightlifting—everything gave me my physique," he said. "My first job in show business, if you can call it that, was at a burlesque house in East Baltimore. I entered a strongman contest and won. I took home the first prize of twenty-five dollars."

"With a body like yours, the prize money should have been so much more," I said, hoping to flatter him but also anxious to get to the studio.

"I wanted to turn my body into that of a Greek God," he said. "I started to model for sculptors for the grand sum of fifty cents an hour. In time I posed for some of the nation's leading sculptors, including Ulric H. Ellerhausen and Augustus Saint Gaudens. That statue in front of the Public Library in New York City is none other than FXB. Today there are public statues of me all over the nation." He crushed out his cigarette and turned with a proud smirk on his face. "Of course, many sculptors wanted me to pose for things that couldn't go on public display, and I was happy to oblige."

"I used to swoon when you came onto the screen," I said. "You were tall, unlike most of the midgets in films today. Your wavy brown hair and those enchanting eyes. I always thought they were blue, and now I see they are indeed. If only films had color. You really have a classic Roman profile."

"Thank you," he said. "Coming from a beautiful tall woman like you, that's very flattering. I like everything big in my life, and I eat big meals. I can eat a platter of fresh corn in one sitting, at least ten ears, but I work off the fat. I even like big animals, big horses, big dogs, even big parrots." To emphasize his love of big things, he let his lavender robe fall open completely to reveal his massive genitalia. Long before it hardened, his cock was a sight to behold. No wonder he was proud of it. A true exhibitionist, he smiled when I seemed in awe of his equipment, little knowing Durango had sampled it all at full mast.

At this point Beverly Bayne, also in her nightgown, came into the room and saw immediately what was happening. The first great love team of filmdom was hardly in a romantic mood that morning.

Francis quickly closed his robe, concealing his awesome display. "You're disgusting," Beverly screamed at him like a fishwife. She was no longer the young, brown-eyed beauty I'd seen in such films as *Romeo and Juliet*.

Rising from the sofa, his robe falling open, he towered over Beverly. He grabbed her, ripping her nightgown from her body, leaving her totally nude, and then plowed his fist into her pretty face. The impact of the blow from this heavily muscled man onto this rather delicate creature sent her sprawling across a coffee table, as blood spurted from her nose.

Suddenly, Lotte became very masculine as I rushed to Beverly's aid but he pushed me back with such power I landed on the sofa, having momentarily lost my breath because of the impact of his fist.

His rage was directed at the object of his love: the weeping and bloody Beverly Bayne. Her screams pierced the early morning air at Bushmanor, their estate, which was furnished with antiques and potted palms. Two male servants rushed out to restrain Francis but not before he kicked Beverly in the stomach, causing another piercing scream.

Seeing that Francis was restrained, I fled from the living room of the manor and ran out to my limousine, ordering the driver to take me to Goldwyn's studio.

In addition to being an exhibitionist, the great Francis X. Bushman was also a wife-beater. I wanted him off the picture, and I knew Goldwyn would agree. That scene had turned me off Francis for life, and I wanted no part of him any more. I was also going to call Ramon and ask him not to take the job of delivery boy for Francis. Let the swollen ego fend for himself. It was up to Beverly if she wanted to stay married to the brute.

After jumping out of the limousine, I rushed toward Goldwyn's offices. His secretary had standing orders that I could enter at any time. I wish I'd knocked and had been more discreet, but I was so upset over the Bushman/Bayne fight that I was a bit hysterical.

Throwing open the door, I found myself in the middle of a screaming match between producer and star. Geraldine Farrar, Goldwyn's leading star, was attacking him with a ferocity she rarely displayed on the screen. Standing idly by as if he weren't concerned with these temperamental and foolish Americans, was Lou Tellegen, her husband.

The French actor, Tellegen, was a well-known name in films but was mostly famous for having appeared in the only movie Sarah Bernhardt ever made. Portraying Queen Elizabeth, Madame Bernhardt starred in *Les Amours de la reine Elisabeth*—"my one chance for immortality." Farrar's fight with Goldwyn was about Tellegen.

"This Tellegen guy here is an unregenerate bounder," Goldwyn charged, ignoring me. "He cares nothing for you, but only the advancement of his own rotten career."

"Lou is a great star, you illiterate moron," Farrar charged. "He's performing brilliantly in *The World and Its Women*."

"Bullshit!" Goldwyn said. "You're a silly little fool. He's upstaging you in every shot. I'm not going to give him star billing with you, so forget it."

"Unless Lou gets equal billing," she said, "I won't complete the picture."

"In that case," Goldwyn threatened, "I will exhibit the first part of the flicker, followed by an announcement on screen that Geraldine Farrar refused to finish the film unless her French frog got star billing."

Farrar stormed out of the office trailed by Tellegen. "I'm finished with this studio," she screamed back at him. "I may not even complete my contract."

"Tear up the damn thing," Goldwyn screamed back at her. "It'll save my studio half a million dollars. Your pictures are lousy. They lose money. No one wants to see a fat over-the-hill opera star, and they certainly don't want to see no French frog."

After Tellegen and Farrar had slammed the door, Goldwyn turned to me and smiled. "The public wants to see the seductive vamp herself, my own favorite, Lotte Lee, who's still a teenage gal and not some overblown matron like Farrar."

I walked over to him and kissed him on the lips. "Oh, Sammy," I said, "your little baby Lotte has a big favor to ask of her daddy."

"I'll move heaven and earth just to get worked over by those succulent lips of yours," he promised.

By six o'clock that evening, Francis X. Bushman was out of the picture. I'd requested Rodolfo to replace him but Goldwyn refused. "No unknowns," he said. "Tellegen is about as unknown as I want to hire. I need a big star to replace that big-dicked wife-beater. That *Joan of Arc* movie was shit. A middle-age opera star trying to play a seventeen-year-old milk maiden."

Later after servicing Goldwyn, I was rushing to my stagecoach but ran into Tom Moore in the hallway. This slightly drunken Irishman lured me into a broom closet where he unbuttoned his fly faster than he ever had.

Twenty minutes later, my mouth still filled with cum, I raced to the back of my limousine. In its curtained darkness, I was taken into a strong man's arms. It wasn't Francis X. Bushman but my director, Billy Taylor, who informed me that Antonio Moreno was going to be signed for the star part so recently vacated.

Pulling me close, he plunged his tongue down my throat and pronounced the taste of my mouth sweet. Apparently, Billy Taylor liked Tom Moore cum as much as Lotte Lee.

*****

Because of the car accident, Olive Thomas and I, as Lotte Lee, never made it up that steep hill to call on Julian Eltinge, the world's leading female impersonator. But I, as Durango Jones, accompanied by Rodolfo, was eager to accept the invitation of the reigning drag queen, because it was almost certain that both of us would soon be cast in his latest film.

As I drove up that hill in my stagecoach, I still found it hard to believe that Charlie, the most famous man in the world, had actually lived with Julian for a year at the Los Angeles Athletic Club, sharing the same bed. At the door to his rented home, Julian greeted us elegantly gowned in white, bejeweled, and immaculately coiffured. Before arriving at Julian's, Rodolfo told me accepting a role with the star gave him "a pain in the heart." He feared his masculinity and his future as a possible screen lover might be compromised by his appearing in a film opposite a drag queen, especially if he were going to be called upon to perform love scenes with actual lip kissing.

I had no such fears. I was now moving freely and easily between the masculine world of Durango and the feminine world of Lotte.

Julian graciously showed us into his living room and offered us drinks, although I noticed he spent more time catering to Rodolfo than to me. When he did try to relate to me, he used our mutual friend of Olive Thomas to get the conversation rolling, saying how sorry he was that Olive and my sister, Lotte, never made it up the hill that night to have a drink with him. "Olive and I are just like sisters," Julian said. "She's Peter Pan and I can't imagine her ever growing up—such a delightful child, playing at being grown-up though she's really not. She skips, not walks, and would probably turn a cart-wheel on the street if she felt like it. She captures youth on the screen like nobody else. Mary Pickford, eat your heart out."

Rodolfo pressed Julian for information about the role he'd be playing. "A small but vital part as my lover, you gorgeous stud," he said, leaning over to give Rodolfo a wet-lipped kiss. I detected a brief flitter of revulsion on his face, but Rodolfo artfully concealed it. By now, he'd become a hardened hustler.

"You have at least five major scenes with me," Julian said, "and this could be a big breakthrough for you. But it'll be some time before the film is released. In the meantime, I suggest you sign up as the lead dancer and go on a tour of Australia with me. I was in the theater the other night to watch the Griffith film. I saw you dance with Carol Dempster, and you were terrific. It's rare to see such magic up on the stage."

Rodolfo was flattered at the offer, even though I was certain he wouldn't accept it. Too many roles were breaking through for him with both Mae Murray and Clara Kimball Young for him to consider becoming just a dancer again.

Finally, Julian turned to me with news of my role. "I like you a lot," he said, reaching out and holding my hand which he eventually placed in his lap. "You're incredibly good looking, much more so than Rudy here." After that mild put-down, he turned to blow a kiss to Rodolfo before facing me again, looking deeply into my blue eyes. "You're not just handsome but drop-dead gorgeous. You're almost too beautiful for a man, and I think that can be a curse for you in films. When it comes to sex appeal, women don't want men more stunning than they are. It makes them feel inadequate."

"Am I still going to be in your film?" I asked, since I had serious doubts at this point.

"Naturally, my pet," he said. "Of course, Rudy's part will be much larger than yours."

"What do I get to do?" The suspense was tearing me apart.

"I appear in the film wearing several beautiful gowns," Julian said, "and I'm always going from one glittering function to another. You'll play my chauffeur. You'll wear an elephant brown uniform and a hat with a brim to cover all that blonde hair of yours so you won't distract too much from me. You'll help me in and out of the back seat of the limousine, taking special care not to mess up my gowns."

"I play the driver," I said, concealing my disappointment.

"Now, now, dear boy," he said, "we'll shoot the picture soon. In the meantime, I wish your sister luck on her film, *Vampira*. I'm sure she'll be terrific. I have only one lingering suspicion, though. If I didn't know better, I could just swear that Miss Lee is a female impersonator just like me. Takes one to know one. I mean, she looks lovely and all, but there are little telltale clues in her photographs that reveal a slightly masculine aura."

Slightly alarmed, I didn't want Julian spreading that view across Hollywood. "I have a dark secret to share, and you must not tell anyone. That goes for you too, Rodolfo. Lotte is really a lesbian—that's what you're sensing."

Rodolfo, no doubt remembering his night with Lotte at the Hollywood Hotel, looked startled.

"That's it," Julian said. "I knew it was something I sensed about her."

Since all of us were hungry, Rodolfo volunteered to go into Julian's kitchen and make some late night spaghetti for us.

Over our second drink, Julian confided fears of his own. "I'm terribly worried about my future in films. My act depends mostly on verbal wit as I poke fun at social hypocrisy. How can I bring all that to a screen that's silent?"

He didn't mean for me to answer that, but broke into a long discussion of the role of female impersonators in the American theater. "Amazingly, audiences don't associate female impersonation with homosexuality," he said. "In those minstrel shows in the early 19th century, a stand-up comedian would come out dressed as a wench in blackface. By the 1880s they were calling them female imps. These imps did everything from toe-dancing to impersonating Sarah Bernhardt."

"But I heard stories that in the early west female impersonators were really prostitutes," I said.

That seemed to displease Julian but he reluctantly agreed. "Of course, there was that too. In honky-tonk towns with a shortage of women, some men dressed in drag and 'worked in boxes,' as it was called then. That meant giving a man a blow-job while still dressed in a gown with makeup and a wig."

Julian didn't know he was hitting close to the real life of Lotte Lee.

"It wasn't until 1910 that transvestites came into their own on the American stage, although I appeared in drag on Broadway as early as 1904. Actually, I'm nearing forty now but I made my drag debut at the age of ten."

Rodolfo called from the kitchen that our spaghetti would be ready soon since the sauce was already made and he didn't like overcooked pasta.

Over dinner Julian kept going with his spin on female impersonation, claiming that the male soprano, Herbert Clifton, had inspired him, as well as another entertainer called "the male Patti." "I also got inspiration from that clothes horse known as 'the Divine Dodson' and also from Karyl Norman who came out on stage dressed as a high yaller gal in a flamboyant costume. My biggest inspiration came from Bert Savoy and Jay Brennan who appeared as a male/female duo. Savoy played the gal's part, and they earned $1,500 a week on Broadway. Savoy walked real swishy, and his line was 'You must come over.'"

After we'd complimented Rodolfo on his pasta and he'd poured us more wine, Julian said he knew this rising star in New York called Mae West. "She claims she's a woman but I think she's a drag queen. She stole Savoy's line but changed it to, 'Come up and see me sometime,' which always goes over big with her audiences."

From what I'd seen of Julian, he did not appear to be a swishy queen but actually promoted a delicate feminine image more than an exaggeration.

"I prefer the soft touch," Julian said, "either when I'm appearing in a bathing suit or doing an Oriental dance, even singing a ballad in a low, sweet voice. I use Lillian Russell as my role model. Right down to the corset."

"Do you ever get heckled?" Rodolfo asked.

"All the time," Julian said. "Sometimes hecklers wait outside the stage door and call me 'Miss Nancy.' Many a heckler has learned that I'm also good with my fists."

After putting the dishes in the sink, Julian directed us to his living room. Before Rodolfo could sit down, Julian came up to him, bestowing another wet-lipped kiss on him. "Darling, be an angel and go into my bedroom down the hallway there. Take off all of our clothes and lie down on the fluffy bed and wait for the arrival of your mama."

Rodolfo appeared as if he were going to protest, but his chest caved in slightly, and I knew he was going to grant Julian his request. He smiled bravely at Julian, his expression dimming as he looked into my eyes. Instead of jealousy, I actually felt pity for him.

When he was gone, Julian turned to me. 'Dear boy, I want to spend the night with your pal, Rudy. You see, I'm what is called a brownie queen. I like to get fucked by Latin men, and I bet Mr. Valentino is great in the hay." He leaned over and wet kissed me on the lips too. "Don't you be disappointed. Before I send you on your way, I'm going to unbutton your trousers and give you a quick blow-job. But for the real action of the evening, I'll be in my back bedroom with my beautiful showgal legs thrown up in the air, getting stuffed with some prime Italian sausage."

Julian kept his promise. After I'd filled his mouth with hot Kansas cum, he'd drunk it slowly to savor its taste and had bestowed endless compliments on me regarding the length and thickness of my penis.

When I'd looked in on Rodolfo in Julian's bedroom to wish him good night, he was lying nude in the center of a bed, stretching his foreskin, hoping to give himself an erection. He'd blown me a kiss. "Call it show business," he'd said.

Out the door and into my stagecoach, I headed down the hill to the home of my husband and new leading man, Antonio Moreno himself. After he'd fucked me repeatedly as was his way, and after he'd fallen into his usual deep sleep, I planned to slip out into the night. Getting fucked was one thing. But I was also a horny cowboy tonight and wanted to fuck someone myself. The Little Tramp would be the target of my attack.

*****

Like a speeded-up camera, my life picked up its pace to a giddy speed. As Lotte Lee, I was on a roll, and all the world opened for me like a flower bursting into bloom on an alpine hill on the first warm day of spring. For Durango, not a lot was happening, and I felt my future roles would be either as a butler or chauffeur. But I couldn't think about that now. That the movie world had not discovered Durango yet was its loss. After all, I was at the height of my late teenage beauty, although rapidly approaching my 20th birthday.

Nights with Charlie were growing more morose. He feared personal revelations in his upcoming divorce from Mildred Harris, and he also suspected he'd be pilloried in the press, as he so often was. He was seriously thinking of abandoning Hollywood altogether and going back to London, but perhaps that was merely a pre-dawn fantasy that he would not act upon.

As Rodolfo rushed from one film to another, nothing much seemed to be happening for him in spite of screen exposure. He simply did not ignite excitement among post-war audiences, and he lived in constant fear that if he didn't find a suitable role, his screen life was going to be over soon.

The other men in my life weren't faring well either. Wally Reid's dependence on drugs seemed to grow daily, and I learned that he was getting morphine from several other sources, not just from Dr. Hutchison.

John Gilbert was getting a divorce from someone whose name I didn't care to mess up my mouth with, and the press reported that he was seen more and more in the company of actress Leatrice Joy.

I made a mental note to get some low down on this Leatrice Joy creature. I was not just jealous of her because of John. I'd heard that both Goldwyn and also Cecil B. DeMille were considering offering her long-term contracts at a huge salary. Was she being groomed as the "next Lotte Lee" before *Vampira* had even flashed on the screens of the world?

Both Durango and Lotte had become the master of the quickie. Increasingly, I slipped off to see William Boyd as a man, but could easily transform myself into Lotte for Tom Mix or even Tom Ince, the latter still talking about starring me in a film.

Doug Fairbanks was heading back to California, and I eagerly awaited the next turn of events with him. Marion kept postponing our movie date, and I feared she was having trouble with W.R., to whom I fed a steady stream of Hollywood gossip, including Francis X. Bushman's violent pounding of Beverly Bayne.

The gossip I supplied him was more tantalizing than what Louella provided. Of that I was certain. Surely Louella hadn't found out that Nazimova was having an affair with Chaplin's estranged wife, Mildred Harris.

I tried to keep the two Richards in my life—that is, both Barthelmess and that hot young stud appropriately named Dix—sexually satisfied, although my schedule as both Lotte and Durango would tax the most overburdened plowhorse in Kansas. Fortunately, men of nineteen, such as myself, are at their sexual peak.

Billy Taylor proved to be a divine director, always photographing me at an angle where I would look like a pretty girl and not a too beautiful boy. For this, I was grateful, and I showed that gratitude in my dressing room, either as Durango or Lotte.

When I was Durango, Antonio Moreno often joined us for a three-way, although I felt more and more he was growing disenchanted with his long-time friend, Billy Taylor. I knew that Antonio was spending more and more time with Ramon. Strangely, I wasn't jealous, as I too was plowing Ramon on the side.

I loved seeing my image as Lotte projected onto the silver screen as we moved through a rapid shooting schedule. In my secret heart I wished that Durango had made it as a star instead of my "sister."

As I dressed as Lotte for a dinner party with Clara Kimball Young, I reflected on the day's shooting. Tom Moore had showed up on the set so drunk he could hardly film our scenes together. Quick-witted Billy Taylor saved the day by hastily rewriting the script, calling for Tom's character to be inebriated.

As Leonora de la Mer, I was to seduce the young lawyer who had come over to have me sign some papers. I'd enticed him to stay and drink with me, as I'd slowly begun a striptease of his delectable whiskey-soaked Irish physique, even though in the film he played a married man. A marriage license did not stop my character of Leonora if she spotted a man she sexually desired.

After Billy had kissed me good-night, at the end of the afternoon, he'd told me he was having dinner with Mabel Normand. He'd invited me to lunch tomorrow where he was entertaining Charlotte Shelby, the mother of Mary Miles Minter.

As if my life weren't complicated enough, I heard over the radio that John Barrymore was heading for California to negotiate the filming of *Dr. Jekyll and Mr. Hyde*. *THE John Barrymore!* He was practically the reason I'd come to Hollywood in the first place. And he was going to be staying at the Hollywood Hotel. I was told he fucked anything that walked. Either as Lotte or Durango I was determined to get him in my bed, no daunting challenge I suspected. I still had my letter of introduction to him given to me by that broken down old actress, Margaret Barker, who'd roomed with Maria Jane and me back in Lawrence.

As I was applying the finishing touches on my makeup as Lotte, Rodolfo showed up at my door. Without saying anything, he took me in his arms and inserted his tongue which I eagerly sucked. Even though we were running

late, that wasn't all I sucked. Feeling his crotch, I knew he demanded immediate sexual satisfaction and I fell on my knees and performed the task. He tasted especially succulent tonight, and later I was forced to rush into the bathroom to repair my face. I decided not to clean out my mouth, as I liked the taste of his semen.

At the splendid mansion of Clara Kimball Young, Swanson, that bitch, and her toad of a husband, Herbert K. Somborn, were already enjoying their second round of drinks as we arrived late.

A servant took me into the living room of Clara Kimball Young, as Swanson and her husband detained Rodolfo in the library. I'd read dozens of magazine articles about Clara Kimball Young, a legendary name in her day. Born in Chicago in 1890, she was already nearing thirty when I met her. That very year she'd made *Cheating Cheaters, The Better Wife,* and *Soldiers of Fortune.* Her latest film, *Eyes of Youth* for Garson-Equity, had a starring role for Rodolfo.

As we talked, I was captivated by her magnetic presence. One critic had called her "the most exquisite work of nature it has ever been my good fortune to behold." With dancing eyes, dazzling teeth, silken tresses, an engaging smile, a sense of humor, and a gracious manner, Clara outshone Swanson, and was indeed a far bigger star than Miss Gloria at the time. Just as Mary Pickford was at the peak of her fame as a youth-child, Clara was in the heyday of her glory, opting to play mature but beautiful women.

She was telling me how she'd launched herself into acting. Ever actor I met seemed to do that. "I toddled onto stage in the third act of a play called *Hazel Kirke,*" she said. "I loved the approval of the audience, so much so a stagehand had to drag me off. Unlike you," she said, reaching gently for my hand, "I was an ugly duckling at the time."

I took this as a signal to assure her how she'd blossomed into a beautiful white swan. She had so artfully arranged herself that she looked unreal. She sat before a bowl of yellow and white long-stemmed roses behind a backdrop of scarlet geraniums. Decked out in jewelry, she wore one huge diamond brooch and one large emerald ring set in diamonds. She even wore a diamond-studded watch, unusual for women at that time.

She sensed that I was eager to be a success in my first film, and she geared our talk to her own early struggles as a Vitagraph player who was known for appearing in short Sidney Drew comedies. Winsomely pretty at first, she seemed ideally suited for ingénue roles until she'd blossomed into a more mature woman.

Although, as she'd often told interviewers, she may have started out at twenty-five dollars a week, she'd quickly turned into the most business-oriented actress in Hollywood, with the exception of that money-grubbing Mary Pickford, a walking cash register. Clara used her box-office clout to get more money not only for herself, but also for her husband, the actor and director James Young, who was nowhere to be seen. I'd heard that the marriage was over.

When Rodolfo entered the room, Clara quickly forgot about me. She seemed enchanted with his continental manners and grace. Holding center stage, she outlined the scenario of the film for all of us. In *Eyes of Youth*, her character envisions a future with a number of different men—one offering love, another fame and riches, and so forth. One of the men would be played by Rodolfo.

Swanson sat nearby. She was all ears and must have remembered everything. Years later when she was the reigning queen of Hollywood, she would take Young's plot and steal the story herself, changing the title to *The Love of Sunya*.

Over dinner Clara kept the spotlight. Somborn was seated on her left—after all, his company, Equity Pictures, distributed her films. Rodolfo was on her right, and Swanson and I sat opposite each other one seat away.

Even before Rodolfo had been signed for *Eyes of Youth*, Somborn was holding out the possibility of another role for Rodolfo in an upcoming picture, *Silk Husbands, Calico Wives*. "Don't you just love the title?" Somborn said, turning to me.

Actually I didn't. My vision was clouded with jealousy. Why did Rodolfo get offered all the roles? Surely I, as Durango, could be a *Silk Husband*. The film, incidentally, was never made, or at least I never heard of it again.

Certainly Rodolfo didn't appear in it.

I'd been introduced to the other guests, including someone named Harry Garson, who was the general manager of Clara's film company. Unlike other dizzy dames in films, including Mae Murray, Clara talked at her candlelit table like a banker. She seemed to know everything about mortgages, injunctions, powers of attorney, and stocks and bonds. She was adamant at continuing not only as a star, but as an independent producer, making her own pictures and retaining a great hunk of the box office receipts.

She held bankers and stockholders in New York in utter contempt. Clara was a formidable woman among men—the first star to form her own company with Lewis Selznick long before Mary Pickford had thought of doing so. Even Charles Ray, whom I'd recently seduced, was reported in the press to be interested in deserting the studio system and becoming his own producer.

There is a certain nostalgic sadness I remember from that long-ago dinner. Perhaps Swanson should not have attended. Years later, when she was shacked up with Joe Kennedy, she tried to emulate Clara Kimball Young and become the producer of her own film, *Queen Kelly*. The silent film, directed by Erich von Stroheim, was never completed and ended up costing Swanson $800,000, a considerable fortune in the late Twenties when stock markets around the world were crashing.

For Clara, it turned out that Harry Garson was her downfall. He became not only her manager, but her lover, persuading her to keep producing her own pictures. The studios in time rebelled, as did the distributors. Though she reigned supreme on the one night I met her, she was in deep financial trouble. All the beautiful jewelry she wore that night, and even what she had in the safe, she was forced to sell.

Though Clara would continue to make films until she appeared as "Fat Pearl" in *Confessions of a Vice Baron* in 1942, her star was dimming. For much of the Twenties she would remain out of work and by 1935 she was appearing as an older extra in such films as the aptly named *Hollywood Extra Girl*. *Kept Husbands*, a film in which she'd appear in 1931, might have been an appropriate title to describe her present living arrangement with Harry Garson.

Although Clara spent most of the evening focusing on her other guests, especially Swanson and Rodolfo, she did come to me to say good-bye after brandy had been served and it was growing late.

On the way out the door, she whispered to me, "Tell me the truth. Isn't Gloria having an affair with Valentino?"

"You've got that wrong," I said in triumph. "I'm having an affair with Valentino."

*****

When Marion Davies pulled up at the Hollywood Hotel in her limousine to take me, Durango, to the movies, I actually believed we were going to watch *For Better, for Worse*, the Paramount-Artcraft film starring Gloria Swanson who was directed by Cecil B. DeMille. In the back seat of W.R.'s chauffeur-driven limousine, Marion was giggling as I slipped in beside her. No sooner had the automobile lurched forward than Marion was offering me a drink of gin from a diamond-encrusted flask.

She was almost giddy in telling me of all the big plans the Chief had in store for her. She claimed W.R. was ready to launch a major studio of his own, and he needed big-time women stars. She even held out the promise that I, as Lotte Lee's agent, might want to speak to the Chief directly. "For all you know, you might come away with a super contract for your sister." She burst into drunken giggles again as she knew perfectly well I was Lotte.

"W.R. is going to produce at least two dozen pictures sooner than later," she predicted. "He's promoting Alma Rubens almost as much as he's hawking me, and I'm getting God damn jealous."

"Who else is he hot for?" I asked.

"Certainly Lotte," she said. "He still talks about his dinner with her."

I could only trust the Chief's discretion to leave out some of the details of that evening.

"He thinks Ethel Barrymore is too much of an artsy stage actress for the screen," Marion said. "But he likes Alice Joyce. He carries on about Elsie Ferguson and thinks her ideal for *Cosmopolitan* melodramas. Phoebe Foster looked like shit in her screen test but W.R. still sees some spark in her." She downed another long drink from her flask. "Personally I think Foster is a cunt. That cow stepped on my toe at a party the other night and didn't even apologize."

At the cinema palace, the manager personally came out onto the sidewalk to greet Marion and me, ushering us into a private booth upstairs where we could watch the Swanson flicker without being seen by the unwashed. Marion was on her way to becoming the uncrowned empress of Hollywood, and I was proud to be seen on her arm, thinking I'd come a long way since leaving the wheat fields of Kansas.

As the lights dimmed and the scarlet and gold curtains were pulled back, the piano music began. Marion tugged at my arms as she rose from her seat. I realized then that the tame sport of watching a movie wasn't in her plans. She didn't want to waste an evening away from W.R. seeing some dumb Swanson film.

Guided by an usher whom she tipped lavishly, Marion and I fled along a second-floor wing and down a spiral staircase and out a rear stage door where a small black private car was waiting to take us off into a night of mystery and romance. By then I figured she'd planned some romantic encounter—pray not with Charlie—and was using me as her beard.

How right I was. We were driven to a mansion in Beverly Hills where we were ushered in through a side entrance. Marion kissed me good-bye and said she'd be down within the hour. "Have a drink and wait for me, sweetie," she said. As she rushed toward the steps, she paused and looked over her shoulder. "Don't worry that you'll be all alone," she said. "Joe knows of your interest and has arranged something." With that piece of enticing information, she hurried up the steps, almost tripping in her too high heels.

A male servant came and directed me toward a suite where he knocked briefly. "Come in," came a strong, masculine voice from inside the bedroom. The servant opened the door only slightly, then turned and discreetly headed toward the rear of the mansion.

Entering the room, I softly shut the door behind me. In the light of the bedroom, I focused on a strapping hunk of man lying nude in the center of the bed, playing with a towering erection. Checking his nether regions before glancing at his face, I only belatedly realized that it was the athletic actor, Richard Dix, whom I'd already seduced and was ready, willing, and able to go the second time around, which I suspected would be even more delectable than the first.

"We'll talk later," he said, smiling at me. "I'll explain how I got here. But, first, don't you think this big dick of mine needs some attention?" He waved it at me.

"You look good enough to eat," I said, wishing I could have thought of something clever to say instead of that dumb remark. I descended on Richard, devouring him. He made my mouth water to such an extent I slobbered all over his cock, and he loved it, arching his back as he fed me his powerful inches. I couldn't pretend that after Francis X. Bushman, Richard reached virgin territory in my throat but it was a powerful invasion nonetheless.

He had good staying power, too, and allowed me to indulge in a suckathon for at least a good twenty lust-filled minutes before eventual eruption came.

After tasting about all he had to offer, I descended on him again for one final drop. The experience had left me weak with emotion and still shuddering with desire for him. At first I was tempted to jerk off but decided I would probably need my load for some other encounter before the night ended.

My eyes were glazed with love for this man as I watched his spit-primed cock slowly deflate. I bestowed kisses on it and on his balls, which I cupped lovingly. It was in gratitude for giving me such a monstrous cocktail. Glassy-eyed, I ran trembling fingers over his chest and long legs, and he kept his eyes closed, enjoying this afterglow. At that moment I wanted to spend the rest of my days with handsome Richard Dix. I had no doubt that with his athletic body, good looks, and personal charm he was headed for big time stardom in

Hollywood. Perhaps he would appear in a film with Lotte after all. I looked forward to that experience.

"One of Joe's spies at the Fruitfly spotted us in a room alone," he said. "Joe offered me a hundred dollars to come here this evening. I needed the money, but…." He looked down at me, then lifted me up with both of his strong hands and pulled me to his mouth where he inserted his tongue, which got the sucking of its young life. "I would have done it for nothing," he said, coming up for air. "I want this to be the beginning of an intense relationship."

Before that relationship could get seriously launched, there was a discreet rapping on the door. No doubt the manservant had returned, just at the moment I was about to ask who this mysterious "Joe" was. After all, he was my patron and I wanted to thank him for paying for such a party surprise as Richard Dix. Joe at least knew my taste in men.

With one long, passionate kiss bestowed by my cherry-red lips on the mouth of this nude stud, I adjusted my black suit and tie, heading for the doorway, but only after a firm commitment from Richard to meet in a few days for another cocksucking session.

Marion was applying some finishing touches to her makeup when I came into the foyer. "Hurry up, sweetie," she said. "We've got to rush back to the theater before the film ends. I want to be there when the lights go on, so this was a real quickie."

As she raced toward the waiting car, I trailed her, still wanting to thank this "Joe" for supplying me with Richard. As Marion started to get into the automobile, "Joe" emerged from the shadows, tightening his bathrobe. He kissed Marion long and succulently right in front of me before saying good night to her.

Only when he turned around did I realize that this was the gangster partner of Samuel Goldwyn. As Lotte Lee, I'd met him that day I encountered Mabel Normand.

"Put it there, kid," he said, shutting the door for Marion. "You're Lotte Lee's brother, aren't you?" he asked, turning to me.

"Yes, I am, and it's an honor to meet you," I said. "Lotte found you extraordinarily sexy. Really a hot man. I can see why." My smile was more of a sexy smirk, or at least I hoped it was.

He leaned and whispered in my ear. "Get your ass back here after you drop Marion off if you want it plowed. I'm hung like a horse. Marion was just a prelude for me. I need to spend the rest of the night fucking some tight teenage boy ass, and you're it, kid."

With that prospect dangling before me like a juicy steak in front of a pack of wolves, I got in on the other side of the automobile just before the driver sped along the boulevards of Los Angeles, back to the cinema palace where Swanson was overacting in the final reel of her flicker.

As Marion and I started to rush upstairs to her private booth, I spotted Louella Parsons heading down the corridor, apparently in the direction of the women's toilet. Even back then, Lolly had weak kidneys. I had thought she was in New York but she must have returned unexpectedly to the coast. As drunk as she was, I knew she would spot Marion right away. Grabbing Marion, I backed her toward the wall and into a dark corner, where I embraced her, pressing my lips onto hers as Louella staggered by.

When I thought Louella was taking a piss, I released Marion, who smiled at me. "Durango, I didn't know you cared. Thank God you're bisexual. We'll have lots of fun and games together, and W.R. will never know."

"I'm as queer as they come," I warned her. "That kiss was bestowed to conceal you from Louella."

"Oh, shit. Even tanked up, she's smart enough to figure out we were slipping back into the theater." Reaching for my hand, Marion raced upstairs toward her booth just as "The End" flashed across the screen and the lights went on.

Emerging from the booth, we encountered Louella climbing back up the steps from the downstairs john. "Marion, Durango," she said in a tipsy voice. "Marion never looked lovelier. Don't you agree, Durango?"

A disaster had been avoided. Louella would surely report to the Chief that she'd seen us at the movie palace. I hoped that was all she'd report. With Louella you never knew. I'd been told that she could drink a whole gallon of booze and still hawkeye some indiscretion in a far

corner of a room.

At the Santa Monica beach house, W.R. was waiting up for our return. After ordering some hot milk for all of us before bedtime, he invited me to stay over, but I told him I had another pressing engagement plus an early morning call.

Marion gave me a light kiss on the cheek, and W.R. shook my hand, walking me toward the limousine waiting to whisk me off into the night. Along the way, I fed W.R. the gossip he so loved, leaving out only one tantalizing detail—that Marion and I had slipped out of the theater so she could go and fuck Joe Godsol.

After thanking W.R. again for his invitation to spend the night, I headed back to the mansion of Joe Godsol. I was eager to sample the cock that had half the showgirls of Hollywood singing its praise.

*****

The next morning I woke up in bed at the Hollywood Hotel, not with Joe Godsol, but with a nude Wallace Reid. The previous night had become a blur, and I could hardly recall exactly what had happened, as I'd consumed a fair amount of booze and drugs myself, especially after Joe Godsol took me to the Fruitfly.

Wally appeared drugged and in the sleep of the dead. With blurry eyes, I rose from the bed, remembering that Billy Taylor needed me on the set of *Vampira* that morning. I looked at myself in the bathroom mirror. I was Durango, and that was good because Wally knew me as a man—not Lotte Lee.

I called down to the front desk and asked reception to have a waiter bring me a pot of black coffee. Before making up as Lotte, I checked on Wally again. He was breathing but appeared dangerously drugged.

Now that he'd discovered the Fruitfly, he'd told me last night that he'd found a constant supply of all the drugs he wanted—and didn't have to depend on Dr. Hutchison any more. I'd been grateful for that bit of news since I was finding it increasingly embarrassing to go to Elizabeth and her father for morphine.

After the waiter had delivered the coffee, I phoned my dear buddy, Rod St. Just, and filled him in on a few details of last night. With Rod, I could reveal all, even Marion's involvement with Joe Godsol. He was also fascinated by my own recent fling with Joe Godsol, especially when I told him Joe knew me as Durango.

"I'm flabbergasted," he said. "The biggest womanizer in Hollywood likes boy-ass on the side. But, on second thought, why am I surprised at anything I hear in Hollywood? Out here, anything is possible every night."

Before hanging up, I got Rod to agree to come over and look after Wally until he woke up. I gave him the number of Dr. Hutchison to call in case Wally took a turn for the worse. "If he is examined by a doctor, he'd better check his rectum," I said.

"You mean, his asshole?" Rod appeared stunned. "I didn't know the virile Wallace Reid went that route."

"It's a long story," I said. "It happened at the Fruitfly. Why don't you visit me on the set later today, and I'll give you the full story. It was a night to remember."

"I'll be over," Rod promised. He also promised to have tea with me in the late afternoon so he could hear all about my nocturnal adventures with Joe Godsol and Wallace Reid.

Billy Taylor had arranged for me to be picked up by a studio driver so I didn't have to appear at the gates as the chauffeur of my own "stagecoach." Kono, I'd learned, would soon be driving Charlie around in his Locomobile, a vehicle I no longer needed. Even though I was "Mrs. Charlie Chaplin," I'd been neglecting my husband. But Charlie always seemed to be involved in his own adventures. If I showed up that was fine with him. If I didn't it seemed all right with him too. I realized that Charlie needed me to fill up only one percent of his life, and that arrangement was fine with me, allowing me to pursue my own adventures both as Durango and Lotte.

As for my own "husband," I was seeing a lot more of Antonio Moreno than ever now that we were working on the same film with Billy. To my knowledge, Antonio still hadn't learned that I was both Durango and Lotte.

Billy had kept my secret.

In front of the hotel, and to my surprise, I found out from the doorman that my chauffeur had been dismissed. Waiting for me in place of the studio car was a lavender-colored limousine. I froze in terror, thinking it was the automobile of Francis X. Bushman. When I spotted two gigantic bull's horns on the hood, I knew it didn't belong to FXB.

Emerging from the back of the limo was Tom Mix attired in lavender-colored cowboy attire from the scarf he wore around his neck to his boots. The only variance was the ten-gallon hat he wore, the color of day-old cream.

"Pretty woman," he yelled out to me in the early morning air. "Get in. My driver will take you to the studio."

I walked over to Tom Mix and planted a kiss on the red lips of this handsome cowboy stud and got in. Sex in the back of a chauffeur-driven limousine on the way to work was not what I had in mind on this particular morning, especially during my "recovery" period from last night, but what woman worthy of her name would turn down the dashing Tom Mix, even if he were dressed in lavender?

The back seat of the limousine was curtained off in black velvet, and it was like a cozy little train compartment where Tom and I could be in private. We took advantage of the situation. After a lot of kissing and tongue-sucking, he came up for air and said, "I woke up this morning with the biggest hard-on of my career. In this town, I've had all the pussy I can handle. For me, only the succulent cherry-red lips of Lotte Lee could satisfy me. I just knew that."

"Time is wasting," I said, getting down on my knees and unbuttoning his fly. Out popped a mammoth erection. He hadn't lied about that. But I wanted his low hangers too, and he was only too willing to give me what I wanted. What both of us wanted.

By the time we reached the studio gates, I had swallowed Tom's second offering of the morning, and how good it was.

Over good-bye kisses, we both promised to get together real soon—and not just for a quickie. "That was worth saving up for," he said, helping me out of the limousine before driving off in a slight fog that the early morning California sun was burning off.

On the set of *Vampira*, the morning shoot would be confusing, as it was a party scene in which all five of my lovers—Antonio Moreno, William Boyd, Thomas Meighan, Richard Barthelmess, and Tom Moore—would appear. I'd appear as Lotte, of course, a woman known intimately to Thomas Meighan and Tom Moore, less so by Richard and Antonio. As for William Boyd, that good-looking mother-fucker took me any way he could get me, either as Durango or Lotte. With my slightly blurred head, I'd have to keep my male and female identities straight.

Before a cow bell rang for a lunch break, I'd danced with all the men in my screen life as Leonora de la Mer, finding that Antonio was by far the best dancer. What he learned on camera with me that morning he would in years to come use to even greater advantage when he danced with Greta Garbo in *The Temptress* in 1926.

After the close-ups were over, Billy Taylor retreated to his makeshift office and dressing room, leaving the final overview of the party scene to be handled by his assistant director. A woman appearing to be about forty years old had come onto the set, and Billy had followed her into the privacy of his own quarters, making me wonder what was going on here. Where is Louella Parsons now that we really need her?

Tom Moore invited me to his dressing room where this handsome hunk told me we could eat lunch with our privacy intact. Just as I was pondering his offer, the very same invitation came in from Thomas Meighan. As I was debating which of the Tom offers to accept, I considered for a brief moment that I might work both of them into an overburdened schedule. At that point, a message arrived from Billy Taylor that he wanted to see me in his office. I assumed that he must have completed his business with that middle-aged woman.

On the way to his office, I ran into William Boyd who looked more dashing and handsome than I'd ever seen him in the tuxedo he was wearing to film the party scene. "Either as Lotte or Durango, I've got to have you before the sun sets in the west," America's future Hopalong Cassidy told me.

That was one invitation I was determined to accept. I kissed him lightly on the lips before continuing my journey toward Billy's office. As I passed by the dressing room of Richard Barthelmess, I spotted Walt Disney leaving the actor's private quarters. Walt smiled at me and thanked me for helping him get a job designing some of the sets for *Vampira*. "It's not my usual thing," he said, "but it's a wonderful change of pace for me, although I don't plan my future in sex films." He looked back at Richard's dressing room. "The atmosphere on this set is so sexy."

Instead of being jealous, I was relieved that someone had temporarily satisfied Richard's libido for the day. Both as Durango and as Lotte, I was too busy. I leaned over and gave Walt a kiss on the cheek. His breath still reeked of Richard's semen. "You and I do cover some of the same ground," I said before rushing off to see Billy.

In Billy's office he was adjusting his attire, which looked almost like an elephant-brown riding outfit. The director was always immaculately dressed except when I ripped his clothes off for fun in the sack. Upon seeing me, he graciously bowed and planted two kisses on each cheek. "I'd go for that mouth of yours with those cherry-red lips, but I don't want to ruin your makeup."

"How kind," I said, with raised eyebrow. "Isn't Mary Miles Minter, Antonio Moreno, Mabel Normand, Lotte Lee, and Durango Jones—God knows how many more—enough to satisfy you, you oversexed limey soldier you?"

"Dear one, when it comes to sex, I have an insatiable appetite," he said.

"I can vouch for that from personal experience." I paused, expecting he had called me into his office to criticize my performance on the set that morning. Unlike the rest of the cast, I was totally inexperienced in acting—in fact, had never had a lesson. I depended entirely on his direction to see me through. He had nothing but praise for my performance, and that came as a great relief.

"Did you see that woman who came onto the set, the one I followed to my dressing room?" he asked.

"The whole God damn party of extras saw her," I said. "Since when did you start fucking mothers instead of hot young stuff like me?"

"Believe you me," he said, "it's strictly a mercy fuck. That woman is Charlotte Shelby, the mother of Mary Miles Minter. She doesn't know I'm banging her seventeen-year old daughter. I throw her a fuck every now and then to keep her satisfied and in line. She's completely smitten with me. Actually I have a hard time getting it up for her." He leaned over real close as if to whisper something to me. "Do you know what fantasy sustains me while I plow her?"

"I haven't a clue," I said. "Mothers do nothing for me, especially middle-age ones," he said.

"I'm older than Charlotte," he said as a warning to me.

"But you're so handsome and virile," I said hoping to cover my indiscretion.

"I can fuck her because I fantasize that my little Mary emerged from that womb," he said. "I know it sounds perverse. But somehow that goads my fantasy, and I can complete the dirty deed I have to perform every now and then with Charlotte."

The assistant director knocked on the door and was invited in. He told Billy he was needed to help solve a problem that had developed on the set. Also his friend and my husband, Antonio, wanted to speak to Billy about some contractual dispute he was having.

"I promised Charlotte I'd have lunch with her, but she's going to have to settle for that fuck," Billy told me after his assistant had left. "Would you fill in for me? Have lunch with Charlotte? You're not due back on the set until two o'clock."

I would have preferred to make those visits to the dressing rooms of Tom Moore and Thomas Meighan, but since Billy was demanding we do the ladies-who-lunch thing, I reluctantly gave in. After all, he was saving my ass by making me look like a ravishing woman instead of a cowboy stud from Kansas, so I figured I owed him a few favors.

"Lunch with Charlotte Shelby it is," I said, concealing the disappointment on my face.

"She's an interesting woman," he said. "Total Southern greed, and I've learned there's no one on earth as greedy as a Louisiana woman unless it's a Canadian like Mary

Pickford, of course."

"I'm sure Charlotte and I will have a gay old time," I assured him, kissing him on the lips. "We have so much in common."

"Exactly what does that mean?" he asked, pausing at the door.

"We both get fucked by William Desmond Taylor."

*****

In my dressing room as I refreshed my makeup before lunching with Charlotte Shelby, a call came in from Rodolfo. He seemed very depressed. "I've got to finish work soon on this film with Julian Eltinge," he said. "The bitch has fallen in love with me, and I don't think I can get it up for her anymore. She's practically old enough to be my father."

"Is it worth it?" I asked. "You've got the part with Clara Kimball Young. The Mae Murray pictures are coming out. You're in a different film every day."

"But nothing is making me the star I want to be," he said. "That's not all. I just found out I am going to make only one-hundred fifty dollars on the Eltinge film. After all the fucking I've done, I'm worth more than that."

"You're priceless," I said, "and I'm getting very jealous."

"Actually Eltinge is jealous of you," he said. "The bitch thinks there's something going on between us."

"Where did she get that idea?"

"Not from me," he said. "She's so jealous, in fact, she's not going to use you in her film."

"Fuck her," I said, "and I had to unbutton my trousers and suffer a blow-job for that shitty bit part."

The hazards of show business, my pet," he said. "I've never told you what I had to do in New York."

"You mean, with the German baron and God knows how many more."

"The German baron." He barely concealed the anger in his voice. "Who in hell told you about that psycho?"

"Hollywood's a small town," I said enigmatically, not outing Mae Murray. "When am I going to see you again?"

"I've got a few more nights with the chubby drag queen, and then I'm going to need the washboard stomach of Durango Jones. Only a big cock, a young body, and blond hair will do after I've finished with lady Julian."

"When you drop her, you'll break the lady's heart," I said. "Charlie Chaplin walked out on her. Now Rudolfo Valentino."

"She'll survive—that one." With promises for an extended honeymoon at our rose-covered love cottage, he put down the phone. I noticed I was late and rushed out the door of my dressing room in time to give Richard Barthelmess a kiss. Wouldn't he be surprised to know Lotte Lee was really his stud boy, Durango Jones? He looked none the worse for wear after his hot session with Walt Disney.

Already waiting at our lunch table, Charlotte Shelby was not a pretty face. She had on only the slightest bit of makeup and had her hair tied unattractively in a bun, which made her look years older. She wore a loose-fitting dress that seemed more appropriate for a revival meeting in the Deep South. It was hard to imagine that she was the mother of golden-haired Mary Miles Minter, the "Crown Princess of Motion Pictures." I guess that made another Mary, Madam Pickford herself, the queen.

After commenting on how lovely "but how tall you are," Charlotte seemed to settle in comfortably with me. Since I was playing vamp parts, she didn't seem to view me as competition for her sweet daughter, whom she assured me would be on the set today if she weren't "suffering from the temper of a balky tooth." Those were her exact words.

"I always wanted to meet your daughter," I said. "I adore her films." What a liar I was.

"That can be arranged," Charlotte said. "With that hair, those blue eyes, and a face made for the camera, she is going far in Hollywood, especially with assistance from that divine Irishman, William Desmond Taylor."

"He's a fabulous director," I assured her. "He's saving me from looking like a donkey's ass on the screen. We're almost finished with *Vampira.*"

"I know," she said with a certain smugness. "You're going to have to get a new director for your next film. William is spoken for. He's set

to direct my Mary in a string of pictures—*Judy in Rogue's Harbor, Nurse Marjorie,* and *Jenny Be Good.*"

"I've seen Mary in the film Billy directed, *Anne of Green Gables,*" I said. "I think it was the best film she's ever made."

"To date, that's true," she said. "But her greatest films are yet to be made. I've negotiated a contract for Mary that guarantees her $1,300,000 over a five-year period for twenty pictures. The deal is with Adolph Zukor who has decided that my Mary is the ideal replacement for the Pickford bitch after she quit Paramount."

"My God, you should be my agent," I said. "I'm getting only two-hundred a week from Goldwyn."

"Mere chicken feed, dear woman," she said. "You've got to be tough with these producers and directors out here. Except for that divine Irishman, William Taylor, all of them have small balls and dicks, unlike the men of Texas and Louisiana where I come from. You should demand a lot more money for your next film, especially if *Vampira* is a hit. William has told me he thinks it's going to create a sensation at the box office."

"That's good news to my ears."

"I'm the guardian of my Mary's money," she said. "Mary is a wonderful gal but not clever at all. She needs me to protect her from men and to look after her money. I plan to invest it so she can live comfortably when she's not working in films any more. Mary's only sweet seventeen. How old are you?"

"Sweet nineteen."

"Get that money while you can," she warned me. As the waiter arrived with lemonade, Charlotte reluctantly accepted the cold drink. When he'd gone she reached into her purse and pulled out a flask, pouring a whole lot of the liquid in the lemonade. "I like my drinks spiked. Nothing like some good Southern bourbon on a hot day. Want some?"

I declined and settled back to eat a light lunch of chicken salad and sliced tomatoes while listening to Charlotte tell about how she and Mary came to Hollywood. As the lunch wore on, she poured from that flask even when her glass was empty of lemonade.

In just months from now, the entire world

would be reading about the life and background of Mary Miles Minter and Charlotte Shelby, but I heard the story on that long-ago afternoon, including some juicy details the hounds of the press never learned.

Charlotte Shelby, or so she said, was born in Shreveport, Louisiana and called "Lily Pearl." She claimed her family was descended from Southern aristocracy, "All plantation owners. When I was known as Mrs. J. Homer Reilly, I gave birth to little Mary in 1902. She was Juliet Reilly back then."

"I had wanted to be an actress myself," she said. "I have two daughters, not just Mary, and I took both of them with me to New York. My other daughter, Margaret, is two years older than Mary. My family was scandalized. Proper Southern ladies don't go upon the wicked stage."

It seemed that in 1908 Charlotte was appearing on stage in Billie Burke's *Love Watches* at the Lyceum. "Mary's career was taking off far faster than mine," she said. "By 1911 my then Little Juliet was Broadway's most prolific child actress. I gave up my own aspirations in the theater to concentrate on Juliet's career. She owes me a lot for that sacrifice." Charlotte's eyes narrowed into a certain ferocity. "In 1912 there was a group called the Gerry Society, and they policed child performers under the age of sixteen. They were a threat to my little Mary—or Juliet as she was called at the time. I had to create another identity for her or else she might not be allowed to work on the stage."

Drinking more from her bourbon, she told me she'd had a sister named Mary Miles who'd married a Minter. "They had a daughter, and named her Marie Milles (with two L's) Minter. Both mother and daughter died some years earlier when they drank apple cider that had been contaminated by a lethal snake's venom. I appropriated Minter's birth certificate and gave my ten-year-old Juliet a new identity as a seventeen-year-old 'midget' now called Mary Miles Minter. My newly christened Mary appeared in the highly successful play, *The Little Rebel*, with the Farnum brothers until she outgrew the part in 1914."

Charlotte said that after Mary appeared in the film, *The Fairy and the Waif*, which Gustave Frohman produced in 1915, she signed with Louis B. Mayer. "The rest has been Hollywood history," she told me. "My personal favorite of her first six movies for Mayer was *Barbara Frietchie* which co-starred Anna Q. Nilsson, although my Mary carried the picture. But when I told Mayer that Mary was flying the coop, he tried to destroy her career. I outsmarted him and signed Mary with the American Film Company. She made a total of twenty-six films for American between 1915 and 1918. All of them were big hits at the box office. But my deal with Zukor is bigger than anything we've seen before."

Charlotte was clearly drunk at this point, and I was anxious to get back to the set, as we had only a day or two to wrap the filming on *Vampira*. Billy Taylor had promised to come to my rescue but he was nowhere in sight.

Charlotte seemed bitter about her time in Hollywood. She'd made a lot of enemies. "Bobby Harron, Jack Pickford, and Mabel Norman have been kind to my Mary and me," she said. "Not those heifers, Dorothy Gish and Constance Talmadge. When my Mary becomes queen of Hollywood, those two bitches will pay and pay dearly. They're jealous of my Mary's incredible popularity at the box office."

Her bitterness toward Dorothy Gish and Constance Talmadge wasn't directed at Billy Taylor. She spoke of the director as if he were a saint. It was obvious that she didn't know that he was fucking her teenage daughter. "Mary has been denied the presence of a father for most of her life," she said. "She's often drawn to older male directors like Henry King, James Kirkwood, and Lloyd Ingraham, viewing them as father figures. Now she's looking upon William as her father. Poor gal."

It was for me to know and Charlotte to find out that Mary Miles Minter viewed Billy Taylor as a hot stud—not just a father.

"People are always gossiping," she said, "linking my little Mary and William romantically," she said. "Those stories are totally ridiculous. There is so much libel and slander spread in Hollywood. Everyone says William is old enough to be Mary's father." She downed the last of her bourbon. She was clearly intoxicated. She leaned over to me to whisper something confidential. "I'm going to tell you something that William doesn't even know. I'm not going to tell him until our honeymoon night. He's promised to marry me, you know."

I not only didn't know that, I didn't believe it either.

"William Desmond Taylor is the father of Mary Miles Minter."

The news came as a shock to me, and I was certain it would be a shock to Billy Taylor too, if not provide him with a stroke. "How could this be?" I asked skeptically.

She related an entirely believable story of how in New York she'd met an Irish gentleman with courtly manners named William Cunningham Deane-Tanner. "Frankly, dear woman," she said, "we had what you young people today call a one-night stand. I thought he was an antiques dealer. He seemed to have a lot of money from some mysterious source in Ireland. Imagine my surprise when I saw William's picture in the papers years later after he'd fathered my little Mary. He'd popped up in the motion-picture colony and now was called William Desmond Taylor. I didn't know it when I first met him, but William was already married to Ethel May Harrison, one of the Floradora Sextettes."

"I wasn't aware that he'd ever been married to anybody."

"He mysteriously abandoned his wife in 1908, and no one knows what became of him. The years between 1908 and 1912 are known as his lost years. He's never told me what he did during that long time before he just showed up one day in Hollywood and started working in pictures."

"Maybe he'll confess all on your honeymoon night," I said a bit sarcastically but she didn't seem to take offense.

"Even though I'm going to marry him, I know there's something wrong with him," she said. "He frequently suffers from lapses of memory. He's often in pain and is sometimes stricken with a facial neuralgia. My theory is that he had a complete memory loss between 1908 and 1912 and didn't even know he was married or that he had another daughter, Ethel Daisy Deane-Tanner, this one by his wife. On our wedding night, I'm going to reveal to him that he has a lovely daughter, Mary Miles

Minter. My former husband thought Mary— or 'Little Juliet'—was his own daughter. No man as ugly as my husband could have been the father of a daughter more beautiful than any angel in heaven."

Before more revelations, Billy appeared to escort me back to the set where I was due for two final love scenes—one with Richard Barthelmess, the other with Thomas Meighan. I was looking forward to both of them, especially the one with Thomas, who was a great kisser. Richard was only a great kisser when I was Durango Jones. He didn't like kissing Lotte Lee at all, and would wipe his mouth after my lips came unglued from his.

Before going back to the set, I stood and watched Billy leading a staggering Charlotte Shelby toward a studio car he'd arranged to take her back to her apartment. I had a strange foreboding about the two of them that day, and it involved more than the upcoming revelation when Billy would learn that one of his young mistresses was also his daughter. It was a lot more than that.

A shiver went up my spine. It was as if I knew in advance that the names of William Desmond Taylor and Charlotte Shelby would somehow be linked one day in one of the major Hollywood scandals of all time.

*****

Five hours later I had fucked Charlie Chaplin as Durango, been fucked by William Boyd, also as Durango, and had sucked off John Gilbert as Lotte Lee. Since Rudolfo was locked in the arms of the aging drag queen for the night, Miss Julian Eltinge, I thought I had earned a well-deserved rest.

At the Hollywood Hotel, the phone rang. Not knowing which of my suitors it was, I picked it up, thinking it was probably my darling Antonio Moreno, although he'd complained earlier that he was coming down with a cold.

It was Rod St. Just, inviting me to join Richard Dix and himself at the Fruitfly. As tempting as that was, I just didn't feel up to another sexual encounter. William Boyd alone would have been enough for one evening, or for several evenings as far as that goes.

I had to turn Rod down most reluctantly, although I told him that Richard Dix was welcome to visit me at the Hollywood Hotel "for breakfast." Since I had no more work on *Vampira*, unless some reshooting was called for, I had tomorrow off. Now that I wasn't going to appear in the Eltinge film, I had no more films scheduled. Goldwyn obviously was waiting to see *Vampira* before offering me another role as Lotte Lee.

There was the possibility that Cecil B. DeMille might have a film for me, depending on how the weekend went at his country retreat. As a final enticement, Douglas Fairbanks had called that he was returning to the west coast to make a film, the threat from Owen Moore having died down. He promised me work on the film for two or three days and also told me he'd like me, as Durango, to "entertain" a very special guest arriving in California from Europe. I'd readily agreed. Doug did not mention Lotte.

If nothing else developed by tomorrow afternoon, I planned to spend the day after Richard Dix left my suite shopping with my friend, Ramon, perhaps going back to his apartment for a roll in the hay. The last time I'd spoken with Ramon, he'd told me that Fatty Arbuckle had invited him—for a fee, of course—to entertain at a very special private party. After all, both Ramon and I were in the entertainment industry, though not always before the camera. We'd both withdrawn from Francis X. Bushman and also weren't open to any more offers to visit the estate of Sessue Hayakawa.

As I retired to bed from which I didn't plan to emerge until morning, I remembered Rod's fascination with what I'd told him about my evening with Joe Godsol. Rod's reaction was one of surprise. "I know almost everybody in Hollywood is gay, except William S. Hart, and you've even had him in disguise, but Godsol is the biggest womanizer on the coast."

I related every juicy detail of Marion's affair with Godsol and how I'd served as the "beard," returning later to take it up the ass from Goldwyn's partner.

"How big is it?" Rod had demanded to know. Everybody talks about it, claiming he's in the same league as Francis X. Bushman."

"Nobody—not even God himself—is in the same league as Francis X. Bushman," I'd told Rod. "Joe may not have the longest cock in Hollywood, but it's as thick as a redwood tree. I don't know how I managed. It's amazing I can still walk."

"I'd love to try to take it myself," Rod had said. "If I couldn't, at least I could take pictures of it."

Rod had been more horrified than fascinated when I'd told him that after our bout in bed, Godsol had taken me to the Fruitfly. When he'd disappeared into a backroom with a young blonde starlet, a woman this time, I had wandered alone in the club where dope, sex, and liquor shared equal billing.

At about two o'clock in the morning, I'd run into Walt Disney again, who thanked me most profusely for Lotte Lee's help in getting work for him. As a special treat, he told me he could get me into one of the backrooms which was off-limits. He'd held out the tantalizing prospect that I'd see a show with a big star unlike any other I'd ever seen on the screen.

The show had lived up to its promise. In one of the backrooms Wallace Reid had lain on a bed while getting fucked by a young actor while six other nude men of various sizes waited to sodomize him. Each of the men who were watching "the handsomest man in Hollywood" get fucked already supported erections.

Walt had whispered to me that between bouts of fucking, he went down on Wally before the enraptured audience, later abandoning the actor to his next attacker. Wally had been given enough drugs to knock him out. Instead of watching like the voyeurs, I'd gone to Godsol and explained what was happening to Wally, fearing that he'd be injured before the rapists finished with him. Godsol, who always traveled with an entourage, had ordered two of his goons to go and rescue Wally and send him back to the Hollywood Hotel with me.

I'd found it amazing that Wally, no longer dependent on me for drugs, still went on making motion pictures with no discernible change in his screen image. Never a great actor, he kept on emoting in his films as he always did, and the public was none the wiser, although Louella had once inserted a "blind item" in her gossip column suggesting that a "major star in

Hollywood" was hopelessly hooked on morphine.

The next morning Wally blamed me for his sore ass and said he didn't even remember being taken to the Fruitfly. He was much too drugged obviously. He'd also informed me that, although he still wanted to be friends and socialize with me, he was no longer interested in any sexual encounters. "I'm just not much interested in sex any more," he'd said, "even with my wife. I don't want Gloria Swanson any more, or any of the thousands of other women who throw themselves at me."

This was one of my first major rejections from a man, and I blamed it on all the drugs Wally was taking. How could he possibly be interested in sex while doped up all the time?

At two o'clock in the morning at the Hollywood Hotel, my phone rang again. Only for Rudolfo would I get out of bed and rush off somewhere in the night. I was too tired. A sexual encounter was the last item on my agenda. After all, the handsome athletic stud, Richard Dix, would be arriving at my suite in only a few hours. At first I was tempted not to answer it. For all I knew, it might be an irate Mabel Norman. Perhaps Gloria Swanson had fled from her ugly husband and needed a place to crash for the night.

At the other end of the phone wire came the voice of William Desmond Taylor. Sex with my director at this hour did not thrill me. Perhaps he'd called Antonio first, finding him sick with a cold. To my astonishment, it was a business call. Up to now I figured that all two o'clock calls in the morning were sexual, never business. But, after all, this was Hollywood where business was conducted around the clock, even back in 1919.

"Please, drive over at once," he pleaded. "I've got to talk to you. Goldwyn has seen a rough cut of *Vampira*. He's screaming at me in his native tongue. The only thing I got in English was that it's a dirty picture, and he's threatening to wreck my career in Hollywood and take away my job of directing the latest pictures with Mary Miles Minter."

"I'll be right over," I said, thankful I could appear at his bungalow as Durango and not in my full Lotte Lee drag.

In the early morning, a fog had settled over

Los Angeles. Such fogs were more typical of San Francisco. Perhaps there was no fog at all. Maybe it was my own brain creating the fog. But I feared that I was in deep shit. Or else Lotte Lee was in deep shit, at least one of us. The career of Lotte Lee appeared doomed before it got launched.

Passing by the bungalow of Edna Purviance, I wondered if Charlie's leading lady was locked in the arms of that darling man, Thomas Meighan. If she were, I envied her.

The living room of Billy Taylor was brightly lit. In those days before air conditioning, his windows were open. As I approached his bungalow, I heard angry voices. Billy's voice was more soft-spoken, almost with a steely control. But the voice of some woman was hysterical, loud, and accusatory.

Who could resist the temptation to stand in the walkway and listen to every tantalizing word? When the woman appeared before the window, I recognized her at once. It was *Anne of Green Gables*, Mary Miles Minter herself, the only real rival to Mary Pickford in Hollywood, and the crown princess of filmdom herself, and the daughter of my recent luncheon companion, Charlotte Shelby.

Since I'd never met her and had only seen her in silent films, I'd never heard her voice before. Believe me when I say that the voice of Mary Miles Minter was not that of the future moppet, Shirley Temple. Even though a teenager, if we could really believe Charlotte Shelby, Minter spoke with the authority of a grown-up woman.

"You've been fucking my mother," she screamed at Billy.

"That's a God damn lie," he answered her back, trying to control his temper.

Only I and God knows who else was aware that Minter's charge was true. I hadn't actually seen him mount that ugly bitch, Shelby, but Billy had admitted to me that he was humping the Louisiana mammy.

"You've promised to marry me sooner than later," Minter said between sobs, "and now I learn today you're fucking Charlotte. I can't believe this."

"You can't believe it because it's a poisonous piece of shit spread by my enemies," he said.

"You didn't know this, you limey bastard,

but I had a spy on the set of *Vampira*," she said. "He saw Charlotte go to your dressing room. She went there to get fucked by you. Everybody on the set of that picture knows you've been carrying on with Charlotte."

I'm an impulsive person but try to keep my emotions under reasonable control. But on that night, I gave in to my impulses. Rushing toward their porch, I knocked on the door of the bungalow. It was already open from the inside but protected by a screen door. "Who's there?" Billy shouted, coming to the door in his pajamas. "Oh, it's you, Durango. Thanks for coming."

Ushering me into his living room, he introduced me to Mary Miles Minter. She looked at me skeptically, seeming to hold judgment until she could determine what my mission was at this ungodly hour of the morning.

"I know who Durango Jones is," she said. "The brother of Lotte Lee. By now, everybody in Hollywood must know that."

"As I came to the door, I couldn't help but overhear your conversation," I said. Unknown to him, I had come to the rescue of Billy Taylor. He'd done me a favor in keeping my impersonation of Lotte Lee under his belt.

"I don't know what you heard, but what business is this of yours?" Minter asked.

"I think I know who is spreading the rumors about Billy and your mother," I said. "It's part of a conspiracy."

"What in hell are you talking about?" Minter asked.

"The night before Doug Fairbanks fled Hollywood to escape a death threat from Owen Moore, he stayed at my cottage until he could catch the morning train," I said. "We got drunk. He told me a lot. He said that Mary Pickford was so jealous of you in *Anne of Green Gables* that she now views you as a serious threat to her career, especially since she's growing out of those little girl parts. She thought Billy's direction of you in that film was brilliant. She fears the upcoming movies in which Billy will direct you. She thinks you might go from crown princess of Hollywood to the queen. You could dethrone her."

"That's true," Minter said, seeming to believe me for the first time. "I'm a much better actress than Pickford. Prettier and much younger."

"Pickford has threatened to do everything she can to destroy your relationship with Billy," I said. "The idea that you two might get married and form a partnership is such a threat to her that I fear she'll stop at nothing to break up the two of you ."

"God damn that bitch," Minter said, "When I run into her, I'll rip every hair off her head, golden curl by golden curl."

Billy got the message fast and went along with me. "What Durango says is true. The worst mistake you could make is to believe every lie that the Pickford camp is spreading. There will be even bigger lies in the future."

"I know Pickford wants to destroy me," she said. "But I could never prove it. If Douglas Fairbanks said that, then I'd believe it. That cow Pickford tells that one everything."

"Let's all sit down and have a drink," Billy said. On his sofa, he handed me a whiskey. But Minter refused any drink and remained standing.

"Fucking my mother was just one of the bones I had to pick you with tonight," Minter said to Billy, momentarily ignoring me.

"What's the other problem?" he asked.

"I've been hearing lots of rumors about you—and not just the ones that involve you and my mother," she said.

"You mean about Mabel Normand," he said, seeming to laugh that off as another lie. "Mabel and I are friends—nothing more, nothing less."

"Cut the bullshit," she said. "Friends? What a howl. Everybody in Hollywood knows you've been fucking Mabel. Maybe not now but you were. Mabel has even admitted that to me. We've discussed the size of your uncut dick. She's got it measured perfectly. We even agreed on what you like to do in bed. You collected her bloomers the first night you fucked her, just as you demanded my pink ones when you deflowered me."

"Okay, I did lie about Mabel," he said. "She and I did get together a few times. But that quickly played itself out. The only man Mabel truly loves is Mack Sennett. Forget Goldwyn. She's just using him. She's still in love with Mack."

"I can believe that," Minter said. "But Mabel Normand wasn't the second bone I had to pick with you."

"If not Mabel, then who?" he asked, downing a hefty swig of Scotch.

"I keep hearing rumors you're a homosexual," she said.

There was a sudden silence in the room. Then Billy laughed as if to indicate how ridiculous the charge was. "You've been to bed with me, Mary. We're going to get married. After a night with me, can you really believe I'm a homosexual?"

She pondered that for a minute, as I thought that Charlotte was right in her assessment of Minter's mental capacity. She didn't seem to be a bright girl.

"Yeah, I guess you're right," she said, dismissing the idea.

"To me," I chimed in uninvited, "it sounds like another rumor spread by the Pickford camp. They'll stop at nothing. Pickford is determined to remain the queen of Hollywood. Who knows what she'll do next to separate or destroy either of you? Perhaps she'll have one of you killed." Considering headlines that would within months flash around the world, that seemed almost like prophecy from me.

"I'm sorry, daddy," she said, rushing into Billy's arms.

I thought it ironic that she called him daddy. Again if Charlotte could be believed, Billy Taylor was her real father.

After they'd kissed and made up, Minter forgave Billy and even apologized for not trusting him. She got up to leave but only after he'd reassured her that he still planned to marry her. Unless he planned to commit bigamy and wed mother and daughter at the same time, Billy was in deep shit.

After Minter told him good night for a million times, and shook my hand, thanking me for my insider information, she left the bungalow, heading up the walk to her waiting car. Acting on another one of my impulses, I excused myself from Billy and ran after her.

She seemed surprised to encounter me chasing her down the walkway. "What is it?" she asked, a bit impatiently. "Did I leave something behind other than my heart?"

"I've got to tell you something in private," I said.

"Haven't you told me enough?" she said.

"With what I've just learned, I won't be able to sleep for the rest of the night." She looked around in the early morning light. "Or what's left of the morning."

It was a chance but knowing what I did, that Billy Taylor was her real father, I had to take a stab at preventing the marriage. "You've got a secret admirer," I said. "He wants to go out with you. Billy musn't find out."

"I'm in love with Billy—and that's that," she said, walking on up the pathway. She paused and looked back at me, as I rushed to catch up. "And just who is this secret admirer?" she asked.

"None other than Charlie Chaplin, the most famous man in the world. King of Hollywood. Surely you've heard of him."

"But he's married."

"He's divorcing Mildred Harris," I said. "He watches all your films. He's really smitten. He wants to date you."

"It's out of the question," she said, walking on before hesitating again. "Charlie is smitten with me? He wants to take me out?" After another moment's hesitation, she said, "You arrange the date. My God, if I could work with Charlie, he and I might become the queen and king of Hollywood." She touched my hand and gently kissed me on the cheek. "Only thing is I must have your absolute promise that you won't let Billy find out."

"Wild horses couldn't drag it out of me," I said.

She walked swiftly toward her waiting car, disappearing into that early morning fog.

Back in his living room, Billy had poured himself another stiff Scotch. He looked up at me as I came in. "Goldwyn wants to see you Monday morning at ten o'clock sharp at his home. That is, he wants to see Lotte Lee. I asked if I could go with you, and he said no."

My heart sank. I knew a dazzling career for Lotte Lee had happened too fast, too soon. In Hollywood, such a rapid rise to stardom is possible, but I feared in my case—or in Lotte's—it was not to be. I dreaded that meeting with Goldwyn.

That's why the weekend invitation to the home of an even bigger Hollywood figure, Cecil B. DeMille, was more tempting than ever. Who knows? After Lotte spent a weekend at

DeMille's country retreat, I might emerge with a contract and a script for my second picture. Who needed Goldwyn?

"I've been thinking it over," Billy said, returning me to reality. "I'm taking my name off the picture. I'm returning whatever salary I got for directing *Vampira*."

"But the picture's got to have a director," I said. "You're a big name. It'll help at the box office."

"The picture was a radical departure for me," he said. "I fear it could ruin my career. On the other hand, it could make your career."

"You mean make Lotte's career?" I said.

"I mean nothing of the sort. I'll agree to list you, Durango Jones, as the director. If the picture flops, you've got nothing to lose. If it goes over big, you'll become Durango Jones, teenage *wunderkind* of Hollywood. Offers will be coming in over the transom."

I poured myself a drink and sat down opposite Billy. "You mean this? It might work. I never thought of myself as a director, but I guess I could do it. I'm not making it on my own as an actor. A bit part that's likely to be cut out of the final film—and that's about it."

"The picture is very, very sexy," Billy said. "I'm going to arrange for you to see the rough cut. Lotte—or rather you, I keep forgetting—photographs beautifully. I disguised any scene where you might look like a boy. It was an artful dodge."

"A teenage Durango Jones directing his sultry vamp sister, Lotte Lee, in her first film," I said, immediately getting sucked up in the Hollywood fantasy I'd secretly had long ago on the fields of Kansas.

"Decades from now," Billy predicted, "modern audiences will not be watching *The Birth of a Nation* or *Intolerance*. They'll be watching *Vampira*. It will become the first cult classic in the history of motion pictures."

At that point I wanted to retreat off by myself somewhere to dream and fantasize. But Billy had other plans for me.

"Before that Minter bitch arrived," he said, "I was immensely enjoying myself and had my pleasure interrupted. Come into the bedroom with me. I met the most adorable waiter at the Alexandria Hotel. He's Mexican, and he's a hot little cunt. I want to share him with you."

"Could it be?" I asked myself. "No, it couldn't," I said to myself before remembering what a small town Hollywood was. Curiosity had me follow Billy to his bedroom where I found my suspicions confirmed.

"Top of the morning to you, Ramon," I said.

*****

Arriving in my "stagecoach" at Paradise, the country retreat of Cecil B. DeMille, I noticed a long black automobile driven by a rather impatient chauffeur ready to haul away a departing guest. A maid opened the door and out came a well-dressed man who introduced himself to me as W. Somerset Maugham. A stately creature, and far from handsome, he appeared to be in his mid-forties. He introduced me to his secretary and companion, Gerald Haxton, an American in his mid-twenties.

After a few words, Maugham asked, "Is *Vampira* as dirty as I hear it is? I can't wait to see it."

"Me too," Haxton chimed in.

"I burn up the screen," I told them, smiling at Maugham. "I think *Of Human Bondage* is the greatest novel I've ever read."

"It was, it was, my darling woman," he said, accepting Haxton's hand who directed him into the limousine.

"Perhaps you'll write a screenplay for me one day," I said.

He leaned out the window. "I'm sure you could play a prostitute. Probably in a setting south of Pago-Pago."

With that tantalizing pronouncement, this fabled writer and his longtime companion disappeared from my life before they'd even entered it.

I was shown to the living room of DeMille, where the director was enjoying his morning coffee and reading a script. He rose to greet me but had to lean up to give me a light kiss on the lips.

After thanking him for the invitation, we talked briefly about why Maugham had come to see him. "He suggested I make a film out of Schnitzler's play, *The Affairs of Anatol*,"

DeMille said. "Maugham wants to write the scenario. I think it would be hard to film but Lasky called from New York. Maugham had already been there to see him, and Lasky is hot for the idea."

I immediately wanted to ask the director if there was a part in it for me, but decided that would be indiscreet.

"Lasky thinks it's wrong for me to be associated too much with the films of one star— Swanson, of course." DeMille said. "He said I should have a different star in every picture. Not only that, he wants to change the title. No more *The Affairs of Anatol* but *Five Kisses*. If I film it at all, I've been considering Swanson for the lead in spite of Lasky's objections. I see Wallace Reid as her leading man."

The mention of Wally's name brought back a painful memory of when I'd delivered his lovesick note to Swanson and her bitter rejection of the star. If they made the film together, would sparks fly?

"The story is bittersweet and intensely sophisticated," DeMille said. "After I see *Vampira*, and if it's as hot as the grapevine has it, I'm considering you for the third lead. It's not the star part, and Goldwyn may see you only in star parts. But the third lead in *Five Kisses* is one of the hottest and most provocative I've read in many a year. It'll become a screen classic."

"What role would I play?" I asked eagerly.

"The part of Satan Synne—don't you just love that name?" he asked. "Your role is that of the wickedest woman in the world. You operate a bordello in New York, catering to 'all known desires.' You palm off all the ugly men on the girls who work for you in the bordello. But if a handsome stud comes into your bordello, you satisfy him yourself. You also get to wear fabulous clothes. Vulgar but fabulous."

"That sounds exciting. I could do that."

"Of course, the script right now is only in general outline form. But it calls for you to seduce two very handsome young men. I'm considering William Boyd for one of the parts. He arrives at your bordello as a rich young Texas millionaire. He's so blond and handsome you seduce him yourself. There's another scene in which a young broker arrives from Wall Street

wanting to get laid. He's very handsome and athletic and you also take him on for yourself. For this part, I'm considering a young actor the photographer, Rod St. Just, has recently introduced me to. I'm quite impressed with this young man and think he'll go far in pictures. His name is Richard Dix."

I did not let DeMille in on my little secret. I too was quite impressed with Richard Dix, especially the Dix part. The idea of love scenes with William Boyd (a repeat performance both on screen and off for me) and with Richard Dix (strictly off-screen up to now) was my idea of movie heaven. At that very moment, I felt there could be no greater pleasure for any woman on earth than to take off the trousers of William Boyd and Richard Dix. What fun it would be to have both of them in my bed at the same time. DeMille told me he was arranging a hunt breakfast for some of his neighbors and that I had about two hours to freshen up. He said I could join him in a cottage at the far end of the property. "The walk will do you good," he said. "My staff will direct you."

After another kiss, he was gone. As a maid appeared to direct me to my bedroom, I spotted Theodore Kosloff out on the sunny terrace performing his morning exercises. He had his shirt off and wore only a pair of tight-fitting shorts that were very revealing of what they were supposed to hide.

I called to him, and he jumped up with the grace of a ballet dancer and kissed me long and hard on the lips, inserting his tongue. At that moment I had forgotten about William Boyd and Richard Dix. I was hopelessly in love with Theodore. "I'm so glad you're here," he said. "Thank God you didn't want to be a ballet dancer."

"And why not?" I said, pretending anger.

"You're too tall. You must be at least six feet tall. I am only five feet, seven inches."

"What you don't have in height you more than make up in inches somewhere else," I said, brazenly rubbing my hand across his crotch.

That caused him to reach out and kiss me again. "That's very flattering," he said. "A lot of dancers in the Imperial Russian Ballet have to stuff a sock in there. Kosloff never has to use a sock. What my audiences see is all me."

"Are we going to be sharing the same bedroom here?" I asked. "If so, DeMille's 'Paradise' would be just that for me."

"So sorry, my beautiful pet," he said. "Of course, I'll slip into your bedroom so you can enjoy my body too, but I am here with the longtime love of my life."

My face reddened. "And who might that lucky gal be?"

"Natacha Rambova."

"I've heard of her," I said.

"She's going to be a big name in films," he predicted. "Not as an actress, although she could do that too, but as a set designer. You can have my body as many times as you want it, but my Russian heart belongs to Natacha."

"When do I get to meet this lovely?" I asked, not wanting to meet her at all. "I wonder if she'll be as lovely when I rearrange her face."

He laughed and kissed me again. "I love it when women—or men for that matter—are jealous of me." He reached to touch his crotch. "Once they've had this, I ruin them for all others."

"That you do, my darling."

"Natacha is the most beautiful student I've ever taught ballet to," he said. "Her complexion is like the world's finest porcelain. Her features are finely chiseled as if created by the grandest sculptor there is. Her auburn hair is angelic. It's parted and coiled in braids on either side of her perfect neck which is long and elegant like that of a swan."

"Stop," I said. "Enough already. She sounds so enchanting I think you're turning me into a lesbian."

"You too are beautiful," he said, holding me close. He whispered in my ear. "In the midafternoon Natacha always retires for three hours of beauty rest in a darkened room. During her beauty rest, you will be feeling the mighty inches of Kosloff plowing into you. A deep, deep penetration that I want to last at least two hours before I pull out."

"I can't wait," I said, giving him a final kiss before heading up to my bedroom to make myself even lovelier than I already was. I had to look spectacular at the hunt breakfast.

Thirty minutes later I felt I had done all I could to create a fetching Lotte Lee. It was then I heard a knock at my door. Thinking it

was Theodore—perhaps even DeMille—I opened the door to stare into the face of a beautiful woman. From Theodore's description, I knew it must be Natacha Rambova.

"May I come in?" she asked, brushing past me. "Since you know who I am, and I know who you are, we can skip the formalities."

"I'm delighted to meet you," I said. "Theodore has told me so much about you, especially your beauty."

She stood in front of a large window, looking out at the grounds beyond. "Why must it always be the beauty of a woman men talk about? In my case, I'd much rather they talk about my talent."

"I understand from Theodore you have that in bundles."

"He is very right about that. I do possess great gifts, and I think the world of films will benefit from the level of artistry I bring to Hollywood."

"I'm sure you're right about that."

She turned and confronted me. "It is no secret that you're having an affair with Theodore." As I stammered to deny that, she said, "Don't even bother telling a lie. I know you're in love with Theodore."

"But I'm not," I protested, "I could fall in love with him. Anybody could. I hardly know him."

"Let's talk pussy to pussy," she said. "I'm glad Theodore is fascinated with you. That makes leaving him all the easier."

"Are you breaking up?" I asked. "I just saw him downstairs. He gave no indication of any trouble between the two of you."

"He doesn't know. I'm going to present you Kosloff on a platter. You see, I have fallen in love with Nazimova."

"But I thought she was in love with Mildred Harris," I said. "Charlie Chaplin certainly isn't."

"Nazimova is merely fascinated by the little Harris bitch," she said. "I will soon eliminate Harris from the picture. I'm going to become the art director on all of Nazimova's films. We have great plans. *Camille. Salome.* Knowing what I just told you, would you like to replace me in Theodore's affections? Help him get over me?"

"He's a gorgeous man," I said. "And so

very sexy. Surely he has one of the most beautiful bodies in the world. But I already have a lover."

"Who?"

"Rodolfo Valentino," I said.

"I've heard of him. Nazimova knows him but calls him a greasy Italian sausage—not her kind of man at all."

"He's very handsome and talented," I said. "I should introduce you some day."

"Perhaps," she said enigmatically. "Please do me a favor. Every afternoon I retire for my beauty rest. Instead of resting, I'll be making my escape. Invite Theodore to your room. *Please.* While he's fucking you, I'll be gone."

"I would be thrilled to become the lover of Theodore," I said. "There might be a problem or two."

"What's that?" she asked.

"Oh, nothing," I said, not daring to tell her I was a man.

"You seem like a nice woman, so I must warn you of something," she said. "Theodore is a true pervert."

"In what way?"

"He's sleeping with two of his pupils right now," she said. "Both are ten years old. One is a girl, the other a boy."

I was shocked, and few things were shocking me any more. "Surely you're mistaken. Fourteen years old, perhaps, not ten."

"No, ten years old." Her beautiful face flashed anger. "I don't know how he achieves penetration if he does at all. As you well know, he has a very large penis. Even a time-tested whore might have difficulty taking that thing."

"I still can't believe it."

"I caught him in bed with both of these children," she said.

"Does he like both boys and girls?"

"What do you think?" she asked. "He doesn't discriminate. For God's sake, he's a Russian ballet dancer. Have you ever known a ballet dancer who limited his fucking just to women?"

"I can't say that I have," I said, as a memory of my brief time with Nijinsky came back.

"Right now I'm living in Theodore's Franklin Avenue house," she said. "But at this very moment Nazimova has sent her friend, Dagmar

Godowsky, over there to pack up all my clothes and possessions. When I return to Hollywood, I'm moving into the Garden of Alla. Theodore will come back to an empty house. The only reason I accepted Cecil's invitation was so that I can get my possessions out of that house without alerting Theodore."

Since we had at least an hour before the hunt breakfast, I invited Natacha out onto my terrace for coffee which we enjoyed after I had summoned the maid to bring it.

Like Mae Murray, Natacha appeared self-enchanted. She could talk only of herself, which suited me fine as I was eager to learn anything I could about this mysterious woman.

To my disappointment, I found out she wasn't a Russian at all. Her real name was Winifred Shaughnessy, the daughter of a federal marshal from Utah whose job it was to enforce anti-polygamy laws in that Mormon state. After her parents separated, she went to live with her aunt, Elsie de Wolfe, a flamboyant lesbian known as America's first interior decorator.

"When Elsie sent me abroad to get a proper education, I met and fell in love with Theodore," she said. "When I joined the Russian ballet, I became Natacha Rambova. Winifred Shaughnessy didn't sound like the name for a dancer in the imperial ballet."

Natacha smiled at me as if I were becoming part of her conspiracy to break away from Theodore. "Back in New York I carried on with Theodore until mother found out. She charged that Theodore was molesting me, a minor. She accused him of statutory rape and went to the police and the press. Our once secret affair became the talk of Broadway. Mother ordered me back home at once."

"Did you go?" I asked.

"Hell no," she said." I fled to Canada where I pretended to be a French governess. Theodore booked passage on a steamer across the Atlantic, a dangerous thing in wartime, and I arrived in Bournemouth where I lived with his real wife. I was so in love with him at the time I was willing to take any risk."

"His wife must have been very understanding." I said.

"She was. When Cecil drafted Theodore to work in films, I hired on as a costume designer. I designed Theodore's clothes for the film, *Why Change Your Wife?*"

My door was suddenly flung open. There stood Theodore in its frame, still attired in those sweaty and tight-fitting shorts, except this time he was holding one of DeMille's hunting rifles. "I called my housekeeper," he said. "She told me that Dagmar has packed all your possessions and moved them out of my house. This is how I am to learn that you're leaving me and moving in with Nazimova. I thought Nazimova was my friend."

Natacha rose and confronted him. "I've had a change of heart. I want the love of a woman, not of a man."

"No woman walks out on the great Kosloff," he said. "When I'm finished with a woman, I'll order her from my house, but only when I'm through with her."

"What in hell are you talking about?" she asked. "I'm no God damn sex slave of yours."

"We are only at Stage Two of our relationship," he said. "I will let you go eventually but only after you have satisfied me in Stage Three."

"Stage Two, Stage Three," she said, totally confused. "You're making no sense at all."

"Remember Stage One?" he asked. "That was when I let you suck me off three times a day. We graduated to Stage Two when I began to fuck your too-tight vagina. You always complained that I was too big for you. That was music to my ears. Every man likes to be told that by a woman."

"What in hell is Stage Three?" she asked.

"That's when I start butt-fucking you." He said. "If you think your vagina is too small for me, I'll have you screaming and kicking when Kosloff's mighty inches penetrate that delicious rosebud of yours."

"You'll never butt-fuck me, you shit," she said. "No man will ever do that to me."

"Why?" he asked. "Because you're a slimy lesbian. I happen to know you've been carrying on an affair with one of my dancers. Anna Fredova is only fifteen years old. You've been licking her pussy. While I was fucking her the other night, she confessed everything."

"You son of a bitch," she said. "How dare you judge me. At least Anna is fifteen years old. I'd think that would be too old for you. You sleep with ten-year-olds. Call me a lesbian,

you scum. What does that make you? A bugger. I know you sleep with every pretty boy in your troupe. You're a fucking satyr. I know you and Cecil bring young girls here for the weekend. But I'm sure Cecil requires them to be a little older than ten years of age. What's next on your agenda? Six-year-olds? In the years ahead will you start frequenting maternity wards so you can get the babies as they emerge from their mother's womb?"

"You're nothing but a disgusting American cowgirl from Utah," he charged. "I tried to make something of you. A grand dancer. But you're nothing but lesbian trash. You have no talent."

That remark seemed to stab into Natacha's heart. She cried out. "I'm leaving you, you bastard." Since he blocked the main door to my bedroom, she raced toward a second door that led out onto the second-tier front veranda.

Before my disbelieving eyes, he took the rifle and aimed it at her. My screams alerted her as he fired. She too screamed as the shot tore through her leg. It was bird shot but seemed to rip into the muscles above her bleeding knee. Finding the veranda door locked, she fled to the safety of my bathroom, bolting the door. By then he was firing haphazardly in all directions.

Rushing toward him, I blocked his advance to the bathroom door and tried to wrestle the rifle from him. I knocked him to the floor but he had very strong and powerful arms, and I couldn't take the rifle from him. From on the floor, he fired one more time, hitting an overhead crystal chandelier. Amazingly, none of DeMille's staff rushed to the rescue. All of them must have left the house to aid in the hunt breakfast.

At the sound of breaking glass, I realized Natacha was escaping through the window of the bathroom and into the rose garden. It wasn't a long drop but she could break her already injured leg.

When he heard her escaping, Theodore sighed, as if admitting she was leaving his life forever. He'd lost her. The fight gone out of him, he released the rifle. He'd be lucky if she didn't go to the police and press charges. Perhaps he'd ruined her career as a dancer forever.

As I lay on top of him, he was breathing heavily. Suddenly, this sometimes charming rogue and handsome devil didn't seem to care about Natacha any more. He possessed almost instant recovery powers.

As I tried to pull myself up off the floor, he held me close to him. He pressed my head onto his, as his tongue darted between my cherry-red lips. All thoughts of the recent violence were seemingly forgotten. Only with Theodore did I realize for the first time in my life the real link between sex and violence. If anything, the recent drama made him more passionate than ever. It must have had something to do with his Russian soul.

"Let's get under the sheets," he commanded. "I want to fuck you."

As I rose from the floor, my wig—normally plastered to my head—had slipped. He rose up beside me, a mile-long erection jutting out of his shorts. He reached up and jerked the wig from my head. "You're not a woman. You're a teenage boy. I thought so the first time I fucked you on that boat. Kosloff has fucked enough boy-ass in his time to recognize one when I see one. Besides, my dick slipped too easily up in you. Most women could not have taken me up the butt like you did, and unlubricated at that, unless they've had a lot of practice. You're Durango Jones. You're not just the brother of Lotte Lee, you are Lotte Lee." He grabbed me and kissed me, reaching to fondle my crotch as if to reassure himself that I was indeed a boy.

"Please don't expose me," I said, whispering into his ear.

"The only thing I'm going to expose is that hot ass of yours," he said. "I'll make you cum when my thick dick goes into you. Then I'll drink your cream. There is no sweeter taste in all the world than that of a corn-fed, flaxen-haired all-American boy."

Stripping off his shorts and pulling off my dress, he ordered me to lie on my belly while he attacked my rosebud with his succulent mouth. He had me squirming and begging for penetration before he'd released me. When he'd wetted me sufficiently, he skinned back his cock and plowed inside. It wasn't a gentle invasion, as he preferred one swift plunge deep into my guts. I screamed at the impact and

pain but he forced my head into the pillow, muffling my outcry. He bit into my neck as he rammed me with the fury of a mighty Russian warrior, taking his prey and asserting a master/slave relationship with his captive from the battlefield. After three minutes, the pain subsided, only to be replaced by the most thrilling of assaults it had ever been my pleasure to receive. By then, I was meeting him thrust for thrust.

In the middle of his delicious attack, I felt my toes—sticking out from the sheets—become encased in a warm, succulent mouth. My feet were getting the assault of their life. Never had they been treated so lovingly. Most men ignored them, preferring other targets of attack. Theodore's tongue was licking my neck, so he wasn't the guilty party doing all that feet-licking and toe-sucking.

"It's only Cecil," Theodore whispered in my ear. "He likes to do the foot thing while I fuck a young girl."

Because DeMille apparently liked to spend a long time at a girl's feet, Theodore with his amazing capacity postponed his climax and maintained fantastic staying power as he continued to plow into me, biting my neck. But time was running out. His eruption finally spewed, as he screamed out into the morning air, biting into my neck so hard I bled. I could hold back no more, and erupted myself into one of the most exciting orgasms I've ever known.

He collapsed on top of me and seemed to go to sleep at once, appearing almost in a deep coma. That made me realize how good it must have been for him, and I just knew he'd be eager to repeat his performance.

I need not have feared he would reveal my real identity to DeMille, at least for that moment. DeMille obviously thought it was Lotte Lee lying under Theodore's body, not Durango Jones.

At some point, having had his fill of my tender feet, the director got up and tiptoed out of the room, gently shutting the door behind him.

After the hunt breakfast, and after a long afternoon in my bedroom with Theodore, I promised to become his boy. He said there were many sexual tricks he'd learned while working in the imperial ballet in Russia, and he promised to try out every one on me in the weeks and months ahead.

The next morning with the promise of future film work from DeMille, and a commitment to Theodore, I drove my stagecoach away from Paradise and headed back to the Hollywood Hotel, wondering if Rodolfo were still with Julian Eltinge.

Back at the hotel, Rodolfo had left me a message. The picture with Eltinge was finished, and he'd been promised two days work with Norman Kerry before beginning his part with Clara Kimball Young. I had almost forgotten about Norman Kerry. Rodolfo said that Norman—"for old time's sake"—could arrange for a bit part for me as Durango in his new film.

The attendant at the hotel desk normally was eager to see me and give me my messages, but he suddenly ignored me and didn't answer my final question. He was used to seeing movie stars come and go in the lobby, but he seemed taken aback at the entrance of this latest guest.

I couldn't imagine what actor was generating so much excitement. Even Charlie Chaplin, the most famous man in the world, didn't generate excitement from the hotel staff which was used to seeing The Little Tramp come and go.

I spun around to discover who was checking in.

Only two feet from me stood the great John Barrymore himself.

Chapter Ten

As I was having breakfast with my divine "husband," the sexy, handsome, and hung Antonio Moreno, I dreaded leaving the comfort of his presence to rush to the Hollywood Hotel where I would have to change into my Lotte Lee drag to confront Goldwyn. Lotte's future film career, if there was to be one, depended on Goldwyn's reaction to *Vampira*. While there, I was also to learn Goldwyn's reaction to the strange request of Billy Taylor to remove his name as director and insert my own—that is, Durango Jones himself in his first screen credit.

I could never make up my mind if Antonio were the better cook, or was it Rodolfo? I finally decided they were both divine in the kitchen, but different, as Antonio prepared dishes from his native Spain, whereas Rodolfo cooked southern Italian but with a certain French inspiration evocative of his mama.

Antonio never told me what he was up to when I wasn't with him, and I too never confided anything. Since we both shared Ramon, he was a safe subject to bring up, but not my other lovers, especially Rodolfo who I suspected would one day become a rival of Antonio's.

As for my encounter with John Barrymore, there was nothing to tell. I'd been in such awe of the great actor that I did not even speak to him, much less intrude on his privacy. Our eyes had met and that was that. Since John was known as a great womanizer, unlike his homosexual brother, Lionel, I suspected I might have to approach him as Lotte Lee instead of

as Durango, although I had that letter of introduction from our long ago boarder in Lawrence, Margaret Barker, the former actress who'd apparently slept with both John and his father, Maurice.

Since one of the reasons I planned to come to Hollywood was to seduce John Barrymore, I wasn't going to allow the actor to escape my net. The question wasn't to be or not to be, but whether my seduction attempt should be made as Durango or as Lotte Lee. That would be tomorrow's problem. I'd heard John tell the desk clerk at the Hollywood Hotel that he was completely exhausted from having made the cross-country trip and didn't want to be disturbed for forty-eight hours.

My dreams about John Barrymore were interrupted by a loud knocking on Antonio's front door. He tightened his bathrobe around his muscular body. He was nude underneath. "Who could that be at this hour?" he asked. "Only Billy Taylor comes calling for a quickie in the morning."

"I'm not up for him this morning," I said. "Besides, he's no longer my director."

"Let's not write him off too soon," he said. "We both will need him in the future, I'm sure."

The loud voices in the front hallway were women who seemed to be returning from an all-night binge on the town. The first to come into the breakfast room was a hell-raising big blonde. "Hello, Sucker!" she called out to me.

To my astonishment, I faced Texas Guinan. Back then she was legendary, the best-known nightclub impresario in America who greeted all her customers with her "Hello, Sucker" remark.

She stood before me, glittering with diamonds from head to foot. "Got any champagne?" she asked.

"Miss Guinan," I stammered. "I'm honored to meet you. I've heard so much about you. I'm Durango Jones."

"Durango," she said, "looking me up and down like Mae West would do with Cary Grant in the Thirties. "Now there's a western name I could wrap my legs around. Texas & Durango, what a team we'd make. 'Cept you're even blonder than I am."

As I rushed to get her champagne, which I knew Antonio always kept in stock, she called after me, "I'm out here on the coast on a little vacation. The God damn 'revenooers' in New York have put a six-month padlock on my club."

"That's too bad," I said, popping open the champagne and pouring her a glass. Since I was soon to face Goldwyn, I opted to join her, thinking the bubbly would boost my spirits.

"Hell, I wasn't selling liquor," she said angrily. "I offered pitchers of water at twenty-five bucks a haul. What my customers mixed into their water, at least the way I figured it, was their own God damn business."

As we sat sipping champagne, I admired her diamond bracelet with what appeared to be a gold police whistle attached to it. "What's that?" I asked.

"I just bought it as a trinket for my necklace of gold padlocks," she said. After downing the first glass of champagne, she jumped up. "I really wowed them last night at the Fruitfly." Her cheeks heavily rouged, her mouth painted a flaming scarlet, she high-kicked in the air to show me she could still do it, as she went into "Give Us a Little Kiss, Will Ya, Huh?" At the end of her number, she planted a lipstick-smeared kiss on my lips. "Anyone for leap-frog?" she asked.

I couldn't believe it. She wanted to play leap-frog at this hour. Since I was only a teenage boy, I said, "What the hell!" As Texas and I in my bathrobe were leap-frogging around the kitchen floor, the second woman was shown into the kitchen by Antonio.

As my bathrobe came open, I landed on the floor with my cock and balls dangling right in front of Pearl White herself.

I'd practically seen every serial Pearl White had ever made at the Patee Theater back in Lawrence. Even then, I never thought I'd actually meet her, especially under these embarrassing circumstances. As I wrapped my bathrobe tightly around me, Antonio introduced me to a woman who at the time was almost as famous around the world as Mary Pickford herself.

Though little known today, Antonio from March 3 to July 20 of 1918, had made a serial with Pearl called *The House of Hate*, with chapter titles like "The Hooded Terror," "The Tiger's Eye," "The Germ Menace," and "The Vial of Death." His advisers had warned Antonio that appearing in a serial with Pearl White would ruin his career as a star of feature films, but it hadn't done so at all.

Seated at the table with Pearl, I offered her champagne. We were joined by Texas who ordered Antonio to cook them up a batch of bacon and eggs.

"This champagne is great," Pearl said. "All Texas here ever gives me to drink is rotgut prohibition likker."

"Pearl is out here making a big movie deal," Texas said. "She's getting tired of being in serials all the time that frighten the pants off a scarecrow."

"With the serials, I'm completely tied up with Pathé," Pearl said. "But my contract allows me to make feature films on the side. I think the world is tiring of my serials. God knows I've faced every danger there is. My agent claims that feature films will save my career. He's hoping that I will take Hollywood by storm."

As we laughed and talked on that long-ago morning, the world seemed filled with hope. For one little hour, all of us dared believe that Pearl White would become the leading star in feature films at Fox in the Twenties. Indeed she would go on to make ten films for Fox, including *Know Your Men, A Virgin Paradise*, and *The Broadway Peacock*. All of them would flop. As her once-fabled career plunged downward, her last appearance before the camera was in 1924 in Paris. It was called *Terror*, and, hoping to capture some of the nostalgia associated with her early days in film, it was released in the United States under the title of *The Perils of Paris*. It too flopped and the great Pearl White, the star of the cliff-hanger, "The Peerless, Fearless Girl" became a memory.

Even with all those Fox contracts looming before her, Pearl appeared despondent over a broken romance, either with her husband or a boy friend. She never said which.

As Antonio came to table with eggs and toast for the women, the wafting aroma of frying bacon arose from the stove. "I've had a hundred strike-outs in the love game myself," Texas said. "Time heals all wounds, and then we find ourselves dead anyway."

Pearl slowly sipped her champagne and looked sadly into my eyes, and then into the glazed eyes of Texas. "Some people call me the queen of Hollywood," Pearl said, "although I think that title belongs to Mary Pickford, and I'm sure Pickford would agree with me. But I feel it's lonely sitting on a throne all by myself. I'd rather a prince be sitting here with me. All the world seems to worship me, but not the one man I want to adore me. I'd give up all the fame and money, everything, for the right man to love me and be by my side."

The screeching wheels of a milk truck in Antonio's back driveway brought us back to the reality of a Los Angeles morning rapidly closing in on us.

Texas reached over and patted Pearl's hand as Antonio leaned over and kissed her forehead. Seeming to forget her romantic woes, Pearl dug into her eggs, toast, and bacon, as did Texas who seemed to have an appetite for food and drink as big as her state.

After all of us chatted pleasantly and over our fifth cup of coffee, Texas rose from the table. "We gotta go," she said. "I want to take Pearl here to mass. Surely somewhere in the giant city of Los Angeles, we can find a mass on a Monday morning."

These two heavily made-up women, in all their night club finery, appeared to be unlikely candidates for attending mass. Antonio asked if I would show them out.

In the foyer, Texas turned to me and winked. In the distance, Pearl and Antonio were talking privately, perhaps planning another cliff-hanger batch of serials.

"I'm sorry to intrude on this little love nest so early in the morning," she said, "but Pearl was in Hollywood and demanded to see her old pal, Antonio." She whispered confidentially to me as she looked back at Antonio. "Marry him, honey. Take the advise of Texas Guinan. You'll find no better man in Hollywood than Antonio Moreno."

After kissing Texas and Pearl good-bye, Antonio whispered to me to join him upstairs in his bathroom shower.

As we stepped outside, a black car was speeding up the driveway. Driven by a woman, the vehicle came to a sudden stop. Out popped a brunette showgirl attired only in lipstick—red high heels and the briefest of G-strings, with two olive-sized pasties that did very little to conceal her ample breasts.

"Texas Guinan," she shouted. "I've been tracking you down all over town. I tried to get an audition the regular way, but couldn't. Desperate times call for desperate means." She reached into the car and hauled out a twelve-foot boa constrictor.

Texas remained calm—apparently, in the state of Texas she'd seen a few reptiles before. But Pearl White, who'd faced every known screen danger a scenario writer could devise, screamed and cowered behind Texas.

"My name's Boa Bubbles," the showgirl said. She tossed the snake around her neck and began a wild tap dance on the concrete, screaming, squealing, and belting out her number. In a final climax, she grabbed the tail of the boa constrictor and whirled it toward us, its head hitting Texas in her bosom. Drawing back, the boa coiled around Miss Bubbles, seemingly feeling it'd earned its keep for the day.

Texas hustled Pearl into her waiting car and got behind the wheel.

"But Miss Guinan," Boa screamed out. "Do I get a job in your club or not? It costs money to feed this monster. I won't even tell you what it eats."

"Great meeting you, Durango," Texas called out. Pearl waved at me demurely.

Her tires spinning in the gravel, Texas Guinan headed down the driveway, yelling one final call to me in her big, brassy voice. "So long, Suckers!"

*****

It was with great trepidation that I, as Lotte Lee, drove to the home of the former glove salesman in the Adirondack foothills, who had become Hollywood's leading independent producer. That was a brilliant achievement for a Jew born Shmuel Gelbfisz in 1879 in the ghetto of Warsaw, the eldest of six children of a struggling used-furniture dealer. His publicists always claimed that the producer had the "Goldwyn touch." But many of his hirelings, of which I included myself, feared his habit of ordering films recast, rewritten, and recut. What would he say to me now that he'd seen *Vampira*? Would he ask for his usual blow-job or else keep both his trousers and his studio buttoned up against another attack by the vamp, Lotte Lee? I was about to find out.

Much of Hollywood viewed Goldwyn as a joke because he ridiculously misused more words than Mrs. Malaprop herself. Goldwyn was famous for his quotes such as "In two words: im-possible," or "If you can't give me your word of honor, will you give me your promise?" I particularly liked, "Include me out," and I also loved, "Anyone who would go to a psychiatrist ought to have his head examined." Aside from that, I remembered his most famous pronouncement, "Pictures are for entertainment; messages should be delivered by Western Union."

Surely he would see *Vampira* as entertainment. With all its scenes of sex and seduction, it would qualify as entertainment. Billy Taylor had taken a daring chance in undressing the men, as *Vampira* showed more exposed male flesh than any flicker to date. As amazing as it now seems, movie directors seemed to believe that audiences wanted to see only female flesh, as in the case of Theda Bara. Billy thought differently. He felt women—and certainly homosexual men—wanted to see on the screen as much exposed male flesh as he dared allow. All the men in the film at some point appeared in a stripped down condition, but, of course, never exposing their genitals or buttocks. That would be going too far. Each man was gorgeous and well built. It was up to Lotte Lee—not the audience for

Vampira—to know what these men looked like when I pulled down their underwear and exposed them to my cherry-red lips off screen.

At Goldwyn's home, a maid ushered me into his living room where I met not the producer, but Mabel Normand once again. "You're a very evasive piece of hot tail," Mabel said, eying me skeptically. "I don't know about you. Every day I hear taller and taller tales about your tail."

"You of all people know how lies and scandal are spread about stars," I said, perhaps a little too defensively, fearing that what was spread about me was indeed the truth.

"Honey, I'm a star," she said. "You're nothing but a too tall and aspirant actress who has made a film that can't be released. Goldfish had it screened for me last night."

"What do you mean?" I asked, filled with a sudden panic. "He hated the picture?"

"Hated is hardly the word," Mabel said. "At the moment he's threatening to destroy the career of Billy Taylor. I love Billy Taylor desperately, but I think he has truly surrendered to his homosexual nature in directing *Vampira*. I was the one who had Goldfish screen the picture with me a second time. It was I who pointed out the subtle or not-so-subtle homosexual implications of the film."

"I have absolutely no idea what you're talking about," I said. "You obviously are doing this to get even with me because you think I'm having affairs with your dear Billy Taylor and even Goldfish himself."

"I don't just perceive, sugar cake," she said, her eyes narrowing with hatred as she focused on me. "I know you're sucking them off, at least Goldfish. He'll settle for a blow-job. But I just know Billy is plowing it to you."

"That's a damnable lie," I said, telling a lie myself. Regrettably, she had nailed me, although I had no idea as to the source of her information. In Billy's case I feared it was his valet-secretary, the mysterious Edward Sands, whom I suspected was a homosexual himself and wanted to keep his boss man for his own sexual pleasure. Billy had more or less admitted to me that he and Sands were fucking. During my several encounters with Sands, I never trusted this ex-sailor, as he seemed to reinvent his background every time I met him. He'd told me three or four stories about his past life, but each version seemed remarkably different from the one before. As a liar, he had a weakness. He never could remember what he had said the day before.

"I'm not as easily fooled as Goldfish," Mabel said. Rising drunkenly—or was it drugged?—from the sofa, she came toward me, stopping only a foot from my body, stretching her neck to look up at me. "I want to go to bed with you."

"Hell, no," I said, backing off. "I'm not a lesbian."

"It's not sexual desire, bitch," she said, "I want to check out your anatomy."

I moved away from her, heading for the door. Even before Goldwyn came down from upstairs, this morning's confrontation wasn't going at all the way I planned. I feared the unmasking of Lotte Lee was about to begin. She'd seen *Vampira* and figured out I was a man after all, something that Billy Taylor apparently had not been able to conceal.

The actress tackled me as I rushed from the room, and I fell banging my head against Goldwyn's liquor cabinet. With the feisty movement she'd displayed on the screen in countless films, Mabel piled on me, pounding her fists into my face. In a rapid jerk, she yanked my blonde wig from my head, even though it was plastered down.

"Just as I thought," she shouted as if she wanted New York to hear. "Lotte Lee is a man."

Goldwyn took that dreadful moment to enter the living room. Mabel got up from my body, while I still cowered on the floor, exposed as a man.

"You're Durango Jones," Goldwyn said, his face a look of pained astonishment. "You're Lotte Lee's brother. Why are you here impersonating your sister? Was she afraid to show up and face me?"

Feeling bruised, I rose from the floor after Mabel's assault. I reached for my wig and placed it back on my head, even if awkwardly.

Mabel looked at Goldwyn as if she couldn't believe his words, much less his perception. "Just how stupid do they get in the Warsaw ghetto?" she asked him defiantly. "Don't you get it even now? There is no Lotte Lee. Only Durango Jones."

"You mean…" Goldwyn stammered and looked as if he might throw up. He stared at me. "You mean you were sent here to play a trick on me."

"That's all it was," I said. "Chaplin wanted to play a joke on you. I went along with it. But when you offered me a movie contract in spite of my height, I went for it. I never thought it would go this far."

He looked furious and for a brief moment I feared he was going to strike me in the face. "Is William Taylor in on this joke?"

"He knows nothing about it," I said, lying. "He would never have gone through with it. He's a very honest director."

"It was a dirty picture anyway," Goldwyn said. "I like family entertainment. This is a film to show at smokers. We'll have to reshoot a lot of it, especially the love scenes."

"What in hell are you talking about?" Mabel asked, confronting him. "The film must never be released. It would ruin you."

"I've got a lot of money invested in this film," he said. "There's a way to save it. Goldwyn can save any film." He looked with a certain bitterness at Mabel. "Except that last piece of shit you made for me. You were so God damned drugged the viewer wouldn't know what in hell you were up to on screen."

"I don't want to continue as Lotte Lee," I said. "The game is over. I've been exposed." I turned to leave.

"Don't go," Goldwyn called after me. "I know how to save this film. At the end we can shoot you taking off your blonde wig. You'll reveal to the audience that you were a man after all. That you were merely fooling them. Julian Eltinge does that all the time."

"Bullshit!" Mabel said. "You don't know what you're talking about. The Lotte character is making love to some of the biggest male stars in Hollywood like Richard Barthelmess. If the audience finds out Lotte Lee is a man, it will ruin their careers once their fans find out that these guys are tonguing a man on the screen."

"You've got a point," he said, looking at

Mabel with a dumbfounded expression on his face.

I used that moment of confusion to flee from the living room and out toward my "stagecoach" in the driveway. Goldwyn ran after me. "Stop!" he yelled. "Wait up."

Behind the wheel of the car, I was tempted to race down his driveway but he caught up with me. "Come back to the studio. I'll think of some way to save the picture. I don't like losing money. I gave you a break, give me one now. Don't leave me now until I've figured out a way."

"No, Mr. Goldwyn," I said. Suddenly he was "mister" again. At this point I couldn't imagine that any intimacy had happened between us.

Sensing what I was trying to blot out of my mind, he stepped up to the car and whispered, "Samuel Goldwyn is not a faggot. But I know how much you want and need it. I'll still let you do that to me," he said, looking down at his crotch, "except you'll have to put on that blonde wig and paint your mouth red before I can get it hard for you."

"Good-bye, Mr. Goldwyn," I said. As he called after me, I stepped on the gas and headed down his driveway as fast as I could without wrecking my car. As I caught a glimpse of him in my rear-view mirror, I could not have known then that it was the last time I'd ever see him.

Ten blocks from Goldwyn's house, I stopped my stagecoach and hopped in the commodious rear where I changed from Lotte Lee to Durango Jones. I always kept some of my Durango clothes in the car in case I needed to do a quick switch, depending on the demands of my date for the evening.

I ripped off my Lotte wig and tossed it on the floor. I'd made my last appearance as Lotte Lee, a name that would surely fade in Hollywood history now that the world would never see her starring debut as a seductive film actress.

Back in the front seat, I headed for the Hollywood Hotel. I had enough money to live on with what I was getting from Charlie and W. R. I didn't need to work in films as Lotte Lee. Actually I had grown to resent Lotte. I wanted to be a big film star but only as Durango Jones. With Lotte removed from my life, I could concentrate on my own career. Of course, certain heterosexual boy friends like Tom Mix and John Gilbert would fall away.

At the Hollywood Hotel, I picked up my messages at the reception desk, noting that the staff looked at me strangely. They should be used to seeing Durango Jones come and go by now. Heading for my suite, I bumped into Blanche Sweet cruising the lobby again for young and impressionable studs who might be in awe of her position as a famed screen actress. Spotting me, she looked away, having long ago given up on the fact I could be used for stud services.

Going down the hallway, I stopped briefly at the door of Jean Acker. But there was no sound coming from the room of Rodolfo's wife. As I turned the key in my door, I heard someone coming out of the room two doors down from Jean Acker. To my surprise, it was the latest star to arrive in Hollywood, John Barrymore himself, my matinee idol now that I'd given up on Francis X. Bushman.

John smiled at me. "Who might you be?" he asked.

"Durango Jones," I said, thinking I should try to find my letter of introduction from his friend, Margaret Barker. Right now, however, I didn't seem to need it.

"I haven't had any satisfaction since the train crossed through Nevada and I made it with one of the married ladies on board." He winked lasciviously at me. "I was actually heading downstairs and out into the day to find some young girl to take care of my always roaring libido." He looked me up and down. "But it seems I have just encountered the prettiest little blond teenage boy in Hollywood, with his mouth painted with scarlet lipstick."

It was only then I realized I hadn't wiped Lotte Lee's lipstick from my mouth.

"I'm going to die on the spot if I can't explode my load into somebody," John said. "I'd had a young girl in mind, but a pretty boy will do just as well the way I feel this morning." He reached for my hand.

My heart beating so fast I feared an explosion, I took his hand as he guided me into his darkened room where he shut, then locked the door behind us.

*****

In John Barrymore's suite, I was nervous but he immediately put me at ease, pouring himself a whiskey and handing me one too without asking if I wanted it.

"I'm out here to sign a contract," he said, "then I have to go back to New York to appear in a play and to shoot a film at the same time."

"You'll be great in both of them," I assured him.

He smiled at me, raising a quizzical eyebrow as he'd done in several silent films. "I can tell that you have a crush on me. Tonight your fantasy will be realized." He grabbed his crotch. "It's full of sperm, all ready for you to suck it out of me."

I thought that rather blunt and not as eloquent as a line I'd associate with the great actor who was also called the great lover. It was so crude, in fact, that it momentarily turned me off, exploding my romantic dreams about him. But the whiskey helped me get over it.

"It's good to get out of New York for a few days," he said. "There's this young actress from Alabama who's chasing after me day and night, begging me to take her virginity. So far I've resisted."

"Is her name Tallulah Bankhead?" I asked.

"That's right," he said. "You've heard of her?"

"Enough to know that Tallulah has already lost her virginity," I said. "I know she fucked Goldwyn when she was last on the coast. She also fucked Charlie Chaplin. She struck out with Tom Moore, though."

"Sorry to hear this news," he said. "Her chief appeal to me as a sexual object is that I'll be the man to deflower her. Now I know the line forms on the right. My sister, Ethel, is also troubled by Tallulah. It seems that when Tallulah isn't chasing after me, she's pursuing Ethel."

"That doesn't surprise me," I said. "I wish I could be more versatile. But I like men, specifically one actor that I dream about nightly."

"Could that actor be John Barrymore himself?"

I looked up at him and smiled, as tears formed in my eyes. I felt lucky and privileged that John was going to present his body to me for my enjoyment and for his own pleasure too.

"You deserve me," he said, pulling off his jacket and tossing it on the sofa. He unbuttoned his shirt and removed it, along with his undershirt, allowing me to enjoy the beauty of his masculine chest and almost perfect physique. He started to unbuckle his belt but looked over at me. "From here on down, the pleasure is all yours."

With trembling hands, I reached for his belt, unbuckling it and then unbuttoning his fly. His trousers dropped to the floor as I reached to pull down his white underwear, exposing two inches of soft uncut cock and a pair of balls, each of which looked like a good-sized egg. I was initially disappointed in the size of his penis, but it looked so tasty I wanted it anyway.

He sat down on the bed as I took off his shoes and socks and then pulled his trousers and underwear off. He spread himself in the middle of the bed as he fondled his cock which had started to rise. It immediately extended to four inches and was quickly beginning to stretch out, as if anticipating what was about to be done to it.

By the time I had engulfed his cock into my hot mouth, it had extended to its full glory of eight inches, having gotten there from unpromising beginnings. It was far thicker than average too.

As he rose to the challenge, so did I. John Barrymore might be a great performer on the stage, but I was a sexual performer in bed, and I was determined that John be the beneficiary of all my recent experiences satisfying Hollywood studs. I attacked him with my mouth and didn't let him up for one entire hour, during which time I tasted every inch of him from the inside of his ears to the toe-jam of his feet. He was one fabulous morsel for my cherry reds to devour. I sucked and licked my way across his fabled torso like a satanic vampire, slurping my way across his adam's apple and down his chest to his balls and beyond to his perfect rosebud which had a marvelous man-musk.

That glorious scent of man-sex filled the air, and John was softly moaning, his eyes closed. His jaw clenched tight, great knots of muscles stood out at his temples. Every now and then he'd deliver a little yelp, and I knew at once I'd hit a particularly sensitive spot to attack with even more ferocity. At one point I'd switched into overdrive, knowing it was time to head home, which in this case meant descending onto his towering cock for the suck of its super-sensitive life.

Long before he descended into the lost years of alcohol and decay, John Barrymore was at his prime, a symbol of male virility and masculinity. His dick exploded in shattering savagery, as if he'd been saving it for a month. It was an orgy of heaving, thrusting, spurting, and splashing, one explosion after another until it seemed as if the nerve endings in his body could stand no more delightful torture.

"My God," he said, sitting up and reaching for my blond hair to pull on it. "I've lost so much cream I think I've ruptured my nuts. Lick them for me to soothe them."

I was only too happy to oblige and took to my assignment so well he had to gently ease my head from his nuts about forty minutes later when they'd gotten what I was convinced was the bathing of their young life.

Some lovers, once they fill you with their creamy contribution, become sullen and want to escape as soon as possible. Not John.

Totally natural in his nudity, he paraded around the room and was very talkative and animated. "Up to now," he said, "my films have been mere fluff. I don't like pansy roles." He looked over at me. "No offense intended. I detest roles like the character of Peter Ibbetson where I'm a marshmallow in a blond wig. That is about to change. I'm out here to sign for a deal to play *Dr. Jekyll and Mr. Hyde*. On stage I get only five-hundred dollars a week, but film producers will pay me one thousand and five hundred a week. I always need the money."

"That sounds like a fantastic role for you," I said, sitting up in bed.

"I see the film as a chance for screen immortality," he said. "Sarah Bernhardt made a film only for that reason. So that future generations could know what she looked like and how she acted. The greatest stage stars will one day be all but forgotten when their audiences die. But a century from now Charlie Chaplin will be a cult figure. After the Jekyll/Hyde thing is released, it will immortalize me long after audiences no longer remember my *Hamlet*."

"Will the film be shot out here?" I asked, hoping for the offer of a small part. The idea of appearing in a film with John Barrymore thrilled me.

"The film will be shot in New York on West 56th Street," he said. "I'll be shooting Jekyll and Hyde during the day and playing *Richard III* at night. I hope the stress won't prove intolerable."

"My God, they sound like the two most strenuous roles of your life," I said. "I've never seen you on stage. The chance to see you in *Richard III* is reason enough for me to make my first visit to New York."

"That's fine with me," he said. "I'll give you some more of this." He reached for his crotch. "But you'll have to pay your own train fare. John Barrymore does not pay the train fare of those who satisfy his insatiable libido."

"I have money," I said, "and I'm dying to see you on stage. I'm sure I'll remember your performance for the rest of my life."

"Don't forget the film," he said with the eagerness of a young boy. "Up to now I've been greater than all of my film roles. One reviewer wrote that in *The Test of Honor*, my first screen drama, I reminded him of Caruso glorifying a song out of Tin-Pan Alley."

"I'm sure that's true." I could not match him in conversation and was reduced to making dumb utterances like a yes man.

"Look at the left side of my face and tell me what you see," he asked, turning his much photographed and much viewed profile to me.

"I see the handsomest profile in all the world," I said.

He then turned his right side to me. "Now what do you see?"

"A very handsome profile indeed," I said.

"Right, but not among the greatest in the world," he said. "My right profile looks like a fried egg. It is hardly my desire to be known as a mere male beauty. Actually I get a great deal of pleasure from disguising my incredible left profile by makeup or facial contortion."

"There is no actor in Hollywood with your versatility," I said.

"I'll show you what I can do even without benefit of makeup," he said. Staring at me was the actor looking like the handsome, intelligent, and charming Dr. Jekyll. He then turned his back to me, covering his face with his hands. When he spun around, his face was hideously twisted and contorted. He'd made his hands clawlike. Without benefit of anything he'd transformed himself into the pointy-headed, fanged horror, Mr. Hyde.

I did what any red-blooded American faggot would do. I screamed in shock.

"No cinematic portrayer, certainly no stage portrait, even that of Richard Mansfield, will top my *Dr. Jekyll and Mr. Hyde*," he said. "I'll go from a doctor of silken suavity to the terror of his alter ego."

"I don't know how you can play such a difficult part in front of cameras during the day and be *Richard III* at night."

He looked at me with a confused expression as if he too didn't know if he could pull off such a double-barreled acting assignment. *"Richard III* will also be a great stretch for me as an actor to turn myself into that lump of foul deformity, that abortive, rooting hog. I'll appear before audiences with long, crow-black hair falling to my shoulders, my mouth twisted in a sly, cruel smile."

Even before beginning what would be the two most demanding roles of his life, he seemed on the verge of a complete physical and nervous collapse. As I was going around the world on his body, twice had he had to reach for a glass of whiskey on his night table to settle his nerves.

"After *Richard III*, I'm going to appear as *Hamlet* on Broadway," he said. "Which brings up a point. I need both your help and advice." Still nude, he went over to his suitcase and pulled out of a pair of green tights. Before putting them on, he faced me with a full frontal. "Take in my entire body before I get into costume." He commanded.

Although I admired his physique, finding it in many places even more chiseled than that of Rodolfo, his cock in repose wasn't as impressive as it should be. I knew, better than anyone at that very moment, how it could rise to an impressive eight inches. But if I'd seen him in a shower, I would not have thought him

well hung at all. I issued words of admiration.

He slipped the thin tights over his nude body. "Look at my basket of goodies now," he demanded of me. "What do you think? I mean the way I fill out the pouch like a ballet dancer or a virile bullfighter should do."

"Considering the length and thickness of your penis, I don't think those tights present you in your fullest glory."

"That's it!" he said, almost shouting. "You've got that right. I'm not presented in my fullest virility and glory of manhood, and my fans are entitled to all that John Barrymore has. Get a sock from that drawer over there and do your magic. Create a penis enclosed in green tights that you as a little pansy boy would be enthralled to view if you attended a *Hamlet* matinee."

After several attempts on my part, the sock was eventually rejected and tossed aside. Both of us feared it might travel during a strenuous performance. Instead of a sock, he went over to a chest of drawers and removed some item. Returning to me, he held it up in front of me for inspection. At first I didn't know what it was.

"This is the kind of male falsies used by some ballet dancers who have a concave where a fully blown cock and balls should be," he said. "They cover their genitals with this so they'll look like male ballet dancers instead of ballerinas." He hooked the device over his genitals, and I helped him pull his green tights over his well-proportioned legs. Once dressed, he stood back from me so that I could inspect him again. "Well, what do you think?" he asked.

"You look like the stud of Hollywood," I said.

"I think so too," he said, admiring his look in a full-length mirror. He went over to his closet and returned with a short, dark green jacket with long sleeves, a costume evocative of apparel in the 15th century. After putting on his full costume, he stared at himself in the mirror before turning to look at me again. "What do you think now?"

"I think you look fantastic," I said.

"I'm not so sure," he said, eying his appearance skeptically in the mirror again. "Perhaps a decadent string bean."

"String bean, my asshole," I said. "You look like the jolly green giant, at least where those basket of goodies are concerned." Some food company decades in the future must have heard of my remark and later capitalized off it in promoting their vegetables.

"The mention of the word asshole has done something for me," he said, reaching out and grabbing me, pulling me close to him. Up to then, I'd sucked and licked every inch of him, except for his mouth. At long last I got to taste his succulent lips and tongue. He inserted his tongue into my mouth.

As many men could testify, no stud ever inserted his tongue into the mouth of Durango Jones without getting a reward. I sucked voraciously, the way I did with all my men. We must have carried on for at least fifteen minutes before his lips departed. As we kissed, we both struggled to free John of his *Hamlet* drag. When he finally pulled out his tongue, he said something unromantic. "They say you should not only brush your teeth but brush your tongue as well. I feel my tongue has been cleaned for a month."

I ran my fingers through his hair and erotically played with his ears before demanding that he kiss me some more. This time our exchange of body fluids lasted longer than before when he abruptly pulled away, as if he'd had his fill.

"I've satisfied myself in that mouth with its cherry-red lips," he said. "But until you mentioned the word asshole, I realized I'd completely forgotten about another part of your anatomy that I bet is itching for an assault. That delectable brown hole of yours. Or is it rose colored?" He tossed me back on the bed and held my legs up in the air. "Grab your ass cheeks and spread them for me," he commanded. "I want to see everything."

I did as instructed, never having felt as nude and vulnerable before any man.

"That looks good enough to eat," he said. He attacked me with his recently cleansed tongue as I moaned in ecstasy. The tongue that had delivered some of the most memorable lines ever uttered on stage had found another calling.

*****

Leaving the suite with a smile on my face, I went downstairs with John to the dining room of the Hollywood Hotel where he'd invited me for lunch. The maître d' showed us to our reserved table where I was surprised to encounter the actress, Jeanne Eagles, waiting for us with the dancer/actor Clifton Webb.

"I slipped away from mumsy for one afternoon," Webb said, "so I could have lunch with the greatest actor of all time, John Barrymore."

John hardly paid attention to Webb's rather sickening flattery. Instead he bowed low and kissed the lovely, delicate hand of Jeanne Eagles. If I didn't know that John had been satisfied sexually, I would have thought that he was putting the make on Eagles. As long as she was in his presence, Webb didn't exist, much less me. After all, I was the only non-star at table.

If John no longer paid me attention, Webb could look at no one else. He was virtually licking his lips. "I must say John knows how to pick them. He's just arrived in Hollywood, and already he seems to have met the prettiest boy on the west coast."

"You flatter me, Mr. Webb," I said.

"You can call me Clifton." He smiled again as I detected a hand placed on my knee under concealment of a white tablecloth.

As I let Webb's hand travel up my knee to the basket of goodies, I was too intrigued with Eagels to care. She was only twenty-five when I met her, and was already famous for having said, "Never deny. Never explain. Say nothing and become a legend." Obviously Garbo in the years ahead must have taken a lesson from my fellow Midwesterner.

Eagles wasn't from the state of Kansas but from Kansas City, Missouri, which virtually made her a kissin' kin of mine. Her hair bleached blonde, she was a stunning, striking beauty with a porcelain complexion and blue eyes.

At one point in the conversation when I thought I might add something, I shared with her the fact that I was from Lawrence, Kansas. "I hate the place," she said, glancing only briefly at me. That ended that attempt to bond on my part.

Even though I didn't impress Eagels, I was mesmerized by her. Even at such a young age, her candle was burning at both ends, to borrow from another writer. She was just months from appearing in W. Somerset Maugham's *Rain*, as the prostitute, Sadie Thompson. Ironically in 1922 she'd be appearing at the Cort Theater at the same time as John, who was playing *Hamlet* in his green and well-stuffed tights.

Although the only time I was to encounter Eagels was during that brief but memorable lunch, I felt she had an aura of melancholy about her, even though it would appear the entire world was opening up for her. With only a decade to live, she too would fall victim to drugs and alcohol like so many other stars of the era. Making her film debut in 1929 for MGM, in W. Somerset Maugham's *The Letter*, she won an Academy Award nomination but didn't live long enough to know if she'd won or not. Late in the afternoon of October 3, she died of a heroin overdose in her Park Avenue apartment and was laid to rest in a Kansas City cemetery four days later.

The romantic history of John Barrymore and Jeanne Eagels intrigued me. By 1911 a rumor was spread that they'd been secretly married, and, of course, it was a stormy union. Any marriage of Jeanne Eagels or John Barrymore to anyone else would be nothing but storm clouds, and of that I was certain. The couple that was so fascinated with each other at that luncheon gave no clue nor indicated in any of their talk that they'd been married to each other.

The talk, however, was of marriage—but not Clifton's. As he fondled my cock, causing it to stretch out into a full erection, he wasn't exactly trying to conceal his homosexuality.

"I'm going to marry Michael Strange," John announced to the table.

"You're marrying a man?" Clifton asked. For the first time at the luncheon, something had caught his interest other than my dick.

"Not at all," John said. "She's a beautiful woman. Only problem is, she's a lesbian."

I was dumbfounded. Why such actors as John or Rodolfo wanted to marry lesbians amazed me.

"I know of her," Eagels said. "She looks like a young Arab boy with dark eyes, brown hair, and olive skin."

"It's like she's in the ring cracking the whip, and I'm jumping," John said. "In some ways I know my outside is masculine but inside I feel my soul is feminine."

That self-appraisal reminded me of Rodolfo.

"I have this need to be dominated but I'm also revolted by that tendency in myself," John confessed. "I turn to Michael because she dominates me. But it also makes me hate her for exposing this need I have. I think the reason I drink is because my masculine side is always fighting with my feminine side."

"All of us need some excuse," Eagels said, downing the last of her whiskey and calling for the waiter to bring her another one.

"When I told Lionel that I was going to marry Michael," John said, his comment was, 'I don't know who is going to kill the other first.'"

"All Broadway is talking about those his-and-hers outfits Michael designs for you," Eagels said.

"I hate to wear such shit but I do so to please her," John said. "Frankly, her designs embarrass the hell out of me. Ethel thinks Michael is making a fool out of me."

"Ethel suspects a lot more," Eagels said. "She also thinks that Tallulah and Michael are bumping pussies at the Algonquin Hotel. Ethel told me that instead of Michael Strange, your future wife should call herself Tom Barrymore."

"The outfits are a bit masculine," John admitted," and thank God for that. She doesn't insist I put on a dress. Her velvet jackets are in the style of Alfred de Musset. We both wear white shirts with wide-open collars—she calls that a Walt Whitman shirt. She also puts heavy riding gloves on with wide cuffs on both of us."

"I guess that would be called the George Sand look," Clifton said, his eyes brightening as he gently caressed the head of my throbbing cock.

"You've got it," John said. "We both wear soft matching hats, and we both carry a walking stick with a heavy knob."

"Sounds grand," I said, like a teenage boy from the Middle West in the presence of these sophisticates of the theater world.

A silence came over the dining table, as

Clifton kept gently fondling me.

"Michael has a young son by the name of Robin," John said. "He always refers to himself as a girl. He spins elaborate fantasies about his adventures as a girl. Actually he imagines himself a princess waiting to be rescued from some dank castle by a handsome and dashing prince. In fact, Robin is in love with me. He always calls me his 'sweet prince.'"

"You'll make a great stepfather," I assured him.

At this point Clifton was practically salivating. He leaned over me and whispered to John, "I can't hold back, and I know you saw him first, but when the waiter isn't looking can I slip under the table and do my thing with Durango?"

"Since you know I don't suck cock, my dear man," John said, "he's all yours. Durango deserves to release a load since I didn't perform that service for him upstairs."

To my shock and surprise, Webb slipped under the tablecloth, unbuttoned my fly, and swallowed me whole in one gulp. This was one experienced cocksucker.

As Webb sucked me, Eagels and John ate lunch as if nothing untoward were happening. They were truly people of the world. As I was being eaten alive, I pondered at the number of times Webb had enjoyed Rodolfo's inches. Webb had danced with Bonnie Glass in New York, and when he got ready to leave, he'd given the job to Rodolfo. Although Rodolfo had never spoken of this to me, I'd heard rumors that Webb had "auditioned" Rodolfo several times before he became the new dancing partner of Bonnie Glass.

As I exploded into Webb's mouth, I was met with a suction pump, draining every drop from me. I tried not to cry out at such a violent explosion on my part, and concealed it with an audible sigh.

When John signaled to Webb that no one was looking, the dancer rose from the floor and seated himself at table, I thought he might go to the toilet to clean up, but he preferred to wipe his mouth with his napkin instead.

"I don't know what you have," he said to me with every intention of it being overheard by Eagels and John. Whatever it is, you should bottle it."

The conversation resumed as if nothing had happened. Over angel cake served for dessert, Webb leaned over and whispered in my ear. "I've had a lot of young men in my day, but none as wonderful as you. I think I'm in love. I want you to come and live with me in New York."

I didn't reject the offer. Neither did I accept it.

I really wasn't thinking of Webb's proposal but of Jeanne Eagels herself. She mesmerized me, and I wanted to ask her so many questions, including what it was like to work with Julian Eltinge when she'd appeared with him as co-star in *The Crinoline Girl*. To me, Eagels in the golden light of the dining room appeared just as she had previously in the film, *The World and the Woman*. Drugs and alcohol were yet to take a toll on her face.

At the time I met her, she was telling us about a new play she was going to do at the Garrick Theater in New York. It was called *The Wonderful Thing*. Then her eyes clouded and her voice became forlorn. "After the run of the play, I think I'll go to Europe for several months to rest and regain my strength." At that point she'd downed four whiskies before calling for the waiter to bring her a fifth.

John had matched her glass for glass while I was still sipping on my first round. Webb leaned over to whisper in my ear. "No whiskey for me today. Only grade A Midwestern cream."

John rose to go to the men's room, and Webb jumped up to follow him. "I've got to go too," he said.

John looked back at Eagels and smiled, then looked at me and winked. "Every time I go to take a piss, Clifton here has to follow thinking he's going to get lucky. All I let him do is take a look—perhaps shake it an extra bit or two for the delight of his eyes." He reached for Webb's arm and pulled him alone. "Come, my dear man, for the John Barrymore unveiling."

At a table with Jeanne Eagels, she used the occasion to reach into her purse and examine her makeup in a small mirror. A lot of her lipstick had rubbed off, and she felt some dire need to replenish it. After she'd finished, she looked at me, seemingly seeing me for the first time today. I could feel the full force of her eyes, the charisma of her personality, and the general magnetism of the woman. "You don't mind, darling," she asked, "if I could borrow John for the evening? After all, we wouldn't want to turn the great lover into a homosexual, now would we?"

*****

After blowing kisses at Jeanne Eagels and the ever-horny Clifton Webb, John asked me to drive him in my "stagecoach" on an urgent "mission of mercy" to call upon a sick and dying friend. This friend, John claimed, was his "greatest, grandest friend on earth. When I die, all I want on my tombstone is that this goddamned son of a bitch knew Ned Sheldon."

At last I found out who the sick friend was. Anyone interested in theater knew the name of Ned Sheldon, as it was as familiar as Tennessee Williams or Edward Albee to future play-goers.

Born Edward Sheldon to a wealthy real-estate family, he'd first gained fame with the play, *Salvation Nell,* which had opened in New York in 1908. That hit was followed by a shocking play called *The Nigger* in 1909, in which the lead character played the governor of a Southern state who learns he had black blood. Plays such as that made Sheldon rich and famous by the age of twenty-five.

As we arrived at Ned's apartment, a guest was already leaving. John introduced me to Charles McArthur, whom the world remembers today mainly for being the husband of Helen Hayes. When I met him, he was already a famous dramatist. He told us he was writing a play, *Lulu Belle,* with Ned Sheldon.

After securing McArthur's promise that he'd write his next play for John, we were shown inside an antique-filled apartment by a maid in a stiff white apron over a black uniform. When we were ushered into Sheldon's bedroom, it was like visiting the shrine of a saint. Before John introduced me, he leaned over the bed of his sick and dying friend and gave him a long, lingering, and wet-lipped kiss of passion.

After the customary amusement with my name of Durango, Ned invited me to sit on the edge of his bed as he held my hand. "I love beauty." He said, "and I'm slowly going blind. Turn your face to the light so I can see it in full sunshine. You are a golden boy. In the years ahead when I will know only darkness, I will remember the beauty of your pretty face and your hair more golden than any American wheat field."

I liked this playwright at once and felt he was an acute judge of male flesh. Perhaps he'd write a play with me as the lead. I'd never even considered the stage before, but that might be my true calling. When John excused himself to go to the toilet, Ned asked me to lean over and kiss him the way his friend had. I obliged somewhat reluctantly, hoping he didn't have any disease that was catching. Before ill health ravished his body, he must have been a dashing and handsome man.

He was clearly an invalid, having been overtaken by a partial paralysis. He told me that his was a most unusual case. "The doctors can't diagnose nor cure me. Day after day I lie in this bed wasting away." His hands and face looked as if they were carved in ivory, although his mind remained razor-sharp.

He tried to sit up in bed. "I adore Jack," he said. "He's the center of my universe. I adore everything about him, even his bad habits. If he wanted to shit in my mouth, I'd view it as nectar from the gods."

Such devotion made me shudder in revulsion.

"Ever since I first met him, the suffering and emotional frustration he's inflicted on me has led to my present illness," he claimed.

"I'm so sorry," I said, not thinking that John could be blamed for what was happening to Ned. "How did you guys first meet?"

"One of my plays, *Princess Zim Zim,* brought us together," he said. "The play was a failure but it marked the beginning of a lifelong friendship during a Boston tryout. Neither of us had known such intensity in friendship—nor will we ever again."

At that point John came back into the bedroom buttoning up his fly. "Ned put the finger of destiny on me," he said. "From the very beginning, he made me realize what I could become as an actor. His love, his friendship, and his belief in me has never wavered. Only last year, a critic in New York wrote, 'The true director of John Barrymore's rich career is none other than Ned Sheldon.'"

"My greatest regret," Ned said, "is that Jack turned down the role of the Reverend Armstrong in a play I wrote called *Romance*. It opened in 1913 and turned out to be my greatest success."

"It was a mistake," John said, "and I know it now. I just couldn't see myself playing a minister in love. William Courtenay was a big hit in the part."

"That's true," Ned said. "*Romance* became my biggest success. At the time my betrothed, Doris Keane, was given the female lead. There are a lot better actresses on Broadway than Doris, but the part was to be her crowning achievement—and in many ways mine too."

The maid brought drinks for us, and Ned and John must have talked for two hours, mostly about his health and John's upcoming role in *Richard III*. Ned seemed rather dismissive of the flickers, as if the art form were aimed merely at children of all ages, whereas serious artists such as John should concentrate only on the theater.

When John told Ned he had to leave, the playwright reached for both of our hands. "There is one final favor," he said, looking at me and not at John. "I'm going blind. For all I know, I won't be able to see a thing tomorrow. There is this request. I want one of my last memory visions to be of John's cock in its full glory, a state I've brought it to countless times in the past. Please position yourself over me and suck off John until he's ready to explode. Then pull out real quick and let me drink John's cream, surely the tastiest in all the world. It's something for me to remember and cherish as my days grow darker."

Without hesitation, John unbuttoned his trousers and presented his cock to me in a flaccid state. I didn't mind giving John another blow-job, but wasn't really comfortable with such an audience. He positioned himself over Ned's face, his cock and balls dangling directly over the playwright's mouth.

Licking my lips, I realized it was show time. I skinned back the head of John's prick and wrapped my cherry-red lips around it, as it

hardened at once. He groaned as I swallowed all of his inches. We seemed to hang suspended over Ned's face. I opened my jaws even wider and lathered John up, increasing my tempo as I slid up and down on his rigid prick for Ned's pleasure.

John seemed to forget all about Ned as he surrendered himself to the joy of the blow-job. Long before his climax, I tasted the first acidic sting of his pre-cum. His blunt head seemed to bruise my tonsils but still I eagerly plunged down on him, taking each stabbing jab with gusto. With my right hand I fingered and lifted his plum-sized balls. I felt them tighten as the hot semen boiled inside him. Then, suddenly, he grabbed me by my blond hair and forced my mouth off him. He yanked back and inserted his cock between Ned's eagerly suctioning mouth where he exploded with a certain violence.

Later, even when I returned from the bathroom Ned's lips still held onto John's cock, now flaccid once again. The playwright didn't seem to want to release John. Finally, John gently eased his dick from his friend's mouth and planted a long, lingering kiss on his lips.

After John had left the room, Ned called me back, requesting that I too plant a final kiss on his lips like John had done. I obliged. As I pulled away, he reached for me, whispering in my ear, "I want you to visit me every afternoon around three until I lose all my vision. I want you to strip and jerk off over my face, splattering your cum all over my lips. I'll go blind with just that memory. You and John scattering your seed over me."

I made no promise to him.

Sensing my hesitation, he called after me in a weak voice, "There's money in it for you."

"Good-bye, Ned," I said. "It was great meeting you." If I were a struggling actor in Hollywood, I might have considered his offer. Instead I thought I might pass it on to Ramon. Ned's request was easier to fulfill than facing that branding iron of Sessue Hayakawa.

The day wasn't over yet. John had other plans for me. Back at the Hollywood Hotel, he told me, "I have this great friend out here. I mean, he's a real ladies' man. Right now he's fucking both Gloria Swanson and Edna Purviance—God knows who else. But he just loves a great blow-job."

"Could your friend be Thomas Meighan?" I asked.

"I see you keep up with the Hollywood gossip," he said. "Tom claims he's found only a few pansies out here who really know how to suck him off. So far no woman has ever pleased him. Edna and Gloria gag when he tries to reach the back of their throats. I'm worn out for today. You've succeeded in satisfying the libido of the great Barrymore himself—no small feat."

"I'd love to meet your friend," I said, intrigued that Thomas had accepted blow-jobs from men other than Durango. Unknown to John, I had already had Thomas, both as Lotte Lee and as my real self at the home of Edna Purviance. "I've seen all his films. He's a favorite of mine."

"I'll call him now," he said. "The only thing I ask in return is that you let me watch, the way Ned did with us today. You see, in addition to all my other bad vices, I'm a bit of a voyeur."

No longer startled by the coincidences of Hollywood, I took a shower. Of course, Thomas Meighan would be a friend of John Barrymore, and, of course, I would already know Thomas both as Lotte Lee and as Durango. Looking at myself in the mirror after the shower, I realized how much easier it was to be me, Durango Jones, and not my sister who was bogged down with all that makeup and drag.

After Thomas arrived, the evening went beautifully. For reasons of his own, he made no mention to his friend, John, that we'd had a sexual encounter before. He was filled with compliments about Lotte's beauty and her acting ability, and told me I was pretty too. "Almost as much as Lotte," he said, "but not quite as pretty as she is. After all, you're a boy, and she's a girl, and no boy can be as pretty as any girl."

I nodded in agreement, although I didn't agree with him at all. Later, after his first whiskey, Thomas stripped and got in the center of John's bed. John pulled off all his clothes and played with himself, as I descended on Thomas, consuming inches I already knew so well. Although the whiskey drinking must have slowed him down a bit, I got my reward of sweet nectar after about thirty minutes of powerful sucking and slurping, with John overseeing every bit of the action.

After sucking Thomas off, I got off him as he retreated to a corner of the room, still not bothering to put back on his trousers. Also nude, John joined him for more serious whiskey drinking. Neither man paid much attention to me. They had a lot of catching up to do.

It was John who got the inspiration at two o'clock in the morning to call two prostitutes he'd regularly used. Thinking of whores, I thought of Maria Jane's long-ago boarder in Lawrence, Kansas—Margaret Barker. That letter of introduction from her to John was hardly needed now. I'd already introduced myself to John.

I'd been a bit disappointed when John had called the hookers. Hadn't I satisfied both Thomas and John? I'd sucked off John twice and been fucked once by him, and I'd sucked off Thomas once and, later at midnight, been fucked by him when John told him my ass was the tightest and most thrilling hole he'd ever known. What did these men want with two whores? John could have had Jeanne Eagels up to his suite but had refused her call earlier in the evening. I truly didn't understand this complicated man, failing to see why he might turn down a beauty like Eagels for some cheap slut.

Later he told me that he'd used up all his semen for the day, and was very satisfied in that department. "But right now Tom and I need the one thing you can't give us, and that's pussy. My buddy and I are serious pussy-eaters. That's something you wouldn't understand, I'm sure."

The night was not over nor lost for me. As I was getting ready to go back to my own suite, John told me that he was practically the godfather of Douglas Fairbanks Jr. "The kid worships me," he said. "Fairbanks Sr. neglects the boy all the time. He's too busy chasing after those golden curls of Mary Pickford." He said he'd promised to take the ten-year-old horseback riding in the Hollywood Hills in the morning. He looked over at Thomas. "Obviously Tommy boy and I won't be in any shape tomorrow morning to go horseback riding, especially after we finish off those two whores due here any minute. Will you go riding with Doug in my place?"

"I'd be glad to," I said. "I know his father, and I hear young Doug's a great kid. Being from Kansas, I learned how to ride a horse a long time ago."

"Good," he said.

Seeing that Thomas was in a stupor, I avoided telling him good morning and headed for the door. John waited for me there and took me in his arms, giving me a long, lingering and wet-lipped kiss like he'd given Ned. Breaking away, he said, "My brother, Lionel, taught me to kiss men like that."

"It's been great," I said, wondering if I'd ever see the great actor again.

A look of concern crossed his famous brow. "I hope you don't mind, but little Doug came to the hotel while you were in the bathroom. His mother brought him over. He was going to spend the night in my suite so we could get an early morning start. I called down and had him sent to your suite instead."

"That is just fine with me," I said. "I'll look after him."

After a final kiss from John, I headed across the hallway to my own suite. I'd never entertained a ten-year-old before.

In the hallway, John called after me. "Thanks for everything. But change that name of Durango. It sounds too phony even for Hollywood. Call yourself Bruce Jones. It'll look better on the marquee." He gently shut his door.

*****

In my own suite, I saw what I presumed to be the young Fairbanks Jr. asleep in my double bed. After cleaning up in the bathroom and taking a much-needed shower, I came out stark naked and gently eased into bed with the young son of the legendary star. I was anxious to see what he looked like in person but decided that would have to wait until morning.

I'd seen photographs of him, of course, and felt he looked like a clean-cut, all-American youth. Sleeping in the same bed with a ten-year-old child was the closest I'd ever come to experiencing fatherhood, as I certainly didn't

plan to have children of my own.

It must have been eight or nine o'clock when I woke up, having barely recovered from my drunken stupor of the previous night. As I opened my eyes into the reality of the morning, I discovered that the sheets had been tossed off me, and that young Doug was sucking dearly on my cock, although managing to take only the first four inches. I could detect his gagging. Even though I presented a formidable challenge to him, he eagerly pressed on, trying for just one more inch.

Looking up at me through his boyish face, we met eyeball to eyeball for the first time. He was a beautiful boy, and I felt he'd grow into a stunningly handsome man.

He raised up slightly, licking his lips. "I like to suck cock," he said. "It's a homosexual period I'm going through. When I turn sixteen, I'm going to give it up and start a new career. I'm going to fuck all the beautiful women in Hollywood."

"That should keep you real busy," I said.

Although young Fairbanks back then wasn't a great cocksucker, he improved greatly over the next few years with lots of experience. In time he'd learn to take all my inches as he grew older. He also turned out to be a prophet. After I'd enjoyed that succulent mouth for years, Doug turned sixteen—and with my blessing—set out to seduce some of the world's most beautiful and glamorous women, from Joan Crawford to Marlene Dietrich.

Except for a brief affair he conducted with Laurence Olivier on their way to Europe in 1932, he didn't go back to male-to-male sex. As he said, it was a "period" he was going through. Well, there was one more time. That was with his new stepfather, Jack Whiting, who looked almost as young and handsome as Doug Jr. himself. Whiting took young Doug to England for George V's Silver Jubilee. Doug became so captivated by the gorgeous, vigorous, and virile Jack that when they went to the steam bath at the Savoy Hotel in London, Doug reverted back to his youthful indiscretions. Apparently, Jack did little to resist the sexual attention of his young stepson.

There was one final time that I know about. When filming *Gunga Din* in 1939, Doug had a brief fling with Cary Grant. But he must have decided to abandon Cary to Randolph Scott, as Doug walked down the aisle that same year with Mary Lee. The year 1939 also saw Doug in a three way with Larry Olivier and Vivien Leigh, Miss Scarlett O'Hara herself.

But it was women who would attract Doug over the years and often get him into trouble. How could he resist Ginger Rogers in 1938 while filming *Having Wonderful Time*, or Rita Hayworth in 1940 while shooting *Angels Over Broadway*?

At the time Doug turned sixteen, he requested that I take him to the photo studio of my dear comrade in heat, Rod St. Just. Once there, Doug demanded that his full and lengthy erection be photographed for posterity. Fortunately he did not have Doug Sr.'s curvature.

How could I have known back then that another nude picture of Doug taken in the early 1960s would practically topple the British government? Margaret, the notorious Duchess of Argyll, the world's greatest nymph, other than myself, photographed Doug masturbating on her toilet. She used an early version of the Polaroid camera. There was also a picture that Doug had taken of Lord Duncan-Sandys, Sir Winston Churchill's son-in-law. He was being fellated by the Duchess who wore only three strands of pearls—nothing else. Regrettably, the Duke of Argyll, in his lonely baronial estate in Scotland, discovered not only these photographs but the diaries of his roving wife. The evidence was introduced to the Edinburgh court, but kept from public view.

Photographed from the waist down, Doug became known in the British press "as the man without a head."

Duncan-Sandys at the time was defense secretary to the government of Harold Macmillan, so this scandal had profound implications. A delegation from London, representing Her Majesty's government, paid a secret visit to me in Hollywood. Obviously word of my notorious past had reached the Queen herself. One of the stories spread about me was that I owned a series of nudes snapped of the young Doug. The British representatives wanted me both to identify the masturbator as Fairbanks Jr. and to turn over copies of the photographs so that they might compare the penises captured on film.

I refused them on both counts. Having known Doug Jr.'s penis for years, I immediately recognized him in the photograph, but I lied to the Brits and told them I'd never seen the man before. I also denied being in possession of any nude pictures of the actor and society figure.

This notorious divorce action was occurring at the same time that the scandal involving the war minister, John Profumo, was unfolding. He was asked to resign in disgrace when it had emerged that he'd lied to Parliament about his relationship with the call girl, Christine Keeler. Doug too was involved in the Profumo scandal.

Lord Duncan-Sandys protested his innocence at the time but threatened to resign from the cabinet on principle alone. He was talked out of that. Coming at the time of the Profumo scandal, his resignation might have been too much for the British people and could have brought down the government. Upper-class decadence had never made such lurid headlines in Britain.

In the decades to come, I met the duchess at a party. We recognized each other as kindred spirits. She confided to me that night that in one twenty-four hour period, she'd sampled ten of Britain's finest studs—and still she wasn't really satisfied. She told me she much preferred giving blow-jobs to men rather than getting fucked. She even offered to go down on me like she had on Fairbanks Jr. and half the rest of the British empire. I spurned her offer.

But I'm getting way ahead of my story. Back at the Hollywood Hotel, young Doug resumed his sucking after our brief chit-chat. I knew Maria Jane would not approve of a ten-year old boy going down on me, and I also knew that the more mature nineteen-year-old Durango should have taken young Doug by the hair and pulled him off me. I didn't. Instead, I gave in.

The kid was getting to me, and there was no way in hell I was going to withdraw from that warm, succulent mouth until I'd shot my load. My God, I realized. I'd become as decadent as Theodore Kosloff himself, going to bed with ten-year-olds. I closed my eyes as Doug struggled to bring me to climax. He did so admirably, in spite of his lack of experience. I exploded in his mouth, and he drank every drop, seemingly wanting even more, although I felt I'd delivered an ample load.

It was the urgent ringing of my phone that finally forced me to withdraw from Doug's mouth. Thinking it might be Rodolfo or even John Barrymore, I picked up the phone to find myself speaking to one of the most famous men in the world. Not Charlie Chaplin, but Douglas Fairbanks Sr.

He explained that he'd just called John's suite and was given my number. "John sounds too drunk to walk," Doug said. "Thanks for volunteering to take my son horseback riding. After you guys finish, send my son back to his mother. As for you, I want you to drop by my house this afternoon. I'm back in Hollywood and I've got a small part for you in my next picture. It's not much but it's something."

I thanked him profusely and learned that the title of the picture was *Till the Clouds Roll By*.

"Was it all right...I mean my son spending the night with you?" he asked.

I paused. Was he implying that I might molest his son? "Everything went grand," I said.

"Fine. I do appreciate your taking care of the boy. There is just one thing."

"What's that?" I asked, trying to sound as innocent as possible.

"Even if you have to go pee, don't take your dick out in front of the boy," he said. "He's showing homosexual tendencies. He was in my private steam bath the other day. I was there with some of my male friends. Doug couldn't take his eyes off our dicks."

"You know yourself that all boys are curious." I said. "He just wanted to compare—that's all. Think nothing of it."

"If you say so." he said. "I figure you know more about these things than I do." Something in the background seemed to be demanding his urgent attention. "Listen, it's imperative that you be here at two o'clock. There's a very special guest I want you to entertain. Remember when you volunteered to do special entertaining for me?"

"I do indeed," I said.

"This is a very distinguished person, and we've got to be very discreet. Do I have your absolute guarantee that you'll never divulge any of the details of the afternoon about to happen?"

"My word of honor," I said. "Won't you tell me who it is?"

"Not over the phone," he said. "Someone might be listening. I'll tell you this: you're in for the surprise of your life. I can only give you a clue. One day he'll reign over an empire on which the sun never sets."

*****

The horseback ride in the Hollywood Hills—that and other things—solidified a bond between young Doug and me that would last a lifetime. We both vowed to live to be a hundred. Regrettably Doug Jr. didn't make it, dying in May of 2000 at age of ninety. I'm still here, although every night I dream Rodolfo is calling for me in heaven. Fortunately, once there, I won't have to compete with Norman Kerry for Rodolfo's affection. Although I love Norman Kerry dearly, he didn't get past Gabriel.

When I left young Doug with his mother, he looked real disappointed, having wanted an invitation to see his father. But Doug Sr. said his afternoon "was reserved strictly for adults."

At Doug Sr.'s house, a servant offered me a drink, and I was told to wait in the parlor. I'd dressed in a dark blue suit, thinking I was being invited to an afternoon garden party. But there were no other guests.

Waiting nervously and uncomfortably, I must have sat in that living room a good hour before a houseboy came and directed me to a sun roof. I knew that Doug liked to stay as brown as a berry. Perhaps he'd lost his sun tan back east and was lying on the roof stark naked getting it back now that he'd returned to California.

On the roof the houseboy pointed me toward Doug and then left quickly, as if he'd been previously warned to divert his eyes. In the center of the roof on a chaise longue lay Doug who looked slightly red instead of berry-brown. Seeing me, he summoned me to him and held out his hand, flashing that smile with those celebrated white teeth, made all the whiter because of the color of his skin. I noticed that his visit East hadn't straightened out that unfortunate curvature of his dick.

"Great to see you, Durango," he said. "We start shooting *Till the Clouds Roll By* in a day or so. The script is great. It's different for me but should be one of my best pictures."

After greeting him, I wanted to ask what role I'd be playing but figured I'd let him bring that up. I looked around for the very distinguished guest, noting a cabana off to the right. Stark naked, Doug rose from his chaise longue and took my hand, leading me over to the cabana. "Your Majesty," he said, may I introduce that young man I've been telling you about, Durango Jones?"

Staring at me was the very young Prince of Wales, a man later known infamously around the world as the Duke of Windsor.

Doug never identified him to me. It was assumed, I guess, that I'd know who the Prince of Wales was.

The Prince did not rise from his cabana or shake my hand. Nor did he even speak to me at first. "He's the golden boy you promised," the Prince said to Doug. "Just like me."

With only a towel covering his genitals, the small, slim figure of the Prince was indeed a golden boy, with a wheat-colored crown of hair. Throughout the British Empire he stood for a symbol of the promise of youth. He was the most sought-after eligible bachelor of his age in the world. In the years ahead, he would be more hotly pursued than even Valentino himself. Women forgave him his habit of falling off horses and devoting too much time to steam trains. The press would dote on his love of the Black Bottom, the Charleston, and New Orleans jazz.

I knew I had to be careful around him. Rumor had it that when crossed the Prince could become a willful, spoiled child.

Doug excused himself and said he'd join us soon in the steam room.

Still fully dressed, I stood confronting the semi-nude Prince. "I can see you have a perfect waistline and are very fit," he said. "The bloom of youth." He slipped his towel down slightly, revealing his waist but still concealing his genitals.

"What do you think of my waistline?" he asked.

"It's like it was carved by a sculptor," I said.

He smiled at me. "That's good. I like that." He raised up slightly and motioned for me to hand him a fan. I didn't know if I were to fan him myself like some Nubian slave. "Men let themselves go to seed early in life," he said. "I'll never do that. A well-toned and carefully nurtured physique is very important to me. Sometimes I stand in front of the mirror for hours at a time looking to see if I have gained one extra inch around my waist. I do at least an hour of calisthenics each morning. The people in my country—yours too—eat far too much meat like beef and consume it with heavy brown sauces. And do the English ever love their puddings. I prefer salads and fresh fruit instead."

"I probably should eat more fruits and vegetables myself," I said, "if I want to stay in perfect shape."

"Promise me you will," he said. "You're perfect now. The idea you will be less than that horrifies me. Always take care of yourself."

"I promise," I said. Believe it or not, that was one promise I'd keep. In the decades to come, I never put on weight, although I fear I have abused my body with drugs and alcohol. But what else were you going to do when hanging out with the likes of Clara Bow, Marlene Dietrich, Frank Sinatra, and Joan Crawford, much less Tallulah Bankhead?

"For breakfast Englishmen eat blood pudding, grilled tomatoes, Cumberland sausages, fried bread, fried eggs, and a host of other horrors like grilled kidneys," he said. "I eat only an apple for breakfast. A salad for lunch. Then for dinner I prefer steamed fish or maybe a small piece of boiled chicken."

As the Prince and I talked about food, I realized on looking back that he was decades ahead of his time when it came to physical fitness. His long-ago diet would still be acceptable today to those who wanted to remain trim and fit.

The Prince might be an expert on diet, but I found all the rest of his opinions pure gibberish. He babbled on, making no sense at all, until he suddenly directed me to remove all my clothing. "Surely you must have heard. Doug said we were to meet him in the steam bath. You don't think you can go into the steam bath dressed in a dark suit, now do you?"

"I guess not, Your Majesty," I said, taking off my jacket. I assumed he wanted me to do a striptease in front of him, and I did just that. I removed each piece of my clothing in my most tantalizing fashion until I was down to only my underwear.

"Please drop your drawers," he said, "unless you are afraid you will not live up to the ideal of the all-American male."

"I live up to the ideal great," I said, dropping my underwear and displaying my cock and balls before this future emperor. As I looked down, I felt my dick had never looked bigger. The hot sun might have stretched it out an inch or two. "My God," he said, "if you weren't such a golden boy, I'd swear you had nigger blood in you. I hear all niggers have penises at least a foot long. That's remarkable if true. I've never seen a nigger nude."

"It's not true," I said. "Some black men have four inches erect, maybe five—some even six, but not all have twelve inches. It's the same with white men."

"That's reassuring to hear," he said, sitting up. "Otherwise, I would get an inferiority complex."

Stark naked, I was led to the steam bath by the Prince, who still retained his towel. In the bath a nude Doug was waiting for us. Their talk was of a big dinner party planned for the Prince that night. I noted painfully that I wasn't invited, although Charlie Chaplin was going to be there. Charlie hadn't invited me either. W. R. and Marion Davies would be there, even Gloria Swanson and Samuel Goldwyn.

After the steam bath, Doug and I showered together, the Prince preferring an enclosed private box which Doug pointed out was usually reserved for women guests who came to take steam baths at his home.

Doug shook my hand several times when he'd dressed and was showing us to a waiting limousine. "I'll see you on the set." He gave me a number to call so I could make arrangements for reporting to work. "It's going to be a big hit," he predicted. "Thanks for taking my son horseback riding." He whispered in my ear after the Prince had gotten into the

back of the limousine. "And please show his Majesty a great time. He's very impressed with you."

On the way to the Prince's suite at the Alexandria Hotel, he abruptly announced, "I hate homosexuality myself and despise homosexuals. Don't you agree with me?"

I didn't know if it was proper protocol to disagree with a future emperor, but I stood my ground. "I don't view people in terms of their sexuality. If I like them, I like them regardless of their sexuality."

"That's a very democratic point of view," he said, settling back in his seat. "I hope you're not so democratic that you believe we should abolish monarchs and their privileges?."

"Not at all," I said, lying. "I believe in kings and queens. I think America should have been a kingdom."

"I think our troops should have fought harder," he said. "We should never have let America slip from our empire."

To that, I had no comment.

"My hatred of homosexuality is like a morphine addict hating the drug but needing it desperately," he said. "I got caught up in this slimy mess of buggery because of my cousin, Louis Mountbatten. While on a tour of the Empire, he forced me to commit unspeakable acts of horror on him, using my mouth. He also buggered me night after night until I became addicted to it and started demanding it. He held the promise of sex over my head like a sword. If I'd been naughty, he withdrew sex. When I'd been good, he'd reward me with a great fuck. Do you think sex should be used like a weapon?"

"I think sex should be used only for pleasure," I said. "But we're in Hollywood, and out here sex is used to get ahead, to sell a script, to promote a film, to seal a deal, to secure a meaty role, whatever."

"That's true, I suppose," he said. "I've become addicted to buggery and have to have it regularly. It was all the fault of Louis. He should not have done to me what he did. Even Edwina Mountbattan found out about it, but I don't feel sorry for her at all. She doesn't lack for companions. She's always taking up with trash for which she needs to be horsewhipped. When Louis and I were touring the Empire, she even fucked this nigger nightclub pianist, Hutch Hutchinson, some stupid name like that. I hear a lot of women go for nigger dick, and until you enlightened me I thought they did so because of the size. Personally, I don't understand how anyone, male or female, could go to bed with a nigger. How does one get beyond the smell without puking?"

I had no comment to make about that either. For a man who would become the head of a world empire of widely diverse people, the Prince certainly held some politically incorrect ideas long before that term was invented.

As I was ushered into his private suite, the first item I noticed was a large perambulator. What did the Prince need with that? Surely he wasn't expecting a child. He asked me to come into his bedroom where without formality he proceeded to remove one of the most beautifully tailored Savile Row suits I'd ever seen. The Prince might be a political idiot with really dumb opinions, but when it came to clothing he could dictate male fashion around the world.

Not knowing what to do and having been given no instructions, I stood forlornly as the Prince stripped for me. This time he did the complete unveiling and I was able to view what must have been the tiniest penis in the United Kingdom. His rod barely emerged from a thick nest of pubic hair. Flaccid, it looked less than half an inch long. Perhaps it would grow a bit when extended, but I wasn't sure about that.

Not at all embarrassed by such a small dick, he walked over to a chest of drawers, removing a diaper and picking up some pins. He then returned to the bed and lay down, demanding that I pin the diaper on him. I did as royally commanded, praying that he didn't plan to do any naughties in that diaper.

Once I got the diaper pinned over the royal genitals and buttocks, he bounced out of bed and demanded that I lie down—face up—on the carpeted floor. A royal command was a royal command and I complied. Fortunately I'd entertained the distinguished visitor from Siam at the home of Sessue Hayakawa, so I'd had some experience in dealing with royalty. Once I was prone on the floor, the Prince took to giggling with delight. He plopped his diapered ass right over my face Again, I prayed

he didn't plan to do naughties. Slowly he began to remove my clothing piece by piece until he had me stripped naked.

After he'd removed every item, he jumped up and raced toward the living room of the suite, calling out for me to follow. Once there, he placed himself in the perambulator and demanded that I push him around the room at headlong speed. We did this for about fifteen minutes while he squealed with delight, although I was getting dizzy.

With enough of that to satisfy him, he asked me to help him out of the perambulator. After I did that, he invited me to pour myself a drink from his bar. He said he was going to the bedroom and would be there for some time, and I was to wait for him.

I didn't now what to expect and at one point thought I'd get dressed and flee the suite. I waited so long that I had time to finish my whiskey and make a call to Charlie, hoping he might invite me as his guest to the Fairbanks party for the Prince that night. Charlie told me he'd "be engaged" for the evening but wanted me to come by at five o'clock before he went out. "I have an itch in a certain spot and only you can scratch it in the right place." I assumed that he meant he wanted me to fuck him.

After agreeing to meet up with Charlie, I tried to reach Rodolfo but couldn't. That man was impossible to find. He contacted you if he wanted to. You didn't contact him. As I was getting ready to call Antonio Moreno or perhaps William Boyd, the Prince's bedroom door opened.

There before me stood the cheapest looking harlot in hell. The Prince was in total drag, and it wasn't elegant. He'd made himself up to look like a whore south of Pago-Pago. It would evoke the many different versions of Sadie Thompson that actresses in the years to come would play in W. Somerset Maugham's *Rain*.

"I want you to rape me," he said. "Pick me up and throw me on the bed and penetrate me deeply. It's important that you rip the garments from me. I must hear the ripping of garments. It's music to my ears."

Wanting to get this over sooner than later, I rose from the sofa and moved menacingly toward the Prince, picking up his slim body.

He pounded his fists into my back and cried out for me to put him down, but I paid no attention. I knew his protests weren't meant to be taken seriously. Tossing him on the bed, I proceeded to rip his garments from him. Curiously enough, all this pretended rape had given me the biggest erection of my career. When I had the Prince totally naked, I hoisted his legs into the air and rammed it in. I figured any rape shouldn't be gentle or pre-lubricated.

In one long thrust I reached his inner depths. He screamed for me to take it out. That made me plunge harder into him. To muffle his screams, I pressed my lips over his, as he broke into a powerful sweat, his body drenched. I pounded harder and harder as he sucked my tongue. His screams became moans of pure joy. When he released my tongue briefly he was amazingly articulate for a victim under assault. "No man has ever gone there before," he gasped. "I feel like I'm getting fucked with a foot-long nigger dick that happens to be on a beautiful golden-haired American boy. Louis only went half as far as you."

When I exploded inside him after a hard pounding of forty minutes, his tiny cock reared its head for an erect two and a half inches and spewed a very weak offering of watery semen.

We showered together, the water raining down just like the shower of compliments he bestowed on my body, especially my cock and balls, and my virility. He even called me a "semen factory." Back in his dressing room, he informed me that, "I can't have a homosexual liaison in my own country. It's too dangerous. News of it might topple the empire. In London I almost picked somebody up. I was looking at paintings in this museum and I spotted this very handsome man. I really wanted to go to bed with him but I couldn't bring myself to speak to him. I think he recognized me. I followed him around—masterpiece by masterpiece—but neither of us spoke. I think at one point he became afraid of me. He fled from the museum and nothing happened."

"It must be very risky," I said.

"It is," he said, "and that's why I'm forced to use prostitutes but only when I'm traveling abroad. Once a male prostitute in Hong Kong didn't satisfy me. I commanded him to eat an excrement sandwich. After all, I have great power and my subjects must follow my command."

I looked startled. "Hopefully, you won't force me to do that."

"Not at all," he said. "I've never been so sexually satisfied in my life. Even with the most skilled of prostitutes, I rarely achieve orgasm. You had me spewing."

His meager offering of semen might have been his idea of spewing but it wasn't mine. I spewed. He didn't.

"Perhaps," I said, leaning over toward him and taking his hand, "if you find a young man who can totally satisfy you sexually, you should make him your secretary. That way, you could have him around at all times, and you'd be a sexually fulfilled person and wouldn't have to suffer the way you do."

"That's a great idea," he said. "I wish it had occurred to me first." He looked into my blue eyes. "I hesitate to ask this, but would you consider becoming my permanent golden boy?"

Even though I had set myself up for that, I hesitated. The prospect of life with the Prince of Wales had some advantages. Maybe secretly at night I could get to wear the Queen's bejeweled crown. But the Prince was so distasteful I didn't think I could pull it off. Besides, as Samuel Goldwyn always said, "I have other fish to milk."

"Let's think about it," I said. "It's such a big decision. I'll call you in the morning. We both will have had time overnight to think about it."

"You're absolutely right," he said. "My mother always told me that I should think overnight about the big decisions in life."

"I'll give it serious consideration," I said.

He jumped up abruptly and I rose too, having heard that you were never to sit in the presence of royalty.

"Do me a favor," he said. "Do you have any money on you?"

"Yes, about two-hundred dollars."

"Good, good," he said. "Please tip the staff for me because I'm leaving early in the morning. I'll pay you back later." He came over to me and kissed my cherry-red mouth. "If you want to become my permanent golden boy, you'll be here at six o'clock in the morning. Don't bring much wardrobe. Once in London, I'll dress you in a complete new look. Get rid of those American clothes and replace them with Savile Row's finest."

"Until then," I said, kissing him for a final time and giving in to his demand to taste my tongue.

After tipping the staff, I headed to Charlie's to throw a fuck to a man even more famous than the Prince of Wales. Halfway there, I knew in my heart I couldn't tolerate the Prince for even a few weeks. Besides I had no intention of forsaking my dream of becoming a movie star.

Over the years, I have on occasion regretted my decision. If I'd packed up and gone with him the following morning, I might have saved him from the clutches of that bitch/whore, Wallis Simpson, who'd been trained in the sexual arts of Fang Chung in China. I might have even saved his throne. But, alas, that was a life I wasn't meant to lead.

*****

The reception desk at the Hollywood Hotel sent up two gifts for me, one from John Barrymore and the other from Samuel Goldwyn. I decided to open the present from John first. He'd presented me with a black and white drawing of himself in the nude by the artist, Kahlil Gibran, a name that sounded Persian or possibly Syrian to me.

At nineteen, I was ignorant of who Gibran was. Today in my dotage I'm not such a fool. When I last had the drawing appraised in 1990, I realized that the jackals who inherit my estate would be in for a lovely surprise.

The second gift from Goldwyn was a check written to Durango Jones for the sum of $250,000, which, if signed, and according to the agreement, would forever discharge his studio's responsibilities to the contract of Lotte Lee. A personal note added by Goldwyn, and endorsed by his attorneys, stated that if I accepted the money, I would "forever more" not be allowed to give any interviews about the Lotte Lee episode or the film, *Vampira*. In other words, this vast fortune—at least back

then—was going to me only if Lotte Lee faded into film history, becoming a little footnote, if that, in the lore of Hollywood.

I held the check up for inspection, not believing my good fortune. Maybe I'd misread the figures. Maybe it was for only twenty-five dollars. There was no mistake. The sum was for a quarter of a million. Since Charlie and W. R. paid all my expenses, and then some, I decided that this money was going to be invested in real estate.

As I'd been warned, Durango Jones wouldn't be young and pretty forever. This money, I just knew, would buy a lot of real estate in Los Angeles. I had my future to think about. I went over to my bar and poured myself a good belt of whiskey. A check like this called for a celebration, even if I were alone. I toasted myself in the mirror. "To the death of Lotte Lee. Long may she live. And to the birth and resurrection of Durango Jones."

Dressing in a dark suit, I headed into my day. My first stop would be a bank where I had to cash that check before Goldwyn came to his senses and stopped payment on it. My next stop would be the shrewdest real-estate broker in Los Angeles. Even on a day of good fortune, there is always a disturbing note. Mine came as I passed through the lobby of the Hollywood Hotel. To my surprise, I spotted the fake German baron sitting in the lobby, his eyes looking up at the room upstairs occupied by Jean Acker. He frightened me. Was Rodolfo showing up here today to call on his wife? Had the baron learned of that and was he waiting here to confront Rodolfo? Did he have a gun and planned to shoot Rodolfo? Brushing aside such thoughts, I realized that Rodolfo and that baron had a long history. I could not even imagine what their relationship was, or what had gone on between them in the past. Actually, on this bright California morning, I didn't want to think about that. I certainly didn't want to think about Rodolfo's wife, the lesbian, Jean Acker. As always, I had no idea where Rodolfo was.

After cashing Goldwyn's check—thank God it didn't bounce—I set up an appointment to see a broker in downtown Los Angeles at two o'clock that afternoon. After all the publicity Lotte Lee had generated, I wasn't certain how I was to make her disappear. I couldn't have her murdered—or something like that. There would be no corpse to show for it.

When I called the Hollywood Hotel for messages, I realized I might have made a mistake in cashing in Goldwyn's check. Calls had come in for Lotte from Cecil B. DeMille, Tom Ince, and John Gilbert. John probably wanted only a blow-job, but Ince and DeMille might have some serious money offers for Lotte. For all I knew, Lotte Lee might have gone on to make millions for either Ince or DeMille, becoming the biggest vamp on the screen.

After the real-estate talk, I decided I needed to line up my love life for the day. Rodolfo would have come first, but he was nowhere to be seen. In that case, I had plenty of reinforcements. Richard Dix on his last visit to me had performed so well that I was tempted to call him for a repeat show. But I had other beaus as well. William Boyd, Antonio Moreno, and Theodore Kosloff all needed attention from me, so it looked like I had a busy agenda.

I planned to spend the early evening at Charlie's and also to set him up with a date with Mary Miles Minter. After all, I had to do something to prevent her from marrying her father, Billy Taylor. It was the least I could do for both of them.

But I couldn't think about all that right now. When my mind wasn't on real estate, I needed to think about how to bump off Lotte Lee without unduly alerting the press.

Remembering I hadn't had breakfast and it was well past noon already, I was suddenly aware of my hunger. Here I was, the most popular teenager in Hollywood, and I had to enter a restaurant alone.

At The Green Hat, I ran into Tom Ince who was leaving the restaurant with Blanche Sweet and Alice Terry. Alice Terry was not the same Alice I'd seen at the Ship Café with Blanche Sweet on the day I came in with Mae Murray and Rodolfo. That actress had been Alice Joyce, who was sometimes confused in the movie-going public's mind, the way latter-day fans would mix up Anne Baxter with Anne Bancroft, two very different women.

Once again Blanche Sweet regarded me as if I were a fool for turning down a chance at her honeypot. Alice Terry, on the other hand, looked at me with a certain smug amusement as if in possession of information I didn't have. How wrong she was. I knew exactly why she had a sneer on that face. Norman Kerry had already told me that Rodolfo and Alice Terry, then billed as Alice Taffe, had an affair while working as extras on the film, *Alimony*. At that point there was no way to know that the names of Valentino and Alice Terry would be immortalized together on the screen in only a few months.

Ince pulled me aside with a sense of urgency on his face. "Mr. Jones," he said rather formally. "Are you Lotte Lee's agent, or are you not? I've left several urgent messages for her to call me. As her agent, you should have returned my calls. I've already heard that Goldwyn has bought her off and she's a free agent. It's about time we got together and made a deal." He stared at me with a certain fury. "Okay?" he said in his harshest voice. "I expect to hear from you by tonight—not later." He glared at me one final time before turning to the ladies, all smiles and charm again.

As I headed into the restaurant alone, the maître d' looked at me as if he didn't want to seat me at all. Apparently, no one dined at The Green Hat alone. Hidden behind a potted palm, I was perusing the menu as the waiter appeared with a note. *"Please join me at table,"* it read. *"Having conquered Broadway, I'm back home. Love, Theda."*

It was with the greatest of embarrassment that I joined Theda Bara at a table in the rear dining room. She'd obviously read of my sister Lotte's attempt to replace her as the vamp of the silver screen. But "the reddest rose in hell" at first didn't mention Lotte.

Theda looked glamorous, wearing a black lace dress with a pearl necklace and a large black hat that partially obscured her face. As I sat gazing into her eyes, I realized that her foreign-appearing seductress charms were becoming a bit ludicrous as the Jazz Age moved in on us, and the reign of the flapper was about to begin.

Theda was filled with stories of how she opened on Broadway in *The Blue Flame* at the Shubert Theater, her appearance causing riots among the public. "Fourteen milk-white horses delivered me back to my hotel," she said.

She told me that the Boston tryout had gone well but her opening on Broadway had been a disaster. "I had a cold and could hardly speak. During my death scene, my leading man picked me up and tossed me onto a sofa. My dress went up over my head. Thank God I was wearing bloomers. Remembering I was dead, I didn't dare cover my legs. The reviews were vicious. One critic, Heywood Broun, wrote, 'At the end of her third act, Theda Bara made a speech in which she said that God had been very kind to her. Probably she referred to the fact that at no time during the course of the night did the earth open and swallow up the star, the authors, the director, and all the troupe.' Most critics asked, 'Which is worse— the play or Theda Bara's performance?'" She looked at me as she sipped her drink. "Did you read what Alexander Woollcott wrote?"

"Of course, I did," I said. "I thought he was ridiculous."

"Quote it to me," she demanded, shutting her eyes.

"If you insist," I said. "He thought it was so bad it was funny. I could go on. Louis Reed said it was the most terrible play within his memory. *The New York Post* said that *The Blue Flame* was received with derisive laughter. But those reviews don't mean shit." I reached for her hand. "The important thing is you're back in Hollywood and ready to take the town by storm again."

"I don't care what the reviewers wrote, I carried on and played to packed houses," she said. "You couldn't believe my lines. 'I'll shake you like I shake my shimmy.' Or, get this, 'You make my heart laugh and I feel like a woman of the streets.'"

"Fuck it," I said. "From what I hear, you've been laughing all the way to the bank. *The Blue Flame* has made you rich."

"It also made me a laughing stock, and I don't think I can be taken seriously as an actress again. I fear I'm hopeless as a stage star. Nonetheless, I'm going to keep touring in the damn thing. I'm pulling in about $15,000 a week. I'll be touring in the turkey at least until 1921. After that, I've got this vaudeville tour lined up. I don't know why. People want to

look at a vampire, I guess. I can't sing or dance and I'm no God damn comedienne."

"Why don't you call it *An Evening with Theda Bara*, and take questions from the audience?" I asked.

"That might not be bad. I could talk about women. I've lately discovered nascent feminism. I'm a champion of women, and I don't think men have treated us fairly. I can also answer questions about my career, about sex, and vampires."

Years later Joan Crawford, Bette Davis, and others were to steal this idea for their own *"Evening with...."*

"There's even talk about putting me on the same bill as Billy Sunday, the evangelist," she said.

"That's a bit much," I said.

"My promoters say I'll make a million," she said. "After Fox dumped me, I can't find work in films but as a sight seen I'm big box office. At least for a while. At least until the public's short memory forgets who Theda Bara is."

"You're immortal," I said. "Your screen memory will live forever."

She reached for my hand, and I knew what was coming. "For me, the Vamp is dead," she said. "I played that on screen until I can play it no more. After all those pictures, there is nothing for me in films. But in all my wildest imagination, I couldn't conjure up that you would become the Vamp, the one who is going to take my place."

"You're joking," I said. "You don't mean me, but my sister, Lotte."

"Don't kid *Cleopatra* or *Salome*," she said, referring to her most famous screen roles. "I've seen it all. Remember, I was born two blocks from the Sphinx, or so my press agents claimed. When I saw those photographs of you as Lotte, I knew it was really Durango Jones."

"Okay, you figured it out," I said. "But I'll tell you something you don't know. Goldwyn's found out too. Lotte Lee is finished. I've been bought out and told to ship my sister out of town."

She looked startled. "I'm sorry to hear that. I was going to lend you all of my old vamp clothes."

"Please keep my secret," I said. "Or

Lotte's secret."

"Even in my autobiography, I'll not mention it," she promised.

She kept her word. I only saw the idol of my dreams one more time before her death to cancer on April 6, 1955. In 1934 she appeared briefly in a Little Theater production of *Bella Donna*, portraying a society divorcée approaching middle age. Nazimova had scored a great success in the play back in 1912, but in the depression-laden Thirties the script had become dog-eared. The show folded quickly but when Theda came out on opening night, I was right there leading the applause which lasted a solid five minutes, interrupting the play.

Backstage Theda and I kissed and became a little dewy-eyed. "I've been getting a lot of offers," she said, "for motion picture work. I'm planning a comeback. I can't decide which script to accept." She sounded very British, having picked up the accent of her husband, British director Charles Brabin.

Those scripts never really materialized for Theda, although there was some talk a few years later of her playing the role of Scarlett O'Hara's mother (eventually portrayed by Barbara O'Neill) in *Gone with the Wind*. When Billy Wilder was casting Norma Desmond in 1949 for *Sunset Boulevard*, he considered everybody from Marlene Dietrich to Mae West, before settling on that grand old bitch, Gloria Swanson. Even Pola Negri and Mary Pickford were interviewed for the part, both turning it down. The role of a has-been actress was perhaps a little too close to home.

Theda Bara was never considered, although no other actress in Hollywood ever rose to such dizzy heights as Theodosia Goodman of Cincinnati, Ohio, with her trailing veils and dubious legends, and no one ever fell so rapidly almost overnight than the eternal screen vamp herself.

Arriving completely exhausted back at the Hollywood Hotel, long after that sad luncheon with Theda, and long after visits to William, Antonio, and Theodore, I was ready for bed, and I wanted to sleep in it alone to recover for tomorrow.

I was confronted with two men, one cute, and the other ugly, who flashed badges and identified themselves as police lieutenants from the Los Angeles Police Department. "Are you Durango Jones?" one of the lieutenants, the cute one, asked.

I admitted to that. To my surprise I noted John Gilbert, more than a little drunk, emerging from behind the potted palms and staring at me from his post in back of the police detectives.

"Mr. Gilbert here has brought it to our attention that your sister, Miss Lotte Lee, has up and disappeared," the ugly lieutenant said. "He suspects foul play, and so do we. Are you aware that Mr. Gilbert called and requested a meeting with Miss Lee tonight at this hotel?"

"I picked up her messages," I said. "But my sister didn't want to be disturbed this evening. I asked reception to call Mr. Gilbert and inform him of that."

"Is your sister hiding in her suite?" the cute detective asked. "If so, may we go up and see her to determine if everything is okay."

"She's not in right now," I said defensively, looking more guilty by the minute. I feared I might be hauled into the station on a murder rap. I turned to John Gilbert. "I'm sorry, I said, "but my sister's planning a tour to launch *Vampira*. She's been too busy to see you.

"I think she's been kidnapped," John said, "and I'm not leaving the hotel until the police get to the bottom of this. You see, Lotte and I were going to elope tonight."

I feared the liquor had taken over John's brain. If he were going to elope with Lotte, he certainly hadn't informed Durango Jones of this spicy bit of information.

"My sister should be back here in an hour or two," I said. "I don't want to hold you gentlemen up." I looked each detective in the eye. "I'll invite Mr. Gilbert up to my suite. When Lotte gets back, they can work everything out, and he can call headquarters to assure you that everything is okay."

"Fair enough," the cute detective said. "After all, we're off duty now, and I've got a hot date."

The ugly detective turned to John. "You'll call and leave word at the station?"

John looked as if he hadn't been completely satisfied but was too drunk to protest.

"Please come upstairs with me," I

whispered to John. I took a firm grip on his muscled arm and directed him to the stairs. At first I detected resistance but he gave in finally, as I slowly helped him up the stairs.

Once inside the darkness of the suite, I turned on only a lamp, its soft glow making the room look a bit eerie. "Lotte has told me what a man you are," I said, tightening my grip on his arm. "You look a little under the weather. To make things easier for you when Lotte returns, let me help you out of all your clothes so you'll be beautifully nude for her enjoyment."

At first he looked reluctant but gave in to my wish. Once I'd stripped him naked, even removing his underwear, I put him to bed and turned out the light, slipping into my combined dressing salon and bathroom. For tonight, I decided not to kill off Lotte Lee so quickly. At least for one more time, I'd get back into my drag so that John could wake up in the morning with Lotte in her wig and red-silk pajamas lying in the bed beside him.

*****

The next morning I woke up before John Gilbert did and rushed back to the bathroom to prepare myself for the nude actor when he stirred in bed. When he finally woke up and saw that it was his darling, blonde Lotte in bed with him, he grabbed me and kissed me, tongue and all, in spite of his slight beard and morning breath. Even before he went to the bathroom, he took his hand and placed it on his raging hard-on, demanding immediate relief before we could get on with our day.

While he was in the shower, I went into a side room where I changed back to Durango, removing all traces of Lotte's makeup. When John came back into the room, he was stark naked. "You're Durango Jones, but where's Lotte?"

"She got a call to go to Goldwyn's house," I said. "About a contract thing. I'm here to gather up some of her papers for safekeeping."

"Watch that Goldfish," he said. "He talks funny but is sharp." Searching for his clothes, he said, "I can't believe how you resemble Lotte. The moment people see you, they know

you're Lotte's brother. You guys are getting more publicity than me. But that name, Durango Jones. It's so corny it's memorable." He turned and looked at me skeptically. "The resemblance. It's amazing."

Putting on only his underwear, he asked me to call down for coffee. "I need to come around," he said. "Too much booze last night."

Over coffee he told me he'd been planning to call me and was glad that we could talk. "I'm really interested in appearing in a film with Lotte. Of course, I can stand on a crate of potatoes so I'll tower over her. But I think her particular kind of blonde beauty in contrast to my dark hair and slightly olive skin would be a dynamite combination on the screen. How does it sound to you?"

"I'd go for it, and I know Lotte would too," I said. "But first we need the right script."

"Perhaps I could come up with something," he said. "I've got two or three guys working on future projects for me."

The coffee pot finished, I asked John if he'd call those detectives from the Los Angeles Police Department and assure them that Lotte was okay. He did that before getting dressed. Once he'd combed his hair in the mirror and adjusted his tie, he asked me to drive him to the Los Angeles Athletic Club. At the club, he invited me to join him inside for a steam bath and a massage.

I gladly accepted, eager to get to know him better now that Lotte was fading from view. Nude and alone together in the steam bath, he asked me the question. "You're a homosexual, aren't you?"

"I guess Lotte has told you," I said, staring deeply into his eyes. "Yes, I am. Proudly so."

"Good," he said. "If you're something, providing it's not a child molester, then don't hide it. As for Lotte, she's told me nothing about you, although I've heard a lot of tales. But a lot of tales—some of them true—are spread about me too."

After the sauna and en route to the massage room, he turned to me and took my hand. "Why don't you give me that massage? I saw the way you were looking at me in the steam room, and I know you want it."

"Your wish, my command," I said as he led me into a private room, where he dropped

Darwin Porter / 301

his towel and lay face down on the bed. Tossing aside my own towel, I began a slow, sensual massage of his body, paying particular attention to his buttocks. Occasionally he would moan softly but made no attempt to stop me even when I got very familiar.

"I want to turn over now," he said. As he heaved himself over, he sported a raging hard-on, the same one he'd presented to Lotte earlier that morning. Without missing a beat, I plunged down on that erection and sucked it like it was one of the world's sweetest lollipops, which to me it was.

After he'd had enough of that, he pulled my head off him. At least I didn't have to worry that my blonde wig would fall off. "What's up?" I asked. "I'm not pleasing you?"

"You're pleasing me too much," he said. "Go on for another minute and I think I'll cum in your mouth. By the way, you suck cock just like Lotte does. It's like getting the same blow-job twice."

"Let me finish," I said, plunging down on him again.

"I want to try something different," he said, rising up and lowering me flat on my back. He eased his body onto mine and descended on my cherry-red lips where he kissed me just like he used to kiss Lotte. "You've really aroused me. I'm not a homosexual either. I've had a couple of blow-jobs from homosexuals, but they don't count. I've never fucked a boy before, and I may never again, but for once in his life Jack Gilbert is going to fuck a teenage boy's ass." He kissed me long and hard, inserting his tongue. He then rose up from me and smiled. "It's for my art, you see. What if I have to play a sodomite one day, and I won't know what the experience is like unless I try it."

John may never have fucked boy-ass before, but he took to it like a Trojan warrior with a teenage boy captive.

As John descended over me, I went wild with need. "It's real tight," he assured me, "the tightest hole I've ever penetrated." But penetrate me he did. Even the big head of his cock wasn't a real challenge for me, as I'd been broken in by experts. He pressed for entry and achieved it almost immediately.

The wonderful head of John's cock was

followed by an equally wonderful shaft, and I took it lovingly and with passion, bucking and moving my body so as to give him the greatest of pleasure, knowing that if I did he might come around for repeat performances.

He filled me with a burning desire, and it was understandable to me how in the years ahead he could make even Greta Garbo or Marlene Dietrich forget about women, at least for an afternoon.

John's balls bounced against me as he fucked me, causing a tingling and erotic sensation to race through my body. I erupted all over his belly long before he exploded deep within me. For some strange reason, he burst into tears.

"You okay, darling?" I asked him.

"These are tears of joy," he said. "When I'm really happy, I cry."

*****

Fully dressed, John and I were leaving the Athletic Club when he remembered he hadn't tipped the attendant. He went over to a booth as I walked by the private rooms and past the showers which were mainly deserted except for three men, all of whom were showering together.

If only we'd had video cameras in those days. I came upon one of the most unusual sights I've ever seen. It still stands out in my memory. There was my former love, Norman Kerry, showering with Rodolfo. That in itself wasn't that big of a surprise. What was, was "the third man." It was the emerging actor and director, Erich von Stroheim. All three of them were paying special attention to their uncut manhood.

That memory still sandblasted in my brain, I drove John to his luncheon date, which was at The Green Hat where I'd encountered Theda Bara so recently.

"I want you to meet the woman I'm going to marry," he said.

"But I thought you were going to marry Lotte," I protested, but only mildly.

"Lotte knows the score," he said. "You don't marry the Lotte Lees of the world. You marry the sweet young girl I'm going to introduce you to."

At a table in the rear, only ten feet from where I'd lunched with Theda Bara, I encountered Leatrice Joy herself.

At that point Leatrice was years away from her eventual position as DeMille's number one star in the late Twenties. There was a slight mannish quality to her, although she had great feminine beauty. She wore her black hair bobbed as was the emerging style, and she set the prototype for a new kind of movie star that Rosalind Russell would carry to its peak of perfection. Unlike an airhead like Mae Murray, Leatrice was ideal on film as the sophisticated and ultra-efficient society girl.

She startled me by wearing a tailored man's suit, and this was years before Marlene Dietrich or Garbo, John's later loves, made such garb acceptable. Apparently, John was attracted to women who dressed like men. Of course, Leatrice in time would also wear women's clothes, and became a virtual showcase for the gowns of Adrian.

Looking at her on that long-ago afternoon at The Green Hat, I could never have imagined that she'd one day dethrone Gloria Swanson as DeMille's favorite leading lady and would star in some of the most celebrated of the director's films, including *The Ten Commandments* and *Manslaughter*.

Over lunch, Leatrice and I talked with warmth and friendliness. Since she wasn't after Rodolfo, I didn't view her as a potential threat the way I had Jean Acker. Either as Durango or as Lotte Lee, I wasn't in love with John Gilbert although I adored having sex with him in both my identities.

Before getting up off that bed in the Los Angeles Athletic Club, he had virtually signed in blood his promise to sodomize me frequently. "It's different from a woman," he'd said. "I'm not saying better, just different. It's another form of sexual expression. I may not indulge in this form of sex with any other boy, but as long as you're around I think I need an outlet like what we just did." Then he'd made a confession. "Subduing a boy like I just did with you makes me feel more like a real man than fucking a woman."

Even back when I first met her, Leatrice Joy was already a familiar face on the screen. Actually she'd made her debut in 1915 as an extra in a Mary Pickford film. As I've often reflected before, almost everyone in Hollywood at one time or another had been an extra in a Mary Pickford film.

Back in Lawrence, at the Patee Theater, I'd seen Leatrice as Billy West's leading lady in a lot of slapstick comedies. If there was one actor in all of Hollywood that Charlie Chaplin hated, it was Billy West who had earned his fame as The Little Tramp's major imitator. West did brilliant take-offs of Charlie both on and off screen. In those Billy West films, Leatrice also appeared opposite Oliver Hardy who always played a comic villain.

Long after Goldwyn had gotten rid of Lotte Lee, he would turn to Leatrice Joy for her box-office appeal. So even though I had reason to dislike her and feel jealous of her, I, as Durango Jones at least, felt only charity for her.

There was a bond between us even if it were only John's noble prick. Perhaps between Leatrice and myself, we could keep John in line and not let him waste his seed on less deserving bodies than ours.

In many ways, Leatrice replaced Lotte Lee on the screen. I've always envisioned that many of the roles played by Leatrice would have gone to Lotte instead. A notable example, confirmed by Tom Ince himself, was *The Marriage Cheat*, which went to Leatrice although Ince told me in 1924 that he regretted that Lotte wasn't around to star in the role instead.

Although our paths would cross over the years, Leatrice apparently never found out about my dalliance with John. If she did, she never spoke of it.

Meeting her at The Green Hat at the dawn of the Twenties, I would later encounter her frequently over the years, although we never became friends and were reduced to kissing air over each other's cheeks. Even now, I recall my last meeting with her in 1951. It was on the set of the comedy, the *Love Nest*, starring the newly emerging star, Marilyn Monroe. Actually Marilyn was a co-star. The leads were played by June Haver and William Lundigan. Leatrice Joy was appearing in a supporting role, playing the character of Eadie Gaynor.

"I still don't respect talkies," she'd told me as I'd waited endlessly for Marilyn to show up. "I think silents are still the superior art form. We lost something when the screen learned to talk. But I still appear in small parts every now and then, as you well know. Really, though, I'm content with being the most glamorous grandmother ever to come out of Greenwich, Connecticut."

As the senile old fool I've become and much to the annoyance of the Bitch of Buchenwald, I'm getting ahead of my story.

Back to The Green Hat and lunch with Leatrice and John. She was filled with excitement about a film, *Water Lily*, she was shooting for Triangle in which she appeared as an Asian woman, if memory serves me. She was also brimming with excitement about a picture she planned to make for Goldwyn called *The Ace of Hearts* starring Lon Chaney.

As thoughts of the roles Leatrice played over the years come rushing back to me, I want to clear up an earlier impression. I did become insanely jealous of her at one point in *Eve's Leaves*, a 1926 release directed by Paul Sloane and distributed by Grapevine Video. I'd come to the set to sample those wonderful inches of her co-star in the film, my beloved blond hunk, William Boyd, and had found that Leatrice had beat me to the seduction earlier in the morning, leaving me with sloppy seconds.

In the case of William Boyd, sloppy seconds were better than nothing. I eventually forgave her, though, deciding that if I'd been fucked regularly by John Gilbert during her marriage to that stud, I could hardly allow one brief fling with William to stand in the way of our long-enduring relationship.

Back once more to The Green Hat for one final time.

In those days, an orchestra played at The Green Hat for dancing in the afternoon. John invited Leatrice to dance to the sound of "Whispering," which in time became known as the love couple's theme song. Leaving me recently fucked but stranded at table, John bribed the orchestra to play it three times before coming back to devour a chef's salad, which, no doubt, he hoped would replace some of the sperm he'd lost first to Lotte and later to me as Durango.

"My mother, Mary Zeilder, is not impressed with Jack at all," Leatrice said right in front of the actor. "She finds him good looking but flashy. The first time I introduced her she detected whiskey on Jack's breath."

"Your mother has a good sense of smell," he said.

"Mary also insisted that I wipe off all my makeup before this luncheon today," she said. "She said Theda Bara had made me up to look like a harlot."

"You know Theda?" I asked rather stupidly, as everyone in Hollywood back then knew everybody else.

"I do indeed," she said. "Jack says I always look like a Madonna, so I figured I'd lose him if I didn't become more glamorous. I called up Theda and she invited me over and helped make me up for this lunch. She darkened my eyes with kohl and a heavy dusting of indigo, which she felt added more allure. Like Mae Murray, I got a scarlet-red mouth painted in a cupid's bow. She applied so much white powder to my already pallid skin that I looked like a cadaver. Theda then took a rabbit's foot, dipped it in rouge, and applied it to my earlobes. When I got home, Mary made me scrub my face."

"You overlooked something," John said.

"What do you mean?" she asked.

"Those ears are still pink" he said. "I didn't want to say anything, but while I was dancing with you I thought you had an infection."

Laughing wildly, our party was interrupted by Tom Ince, dining at The Green Hat for the second day in a row. Fearing a scene, I jumped up to corner him. "Lotte's dying to see you," I said. "Something's come up. It's really major. Can she meet you for cocktails at your place at seven o'clock tonight?"

"She sure as hell can," Ince said. "Make sure she's there, and I want an explanation as to why she hasn't returned my calls."

"She'll make it up to you," I said near his ear.

After kissing Leatrice on the hand and shaking John's hand, Ince turned and looked at me with a stern glare before departing with his luncheon guest.

This time it was Marion Davies, without W. R. Marion rushed over and kissed me on the lips, promising she'd call me for another movie date in a few days. W. R., it seemed, was heading back to New York and she claimed we'd have much longer this time." She whispered in my ear, "Joe has another surprise for you."

"Richard Dix would be terrific in a sequel," I said, remembering the first time I'd visited Godsol's mansion.

"Joe said he thinks you'll find this one even better."

I returned to table trying to think of anyone I'd ever heard of who'd arrived in Hollywood that would be better in bed than the athlete, Richard Dix. No one came to mind.

Over dessert and coffee, Leatrice and I discovered we had one more common bond— and not just John Gilbert. It was Ramon Samaniego or Novarro as he was later to call himself, my dear little on-again, off-again fuckmate whom I shared with Antonio Moreno and Rodolfo at certain times.

"Ramon," she confided to me, "used to pose nude at the J. Francis Smith School of Art and Design in downtown Los Angeles. Don't tell this to my beau here." She looked directly at John. "But I posed nude too. Once Ramon and I posed nude together as Adam and Eve. At night Ramon was a café singer. 'Poor Butterfly' was his most requested song."

I knew that Ramon had been a grocery clerk and a bus boy, even a singer, but the nude modeling came as a surprise.

I decided to hunt around and acquire one of the nudes he'd posed for, although I knew I could see the real thing any time I got on the phone. I'd never known Ramon to turn down a request if any man wanted to fuck him, especially Rodolfo, Antonio, or me.

Appearing at our table uninvited was Maurice Tourneur, the famous French director who was the toast of Hollywood. At first I thought he might have spotted me and was coming over to discover me personally and cast me in his next film. He kissed Leatrice on the hand, then faced John without a handshake.

Every actor in Hollywood wanted to work for Tourneur, who'd given up a career as a painter to direct films. He was known for his unprecedented use of light and shade in film. The only thing that bothered me about working with Tourneur was his celebrated quote, "Actors in films are incidental."

I knew John had worked for Tourneur in *The White Heather* opposite Mabel Ballin. The director had signed John to a permanent contract, but had not honored it.

The strain between John and Tourneur was obvious. At one point John balled his fists as if he were going to bash in the director's face. "You lied to me," he accused the director in a voice so loud half the tables nearby turned to look. You left Olivia and me with nothing. I had to send her back home to Mississippi."

Olivia was John's first wife, although I never paid much attention to my beau's wives or girl friends unless directly confronted with them.

"I practically starved to death," John said, "and all because of you. If Sessue Hayakawa hadn't given me work in *The Man Beneath*, I think I would have gone under."

"I had to cut back on expenses," Tourneur said apologetically. "Please understand. But I want you back for another film."

"You can go to hell!" John said. "I'm considering bashing your face in."

"I want you for *The Glory of Love*," Tourneur said. "It'll star Lon Chaney."

I was surprised that both Leatrice and John were being offered roles in different pictures but each with Lon Chaney. Another bit of evidence about what a small town Hollywood was back then.

Although John had sentenced Tourneur to hell on that day, he did accept a part in the picture, *The Glory of Love*. But it wasn't released until the year 1923, and by then it had changed its title to *While Paris Sleeps*.

After Tourneur had departed, John turned to face Leatrice, then me. "I hate that man's guts. But he is the most talented fucking director in Hollywood. The man's a genius."

At that point the *maître d'hôtel* came over to our table. One of us was wanted on the phone, and I assumed that it was one of the stars, Leatrice or John. The call was for me.

On the other end of the line was Rodolfo himself. He said the receptionist at the Los Angeles Athletic Club had told him that I was seen leaving the club with John Gilbert. I didn't tell Rodolfo that I had seen him in the shower with Norman Kerry and Erich von Stroheim, although I suspected he'd spotted me with his eagle eye.

He said that same receptionist had made a reservation for us at The Green Hat, so he knew where to call me. He asked that I meet with him at three o'clock at Norman's house. Mr. von Stroheim might also be there," he said. "We're having lunch now, and he mentioned that he might like to star your sister in one of his films. He's fascinated by Lotte. Mr. von Stroheim is going to become the biggest director in Hollywood, so you'd better get on that. He can do a lot more for Lotte than William Desmond Taylor."

"That's great," I said, hesitating briefly. "How are you, Rodolfo?"

"Everything's going well. But I miss my little baby, namely you."

"Is the thing with Julian Eltinge over?"

"Nothing had ever begun with that chubby transvestite," he said. "I've been used like a cheap hustler. As I predicted, appearing with that one won't help my career at all."

"I wish Norman and Mr. von Stroheim weren't going to be there this afternoon," I said. "I'd rather be alone with you."

"I'll set that up now that I'm free of Eltinge," he promised. "But Norman's picture has come through, the one I mentioned to you. He's got parts for both of us." I'll be his brother. I'm not sure what your role will be."

"It figures," I said with disappointment in my voice. "What's the name of the flicker?"

"*Passion's Playground*," he said. "The story of our lives."

*****

At the home of Norman Kerry, Rodolfo's on-again off-again patron, Norman rushed to greet me, whiskey heavy on his breath. "Glad you could come," he said. "I hear Lotte Lee's *Vampira* will burn up the screen. You should have gotten Goldfish to cast me as one of her lovers."

Even though we were getting ready to shoot *Passion's Playground*, I looked Norman over carefully as we made small talk. At that moment, I could not imagine that I was ever infatuated with him. No longer the dashing movie star I had at first envisioned, he looked older, paler, less sexy, and balding. He really didn't have the body to appear as one of *Vampira's* half-dressed male lovers. He no longer had power over me—in fact, I was certain I had more money in the bank than he did. Nonetheless, I was extremely gracious to him and even pretended I still hadn't gotten over "my broken heart" after he'd unceremoniously dumped me.

"I hear you and Lotte are going to take Hollywood by storm," he said. "I'd better get on the good side of you. Perhaps you'll consider starring me in Lotte's next film. I can just see the marquee, 'Norman Kerry and Lotte Lee starring in *Love's Dashed Hopes.*'"

It wasn't only the billing that was wrong in that picture, it was the whole idea. Sooner than later Norman would learn that Lotte had gone bye-bye.

Walking into Norman's sunken living room, I was mildly surprised to spot Rodolfo in the distance, parading nude around the pool. At one point he got on the jumping board, bouncing up and down, his cock and balls dangling, and plunged into the water. It was an extremely hot day, and I wished I could have joined him, as I was wearing a dark suit and tie.

Norman brought me over to a corner of the living room where a shirtless Erich von Stroheim was having a cognac as he fanned himself. "California is nothing but a desert," he said, not bothering to get up nor to shake my hand. "Take Austria—now that's a country with a perfect climate. The winters ideal for skiing, the summers like the breath of spring."

"I'm honored to meet you, sir," I said, as Norman waddled off, drink in hand, to check out his Latin lover boy in the pool.

Over drinks, von Stroheim sketched out two or three very rough scenarios where he might star Lotte in a film. "If Goldfish thinks *Vampira* is decadent," he said, "he hasn't seen von Stroheim at work. I am the only director in Hollywood who understands decadence. Out here in California it is merely sin. Only an old continent like Europe truly understands the meaning of decadence."

Deep into several shots of cognac, von Stroheim revealed his dream to have become another Douglas Fairbanks or even a J. Warren Kerrigan. The handsome Kerrigan, already famous as "The Gibson Man," always played the classic virile and virtuous hero. John Gilbert had appeared with him in *Sons of Men* in 1918. "I wanted to be the knight in shining armor who rescues blonde-haired damsels in distress," von Stroheim said. "I wanted to chase after the villains, not become the man you love to hate. Alas, my looks are against me. Film directors think all von Stroheim is good for is tossing babies out of windows or shooting old men in the back. Moviegoers think I'm ugly, so I try to behave on the screen like they expect me to. Do I want to become the Hun monster on screen or do I want to be a do-good actor who will be assigned to obscurity? For me, the struggle is almost over. I'll take a lesson from *Paradise Lost*. Milton let Lucifer decide it was far better to rule in hell than be a manservant in heaven." He suddenly stood up. "Look at me. What do you see?"

I said nothing but noted his aristocratic sneer, his dueling scars, his bull neck, his brutal scowl, and his cropped head, along with a stiff military bearing.

"Who else but von Stroheim could play the loathsome Hun to the unwashed masses of America?" he asked. "What red-blooded American soldier wouldn't want to rescue a lovely Red Cross nurse from my lascivious embrace? I am nothing but a repulsive beast. My leer is sadistic, and even my monocle is 'undemocratic,' as one reviewer put it."

"You actually aided America's cause in the war," I said. "At least back in Lawrence, Kansas."

"What is that supposed to mean?"

"Army recruiters set up posts outside movie theaters," I said. "After seeing you play the dreaded Hun, they got a lot more young men to sign up to fight the Kaiser."

"How perfectly delightful," he said, flashing that famous sneer and brutal scowl.

In the distance we could see Rodolfo emerging from the pool. With gaping mouth, Norman was waiting for him. He directed him to lie down on the chaise longue where he proceeded to plunge down on his cock.

Von Stroheim seemed to look on with approval. This was the type of American decadence he preferred. "Are you a homosexual too?" he asked me.

"Yes," I said as proudly as I could.

"That's perfect," he said, "for a small but vital part I have in mind in a film I'm contemplating. I'm working on the scenario right now. In the scene a beautiful golden-haired boy is drafted into the Army. Back in Vienna they are used to getting women whenever they want them. But in this remote outpost, the boy starts to look good to them. One drunken night they tie him up and proceed to sodomize him. Of course, on the screen I can show only the boy's face as he's getting penetrated."

"You want me to play the boy?" I asked.

"You'd be perfect for the part," von Stroheim said. "Only problem is I don't want you to act out the penetration. I want each of the men playing the soldiers to actually penetrate you. You won't have to fake your expression before the camera. It will be genuine."

"How do you expect that to get by the censors?" I asked.

"The censors?" he asked with contempt. "All my life I'm sure I'll be hounded by the censors. I try to bring realism to the screen. All Hollywood seems to want is stupid fantasies like the movies of Mae Murray."

Having presumably unloaded an explosion of cum in the gut of Norman, Rodolfo strode into the living room, a towel around his waist. He kissed me on the lips right in front of von Stroheim who seemed to find amusement in this American attempt at "decadence."

I joined Rodolfo and Norman around the chair of von Stroheim. It was more like a throne. As von Stroheim drank more and more, and continued lecturing us on how stupid Hollywood was, I could easily see that he was slowly passing out. When the cognac bottle grew low and his opinions less blistering, Norman motioned for Rodolfo and me to let him sleep, as we tiptoed out of the living room, directed by Norman to his darkened bedchamber off the main hallway on the ground floor.

In the bedroom a scenario unfolded that Norman had already outlined to me during one of my first meetings with him. Von Stroheim wasn't needed to direct this picture. Norman fancied himself as both director and star, with Rodolfo and I merely co-stars. He went down on Rodolfo's cock, getting it raging hard before guiding it deep inside me.

"Ride 'em, cowboy," he directed Rodolfo as my Latin lover did as instructed. I reached for his head, pulling him down on me for a long, lingering kiss and a lot of tongue sucking.

As Rodolfo reared back slightly in extreme ecstasy, I sensed that Norman was attacking his rosebud with fury. This caused Rodolfo to ride me all the harder. When he exploded within me, eventually pulling out, Norman was waiting like an attack dog. He descended on me like a suction pump, cleaning me out completely and drinking all of Rodolfo's second explosion of the day.

Norman himself then mounted me as Rodolfo took up his station at Norman's anus. From Norman's cries of pleasure and joy, I assumed Rodolfo was good at that job, at least I always thought he was. It was, in some respects, one of his favorite forms of sex, although he'd claimed to me he liked to indulge in "rosebud kisses" only with me.

Perhaps he was a liar. At this point in our relationship, I didn't expect truth from Rodolfo, and, in fact, found that his lies had taken on a kind of sexual allure for me.

When Norman exploded in me, Rodolfo did not proceed to clean me out. He didn't go that far. Since I hadn't been satisfied, both Rodolfo and Norman descended on me, licking, sucking, tasting, until I was screaming with delight. I felt I was being worked over by the two most talented tongues in Hollywood.

Having licked my entire body surface from ears to toes, each one took turns sucking me off. As Norman plunged down on me, Rodolfo went for the balls. At some point they would reverse positions. Rodolfo was the lucky one who was sucking me at the moment of eruption. But Norman forced him off me, claiming the last spasm for himself.

At the sound of loud clapping, I looked up, as did Norman and Rodolfo, to see von Stroheim standing at the bedroom door. How long he'd been there I couldn't tell. Long enough, I figured.

"You little pansy boys are very good," he said. "I wish I had captured it on film. Perhaps I was wrong. America is a very decadent country after all."

Norman was the first off the bed, generously offering von Stroheim my body as if it were Norman's to give. What did he think, that I was some sex slave of his?

Von Stroheim graciously turned down Norman's offer. "I like to watch men having sex. I have even watched animals having sex. I've also watched women having sex with animals. But when it comes to sex, I prefer women. However, I will give the pansy boy a thrill he'll never forget. A deep kiss from the Hun, the beast himself."

On the bed he lowered himself over me, opening his mouth and sticking out his tongue as he pressed against my cherry-red lips. As always, when presented with a man's tongue, I sucked voraciously.

Von Stroheim turned out to be a prophet. Although kissed by thousands of men in the years ahead, from Cary Grant to Randolph Scott, from Errol Flynn to Tyrone Power, no kiss was ever quite as memorable as that one bestowed on me by von Stroheim himself.

*****

Later, in my Lotte Lee drag, I sat across from Tom Ince little knowing the dramatic events that would happen to both of us, all of which would become Hollywood lore and gossip for years to come. But back then, at that very moment, the dying afternoon sun cast a melancholy glow across the coast. To me, there's nothing like a California sunset. As we stood on Ince's terrace, this one was the most dramatic I'd ever known. I even saw "the green flash" as the sun went down, that phenomenon that Ernest Hemingway would write about in years to come.

"You're too hot for Goldfish to handle," he told me. "That's why he's bought out your contract. All Hollywood is talking about it. I hear *Vampira* is the sexiest film ever made. I predict it'll cause riots across the country."

"I'm not too hot for you to handle, am I?" I asked seductively, kissing his ear lobe and cuddling into him as best I could, even though I was taller. I was fast learning that some men don't object to a woman being taller, a case we were to see more dramatically in the decades ahead when Mickey Rooney wed that tall and statuesque brunette from North Carolina, Miss Ava Gardner, Southern accent and all.

After the sun had gone down, and over our second drink, I confided to Ince why I was leaving Hollywood. "You must never breathe a word of this to anybody," I said, "but the Prince of Wales has fallen for me. He wants me to come to England where he's going to install me in a country house in Essex. He'll visit me there."

Ince was in a state of total shock. "I heard he was in town. I wanted to meet him. But that Fairbanks son of a bitch didn't invite me to his party."

"Of course," I said, "I don't expect to become the next Queen of England. "My..." I hesitated. "My past wouldn't allow that. The very making of the film *Vampira* would disqualify me to become queen. But a gal can do a lot worse than be the mistress of the world's most eligible bachelor, and a filthy rich one too."

"You should insist that he give you a lot of jewelry," he said. "A lot. You'll need to polish those gems when you're old." He looked deeply into my eyes. "I can't imagine you ever turning old, though. To me, you'll be forever young."

I took his hand and kissed his inner palm. "I'll return to Hollywood on very private visits," I promised. "Let me call you and get together with you during those times."

He pulled me close to him and kissed me, as I opened my mouth to receive his tongue. I was becoming known for my tongue sucking almost as much as I was celebrated for my blow-jobs.

"I've got to go soon," I said to him, "but before I do, I desperately need to taste you. To feel that big cock all the way down my throat. To taste that delicious cum you manufacture in buckets."

My request had the desired effect. As I felt between his legs, I could hold his growing hardness. Within moments, I was on my knees in front of him, unbuttoning his fly and removing his magnificent and now fully erect cock. It tasted just as good as it looked. Not knowing when I would be able to service it again, I sucked him as if he were the last man in the world. When he erupted, I drank him dry. He then reached down and pulled me up to his face where he kissed me, tasting his own semen as his tongue probed my mouth.

After I'd retreated to his bathroom to make myself as alluring as I was pre blow-job, I came back onto the terrace, finding him still seated with his fly unbuttoned. I bent down and planted a final kiss on his thick uncut cock, then buttoned up his trousers for him.

"I'm as disappointed as hell," he said, standing up, taking my hand, and walking me over to the edge of his terrace which overlooked an ever-darkening sky which was still streaked with red from the setting sun. "I wanted us to get to know each other a lot better. I think if you had stayed in Hollywood, I might have asked you to become my steady girl. I've even had dreams about asking you to marry me one day. I'd get rid of other wives or girl friends and save all my loving for you."

I kissed his lips tenderly. "My one reason to return to Hollywood on very private visits is to tongue you to death."

"You know if you stayed around, I'd want more," he said. "A hell of a lot more. I'd want to lick and bite your breasts. Lick your asshole before plugging it, and eat your pussy before fucking it all night."

"Stop it!" I said, "You're getting me hot and bothered."

"Then spend the night with me" he said, holding me close and kissing me long and hard again.

"I can't," I said. "I've got some very important business to take care of. I'm packing tonight and leaving first thing in the morning. People are waiting for me."

"Your disappearance will be the talk of Hollywood," he said. "It'll get into the papers."

"I'll disappear and become a Hollywood legend," I predicted. "My brother, Durango Jones, will stay here. Promise me you'll get him a film role whenever you can."

"For you, baby, anything," he said. "Have Durango give me a call. I hear he's a homosexual."

"You got that right." I kissed his lips gently. "Believe it or not, but Durango gives an even better blow-job than I do."

"That's not possible," he said.

"Try him out some day," I said. "Since I won't be here to service you myself, I need to have Durango serve as my proxy."

He laughed softly. "No way. I've never done anything like that with a man. I never will. Tom Ince is strictly a treat for the ladies."

"Don't be so sure," I said. "Durango's a very beautiful boy. Check out those cherry-red lips of his. Some lonely, rainy night when Tom Ince gets really horny and starts to miss his Lotte, all he has to do is pick up that phone and dial Durango. He'll even wear lipstick and put on Lotte's wig for you."

"He'd do that?" he asked with a look of astonishment on his face.

"For you, and if I told him to, he would do that."

"That's a very interesting offer, but I'm too much of a he-man to consider it."

I kissed him again. "You're such a he-man that you will definitely consider it. Homosexuals don't go for weak, ugly men. They prefer virile men like you. Real good looking like you." I reached for his crotch. "And hung. Durango is also an expert at licking those big balls of yours, and he can eat out that delectable ass of yours all night. He loves to get fucked. Men tell me he's better than a woman."

"He likes to get fucked?" Ince looked confused. "I don't know...." He paused as if not knowing what to say next. "I'll have to think about it."

"You do just that."

Over a cocktail, I bid farewell to Tom Ince, knowing that Lotte would pay him a return visit whenever I wanted him again. What I really wanted was to have him as Durango. That way I could take off all my clothes and get real down and dirty with him.

"Please come back to Hollywood soon," he said as I headed for my "stagecoach."

"You can reach Durango at the Hollywood Hotel," I said. "He'll be waiting for your call."

"He'll probably have to wait for a very long time," Ince said. "I'll call him when I can fit him into a picture. I'll give him some work from time to time. But it'll be strictly business. In other words, no monkey business between us. You can count on that. Tom Ince doesn't go that route."

"Sorry to hear that," I said, kissing him again on the lips. "I've given my brother a blow-by-blow description of your physical assets, and he's dying to sample them for himself. We often share men."

"You do?" he asked skeptically.

"Yes, the biggest studs in Hollywood, all he-men like yourself. A man isn't really a man, certainly not a sophisticated one, until he's shown his complete dominance over another male. As you know, it's a tradition that goes back to ancient times."

"I don't know, I'll have to think about it." he said, repeating himself.

He grabbed me and kissed me for one long time. The kiss seemed to go on forever before he let me go with promises to meet again in a few months upon one of my returns from England.

Back at the Hollywood Hotel, I had to transform myself quickly into Durango Jones. I had promised to pick up Norman Kerry and Rodolfo and drive them to a party at the Garden of Alla where Nazimova would be entertaining the elite of Hollywood.

Scanning my messages, I read the most recent one first. It was for Durango Jones. Tom Ince had just called requesting that my brother ring him up tomorrow. For a call back he gave not the number at his studio, but his unlisted home phone.

*****

Arriving at the Garden of Alla with Rodolfo and Norman Kerry, I let them out near the side entrance as I went to park the car. Many stars on off-the-record visits entered this way. But stars who wanted to be photographed went through the front entrance, and this is where I was determined to go, having decided that if I'd been invited to a party at Nazimova's, I didn't want to keep that secret from the world.

Three movie stars were holding forth and at first I couldn't see who they were. Edging closer, I recognized the trio: Dorothy and Lillian Gish accompanied by Mildred Harris, the real Mrs. Charlie Chaplin who looked like some little golden girl, far more fetching than either

Mary Miles Minter or Mary Pickford.

"Dotsie and I never stay up late," Lillian was telling the press. "You can't fool the camera. It will show up in your work the next day."

Dorothy started to say something, but Lillian hushed her up. Seeing the sisters together, as I had before, it was clear that Miss Lillian commanded the Gish army. "As far as the press is concerned, I think you should stop reporting about the alleged high salaries we make. Except for Mary Pickford and one or two others, none of us really take home as much pay as you say."

"What about Nazimova?" one of the reporters called out. "I hear she takes home $13,000 a week."

Not directly answering the question, Lillian said, "Nazimova is a wonderful actress because you never catch her acting."

As the Gish sisters excused themselves, Mildred Harris stepped into the spotlight. "The Gish sisters are sweet, nice girls. They would be a credit to any profession." A scornful curl of her lip appeared. "You should write about these fine examples of the moving picture industry—and not always splash stories on the front page about actors who do unspeakable things like take morphine or other drugs or who engage in perverted sexual practices. Norma Talmadge is another example of the fine morality of the movie colony."

Invariably the press wanted to question her about Charlie, and Mildred was surprisingly straightforward in her answers. "Mr. Chaplin is far too temperamental to be married to anyone. He is never satisfied or contented for long, and I can't stand that in a person. I like him and I respect him, but I just feel I'm too young to waste my life trying to understand why he wants so many different things. I can't live like that."

"I hear he's a Socialist," a reporter asked. "Is that true?"

"I have no knowledge of Mr. Chaplin's politics," she said, seeing me among the gathering. She reached for my hand, bringing me into the spotlight. As the photographers snapped, she kissed me lightly on the cheek, pretending some affection that didn't exist between us. As the press started to quiz me about *Vampira* and my sister, Lotte Lee, Mildred grabbed my arm and ushered me into the safer precincts of Nazimova's home.

Once inside the door and out of hearing distance, she confided, "I lied to the press. Charlie used to invite all these Socialist friends of his to our house. But I'd hide upstairs in my bedroom and lock the door."

"Did you think they would bite you?" I asked.

She didn't seem to hear me but rushed toward a waiter demanding a drink.

Over drinks she called me over toward some potted palms away from the rest of the party. "I've just come from Charlie's. He's furious with me. If Kono hadn't been there, I think he would have beaten me black and blue."

"What made him so mad?" I asked.

"I've been meeting with Louis B. Mayer," she said. "I plan to bill myself professionally as Mildred Harris Chaplin. I'm his wife. I have that right. But Charlie told me I was merely a dim-witted, mediocre actress trying to capitalize off the name of a film genius. He's even hired spies to try to catch me in bed with another man, but I've eluded him so far."

She downed her whiskey and called for another round. Unless she'd been drinking before, she was already intoxicated after the first whiskey. "Charlie's a fool. If he tries to blackmail me about my affairs, I'll name Edna Purviance as the other woman. The scandal might ruin his career." She looked defiantly at me. "Don't worry, I won't tell the press Charlie's having an affair with you. If word of his homosexuality leaked out on top of everything else, it would be the end of his career."

"To what do I now owe this generosity on your part?" I asked.

"Darling, you've been in Hollywood long enough not to be naïve," she said. "If I reveal that sordid story about Charlie, he's threatened to file a counter claim that I've been sleeping not only with the Gish sisters, but Nazimova. These charges of homosexuality would finish both of us off, don't you see?"

I saw more than clearly as she looked smugly at me. "I'm going to tell you a secret about myself that is so scandalous that I dare you to repeat it. A revelation like the one I'm about to make to you would drive Charlie insane. For all I know, he might kill himself."

"What is this tantalizing news?" I asked.

"I'm having an affair with a man almost as famous as Charlie Chaplin," she said with a defiant pride.

"That could only be one person in the world," I said. "Douglas Fairbanks himself. Does Mary Pickford know?"

"Hell, no, and why should the bitch know?" she asked. "Her divorce is coming through from that drunkard, Owen Moore. And Doug's also getting an expensive divorce. If my plans go right, I'm going to prevent his marriage to Mary Pickford. I'll go from being Mrs. Charles Chaplin into becoming Mrs. Douglas Fairbanks Sr."

"Then you could be known as Mildred Harris Chaplin Fairbanks," I said. "They'd really line up at the box office then."

"Don't be sarcastic, you little faggot," she said, finishing off a second drink in rapid-fire order and demanding another one. "The only thing I don't understand is why Mary Pickford gets off so much on that curvature of Doug's dick. Her vagina must be built crooked. He hurts me during penetration. Charlie hurts, too, but for a different reason. He's just too big."

I didn't plan to spend the entire evening with Mildred so I tried to excuse myself, but she grabbed my arm, holding me back. "When I was growing up, I felt the world was a fairytale, and I was a beautiful princess waiting to be rescued by a handsome prince in shining armor. Instead of that prince, I got Charlie Chaplin. Now Doug can play a prince and make it believable. Charlie can do nothing but The Little Tramp in baggy pants. Those pants used to cover underwear that I mended at night for him. He demanded that as his wife I mend his underwear. His socks, too. Here he is, one of the richest men in America wearing mended underwear and socks."

"He's thrifty," I said. "An impoverished childhood. It makes you stingy."

She grabbed hold of my arm again with a kind of desperation. "Believe it or not, I still love Charlie. I've even turned to this religious sect. They preach the gospel of positivity. We're taught to wipe all negative thoughts from our lives and approach everything with a bright,

sunny smile."

"Your recent meeting with Charlie didn't sound like a sunny smile," I said. "You want to use his name professionally—and all that."

"It's just an attempt on his part to prevent me from working as an actress," she claimed. "He opposes me on everything, even my religion. He told me I was irredeemably stupid. He's an atheist, you know. When our baby son died, he went ape-shit when I invited people from my church to the funeral. He even attacked the undertaker for fixing an artificial smile on the infant's face. After that, I tried to adopt needy children. He opposed me on that. He attacks my decorating. He said my idea of luxury is what Marie Antoinette would have done if she'd hired Flo Ziegfeld as her decorator. Calla lilies are my favorite flower, and I used to fill our house with them. Guess what? Charlie detests calla lilies."

As far as I'm concerned, you and he had better get a divorce sooner than later. After all, you're not living together."

"That would certainly serve your interests," she said. "Charlie will have to agree to some financial settlement, or else he's going to be in deep shit. Tell him that. He's hoping that I'll get involved with another man and will file for a divorce to marry someone else. That way, Charlie can look like the victim. He just loves to play the victim."

At that point the Gish sisters arrived to rescue their favorite girl, Mildred herself. Lillian directed all of us to the buffet table Nazimova had arranged for her guests. I looked around but Rodolfo was nowhere to be seen. "Dotsie" went for a large plate of shrimp and a bowl of avocado dip with sour cream. Lillian went over and gently took the plate from her. "I'll select something for you, my dear," she told her sister. Lillian filled a plate with a salad of iceberg lettuce and bell peppers with no dressing, and added a boiled egg without mayonnaise. For her drink, she selected a small tomato juice. Dorothy looked heartbroken but gave in to her sister's wishes.

I rescued that plate of shrimp and avocado that Lillian had rejected for Dorothy. Mildred preferred nothing to eat—only whiskey.

Lillian, I learned, liked to dominate

conversations. The only subject she talked about was acting. "I used to think that to act on the silent screen you had to beat your breast and tear at your hair to show emotion. That changed when I visited England during the war. I was in Whitechapel at the time of an air raid. A Zeppelin dropped a bomb on a kindergarten, killing nearly a hundred children. Frantic mothers searched the ruins for their loved ones. I couldn't help but notice the terrible strain on their faces. I studied their emotions in great detail. It was on that very day, that horrible day, that I learned how to present real emotion on the screen."

"That's just great," Nazimova said, moving up behind Lillian. "You'll really have something to get emotional about if you completely tie Mildred up for another weekend with the two of you. I haven't objected to Mildred spending a weekend away with you two pussies, but if I invite her for a weekend, I expect her to accept my invitation—not yours."

I looked at Mildred, who seemed to be beaming at all this attention from three world-famed film stars.

"I know I'm a guest in your home," Lillian said, "and I speak for Dotsie when I say this, but we feel that you're putting a lot of wrong ideas into Mildred's head. Frankly, my dear, you're a bad influence, and we can't allow you to gain such power over her. You've ruined the lives of other girls. We simply cannot tolerate your destroying Mildred's life, too."

"Charlie Chaplin, not Alla Nazimova, has destroyed Mildred's life, you D. W. Griffith cow," Nazimova said. "Please get out of my house, and never darken the door of the Garden of Alla again."

"Come, Dotsie," Lillian said. She reached for Mildred's arm. You're coming too." It was more of a command than an invitation.

Mildred grew defiant. "I want to stay and enjoy the party," she protested, almost like a little girl. She linked her arm with Nazimova's and stared back in a kind of drunken stupor at both Lillian and Dorothy. "Besides, both of you are boring in bed. Nazimova takes me places where I've never gone before sexually."

Lillian regally faced both Nazimova and Mildred. "As for both of you, you are dead as far as the Gish sisters are concerned," she said.

"We don't want to see either of you again." Noticing me, Lillian kissed me lightly on the cheek, a birdlike kiss, which was followed by the almost identical kiss from Dorothy. Lillian whispered in my ear, "You've probably heard men fight over women or men fight over other men, but to hear women fighting over women is probably a first for you. Chalk it up to experience, my dear." The sisters departed arm in arm.

"I need another drink," Mildred said after they'd gone. Her eyes frantically searched the floor for a waiter.

"Let me provide it," came a dramatic and slightly familiar voice emerging from the darkened library. It was Natacha Rambova attired in red silk like an Asian princess with a string of white pearls laced through her hair and a diamond-studded gold medallion glued to her forehead. She walked with a slight limp, no doubt from Theodore Kosloff's buckshot at DeMille's Paradise. In her hand she carried a tall cocktail, which she poured over Mildred's blonde curls, sending her screaming toward the bathroom.

Natacha confronted Nazimova. "The Chaplin bitch gets kicked out of this house tonight," she demanded, "or else I'll leave. You cannot have both Natacha Rambova and Mildred Harris too. Do you want a diamond or a cheap rock? You decide and decide now."

Nazimova looked deeply into Natacha's eyes for a long, lingering moment as if remembering previous times alone together. When she spoke it was in a relatively subdued voice. "I'll go right now and tell Mildred to leave the Garden of Alla. I'll send her back to the Gish sisters where she belongs."

Looking triumphant at Nazimova's departure, Natacha knew she'd won her victory. After that last embarrassing encounter we'd had with Theodore Kosloff, I felt she was relishing her victory over Mildred Harris.

"How's your leg?" I asked.

"No permanent damage," she said, "but I should have sued the bastard. Nazimova talked me out of it because Theodore can be helpful to her with her future films. To Nazimova, that is more important than prosecuting someone for filling my leg full of buckshot."

Out of the shadows, appeared Rodolfo

without Norman Kerry.

Startled, I turned around to greet him. "Rodolfo Valentino," I said, "meet Natacha Rambova."

The very moment I introduced them, and had witnessed a look exchanged between them, I knew that I had made the mistake of my young life. But could I have known back then that I had introduced Rodolfo to the one person who would do more than any other to destroy his life and career?

Durango Jones's (Annotated) PHOTO ALBUM

Winston Churchill (1874-1965) and Charlie Chaplin shared something in common: Both had horse cocks. Referring partly to Chaplin's legendary egomania, his genitalia, and his incendiary views on recent British politics, Sir Winston said that Charlie should play Napoleon and include a scene of the French dictator nude in his bath.

Tom Mix (1880-1940) was "King of the Cowboys" for more reasons than one. Partly because of his former stints as a soldier, western marshal, rodeo star, and bronco buster, I always made it clear that he could put his boots under my bed any night he wanted. Before Tom, cowboys didn't wear lavender and purple outfits. After the example he set in some of his films, such color variations became more popular. Above, in a rare photo without his pants, he had to wear a jock to keep his six-shooter from hanging out the left leg of his boxers. The pretty girl is amused.

Much more handsome than this picture, movie director Tom Ince (1881-1924) should not have accepted the invitation of William Randolph Hearst and Marion Davies to go sailing on their yacht, *Oneida*. He never lived to tell about it. A massive cover-up followed his death, and--according to some--the career of Louella Parsons was launched.

My Romeo, my Don Juan, John Barrymore (1882-1942) once confronted me with a burning question: In his green tights, he bluntly asked if he should stuff his crotch. I added a sock to his groin area and box office receipts soared.

Julian Eltinge (1881-1941) was the most famous female impersonator in America. He shared a room at the Los Angeles
Athletic Club for nearly a year with Charlie Chaplin. Valentino
appeared in a film with this grand lady, but only after lengthy
auditions on a casting couch.

Tom Moore (1883-1955) was the handsomest and best hung of the three Irish-born Moore brothers, each a movie star in his own right. His brother Owen was married to Mary Pickford. Tallulah tried to bed Tom, but I got him first.

"*The Self-Enchanted*" Mae Murray (1883-1965) befriended Valentino when he got into trouble with the police in New York. He tried to seduce her, but "*The Merry Widow*" had other beaus. Murcurial and beautiful, she had had too much champagne when this photo was taken.

Douglas Fairbanks, Sr. (1883-1939) found in the movies a thousand ways to use and show off that marvelous gymnastic physique of his. Until I met him, I'd never before encountered a circumcized dick.

In *Thief of Baghdad*, Douglas Fairbanks, Sr. always had a gleaming smile of chicklet teeth underneath a black moustache. Doug liked action and dizzy stunts both on and off the screen. In my drag incarnation as Lotte Lee, he let me "break in" his son, the Divine Doug, Jr.

Filmdom's first matinee idol, Francis X. Bushman (1883-1966) was called the handsomest man in Hollywood. A self-acknowledged exhibitionist, the former sculptor's model once proclaimed, "if you've got a cock the size of the Empire State Building, why keep it a secret?"

Here, (left photo) Francis X. Bushman launches a trend that eventually led to an appreciation of men who look like well-muscled bears. He was the first Hollywood star to have a dildo modeled from his gargantuan penis. The Bushman dildo sold like hot cakes--but put a few overly ambitious young men in the hospital.

In the world's first cinematic version of *Ben-Hur* (1925), Francis X. Bushman (left) in full uniform fetish, wraps a whip around the neck of Ramon Novarro (1899-1968). Long before Novarro became a famous actor in his own right, Francis claimed we were the only guys in Hollywood who could take all of him.

It was a bit of a stretch to call screen vamp Theda Bara (1889-1955) "the wickedest woman on earth," but this sex goddess of the Silent Screen frequently lured men to their downfall. Dubbed "the reddest rose in hell, and "a sex bitch," Cincinnati-born Theodosia Goodman was despised by many Puritans after World War I. According to her press agents, she was born "within the shadow of the Sphinx."

After he penetrated me for the first time, Spanish actor Antonio Moreno (1887-1967), star of films that included *The Temptress* (1925), announced that he'd just become my new husband. He always bragged--accurately--that he didn't want to pull out until he'd climaxed three times. Viva España!

(Right) Wallace Ried (1891-1923), the strapping star of such films as *The Birth of a Nation*, had youth, charm, good looks, perfect manners, and a fine physique. He was also addicted to morphine, which caused his early and scandalous death.

"ELMO THE FEARLESS"
Universal's Thunderbolt Serial
Starring
ELMO LINCOLN

(Left) Tarzan of the Apes, Elmo Lincoln (1889-1952) was in an inch-by-inch race for the title of who had the largest cock in Hollywood. In a foot-long war whose contenders were eventually limited to Elmo and Francis X. Bushman, it was hard to determine who was King of the Jungle. Everybody in Hollywood seemed to develop a strong opinion about it.

(Right) When Wallace Reid appeared in James Fenimore Cooper's *The Deerslayer,* no male star had ever shown such nudity on film. Later, gay men in the showers discovered that Reid had the world's most beautiful cock.

This photo (left) shows Wallace Reid with his dog and rifle. What it doesn't show is the always-reliable six-shooter in his pants. Drug-addicted, and to an increasing degree impotent, he once offered himself as a sexual smörgåsbord for a coterie of gay men in a Los Angeles bar.

Six feet tall and 180 well-muscled pounds, Minnesota-born Richard Dix (1893-1949) excelled in sports, expecially football and baseball. His rugged good looks and dark features made him a bedtime favorite of mine.

"America's Sweetheart" was anything but. Dressed here as a little girl, Mary Pickford (1893-1979) liked alcohol and men in that order. She and I shared many things in common, including (continued below)....

Sincerely
Mary Pickford

...all three of her husbands, Owen Moore, Douglas Fairbanks, and Buddy Rogers. I even managed to hop into the sack with her brother, Jack, and her two brothers-in-law, Tom and Matt Moore.

Snatching him from the arms of Dorothy Gish, I had to strip down D.W. Griffith's leading male star of the teens and see what all the excitement was about. Bobby Harron (1894-1920) rose to the occasion, just before his tragic suicide, an event whose publicity was at first suppressed, and then clumsily spin-doctored by the studio.

Depicted here as a sea nymph and festooned with kelp, Olive Thomas (1894-1920), the sprightly Ziegfeld Follies' queen and film star, died of a mysterious poisoning, perhaps self-inflicted, at the Ritz Hotel in Paris. She was married to Mary Pickford's brother, Jack Pickford, who--despite ample evidence to the contrary-- was often referred to as the "Ideal American Boy." I found Olive's brothers much hotter than her husband.

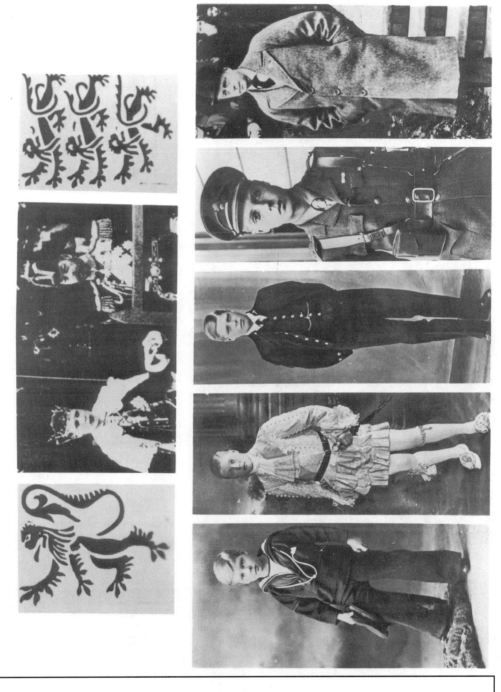

Despite the romance he evoked for millions of women worldwide, Prince Edward of Wales, later King Edward VIII and--after his abdication--Duke of Windsor (1894-1972) was sexually ambivalent and considerably lacking in virility. More stylish than any other man of his era, he most definitely had the world's tiniest penis.

(Left) Rochester-born Norman Kerry (1894-1956) was the Silent Era's equivalent of Errol Flynn. Dashing and handsome, he cut a striking figure as a swashbuckler. He was also Valentino's lover in the pre-shiek era.

(Right) Modest, unassuming, and good-looking without being strikingly handsome, Richard Barthelmess (1895-1963) got his start posing for full-frontal nudes that were distributed as naughty French postcards. He was an appealing and virile hero, both in films for D.W. Griffith and in bed with me.

A broad-chested, handsome blond, William Boyd (1895-1972) thrilled children throughout the 1950s as Hopalong Cassidy. But he was hopping on me long before that. A hell-raiser in his youth, he was later marketed by Hollywood as a standard for "clean living."

Going down on Ohio-born William Boyd (known to a generation of children during the Cold War as Hopalong Cassidy) was always convenient for me, since he was always appearing in films with my other lovers, including Valentino, Thomas Meighan, and Ramon Novarro.

"The epitome of gallantry and fair play," William Boyd (Hopalong) lived up to his reputation. A knockout in Hollywood films, he always thanked me kindly as I rose up off my knees after plunging down on him.

William Boyd was all man. Quick on the draw with his six-gun, he was a man who liked to take his time when he unbuttoned his fly and pulled out his eight-incher.

Wearing a bit too much lipstick here, William Boyd was a beauty in his pre-Hopalong days. Ironically for an actor playing a cowboy, he was one of the world's worst horsemen, but whenever he rode me, it was a ride down heavenly trails.

(Left) Marion Davies (1897-1961), mistress of William Randolph Hearst, was a lot smarter and more talented than Orson Welles made her out to be in *Citizen Kane*. Marion--depicted here as *Blondie of the Follies* (1931) --was carrying on with Chaplin, usually maneuvering her way around her old man's private dectectives.

Like the butterfly, her life was too short, but the charming and nymphomaniacal Barbara LaMarr (1896-1926) gave off a beautiful glow, even under this heavy head dress. She finally succumbed to drug addiction before the age of 30. In the words of Adela Rogers St. Johns, "She died because the tale was told."

Film director and noted lothario William Desmond Taylor (1872-1922) liked to watch whatever entertainment my then- "husband" Antonio Moreno and I devised. An insatiable voyeur, he often took me to all-male opium dens where love cults smoked dope and conducted orgies. A .38-caliber bullet aimed at his heart proved to be this British Romeo's "kiss of death." The case eventually evolved into a world-class scandal and one of Hollywood's most famous unsolved murders.

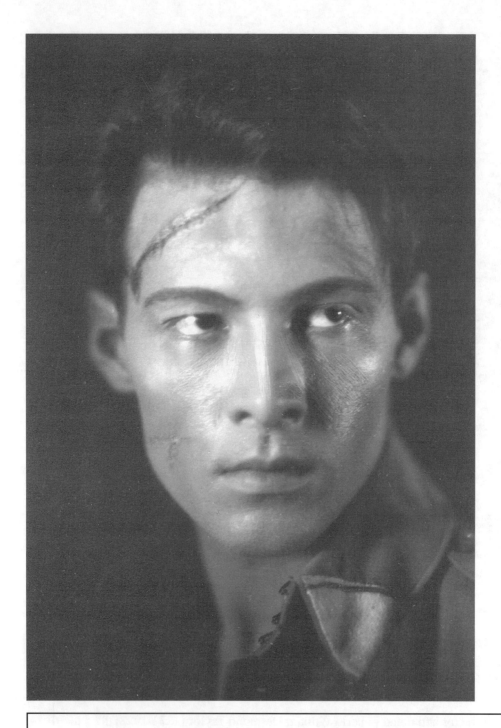

Here, in a particularly sensitive portrait, the on-again, off-again love of my life, Rudolph Valentino (1895-1926) hustled his way through the male and female bordellos of New York before Hollywood discovered his remarkable photogenic flair. America swooned over his portrayals of exotic swashbucklers who weren't averse to raping and pillaging. He often rehearsed this persona with me, in bed, polishing his sex appeal for movie scenes whose filming was scheduled for the following day.

The *Young Rajah* (1925; right) was the least successful movie Valentino ever made after he was widely acknowledged as a star. But did he ever get to dress UP! At one point, he appeared covered in white pearls, wearing only a loincloth. Gay America loved it, but the straights howled in protest. As gloriously seen in a state of partial undress (left) in the same film, Valentino was the first actor to appear in a bathing suit with his cock and balls clearly defined. Basket devotees across America stole this still whenever it was displayed as a "teaser" at their local cinemas. Shortly after its release, the allure of surfing caught on across the country.

(Left) As Julio in *The Four Horsemen of the Apocalypse* (1921),, Valentino became a household word after years of struggling, including hustling both men and women. His first wife, Jean Acker, wasn't putting out for the great lover. But I was. His favorite sexual diversion? An "around the world."

Valentino was proud of his body and his physical prowess and took every chance he could to display his manly assets. But here (right), except for his smoldering eyes, he covers up for *The Hooded Falcon,* a film that was never made. He'd wanted to play El Cid, and "surpass" Douglas Fairbanks, Sr. in exotic mystique. Alas, at least in this instance, that wasn't meant to be.

(Left) In *A Sainted Devil,* (1924), Natacha Rambova was accused of designing costumes "for men who were not men." Playing a drunkard, Valentino appeared in sparkling bolero, knickerbockers, and silk stockings. The first time he penetrated Natacha, she fainted, but fortunately, I was available to fill in.

(Right)   In *The Sheik* (1921), Valentino's role as lover helped coin a new word in the American vocabulary. Women and gay men swooned over him. At the dawn of the Roaring 20s, America was ready for a fiery sex god, and Valentino was "it."

RUDOLPH VALENTINO - A5

When he wasn['t]
making love[,]
Valentino was [a]
great cook (see[n]
here airing his spa[-]
ghetti). His int[i-]
mates knew h[e]
liked a good pla[te]
of pasta bette[r]
than a woman, e[s-]
pecially the tw[o]
lesbians he ma[r-]
ried but didn't be[d]

Showing basket, Valentino posed with Pola Negri (1894-1987) after winning a costume dance at Los Angeles' Biltmore Hotel in 1926, shoutly before his death. The bullfighter's costume was the same he'd worn in the 1922 film *Blood and Sand*.

Valentino and Natacha Rambova (1897-1966), his imperious second wife, posed like royal personages hoping for their imprimatur on stamp or coin. In this profile, they are like twins. Even the smooth glossiness of their preferred hair styles resembled each other.

(Left) Valentino was self-conscious about the scar on his right cheek, and consistently refused to discuss how he got it. Here, make-up conceals it. Hollywood gossips claimed it was the result of a particularly unsavory (and undocumented) night on the town. But in this posed portrait, the scar would have gone well with the pirate-inspired head-dress.

Nostils flaring, Valentino was a fiery continental lover--intense, passionate, obsessive. Eyes bulging or narrowing, depending on his mood, he had the look and stare of a panther stalking its unsuspecting prey. He delivered a deep penetration.

For the audience who watched *The Adventurer* (left) in 1917, Charles Chaplin (1889-1977) wasn't afraid to camp it up, and could always get a laugh when he played his roles effeminately. He could also be a woman, in full drag, in bed.

The Little Tramp (right) caught in a gay mood. Charlie Chaplin, in his 1964 autobiography, decided not to write one word of truth. He had a lot to cover up, especially his relationship with me and his excessive fondness for little nymphets.

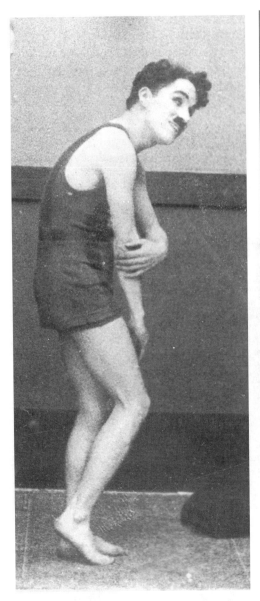

(Left) Shown here in a scene from *The Cure* in 1916, "bathing beauty" Charlie Chaplin demurely covers his genitals. The Little Fellow wasn't little when he disrobed. As I once told some of my gay pals, most of the meat on Charlie's body went into his cock.

(Right) Charlie Chaplin impersonated *A Woman* (the title of this 1915 short film) but perhaps forgot to remove his moustache. He picked up tips on dressing in drag when he spent a year of his life sharing a room with the world's leading female impersonator, Julian Eltinge, whose picture appears earlier in this album.

Fans swooned over Rod La Roque (left; 1898-1969), not only Swanson, but Pola Negri, who despite the fact that she was a closeted dyke, was always trying to steal men from me, especially Valentino. Ironically, Rod later made a serious play for Gary Cooper.

Thomas Meighan (below; 1879-1936) was a real man, not one of the "gay husbands" for whom movie roles were written so often in the 1920s. Six feet tall, with piercing blue eyes and a strong jaw, he had a ruggedness he liked to show off both on and off the screen.

Rod La Roque was such a girl, but he eventually proposed marriage to Gloria Swanson and later married Vilma Banky. He attracted world attention playing Richard Dix's brother in DeMille's *Ten Commandments*. I managed to seduce both the Rod and the Dick, in an era when phallic-sounding names were all the rage for male stars in Hollywood.

"Clothes Cow" Gloria Swanson (1899-1983) spent $10,000 a year on stockings alone, a fortune in the early twenties. She lied in her autobiography when she claimed she never screwed Valentino. Her only film with Rodolfo, *Beyond the Rocks* (1922), has disappeared except for the stills.

Metro claimed that their budding star, Ramon Novarro (1899-1968), was "Michangelo's David with the face of an El Greco Don." The "too beautiful" Ramon loved to be topped, especially by me, but also by Antonio Moreno and his arch-rival, Valentino.

A very young Ramon Sameniegos (later Novarro) poses as "Ali" in *A Lover's Oath* (1925). Before his tragic death, caused by a hustler who stuffed Valentino's Art Deco dildo down his throat, Ramon was a sweet adorable youth. We turned tricks together, once jointly with the Prince of Siam during his visit to Hollywood.

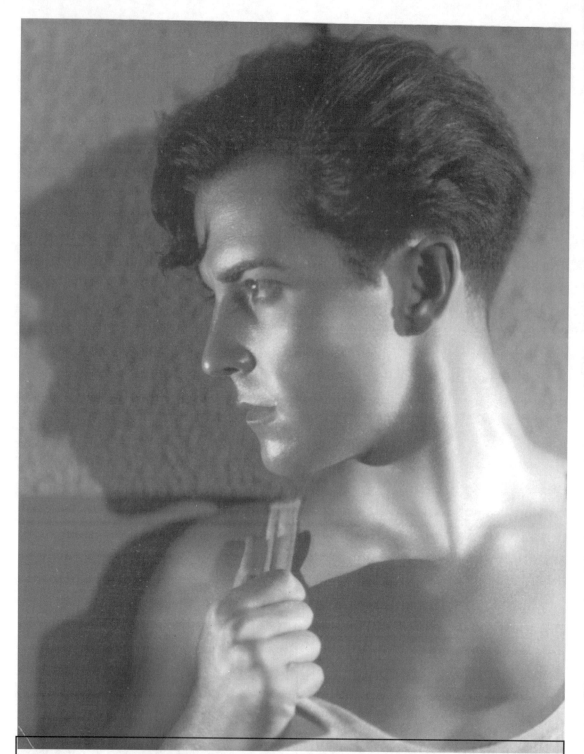

When Valentino's hot-blooded tango caused a sensation in *Four Horsement of the Apocalypse* (1921) Hollywood went wild, and immediately began looking for a Latino equivalent. Their answer was Ramon Novarro, photographed here in a way that evokes the sultry passion that Valentino might have inspired had he posed in a strapless T-shirt.

We begged Ramon Novarro to butch it up a bit, but this Mexican-born beauty was defiant in posing "my way." He penis was as long as Valentino's, but not as thick. Nonetheless, it was viewed as a delectable *burrito* ever ready for action.

"The noblest Roman of them all," Ramon Novarro as *Ben-Hur* (1925) was both a romantic lover and a swashbuckling hero. Billed as "a second Valentino," he plays golf in Rome, in a stripped-down version of gladiator fetish, during the filming of the epic.

Ramon Novarro in a publicity still for *Ben-Hur,* released in 1926 by MGM. Even his pubic hair was showing, a first ever for a film star. The caption read, "This photograph proves rather conclusively that he has no intention of ever joining a monastery."

With its S&M implications, *Ben-Hur* was
the role of a lifetime for Ramon Novarro (right), and
the cinematic comeback for horse-hung but faded matinee
idol Francis X. Bushman (left). Here, they glare at each other,
perhaps re-activating the sexual role-playing they'd enjoyed
together during their heyday six years
before.

There was a playful, lighthearted, mischievous, tongue-in-cheek quality to that roguish flirt, Ramon Novarro. He always had an impish glee in his eyes when you were about to top him. That's me, incidentally, in the background.

Long before Dietrich and Garbo pawed his handsome male flesh, John Gilbert (1899-1936) was dropping trou for me at the Hollywood Hotel. He excelled at romantic fare, both on-screen and in the bedroom. Here, in views both with and without mustache, he shows some of the charisma and charm that audiences swooned to in films that included *The Merry Widow* (1925), *The Big Parade* (1925), and *Flesh and the Devil* (1926). With me, he always requested his favorite sexual passion--an "around the world" delivered with enthusiasm by my cherry-red lips. What was known to the Hollywood community, but not to general-release audiences nationwide, he had an inordinate fondness for orgies and alcohol.

Clark Gable (1901-1960) was not a great lay, but I found him so remarkably handsome, it didn't matter that much. His rugged good looks and devilish grin won me over. He admittted to being a bad lover, claiming he needed more practice.

Years before he began making offensive, anti-gay remarks, a young Clark Gable wasn't opposed to hustling a john for a buck. He insisted that tricks pay at the rate of $10 per inch, which brought him $50 a throw.

Strong and straight-arrowed, the quint-essential American hero, Gary Cooper (1901-1961) could also camp it up a bit. When he was working his way up the Hollywood ladder, he wasn't averse to an occasional male-to-male affair, even though he ferociously pursued women.

When I first met Gary Cooper on the fields of Kansas, long before he became a star, he was known only as "Frank." He liked dating me because I would do to him what no girl would ever agree to do.

Long, lean, and lanky, Gary Cooper was a great beauty in his day, especially when lipstick was applied to his mouth. After a photo session, I liked to work the lipstick off that mouth.

Gary Cooper isn't really comparing his dick size to a wagon wheel, even though he was known as "The Montana Mule." I had to fight off Rod La Roque for his sexual favors. With Gary, it was always "High Noon."

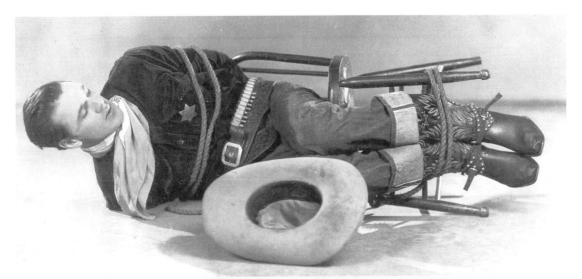

(Right) Under a ten-gallon hat, his lips painted in scarlet red, cupid's bow style, Gary Cooper was still searching for an image when this portrait was shot. Before this, he'd tried to imitate Valentino.

(Above) All tied up and ready for bondage, Gary Cooper lived for some of his early years in Hollywood with an openly gay millionaire size queen. Of that experience, Coop said, "A cowpoke's got to do what a cowpoke's got to do."

(Above) Long before my beloved Joan Crawford got to sample his delicious meat, I was going down on a teenage Douglas Fairbanks, Jr. (1909-2000). This young actor became an American Prince of Wales. He had a magnificent body.

(Left) Buddy Rogers (1904-1999) was Mary Pickford's third husband. But America's "boyfriend" was also my boyfriend way back in Kansas. He was more macho than this bathing beauty photograph suggests.

Whenever his date for the evening wouldn't put out, young Douglas Fairbanks, Jr. would come knocking on my door for "relief." I'd gladly oblige, since he had two inches more than his father, and didn't suffer from his famous dad's curvature of the dick.

The End

Chapter Eleven

The long-anticipated Twenties arrived with a bang. I had nothing but high hopes for all of our futures, not knowing then that many of us were to embark on a series of almost unexplainable tragedies that would become part of early Hollywood lore forever.

New Year's came rushing in at The Wallace Reid Ball at the Alexandria Hotel, co-sponsored by Dorothy Reid, his wife, and Mary Miles Minter. I'd wanted to go with Rodolfo but he hadn't called all day, and I suspected he'd disappeared with Natacha Rambova.

The list of patronesses included some of the biggest names in Hollywood. I drove Charlie to the event, even though Mildred Harris Chaplin was there. The two avoided each other all evening.

Charlie and I made the rounds, seeing Mary Pickford, Clara Kimball Young, Anita Stewart, Viola Dana, Mary MacLaren, Bessie Barriscale, Gloria Swanson, and Ruth Roland. When we ran into Edna Purviance, Charlie gave her a light kiss on the lips. She was with Thomas Meighan who gave me a hug and whispered a thank you for that night I'd spent seducing both him and his cohort, John Barrymore, at the Hollywood Hotel. Mary Anderson, Edith Roberts, Peggy Hyland, and Marguerite Livinston—all the big names of the era were there, except Douglas Fairbanks who chose not to appear in public with Mary Pickford that night. Later I spotted him sneaking off with Mildred Harris.

Right before the beginning of the year, only five minutes before midnight, I introduced Charlie to Mary Miles Minter. Although as I've pointed out, Hollywood was a very small town back then, the two actors had never met. Mary was Charlie's type. The two seemed to fall in love upon meeting each other. I hoped I was doing the right thing in bringing them together. I felt I had to do something to prevent Billy Taylor from marrying his daughter.

In the men's room right after midnight, Charlie told me, "I've got to have her. Where have you been hiding her? Believe it or not, I've never seen one of her films. Don't tell her that. You don't mind if I desert you tonight? A pretty boy like you won't be alone for very long."

I told him to go and have fun and that we'd meet for lunch tomorrow. Not knowing why I, the most popular boy in Hollywood, should be alone on New Year's Eve, I headed out of the men's room just as two handsome men were coming in. It was Ramon Novarro and Richard Dix. I couldn't believe that Ramon. He'd become friends with Richard Dix too. *My* Richard Dix.

They invited me back into the urinal where I was propositioned. Ramon suggested we split the party and head for his apartment where we could bring in 1920 with a three-way.

In my "stagecoach" and on the way to Ramon's, I lowered the windows to breathe the air. It was 1920. People were talking about "the facts of life." Skirts were getting shorter, and necklines were more daringly down. Durango Jones was set to become the biggest male star in Hollywood. I could feel that Ramon Novarro was thinking that he was going to become the biggest star in Hollywood. Looking over at Richard Dix, I felt he too planned to become the brightest and best of all the stars. It was going to be a heady decade. But, first, we had some major kissing, sucking, licking, and fucking to do. Three hot and horny studs were setting out to bring in the New Year in style.

That evening set a pattern that would last for years. Ramon and I discovered that even though we had great sex together, we had even better sex with Richard Dix in the bed with the two of us. Ramon Novarro, Richard Dix, and Durango Jones, beginning January 1, 1920, became one of Hollywood's closeted but infamous *ménages à trois*, rivaling the Gish sisters and Mildred Harris.

Work came the very first week, although stardom still eluded me as it did for Rodolfo, even though he was actually co-starring in major release films. As he so often pointed out to me, the "movie public talks about everyone else in the picture but me."

I tried several times to find out how his friendship was going with Natacha Rambova, but he told me to mind my own business, which I did. I had a career of my own to think about, and in some ways I preferred to spend my evenings with Antonio Moreno or William Boyd—even Richard Barthelmess—than I did with Rodolfo. He was growing increasingly moody and hostile, and he was quick to anger, especially when he felt Hollywood didn't appreciate him.

The first week of January, I reported to the set of *Till the Clouds Roll By*. My part consisted of a walk through an office carrying a stack of files. Presumably I was a file clerk, or perhaps a secretary. The director never fully explained my role. In gratitude for my having entertained the Prince of Wales, Douglas Fairbanks Sr. paid me seventy-five dollars for a day's work. That's not as low as it sounds, since many extras in the film got only five dollars a day.

The jauntiest movie Doug ever made, and his second for United Artists, *Till the Clouds Roll By* was jointly released by Mary Pickford, Charlie Chaplin, and D. W. Griffith.

Before switching to swashbucklers in the years ahead, Doug spoofed psychiatry in the film which is notable today mainly for some trick effects that remain baffling as to how the director pulled them off. Since I wasn't on the set that much, I don't have a clue. In the film Doug doesn't sit still for a minute, but bounces all over the place. When he proposes to a girl, he is seen hanging by his feet. When she accepts his proposal, he is shown swinging back and forth on the side of a door in glee. The psychiatrist who motivates the plot is revealed to be a lunatic escaped from an asylum.

Viewed today, the film is mainly an exercise in acrobatics for Doug. He struts his greased-lightning stuff aboard a ferry, atop a speeding train, and in the deluge of a raging flood. The romantic lead was played by Kathleen Clifford, who isn't exactly the first actress you think of when you cite favorites of the silent screen. Victor Fleming, the director, earned greater fame in the years ahead when he was called in to replace George Cukor, whom Clark Gable had denounced as a "faggot" on the set of *Gone with the Wind*.

As for that picture with Norman Kerry, *Passion's Playground*, I got three days of work as an extra. I was paid a grand total of thirty dollars. I don't know if a copy of that stinker still exists today, and I trust it doesn't. Norman showed up for work every day completely inebriated, marking the beginning of his descent into alcoholism. Even though half-drunk throughout the entire shoot, he still came across as wooden on the screen.

Completely miscast, Rodolfo struggled through the flicker as best he could. I had nothing to do but walk across the set a few times. Originally I thought I was going to be cast as Norman's other brother, but the part was cut at the last minute. The idea that Norman Kerry, Rudolfo Valentino, and Durango Jones were brothers was a bit ludicrous. Rodolfo was completely unconvincing as Norman's brother as well but his role was retained thanks to the older actor's influence and his continued infatuation with his Latin lover.

The less said about *Passion's Playground*, the better.

And then one night tragedy struck, the first of a chain of deadly events among young Hollywood stars that would either destroy our lives completely or darken our days for the rest of our years, even though a few of us managed to live until we became old. But many of us were struck down in our prime at the peak of our beauty and fame. Not me, of course, but so many others that I loved.

The press thought the tragic events about to descend on Olive Thomas—more about that later—were the first real Hollywood scandal since the birth of the films, but there was one tragedy that happened right before that. All this time I have remained silent over the years about it, even though in the decades ahead I became the best known male gossip columnist in Hollywood.

Little Bobby Harron was feeling despondent when I'd encountered him at the studio. He'd been dumped by Charles Ray and felt that Richard Barthelmess was set to replace him on the screen in major parts that he felt rightfully belonged to him, considering those long early years spent before the cameras of D. W. Griffith.

He was nervous about being seen at the Hollywood Hotel going up to my room with me. Rumors were already circulating that he was a homosexual. I asked him to come by my rose-covered cottage in back of the house occupied by Elizabeth Hutchison whom I had not seen in several weeks. The one time I had encountered her was one late afternoon when I drove up. She was in her garden picking flowers. Although she said, "Hi, Durango," she quickly retreated inside her back porch doors and didn't engage me in conversation. It was as if she looked guilty about something and didn't want to confront me. What could she possibly have guilty feelings about?

In bed that night, Bobby had been more passive than ever. He lay almost motionless, claiming he wanted me to use him for whatever purposes I desired. "Satisfy your lust on me," he'd said. Obviously that was an invitation to fuck him, which I did admirably. But it wasn't all that much fun. He'd seemed to view my penetration of him as a punishment. Instead of being a pleasure, the sex had seemed like an instrument of discipline for him, something to be endured. Yet when I'd climaxed inside him, he'd erupted himself, indicating to me that he must have enjoyed it. I held him a long time, kissing him tenderly, before pulling out. Bobby

was the one lover I had that I never really knew. It was as if he lived in a very private world of his own, and I was never invited there to join him.

As we were having a drink in the kitchen, there came a loud rapping on my front door. I excused myself and went to answer it, finding Wallace Reid standing there clad only in his underwear. "Are you alone?" he asked, a desperate panic reflected in his face.

"I will be soon," I said, telling him to wait by the side of the house. Back in the living room, I told Bobby there had been an emergency up front in the main house and that he was to leave at once. Since I had driven him to the cottage in my "stagecoach," I called a taxi for him and told him to wait across from the house of Francis X. Bushman. Bobby did as told, kissing me on the lips and thanking me and asking me to get together with him in a few days.

Once Bobby had disappeared from sight, I went around to the side of the house and asked Wally to come into the living room. "What on earth is the matter?"

He was sobbing. "Something terrible has happened. I've been horrible to you and I feel such remorse. You're my best friend."

Best friend or not, I remembered that when I came upon him at his New Year's ball, he and his wife, Dorothy, had virtually ignored me. He only smiled briefly before turning to chat with Gloria Swanson. I overheard them talking about the possibility of making a picture together. This was the same Gloria Swanson who had dismissed Wally's love note with such contempt only weeks earlier. Hollywood was nothing if not totally two-faced.

He kneeled down before me as I sat in an armchair, then took my hands and looked imploringly into my eyes. "I'm going to ask you to do the biggest favor of your life for me. It will save my career. It will earn my eternal gratitude. Only you can save me."

"What on earth are you talking about, and what are you doing running around half-dressed in my yard at this time of night?"

"Elizabeth Hutchison is dead," he said, standing up. "She died while we were having sex. Went into one of her fits or something."

I jumped up. "My God, are you sure? Let

me go and try to help. Maybe there's still life in her. Let me call her father at once. He's a doctor."

He restrained me, using a powerful grip. "I told you: she's dead. There is nothing you can do to save her. I've been with her for the last hour, crying and sobbing over her dead body. She's as cold as ice."

I started to cry and he went over to the counter and poured me a glass of brandy. "Here," he said, "belt this down. It'll steady your nerves for the favor I'm about to ask. Now come and sit down on the sofa with me. I'm going to look deep into your eyes as I talk. You've got to listen to every word. This is the most important night of my life. Only you can save me."

On the sofa, I didn't say a word but listened to him intently, as he told me that he was not a homosexual and had come to resent me for luring him into that lifestyle, using the morphine as bait. He had snubbed me at the party because he wanted to blot out our sexual episodes together.

When he'd first met Elizabeth, he'd been powerfully attracted to her and had arranged secretly to meet with her every few nights for sex. They'd had a great sex life together and she'd satisfied him and he'd pleased her greatly. Perhaps that explained why she'd looked so guilty when I encountered her in her rose garden." I told Elizabeth that you're in love with me, and she agreed to keep our affair a secret."

He said that when he was fucking her earlier that night, she'd gasped and cried out. At first he felt that was because she was so enjoying his penetration of her. But when she didn't move in the next few moments, he'd pulled out of her. He couldn't hear her breathing or feel her heart beating, and he knew at once that she was dead.

"What do you want me to do now?" I asked. "It's too late for anything."

"Like hell, it is," he said. "It's not too late for a cover-up. I want you to call her father and explain what happened. But instead of me, I want you to claim you were having intercourse with Elizabeth when she died. She's a single gal, you're a single boy. These things happen. With you, it would be a quiet burial. Chances

are her father will never release the details that a seduction was going on at the time of death. He'll view it as an accident. He won't want to blacken the good name of his daughter. But if the press discovers that it was Wallace Reid who was fucking Elizabeth at the time of her death, it will make headlines around the world. Don't forget, I'm the fourth most famous star in Hollywood, right up there after Chaplin, Fairbanks, and Pickford."

"I could never forget that," I said, sighing.

"Will you do it?" he asked eagerly, taking my hand and, in his desperation, squeezing it hard.

"I don't know," I said with great hesitation, wishing I'd never gotten mixed up in this rotten mess in the first place. "It would be awful hard to do that, to call Dr. Hutchison."

"Call him you must—and take the blame," he commanded me. "Look up at me. What do you see? The handsomest man in Hollywood, a strapping, virile God of a man. Listen to me, sweet cakes. If you do what I'm asking, Wallace Reid will belong only to you from this day forth. You can have me any moment of the day or night. I'm all yours. You said yourself I have the world's most beautiful dick. That cock will belong just to you. For you, I would even give up fucking my own wife, not that that would be much of a sacrifice since I'm not enjoying screwing her all that much more."

"I don't know," I said, turning from him.

He moved toward me, taking me in his arms and planting his lips on mine. At first I tried to break away, but what is a faggot from Kansas to do when the world's handsomest man takes you in his arms? You give in—that's what you do.

"Oh, Wally, I still don't know," I said. "I want you and everything…"

He interrupted me with another kiss. "I'm yours. All yours. Exclusively yours. No other star in Hollywood will be faithful to you. Wallace Reid will be faithful. Nobody will get the body of Wallace Reid but Durango Jones. I'll be your property for the rest of my life."

"I don't like this kind of bargaining," I said. "I feel I'm not winning you because you want to be with me but I'm getting you by default."

"Go on," he ordered me, "reach inside my

underwear and feel everything."

I didn't obey him at first.

He bit into my ear real hard. "I said reach inside my underwear and feel everything."

It was an invitation I couldn't resist. I reached inside and fondled him, and couldn't take my hands from him. At that very moment I felt I loved him even more than I loved Rodolfo. "Go on, admit it," he whispered in my ear. "You want those goodies and you want them all for yourself. You're a homosexual and no homosexual in his right mind would turn down Wallace Reid. You're not that crazy." He pulled me by the hair, turning my lips up to his and tightening his arms around me, as his tongue went into my mouth.

No man had ever given me the gift of himself before. Rodolfo had Natacha and everybody else. Charlie had his little girls. William Boyd and even Antonio had so many others, I never knew. John Gilbert was going to marry Leatrice Joy. Only I had Wallace Reid, one of the world's most desirable men. It was said that millions of women around the world went home to their husbands, dreaming he was Wallace Reid. I could well imagine that most of the world's gay men felt the same way about Wally as did those love-starved women.

When he finally let me go and I'd reluctantly pulled my lips from him, I looked deeply into his eyes. "I'll make that call now to Dr. Hutchinson."

*****

At this point everyone's world speeded up, as new stars emerged overnight. But many members of the old guard, including Theda Bara, either saw their careers collapse completely or else they went into slow decline, as evoked by William S. Hart. Pickford, Fairbanks, and Chaplin still reigned supreme, but new stars were on the horizon. Within months, the public would flock to see films starring Rudolph Valentino, Ramon Novarro, John Gilbert, and Barbara LaMarr. Mae Murray and Gloria Swanson were no longer "discoveries," but became reigning queens of the cinema. It was a new and exciting time, but not for all of us.

In an attempt to embarrass Goldwyn with his financial backers, Joe Godsol ordered that a copy of *Vampira* be sent to Chicago for its premiere. Why Chicago I didn't know, except Godsol had a lot of connections there.

The first night of its screening provoked a virtual riot. Many patrons stormed out of the theater, I was to learn later to my horror. Many members of the audience laughed at the sex scenes and the display of male nudity.

William Desmond Taylor's name had been removed as director. Durango Jones had not been substituted instead. The name of "Bernard McCarthy" appeared as director of the picture, although he'd had nothing to do with the film, if indeed he existed at all.

The picture immediately ran into trouble with state boards who wanted to censor it. Godsol decided to release it to only a select number of theaters across the country to gauge the general reaction. It was all unfavorable. Individual exhibitors took it upon themselves to drop entire reels out of the film, claiming they were offensive. The manager of the Strand Theatre in Omaha, Nebraska, showed the film in its entirety. But some members in the audience fired bullets at the screen, indicating their reaction.

On top of everything else, a little old lady in Wilkesboro, North Carolina, claimed that the film was plagiarized and sued us to prevent our showing it. She said she'd published a novel in 1908 about a female vampire who hired five male servants and systemically killed each one of them by sucking the blood from them. This would-be novelist seemed to misunderstand the actual plot of *Vampira*. I didn't play a real blood-sucker. The only blood I removed from my servants was in their semen, a point overlooked by the other vampire writer. Nonetheless, both Godsol and Goldwyn prepared to go to court to defend the film. The financiers who backed both men frantically ordered that *Vampira* be removed from general release. Goldwyn, and I never knew this for sure, was said to have destroyed all copies of the film except one that was allegedly possessed by Joe Godsol, who didn't like the idea of losing money on any film. In a call to me inviting me over to visit him with Marion Davies, he confirmed that he had the one copy left. He'd heard of Lotte's disappearance and had wanted her to accompany him to Paris where he planned to release the film on the continent.

"Europeans can appreciate a film like this," he said to me. "Americans are too provincial. Mary Pickford's about as sexy as they can take." Since Lotte wasn't available, he invited me to go to Paris with him, as her agent. "You're my second choice. I never did get into your sister's honeypot, but the most delectable boy-ass in California—namely yours—is a wonderful substitute."

"That's very flattering," I said.

"Confess up," he told me. "Don't I have the biggest dick you've ever been fucked with?"

"God damn yes," I said, lying. Godsol might not have the longest dick that had ever fucked me, but he certainly had the thickest. I feared he would stretch Marion out so wide she'd never be satisfied with W.R. again.

Not knowing of Godsol's plans to release the film on the continent, Richard Barthelmess told the press he wasn't actually in the movie. He claimed his alleged part was played by his younger brother who bore an amazing resemblance to him. Tom Moore was too drunk to care, and William Boyd treated it as a bit of a joke, a curious detour he'd made before the start of a legendary career. Thomas Meighan never spoke of the film to the press and always refused to answer any questions about it. In his film biography, *Vampira* has been omitted.

Because of all the controversy surrounding *Vampira*, there was a tremendous demand from the press for interviews. But I held these news hounds at bay, claiming that Lotte Lee had gone on a very long and extended trip to the Far East with an "admirer," suggesting that he was some wealthy maharaja who was showering her with her weight in gold and diamonds.

When the press grew more persistent, I even admitted that this maharaja might be planning to marry her and that he'd bought up all copies of *Vampira* because he didn't want his future princess to "be on display in the cinema," considering it a vulgar profession, not worthy of a fine lady such as my sister.

But I'm getting ahead of my story, as I was so harshly reminded by the Bitch of Buchenwald.

On the very night I was to join Mary Miles Minter and Charlie Chaplin for dinner at the Alexandria Hotel, The Little Tramp made a major confession to me. "I'm in love," he said.

At first I was startled. Having just won the heart of the fourth most famous male movie star in the world, Wally Reid, I had now captured the first most famous male movie star in the world. This was a spectacular achievement for a golden-haired youth from the wheatfields of Kansas. Even if I couldn't make it as a film star myself, I could at least win the hearts of the idols of the screen.

I looked deeply into Charlie's eyes. "I've fallen for you too," I said. "I don't know how it happened. Our love-making has always been great. I've come to love the man behind that big dick."

"Don't be a fool," he said, breaking away from me. "I'm not in love with you. I keep you around—and pay you better than anybody else—for sex. You take care of that disgusting homosexual nature of mine. I abhor it but I keep returning for more. I'm in love with someone else."

"You've just met Mary Miles Minter," I protested. "How could you be in love with someone you just met?"

"I'm not in love with Minter," he said in exasperation at my stupidity. "I'm going to the hotel tonight to fuck her. The woman I'm in love with is Florence Deshon."

"Who in the hell is Florence Deshon?" I asked. "I've heard of Florence Vidor. Who's this other Florence? A city in Italy?"

"Don't be a smart-ass," he snapped at me in anger. "Flo is an aspiring stage and screen actress. Goldfish has signed her to a contract at four-hundred dollars a week. There's talk that she's going to replace Lotte Lee on the screen."

Charlie was really making it tough on my ego. Goldwyn gave Lotte only two-hundred a week. Of course, Deshon, or so I doubted, would not make off with $250,000 like I did.

"Goldfish is going all out for her," he said. "Dressing room and everything. He's redecorating according to her likes. Sunflower yellow walls, red gingham curtains, and wicker furniture painted just the right shade of ivory."

"How nice," I said, growing more furious by the minute.

"He's even given her a thousand dollars for wardrobe expenses," he said, "even though Flo is responsible for her own clothes."

"Why is Goldfish being so generous?" I asked. "Could it have anything to do with the intervention of the great Charles Chaplin?"

He smiled at me. "I think you're jealous. You've nailed me. The thousand dollars came from my tight pocket. Flo has suffered for her allegiance to socialism, and I wanted to help make up for it in some way. Actresses like Mildred Harris are empty headed. Flo reads Li Po in translation. Her favorite author is John Milton."

"An actress with an intellect." I said. "A first for Hollywood."

"You've got that right," he said. "She's adored by my friends, at least those with some intelligence. Theodore Dreiser dotes on her."

That impressed me, and I was growing more jealous of Florence Deshon by the second. Several times in the past Charlie had hinted that I didn't have the intellectual capacity to dine out with his "more educated friends."

In time I would find out that Charlie hadn't lied about Deshon's friendship with Dreiser. In his 1929 novel, *A Gallery of Women*, the novelist based his character of Ernestine De Jongh on Deshon, whom he described as "sensuously and disturbingly beautiful and magnetic."

How could I compete?

"Flo has a bit of a wayward spirit," Charlie said. "She's sculpturesquely beautiful."

"And young?" I asked sarcastically.

"Very young," he said. "She also has another suitor in Max Eastman. Max and I vie for her love."

"May the best man win," I said, not meaning it.

Getting dressed upstairs, I felt dejected and alone that I could no longer be Lotte Lee and that others were taking my place. Charlie certainly wasn't kicking me out, and I was in fact fixing him up with another woman, Mary Miles Minter. That was always understood in our relationship. I wasn't jealous of him for fucking Marion Davies, as I genuinely liked her. I was hardly jealous of Mildred Harris, and in fact viewed her as pathetic. But there was something about Deshon that intrigued me and

made me turn green with envy. Apparently, she had a first-rate mind, and Charlie was a sucker for that. He turned to me or the likes of Mary Miles Minter, even Reatha Watson, for sex, but Florence Deshon gave him both sex and intellectual stimulation.

Suddenly Charlie, stark nude from the shower, his big dick protruding, came into my bedroom. He was still drying himself off.

"Just to stimulate your own mind a bit," he said. "I've arranged a surprise for you. Before meeting Minter, we're going to have a drink with Frank Harris." He smiled smugly. "I know your first question. What films has Harris made? I'm sure you've never heard of him.

"If we mean the same person, I certainly have heard of Frank Harris," I said proudly. I'd first heard mention of him back in Lawrence, Kansas, when I'd visited my friends, Martha and Henry Ingalls, on their front porch. Frank Harris was one of the great editors of his day— *Saturday Review* and all that.

But what I'd really remembered about him was that he'd written two scandalous books. One about Oscar Wilde, another about *My Life and Loves*. The latter was so shocking in its revelations that it had never been released in this country. I couldn't believe I would actually be meeting this towering literary figure. Back in Lawrence, Kansas, when Mr. And Mrs. Ingalls had first told me about him, their tales of Harris had made such an impression on me that I often blamed him for interesting me in sex. The night I'd heard about Harris had also been the night I'd learned that certain boys—and not just female whores—charged for sex. That had made an enormous impression on me, as I'd set off on the Santa Fe, leaving the wheatfields of Kansas for the fleshpots of Hollywood.

"Frank is my idol," Charlie said. He'd never told me that before. In fact, until that very moment I never knew that Charlie had any idols other than The Little Tramp.

"Frank, or so I'd heard, was always in financial trouble," Charlie said. "Sometimes he couldn't pay his staff at *Pearson's Magazine*. He was always publishing appeals for contributions. I sent him a generous one, and he sent me both volumes of his book on Wilde in gratitude."

Still naked, Charlie rushed to his own bedroom and returned with a handwritten note. "He sent this to me last August to thank me for my contribution." He looked at the note reverently, handling it like it was a precious gem. He read it to me:

To Charlie Chaplin—
One of the few who has helped me without knowing me, one whose rare artistry in humor I have often admired, for those who make men laugh are worthier than those who make them weep.
From his friend, Frank Harris.

Charlie seemed genuinely moved by this. Anyone he considered an intellectual and who regarded the little cockney tramp from the East End of London with respect always won his heart. He appreciated these so-called intellectuals more than he did his millions of movie-going fans. How unlike Joan Crawford, another film icon who at the moment of my talk with Charlie was in some laundry somewhere dreaming of the days to come when she'd bounce onto the screen as one of America's dancing daughters.

I stood before Charlie in my underwear, and apparently the sight of my beautiful, golden body temporarily made him forget both Frank Harris and Florence Deshon.

"I want you to take me to bed and fuck me," he said. "I can't drop my seed because I need it for later in the night with Minter. But if you fuck me, it'll take away all my homosexual urges for the night, and I'll be an unrestricted heterosexual for the rest of the evening."

*****

An hour later, our dirty deed done to Charlie's complete satisfaction, he had nothing but praise for me as I drove him to the Alexandria Hotel for our meeting with Frank Harris, to be followed by a dinner in the main restaurant with Mary Miles Minter.

Charlie had asked me to accompany him to his meeting with Minter. I was serving as a

"beard" again. He didn't want to be seen dining alone with Minter weeks before his divorce from Mildred Harris, and he also feared that a jealous William Desmond Taylor might show up unexpectedly and either beat him up or fire a shot at him.

Over drinks with Frank Harris at the Alexandria Hotel, Charlie, for the first and only time I'd seen him in life, became the fan—not the idol—and let the editor and writer do most of the talking. Even though I was thrilled to meet such a literary legend, I had long ago learned that when you dine out as the companion of a famous person, you are too often ignored. Years from now, such people would be called "walkers."

On the way to the hotel in Charlie's Locomobile, he claimed that Florence Deshon found Frank Harris "an unstable quantity" in her mind. He seemed overly impressed with his new girl friend's pronouncement, even though I wasn't certain what she meant.

When Frank Harris stopped pontificating, Charlie told him of his upcoming divorce and how hard it was to work out a settlement with Mildred Harris, or Mildred Harris Chaplin, as she now billed herself. A brilliant mimic, he captured her mannerisms and voice perfectly. "My attorney won't let me take fifty thousand," Charlie said, imitating Mildred. "He says that amount is chicken feed. He demands that you give me one-hundred thousand. All this bickering over money is causing my health to fail." He resumed his natural voice. "In revenge I called her back and offered $500,000. I let her rejoice in that for a few moments, and then I phoned her again saying my lawyer had nixed that offer. A year's earnings for what amounted to only a week's real marriage—that's ridiculous. Then I put down the phone to let her stew."

Frank Harris sipped his drink and leaned back, observing Charlie closely. "I noticed that little smile on your lips as you told me this. There's just a bit of acid contempt for the female nature in you and I like that."

"I'm sure no one knows women more than you do, Mr. Harris." That was my learned observation, my only one, for the evening.

"For a potential mistress, I judge them of course to see if they have long lines and slight curves on a lovely body," he said. "I can tell at once if a woman is the very highest of the pleasure-giving type. In bed, I rate them on their ability with the cinder-shifting movement."

I didn't know what that vaginal reference meant, and I suspected Charlie didn't either, although he nodded his head in agreement.

Over a second drink, Harris, for no apparent reason, extended an invitation for Charlie to visit Sing-Sing prison with him. "Once there, I can arrange with the warden for you to get a glimpse of an electric chair. I bet you've never seen one of those before."

Like a little kid being invited to the circus, Charlie gleefully accepted his invitation for reasons known only to him. I wasn't invited to accompany them, which was just as well with me. I had no desire to see convicts, a prison, and most definitely I didn't want to look at an electric chair. Even back then, I was no great devotee of capital punishment.

"Among women," Harris observed, "I have found that the women who make the greatest lovers are those who have spent time in prison."

When Harris spoke of literature in front of Charlie, Charlie pretended he'd read a great many books that he hadn't. I personally had seen Charlie in his library. He had an amazing gift of turning the pages of a book rapidly, glancing at a key paragraph here and there, then claiming he'd read the entire book.

Frank Harris was, as Mr. And Mrs. Ingalls had described him—short and thick set, although I found he had a rather noble head and well-defined features, obscured somewhat by the kind of handlebar mustache worn by members of barbershop quartets. He appeared to be in his sixties with a deep, resonant voice.

From literature, Harris switched to politics. Like Charlie, he was a socialist, although he thought Bismarck was the greatest man who ever lived. He didn't explain why, looking at Charlie as if his remark should be taken as gospel. Almost as good an actor as Charlie, Harris did a brilliant impersonation of the German leader that had Charlie roaring with laughter. I smiled politely.

The talk inevitably led to Oscar Wilde and the two tomes Harris had written on that tragic figure. Harris claimed that the "chief influence of my life," at least in the early 1890s, was

Wilde. "After that, Whistler, but Wilde came first," he said.

Harris was filled with anecdotes about Wilde. Suddenly, the conversation fascinated me. Here I was sitting with the world's most famous man, Charlie, having a drink with the world's most famous editor, Harris, talking about the world's most famous homosexual writer, Wilde. Harris had actually known Wilde. I couldn't believe that I was actually meeting someone who had been a friend of the disgraced writer.

"From 1885 until the date of his arrest," Harris said, "I dined with him about once every fortnight. He was the best conversationist I have ever known, a born story-teller, far more than Kipling. He could deliver the most devastating portraitures of people. His imitation of Queen Victoria was priceless. I still recall him. That eloquent tenor voice, those laughing eyes—that is, before they grew sad—and a sudden sentence that would illuminate a whole situation. I remember one day in Westminster as we were strolling by the House of Parliament. Both the suffragettes and the unemployed had joined forces to attack the government. Oscar looked at them and said, 'I see the unemployed has joined in protest with the unenjoyed.'"

From Oscar Wilde the talk over drinks drifted into homosexuality. "Come on, Frank, you're so honest in your *Life & Loves*, but why didn't you come clean about homosexuality? Didn't England's most famous womanizer dip into it once or twice?"

Charlie was being provocative but Frank Harris, unlike most American men at the time, didn't become hysterically defensive. "You have certainly nailed me to the wall with that one," Harris said. "My autobiography is supposed to be the most honest ever written, but even I, author of two tomes on Wilde, couldn't bring myself to relate the one or two times I've come even close to a homosexual experience. Except for some silly schoolboy stuff—all English schoolboys indulge in a bit of buggery you know—I have had one or two experiences. One time was when an assistant editor invited me home to meet his wife, whom he described as one of the loveliest of English school girls. After dinner and over a few drinks, he asked me into his bedroom to spend the night with him and his wife. It turned out that he wanted me to bugger both of them. I was so aroused at the prospect of getting to fuck his wife, that I obliged."

"Although approached constantly in my early days in vaudeville, I've had only one homosexual encounter in my life," Charlie told Harris, then glanced at me as if to remind me to keep my mouth shut. "It was one night in New York. To avoid some process servers who were after me at the time over some dumb law suit, I changed hotels every night. One night I checked out of a hotel, called a taxi, and went around to various hotels, but found all the rooms taken. It was then that the taxi driver, a real brute of a man, invited me back to sleep at his apartment in Brooklyn with his family. At first I was afraid to accept but in desperation I agreed to it. He took me inside his darkened apartment and led me into a backroom with a large double bed. In that bed was one of the most beautiful young boys I've ever seen in my life. The boy, his son, was fast asleep. He picked the boy up and flopped him over to the edge and invited me to drift off to dreamland. At about four in the morning, I woke up as his young son was going down on me. I was already hard. I'd been so out of it I hadn't even felt his mouth on me at first. The boy was good and I was nearing climax. I decided to keep my eyes closed and let the boy enjoy himself."

At that point a very lovely young red-haired woman arrived and walked over to our table, kissing Harris on the lips. Even at his age, the author could still attract the lovelies. He didn't bother to introduce her to us, although it was clearly obvious she wanted to meet the great Charles Chaplin.

Before Harris had disappeared upstairs with his redhead, Charlie nudged me that Mary Miles Minter was heading toward our table.

*****

In the dining room, when Charlie got up to go to the toilet, Minter confided in me that Charlie had taken her home that first night and

fucked her. "It wasn't only a new year which had come, Charlie did a lot of cumming too. My God, he's got a big dick—far more than my beloved Billy Taylor."

Before Charlie returned, Mabel Normand came into the restaurant alone. No doubt planning to meet her date for the evening.

Spotting Minter and me, she staggered over to our table, looking drunk or drugged, certainly belligerent. "I see you two little lovebirds have found each other," she said, placing her hand on her hip the way I'd seen her confront a female rival in one of her films whose name escaped me. "Mary Miles Minter and Durango Jones. Combined, the two of you are more of a bitch than Mary Pickford."

"Miss Normand," Minter said, "I have great respect for your talent on the screen in spite of that last disastrous turkey you made. To me, you represent old Hollywood like Theda Bara, and I respect what you've done in the past. Why don't you just gracefully bow out of pictures now? That way, the public will remember you at the peak of your glory when you weren't drugged?"

"Why you little bleached-blonde cunt you," Mabel said, her eyes literally dancing with ferocity. At that moment the waiter arrived with three bowls of soup, which back in those days came free at the beginning of every meal.

Mabel reached out toward the tray, picked up a bowl of soup, then tossed it into Minter's face. Jumping up from table, Minter ran screaming from the dining room toward the toilet, as two waiters trailed her offering their assistance.

"My God," I said to Mabel. "You're a fucking maniac. I hope that soup was tepid. She might be permanently disfigured."

"Fuck you!" Mabel said. "As for Lotte Lee—namely you—that drag queen career came to a beautiful end, didn't it?"

"You're a monster!" I said.

As I watched Mabel stagger off toward her table, I couldn't help but reflect that up to now I'd read only good stuff about her. It seemed that everybody who ever met Mabel Normand sang her praise, especially co-workers. I'm sure she was as wonderful as they described, but my own experience with Miss Normand suggested she was the equal of either Tallulah Bankhead or a latter-day Joan Crawford on a bad Rose Garden night.

As I was dipping my finger into the soup, finding it lukewarm (thankfully for Minter), a woman attendant came to my table and informed me that our guest of honor had been taken upstairs. "She's not burned," the attendant said, "only her pride injured. She told me to tell you to send Mr. Chaplin up to her room after he dines. She won't be joining the two of you for dinner."

I thanked her and stood up to welcome Charlie back from the men's room. "Where's Mary?" he asked.

"I'll explain everything."

He seemed to assume that she had gone "to powder her nose," as the expression was back then. Completely wrapped up in himself, he whispered an incident to me that had just happened to him in the men's room. "It felt so good that I've been carrying around your cum all night. But nature called and I had to go to the men's room to lose that delicious stuff and some less delicious stuff. While I was in one of the stalls, a guy from some cornfield stuck his head under my stall and peered up at me as I was taking a crap. 'May I have your autograph, Mr. Chaplin?' he asked." Charlie burst into laughter at the experience. "The price of stardom, my pet."

After telling him of the incident with Mabel Normand, he looked over at her table, where she spotted him and waved back at her former co-star in comedy. Fortunately, the dining room was just filling up and was almost empty when the bowl of soup incident occurred. Charlie was eager to go upstairs to comfort Minter, but I assured him she had requested an hour or so alone before receiving him. "She's got to collect herself," I said. "You know how women are."

In retrospect if I had known what was going to happen later in the evening, I would have let Charlie go upstairs without dinner. To my astonishment, Billy Taylor was seen walking across the dining room heading for Mabel's table. He didn't seem to notice Charlie and me, and I was not eager to encounter him either. Since the disaster of *Vampira*, he wanted to forget about me for a while. Antonio Moreno told me he hadn't called him either.

Billy was spending much of his time with Minter—that is, when she wasn't with Chaplin, and obviously, if this night could be a barometer, the rest of his time with Mabel Normand. I was certain that he was still seeing Charlotte Shelby on the side for those mercy fucks.

For yet another astonishment of the evening, I looked up to see Louis B. Mayer escorting Mildred Harris Chaplin to table. Both Mayer and Harris walked right by our table, without looking down at us. Mayer and Chaplin knew each other, and also hated each other. There were as many feuds in Hollywood back then as there are now.

As we enjoyed dinner, a delicious western steak, Charlie didn't mention Harris or Mayer, even though he kept glancing over at their table.

When I got up to go to the men's room, I took the long way around deliberately to avoid running into either Mildred Harris or Mabel Normand.

To my surprise I encountered Jack Pickford dining behind a potted palm with his wife, Olive Thomas. We exchanged the obligatory kisses, as they told me of their plans to go to Paris. I said that I too would be going to Paris with Joe Godsol and perhaps we'd meet up there. Olive looked shocked. It was only then I remembered that Jack had told me that Olive was having an affair with Godsol. Since her husband knew this, I was somewhat taken aback that she seemed surprised we were sailing over to Paris together. Recovering quickly, she told me to call her at the Ritz Hotel when I got to Paris. "We'll be there before you and Joe."

A waiter came up and Jack was distracted as he placed a dinner order for the both of them.

"Joe didn't tell me he was going to Paris," she whispered with a certain fury. "He's fallen for another woman. I don't know who it is, but when I find out there's going to be one whore walking around Hollywood with her hair snatched bald."

Could this be a fate that awaited Marion Davies? I wondered to myself. I suspected that Jack accepted Olive's relationship with Godsol as long as Jack felt it was a casual affair. But from the look on Olive's face, I knew she'd fallen desperately in love with Godsol.

Having known both Jack Pickford and Joe Godsol intimately, I feared that Godsol's thick dick had spoiled Olive for Jack's more parlor-sized assets.

As the waiter left with their dinner order, Jack turned his attention toward us again, and the subject of Joe Godsol was abruptly dropped.

As I promised to get together with them soon, Jack called out to me. "So sorry to hear about Lotte's picture. A damn shame." He let me know that Owen Moore was also going to Paris with Olive and him. That I found completely baffling. Jack was, after all, the brother of Mary Pickford, his main support in Hollywood, and here he was in an act of flagrant disloyalty going to Paris with his brother-in-law in the middle of this messy divorce where Owen was making a lot of financial demands on his wife.

Back from the toilet after taking a leak in the presence of an appreciative male diner, I headed for Charlie's table. Jack motioned for me to come over to his table again where he handed me a note. "Give this to Charlie," he said with an impish grin, making me realize how drunk he was.

"Jack's still a little boy playing games," Olive said with a slight contempt. "But let him have his fun."

"Don't tell Charlie where you got the note," Jack said, insisting that I promise.

"Sure thing," I said.

"You took long enough," Charlie said in an accusatory voice as I sat down opposite him. "Showing off that big thing in the toilet?"

"Nothing like that," I said, handing him the note. "A waiter gave me this. Said to give it to you."

"Fans," he said, reading the note, then crushing it in his fist, a mask of fury coming onto his face so severe it scared even me. I had no idea of what the note contained, and didn't pursue it.

He looked over at Mayer. "That God damn little Jew bastard," he said under his breath. "I could kill him. From the beginning, Mayer has tried to fuck with me. It all started when he proposed a six-picture contract at fifty thousand dollars per film with Mildred. The cheap shit was going to make her a co-pro-

ducer. That way he could release her films as a Chaplin-Mayer production, trading off my name. The little shit has also pursued Mildred. He wants to fuck her." He looked with disgust at their table again. "I'm sure he has—many times."

"I didn't know they were carrying on," I said. I was familiar with some of Mildred's sexual liaisons, including some lesbian dalliances as well as some heterosexual flings, such as the one with Fairbanks, but the Mayer link came as a surprise until I remembered that Mildred Harris got her start in the Babylonian orgy scene in D.W. Griffith's *Intolerance*. It must have been type casting.

Mayer got up and headed for our table, and I feared the worse. He was only stepping into the foyer, no doubt going to the men's room. Charlie jumped up and chased after Mayer. Fearing trouble, I too got out of my seat and trailed Charlie.

In the lobby, Charlie confronted Mayer. "I got your God damn insulting note."

Mayer looked at The Little Tramp with disdain. "I don't know what in the fuck you're talking about. Are you drunk?"

"Take off your God damn glasses," Charlie demanded. When Mayer complied, handing them to a waiter, Charlie socked him.

A big mistake. A former junkyard dealer in Haverhill, Massachusetts, Mayer had handled a lot of heavy metal in his day. With one fist he plowed into Charlie's face, sending him sprawling backward into a potted palm with a bloody nose.

A newspaper reporter just happened to witness the incident, and tomorrow's headlines would hear of this "fistic encounter," as it was called, with Charlie clearly the loser and the humiliated one, as he was so often in his films.

Rescuing Charlie from the pot, I took him to the toilet where, with the help of a black attendant, we got him cleaned up and ready to go upstairs to confront the second battered party of the evening, Mary Miles Minter.

Back in the restaurant, I found that Charlie had left me the tab, a trick no doubt learned from the Prince of Wales. Sitting quietly and alone, I finished my steak and even ordered dessert, a baked Alaska.

For me, the evening was rescued by Jack

Pickford. He was highly amused at what had happened between Charlie and Mayer, and invited me to join Olive and him for a three-way back at their home. "I know you don't like to fuck women," he whispered, "but while I'm going down on Olive, you can go down on me. Then when I fuck her, you can eat my ass."

That was such a delectable invitation I couldn't turn it down. I promised I'd meet them outside after tipping the waiter. After my little session with Olive and Jack, I planned to call on either William Boyd, Richard Dix, or Antonio Moreno, depending on who was available. If none of the above, then Ramon Novarro. As for Rodolfo, who knew where he was? The obvious answer was in the arms of Natacha Rambova.

As Durango, I also had returned the call of Tom Ince with a promise to get together. I hoped that he would offer me two opportunities—a picture I could appear in, even if a bit part, and a chance to get fucked in the ass.

Mayer, who had returned to the table with Mildred Harris, got up and took her hand. Linked arm and arm, he escorted her by my table. Mayer ignored me and would never speak to me again until I'd become a powerful gossip columnist and he'd been forced to deal with me. On the other hand, Harris looked at me with contempt. "You're disgusting," she said, before exiting with Mayer, the future head of Metro-Goldwyn-Mayer.

Except for her screen appearances, which would be frequent throughout the Twenties until she started playing uncredited roles in the Thirties and Forties, I would never encounter Mildred Harris again except once.

It was on the set of *Night Nurse* in 1931, when I'd been assigned to interview its two emerging co-stars, Barbara Stanwyck and my former trick, Clark Gable.

At first Mildred didn't recognize me, and she'd changed enormously. All those years with the bottle hadn't improved her looks but had made her so much mellower. She spoke nostalgically of Charlie, claiming she still loved him. "That one-hundred thousand dollars he gave me in the divorce didn't last long," she said. "Not after my attorneys took their cut. Within a year I was bankrupt, and as you well know

that career that looked so promising for me in 1918 didn't happen either."

Although she'd remarried and had given birth to a son, Mildred Harris had become reduced to acting as a foil for The Three Stooges. I last saw her on the screen in 1944 in an uncredited role as the wife of a marine colonel in a film called *Hail the Conquering Hero*. She died in Hollywood that same year. The newspapers blamed her death on pneumonia but I knew the real reason was acute alcoholism.

Once and for no reason at all in 1951, I went to the Abbey of the Palms memorial burial grounds in Los Angeles. In case anyone's interested, what's left of this once-beautiful film star lies in her dusty tomb, number 740, second corridor on the left.

*****

At long last just when it appeared that stardom would never come to Rodolfo, his lucky break came. He'd been thinking of giving up films—or as he put it, "films gave up on me"—and returning to Italy to become a farmer.

Metro had purchased the film rights to *The Four Horsemen of the Apocalypse* by Vicente Blasco Ibáñez. The four horsemen in the title, of course, stood for Conquest, War, Famine, and Death. The novel released in 1918 was a sweeping epic covering the tragic events of the First World War, as they affected the lives of a Spanish family living in Argentina. The family had inter-married with the French and the Germans, so the war raging in Europe divided their loyalties.

The book had been eagerly read by Rodolfo, in Spanish no less, and he felt he was an ideal choice to play the role of Julio Desnoyers.

He was already in New York filming another one of those forgettable Valentino films, this time co-starring Margaret Namara. Again, he was cast as a heavy. The film was entitled *The Great Moment*, but it was hardly that for him, even though he was making $350 a week, his highest salary ever.

In some releases the picture was called *The*

Wonderful Chance. In it, Rodolfo played a gang leader in a straw boater. He had a cigarette dangling from his mouth through a lot of the picture, and the mustache he'd grown made him look Chaplinesque.

When he wasn't needed on the set of that picture, he went to the Metro offices in New York, where he met the production manager, Maxwell Karger, and virtually begged him to cast him in the part of Julio. Karger informed him that some of the biggest male stars in Hollywood coveted the part, and he also told Rodolfo how disappointed he'd been in some of his other film work. "Stick to playing heavies," Karger had said. "You're lucky to get work."

That night Rodolfo called from New York telling me how bitter it was to return to the city that had been the scene of so much humiliation and defeat for him. Once there he'd had to face the most painful loss of his lackluster film career, the role of Julio. Apparently, other people at Metro agreed with Karger's harsh assessment. One assistant, Jeffrey Koeher, was quoted as saying, "I can't see a heavy like Valentino playing a romantic and sensitive youth with innocent charm."

Not knowing of my connection with Rodolfo, Antonio Moreno spent virtually every night back in Los Angeles discussing his dream of playing Julio himself. "I'm the only real Spanish male star in Hollywood," he said. "That role has Moreno written all over it."

When I wasn't in Antonio's bed, I heard a different type of pillow talk from Ramon Novarro. He claimed, "I was born to play Julio. The role will make a big movie star of me." It probably would if Ramon had been cast in the part.

Rodolfo called again the following night, and I could immediately detect the dejection and disappointment in his voice. One of the films he'd made with Mae Murray, *The Delicious Little Devil*, had opened in New York. Even though a co-star, Rodolfo's name wasn't on the marquee. "Only one newspaper mentioned me," he said. "The reviewer wrote, 'A young Rudolph Valentino appears opposite Mae Murray in the picture.' That was it! That was all he said. Not even a vicious attack."

All was not lost, I was to learn. The very next night, when Rodolfo was in his greatest despair and almost suicidal, the most important phone call of his life came into his hotel. It was from June Mathis, inviting him to the Metro office the following morning.

One of the most important women script writers in the history of Hollywood, and the most powerful, Mathis had seen Rodolfo in *The Eyes of Youth*, cast opposite Clara Kimball Young. Mathis had written the script for *The Four Horsemen of the Apocalypse*.

Rodolfo didn't sleep all night and arrived an hour early at the Metro office in New York. He was dressed in a blue serge suit with a white silk handkerchief, a gift from his late mother, in his lapel pocket. In a pale gray Homburg, a Chesterfield overcoat, and a white silk scarf, he cut a dashing figure walking through the snow flurries of New York.

At the Metro office, Mathis didn't say anything at first, but looked him up and down, then took him by the hand and led him into Karger's office, scene of his earlier rejection. "Max," she said, looking over at Rodolfo, "we have found our Julio."

Rodolfo was overjoyed. Obviously Mathis had approved of what she'd seen.

Metro assigned the young, adventuresome, and creative Rex Ingram to direct the picture. He had already selected Alice Terry, his fiancée, as the female star of the film. Ironically, Rodolfo had been the lover of Terry when they'd appeared as extras together in the film, *Alimony*. Again, Hollywood continued to be a small town of coincidences.

Ingram bitterly opposed the casting of Rodolfo, preferring a well-known leading man of his day, Carlyle Blackwell, for the role of Julio. Terry pushed for Rodolfo, and Mathis stood her ground. Over violent protests from many officials at Metro, Rodolfo finally got the part at the same salary he'd been making in New York: $350 a week.

When I later met Mathis in Hollywood, I found her to be a plain, even an ugly woman. I suspected Rodolfo had engaged in the same type of casting couch audition he'd done so well with Julian Eltinge. Rodolfo adamantly denied that, however, and accused me of not having the faith to believe that a hawkeye like Mathis would select him for his acting talent "and not this thick dick I carry around with me."

Before returning to Los Angeles, Rodolfo called me for a final time. This time he was hysterical, with a kind of stage fright, fearing that he would photograph badly in a major release film because of his physical defects—a cauliflower ear and a scar on his face. As a villain, that was all right but he feared his appearance would work against him as a romantic lead. Mathis, he claimed, had already tried to assure him that these so-called defects would only add character to the role of Julio. But Rodolfo wasn't so sure that American women would "accept a scar face."

Rodolfo's fears were in vain. As filming began, there was a buzz at Metro after only the first week of shooting. Rodolfo, according to witnesses, was acting and photographing brilliantly. In no small way he was aided by the great cameraman, John Seitz, the same man who photographed Gloria Swanson so fantastically in 1949 in *Sunset Boulevard* when she told DeMille she was ready for her closeup.

Even though Ingram was photographing the fragile beauty of Alice Terry behind gauze, Rodolfo was clearly stealing the picture from her. Mathis convinced the powers at Metro to enlarge Julio's role. Each day Ingram felt the film was becoming less and less a vehicle for Alice Terry and more and more a showcase for Valentino.

Garbed as a gaucho, dancing the tango, or in the trenches as a war-weary soldier, it was clear that Valentino was the rider in control of *The Four Horsemen*. The picture was running up costs of $800,000, a staggering amount of money in those days, setting off alarm bells in the office of Marcus Loew, Metro's major stockholder.

Even though impressed with Rodolfo's performance in the film, or what he'd seen of it, Loew was still skeptical, not believing Rodolfo could ever be developed into a major star. "Can you imagine Mary Pickford falling for a guy like Valentino?" he asked Mathis. "Richard Barthelmess maybe, but not Valentino."

When I was allowed to visit the set, I encountered Bridgetta Clark, who used to live next door to Maria Jane and me in Lawrence, Kansas. It was Bridgetta's letter to Maria Jane, inviting us to Hollywood, that sent me rushing off on the Sante Fe. Bridgetta had also arranged for Rodolfo to become my roommate. In the film, she played Julio's mother.

Since I'd arrived in Hollywood and had fallen into a man-trap, I had sadly neglected Bridgetta but tried to make up for it. I invited her to lunch where over a turkey sandwich, she confronted me. "I was shocked to read in the paper that you have a sister calling herself Lotte Lee. I've known Maria Jane all my life, and she never mentioned any daughter to me."

"It was a scandal she wanted to conceal." I lied. "Lotte is only my half sister. One time Maria Jane, otherwise a God-fearing Christian woman, made a big mistake, one she lived to regret the rest of her life, fearing it would deny her entrance into Heaven. My father never found out. I can't stand talking about it."

Bridgetta leaned over and kissed me on the cheek, taking my hand and holding it fondly to give me comfort. "I understand, you dear boy. I wish Lotte well."

During the thirteen weeks it took to film the horsemen picture, Antonio ranted nightly that he hated Valentino. He still hadn't learned of my own involvement with the emerging star. "I am Julio," he would shout. "The role belonged to me—a real Spaniard—and not some immigrant WOP."

In another case of a dashed dream, Ramon got a call from Metro to appear the next day on the set of *The Four Horsemen*. That was during the first week of shooting when Metro had not announced the casting of Rodolfo. Ramon went into hysterics of joy, immediately assuming he'd been summoned to Metro to sign a contract to play Julio. "I've got the part," he'd shouted at me over the phone and between sobs of sheer delight.

Regrettably, when he'd shown up at Metro, he learned he had been wanted to play an extra in the film. He'd also learned that Julio would be played by his sometimes lover, Rodolfo. I own a still from that film, showing the two of them in the same frame. Apparently, it was the only picture ever taken of them together, as they preferred to meet in secret over the next few years. Decades into the future, Ramon would deny over talk radio that he had ever met Valentino, which can be filed with Gloria Swanson's denial that she ever fucked Valentino.

After the third week, Ingram invited Rodolfo and Alice Terry along with Bridgetta and me to see the rushes.

The moment Rudolph appeared on the screen in a closeup that would make Lillian Gish envious, I knew that a new star had been born. His glistening white teeth were clenched around a cigarillo, and in the words of one observer, "the smoke puffed boldly down his nostrils like a stud stallion on a frosty morning."

Rodolfo handled a cigarette on screen like no one before or since in film history. Forget all that Bette Davis huffing and puffing. Rodolfo taught the world how to smoke a cigarette with sex and sensuality. His only rival in that department in the years ahead would be Marlene Dietrich. If only the two of them could have appeared together with cigarillos aglow on the silver screen!

Every emotion seemed to flicker over Rodolfo's olive-toned skin. There was male sexual energy on screen like I'd never seen it before, certainly not in the roles played by Bobby Harron, Charles Ray, Norman Kerry, and the like. Rudolph Valentino up there on that screen was irresistible, as if there were something illicit about him. In a scene with Alice Terry, he kissed a lump of sugar before dropping it into her tea, and I sighed.

It was the tango dance I'll always remember, knowing how good he was at it, having watched him in the light of a dying afternoon with Mae Murray. Dressed as a gaucho with a flat-rimmed hat, Rodolfo lit up the screen with his costume, a loose blouse with vest and wide, floppy black pants tucked into shiny boots.

Seeing a tango dancer he likes, he heads for the dance floor, cutting in on an outclassed male extra as the camera moves in on Rodolfo. Even the slightly natural droop he always had over his right eyelid was perfect for the role, establishing his woman-killing menace qualities. When the man protested, Julio removes his coiled stock whip to crack the air. He grabbed his prize and guided his woman of choice into a lazy tango, clasping her tightly to his body. At one point he inserted his leg between hers like he was humping her. Spinning, twirling, dipping, and bending, Valentino was clearly making film history. In years to come Fred Astaire or Gene Kelly would dance on screen. Valentino's tango wasn't about dance—it was about sex.

At the end of the dance, he pressed his lips brutally over his female partner's. Even before the picture's release, I could just imagine the swoons of millions of women around the world—and gay men too. Rodolfo would appeal to homosexuals as much as he did to women.

As the rushes ended, I sat in a daze in the darkened booth. I was so stunned by what I'd seen on the screen I could hardly speak. The face projected on that screen was different from all other cinema faces. Unique, Rodolfo looked like no other star. In the decades to come, the same would be said of such stars as Robert Mitchum, Audrey Hepburn, and Lauren Bacall. Unlike many actors of his day, Rodolfo was not overly powdered, overly mascaraed, or overly lipsticked.

That very night after watching the rushes, I returned to the cottage with Rodolfo. It was to be our final night there. After the death of his daughter, Dr. Hutchison had asked me to move, claiming he was going to sell the property and didn't want to see me again. In some vague way, I think he suspected that Rodolfo might have seduced his daughter and contributed in some way to her death.

All through the night I worshipped Rodolfo's body with my lips and tongue, not knowing when I'd get a chance at it again. I feared I would lose him soon if I hadn't already. Not just to Natacha Rambova, but to his future stardom.

When morning came, he got up early and made coffee for us, the final cup we'd enjoy in our rose-covered cottage. Over coffee, I invited him to move into the suite at the Hollywood Hotel with me, forgetting for the moment that I was directly across the hall from his wife, Jean Acker, if she could indeed be called that. He turned me down, saying that Natacha had made "living arrangements" for him. I noted that he didn't give me his new address.

"Hollywood is a small town," he told me, "and I can't let it be known that I'm living with a man, especially in a hotel. There was a lot of talk about Norman Kerry and me doing that at the Alexandria, and I can't allow gossip like that to harm my future career. When I was a struggling actor, it was different. I'm even going to stop seeing Norman. I don't need him any more. If anything, his own career is in trouble, especially with his showing up drunk all the time."

"What you're also saying is you don't need me any more either," I said, tears welling in my eyes. He was the only man in the world who could break my heart, and he was doing just that.

"I'll still drop around from time to time," he said. "We'll still be friends, even lovers at times. From now on, it will be only a sometime thing between us. No waiting up for each other at night. I'll be with Natacha every night she wants me. If she doesn't want to be with me one night, who knows? You might get lucky."

"So she'll be your future fuckmate?" I asked with a certain contempt in my voice, even though I feared that was the worst note to sound at a time like this.

"That's not part of our life yet," he said, although I wasn't convinced.

Dressed in a business suit, he surveyed the cottage for one final time. "This has been our happy nest. We've known good times here. But right now I've got to report to the studio. I'm making a picture *Unchartered Seas*, with Alice Lake. Wesley Ruggles is the director. The flicker's pretty trivial, about some gold-hunters heading north to Alaska. At least I don't play the villain and I win the hand of Miss Lake in the final reel." As an afterthought, he turned and looked back at me. "Anything happening in your career?"

"Not much," I said. "Joe Godsol is taking me to Paris to try to get a continental release for *Vampira*."

"Too bad about your sister's film," he said. "I heard she's skipped town in embarrassment. Sorry I didn't get to meet her."

I smiled at that, regretting that his parting words to me were a lie. He not only had met my "sister," he'd gone to bed with her. "Are you still seeing Swanson?"

"No, she smells funny," he said. "I'll see her only if we make a picture together. Natacha says I may get cast opposite Nazimova in *Camille*. Who knows at this point?"

"What about Mae Murray?" I asked.

"Mae and I will always be friends," he said.

"And Jean Acker?"

"She's dead for me," he said. "We're getting a divorce. I've asked Natacha to marry me."

That didn't come as a surprise to me, although it hurt to hear him actually say it.

"Don't worry about work for yourself," he said. "I'll help you out from time to time. We'll keep in touch."

He didn't know and I hadn't told him that I had become independently wealthy. If my plans worked out, I might end up owning a block of Los Angeles real estate with the money I'd picked up from Goldwyn.

"One day there will be a knock on the door of the Hollywood Hotel, and your Rodolfo will be there for you."

"I'll wait for that moment."

He winked at me like he'd winked at Alice Terry in a scene from *The Four Horsemen*.

And then he was gone.

*****

Forgetting about Rodolfo was made easier for me when I was welcomed into the arms of Theodore Kosloff, William Boyd, and Antonio Moreno, with Ramon Novarro occasionally tossed in on the side. All of these men were great lovers, but none of them hit the spot like Rodolfo. But what did I really need with a self-enchanted actor who spent as much time gazing in mirrors as he did looking at me? I also felt there was little future in chasing after a man who went around proposing marriage to lesbians.

I tried to forget about Rodolfo as I packed my possessions and moved out of the cottage, putting all my stuff into my suite at the Hollywood Hotel. I could easily afford the cost of the suite even though Goldwyn had stopped paying for it. Obviously Goldwyn thought he'd given me enough money.

After an initial invitation to me as Durango, Tom Ince had called back and abruptly cancelled. I guess he'd changed his mind. Back at the Hollywood Hotel I received another call from him, letting me know he wanted to see me after all. This time I turned him down, using my immediate departure as an excuse. "It's probably not a good idea anyway," Ince said. "That tall, statuesque sister of yours has put a lot of crazy ideas in my mind, stuff I shouldn't really be thinking about. It's all crazy. I'm not into a lot of the shit she was talking about."

"I've got an idea," I told Ince. "Think about it while I'm in Paris and we'll get together when I get back. You don't have Lotte, but you've got me, and you're the one man in Hollywood who can get me a job every now and then. I'd really appreciate that."

"I'll do my best," he said. "I could get a lot of roles for you if you weren't so God damn pretty. You're so fucking pretty that to bring you on the screen almost requires some explanation. Tell me the truth. Doesn't everybody you meet comment on how pretty you are? You're not handsome. Tom Ince is handsome. You're fucking beautiful. Hell, you're even more beautiful than Lotte Lee, and she was the prettiest gal ever to hit Hollywood."

"Then make a star out of me."

"I'll think about it," he said. "But there's one hitch."

"What's that?" I asked.

"Have you ever heard of the casting couch?" he asked.

"I certainly have and I can't wait to lie on it."

"I'll be dusting it off while you're in Paris," he promised. With that pronouncement, he put down the phone. Not even a wish for bon voyage.

In the late afternoon, I found I was packed and ready for Paris. Godsol and I were to take the train from Los Angeles to New York where we'd sail for Europe, as Jack Pickford, Olive Thomas, and Owen Moore had so recently done. Before departing, Jack had informed me that Owen would be on a spending spree, as his sister Mary had recently settled one-hundred thousand dollars on Owen to get rid of him.

At ten o'clock I was supposed to pick up Marion Davies and drive her to the home of Godsol where I'd been told that a "surprise" waited for me. Calling Richard Dix, I invited him to the Ship Café for dinner. I was growing

fonder of him all the time. I figured we could have an early dinner and go back to the Hollywood Hotel for a little intimate get-together, and I'd still have time to drive out to Santa Monica and pick up Marion.

After Richard Dix accepted my invitation, I called Richard Barthelmess for a final adieu, promising to bring him a lovely gift from France. Later in the evening, after I'd left Godsol's home, and dropped Marion off, I wanted to spend the rest of the time before my train departure in the arms of Antonio. According to Kono, Charlie was already engaged, having dinner that evening with his new love, Florence Deshon, while pumping his iodine-coated dick to Mary Miles Minter on the side.

As I was getting dressed for dinner, the head receptionist at the hotel called up, announcing that Wallace Reid had arrived and would like to come up to my suite. I told him to send Mr. Reid up. When Wally arrived, he came into my sitting room and reached out for me, sobbing and taking me in his arms. "I've not come here for any love-making," he said. "I want to be held. I desperately need a friend, and you're it."

He lay on the sofa with me for at least thirty minutes as I held him tenderly stroking his hair. "I don't have anybody to turn to. Dorothy doesn't understand me at all. All she does is criticize me. She complains about all the people who hang on to me. I make loans to them all the time. They never pay me back. They're just using me. Dorothy is using me too. She's only interested in my money and her own career. The studio is using me, rushing me from one picture to the other and not paying me enough."

At one point Wally volunteered that I could use him if I wanted to, but he feared he might not be much good to me as a stud. "More and more I can't get it up," he said. "I fear I'm becoming impotent. The other night Dorothy wanted me to go to bed with her, and I did. Nothing happened. She played with me for a long time, and I managed to rise an inch or two, and then I lost my hard-on. What's happening? Do you think it's stress?"

I feared it was a combination of both stress and his increasing drug dependency. Before leaving the hotel, I told him I'd never use him sexually unless he wanted love from me.

"But we had a deal," he said. "I'm a man of honor. You'll see that I am."

When he left, he kissed me for a long time at the door. He never mentioned the death of Elizabeth Hutchison, and I too would never speak of that night again. It was as if she'd never lived. What could have exploded into one of Hollywood's biggest scandals died with a whimper. I never knew what Dr. Hutchinson thought. I was certain that he'd examined his daughter and suspected she'd been having intercourse at the time of her death. If he suspected Wallace Reid, or even Rodolfo, I knew he did not want to taint the memory of his beloved daughter, or have a police investigation lead to the discovery that he was supplying morphine to Wally. It was a story that was never to be told, until now.

Later, dinner at the Ship Café with Richard Dix had gone beautifully. We'd not only enjoyed a good steak, but were so star struck that we delighted dining in an atmosphere where movie stars paraded in and out. After dinner, I paid the bill and headed out the side door into the parking lot.

Suddenly, I spotted Rodolfo arriving in his car with a passenger. He didn't see me, and I slipped behind an automobile taking Richard with me. I told him to be quiet.

Rodolfo's passenger wasn't a woman. I'd anticipated Natacha Rambova. As Rodolfo stepped into the porch light of the café, I noticed he was wearing a suit tailor made for him, and looked stunning the way a rising star at Metro should.

The other figure got out of the car slowly. It was a man but I couldn't make out his features until he too emerged into the light of the café. His face looked strangely familiar but I couldn't place it. It was only after the two men had gone into the café, and I had driven off with Richard, did I remember where I'd seen that man before. He was the fake German baron who'd spied on Gloria Swanson and Rodolfo in the Hollywood Hills, and the former patron of Rodolfo in New York during his hustling days.

After depositing Richard with a good night kiss, and a promise to get together as soon as I returned from Paris, I drove into Santa Monica where I picked up Marion Davies. She was all bubbles and giggles, and seemed liberated to have W.R. back on the east coast for a few weeks.

As we turned a corner on Sunset Boulevard, she looked behind to a large black automobile following us. "W.R. is having me followed," she squealed with delight. "He's spying on me."

Instead of being angry, she seemed to delight in the chase, almost as if we were playing cowboys chasing Indians on the silent screen.

"Quick," she shouted to me as we turned a curve. "Turn into that driveway real fast."

I madly swerved the car, almost wrecking it, and turned into the driveway of some unknown mansion, cutting off my lights. Marion looked back and on the highway spotted W.R.'s boys rushing by in mad pursuit of us.

"Let's wait about ten minutes until they have long gone," she said. "Then let's go on to Joe's. It'll be fun for both of us. As I told you, he's lined up a very special prize for you this evening."

While we waited, I invited Marion out of the car and lit a cigarette for her, enjoying one myself on the darkened grounds of this newly built Hollywood mansion. Stars were just beginning to erect lavish mansions along the boulevard. Maybe Harold Lloyd or some other big star lived here. I took in the mansion carefully, almost fantasizing that it belonged to me.

I realized I could have bought it with the money Goldwyn had settled on me, but I preferred business real estate in downtown Los Angeles. I truly believed I might never get another load of money. I would continue to live modestly in hotels, investing whatever money I earned into tangible assets for my old age, as the mother of the Gish sisters had warned me.

As I smoked the rest of my cigarette and looked at the mansion, it made an indelible impression on me. I never found out who lived there, but in 1950 I saw it photographed to perfection in the film, *Sunset Boulevard*, starring Gloria Swanson. Long before William Holden, the co-star of that Billy Wilder film, drove his car into that driveway to escape his creditors, Marion and I found refuge in that same driveway fleeing from W.R.'s spies.

When we finally arrived a little late at Godsol's mansion, he was waiting for us and his servants had prepared a late-night spread for us. As always, his bar was fully stocked.

As a maid helped Marion remove her wrap and directed her to the ladies' room, Godsol whispered to me, "Enjoy yourself tonight, kid. I've got to pay all my attention to Marion. Don't be disappointed. I've arranged for you to have fun too. As for me, you'll have me in that train compartment all the way to New York. Once there, I'll have to devote my attention to showgirls. But you'll have me on that boat ride across the pond all the way to Paris where I'll have to give the showgirls a break again." With that, he was gone, rushing to bestow a kiss on Marion, newly emerged from the toilet.

I headed for the bar, drawn there not only by the urgent need for a whiskey but by the waiter behind the counter. He was so strikingly handsome that he evoked an actor who would emerge in the years ahead, namely Rory Calhoun, who would one day appear in *The River of No Return* with Marilyn Monroe and Robert Mitchum. I was certain the bartender was going to be my party favor of the evening. As he smiled and gently caressed my hand as he handed me my whiskey, I was convinced he was my date for the night.

"I saw that incredible car you and Miss Davies drove up in," he said. "It's fantastic. Mind if I look at it later?"

"Be my guest," I said.

"Hey, that's terrific," he said. "I'm all excited."

"I love the car too," I said. "I'll even let you drive it later. We'll go for a spin."

His eyes lit up as if I'd bestowed the greatest of all gifts upon him.

"My excitement is in meeting you," I said. "It's my last night in Los Angeles before heading all the way across country to New York. Joe and I are going to sail for Paris. I've never been to Europe before."

"Gosh, I've never been anywhere other than to San Diego," he said. "I wish you guys could take me with you."

"I wish we could too," I said. "I'm Durango Jones."

"I know who you are," he said. "I've seen your picture in the papers. I'm Brian Drummond."

"I bet you want to become a film star," I said. "You certainly have the looks for it."

"Thanks," he said, "but when it comes to looks, Durango Jones has every guy in Hollywood beat. Forget that Wallace Reid. He's no longer the handsomest man in town. You are."

I smiled into Brian's eyes. I'm going to make you eat those words later tonight."

A tap on the shoulder and I whirled around to face a young man introducing himself as Reginald Denning. "Joe says I'm to keep you entertained tonight, and here I am."

I cast a soulful eye at that delectable Brian Drummond before I was ushered away to a far corner of the living room to meet the real party favor of the evening.

Reginald was unlike any hunk I'd ever seduced before, completely different from Godsol's last party favor for me, Richard Dix, another actor whose recent explosion of cum had settled comfortably into my stomach.

Reginald spoke with a pronounced British accent. "I'm broke and I'm just doing this sort of thing to earn some extra money."

"A pretty boy's got to do what a pretty boy's got to do," I said, toasting him as Brian brought him a drink. Brian was cold and reserved in front of Reginald, but Brian's eyes danced when he gazed into my face.

Reginald had "star" written all over him, as did my last party favor, that athletic hunk, Richard Dix. But it was obvious to me that Richard and Reginald wouldn't compete for the same roles.

If anyone today still remembers the dashing and handsome Reginald Denny, they recall him as a Rex Harrison type. Reginald is known for his fabulous *My Fair Lady* success on the New York stage. On the late, late show he is still seen in a score of comedies playing a slightly foolish Englishman, or is depicted as "the other man," cast as the perfect gentleman who steps aside rather nobly in the final reel allowing the more dashing male co-star to carry the girl off into the sunset.

At the time I first met him, Reginald projected a completely different type—the strong, virile hero full of cum and vigor. A man of action. He was negotiating with Universal to appear in a series of "Leather Pusher" films, two-reelers which would be released in the early 20s.

Reginald played a boxer in black trunks which showed off his manly chest and a great set of legs, all resting under his handsome face with its striking Roman nose and lips almost too perfect to be on a man unless sculpted by Michelangelo. He also had beautiful eyes that would focus on you, making you think, if only for a moment, that you were the most important person in the world.

Amazingly in the years ahead, after those leather pusher films, Reginald became the rival of Doug Fairbanks on the screen. Depicting an ebullient and breezy personality, on screen as in real life, Reginald appeared in comedy after comedy that were popular at the box office. There was a difference, however. Doug's films were often fantasies, whereas those of Reginald were more down to earth.

With the advent of talkies, Reginald faced a problem. He had not lost that unmistakable accent of a brisk young Englishman. In silents he could play a strapping all-American youth. But in talkies the parts had to be doctored, identifying him from the very beginning as an Englishman, or at least someone from Canada.

Reginald and I eventually drifted off to the bedroom where I took pleasure in stripping him and sampling every inch of his beautiful body with my lips and tongue. That man tasted good. Unlike Richard Dix's more masculine aroma, Reginald tasted like he'd just emerged from a spring bath. With some reluctance he let me kiss him and with a lot of coaxing he finally stuck his tongue in my mouth, which I sucked like the sweet lollipop it was. That Reginald Denny tasted good.

At the very first, he told me he didn't let anybody fuck him. "I tried that once with John Barrymore. He's a great friend of mine. I didn't like it at all. John's a real animal. I ended up bleeding."

Reginald didn't really need to tell me what it was like to be fucked by John Barrymore. Been there, done that.

Before coming to Hollywood, he'd been the brigade heavyweight boxing champion of the Royal Flying Corps, and he'd even survived a mutiny aboard a United Fruit boat, the *Taloa*. I wanted to ask him how he knew John Barrymore, but was too polite to inquire.

Reginald finally agreed upon an "around-the-world," climaxing in a super-colossal Durango Jones blow-job special that caused him to erupt and explode in my mouth. After it was over, I felt a little awkward, thinking I had sexually exploited him when it was unnecessary to hire men to have sex with me. I had half of the hunks of Hollywood willing to give it away for free.

As I was putting on my clothes, a nude Reginald rose up on the bed. Did I detect that he was also rising again to his full mast of seven and a half rather thick inches? "It's just an idea I have," he said. "I've never done this before, and I may never do it again. My ambition is to marry some nice girl and settle down with her. But—just this once, never again—I want to fuck you. Just like John fucked me. But I won't make you bleed, will I?"

I didn't even answer him, but showed my willingness to participate by getting under him on the bed. Although he had some initial difficulty entering me, he later proved he was born to fuck. He'd obviously fucked before, many times, and was good at it, tantalizing me at one moment, plunging deeper in the next, then plowing in for the final rodeo ride to his climax. When it was all over and I was in the shower with him, washing his back and other private parts, he told me it was "just like fucking a woman, only much tighter."

Later, as we were dressing, I learned that Godsol was paying Reginald one hundred dollars for his masterful performance. I slipped him another fifty dollars out of sheer gratitude. He thanked me generously, although it was understood that we wouldn't be contacting each other again.

"This is not my usual line of work," he said to me, giving me a light kiss on the lips and thanking me for the money before disappearing into the night and whatever life Reginald Denny was living in his pre-fame days.

Except for his appearances on the screen, I would never see him again until I showed up to work on the set of *Sporting Youth* in 1923. My salary as an extra was ten dollars a day, a sum far less than what Reginald had earned for that encounter with me at Godsol's mansion.

In that film, I appeared with a heavy coating of Max Factor 28, which gave my pale complexion a dark, ruddy color. I'd lined my eyes with mascara and coated my mouth with heavy lipstick. I'd combed my blond hair until it was lustrous, put on a blue serge suit, and was set to appear in that picture directed by Harry Pollard. The script was similar to the auto-racing films starring Wallace Reid. The talk on the set that morning was that Reginald was going to replace Wally as the romantic lead.

When I encountered Reginald, he made no mention of our meeting several years previously in the bed of Godsol's mansion. His brief hustling period seemed a painful memory to him, I was certain, and I had no intention of reminding him. By then he was a big star, and I was still an extra.

He immediately told me that he was seething with frustration. He'd had a big fight early that morning with Pollard and wanted to walk off the picture. "Pollard doesn't have a well-defined comic sense," he said to me. "He plays everything too broad."

Pollard, or so I heard that morning, was furious that the female co-star part hadn't gone to his wife, Margarita Fischer. Reginald had insisted on Laura La Plante, a beautiful blonde and the reigning female star at Universal.

Reginald seemed to want to get rid of me, and quickly pushed me off onto Miss La Plante who was charming and gracious in her blue-eyed way. By then I was used to meeting reigning movie queens, blonde or otherwise. I'd always been impressed with her beauty, as shown to the public as Tom Mix's leading lady and as the daughter in the *Bringing Up Father* series. Her girl-next-door charm was against the fashion of the day. She'd been fed on corn and milk, and, unlike Theda Bara, did not pretend to have friends who were vampires in Transylvania.

La Plante, though charming, was the single most inarticulate actress I'd ever met. She steadfastly remained the simple girl she was,

ignoring fads and fashions. In the ambition-crazed hurricane of Hollywood, she was like a refreshing, but not threatening, spring breeze.

Like me, she came from the Middle West. Born in St. Louis, Missouri, she'd known poverty and hard times, and had struggled in films since 1919 until she'd achieved stardom in the jazz age. I had recently seen her in *The Ramblin' Kid* where she'd played Hoot Gibson's Eastern-bred sweetheart. She'd even been a Wampas Baby Star.

But her big break was just going before the camera, and that was *Sporting Youth*. In all my years, I've never met a star like Laura La Plante. Unlike Gloria Swanson or Mary Pickford, she appeared neither egomaniacal or financially greedy. "I need the money," she said. "A job is a job whether it's being a movie star or being a housewife. Movie stars are just like anybody else except they got lucky."

Miss La Plante was called to the set and excused herself. "Oh, by the way," she said. "Reg is a real sweet guy. He's got a nice wife, too. Would you like to meet her? She's coming our way."

I didn't look back as I had little intention of meeting Mrs. Reginald Denny, although I knew from first-hand experience she was getting properly plowed by her husband.

I worked all day on that picture and did indeed collect my ten dollars at the end, but not much of me appeared in the final cut. A brief glimpse of the back of my head, and with a bad haircut at that. After *Sporting Youth*, I changed barbers.

While memories of Reginald Denny danced in my head, the Bitch of Buchenwald interrupted me, warning angrily that I was getting ahead of my story.

Back to Godsol's mansion. Marion sent word to me that I was to go home and that a chauffeur would deliver her back to Santa Monica. Glad to be freed of the escort assignment, I headed for my "stagecoach." In the back seat I encountered a sleepy Brian Drummond. "I'm ready for that spin you promised me."

I drove him directly to the Hollywood Hotel. Once there, I looked into his dreamy blue eyes and invited him up to my suite. "Thought you'd never ask," he said.

That early morning romp in the hay with Brian was a refreshing change of pace. After all, I didn't always have to confine my fucking to stars or future stars. A young man destined to work as an extra could be fun too.

*****

City of light, city of dreams, I'd made it to Paris. I'd even seen New York. Although Godsol on the train ride across America split me open every night and at least two times during the day, I arrived in New York reasonably intact. At least John Barrymore thought so.

As for Godsol, I didn't see him until we were ready to sail for Paris. He claimed during his time in New York he'd battered ten showgirls. If most men told me that, I wouldn't believe them. In Godsol's case, I was a believer.

Sea air must have agreed with Godsol. On the transatlantic crossing, he was a battering ram. He'd fucked the juice out of me so many times I had to consume extra protein to replenish my supply. Godsol claimed he'd ruined me for all other men, a reference to the "milk bottle" he carried between his legs. That would certainly be true in the case of Jack Pickford or Owen Moore. If either of them penetrated me, I would hardly feel it.

Godsol had arranged for a guide for me, a handsome French boy whose physicality evoked that of Alain Delon as he'd appeared—decades later—in *Purple Noon*. This charming Frenchman spent the next three days showing me his Paris and acquainting me with all his body parts. As for Godsol, he just disappeared during the whole time, not even coming back to our suite at the Ritz Hotel.

Over breakfast on the fourth morning, a note was delivered on my tray. It was from Olive Thomas, telling me that she'd returned from the châteaux country with Owen Moore and her husband, Jack, a real gathering of the extended Pickford family, or at least some in-law branch of it.

I didn't know then if Mary Pickford's divorce from Owen had come through. Olive's main concern seemed to be to reach Godsol. Apparently, she'd called the Ritz and had left repeated messages for him, none of which had been returned. She wanted me to come by her suite at ten that morning to see her. Her note sounded desperate.

It was with great reluctance I had to cancel my date with the Alain Delon look-alike when he came by the suite at nine. However, I saw to it that he got his day's pay. Before leaving the suite, he certainly earned it as I was particularly sex crazed that day. I'd found myself missing the pounding I'd received from Godsol on the train and the ship.

At ten o'clock I was ushered by a French maid into the suite of Olive Thomas who was having her breakfast alone. Apparently, both Jack and Owen were sobering up from a particularly raucous night on the town.

Dressed entirely in white, she was a vision of loveliness. She'd just made *The Flapper* and it was playing to packed houses across America. Studio executives were predicting that Olive would become the reigning queen of the screen in the 1920s. Before sailing to Paris she'd completed *Everybody's Sweetheart*, and it too, or so it was believed, was headed for big success at the box office.

Over coffee she told me she was hysterical over the disappearance of Godsol. Personally I thought he'd run off with some showgirls from the Folies Bergère but she feared he'd been abducted.

"Joe has fucked over a lot of people in Paris." she said. "Really swindled them and that goes for the French government. I think we should go to the police. For all we know, he might be dead."

Since I didn't really believe that, I tried to reassure her that he was all right, vaguely remembering that he'd told me he had some important business to attend to and would be back at the Ritz "in a few days." That bit of information plucked from my inventory of lies seemed to ease Olive's concern for a brief few hours, at least enough time to allow us to go shopping.

At lunch at Maxim's, Olive confided in me the way two loving sisters might, or at least two friendly girl friends. She didn't seem to relate to me as a man but treated me like a woman. I thought I'd better check my appearance in one of the thousand mirrors at Maxim's. Had I not gotten out of my Lotte Lee drag?

"The press wrote how happy Jack and I looked when we sailed from New York," she said. "Still America's most ideal couple. As for Owen, he stayed below. We didn't want to explain why Jack was sailing with his estranged brother-in-law, right in the midst of a messy divorce from his beloved sister."

Before the appetizer was served, Olive had confided her entire plan, which would begin with a divorce from Jack Pickford. She claimed that Godsol had fallen "desperately in love with me." As far as I could detect, the reality of the situation was the exact opposite of what she'd described. It was she who had fallen desperately in love with Godsol.

Filled with schoolgirl fantasies, she said that after her divorce and subsequent remarriage, Godsol had promised to devote the years ahead not only to making love to her but "making me the biggest star ever to set foot in Hollywood." She reached to take my hand, clinging to it with a kind of desperation. Not seeming to know what she was doing, she dug her nails into my hand. I'd never seen her so agitated. She was talking about a glorious life waiting for her, but her physical actions seemed just the opposite of such a hope. She was a bundle of barely controlled hysteria.

I learned she was going to file for that divorce from Jack on her return to America. "He doesn't know what I'm going to do. I'm telling him tonight. I've got stuff on the Pickfords that would ruin them and destroy Mary's career. It's blackmail but I want money—a lot of money." A steely determination came across her face. "Owen settled for one-hundred thousand dollars. I'm demanding three million. If I don't get it, Mary Pickford is cinema history. Dust, baby. Jack, my darling heroin addict of a husband, is so easy to destroy he's almost not worth bothering with."

Alarmed, I asked her, "Does Jack even have an inkling of what you're planning to do?"

"He's too drugged most of the time to suspect anything," she said. "He doesn't even know about my plans to wed Godsol. Tonight when I confront Jack, I won't tell him either. The talk will be only about money. Olive Thomas is not only going to be the biggest star in Hollywood but she's also going to become one of the richest women in America. Mary is going to pay so much her hair will become uncurled."

As we walked along rue du Faubourg-St-Honoré, Olive was inspired by her upcoming dream—to marry Godsol, to become Hollywood's brightest star, and to loot Mary Pickford's bank account. I wasn't even certain that Mary had three-million dollars stashed away, but Olive assured me she did.

At three o'clock, she called the Ritz Hotel to see if Godsol had returned or left a message. So far, nothing. Covering her disappointment, she spent the next half hour discussing Godsol's sexual prowess. "He's got the world's biggest cock. It's at least eight inches thick and a foot long."

From personal experience I knew she was exaggerating just a bit there—not about the thickness but about the length. She'd obviously never seen the cock attached to one Francis X. Bushman.

"After going to bed with Joe," she said, "how could I ever be satisfied with Jack again? If he ever penetrated me again, it would be no more than a pin prick." I felt she was being a bit unkind to Jack. He was hung like any normal man, maybe with an inch to spare. Of course, he wasn't in Godsol's league but he was no midget either. A lot of women would be satisfied by the prick of Jack Pickford but I wasn't going to challenge her on that point.

As we continued to purchase more clothing than either of us really needed, I felt we shared some strange bond, although of what nature I could not divulge. Olive Thomas and I were probably the only two people in Hollywood who knew the private parts of both Jack Pickford and Joe Godsol, as those two didn't move in the same sexual circles.

It was in the early evening that I came to realize what had been obvious but had escaped me up to now. Olive Thomas was a hopeless cocaine addict, her husband preferring heroin.

Back at the hotel, there still was no message from Godsol. Jack and Owen had left a note before disappearing into what they called "the opium dens of Paris."

"Fuck Joe Godsol," she shouted. "Fuck

Jack Pickford. Fuck Owen Moore. They think only men can have fun in Paris and get into trouble. Olive Thomas can beat them on all fronts. You stay right here. I'll be ready in an hour." She slammed her bedroom door while I poured myself a whiskey. I knew she was not only going to get dressed but consume cocaine before emerging to go out on the town.

When she came out of her dressing room, she was almost inarticulate, her face dazed. She also seemed paranoid, claiming she feared that someone was lurking in the closet with a gun to assassinate her. "Mary may have learned that I'm going to blackmail her," she stammered, having a hard time getting the words out. "She is planning to have me murdered. I just know it. I may never leave Paris alive."

After I'd checked the apartment thoroughly, I assured her no one was there. She didn't believe me. The way she looked at me through her drug-induced haze, I suspected she didn't trust me either.

It was one of those wild Parisian nights that only happened in the Roaring Twenties. Forget the Folies Bergère. Olive wanted to plunge into the *bas-fonds*. Her love of gangsters drove her to the hangouts of the Parisian underworld. At both the Jockey and the Maldoror, two notorious dives of the time, she met the gangsters of her dreams.

At both clubs, especially the Jockey, she continued snorting cocaine. One tall man from Marseille exposed her breasts in the Jockey, kissing, fondling, and licking them, while his friend fingered Olive under the table, in effect masturbating her.

Back then the most notorious club in Paris, located in Montmartre, was called "The Dead Rat." If a couple, a threesome, or whatever, found someone in the main room they wanted to take to bed, there were some compartments in the back which could be rented for a few francs, the doors locked, and no questions asked. Both homosexual and heterosexuals patronized the dive. Enlisted men in the underpaid French armed forces often came here to earn extra money hustling among the rich Parisians, both men and women, who were patrons.

After about thirty minutes in the club, Olive disappeared with two men who looked more Algerian than typically French. She was in the compartment in the rear almost an hour with the two men. When she rejoined me, she claimed she'd had "the time of my life." Her consumption of alcohol, cocaine, and, I suspected, heroin continued throughout our night prowl. She didn't appear to be a woman desperately in love with Godsol. But then I knew I couldn't believe anything she said. She was completely deranged and growing crazier and more paranoid by the minute.

When she had me call the Ritz, I learned that Godsol had reappeared. Getting through to him, he ordered me "to get your ass back here. I'm having a party." He also told me he'd had great luck in getting *Vampira* distributed. He'd shown it to some French exhibitors, and they thought it would be a sensation on the continent, making millions. "Forget America, they told me. This film is going to make Lotte the biggest star in Hollywood. I'm also going to make her my mistress and take over the direction of her career from Goldwyn. I don't know where in the fuck she is. But you're going to find her and bring her back to Hollywood."

The question of Lotte Lee was tomorrow's problem for me. Right now I had to deal with Olive. I told her that Godsol had returned, and she demanded to be taken back to the Ritz at once to confront him about his disappearance. She also told me that later she was going to present her blackmail demands to Jack.

I begged her to wait until morning. "Jack will be in rough condition when he gets back from wherever he went with Owen. It's not the time for the two of you to negotiate anything. It's too explosive. Come on, Olive, you've had a lot of drugs. He has too."

Who in hell do you think you are?" she asked, turning on me in bitter rage. "I'm the biggest star in Hollywood. I know what I'm doing."

At the Ritz, she headed for the suite that I, at least in theory, shared with Godsol. As I turned the key and went inside, we were greeted with a wild party. The suite was packed with people, both Americans and French. It looked for a moment as if Godsol invited the entire crowd of patrons from the Moulin Rogue here.

Olive searched desperately for Godsol,

heading to our bedroom whose door was unlocked. I heard her scream as she rushed back into the living room of the suite. At the door I confronted her, trying to calm her. She slapped my face. "You've betrayed me too. Everybody's against me. Everybody's plotting against me. I'm not safe. They're going to kill me."

As she rushed down the hall, I ran after her. Catching up with her, I grabbed her arm. She turned and slapped me real hard again. "Get out of my life, you double-crossing faggot. I don't ever want to see you again."

Back in the suite, I wove my way through the party-goers and headed for our bedroom. There on the wide double bed, a nude Godsol was fucking a showgirl from the Lido, or at least I thought that's where he'd found her. Two other nude women lay on each side of him, playing with themselves as they waited their turn.

I closed the door to give them their privacy.

It was no dope for me that night but I consumed more than my fair share of alcohol before awakening to a persistent knocking on the door. I noticed it was nine o'clock in the morning. Everybody except one person among the party-goers had cleared out of the suite which was in shambles, with liquor glasses and empty bottles everywhere. I looked into the face of the nude man beside me. It was the Alain Delon look-alike tour guide. God knows what he had done that night.

One of the bellhops was delivering a Marconi Radiogram from Myron Selznick to Joe Godsol. I tipped him, then rushed into Godsol's bedroom to give him the message, thinking it might be important. The Lido girls had departed. A nude Godsol lay sprawled on the bed and cursed me for waking him up. "Read the fucking thing to me," Godsol said. "What in hell does that shit, Selznick, want?"

As I read the words, I could not believe them. Olive Thomas, barely alive and barely breathing, had been found that morning by a room service waiter. Her nude body was spread out on the floor on a sable opera cape. In her hand she clutched a bottle of toxic mercury bichloride granules, some of which she'd consumed. She'd been rushed to the American Hospital at Neuilly, where she was in a coma.

Searching Godsol's face for a reaction, he sighed, "Oh, shit," then turned over and fell back into a deep sleep.

At the hospital, I encountered Jack Pickford accompanied by Owen Moore. The story was just breaking around the world, and newsmen were hounding Jack wherever he went. He required police protection just to get to the hospital. Safely inside, he told me that French doctors held out little hope of Olive's recovery. "She's going to die any minute now," Jack said. "It's all over for her."

Dr. Joseph Lynn Choate, of Los Angeles, who'd been staying at the Hotel de la Grand-Bretagne in Paris, was a close friend of the Pickford family and had been summoned to the hospital for consultation. He told Jack, "Prepare yourself for her death." When I confronted Jack in a private room, I demanded to know what had happened early that morning. He was eager to learn of Olive's exploits the night before, particularly at "The Dead Rat," but would reveal nothing about what went on later in the suite at the Ritz. "Owen was passed out," Jack said. "What happened in those early morning hours is a secret between Olive and me. Olive won't be talking, and I'll take what really happened that night to my grave."

Five days later, following terrible suffering, a hospital spokesman announced that the American movie star, Miss Olive Thomas, wife of Jack Pickford and a Selznick Pictures star, was dead.

After questioning by the police, Jack was free to go. He invited me to sail to London with Owen and him, where we'd later book passage to cross the Atlantic again back to New York.

I agreed to go. First I returned to Godsol's suite. He was gone. I searched a little alcove where he kept his business papers. There I found his copy of *Vampira*, which he was going to have duplicated at a studio in Paris.

Packing my luggage I checked out of the hotel with what I believed was the last copy of Lotte Lee's *Vampira*. I kept it all through our London sojourn and half way across the Atlantic. Near the spot where the *Titanic* sank, I threw the film overboard, a decision I was to regret for the rest of my life.

Vampira was no more. Down to the bottom of the sea went the career of the film actress, Lotte Lee. I cried as I watched the film whirl through the air.

To this day, I secretly pray that somewhere and somehow one copy is still preserved. Perhaps it'll turn up in some old film house in Chicago or even Nebraska. I killed Lotte Lee but at the very moment I did I wanted to rescue her from a watery grave. Too late, my decision had been made. I turned from looking at that sea that had claimed so many lives among the *Titanic* passengers and headed back to the ocean-floating suite I shared with Owen Moore and Jack Pickford.

Jack dreaded facing the press in New York and was drunk and drugged for most of the sailing as was Owen. Owen was fast going through that one-hundred thousand dollars that Mary Pickford had given him, I feared he'd be bankrupt in a few months.

When Jack had originally sailed from New York to France with Olive, he'd announced to the press that the trip was to be "our second honeymoon."

That honeymoon from hell had come to an end.

*****

In spite of Olive's death, I actually enjoyed New York, even though I felt I should be in mourning. But I'd seen Olive for only a few times and was hardly a close friend of hers. Her tragic loss saddened me, because I felt she could have gone on and been a great star for the Twenties. All those flapper parts that later went to Colleen Moore and Clara Bow could have been played by Olive Thomas. She was the original flapper. That afternoon, by myself, I went into a theater near Times Square and saw Olive, alive again and engaging on the screen in *The Flapper.* Announcement of her death had caused a morbid interest among viewers, and the theater was packed.

John Barrymore was too busy to see me, except between his matinee and evening performance. Although I would have liked to spend a night with him, I took what was offered, even though the invitation wasn't particularly a romantic one from the Great Lover. His actual words were, "I want you to come over and service me even though I'm a bit sweaty."

All was not lost, however, as John told me that Thomas Meighan had arrived in New York that afternoon. I was assured that Thomas would like to entertain me and take me out to dinner. I left a message for Thomas at his hotel and waited by the phone. When it hadn't rung by eight o'clock, I thought I might leave my suite and drift off into the night. I didn't know where Jack Pickford or Owen Moore were. Both men had disappeared after arriving at the pier. Jack didn't even tell me at what hotel they would be staying. He said, "I don't want the press to find out." He could at least have told me. Although we shared quarters on that ship making the transatlantic crossing, Jack and Owen seemed to have other business to attend to in New York and left me to fend for myself.

Just as I was dressing to leave, the phone finally rang. It was Thomas Meighan. He'd already talked to John Barrymore and said he'd be delighted to go to dinner with me. Later, after a fabulous dinner, I was invited to spend the rest of the night in the Thomas Meighan suite. Since I was locked in the arms of one of Hollywood's leading male stars, I forgot all about the rejection from Jack and Owen. One Thomas Meighan made up for one-hundred Jack Pickfords. Thomas had taken the train to New York to be a pallbearer at Olive's funeral, as he was a close friend.

The next morning, Thomas and I arrived at a simple Episcopal funeral service with the Rev. Dr. Ernest Stirce officiating. There was a crush of mourners drawn not to pay homage to a fallen star but to gaze upon all the other stars expected to attend the funeral. Hundreds of people, nearly all from the film colony in New York, turned out for the funeral.

Thomas was allowed in through a side entrance, and he let me go with him. Floral tributes poured in from everywhere, and never had I seen so many roses, lilies, and orchids. The largest wreath was from Mary Pickford who never had to face that blackmail threat from Olive. From the Selznick studios came another giant wreath inscribed, "Our Pal Ollie."

Outside I heard that mounted policemen had to force lanes through the throng so that mourners could enter St. Thomas's. A male choir sang "I Need Thee Every Hour." As the music died, the organ pealed a funeral march. Thomas had excused himself earlier and now he reappeared as a pallbearer, carrying Olive's casket blanketed in purple orchids and topped by a spray of yellow and brown orchids, a gift from Jack Pickford, I was told. Other pallbearers included Allen Crossland, William Kelton, Harrison Fisher, Harry Carrington, Gene Buck, and the soon-to-be famous Myron Selznick.

Following the casket was Jack himself and his mother, Charlotte Pickford. The mother of the dead screen star, Mrs. Van Kirk, accompanied them, as did Jimmie and Willie Duffy, brothers of the late star. Memories of my sexual encounter with these brothers couldn't help but race through my mind. I recognized Mr. & Mrs. Lewis Selznick, and their other son, David Selznick, along with George Derr, William Semon, and others.

An usher had placed me in a pew next to Irving Berlin, who said nothing. On my left a spot had been reserved for a late-arriving guest. Dressed entirely in black, and wearing a veil and dark glasses, Mabel Normand was shown in, taking the seat beside me and giving me only a glancing nod.

After the service and en route to Woodland Cemetery, Mabel sat beside me in the back seat of a big black limousine. "I'm sorry about what I did to you in front of Goldfish."

"It's too late for that now," I said. "I have mixed feelings about Lotte. What I really want to do is make it on my own—not pretend to be somebody else, especially a woman."

"I understand that, and I think you'll go on from all this and become a big star in your own right," she said. "If you do that, then I'll never regret what I did." She seemed extremely agitated and her whole body quivered. She nervously tried to light a cigarette for herself, having refused my offer of a light. Eventually she handed the cigarette to me, her hands shaking, and asked me to light it in my own mouth. "I'm

just not myself any more. Too much drink. Too many men. Too many drugs. Before leaving Hollywood, I begged Billy Taylor to marry me, thinking if I settled down with him, I might chase away my demons in his rose-covered bungalow. He turned me down."

"He turned you down because he can't make up his mind about what he wants," I said.

"Neither can I, but I'd better make some strong decisions, sooner or later. Olive's death came as a shock to me but also a wake-up call. When I get back to the coast, I'm going to check into the Glen Springs Sanitarium. I need help."

After Olive was laid to rest, Mabel disappeared without saying good-bye. Unexpectedly, she called me the next morning and invited me to attend an auction of the personal belongings and effects of the late Olive Thomas Pickford. She was shocked that Jack Pickford had arranged an immediate auction of Olive's effects and personal belongings at 115 West 32nd Street. Many theatrical celebrities attended, including producer Lewis Selznick, to whom Mabel introduced me. Mr. Selznick obviously didn't think I was immediate star material, even though I slipped my card into his suit jacket. He never called.

At the auction, Mabel purchased a 14-karat gold cigarette case for $50, a toilet set of 20 pieces for $1,425, a diamond pearl brooch and sapphire pin and a platinum set with star sapphire for $425.

Over lunch that day, Mabel confided in me that she felt a great affinity with Olive. "We both came from the same lower class Irish-American trash. We also shared so many personality traits—namely we were two mixed-up twats. We never saw enough of each other. If I were in Los Angeles, she was in New York or vice versa. But the times we were together made up for the times we weren't. Her loss is a loss to the entire film industry. She would have gone on to become a big star."

After several drinks, Mabel became enraged at Jack for staging an auction of Olive's jewelry which she'd carried to Paris with her. The personal effects had been gathered up from an apartment they had temporarily rented in New York. Apparently, Owen and Jack were staying there during their sojourn in New York, and I wasn't invited to live with them. Not that I cared at that point. I had Thomas Meighan. What self-respecting faggot would run off with Owen Moore and Jack Pickford when Thomas was waiting in the bed?

Mabel reached over and gripped my arm real hard. I was amazed at her strength. "I want you to tell me what happened and tell me the truth. No lies. No cover-up. Did Jack Pickford poison Olive or have someone do it for him? I know what Olive was planning to do with Mary. The blackmail. I know everything."

"I honestly don't know the answer to that but until the day I die I'll suspect Jack of poisoning his wife."

"I will too," she said, as a melancholy sadness descended over her. That same melancholy sadness would remain with her the rest of her life, in spite of her attempts at fun and frivolity. I think she saw in Olive's untimely death her own upcoming demise at too young an age.

As I stood on Fifth Avenue kissing her goodbye in the fading light of an afternoon, the wind must have blown in from Canada. Winter seemed to have come three months early to New York, and I was anxious to go back to the warmth of California. I stood for a long moment watching Mabel walk alone down the avenue. A few fans recognized her and tried to slow her pace to ask for an autograph but she ignored them, pressing on into the windy but dying afternoon.

I was never to see Mabel Normand again, except for one more time and that was a night I'd like to forget.

Mabel's biggest scandals were ahead of her. Olive's death seemed to set off a string of tragic events that would engulf all of us, some fatally.

As the years went by, I would occasionally think of Mabel again as I read of some difficulty she was having in the newspapers. And then on the morning of February 23, 1930, a newspaper was thrown on my doorstep announcing that the "Queen of Comedy" was dead in Monrovia, California, presumably from tuberculosis, but I knew that Mabel really died of a broken heart. In the Twenties her career never achieved the luster it had in the Teens.

She'd stumbled in and out of a few mediocre films, appearing for the last time in the 1927 release, *One Hour Married*. Her 1922 film, *Oh, Mabel Behave* seemed to have sounded a warning call she didn't heed. The "Female Chaplin" had died at the age of thirty-five.

I learned later that day that Mabel had begged to be taken home to die. Her attending physician was Clifford Loos, brother of the famous Anita Loos. Since Mabel was too sick to be moved, a portable screen was brought in from her bedroom in Los Angeles. Thinking she had been returned to the womb of her home, she died in peace.

Memories of Mabel came rushing back to me when I attended the Broadway musical, *Mack and Mabel* in 1974, with lyrics by Jerry Herman. But Bernadette Peters was no Mabel Normand.

When I saw Owen Moore and Jack Pickford off at the train station in New York, I didn't know at the time that it was the last time I'd see either of them. When all of us got back to the coast, we never contacted each other again.

Owen would live until June 9, 1939, dying in Beverly Hills of a heart attack. When he'd appeared briefly in *A Star is Born* in 1937, he hadn't made a film since the 1933 Mae West vehicle, *She Done Him Wrong*.

Jack went to his grave January 3, 1933 when, ironically enough, he'd returned to Paris. He kept his promise and never revealed what really happened between Olive and himself on that fatal night in 1920.

Like so many others, such as Theda Bara, Jack's film career virtually ended in the Twenties, although he made a few lackluster productions, last appearing on the screen in 1928 in *Gang War*. He was to marry another famous star, Marilyn Miller, a Follies girl like Olive. Jack would even marry a third Follies girl, Mary Mulhern, before ending it all. As the actor Donald Crisp put it, "Jack was a drunk before he was a man." Mary Pickford's attempt to get work for Jack as either an actor or a director finally failed to. Her brother was reduced to performing antics at Pickfair like walking arm in arm with Bea Lillie, both fully dressed, into the swimming pool.

When Jack finally went through his trust

fund of $100,000, willed to him by his mother, he was reduced in the end to serving as a bootlegger for his sister Mary, who was increasingly becoming an alcoholic, much to the horror of her husband, Doug, who abhorred alcohol.

After a final night with Thomas Meighan, I had decided to stay on in New York for a few days following Olive's funeral. I was secretly hoping to see more and more of John Barrymore. But more and more became less and less, as the actor had far more interests than me to deal with.

Rodolfo had Natacha Rambova, Charlie had his Florence Deshon, and I didn't have much waiting for me back on the coast, except an increasingly morose Wallace Reid.

Antonio Moreno was still there but in the last few weeks he'd seemed distracted by some other relationship and was often not available. Ramon Navarro was available when he didn't have another conquest for the evening. There remained William Boyd and Richard Dix, but like Charlie and John Barrymore, they had a lot of other interests.

On the day in New York when I felt my most despondent, I ran into Bobby Harron on Fifth Avenue.

That very year, Louella Parsons had written that "Bobby Harron will go a long way in pictures of the Twenties, this young pioneer with the laughing brown eyes and the boyish, happy disposition."

Louella got it wrong.

*****

D.W. Griffith's mainstay for juvenile leads, who had shown so brightly in such classics as *The Birth of a Nation* and *Intolerance*, was not in a happy mood. Bobby Harron was another big star who faced the prospect that he could not transfer his stardom of the Teens into the Twenties.

I invited him back to my suite where he didn't want to have sex but preferred to be held in my arms while he sobbed. He seemed to be fading away with a broken heart. For some strange reason, as if to humiliate himself,

he'd arrived in New York on the eve of the world premiere of *Way Down East*, Griffith's latest film.

Bobby had coveted the male lead in the film but it had gone to Richard Barthelmess who now seemed to be the director's new favorite. Louella Parsons had once written that "Bobby Harron has no envy in his heart." Did she get that wrong! His hatred, resentment, and jealousy of Richard Barthelmess seemed to seep out of every pore in his body.

Before leaving Hollywood, I'd heard that Barthelmess was set for major stardom. Master director Henry King and Charles Duell were joining resources with him to form Inspiration Pictures, Inc., a major player in Hollywood until 1931. In time, Barthelmess would become that company's major star, hitting it big in the landmark film, *Tol'able David* in 1921 along with another King discovery, Ernest Torrence.

Over the years I was to follow avidly the career of Dick Barthelmess. I thrilled to him in *The Bright Shawl* in 1923 with Dorothy Gish and Mary Astor, and *The Enchanted Cottage* in 1924 with May McAvoy, the "star-eyed goddess," as Carl Sandburg called her, who stood only four feet, ten inches. She went on to star in forty films for every major Hollywood studio until sound ended her career.

Eventually starring Lillian Gish and Richard Barthelmess, *Way Down East* would in later years be cited as one of the twenty greatest classics of the silent screen, and it also was one of the most financially successful box-office hits Griffith ever made. Bobby's instincts as a showman had been right. If he'd appeared opposite Lillian in this film, he might have launched himself successfully as a more mature star of the Twenties, because he was rapidly ceasing to look like a juvenile. He faced the same dilemma that Mary Pickford did. She was no longer the little girl with the golden curls, although she'd continue to masquerade as such, and Bobby was no longer Griffith's "innocent boy" but had grown into a man.

He nervously paced the floor of my suite. "I was meant to play the part of David Bartlett, the honest farm boy who really loves Anna, Lillian's role, and finally wins her. The role has Bobby Harron written all over it. I would be a son rebelling against the puritanical bigotry of my father, Burr McIntosh. The mother in the film, Kate Bruce, has practically been a real mother to me all during the Biograph years."

To me, the story was a hoary old melodrama that had long passed its prime on the stage. Griffith had purchased the rights for $175,000, an outrageous amount of money to pay for screen rights back then. The story still retained many aspects of the Victorian era and wasn't modern like *Vampira* or other films contemplated by Erich von Stroheim. Lillian Gish with her brilliant acting rescued the film. Even John Barrymore was to remark later that in her role as Anna she "surpassed Eleanora Duse and Sarah Bernhardt."

"What poured salt on my wounds is that D.W. even cast Barthelmess' wife, Mary Hay, in the film in a supporting role," Bobby said. "Barthelmess has decided to deal with his homosexuality by parading a wife out before the press. He hopes that will end speculation about his sex life. As you know there is more and more talk about me, but I'll never marry."

The film, when shown today, usually is part of a review of the silent era and features the dramatic climax when Lillian rushes distraught into a blizzard. She collapses on the frozen river and is trapped on an ice-floe as the ice breaks. She is rushing to her death toward the falls until rescued by Barthelmess, upon whom the sun was now shining in Hollywood. He no longer had to earn money by posing for frontal nudes for French postcards.

At the height of Barthelmess' screen career—and the inauguration of the Oscar awards in 1928—he was nominated for best acting in *The Patent Leather Kid* for First National and *The Noose*, also for First National. Before the debut of the 30s, he was still appearing in films but Gary Cooper and Clark Gable had come along by then, and Barthelmess could no longer claim title to "The most beautiful face of any man before the camera."

I remember attending the premiere of *The Spoilers* with Marlene Dietrich in 1942 (she was also the star of the film, with Barthelmess as a supporting actor) and seeing Barthelmess' farewell appearance in *The Mayor of 44th Street* made for RKO in 1942 and starring George Murphy. After a stint as a soldier during World War II, Barthelmess settled on the East coast, there to die of cancer on August 17, 1963 in Southampton, Long Island.

When I learned of his death that day, I remembered that I had planned to bring him back a present from that trip to Paris I took with Joe Godsol. I never bought the present and never called Barthelmess again. It seemed disloyal to Bobby to do so.

At my hotel suite in New York, Bobby wanted a drink and I went over to a liquor cabinet to get him one. To learn that Richard Barthelmess had married didn't come as a surprise to me. I'd banged the actor but felt no magic in the romance the way I did with Richard Dix and William Boyd. Barthelmess was a definite bottom, and I didn't know how his wife coped with that. I was happy to surrender him to Walt Disney whom I'd seen on the set of *Vampira* emerging from the actor's dressing room.

Downing half of his drink in one gulp, Bobby said, "Barthelmess not only ruined Dorothy Gish's affection for me, but he also is having an affair with Charles Ray. Charles, as you know, is the only man I've ever loved."

The mention of that actor's name brought back my encounter with him in a three way with Bobby. I was also happy to relinquish Charles Ray to Richard Barthelmess, as Ray was one actor I didn't plan to pursue either. As a star-fucker, I had begun to discriminate, whereas when I'd first arrived in Hollywood I was willing to go off into the night with any star regardless of whether I was personally attracted to him or not.

"I'm going to tell you something I've never told anybody else in the world," Bobby said. "I tried to come between Charles and Barthelmess. I figured that I could break up the thing with Charles by getting Barthelmess to fall for me. Only problem is, my plan backfired. Getting Barthelmess to bed is no hard job for any good-looking young man. My humiliation came when he wanted me to fuck him. I couldn't even get it up. He laughed and mocked me. If that weren't enough, he called Charles in front of me and made fun of me. I ran from his bedroom but what I really wanted to do was shoot him in the head."

"Forget it and go on," I said. "Bobby Harron can have almost any man he wants in

Hollywood, and I'm sure of that. Far better men than Charles Ray or Barthelmess. I'm confused, though. Do you love Charles Ray or are you really in love with Dorothy Gish, as everybody says. Or are you in love with both of them?"

He looked baffled as if the question had never been asked. "I love both of them. With Charles, I feel this passion, this incredible passion, where I want him to possess me, force me to do his bidding. I want him to treat me like I'm his woman and make me do things that I think I don't want to do, but when he makes me do them I love it."

I more or less understood that, and could recall a few episodes in my own life where I felt the same way about a man.

"As for Dorothy, I don't want to have sex with her," he said. "I think she's really in love with Mildred Harris. I want to put her on a pedestal and worship her. Bring her flowers. Maybe kiss her hand. But nothing more than that."

"I see," I said, not understanding at all, and fearing that Bobby was a hopeless case. I never understood men who struggled with their homosexuality. I just accepted mine from the beginning and set off to have fun, without giving a second thought that I might be queer and that the world would condemn me. To hell with that!

Over dinner Bobby and I talked more about the one picture where he'd actually co-starred with Barthelmess, *The Girl Who Stayed at Home.* The female leads in the film were Carol Dempster, whom I'd met when she'd danced with Rodolfo, and Clarine Seymour, the small, dark, and vivacious star who had been working in comedies for Hal Roach. Griffith, or so I was led to believe, was having affairs with both Dempster and Seymour. To use a term from a movie decades in the future (1950), Seymour was Eve Harrington to Dempster's Margo Channing in *All About Eve.*

I tried to reassure Bobby about his acting skills. He had played the brother of Barthelmess in the *The Girl Who Stayed at Home.* In it, both brothers faced upcoming conscription into the army and active war service. Barthelmess played a serious and up-

standing youth, and Bobby was cast as a lounge lizard with a "killing slouch," and a weird walk that film critics of the time called a "crablike scuttle."

As the character of "Cutie Beautiful," Seymour stole the film from Dempster. Bobby's light comic touch as the lounge lizard also stole the show from Barthelmess. "Barthelmess gave a real fussy, jumpy performance," I said. "Dempster did too. That film belonged to you and Seymour, not Dempster and Barthelmess."

For a brief moment, Bobby found comfort in those words. "Clarine is in New York to attend the premiere. She's staying with Griffith in his suite. They're carrying on, you know? When you meet her, please tell her what you just told me."

"I'd be glad to," I said. "Cheer up. You can get by without the sponsorship of either Dorothy Gish or D.W. Griffith. You can make it all on your own."

"We'll see," was all Bobby said. He was staying at the Seymour Hotel, and he invited me back there to get ready with him.

Dorothy Gish had invited Clarine Seymour, whose name had no relationship with the hotel where Bobby was staying. Bobby and Clarine Seymour were asked to join Dorothy's sister, Lillian, at Mamaroneck, where *Way Down East* had been filmed. "I'll call Dorothy," he said. "I'm sure she'd be delighted to include you."

I accepted the invitation, having little else to do, and Bobby called Dorothy and confirmed it. When he put down the phone, he said, "Even though Lillian and Dorothy invited me out to see them, they're still cold to me. Dorothy seems to be falling in love with this guy, James Rennie. At least she had the good sense not to fall for Barthelmess."

I was surprised to learn that D.W. Griffith would also be at the house of the Gish sisters. "I thought you guys were finished."

"Not really," he said. "I'm still under contract to him. He's sent me to Siberia, though. Instead of starring me in his own pictures, he's lent me out for four low-budget comedies at Metro. They're each budgeted at $25,000. I've just finished the first one, *Coincidence.* A real second-string affair directed by Chet Withey. Richard Barthelmess is co-starring with

Lillian Gish in the biggest production of the year and I'm in a second-rate comedy."

To make matters worse, the phone rang. Bobby picked it up and after a long minute a look of deep anguish came over his face.

"What's the matter?" I asked, when he put down the phone.

He went over to his suitcase and pulled out a pint of liquor, pouring himself a stiff drink in a dirty glass by his night table beside a rumpled bed. "That was Chet Withey out in Westchester," he said. "They've just shown *Coincidence* to a group of distributors. All of them turned it down. And this was the picture that Withey said was going to make me a big star in my own right without Griffith. It's made me a big movie star all right. They can't even find a distributor for the fucking turkey. *Coincidence* is going to ruin my career. I'm washed up."

I didn't know what to say and was almost grateful when the phone rang again. Bobby reluctantly picked it up. It was Dorothy Gish calling from the lobby. She and Clarine Seymour were waiting downstairs in front of the Hotel Seymour, whose name, as I mentioned, had no connection to the actress herself.

Having already met Carol Dempster, the rival mistress of D. W. Griffith, I was introduced on the sidewalk to the woman who might become her replacement. Dorothy Gish was there too, giving me another one of those birdlike kisses the famous sisters specialized in. I couldn't imagine Dorothy ever giving a man a real kiss. I figured that when she wasn't busy making love to her sister, Lillian, or else Mildred Harris, she would deliver her love to this Rennie character.

When Dorothy got out of the car, she'd left the rear door slung open onto the busy street. Suddenly, a fast-speeding taxi came along, banging into the door and shattering its window before disappearing around a corner.

A Japanese chauffeur jumped out of Dorothy's car and started screaming. Had Charlie set off a vogue among stars to hire Japanese chauffeurs? The driver didn't seem as upset by the dented door as he was by the shattered glass. "It's a bad omen," he shouted at Dorothy." It means anyone who drives in this car today will meet an untimely death."

"Bullshit!" Bobby said, becoming a real man for a change. "I'll drive the God damn car. Get in Clarine. She took the seat up front with him.

The Japanese chauffeur stormed into the hotel yelling back at Dorothy, "I no drive that vehicle. It carries the curse of death."

I held open the back door for Dorothy, as the car had not been seriously damaged. I noticed a slight hesitation in Dorothy's voice. She held back and reached for my hand. "Oh, Bobby," she said, "go on without us. Tell Lillian and D.W. we'll take a later car. I just remembered I have a press interview."

Waving good-bye, I stood with Dorothy and watched Clarine Seymour and Bobby Harron drive off in the damaged automobile, not knowing that I would never see either of them again.

Dorothy invited me to accompany her to the premiere of *Way Down East* tomorrow night. For some reason, and I still don't know why, I graciously bowed out of the invitation, although it was the kind of offer that would normally delight me.

I wanted to flee from New York, as I felt a sense of danger. The prediction of that Japanese chauffeur had strangely disturbed me. Being a faggot was difficult enough but being a superstitious faggot was too much, or at least that's what I told myself. Nevertheless, his words sounded like a warning in my head. I feared disaster around every corner.

As it turned out, Dorothy hadn't lied. She actually did have a press conference she'd forgotten about. After a dinner with her, I planned to take the train to Chicago in the morning en route to Los Angeles.

Two calls came in after midnight, the first from Dorothy. "Something terrible has happened," she said, sobbing into the phone. "Clarine was stricken and taken to the hospital. Her mother just called me. She died in the operating room. Strangulation of the intestines."

After exchanging condolences with Dorothy, I was more determined than ever to escape from New York. Maybe Bobby was next. Maybe the Japanese chauffeur was right in predicting disaster.

The second call that came in was from

Rodolfo, phoning from Los Angeles. *The Four Horsemen of the Apocalypse* had made him a big star, but he decided he had time in his life for me after all. "There are things I get from you I don't get from anybody else," he told me.

Tears welled in my eyes. To have been dumped by someone who was calling to take you back thrilled me as nothing else. The other men in my life didn't have what Rodolfo had. "I'll still have women in my life, especially Natacha, but I want you to be there waiting on the sidelines for me when I need you. When I need you, I want you to drop everything else and come to me. Will you agree to that as part of the terms of taking you back?"

"I promise," I said, being a total fool and knowing how silly and ridiculous I was but agreeing to those conditions anyway.

On the train to Chicago, I thought of nothing but Clarine Seymour, an actress I didn't know. She seemed to have everything—or had everything. After she'd appeared in *The Idol Dancer*, whose premier was only a month ago, she'd been signed to a four-year contract, assuring her of two-million dollars in income. And she was only twenty-one, not much older than me. In one afternoon her dream of stardom and screen immortality had turned into a nightmare of death.

When the newspapers were brought aboard the train in Chicago, Clarine Seymour had faded from the headlines. Bobby Harron had replaced her in the news. He'd died at Bellevue Hospital in New York, having been rushed there when he'd been found shot in his hotel room.

Had he committed suicide on the eve of the premier of *Way Down East*?

All the way to California I thought of nothing else but Bobby. Had Dorothy rescued me from the jaws of death? Had the Japanese chauffeur been right? Obviously he was. Clarine Seymour and Bobby Harron had stayed in the doomed car and died within hours.

To this day I'll never really know if Dorothy Gish saved my life that fateful day. If she did, I'll be forever grateful, having no way of knowing what would have happened to me if I'd ridden off with Bobby and Clarine Seymour.

For years to come I'd always raise a champagne toast to Dorothy and another to Clarine Seymour and Bobby Harron on the anniversary of their deaths.

If I thought my life had been a thrill a minute since arriving in Hollywood, I was to find upon my return that bigger and more exciting surprises awaited me.

Chapter Twelve

The official scenario presented by the studio about the death of Bobby Harron was no more convincing than the actor's last film, *Coincidence*. One of the studio's representatives claimed that Bobby had purchased a revolver at some earlier time from a man in need of money. So the story went, he'd put the weapon in his dinner jacket pocket and had forgotten about it. On the evening that he was to attend the premiere of *Way Down East*, he'd taken the dinner jacket from his trunk. The weapon had fallen to the floor and discharged.

Hearing the gunshot, one of the staff members at the Seymour Hotel had used a pass key to gain entrance to Bobby's bedroom. He'd found Bobby on the floor bleeding severely. Taken to Bellevue Hospital, Bobby died a few hours later at the age of 26.

Could anyone possibly believe that story? By the time I arrived back in Los Angeles, the movie colony was abuzz with talk of Bobby's suicide. Richard Barthelmess was hounded by the press for comments, but he'd left town for a few days. Both Lillian and Dorothy faced the press—D. W. Griffith did not—and spoke in their usual wondrous glow about Bobby, not revealing their conflicts with him over the years.

The very afternoon of my return, I went with Antonio Moreno and Billy Taylor to a memorial service for Olive Thomas, Clarine Seymour, and Bobby himself. Billy addressed the audience of Hollywood elite assembled on one of the Brunton Studio stages. Not only stars attended, but producers, stage hands, cameramen, and a representative medley of the Hollywood colony. Pews were borrowed from the prop department.

Many members of the audience got up and remembered Clarine, Bobby, and Olive through tear-dimmed eyes. After Billy had spoken of "sweet little Clarine Seymour, radiant with youth; true-hearted Bobby Harron, and generous, great-hearted Ollie Thomas," the solemn harmonies of the Grauman's Symphony Orchestra, and the choir of St. Paul's Pro-Cathedral echoed across the stage.

Although I'd promised to bring a gift for Richard Barthelmess upon my return from France, I never called him again, and he never made an attempt to get in touch with me. For all I could care, he could spend all his evenings in the arms of his devoted wife.

Back at Billy's bungalow, Antonio and I relaxed with the director. "We went too far with *Vampira*," Billy confessed. "Years from now Hollywood will make movies like *Vampira*. We were just decades ahead of our time."

Antonio agreed that it "was one hot picture." He also confessed that he got a hard-on three times while watching the flicker. He leaned back in his chair and spread his legs. "Speaking of hard-ons, anyone want to sample a thick Spanish sausage?"

Even though we'd just returned from a memorial service at which Billy had been the major speaker, I took Antonio into Billy's bedroom where I proceeded to strip him down. As always, the director and voyeur, Billy himself, was there to oversee the action as he too took off his clothing. As I sucked off Antonio while Billy plugged me from the rear, I knew I'd arrived back in Hollywood where there was always more sex off the screen than on the screen.

With everyone's libido satisfied, I could drive my "stagecoach" back to the Hollywood Hotel where I planned to call on Charlie in a few hours if he wanted to see me. After all, I was his "wife." If Charlie wasn't at home, Kono could fill me in on the details.

There were two men I wanted to speak to: Tom Ince and Rodolfo Valentino, and not necessarily in that order. Ince remained my one hope of getting work in films as Durango Jones, and Rodolfo still owned my heart. Surely there wasn't a homosexual male in the world who could be pounded nightly by Rodolfo and who could forget him easily.

Luck was on my side. There were messages from both Rodolfo and Ince, among others, including an invitation to visit W. R. and Marion at one of their countless parties. William Boyd had called, as had Rod St. Just, Richard Dix, and Ramon. I returned several of these calls but found only Ramon at home. He'd fallen in love with some actor who he was dying for me to meet. "His name is Rod, too."

"What an intriguing name," I said.

"Rod is very handsome," Ramon said, "and he's dying to meet you too. He's seen your picture in the paper. He likes me a lot but I have dark hair. What Rod really desires is a blond boy like you."

Before ringing off, Ramon invited me to a midnight party the following night. The word was out that it was going to be the most notorious party in Hollywood history. That I had to attend, unless Rodolfo had other plans for me. I asked if I could bring Rod St. Just, and Ramon said he thought it would be all right.

I'd show up with my "Rod" and Ramon would be there with his mysterious new lover, also called "Rod." No doubt there would be a lot of other Rods on exhibit at this party. Ramon agreed that Rod St. Just and I could arrive at his apartment at ten o'clock so all of us could get acquainted before heading for Arbuckle's night of debauchery.

Before ringing off, Ramon assured me that

his Rod was "going to become the biggest star in the history of Hollywood. Rather, the second biggest star. I'm going to become *Numero Uno*."

Arriving unannounced at my suite at the Hollywood Hotel, Wally Reid bounded up the steps and into my heart again. He took me in his arms and held me for a long time, kissing me hard. But I could tell he was agitated and nervous, as he kept pacing about the room, slapping his hands together and breathing heavily. "Glad you're back," was all he said after releasing me. At a knock on the door, he raced to answer it. I thought it might be room service. He reached into his pocket and pulled out some money, handing it to the person at the door. He'd received something in a brown paper bag. Shutting the door, he glanced quickly at me before excusing himself to go into my bathroom where he was gone about thirty minutes.

When he came out, he was more in control of himself. I just knew he'd consumed morphine. "I can't do this at home around Dorothy," he said. "She's getting really suspicious. Complains all the time that I don't love her. Our sex life together has ceased to exist. We're just hanging on to the marriage—that's it."

Wally asked me to drive him to a press conference that his studio had arranged for him with a lot of out-of-town movie writers visiting Hollywood. These journalists demanded that interviews be set up with "all the big stars," and they'd lodged complaints with the studios that they were not fed enough data. Hollywood studios, they charged, spent too much time catering to reporters in Los Angeles and New York and ignored the great American heartland.

Wally's job was to help remedy that situation. "I just had to have a fix," he said to me en route to the press conference. "I was shaking all over and not able to face the press or anybody else for that matter."

Once we arrived at the studio where the press conference was to be held, Wally had become his screen image again—the handsome, clean-cut American male. He went and shook the hand of every journalist, making eye contact.

A studio rep whispered to me, "Men love him, boys, old people, children. As for the women, need I say more?"

Before the press, Wally fended questions about how he handled all the female adulation heaped on him. "It's a nuisance," he said rather bluntly. "Being called a matinee idol is a deadly insult. This thing about the women liking me is bunk. If I have any popularity it is as much with the male element as with the schoolgirls. It never flatters me to hear that a lot of schoolgirls want my picture or that some man is jealous because his wife visits the theater where my picture is showing. I would much rather hear about a picture that has good acting and direction."

The studio rep nudged me as if finding Wally's remarks too incendiary.

"I really want to be a director, and I still do," Wally told the press. "Being a leading man was never my dream. I actually directed my wife, Dorothy, once in a film, and she obeyed me to the letter. When I'm directing, my word is law, and that's as it should be. The director should be the general in total command."

He told the writers that he was seriously considering drama. "But I'm a little worried," he confided. "The public expects to see me in comedy, not shedding enough briny drops to fill an ocean. I'm not very fond of gloom myself, and I think I understand how my friends in the small towns feel."

Although at first taken back by his comments about adulation, the press was eventually won over. "The habitués of Main Street are very important to me," Wally said. "Whereas the average motion picture star is more concerned with what New York thinks of his film, I am far more concerned with how one of my flickers goes over in Keokuk, Iowa, or Oskaloosa, Michigan. These are the real people responsible for my popularity, and I'll never forget that."

The press burst into applause. Wally had pulled it off.

Back in my stagecoach, we drove back to the Hollywood Hotel. In the room Wally ordered me to strip him down. "I'm real worried," he said. "I'm losing interest in sex and I used to think of little else."

In my bed, I used my lips and tongue to reacquaint myself with every inch of his body. But I couldn't help but notice that he didn't produce a full erection. After I'd struggled in vain to get him fully hard, he looked up into my eyes with great tenderness. "Fuck me hard— that's what I really want."

That is what I did, and that is what I would continue to do until the very end.

*****

Arriving at Charlie's house, I got an update on what had happened to him from his chauffeur, Kono, who was hobbling around and could at least drive a car again. It seemed that The Little Tramp had fled east to escape process servers.

Attorneys for Mildred Harris, teaming up with studio chiefs at First National, had petitioned the Los Angeles Superior Court to seize the negative of his latest film, *The Kid*, with Jackie Coogan, another "little fellow." Packing the negative into coffee cans, Charlie had fled by train to Salt Lake City where he'd rented a hotel room and had begun cutting the negative, turning 400,000 feet of raw film into 5,400 feet of finished product.

First National was claiming that it would give Charlie only $405,000 for the film, and he'd already put half a million of his own money into it, plus a year of his life.

From Kono, I learned other painful news. Charlie had driven Florence Deshon south to Tijuana where he'd arranged for her to undergo an abortion. The Little Tramp couldn't have the world learn that he was the father of her child while he was still legally married to Mildred Harris. Upon Deshon's return to Los Angeles, Kono had noted that she was growing increasingly ill. Nonetheless, she had agreed to go by train to Salt Lake City with Charlie, even though it should have been obvious to anyone she was in no condition for such an arduous trip.

From what Kono had learned, Deshon had grown sicker by the day as all of Charlie's attention was devoted to *The Kid*. One of his assistants, Alf Reeves, had come to Salt Lake

City and had arranged for a sneak preview of *The Kid* in the city's biggest movie palace. Charlie had called Kono and claimed that the audience was "hysterical with praise" for the film.

With the cut negative in hand, Charlie had headed east, taking an increasingly ailing Deshon with him. Once on the east coast, he'd rented a vacant film studio in Fort Lee, New Jersey, where he'd continued last-minute editing on *The Kid* and had also continued to battle First National over money.

Kono told me that Deshon by then was losing weight and had turned yellow. Amazingly, Charlie had not secured medical attention for a woman who seemed to be dying right in his studio where all of them lived. Finally, in desperation and in a last-minute attempt to save herself, Deshon had fled Fort Lee and escaped to Croton-on-Hudson to rejoin her former lover, Max Eastman.

Apparently, as soon as Eastman saw his former mistress, he'd called his friend and physician, Dr. Herman Lorber, who came immediately. After examining her, Dr. Lorber had ordered that she be taken at once to a hospital for an operation. "She has only hours to live, if that," the doctor had told Eastman. "Blood poisoning can set in at any minute."

On the operating table, doctors learned that the Mexican abortion had been botched. Part of the dead fetus had remained inside the actress. In the end, the would-be child of Charles Chaplin and Florence Deshon was disposed of between Tijuana and New York State.

Kono gave me a number at which I called Charlie who was at first reluctant to answer the phone until he'd discovered who it was. He greeted me warmly, welcoming me back from Paris but making no mention of the death of Olive Thomas or my own involvement in the tragedy. He assured me that Deshon was recovering satisfactorily at Eastman's home, and could not make up her mind which lover to select, Eastman or himself. He also said that Mildred Harris had finally agreed to the terms of his settlement, and his divorce was now under way. Without saying it to him, I felt that left me as the only "Mrs. Charles Chaplin" in the field.

Charlie promised to return to the West Coast soon, claiming that I was "the only boy in my life—there may be other women, but you're the only boy. So in my way I'm true to you." With that assurance, he hung up the phone, pleading that he was too busy to talk any more.

Florence Deshon had hardly played her final reel in Charlie's life. In time I came to realize that she'd been the most important woman in his life, other than Oona O'Neill, his final and lasting bride. Remarkably, in *My Autobiography*, Charlie made no mention of Florence Deshon at all. One of the most important and dramatic relationships in his life simply didn't exist for autobiographical purposes.

While at Charlie's house, I called Rodolfo on the set of *The Conquering Power*, directed by Rex Ingram. *The Four Horsemen* was playing to packed houses across the country, earning rave reviews and on its way to making four-million dollars, an amazing figure for a film back then. In spite of that, Metro still didn't seem to realize what a star they had in Valentino. With Rodolfo's beloved June Mathis in charge of the script again, *The Conquering Power* looked like another hit for Rodolfo. Mathis had adapted it from Balzac's *Eugénie Grandet*.

The film co-starred Ingram's woman, Alice Terry, who'd appeared in *The Four Horsemen*. Later, I ran into Terry briefly on the set, but she and I never bonded, although I would encounter her for years. I was being completely unreasonable but I was jealous of her for getting into Rodolfo's trousers when they worked as extras on the film, *Alimony*.

When I arrived at the studio, Rodolfo was filming, cast in the role of a pampered playboy. He looked startlingly handsome and sophisticated, and the camera seemed to be having a love affair with him the way it would in decades to come with Marilyn Monroe.

The scene depicted Rodolfo arriving in a custom-made automobile in a poor village of peasants. His chauffeur braked the car and jumped out to open the rear door for Rodolfo who emerged into this sea of awe-struck villagers. An old man was begging on the street. With a sensual sneer, Rodolfo cast a disdainful look at the man. Instead of the money pleaded for, Rodolfo deposited ashes from his onyx cigarette holder into the beggar's ear trumpet. Where had he learned that trick? No doubt from Erich von Stroheim himself.

In a tailor-made suit from Savile Row, and under a bowler hat, the sleek and sexy Rodolfo made his way through the village with an ebony cane crowned with a pearl-studded handle. He held a well-manicured white poodle on a gold leash.

My darling Rodolfo, it was plain for me to see, had arrived at his lofty goal of stardom. Rex Ingram was allowing Rodolfo to steal the picture in spite of his dedication to his bedmate, Miss Alice Terry herself.

Rex Ingram, who seemed instinctively to know of my role in Rodolfo's life, joined me for a drink as he shut down the set for the night. Rodolfo rushed over to give me a welcome back hug before excusing himself to get out of costume and to take a shower.

"Believe it or not, Valentino is not the star of this picture," Ingram said when Rodolfo had left.

"You could have fooled me," I said. "Of course, your Alice Terry is the star and rightfully so. She's terrific." I had really learned to lie.

"No, I mean it," Ingram said. "Officially Ralph Lewis plays the lead. He's cast as the old Grandet who loses his marbles over his desire for gold."

I'd seen this character actor on the screen before, but even so, knew that Rodolfo was the real star. In spite of what he said, Ingram knew that too. The film virtually showcased Rodolfo as no male actor had ever been depicted before. The camera followed Rodolfo from his two-toned shoes to his plastered down hair with love and devotion, the way D. W. Griffith might linger over the likes of Mary Pickford or Lillian Gish.

Then the director said something that utterly astonished me. "I think Valentino is a flash in the pan. He may be able to do one or two more films for Metro, then that's it."

"But his performance—your direction— in *The Four Horsemen* is terrific," I protested. "People swoon when he's on the screen."

"The public will quickly tire of his male prancing and strutting," Ingram said. "I have recently met an actor who I think will dominate films in the Twenties."

"Who might that be?" I asked, already jealous of Ingram's new discovery even before I'd heard his name.

"A Mexican kid," Ingram said. "Better looking than Valentino and a lot better actor, or so I'm told. I'm going to devote the years ahead to making a star of this Hispanic kid— not Valentino."

"Could this Mexican kid be Ramon Novarro?"

"Yes, how did you know?" Ingram asked.

"A lucky guess on my part."

At that moment Alice Terry came up to rescue Ingram and take him off for the night. She looked at me with a glance of sparkling rivalry as if to say that Rex Ingram was one man in Hollywood I wasn't going to steal from a female embrace. If everything went right tomorrow, I'd have my own director, Tom Ince, and didn't need to rely on the good will of Ingram.

At a tap on the shoulder, I turned around to stare into the dancing eyes of Rodolfo. I'd never seen him like this before. Stardom had made him more dashing and confident than ever. Even though he'd changed from the playboy dandy wardrobe he'd worn in the film, he was still dressed as a dandy in his street clothes.

"I'd kiss you," he whispered in my ear, "but I don't want anyone to see us. Can you wait until we're alone together?"

"It'll be hard," I said, "but I'll try." I complimented him on his new wardrobe.

"It was selected by Natacha," he said. "She has more taste than anybody in Hollywood. From now on, she's in charge of my wardrobe, both on and off the screen."

"How nice," I said, trying to conceal my jealousy, which had flared up again. "And where is Miss Rambova tonight?"

"She's been invited to a party Nazimova is giving at the Garden of Alla," he said. "Only women, and beautiful women at that, are invited. That leaves me free for the evening."

I linked my arm with his. "Let's call it boys' night out," I said.

*****

At the Hollywood Hotel where I'd taken Rodolfo for dinner, he tipped a member of the staff ten dollars to learn that Jean Acker no longer occupied the suite next to me. Although she wouldn't let Rodolfo into her room on his honeymoon night, she'd been living there with the actress Grace Darmond. Both Darmond and Acker had moved to an apartment somewhere in Los Angeles, address unknown.

As he headed into the dining room, Rodolfo said to me in a soft voice, "The pussy denied me is being well serviced by Darmond, and of that I'm sure."

I said nothing, enthralled as I was to have Rodolfo back in my life at least for a night where I would not have to compete with the likes of Natacha Rambova. There was a certain irony in the situation. I now had Natacha's man, Theodore Kosloff, and Natacha had snared my man, Rodolfo. It was like we were trading partners, establishing a role model that future stars would follow. Fernando Lamas and Lana Turner with Esther Williams and Lex Barker, who in time became Fernando Lamas and Esther Williams with Lana Turner and Lex Barker. Of course, I didn't really have Theodore except sometimes. He turned to me whenever he wanted "real sex," amusing himself at other times with the children he so adored.

Maria Jane always told me, "When you live in glass houses, don't throw stones." I could no longer condemn Theodore. Instead of spending Saturday mornings with Wallace Reid, I was now taking young Doug Fairbanks Jr. riding into the Hollywood Hills. We were doing that and other things while young Doug worked through his "homosexual period."

Dining with Rodolfo at the Hollywood Hotel wasn't the same any more. For one thing, the maître d' who up to now had virtually ignored us, directed us to his finest table where a spotlight shone down. Rodolfo, because of his appearance in *The Four Horsemen of the Apocalypse*, was being treated like Mary Pickford. It was a time when stars were made overnight. His stock was on the rise. Metro didn't realize it, but the world was telling Rodolfo that he was heading for super stardom.

As for me, I would continue as the richest extra in films. Since news of my real-estate purchases had spread, rumor had it that I was the son of billionaire parents from the Midwest who worked not in films to earn a living, but as a way of getting close to the male stars so I could seduce them. Rod St. Just claimed that another tantalizing rumor was spread about me—that if a straight man spent one night in my arms, he'd be homosexual by the next morning. I suspected Rod of having spread that rumor himself, but it was hardly doing me any harm. Not when I was going to bed with the likes of William Boyd, Richard Dix, Wallace Reid, Antonio Moreno, and Ramon Novarro, plus my regulars such as William Desmond Taylor and Charlie Chaplin.

The Little Tramp, it was true, had less need for my services lately while caught in the throes of the divorce from Mildred Harris, the romance with Florence Deshon, and an off-the-record affair with Mary Miles Minter. As long as he kept to women, that was all right with me. If I learned that Charlie was dating another boy, that's when sparks would fly and there would be one less fairy in the kingdom of Hollywood when I finished off the boy-whore. So far, I didn't have any competition in that department, and both Stella Dallas and Kono had confirmed that for me.

"When you're around, Charlie is abnormal," Kono had told me. "When you're not around, Charlie becomes normal again." I didn't entirely agree with Kono's assessment. Back in Kansas we thought men were abnormal who screwed twelve-year-old girls.

As Rodolfo got up to go to the men's room, I read my messages. Godsol had left a long, detailed message, telling me to call him. He claimed that his lone copy of *Vampira* had been stolen from the Ritz Hotel in Paris, and he was threatening to sue the hotel if it couldn't be found. He urged me to call him at once. It was an emergency.

I told the maître d' to tell Rudy that I would be right back. I raced up the steps to my room and called Godsol. Fortunately, he didn't suspect me of stealing the film. On the phone, Godsol told me, "I know this is going to break your heart. You had everything riding on getting that film released in Europe, and I was going to make Lotte a star. As her agent, you stood to make millions."

"Are you sure it's lost?" I asked, pretending to be on the verge of tears. "If so, everything is gone for Lotte."

"The God damn print is lost," Godsol screamed on the phone. "I know who did it. It was that fucking tour guide I hired for you."

Memories of that Alain Delon look-alike crossed my mind.

"I know these thugs in Paris," he said. "They grabbed the boy and took him to this warehouse in a suburb. Even under torture, he denied stealing the film. It was too bad what happened."

A growing panic gripped my body. "What happened?"

"The boys got a little rough," he said. "You know French thugs. They were just trying to torture him to get him to tell them where *Vampira* was, but they went too far. The boy died while strapped up. They tossed his body in the Seine. Happens all the time in Paris."

I gulped, as a little sigh escaped my throat. I couldn't say anything. The horror was more than I could imagine. It was then I realized that if Godsol knew I'd destroyed the last copy of that film, he'd have me wiped out too.

Fortunately, I didn't have to react, as he kept on talking as if disposing of bodies was a relatively routine occurrence in his life. "Hey, kid," he said before ringing off. "I'm going to be at my place all tomorrow afternoon. Get over here. Last night I fucked three broads, but now I need to split open some teenage boy ass as a diversion."

Promising him I'd be there, I put down the phone and raced back to my table with Rodolfo, as memories of that murdered French boy stabbed at my heart. In some way I felt responsible for his death, although Godsol had something to do with it too. I was determined from that night on never to defy Godsol or deny him what he wanted.

Throughout my long years in Hollywood, I never confided in anyone that I destroyed *Vampira*. Even when quizzed by Rod St. Just, I never admitted anything. Only now am I confessing to the Bitch of Buchenwald, who is looking at me as if I'd be capable of doing anything, including the torture and murder of that poor French boy. The tension between the Bitch of Buchenwald and me is growing more severe by the day.

Earlier in my memoirs I had deliberately promised to add a few episodes in my life that I might normally have suppressed. This was done to spite her. One such episode was the affair with the underage Fairbanks boy. The next morning after I'd dictated those sordid details, she'd shown up at my home more hostile than ever. "Back in the old country," she said, "a man caught having sex with a young boy was immediately taken by the villagers to a tree. They stripped off his clothes and castrated him."

After that tidbit of information about her ancestral background, we resumed my dictation. I was back at the Hollywood Hotel for that dinner with Rodolfo and my post-Paris reconciliation with the dashing, young, and emerging star.

At our table, where the bright light shone, I feared I'd lost Rodolfo once again to another woman. A vivacious young girl, who bore an amazing resemblance to Mary Pickford as she appeared in 1914 films, was at the table with Rodolfo, laughing and talking with him as if they were lovers. When I came back, Rodolfo got up and grandly introduced me to Patsy Ruth Miller.

After about fifteen minutes of talk, I came to realize that Patsy wasn't a potential rival of mine but was a friend of Rodolfo's. "He's like a kid brother to me," Patsy claimed.

Jeanne Eagels had not been impressed by our common Midwestern heritage, but Patsy was. She was from St. Louis and claimed she'd been "stage-struck" all her life. She wanted to be a film star, and had attracted the attention of Nazimova at a party. Apparently, it was the same party where I'd gone with Norman Kerry and Rodolfo and ended up coming between Mildred Harris, Natacha, and the Gish sisters.

"I must have caught Nazimova's eye that night," Patsy said. "She's offered me a small part in her upcoming film, *Camille*. It's almost definite that Rudy is going to play opposite her in the role of Armand."

I looked at Rodolfo in astonishment. Could that possibly be true? I wasn't certain because Nazimova's appraisal of Rodolfo seemed to change every day. Natacha apparently was urging Nazimova to cast Rodolfo in *Camille*.

"Please don't get the wrong idea," Patsy said to me. "Nazimova may have been attracted to me, but I assured her I don't go that route. In fact, I'm here waiting for my dashing cowboy date for the evening. Since I'm from the Middle West, I don't go in for those kinds of things. There are no lesbians in St. Louis. We just don't do that. But Nazimova is giving me the part anyway."

I wished her luck. It seemed that I was always hearing about other actors getting parts, not me. I observed Patsy carefully. If anything, she looked like a clone of Mildred Harris instead of Pickford, as I had originally assumed. I couldn't believe she'd even be another Mary Miles Minter clone. Hollywood was filled with that type. To me, her dreams of stardom were never to be realized.

How wrong I was. Although relatively unknown today, Patsy Ruth Miller would in the Twenties become the top female star at Warner Brothers, all five feet, two inches of her. From Wampas Baby Star, she landed the coveted role of Esmeralda opposite Lon Chaney in the spectacular production of Victor Hugo's *The Hunchman of Notre Dame*. It seemed that everybody but me was appearing in films with Lon Chaney. She became known for romantic farces which were a Twenties precursor of the screwball comedies of the Thirties, the kind that starred Cary Grant or Carole Lombard. Patsy became an excellent foil for the likes of Monte Blue, Glenn Tryon, and Edward Everett Horton. She even starred in the sophisticated comedy, *So This is Paris*, Ernst Lubitsch's most popular silent film. The future queen of Hollywood, Myrna Loy, appeared in support of Patsy in the 1926 film, *Why Girls Go Back Home*.

Patsy would in time even appear opposite Matt Moore, one of those Mary Pickford brothers-in-law I'd seduced at the Santa Monica beach house. The film was *The Wise Virgin*, but by then Matt wasn't as cute as he'd been when I got his trousers off him.

Patsy would also appear opposite Norman Kerry playing the romantic lead, of course. As if Patsy were on a mission to appear opposite all my former conquests, she even co-starred with Richard Barthelmess in *The White Black Sheep* in 1926. Since I was still—technically at least—an agent for the stars, I should have signed Patsy up as my new client.

Rodolfo was informed by a member of the staff at the front door that a "Miss Natacha Rambova" would like to speak to him on the phone. While he was gone, Patsy got personal. "Rudy is in love with Natacha, but he's doing it all wrong. He teases her and indulges in tomfoolery which he thinks will make her laugh. He doesn't seem to realize that the way to Natacha's heart is to take her seriously as an artist. He's starting to take my advice, and it's working."

"Exactly what does that mean?" I asked, growing more jealous of Natacha by the minute.

"There's an enforced gaiety about Rudy because he wants everybody to like him," she said. "But I think Natacha is beginning to see below the surface. She sees the lonely and sad young man that dwells behind the laughter. I think it's not like a typical man and woman love thing. I think Rudy is touching some maternal instinct in Natacha. She's finding a man who appreciates beauty and culture, and Natacha devotes her life to beauty and culture. In many ways, she's not like an American woman at all, but a continental creature."

"Such a lovely one," I said, not meaning it at all.

"They exchange many experiences from time spent in Europe," she said. "I often see them talking together. Sometimes they speak in Italian, sometimes in French. Rudy and Natacha speak both languages."

"How fortunate for them," I said, downing my entire glass of liquor and ordering another one at once.

"They're always talking of going to Europe together," Patsy said. "Natacha is so talented. She can turn a sow's ear into a silk purse. I went to dinner at her bungalow at 6612 Sunset Boulevard. She's living on very little money. But she'd taken flea-market items and packing crates and cleverly transformed everything into chinoiserie. She's lacquered everything in red and black. Rudy is often there helping her paint. Sometimes he cooks these fantastic meals and invites guests like Nazimova and June Mathis. Paul Ivano is often there."

"Who, pray tell, is Paul Ivano?"

"He's this French-born cameraman," she said, "although I hear he's a Serb. Nazimova has taken him as a lover, although he's only half her age. She adores him."

"I thought Nazimova liked women," I said.

Patsy giggled. "You'd better get the Kansas cornsilk off your ears. You've been in Hollywood long enough to know that people out here sleep around. A woman wants a woman one day, a man the next. I hear the biggest womanizers in town like a boy every now and then, even Charlie Chaplin. Someone told me that such stars as Mabel Normand have a lesbian streak that comes out every now and then. I hear that the Gish sisters are also lesbians, but that I can't believe. They're too pure."

Striding across the room in a ten-gallon hat was Tom Mix. Patsy jumped up and raced to give him a kiss on the lips. "This is Tom, my date for the evening."

I shook hands with Tom Mix, who said he was sorry to learn that Lotte Lee had had a bad experience with *Vampira* and had fled Hollywood. "I hear she could have been a great star." Before escorting Patsy to her table on the other side of the room, Mix turned to me and spoke softly. "If you hear from Lotte, have her call me." Fortunately Patsy was talking to the maître d' about what was fresh on the menu and was out of hearing range.

"Lotte is really crazy about you," I said. "I'll tell her I saw you when I speak to her again."

Rodolfo returned to table and was rhapsodic. "Nazimova has cast me as Armand. It's definite. I'm going to be the co-star of *Camille*."

He ordered champagne from the waiter. "The future belongs to me." As I drank his champagne, I could only note that he said the future belonged to "me" and not "us." Even though I was supposed to be dining alone with Rodolfo, I got little of him for myself. He'd reached the pinnacle in Hollywood where other stars dining at the hotel stopped by his table to congratulate him on his recent success in *The Four Horsemen*. Even sad-faced Buster Keaton came over, offering his best wishes to

Rodolfo but giving me a rather weak and wet-palmed handshake. With his dead-pan face, he shared in Rodolfo's good news that he'd been cast opposite Nazimova in *Camille*.

Patsy rushed over to greet Buster Keaton and invited him to join Tom Mix and her at their table. I was amazed at how fast Patsy was moving up the Hollywood ladder. She'd just arrived in town and already she knew Nazimova and Buster Keaton, not to mention Tom Mix, her date for the evening. Blowing kisses to Rodolfo, she took Keaton by the arm and escorted him over to drink and dine with Mix.

When Mae Murray walked into the room in a glittering gown of scarlet with sequins, Rodolfo jumped up and raced toward her and her husband, Bob Leonard. Rodolfo invited them to join us at the table. Mae was thrilled for Rodolfo, and shared in the just announced news that he was going to play Armand in *Camille*.

My reunion with Rodolfo wasn't going at all the way I planned. Rodolfo and Mae virtually ignored me, as they were caught up in their shared glory of their own glittering stardom. Wandering alone to the men's room, I stood at the urinal to piss out some of the champagne. I felt as sad and lonely as Rodolfo must have felt when he'd first arrived in New York as an immigrant with no money.

But my luck changed real fast. Coming into the men's room was Tom Mix who winked at me as he took the urinal next to mine. He pulled out that dick as big as his horse's and let me take in the show. He even removed his hand from his prick so I could get an uninterrupted view.

"Lotte never said anything to me," Mix said. "But I've been hearing rumors around Hollywood about you. All the guys are talking."

Taking my eyes off his cock for just a moment, I looked him squarely in the eye. "Everything you've heard is true. And more." When I looked down at that cowboy dick again, it had stopped dripping and was on the rise.

*****

Once in the toilet booth alone with Mix, I looked for only a brief moment at the dick hanging out in front of me before reaching in to free the cowboy's big balls. My own cock swelled painfully in the tight confines of my trousers, but I knew I had to wait for my relief until I was with Rodolfo later in the evening.

With his large right hand, Mix cupped the back of my head and pressed my face tightly against his crotch. I needed no more urging than that. The prick hardened as I licked his balls, taking in his sweet male aroma. Overcome with a wild need, I moved my lips over the head of his prick, swallowing it inch by inch as I took in the whole monster. He'd buried his cockhead deep within my throat, as I went to work on him. I tasted his smooth skin as it rode across my mouth. His size was a challenge for me but I was now so well experienced that I could handle it. I was not a gagger. That cowboy's hips moved in perfect rhythm as he continued to feed my mouth, which had become a suctioning pump. His sighs and groans of pleasure were growing louder and louder, and I feared someone would walk into the men's room at that very moment of white heat, spoiling our fun.

My hot lips gripped him as his strokes speeded up in tempo. I moved my hands around to press against the driving mounds of his ass. Wherever I felt, except for his dangling balls, I met firm flesh. He pressed harder into me, battering against the back of my throat.

With all the wonderful sensations going through me, I was able to forget all about Rodolfo and Natacha. All I could think about now was the sheer joy of having this cowboy in his prime. Only his need and my own desires were real and his strokes grew still deeper and more vigorous.

That wonderful and anticipated moment came, as his cock pulsed and then released its load. The volume and sweetness delivered was like a dream for me. Mix was gushing, and it was plentiful as I sucked with fury, pressing my mouth to the pit of him and drinking fully of all he had to offer, which was a lot.

His cock was neither drooping nor completely satisfied as Mix stepped back. This was just a temporary relief, and I knew he wanted more. But both of us, without saying so, feared we'd been gone too long in the toilet. We'd pressed our luck to the limit.

The smile on Mix's face told me what I wanted to know. Buttoning up his trousers, he said, "I hear you're living at this hotel. I like women. I like to fuck women. But I'm also a wild rodeo rider. If you don't mind, I'd like to call on you privately—and always late at night—for you to show me what you can really do when we have more time. I bet you know a lot more tricks other than giving the world's greatest blow-job. Up to now, only amateurs have worked me over."

"Any time, cowpoke," I said. "You're right. I've got some hot surprises for you." Both of us were standing at the sink when Buster Keaton rushed in, unbuttoning his trousers and taking out his dick even before reaching the urinal. "I have to go and go real bad," he told us, "but I was stopped four or five times on the way here."

Ever the opportunist, I took one look at Keaton's meat displayed at the urinal before leaving the toilet with Mix. Since I am the only person still alive in the world who knows what Keaton's dick looked like—at least soft—I will go to my grave and not divulge his secret. For only this one time, the Bitch of Buchenwald thanked me for my good taste, something she claimed I hadn't demonstrated up to now in my memoirs.

The Bitch still hadn't recovered from one of my first descriptions about an event back in Lawrence, Kansas, when I actually admitted I'd drunk Frank's piss. He was my first boy friend, and I didn't know the limits of homosexual love. Fortunately, no boy friend other than Frank ever made that request of me.

Almost every day that went by I thought of Frank, and wondered what had become of him. I'd heard that Montana was an underpopulated state. Perhaps I could go there and knock on every door, hoping to find him and bring him back with me to Hollywood. I bet he'd filled out and was handsomer and sexier than he was before.

I felt a sense of shame as I emerged from the toilet with Mix. Not at what we'd done there. But here I was dreaming of a Montana cowboy when I had America's sexiest and most romantically dashing cowboy on my arm, and, dare I mention, a belly filled with his cum.

On the way back to Rodolfo, I stopped briefly at the table where Patsy Ruth Miller sat. If she thought we'd been away too long in the men's room, she made no mention of it. Perhaps she thought both of us needed to take a long crap and found ourselves a bit constipated.

As I told them good night, I imagined that before too long Patsy would be appearing as Mix's leading lady. How right my instincts were. I recalled that a few months later as I sat in a movie theater watching Tom Mix and Patsy in *For Big Stakes*. Patsy even went on to appear opposite Hoot Gibson in *Trimmed*, which had nothing to do with circumcision. The ironic thing was, she couldn't even ride a horse at the time, although she learned from the master, Tom Mix himself. I decided not to be jealous of Patsy providing Tom Mix would live up to his promise and keep making those late night calls on me. Mix may have faded from Lotte's life, but not Durango's.

Valentino, the star, emerged over the dinner table. First he called the maître d' and denounced the chef of the hotel for not putting spaghetti and meat sauce on the menu. "It's my favorite dish," Rodolfo said. "When and if I decide to come to this dump again, I want to see it on the menu."

The maître d' assured him the dish would appear. Having won that victory, Rodolfo pressed his demand for some Italian wines on the menu. "This wine you have now is mere grape juice." Again the maître d' assured him he'd have the chef order some Italian wine.

During the course of this interchange, Rodolfo had worn a monocle like the character he played in *The Conquering Power*.

When the maître d' had gone, Rodolfo looked at me—still with his monocle in his eye—with an icy glaze. "When I arrive on that Metro set in the morning, Rex Ingram will wish he was never born. I may even end his career as a director."

It was taking me some time to get used to the new Valentino, formerly the poor Italian immigrant and now the world's leading romantic hero.

After dinner, Rodolfo came up to my suite.

Thinking at long last I'd have some time with him, I resented the ringing of the phone. I resented it even more when I found out it wasn't one of my beaus, but Natacha calling for Rodolfo.

Later I found out why she'd called. Nazimova was anxious for him to finish shooting his current picture so that the filming of *Camille* could begin at once. Natacha had also, at least according to Rodolfo, figured out a way to disguise his cauliflower ear with makeup. Not only that, but she wanted to curl his hair for the role of Armand and get rid of its glossy straightness. I thought he'd balk at that, but he'd given in to her.

Just as I had managed to get his shirt off, and was paying special attention to sucking on his tits, the phone rang again. This time he didn't even wait for me to answer it, but picked up the receiver himself.

Natacha was on the phone again, acting as Rodolfo's financial adviser. For his work on *The Four Horsemen*, Rodolfo had received $350 a week at a time many stars were drawing one to five thousand dollars a week. Even Nazimova, as the press had duly noted, was pulling in $13,000 a week. Pickford, as always, was making far more. Natacha was urging Rodolfo to go to the office of Maxwell Karger, the Metro production manager, visiting from the east coast. Karger had originally rejected Rodolfo for the role of Julio until June Mathis had intervened.

Putting down the phone, he turned to me. "Natacha is right. I'm being underpaid. I can't make ends meet on my salary."

Without saying so, I knew that his expensive tailor-made clothing and his sudden habit of acquiring antique pistols and swords were causing him to go deeper and deeper into debt.

Impulsively and spurred on by Natacha, Rodolfo against my advice called Karger at his hotel. He was staying at the Alexandria, and apparently Rodolfo had awakened him from a deep sleep. I heard Rodolfo telling Karger that *The Four Horsemen* was playing to packed houses across America, and it was saving Metro from bankruptcy, which was true. To my embarrassment, Rodolfo even pleaded for just a $50-a-week raise. By the look on his face when he slammed down the phone, I realized Karger had turned down this reasonable request, which meant that the top brass at Metro considered Rodolfo a "one-hit wonder."

A look of steely determination came across his Mediterranean features. He almost glowed with a kind of fierce resolve. "Tomorrow morning I'm going to arrive late on the set. Let Rex Ingram start the picture without me, or write in an extra scene or two for his precious treasure, Alice Terry. I'm walking into the office of Jesse Kasky at Famous Players. I'll see what price tag he puts on my head. Natacha says I should demand at least a thousand dollars a week. Metro and I are through."

It was way past midnight and I still hadn't bedded Rodolfo. Acting on an impulse, he placed another call. "To a friend of mine," he said. "He's in Hollywood for a few days."

Getting the great French filmmaker, Abel Gance, on the phone, Rodolfo pleaded with him to let him return to Paris with him. "I could go over big in French films," Rodolfo said. "I understand the French. My mother was French. Americans don't appreciate my art form. I want to return to Europe. I should never have left."

Gance apparently told Rodolfo that he was doing very well in Hollywood and to stay where he was. When he'd put down the phone, he felt rejected. "Gance told me he has nothing for me in French films."

Even though his character of Julio was the sensation of movie audiences across the country, and even though he was appearing in a major release film for Metro, and even though he'd been offered the coveted role of Armand opposite Nazimova in *Camille*, Rodolfo spent the rest of the early-morning hours pouring out his frustrations.

His great concern was about Natacha. "I love her but it's a love that's not returned. I make a fool out of myself around her, and she ignores me unless our conversation is about her career or my career. When the conversation turns personal, such as my romantic interest in her, she becomes as chilly as an Arctic night."

For me, the evening drifted into morning and a total disaster. It hardly lived up to my fantasy of what our reunion was going to be like. I was back in Rodolfo's life in some limited capacity, but it was increasingly clear to

me that I was some sort of friend to be with on occasions, perhaps to have sex with. But his heart and his emotions were wrapped around that scheming Natacha Rambova, as she called herself. I thought her real name of Winifred Shaughnessy fitted her better.

At dawn's early light, I'd gotten Rodolfo undressed. He'd curled into a fetal position and was crying and sobbing for more than an hour. I felt at times he was almost suicidal. I couldn't really understand it. It appeared that all his hopes and dreams of stardom were coming true, but nothing going on in his life satisfied him or fulfilled him in any way.

He was a bundle of frustration and despair, and cried out for the protective arms of his "beloved" mother and his "beloved" country of Italy. As soon as he could find time in his busy schedule, he promised himself to return to his hometown. He invited me to go with him, and I agreed to that

"The people will welcome me as a conquering hero," he predicted. "The first son who ever made good from that region. My people are a warm and friendly lot. You'll be received in all their homes. It will be the crowning glory of my life to return to my hometown as a big American film star."

Indeed, that journey through Italy was one trip we'd take, but much later in Rodolfo's short life than either of us ever planned.

Finally he drifted off to sleep. I felt his despair had consumed me too, and I couldn't sleep. My own career was a disaster unless Tom Ince would come through for me. Fortunately, I was better off financially than Rodolfo, and I didn't have to worry about how I was going to pay my hotel bill or restaurant tabs, much less buy gasoline for my stagecoach. In spite of Charlie's financial troubles, he was honoring his commitment to me, as he did throughout the rest of his life.

Around seven o'clock there was a knock on my door. At first I thought it might be Tom Moore or one of Lotte's old beaus. I shut the door to our bedroom, knowing that at long last Rodolfo had fallen into a coma-like sleep. Tiptoeing across the suite, I responded to the urgent knock and threw open the door to find an unshaven and badly shaken Wallace Reid. Without being invited in, he rushed into my suite. He was perspiring heavily. Fearing he'd discover Rodolfo in the next room, I ushered him into my dressing room next to the bathroom.

He was shaking violently, and I asked him if he wanted me to take him to the hospital.

"Hell, no," he said. "I have to have morphine. Call Dr. Hutchison. I'm coming apart."

"There's no way in hell I can call Dr. Hutchison," I said. "He doesn't want to speak to me ever again. I'm sure that holds true for you too."

"You've got to do something for me—and quick," he said. "I feel like I'm bleeding inside. It's never been this bad."

I directed him to a cot I used for emergency guests, and covered him in a blanket, as he claimed he was freezing to death although the room was toasty warm.

In desperation I turned as I always did to the one man in Hollywood who could solve everything for me from getting a minister to marry Charlie and me to securing Wally his morphine fix. The evidence was clear. Wally could keep himself under control only with the drug in him. There could be no more withdrawals for even a day or two. The morphine had to be there and supplied freely every day. Rod St. Just picked up the phone and learned of my predicament. We both agreed that Wally had to have morphine, or he might die. Rod claimed he'd come to the hotel after visiting a friend's house.

"Will you have the morphine?" I asked rather desperately.

"I'll always be there for you," he said.

While waiting for him to come and rescue Wally and take him off my hands, I felt the incredible irony of my situation. Here I was at my hotel suite with America's two leading heartthrobs, Rudolph Valentino in one room and Wallace Reid in the alcove bedroom. One was lying on tear-drenched sheets in his fetal position, and the other was shaking violently under a blanket imagining that demons were trying to break into the suite.

At that moment I felt no passion for either man, but an overwhelming sympathy. For the first time in my life since leaving Kansas, I questioned the pursuit of stardom itself. Rodolfo and Wally were stars, but what had it really gotten them except a bath in a pool of chaos?

*****

When he'd played a villain in a dozen or so films, Rodolfo had been known as one of the most cooperative and easy-to-handle actors in the business. When Rex Ingram had directed him in *The Four Horsemen of Apocalypse*, Rodolfo had followed directions perfectly and performed any task to the director's specifications and satisfaction.

After leaving the office of Jesse Lasky at Famous Players, Rodolfo had been promised a contract for five years, with a starting salary of $500 a week, $150 more than Metro was paying him. Before signing, Lasky's legal department had to discover if Valentino was free to walk out on Metro after the finishing shots were concluded on *The Conquering Power*.

In my stagecoach, I drove Rodolfo back to the Metro lot where Ingram was furious that he hadn't showed up until nearly eleven o'clock when he'd been ordered on the set at seven. Rodolfo offered no explanation to his director and went at once to his dressing room, where I followed him to help prepare him for camera.

Without knocking, Ingram stormed into the dressing room, catching Rodolfo in his underwear. "Do you know what you're costing us in production overtime?" Ingram shouted at him.

Rodolfo turned on the director like a miniature Vesuvius. "Why bother to shoot any scenes with me? They'll just end up on the cutting room floor. I've heard what you're doing. You don't want me to repeat my success in *The Four Horsemen*. I stole the picture from your fiancée, Miss Terry. I'm also stealing this picture from her. You can't stand for that. Any time I look great on the screen, I heard you were exercising your right of severe pruning."

"I have a director's right," Ingram said, "but it's not because of Alice. Your fashion-plate character with a monocle and a dog on a leash is too flashy and has gotten in the way of the plot. I had to cut some of your scenes."

"And why don't you get the fuck out of my dressing room and let me put on some clothes?" Rodolfo asked as he moved threateningly toward Ingram, who retreated to the door which was soon slammed in his face.

Both on and off the set that afternoon, Rodolfo became his character in *The Conquering Power*, being an overriding and overdressed boor who attacked waiters in restaurants, denounced cab drivers, and shoved "peasants" aside with his pearl-studded walking cane. At one point Ingram became so violently disturbed in his attempt to direct Rodolfo that he stormed off the set, turning the job over to his assistant director. As the star of the picture, Alice Terry tried to intervene, hoping to make peace between her future husband and Rodolfo, her discarded lover.

Terry could not console Rodolfo. "He's photographing you through gauze, God damn it," he said. "I guess he wants to soften your contours to make you look ethereal and to complement your fragility. But he's photographing me harshly, emphasizing my cauliflower ear and my scar. I'll look grotesque on the screen, like some monster. He's doing it to ruin my career. He hates me. He's jealous of my success. He wanted everybody to talk about his direction and your beauty in *The Four Horsemen*. But the public is going to see the film for one reason, and that it to see Valentino on the screen."

Terry tried to laugh off his remarks and dismiss his charges. "Rex thinks you're wonderful," she said but was not convincing.

In spite of Terry's soothing voice, Rodolfo grew more belligerent as the afternoon wore on. Screaming for the wardrobe woman, he berated her in front of the cast, ripping at the lapels of his 19th-century coat. "These lapels are too wide," he shouted at the elderly woman. "You look old enough to have lived in the 1800s. Don't you know they didn't wear lapels this wide? You were there." He ripped off his jacket and tossed it at the woman, who ran, coat in hand, retreating from the stage.

After she'd fled, Rodolfo walked around the set, meeting each juicer personally, making a circuit of the lights. "I don't know which one of you is responsible for lighting and ruining my appearance. The aim of this picture is not to make Alice Terry more beautiful than she is, the aim is to light the set so that I can thrill the audiences who are clamoring to see me on the screen in my next role after Julio."

Matters grew worse when word reached the set that Ingram had stormed into the office of Karger demanding that Valentino be replaced as a star of the film. Karger turned down Ingram's request but headed for the set, claiming he personally would deal with "that stupid WOP."

Karger called Rodolfo aside for a disciplinary talk. The production chief was not going to take him off the picture but demanded that Rodolfo apologize to Ingram, and that Ingram apologize to Rodolfo. As if to sweeten the package, Karger said that if Rodolfo would cooperate until the shoot was finished, he'd grant his request of a fifty-dollar a week raise.

After he'd left, Rodolfo came to me in fury. "Karger thinks he can win me over by tossing a tired old bone with no meat on it to his little lap dog. Valentino is no lap dog, who'll lick his God damn hand for a lousy fifty dollars. That raise was even more humiliating than not getting a raise. It was a cruel and callous insult to my manhood and to my ability as an actor."

Only the arrival of June Mathis on the set seemed to cool off Rodolfo's temper. The screenwriter assured him that he had only days left to finish the picture, and she promised to be a buffer between him and Ingram. She also told him that Ingram was too fine a director to deliberately sabotage his performance in the film. "I've seen the rushes," Mathis said. "Ingram has made some errors in photographing and directing you, but I feel they were not intentional."

When Mathis and Rodolfo retreated to his dressing room, I encountered Ingram coming back on the set. "That God damn Karger wouldn't give in to my demands. I wanted to scrap this fucking picture and start all over again. I begged Karger to replace Valentino with my new discovery. I was going to give the role to Ramon Novarro."

As I retreated from Ingram, that was one startling piece of news I didn't plan to share with Rodolfo.

Mathis emerged from Rodolfo's dressing room, assuring me that he'd cooled down and would complete the picture with Ingram. She'd also heard the good news that Jesse Lasky was going to combine his company with that of Adolph Zukor's to form Paramount Pictures. "Rudy will be a big star at Paramount. Metro has treated him badly. It's time to go."

To make matters worse, Natacha Rambova arrived on the set, carrying a small package. She kissed me on the cheek and thanked me for taking Theodore Kosloff off her hands. "After that morning at Paradise, he has never called again. I could have sued him. I feel like a free woman for the first time in my life. Rudy is trying to put me in slavery and bondage again, but I won't give in to him. I'm not going to free myself from one imperial boy friend to become the acolyte of another colossal ego. Italian men have egos as big as Russian men."

In the dressing room, Rodolfo rushed to kiss Natacha but she turned from him. "Now, now," she said, "don't get carried away. I've artfully made up my face, and I don't need you to spoil my looks."

Dejected, he turned from her and looked at himself in the dressing room mirror, checking his own makeup. "The day has been fantastic," he said. "Lasky is going to sign me on at $500 a week."

"That's ridiculous," Natacha said, not viewing this as good news at all. "I told you to hold out for one-thousand or else nothing. Studios have got to learn to respect artists, and you can help that cause by demanding that you be paid a decent wage."

"It's too late now," he said, looking disappointed at her reaction.

"If you gave your promise, you'll have to keep it," she said. "But you're a fool to let them take advantage of you that way."

"You'll be the greatest star at Paramount," I interjected. "You're on your way to becoming the biggest star in Hollywood. One more great success at the box office and you're going to be making as much as Mary Pickford herself."

Rodolfo seemed to delight in my words and the golden prospect it held out for him.

"Bullshit!" Natacha said, turning on me with more ferocity than I'd ever seen in her before. She unwrapped the package she'd been car-rying and turned her back to me. "Nazimova knows everything happening at Metro. She's even learned the first picture Lasky is going to star you in." She tossed a pulp fiction book on the floor in front of Rodolfo.

It was a book being read behind closed doors and described in newspapers in what I later learned was slightly flawed grammar as *le grande scandale de tout le monde.*

The title was *The Sheik.*

*****

The following night was to be one of the most glittering in Hollywood history, and later, for me at least, one of the most notorious. It began innocently enough at the Ship Café, which was rapidly becoming my hangout. (Every now and then, just for fun, I like to use an expression not *au courant* at the time.)

After he'd paid a two-hour visit to my suite at the Hollywood Hotel, I'd invited William Boyd for dinner, feeling that my handsome leading man and later cowboy star needed a big, juicy steak to replenish his system after I'd drained him dry. William liked to plug every orifice before he was finished with you.

I knew that after leaving me, William had a date with a woman, but we never spoke of such matters. I told him absolutely nothing about my private life, and he revealed nothing either. To be brutally honest, we didn't have much of a social relationship. Our "friendship" took place in the bedroom. If we socialized at all, it was over dinner. If that dinner were at the Ship Café, our entire conversation consisted of comments on the stars arriving and going and our digs about their entrances and exits. What neither of us said was that one day each of us wanted to be the star making the glamorous entrance or exit.

Rushing back to the Hollywood Hotel I put on the loin cloth I'd worn the night I'd first met Rod St. Just at the home of Theda Bara where I'd posed with her dressed as the serpent of the Nile, Cleopatra. Theda had called and invited me to the ball at the Ambassador Hotel where all the Hollywood elite would turn up later in costumes. Actors like Gloria

Swanson and Thomas Meighan would be there, as well as writers such as Elinor Glyn who was to label a future screen star, Clara Bow, the "It Girl" and write a picture for Rodolfo and Gloria Swanson called *Beyond the Rocks*. Some of the biggest producers and directors would be there, from Samuel Goldwyn to Louis B. Mayer. Charlie had invited Mary Miles Minter. Dorothy Gish would show up with Richard Barthelmess, and Doug Fairbanks Sr. would make one of his first formal appearances escorting Mary Pickford to the delight of photographers who weren't as aggressive as the paparazzi of today.

Theda had wanted me to dress in the same loin cloth I'd worn to pose with her dressed as Cleopatra. I thought it was a great idea, as my body was beautifully tanned. Standing nude in front of the mirror, I looked like the California golden boy I so aspired to be. Appearing practically naked at the ball would definitely attract some attention to me, and I suspected I'd be signed to a big film contract before the night had ended.

With Theda dressed as Cleopatra, I drove her in my stagecoach to the Ambassador Hotel. I'd had to wear outer clothing to get through the lobby but once at the hotel I retreated into the men's room and emerged wearing only the very revealing loin cloth. Taking Theda by the arm, we entered the ballroom expecting our grand appearance would dominate the gala. Our timing could not have been worse.

Also making their entrance at the same time was Rodolfo escorting Natacha Rambova. To my horror, I saw that Natacha too was dressed as the Queen of the Nile. When Natacha glared as Theda, I knew Natacha felt that there could be only one Cleopatra at the ball. Rodolfo winked at me, but Natacha said nothing, standing there glaring. I made an attempt to introduce Theda to her but Natacha took Rodolfo's arm and pulled him away to the other side of the ballroom. Theda looked embarrassed at this humiliation, but masked her concern with a smile.

Rodolfo had never looked more stunning. He'd come dressed in his Argentine gaucho costume, the same one he'd worn as Julio in the early sequences of *The Four Horsemen of the Apocalypse*. Since that film was the biggest hit in America, and virtually everybody at the ball had seen it, Rodolfo could not have made a better choice. In fact, I'd say that his reign as the King of Hollywood began the night he escorted Natacha across the floor of that ballroom. Even the Metro producers and directors must have realized by then that they'd let a major star escape from their clutches.

Only months before the ball, Theda had reigned as one of the queens of Hollywood, sharing a shaky crown with the likes of Mary Pickford. On the night of the ball she stood as a painful example of a has-been, which up to then had been a rarely used word. Goldwyn, only weeks before, had uttered a line that would become the motto of Hollywood, "You're only as good as your last picture."

Directors and producers who'd worked with Theda in the past acknowledged her, but it was obvious they were eager to remove themselves from her presence as soon as possible. Louis B. Mayer, Goldwyn, Cecil B. DeMille, and others were anxious to meet and socialize with the up-and-coming stars, not walk down memory lane with a woman formerly billed as "the reddest rose in hell." Theda Bara was a fallen star. New names like Colleen Moore, Vilma Banky, Nita Naldi, Lila Lee, Doris Kenyon, and Agnes Ayres loomed on the horizon.

No producers or directors approached me, but when I had to go to the men's room at least five young men followed me in for the unveiling, and I trust they were duly impressed. All that attention at the urinal made me swell up two or three inches, and I had a hard time pissing in front of such an appreciative audience. I must have received at least twenty offers before the night ended, but not one film contract from a producer or director.

Theda and I joined the throngs on the floor for the fox trot and the waltzes. But when the band struck up the stirring rhythms of a tango as authentic as those played in Buenos Aires, we retreated back to our table, as did most of the other dancers.

Like the parting of the Red Sea, the masqueraders moved aside to welcome Julio and Cleopatra onto the ballroom floor. Their presence was overwhelming and stunning, two stars shining brightly in the spotlight. As Rodolfo led Natacha through the steps of a hot tango, it was obvious both of them were among the most skilled dancers in the world, at least when it came to doing the tango. The drama of their dance matched what Rodolfo had displayed on the screen in *The Four Horsemen*, and all those years with Theodore Kosloff had taught Natacha had to keep an audience spellbound.

Rodolfo had seemed in a state of ecstasy as he danced before the Hollywood elite with the girl of his dreams. The fame that had eluded him for so long had now descended upon him. The world belonged to him and to Natacha. The dance ended as he took the former Winifred Shaunessy into his arms and kissed her in front of the entire ballroom audience. John Barrymore could move over. The screen world now had a new "Great Lover."

Later as Rodolfo cornered me and I congratulated him, he seemed thrilled. "My darling Natacha let me kiss her for the first time. She kissed back. Right on the lips. Good and hard the way you of all people know I like to be kissed." The news stunned me. Rodolfo and Natacha had only reached the kissing stage of their relationship? He was sharing his excitement of the kiss with the wrong person. Natacha might have kissed him, but I'd let him fuck me. I'd sucked his tongue. I'd fucked him. I'd eaten his rosebud, devoured his toes, and licked his armpits. What was all this shit about a stupid kiss? I was angry but tried not to show it.

Coming up behind me, Theda apparently had had enough rejection for one night. She looked first at Rodolfo. "You dance the tango beautifully. But take the advice of an outgoing Cleopatra. That Serpent of the Nile is dangerous. A young man can drown in the Nile or else be devoured by crocodiles."

Taken back, Rodolfo didn't know what to say. Theda turned her attention to me. "Take me home. The Vamp is a little tired of vamping tonight."

After I'd put back on my outer clothes for street wear, I escorted Theda home and kissed her good night right on the lips. Her final words to me were, "Some of us have to park our barges along the side of the Nile and make room for a new queen."

For me, the night wasn't over. Another invitation loomed. Ramon had assured me that my loin cloth would be all the dress I needed for this private party. It was "for gentlemen only," and some of the guests had come all the way from New York to attend. There was a rumor that one gentleman had sailed over from London and taken a train across America to visit. Ramon had heard that W. Somerset Maugham, whom I'd met only briefly, would be there. I wasn't sure that Ramon knew exactly who Maugham was, only that "he sounds important."

As I pulled up to the site of the party, I recognized the address at once. It was the same mansion owned by the two queens, the Liberace and Clifton Webb clones, who'd sponsored Nijinsky's farewell performance danced in the nude for a finale. I knew these gentlemen gave quite a party, and money was no object. I didn't know what to expect, but I was thrilled to be invited.

As I was shown in, I greeted my hosts who directed me to a side room where I was told to remove my outer garments. "The loin cloth Ramon told us about will be sufficient," one of the gentlemen said. "As the party wears on, even the loin cloth will have to go."

Making my entrance, I was immediately introduced to Ramon's new friend, and, I presumed, his new lover. That is, his lover when he wasn't getting plugged by William Desmond Taylor, Antonio Moreno, Rudolph Valentino, and countless others."I'm Rod La Rocque," the young man said. He appeared to be about twenty-two. "Ramon has told me so much about you."

Staring at me was a handsome, dashing man who was destined to become my lover, my bitter rival, my lover again, and eventually an old friend with shared memories. Naturally, he was an actor. What handsome young man in Hollywood at the time wasn't an actor?

Like every actor I met at the time, the conversation consisted only of autobiographical references. I took in his good looks and found them most agreeable. His dark continental features gave him the possibility of becoming a Latin lover on the screen. Rod had an amusing combination of high spirits and a casual, carefree manner that I found quite endearing.

He was from Chicago, as I learned, the

son of an Irish mother and a French father. "As an early teenager I wanted to go on the stage and I did, performing boy parts for $1 a night. Then I learned about the films. I got a bit part in *The Snowman,* directed by E.H. Calvert. That brought me in $3.25 for a day's work. So I figured being in films is better pay than being on the stage."

He told me that he'd worked at Essanay and had gotten to know all the big stars. "I even know Charlie Chaplin and Francis X. Bushman," he said. "Perhaps I'll introduce you to them." He leaned over and kissed me on the lips. "That is, if I like what I find in that loin cloth, and from the bulge I think it will be most satisfactory. Actually Ramon has already described what's there in detail."

Rod, who had the same first name as my beloved friend, Rod St. Just, couldn't stop talking about himself, and I was his eager listener, because I felt an attraction to him. I just knew he'd be a bottom.

"At Essanay I worked in bit parts under the Black Cat Productions moniker," he said. "Every day I was talking to the likes of Bryant Washburn, Ruth Stonehouse, Gloria Swanson, all the big names. I got more money and better parts when I appeared in *Money Mad* and later *Uneasy Money.*"

"What happened when Essanay folded?" I asked him.

"I followed Calvert to New York and took a room at the YMCA with another actor, Ralph Graves," Rod said. "I'm sure you know who he is."

Of course, I knew who Ralph Graves was. Everybody knew of him. He'd appeared in *The White Heather* with Mabel Ballin. John Gilbert had played the supporting lead.

"Ralph can throw a mean fuck to a faggot like me," Rod said. "I got me an agent, Eddie Small. His name may be small but he represents many of the stars like May McAvoy and Norma Shearer. He got me a part in the Billie Burke picture, *Let's Get a Divorce.* I made three films for Goldfish, *The Venus Model, A Perfect 36,* and *A Perfect Lady.* You perhaps saw me recently in *The Trap* which I made at Universal. My latest film which will be released any day now is *The Garter Girl* for Vitagraph. I'm terrific in it. You've got to see it."

Rod had backed me in a corner and I really wanted to circulate until I decided I could do no better than him. I surveyed the crowd in the distance. Some of the more scantily dressed men had come directly from the ball at the Ambassador Hotel. The atmosphere reeked of an orgy about to happen.

"I've finally settled on the name Rod La Rocque," he said. "Before that I was credited as Roderick La Rock, Rodney La Rock, Roderick La Rocque, Rodney LaRocque, and Rod LaRocque."

"Stick with Rod La Roque," I advised him. "If you can act as good as you look, I predict you'll be the next Valentino." Even as I said that, I realized how ridiculous it sounded. Rodolfo had hardly emerged and already there was talk of who was going to be the next Valentino. Ramon certainly could fit that bill, and I suspected Rod La Rocque could too. In the months ahead, I was to learn what a prophet I was.

It was party time at the mansion, and, even though I knew I wouldn't be treated to such a show as Nijinsky's farewell to dance in the nude I expected some major entertainment had begun.

The sixty or seventy guests had assembled near the grand staircase in the mansion. Several of the guests had dressed in drag, and others appeared as slave boys and were practically as nude as I was. Rod told me that later there was going to be a "slave auction," and the hosts wanted to sell him to the highest bidder, but he'd already turned down their offer. "Instead of making some bucks tonight, I want you for myself—and for free."

"It's a deal," I said.

"This is the *pièce de résistance* of the evening," Rod predicted. A jazz drummer had been hired to play, announcing that the evening's festivities had begun. A spotlight suddenly threw a glare onto the wide staircase.

Down the stairs marched eight handsome men, all clad in loin cloths like me. Presumably they were masquerading as Roman centurions, and would themselves be auctioned off later to the wealthy but older men at the party.

On their shoulders they carried a silver coffin, which they placed on a large table in front of the party. One of the hosts announced, "We have selected the most delectable boy in Hollywood to open the auction. Usually we save the best for last. There will be other auctions later this evening, but we wanted to launch our little gathering by offering the best first."

I was offended, thinking that I was the most delectable boy in Hollywood—that is, if you liked blonds.

Rod seemed in the know about something. "You're really going to get a kick out of this," he whispered in my ear.

"For our other auctions, we are going to have the 'slaves' appear on our little stage in the rear," the party host said. "They will be fully nude, and one of our staff members will masturbate them to a full erection before the bidding begins. But in this case we want you to buy sight unseen. You have only our promise that what you're bidding for is grade A prime."

The bidding began and mounted quickly, the top offer of a thousand dollars being placed by the so-called nobleman who'd sailed over from London. When the bidding ceased, one of the Roman "centurions" opened the coffin. As the lid came open, a young man emerged from the coffin but before we could see him fully the lights were turned off. The audience gave off a universal sigh of disappointment. But they weren't disappointed for very long. When the lights came on again, the nude young man in his full glory stood before the appreciative audience. Catcalls and whistles filled the air.

It was only then that I noticed who the boy slave was. It was my darling friend and the future movie star, Ramon Novarro himself.

*****

By ten o'clock that morning, I had not even separated my body from that of a nude Rod La Rocque, who was still sleeping peacefully in my much-used bed at the Hollywood Hotel. I didn't want to imagine what that English nobleman who'd purchased Ramon was doing to him. Anyone who allowed himself to be placed on the block at a slave auction deserved what they got in my view.

It is true that I got to sample the sexual charms of Rod La Rocque long before Gloria Swanson, Vilma Banky, and Pola Negri tested and tasted his seven inches. It's also true that my sexual experience with him was different from any other bedmate of mine.

The excitement in going to bed with Rod was his almost hysterical desire for me and his eagerness to please. He hit pleasure points in me I had not known were hot spots.

Although, as I'd suspected, he was the ultimate bottom, he wanted to please as a sexual partner as no other man had. When I was fucking him, he not only goaded me on but the look in his bright eyes told me that I was transporting him into a celestial orbit.

Knowing how much I was thrilling him made it all the better for me. For the first time in my sexual life, I was getting off on the pleasure I was giving another human being. When I'd erupted within him in the early morning hours, he'd descended on me like a lapping dog and had licked me clean long before I could go to the bathroom.

"Please, please," he begged before I fell into a deep sleep, "do that to me again and again. Your cock has found its nest in me." What he didn't say but what was obvious was that he'd climaxed twice while I was pumping him. This flattered my male ego which was in need of restoration after my drag act as Lotte Lee. Through Rod, I was establishing my identity once again as a Kansas cowboy from the wheatfields.

After a late brunch at the hotel, I drove him back to his apartment, promising to get together the following day when we visited Ramon and learned of his adventures. I stepped inside Rod's apartment and gave him a long, lingering kiss before telling him goodbye.

Back in my "stagecoach," I headed for the mansion of Tom Ince. After a night with Rod, I was hardly desperate for sex. As Lotte I'd found Ince attractive but his real appeal for me was my long-held belief that he could turn me, Durango Jones, into a film star. I expected resistance from him but felt I could win him over. There was also a hidden agenda. I wanted to seduce him as Durango, as I felt very competitive with Lotte and hoped to sample some of the same men my "sister" had deflowered.

As I sat and had a drink with Tom Ince, I realized I hardly knew him. My sexual encounters as Lotte Lee at his party for the cowboys didn't count. From his nervousness and awkwardness, I sensed that he was confused about why I was even here.

I immensely admired his talent as a producer, director, screenwriter, and actor. He was, in fact, the most "Renaissance man" in Hollywood, dwarfing the talents of Billy Taylor and others. I'd seen his epic, *Civilization*, three times at the Patee Theater in Kansas and felt it was on par with Griffith's *The Birth of a Nation*. John Gilbert had appeared as an extra in *Civilization*.

It was only the dawn of the Twenties, and Ince was already hailed as one of the most influential figures in the history of American cinema, having discovered or else advanced the careers of Mary Pickford along with her then husband, Owen Moore, as well as William S. Hart, John Gilbert, Sessue Hayakawa, and Charles Ray. To my astonishment, I realized I knew all of those performers intimately, even though bedding them had done nothing to advance my own career.

"I'm sure Lotte has told you about my proclivities."

"She did mention it," I said.

"I know that labels me a voyeur, but all film directors are voyeurs," he said. "Our job is to oversee the action of others, even the sex scenes. I think it only natural that I look through my peephole in on some scenes of bedroom action. What excites me is that the parties on the other side don't know I'm overseeing their most private moments."

"I can see the fascination for you," I said, trying not to sound too judgmental. "The difference between that private little custom of yours and your directing actors before a camera is monumental."

"I'm glad you understand that," he said. "I've had an instinctive hunch about you even before you went to Paris. What you don't know about me, is that I have this vision thing of foretelling the future. I can sense danger even before it happens. One time when some-

one very close to me was about to be murdered, their image appeared to me in a vision on a bright, clear Sunday morning when I was wide awake in my study. I saw my friend dressed in a dark blue suit with a distinctive emerald green tie. He was murdered the next day but he'd appeared as real as life in my study the day before, even though I was on the east coast and he was on the west coast. When I attended the funeral, I cried out. When I looked down at my friend in the coffin, there he was dressed in that same dark blue suit and emerald green tie."

"That's spooky," I said. "Seeing the future would frighten me. I think deep down I don't want to know. I met Winston Churchill at W.R.'s place in Santa Monica. Churchill told me we shouldn't be afraid of the future but should welcome its surprises as they come along."

"That's the way it should be but when you have this gift as I do, there's nothing you can do about it," he said. "You may think I'm bullshitting you but I'm telling the truth. I foresaw the disaster of Olive Thomas and even called her and warned her not to go to Paris."

"Did she listen?"

"Not at all," he said. "She laughed at me and called me a superstitious fool."

"Do you see disaster waiting for a lot of other stars?" I asked him, not really wanting to know.

He settled back with his drink. "As a matter of fact, I do. But I don't want you to tell any of them. I see even great scandal or an untimely death looming for Fatty Arbuckle, William Desmond Taylor, Mary Miles Minter, Mabel Normand, Charlie Chaplin, and especially Wallace Reid."

"My God, I either know or have met all of those people." I hesitated before asking my final question. "There is one name not on that list. Did you leave him off because you predict for him a long and happy life?"

"I know who you are referring to." He said. "Rumor has spread through Hollywood that you're keeping company with Valentino when he's not with that dyke, Natacha Rambova."

"We know each other," I said.

"For that very reason, I didn't mention him,

but if you insist."

"No," I said, rising unexpectedly. "I don't really want to know."

"Suit yourself," he said.

"I think you've answered my question," I said. "I don't really want to hear any more. If this crystal ball gazing keeps up, I'll be asking you questions about my own future, or even your future—that is, if you can look ahead into your own future."

A look of sad melancholy came across his handsome features. "I'd rather not contemplate my own future. But, as for you, I can reveal yours. You'll have a long and happy life. It'll have its pitfalls and tragedies, but it'll be played out against some of the most fabulous figures of the 20th century. You'll have many, many lovers, far too numerous to even contemplate at this point."

"You said earlier you had this instinct about me. But you didn't really explain that. I'm all ears."

"I'm looking for someone who will be very discreet," he said. "I have need of such a person in my life. Lotte told me you'll fit the bill. In other words, I'm tired of looking in on a hot scene in my bedroom, spying on two lovers, and jerking off for my own pleasure. I need a hot, sucking mouth on my dick while I'm viewing the action of two lovers, being, if you will, a spy in the house of love."

"You've got your man," I said. "If there's one thing I know how to do, it's suck cock."

"Your reputation has spread throughout Hollywood," he said. "I'm sure you get many offers, even from heterosexual guys."

"I've had a few," I said, rather modestly I thought, considering my string of seductions as Hollywood's first star-fucker.

"There is one thing I need you to do for me, and that's to serve as a beard for me. I've fallen in love with this woman, and we have to be very discreet. My career could be ruined. So could hers if word got out."

"Surely you don't mean Mary Pickford?" I said.

"Mary's true to Doug, even though the bastard is fucking Mildred Harris on the side," he said. "But I'm sure Mary doesn't know that. She's gotten rid of a drunken husband and replaced him with one who doesn't drink but who has a roving eye."

"Poor Mary," I said.

"She's got booze and her billions to keep her company."

"Who is your lady love?"

"Marion Davies."

I was astonished, even though I knew that Marion was cheating on W.R. with both Charlie and Joe Godsol.

"Marion says you'd be the perfect beard for us," he said. "W.R. trusts you. You're on his payroll, I've learned."

"Of course, Marion knows how discreet I can be," I said. "I'm sure she has told you that already."

She has indeed," he said, "and for the little favors you'll do for me, I'll get you parts in films. They won't be the leads in big epics but you can stay employed in the film industry, which I suspect you're doing just for your own entertainment. Another rumor has spread about you. You're not just Hollywood's greatest cocksucker, even rivaling the talented mouth of Rod St. Just, but I hear you're very, very rich."

"My cocksucking abilities haven't been exaggerated, as I hope you'll see for yourself later this afternoon, but my wealth has." Since I didn't have Tom Ince's gift of prophecy, I could not have imagined then that the seed of my future wealth would be planted on his grave.

The sound of an automobile loudly coming to a fast stop in the graveled driveway distracted us. "That could only be John Gilbert," he said. "We saw John perform with Blanche Sweet. But I have a young thing lined up for him this afternoon, the most beautiful girl in the world. She says she's only fifteen. John, like Charlie, prefers them young. She's already in the bedroom lying nude and asleep just waiting to be deflowered. I'm getting hard thinking about it already."

"When it comes to fucking, John's your man," I said, speaking from personal as well as voyeuristic experiences.

John Gilbert arrived with a kiss for me as Durango right in front of Tom Ince. John had seemingly gotten over Lotte and had replaced her with Leatrice Joy, but still left a little time every now and then for me in his life. Privately he liked to call me his "boy pussy," which wasn't as politically incorrect and objectionable a term back then.

Instead of wanting to talk about sex, John was thrilled with the prospect of shooting moving pictures in color. Of course, Technicolor was years away but John had been working in the studios of Maurice Tourneur. In the laboratory John had seen films hand-tinted in blue, rose, or amber. "Tourneur says that color will create the desired mood you're going for," John said. "Color will actually help the actor. I've been working eighteen hours a day in that studio."

Ince was very skeptical of color, feeling that there was nothing purer than black and white. He defended his actors, claiming if an actor were good he and she would depict the desired mood. "And you don't need rose, amber, or blue film to do it either."

I'd never seen John so thrilled with the idea of movie-making. He told us he wanted to make his own movies one day. "I'm not only starring in films for Tourneur, I'm in the cutting room, as I told you. I'm even his assistant director. Get this. He's even asked me to adapt Robert Louis Stevenson's *The Pavilion on the Links*, which Tourneur wants to retitle *The White Circle*. Now I'm a fucking writer too. Naturally, I'm still a movie star. Tourneur has just lined up another big film for me, *Deep Waters,* starring Barbara Bedford. There's a girl signed to do it with us who I hear is terrific. She's said to be a replacement for Lotte Lee." He turned to me and smiled, blowing me a little kiss. "Not that anyone could ever replace our dear Lotte."

"Who is this broad?" I asked, trying to conceal the jealous greenness of my face.

"Florence Deshon," he said matter-of-factly. "Chaplin's money is behind her. He's not only fucking her, but going all out to make her the biggest female star in Hollywood. I think he's doing it deliberately to sabotage Mayer's plans with Mildred Harris Chaplin."

"Perhaps when Florence Deshon samples the virile charms of John Gilbert, she'll forget all about Charlie Chaplin," I said.

"Perhaps," he said, winking at me just as Rodolfo did. "It wouldn't be the first time Charlie and I have sampled the same twat. I had Mildred Harris screaming for joy when I

fucked her every day of our shoot on *Golden Rule Kate.*"

"That one was made for me," Ince said. "Reginald Barker directed. You were very good in that, but the picture went to Louise Glaum and Gertrude Claire because your role wasn't big enough." Ince congratulated John on all the success he was having, then told him what his reward was. "The most beautiful girl in the world awaits you. I've stripped her nude and tossed rose petals on the bed. She's one sleeping beauty I know you'll arouse."

John frowned. "You know me, always ready for the occasion. I'd normally be hard right now thinking of the prospect, but I'm completely exhausted."

"God damn it," Ince said, looking at me as if he'd have to disappoint me. "I'll have to fuck her myself, although I got my fill of her last night."

"Sorry about that, old chap, but I need to go sleep somewhere alone for a little while," John said. As Ince went to pour himself a drink, John whispered to me. "Come and visit me in about three hours. I'll be completely nude. What I want today is to be licked erotically all over. I'm too tired to do much humping. I haven't slept in days."

When Ince returned, John slapped him on the back. "All is not lost. I've got a replacement waiting in my car. Mind if I bring him in?"

By all means, Ince said, his face lighting up at the prospect that he'd get to see another handsome young man like John fuck the most beautiful girl in the world.

John was gone for just a few minutes and returned with Lon Chaney.

I was shocked to see Chaney here and under these circumstances, although I knew he was working with John on the film, *The Glory of Love*. In the film, or so I'd been told, Chaney played an old sculptor who falls in love with his model. As an American tourist, John eventually would win the girl in the final reel. Ironically the film would not be released until 1923 under its new title, *While Paris Sleeps*.

These three presumably heterosexual men treated me somewhat like a girl as they chatted briefly. Ince seemed to bring a spark of life to the sad-looking face of Lon Chaney, whose dead-pan was almost as great as that of Buster

Keaton. Although Chaney, when I met him, was only thirty-seven, his face was lined and marred like that of a much older man.

As John retreated upstairs to an empty bedroom for sleep, and Ince went to take a telephone call from his studio, I found myself alone on the sofa with Lon Chaney. Since he at first had nothing to say to me, I decided I'd have to spark the conversation.

I told him about my mother, Maria Jane, and of my growing up in Lawrence, Kansas, and the visits to the Patee Theater. "My mother wouldn't go see many films, especially those with Theda Bara, but she always went to see your movies because she knew they would be decent entertainment for the entire family."

"That's very nice," he said, letting me know that I hadn't hit upon a subject that particularly interested him.

"She loved you as the cripple in *The Miracle Man*," I continued. "It was the last movie we ever saw together." That seemed to spark a bit of interest in Chaney. "Maria Jane said you were probably deep down a very nice-looking man who disguised your handsomeness behind grotesque makeup. She thought you were afraid to be yourself, and that you just tried to hide behind makeup."

The subject of mothers seemed to stir some nostalgia in him, and his hardened face became less bitter. His eyes lit up as much as it had when Ince had brought up the possibility of his deflowering the young maiden who lay nude in the upper bedroom.

"Your mother must be a great audience for pantomime," he said, "for that is what I do. It is my life, in fact. Between pictures, there is no Lon Chaney. There's nothing for me but my faces and the camera. It's a lonely life, really."

"But I thought you were married."

"I was to Cleve Creighton. We were married in 1905 and divorced in 1914. Last I heard she was cooking for the hired hands on a bean ranch near Oxnard. She was a cabaret singer at one time. Lovely voice. But I found out she was nothing but a whore. I left her and took our two-year-old son with us. When I became a film star, she came to Hollywood and broke into my house. She wanted money but I called the police and had her run out of town."

"I hear you're happily married now," I said, although wondering as I did what a happily married man was doing at Tom Ince's house getting ready to deflower a young maiden.

"My new wife, Hazel Hastings, is much better than the first," he said. "I was attracted to her because she had a previous husband who had no legs. Ran a cigar store in San Francisco. I always feel kindly about people who befriend the disabled. Both of my parents were deaf-mutes. I owe my present success to my mother. I became 'The Man of a Thousand Faces' because of her." An expression of great love and devotion came across his face. "She spent most of her time in bed. A real invalid. She couldn't see films or even know what was happening in the world. We were so desperately poor we couldn't even afford radio. I began to create characters and stories for her. I acted out in front of her what I'd seen that day. I imitated a lady fighting with the butcher over a leg of mutton. A fat woman passenger fighting with the streetcar conductor for going so fast she'd lost her picture hat in the wind. An angry coach balling out his team over losing a game. A dancer at a vaudeville house. For that, I even put on an old hat and pulled together a dress out of a worn-out curtain. I used a dish towel for my wig. My mother's face would light up. My pantomimes were the only joy in her life. She was my first audience and she inspired me to go on."

"I think it's wonderful how you have such a feel for people who are born different." I said. "When I was growing up, the kids would make fun of me for being different. They said I was too much of a sissy."

"That's one deformity I don't appreciate," he said, his face growing stern. "I sympathize with people with real deformities. I have no sympathy with he-vamps who entice men into perversion when they can't get a woman to satisfy them."

Personally insulted, I welcomed the presence of Ince telling Chaney that he could go upstairs into the room where the girl still lay sleeping. Ince had just checked on her. "It's going to be a thrill," Ince said. "I want to hear her scream when she wakes up and finds herself being penetrated by *The Miracle Man* himself."

"I can top that," Chaney said. "Some directors are talking about making *The Hunchman of Notre Dame* one day with me playing Quasimodo. Even without props and makeup, I can transform myself into a monster. I think I'll wake up your little beauty so she can discover in horror she's getting fucked by Quasimodo himself."

After Chaney had left, Ince seemed titillated at the voyeuristic possibilities. "We should make a film of it. Call it *The Beauty and the Beast.*"

He directed me upstairs and into his private viewing room with its peephole to invade the privacy of Lon Chaney and the beautiful girl. He said I could look first. As I took in the room, I saw Lon Chaney stripping, and, as he did, he seemed to be physically transforming himself into a deformed monster. Fully hard, with a thick seven inches, he pounced on the sleeping girl like an animal in heat.

She woke up screaming at the rape and tried to fight him off, but he overpowered her. I got only one look at her anguished face before he covered it with his lips, which were slobbering and drooling with saliva.

"Let me see now," Ince said, placing his hand on the back of my head and pressing me down low on the floor to his crotch. He already had his monster dick out, roaring hard and waiting to be sucked. Unknown to Ince, I'd gone this route before, and I swallowed him whole in one gulp. As I licked and polished his shaft, it was one whole minute of delicious slurping before I realized that I'd seen that face before.

It was Charlie's conquest from the schoolyard, Reatha Watson herself. Or had she started calling herself Barbara LaMarr?

*****

After the super horror show staged by Lon Chaney for Tom Ince's benefit, even though the "hunchback" didn't know that, Ince went to bed to rest up for a big Hollywood party he was throwing that night. I still had three hours before I was to call on my sleeping beauty, John Gilbert himself.

When Chaney came out of the bedroom,

he didn't want to speak to anybody and demanded that I call him a taxi at once. "I've got to get home to my wife," he said. "She's preparing this big meal for me."

When he'd gone I spotted Reatha (or was it Barbara now?) sitting out by the pool, wearing a white bathing suit. As I approached her, she looked calm and assured, showing no sign that she'd just been raped by a hunchback. She also looked four to five years older than when Charlie had abandoned her at the schoolyard.

"Durango," she said, shielding her beautiful violet eyes from the sun when she looked up at me. "I called that number you gave me, but it's been disconnected."

"Great to see you, Reatha," I bent over to kiss her.

"It's now Barbara LaMarr, baby," she said, flashing her stunning porcelain smile at me. She was the single loveliest creature on earth.

"I'm living at the Hollywood Hotel," I said.

"A working gal, just like me, huh?" she said. Fortunately, pictures didn't have sound then because Barbara had a crudeness, even a vulgarity, to her voice, that was no match for her stunning but fragile beauty. Like so many stars of that era, the voice didn't match the face. The same was true of John Gilbert, lying nude in the next room. He was a handsome and virile man, but his voice was "light," not effeminate.

Barbara made no mention of her deflowering by Chaney, treating it as if such an event was a daily occurrence in her life.

Over drinks, we chatted intimately, as she filled me in on the details of her past life. Regrettably, those details, as I was to learn, changed from day to day. Throughout my friendship with her, which was to last until the final day of her too brief life, she constantly rewrote her autobiography in her mind.

"I want to live with a whirlwind intensity," she said. "You see, I'm a poet, and I want to create beautiful verses. But I know that beautiful verses can only come from the pain and horrid experience of life. I suffered in my life because I want my poetry to be great."

"I didn't know you were a writer."

"Darling, I'm much older than you think," she said. "I was just pretending to be a schoolgirl when that fucker, Chaplin, picked me up.

Actually I was born in 1896."

By a quick calculation I figured that she was now twenty-four years old, although she hardly looked it. She was about ten years older than I thought she was when I'd first met her. "Why were you pretending to be a schoolgirl?" I asked, completely dumbfounded.

"I was hiding out," she said. "A long story. I was no virgin when I met Charlie. I let him think that. I'm an actress and a great one. I've been married a few times."

"A few times," I said, completely astonished at what she was revealing to me.

"The first time to a guy named Jack Lyttle," she said. "His name was the only thing little about him. He was a young rancher who used to spot me out in the fields. One day he came along on his horse, swooped me up in his arms, and carried me away. I married this cavalier. But only a few months later he died of pneumonia. I was a widow at sixteen."

"I'm so sorry," I said.

"Don't worry for me," she said. "Life's too short. I remarried right away to a Lawrence Converse. He was a handsome young lawyer in Los Angeles. He was rich. Came from a great family. He was well educated. Encouraged me in my writing. He was too perfect. When the announcement of our wedding appeared in the Los Angeles paper, the first Mrs. Lawrence Converse showed up in court with their three children. He'd fled his household and had committed bigamy when he'd married me."

"Did he go to jail?" I asked, not knowing if she were really telling the truth.

"You won't believe this," she said, "but it's all true. His defense was that when he met me, he found my beauty so overwhelming it wiped out his previous memory. In his amnesia he married me. He claimed I'd cast a magic spell on him like a witch, and he'd developed this obsession for me. His attorneys said a blood clot was causing this amnesia. He was operated on to remove the clot and died on the operating table."

"Oh, my God," I said, "I can't believe all this happened to you."

"All that had happened to me by the time I met you in the schoolyard," she said. "I had to run away. Since I had to make a living, I got this job working as an interpretative dancer at private clubs. I've been arrested once or twice. Ince has hired me for the party tonight. Stick around and see for yourself. After my dance, I'll go to bed with the guests Ince selects for me."

"The widow Barbara LaMarr," I said, sighing in exasperation.

"You haven't heard anything yet," she said. "I even took a third husband, Phil Ainsworth. I met him on one of my dancing gigs. I don't know why he married me, but he did. Two nights after our marriage, I caught him in bed with another chorus boy. He was homosexual." She reached over and patted my cheek. "Just like you, babycakes. I have nothing against homosexuals except I don't recommend a woman marry them. They made great pals, though."

"For God's sake, why in hell did you marry all these guys?" I asked. "Take them to bed and call it a night."

"I even married another guy," she said. "Ben Deely. I was on the rebound from Phil. Ben's a comedian. He was more of a comedian in bed than he was on stage. He was also an incurable alcoholic. He never got it up for me on our married night. I left our hotel room and found other men for the night who had no trouble satisfying me—that is, if any man can truly satisfy me."

"I can't believe it," I said. "You're still a baby but with four marriages."

"Men and writing, my true passion in life," she said. "I've already written some movie scenarios which I've sold to Fox."

"That's terrific," I said.

"But wherever I go, people tell me I'm too beautiful to be behind a camera. One day I met Mary Pickford. She told me my 'vibrant magnetism should be shared by film audiences.' You don't think she's a dyke, do you?"

"Not a chance," I said.

"Her boy friend's coming here tonight," she said.

"Surely you don't mean Douglas Fairbanks?" I asked.

"Who else?" I've been fucking him a lot— that is when he isn't pounding Pickford or Mildred Harris. He's promised me a screen role. As a wicked vamp, naturally. I may get a job before Doug comes through. It's in a picture called *Harriet and the Piper*. It's almost certain. The script is no good. I'm going to call myself Barbara Deely in the billing. I'll save the LaMarr until I do that picture with Doug."

"I can't wait to see it."

She claimed she'd done film work before. "I've even filmed some quickie westerns in Arizona."

"I had no idea you were in films before."

"The parts were shit," she said. "I don't want to talk about them. I did some other film work too. Not feature films. These were dancing shorts. I did some with Clifton Webb, the hoofer. Do you know of him?"

"I've heard of him," I said, remembering that luncheon date with John Barrymore and Jeanne Eagels.

"He's a homosexual, you know."

"I had heard that."

"I also did some dancing shorts in New York with Valentino," she said. "He's an amazing dancer. I adore him. What a sensation he's become. You've seen *The Four Horsemen* thing, haven't you?"

"I have indeed like the rest of the world," I said, trying to suppress my jealousy.

"I finally reached him to tell him I'm back in Los Angeles," she said. "We had this torrid affair in New York. I just love his Italian sausage. He's a great fucker. He called me back the other night. We're going to meet tomorrow night to resume our hot nights in bed. Once you've been fucked by Valentino, you remember it."

"From what I've heard, that's true." I said.

"I've also met Louis B. Mayer," she said. "He's hot for me. I've fucked him several times. He's promised to make me a big star. How can I lose? I've got Louis B. Mayer, Douglas Fairbanks, and even Mary Pickford predicting major stardom."

For that one moment, Barbara reminded me of Mae Murray, as both shared a kind of self-enchantment.

So many actresses I met in Hollywood were dreaming of super-stardom long before that term came into vogue. But in Barbara's case I felt the dream might be realized. She could indeed light up the silver screen. Another star in the years ahead would capture some of Barbara's beauty. Hedy Lamarr was almost as beautiful as Barbara, but had a dead-pan expression, unlike Barbara's more expressive face. Louis B. Mayer himself had changed Hedy's name from Kreisler to Lamarr in honor of his long-ago girl friend. Elizabeth Taylor at the peak of her beauty was the only other star who captured Barbara's gorgeous essence on the screen, a rich beauty of haunting quality. Barbara had jet-black hair, big violet eyes, as large as Joan Crawford's, and a delicate light skin like a porcelain doll.

"I think you're going to make it," I assured her. "You're going to get two kinds of fans, one who'll say you're a hot-looking babe, and another who'll claim yours is the face to launch a thousand dreams."

"Darling, everything you say about me is true, I just know it, but there will be one final title for me. I intend to become the ultimate jazz age goddess. It will happen fast and soon, and I'll have to write my own autobiography before it's too late. I'll call it *Young, Beautiful, and Damned.*"

As one drink led to another and another, Barbara and I got to know each other. I felt an instant friendship and bond with her like the one I'd established with Rod St. Just.

Barbara told me she fell in love immediately. "I don't believe you have to get to know a man. If he's going to be your lover, you'll know it at once. I don't see all this shit about waiting around to make up your mind. Life's too short for that."

As she talked, Barbara seemed to weave her belief that life's too short into almost every one of her utterances. As I got to know her better, she repeated that conviction over and over in the course of a day.

"I've never been in love with just one man," she said. "Certainly with none of my husbands, even if one or two of them were criminally handsome. I'm in love with love."

We talked of vamps on the screen, as I told her about the ill-fated career of my sister, Lotte Lee, never admitting that I was, in fact, Lotte Lee.

"I'm sorry I didn't get to meet Lotte," Barbara said. "I suspected she might be a blonde version of me. If I become a vamp on the screen, I won't be like Theda Bara. Not at all.

Theodosia Goodman from Ohio. She's all manufactured. I'll be for real. Bara is the same old wicked slut on the screen in every movie she makes. 'Kiss me, my fool.' How ridiculous! My vamping will be more graceful, more youthful, certainly more believable. Of course, I won't be Mary Pickford either. Dear sweet Mary, the little girl who never grows old. No one will ever compare me to her. The only thing Mary and I share in common is that we both have vaginas that can accommodate that unfortunate curvature of Doug's dick."

Over her drink, she desperately reached out for my hand. "I believe you should live every moment to the fullest. This is our only time around. There is no hereafter. There is so much to see and experience right now—our only chance. I feel I won't be able to do it all. Sometimes I wake up in the middle of the night drenched with sweat, thinking the end will come too soon. I sleep as little as possible. I'm too afraid I'll miss something."

Before the afternoon had faded, before the Hollywood party had begun, and even before I descended on John Gilbert, I'd agreed to let Barbara move in with me at the Hollywood Hotel.

She kissed me on the lips. "I feel you're just like me. If you thought your life was going good before you met me, you'll learn just how good it can get."

In front of me, she pulled off her white bathing suit. She stood fully and beautifully nude. "We'll have such fun times. Men, Men, Men."

To me but also to the rapidly dying afternoon sun, she shouted. "Lovers, lovers, lovers. They're just like the red rose. More beautiful by the dozen." With that pronouncement, she plunged into the pool.

Moving Barbara LaMarr into my suite began a period of descent into drugs and alcoholism that were already there waiting for me but which I'd never succumbed to before. I don't blame anybody but myself for my fall. Perhaps if I'd found work as a film star, and not those damn extra bits, I would have avoided drink and drugs. Often I slept until one or two o'clock in the afternoon.

Knowing I had money coming in, I felt I didn't really have to get up at five o'clock in

the morning and go to some set where I'd mill around all day in the hot sun and find I'd been cast as part of a crowd scene. One time I was one of the rabble screaming for the head of Marie Antoinette at the re-created Place de la Concorde in Paris; another day I was a cowboy out in some sagebrush country being served a lunch of pork and beans poured out of a tin can and heated in a big black iron pot of dubious hygiene.

When Barbara, without an invitation, walked in on John Gilbert and me that afternoon at the house of Tom Ince, it began a sexual pattern that would become the whispered gossip of Hollywood. I couldn't pretend I'd never had a three-way with a man and a woman before. The memory of such a sexual encounter between Olive Thomas and Jack Pickford was all too vivid in my memory.

I didn't think I needed to work as a team with Barbara until I, in time, saw that many men in Hollywood were eager to sample "the world's most beautiful girl" and "the world's most beautiful boy" at the same time. The possibilities were endless for three ways, as Barbara and I could team up with Rodolfo, Richard Dix, William Boyd, Tom Mix, Joe Godsol, Douglas Fairbanks Sr., Theodore Kosloff, William Desmond Taylor, Wallace Reid, Tom Ince, Tom Moore, and—dare I consider the possibility?—Charlie himself. As for Ramon, Rod La Rocque, and Antonio Moreno, I thought it best to keep things as they were. With those men, it was strictly male-to-male bonding.

John was fucking me at the time Barbara entered our bedroom. But when he looked up to discover this lovely creature standing nude in the room, he invited her to join us in bed. At first I resented her presence until I discovered that I was very much a part of the action. John had recovered his energy and he'd climaxed in me just at the very moment he was licking Barbara in all the right places.

Because of John Gilbert's penchant for breaking into our act, we'd had our routine perfected by the time Rodolfo slipped into my suite at the Hollywood Hotel. Barbara told him I was gone, even though I was secretly hiding in my dressing room. To his apparent surprise, she said I was out of town and had allowed her to use my suite until she could find a place of her own.

An hour later, when Rodolfo was humping Barbara, and on a signal from her, I slipped into the bedroom with a raging hard-on which I plowed into Julio of *The Four Horsemen*. At first he gasped in surprise until he saw who it was. "Ride 'em, Durango," he said, humping Barbara all the harder.

Later, after all of us had showered, Rodolfo announced what a great time he'd had. All of us piled into the bed together.

I was the first to wake up, and, as I did, I discovered a hastily scribbled note from Barbara. She had a "mission of mercy" to perform and wouldn't be back until much later that afternoon. That was to be a pattern repeated during all the short years I knew her. She never announced where she went, and I never inquired.

In the weeks ahead, Rodolfo was playing Armand opposite Nazimova in *Camille*, and that consumed him with a passion. I still saw him alone or with Barbara, but it was clear that he was under the domination of Natacha Rambova and only visited with me when they'd had a fight, which was often, or else when he could no longer tolerate the overweening presence of the combined armed forces of Natacha and Nazimova, two powerful Amazons in spite of their small size.

One afternoon on the set of *Camille*, when Rodolfo wasn't needed for a shot, he said, "It is not sex that draws me to Natacha. I have never bedded her. I find protection in her strong will. She can make decisions for me I can't make for myself. I have not known a womblike love like this since I left my beloved mama in Italy. I feel Natacha can guide my career. She has great artistic taste."

An hour later I was talking to Natacha, and indeed sensed more and more that she was a woman of powerful will and self-direction. Rodolfo was often amused by simple pleasures such as horseback riding and cooking a spaghetti dinner. When he wasn't brooding, he could be playful like a child.

Natacha was the exact opposite. Like Nazimova, she had absolutely no humor at all and viewed herself with a deadly seriousness, One thing she held as absolutely sacrosanct was

the advancement of her artistic career, which I suspected was the main reason she was with Rodolfo in the first place, thinking his stardom would promote hers.

If opposites attract, the two of them had found their soul mates. Rodolfo adored "bambini" and wanted to have a brood of his own. Natacha detested children. He had continental graces and was often ruled by his passions. She was, as she often said herself, "cold as the tit of a witch." If she had any passion at all, it was directed toward Nazimova but mainly toward herself. Every day she showed up in a new costume. She dressed to be admired. I'd never seen her when she wasn't dramatically costumed, with her hair parted in the middle, a mass of floaty draperies and long beady necklaces.

Years later, in 1941, when Nazimova was playing the role of the mother in the remake of Rodolfo's *Blood and Sand*, this time starring another lover of mine, Tyrone Power, she claimed she had discovered Valentino and cast him in *Camille*. She stated falsely that he'd gone from *Camille* into *The Four Horsemen of the Apocalypse*." Sixteen years must have dimmed Nazimova's memory. He'd already created a sensation as Julio in *The Four Horsemen* before filming *Camille*.

On the set of *Camille*, it seemed that Ray C. Smallwood wasn't the director at all. That role was performed by Natacha herself. In the film Valentino became notorious for his popping eyeballs and elongated penciled eyebrows, a look Natacha encouraged and one for which he was later ridiculed, as it greatly feminized him.

When Rodolfo became too love sick on the set, gazing haplessly at the incomparable "beauty and brains," Natacha herself, Nazimova came up to him to bring him back to reality. "You can't have her goodies," Nazimova said, standing before him, hand on her hip. "Why don't you fuck me instead, Armand?"

When he wasn't with me, Rodolfo became friendly with Nazimova's young lover, Paul Ivano. They often went off together to box, ride horseback, play tennis, and drive dangerously in junky cars.

Natacha told me the two men were having an affair, but that did not make her jealous. "I find it amusing the way you men carry on," she said to me. "Such boys. It's like Kosloff and his ten-year-olds. Which reminds me, gossip has it that you yourself are having an affair with a ten or twelve year old—Douglas Fairbanks Jr."

"That is the biggest God damn lie ever told in the history of Hollywood," I said to her before heading to my "stagecoach."

She called me back to her dressing room. "Don't be offended," she said. "Natacha accepts all forms of human love. Nothing is foreign to me. The sin is not who you love but not loving at all."

In her dressing room, Natacha showed me the preliminary sketches for *Salome*, based on the Oscar Wilde play. "It's Nazimova's next film, and I'm already designing the costumes. Nazimova is offering a leading role to Rudy. The play will have an entire cast of nothing but homosexuals, in tribute to Wilde. We're going to ask you to appear in it. You'll play opposite your darling and my former love, Theodore Kosloff. You'll be a slave boy and he'll play a Syrian soldier, your master."

The prospect of that filled me with excitement. For a role like that, I would get out of bed in the morning.

From what I could tell after having made several visits to the set of *Camille*, the part of Armand called for Rodolfo to stand around as Nazimova preened in such costumes as a lizard-tail opera dress. About all he got to do was to kneel down to worship her, begging her to be "your servant, your dog."

In spite of being given such ridiculous lines, word spread through the set that "Valentino was stealing the film from that dyke." That Nazimova could not allow. As she viewed the rushes, it was obvious that Rodolfo was walking away with the picture. When Rodolfo wasn't stealing the picture from Nazimova, Natacha's set was. The whole film was taking place in some Art Deco no man's land—or, in this case—no woman's land. At times Nazimova seemed swallowed up by Natacha's costume designs. One day Nazimova appeared on set in a gown designed of camellia patterns and a black fur train that blossomed open just like a Chinese fan. This extraordi-

narily slim woman seemed lost under a huge curly black wig, her face as pale as death, and her mouth painted scarlet like Mae Murray's fabled bee-stung lips.

Over coffee, I told Smallwood, the so-called director, "Valentino has an animal cunning. No woman—or man either—can steal a picture from him."

"You're right," Smallwood said. "Nazimova knows that and she's enraged."

When I remember the film today, and I often do, I can still see Rodolfo playing Armand at the gambling casino. He thinks Marguerite, played by Nazimova, has betrayed him, and he becomes the brutal avenger, making her submit to him. Obviously he'd carry this technique to far greater glory in *The Sheik*, but *Camille* was his macho launching pad.

Subjecting the Nazimova character to public humiliation, he approaches her, seizes her, pins her arms behind her, and plants a deep kiss on her red lips. He then tosses all the money he'd won into her face. Months later, when American women saw that scene, they swooned at the "cruel" Valentino, wishing some man would dominate them so totally.

Fortunately that scene remained and didn't end up on the cutting-room floor. The one scene that should have belonged to Nazimova—her deathbed scene—went to Rodolfo. At her bedside, he played his role of Armand so perfectly that he even moved the hard-hearted crew to tears. Seeing the final rushes, Nazimova had been horrified that he'd even stolen her biggest moment from her. Unbearably autocratic and temperamental, she ordered that all the close-ups of Rodolfo be cut from the death scene.

Camille would mark the end of Nazimova's reign at Metro. New stars, such as Mae Murray, were waiting to pick up the crown. Studio officials at Metro could no longer tolerate Nazimova's whims, demands, and vagaries. All the "iris" effect of the sets and the extremely soft-focus photography could not disguise the fact that Nazimova was an aging woman in her forties, too old to play Marguerite. All the rice powder in the world couldn't hide the pock marks of a childhood illness, the pits of which seemed to deepen as she aged. Rodolfo, however, looked gorgeous, and the failure of the film at the box office did not harm his career which was about to take off like a skyrocket.

But the worldwide fame of Valentino was almost cut short on the final day of shooting. In spite of the fact she'd closed her bedroom door to him on their wedding night, and had never really been his wife, Jean Acker filed for divorce. Right on the set, Rodolfo was served notice of the suit against him for separate maintenance. Twisting reality, she charged in her brief that he was the one who'd deserted her. "He refused to live with me," she'd told the court, "and has never supported me, his legal wife." She was demanding $300 a month for living expenses and $1,500 to pay her lawyers.

On hearing this news, Rodolfo had become hysterical, storming off the set in the most violent rage I'd ever witnessed before or since. "In Italy, no woman could get away with this," he shouted. "America is disgusting to allow a woman to lie like this."

In a dramatic gesture, he raised his arms to the heavens. "If there is a God, let him strike the bitch down for her lies against me. She deserted me. I pleaded with her." He burst into tears, almost becoming Nazimova herself or at least Natacha Rambova and not the strong macho image of Valentino. Locking the door, he refused to see anybody. I pounded loudly but he wouldn't come to the door. I listened at the door but no sounds came from within.

I went to the director, Smallwood, and begged him to order two stagehands to break in the door. I thought Rodolfo might poison himself or something, as he looked that distraught.

When the men bashed in the door, I ran inside to discover Rodolfo lying nude on the floor, both wrists cut.

He was as still as death itself.

Chapter Thirteen

VALENTINO LIVES!

That was the word that emerged from the hospital where Rodolfo had been secretly taken after his suicide attempt. Nazimova, fearing a scandal, ordered that all the news be suppressed. She didn't even want Natacha to go to the hospital, fearing someone might recognize her, as she was already famously linked with Rodolfo. "Madam," as Nazimova was known on the set, sent her lover, Paul Ivano, and myself.

Rodolfo was alone in an emergency room with a Dr. Brian Sheehan for an hour. At the end of the session, the doctor emerged into the waiting room and asked Ivano and me to follow him into his private office.

I couldn't help but notice that Dr. Sheehan was handsome enough to be a movie star himself, standing six feet two, all blond with eyes of blue.

"Will he be okay?" I asked, urgently imploring this dazzling looker for information.

He smiled at me, flashing real teeth whiter than any dentist at the time could create.

"He'll be just fine," Dr. Sheehan assured both Ivano and me. "The cuts on his wrist are completely superficial. He sliced himself so delicately that a razor's nick is sometimes deeper when you shave. If he bled as much as you reported, he must have forced blood from his wrists. He is, after all, an actor."

"Can we go in to see him?" Ivano asked.

"Sure," Dr. Sheehan said. "Valentino is as healthy as we are. Maybe more so." He winked at me.

Ivano thanked the doctor and headed for Rodolfo's room, as I waited behind to talk to this medical wonder.

"I'm not absolutely sure what that wink meant." I said.

"It meant that Valentino is one healthy specimen," he said. "I gave him a complete physical. As I stuck my finger up his asshole— for purposes of a medical examination, of course—he got immediately hard and was moaning in passion as I fingered him harder. I kept pumping my much experienced finger into him, as I went down on him. I'd hardly gotten all of him swallowed when he shot off into my mouth. Tasted good too."

I was shocked. Up to now I had viewed doctors as revered figures, men you respected like priests or sheriffs. In time, I was to learn what priests and doctors were really up to, but Dr. Sheehan was my first revelation. Maria Jane had once told me that doctors did not have sex lives, and therefore it was proper for women to undress in front of them, because they did not appreciate the female figure. In Dr. Sheehan's case, I think Maria Jane was right. Dr. Sheehan might not appreciate female bodies, but I felt he'd like to give me a physical examination at that very moment. I stammered, not knowing what to say at first. "Nazimova's paying for this, and she wants utter discretion."

"I understand," he said, smiling at me. "As you get to know me, and I hope you will, you will find that Brian Sheehan is the most discreet doctor in Hollywood. "You see, I don't want to work the graveyard shift at hospitals all my life. My dream is to set up a private practice catering just to the film colony." He reached into his top desk drawer and handed me his card. On the back of it he wrote his private home number. "You can call me day or night, especially at night."

I stood looking deeply into his eyes, not believing this was happening. I'd never seduced a doctor before. "I've lost my former doctor in Hollywood, and I'm shopping around for another one, especially one who can be discreet."

"Test me on the Valentino thing," he said. "If word of his suicide attempt doesn't get out, at least from these quarters, you will know I'm your man."

It was at this point I decided to get provocative. "Even without testing you, I know you're my man."

"I'll hold you to that," he said, moving closer to me. "You see, some blonds like Latin types; others like men of ebony. But I'm a blond who likes fellow blonds, although in desperation I take what I can get."

"I'm versatile," I said, "but blond is my favorite color too."

"Time for me later," he said. "Right now I have surgery to perform. You'd better rush to your lover boy before Ivano takes him away from you."

"But Ivano is Nazimova's lover," I said in way of protest. "He's not a homosexual."

"Honey, I don't know how long you've been in Hollywood, but Ivano is as pansy as we are." He leaned over and kissed me on the lips. "I'll expect your call. Sooner than later." With that invitation, he was gone from my life.

But not for long. I'd have need to call on Brian Sheehan again and again throughout my life, both for social and professional reasons. In fact, I single-handedly built up his star-studded clientele, and throughout his life he kept his word, remaining discreet until the end, although many a publisher offered him top dollar for his memoirs.

Whenever one of my star-studded group in the years ahead needed medical attention, we called Dr. Sheehan. It was to Dr. Sheehan that I took Greta Garbo in for a total of eight abortions. Did you hear that count? Eight! Rubbers back then weren't as reliable as today's Trojans. Presumably, it was John Gilbert who caused those eight pregnancies, as

he was a virile man in spite of his squeaky voice. But with Garbo you never could be sure.

When I walked in on Ivano and Rodolfo, I could have sworn that I'd interrupted a lovers' quarrel. Even though Natacha had told me Ivano and Rodolfo were having an affair, it had not really registered because somehow I didn't believe it. At best, I felt they might have slept together once or twice when they'd gotten drunk. Rodolfo had so many affairs I couldn't take a minor involvement with Ivano seriously—that is, if there were any romantic links at all.

I was about to learn differently. Ivano pulled himself up from the bed where he'd been hovering over Rodolfo, no doubt kissing him. "You might as well know," Ivano said to me. "Rodolfo tried to kill himself not because of the Jean Acker divorce, although that is troublesome enough, but because I broke off with him this morning."

I walked over to Rodolfo and looked down at him. His face confirmed what Ivano said. "It's true. I've fallen madly in love with Paul here, and now he's leaving me for another man."

"I thought you were in love with Nazimova," I said, confronting Paul.

"Nazimova is not always available," he said. "In fact, she's almost never available. She's got her girl friends and also her 'husband,' as she calls him. Charles Bryant."

"You mean her business manager?" I asked.

"She just pretends to be married to Bryant," Rodolfo said, sitting up in bed, looking perfectly well. His wrists weren't even bandaged. The wounds were so minor a band-aid sufficed.

"Bryant was an actor when she toured with him in 1902," Ivano said. "He fell in love with her, but they weren't compatible. They tried. But their physical union was never consummated."

"For God's sake, what was the matter?" I asked.

"Bryant's too big for her," Ivano said. "She's very small down there. He practically ripped her apart the first time they tried it." He smiled at me. "However, I found that Bryant wasn't too big for me."

I looked at him, then at Rodolfo. I didn't

really understand the Hollywood I'd stumbled into. Everybody seemed to be in love with everybody else. It made no sense. I took Rodolfo's hand. "I thought you loved Natacha."

"I do," he said. "That is a pure love. But a man needs love and passion in his life. You must understand that."

I cast a jealous glance at Ivano, then looked deeply into Rodolfo's eyes. "I thought I gave you some of that."

"You do," he said. "But I need more. You can supply the sex. At that, you're better than anybody I've ever tried in Hollywood, man or woman. But I need mercurial personalities around me. I need men or women who can make me suffer. You never make me suffer because you're always there for me." He reached out and took Ivano's hand. "Paul makes me beg for it. Sometimes he doesn't grant it and breaks my heart. He causes me the great pain I need to endure as an artist."

I withdrew from Rodolfo as a nurse entered the room, telling us we had to go and let her patient get a good night's rest. Defiantly and right in front of the nurse, I bent down and kissed Rodolfo gently on the lips. "Good night, sweet prince," I said. "I'll be here first thing in the morning, tending to your needs."

"The patient will be dismissed at eight o'clock," the nurse said abruptly, looking at us with disgust. She apparently assumed that all of us were foreigners, and from the look on her face I suspected she felt this was how all exotics behaved.

"Will you be here for me, Paul?" Rodolfo asked.

"I'll be your friend—that's all," Ivano said. "The physical thing between us has got to stop. Too many people know about that. As a boy, I must belong only to one man at a time. I now have the promise of someone in my life. Between Nazimova and my new male lover, I have a full agenda. There can be only one man and one woman in my life at the time."

"Is that your final word?" Rodolfo asked.

"I've made up my mind," Ivano said, before walking out of the room.

"The little shit," Rodolfo said after he'd left. "To think I tried to commit suicide over that one. He's not worth it."

"How quickly we fall in and out of love," I said sarcastically.

"Darling, I'm an artist, and that's what artists do," he said. "I'm temperamental. Controlled by my emotions. If you were an artist, you'd understand that. As it is, you're nothing but a good, reliable, corn-fed farm boy from Kansas, wherever in the hell that awful place is." He reached out and pulled me down to him and kissed me hard. "Good night. Come by in the morning and pick me up. In the meantime, I want to catch up on my sleep."

As the nurse peered into the door again, I retreated at once, fearing she'd bodily kick me out. In the hallway Ivano was waiting. "Let's go for a drink, pretty boy," he said, "And get to know each other. You're very attractive."

"I thought there was room for only one man in your life," I said.

"My sugar daddy is on his way by train from the east coast to reclaim me right now," he said. "The way I figure it, his train must be going through the cornfields of the Middle West, so you and I have plenty of time."

Over drinks at the Ship Café, Ivano told me of his ambition to become the greatest cameraman in Hollywood, and of his belief that his new male sponsor was going to help launch him into a big time Hollywood career.

"Please tell me who it is?" I said. "The suspense is killing me."

"You'd die," he said. "Just up and die. You could guess all night, and never come up with the right guy."

"If we can't talk about your new lover, then tell me about Natacha and Theodore Kosloff," I said.

"You mean the buckshot thing?"

"Exactly," I said. "You know about that."

"Honey boy," he said, "I was there to help pick the buckshot out of her knee. What a son of a bitch he was to have done that to her. Nazimova was furious, but not mad enough to fire Kosloff from *Salome*." Nazimova understands a lover's quarrel."

"Bullshit," I said. "A lover's quarrel. He might have killed her."

"Natacha was injured but she never intended to sue. First, she feared the publicity. She didn't want scandal attached to her name just as it was announced that she was going to become Nazimova's new artistic director. Also, Nazimova and Natacha are very career oriented. Both of them figured they would have need of Kosloff's services, like on their upcoming film, *Salome*."

"I've been promised a role in that one," I said. "I'm going to be Theodore's slave boy. He's going to play a Syrian soldier."

"Lucky girl," Ivano said. "I'd love to be a slave boy to that one. Natacha says he's really hung. I've seen him in ballet tights, but you can't really tell about a man until you see it fully hard. My new lover's got a big one. I like them big. Men built like Valentino. But that Charles Bryant's got him beat by a long shot." He reached over under the table and felt me. "Rudy says you've got a big one too. Want me to try it on for size tonight? I feel it getting hard just at my touch."

"I'd like to go back to your apartment and fuck you," I said. "If you could make Rodolfo fall in love with you, you must be very special indeed."

As we left for our night of adventure, I noticed that fake German baron sitting by himself in the far corner of the café. Had he given up on stalking Rodolfo and had taken to stalking me now? He sent shivers down my spine. I felt if there were a vampire in Hollywood, it was this pseudo nobleman, not poor Theda Bara. I was going to confront Rodolfo about his mysterious baron. Maybe eventually I could force Rodolfo to tell me the truth about him. I felt both Rodolfo and I were in some sort of danger from him, even though I'd seen Rodolfo enter this same café with him.

That promise of love held out by Ivano didn't happen. I managed to fuck him all right, but it was not memorable. He had genitals of average size, maybe an inch or so less, and he liked to be penetrated but he lay back on the bed like a cadaver in a morgue. I imagined fucking him would be the same as plowing Natacha. I did lure an orgasm out of him, and he'd kissed me more passionately at the end than when I was having sex with him, assuring me I was the "best ever." Maybe he meant it. But I was not tempted to repeat it.

After we'd snorted some cocaine, I did agree to be his sometimes lover—that is, when his evenings weren't occupied with this big male

star heading to Los Angeles on the Santa Fe, the same train I'd taken from Kansas to my dream of glory and fame in Hollywood. Ivano moved in the same power circles I did, and I felt I'd want to bed him for that reason alone.

Long after his passion for me had faded, I was to see and know Ivano for years. He actually did become a cameraman, though hardly the great one he'd envisioned on that long ago night when I'd first seduced him.

His last big picture was *The Shanghai Gesture* in 1942 when Josef von Sternberg wasn't getting Marlene Dietrich as his star but ended up with Gene Tierney, John Kennedy's future girl friend. I was on the set to suck off Victor Mature, who was also sharing his notoriously big cock with Ivano. That was the last "A" picture Ivano shot. In the years ahead he was assigned to "B" movies like *Spider Woman Strikes Back,* made in 1947.

Mostly I knew him in the Twenties, and only ran into him a few times in the Forties. Actually, our friendship had more or less ended in 1935 when he'd married a woman named "Greta" (no, not that one).

Occasionally I would encounter Ivano over the next two decades during my gossip columnist days. I saw him even less in 1970 when he retired from pictures, or else films retired from him. Actually our reunion was only on one occasion shortly before his death in 1984 at the age of eighty-four.

Paul Ivano had outlived all the fabled people who'd passed through and touched his life— Natacha Rambova, Alla Nazimova, and Rudolph Valentino. Even that big-time star and former male patron of his had passed on seven years before.

In time, I did find out who that big male star was who was sleeping with Ivano, and the news hit me with the same impact it would have had I learned Paul Ivano and Winston Churchill were lovers.

*****

Before going to the train station in Los Angeles to pick up Charlie on his return from New York, I stopped by the hospital to rescue

Rodolfo. Surprisingly, he didn't want to be taken home but preferred to remain in the clinic. He told me he appreciated the "womblike comfort" of the place, and found it a perfect retreat.

Natacha had visited secretly and warned him that if he made *The Sheik*, his future career would be destroyed. That had sent him into a deep depression, fearing he had to honor his commitment to Paramount in spite of Natacha's warnings.

Brian came into the room, and Rodolfo begged for some sedative that would knock him out and help him get over his depression. He certainly didn't have to be hospitalized because of those Band-Aids on his wrists. Ever ready to cater to the stars, Brian agreed to give him a sedative and let Rodolfo remain at the clinic as long as he wanted.

After kissing Rodolfo goodbye, a real wet one, I went to Brian's office where I gave him an even wetter kiss. Then it was over to Charlie's house to pick up Kono to take him to the train station to greet Charlie upon his return.

It was a different Charlie waiting at the station in Los Angeles where Kono and I stood on the platform to welcome him home. He shook my hand but seemed embarrassed to see me. "One chauffeur is enough," he said brusquely as if to dismiss me. "Both of you didn't need to show up."

Taken aback at his rudeness, I was shocked to be demoted to the role of his chauffeur again. I thought I shared a tiny part of his heart, but now feared I no longer could claim such territory. I was hurt and confused. At least he let me ride in the back seat with him, but did not make eye contact.

Maybe his heart did belong to Florence Deshon. He leaned back in his seat and closed his eyes. "I gave Florence a choice," he said. "She could have either me or Max Eastman. She chose Eastman."

"I'm sorry," I said, reaching for his hand to comfort him.

He quickly removed it, folding his arms to prevent me from touching him. "Don't feel sorry for me," he said. "I can have her back if I want her. I spent a night at a Chicago hotel. I called her. She was hysterical, claiming she'd made an 'absolutely insane' mistake. Their first night together Eastman and Florence launched World War I. It seems he didn't want her back but was secretly hoping she'd chose me over him. She's heading on the train for Los Angeles now. Should be here tomorrow."

"Then you've won," I said. "I'm happy for you."

"Just who in hell do you think you are, feeling happy for the great Charlie Chaplin? Charlie Chaplin will be the only person in the world to determine when he's happy and when he's sad as a clown. I've decided I'm unhappy. At least where Florence is concerned. While I was waiting for Florence to make up her mind. Correction. I wasn't exactly waiting. I've fallen in love with another actress, May Collins."

I settled back into my seat, figuring if he wanted to tell me about Miss Collins he would.

After a long silence, he spoke. "While I was in New York, Sydney, my half-brother, hired May to answer my mail. She's plump, round, bright eyed and bushy tailed, rosy faced, and filled with cheer—not my usual type." He unfolded his arms and for the first time reached for my hand. "But, as you of all people know, I demand variety."

The rest of the ride was filled with talk about Jackie Coogan. Charlie seemed to resent Coogan's success in *The Kid*, feeling it detracted seriously from his own performance. "The little prick tried to steal the film from me."

The Kid did, in fact, launch Jackie Coogan, and over the next four years he'd star in nine pictures from *Peck's Bad Boy* to *Oliver Twist*, earning upward of $2 million which wouldn't be there in the bank for him when he grew up. After this meteoric rise his career nose-dived, until he made a comeback as the bald-headed, demonic Uncle Fester in the *Addams Family* television series.

Not knowing what else to say, I asked if First National had met his price for *The Kid*. "They finally offered me one and a half million, which was my price all along. As you know, it's racking up record receipts around the world."

Leaving Barbara LaMarr to her own amusements at the Hollywood Hotel, I opted to spend his first night back with Charlie. Immediately when he'd gotten home, he rushed to his bedroom and locked the door.

When Kono came in, carrying luggage, I turned to him. "What should I do? Stay or leave?"

"Don't ask me." he said. "I know about normal love. I don't know about abnormal love. You pansy boys must decide these things for yourself."

I decided to stay. By ten o'clock Charlie had not emerged from his room. I went to his door and rapped loudly. There was no answer. I tried the door but found it locked. As I was returning to my own bedroom, I heard him unlock his door. He came into my darkened room stark naked.

"We've got to talk," he said. "I don't mean to break your heart, because you've served some very useful purpose for me, for which, I must say, you've been rewarded like I've never rewarded anybody else in my life. You know one of my darkest secrets." He coughed slightly. "About the Black Panther side of my nature. That stupid marriage to you. I must have been out of my mind. You know things that could ruin my career forever and make me the laughing stock of America."

"I'll never tell."

"If you ever do, your weekly check disappears," he said.

"I'm not a blackmailer, Charlie."

"Fine," he said, turning to leave. He hesitated a moment before spinning around to confront me. "Why don't you leave tonight? I've bought that stagecoach for you. If the motor is working, you can go back to the Hollywood Hotel. I'll have no more need of your services."

"I will," I said, getting up from the bed to dress. "But I thought we had something more. Was I just someone who provided services to you?"

"You've got that right." he said. "I don't love you. You're a homosexual. I'm not. I love women. In fact, I have so many women in my life I'm very confused. All of them are causing me trouble."

"Being with you has meant a lot to me," I said, tears welling in my eyes. I couldn't believe it, but I was actually crying over the loss of Charlie Chaplin. Me, who had Wallace Reid and Valentino, plus a few others.

"With you, I explored this disgusting side of my nature to the fullest," he said, "and I'm ashamed of myself and what we did together. If you stay here, you'll remind me of my dark side every day of my life, and I want to forget it."

"I'm leaving," I said, choking on my tears.

"You must," he said, "because I'm expecting someone right now. I don't want you here when my new love arrives."

"You mean May Collins?" I asked.

"You might say that—then again you might not."

"I'll get out real quick," I promised.

He headed for the door, but turned and looked back at me. "You're losing me but you're getting all that glorious money coming in every week. I'm sure it'll help you get over me as you count it every night." Again he started to leave the room, but paused. "One more thing. Forget that pursuit of stardom. You have no talent. Charlie Chaplin has talent. Why don't you take up some other profession? Not blackmailing, but real estate."

With that hurtful pronouncement he was gone.

*****

It was very late on the same night after leaving Charlie's that I was still awake at my suite at the Hollywood Hotel. If anyone, other than Rodolfo himself, could cure me of my heartsick blues, it was Theodore Kosloff who I had called earlier when Barbara LaMarr was still in the suite.

To lure him away from his kiddie harem, I had promised him both Barbara and myself. But when he'd arrived two hours late, Barbara had long ago skipped out, claiming she'd been invited to a special party in Los Angeles for Louis B. Mayer. Who knows what that party was, or even if Mayer would be there?

As always, Theodore did not believe in a lot of preliminaries before sex. When he wanted sex, he signaled his desire not by kissing, as some lovers do, but by biting viciously into my neck, like an animal asserting its dominance. Although painful, it was inevitably erotic for me. With Theodore Kosloff on top of you, it was homosexual heaven.

No wonder Natacha had fled from him. He didn't want intercourse: he wanted rape. If you weren't into his type of rough love-making, it would be thirty to forty minutes at the bottom of hell. But I was into it and always left his bed—or my bed—completely satisfied, wondering how any man could ever thrill me again after my having known the mighty inches of that great Russian dancer. Nijinsky had become but a distant memory.

Shortly after Theodore left to pursue whatever it was back then that he was pursuing, a call came in. It could be from anyone. Was I up to taking on another lover after having been so thoroughly deflowered by Theodore?

It was from Marion Davies, who was hysterical, crying and screaming over the phone. She'd had a big row with W.R., who'd accused her of fucking Joe Godsol. Although Marion and I had been discreet about her visits to Godsol, the financier had not kept his trap shut. He'd bragged to several men how he'd fucked Marion, and word had reached Louis B. Mayer who had tipped off Hearst to what was going on. Marion said he'd walked out on her after the fight. Their famous relationship was over.

"Not only that," Marion said. "I'm pregnant."

"Oh, fuck," was all I managed to say.

"Not by W.R. but by Joe," she claimed. "W.R. has been impotent for the past few months. All we do is some heavy petting."

"What are you going to do?"

She told me she was going with a sister to Tijuana to face "one of those hog butchers down there."

"Don't, it's not safe," I said. An idea was forming in my head. I told Marion I'd be in touch with her within the hour. Immediately after hanging up, I called Dr. Sheehan at the private number he'd given me. He'd already handled Rodolfo's suicide attempt. Why not an abortion for Marion Davies?

Reaching a somewhat sleepy Brian at his home, I gave him a full report, and he immediately volunteered to perform the abortion. Marion was all too happy to learn that the abortion would be performed in a safe and sanitary hospital right in Los Angeles.

Only Dr. Sheehan would know the truth. Other members of the staff would be told that Marion was having some "female problems" and some difficulty with her urinary tract—nothing major, nothing to alert the press about. The staff would be informed that the surgery was very minor and Miss Davies would be released the following morning.

If the character of Dr. Kildare had been created at the time, Brian Sheehan could have played the role instead of Richard Chamberlain. Brian was the model of decorum as he examined Marion while I waited in the next room. He'd booked the adjoining room for me at Marion's request as she wanted me nearby in case there were any problems.

I'd taken her to the hospital, and she'd been nervous and strained, not only about her breakup with W.R. but about the upcoming operation. This was to be the first of several abortions she'd have in the years ahead.

"My career would be ruined if I had a baby out of wedlock," she said, and I knew that was true. It was still a world where even the exposure of Francis X. Bushman's divorce and subsequent marriage to Beverly Bayne had ruined both their careers. An abortion was not acceptable. Even Mary Pickford and Doug Fairbanks feared for a time their joint divorces would spell the end of their careers.

Around four o'clock in the morning Brian came into my hospital room where I'd been waiting anxiously. "It went well," he said. "She's resting now."

"Thank God."

"Thank someone." He walked over and planted a tender kiss on my cherry-red lips. "I think you've launched me into that career I've always dreamed about. Doctor to the stars."

Right in front of me, he peeled off his white uniform and stood stark naked, as if awaiting my approval. "Am I allowed to whistle in a hospital?" I asked. This guy was in the league of William Boyd or Richard Dix, not Bobby Harron or Charles Ray. Brian was prime grade A meat, unlike Paul Ivano.

When Brian headed for the bathroom and a good, cleansing scrubdown, I followed him to help out. I viewed it as training for my role as the slave boy in *Salome* when I'd have to tend to that luscious body of Theodore Kosloff.

But thoughts of Theodore vanished as I washed Brian, starting with a scrubdown of his back but moving on to other more private parts. Even before leaving the bathroom, I'd given him a thorough medical examination, and he'd passed the test beautifully. Later, after we'd dried off, he gave me the first of what would be a series of rectal probes that would continue for years and years. I had found my own private doctor.

Still asleep, I woke up in the hospital room to someone's nudging. It must have been noon. Opening my eyes and expecting Brian, I encountered the face of the Chief himself. In a change of heart, W.R. had decided to forgive Marion and had had her whereabouts tracked to the hospital. "Marion has told me everything," he said. "You did well, boy. You earn that paycheck I give you. Marion's being loaded into a limousine right now."

"I hope she's okay," I said.

"She'll be fine," he said. "If word of this got out, it'd ruin the career I'm so carefully building for her." A bitter frown crossed his brow. "I could just imagine what my enemies would do with this information."

Getting out of bed stark naked, I paraded in front of W.R. as I put on my clothes.

"You believe in sleeping with nothing on," he said. "Just like Marion, my little Rosebud. I always wear pajamas myself. I figure the more I cover of my pear-shaped body, the better I look."

He shook my hand at the door and invited me to go with him this weekend to the construction site of San Simeon, some grand castle he was building somewhere north of Los Angeles. I thought he was living luxuriously in Santa Monica and didn't know why he needed a grander place, but I could never figure out the workings of his mind.

"Marion wants me to invite Tom Ince," he said. "I understand you know him. Great guy. He and I might go into the picture business together."

Without confiding anything to W.R., I knew what that meant. Marion's dalliances with Charlie and with Joe Godsol were now too obvious. Tom Ince was her next victim.

Hearst had an amazing way of forgiving Marion's suitors. He'd already forgiven Charlie

and continued to entertain The Little Tramp. In time he would forgive Godsol. In the months ahead as Marion's *When Knighthood Was in Flower* became the third biggest box office success of 1923, Hearst broke off from Adolph Zukor and launched his own distribution company, calling it Goldwyn-Cosmopolitan. His partner? None other than thick-dicked Joe Godsol, head of Goldwyn Pictures.

Godsol even tried to sell Goldwyn Pictures to Hearst. Short of cash, W.R. regretted it but had to turn down the offer. Marcus Loew was only too willing to buy into the deal. Loew combined Metro Pictures with Goldwyn Pictures, and Louis B. Mayer was named as general manager. Metro-Goldwyn pictures was launched (Mayer got his name tacked on much later). The distribution company of Hearst and Godsol eventually emerged into this new entity created by Loew.

That picture deal was a futuristic tidbit I tossed in to annoy the Bitch of Buchenwald and throw off her recording of events in sequence.

"Back to the hospital and this child murderer you got involved with," she warned me, as my memory went back to a somewhat pathetic W.R. Hearst standing in that forlorn hospital room with me.

At the door W.R leaned in so close to me I thought he was going to kiss me. Far from it. He wanted to whisper something confidential. "Why don't you invite your sister along to San Simeon?" he asked. "I know she's in hiding. But it'll be a very discreet weekend—no photographers, no press, no Lolly Parsons."

"I'll see what I can do."

He looked at me with the ferocity he might give one of his managing editors who'd displeased him. "At the money I'm paying you, I expect Lotte Lee to be at San Simeon, if only for an hour or two."

"That I could arrange," I promised, as a plan formulated in my brain.

"You see," he said, still leaning in close. "I've been having a few problems." He looked at me, all ferocity gone. If anything he looked like an overgrown child asking to be forgiven. "You know. You see, it's like this. Men have these problems from time to time. I've been having them with Marion. But with Lotte I didn't have that problem. Your sister really got a rise out of me. I've got to have her back. I go around feeling I need satisfaction, and I can't get it." He looked at me one final time before leaving, and it was obvious he was issuing a command.

If I wanted my paycheck, I'd deliver Lotte Lee to him. "See you this weekend. Meet me Friday afternoon at three o'clock at the Santa Monica place. Until then." At the door, he hesitated. He reached into his pocket and pulled out an envelope. "There's one-thousand dollars there. In one-hundred dollar bills. Give that to your Dr. Sheehan. Tell him we want to retain him as our private physician."

"He'd be delighted."

With that he was gone, and I'd hardly had time to brush my teeth before Brian came back into the room. Dressed in his street clothes, not his usual white uniform, he told me he had the day off and would like to spend it with me.

He said he'd checked on Rodolfo, who still wanted to stay at the clinic a little while longer. "Does he want to see me?" I asked eagerly. Brian told me Rodolfo didn't want to see anybody, and had even turned down a visit from Natacha Rambova herself. "He must be depressed," I said, "because he's always there for that one."

I presented Brian with the money W.R. had left for him, and the doctor was like a kid at Christmas, that is, a brat whose parents had been particularly generous to him. "I've never made this much money before," Brian said, counting every dollar. "All this has convinced me I've chosen the right direction to go as a doctor and you're my boy, the one who really got me started." He headed for me, wetting his lips as he moved closer.

Over lunch at the Ship Café, Brian told me of a recent operation he'd performed on Virginia Rappé, a two-bit actress whom I'd never met but whose name was familiar with me. One of my unkindest critics once called me a "boy Virginia Rappé, a reference to the fact I slept around with any male star who asked. Her name was pronounced RAP-PAY, and she was already a notorious figure in Hollywood. Brian told me that before coming to him she'd already had four abortions performed on her before the age of sixteen. He'd performed the

fifth.

"I understand that she was kicked off the Keystone lot because she was spreading gonorrhea."

"That was true," Brian said. "Both Rappé and her lover, Henry Pathé Lehrman, had gonorrhea. Mack Sennett had the lot fumigated when those two left. But it came too late for him. She gave him this little venereal problem, too, and Sennett passed it on to Mabel Normand, or so I heard."

"Oh, shit," I said, fearing she'd passed it on to William Desmond Taylor who might have passed it on to Antonio Moreno and me, maybe even to Mary Miles Minter and her mother, Charlotte Shelby.

"Don't worry," he cautioned me. "You don't have a venereal disease. No symptoms, whatsoever." His eyes sparkled. "However, I should test your other friends. Maybe you could send each of them to me privately. I could check on their health and maybe they would become my clients."

"I'll do that." I said. "It's for their own good. All of us need a doctor who can be very discreet and who we can call in the middle of a dark night when we've shot someone."

"Rappé knows this witch, Maude Delmont, sometimes called Bambina," Brian said. "The LA police have filed 50 counts against Bambina. Extortion. Bigamy, Fraud, Racketeering. She's also a professional co-respondent for blackmailers."

"What does that mean?" I asked. "She traps someone trying to get a divorce, is caught having sex with them, and then is named as a co-respondent."

"You got it," he said. "A lovely woman."

"What a way to make a living," I said.

"I don't want to get involved, but while Rappé was in the hospital with Bambina, I secretly overheard them talking about a scheme that involves Fatty Arbuckle."

"I know him," I said. "Not very well."

"If you do, you might warn him," Brian cautioned." He's having a big party at the St. Francis Hotel in San Francisco this weekend. Arbuckle is going to be set up. Bambina is going to be there 'escorting' Rappé. This hag, Bambina, is going to encourage Arbuckle's friends to fuck Rappé. Arbuckle has this

Francis X. Bushman dildo which I understand Fatty likes to insert into women. Young boys, too. He's impotent and apparently gets his kicks inserting large objects into his victims."

"I've heard that," I said, reluctant to admit that it was I who'd delivered the mighty Bushman dildo to Arbuckle.

"Those two are scheming," he said. "Rappé's vagina has hardly healed from the recent abortion. Bambina is goading her into intercourse. Maybe she's even going to ask Arbuckle to shove the dildo into Rappé. Bambina warned Rappé that she'll bleed but can be taken to a hospital. The bitch has convinced this young girl that if she'll suffer through this—the blood and everything—that they'll be able to blackmail Arbuckle for $50,000, even more if some prominent friends of Fatty are there who can also be blackmailed."

"I'd better warn Arbuckle," I said. "He's vaguely connected with a friend of mine by the name of Ramon. He's Mexican. Arbuckle wants Ramon to perform with the dildo for some of his homosexual friends."

"Tell your friend to head back South of the Border," Brian said.

"I'll contact Arbuckle and warn him," I said. "I don't know if he'll listen. He's one crazy pig. He's not only fat around the waist but fat in his pig head too."

"I'm just passing this on to you" he said, "because I think this bigtime—big in more ways than one—film star is heading for a fall. He'd better call off that whole San Francisco thing."

"I'll see what I can do, although I don't like this Arbuckle creature at all. He's coarse and vulgar, but a lot of Hollywood stars like him, especially Chaplin and Mabel Normand."

"Remember, don't involve my name at all," Brian said. "I'm trying to make a name for myself in Hollywood as a doctor who can be discreet. If word gets out that I stand in the ward behind a curtain and listen to the secrets of my patients, I won't get off the ground as a doctor to the stars."

"Oh, yes, you will," I said. "One of your next assignments will be to cure the impotence of W.R. Hearst himself." I smiled and reached for his hand under the table. "Of course, I'll have my own role to play in that." Brian looked puzzled, but I could hardly tell him that I was bringing my famous—now notorious—sister, Lotte Lee, out of retirement for an appearance at San Simeon.

Before leaving the Ship Café, Brian called in to check with his clinic. He learned that Rodolfo on a sudden impulse wanted to be checked out of the ward and was claiming that he was being held there against his will. "I'm a prisoner," he'd told the staff repeatedly.

When Brian related all this to me, I suggested we'd better get over there and release Rodolfo at once. "He's got a temper that one—and he's impulsive too. He demands instant gratification. If he doesn't get it, he can be a very naughty boy."

"Don't worry about it," Brian said in his self-assured way. This was one doctor with perfect bedside manners. "Lets drive to the hospital and check him out. Take him home." He looked over at me. "Wherever his home is these days. With you or Ivano?"

"I don't think with me," I said. "Maybe not even with Ivano any more. Maybe with his lady love, Natacha Rambova."

"He seems to go in all directions," Brian said.

"Does he ever."

At the hospital, Rodolfo was fully dressed and waiting impatiently for us. He said he wanted to be taken to the apartment of Paul Ivano. "Paul has found some very big shot star to take care of him."

"Who could it be?" I asked, thinking I'd made the rounds of all the hot shot stars in Hollywood. "You don't mean Nazimova?"

"We know who Nazimova is," Rodolfo said, his patience growing thinner with me. "Someone else. A male star."

I was completely puzzled. As Brian checked his wrists, Rodolfo gave me a hastily scrawled phone number. "Paul said he's to be called at this number late tonight. It's a new phone number. Just installed in his private quarters. I'm to give the number to nobody. I was supposed to call him and report on my condition, but I can't bear to talk to him at this point. You call him for me. You tell him I'm fine. I want to forget all about this suicide thing. I fear I'll never be able to face Natacha again."

At Ivano's bleak and rather sparse apartment, I put Rodolfo to bed as he was complaining of a headache and still felt drowsy from the sedative Brian had given him just before checking him out. I kissed him good-bye as he took my hand and pressed it against his crotch. "Come by in the morning," he said, "and I'll give you this because I know that is what you want. Natacha and Paul are interested in my art, my soul, my inner feelings. With them I talk art and culture. We talk of Europe. My home country. With you, it is sex. The other night you watched as I fucked Barbara LaMarr. You even want to know what I do privately with a woman, and now you do. But for you it is always Valentino the sex machine, not Valentino the man, the artist."

"That's not true," I protested. "We have a lot of sex when we're together. But our relationship is more than that."

"Is it?" he asked, raising one of his recently plucked eyebrows. "Please leave. I need my sleep. Don't come around until ten o'clock. I won't be ready for you until then."

Dismissed like a servant, I left, shutting and locking the door. I headed for my stagecoach where Brian was waiting. I looked at him and smiled.

"Valentino okay?" he asked.

"Physically fine, but a little messed up in the head."

"All the stars are," he said. "I can deal with them."

"You want to be a doctor to the stars?" I asked.

He looked at me as if he hadn't understood me. "You know I do. You're going to help me meet them?"

"Can you get hold of any morphine?" I asked.

"All I want." he said. "You hooked on it or something?"

"If you can get morphine, you can start treating one of the biggest stars in Hollywood."

*****

Fortunately when I called Wallace Reid, I found that his wife, Dorothy, was out on some sort of mission and he had his house to himself for a change. He wanted to see me right away.

I explained I was with a Dr. Sheehan, and he seemed delighted, understanding the implications at once.

When we arrived at Wally's house, he came out to greet us, wearing only a pair of tight-fitting swimming trunks. In spite of his drug dependency, he looked handsome and virile but on edge. Inside his home, as we shared a drink, he asked if he could speak frankly in front of Brian, and I assured him that the doctor was aware of his condition and was anxious to help him.

"Bennie Walton was arrested last night," he said. "By the Los Angeles police. His name, it turned out, was Thomas H. Tyner. He was caught with seven bundles of heroin and a large supply of morphine for me. When he was arraigned before the U. S. commissioner, Tyner said he was delivering some of the dope to one of the best known picture stars in the world. Guess who turned him in? Dorothy."

"Will this make the papers?" I asked, growing alarmed for him.

"I don't know," Wally said. "Dorothy claimed she was doing this to help me. But she may have ruined my career."

Brian studied Wally closely, and it was obvious he was impressed with the actor's beauty and facile charm. Wally smiled a lot when meeting people, even when discussing something unpleasant. It was the kind of smile that made a homosexual male experience meltdown.

"I will personally go to the police," Brian said. "With your permission, I will explain that I, as your doctor, am giving you small dosages of morphine to cure your pain. On the way here, Durango told me about your physical injuries. I will maintain that with me legally administering proper dosages of morphine as needed, you have no need to turn to dealers for your supply. I have other patients on morphine. I'm sure the police will believe me."

"Do you think we could get away with that?" Wally asked, his eyes brightening in hope.

"I have no doubt," Brian said. "Is there no way to keep your wife from interfering?"

"She's half crazed about my drug taking," he said. "She feels that only she can break my habit."

"Sounds to me like she's going to get you in a lot of trouble," I said. "You'd better stop her sooner than later. Surely you have a way to exert power over her."

Wally finished his drink and leaned back in his chair. "I do have some power over her," he said. "Remember that girl who hid under our bed while we were going at it?"

"Of course, I do, although I'd rather forget it," I said, turning to Brian to explain the details of that embarrassing encounter.

"She denounced us as perverts, but later made contact with me again," Wally said. "I was flying high and went for her this time. We not only had sex but the end result was a baby daughter. Dorothy wants me to adopt it. So far I've refused. I'll agree to the adoption— something she wants desperately—if she'll stop interfering with my habit."

"Go for it," Brian said. "If it'll work."

"It'll work all right," Wally said with a kind of despair. "With that baby daughter running around the house, Dorothy knows it will remind me of my indiscretion. In some way, and I'm convinced of this, she thinks that reminder will keep me in line in the future."

Wally consented to go into the bedroom with Brian for a physical examination before the doctor administered morphine. "Before we go in," Brian said to Wally, "I must warn you in advance I'm a homosexual man who has always found you the sexiest male on the screen. I can't pretend my exam of you won't cause a certain excitement in me."

"Be my guest," Wally said, taking his hand and leading him to the bedroom.

In about thirty minutes Brian called through the bedroom door for me to come in. As I entered the room I was shocked to see him fucking Wally. Seeing me, Wally called out for me to come to him. As I stood over him, he reached for my trousers, unbuttoning me and pulling out my cock, which he put into his mouth and started to suck voraciously.

Over Wally's body, Brian and I kissed, taking turns sucking each other's tongues. It was one hot session. I loved it and didn't want it to end. But when I detected Brian was nearing an explosion, I too erupted within Wally's mouth. He sucked every drop, a generous load, I thought, but he seemed to want more.

He hadn't had his fill but we feared that Dorothy might be arriving at any minute so we dressed.

Still nude, Wally stood at the door, kissing me good-bye. "Thanks," he said, while Brian was in the bathroom. "You've hooked me up in more ways than one. As you always do. The sex was great."

"But you didn't get off," I said.

"I'm not doing much of that any more," he said. "My problem with getting a hard-on continues. The only way I can have fun now is to suck and get fucked. Just like what you guys did to me. It's my only sexual release. I know you rescued me from the Fruitfly when you thought all those guys were taking advantage of me. But I loved it. Really I did."

"Your secret is safe with me," I said, greeting Brian as he emerged fully dressed from the bathroom.

"You've got yourself a new doctor," Brian said to Wally. "One known for his rectal probes."

"You'll be the busiest man in Hollywood," Wally predicted. "When word gets out."

No longer edgy, Wally looked at ease as he waved good-bye. We left just in time, as we passed the stern-faced and disapproving Dorothy driving up to the Reid garage.

Our day wasn't over yet. After calls to Antonio and Billy Taylor, it was agreed that both men would meet at Antonio's home to be examined by Brian. Equally concerned, the men were only too anxious to get a check-up.

Sitting in Antonio's patio, I told both Billy and Antonio of the Virginia Rappé story and of our suspicions that Fatty Arbuckle was going to be set up as a blackmail target in San Francisco during his upcoming weekend.

Through Billy's link with Mabel Normand, there was fear that Rappé's gonorrhea had spread to other members of the film colony.

After a thorough examination of each man, Brian pronounced them in fine health with no sign or symptoms of the disease.

"I don't know why I haven't caught it from Mabel," Billy said. "No more sex with Mabel. I'm cutting her off." He turned to Brian. "I'm going to talk her into coming to you for a cure. Mabel doesn't like to go to doctors, but in this case what alternative does she have?"

Brian smiled at me before looking over at Billy and Antonio. "I'd like to be a doctor to you gents. I feel you'll have need of my services in the future."

"You've got yourself a deal," Antonio said, standing up to shake his hand. Billy too stood up and shook Brian's hand, agreeing to become his patient.

Right in front of the two men, Brian kissed me on the lips. Earlier he'd called the hospital and found there was some sort of emergency. He'd have to report to duty.

"Never marry a doctor," I said, kissing him good-bye and waving him off in the driveway. As I returned, both Antonio and Billy were caught kissing each other. "Well, well," I said, "is this a limited invitation only party, or can Kansas cowboys join in the fun?"

All I remember were two men moving in on me, carting me off to the bedroom as my clothing was already being removed and tossed aside.

"Now that we've been pronounced healthy specimens," Antonio said, "let's take advantage of it."

Indeed that is what happened, and it was growing late when I arrived back at the Hollywood Hotel. Barbara LaMarr was not there but had recently visited, as wet towels were thrown about the suite, the entire place in disarray. Barbara had gone off on another one of her adventures. She didn't really live here with me but used it as a powder room for changing between "engagements," whatever her engagements were.

I called Ramon but got Rod La Rocque instead. He had a cold, but said he'd been invited to go with Ramon to the Fatty Arbuckle weekend in San Francisco. He was real disappointed that he couldn't go because he'd heard that after midnight there was going to be some hot private shows similar to the recently staged slave auction where Ramon had allowed himself to be auctioned off to the highest bidder.

Believe me, you're lucky you have a cold," I said. He told me that Ramon was dining at the Alexandria Hotel with the Fatty Arbuckle party and that later all the gang would pile into two cars and head north for the long trek to San Francisco, getting as far as they could on the first night.

After checking messages, I too decided to go to the Alexandria Hotel to see Ramon if he were there.

In the dining room of the Alexandria, Fatty Arbuckle was being his most obnoxious and boisterous self. I'd heard that he'd been drinking a lot lately and was almost desperate to make people laugh, doing anything for a gag. Increasingly, he was becoming more of a monster than he already was. Ramon was dining at a table filled with people I didn't know, except for Fred Fischbach who was said to be living with the comedian.

Fred Fischbach was a well-known Mack Sennett director at the time. He'd been one of the original Keystone Kops. The only other party I recognized was Lowell Herman, an actor who'd made his motion picture debut opposite Mary Pickford in the 1914 *Behind the Scenes*. Was there any actor in Hollywood who hadn't made his debut with Pickford? I'd recently seen Sherman as the suave rogue seducing innocent Lillian Gish in Griffith's *Way Down East*.

Virginia Rappé and that blackmailer, Bambina (also known as Maude Delmont) weren't in the dining party. Arbuckle invited me to come to San Francisco with them, and Ramon seemed especially eager to have me go too, but I turned down the offer. In later years I regretted it, as it would certainly have added a spicy weekend to my memoirs. But I had my own spicy weekend coming up at San Simeon.

When Ramon later got up to go to the men's room, I used this as an opportunity to see him alone. Confronting him in the toilet, I denounced him as "little fool." His Mexican temper flared but subsided when I told him that Arbuckle was going to be set up for blackmail. I explained about the Rappé abortion and what her condition was, and also told him anything wicked I could about this mysterious Bambina.

As Ramon and I stood together at the urinal relieving ourselves and checking each other out, I said, "You've got a big career ahead of you. I think Ingram is going to make you a star. Another Rodolfo. But any involvement in scandal now will wreck it for you. The whole town's already talking about that nude boy in a coffin story. Fortunately, your name hasn't been linked to that party, but you've gone too far. You've got to lay low." I sounded like some character in one of those gangster movies that would be made a decade or so later.

Ramon agreed to cancel the trip and to warn Arbuckle not to take Rappé and Bambina north to San Francisco with him. "That will take some persuading," Ramon said. "Fatty told me he's been trying to get into Virginia's bloomers for five years."

"I thought he was impotent," I said.

"When Fatty can't get it up, which is most of the time, he has his instruments. I know he's packed the Bushman dildo in his luggage. He's going to try it out on Rappé in San Francisco. I think he wants to use it on both Rappé and me. Hopefully not at the same time."

The sound of Arbuckle's laughter could be heard as Ramon and I walked into the dining room together. The "Prince of Whales" was having a jolly good time at anybody's expense. Perhaps his pie-throwing days at Keystone had made him demented. When the waiter arrived with a plate of chicken à la king for him, Arbuckle took the plate and tossed it in the waiter's face, presumably for a laugh. But the movie cameras weren't on Arbuckle, and no one seemed amused. Crying out in pain, as the dish must have been hot, the waiter ran from the room in humiliation. Arbuckle was the only one at table laughing until the others reluctantly joined in.

I turned to Ramon. "I'm getting out of here. You deal with Arbuckle if you want to. It's not my scene."

As I was leaving, I encountered the actress, Lila Lee, entering the hotel. She had appeared with my lover, Thomas Meighan, and Gloria Swanson in *Male and Female* directed by Cecil B. DeMille. I'd read that Lila had just returned from Chicago after filming scenes with Arbuckle in *Freight Prepaid*. Introducing myself, I learned she'd been invited to join the Arbuckle party in the dining room. I warned her that Arbuckle seemed out of control and described the incident with the waiter.

She looked surprised at first, then accepted my story. "You should hear what he did in Chicago. On second thought, if you've got any place better to go, let's go." She took my arm

and we headed for my stagecoach. "I don't think Fatty is my cuppa tonight," she said. "Let's you and I go somewhere and get real drunk. You can tell me the real story of Lotte Lee. I'm dying to know what happened, and I don't believe a thing I've read in the papers. Many fans got me mixed up with Lotte. Lila Lee and Lotte Lee. The names are too close. Thank God she retired from the screen or I'd have to live up to her reputation."

Over drinks at the Ship Café, Lila and I became instant friends. That sometimes happens. She felt rebellious tonight because she'd learned that her husband, the famous actor James Kirkwood Sr., was off fucking Mary Pickford.

"I knew that Doug played around, but not our dear, sweet Mary," I said.

"Pickford can't keep her hands off my husband," Lila said. "They've been fucking for years."

After six drinks, I told Lila that this was going to be the start of a beautiful friendship for us. Decades from now, Humphrey Bogart stole that line and repeated to Claude Rains in the final reel of *Casablanca*.

When Kirkwood Sr. wasn't fucking Pickford, he managed to sire a son, Kirkwood Jr., who would grow up to become a novelist and co-author of *A Chorus Line*.

Fifty years from the night I met her, I invited Lila for dinner in Key West. She maintained that we went to bed together on the first night. I didn't remember it that way at all. But then I've tried to blot out a lot of my experiences with women. It's hard enough to keep the male lovers "straight" in my increasingly befuddled brain.

*****

The next morning, when I went to Paul Ivano's now largely abandoned apartment at the corner of Hollywood Boulevard and La Brea to check on Rodolfo, he was in a state of great agitation. Ivano, or so Rodolfo said, was supposed to be available to photograph him in some costumes designed by Natacha for a future film production. Ivano had called and abruptly cancelled, claiming "something had come up." He had to leave town with his "new patron," whoever that was.

I soothed Rodolfo's nerves but only after checking his wrists. Brian had been right. The attempt at suicide was a fake. Each of Rodolfo's inner wrists appeared as if he'd received a light scratch from a cat, and he was healing fast.

I told him that I was a personal friend of the finest photographer in town, Rod St. Just, who was far better qualified "to take any photograph" than Paul Ivano was. On hearing that, Rodolfo relaxed.

It was as if he could not disappoint Natacha in any way, as she had her heart set on dressing Rodolfo up in her costumes and having him photographed that very day. "You must understand," he said to me, "Natacha and I, unlike you, are artists. Artists get an inspiration and must act on it that very day. Tomorrow her inspiration may desert her. That's why it's important that these photographs be made today."

After I'd made the arrangements with Rod, Rodolfo called Natacha and she agreed to meet him at the photography studio. Over the phone, Rod was excited about the project as he had longed to meet Rodolfo and was especially thrilled to get to photograph him in the flesh. "And I hope he does expose some flesh," Rod had whispered to me over the phone before hanging up.

On the way to Rod's studio, Rodolfo filled me in on the background of the shoot. Natacha had been very disappointed over Paramount's selection of "that pulp fiction trash," *The Sheik*, as a starring vehicle for Rodolfo. She and Nazimova had schemed to develop more artistic projects for Rodolfo. Nazimova had hired Ulderico Marcelli to write a musical score for the upcoming film *Salome*. Marcelli's score had drawn much of its inspiration from Debussy's *Prélude à l'Après-midi d'un faune*.

Nazimova had already asked her would-be lover, Charles Bryant, whose dick was too big to penetrate her, to find a screenwriter and fashion a play based on this lascivious faun that Nijinsky had created for Diaghilev's Ballets Russes. Natacha, it seemed, had been enthralled when she'd caught a performance of this work in London's Covent Garden shortly before the start of the world war. To inspire a potential screen writer, she'd wanted Rodolfo photographed in costume as the faun. Little could we have known on that day what a scandal this would become.

Arriving at the studio before Natacha, I introduced Rodolfo to Rod St. Just, who seemed enthralled with him. Rodolfo was completely comfortable with the attention he generated from homosexual men, and, in fact, always seemed to enjoy it. If he had a problem, it was with the attention he received from women. He always appeared a bit bewildered about Natacha's intentions and motives, and remained completely confused about why Jean Acker had married him and was now divorcing him after a marriage that was never consummated.

Natacha arrived with Patsy Ann Miller, who was serving as her assistant prop woman that day. Patsy carried the costumes and two makeup kits into Rod's studio. Natacha carried nothing. After a huddled conference with Natacha, Rodolfo kissed Patsy goodbye but told her he couldn't take these pictures in front of her, as he viewed her as a good friend and that he "would not be natural posing with you in the studio."

"Bye, guys," Patsy said. "I'm disappointed. Seems I'm missing the greatest show in town."

Introduced to Rod St. Just, Natacha treated him like a stagehand. "I'd feel more comfortable if Paul Ivano were taking the pictures. I can work well with Paul." She glared at Rod. "Natacha does not like to work with strangers."

If any man in Hollywood could deal with colossal egos, it was Rod. He treated Natacha with great respect, deferring to her judgment at all times throughout the shoot, even though he knew more about photography than this art director ever would.

While Rod set up his camera, Natacha ordered Rodolfo into the dressing room. She asked me to join them, claiming she needed an assistant. My job was to carry in the costumes and props, "and whatever else Natacha decides for you to do." Once inside, she shut the door and began to open up her set of cosmetics and to rummage through the costumes, which seemed made of deer skin. She ordered Rodolfo, "strip off every piece of your clothing." She turned to me with a smug smile. "Rodolfo looks good in clothes. But he looks even better with absolutely nothing on at all. I can't wait for the day of liberation when men and women are allowed to appear completely nude in films and on the stage."

Natacha was years ahead of her time. Many actors at that time and in the years ahead resented it when they were ordered to strip naked in front of directors. Not Rodolfo. He enjoyed taking off all his clothing in front of Natacha and me. If anything, it was a sexual thrill for him.

The first costume Natacha settled on was a tiny fig-leaf pouch held together by a thin harness with a furry short tail at the other end evocative of a faun's rear end. Handing the pouch to Rodolfo, Natacha ordered him to put it on.

"I can't fit into that little thing," Rodolfo said. "It's an insult to my manhood. I have a monstrous cock and a big set of testicles."

"Any man can fit into that," Natacha said. "Even Theodore Kosloff, and his endowment is legendary. The fabric will accommodate your size." She turned to me like a Russian empress directing her troops defending St. Petersburg. "Put the costume on Rodolfo."

I was only too glad to obey this Amazon's command. I asked Rodolfo to step into the harness while I artfully arranged his genitals. The fig-leaf pouch actually accentuated the size of his cock and balls, making him look obscenely sexy the way I liked him. Just as I was really getting into my job as assistant wardrobe mistress, Natacha emerged with two jars of body paint. One jar was black, the other white. Naturally she handed me the black one, as it was the messiest and least desirable paint to work with.

"We'll paint our faun now," she instructed. I dipped into the paint, and we brushed alternate sections of his beautiful body.

When it came to body paint, Natacha was one of the greatest *artistes* of Hollywood. She was precise in her movements, as she applied the paint over his well-developed legs and around his lower abdomen. She directed me as if she were Theodore Kosloff himself issuing instructions to the Imperial Russian Ballet. I particularly liked applying the paint to the delectable cheeks of Rodolfo's ass and rubbing his chest and in between his legs near his crotch.

All this attention from Natacha and me was having a pronounced effect on Rodolfo. If he thought that fig-leaf pouch a bit skimpy when he was completely flaccid, it was reaching the bursting point as he felt Natacha and I erotically applying the body paint to him. Natacha reached down, took her hand and removed his penis from the fig-leaf pouch. "We cannot stand for this," she said. "It is completely unprofessional. Thank God Nazimova isn't here today to see such conduct."

Fully freed from its pouch, Rodolfo's cock rose to its impressive and final length. "I simply cannot have this," she said. She got up from his body and stared down at me. "I'm going into the studio to help Mr. St. Just with the light metering. Valentino must be photographed in just the right kind of light. I want the faun captured in a kind of morning's glow when the first light of a bright new day is breaking through an enchanted forest." She looked at me sternly. "When I come back into this dressing room, I want that cock deflated." She stamped her foot in a petulant manner, which was the beginning of a habit that would last the rest of her life when issuing one of her many commands to her underlings. "Flaccid," she yelled at me. "I want that cock drained of its blood. Soft. Do you understand that?"

"Your wish, my command," I said. When she'd gone, I descended onto Rodolfo's towering erection, sucking, loving, and devouring him as if he were the world's tastiest treat, which to me and on that day he was. Although thousands of dicks would pass through my mouth, there are few I can recall with the exact flavor and texture on that day I fellated Rodolfo.

When Natacha returned, Rodolfo was at rest, although the pouch still looked rather fully packed. The black and white body paint had dried on his body. She reached into a cosmetic kit and removed some putty. With the skill of a sculptor's hands, she applied putty to the tips of his ears, giving them points like a faun. After she'd finished, she stepped back to survey her makeup. She reached for a jar of petroleum jelly and directed me to apply it to his face, his chest, his legs, and his arms, even his buttocks. When I'd completed that job satisfactorily, she took out a brush with delicate bristles and painted one long black eyebrow directly over his eyes. Picking up a comb, she dipped it into a glass of water and parted his hair down the middle. At the top of his brow, she coiffed his locks into two devilish curls.

In the studio, Rod was waiting, as Natacha commanded me to hand Rodolfo a flute and a cluster of grapes like Bacchus might have held. The grapes were placed around his crotch.

Natacha stood back and critically judged her handiwork before pronouncing Rodolfo camera ready. "You will become Natacha's greatest creation," she said, addressing no one in particular. It was as if she were really talking to herself.

I was awed at the lusty, lascivious faun Rodolfo had become. Just for fun, I still held some of his recently spewed cum in my mouth, savoring the taste of it and reluctant to swallow it since I didn't know when he'd replenish the supply.

Rodolfo struck one pose after another. It was obvious to all of us that he was perfectly cast as the devilish faun. Had Diaghilev seen Rodolfo that day, his lust would have been directed at Valentino and not at Nijinsky. I felt honored having known the essence of both Valentino and Nijinsky.

For one moment Natacha seemed frozen in excitement. "These photographs will prove that Valentino and I are the perfect *anima* and *animus*. At last I have found a male body that can live up to my fantasies." She ordered Rodolfo to play the flute, as she came up with five final ideas for the shoot.

After the session, she directed me to pack up the costumes and makeup kits, delivering them in a few days back to Nazimova's Garden of Alla. "All we need is a script," she told us. "Rudy will star as the faun. It will be the greatest artistic achievement of his career."

Regrettably, the script was never written, the film never made. Rodolfo pleaded with Natacha to stay and be with him that day but she claimed that she had to spend the rest of her time working in Nazimova's studio on the costume designs for *Salome*. "We are making a masterpiece," she said to Rodolfo. "Perhaps she'll offer you a starring role." That seemed to make Rodolfo's face light up momentarily, although a look of dejection came over him when she left through the front door, without so much as a thank you, a kiss, or even a farewell greeting. She was all business.

After she'd gone, Rodolfo turned to Rod. "I saw that you have many dozens of props back there in the dressing room. The faun is okay. But what I really want to play is an American Indian."

Why he wanted to play Indian I didn't know then and never figured out. But that had been his dream.

Rod assured him he had the perfect wardrobe. "I'll make you the sexiest Indian that ever rode across the American plains."

Back in the dressing room, Rod too ordered Rodolfo to strip. In front of two homosexual men, Rodolfo peeled off his faun's costume, even the fig-leaf pouch and busy white tail with the skill and artistry of a male stripper. He was obviously enjoying his appreciative audience.

Rod had never seen Rodolfo's genitals before. Rodolfo stood completely nude in front of him, enjoying our inspection of his paint-smeared body. He reached for his cock and fluffed it up a bit, as it rose an inch or two before our eyes. "I always skin back the head," he said, pulling back his foreskin to reveal his large purplish head. "I find homosexuals like to see the head of a man's dick all uncovered. It excites them."

Although Rodolfo could have bathed himself, Rod and I were only too glad to get him in a bathtub to personally clean off the body paint. We didn't miss any parts as we scrubbed him, removing all the paint and having him stand up in the tub as we hosed him down.

I dried Rodolfo's body as Rod went for the costume of an Indian brave. No Indian had ever appeared on film as scantily clad as that costume Rod selected. He personally fitted the pouch onto Rodolfo. Since his genitals were clearly revealed in a leather pouch, Rod took a piece of leather and draped it over the strap holding the precious goodies.

He then procured a braided black wig which he had Rodolfo wear. Once the wig was fashioned over him, Rod placed a band around Rodolfo's brow, with a feather sticking up from his head. He let me help Rodolfo into a pair of leather moccasins. As I did, I kissed his feet. Rodolfo was clearly being worshipped by two admirers, and he was enchanted by the experience.

Instead of an Indian brave, Rod may have created the screen's first "he-vamp," an expression that was just coming into vogue. The pictures he took later of Rodolfo as the Indian brave were so provocative that in the years to come when male striptease finally arrived in America, many "artists" appeared on stage dressed as Rodolfo's sexy Indian of long ago.

At the end of the shoot, Rodolfo thanked Rod for the photography. "I don't just want to thank you but to actually show my gratitude." In front of us, he removed all his Indian drag and even kicked off his moccasins. He reached for his foreskin again, skinning it back to expose the head. "Natacha may have no need of me today, but I'm sure both of you gentlemen can devise something amusing to do with the screen's greatest lover."

*****

The next day word of Rodolfo's photo shoot spread across town. After I'd gone down on Theodore Kosloff at his town house and had been brutally fucked by him, he demanded that I set up an appointment to take him to the studio of Rod St. Just. Theodore wanted to be photographed in some of his most daring pouches and ballet tights. "I need to be captured in my full male glory while I'm at my peak," he said. "Perhaps I'll leave a treat to posterity. I might let your friend photograph me completely nude. And hard. It's important that I leave a gift of myself to future fans."

After agreeing to set up a date with Rod, I kissed Theodore as if he were the only man on earth, as if it was my last kiss before dying. Then I rushed out to get into my stagecoach. Fantasies of grand castles as San Simeon danced through my mind. I'd never spent the night in a castle before. Only in my dreams. I wondered what handsome young Prince Charming would be waiting at the castle to deflower me that night.

Fantasies were one thing, reality another.

The invitation to visit San Simeon was grotesquely premature. I arrived with W.R., Marion, and Tom Ince expecting that a grand castle had been constructed at "the loveliest spot in the world," as the Chief called it. It was located at Camp Hill, some 1,600 feet above sea level, above the old whaling village of San Simeon. You reached it after an adventurous, bumpy ride along some five miles of rocky road that was more like an interconnected series of rutted cow paths. A recent rain had made the so-called road even more treacherous. Except for some oak, laurel, and sage, the land of steep, rugged ridges and peaks had turned yellow or even brown in the heat.

Hearst's wife, Millicent, had recently decamped with their sons, returning to New York. This was Marion's first visit. Since not even the guest houses had been built, W.R. showed us to the tents where we'd be living. Tents? I was stunned, having expected so much more luxury. Admittedly, they were the biggest tents I'd ever seen, fit for an Arabian sheik of some rich Oriental dynasty. You didn't find many tents in those days with private showers for guests, but these tents were the world's most luxurious.

I was to share a tent with Tom Ince, a pleasure I was looking forward to, and W.R. and Marion would be in the main tent that was large enough to contain a dressing room for her. Some servants were readying a third tent. W.R. winked at me when he announced that the identity of his third party of guests would be kept a surprise until they actually arrived. He smiled enigmatically at Marion. Surely W.R. had not invited Joe Godsol to the camp-out.

W.R. spent the rest of the afternoon showing us the grounds and talking of the difficulties in erecting his "dream house." Marion spent the time complaining that she wanted to return to Los Angeles. To my surprise, I found that W.R. had booked her into the Hollywood Hotel for a few months so she could be closer to her film work. Santa Monica was viewed as too distant for a daily commute. Marion looked forward, or so she said, to being close to me. She giggled at the prospect of the future fun and games we'd have. "We girls will get to know each other much better." Marion didn't seem to realize that I was not a girl, even though I'd impersonated one for a time.

W.R. claimed he was going to improve the road, and that all the building materials had to be hauled up to the summit. Perhaps if he'd chosen to build a castle at the North Pole, it would have been easier. Building supplies had to be shipped in from San Francisco by boat. Some workmen stayed for only a week before quitting. Others arrived, looked around at the job site, then fled before unloading their luggage.

Temporary shacks and tents gave the site the look of a military encampment. Water had to be piped in from natural springs down below. Ditch diggers used pickaxes to open crevices in the rugged earth in which they inserted sticks of dynamite. When big holes had been blown into the hillsides, topsoil was shipped up from below so that landscaping could proceed. It was a daunting task, and already the talk was of "Hearst's folly."

Although San Simeon was to become in time a permanent residence for Marion, she wanted no part of it on the first day she saw it. She prevailed upon W.R. to let Tom Ince take her back down the hill where she wanted to check into a little inn about three miles from the village of San Simeon.

Very reluctantly it seemed, W.R. let her go. Ince suggested that he could spend the night at the inn to be near Marion should she need anything. But W.R. objected and Ince obviously decided that if he insisted, it would tip off W.R. about his illicit relationship with the Chief's already illicit mistress.

I was disappointed but had to face the reality of the situation. Tom Ince would rather spend the night with Marion than with me. Nonetheless, upon his return, I planned to do my best for him to help him forget about Marion for one night at least. W.R. informed Marion that he'd sent for her maid who would be arriving at San Simeon shortly, attending to the star if she needed anything.

After W.R. finally released me for the af-

ternoon, I retreated to my lonely tent to shower and make myself lovely for the dinner that night which would be served in a main tent at communal tables set with catsup bottles. The workmen would eat after we were finished. W.R. was alone in his tent, I alone in mine, and the second guest tent was still unoccupied. The mysterious guest or guests hadn't been revealed to me.

An hour before dinner, a loud motor sounded right outside my tent, and I thought that either the mystery guests had arrived or else Tom Ince had returned from down below, no doubt having welcomed Marion to the inn with a good pumping job. Not wanting to be too eager, I stayed in my tent, hoping to peer out. Before I could play Peeping Tom, I recognized a voice that was unmistakable. It was that of Charlie Chaplin.

Checking my appearance in a mirror in the tent, I too emerged into the fading afternoon, hoping I looked even more golden than the California sun. Charlie was introducing Hearst to a companion. Instead of one of his actresses, the companion turned out to be Paul Ivano. I was shocked, stunned, and rather furious. Charlie had lied that he was giving up homosexual affairs.

Before leaving for San Simeon I had called Ivano at his unlisted Los Angeles number that Rodolfo had given me. Ivano was upset when I called him, saying that number had been given "only to Rudy" and that I wasn't to call him again. I'd heard him yell out to someone in the background.

"Rodolfo's fine," I'd said, hoping to reassure him.

"That's great," he'd said nervously, putting down the phone.

Now I realized that it was Charlie himself who was in the background. The phone no doubt had been newly installed in Charlie's home so that Ivano could receive his private calls, a luxury that I wasn't afforded during the short period that I lived there.

Charlie appeared distressed at my presence at the camp. Obviously W.R. had not told him. "Durango," Charlie said, extending his hand. "What a delight. It's been a long time."

Not knowing of my past relationship with

Charlie, Ivano seemed genuinely glad to see me, as he felt he had someone to talk to when Charlie was huddling with W.R. I greeted Ivano as warmly as I could, considering the glacial windstorm raging in my heart.

Charlie quickly excused himself, ordering his tag-along, Ivano, to go with him to their own tent to get ready for dinner.

W.R. turned to me as if we were involved in some conspirational intrigue. "Originally when I called Charlie, I invited him to bring you. But Charlie told me you left him for another bigtime movie star. He wanted to bring his new boy instead. Marion told me that, unlike heterosexual couples, homosexual men change partners all the time."

"At least I do," I said. "But I'm surprised. If you knew that Charlie and I had broken up, why did you invite me? Wouldn't that be embarrassing to bring two lovers together who'd recently separated?"

"Not at all," he said. "Marion said that with you boys it didn't matter. Let's face it: it's not like inviting Millicent and Marion to the same party, now is it?"

Not wanting to argue with the Chief, I pretended to agree. He called me into his tent. I'm so glad you're on my payroll, because I have a rather delicate favor to ask of you."

"At the money you pay me, I'm willing to do anything."

"Marion is spending a lot of time with Tom Ince, and I'm beginning to get suspicious," he said. "I deliberately invited Ince up here with you, and I deliberately planned for you to share a tent with him. You see, I understand from sources that Tom Ince is secretly homosexual. Before the night is over, I want you to make a move on him. If he responds, and I think he will, I'll know I'm right. If I'm right, I don't have to be worried if Ince and Marion are together. I'll just have to keep Ince away from my sons—and that's all."

"He's very handsome, and I'd love to make a play for him," I said. "I've heard he's secretly homosexual too. I don't know if Marion has told you but certain homosexual men will even marry to cover up their perversion."

"I had heard that," the Chief said, "but I still find it hard to believe."

Before letting me go, he called me back.

"You know, you're supposed to tell me everything."

I stopped in my tracks, as panic came across me. Was I going to lose my five-hundred dollars a week? Had W.R. found out about my taking Marion to the home of Joe Godsol?

"Charlie told me you broke up with him," W.R. said. "Sent him away. At first I found that hard to believe, until Charlie informed me that the man you deserted him for was also one of the biggest stars in the world. Charlie wouldn't tell me. But the old fellow journalist here wants to know. Naturally, it will be a secret between us. It'll never see print in any of my papers."

"I'll tell you but no one else must ever know," I said. "I'm sorry to hold back on you, but I couldn't bring myself to tell anyone for fear word might get out."

"Believe you me, you have my word of honor," he said.

"Douglas Fairbanks," I said.

He looked at me long and hard. "Doug. Our Doug? Mary must never find out. You're standing there telling me that you've gone to bed with Douglas Fairbanks. I'll certainly keep that under my hat. The American film industry would be devastated economically around the world if word leaked out that two of our biggest stars, Charlie Chaplin and Doug Fairbanks, engaged in homosexual sex with young boys. The world must never know." He looked shaken. "Our third biggest star is Wallace Reid. We don't have to worry about him. I hear he's fathered a baby out of wedlock, and his wife wants to adopt this little bastard girl. All the girls are after Wally, and I know he has had numerous affairs. No one ever called Wallace Reid a homosexual. At least there is one big star in Hollywood living up to the image of a clean-cut all-American male."

"I don't know him," I lied, "but I understand you're right about that."

"This new Italian boy, Valentino," W.R. said. "I hear half the women in Hollywood are after him, even Nazimova. Marion told me that if anyone could cure Nazimova's unfortunate lesbianism, it's Valentino."

"You've heard that right," I said. "Valentino

was a gigolo in New York. A guy like that is used to pleasing ladies."

"Wallace Reid and Valentino will help make up for some of the sins of Charlie and Doug. If you find out that Tom Ince is homosexual, then I'll think this is a perversion that can be spread like tuberculosis."

"I'll let you know in the morning." I said, retreating before he called me back once more. I knew what his next question would be, and I was prepared for it.

"I just pretended that I didn't want Marion to leave our camp site tonight," W.R. said. He giggled to himself. "I'm a pretty good actor myself. I knew that when she saw how primitive the conditions are here, she'd want to retreat down below."

"That means Lotte is allowed to make an appearance later tonight," I said. "I hope you'll let her come directly to your tent.

"I've been thinking of nothing else," he said. "Tell her to show up around midnight. Everybody will be asleep by then. I'll leave my tent door open."

"You've got yourself a night visitor," I said. "Pocahontas herself, slipping into your Indian tent." At last I was free to go. I'd packed my Lotte drag with me, and before Ince came back to the tent I'd checked to see that it was ready for audition later tonight. Of course, I'd have to satisfy Ince and make sure he was in blissful, heavenly sleep before slipping off to play Lotte. I'd have to be careful getting dressed so that Ince wouldn't see my transformation.

Before dinner I went by myself for a long walk in the hills, figuring out for the first time the beauty and majesty of such a setting, and understanding why W.R. had selected it for his Shangri-La.

As I climbed up on a rock and looked down, I spotted Charlie a few feet below. I called out to him.

"Sorry about all this," he said, coming up to me. "It's obvious now: I lied to you. I wanted to break off with you but didn't want to hurt you. I never knew you would be here or I'd never have come. I've just talked with W.R. He planned it this way. You see, he's taken an instant dislike to Paul. He wants me to get rid of Paul and patch up things with you again."

"I'd like it if you would do that too," I said. "I'm certainly willing. I do love you."

"Don't be nasty," he said. "Right now I'm in love with Paul Ivano, among others. May Collins, at least I think so. Maybe even Florence Deshon. There are a couple of others. With Mary Miles Minter, it's just for sex. There is my darling little twelve-year-old, Lita. I'm sure you've heard about her. I did feel something for you once, but I find that where love's concerned, I have a short attention span."

"I understand," I said. "This sounds like a silly commitment, but I mean it. If you ever need me, I'll be there for you. Just call."

"You must be surprised to see me shacked up with Nazimova's boy," he said.

"I was a bit shocked," I said. "I keep asking myself what does he have that I don't."

"You have the looks," he said. "Paul is quite plain. You've certainly got the body too. And the cock. Your cock is about as big as mine. But, and this may shock you, all men don't want lovers with big cocks. You actually hurt me when fucking me. Paul's just right. The perfect size for me. I feel comfortable with his. With you, I thought I was getting plowed, and I had a loose stool for two days every time you fucked me."

That was one graphic detail Charlie could have kept from me. At the sound of a dinner bell, I said, "I guess we'd better haul ass. As you know, W.R. doesn't like his dinner guests to be late."

"I know that." He walked along briskly with me. At one point as we neared the camp site, he reached out for my arm, restraining me. "I'm willing to make a concession. I know you're in a period of withdrawal from me. If he wants, I'll suggest to Paul that you come to our tent late tonight. Say, around midnight, when everybody has retired. We could have a three-way. I'm sure Paul would be into it."

"Sorry, my dear friend," I said as graciously as I could since I was still on his payroll and didn't want to offend. "But I'm booked up at that hour. Besides, I couldn't stand sharing you."

That seemed to flatter his male ego. "Who are you booked up with, if you don't mind my asking? Tom Ince? I've heard stories about him."

"You won't believe this," I said, "but it's the absolute truth. William Randolph Hearst."

*****

Dinner at San Simeon brought together unusual couplings—Charlie and Paul Ivano, that little whoring bitch moving onto my turf, plus Tom Ince and myself. Presiding at the head of the table was W.R., looking forlornly alone, perhaps dreaming of a midnight visit from that vamp, Lotte Lee herself. Charlie had little to say to Ince, Ivano, or myself, directing all his political talk to W.R. It was just as well that dinner conversation wasn't personal that evening, considering all the secrets we wanted to keep.

An hour later, alone in the tent with Ince, he headed for his luggage where he removed some bootleg whiskey and poured a drink for both of us. "I love the Chief dearly," he said. "but sweetened ice tea at dinner is not my idea of a good time."

As we drank and talked softly, he told me that he had fallen "madly" for Marion and that they had made love at the inn, as I suspected. "She's very seriously considering leaving W.R.," he said. "Their sex life has dried up. He knows Marion is running around. He's found out about Charlie. Also Joe Godsol. She thinks he's going to kick her out at any time."

"Do you think you'll marry her?" I asked.

"I love Marion but marriage is out of the question," he said. "We don't need W.R.'s money. Besides, he doesn't give her that much anyway. I can turn Marion into a bigger star than she already is. Her pictures and my pictures will make us a fortune."

"If you're planning to team up, why not marriage?" I asked. "Don't get me wrong. I'm not urging it."

"I'll not leave my wife," he said. "Marion is not the type of gal you marry. For marriage, you find someone far more respectable than that. Marion is a courtesan. She's someone to have fun with, maybe a lot of fun—she is after all, a lot of fun—but you've got to keep your options open. When my thing is over with Marion, and you know it will be some day, I

want to walk out with no strings attached if that's how I feel."

"I thought you said you loved her."

"Love, yes," he said. "That doesn't mean I'm devoted to her. The only person in the world I'm devoted to is Tom Ince."

Over our second whiskey, I told Ince about W.R.'s secret suspicion that he was a homosexual. "W.R. told me to try to seduce you tonight. That's why he moved us into the same tent together. He feels if I secretly find out you're a homosexual, it will then be safe to trust Marion with you."

Ince smiled, amused and intrigued with the suggestion. "In that case, let's put on a show for him. He's in the tent next door. We're whispering now, but when we have sex together, let's be real vocal. I'm sure he'll be listening."

"Does that mean you're going to have sex with me?" I asked. Something better than me getting down on my knees while you watch someone fucking in the next room."

He leaned over and kissed me lightly on the lips. A smug look came across his face. "A little better than that."

He stood up, a bit drunk. "You know, you've never seen me completely nude before. Tonight you're in for a treat. Marion told me that most homosexuals don't get to see a man completely nude since that kind of love is conducted mostly in cars or in toilets." He slowly started to remove his clothing. He was clumsy at it, having none of the striptease skills of Rodolfo but I was anxious for the unveiling. His was a strong, masculine body. He might work out at an athletic club. He removed everything but his underwear.

"Let me take off the final item," I said. "I'll be appearing in Nazimova's *Salome* soon, but right now let's launch the film by your dropping the seventh veil." I pulled down his shorts to reveal his thick penis upon which I descended to plant tiny kisses and tongue licks.

In our makeshift bed, as I was going down on Ince, he was moaning loudly, because I felt he genuinely enjoyed the blow-job but also because he suspected it might be music to the ears of W.R. in the tent next door. At one point Ince reached down and pulled my head off him, just as I sensed he was nearing a climax. "I want to do something different tonight," he said.

I didn't need any more instructions or signal from him. I lay on my back as he reared up over me. Reaching for him, I guided him inside. As thick as he was, I didn't need lubrication. I was a natural. After all, I'm sure boys in the Middle Ages didn't lubricate themselves either.

When Ince inserted himself into me, inch by enticing inch, I thought I'd fallen madly in love. All thoughts of Antonio, Rodolfo, and Wally vanished from my head. I wanted only this man on top of me. When Ince had fully entered me, and I felt his big balls banging against me, he lowered himself onto my face, his tongue sticking out even before he'd met my lips.

When he withdrew from me, that same tongue went inside my left ear. "That's the most incredible sensation I've ever known," he whispered. "I thought fucking a woman was the world's greatest thrill. Now that's number two." With that glorious news, he started to pump and pound, and I reared up to meet him inch for inch as my hands traveled across his body, always settling in to weigh and fondle his balls, one of my favorite parts of him, then and in the months ahead when I would devote far more attention to them than I did on that long-ago night at San Simeon.

When he finally erupted in me in about twenty minutes, he cried out. I locked my arms around him and sought his mouth. The pounding I'd gotten from him caused my own eruption. He must have lain on top of me for a good fifteen minutes before finally pulling out. I used all my rectal muscles to keep him inside me, fighting his withdrawal, but he overpowered me and I was forced to surrender my prize.

As he cleaned up while I waited to use our makeshift bathroom, I felt that Tom Ince and I had discovered a new expression of sex which no longer would be confined to my being down on my knees in front of him. Of course, in the months ahead there would be that too.

When I came out of the bathroom fully showered and looking lovely, he was lying nude on our bed smoking a cigarette. "That symphony was played out with the great W.R. listening in," he whispered confidentially. "That

was one of the greatest sensations of my life. I'm going to sleep now, but I want to repeat that again at about six o'clock in the morning. I met two of the workmen. We're going fishing, since tomorrow's Sunday."

On the bed I kissed every inch of his body, almost worshipping him for the good time he'd shown me. At one point he said to me in a very low voice, "Don't get the wrong idea. I'm not a homosexual. I'm strictly a man for the ladies. But I love sensation, especially a sensation like that. I've never experienced anything quite like it. So we'll keep doing it with the total understanding that you and I both know I'm not a homosexual."

"It's for the sensation thing," I said, taking time off from licking his balls to answer him. "I know that. You know that. So we don't have to speak of it again." With that assurance from me, as false as it was, I let him drift off into blissful sleep. When he was snoring peacefully, dreaming either of Marion or me, I slipped back into the bathroom with a special suitcase I'd brought along, containing Lotte Lee's wardrobe.

Tom Ince had exhausted Durango Jones, but I found renewed exhilaration dressed as Lotte Lee. As I slipped into W.R.'s tent, my task was a daunting one. The Chief was already old and from what I understood impotent, so Lotte's work was cut out for her. I'd have to convince myself that this flabby, pear-shaped man with the light, squeaky voice and a penis less than impressive was my dreamboat. The task would bring all the actress skills Lotte possessed. Even though I didn't get much of a chance to show the world I could act on the screen, I'd have to make up for it in my personal life.

As I sat talking with W.R. and stroking his withered hand, I realized I'd retired Lotte too soon. Originally after the demise of *Vampira*, I'd told myself I'd never dress up as Lotte again. I was wrong.

W.R. was clad in a pair of emerald-green pajamas, a gift from Marion, no doubt. As he shared with me his dreams of building his castle at San Simeon, and all the art he planned to purchase in Europe and transport up that rock hill, I felt nothing but a tender compassion for him. He might be a ruthless press baron. He might even be a monster. But he showed none of that to me that night.

I felt that Marion had seriously hurt him and wounded his pride. I hoped to restore some of his manhood to him, and I knew I had to make all the moves. When I whispered to him that I wanted the candlelight doused, he readily agreed but warned me not to expect too much from him. He repeatedly thanked me for coming up from Los Angeles. I told him that I was secretly living in Florida and had to return before dawn the following morning, and he made me promise to visit him either in New York or Los Angeles as soon as I could arrange it.

At this point in my dictation, the Bitch of Buchenwald intervened. "It was all I could do to take down that filth with Mr. Ince," she said. "You don't even respect the poor man's memory to let him rest in peace with his own dirty secrets." A stern, almost frightening look came across her face. "All of us—yes, even me—have secrets which we don't go putting in books. Anyway, I took down every word of the smut you dictated. But I want you to know this. If you for one moment think I'm going to sit here and take down what Lotte Lee did to that old fellow, William Randolph Hearst, you'd better get yourself another girl. I refuse to do it."

"Perhaps you're right," I said, and meant it. This was the first time I'd ever agreed with the Bitch. Instead of a blow-by-blow description, I'll cut to the chase.

W.R. took a lot of tender, loving care, and much encouragement from Lotte, but he did achieve orgasm. The job wasn't as repulsive as I'd feared. Believe it or not, in sharing such an intimate moment with him, I felt a loving compassion for him. I knew that a large part of America considered him a son of a bitch, but I found that with his pajama bottoms off he was a vulnerable and kind man who had pride, who could be wounded, and who was in dire need of some woman telling him how terrific he was in bed. That Lotte did. He was so happy when he'd erupted in my mouth that he was almost overflowing with tears of joy. I could tell it in his voice even though I couldn't see his face.

After I'd straightened up in Marion's makeshift dressing room, W.R. in the main part of the tent had lit a lonely candle. I kissed him good-bye and promised to meet with him as soon as it was possible. Durango, I told him, could arrange our meetings.

Before I got out of the tent, he called me back to him to take me in his arms and kiss me tenderly for one more time. "I feel terrific," he said. "You did that for me. I want to ask you something. No, no, you don't have to answer me right this minute. But I want you to think it over very seriously and let me know your answer in a few weeks."

I looked astonished. This time I couldn't outguess him. I had no idea what he wanted of me other than a few repeat performances.

He took my hand and held it up to his lips tenderly. "It's such a beautiful hand," he said. "But it looks raw and vulnerable. I have something for it." He went over to his makeshift desk and removed a ring which he placed on my finger. The rock weighed down my hand. "It belonged to my mother," he said. "It was once owned by Catherine the Great of Russia."

I looked at the stone in the dim light and was stunned, not knowing that diamonds came that big.

"I want you to have that ring and wear it always," he said. "It was for tonight. I'm truly grateful."

Tears came to my eyes, tears of pure joy. I sensed a hesitation in him. "There's more," I said. "You want to say something. Please, please. What is it you want to ask me?"

"No one must know this, but I can tell you after what we've shared. I go back and forth. At one minute I'm determined to leave Marion. At other times I want to hang on to her in spite of her drinking and whoring." He spoke slowly as if his own words were causing a pain in his heart. "It's this love/hate thing I have with her. She's screwing around. Maybe not with Ince after the sounds I heard coming from his tent with your brother, Durango. But others. Godsol, Charlie, who knows? I can't abide a woman who is a lush, and Marion drinks like a fish. I'm considering ending it all between us."

"I'm sorry to hear that, W.R.," I said. "Marion's a great gal. I think you two make a wonderful couple."

He took my hand, the one with the heavy

stone on it he'd so recently given me. He held my hand up to his face, kissing my inner palm in a tender, gentle way. "I'm afraid to get rid of Marion. I'd be lonely without her. But if you would agree to replace Marion in my affections, I'd have the courage to let her go on her way." A disturbing look crossed his brow, as if he instinctively knew he'd have to sweeten the deal with me. "I could make a big star out of you. I know Goldfish screwed up, but I know where he went wrong. With me, your name would be up in lights just like Marion's is."

"No stardom," I said. "I've abandoned that prospect for myself. But to the more serious part, I'll think it over. I think I fell in love with you tonight, and I truly want to be your woman. But there are problems."

"Don't get me wrong," he said. "I don't want to mislead you. I'll never divorce Millicent. It will always have to be a secret affair."

"I understand," I said, "and I'm honored to be asked. I feel I don't deserve a man as great as you."

"You deserve me more than Millicent or Marion," he said.

I told him I'd convey my answer through Durango. Suddenly, W.R. became very inquisitive about how I'd gotten up the hill and how I'd get back to Los Angeles. I told him that I was walking back down the hill for about five-hundred feet where a driver was waiting to take me back to Los Angeles. I thanked him for the beautiful gift, the loving, and the stunning proposition. I kissed him several times very tenderly on the lips, and let him feel my tears being shed at our parting.

Once out of his tent, I slipped back into the quarters I shared with Ince. He was still snoring lightly, lost in the dreamland I'd sent him to as Durango. In the makeshift bathroom, I removed all traces of Lotte Lee. Her wardrobe was gently folded back into her suitcase. By candlelight I checked my face in the mirror. I had transformed myself into Durango again.

With Ince at my side, I drifted into sleep. When I woke up, it must have been six o'clock. True to his promise, Ince was moving in on me, and I was suddenly awake to welcome the invasion. If anything, I enjoyed it more than the

night before. Tom Ince and I were those rare individuals whose body chemistry seems to explode when mixed together. In other words, he loved to fuck me and I loved getting fucked by him. The sensation was quite different from anybody else, and I never knew why regardless of how many times we'd repeat the act in the future.

Durango Jones was not the kind of boy a man would invite fishing, so when he'd dressed and left after some long, lingering kisses, I turned over in bed to get my beauty sleep. I wanted to look especially radiant in the morning if for no other reason than to make Charlie jealous that he'd dumped me for that ungainly Paul Ivano, with his average sized dick.

The sun seemed to have risen to its midday position in the blue California sky when I finally did wake up. I slowly opened my eyes feeling I'd successfully pulled off the previous evening which had the potential for a real disaster if only one element in my carefully conceived plan had gone wrong.

I stretched out in the bed, finding the tent hot. Sometime during the morning I had kicked the sheets off me. Fully nude, I felt my own arousal. I was almost tempted to jerk off, but felt I'd better save my juice in case there would be more action for me later in the day with Ince.

All of a sudden I felt the presence of someone in the room with me. I jerked my head to the right to discover W.R. sitting in a chair inches from my bed. "Good morning," I said. I reached for the sheet to cover my nudity.

He also reached over and pushed my hand gently away from the sheet. "You have no secrets from me. I must have been sitting here for more than an hour looking at you sleeping. It's time for lunch. I came to your tent to get you."

"You should have awakened me," I said, embarrassed.

"You don't awaken one of Botticelli's angels," he said, getting up slowly. "Charlie and his friend have already gone. They're heading for Europe."

That news stunned me.

"I'll have to talk to Ince and reprimand him," he said. "He went fishing with two of my men. I don't allow fishing and hunting on my grounds." He turned back and smiled at me.

"I've saved a place for you at lunch sitting on my right." With that, he walked out of the tent, not looking back.

Still nude and still a bit aroused, I sat up in bed, looking down at my own body as the golden light of the already well-established day shone in on me.

Ever since, I've wondered why William Randolph Hearst spent an hour of his time looking at me sleeping peacefully in the nude on that long-ago morning.

*****

W.R. ordered his driver to stop by the inn to pick up Marion. "The news world has changed since we went up to Camp Hill," he said enigmatically. Getting into the limousine, Marion wasn't her usual gay (the word meant something different back then) and radiant self.

She had little to say to W.R., other than a "good morning," and he virtually ignored her. It was clear to all of us, especially Ince himself, that the party was over. If Charlie and Paul Ivano were in the car, the tension might have been unbearable. I'd been involved with W.R. as Lotte Lee, and I'd had an affair with Charlie who had also had an affair with Marion, who was conducting a longtime affair with W.R. and also a short-term affair with Ince. I'd slept with Ivano who was now sleeping with Charlie—that is, when Charlie wasn't sticking that iodine-coated big dick into little girls.

Ince, Marion, and I were surprised when W.R. ordered his driver to head for his offices in San Francisco, specifically the *Examiner*. Up to then, I thought we'd be driving back to Los Angeles. "I personally want to direct coverage of this story," he said, as his eyes danced with glee. "I'm going to sell some papers, even more than I did at the sinking of the *Lusitania*. Wait till you guys hear what's happened to Fatty Arbuckle. He's been arrested on a charge of murder."

I sat back sighing in relief that Ramon and I hadn't accepted the comedian's invitation to come to San Francisco for a good-time weekend. I'd obviously been much safer at San Simeon. "Who was the victim?" I asked.

"A little teenage girl," W.R. said. "By the name of Virginia Rappé."

The name was more than familiar to me. Arbuckle had already been warned about her. At the moment of her death, thousands of Americans were buying a piece of sheet music. On the cover was Rappé in a sunbonnet with a smiling face. The hit song of the day was, "Let Me Call You Sweetheart." The idea that Arbuckle would murder Rappé struck me as far-fetched, unless she'd tried to blackmail him and he'd reacted violently. After all, he was the kind of butterball who'd toss a plate of hot chicken à la king into a waiter's face for a laugh.

At the time of Rappé's death, Arbuckle was at the peak of his popularity. Paramount's Adolph Zukor had offered him a million dollars a year to make films, a staggering sum in the early Twenties. Zukor also wanted to make sure the comedian earned his money and had cast him in so many films that Arbuckle's head was spinning. At one point he was running from one stage at a time, appearing in three films at once. Exhausted by eighteen months of constant work before the cameras, he had gone with his friends to San Francisco for a three-day vacation of "fun and games."

I was sitting beside W.R. and I could see the stories about Arbuckle already being written in the Chief's head—if not the stories, then the headlines. The master yellow journalist was plotting, and I knew he'd exploit this scandal to the fullest, as he would others in the future. I was also to learn firsthand that the Chief was a master of the cover-up too, especially if the scandal involved Marion and him.

W.R. did not go to his home in San Francisco but instructed the driver to take all of us to his office at the *San Francisco Examiner*, where he immediately launched the direction of the coverage of the story personally. Ince, Marion, and I remained in the executive suite for at least three hours, while each salacious detail upon juicy detail of the case unfolded.

Arbuckle's new $25,000 Pierce-Arrow had made the dash up the west coast from Los Angeles to San Francisco, carrying, among others, his two friends, Fred Fischback and Lowell Sherman. There his party had checked into rooms 1219, 1220, and 1221 of the St. Francis Hotel. Ramon had told me that the Arbuckle party had left Los Angeles in a two-car caravan that also transported Virginia Rappé and "Bambina" (a.k.a. Maude Delmont). But the story breaking in San Francisco was that Rappé and her companion, Bambina, were already in San Francisco at the time, and had casually been invited to come up to the Arbuckle suites to party. That contradiction was merely the beginning of a series of contradictions that plague the retelling of the case even today. Contradictions is the kindest word. Lies might be more accurate.

The Arbuckle camp claimed that he had decided to leave the party at 3pm when it was already four hours old, and had gone to take a crap before changing into his street clothes. He was wearing only the bottoms of his pajamas. That version had him walking into the toilet, where he had discovered Rappé passed out on the tile floor. He was said to have picked up her limp body and to have carried here into his bedroom where he'd placed the body on his bed. Reportedly, Arbuckle had returned to the party at 3:10pm, claiming that Rappé was in acute pain.

That was the most sanitized version put out. In contrast, colleagues reported that Arbuckle had been pursuing Rappé ever since they'd both worked at Essanay together. Many of his fellow workers reported that he'd always cast his "roving eye" on the beautiful actress and had at one time asked her to appear in one of his comedies.

At least fifty studio hands at Essanay could verify that. But Fischback told the press that Arbuckle had at first been reluctant to attend the party because he feared it might be raided considering the "lowly reputation" of Rappé and Bambina. Again, that meek little response didn't seem to match Arbuckle's reputation for a wild orgy-throwing type of guy who liked lots of nudity at his previous and also notorious parties. And it certainly didn't match Ramon's story that Arbuckle had transported Rappé and Bambina to San Francisco in his two-car caravan. It was also doubtful if Rappé and Bambina enjoyed such a reputation all the way up in San Francisco that their mere attendance at a party, assuming the police even knew about it, would

precipitate a raid. Almost no one in the world was that notorious.

Also Fischback's version didn't match the story of my favorite doctor, Brian Sheehan, who'd overheard Bambina and Rappé planning to go with the comedian to San Francisco where they hoped to set up a compromising situation with Arbuckle that would put him in a position where he could be blackmailed. Bambina had wanted, at least according to Brian, to have Rappé endure some form of intercourse shortly after her abortion which might cause her to bleed and suffer internal injuries. Bambina, Brian claimed, had told Rappé that if she could endure that momentary pain she might make enough money to live comfortably the rest of her life.

Other witnesses at the party were reporting a different version, claiming they'd seen Arbuckle grabbing Rappé and steering her toward his bedroom. He'd looked back at his fellow party-goers and cast the same leering wink so familiar to his movie fans. He'd yelled back at the showgirls and male revelers at the party, many dancing the shimmy, a lot of the women topless. "This is the moment I've been waiting for for five years."

Screams and piercing moans were reportedly heard from the Arbuckle bedroom. Bambina charged that she'd kicked at the door with her shoe but found it locked.

Arbuckle had emerged later, his pajamas ripped. He'd worn Rappé's squashed Panama hat on his head set at a jaunty angle. "Get her out of here. She's a screamer." He called back into the room. "Shut up, bitch, or I'll toss you out the window."

Bambina told the police that when she'd entered the room she'd found Rappé nude on the bed, clutching her stomach and screaming in agony. Bambina had admitted to having ten gin-laced "Orange Blossoms," so she was hardly the most reliable of witnesses. Bambina said that Rappé had looked up at her, saying, "I'm going to die. He stuck it in me. I'm bleeding down there. Make Arbuckle pay for this." Bambina reported that Rappé's clothing had been ripped apart, her blood-soaked panties tossed on the floor.

Amazingly, no one thought of calling the house doctor, who was on the ground floor below. The failure to summon a doctor was just one of the bizarre events that were never fully explained.

When Fischback came into the Arbuckle bedroom and saw Rappé, he'd convinced the drunken revelers to immerse the actress into a tub of ice-cold water. Bambina had staggered into the living room of the suite to get the ice. Three of the men carried the nude girl back to the bathroom where they'd lowered her into the arctic bath, causing her to scream all the more.

At long last, H.J. Boyle, the assistant manager of the hotel, was summoned. Instead of calling a doctor right away, he suggested that she be transferred to room 1227. "That will be more discreet," Boyle told Fischback. "It wouldn't be proper to have her discovered in Arbuckle's bedroom if something goes wrong with her."

In time, and no one seemed to remember for certain, Dr. Arthur Beardslee, house physician for the Hotel St. Francis, was called in. In later testimony when Dr. Beardslee was reached at his vacation retreat in the Sierra Nevadas, he wasn't certain when he'd been summoned to Rappé's bedroom. He'd examined Rappé and found that she "showed symptoms of an internal injury." Could that have been from Brian's abortion or Arbuckle's dildo rape? Beardslee detected bruises on her but claimed those might have been caused by manhandling from the ice-cold bath the drunks had dumped her into. He also testified that he'd had to administer three hypodermics to quiet her down. Amazingly, Dr. Beardslee had not ordered that Rappé be moved to a hospital. After he'd left the room, Bambina had remained by her side and had continued to drink the gin-laced "Orange Blossoms" to which she was addicted, along with her other favorite sports of blackmailing and racketeering.

Again, and no one knows for sure, but somebody at some point called an ambulance and had Rappé transferred to the Wakefield Sanatorium, a hospital where movie stars often went when they wanted a pregnancy terminated instead of heading south for the more unsanitary conditions found in Tijuana. Reportedly, Rappé's final words were, "Arbuckle did it to me. Make him pay."

She then lapsed into a coma from which she never recovered. The actress would never appear in the aptly named *Twilight Baby*, her upcoming picture on which she'd already signed a contract.

Arbuckle was already heading back to Los Angeles when he'd learned of Rappé's death. An order was issued for his arrest on a charge of murder. The penalty for murder in California? The gas chamber.

L'affair Arbuckle had begun.

So had a cover-up.

An anonymous caller had sent Michael Brown, the deputy coroner of San Francisco, racing to the Wakefield Hospital where he'd discovered a male orderly emerging from the elevator. He was heading for the hospital incinerator with a sealed glass container which was then requisitioned by Brown. He'd discovered that it contained the "injured female organs" of Rappé.

Dr. Shelby Strange performed the autopsy, finding that Rappé's death was caused by an "extreme amount of external force." In a second postmortem examination, Dr. William Ophuls discovered "bruises on the body, thighs, and shins, and fingermarks on Rappé's upper right arm."

The official announcement of death was that Rappé had "died of peritonitis, brought on by the rupture of her Fallopian tubes, complicated by pus accumulation in the tubes from gonorrhea." Bambina, both to the press and to the San Francisco police, had a different charge, claiming that Arbuckle had raped Rappé, causing her death. Why Bambina, given her past record, wanted to call undue attention to herself remained a mystery. She told the press that she was a "professional dress model."

The country buzzed with speculation about that "external force." The word was, that "everybody" knew Arbuckle was as heavy hung as a whale. Bambina only fueled speculation in that direction when she'd told her "dress model" friend, Alice Blake, that she, Bambina, had gone to bed with Arbuckle, and "I can well understand why he'd be capable of inflicting damage on Virginia's insides." Other reports were that he'd brutally crushed Rappé to death with 300 pounds of fat riding on top of a teenage girl who weighed less than a hundred pounds.

This report of the Arbuckle "whalelike penis" struck me as a joke. Me, of all people, who knew more about the size of movie star cocks than anybody, with the possible exception of Rod St. Just. All the women I'd talked to about Arbuckle had spoken of him as "Princess Tiny Meat," an expression only then gaining in vogue. I'd never viewed the Arbuckle penis hard, but I'd seen it flaccid. There is no way that a whale penis could rise from such unpromising beginnings.

The penis theory quickly gave way to the bottle theory. Word spread that Arbuckle was impotent and often liked to insert Coca-Cola bottles into women in lieu of feeding them his own pork. Some claimed he preferred champagne bottles to coke bottles. Considering the size of a champagne bottle, the coke bottle gained in popularity.

The details of what actually happened at the St. Francis Hotel will never be completely known. The only conclusion to be drawn is that everybody involved in the case, regardless of how remotely, lied and continued to lie, taking the actual facts to their grave—each and every one, including Arbuckle himself.

The San Francisco police detective sent to investigate the case wasn't much help either. When he'd arrived at the Arbuckle suite, he found Bambina dancing in pajamas belonging to Arbuckle's friend, Lowell Sherman. Bambina claimed the detective was "robustly handsome," and the two of them finished off what was left of the bootleg gin and orange juice.

Sherman shed no light on the case at all, fleeing to Chicago where there were no legal means the district attorney in San Francisco could use to make him return. Reached in Chicago by the press, Sherman claimed it was just a tame party where a few good friends in the film industry got together to share a few laughs. He said that "Mr. Arbuckle and Miss Rappé conducted themselves properly at all times." He also claimed everyone at the party was well dressed—that there was no nudity at all. He further stated that Arbuckle attended the party in a suit and tie and not in pajama bottoms as had been reported. So much for Sherman's memory, which was in complete

contradiction to everybody else's.

San Francisco in those days was where members of the movie colony went "to raise hell," and the Arbuckle party wasn't actually the "church social" as remembered by Sherman.

Arbuckle's other friend from the Mack Sennett era, Fischback, changed his story so many times over the years that he himself lost track of what he'd said, as did Bambina herself. Each day she seemed to come up with a different version of "what actually happened."

At the offices of the *San Francisco Examiner*, W.R. was in total control, ordering extra editions of his newspapers to be printed. He might have been timid and even a bit shy when Lotte Lee had coaxed him into removing his pajama bottoms the night before. But at the *Examiner*, he was a general directing his troops into battle. He ordered his reporters to dig up the most lurid details of Arbuckle's private life. Talk of banner headlines filled the newsroom. He'd taken delight when word came in that the *New York Times*, which printed only the news fit to print, was "going all out" to incriminate Arbuckle in their press coverage. The action by the Times seemed to justify journalistic excess to W.R.

I asked a Hearst assistant editor to get me into the private office of W.R. for an important message I had to convey to him. I was ushered in at once. I told the Chief about Brian Sheehan who had administered the abortion to Marion. I reported that he had heard Rappé and Bambina plotting to blackmail Arbuckle and that shortly before going to San Francisco, Brian had performed an abortion on Rappé.

"We must not involve Dr. Sheehan in this scandal," W.R. said. He looked at me and smiled weakly. "We might find him useful at some future date."

As the news emerged that day and in the days ahead, the reaction of the public across America was swift and brutal. Initially the most hostile reaction came from women's groups condemning Arbuckle for his "immorality."

Shortly after the day's papers were printed, the comedian had been "tried" and found guilty in the public mind. Arbuckle had gone from the fat guy everybody liked to "the butterball you like to hate."

In Hartford, Connecticut, a movie theater

showing an Arbuckle comedy was raided by a group of women vigilantes, who disrupted the film by throwing rotten eggs at the audience. The Apollo Theatre in Jersey City announced a future ban on all Arbuckle films, either those made previously or likely to be filmed in the future. In the interest of "public safety," Arbuckle films were withdrawn in such places as the Maverick Theatre in Thermopolis, Wyoming. "Cowboys" had raided a movie house, seizing Arbuckle's latest film and burning it in front of a crown of rabble-rousers hooting and howling their approval.

Some movie exhibitors tried to re-release films that Rappé had appeared in, but those too ran afoul with the pressure groups. The Committee of Public Welfare of the Theatre Owners of America denied release of any Rappé films, claiming that the actress was "one of a mere handful who do not enjoy an enviable reputation for industry, citizenship, and morality."

Adela Rogers St. Johns, my former next-door neighbor, was a bit more blunt, claiming that Rappé was "a parasite, a studio-hanger-on, who used to get drunk at parties and start to tear her clothes off. She was an amateur call girl."

St. Johns, a usually reliable source—at least a lot more so than Lolly Parsons of the weak kidneys—almost got it right. The police in Los Angeles discovered that Rappé was no "amateur call girl." She'd once worked as a teenage prostitute in a "house of ill repute" run by her own mother, who was also her "lesbian lover."

In Los Angeles, Clergyman Bob Shuler of the Trinity Methodist Church denounced the end of America unless it rid itself of "films, dancing, jazz, evolution, Jews, and Catholics." At New York's Calvary Baptist Church, the Reverend Dr. J. R. Straton attacked the "sordid divorce" of Charlie Chaplin, and "the even worse divorce of Doug Fairbanks and Mary Pickford."

Those were the first clues that the Fatty Arbuckle case would not be just an indictment of the comedian, but the whip used to beat the entire film industry.

Few people in the film industry would escape from the far-reaching implications of the death of a teenage prostitute. It would lead to censorship in pictures and a "clean up" of our fair town which upset me a lot, since I had been—almost more than anybody with the possible exception of Barbara LaMarr—enjoying the decadence. It was the prospect of decadence that had driven me from Kansas to Hollywood in the first place.

At first a star like Gloria Swanson didn't see how the arrest of Fatty Arbuckle would affect her life, but the imperial diva soon got the message. She was involved in her own messy divorce, while carrying on an affair with a married man at the same time. Swanson denounced Arbuckle as a "fat, coarse, and vulgar man," and claimed she wouldn't go to bed with him. She didn't want the sudden glare of the Arbuckle scandal to cast a light on what was going on behind her own closed doors.

Charlie had fled to Europe with Paul Ivano, thinking—erroneously, it turned out—that the Arbuckle scandal would not directly harm him.

In Los Angeles, Rappé's so-called friend, Henry Lehrman, threatened to kill Arbuckle if he were acquitted for the "murder" of the young actress. He issued this quote to the press, "Arbuckle is the result of too much ignorance and too much money. When I used to direct him I had to warn him to keep out of the gals' dressing rooms. He's a disgrace."

Back in Los Angeles, Barbara LaMarr and I, along with some 8,000 others, attended the funeral of Virginia Rappé. The funeral on September 19 was at St. Stephan's Episcopal Church of East Hollywood. In a public display, Lehrman had sent $1,000 worth of tiger lilies—the exact floral bill announced to the press—to drape across Rappé's coffin.

Actually I was there on official business. W.R. had asked me to attend as a mourner, hoping that I could pick up some insider information, as he'd become impressed with the data I was acquiring. Since I was on his generous payroll, I could hardly say no. Besides, I, along with Barbara, was very curious. I expected to encounter Bambina at the funeral, but after causing all that eruption in San Francisco, she seemed to have disappeared.

Actually I did manage to get some information that led to an amusing feature story in the Hearst papers. In spite of all those tiger lilies, and even the grandstand threat to kill Arbuckle, Henry Lehrman did not bother to show up at the funeral. From a bellhop at the Hollywood Hotel, I got all the details. During Rappé's funeral, Lehrman was shacked up in one of the upstairs bedrooms with a Follies showgirl, Jocelyn Leigh. I even managed to get an interview with Leigh, who claimed that she'd fallen madly in love with Lehrman. "Rappé's loss is my gain, and what a gain," Leigh told me. "He's more man than I'm used to." Unlike most people issuing comments about the Arbuckle case to the press, Leigh must have meant her words. Within six months, the showgirl had married the director as Virginia Rappé became a distant memory for them.

I pulled another coup when I learned from the funeral director that Lehrman had ordered a stone for Rappé but then refused to pay for it. I called W.R. who told me to post the two-hundred dollars for her stone, which he'd then announced in his yellow press had been a gift of the Hearst organization "to a poor and unfortunate waif who had innocently stumbled into the moral depravity of Hollywood, where she'd been the hapless victim of lust and sexual perversions so rampant there."

Returning from the funeral, and heading for the Hollywood Hotel, Barbara and I decided that we wouldn't let the new morality creeping through Hollywood affect the way we'd lead our lives at all. "When you're young, hung, and beautiful like me," I told her, "I plan to keep doing what I do best. Having a good time. I've got no career to protect, really."

"I'm young and beautiful too," Barbara said. "In my case, skip the hung." Regrettably, Barbara followed my hazardous plan which worked for me, but didn't at all for her.

I was out of the star category, but all future contracts, even or especially those of Gloria Swanson, contained a morality clause. This new action was directly traced to whatever happened between Fatty Arbuckle and Virginia Rappé in that hotel suite at the St. Francis Hotel.

Rappé's funeral hardly ended the Arbuckle scandal.

It had just begun.

*****

Just like the movies itself, the Arbuckle scenario unfolding in San Francisco needed an ambitious and half-crazed district attorney who aspired to higher office—in this case the governorship of California. That lunatic appeared in the person of Matthew Brady with dragon-fire breath. He launched a trial that generated as much publicity as did the 1994 trial of O.J. Simpson when he'd slashed his wife, Nicole, and her waiter friend to death—and got away with it.

Luckily for Arbuckle and unluckily for Brady, the case began to unravel at the very beginning. Bambina lived up to her reputation as the biggest liar in Los Angeles. She was to be Brady's star witness—in fact, she'd been the one who'd filed the original charges against Arbuckle—but she changed her story every time she told it. Brady also learned that she was a bigamist and couldn't be put on the stand for that reason, as her testimony would be discredited.

Not easily surrendering, Brady pressed on, using what the press called "third-degree methods" to get another witness, a local chorus girl named Zey Prevon, to testify. She'd attended the brawl at the St. Francis. He threatened to have her charged with perjury if she didn't agree to sign a statement alleging that she personally had heard Virginia Rappé cry out that, "Fatty hurt me," presumably by inserting some large and blunt instrument into her vagina.

Could it have been the Francis X. Bushman dildo? I went to W.R. and told him about the dildo. He sat back in his chair calmly and said, "I wouldn't want to embarrass Francis by publishing something like that. He has trouble enough with his career and that Beverly Bayne. Perhaps we can suggest a large bottle instead. You must realize that the average American in this country has never even heard of a dildo." I figured that W.R. knew more what to write in his newspapers than I did.

The presiding judge, Sylvanin Lazarus, found the district attorney's case so weak he had the charges reduced from murder to manslaughter. If there weren't such pressure on the judge, he might have dropped the charges altogether. Fearing a public uproar across the land, he dared not go that far.

Some Hollywood stars wanted to go to San Francisco to stand as a character witness for Arbuckle but their attorneys persuaded them not to, fearing the violent "anti-Hollywood" resentment there.

Arbuckle's boss, Joseph Schenck, tried to bring pressure on Brady but failed miserably. If anything, his hint of a bribe only infuriated the district attorney. Schenck later told friends that if the scandal had erupted in Los Angeles, he could have bribed his way out of it.

Schenck was from the old school where "hush money" solved all problems. It had happened before with Arbuckle. On March 6, 1917, a drunken bash was staged at Brownie Kennedy's Roadhouse in Boston to celebrate Arbuckle's signing of a $5,000-a-week contract with Paramount.

A dozen party girls were hired for the night for a collective fee of $1,000. A bluenose maid peeked through an open transom just as Arbuckle and his showgirls were stripping for action. She called the Boston police and the party was raided, netting a trio of the biggest names in Hollywood, film moguls Adolph Zukor, Jesse Lasky, and Schenck, plus Arbuckle, of course.

The flamboyant Boston mayor, James Curley, was all too happy to get his district attorney to drop charges once $100,000 of money shipped in from Hollywood in unmarked bills exchanged hands. The movie magnates wrote the bribe off as "production expenses."

Failing to bribe Brady, Schenck conceived another public relations maneuver. He called Arbuckle's estranged wife, Minta, living on the east coast, and agreed to pay her way across country by train if she'd go to San Francisco and stand by the comedian "as his faithful wife" during the trial. It would generate favorable publicity, Schenck accurately predicted.

Unemployed at the time, Minta gladly accepted the deal. After she'd appeared in some two-reelers with Billy Quirk, exhibitors pronounced her "box-office poison," evocative of a much later charge made in the 1930s against Katharine Hepburn, Joan Crawford, and Marlene Dietrich.

Her Keystone Kops career over, Minta faced a stonewall when she applied for jobs, even when she'd billed herself as "Mrs. Roscoe Arbuckle" and had a resumé that included film work with not only her husband but Charlie Chaplin and Mabel Normand.

Once in San Francisco, Minta found that no hotel would give her a room, even if they had plenty of vacancies. Her picture had been plastered across newspapers throughout America. At lobbies she'd entered, she was often greeted with catcalls. Some guests even launched into a refrain of "Carry Me Back to Old Virginny." Others yelled out, "I'm Coming, Virginia." Everyone seemed to be conspiring to mock her husband's ill-fated adventure with Virginia Rappé.

The first trial began on November 14, 1921, with Arbuckle under police escort arriving at the courthouse in San Francisco, where women's vigilante groups waited to spit on him. And did in spite of police attempts to hold them back. Covered with spit, the comedian entered the courthouse where on the very first day the district attorney's case started to fall apart. Evidence was presented that Zey Prevon had been threatened by the district attorney. Prevon made a better showgirl than an eyewitness. Originally she'd claimed that she'd personally seen Rappé writhing on the floor of the hotel suite, crying out, "He killed me. Arbuckle did that."

Within days her story had changed, Prevon now maintaining that she hadn't actually seen that herself, but had merely been "told by Bambina," who, it seemed, had urged Prevon to claim that she'd actually been in the room herself. Zey Prevon later told the press that, "Virginia Rappé went into the bedroom with Fatty because she wanted to."

Zey Prevon was good at two things—dancing in the chorus and disappearing. When he would later need her, Brady couldn't find her. Fearing the police had stationed a plainclothes detective in the lobby of her San Francisco hotel, Prevon had lowered herself by a sheet rope through a third-floor window and into the courtyard. Reportedly, she had fled to the Deep South, eventually checking into a seedy hotel in New Orleans. It was later reported that she'd made it to Miami where she'd boarded a boat headed for Cuba.

Throughout the trial, Arbuckle remained steadfast in his testimony that he'd merely tried to bring aid and comfort to Rappé whom he thought "had had too much to drink and would sober up in the morning." Like an actor preparing for a stage play, he'd been carefully rehearsed in his testimony and never deviated from his story, unlike Bambina who kept changing her version of the events every day.

Medical experts for both the prosecution and the defense agreed that Rappé had died of a ruptured bladder and that there were signs of acute peritonitis. The testimony then got murky, some doctors claiming that an "outside source" had caused the bladder to rupture, others maintaining that it was the result of "internal complications."

Arbuckle's attorney, Gavin McNab, attacked the police department of San Francisco, claiming they were involved in a deliberate conspiracy "to hang Arbuckle." McNab called the case "the shame of San Francisco, with perjured wretches on the stand trying to deprive this stranger within our gates of his liberty."

On December 4, after 22 ballots, the jury returned its verdict, announcing that it was hung ten to two for acquittal. One of the hold-out jurors, Helen Hubbard, told the press that, "No amount of evidence can make me change my mind." She also claimed that, "From the beginning, I intended to vote for conviction from the moment I'd first heard that the scumbag had been arrested. I also hated all his pictures." No one thought to ask Hubbard at the time why she attended "every Arbuckle film ever shown," if she despised them so. It was later revealed that she had some bizarre sexual hangup or attraction to "fatsos."

One of the mysteries at that trial, widely speculated about in the press, was what had happened to the "bloody bottle" that Arbuckle had allegedly used to penetrate the vagina of Virginia Rappé.

At last the story can be told. While Paul Ivano and Charlie toured Europe, I received a call from Kono to come to Charlie's house. It was most urgent that I do so, and nothing more could be said over the phone. Since I was pulling in $1,000 a week from Charlie, I was willing and able to perform any task he demanded, the way I would do for W.R. who was paying me only half as much.

Once at Charlie's house, I learned that my mission, should I choose to accept it, was to drive to the St. Francis Hotel in San Francisco where I was to pick up a suitcase from a bellhop named "Tom-Tom." In return for the suitcase, I was to give Tom-Tom ten-thousand dollars, all carefully packaged into a series of twenty-dollar bills.

I didn't have to be Sherlock Holmes to understand that that suitcase obviously contained Rappé's torn clothing which had mysteriously disappeared and maybe even the bloody Bushman dildo. Tom-Tom, it seemed, was willing to part with the suitcase if I delivered the money.

"Why would Charlie put up this money for Arbuckle?" I asked Kono. "We both know how cheap he is."

"Charlie thought it would be more discreet," Kono said. "Since you know so many of Charlie's secrets, I can tell you this one, too. When he worked at Essanay, Charlie too was involved with Virginia Rappé. He too picked up something nasty from Rappé. That explains why he always covers his dick with iodine before he penetrates a woman. After Rappé, he considered iodine a medical precaution."

When I met the blond-haired Tom-Tom, a hot-looking guy who stood six foot two, I fell immediately in love with the Adonis. As with Lila Lee, it was the beginning of a beautiful friendship that would last for years. In the years ahead, I sent my favorite homosexual stars to the St. Francis to enjoy the services of Tom-Tom. When he grew a little long in the tooth and retired from that profession, he furnished young boys to the stars who visited San Francisco.

When I became a gossip columnist, Tom-Tom kept me supplied with the juiciest tidbits happening up there, especially when a member of the film colony would drive north for an off-the-record weekend.

That Tom-Tom was quite a guy, and became legendary for his thick ten-inch dick which he would gladly whip out for a guest at the hotel if requested. He even put on shows for those who'd never seen a man auto-fellate himself before.

It was difficult for me to leave the arms of Tom-Tom, but I drove back to Los Angeles in Charlie's Locomobile with the suitcase intact. At the Hollywood Hotel, I called Kono to tell him that I had burned the contents of the suitcase en route to Los Angeles when I'd stopped at a little inn with a fireplace.

I lied, of course, figuring that it was wrong to destroy this piece of Hollywood history. Years from now, that collector of Hollywood memorabilia, Debbie Reynolds, would have understood my position. That suitcase remains today locked safety in my Los Angeles home. No doubt it will come as a surprise package to my heirs.

Like a bloodsucker, Brady hung onto the case, trying Arbuckle for yet a second time. This time the district attorney had better luck, as he capitalized off a major mistake made by the Arbuckle lawyers. The defense did not bring Arbuckle to the stand. In complete contempt of the prosecution, the defense even refused to present closing arguments, which was unheard of in a murder case.

The jury, assuming no doubt that this bizarre action was an admission of guilt, voted ten to two for conviction. Fortunately, for Arbuckle it was another hung jury.

The third and final trial was ordered by Brady, and this time the defense wasn't about to repeat its mistake of the second trial. Arbuckle's attorney, McNab, blasted into the prosecution time and time again, pointing out the weakness of Brady's case. By then, Zey Prevon, Brady's main witness, was no doubt already safety in Havana working in some Cuban bordello. Even if she were an unreliable witness, her disappearance was a fatal blow to the Brady case.

Finally, on April 12, 1922 Arbuckle was acquitted. The jury, in a statement, said that, "The happening at the hotel was an unfortunate affair for which Arbuckle, so the evidence shows, was in no way responsible."

The acquittal came too late, as the damage to Arbuckle's career was lethal. He returned to Hollywood to find himself a pariah in the motion-picture industry. That dirty little $100,000 a year "censor" of the film industry, Will Hays, blamed Arbuckle personally for "the ills of Hollywood."

As a screen comedian, Arbuckle was not employable, and he was also deeply in debt to the tune of $700,000 in attorney's fees. He was momentarily rescued by Buster Keaton who generously paid many of Arbuckle's bills. His friends even raised money to send him on a trip to Asia, but foreign fans booed and threatened his life at one point. Arbuckle at the time of his cruise was still known all over the world, and was in fact one of Hollywood's five most famous film stars.

When the comedian returned to America in 1923, the director, James Cruze, snubbed the ban on Arbuckle and gave the actor work, casting him as himself in a spoof of the film industry, called *Hollywood*. As if mocking his own hapless predicament, Arbuckle was depicted waiting outside casting offices but never getting a job. When he did get some work from time to time, Arbuckle was forced to use the pseudonym of William Goodrich.

Another breakthrough occurred in 1924 when the ever-loyal Buster Keaton decided to hire Arbuckle to direct *Sherlock Jr.*, his latest comedy. But the stress of the job proved too much to the increasingly alcoholic Arbuckle, and Keaton reluctantly had to take him off the picture.

Hollywood proved that Goldwyn was right when he'd uttered those soon-to-be-famous words that you're only as good as your last picture. Arbuckle was viewed as a fat, out-of-work drunk who'd beat a rape and murder charge.

His wife, Minta, eventually filed for divorce in Rhode Island, claiming that her husband had deserted her in 1917. Privately to friends she said she was tired of apologizing to all those persons whom Arbuckle offended drunken night after drunken night. "But mainly," she said, "I've grown weary of apologizing for myself to myself."

What Minta didn't tell the press was her real reason for divorcing Arbuckle. Amazingly, during his first trial in San Francisco, when he faced the prospect of the gas chamber, Arbuckle had fallen in love with another woman. Her name was Doris Deane.

After his divorce from Minta, Arbuckle married Deane at the home of her mother in San Marino on May 16, 1925. But his second marriage drifted into the same problems as did his marriage to Minta—drunken nights, verbal attacks, the occasional throwing of furnishings and the bashing of household goods.

The problem of impotence plagued the marriage as it had with Minta. The new Mrs. Arbuckle told all who were interested in rather blunt language that, "Fatty can't get it up—not that there's much to rise." Arbuckle heard that she'd laughingly told friends at a Hollywood party, "No wonder Fatty had to use a coke bottle on Virginia Rappé."

When she'd returned home from the party that night, he'd beaten her severely. She'd called the police, only to have Keaton intervene and get Arbuckle off. The arrest cost Keaton some money. How much I never knew.

Surprisingly, a job offer—his most important since the trial—came from an unlikely source, W.R. Hearst himself. Even though W.R. had pilloried Arbuckle in his yellow press, the Chief asked Arbuckle to direct Marion in her upcoming film, *The Red Mill.* When confronted with Arbuckle, W.R. said, "I don't care what you did," implying that he was guilty. "I was only trying to sell newspapers. Now I'm trying to get a film made for Marion."

Arbuckle, working under the name of William Goodrich, took the job in spite of his misgivings about Hearst. The comedian carried it out professionally unlike the time Keaton had hired him. Nonetheless, W.R. hired master director King Vidor to drop by the set every day "to keep an eye on Fatty" during the filming.

That soggy, stodgy mess, *The Red Mill,* bombed at the box office, and W.R. never hired Arbuckle again. As for Marion, she told me she hated the film from the very beginning and had tried to persuade W.R. not to make it. She claimed she'd also made a mistake when she'd laughed at the jokes Arbuckle was constantly telling her on the set. From afar, W.R. had incorrectly assumed that Arbuckle and Marion were making fun of him.

Unlike W.R., Charlie never offered Arbuckle work even under his pseudonym of William Goodrich. Yet Charlie constantly claimed that his comedian friend had been framed in "the San Francisco mess." Nonetheless, in spite of this rejection by Charlie, and

in spite of Arbuckle's frequent requests for work from Charlie's studio, Arbuckle remained "eternally grateful" to Charlie for bribing Tom-Tom to hand over that little suitcase of Virginia Rappé "goodies" which might have incriminated Arbuckle.

Finding no more work in Hollywood, Arbuckle got a starring role on Broadway, appearing in *Paris Bound*, that farce of "borrowed babies" which was a revival of a 1910 comedy by Margaret Mayo. The juvenile actor, Humphrey Bogart, who would go on to greater things, appeared in the play with Arbuckle but even Bogie couldn't save that stinker. It lasted only twelve performances.

When Arbuckle returned from his Broadway fiasco, nothing had changed in the Fatty/Doris household. If anything, matters got worse—the drunken brawls, the continued impotence, the beatings. In August of 1928 the second Mrs. Roscoe Arbuckle was granted her divorce.

When I encountered her a year later at a Hollywood party, she claimed that, "Fatty is a sweet man," even though she'd charged him with beating her. "He wouldn't even undress in front of me—a really shy man." Unknown to her, she was talking to a man who'd seen Arbuckle sans clothing. I fully understood why he didn't want to take off his clothes in front of a woman. "I think my marriage to him offered him no solace," Deane said. "He found that only in the bottle."

As debts mounted and jobs completely disappeared, Arbuckle secured some backers and opened the Plantation Café on March 27, 1929 along Washington Boulevard next to Culver City. Mabel Normand rallied to the support of the club, sending a larger-than-life floral sculpture of Fatty himself for the club's opening night.

I showed up on opening night with Clara Bow, the "It" girl who had become my friend, replacing Barbara LaMarr in my life. Even Charlie, accompanied by me, made a few appearances.

But Black Tuesday (October 29, 1929) signaled the club's demise. The crash heard on Wall Street that afternoon eventually came down on Arbuckle, who watched patronage decline. For the next few months, the club lingered on before closing its doors forever, even with "the great Fatty Arbuckle" offering free entertainment nightly. Eventually no patrons in Hollywood wanted to see Arbuckle even if they didn't have to pay for a ticket.

"The bottle" had become forever etched in the public brain. Whenever there was mention of Arbuckle's name, even at the Plantation Club, drunken revelers held up champagne bottles for Arbuckle to autograph. Swallowing his pride, he signed his name. He even took one of those bottles home with him, racing up Sunset Boulevard, drinking as he did. He'd already been staggering drunk when he'd left the club. Spotting a traffic cop signaling him to pull over, Arbuckle had tossed the bottle into a hedge of bushes. "There goes the evidence," he shouted at the cop, who arrested him anyway. Buster Keaton, once again, came to the rescue to get Arbuckle out of jail.

Positive feedback came on the tenth anniversary of the Virginia Rappé scandal. In a poll of its readers, *Motion Picture,* a leading film magazine of the time, asked its readers, "Doesn't Fatty Arbuckle deserve a break?" The response from fans was overwhelmingly positive in Arbuckle's favor, readers claiming they wanted to see his return to the screen.

Impressed by that response, Jack Warner signed Arbuckle to star in six two-reel short comedies. Times were starting to look good, enough so that Arbuckle, in spite of his impotence, decided to wed for a final time. The minor and rather untalented actress, Addie Oakes Dukes McPhail, became the third Mrs. Roscoe Arbuckle on June 21, 1932.

Jack Warner had been so delighted with the Arbuckle two-reelers that he'd offered him a contract to make a feature length film. Arbuckle was delighted. I was at Charlie's house—The Little Tramp and I had long ago made up—when the call came in from Arbuckle in New York, telling Charlie of his new contract. "I'll do what no one in Hollywood history has ever done before. I'm going to return."

"I don't like the word return," Charlie had told Arbuckle on that day. "I prefer comeback."

Ironically, Gloria Swanson, playing Norma Desmond in the 1950 film, *Sunset Boulevard,* reversed Charlie's words, telling William Holden, playing Joe Gillis, that she hated the word "comeback," preferring a "return" to pictures.

Sadly, Arbuckle died the next day of a heart attack. Buster Keaton told the press, "It wasn't the stroke that killed him. What he really died from was a broken heart."

The funeral was held at the same parlor that eventually hosted the riots associated with the Rudolph Valentino funeral. Spectators, mostly curiosity seekers, flooded into the Gold Room at Campbell's funeral Home in New York on July 2, 1933 to catch their last glimpse of the notorious Fatty Arbuckle. Pallbearers included Bert Wheeler and Bert Lahr.

The body was shipped by train across country for burial at Forest Lawn where it rests today. After the burial and after the crowds had departed, a still unemployed Minta, his first wife, was spotted the next day at the gravesite laying a yellow rose on his tomb. She was seen kneeling and praying, perhaps not only for Fatty but for the "promise of work tomorrow."

As I dictated the Arbuckle saga to the increasingly hostile Bitch of Buchenwald, she turned on me at one point. "You should have been arrested for concealing state's evidence," she charged. "The contents in that suitcase could have sent Arbuckle to the gas chambers."

The mention of gas chambers brought a particular delight to the wrinkled and bitter face of The Bitch. "Even now, you are trying to perpetuate the lies. I don't think you have come clean at all about the Rappé thing. You've distanced yourself too much, and you are still protecting that pervert, Ramon Novarro, whom I understand was killed by a hustler who stuffed an Art Deco dildo down Novarro's throat. A dildo Valentino had modeled from his own penis, and one he'd used on Novarro several times."

"I don't know what you're talking about," I said, stammering, figuring I'd given potential readers many juicy details about the Arbuckle case, stuff that has never been known or published before.

"The cover-up continues," she claimed.

"What damn cover-up are you talking about?" I demanded to know.

"You're an old and dying man," she said. "In a few weeks, maybe a few days, you will be dead, and I won't be forced to sit here and listen to you dictate your smut. You will have departed the earth forever, leaving behind only this vulgar memoir, a record of your debauchery and depravity. Here is your chance to set the record straight and deliver the truth, something you haven't done up to now."

"Once again, what in hell are you talking about?" I asked, growing increasingly agitated and reaching for my pills, fearing she was about to deliberately bring on a stroke.

"The truth, you senile old fool," she said in the harshest tone she'd ever directed at me. "I have no doubt that you and your fellow pervert, Ramon Novarro, accepted Arbuckle's invitation and attended that party in San Francisco."

"I was at San Simeon," I protested.

"Of course, you were at San Simeon," she said. "But I'm sure it was a week before the Arbuckle scandal. You have deliberately confused the dates to mislead the reader. You and Novarro were in San Francisco on that fatal weekend. Nothing you can say, other than a complete admission, will make me change my mind."

"You're a liar," I said, rising from my chair until a nagging cough returned me to its protection.

"I suspect that once in San Francisco, both you and Novarro were penetrated by that dildo. Arbuckle used it on both of you before he used it to kill that poor, innocent girl, Virginia Rappé. For all I know, Arbuckle ordered you to penetrate Virginia with the dildo. He probably sat by the bed trying to get an erection, thinking the scene would get a rise from his little peepee. That is what I think happened."

With that, she rose from her chair. "I have already stayed here in this den of depravity where all sorts of Sodom and Gomorrah activities have taken place over the years. I was due to leave at five o'clock. It is now three minutes past five. I'll see that your office is billed for your keeping me overtime which is against the agreement I made with them."

After she'd departed, I sat alone in the library for a long time, watching the sun die over the Pacific. At one point, I wanted to call my houseboy and order him to bring the Rappé suitcase to me. In all the years I've owned it, I have never opened it, even on that day I purchased it from Tom-Tom and drove it back to Los Angeles. Finally I decided I didn't want to see what was inside.

As the night slowly approached, I reflected on the words the Bitch of Buchenwald had stabbed me with. Her projected scenario wasn't exactly what had happened back at the St. Francis. But she'd sensed that I had not been completely candid in my dictation.

There was a cover-up on my part, even at this late day. I wanted to protect the memory of someone I once loved, Ramon Novarro. He's long dead and gone, as I will soon be, but that horrible Buchenwald slut had nailed me. I hadn't told all I knew about the Arbuckle scandal, even though I'd revealed a lot.

If I had come clean with everything, the whole history of Hollywood scandals would have be to rewritten.

A man has got to keep some secrets close to his chest—to keep something of himself, a space reserved for his personal privacy and his alone, even when writing a "tell-all" memoir. After all, I can't share everything with the world.

I am the last man on earth who knows all the most intimate details of the Fatty Arbuckle case, and I'll go to my grave never revealing exactly what happened that day that began on September 3, 1921.

Tomorrow when the Bitch of Buchenwald arrives, I won't mention mention our mini-scandal over Fatty Arbuckle. I'll go back to another time when Marion Davies, Tom Ince, and even W.R. himself returned to Los Angeles. It was like coming home again. San Francisco wasn't my kind of town.

I belonged back in Hollywood, that "cesspool of depravity" being denounced in pulpits across the nation.

*****

Even though cut off from Charlie personally, I was more eager for news of his trip to Europe with Paul Ivano than I was to hear of the latest conquests of Barbara LaMarr.

Already the future Hollywood gossip columnist was growing inside me. In the weeks ahead, I kept visiting Kono secretly at his cottage. I'd always arrive with a present in hand. It was understood that those presents were really bribes to get him to talk of Charlie, although we never called them that. I was "always in the neighborhood," when I dropped in, and I always "saw this delightful item in a store that I know you and your lovely wife will adore."

Paul Ivano also fed me a constant array of insider's stuff in letters that arrived almost daily. Amazingly Ivano was completely unaware that I was the boy who he had replaced in Charlie's affections. Ivano vaguely spoke of there having been someone else, but he didn't know who it was. For a while, he suspected it might have been Ramon Novarro. Charlie wasn't talking.

Although Kono and I had developed a rather friendly, confidential relationship, I learned that the chauffeur detested Ivano. Ivano treated Kono like a servant and not the "Japanese aristocrat" he aspired to be.

While Charlie and Ivano were in Europe, I learned from Kono what had gone on before The Little Tramp had sailed to London.

It seemed that Florence Deshon did arrive in Los Angeles just in time to read a report from Charlie's studio that he was to wed May Collins. But two weeks after that report, Charlie was telling Kono that he couldn't stand to be in the same room with Collins, which made it a little difficult since she was living in his house and still performing duties as his secretary.

Once back in Hollywood, Deshon learned painfully, as Mildred Harris Chaplin would, that there was little interest generated among producers about her once-promising movie career. As word leaked out that she was no longer the mistress of Charlie Chaplin, the contracts dried out. She got a small paying job appearing on stage at the Pasadena Playhouse. But in time she drifted back to New York where she'd checked into the Algonquin Hotel. She found the hotel too expensive and was pursued nightly by Tallulah Bankhead. Moving to West 11th Street in Greenwich Village, she searched for work on the stage, finding none.

One day she'd gone into the kitchen of her little apartment and turned on the gas, lying down on the linoleum floor to die. When Eastman heard she'd been found and rushed to St. Vincent's Hospital, he went to her side. Learning that a blood transfusion might save her, he volunteered to give blood as his former mistress had the same type as he did. According to Kono, Eastman later called Charlie and told of how he'd lain by her side, as his blood was transferred into her. "I could hear her ragged breathing and knew her body had given up even though I was pumping fresh blood into her, her blood mingling with mine," Eastman had said.

Florence Deshon died a suicide and Hollywood made little note of it, unlike the case of a real star like Olive Thomas.

Although Charlie made no mention of Florence Deshon in *My Autobiography*, as I've already pointed out, he did use her suicide for dramatic purposes in his future film, *Limelight*, depicting a troubled young ballerina who turns on the gas to commit suicide in her London flat. In the film it is Charlie who saved her life. But in real life it was Charlie who might have been the cause of Deshon's death.

Before sailing to Europe with that boy whore and double-crosser, Paul Ivano, Charlie continued to involve himself in one scandal after another, many of which, fortunately for Charlie, didn't make the newspapers.

A few months earlier I'd seen him at the Ship Café as the escort of an aspiring actress, Claire Windsor. Her real moniker, or so I'd learned, was Olga Cronk. It was obvious why she'd changed her name. A fragile-looking blonde, she was rumored to have a two-year-old son but there was no daddy. Kono suspected it belonged to Charlie because he had told Kono he liked to have "natural sex" with Claire; otherwise he couldn't enjoy the full sensation of intercourse.

The headlines in Los Angeles reported that Windsor had been kidnapped while horseback riding in the Hollywood Hills, as she'd followed the same route that Gloria Swanson and Rodolfo had done the day I, along with the mysterious German "baron," had spied on the two lovers. Charlie announced to the press he was putting up $1,000 in reward money, and he set out for the hills himself, leading a search party. Windsor was found under a tree later that afternoon. She appeared dazed and claimed she was suffering from amnesia.

Kono didn't buy that, although Charlie at first had seemed convinced. Later Windsor came to Charlie's house, demanding to see him. Before that evening had ended, Charlie had agreed to make a $10,000 settlement on Windsor "and your brat," providing she'd agree to stay out of his life and away from the press forever. Her faked kidnapping had paid off.

As if all these women weren't enough in his life, Kono reported that Charlie had fallen for a twelve-year-old girl to whom he'd offered a bit part in his two-reeler, *The Idle Class*. He'd even hired her mother for a bit part in the film too. Charlie had told Kono, "I've got to have this girl," who turned out to be Lillita McMurray, a child of Mexican and Scottish background. She was called "Lita" by her friends and was to prove one little girl Chaplin wouldn't be able to get rid of as easily as he had the rest, even Mildred Harris.

If all these complications weren't enough, Charlie learned that his emotionally disturbed mother, Hannah, was en route from England to Los Angeles. His brother, Sydney, had arranged for her to stay in a cottage in Santa Monica, because Charlie didn't want to be under the same roof with her, blaming her for "darkening" his childhood.

It was at this point that Charlie had announced to the press that he was going to close his studio and head to Europe "for a sentimental journey long postponed." He left out the little tidbit that Nazimova's boy friend, Paul Ivano, would be sharing his bed. Nazimova herself was raging in fury, but since Charlie knew many of her own dark secrets she kept her mouth shut in spite of her jealousy. Besides, Natacha Rambova, in spite of her nonsexual link to Rodolfo, seemed to keep Nazimova's libido in check.

In the Los Angeles papers, I read about Charlie's good-bye party at the Elysée Café, at which Doug Fairbanks and Mary Pickford attended as guests of honor. Charlie had dared appear at the party with Paul Ivano. It was fairly safe for him to do that, as it was assumed that he was considering hiring Ivano as his cameraman. Charlie's reputation had been secured as a womanizer and a deflowerer of young maidenhead. Very few people, even among the Hollywood elite, knew of his homosexual liaisons.

What Charlie and Paul Ivano did in New York en route to London, neither one of them cared to divulge. The next word Kono and I heard was that they had boarded the *Olympic* and were sailing to Southampton where, it had been reported, the English were viewing the return of their home-grown boy, Charlie, as "the Second Coming." After arriving in England and making his way to London, Charlie and Ivano had checked into the Ritz Hotel. The Los Angeles papers carried pictures of Charlie, minus Ivano, waving like royalty to his fans from the balcony of his suite at the Ritz.

From Kono I learned that the elite of England was inviting Charlie to parties and dinners. In the *chiaroscuro* atmosphere of the Garrick Club, he was photographed with Sir James Barrie, and no doubt they talked of Paramount's plans to film *Peter Pan*. He was also photographed with the celebrated architect, Sir Edwin Lutyens, who had just come from Buckingham Palace and a meeting with King George V and his Queen.

What does a great architect say to royalty who ruled an empire on which the sun never set? According to Ivano, Lutyens had amused the King and Queen with a workable miniature toilet about six inches high with a cistern. The King and Queen had been charmed by this little dollhouse toilet and had spent their time with Lutyens flushing it.

While in England, H.G. Wells had introduced Charlie to Rebecca West. Charlie had claimed to Ivano that he'd seduced the great Rebecca West on their first night together, an unlikely mating.

Although Paris turned out to welcome Charlie, as they would a future comedian, Jerry Lewis, Charlie arrived in Berlin to find he was virtually unknown to the general public. Of course, film industry people knew who he was. But he couldn't even use his influence at the Hotel Adlon to get a room for Ivano and him.

At the fashionable Kaiser Restaurant, he was given the most undesirable table in the house by the kitchen door. Al Kaufman, an executive for Paramount, recognized Charlie and invited him to one of the decent tables.

There Charlie was to meet the actress, Pola Negri. Kaufman was in Berlin negotiating a Hollywood contract for her. Born in Poland on the last day of 1894 (or 1901 as she'd later claim), Negri grew up in poverty but had found success as an actress at the studios of German director, Ernst Lubitsch. Her 1919 *Madame Du Barry* had scored a great success in the United States when it was released under the title of *Passion*.

Minxlike Pola, or so it was reported, couldn't speak English at the time. The only words she could say to Charlie, was "Jazz boy, Sharlie," which she apparently had repeated endlessly to him in lieu of conversation.

I devoured all news I could read about Negri, suspecting she'd already become another one of Charlie's women. One critic called her, "all slink and mink." But I relished a comment from another commentator who wrote, "With Pola Negri, you get the feeling that the back of her neck is dirty." No doubt this was a reference to her "earthly quality."

I had no idea where Charlie had stashed Ivano, as he never appeared in any of the news pictures sent back to Los Angeles.

In Negri's photographs in Berlin with Charlie, a blond German Adonis was always depicted glowering in the background. Many editors cropped out his presence. But when at last I saw a full photograph of him, I was dazzled.

In time I was to learn a lot more about this discarded lover of Pola Negri's. He was a German with a profile of classic beauty by the name of Wolfgang George Schleber. Negri had labeled him "Petronius," because she considered him the living incarnation of the hero of the novel, *Quo Vadis?*

I was so taken by the looks of this man that I found it hard to believe that Negri could be smitten with *The Little Tramp*, and neglect this Teutonic wonder who could later be a poster boy depicting Hitler's ideal man of "the master race."

When I did finally get to see a full picture of Petronius that editors hadn't cropped I too fell in love with him if only from afar. At least I could dream.

The closest American equivalent of this blond beauty was Dr. Brian Sheehan. In fact, looking at pictures of Petronius made me hot for Brian all the more.

In time, I would not only meet Petronius, but be his host when he finally arrived in Hollywood to see what the excitement was all about. Before the end of his second night in town, he'd learned what happened to a handsome, hung, and blond German stud who accepted an invitation to be the houseguest of a homosexual man. My neck wasn't dirty like Negri's, at least according to Petronius, who'd spent part of the night licking and kissing it as he plowed into me. Negri's rejects could put their shoes under my bed at any time.

"Leave this smut about Petronius for another day," the Bitch of Buchenwald reminded me. Once again I was racing ahead of my story. "We do not need to hear of this future Nazi," the Bitch said. "Only eyes that blue could have dropped the gas pellets." I looked at her sternly, thinking that Petronius in time to come might have indeed dropped those pellets. But she'd rounded up the bodies to peel off their skin to make lamp shades.

Back in Berlin, and back to my story. Negri told the German paparazzi of her day that Charlie brought out "a wonderful maternal instinct in me." Yeah, right.

Long before arriving in Hollywood, Pola Negri established her credentials as the biggest female liar in Hollywood even before she got there. She too would write an autobiography, modestly called *Memoirs of a Star*. It had about as much truth in it as Charlie's *My Autobiography*. Some of the space in Negri's tome was devoted to proving that "at heart" she wasn't a lesbian.

Even before Charlie left Berlin, word had reached Hollywood that Negri was abandoning her film career in Germany to "take California by storm." Already before landing, she was hailed as "the Theda Bara of the Twenties."

Having never met her, I knew instinctively that she was going to become a distant rival of mine, like Gloria Swanson. I suspected that Miss Negri and I would be competing for the same man or men.

But other than Charlie, which one?

Chapter Fourteen

At the dawn of the Twenties, handsome hunks from all over America were arriving by the hundreds at the Los Angeles train depot, many of them with only five dollars in their pockets. All dreamed of stardom. Homosexual men, often claiming they were highly connected with the film industry, were laying in wait for them. It was a bountiful harvest.

Most of the young men wanted to be either the next Rudolph Valentino or the next Wallace Reid, and a lucky few actually did achieve that dream. Those directors and producers who liked men found their casting couches wore out quickly. These young men were "willing to do anything within reason," as the good-looking actor, Robert Ellis, told me as I was hauling him back to the Hollywood Hotel in my stagecoach for a workout with Barbara LaMarr and me.

In spite of his morphine addiction, Wally Reid was still holding his position as a major star at the box office. He remained the king of Paramount. The reigning queen? Who else but Gloria Swanson? She was appearing opposite Wally in *The Affairs of Anatol*. But by the time they came together in a picture, Wally had lost all interest in Swanson, and he appeared wooden and a bit dazed in the movie, although no reviewer commented on that.

The careers of Joe Godsol's "party favors" to me, namely Richard Dix and Reginald Denny, were starting to march. Some older and more established stars such as Beverly Bayne and Francis X. Bushman had returned to the stage when their presence was no longer desired by producers.

A trade journal revealed that the top fifteen male stars at the box office were: Wallace Reid, Charles Ray, Thomas Meighan, Eugene O'Brien, Douglas Fairbanks, William S. Hart, William Farnum, Tom Mix, Tom Moore, Harrison Ford, Richard Barthelmess, Bryant Washburn, Charles Chaplin, Earle Williams, and Harold Lloyd. I'd had sex with nine of them—not bad, not bad at all for a star-fucker.

Every day you picked up the paper you read of another actor who had been "discovered," rescued from the role of an extra or else with no previous experience, and placed in a starring vehicle. Such was the case of my divine silver blond, William Boyd, who found himself cast opposite Mary Miles Minter, the slut, in *Moonlight and Honeysuckle*. As if Chaplin, William Desmond Taylor, and countless others weren't enough, Minter went knocking on William Boyd's dressing room door the second day of the shoot. She asked him if he'd like to sample some of her freshly brewed coffee. Inviting her in, he locked the door behind her.

Later as William was letting me tongue his tits at the Hollywood Hotel waiting for Barbara to return, he said he never got around to tasting Minter's coffee.

Even sports figures were arriving in Hollywood to try their luck in the movies. Such world famous legends as Jack Dempsey, Babe Ruth, and Georges Carpentier also got off that train to make their film debuts, although in time it would be revealed that acting wasn't their major talent. But I do remember standing in the shower between beefy Tom Mix and beefy Jack Dempsey following a workout in Mix's gym. Dempsey might be a world champ, but when facing Mix in the shower, it was my cowboy who scored the knock-out punch.

Working as an extra I got to renew "old acquaintances," as when Ince got me a bit part in *Everybody's Sweetheart*, starring Elsie Janis and Matt Moore, later released by Selznick. On the set, Matt spoke lovingly of having met my sister at the Santa Monica beach house and what a "wonderful time" they'd had there.

Matt, although he was cute and cuddly, wasn't worth my pursuing as Durango Jones. I figured having seduced him as Lotte Lee was enough of a challenge.

Sometimes I'd meet an actor on the set which would lead to a one-night stand, often not even that, perhaps hurried sex in a closet. That's how we did it back then.

One memorable encounter was with Lou Tellegen, the actor who'd appeared opposite Sarah Bernhardt when she'd starred in a film as Queen Elizabeth. I'd encountered him before in Goldwyn's office when the producer was fighting with his girl friend and future wife, Geraldine Farrar. For at least two years, the Farrar/Tellegen romance sold a lot of movie magazines.

Once again my ever-faithful Ince had gotten me a bit part in *The Woman and the Puppet*, which starred both Lou Tellegen and Farrar. I appeared briefly in a background scene where Farrar is caught between Macey Harland and Tellegen.

Throughout the day the raging fight between Farrar and Tellegen was the talk of the set. Tellegen had been drinking heavily all day, and at one point he'd accused Farrar of sleeping with Owen Moore, Mary Pickford's discarded husband. In turn, she accused him of sleeping with Betty Compson, the Paramount star. Who cared? Everybody was sleeping with everybody else back in those days.

Heeding a call of nature, I headed for a barracks-like set of buildings containing the men's toilets. Although I actually planned to relieve myself, there was that slight bit of titillation I always experience, then and since, when entering a men's room.

The urinals were empty, as I positioned myself in the center. A man dressed as a soldier with gold buttons, stripes, and a military hat took the stall right next to mine, even though there were eight urinals in all. He obviously didn't want privacy.

When I turned around, I spotted Lou Tellegen, who'd spoken to me on the set several times in the past few days. He seemed to know of my reputation. But, then, what Hollywood stud didn't? Even though I'd never had a real part in a film as Durango Jones, I was a bit of a legend myself. At least I could attract some attention from so-called straight men who if nothing else were curious.

I couldn't help myself but when Tellegen pulled it out, I inspected it fully, finding it quite thick and perhaps three and a half inches long, with a lot of meaty promise. He pissed like a horse, as my eagle eye took in the show. At one point, he pulled back the wrinkly foreskin and exposed a large, plumlike head. Perhaps he heard my barely audible sigh. After finishing, he stood there longer than necessary shaking himself. When I looked into his face, he winked at me. Even though by now I was a hardened whore and not the innocent child who'd arrived on the train from Kansas, I flushed in embarrassment.

"I think you like what you see," he said. "It's okay with me. A man's got to get it wherever he can, especially if he's married to a bitch who keeps a tight lock on her pussy."

"Let's go into that booth over there," I said, reaching for his hand and guiding him—his dick hanging out—into the booth where I locked the door behind us. I reached inside to remove a pair of respectable looking balls onto which I planted tongue lashings to get the party rolling.

"I know you pansies make the greatest cocksuckers in Hollywood," he said, flashing a smile as he reached out and cupped the back of my head, pulling me up from his balls to a much larger target. He wasted no time with preliminaries but guided his cock between my cherry-red lips where I proceeded to live up to my reputation.

My knees were quivering in anticipation of his oncoming climax, which was arriving much too soon for me. I was enjoying this tonguing and sucking, and wanted it to continue even though I knew he was due back on the set for a love scene with Farrar. I managed to hold him back for about five minutes but I was just too good at my work. Tellegen exploded in my mouth, and I devoured his every drop, wanting a repeat performance which I didn't get.

Buttoning up his trousers rather quickly, he looked down at me and patted me on the head like a lap dog. "You're good," he said. "Let's do that again sometime. Perhaps in a setting that's more romantic than this stinking toilet." And then he was gone.

Even though I'd fallen madly in love with him at that point and planned to rescue him from the clutches of that cow, Farrar, I never saw Tellegen again.

But I vividly recalled the taste of him when I read the front pages of the Los Angeles papers in 1935. Tellegen had committed suicide. Not only suicide, but *hara-kiri*.

He was found nude in his Hollywood apartment with a pair of gold scissors, a gift of his former wife, Farrar, who had the scissors initialed "LT."

Surrounding Tellegen were his most favorable press clippings from the movie mags of his heyday, which had been filled with pictures of Farrar and himself when they'd been hailed as "Hollywood's two love birds." There were two posters found beside Tellegen, one advertising his box office hit, *The Long Trail,* and another promoting his second big attraction, *The Redeeming Sin.*

The Los Angeles police reported that Tellegen had apparently squatted Japanese style in the center of the room with his beloved souvenirs. He'd taken the gold scissors and had eviscerated himself with the instrument, even stabbing into his heart and laying it bare.

His rotting body had been found two days later, surrounded by blood-soaked memories of his glory days as a star. The papers referred to him as a "has-been."

At this point the Bitch of Buchenwald interrupted my dictation, claiming I'd wandered off into a "byway" again.

That weekend, after my "work" (if you can call it that) on the Farrar flicker was finished, I headed for the home of Tom Ince, as I so often did. Little did I know that for the next forty-eight hours, I would fall madly in love with a new Ince discovery, Lloyd Hughes. I'd first discovered Hughes myself when Ince let me look through his peephole as Hughes plowed it to the big-time star, Bessie Love.

I liked what I saw. Durango Jones wanted to be where Bessie Love was. Sensing my excitement, Ince arranged for me to share a bedroom with Hughes that night, and he must have suggested to Hughes that if he wanted to break into pictures, he'd have to satisfy me first even though I was a man. "You've got to fuck more than women in this town to get ahead," Ince had told Hughes, or at least that's what the young actor claimed when he came to my bed to begin the fun.

Within two days before he departed, I had thought he was the most divine creature I'd ever seen or known, forgetting Rodolfo and Wally for the moment. Wondering when I'd see him again, I was a bit forlorn as I sat alone by Ince's pool.

Walking toward me in a tight-fitting two-piece bathing suit was a man of such stunning beauty that I forgot all other lovers. Ince had sent him out to talk to me. I don't know what else the producer had told the young actor, Cullen Landis, but I found him most cooperative and even eager to enjoy an afternoon siesta in my bedroom now that Hughes had vacated and made room for another man.

As I looked at those biceps and that promising bulge emerging from his brief trunks, I didn't think Cullen Landis and I would get much sleep that day. He had to leave by five o'clock, however, as he was due on a set somewhere down the coast near San Diego and had to head out early if he wanted to get checked into a hotel where he'd be ready for an early morning shoot.

By the time he'd left I'd fallen in love with this Greek God. Facing the night all alone, I was relieved when Ince told me I'd be sharing my bed with an up-and-coming actor, named "Bull" Montana, an emerging star at First National. It was late by the time Bull arrived at Ince's mansion but I'd left the light on. When Bull opened the door at midnight, I saw a big man with a bull neck. He wasn't a pretty boy like Hughes or even Landis, but he was strong in the tradition of Francis X. Bushman. After a night with the aptly named Bull, I would rec-ommend that anyone contemplating going to bed with him work out for a week with the Francis X. Bushman dildo before allowing this cowboy inside.

Since I'd been so intrigued with Lloyd Hughes and his thick, eight-inch, straight-as-an-arrow cock, I was delighted when Ince got me a bit part on the new Mary Pickford Film, a remake of one of her earlier successes, *Tess of the Storm Country*. Hughes would be play-ing her leading man.

I hadn't seen Mary since her wedding to Doug, and was anxious to renew my acquain-tance with her. All the papers had been filled with stories of her marriage. In spite of the Arbuckle scandal and the condemnation of Hollywood from various pulpits, "America's Sweethearts" were even more popular after their wedding than before. Mary had found her heart's desire, who just happened to be the most popular man on earth. Although they feared their divorces might destroy their ca-reers, as it had for Francis X. Bushman and Beverly Bayne, it hadn't at all.

Encountering Mary the first time on the set, she said, "I fear this movie might play to empty houses. Doug felt we might have gone on and lived as secret lovers, the way we were the day we met you. I felt it was wrong to put our joint careers at risk. But once he threatened to leave me, I gave in."

I learned that all was not going smoothly, at least with the law. Mary had gotten her di-vorce in Nevada, with its relatively liberal di-vorce laws, and had tried to meet that state's three-month residency requirement by board-ing at a ranch, in the tiny village of Genoa with her mother, Charlotte.

At one point Owen had arrived at the ranch to sign some legal papers Mary wanted his signature on. But when the district attorney in that area of Nevada had read of Mary's marriage to Doug, he'd challenged her in court, claiming she had no intention of becoming a permanent resident of the state as she'd claimed in court. He also said that Owen's appear-ance at the ranch had represented "collusion." If the district attorney's charges were upheld, Mary's divorce from Owen would not be vali-dated and her marriage to Doug would expose her to a charge of bigamy.

Those problems aside, there was no evi-dence that the marriage had destroyed the box-office clout of a couple which was increasingly referred to as "the King and Queen of Holly-wood." In spite of the Arbuckle scandal and the subsequent outrage, the moral tone of America in the early 1920s had become con-siderably more liberal than it had been during the pre-Edwardian years.

The Jazz Age had arrived. Freudianism was in vogue, as was Darwin's *Origin of the Species,* challenging traditional religious values. Resting in their graves were such staunch fig-ures as Queen Victoria and William McKinley.

The use of contraceptives was on the rise, as Americans, both men and women, became more sexually liberated. In the wake of the Arbuckle scandal and noting how many news-papers that case had sold, W.R. made sex and scandal a regular feature of his newspapers. Lolly Parsons of the weak kidneys wrote that Doug and Mary "were the modern fulfillment of every love story since Adam and Eve."

As usual, Lolly got it wrong. Even on their honeymoon, Doug had demonstrated exces-sive jealousy where Mary was concerned. Apparently it was a marriage based on a double standard, as he had no intention of giving up his extramarital affairs with starlets.

On their honeymoon in Europe, Doug had demanded that Mary was never to do any "twosing" with anybody on the dance floor but himself. That led to her being placed in the position of turning down a request for a dance from the Duke of York (later King George VI), although His Majesty later forgave her.

I decided that Doug didn't know about Mary's continuing affair with the actor, James Kirkwood. Although infrequent, it was defi-nitely a love affair. Yet another affair was about to bloom. When Mary confronted the drop-dead gorgeous hunk from heaven, Lloyd Hughes, I couldn't blame her for being awed by his male beauty. I'd had the same reaction to him, so I could hardly fault Mary for feeling as I did. Even if she did have Doug Fairbanks at home, what woman, or even what homo-sexual man, could resist Lloyd Hughes? You swooned if you saw him with his clothes on. But you fainted when you saw him with his clothes off.

As each day went by on the filming, Mary was spending longer and longer lunches with Hughes in her dressing room. The actor was flattered by the attention of the queen of Hollywood, although later that night as he let me fuck him, he told me he didn't find Mary sexy at all.

Perhaps Mary would have gotten away with this little indiscretion had it not been for Hedda Hopper visiting the set. She had a bit part in a film next door. Like a future Lolly Parsons, Hopper spotted Hughes emerging from Mary's dressing room, and she accurately surmised what had taken place there.

Unlike me, Hopper couldn't keep a secret under her picture hat of red cabbage roses. She went to Doug the next day and told him of her suspicions about Hughes and Mary. "Robin Hood" exploded, going so far as to arrange for two hit men in New Jersey to take the train from New York to Los Angeles to kill Hughes.

Fortunately blabbermouth Hopper told several other people of this, and word quickly reached Hughes and Mary on the set. The next morning Mary called me to her dressing room. "You've been privy to my secrets before," she said, welcoming me warmly. "I must ask you to do one more favor for me. Doug has already told me how accommodating you are." She paused as if embarrassed. "I mean, the Prince of Wales thing. Come to Pickfair tonight. We're having some people in for dinner. Lloyd will be there."

I was astonished that she'd invite Hughes. Doug might beat him up…or worse.

Awkwardly, Mary finally revealed to me what she wanted me to do. "Lloyd has told me about that thing between you and him at Tom Ince's house," she said. "I understand how you boys will play around when there are no girls present."

If she believed that, she didn't understand anything at all.

"Please, don't take offense," she said. "I don't condemn such practices. Lloyd has to have some relief, and I prefer he do it with a man instead of another woman. Of course, for real sex he'll turn to a woman."

Although it took Mary at least fifteen minutes to get around to her specific request, she finally made her point. At night before dinner,

Doug always used the steam bath. She wanted Hughes and me to go into that bath before Doug. When Doug would walk in later, she wanted me to be going down on Hughes. In Mary's view, when Doug saw that Hughes was homosexual, and was secretly in love with me, he would not be suspicious of them any more.

The whole plot seemed far-fetched and ridiculous to me, but then I was unfamiliar with how the minds of straight couples operated.

I was only too eager a few hours later to sample the attractions of Lloyd Hughes, as I found I couldn't get enough of him. As Mary had ordered, we both paraded nude into the steam room at Pickfair, Hughes sitting on one of the upper marble tiers. On the tier below I removed his towel and went to work to get a rise out of him, and was it ever magnificent.

Just when I'd forgotten all about Doug and was enjoying my slurp session, Doug came into the steam room stark naked. He didn't say anything at first, and I didn't stop as I was too much into it. "Carry on, boys," I heard Doug say. "Don't let me stop you."

Taking a seat on a marble slab right near Hughes, Doug dropped his towel and peered down at the action. Like an intense director, he didn't take his eyes off of us even though I managed to hold off Hughes' eruption for at least another ten minutes.

Finally, my mouth dripping with cum, I rose from Hughes' loins and flashed a smile at Doug, asking him if he wanted a sample. I noticed that his crooked dick had risen at least two and a half inches as he'd overseen the action. "Better not," he said, getting up and reaching for his towel. "I'm tempted but I don't think Mary would approve."

Hughes' life had been saved, and in the months ahead Doug referred to us as "an item." Since he felt that Hughes was a homosexual, which I suspected he really was, Doug didn't think he had to worry any more about Mary and the young actor.

Mary was so grateful to me that she issued a steady stream of dinner invitations for me at Pickfair, that ersatz hunting lodge that Doug had remodeled for his new bride. An invitation to dinner there was a certificate of success in Hollywood. You ordered from a printed menu but got no wine with your meal, at least in the early days. Mary might be a secret drinker, but that was only after the dinner guests had departed.

My major obstacle while dining at Pickfair was Mary's white-haired terrier, Zorro, who bit my ankles, often severely. He bit not only me, but kings, princesses, oil billionaires, and ambassadors. He bit anything that moved. Finally, I tamed the beast by bringing it some freshly ground sirloin wrapped in plastic.

"You're the only person Zorro doesn't bite," Mary said, noticing the dog licking my hand. That seemed to ingratiate me more than ever with her. "I don't understand it," she said. "Zorro costs me a fortune in claims from hotel maids, delivery men, even a policeman who dared stop me for a traffic ticket, claiming I was speeding. Zorro must have resented his accusation and proceeded to make mincemeat out of that cop."

Between the parties thrown by Marion Davies and W.R., and those dinners at Pickfair, you got to meet the world. At Mary's, the Queen of Siam might be in the bathroom "refreshing myself," or else you found yourself in Doug's steam room sitting next to the Duke of York (yes that same Duke of York and future king that Mary had refused to dance with). I noticed when I was in the steam bath with His Majesty that the Duke didn't share the same proclivities as the Prince of Wales. He did stare at my penis, though, and I think he was impressed with it. His own penis was as tiny as that of the Prince of Wales. It must be a genetic flaw in the British family, I assumed.

For his amusement in Hollywood, the Duke of York liked to trail Doug to his movie set. He was particularly fond of watching stuntmen crash through windows made of fragile sugar which evoked glass. The future king tried that a few times himself, always ending up licking the glasslike shards of sugar as if they were lollipops.

One night at Pickfair you might be seated next to the Duchess of Alba, or Henry Ford and his wife, Clara. You might even turn around to find yourself staring into the ugly and mischievous face of Albert Einstein. The genius insisted later on a parlor game. He assigned each of us a profession and demanded that we speak five minutes in the character of the role

we were assigned. Regrettably, he assigned me the role of a British labor leader, and I struggled through five minutes of inane chatter before giving way to Lloyd Hughes, who'd been assigned the role of a manufacturer of children's toys.

Sometimes when I didn't have Hughes for the night, I'd get lucky with one of Doug's guests. That happened the night the world famous champion hurdler, Charley Paddock, arrived. That athlete had great legs. Alone and nude with him in the steam room, I discovered a "third leg" that Charley had. Under my intense scrutiny, it rose and rose to its impressive peak, but I managed to deflate it before any of Doug's other guests came into the steam room and interrupted the session.

My favorite dinners at Pickfair were with Mitchell Leisen, a sensitive homosexual art director who had won the favor of Doug and Mary. On the nights Leisen was the guest of honor, only men of a certain persuasion were invited. With his crooked dick, Doug paraded nude into his steam room, not adverse to showing off his physical attributes to homosexuals.

Later, Mary would sit at the head of the table, presiding over this gathering of "men kissers," as she sometimes called us. Over the years, I never really understood how she felt about homosexuals. She found gay men amusing and her indulgence of them went beyond mere toleration. My guess was that she viewed homosexual love as not a serious commitment, the way it could be between a man and a woman. It was something men did in locker rooms and toilets for emergency relief, or when sent to film a western in a remote location where no women were available.

As we were seated in the parlor one night, talking to Lord and Lady Mountbatten, along with the Duke and Duchess of Sutherland, freshly arrived from England, Doug flew into a rage at his Japanese valet. He screamed, shouted, and denounced the servant in front of his stunned guests. Grabbing the lightweight valet by his heels, Doug picked him up and swung him into the air, as the Japanese boy went spinning around Doug's head. Lady Mountbatten regarded it with cold-faced detachment, no doubt presuming that is what Americans did at home, especially if they were exhibitionistic movie stars. But the Duchess screamed in fright. When Doug let the boy come out of orbit, the guests were told he was a trained acrobat and that it was only a stunt.

Sometimes Jack Dempsey would come over, and Doug was fond of lifting the champ up on his shoulders for a photographer. Once he even hoisted both Charlie Chaplin and Mary Pickford onto his shoulders for the benefit of the camera.

It was all fun and games, and even the "homosexual thing" never caused any problems after that incident with Lloyd Hughes. That is, until one day. After I'd taken Doug Jr. horseback riding in the Hollywood Hills, Doug Sr. invited both of us to Pickfair. Doug Jr. was excited because he felt that Mary was jealous of him, "Since I'm Beth's son—not hers—she doesn't want to be reminded that dad had another wife before her."

Doug Jr. became even more excited when he learned that Bill Tilden, the greatest tennis player of all time, was being entertained at Pickfair and wanted to pass on some "tennis secrets" to young Doug, whom he'd specifically requested to meet.

"Big Bill" Tilden was always getting photographed in the sports pages. He'd already starred in several silent films. Doug invited him to join us in the steam room but he seemed painfully shy. I later learned that he never stripped in a locker room or shower and often had body odor because of that. I also learned, much later that is, that his mother had tried to feminize him and had called him "June" until he turned twenty-one.

Doug Jr. showed up on the courts looking like a prepubescent Ganymede in clinging blue seersucker tennis briefs. Until he came along, men wore only whites. I couldn't help but notice the glimmer in Tilden's eye.

In time, Tilden would be a great success on the Hollywood courts, playing with Rodolfo, Greta Garbo, Clara Bow, Ramon, and Louise Brooks, Joan Crawford, and even Chaplin himself.

Doug Sr. played the first game of tennis with Tilden but the pro beat d'Artagnan's musketeer so badly he retreated back to the main house with me to talk to Mary.

When Beth, Doug's former wife, called to ask why Doug Jr. hadn't returned home, Doug agreed to send the boy over right away, asking me to drive him, which I agreed to. Doug Sr. left to retrieve his son, and had been gone for about ten minutes when Mary and I, sitting on her veranda enjoying the late afternoon sun, heard shouts coming from the tennis courts. "Go see what's happening," Mary urged me.

Racing to the courts, I saw Doug Sr. beating up Tilden who lay sprawled on the court, offering no resistance. I pulled Doug off the tennis pro. Doug rose to his feet, "Get that pansy asshole off my grounds. *Now.*" He turned in anger and disgust, heading back to the house.

Without saying anything or even looking at Doug Jr. or me, Tilden left the courts and headed for his car.

As Doug Sr. came out to see me off in my stagecoach with his son, he leaned into the window and pointed a finger at Doug Jr. "Just let me catch you doing that one more time, and you won't have a weenie to play with. I'll cut it off." He slapped my arm. "Thanks, Durango. At least there's someone in Hollywood who can be trusted with my son."

Before we were out of the driveway, Doug Jr. told me how his father had caught him alone with Tilden. "He had my trousers down and was playing with it. I really enjoyed it. You don't touch me there. Bill says I have a nice one. He said it'll grow big one day just like my daddy's. We were having such fun, and then Dad came and spoiled everything."

I said nothing but drove in silence, delivering Doug Jr. home.

Before we pulled into his driveway, Doug Jr. looked at me defiantly. "I'm going to call Bill up and arrange to see him in secret. He loves my privates. I'm grown up. I can do what I want to do."

"We'll talk about it," was all I said, feeling embarrassed and defeated at what had happened. I knew that Doug Jr. really wanted to be with Tilden, and the tennis pro certainly wanted to be with this beautiful boy. But I didn't want to know any of the details if they did get together. I had my own problems.

My main concern was Barbara LaMarr, who was really out of control. The manager of the hotel was constantly complaining to me about the number of men arriving at our suite. "I can't believe it's just for cocktails," the manager had said.

One of those men was Doug Sr. himself. After Barbara had finished filming *The Desperate Trail* with Harry Carey, Doug had cast her in his film, *The Nut*, which fully launched a two-year affair between the two of them, in spite of his storybook marriage to Mary.

It seemed to be love on Doug's part, but not on Barbara's. I don't think she ever really loved just one man. Much of their affair was conducted in my suite at the Hollywood Hotel. That was one duo that never became a three-way with me. Between Doug and me as Durango, it was strictly a hands-off policy, although he often walked around my suite with a crooked hard-on.

Doug deliberately exaggerated his friendship with me to conceal his involvement with Barbara. He told me he loved Mary, and that they "were real good together," but that there was another side to him—"a dark side, just like Charlie has"—that demanded more. "I do down-and-dirty things with Barbara that I can't with Mary," he said. He smiled at me and kissed me lightly on the cheek. "You're a great guy to cover for us this way. If only I was like you and didn't go for women so much, you might get to know the great Fairbanks dick in a very intimate way, the same way you know the dick of Lloyd Hughes."

As he headed to our bedroom to pump that dick into Barbara, I smiled to myself with a certain satisfaction. Little did Doug know that I, as Lotte Lee, had already enjoyed those mighty d'Artagnan inches.

Doug not only loved Barbara, but he liked her work so much in *The Nut*, he cast her as Milady de Winter in his upcoming production of d'Artagnan's *The Three Musketeers*.

Barbara played the role beautifully. The film showcased both her acting and looks, enough so that she attracted the attention of the director, Rex Ingram, who'd directed his wife, Alice Terry, and Rodolfo in *The Four Horsemen*. Ingram asked Barbara to appear as a secondary lead in *The Prisoner of Zenda*, which he had conceived as a showcase for his Miss Terry who would be the star, of course.

Barbara felt that Rodolfo had stolen the show from Terry in *The Four Horsemen* and now Ingram was setting his wife up for another film to be stolen from her. "I'll be the real star of *Zenda*," Barbara had predicted.

Later that night she told me that she'd met the young man who'd played opposite her. "He's divine," she said, "and I can't wait to go to bed with him. He's absolutely gorgeous. I've already fallen for him but so far he has resisted me. No man resists Barbara LaMarr for long. He's from Mexico. Real sleek, dark haired, and very good looking."

Who is this Adonis?" I asked, growing jealous already.

She looked at me and smiled. "His real name is Ramon Samaniego. But he's billing himself as Ramon Novarro."

*****

In spite of often violent objections from Natacha Rambova, Rodolfo moved ahead with plans to appear as Ahmed Ben Hassan in Paramount's *The Sheik*, that torrid novel about miscegenetic love written by E.M. Hull in England. Originally readers thought the author was a man. When the press discovered that E.M. stood for Edith Maude, and that the novel had actually been penned "by a gentle Englishwoman," sales of the paperback skyrocketed. Reviewers might have thought it a "paltry tale without merit," but readers, especially women, wanted to learn of this tale of illicit passion, even or especially if it were being denounced as pornography.

At Paramount Jesse Lasky was adamant that his new star, Valentino, appear in the film, although Lasky hadn't read the scenario. Jesse Lasky didn't read novels, and at times didn't even scan a two-page synopsis of a novel prepared by a $25-a-week reader. He called "one of my gal Fridays" from the story department and had her explain the story to him. In the book, Lady Diana is abducted by a Sheik who at one point is referred to as "a damned nigger." However, Lasky was relieved to hear that the Arab, Ahmed, was really Viscount Caryll, Earl of Glencaryll, who'd been abandoned by his Scottish parents of noble birth and left, accidentally perhaps, in the Sahara desert. That seemed to make the plot all right. The "gals" in Lasky's story department told the studio boss that the novel had left them "quivering."

Originally Lasky had considered, if only briefly, some of his other stars. Wallace Reid. Much too clean-cut and all American. Thomas Meighan. Again, too whole, pure, and all American. Even an aspirant Rod La Rocque was considered but rejected as too suave and continental.

June Mathis, who'd penned the brilliant script for *The Four Horsemen*, had recently transferred from Metro to Paramount, following in Rodolfo's footsteps. But after working on the script of *The Sheik* for a few short weeks, even she bowed out, finding it not to her liking. Nonetheless Rodolfo signed for the role, cast opposite Agnes Ayres who would get star billing along with Adolphe Menjou, cast as Vicomte Raoul de Saint-Hubert.

One foggy morning after I'd spent the night with Rodolfo, I kissed him good-bye at the Hollywood Hotel with a flutter in my heart. He was heading for Yuma, Arizona, which would double for the Sahara in the film. Even to the very end, Natacha continued to raise violent objections to his playing the role. Her departing words to him had been, "The characters are pathetic puppets. This film will mean the end of your short-lived career."

He heard a different story from me. I predicted it would make him the greatest star in Hollywood. I had read the book and had fantasized about getting captured by a handsome sheik and taken to his desert oasis where he raped me repeatedly. I figured that if the idea even vaguely appealed to me, women across American would swoon at the prospect.

In spite of my enthusiasm for the project, Rodolfo never contacted me during the rest of his time in the desert on location. The press, however, had discovered the film before it was even made. Almost daily some story appeared in the newspapers. There was mounting excitement, just as there had been before the release of *The Four Horsemen*.

Weeks later my first news of the film had come at a dinner party Theodore Kosloff had given for his best friend, toe-sucking Cecil B. DeMille.

Over an after-dinner brandy, DeMille said he'd seen a rough cut of the picture with Lasky. "It's a very stupid, uninteresting picture, with not a moment of reality, and it bores me throughout," DeMille said. "There are some of the most beautiful shots of Arabs riding for so long that I could take little naps and wake up to find them still riding." He bet Theodore one-hundred dollars that the film would bomb at the box office.

That forecast from an acute judge of motion pictures made me feel the film was doomed. Perhaps I'd offer Rodolfo a chance to buy that farm in Italy after all. I had the money. He could take me to his native region of Italy where for $10,000, or so I understood, we could become landowners. Maybe that would make him happy. At least it would get him away from the cynical clutches of Natacha Rambova.

When Nazimova presented me with the script of *Salome*, she told me she too had seen an early cut of *The Sheik*, denouncing it as a "crude comic-strip." She also predicted that "Valentino is ruined in films."

Rodolfo was back in Hollywood for two weeks before he contacted me. I had seen Natacha who told me that even though he'd called her she was refusing to see him. "I can't stand failure," she said, "and he's a failure."

Where was he? He wasn't at the apartment of Paul Ivano. The rumor mill placed him at the home of his co-star in *The Sheik*, Agnes Ayres. Members of the crew on *The Sheik* reported that they'd returned to Hollywood together and had shared the same compartment on the train heading west.

I never found out the truth of that. When Rodolfo finally called me at the Hollywood Hotel and asked to come by, he didn't want to explain any of the press speculation about himself and Ayres. All he had to say on the subject of his co-star was, "I stole the fucking picture from the bitch."

Once back in Hollywood, Rodolfo had another woman to deal with, more frightening to him than either Natacha Rambova or the estranged Agnes Ayres. It was his real wife, Jean Acker, who had forced him into court for a showdown divorce, with the press invited. From the outset, it was clear to Rodolfo that she wanted to force him into a settlement.

On the stand she was no better a witness than she was an actress. Her most convincing testimony was her claim that Rodolfo had entered her bathroom and had hit her with his fist and knocked her down, leaving her nose bleeding. But instead of the shocking allegation she'd hoped it would be, it sounded like a publicity stunt sponsored by Paramount to promote Rodolfo as the rape-minded abductor in *The Sheik*.

This reported violence by Rodolfo only intensified the interest of female fans who expected him to "manhandle" Agnes Ayres on screen. Whispered charges of wife-beating had dealt a fatal blow to the career of Francis X. Bushman, but had made Rodolfo appear as a potential "sexual menace" who might cause a stampede at the box office by horny women willing to pay good money to see the Great Lover do his thing.

In another attempt to embarrass him, Acker produced the Rod St. Just photographs of Rodolfo dressed in the costume of the faun with the bushy tail. Natacha had ordered dozens of reprints of these photographs, of which she was very proud, and had distributed them throughout the town, copies somehow falling into the hands of Acker's attorneys.

"This is how my husband dressed in front of his mistress, Natacha Rambova," Acker charged from the stand. "In skin-fitting fur tights playing a flute. He does that in lieu of working hard to earn money to support his real wife."

Embarrassed at the campy photographs, Rodolfo tried to explain to the court that he was merely doing a costume test for a projected film, called *The Faun Through the Ages*." He left out the fact that no such film project actually existed. Acker's lawyers searched for missing photographs, perhaps a matching nymph enacted by Natacha Rambova herself, but none ever surfaced because they didn't exist.

Natacha had predicted that the release of *The Sheik* would destroy him, but Rodolfo feared Acker's testimony would finish off his career before that.

On the stand, Acker testified that Rodolfo had told her that he wanted to be her dear friend, but not her husband. She claimed he said he couldn't allow "a mere woman" to stand in the way of his career. She appeared ill and distraught, sometimes vague and confused in her testimony. She reported that she'd repeatedly begged Rodolfo for money, but was turned down. She wanted the court to force him to give her $300 a month in alimony.

When asked why she'd married Rodolfo in the first place, she claimed she'd wanted "to make a man out of him." Rodolfo winced at this testimony. Acker went on, "I did not want him at my hotel. He was unknown at the time. My friends said he was a bum, a man who was known for preying on women and getting them to support him. I could not have such a man coming to the Hollywood Hotel to embarrass me. I was working for Metro at the time. An established actress. I think he married me for my money because he was used to having women support him. I learned later he was but a gigolo in New York. I had to buy his clothing, even his underwear."

I took particular offense at Acker's last testimony. It was I who bought Rodolfo's underwear, even fitting the briefs on him personally.

Acker just managed to get through her own testimony but began to melt down under cross examination by Rodolfo's attorney, W.I. Gilbert. He immediately attacked the actress for not allowing Rodolfo to visit her on her film location at the remote Lone Pine, and produced bills totaling a hundred dollars, which Rodolfo had spent on telegrams to Acker pleading with her to let him visit her on site.

He even produced a copy of the letter that I had personally delivered to Acker in Lone Pine when she was shacked up with her lover, Grace Darmond. Another telegram from Acker was revealed in which she claimed that the hotel had room only for film crew members. Yet, it was shown, Acker entertained Grace Darmond in her private quarters and in her bed, but yet had no room for her husband. Acker countercharged that the film company would not allow visits from husbands or wives. An official from the Arbuckle film testified that there was no rule about visitation rights. In front of the court, Acker had been caught perjuring herself.

Acker was called back to the stand to produce bills showing where she'd spent money on clothing and underwear for Rodolfo. She could produce no bills and could not remember the names of the stores where she'd made such purchases. It was clear she was perjuring herself again. In her final statement in lieu of clothing bills, she claimed that "Mr. Valentino used too much of my expensive perfume." The courtroom burst into laughter at that, as Rodolfo sank even lower in his seat. Even the expensive perfume was used against her, when Acker was forced to admit that she couldn't personally afford the luxury and that the scents so generously used by Rodolfo had been a gift of either Nazimova or Grace Darmond.

On the stand, Rodolfo told of that night at the Hollywood Hotel where he'd "stood for hours" outside Acker's door wishing to be admitted to the bridal chamber. Fortunately, he didn't tell where he really spent that honeymoon night—in the suite of Lotte Lee across the hall.

Rodolfo told the court that he could not understand the "enigmatic conduct" of his wife ever since their wedding. Throughout this testimony, Acker took "medicinal powders" in front of the court, hoping to prove how sick she was.

Hearing enough, the judge adjourned the court but postponed a ruling on the case. Finally on January 11, Rodolfo faced Acker once again before Judge Toland who ruled that Acker had "deserted" her husband which alone entitled Rodolfo to a divorce. However, he postponed his ruling on the alimony until "Mrs. Valentino recovers her health. I want to see if she is able to work again." He denied her requests for attorney's fees.

Acker retreated to the apartment of her lover, Grace Darmond, where she allowed only one reporter into their chambers, claiming she was destitute and unable to work. In time, the judge ordered Rodolfo to make a one-time settlement on her for $12,100.

Even though it was illegal because of a ban on alcohol, I threw a champagne party for Rodolfo at the Hollywood Hotel where I invited the new stars of *The Prisoner of Zenda*, Barbara LaMarr and Ramon Novarro. It was a gay and happy night in more ways than one. Richard Dix showed up, and Barbara snared him at once, leaving Rodolfo and Ramon for

me, a delectable treat for me to enjoy later upstairs.

Natacha Rambova seemed to have disappeared from Rodolfo's life, and now the Acker divorce was laid to rest.

How wrong I was.

*****

When Nazimova set out to film the long-delayed *Salome*, she demanded that all members in the cast be homosexual, in tribute to Oscar Wilde who'd originally written the play in French, intended for Sarah Bernhardt. The English translation, upon which the film was based, was by Lord Alfred Douglas, Wilde's lover and the son of the Marquis of Queensbury who had originally brought the charges of sodomy against Wilde leading to his trial, imprisonment, and ruination.

The illustrations for the play—published in purple wrappers—had been done by Aubrey Beardsley. In London, the Lord Chamberlain had ordered that many of the illustrations be withdrawn on the grounds of "obscenity." Although the Wilde trial and tribulations were long over, a dark shadow was cast over the film even before shooting began.

Little did Nazimova know that this flicker would spell the end of her spectacular reign as the "goddess of film." Metro had kicked her out the door in spite of the fact that most of her films had made money for the studio. Even though her accountants had warned her that her lifestyle was "lashed with extravagances," she still had $300,000 in the bank, on which she was able to borrow $100,000 more. She announced that she personally would finance the filming of *Salome*, predicting that it "would become the most artistic film ever made in the history of Hollywood."

Even though I was hardly needed on the set, having only two scenes in the movie, I showed up every day, having little else to do. Encountering me on the first day of the shoot, the imperial Nazimova said, "I'm afraid of nothing in word or deed." She paused as a makeup artist held up a mirror to her features so she could inspect his work. A small gasp escaped from her throat. "Except of ugliness, of growing old."

As a stage actress in 1906, Nazimova had fallen in love with Wilde's play and had always wanted to make it into a film. At long last that dream had been realized. The filming of *Salome* had begun as Charles Bryant, her "husband," called for "Lights. Camera. Action!"

Wilde had announced that he was writing a play about "a woman dancing with her bare feet in the blood of a man she has craved for and slain." To this fable of forbidden love, Nazimova had combined her own fantasies—and those of Natacha Rambova. No work before or since had given such free rein to Natacha's romantic costumes and sets based on Beardsley's original designs.

Although forty-three years of age, Nazimova made a tragic decision. She would play Salome as a fourteen-year-old girl. When she'd looked in that mirror, Nazimova had not seen a middle-aged woman staring back at her, an actress who'd reached that day in her career when all the makeup in Hollywood couldn't fool the film-going public into thinking Nazimova was a virginal teenager.

After a night spent in the arms of Theodore Kosloff, he and I arrived on the set the second day and headed immediately for his dressing room. He was to portray a Syrian captain of the palace guard, who, in theory at least, was lusting for Salome as played by Nazimova. I was to be cast as the beautiful slave boy and personal body servant of the Syrian captain, a role tailor-made for my special talents. Even though small, my part in the film would surely attract such attention that I would be instantly discovered and made a star just like Rodolfo himself, or even Ramon who was appearing in *Prisoner of Zenda* with Barbara LaMarr.

On that long-ago day, I felt that stardom awaited all of us, coming to Richard Dix, Reginald Denny, William Boyd, John Gilbert, and a host of others. As for Richard Barthelmess, Charlie, Doug, Mary Pickford, and all the rest, their most spectacular performances were still in front of them, and for some that was true. For others, their greatest days were behind them, as the parade had passed them by at the end of World War I.

When Theodore was shown the costume Natacha had designed for him, he called it "ambisexual." On the same set, Natacha was refusing to speak to Theodore, no doubt still remembering their last encounter at DeMille's Paradise retreat where the impulsive Russian had shot buckshot into her knee. A wardrobe man (not the usual woman this time) fitted Theodore into his black tights. The dancer wanted "my natural bulge" to show and insisted on wearing nothing underneath his tights "but my own flesh, of which I am amply endowed." The wardrobe man placed a beaded necklace around Theodore's manly chest before draping a fishnet hood over him. A makeup artist arrived, the same one who had held up the mirror for Nazimova. He painted Theodore's nipples purple. The nipples showed through the fishnet and looked succulent like ripe berries ready to be plucked. That I would do later when I wiped that body paint off.

On the set I encountered the "beautiful ladies" on Herod's court. All of them were men dressed as women and sporting wigs that would have made Madame Du Barry proud. Mostly my eyes were drawn to the other male members of the cast, who obviously had been selected for their beauty and endowment. That was one coterie of hot men walking around the set of *Salome* that day.

The black slaves with their masculine physiques appeared in white wigs with curls to rival those of Mary Pickford. The silver lamé loincloths on the "slaves" evoked my own pouch worn in that revealing photograph Rod St. Just had taken of Theda Bara and me.

The Roman "soldiers" appeared in sleeveless armor to better show off the muscles of their bare arms. Their metallic skirts ended just at their crotches, and they were bare-legged, and wearing only sandals.

The black executioner, in the role of Naaman, was a stunning Mandingo. Actually it turned out that he was a gigantic white man whose body had been covered in gleaming black body paint. He appeared with a three-foot-long silver sword which would later be used to chop off the head of John the Baptist. His satin loin cloth was fully packed, and it was obvious why Nazimova had selected him to play the role. His string of white beads were as big as ostrich eggs, matching the size of his testicles which the loin cloth clearly outlined in all their magnificence.

Back from Europe, Paul Ivano appeared on the set with a broken heart. He was assistant cameraman. The job of chief cameraman had gone to Charles Van Enger, a credit Ivano clearly wanted but Nazimova had turned him down. I pretended to be sympathetic to Ivano's plight, although still raging with jealousy that he'd gone to Europe with Charlie who should have taken me.

"Charlie has dumped me," he said, looking forlorn. That came as no surprise to me. Charlie eventually dumped everybody. Ivano poured out his heart, claiming that Charlie had neglected him in Europe, as he'd conducted affairs with Rebecca West in England and Pola Negri in Berlin. He'd also involved himself with teenage girls in every capital of Europe. In Paris, Ivano said he'd caught Charlie in bed with two girls who looked no more than twelve.

Since I was being extra friendly with Doug Fairbanks Jr. at the time, and my lover, Theodore, was conducting fun and games with ten-year olds, I kept my mouth shut, not wanting to condemn Charlie for his pastimes.

"Where's Charlie now?" I asked. "Back at his studio?"

"Not at all," Ivano said. "He kicked me out and went off to Catalina Island with Peggy Hopkins Joyce."

The name of this international tramp was all too familiar to anybody who read the gossip columns of newspapers. She'd achieved international notoriety by marrying, then divorcing five multi-millionaires in quick succession. Joyce, it seemed, had arrived in Hollywood seeking a rich sixth husband, and had targeted Charlie as her next big game. She'd announced to the press that after marrying one of her husbands, she had locked her bedroom to him unless he wrote out a check for half a million dollars. Then she let him in. Even so, she said she'd hit him over the head with a champagne bottle which "he seemed to like."

Ivano's beady little eyes focused in on me, suspecting that I was enjoying his tale of woe and not in total sympathy with his plight. "Don't think Peggy has spared your man either."

"My man?" I asked in astonishment, not really certain who my man was. "Guess whose boat they took to Catalina Island?"

"I'm all ears."

"Tom Ince invited them to go on his boat," Ivano said. "I understand from Kono that Peggy is carrying on with Ince too. She's fucking both Charlie and Ince and trying to decide which one to marry."

That didn't delight me at all, as I was furious. She was enjoying two men, both Ince and Charlie, that rightfully belonged to me, or at least that was what I thought back then. Ivano apparently had still not learned of my own involvement with The Little Tramp, although he'd known at the Hearst campsite that Ince and I were kissin' cousins.

I too had been dumped by Charlie, but since I was on his payroll The Little Tramp felt he could call on me at any time to perform certain services for him, including driving up to San Francisco to pick up Virginia Rappé's belongings from that gorgeous bellhop, Tom-Tom.

Ivano was installed once again as "Nazimova's boy" at the Garden of Alla. I learned that big-dicked Charles Bryant, Nazimova's "husband," had finally had enough and had moved out to the Hollywood Athletic Club. Bryant, in theory, was the director of *Salome*, although the entire cast knew that the real director was Nazimova, the "Queen who could do no wrong."

Eventually Natacha introduced me to Bryant, who invited me to lunch. Over a corned beef and pastrami, I learned that he was fed up with Hollywood and planned to return to New York as soon as production work on *Salome* shut down.

It was at this point in my narration, that I became aware of the beady gas-chamber eyes of the Bitch of Buchenwald glaring at me. "Go on," she said. "Let's get it over with. Tell us about your affair with Charles Bryant. But, for God's sake be brief and spare us some of the more gory details."

The Bitch had nailed me again. I was more than a little intrigued with Bryant. He was tall and ruggedly handsome, with a well-built muscular body. Being a homosexual male, I had been immensely intrigued to learn from Ivano that Bryant's prick was so large that Nazimova could not endure penetration from him, preferring Ivano's more parlor-sized dick.

It didn't take me long to find out that Bryant liked to fuck teenage boys, at least those he didn't bloody and send off to the hospital emergency ward. At his little cramped room at the Hollywood Athletic Club, I learned after the first week of shooting *Salome* that Ivano had not exaggerated the endowments of Bryant. I'd rate him somewhere between Charlie and Francis X. Bushman, which is high praise indeed. Charles Bryant was definitely in the major league among Hollywood dicks.

In me, he found an experienced star-fucker who took it inch by inch like the proud man I was. In fact, before I left his bedroom that early morning I had enjoyed Bryant three times, and was only too eager to accept his invitation to return the following night and for several nights thereafter. Even though I had Theodore, and countless others, panting for me, I devoted a great deal of my time to Bryant, wanting to enjoy him to the fullest before his upcoming departure for New York.

As I later told Rod St. Just, "Bryant has more than all three Moore brothers, Tom, Owen, and Matt."

With a sore ass, I appeared back on the set of *Salome* to watch Nazimova emote before the cameras for her "Dance of the Seven Veils." The star appeared in a multilayered, diaphanous gown trimmed in pearls with a six-foot train and a veil. She wore a headdress from which two wire-like antennas radiated, holding the seventh veil. This was clearly the most spectacular costume in a film filled with actors in spectacular costumes. Suddenly, in front of the cast, Nazimova exploded, denouncing Natacha who ran from the set in tears. Nazimova ripped at her clothing, tearing it to shreds. She screamed to Bryant that she couldn't dance in all of this fabric which had been expensively imported from Maison Lewis in Paris.

Apparently, much later Natacha and Nazimova patched up their lovers' quarrel that night. The next day Nazimova appeared on the set with a different costume for the "Dance of the Seven Veils." Natacha had given in to Nazimova's demands. The star appeared in a costume designed to show off her figure. It was like a bathing suit, hugging her trim figure and modest breasts and revealing her creamy thighs. A bejeweled and feathered headdress crowned her frizzy hair. A pair of flat slippers finished off the outfit. Natacha had insisted that incense pots be lit during the filming of the dance.

At one point while Ivano and Van Enger were setting up the cameras, Nazimova appeared before Theodore and me. She explained that the rubber lining which clung to her body in the "bathing suit" was made by a manufacturer of tires for automobiles. "Do you like my figure?" she asked.

"If I were a certain kind of man, I'd rape you on the spot," I said.

She smiled, "So many men have tried," she said. "So few have succeeded."

I suspected she included Charles Bryant in that list of failures.

"I'll tell you guys how I keep my youthful figure even at my age," she said. "Both of you will need to know this when your bodies aren't as golden as they are today. First, I get up early. I drink only hot water for breakfast. At lunch I have a three-minute egg and a piece of dry toast. For dinner I order a small salad of fresh field greens—no dressing—and one steak that can be consumed in four bites. That's it. Now you know Nazimova's secret." Bryant came for her to summon her back to the set.

"I know exactly why Nazimova wanted Natacha to create a new costume for her," Theodore said to me when the star had departed. "She fears that all these scantily clad homosexual men will steal the show from her the way Valentino did in *Camille*. She wants to show she's got a figure too."

To accompany her dance, real dwarfs had been hired as an "orchestra." These little men appeared in towering helmets, half their size, from which metallic flames shot. Herod's soldiers showed up in form-fitting black leotards, which Natacha had insisted they wear over nude bodies. She wanted "the natural man to show through." It was reported that on that day of shooting, a lot of fat sausages were ordered early that morning at the studio cafeteria.

Nazimova also demanded that the actors in Herod's court appear as effeminate as possible to emphasize decadence. That wasn't too much of a stretch for these "girls" pretending to be courtiers.

Finally, after hanging out on the set for days, my chance to appear before camera came. I was dressed in a silver lamé "grape leaf." The homosexual implications between Theodore, as the Syrian captain, and me, the slave boy, were all too clear even to the unsophisticated movie audiences of that day. The plot called for Theodore to summon the most beautiful boy captured in a defeated army on a nearby battleground. As that boy selected, I was brought to his headquarters where I had been strung up against a wall, my hands and feet bound.

The tiny little G-string did little more than cover my asshole. The suggestion was that the captain wasn't really interested in what I looked like from the front, only the rear. It was obvious how the captain planned to take his pleasure later from the new slave boy. Sodomy was his game, and I was his delectable target.

In a scene shot the following day, I was again scantily clad, this time in the same gold loin cloth I'd posed in with Theda Bara. Apparently after a blissful night where it was suggested that the captain had "tamed" me in his bedroom, I was summoned to give him a rubdown in a gold tub. I sensually rubbed his back as we exchanged leering, lustful glances. Nazimova said that I was to suggest with my eyes that I had been enthralled the night before with my new master, and now eagerly sought his embraces. Nazimova instructed Theodore that he was to suggest in his eyes that he had other plans for me when I finished bathing him and drying him off.

Years from that day, Tony Curtis and Laurence Olivier in *Spartacus* would repeat a scene similar to ours. But Theodore and I made mincemeat out of Olivier and Curtis. Some of the homosexual extras told me they got hardons watching Theodore and me emote.

To make the scene more realistic, Nazimova had insisted that Theodore actually step nude into the tub, where as Olivier, or so I was to learn decades later, wore a bathing suit in *Spartacus*. Theodore was only too willing to appear stark naked in front of the homosexual cast. He had nothing to be ashamed of. For greater verisimilitude, Nazimova had demanded that I reach into the sudsy bath water and apply soap to Theodore's genitals. I was

only too glad to do that, and was delighted to note that my fondling of him produced a hardon, which I would have to satisfy later in his dressing room.

Regrettably, my scenes with Theodore were too realistic and suggestive, at least in view of the Hays office. Hays himself denounced us to his cronies as "two pansies making love to each other on the screen." In the wake of the Arbuckle scandal, he claimed that our film could not be released unless Theodore's scenes with me ended up on the cutting-room floor, which is what happened to them. Just as I lamented my tossing away the final copy of *Vampira*, so I wept over the eternal loss of my scenes in *Salome*. I'm sure that future generations would appreciate the white heat Theodore and I generated before those long-gone cameras.

The Arbuckle scandal could not have come at a worst time for a production crew filming a play based on a work by Oscar Wilde. Even though filmed on a closed set, word had leaked out to the press that there were scenes of necrophilia in the movie. Originally there was, and it was ghastly. As Salome, Nazimova had been unsuccessful in luring John the Baptist to her bedchambers. She called for his death, and his severed head is brought to her on a silver platter.

Only the head of the actor playing John the Baptist was photographed. He was standing on his own feet, and his head had been fitted through the center of the platter, making it appear severed from his body. Sensually, Nazimova kissed the lips of the supposedly dead saint. It was a long, passionate kiss with tongue that even shocked the film crew. In the film, Herod, seeing this "morally disgusting" scene, ordered that his guards crush Salome to death with their shields. That was allowed to stay in the final version, but the outrage coming from the Hays office forced Nazimova to order that the scene be reshot by Paul Ivano and Charles Van Enger. In the new version, instead of the silver platter, soldiers arrive carrying the shield of the executioner, Naaman. You don't actually see the head of John the Baptist depicted, but his presence is symbolized by a mystical light emanating from the shield.

Remembering that parts of Theda Bara's

earlier version of *Salome* had been banned across America, Nazimova appeared before the press in an attempt to tone down some of the gossip about her own version. She actually tried to convince the press that her film wasn't about a *femme fatale* who caused the death of a saint. "Salome was the purest creature in Herod's court," Nazimova told the press. "She was uncontaminated like a flower growing on unfriendly soil. She saw but didn't understand the decadence around her. She loved—her first time—and that love was rebuked by John the Baptist. She was impelled to ruin the life that might have saved her. If in her ignorance she destroyed her idol, she was not the first woman to do that—nor the last." In saying that, Nazimova overlooked the fact that most women rebuked in love don't order the head of the man who rejected them to be brought to them on a silver platter.

On the last day of the shoot, and to my shock and surprise, Rodolfo appeared on the set arm and arm with Natacha. And I thought the love birds had flown in separate directions. My heart was crushed upon seeing them together, although I had Theodore, and several others, including William Boyd, keeping my bed warm at night.

Like a queen summoning a servant, Natacha motioned for me to come over to them. I was wearing my gold loin cloth, and Rodolfo still seemed appreciative of his golden boy. He gave me a brief hug before commenting on how spectacular I looked as the slave boy.

"Don't worry, darling," Natacha said to Rodolfo. "There is no need for you to be jealous of Durango. Wait until you see the costume I have designed for you in an upcoming production I'm going to insist that Paramount star you in. You'll get to show off your assets as well."

Rodolfo took my arm as if to hold me down. He looked into my eyes as if he were going to tell me something, and I was going to accept it without question. "I've asked Natacha to marry me."

Like a firestorm from hell, those words came raining down on me. As an actor, I offered my congratulations but hid my real feelings. This hasty marriage proposal evoked an image of him at the Garden of Alla party proposing marriage to Jean Acker. I immediately protested. "You can't marry anyone for a year after your divorce. It's the law in California."

"Don't worry," Natacha chimed in. "Dagmar Godowsky told us how we can circumvent the law. She slipped off to Mexico and married Frank Mayo."

That came as another surprise to me. I always thought Dagmar was a lesbian. For that matter, I naturally assumed that Natacha was a lesbian too. What would Nazimova say about losing another one of her girl friends to Rodolfo? But, then if Nazimova were a lesbian, what was she doing with Paul Ivano? Long before the days of Greta Garbo and Marlene Dietrich, I had not fully appreciated bisexuality in women, although I seemed to understand it in men.

Rodolfo released my hand. "I want you to drive us to Palm Springs for a pre-wedding party before we go to Mexico," he said. "In your stagecoach. It'll be most fitting."

I kissed both Natacha and Rodolfo on the cheek, lingering a bit longer on his cheek than hers. Ivano called me to the set for my final scene with Theodore, and I was off, holding back my tears. I feared once Natacha got her clutches into Rodolfo, I'd never get to have him in my bed again.

A few days later, with *Salome* in the can, I set off in my stagecoach, driving the Valentino/ Rambova wedding party to Palm Springs. Dagmar and her girls followed in a car behind me. Where was Dagmar's new husband, Frank Mayo? I wondered about that but didn't dare ask. Natacha sat up in front seat with me, with Ivano on her right.

In the back sat a sullen Charles Bryant. When he learned that Ivano was coming along he at first refused to go. But one didn't refuse Nazimova for long. She insisted that he accompany her to the party. Nazimova sat between Bryant and Rodolfo, with Rodolfo on her left.

I smiled, laughed, and joked, but my heart wasn't in this wedding party. I felt a sense of approaching doom like a thunder cloud beginning to amass in a far and distant corner of the sky, but one that would grow in size to rain down torrents on our heads.

*****

The drive to Palm Springs was not without its arguments. Impulsively Natacha reached back and mussed up Rodolfo's hair. He exploded in fury. Even while making mad, passionate love, he didn't like his hair messed with, preferring to keep it so combed down and flat that the effect was like shiny black satin, as all the film reviewers of the time noted.

"Please don't do that," he yelled at her. Nazimova came to the rescue, reaching for a makeup mirror she always carried in her purse. She held up the mirror while Rodolfo removed a comb to restore his hair to that plastered look.

"I want you to be wild and free," Natacha said. "Do you think Lord Byron wore his hair slicked down like you?"

For the rest of the night ride into Palm Springs, Rodolfo remained silent. He was still fuming about his hair. He'd let you bite and pull on his pubic hair with your teeth, but he wouldn't let you touch his coiffure. His marriage seemed headed for a disastrous course even before the wedding ceremony.

It was shortly before midnight as I pulled into the driveway of the villa at Palm Springs. The mansion was said to belong to a lady friend of Dagmar Godowsky's. This hostess had generously lent it to us for the pre-wedding party. The place was beautifully furnished, but all the servants had retired for the night, leaving only the lights on to greet us.

Our hostess, or so I as told by Ivano, was married to an oilman in Texas and had two children but liked to slip off to this retreat in Palm Springs to entertain girl friends, which included Dagmar, Nazimova, and Natacha.

Rodolfo changed his clothes, dressing casually in a pair of slacks. Barefoot, he headed for the kitchen where he announced he'd found fresh supplies. As Ivano and I set the table for the ladies, Rodolfo prepared the finest *bisteca Milanese* I've ever tasted, followed by fresh peaches he'd lightly cooked in a Vino Rosso.

At the table, over brandy, Nazimova produced some reviews she'd culled from the papers in Los Angeles. These were advance previews from a press party staged by Jesse Lasky on the dawn of the opening of *The Sheik* across the nation. The first one, written by a male reporter in Los Angeles, said, "Since the torrid tango dancer with the slithering hips has put on a sheik's kimono, I predict our womenfolk will leave the dirty dishes in the sink."

That was but a harbinger of how men in America would regard the screen's new lover, and Rodolfo winced as Nazimova went on and on, producing more reviews. She thought it'd be a delightful surprise to Rodolfo, but he acted as if mortally wounded. He was also embarrassed in front of his bride to be, fearing she was right all along about that pulp fiction trash, *The Sheik*. Finally, he slammed down his wine glass and headed for the bedroom, muttering something about "parasitic gossipmongers."

Later that night I shared Rodolfo's bed, as Nazimova retreated to the master bedroom with Natacha. Dagmar and three of her girl friends shared a larger room in a cottage in back. Paul Ivano was assigned yet a second cottage, which was the smallest of the lot, looking like an oversized dog's house. To my dismay, I found out that Rodolfo had originally asked Ivano to share his bedroom, but the cameraman had turned him down. Second choice or not, I was going to make the most of the occasion.

Stripped totally naked, Rodolfo paced the room, even running his fingers through his hair and mussing it up himself, something I'd never seen him do before. He must really be distraught. "Even though my name is up in lights across America in *The Four Horsemen*, and even though *The Sheik* will make me known all over the world—I just know that it is not enough for Natacha," he said. "She does not view it as an artistic triumph for me. She would rather that I wrote poetry or grew the most beautiful flower garden in Los Angeles, anything but becoming a big-time film star in what she feels are inferior products."

"You will never please her, so don't even try," I cautioned him. "She's part of an artistic elite doomed for failure. Frankly, I think *The Sheik* will become the biggest film in America. From what I've seen of *Salome*, I'm not even sure it'll find a distributor."

"One can be an artistic success without being a commercial success," he said. "There is nothing wrong with that."

"Yes, there is," I said. "It's called paying the bills. Putting beefsteak Milanese and burgundy peaches on the table. Stuff like that. Your fancy clothes. Your car."

He went over to his suitcase and removed a present. "Open it," he said.

Knowing it wasn't for me but for Natacha, I opened a box to discover an emerald brooch and a gold compact inscribed, "To Natacha from Rudy with All His Love." I rapidly closed the box. It was too painful to look at. I wanted him to buy gifts for me, not Natacha Rambova. "Such expensive gifts," I said. "You know you can't afford them."

Before the words were out of my mouth, he slapped my face. Immediately he was apologetic. "How can I make it up to you? I'm so sorry. I am out of control these days. I don't know what's happening to me."

"There is a way you can make it up to me," I said, rubbing my face.

"I'll do anything."

"Take me to your tent like you did Agnes Ayres in *The Sheik* and rape me."

He looked at me as if he hadn't heard me correctly, then broke into laughter, his tension fading. He picked me up in his arms and carried me to bed and bliss. All thoughts of Natacha faded as he moved over me. I welcomed him, reaching up to bring his lips down to mine. With my right hand I cupped the back of his neck, taking special care not to muss his hair, as his lips and tongue descended on me. I could feel him growing hard against my nude stomach.

An hour later, still locked into his arms, I wanted to hold onto Rodolfo forever. The thought of surrendering him tomorrow to Natacha was more than I could stand.

It must have been three o'clock in the morning, as both Rodolfo and I were asleep, that I heard a loud pounding on our French doors that led to an open terrace. I recognized Ivano's voice. He was screaming for us.

Jumping out of bed and reaching for a towel, I turned on the porch light and opened the doors. There was Ivano standing nude on the terrace, with wounds on his legs, chest, and arms. He was bleeding heavily.

"Charlie did this to me," Ivano shouted so loud that he began to wake up the rest of the household. "He broke into my cottage and attacked me with a razor. I'm dying." Ivano fainted.

Suddenly, I was aware of a presence behind me. It was an astonished Rodolfo. "Bryant did this? I can't believe it."

"Not Charles Bryant," I said. I think he means another Charlie."

The next three hours passed as in a nightmare. First there was the madcap rush to get Ivano to the local hospital, where the medical staff alerted the police. Since Ivano had been given a heavy sedative, he could not talk to the police.

Fearing scandal, Rodolfo, Nazimova, and Natacha refused to go anywhere to help Ivano. Rodolfo had checked and found Charles Bryant asleep with one of Dagmar's lovelies, who apparently dug both men and women. That woman claimed that, "Charlie has been with me all night. There was no way he could have attacked Paul."

I was hoping to hush the matter up, reporting to the police that some intruder must have entered the grounds of the villa with robbery on his mind. Discovering the cottage occupied, he'd taken a razor and slashed Ivano.

The policeman who interviewed me seemed very skeptical of my story. "I think there's more to it than that," he said. "I'm going to grill Ivano in the morning. We want to get to the bottom of this. Frankly, I think you're covering up for a big-time movie star. I hear that Rudolph Valentino and Nazimova are occupying that villa. Didn't that pansy, Valentino, attack Ivano? One of the lady guests we questioned broke down and confessed that Ivano and this Valentino boy are lovers. Isn't this about a homosexual lovers' quarrel."

My heart sank, as I feared that an innocent Rodolfo was going to be involved in another major Hollywood scandal just as *The Sheik* was about to open across America.

Arriving back at the house at six o'clock in the morning, I found that Nazimova and Dagmar had fled along with Charles Bryant and a bevy of lady friends. Natacha remained. Even though I pleaded with her to call off the wedding, she was adamant, demanding that I drive them to Mexico.

After bitter arguing, I finally agreed but only

after I called Brian Sheehan in Los Angeles, telling him what had happened. The trustworthy doctor agreed to drive to Palm Springs, since Ivano was his patient, and to bring him back to Hollywood for treatment. After thanking Brian profusely, I headed for Mexico with Natacha and Rodolfo. So much for the gay wedding party.

No one wanted to discuss Ivano, so the talk was of Rodolfo's latest movie, *Moran of the Lady Letty*, in which Dorothy Dalton was the star. Rodolfo, listed as a "featured player," was her leading man. He was cast as a wealthy young man of leisure in San Francisco who is shanghaied onto a rough-and-tumble boat that heads out to sea.

"You are a woman's actor," Natacha protested. "Suited only for boudoir roles, not this action adventure piece of trash. You should appear only in costume dramas—not modern dress pieces."

Later, when I had a chance to see the film, I agreed with Natacha. Rodolfo had been miscast, but Jesse Lasky at the studio had insisted that Rodolfo star in the picture, with Dorothy Dalton playing the skipper's daughter. At least according to the script, she is supposed to fall in love with Rodolfo. Dalton had a rather masculine face and appeared in men's clothing in the picture. When Rodolfo kissed her, she seemed repulsed. I suspected she'd rather be kissing one of the Gish sisters, certainly Mary Pickford, and maybe even Nazimova.

Lasky had told Rodolfo that as studio chief he feared a "backlash" when *The Sheik* was released throughout America. He never fully explained what he meant by that. "It's important," Lasky had said, "that you be seen on the screen as a man among men, showing off your manliness. American men might resent your amorous conquests. Already some of them are referring to you as 'that dago.'"

In the film Rodolfo certainly showed off his manly quality, his muscles rippling under his sailor's singlet. He revealed an impressive basket when he hoisted up his bellbottoms. He threw punches at the villainous captain, and climbed the ship's riggings as if he were Douglas Fairbanks. In some scenes he appeared as stone-faced as William S. Hart, his eyes narrowed to distrustful slits, his cheeks like marble.

As for the future, Lasky had signed him to appear as the matador in *Blood and Sand*, opposite Nita Naldi and my new friend, Lila Lee. He was also set to appear in a "program feature," *Beyond the Rocks*, co-starring Gloria Swanson whom he'd fucked in the Hollywood Hills that day the fake German baron had spied on the lovers.

"Blood and Sand is glamorous corn," Natacha said, "and is all right for you. But *Beyond the Rocks* is trash."

Arriving in Mexicali, I found that Natacha had already made elaborate plans for the wedding at the home of the town's mayor. His name was Otto Moller, which didn't sound very Hispanic to me. The tequila was already flowing as I drove up to the impressive villa where a string orchestra played ceremonial music on the front porch. The town band had also turned out to play in appropriate military music. *The Four Horsemen* was showing at theaters in Mexicali, and the local papers had written that Valentino was "the new Mexican star of Hollywood."

The mayor himself performed the wedding ceremony, followed by a banquet of Mexican dishes. Dancing, drinking, and singing lasted throughout the hot afternoon, and I welcomed the coolness as twilight approached.

I was instructed by the mayor to drive to a villa outside of town where the honeymoon night would take place with just the three of us. Throughout this whole ceremony I'd felt unneeded and unwanted except as a chauffeur. I was bitterly disappointed that Rodolfo was marrying Natacha, although I felt I had to pretend to be her friend. If I fought with her, I knew Rodolfo would cut me off completely. After that night of passion with him, I didn't think I could stand to see that happen. I would not be the only homosexual in history who stood idly by and watched the man he loved marry a woman.

At their wedding supper on their honeymoon night, I asked to be excused, giving them their privacy. Both Natacha and Rodolfo insisted I stay with them. Actually they demanded it, as if they didn't want to be alone together.

Over wine Rodolfo spoke of nothing else but his love for Natacha. "When I take her in my arms, I discover life itself," he told me. "She is the only woman who has made me feel whole as a man. No other woman has stirred up such ecstasy in me. All the other women in my life were stuffed with sawdust."

I contrasted this statement with what Natacha had told the press earlier that afternoon. She said she'd married Rodolfo "not for romance but for congeniality."

Retreating to a distant wing of the house, I prepared to sleep alone as I recalled Rodolfo's first honeymoon night at the Hollywood Hotel when I, as Lotte Lee, had snared him in the wake of his rejection from Jean Acker.

At about three o'clock in the morning, I was awakened by Rodolfo, just as I'd previously been awakened by Paul Ivano in Palm Springs. "Get up!" he shouted at me. "I've killed Natacha."

Rubbing my eyes, I turned on a night lamp only to discover Rodolfo standing over my bed with a full erection. "What in hell are you talking about. You've murdered her?"

"No, you fool," he said, grabbing my arm and yanking my nude body from the bed. "When I penetrated her, she passed out. I can't revive her. I fear she's dead."

"Stay here," I commanded him, rushing without my clothes to the bed of Natacha on the other side of the house. There I found her lying on top of the sheets stark naked. I felt her heartbeat, realizing she was still alive.

She'd unbraided her hair and it flowed over the mauve-colored bedsheets and pillows. She looked like what I fantasized some medieval princess in a fairytale to be.

I rushed to the bathroom, finding a sponge, which I wet in the sink. Returning to the bed, I rubbed the cold sponge over her nude body. After a minute, I could hear a moan escaping from her throat. As her breathing returned to normal, she opened her eyes to discover me applying the wet sponge to her nude body. At first she said nothing but appraised my own nudity, seemingly trying to recollect what had happened.

She slowly sat up in bed and regarded me with a steely look of such ferocious determination that I too felt I'd faint. Only the great Nazimova herself could stare down someone like Natacha Rambova.

"You tell *The Sheik* that if he ever attempts to penetrate me again, I will take the largest knife I can find in the kitchen and castrate him," she said. I feared she meant that. "Thank God the screen, unlike the stage, is silent because otherwise I will turn Rudolph Valentino into a boy soprano. Tell him never to enter my bedroom again. It's not to be that kind of marriage."

Rising from her bed and tossing the wet sponge to the floor, I retreated back to my own bedroom where I confronted Rodolfo lying nude on top of my sheets. "I have revived the corpse," I said. "She had only passed out."

"That's good to know," he said in such a matter-of-fact tone that I felt either he was insane or else I was for coming between these two lovers.

Amazingly, Rodolfo had still maintained his erection. It was as if that encounter with Natacha, as bizarre as it was, had sexually aroused him. He looked first at his impressive erection, then at me. "If you're seeing what I'm seeing," he said, "I suggest you'd better do something about it."

I stared at his hard-on, then gazed deeply into his eyes, as I slowly moved toward his bed to take possession of that towering monument of flesh.

Once again, I became the "bride" of Rodolfo on his second wedding night.

*****

The shit had hit the fan by the time I drove the new bridegroom, rising star Rudolph Valentino, and his little "Mexicali Rose," Natacha Rambova, into Los Angeles. We stopped first at my suite at the Hollywood Hotel because Natacha, still furious at Rodolfo's attempt to penetrate her on her honeymoon night, refused to speak to him all the way up from Mexico. Some honeymoon.

At the suite, Barbara LaMarr had moved out, leaving me a note thanking me for my hospitality. Now that she'd become a movie star, she'd secured her own home with her first earnings.

Ramon had left several eager messages

proclaiming his good fortune, and repeatedly inviting me to the studio where *The Prisoner of Zenda* was being shot. "I can't believe it," he wrote in a note left for me at the hotel. "Ramon Novarro is now a movie star. Barbara and I are almost too beautiful on the screen. I only wish that I'd retained my own name for immortality—Ramon Samaniego."

Ramon's message was near the top. There were at least twenty-five others. After using the bathroom, Natacha took French leave. We found out later that she'd ordered a bellhop to place her luggage in a taxi where she'd headed for the Garden of Alla without inviting her new husband.

I immediately placed a call to Brian at his doctor's office. I was eager for news of Paul Ivano. Getting Brian on the phone, he told me that he'd driven a heavily bandaged Ivano back to Los Angeles. "He'll be scarred for life," Brian told me. "Some of those cuts were pretty deep."

"Is he okay?"

"He's coherent, but I'm a little suspicious about his story of the attack," Brian said. "He told me what happened two or three times when I drove him back. But several key points were different every time he told the story."

"Why would he lie about something like that?"

"He did swear out a complaint against Charlie Chaplin before leaving Palm Springs."

"Oh, my God," I said. "Has it reached the papers yet?"

"I don't think so," Brian said, "but it will. A story like this will be sensational. It'll be heard around the world."

"I've got to get in touch with Charlie," I said. "Where's Ivano now? I'd like to see him."

"He's resting here at the clinic," he said. "I have him under observation. He's badly wounded but he's also a bit deranged. I think that an attack that brutal has dislodged his brain. I know that's not an official medical analysis. But there's something more here. Doctors are supposed to be scientists, but with Ivano I'm going on my intuition. We haven't heard the full story yet."

After putting down the phone, I immediately dialed Kono and told him of the latest threat hanging over Charlie's head. I asked to speak to Charlie if he'd come back from Palm Springs.

Kono became hysterical. "This will ruin Charlie," he said. "It's a lie. It could not be." Kono claimed that he'd spoken to Charlie at least twice a day on Catalina Island. "There's no way in hell he could have gone from Catalina all the way to Palm Springs and all the way back between our phone calls."

I told Kono to tell Charlie what had happened—or what was about to happen—and to call me at once at the Hollywood Hotel. "Tell Charlie I'll be there for him," I said before ringing off.

As I went to take a quick shower before returning my messages, Rodolfo made a few phone calls himself. He still hadn't decided where to live. I invited him to stay here at the suite with me, since Barbara had hastily departed for new adventures. During all the time she'd lived with me, she'd been more like a sometimes visitor than a roommate. He thanked me but still wasn't certain what he was going to do.

When I came out of the shower nude, drying myself, I confronted an ashen-faced Rodolfo. "What's the matter?" I asked.

"I'm ruined," he shouted. "This awful judge, a man named John W. Summerfield, has told reporters that my marriage isn't valid in California. He said I am entitled to a divorce from Acker only after a year has passed. I'm going to be arrested for bigamy."

I was stunned. "Oh, my God," was all I could say. I was becoming an expert at uttering those words of astonishment.

Rodolfo immediately called Jesse Lasky at Paramount. I heard him tell the studio boss that he was leaving at once for New York "until this thing blows over." After a lot of shouting over the phone, Rodolfo came into my dressing room. "Lasky says I can't run to New York. I ran from New York to Los Angeles when I'd gotten into trouble there. But he said my running from Los Angeles back to New York won't work. He said I'd be sought as a fugitive from justice. He also told me that he'd just spoken to that czar of the industry, Will Hays, who demanded that Lasky blacklist me. I fear I've made my last film."

Sitting down before my makeup mirror, Rodolfo seemed paralyzed. I'd forgotten about Charlie's troubles. For the moment Rodolfo's dilemma seemed more serious.

Nazimova called to tell me that Natacha had heard the news and feared for her own arrest on a bigamy charge. "Dagmar and I are disguising her right now to put her on a train to New York," Nazimova said. I warned her about Lasky's fear that Natacha might be considered a fugitive from justice and a bigamist.

"That's bullshit," the actress said. "You're talking to Nazimova. I've always fled towns when I've run into trouble. It has worked for me, and it'll work for Natacha. What do you propose? That she stay in Los Angeles and be thrown in jail as a bigamist? Now get Rodolfo on the phone. Natacha has agreed to speak to him."

When he came back from the phone, he told me that Natacha had decided that both of them should flee the United States. Her exact words were, 'Provincialism reigns over democracy.' She wants us to return to Europe to make films there."

"That's ridiculous," I said. "You stay here. We'll fight this thing and see it through. You're going to be the biggest star in Hollywood. If you run now, everything will be lost."

The more I talked to him, the more convinced he became that he must stay and ignore Natacha's advice. Even so, he called Lasky again. For some odd reason, Lasky asked to speak to me. I picked up the phone, knowing that whatever Lasky had to say to me, he wasn't offering me a movie role.

"His first words to me were, "Keep your lover boy's ass in town."

Up to then I had no idea he knew anything about my relationship with Rodolfo.

"My publicity department can put the right spin on this," he said.

That was the first time I'd ever heard the word "spin" used in that connection. Lasky might have invented "the spin."

"Even before the release of *The Sheik*," he said, "Valentino is known as a lover. My boys will depict him as an impulsive and young romantic desperately in love with the girl of his dreams. We'll leave out mention of the fact that the bitch is a dyke. We'll claim Valentino

didn't mean to break any American law. He's an Italian and doesn't understand our way of doing things. If he runs now, the charge of moral turpitude—that's what bigamy is called—will plague him forever. It'll prevent him from ever returning to this country. I'm not Metro. I think Valentino will become Paramount's biggest star. Bigger than all of our other stars. Even Gloria Swanson. Tell the dago to stay put." He rudely slammed down the phone.

About fifteen minutes later, Rodolfo's attorney, W.I. Gilbert called, assuring him that Thomas Lee Woolwine, the district attorney of Los Angeles, wasn't going to make any trouble for Rodolfo. It seemed that Woolwine was having his own legal difficulties. A recently discharged employee, Ida Wright Jones, was bringing America's first case of sexual harassment against him. She was claiming that over a period of years she'd been forced to have sexual relations with Woolwine in order to keep her job as his secretary.

So much for a lawyer's advice. While Rodolfo was still at the Hollywood Hotel, Woolwine sent two deputies to arrest Rodolfo. I discovered them when I answered the loud pounding on my door. The men pushed me aside and entered my suite where they proceeded to handcuff Rodolfo.

Rodolfo was in tears. As the men led him from my suite, I promised I'd call his lawyer and get what help I could for him.

"Don't worry," I said. "We'll work this out." Actually I wasn't convinced we would, having learned that Woolwine was up for re-election as district attorney. Perhaps he hoped that "bagging" Valentino in a widely publicized case would distract voters from his own nagging problems with that Miss Jones creature.

Even though a Sunday district attorney Woolwine was in his office, directing the Valentino case personally. When W.I. Gilbert, Rodolfo's attorney, and I arrived, he told us that Rodolfo had pleaded guilty to a charge of bigamy before a justice of the peace and that bail had been set at ten-thousand dollars. Woolwine demanded that either Gilbert or I post the bail money or else "Valentino will go to jail."

Gilbert protested that "there was no way in hell" we could raise that much money. I made an emergency call to Jesse Lasky, reaching him at his home. After explaining our dilemma, I begged him to instruct Paramount to raise the money for Rodolfo's release. "Dream on," Lasky shouted at me into the phone before slamming down the receiver.

Woolwine even turned down Gilbert's request to see Rodolfo in his cell. "You can see him Monday morning at eight o'clock—not a moment before," Woolwine said. "Attorneys can only visit clients during regular weekday business hours." With that pronouncement, he ushered us from his office.

Returning to my hotel, I was determined to raise that bond money myself. I figured I'd be at the bank first thing tomorrow morning. Even after my investments in real estate, I still had about twenty-thousand dollars in savings, although only one thousand in my checking account. I could raise the bail, even though it meant Rodolfo had to spend a night in jail.

I was amazed that Lasky would let his major new star rot in jail overnight, unless the chief was trying to warn Rodolfo of the consequences of taking any major action in the future without the studio's approval.

Even before picking up the phone, I detected the urgency of its ringing. As I said hello, I encountered a distraught Charlie Chaplin calling from Catalina Island.

*****

As I fed Charlie all the details I could muster, he was growing increasingly alarmed. The long shadow cast by the Arbuckle scandal fell over all the stars of Hollywood. For some reason, perhaps his colossal ego, Charlie had seemed to feel he was immune. How else could that explain why he was seen by several visitors romping in the nude on Catalina Island with the notorious Peggy Hopkin Joyce?

Amazingly, he'd always rescued himself from trouble before, especially in the case of that Mexican girl, Dolores del Rio. But the Ivano scandal that threatened to erupt was more deadly. It would brand Charlie a homosexual before the world.

"I made a mistake in running off with Paul and dropping you," he said. "A big mistake. I want you back."

I hesitated only a moment. In spite of his big dick, I had handsomer lovers with better bodies. It was the money thing, stupid. A thousand dollars a week was a dream salary back then. Until Paramount raised Rodolfo to $1,250 a week, he wasn't making that much money, and he was already a major star, about to become even bigger when *The Sheik* opened across the country. I will always be there for you, Charlie," I said with all the passion and conviction I could muster, even though I felt bitter toward him for his betrayal of me with another man. A petulant note crept into my voice. "What about Peggy Hopkins Joyce."

That's over," he said. "I caught her in bed with Tom Ince. She was so furious at me that she picked up a champagne bottle and hit me over the head. She'd done that to one of her husbands before, claiming he liked it. I didn't like it at all. It hurt like hell but didn't knock me out. I grabbed her from Ince's bed and carried her nude body on deck and tossed her overboard. We were in port so I walked off the boat at that point, and don't know if the sharks got her or not. I'm at this little inn in Catalina now, and I'm heading back to Los Angeles just as soon as I can arrange a boat out of here."

"I don't know how much you know," he said, "and I don't want to go into too many details over the phone. But Paul hired a photographer friend of his to trail us from London to Paris to Berlin. He took secret pictures of Paul and me. Pictures that if published in newspapers would be misunderstood by the American public."

"I understand."

"Before I get back home, I want you to go to Paul the way you did with the Mexican *puta*. I want those pictures back. Get them for the cheapest price you can. But get them back. I'll be ruined if you don't."

"What about the knife attack?" I asked. "The police complaint."

"The God damn thing has to be withdrawn as part of a deal," Charlie said. "How could I attack the little pansy with a razor-like knife if I'm on Catalina with Ince and that Peggy cunt?" If I had to in court, I could prove I was here all the time, but the publicity would ruin me any way."

"Then who attacked him?" I asked.

"How in hell do I know?" he said, his voice the angriest I'd ever heard it. "I think some burglar broke in and assaulted him. Paul saw this golden opportunity to make his blackmail demands all the hotter for me. I was framed."

Those words, "I was framed," said to me by Charlie on that long ago day would be repeated ever so often in the years ahead, when he was indeed framed time and time again. The price of fame. Ain't it a bitch?

After agreeing to meet with Charlie that evening if he got back in time, I headed for Brian's clinic, forgetting momentarily about Rodolfo in that stinking jail cell. Since there was nothing I could do until morning, I hoped to blot him out of my mind.

At Brian's office the doctor welcomed me into his warm embrace, and he was so charming and handsome that I would have loved to spend the rest of the day and night with him if I had sex on the brain. "Can I see Ivano?" I asked, breaking away.

"Sure," he said. "Alone or with me there?"

"I'd better talk to him in private," I said. "Some real nasty business going on here."

"That's what I think," he said. "When I meet people I always have my shit detector on. I think Ivano has got more shit stuffed in him than a barnyard."

After promising Brian to spend the rest of the afternoon with him, I headed for Ivano's private room where I found him sitting up in bed listening to the radio.

Not even bothering to ask him how he felt, I immediately got down to business. "Exactly what have you got and what do you want?"

"You certainly believe in coming to the point," he said. "I thought you were my friend."

"I am your friend," I said, lying "I'm also a friend of Charlie Chaplin's."

"Charlie?" he said, sitting up in bed and looking astonished. "So that's why you're here. You were Charlie's boy before I replaced you. I knew it was somebody in the film business. I never suspected you."

"For a while you managed to capture Charlie's heart and also Rodolfo's," I said. "I've gone to bed with you. Frankly, I don't know what the attraction is. I could see why Nazimova was attracted to you, though. Your dick's tiny enough to penetrate even the smallest of vaginal openings."

His face assumed a bitterness and fierce determination that dramatically altered his appearance. The transformation wasn't as great as John Barrymore going from Dr. Jekyll to Mr. Hyde, but it was a frightening change in his personality. I realized I didn't know him at all in spite of having gone to bed with him. That had meant nothing.

"If we're going to turn this friendly little chat into personal insults, I can play that game too," he said. "I have fifty photographs snapped of Charlie and me in Europe. Even to the untrained eye, we appear as homosexual lovers which we were. One of them shows me kissing Charlie."

"I can't believe Charlie would allow himself to be photographed with a young man kissing him."

"Charlie didn't know there was a photographer lurking there," Ivano said. But I did. At the right moment I leaned over and kissed Charlie before The Little Tramp knew what was happening. It was immortalized on film."

"You're a common blackmailer."

"And what do you think you are?" he asked. "Some Presbyterian deacon? You're known all over this town as a boy whore. I'm sure you've been involved in dirtier deeds than I ever dreamed of. You're fucking just for the money—everybody knows that. I'm doing it to advance my career as a cameraman. I also want to become a producer."

"And just how do you propose to do that?"

"I want one-million dollars from Mr. Chaplin," Ivano said. "Or else his career is history."

"He will never give you that," I said. "You're out of your mind. Besides, he's got witnesses that he never left Catalina Island during the time of your attack. Tom Ince, for example."

"He'd have to prove that at a trial, and at such a trial I'll produce the pictures and tell of my relationship with Charlie. Even if Charlie is found innocent, his career would be over. There's more. When Charlie was a little drunk and asleep on the rooftop of a Berlin solarium,

I slipped and took nude pictures of him. If he fucks with me, and doesn't pay up, he'll be the first movie star in history who has suffered having nude pictures of himself released to the press. The whole world will get to see his big dick."

"You rotten piece of shit." At that point I wanted to strike Ivano, even though his body was bandaged. I resisted the impulse.

"There's more," Ivano said, almost rearing up from the bed at some revelation he was about to make to me. "In Paris, Charlie and I visited some real low dives, including a club that Olive Thomas went to right before she was murdered. At this club you can get anything you want for a fee. Charlie went there to be hooked up with French girls. He was tired of fourteen-year-old nymphs. He wanted to try a ten-year-old, even an eight-year-old if she could be found and was the right type for him. Instead of that, I had the waiter drug Charlie's drink. We were in one of the backrooms. After Charlie was in a coma, I pulled off his clothes and mine too. My photographer friend came into our private compartment and took pictures of Charlie taking it up the ass from me. I have a great shot of myself going down on The Little Tramp. When he woke up the next morning, he was none the wiser."

Without saying anything, I knew he was telling the truth. If I demanded it, I just knew he could produce copies of the incriminating pictures. Charlie, I feared, had wandered into a trap from which there was no exit, other than parting with megabucks, including his financial windfall from *The Kid*.

When I didn't say anything, Ivano went on. "I've also notified Louella Parsons. She's here from New York doing some post-Arbuckle stories about how that scandal has cleaned up the lives of the stars, even the films themselves. Wouldn't Lolly love to break this story about Charlie? It would be read with more interest than the Arbuckle case. Hearst would have a field day. It would be his way of getting back at Charlie for fucking his whore, that drunk, Marion Davies."

"How much does Miss Parsons know?" I asked.

"She knew a lot even before I contacted her," he said. "She'd been hearing reports from Europe about Charlie and me. Sent by anonymous sources." A smirk came across his face. "You could never guess who those anonymous sources were, now could you?"

"I have an idea," I said, feeling that the rope was tightening around Charlie. At that moment I saw no way to untie him from this sordid mess. At the same time I had a bitterness of my own. It was fueled by jealousy. If Charlie had taken me to Europe instead of Ivano, I knew this would never have happened. "Why are you involving Louella Parsons before Charlie has had a chance to respond to your demands?"

"Insurance, sweetheart," Ivano said. "Sweet insurance. Charlie attacked me in Palm Springs and tried to kill me. I've left instructions with my attorney that if Charlie tries to kill me again, or succeeds in having someone do me in, all the pictures along with a full handwritten confessional from me will be shipped directly to Parsons herself. When Charlie was cavorting with Rebecca West, Pola Negri, and those teenage gals, I was recording all the details of my most intimate life with him."

"If Charlie will meet your demands, will you agree to turn over your confessional, the photographs, everything? Will you withdraw the complaint in Palm Springs? Call off that hound dog, Louella Parsons?"

"For a million dollars, baby, there isn't much that Paul Ivano won't do."

"That I believe," I said, getting up from my chair by his bed. "Don't do anything until Charlie has had a chance to meet with his lawyers. Give him time to respond."

"I'm very patient," he said. "But Louella is beating down the door. I'll give Charlie forty-eight hours."

At the door, I paused and looked back at this little schemer. "Exactly what will you do with one-million dollars."

"I'll launch myself as a producer," he said. "I'll be the first producer in Hollywood who is also his own cameraman. Nazimova has agreed to sell me the distribution rights to *Salome* for half a million, a good deal as far as I'm concerned since she's already invested $400,000—the last money she has—in the film. I think *Salome* is going to be a big hit. Even after buying the film, I'll still have half a million left. With that delicious green stuff, and with all the money I'll make from *Salome*, I'll be the town's next Samuel Goldwyn. With me as cameraman on any picture I want to shoot."

After leaving Ivano, I was deeply churning inside as I drove back to the Hollywood Hotel with my doctor at my side. Brian Sheehan was becoming known in Hollywood for his "bedside manner."

Waiting in the lobby for me was Dagmar Godowsky, Nazimova's beloved friend who'd attended the Palm Springs wedding party with me. Brian was already familiar with this silent screen vamp. Everybody in Hollywood knew that the actress from Lithuania was the daughter of Leopold Godowsky, one of the half-dozen great pianists of the 20th century. Rodolfo's future leading lady in *The Sainted Devil* was distraught. She asked to come upstairs to my suite as she had something personal to tell me. I assured her as we went up that she could trust Brian, who had driven to Palm Springs to bring Ivano back to Los Angeles.

I must speak to you about Paul," she said, once the doors of my suite had been closed. "Nazimova must not know I'm here. I don't want to be dragged into this mess, but I'm still loyal to Charlie, and I want to help him if the situation gets desperate."

Being very careful what I said, since I didn't know the extent of her knowledge, I ventured one question. "Is Nazimova aware of the demands Paul is making on Charlie?"

"She knows everything," Dagmar said, as Brian went to pour her a drink. Dagmar's fondness for bootleg gin was already known in Hollywood. She'd missed her opening night of *The Rat*, the play by Ivor Novello and Constance Collier, when she'd encountered a bottle of gin.

After she'd downed her first drink and asked Brian for another, I seated her on a sofa. "I didn't know you even knew Charlie. Why are you wanting to help him? I thought your loyalties were still with Nazimova."

"I'm in love with Charlie," she said, on the verge of tears. "You don't know this, but Charlie asked me to marry him before he was tricked into marriage to that bitch, Mildred Harris. When Charlie married her, I turned to Irving Thalberg for comfort. But during our

affair, he was sick most of the time. Only my chicken soup—the recipe from my father, Leopold—cured him, not the medication from his stupid doctors."

I'd never heard any of this lore before. "What can you do to help Charlie? Paul's backed him into a corner."

"I know that," she said. "But what Paul doesn't know is that I know who attacked him with that knife or razor."

Both Brian and I grew suddenly silent.

"I couldn't sleep," she said. "I'd satisfied all my little maidens for the night, but the drive from Los Angeles had upset me. I think I'm in love with Natacha Rambova, and I was very upset that she was marrying Valentino."

"You saw the attacker?" Brian asked.

"I did indeed," she said, finishing off the second gin. "I was wandering alone in the garden when I saw Paul in his pajamas emerge from his small cottage. He didn't see me, and I didn't call attention to myself. I'm a bit of a voyeur. Paul is known for his moonbaths."

"What's that?" I asked.

"Instead of a sunbath, Paul believes that a moonbath makes you more spiritual and connects an artist more with his soul. I'd heard about his moonbaths for months but saw this as a chance to see first-hand what they were all about. He stripped off his pajamas and stood stark naked in the moonlight. It was a full moon, and I could see him almost as if it were day."

"Then what happened?" I asked. "You saw the attacker?"

"As clearly as I see you," she said. "Paul reached down and removed something from a little case he'd brought from his bedroom. It was either a razor or a knife. He started to slash his body."

"Oh, my God," I said, uttering my by now famous statement of shock. "Why didn't you do something?"

"I was going to rush toward him to prevent him from killing himself, but everything happened so quickly and I was in a state of shock. After slashing himself, he ran toward your bedroom window and screamed out for help. That's when I saw you coming to his rescue, and I fled back into my own bedroom, not wanting to get involved."

"Paul slashed himself?" I sat down, enjoying some of that bootleg gin for myself.

"A man will do a lot for a million dollars," Brian said.

I sat there for a long time, holding Dagmar's hand. Neither of us said anything. Finally, I spoke, "You may have saved Charlie's skin."

"I'm not doing this for my health, and when Nazimova finds out, I'll be banned from the Garden of Alla," she said. She wants Paul to get that money from Charlie so he can buy the distribution rights for *Salome*."

Dagmar stayed for another hour, during which time she had a lot more gin and also agreed to enlist the services of Brian as her own doctor. His movie-star list of clients was growing almost daily.

Dagmar agreed to go with us to the police in Palm Springs and reveal in a signed affidavit what she knew.

At the door as she was leaving, she turned to me with what I feared was a request. I prayed it wasn't for more money from Charlie. "There is a condition attached to my willingness to testify in Charlie's behalf."

Staring at this vamp who'd entertained the likes of Thomas Mann, Sigmund Freud, Ignace Paderewski, Sergei Rachmaninoff, and Gustav Mahler, I asked, "What is it?"

"In exchange for my help, Charlie has got to agree to become my boy friend again."

*****

The next morning Rodolfo was released on $10,000 bail I posted. The district attorney had made his headlines and distracted the voting public from his own record of sexual harassment. It was a day to remember.

Although Jesse Lasky had refused to post bond, other friends came forward and offered to help Rodolfo. But it was too late. Nonetheless, Joseph Schenck announced he'd post bond for up to $200,000 if needed. The screenwriter, June Mathias, offered to put up some money. Even Thomas Meighan, who hardly knew Rodolfo, offered financial help by agreeing to turn over his gold coin collection. Thomas hardly knew Rodolfo and was totally unaware that in private Rodolfo was bitterly critical of his old-fashioned looks and "Victorian acting style." When I spoke to Thomas, he felt that Rodolfo was being treated unfairly. Being the decent man he was, Thomas wanted to come to Rodolfo's assistance. I assured Thomas that the bail had been raised.

With W.I. Gilbert, Rodolfo's attorney, leading the party, Rodolfo and I rushed past a barrage of bloodthirsty reporters screaming for his attention. Gilbert had told Rodolfo not to talk to the press, but he was in no mood to listen to his attorney. "It will be proven that I have done no wrong," he said to the reporters. "My name will be cleared. I am not a bigamist." Those words rang out clear and true, but then he appeared muddled as he launched into a story where he'd attended weddings in New York only a week or so after a divorce had been granted. He claimed that he felt the same laws applied in California. "I thought this was America, one country." His face turned bitter. "Now I know otherwise." He claimed he would "continue to be a law-abiding citizen."

As Gilbert was ushering Rodolfo into my car, a particularly obnoxious red-haired male reporter ran up to Rodolfo. "What's the matter, Great Lover?" he shouted. "Did your second bride run out on you, or what?"

It was all Gilbert could do to restrain Rodolfo from slugging the man and getting himself arrested on an assault and battery charge.

Discovered by scandal-hungry reporters when her train reached Chicago, Natacha blamed "an enemy" for causing all the trouble, but did not identify the person. To escape, she fled to the baggage car where she was discovered once again, having to run away and lock herself in a private compartment. The press found her to be a "prize filly," and wrote extensively of her dress, commenting on "form-fitting garments that left little to the imagination."

Rebuffed, reporters began to dig furiously into the background of Natacha, finding out that she was actually Winifred Shaughnessy, the stepdaughter of the cosmetics magnate, Richard Hudnut. Before all the stories started to appear about Natacha, much of Hollywood up to then thought she was a dancer from the Russian Imperial Ballet.

On the way back to my suite at the Hollywood Hotel, Gilbert reported that most of the support for Rodolfo was favorable, with one exception. Death threats had come in from the Ku Klux Klan.

When Gilbert had left and we were alone in the hotel suite, Rodolfo burst into tears in my arms. I'd never known such sobbing in a man before or since in all my one-hundred years on this earth. He was inconsolable in his grief.

He'd been jailed before in America—once in the fetid Tombs in New York—when he was but a struggling immigrant. But to have been imprisoned as the megastar, Rudolph Valentino, seemed to have destroyed his self-esteem.

Thanks partly to his mercurial personality, I knew two men—the pre-jail Rodolfo and the post-jail Rodolfo. They were remarkably different. The night spent in the Los Angeles jail changed him for all time. It was the beginning of a serious mental deterioration that I noticed in him when no one else seemed to.

Hollywood was long accustomed to stars like Mae Murray behaving erratically, so the changes occurring in Rodolfo's character went virtually unnoticed, except by me who remained close to him in spite of Natacha. With the wave of her magic wand, the imperial princess, Natacha Rambova, could have banished me from Rodolfo's life, and he would have willingly obeyed her command. For some reason, she never did, and I went on with Rodolfo until the end. Amazingly, she seemed to offer no objection to our relationship, assuming she knew the full extent of it.

Thrown into a prison with the low lives of Los Angeles, a terribly shaken Rodolfo in his fancy dress street clothes had become an immediate target for the drug pushers, gamblers, vagrants, petty thieves, and muggers of that day. Some of this motley crew had known who he was. In those days everyone from lorgnette-wearing society matrons in Southampton to the beggar in the gutter went to the same movies, and many men locked in Rodolfo's cell had seen *The Four Horsemen of the Apocalypse*.

"I shouted at the guards and tried to pull the bars loose with my bare hands," Rodolfo said. "I screamed at the guards up and down the corridor. I told them they were imprisoning me only because I was a film star and world famous. I swore revenge against the district attorney. I think I got so upset, I started bab-

bling in Italian without knowing what I was doing. The guards just laughed at me. Later they brought all the prisoners coffee—no dinner. Not that I wanted any food in that rat-infested dump. The whole cell had eight other men in it. It smelled like the foulest latrine. I threw my coffee on the floor."

At that point, he broke into sobbing again. "I can't tell even you what happened to me that night." As I tried to put my arms around him, he pushed me away, sending me sprawling onto the floor. "Get out of my room. Leave me alone. God damn you Americans. God damn all of you. I'm going back to my own people."

I quickly retreated from my own bedroom to let him have time alone. In the living room of the suite, I dialed my ever-faithful doctor, Brian Sheehan, and asked him to come over to the hotel to see Rodolfo. "He's in a bad way," I told Brian. "You'd better look at him."

Brian arrived less than an hour later. He was dressed in street clothes as I'd reached him at home, and he'd rushed over without bothering to dress more formally. When I knocked on the bedroom door, there was no answer. Fearing Rodolfo had killed himself, I tried the door, finding it unlocked. Curled up in a fetal position in the center of the bed, Rodolfo looked up at us. He was sucking on his thumb. "If only my mama was here to be with me now," he said after taking his thumb out of his mouth. He'd taken off all his clothes and lay nude on the bed.

When Brian moved in to examine him and feel his pulse, Rodolfo stretched out on the bed. He flipped his cock at us. "Go on, pansy boys. Eat me. Devour my flesh. I know that's what you want. That's what all the world is screaming for. To get fucked by Rudolph Valentino."

As I stood in astonishment, Brian paid no attention to Rodolfo's words and proceeded with the examination. Suddenly, Rodolfo flipped his body in bed. He arched his ass in Brian's face. With both hands, he spread the cheeks of his ass.

"I was raped," he shouted. "Three times in that God damn cell. The bastards held me down, pulled down my trousers, and raped me. The other shitheads stood around watching and taunting me. I heard them say all the names.

'Pretty boy.' 'Little pansy boy.' 'Stinking dago.' As the first son of a bitch penetrated me, he bit into my neck so hard I thought he'd kill me. Right in my ear, he shouted, 'Let's give the little powder puff what he wants, a dick up his ass." When he'd finished with me, another piled on me and was even worse than the one before. A third had attacked me before my screams alerted the guards. When they saw what had happened to me, they just mocked me. I begged them to transfer me to another cell but they wouldn't. All night the drunks and vagrants taunted me. But at least they let me alone. They didn't attack me again."

"I want to examine you thoroughly," Brian said to a more compliant Rodolfo. He called for me to come and join him in the bed and hold his head in my lap as the doctor inspected every inch of his body, including an anal probe with rubber gloves.

As that examination was going on, Rodolfo looked at me through teary eyes. "You're never to fuck me again," he said. "Do you understand that? No man will ever fuck Rudolph Valentino ever again. You can take me down your cocksucking throat. I'll fuck you and be brutal about it. But on my mama's grave, I swear that I will kill the first man who ever penetrates me again."

If America could only look in on that scene going on that day at the Hollywood Hotel, they would surely be shocked. As it was, much of the country was enthralled at a different scene. Several scenes in fact. Rudolph Valentino burst upon the public in his most memorable role— *The Sheik* opened to standing room only.

Whether the plot was nonsense, as most critics claimed, it touched upon a fantasy in the film-going public. Almost overnight, a line uttered by Rodolfo became famous. "Lie still, you little fool." His words to Agnes Ayres flashed across the silent screen, and women swooned.

When he rescues Ayres from a bandit attack and hauls her off to his tent, she demands to know in a card title why he has brought her here. Valentino sneers at his captive as she struggles in his muscular arms. "Are you not woman enough to know?" It was reported that many women fainted at witnessing that scene. Playing a French writer, Adolphe Menjou ex-

plains to the audience: "When an Arab sees a woman he wants, he takes her."

The role marked the beginning of what became Rodolfo's exaggerated acting style. His flaring nostrils, dilated eyes, and flashing white teeth were commented upon by most reviewers. Regrettably for Miss Ayres, most critics found her "drab and irritatingly unemotional" when stacked against that raging seducer, Valentino. Throughout America police searched for runaway young girls, fleeing to the burning sands of the Sahara Desert to find the sheik of their dreams. "The Sheik of Araby" became the most popular song in the country, and billboards across America proclaimed, "Shriek for the Sheik Will Seek You Too."

As Natacha remained on the East Coast with her parents, Rodolfo lost himself in his work—and there were plenty of screen roles for him. No longer was he the "villain" actor knocking on studio doors, hoping to get a five-dollar-a-day job as an extra playing some criminal in the background. He was now a major star for Paramount. It seemed only natural for Jesse Lasky to cast his biggest male box office attraction opposite his leading female star—Miss Gloria Swanson herself.

Directed by Sam Wood, the film was based on Elinor Glyn's bad novel of 1906, *Beyond the Rocks*. Glyn had become famous in Hollywood for determining who had "It" and who didn't. In her view, Valentino definitely had "It," and she often referred to him as a "he-vamp." In typical Glyn style, her scenario was a romantic triangle set in the Alps. Swanson played the young wife of a wealthy but moronic husband in his late 50s, whereas Rodolfo was cast as the dashing "other man," Lord Hector.

Much to the chagrin of an increasingly addicted Wally Reid, Glyn announced to the press that Valentino had now replaced Reid as the greatest lover of the silver screen. Ironically both men were in current movies that co-starred Gloria Swanson, Wally having made *The Affairs of Anatol* with Swanson. Cecil B. DeMille had directed that one, which surprisingly had also co-starred my dancing Russian knight, Theodore Kosloff. Even Agnes Ayres, Valentino's tent mate in *The Sheik*, was in it, too.

Although Swanson attempted to look

vampirish in the film, Wally's sexual interest in her had long ago vanished, as had Rodolfo's. After making the film with her, Wally told me, "I'm glad she didn't read my love letter to her that you delivered. In looking back, I think my hard-on would have gone soft the moment Gloria dropped her drawers. She's more man than I am."

On the set, Swanson was involved in another one of her many affairs and had seemingly forgotten that she'd once discussed marriage with Rodolfo while horseback riding and fucking in the Hollywood Hills. He later admitted that they had had a brief affair, but confided to me that, "Fucking Swanson, even though she's still young, is like screwing a very old sailor."

The only memorable thing in that "lost flicker" was the 18th-century clothing Swanson and Rodolfo got to wear in flashback scenes written by Glyn. Rodolfo was delighted to appear in the 1700s waistcoats designed by Natacha before her hasty departure for New York. As for Swanson, she continued to live up to her reputation as the most overdressed star in films. That title obviously was held before the arrival of Pola Negri from Berlin. Never had Swanson appeared in so much velvet, sable, chinchilla, and silk ruffles, plus a million dollar's worth of precious gems.

All this incredible wardrobe only emphasized the cheap sets Jesse Lasky had authorized. Even though the studio boss proclaimed that *Beyond the Rocks* would out-gross *The Sheik*, he didn't want to invest much money in production.

In the wake of the Arbuckle scandal and the attempt of the Hays office to clean up films, an order went out that no kiss could linger longer than ten feet of film. A separate version of a kissing scene would be shot for European audiences, allowing the actors a longer smooch. In spite of their former passion for each other, Swanson openly mocked Rodolfo in his love scenes. When she'd filmed an abbreviated American kiss scene, she broke from him and spoke loudly in front of the cast. "That kiss was so short that Valentino could hardly get his nostrils flaring." She turned to him. "Don't put so much garlic in your spaghetti tonight. Your breath stinks." Leaving him humiliated, she

grandly walked away, heading for her dressing room.

But her imperial manner lightened considerably when the crew was taken to Catalina Island, scene of Charlie's recent escapade of cavorting in the nude with Peggy Hopkins Joyce.

Swanson dreaded her first scene on the island as she always had a fear of drowning in the ocean. The director, Sam Wood, demanded that she plunge into the murky deep when her rowboat tipped over "beyond the rocks." The hero, Rodolfo, dashed into the ocean to rescue her, bringing her unconscious body back to shore. Swanson flubbed the scene so many times, and so many retakes were necessary, that I feared both stars would come down with pneumonia.

Dinners for the cast were more lighthearted, once the shooting of the day was over. For a few nights at least, Rodolfo seemed to forget all about Natacha and the bigamy charges facing him. One night as I was walking up to the bedroom where I'd seduced William Boyd, and which I now shared with Rodolfo, I actually saw Swanson and Rodolfo—two of American's biggest romantic stars-engaging in a pillow fight in the corridor.

How could *Beyond the Rocks* fail? It had the "sultry glamour" of Gloria Swanson, the "steamy Latin magic" of Valentino, and the "rapturous love story" of Elinor Glyn. Even a tango sequence was thrown in. Swanson appeared on the set and looked dazzling in a gold-beaded and embroidered lace evening gown that shimmered in the lights. But her tango with Rodolfo was weak lemonade to the dance as performed on that deserted studio floor by Mae Murray and Rodolfo on that long-ago afternoon.

In the wake of the popularity of *The Sheik, Beyond the Rocks* opened with Paramount's two biggest stars, Gloria Swanson and her leading man, Rudolph Valentino. The public took little notice of this film, all copies of which have disappeared. So you have only my word for what a lousy flicker it was.

Rodolfo returned to the mainland to face the charge of bigamy in the court of J. Walter Hanby, justice of the peace. The "wedding party" coterie from Palm Springs was called to testify—all except Paul Ivano. Wanting to keep his knife attack out of the papers, everybody, from Nazimova to Rodolfo to Dagmar, agreed to forget that Ivano had been with us.

Nazimova had been arrested at the train station while attempting to flee Los Angeles for New York. Too heavily veiled, she just called attention to herself and alerted the suspicion of a detective. Apparently, she feared any involvement in the Valentino/Rambova case might lead to her deportation. Forced to testify, she claimed that Natacha had slept in a separate room in Palm Springs because she was sick. I was forced to testify that I shared a room with Valentino for the night, although no one seemed to draw any sexual references from that. Men in those days commonly shared bedrooms, and few were the wiser in those innocent times.

As presented to the court, Rodolfo and Natacha did not share a room. Then a bright light finally dawned on the judge who brought an end to that whole line of questioning. It had been erroneously assumed that Mr. And Mrs. Valentino were in Palm Springs on their honeymoon night—not in Mexicali. When this misconception was uncovered, all testimony about the Palm Springs celebration was dropped. Since there had been no wedlock at the time, it was not significant if their relationship had been consummated or not.

When the question finally rose as to where Valentino had actually spent his honeymoon, I was called to the stand through an arrangement with his attorney, Gilbert. I claimed that after the wedding ceremony in Mexicali, I drove both Miss Rambova and Mr. Valentino to the Barbara Worth Hotel in El Centro, California, where she wanted to rest. I then testified that I took Mr. Valentino back to Los Angeles for a business meeting the next morning with his attorney, claiming that except for the drive from Mexicali to the hotel the couple had not been together on their actual honeymoon night. "The only intimacy I saw between them," I said, lying to the court, "was a light kiss bestowed by Mr. Valentino on the cheek of Miss Rambova after we'd let her off at the hotel."

On June 5, the judge dropped the bigamy charge. A gleeful Rodolfo issued a statement to the press, thanking the American people for making me "the lover of the screen. I will say that the love that made me do what I have done

was prompted by the noblest intentions that a man could have. I loved deeply, but in loving I may have erred." He stated his intention of marrying "Mrs. Valentino" when a year had passed, claiming defiantly that such a delay "will not in any way diminish our love and eternal devotion to each other."

Again, as a means of forgetting his romantic complications, Rodolfo rushed into a new film, *Blood and Sand*, the first movie in which he was the major star instead of ladies like Nazimova or Gloria Swanson. His leading ladies this time were Nita Naldi and my recent favorite friend, Lila Lee. *Blood and Sand* was ideal for Rodolfo as once again he got to be a Latin Lover, and even treated viewers to another of his famous tango dances.

Wearing the tight pants of the matador he played in the film, he had never looked sexier, especially when his card title proclaimed, "I hate all women…but one." Strutting about in his suit of lights and twirling his cape, he was in rare form, sexy and confident in his virility as was often outlined in those toreador pants.

As Juan Gallardo, the bullfighter, he accepted the sexual challenge of the vampire widow, Donna Sol, although this scene with Nita Naldi with a rose in her teeth was a bit much, causing future audiences to giggle. That was dangerous territory for Valentino, the screen idol. The worship of a romantic hero can easily turn into ridicule if the vamping is laid on too heavy, as John Gilbert was to learn in his first major talkie.

Rodolfo accepts the rose from Naldi, then pushes her away, fending off her attempt at seduction. Finally, he succumbs to her charm and takes her in his arms in a brutal embrace, loving and kissing her, even though calling her, "You serpent from hell."

The audience knows he's going to fuck her. He conveyed that magnificently in the scene, with a dose of sadism and a dash of spice suggesting an upcoming rape. It was one of the great battle of the sexes on the screen. Even though the screen was silent, Rodolfo and Naldi seemed to hiss like a snake and vamp so much it would make Theda Bara blush.

As he twirled Naldi around in his arms, he seemed to be dancing the ritual dance of seduction. But in viewing the film today it appears that he is actually making love to himself, his male beauty and virility and that love affair just between him and the camera, Naldi a mere prop.

Throughout the shoot, Rodolfo was in constant conflict with Fred Niblo, the director. Rodolfo used to be cooperative, agreeing to almost anything a director suggested. But on the set of *Blood and Sand*, he often refused to do a scene as directed, because "Natacha would not want it this way." Rodolfo never overcame his major objection, which was that the film was being shot on a Hollywood backlot, although he said that Lasky had originally promised to send the entire production to Spain. Natacha had wanted George Fitzmaurice, a sometimes friend of Rodolfo's, to direct the film and was disappointed when the assignment went to Niblo.

Rudolfo continued to challenge Niblo's direction, citing the serious reservations of Natacha. When that didn't work, he declared to Fitzmaurice that "A real director would never shoot a scene so stupidly." In the white heat of a California afternoon, that seemed to produce a stroke in Niblo. He grew to detest Rodolfo more and more each day, and the feeling was mutual.

The trouble had begun on the first day of the shoot when Rodolfo broke into a screaming rage when he'd discovered that he'd been assigned one of the smallest dressing rooms on the lot. There wasn't even a private bathroom. He was getting so many calls from Natacha that day that Niblo ordered that "Valentino's messages be restricted." This caused another eruption from Rodolfo who stormed off the set, refusing to work for the rest of the day.

June Mathias, his ever-faithful screenwriter friend, adapted the bullfighting story for the screen from the Blasco-Ibáñez novel. Documentary footage of real *corridas* in Andalusia would be added to the faked scenes in the film.

One of the highlights of the film was Rodolfo getting dressed in his "suit of lights" before four men. He played it seductively and provocatively, the tight pants showcasing his firm ass, muscular legs, and basket. He'd grown his sideburns long and played the role with gusto— that of a matador trapped between love for his trusting wife and his sexual desire for the se-

ductive tramp as played by Naldi.

Naldi had long gotten over her previous life as a little girl being raised in a convent in New Jersey where her great aunt was a mother superior. Naldi played the role with sultry passion, in spite of her Catholic upbringing, which press agents wanted to conceal. They got carried away, however, when they claimed she was "distant relative" of Dante's beloved Beatrice.

On the set I quizzed Naldi about her role as the Spanish dancer in *Dr. Jekyll and Mr. Hyde*," with John Barrymore, who'd told the press she was a "dumb Duse." She spoke lovingly of John, however, claiming he was a great lover. She whispered a confession to me. "I've had Barrymore. He's called The Great Lover. Now Valentino is called The Great Lover. I'm anxious to sample the things I see outlined in that matador's costume. I'll make him forget all about Natacha Rambova. After I've had both Barrymore and Valentino, I'll let you in on the secret of who is the Great Lover."

That whoring bitch, Naldi, was too late. I could already answer that riddle for her.

Although it was hushed up at the time by Jesse Lasky, Rodolfo almost made the headlines again. He even came very close to spending the rest of his short life in San Quentin. In a way, Niblo had provoked a confrontation. He not only had assigned Rodolfo a cubicle as a dressing room, one without a toilet, but had cursed him out when Rodolfo had emerged from the public shower, claiming that Rodolfo was using too many towels and not leaving enough linen for other members of the crew.

As Niblo angrily stormed away, having insulted Rodolfo in front of the crew, Rodolfo picked up one of the *banderillas* one of the cast was using and raced toward Niblo to plunge it into him. Had a dress extra not screamed for the director to watch out, Niblo might have been killed.

As it was, he whirled around and the *banderilla* cut into his left arm. Seeing him fall to the ground, Rodolfo seemingly came to reality and retreated back to his dressing room.

Lasky was summoned to the set where he ordered production halted for two days, as his director was carried off to a hospital clinic. Lasky was then seen heading for Rodolfo's dressing room for "a talk with this temperamental dago." The incident never got to the press.

With *Blood and Sand* wrapped, Rodolfo had time between pictures. He decided to disguise himself and take the train to New York City. From there, he'd drive to Foxlair, in New York State, the summer home of the Hudnut family where Natacha was "in seclusion" with her parents.

I was astonished at his disguise when he asked to be taken to the train station. He wore a fake heavy beard, his now famous eyes hidden behind a monstrous pair of dark goggles. A gray flannel cap hid most of his face, and he wore a tweed golf suit with a golf bag slung over his broad shoulders.

As I watched him leave, I was sad. We were no longer lovers. Not really. I still had sex with him, but it was different. He did not reciprocate, but laid back and demanded that I worship him. He had truly started to believe his press clippings, at least those written by women. One reporter called him a "male Helen of Troy." Another, the "Romeo of all the ages, the deathless troubadour at every lady's balcony window." Yet another said he was "every woman's husband by proxy."

The night before he'd left for New York, he'd lain nude in my bed, demanding that I make love to him with lips and tongue. He was no longer a lover, but some Oriental potentate with a slave boy. He still kissed me, but it was like he was bestowing a favor on me. "You are one lucky homosexual boy," he said to me. "Just think, half the world is wanting Valentino to make love to them, and you've got me. I hope you appreciate what I'm doing for you."

That opinion was said to me as I attacked his rosebud which he wanted endlessly licked, viewing that as something only the "most Godly" of men should receive. As I heard his moans of passion, I'd wanted to tell him it was not what he was doing for me, but what I was doing for him. Since my mouth was fully occupied, I kept at my task and said nothing.

After Rodolfo had departed Los Angeles in that stupid disguise, I returned to the hotel where Wally Reid was waiting. I'd called him earlier because I wanted to be with him, as we'd become quite tender together. Some-how I felt that being with Wally would make up for the increasingly brutish behavior of Rodolfo.

In my suite, Wally broke down and cried. They were tears of joy. One Los Angeles news reporter had written that morning that movie fans should forget this "fancy man," Rudolph Valentino. The reporter said that Wallace Reid was still "the Sheik Supreme of Feminine Hearts."

*****

As the Bitch of Buchenwald arrived for dictation, she was in an especially foul mood. No doubt if she had held her former command post, she'd order a whole convoy of prisoners stripped for her inspection. Surely she'd select thirty with the most beautiful skins for her lampshades.

"We've heard enough about this Valentino dago," she said. "Back to the cocksucking Paul Ivano and that child-molesting Little Tramp. Give us the juicy details, you old fart, before you expire right here in your library."

I obeyed her orders, fearing a dreadful fate if I didn't.

Back at Charlie's house, Kono, no doubt fearing for his job if Charlie were exposed, was in a particularly compassionate mood toward me. He even made some Japanese tea, which he shared with me as I sat in Charlie's favorite chair. He had long since ceased to think of himself as Charlie's servant—rather his "trusted friend and confidante."

I told him of all I knew of the blackmail and extortion demands, including Dagmar's claim that she'd seen Ivano perform a self-mutilation in that garden in Palm Springs on the moonlit night.

Like an Oriental wizard, Kono accurately got to the point. "Dagmar Godowsky's evidence could force Ivano to drop the charges filed with the police, which are very serious and could not only lead to Charlie's public humiliation but his arrest, trial, conviction, and jailing. We both know that it wouldn't be just one night in jail either, like that Valentino guy. If convicted of such an assault, Charlie could be sentenced to San Quentin for possibly ten years."

"Even if the assault charges against him are dropped," I said, "Ivano still has the photographs. They're worth a lot of money. They, too, could ruin Charlie."

"He's going to have to pay to get them back, and pay out a lot," Kono said. "Everybody wants Charlie's money." He looked at me as if I too were one of the blackmailers. "Even you."

"Cut the shit," I said, reacting angrily. "You're one of the money-hungry horde too. Charlie has told me that the only way he keeps your loyalty is to buy it. He toys with you, claiming you'll inherit one-quarter of his estate if you stick with him. Don't kid yourself into that bit of foolishness. Charlie will outlive all of us." In that prediction I was only half right, living long enough to attend both of their funerals.

When Charlie arrived two hours later from Catalina Island, he was ashen, looking almost ill, and seemed smaller than I'd ever seen him, as if he were gradually shrinking within his own skin. Once Kono had left the room he impulsively reached out for me to take me in his arms. There was no passion. It was the embrace of friends. More than any threat he'd faced before, he feared the Ivano blackmail would lead to his downfall.

When we went to his library so we could talk privately, he told me of his scheme. "I'm leaving Los Angeles, perhaps by tomorrow morning. I've decided how I can avoid paying Paul anything."

"How do you propose doing that?" I asked. "Flee to Fort Lee, New Jersey, the way you did to escape that pack of hounds Mildred pursued you with."

"Nothing like that," he said. "Paul can only threaten to blackmail me if I have a career to protect. I want you to pretend to negotiate with Paul. Stall him. In the meanwhile, I'll raid all my assets, put them in gold coins, and flee to some neutral country. I'm seriously considering Switzerland. With what money I have, I can retire comfortably even though I'm still young. I've already made my major statement in films, and I'm semi-retired now anyway—nothing like the factory I used to be in where it

seemed like I was making two films in a week."

"His demand of a million dollars is ridiculous," I said. "I'm sure all blackmailers start at some outrageous price and negotiate downward from there." Since coming to Hollywood, I had become an expert at blackmail.

"I don't want to give him a cent," Charlie said, "and I'm not going to." Even as he said that, he seemed to realize how ridiculous his opinion was. "Okay, deal with him, but get him down. The highest I will go is ten-thousand dollars."

Realizing how unrealistic Charlie was about money and bribery, I said, "You'll never get out of this that cheaply. There's no way."

He reached for my hand and squeezed it so hard he hurt me. It was a signal as to how desperate he was. "Get me out of this like you got me out of that Mexican *puta* thing. You did it once. You can do it again. After all, that's what I'm paying you for."

Kono knocked on the door, then entered abruptly. He looked nervous as if he had some bad news. "I've just spoken to Miss Louella Parsons," he said. "She's on her way over here, and she said to tell you that if you're not here when she comes over, your career is history."

As we waited for the arrival of the dreaded gossip columnist, Charlie spoke of the two of us for the first time. After all, this was my first appearance in his life after I'd been dumped. "I want you back," he said, "but we'll have to have an understanding. There will be women, lots and lots of women, the younger the better, in my life in the future. But from now on, you'll be the only man. I promise you that. No more Paul Ivanos. I can't ever take a risk like that again. That dirty little blackmailing shithead. I wish him dead."

"I can deal with the women," I said, as if I were still in love with Charlie, which was a bit of a stretch. The sex with him was good, but I had many other beaus for that. While he was out with his women in the future, I'd be out with Richard Dix, Antonio Moreno, William Boyd, and hopefully, Rodolfo himself.

"I know there will be many unwanted pregnancies," he said.

"Why don't you use some protection?" I asked. "Contraceptives aren't reliable but they're better than the raw thing."

"Like shit they are," he said. "At least not for me. If I'm forced to wear a condom with a woman, I can't even sustain an erection. I detest rubber and all rubber-like products. There will be a string of abortions in my future, all of which I want you to arrange. We'll need to make contact with a very good doctor. A very discreet doctor."

"I have such an arrangement now," I said. "Dr. Brian Sheehan. He performed that abortion on Marion, and everything went perfectly. He was the one I told you about who drove Ivano back from Palm Springs. Even on the ride back, he found inconsistencies in Ivano's story."

"Thank God Dagmar Godowsky told you about that," he said. "I'll owe her a few mercy fucks since you told me earlier that she wants me back as a boyfriend. I have no intention of taking Dagmar back, much less marrying her. I was in love with her a few weeks before I was tricked into marriage by my bitch ex-wife, that little slut, Mildred Harris. I'll try to be with Dagmar just enough to shut her up. But I've lost all sexual interest in her."

As we heard Louella come to a screeching halt in the driveway, Charlie jumped up, appearing nervous. I noticed that beads of perspiration had formed on his brow. "Bribe the bitch if you can, and I know you can," he said, the agitation mounting in his voice. "I can't stand the cunt. But we'll have to give in to her demands. Just get her down as low as possible, the way you'll have to do with Ivano."

"You're not going to Switzerland then?" I asked. "You're staying here to see it through. You're not running away."

He looked vague, as if not remembering his threat to flee to Switzerland. "Did I say Switzerland?" he asked. "I meant Jamaica. I hear in Jamaica you can get beautiful young girls real cheap. No questions asked. In some cases I hear their fathers sell them to wealthy Englishmen for very little money. Who said slavery was dead?"

Charlie and I were interrupted when Kono showed Louella into the room. Even though young, she was a fully grown witch, a presentation she'd perfect in the decades to come.

Over drinks, Charlie and "Lolly" exchanged pleasantries until venturing into jointly shared stories about their kidneys. Knowing of Louella's tendency to pee in her pants, Charlie too claimed he couldn't control his bladder. "Sometimes I have to get up ten times or more in one night to urinate." I knew from sleeping with him that that wasn't true. But he'd accurately sensed that Louella would be a sympathetic listener to that.

"I've got the same problem," she said, "except I don't often make it to the toilet. Every evening I go out I always carry along two or three changes of drawers with me."

After those medical bulletins, Charlie gracefully retreated to his bedroom for the night. Without a word being spoken, it was obviously understood by Louella that I would remain behind to discuss the actual terms.

When Charlie had gone, Louella looked over at me. She held up her empty glass. "I've been sitting here for four minutes staring at nothing but a melting ice cube in my whiskey," she said.

I immediately summoned Kono who appeared and took the glass from her and came back shortly thereafter with a refill. She looked at him in disappointment. "The whiskey is fine," she said, "but right now before I get down to business with Durango I have a desire for a double martini." She took one big gulp from the whiskey before Kono went to fill her second order.

For seemingly no reason, Louella launched into a story about her past, set in the time when she was leaving Chicago and heading for New York. "My mother said the only person she knew in New York was Charlie Chapin, and she agreed to set up a meeting between us."

At first I thought she meant "Chaplin" and had failed to pronounce his name correctly because of her heavy drinking.

"Chapin was the meanest man in New York," she said. "The editor of *The New York World*."

By then I knew she was talking of some other man, not my actor friend.

"My first meeting with Chapin went beautifully," she said. "I was quite a glamour gal then." She ran her hands down her waist. "Still am as you can plainly see. He was real smitten with me. Expensive dinners. Broadway shows. Cozy horse-and-buggy rides in Central Park.

Within the first week I was falling in love with him. Then I spoke to my mother and my Aunt Hattie back in Chicago. Over dinner one night Chapin had claimed that my Aunt Hattie was the only woman he'd ever loved." By the time Kono had arrived with the double martini, Louella had already finished off the whiskey. "My mother asked me about Chapin's wife and had I met her."

"I can see you thought he was a bachelor," I said.

"I did indeed," she said with a bit of indignation in her voice. "After all, I'm a good girl. The next time I went out with Chapin, I demanded to be introduced to his wife. I heard she was a lot older than he was, and even then Chapin wasn't a spring chicken. I wondered how strong the marriage was. I never got to meet the poor old bag."

"He decided against it?" I asked.

"My Sunday luncheon with his wife never came off," she said, "because he murdered the hag before we could get together."

That was a bit shocking to me. Even then, Louella, drunk or not, could spin a good yarn.

"My boss insisted that I go into hiding at the Astor Hotel until the case blew over," she said. "I wasn't directly involved in the murder but there was talk that Chapin killed his wife so that he could be free to marry me."

"Did the police want you for questioning?"

"They did indeed—that is, if they knew where to find me" she said. "Finally, the police got to the bottom of it. Chapin was deeply in debt and had been pawning his rich wife's jewelry. There was another woman, a cute redhead. But she'd dumped Chapin for another man. Chapin had been buying expensive gifts for this whore with the money he'd gotten pawning his wife's gems. He was so generous that he even bought the redhead's mother a $200 pair of false teeth. When the redhead dumped him, he stormed over to the mother's house and found the false teeth resting in a glass of salt water in her bathroom. He flushed the teeth down the toilet."

"An amusing story," I said, "if a murder weren't involved. So you were almost involved in a scandal of your own. Not as much fun as reporting about scandal, is it?"

"How true," she said, settling back into her seat and studying me carefully through her bleary eyes. "As far as that scandal was concerned, my involvement in it was hushed up. How it was hushed up is really none of your business. I'm only relating this story to you to suggest that Charlie Chaplin with an "L" can also hush up the Paul Ivano scandal before it even breaks."

"I understand perfectly," I said. I too studied Louella. Behind that distorted, alcoholic-soaked face, I detected a fierce ambition, rivaled only by the crazed compulsion of Gloria Swanson to rule over Hollywood. "I don't know what Paul Ivano has told you," I said on the edge of my seat. "He's an unreliable witness. He recently tried to commit suicide in Palm Springs. He's very unstable. A liar, really."

"We're all liars, darling," she said. "Even me at times. I've been known to print information in my column even when I knew it wasn't truth if it served some purpose of mine. Imagine me doing that. But I know plenty about Ivano and Charlie." She looked at me like a prosecuting attorney. "So, Charlie is a pansy, a little fairy boy. My readers think of him only as a child-molester. Now I can add homosexual to the laundry list of charges."

"Perhaps it won't be necessary to inform your readers of certain of Charlie's proclivities," I said.

"You mean, I should deal only with the news fit to print."

"You got that right."

"That could be arranged," she said rather coyly. "I guess everybody has his price. Make that *her* price."

"If you don't mind my asking, what is your secret dream?"

"To become the richest and most famous newspaperwoman in the world," she said. "After that, to marry a handsome nobleman."

"Again forgive me, but do you mind if I ask you how much money you make a week?"

"One-hundred dollars, she said between sips of her martini. "That's pretty good pay for a gal in my line of work."

"What say that tonight we at least launch you toward your goal of being the richest, if not the most famous, newspaperwoman in the business."

"I'd say you and I talk the same language."

"How about $50,000 deposited tomorrow in the bank of your choice?" I asked.

"I would call that a blessed event," she said. "My agreement would be never to mention the name of Paul Ivano in my column ever again, even if he becomes the king of Hollywood." She smiled showing teeth that were already beginning to rot at her early age. "I'll go back to reporting scandals about my loved ones—Dick Barthelmess, the Talmadge gals, Monty Love, Barbara LaMarr. The stories I'm hearing about that LaMarr creature! Mabel Normand went to a clinic to dry out but is taking dope again."

Louella stayed for no more than fifteen minutes once our deal was concluded. As she was leaving, she wet-lipped me on the mouth, making me think she was sexually attracted to me, at least a bit.

"I hope you're not one of those boy whores like Paul Ivano."

"I'm strictly a man for the ladies," I said, lying.

"I figured that," she said. "In that department you can't fool Louella, although many actors have tried. "Tell me the truth. What fair lady are you fucking now? I swear I won't print anything. It's for my own curiosity."

"Blanche Sweet," I said, another lie.

"I got that wrong," she said. "I figured it was Marion Davies. I've even seen the two of you together, but I'm certainly not going to publish that. I still think I might go to work for W.R. one day. As for Blanche Sweet, that's no distinction. All the men in Hollywood are fucking that one—at least those who aren't homosexual like Antonio Moreno and that new kid, Ramon Novarro."

Hoping to get rid of her, I stood at the door, taking her hand and planting a kiss inside the palm, as the screenwriter, Elinor Glyn, had instructed aspirant Hollywood Romeos to do.

She giggled. "If one night you want a real number, call me." She handed me a card. "Anything Blanche Sweet has, I've got more of." She hesitated again, the promise of romance dying as the prospect of a scoop occurred to her. "I want you to tell me the real story of what happened to Lotte Lee. I don't believe one word of all that crap you've been giving out to other reporters."

After Louella had left and before retreating upstairs to Charlie's bedroom, I called the reception desk of the Hollywood Hotel for my messages. That was at a time Rodolfo was still staying there in the suite with me, and before his departure for New York and the much-used arms of Natacha Rambova.

One of the calls was from Marion Davies, who W.R. had installed into the Hollywood Hotel in a suite next to mine. I had vaguely talked to Marion about getting together for dinner the first night in the hotel. But it wasn't a firm commitment, and all the charges against Charlie or Rodolfo had certainly distracted me.

I telephoned her suite and she picked up the receiver, sounding drunk over the phone. After a few preliminaries, she confessed that she'd had the "fucking of my life."

"Tom Ince strikes again," I said.

"Ince is good, but he's not as good as what I just had."

"I know it wasn't Charlie," I said. "He's been with me"

"The living doll I just made it with would make me forget all about Tom Ince or Charlie, even W.R. himself," she said. "For a chance at that dick I just had in every one of my holes, I'd go so far as to sell my jewelry." When I found you had gone somewhere, I wandered downstairs to the bar. And there he was. Every woman in America is dreaming of going to bed with the Sheik of Araby."

I supplied his name for her. "Rudolph Valentino."

*****

It was late when I returned to the Hollywood Hotel the following evening to discover a visitor waiting for me in the lobby. It was Charlotte Shelby, the mother of Mary Miles Minter. As Lotte Lee, I'd had lunch with Shelby on the set of *Vampira*, filling in for Billy Taylor.

"I've been waiting three hours," she said, coming right up to me and reaching out to shake my hand. "I'm Charlotte Shelby, a friend of your sister, Lotte Lee."

She could hardly have known that I was

Lotte Lee, and Shelby was no friend of mine. I considered her dangerous, and wondered what mysterious reason compelled her to seek me out. "I knew you right away from seeing your picture in the paper," she said. "They say my Mary is the prettiest gal in Hollywood. Well, Charlotte Shelby says you're the prettiest man, and I've known a few of those devilish critters in my day—not many, but a few."

"Mrs. Shelby, it's an honor to meet you," I said. "I'm a fan of your daughter's. Her pictures are wonderful, far superior to those of Mary Pickford. Your Mary also photographs better than Pickford." With those words, I knew I had won the heart of Mother Shelby.

She smiled and hooked her arm in mine. "I hope you don't mind if we retreat to the bar for a little bourbon and branch water," she said. "This is one thirsty swamp bitch from the bayous."

"Be my guest," I said, acting as gallantly as I could. "I'm sure you're here on a mission tonight, Mrs. Shelby."

"Call me Lily Pearl," she said. "My best buddies have called me that ever since I was knee-high to a possum."

In the bar, Lily Pearl ordered colas with lots of ice. As was the custom, serious drinkers brought their own booze in flasks, which they poured into their soft drinks after the waiter had left. Lily Pearl carried enough bourbon with her to last all the way to Louisiana, even if we decided to take a hayride back there instead of the train.

She might act like a drunken swamp bitch, but to hear Lily Pearl tell it, she was the offspring of landed gentry. "I am descended from slave owners," she said. "My great-grandfather originally had the biggest plantation in Mississippi. He was a cruel master, but he whipped those darkies into a working crew that grew more cotton than any other pack of niggers in the Delta. His secret?" She downed more of her drink. "Frighten the hell out of them. If one of them got out of line, he would summon all the niggers on the plantation. In front of all of them, he would heat up a cocktail of pure scalding lead and force the errant darkie to drink it. To escape a fate like that, the darkies would be out the next morning practically praying for that God damn cotton to grow."

"Now, Lily Pearl," I said, growing a bit impatient, "I know you didn't bring me here to enthrall me with romantic stories about the Old South." I stared into her glazed eyes. "Let's dig into the pie and see what you're slicing off for me."

"Speaking of food," she said, "that reminds me of the time I met Louisiana's literary sweetheart, Lulu Belle Broyhill. She'd written a cookbook. I loved one of her recipes. It was for some sort of road kill. Her only instructions were, 'Cook as you would blackbird.'" She laughed at her own humor before her face stiffened into a grimace. "You've got one thing right, boy, and it's this—Lily Pearl is definitely here on a mission. I have two very tricky challenges to place before you. Before I can talk about them, I think that waiter needs to bring up some more cola."

After another drink, Lily Pearl got around to the reason for her visit. I realized that it takes Southerners a while to get to the point. "First, let's get the dirty business out of the way before I reward you with the goodies. As I'm sure your sister has told you, I'm planning to marry William Desmond Taylor. But there's a problem. Even though he behaves like a perfect gentleman around me and my Mary, I keep hearing reports that he's one big sinner. Not just going to a dope parties here and there, but making regular appearances at sex orgies."

"You know how people exaggerate," I said. "Everyone tells tall tales out here just like they do in the Old South where you come from."

"I guess I'm not making my point clear enough," she said. "I'm hearing stories that William is a homosexual. That he screws women for the sake of appearances, but what he really prefers is some teenage boy ass."

"I don't know Mr. Taylor well," I said, "but that sounds like pure Hollywood bullshit. Since coming to Hollywood, I've heard about every slander and libel that was ever made up about everybody out here. Most of it—in fact, nearly all of it—is simply a bald-faced lie, nothing more."

"That's very reassuring," she said, "but I'm not convinced that all these stories about William aren't true. At least some of them. The whispers keep cropping up. They keep getting worse and worse. You know what I say?"

I completed her sentence for her. "Where there's smoke, there's fire."

"Exactly," she said. "I was madly in love with this handsome devil in New Orleans," she said. "Real crazy about him. He was a perfect gentleman and everything. Even though I gave him a million golden opportunities to get into my drawers, he never went for the honeypot. Of course, he bragged to all his fellow bubbas that he was banging me every night. As it turned out, he was dating me for show. He eventually got caught fucking a little black boy up the ass. It seemed he preferred those dark holes of Calcutta to what I had to offer him. I don't want to make the same mistake, lusting after another God damn pansy. If you ask me, guys like that should all be rounded up by the government and castrated. That would cure them of their habit of cornholing."

"Seems like a harsh punishment," I said, trying to figure out a way to escape from her clutches.

"I want you to do a big favor for me," she said. "You're a mighty pretty teenage boy. I want you to visit William in his bungalow. After a drink ore two, make yourself available to him. I'm sure you know how to do that. If he doesn't respond, just out and out proposition him. To put it in blunt words, ask him to sodomize you."

"I don't think I could do that," I told her. "I'm not that kind of guy."

"I don't mean you actually have to go through with it," she said. "All I'll need to know is this: Did he accept your proposition? If he makes a pass back at you, then get the hell out. Run for the hills. You'll have found out what I want to know."

"If I do this for you, what are you prepared to do for me?"

"I like a boy who can bargain," she said, smiling in some sort of imagined triumph. "For your help in smoking out Sweet William, I'm going to arrange for you to date my little cherub, the great Mary Miles Minter herself, the Princess of Hollywood. You and she are about the same age. All the motion-picture magazines will pick up on it. You'll replace Douglas Fairbanks and the Pickford bitch as America's sweethearts. Maybe you two will get married one day. I can just see the offspring you lovelies

will have. I bet even your children will grow up to become movie stars."

"Let's don't rush this thing," I said, "We haven't gone out on our first date yet, and already you're talking about children."

"I do get carried away, but I've really been fantasizing about this. I want Mary to give up her fascination for older gents and date someone her own age. These older men like James Kirkwood are just exploiting her. There's no future with these old goats. Mary belongs with a young and virile man like you."

"That's very flattering," I said, "but what makes you think she'll go for me?"

"I've already discussed it with her," she said. "She thinks you're very handsome and she'd would love to go out with you. Imagine the publicity you'll get dating my Mary. It could mean your big break into pictures. With all the publicity generated by your being seen with my Mary, some producer is bound to take notice of you and cast you."

"That didn't do much for Lotte," I said.

"*Vampira* was a dirty picture," she said. "I warned William not to make it. I always insist that my Mary appear in pictures that the entire family can go to see. I'm sure you'd look wholesome on the screen. All the young gals will fall for you, and all the mothers—myself included—will want you for a son-in-law."

Actually, the more I thought about it, the more possible such a scenario seemed. All the homosexual actors in Hollywood either dated or married women. My going out with Minter would make us the darling of the fan magazines. The question was, could I stomach it? "I'm going to accept your offer," I said, getting up. "First, I'll arrange that rendezvous with Mr. Taylor and report back to you. Then I'll make you keep your promise to let me date your beautiful daughter."

"Regardless of the outcome with William, consider the offer of my daughter a done deal," she said, standing up on wobbly legs.

I looked at Charlotte with a heavy heart. If dating Mary Miles Minter was the first step on the road to stardom, I would have to take it, as hazardous and slippery as that step was.

"I can see it now," Charlotte said, a bright light gleaming in her glazed eyes. "It might even be a double ceremony. The press would love

to cover it--a blow-out to rival the death of
Jesus Christ! The simultaneous weddings of
Mr. William Desmond Taylor with Miss Char-
lotte Shelby, and Mr. Durango Jones with Miss
Mary Miles Minter."

Chapter Fifteen

Even though Charlie threatened to commit suicide, he was forced to turn over $100,000 to blackmailing Paul Ivano. Fierce negotiations were required. Had Dagmar Godowsky not stepped forward as a possible witness, Ivano might have gotten more money.

At first Ivano had had Nazimova's backing, thinking Ivano could use the money to buy the distribution rights to *Salome*. But Charles Bryant, her "husband," was finally able to convince her that she too would be taking part in a blackmail of Charlie, and there was no way she wanted to be implicated in that. Coming so soon after her involvement as an eyewitness in the Valentino bigamy charge, she felt a possible second scandal might lead to her deportation for certain, as she was never sure of her legal status in this country.

As for me, I wasn't particularly concerned with what happened to *Salome*, as I was furious with the Hays office for demanding that my scenes as the slave boy with Theodore Kosloff be cut from the film before it could go into general distribution. In my slightly self-enchanted view, those scenes were the best thing in the film, certainly the hottest. Nazimova might have thought her dance of the seven veils was sexy, but Oscar Wilde as the playwright would definitely have cast his vote for the sexual chemistry between Theodore as the Syrian captain and me as his virtually nude slave boy.

Coming in the wake of the commercial failure of Nazimova's *A Doll's House*, the aging actress began shopping *Salome* around to various distributors. At the suggestion of both Bryant and Ivano, she screened it to critics who were equally divided, either dismissing it completely or else praising it as an artistic success. In *The New Republic*, Thomas Canen wrote, "Try as she will, Nazimova cannot be seductive. The deadly lure of sex, which haunts the Wilde drama like a subtle poison, is dispelled the instant one beholds her puerile form."

Allied finally gave the film a restricted release in February of 1923, using Natacha's poster to promote the flicker. She used Nazimova's face in her drawing of the moon that hangs above Herod's palace like "a dead woman" in the sky. In the original Beardsley poster, he used the face of Wilde.

Nazimova didn't look like a sinister fourteen-year-old, but more or less like a middle-aged woman attempting an impersonation of adolescence. That pre-Jean Harlow platinum blonde wig she wore in her "bathing suit" for the Dance of the Seven Veils, was a hideous mistake, and Nazimova needed Isadora Duncan to pull off that dance routine. The high point of the film was Nazimova, dressed in an elaborate turban and cape of peacocks, waiting outside the cell of the John the Baptist about to face beheading from the powerfully built executioner. Her eyes practically dilate in orgasm when she hears the head fall from her would-be lover. When no audience could be found for *Salome*, Allied put it on the shelf where it would forever linger.

Once one of the highest paid stars in Hollywood, Nazimova found herself broke. There were no immediate offers for movie work. One year later she was burlesquing Salome's dance in the film, *The Redeeming Sin*. Perhaps the low point in her career was when the once great star was cast as Jack Pickford's mother in *My Son*, which had a modest success but didn't lead to any more movie offers for this fallen star. *Variety* claimed that Nazimova's "grimaces in close-up are not at all pleasant to see."

She did live on in political memory as the godmother of a girl born Anne Frances Robbins to one of her former lesbian lovers, Edith Luckett, who'd once toured with her in that stinker of a play, *'Ception Shoals*. Born to parents who ran a boarding house in Washington, D.C., Edith soon deserted Nazimova. Edith invented an aristocratic Southern plantation background for herself and married the son of a real aristocratic New England family, Kenneth Robbins, an insurance salesman. Their daughter, Anne Frances Robbins, later became Nancy Davis, the actress and fellatio queen of Hollywood rivaling a position I held, and even later Nancy Reagan who ruled the White House in the 1980s. In the late Thirties and early Forties, I, too, had made a play for "Ronnie," losing him finally to that mean bitch, Jane Wyman.

As for Chaplin, the blackmail from Ivano and the threat of a scandal so great that it would have destroyed Hollywood's leading career panned out. Of course, money had to exchange hands.

After paying out $100,000 to Paul Ivano, plus another $50,000 to Lolly Parsons, Charlie went into a long, sulky period. He had a pistol concealed somewhere in his bedroom, and constantly threatened to fire a bullet into his head, but neither Kono nor I seriously considered these threats.

For a few weeks, his appetite for sex with a man or a woman had diminished in his post-blackmail depression. Sometimes he would just want to be held in my arms, and at other times he wanted to be left alone to think about what his next career move was going to be in Hollywood. He grew increasingly paranoid that everyone he knew—or didn't know—was plotting to get his money. Perhaps that wasn't

paranoia. It might have been a realistic look at the events.

With all that murk and scandal behind me, beginning with Olive Thomas and going on to Fatty Arbuckle, to be followed by Charlie and Rodolfo, I was at last free to pay some attention to the great success that had come to my friends, Barbara LaMarr and Ramon Novarro. At long last, before filming was completed, I headed for the set of *The Prisoner of Zenda*.

Rex Ingram, Rodolfo's former director, seemed fated to cast his wife, Alice Terry, in roles where she'd be overshadowed by her co-stars. Such was the case with Rodolfo in *The Four Horsemen of the Apocalypse*. Such was also the case in Alice Terry's latest vehicle, *The Prisoner of Zenda*, with co-starring parts going to Barbara and Ramon, who had achieved the one thing that had eluded me in Hollywood—movie stardom.

Even though happy for both of their successes, I was still a bit jealous, although I concealed that when I went to the set to visit them.

Since Barbara and Ramon were shooting, I got to renew my acquaintance with Alice Terry, who, surprisingly did not speak of Rodolfo, although he dominated the news. Resting between takes, she had removed her blonde wig. Since her husband, Ingram, had wanted to follow accurately the script of *The Four Horsemen*, he'd asked her to cover her naturally auburn hair with the wig, and the effect made her look so stunning her fans expected it of her since.

"Always the damn wig," she said. She claimed that she didn't know if she wanted to continue as a Metro star but perhaps should go to Paramount. "I love working with my husband, but it might be better for us to break up. If he plays me up too much in a picture, people will say that he's pushing his wife. I'd like to see what I could do without his help."

After finishing his work before the camera, Ramon rushed over to me. I'd never seen such an excited, eager face. It was as if stardom meant everything to him and had opened up a new and glittering life for him, which could only mean happiness and success at every turn. He was also delighted to have met Barbara, with whom he'd formed an instant friendship. "She came on to me real strong at first," Ramon confided. "Like she does with most men, even Rex Ingram. Don't let Alice know. One night we got drunk together, and I told her my little secret. We've been girl friends ever since. What do you think of her, your former roomie?"

"I think if Cleopatra had been living in the Twenties, she would be Barbara LaMarr," I said. "In fact, I suspect that Cleo has come back to life as Barbara. The Queen is hoping bad luck won't follow her into this new life."

He looked sad. "I haven't known her for long, but from what I've heard I wonder how happy her life will be. Barbara is a candle burning at both ends. I fear no one is around to save the wax."

At that point a radiant Barbara rushed over to kiss me. "Have you heard the good news?" she asked, bubbling over and looking as young as the girl Charlie had picked up in the school yard.

I congratulated her on her incredible and virtual overnight success. "Rex thinks there is real chemistry between Ramon and me on the screen," she said. "He's going to co-star us in *Trifling Women*. No Alice Terry this time. Rex is writing the screenplay himself."

"It's another one of those old-fashioned Theda Bara type vampire things," Ramon said. "But we think it'll go over at the box office."

"Theda Bara was too wicked," Barbara said. "I mean, a bit much. Pouring poison into the coffee cup of her victim. Shit like that. She was also portrayed as too exotic. I want to show the world that homemade American vampires are even more vampish and sexier than the foreign ones."

Since *Trifling Women* has been lost to history, I will quote what an assistant filmmaker of the time, Michael Powell, said about it. He called it "moonlight on tiger skins and blood dripping onto white faces, while sinister apes, poison, and lust keep the plot rolling." I couldn't have summed it up better myself. Nonetheless, *Trifling Women* was a big success at the box office.

Ingram viewed it as his revenge on Rodolfo. The director still bore a deep grudge against Rodolfo and was elated when he read in *Photoplay*: "It seems that Ingram has done it again by casting Ramon Novarro in *The Pris-*

oner of Zenda. He no longer needs Valentino. From what we hear, this new young man who hails from Spain (sic) threatens to become even more spectacularly famous than Rodolf (sic) Valentino. Novarro, Rex Ingram's latest discovery, was recently known as Samantyagos (sic)."

Both Barbara and Ramon were filled with stories of their adventures, although hearing of them made me a little sad, as my most recent film work, like all my other work, ended up on the cutting-room floor or with only the back of my head showing.

"At first Rex didn't think I was the type for Zenda," Ramon said. "He saw the role of Rupert of Hentzau as tall and blond, about 35 years old with a mustache and beard. I reached into my makeup kit, applied a false beard and mustache, and did a transformation. I got the part."

"At Ramon's first test," Barbara said, "he still looked too young. Rex came up with an idea of having him wear a monocle. It made him look more mature. Rex had Ramon practice tossing the monocle and catching it in his eye. Ramon was perfect. The role of Rupert was then assured for him."

"I almost walked off the set and ruined my big chance," Ramon said. "The scene called for Barbara playing Antoinette de Mauban to slap me. We went into twenty-seven takes and still Rex wasn't satisfied. My face was getting redder and redder and started to swell, and I thought Rex had it in for me. I threatened to leave after only one more take. Barbara slapped me again, harder than before, and Rex yelled cut. I raced to get an ice bag."

For later that night, Barbara and Ramon invited me to a studio party being thrown in their honor. But I'd already accepted an invitation from Charlie. He didn't want to be seen in public with a woman, hoping to live down some of the scandalous headlines from Catalina Island he'd made with that man-chasing Peggy Hopkins Joyce. Rephrase that to rich man-chasing Hopkins. She never slept with poor men. If she did, she didn't marry them.

Charlie had been invited to appear at a benefit for the Actors Fund in the Hollywood Bowl, staged under the sponsorship of the Motion Picture Directors Association. All the major stars were asked to appear as Shakespearean characters. Charlie, for some reason, chose to appear as Romeo.

At the entrance to the bowl, a limousine in back skidded and plowed into Charlie's Locomobile, which Kono was driving, having resumed his duties as chauffeur.

"Oh shit, there's probably some big star in that car," Charlie said. "Pickford. Fairbanks. Maybe both." He jumped out before any of us could even register the impact of the crash, and raced back to the limousine. Through the window I watched him throw open the car door of the limousine which had crashed into us.

Getting out to join him, I saw him peer into the darkened car.

Seeing its passenger or passengers, I heard him say something real surprising. "What a fortunate accident." Why would he call any accident fortunate?

Emerging from the back of the limousine, the face of the occupant was immediately familiar to me. It was Pola Negri, who'd recently arrived from Berlin and was already appearing in screaming headlines with Gloria Swanson. The subject involved a feud which both actresses were denying but one which was just as intense, and just as newsworthy, as the feud, decades later, between Bette Davis and Joan Crawford.

Negri was wearing a costume of Shakespeare's Cleopatra, which looked like something that had been rescued from the prop room of the old Theda Bara movie. She was bejeweled and virtually nude. Charlie kissed her on the lips. He turned to me. "Miss Negri, Durango Jones."

"What a quaint name," she said in heavily accented English. "A cowboy name." To my astonished eyes, she pretended to gun me down, making a six-shooter with her hand, a piece of action no doubt seen in a William S. Hart movie.

Before I could lie and tell the bitch how honored I was to meet her, she turned to Charlie as he took her hand and told her, "You don't know how I've been dying to get in touch with you."

"Ever hear of a phone, Charlie?" she said, a bit sarcastically, I thought.

Suddenly, she ignored Charlie and turned her attention to me. "Don't you think I'll create a sensation tonight?" She seemed to model the Cleopatra costume just for me.

"All of Hollywood is dying to lay eyes on you," I said, more or less avoiding a direct answer.

"Please join us," Charlie said to her.

For the rest of the evening, Charlie was lost to me, focusing his entire attention on Pola Negri, whose charms escaped me. He invited her to join us for a large party at the Cocoanut Grove, later that evening, but she declined, saying she had to get her beauty sleep in order to face the photographers tomorrow.

Two weeks later at a dinner party at the home of Pola Negri, I befriended her maid, Lena, who was also her butler, chauffeur, secretary, and private chef. "In the middle of the night as Miss Negri was sleeping, I heard this loud noise," Lena said. "The dogs were barking like crazy. From your movies, I knew you still had wild Indians out here in the west, and I just knew it was an Indian raid on our house. Miss Negri threw open her window to discover that Charlie had hired a ten-piece Hawaiian band to serenade her all night. We were kept awake all night while Mr. Chaplin slept peacefully, I'm sure."

From my personal knowledge, I didn't know if Charlie slept all that peacefully. He did let me fuck him, but all during our mating ritual I felt he was dreaming of this Polish bombshell—and not of me.

Knowing what I know now, I would, if I had the power, have shipped Pola Negri back to Berlin. Charlie, as mentioned, wrote *My Autobiography* and Pola Negri penned *Memoirs of a Star*. Both were pieces of fiction. In Charlie's tale, he claims that he reunited with Pola Negri when seated next to her box at the Hollywood Bowl, leaving out the car incident. Negri claimed she was cool toward Charlie, but in his version she's practically hysterical at encountering him again. "Chaarlee!" he quotes her as saying, Why haven't I heard from you. You never called me up. Don't you realize I have come all the way from Germany to see you?" He also claims he had seen her in Berlin for only twenty minutes, which was such an obvious lie.

I sensed Charlie was heading for big trouble

with Miss Negri. But he wouldn't listen to me, claiming I was jealous. The following night, as I could have predicted, Miss Negri called and I answered the phone. She was rather dismissive of me. She seemed a bit aware of Charlie's homosexual tendencies. "Are you the new boy who has replaced Paul Ivano in Charlie's life?" she asked.

"I'm his secretary." I said.

"Secretary?" she asked skeptically. "In Europe we call it lovers. But that's not why I'm calling. I'm having a dinner party at my beautiful rented house in Beverly Hills. I want Charlie to attend. It will be a spectacular event. I'm inviting all the big stars, even Pickford and Fairbanks. All of them are clamoring to meet the great Pola Negri, since my reputation as the rage of the Continent has preceded me."

The more she talked, the more flabbergasted I was at her command of the English language. Although still heavily accented, she made her points in English rather well. From Berlin, we'd heard that she knew only a few words of English, perhaps another lie spread by Ivano.

"Darling," she said, "I am so very sorry that I cannot invite you. We're not inviting secretaries to the stars. Only the stars themselves."

"I see," I said. "I'll convey your invitation to Mr. Chaplin."

"As a good secretary is supposed to," she said, before rudely hanging up on me without even saying good-bye.

I'd had my first phone call from Miss Negri. Regrettably, it would not be my last.

*****

In her suite at the Hollywood Hotel, Marion Davies thought she had a dilemma. I faced one too. How could I remain her friend when she was standing before me telling me that she'd fallen in love with Rudolph Valentino? "He's even teaching me how to do the tango, although I'm not very good at it."

I didn't know how she planned to deal with W.R. in her life, and if Rodolfo had fallen in love with Marion too. Perhaps he planned to wed Natacha Rambova again when it became

legal and take Marion as his mistress. Although Marion knew of my sexual relationship with Charlie, I don't think she was aware of my love for Rodolfo. She had to know that the star was sharing a suite—and perhaps the same bed—at the Hollywood Hotel with a homosexual male, namely Durango Jones.

Finally, that point seemed to occur to her soggy brain, as she looked as if she'd been drinking all day. "I don't know how you can keep your hands off of Rudy and share the same bed," she said. "Does he sleep in the nude? Have you ever seen him without his clothes? He's got a terrific body—not to mention his fabulous cock. Rudy doesn't have one quite as big as Charlie's, but he knows how to use it better than The Little Tramp."

"I've not seen Rodolfo in the nude," I said, lying. "He sleeps in pajamas and bathes with the door shut. We're just good friends. You know what a womanizer he is. To tell you the truth, I can't think of any man but my own beau. The new love of my life."

"Care to tell me about him, sugar?" she asked. "Is he a famous star?"

"He's going to be a famous Hollywood doctor," I said. "He's Brian Sheehan, who performed that little job on you at the hospital."

"He's a living doll if you prefer them tall, devastatingly handsome, blond, and blue eyed," she said, heading for the bar and another drink. "Frankly, I prefer the more continental Latin type like Rudy. He's so suave. Charlie's idea of romance is to hop onto a woman, pump her a few times, and jump off, after he's quickly satisfied. Tom Ince likes to take his time, but you know that everything he does is for his own pleasure—and not the lady's. As for W.R." She paused as if not wanting to complete her assessment of the Chief's sexual prowess. "He's a very gentle, very kind lover. But Rudy makes me feel all woman. He doesn't climax until he knows I'm completely fulfilled sexually."

At that point, I almost blasted off at Marion, accusing her of stealing my boy friend and telling her that our friendship was at an end. I had been able to handle all of Rodolfo's other involvements with both men and women, ranging from Tallulah Bankhead to Barbara LaMarr, from Norman Kerry to Ramon Novarro, even Natacha Rambova. But I was absolutely furious at Marion. It's not that we hadn't shared boy friends before—Tom Ince, Charlie Chaplin, and, if we could call W.R. a boy friend, the Chief himself.

But her pawing of Rodolfo's delectable flesh pissed me off. I was enraged and wanted revenge. Much earlier in this tome I mentioned that I had originally planned to leave out a few scandals—notably my involvement with Douglas Fairbanks Jr. at an age when he was jail-bait. Another thing I planned to leave out was how I betrayed Marion Davies, which in looking back I realize was a big mistake. I'm not proud of it, but I did it and I'm very sorry now.

It happened this way, and I'm confessing up, even though I fear I might lose what final sympathy any reader might have for me. The Bitch of Buchenwald reminds me every day that if I publish these confessions, I'll be listed among the all-time whores of Hollywood, dimming in comparison the sexual escapades of Ava Gardner, Marilyn Monroe, Lana Turner, and even Joan Crawford herself.

At a knock on the door, Marion staggered to answer it, letting into the suite her female hairdresser, who looked like a stern librarian, and her "beautician," who appeared to be a young and very queenly Fatty Arbuckle type. She pleaded with me to stay and to answer her phone, while she retreated into her dressing room to make herself beautiful for the night. Since W.R. was somewhere east of California—she wasn't sure—she'd invited Tom Ince to accompany her to a party.

Enraged with jealousy over Rodolfo, I felt like a secretary as I took Marion's messages. The first was from Frances Marion, one of the great women screenwriters of her day who had written such scenarios for Marion as *The Cinema Murder* and *The Restless Sex*, both released in 1920. The next call was from Mary Pickford, about a dinner invitation.

On yet a third call I was confronting, at least over the phone, a hysterical Lillian Gish, who seemed surprised that I was picking up Marion's calls. Although the portrait of Lillian is usually that of a sweet and adorable rose, she was thorny as hell itself. Screaming into the phone, she claimed that Marion had "seized" the only dressing room at the studio with a toilet.

"Marion then dumped all my possessions outside my own bungalow and changed the lock," Lillian said. "It's my dressing room, assigned to me by Louis B. Mayer himself. There's going to be a showdown in the morning in Mayer's office. I don't give a damn who Marion is the mistress of. I'm the biggest star at Metro, and that untalented courtesan had better face up to that. If she doesn't I'm going to snatch her bald, blonde hair by blonde hair." She slammed down the phone.

After that, I called down to the desk for my own messages, discovering one to attend a private party at the bungalow of William Desmond Taylor. Antonio Moreno had called after Billy Taylor, inviting me to go with him. After the failure of *Vampira*, Billy had been more or less avoiding me but he was growing friendlier in the past few weeks.

John Gilbert had called too, and I did return that one, thinking this handsome matinee idol was inviting me out on a date. But, to my surprise and displeasure, it was to tell me he'd fallen in love. "You mean with Leatrice Joy?" I asked.

"I guess I still love her." He said with some hesitation. "No, no, not Leatrice. I'm in love with Lillian Gish." Not wanting to learn the details of this unrequited romance, I begged off, claiming I would call him tomorrow. Before putting down the phone, I chastised him. "First, Leatrice Joy. Now Lillian Gish. That leaves no time for me."

"I'll pick you up at ten in the morning," he promised. "We'll go to the Los Angeles Athletic Club. You'll find there's still plenty left for you, baby."

Thinking Marion did nothing when she was alone but receive phone calls, I picked up the receiver again to discover W.R. himself on the line. He was calling from Kansas City and said, "I'm glad you're on the phone. I'm livid with rage. From two detective agents I've gotten reports on Marion. One man was seen leaving her suite at four o'clock in the morning. Another man stayed until five o'clock. I can't believe these were harmless social visits at those hours."

"Do you know who the men were?" I

asked.

"Hell, yes," he said. "Low studio grips. No one even important, like Charlie. Of course, I had suspected Ince but after your night with him, I know his sexual interests lie elsewhere."

And then I did it. "You're paying me, and I'm supposed to report on her. I hate to tell you this. But she has bagged a big one. Her latest romance is with the Great Lover himself, one Rudolph Valentino."

There was a long pause at the other end of the phone. At first I thought he might not have heard me, because of a bad connection.

"That's it," he said. "I don't like to use clichés, but it's the final straw. Marion and I are history. Is she there?"

"She's in her dressing room getting her hair done," I said.

"Order her to the phone," he said. "I'm telling her that I'm on my way back to Los Angeles where we'll conclude our affairs. I mean, business affairs. I won't mention the Valentino thing to protect you, because I'll need you as my informant for many a year to come. But I have to tell Marion that it's over between us."

Then I did another stupid thing, like my so-called marriage to Charlie. Even as I said the words, I knew I was entrapping myself. Somehow the words seemed to spew out of my mouth without my even thinking. I think I was experiencing meltdown in the phone presence of such a fabled and powerful world figure. I hadn't succumbed to the kinky Prince of Wales, and he might one day be the Emperor of India, but this newspaper baron—at least in the way I felt at that very moment—thrilled me with his awesome power, especially if I could replace Marion in his affections. "If it'll help I have good news from Lotte," I said. "She's accepted your offer and wants to see you as soon as you're back in Los Angeles."

"That's all I needed to make my final decision," he said. "Tell Lotte I'm there for her. Instead of building up Marion as a movie star, I'll devote my future star-building power to Lotte. She's a dear, dear girl."

"Thanks, W.R.," I said. "I think the two of you will be very happy together. She's so attracted to you."

"I wanted Marion to be attracted to me," he said, "but she obviously prefers the muscles of that WOP, Valentino, to me."

"Lotte doesn't judge a man by his body," I said reassuringly. "She looks for the inner person, not muscles. She's a true woman."

"That's how it should be," W.R. said. "Men are attracted to shapely legs and big bosoms, but women should not evaluate men in physical terms. It's not right."

"I'll put Marion on the phone now," I said, "and I'll retreat from her suite. I want your talk with her to be private, and I don't want to be here."

After promising him I'd see him as soon as he returned to Los Angeles, I retreated to Marion's dressing room where I informed her that W.R. was on the phone.

"Tell the son of a bitch I'm having my hair done," she shouted at me. "If fatso wants to talk to me, he can bloody well call back when I'm free."

She'd been around Charlie long enough to use the word "bloody." I faced her firmly. "This is one call you'd better take. I'll ring up tomorrow. I'm going to a party."

She seemed to sense something in my eyes, and knew instinctively that this was one phone call from W.R. she couldn't put off. As I retreated down the hall to prepare myself for the party with Billy Taylor and Antonio, I heard Marion screaming into the phone at the Chief. Safely inside my own suite, I shut the door, blotting out the phone conversation of what was being said between America's most famous "illicit" couple.

Arriving with Antonio at the bungalow of Billy Taylor, I learned he'd invited us to a party staged by Sessue Hayakawa at a private club called "The Green Jade." When we pulled up in my stagecoach and were invited inside, it was like entering a Chinese opium den.

It was some sort of cult gathering with a lot of young and beautiful boys that ranged from Chinese to Senagalese, from Mexican to the Canadian north woods, and also with a lot of cornfed boys like myself. Many of the older guests, who were clad in red silk kimonos, were heavily painted in shades of purple, scarlet, and magenta. Before entering, each of the teenage boys was given only a brief loincloth to wear.

Regrettably, I am not sure what happened throughout the evening, as I'd never inhaled the sweet smell of opium smoke before, certainly not back at Maria Jane's in Lawrence, Kansas. All I remember is that my eyes became glazed by its effect, and when the actual "rites" of the evening began, I was too far gone to care.

I did recover once to discover Hayakawa licking and sucking my face before he went to my nether regions for greater exploration. He was followed by a long line of cult members who wanted to taste and sample me when they weren't involved with one of the more exotic boys. Only Ramon wasn't at this gathering. After the Arbuckle scandal, he'd decided to be more discreet now that he was a full-fledged movie star.

I do remember that the cult, most of them actors in various Hollywood studios, demanded that each of us swear that we'd turn for "companionship" only to other members of the cult, and that our "solace," other than sex with each other, would be the opium pipe. By then, I was agreeing to anything, having no intention of keeping my pledge. It wasn't a blood oath anyway. This bond we swore was said to be as "old as Sodom."

When I got back to the hotel, shortly before dawn, I found a note Tom Ince had written to me waiting at the desk. "Better look in on Marion," he said. "I dropped her off here but she was acting strange all evening. W.R. has dropped her. She's half crazed."

Even before going to my own suite, I went to Marion's door and pounded loudly, thinking she might be asleep and didn't hear me. When no one answered I went back to my room and called her. No answer.

Back at her suite, I heard music playing from the living room of her quarters and also saw through the transom that the lights were on. I pounded again, and still there was no answer. Trying the door, I found it unlocked.

Invading her private quarters without an invitation, I called out her name. "Marion." There was no sound other than the radio playing "sleepy time" music.

As I passed through the foyer, I peered into the living room. There on the floor lay a nude Marion, her eyes shut as if in death.

*****

Unlike Valentino, Marion's suicide attempt was for real. I feared she'd taken some kind of drug or even poison. After placing an urgent call to Brian Sheehan, I picked Marion up off the floor and tried to walk her around the room. She appeared in a coma and was so lifeless I could hardly support her body.

If the death of Virginia Rappé and the Arbuckle scandal had made headlines around the world, I could just imagine the "second coming" headlines that the death of the world's most famous mistress would generate. W.R. wouldn't be able to suppress that story.

In record time for that era, Brian arrived at Marion's suite with two assistants. He had her body removed to the bedroom where he disappeared with his aides, ordering me to stay outside. The most awful sounds of vomiting and retching came from her bedroom, as I stood paralyzed outside the door, wondering what her fate was. There was no way I could speak to W.R. as he was at that moment on a train heading for Los Angeles.

In what seemed like less than an hour, Brian came out of Marion's bedroom. There was blood on his white shirt. "She's going to live, but she's in a bad way." He went over to the phone and telephoned his clinic, ordering an ambulance sent to the hotel.

"W.R. will chop off heads if this leaks to the press," I said.

"I know that," he said, "and that's why I'm committing Miss Davies to the clinic under an assumed name. My career as a Hollywood doctor will end overnight if I can't cover this up." A sound that was almost like a gurgle came from Marion's bedroom, and Brian rushed in to be at her bedside. When the ambulance attendants came for Marion, I stood aside, as she was taken away to the clinic and seclusion.

At the door when all the staff had left, Brian gave me a quick kiss on the lips. "If anyone calls, tell them that Marion left for San Francisco for a few days. That's a story anybody will believe."

"Thanks, as always, for being here for me," I said, regretting to see him go, as he offered me comfort somehow and I felt dreadfully alone at that moment. For want of anyone else, I went to the telephone to place a call to Tom Ince, knowing he was the last person who'd seen Marion before her suicide attempt. He might give me some clue about her condition in the hours leading up to her attempt to do herself in.

I dreaded W.R.'s arrival in Los Angeles, and wondered how I'd handle that commitment I made for Lotte Lee, who I kept bringing back to life after having, in theory at least, killed her off.

After a reassuring call from Brian that Marion was resting comfortably, "though pale as death," I had breakfast with Tom Ince. In spite of his private habit as a voyeur, he was solid and reliable in all other aspects. All he could tell me was how bitter Marion had been at getting dropped by W.R. She had thought that their relationship would continue until the death of either one of them.

Apparently, W.R. had promised "big things" for her, both in her career and in her private finances. He'd promoted her career, but except for some jewelry the cash had not been delivered. "She feels used and abused after being dropped like this." He told me that Marion also feared that her career would fade once the studio learned she didn't have W.R.'s backing or the free publicity machine generated by his newspapers, which promoted each of her pictures for free.

An hour later Brian called to tell me that Marion's condition was stabilized but that she'd require several days of rest. She was conscious but incoherent. He was cutting her off from all calls until her mental condition was restored.

"So far, W.R. doesn't know about this?" I said.

"To my knowledge, not a thing," he said. "You should meet him at the station. Tell him everything so he'll be prepared if word of this gets out."

After thanking Brian profusely, I hung up, figuring there was nothing I could do for the moment.

Confused and bewildered, I didn't feel in control of my own life. My world seemed to spin around the lives of other people, as if I existed only to respond to a crisis. As if to reinforce my opinion, a call came in from William Desmond Taylor, asking me to come to his bungalow at 404-B South Alvarado Street, an address soon to become famous across America. He said he had also asked Antonio Moreno to come over too. In normal times, this was a sexual solicitation but I sensed there was some major problem brewing. Although he couldn't speak on the phone, I detected a sense of fear in his voice.

At the bungalow, I encountered the young black man, Henry Peavey, who had replaced Edward Sands as Billy's manservant. When I was shown into Billy's library, Antonio was already there.

Billy was on the phone speaking to someone. It later turned out to be his accountant, Mrs. J.M. Berger. I was startled to hear him say, "Look out for my affairs if anything happens to me. I fear the worst."

From the look on Antonio's face, I too feared the worst. When Billy put down the phone, I confronted him. "What in hell is going on?"

"A lot," Billy said in a courtly manner, although he was sweating profusely. Usually even if fully dressed in a business suit on a hot day, he appeared calm. Not this morning. "My man, Peavey, was arrested last night in Westlake Park. The charge is 'social vagrancy,' and I've posted bail for him. But there could be a scandal."

"Let me figure this one out," Antonio said. "You sent Peavey to the park to bring back a hired stud or maybe two for the night."

"A harmless diversion," Billy said. "After all, Westlake Park is where the best looking men—all out-of-work actors—go in California. Usually when I'm a bit horny at night, and one or both of you guys isn't available, I send Peavey up there to secure some fresh meat. This time the best-looking man was a detective. In his report he said that Peavey was acting 'lewd and dissolute.'"

"He didn't tell the police he was pimping for you?" I asked.

"My good man," he said, "for five-hundred dollars Peavey can be very discreet."

"Then the whole thing looks like it'll blow

over," Antonio said. "Peavey might get off completely—three months in jail at the most."

"There's more," Billy said, "a whole lot more." A look of acute distress came over his face. "I haven't been seeing a lot of you chaps lately—it's been one thing after another. But I've called you here today because I trust you as good friends. I am in deep trouble. Trouble so deep I wanted to handle it myself. But I can't. It's too much."

"There was a long silence in the library before any of us spoke. It was Antonio who broke the stillness in the air. "What have you done?"

"I've murdered a man," Billy said. "Edward Sands."

"Your former secretary?" I asked. "I've met him."

"Me, too" Antonio said. "Why and how did you do this?" He said that in a low voice as if he were used to hearing murder confessions as part of his daily routine.

"Close the door." Billy said to me. As I walked over, I noticed that Peavey was sitting in the next room, having removed his sewing from a satchel. He was surrounded by beautiful pillow tops, exquisite doilies, and other crochet work and tatting. I felt he'd positioned himself here to eavesdrop on our conversation.

"I've never come clean about my relationship with Sands," Billy said, "He and I were lovers, as I'm sure you know. His real name is Edward F. Snyder, but he seems to come up with a different alias every week. He constantly reinvents himself. He enlisted in the military seven times, each time under a different name, of course. Four times he deserted and twice he was kicked out. In 1915 when he first enlisted in the Navy at the age of seventeen, he was court-martialed for fraud and embezzlement. I should never have gotten mixed up with that lunatic bloke, but I did and I can't change that now."

Billy sat back in his chair and told us the amazing story of his involvement with Sands. He said that his former secretary had forged checks, illegally drawing money out of Billy's bank account. "He wrecked my car while driving drunk," Billy said. "Twice he's broken in, after I fired him, to steal money and jewelry. The last time he broke in here—it was right before Christmas—he stole much of my good clothing and my entire stock of special gold-tipped cigarettes. He took his time during the last robbery, even cooking a dinner for himself. Each week since that robbery I returned home to find the butt of one of my gold-tipped cigarettes on the front doorstep. That was his way of letting me know that he was out there, and that he could move in on me at any time."

Billy reached into his desk drawer and removed a small handwritten note, which he passed on to me. I glanced at the note. The words were: "I promise to be your servant for life. I will always be your slave. Eternal love, Edward." Without commenting, I passed on the note to Antonio.

"He fell in love with me, but when I swore out a warrant for his arrest for that first robbery, he turned viciously on me and started the break-ins and the intimidation," Billy said. "Several of my neighbors, including Edna Purviance next door, claimed that they had seen Sands standing across the street late at night. Just standing there smoking a cigarette under an electric light and not even bothering to conceal himself. It was as if he wanted someone like Edna to see him and report back to me."

"Oh, shit," Antonio said, handing the note back to Billy. "Sands was a real nut case."

"He broke in here and robbed me again two nights ago," Billy said. He even left another note. This time Billy did not read me the note but picked it up from his desk and read it to us. "It's clearly Sands' handwriting, even though signed Jimmie Valentine. This note says, 'I got your things again this time, but next time I'll get you.' He took more jewelry and clothing."

"Did you think of going to the police?" I asked.

"Not this latest time," Billy said. "I feared it was too dangerous. Sands called me only yesterday morning, demanding $200,000 in blackmail money, which I didn't have. He threatened me. He said if I didn't raise the money at once, he was going to the press and tell everything he knows about my frineds and me. After that Arbuckle thing, the press is hot for more Hollywood scandal."

"Antonio jumped up in his nervousness. "I didn't know a God danmn thing about this. It could have involved me. Sands knew about our affair."

"Sit down, my darling boy," Billy said. "It's been handled. "It's true that Sands did know everything. He had the room next to my own bedroom. I found out that he'd removed a knot from a pine board and could see all the action in my bed. As you know, I like my sex with the lights on so that I can see everything."

Neither of us said anything for a minute. The screech of the wind blowing in from the colder north grew louder, followed by a mutter of rain which came down slowly at first. Billy's tin roof seemed to magnify the sound of the rain. The volume increased until it sounded like torrents raining down on our heads. I knew Billy was leading up to something deadly serious, in spite of his assurance that the "matter" of Edward Sands had been dealt with.

"He saw me go at it with Mabel Normand, Mary Miles Minter, Betty Blayne, Margaret Gibson, Ethel Clayton, Elsie Ferguson, May McAvoy, Myrtle Stedman, Lila Lee. Oh God, you won't believe this. But Sands even saw me fuck a very drunk Jack Pickford one night. Sands knew all about the sex parties, the drug parties. Yes, he saw me fuck you, Antonio, and also Ramon Novarro, a little Hispanic rosebud all of us are very familiar with. He knew about those all-male love cult parties staged by Sessue Hayakawa. For one week, I hid out here banging Mary Pickford. Sands saw it all."

"Billy," Antonio said, "it's been too much. It was bound to go wrong somewhere."

"God damn yes," he said, sitting up tensely in his seat. "Sands once saw a three way I had in my bedroom with Edna Purviance and Thomas Meighan."

"What did you plan to do?" I asked. "Go around to all your movie star friends and try to raise that much money."

"I knew that wouldn't work." Billy said.

"Sands was so mentally unbalanced that you couldn't enter into any agreement with him, and have him stick to it. When I used to go off with a woman—and he told me this months later—he would get insanely jealous and get even. He claimed he'd go into a toilet, piss into a cup, and put that urine in my soup and I was never the wiser. Believe it or not, he once

threatened to kill Peavey when the two of them worked here together for a brief while. I innocently told Peavey that he made the best rice pudding I had ever tasted, forgetting for a moment that Sands viewed rice pudding as his own dessert specialty." Billy reached into his desk drawer again, this time removing a revolver. "I purchased this German Lueger with a shoulder piece when I once lived in New York. I figured if I were heading for the Wild West, it might come in handy."

Antonio's face brightened, as my own stomach turned into a cold knot. "You killed Sands," Antonio said, repeating what Billy had already confessed to. It was said as if stating a matter of fact. It didn't sound like an accusation at all.

"Precisely," Billy said. "It had to be done. I simply couldn't allow Sands to wreck more careers. I couldn't let him turn Mary Pickford's career into another Arbuckle scandal, or destroy the careers of Mabel or Mary Miles Minter. I agreed to meet Sands at a little summer amusement park outside of Los Angeles in the mountains. It was closed for the winter, and I knew the place would be deserted. I told him I had all the money on me. He agreed to this clandestine meeting. I drove out there and, true to his word, Sands was waiting for me. He confessed that the car he drove to meet me in had been stolen so it could not be traced to him. I had him get in my car, and I drove him to a deserted spot along a mountain road about two miles away. He demanded the money. I told him it was in my trunk. I got out of the car and he followed me. Instead of pulling out the first bundle of hundred-dollar bills like he expected, I removed my revolver and shot him up close. When he saw the gun, he cried out, 'Don't, Billy, don't do it. I'll go. Don't kill me. I'll go away. Never bother you ever again.' Those were his last words, and indeed he'll never bother me again. My last memory of him was shouting out those words from cracked, dry lips that will remain forever shut with all his blackmail evidence. He died instantly."

"What did you do with the body?" I asked.

"I dragged it to the edge of a ravine where I attached his arms, legs, and neck to rocks, using some rope I had brought. Then I pushed his body over the edge. It plunged down the cliff and disappeared into the lake."

"It sounds like a movie scenario," Antonio said.

"You're right about that," Billy said. "It was a scene from a film I shot about three years ago—one of those quickies. The name escapes me. It was a case of real life imitating art."

"Sands was a drifter," I said. "No one will even know he's missing. If his name comes up at all, people will assume he's fled Los Angeles for another town. If the body is never found and not traced to you, a sound possibility, you're home free. You may have saved a few careers in Hollywood, especially Antonio's and certainly your own."

"What I don't understand is why you're telling Durango and me," Antonio said. "If you did this thing, why not keep it a secret? Seems to me the less people who know about this, the better."

A frown crossed Billy's features. "I wasn't alone when I went to that remote spot to meet Sands. I was with Mabel Normand."

"Mabel?" Antonio asked, as an incredulous look crossed his face. "Why in hell did you take her?"

"Mabel had raised fifty-thousand dollars on her own," Billy said. "She thought she could talk Sands into settling for that much. She had agreed to go with me and hid on the floorboard in back of my car. She covered herself with a blanket."

"But you didn't let her negotiate," I said in way of a mild protest.

"I left out one thing," Billy said. "When I got to that fun fair, Sands had upped his demands to half-a-million dollars. I realized then there could be no negotiation. Any agreement entered into with Sands would be violated by him the next day. He'd ask every penny that we not only had in the bank, but would make in the future. All of us would be slaves to him for life." He looked over at Antonio. "Would your fans like to think that the great lover of the screen was a secret homosexual?"

"I think Valentino has that honor," Antonio said, growing more uncomfortable by the minute and appearing as if he wanted to escape from the bungalow.

"Mabel did not take part in the killing," Billy said. "But she's trying to take advantage of what she knows. I had quit having sex with her when I learned she might have a venereal disease. To some degree, I've also encouraged her drug-taking. She had dried herself out at a clinic, but she's back on the stuff. As you chaps know, I take a few drugs myself. In my case, it's purely recreational. Mabel, however, is an addict."

"What does she want?" I asked.

"She wants to marry me," he said. "She wants control of my life. She wants me to call Mary Miles Minter and break it off. Break it off with all the women in my life. She even wants me to give up my secret life as a homosexual, and you of all guys know I can't do that."

"Are you giving in to her demands?" Antonio asked.

"I don't know what to do," Billy said. "I'm in deep shit and terribly confused. I want to let you chaps in on what's happened to me. I'm coming unglued. I can't think straight." He looked up at us with large, imploring eyes.

Before either Antonio or I could even begin to try to come up with an answer to that, there was a light rap on the door. Billy got up from his desk and opened the door to discover Peavey standing there. "Mr. Taylor, sir," he said. "A Mrs. Charlotte Shelby is here to see you."

"Fuck," Billy said. "The last person on earth I want to see now is Charlotte Shelby."

About the last person I wanted to see was Charlotte Shelby too. Even though she'd made repeated calls to the Hollywood Hotel, I'd never returned them and had not spoken to her since our last meeting in the hotel bar where she'd gotten drunk.

The idea that I was to "smoke out" Billy Taylor and determine if he were homosexual grew more ridiculous the more I'd thought about it. At any rate, I never planned to tell Shelby what I already knew. Although it had seemed like a good idea at the time, the prospect of dating Mary Miles Minter for publicity purposes to advance my career also appeared more than I could stomach.

"I don't know how to handle this." Billy said in a whisper, "but I'll leave the door open in case you chaps need to come to my rescue. Charlotte has a wild and violent steak in her. You know these swamp bitches from the Louisiana bayou country. They kill alligators and eat their tails for breakfast. She's likely to try to do anything to me. But, first, I'd better find out why she's here. I know I'm not going to like it."

Like some innocent animal, Billy looked back at us as if he were about to be slaughtered, even though he was a killer himself.

*****

Like voyeurs privy to the secret life of William Desmond Taylor, Antonio and I sat in the library listening to the confrontation between Charlotte Shelby and Billy. Even though I'd known that the two of them had had an affair, that lovefest was now at an end and had turned to bitterness.

"You've lied to me from the very beginning," Shelby was telling Billy. "I believed all your lies, including the biggest lie of them all—that you loved me and only me."

"You're a fine filly of a woman," Billy said in his usual courtly manner with women. "I've always lied…" He paused as if caught in a Freudian slip. "What I meant to say was, I've always admired and respected you."

"I heard you the first time," Shelby said. "Cut the bullshit, Taylor, I'm not here to listen to any more of your lies. I've forced the truth from Mary. She's told me everything."

"Everything?" Billy's voice sounded weaker, like a victim about to be shot, one who finally surrenders to the inevitable.

"You might call it the war of the roses," she said.

"What in hell are you talking about, woman?" Billy asked, his voice regaining its strength.

"My Mary uses the same florist you do," she said. "Only this morning she learned that you sent Mabel a dozen American Beauty roses. As an afterthought—no doubt feeling guilty—you sent my Mary only three roses, and not the shop's best ones either. The loveliest flowers of all you reserved for Mabel. The florist told Mary everything."

"That means nothing," he said. "Mabel's recovered from a certain illness."

"Gonorrhea, you mean," Shelby said. "Everybody in town knows Mabel came down with a venereal disease. You could have picked up the disease from Mabel and passed it on to me."

"I'm disease free," he said. "If you don't believe me, you can call my doctor, Brian Sheehan. I was introduced to him by Durango Jones. I'll give you his number."

"That won't be necessary," she said. "I've already been examined. I did not get any filthy disease from you. If I had, I would have known where it came from. I've had no relations with any man but you. You have been the love of my life. Until this morning, I took you at your word that you were going to marry me just as soon as you made a few more films and saved some more money."

"What happened this morning that led you to another opinion about us?" he asked.

"I was eating breakfast with my other daughter, Margaret, when we heard the sound of a bullet going off in Mary's bedroom," Shelby said. "We ran into Mary's room and found her lying on the floor, the gun still in her hand."

"My God, is she dead?"

"She didn't fire my gun—a .38 caliber revolver—into her body but into a wall," Shelby said.

"Was she playing some sick joke on you and Margaret?" he asked.

"Hell, no," she said. "Don't you see—and you're supposed to be so smart. She was crying out for attention. She was warning me that she could easily commit suicide."

"You'd be hard up without your bread winner, wouldn't you?"

"You bastard!" she said. "I could kill you right now if I had my revolver with me. When we got Mary settled down, she confessed that you had broken off with her. That you planned to marry Mabel Normand instead. Until that very moment, I had been the most stupid woman in Hollywood. I did not know you were carrying on with my daughter. I believed you when you said you had only a fatherly interest in her. I was dumb because I loved you. It's true: Love is blind. Now I know you were fucking me just to get close to Mary."

"I detest you," I heard Billy say in a voice completely foreign to him. It was as if some demon lurked inside his body and was now speaking for him. "Do you think for one moment I wanted your tired, old, and used-up body? You and I are about the same age. I like young, sweet girls like Mary. I like Mary's body—the sex with her. But for true love, I gravitate to Mabel. With her, I have great sex and mental companionship too. Mary is just a silly little schoolgirl—nothing more."

For a long moment there was no response from Shelby. "So you're the pervert you're rumored to be," she said. "Nearly everybody in town says what a fine and upstanding gentleman William Desmond Taylor is. So courteous. So gracious. So intelligent. So charming. But then we hear other reports. That he's a secret homosexual. That he attends dope parties. That he's part of an all-male love cult. For the first time, I'm seeing the real William Desmond Taylor. I know now all those rumors about you are true."

"Just what do you plan to do about it?"

No response came from Shelby, and Antonio and I could just imagine the look on her face. Apparently, both Billy and Shelby were standing and confronting each other, not knowing where to go. "My daughter was a virgin before she met you and you ruined her."

"To use your favorite word, that is pure bullshit," he said. "Your precious daughters aren't as innocent as you'd have us believe. When James Kirkwood directed them in that 1916 flicker, *Faith*, he fucked both your daughters."

"That is a damnable lie," she said. "Besides, James is married to Lila Lee and has this thing on the side with Mary Pickford."

"Do you think that being married to Lila Lee and seducing Mary Pickford prevents him from banging Mary and Margaret? You don't know this but your Mary has already had her first abortion. The father? James Kirkwood."

"I will confront Mary with this," she said. "If I find out you're lying, I'll come back here and shoot you for defaming my daughters."

"I'm telling the truth, something you don't know how to face," he said.

At this point we heard someone enter and come in through the front door. "My darling Billy," she said in a warm, loving, even seductive voice. But when she spoke to Shelby, her voice was angry and bitter. "Mother, Margaret said you'd gone here."

I knew at once that Mary Miles Minter had arrived on the scene.

"It's showtime," Minter said. "Time for all of us to come to our senses. I'm the youngest here, a child really, but I've got to supply the adult brains."

"Just what is that supposed to mean, my precious rose?" Billy asked her.

"Did you propose marriage to Mabel Normand?" Minter asked like a prosecuting attorney."

"I think I did," he said.

"You think you did." The same angry voice that Minter had used on her was now directed at Billy. "You know God damn well you asked Mabel to marry you. Hopefully, she'll not be too doped up to stand up straight before the preacher."

"Mabel hasn't accepted my proposal," he said.

"Nor will she," Minter said. "Get Sennett's cow on the phone and tell her the marriage is off. You're marrying me instead."

"Forget it, Mary," he said. "I'm too old for you. You don't know your own mind."

"I know my mind better than you two," Minter said. "I'm determined to force you to marry me—or else you'll face a jail term. I'm a minor."

"You can't prove anything," he said.

"Don't be so sure about that," she said. "I'm pregnant with your child."

There was a long pause, as if each of the unholy trio were digesting that latest bit of information.

It was Shelby who broke the silence. "You can't marry him. You can't have his child. You'll have to have it aborted like you did James Kirkwood's brat."

"How in hell did you find out about that?" Minter asked her mother before apparently turning on Billy again. "You told her, you shit."

"I didn't want Miss Shelby here to think you were as innocent as you pretend," he said.

"You can't have that baby," Shelby said,

"because William Desmond Taylor is not only your lover, he's your father."

Again, a long silence followed this latest startling news, a kind of early radio soap opera. "You're a liar," Minter charged. "You're only saying this to break us up. He's not my father."

"But he is," Shelby said.

Minter confronted Billy. "Could what she says even remotely be true?"

"The timing is right," he said. "We did have this very minor involvement in New York. The year would have been right, but for all we know Charlotte here was involved with a lot of other men. The casual way she picked me up suggests how promiscuous she was at the time."

"You're Mary's father," Shelby said. "You can't marry your own daughter. The child can't be born. It'll be deformed—I just know it."

"I don't think either of you fully comprehend just how determined I am to become the second Mrs. William Desmond Taylor. Get Mabel on the phone. Invite her over later tonight for a farewell talk. Break off your engagement. Tomorrow morning I'm announcing to the press that William Desmond Taylor has proposed marriage to me, and I've accepted."

"The marriage will never happen," Shelby predicted.

I heard Billy placing a call to Mabel. "Is Miss Normand in?" he asked. "Please leave a message for her. Tell her it's most urgent I see her. I want her to call me later. I want her to come by my bungalow."

When he put down the receiver, Minter said, "You've done the right thing. I was going to claim to the press that you raped me one night after I stayed late after you'd directed me in a picture. All the world will believe the sweet-faced and innocent girl with the golden curls, Mary Miles Minter. I am America's princess. I'll tell the press dogs that I was saving my virginal self for a Prince Charming to come along, and you moved in on me and took away my innocence and the one thing I wanted to bring to my marriage—my virginity."

"I believe, my dear, you would actually do that," he said.

Shelby hadn't spoken for a few moments, but when she did, her voice had a determina-

tion to it that was frightening. "It seems there is nothing more for me to say. I've told you the marriage will never take place. Your bastard child will never be born. Apparently, neither of you believe me."

"I have no choice," he said, "but to give in to Mary. I've worked too hard for my career. I can't just abandon it. If the press learns of any of this, this scandal could become bigger than the Arbuckle thing."

"Mary," her mother said, "I'm giving you one last chance. Walk out that door now."

"You don't love me," Minter said to her mother. "You never did. I'm the goose that lays the golden egg. You're interested only in seeing how much of my money you can steal and salt away."

"That's not true," Shelby said. "Of course, I love you. You're my own daughter. I gave up a promising career on the stage for you. I've devoted all the time since to promoting you and your career, forsaking my own."

"You were an untalented actress who couldn't find work most of the time," Minter said. "You devoted your career to me so you could steal my money. And I've made it for you. I've your million-dollar baby. But all that is going to end soon. When Billy marries me, I'm not only turning over the direction of my career to him, I'm turning over my finances as well. After all, he'll be my husband. As for you, mother, I hear there is an opening for a good maid or two down at the Alexandria Hotel."

"Is that your final word?" Shelby asked.

"The last rites, mommie dearest." Minter said. Shelby said no more but Antonio and I heard the door slam.

"You're absolutely certain that you want this?" Billy asked.

"I'm deadly certain," Minter said. "Dump the Normand bitch tonight. In the morning read about my press conference announcing our upcoming marriage. I've got a God damn baby growing inside me, and I need you to get that ring on my finger sooner than later. What would my fans think if they learned their innocent baby girl on the screen—namely this hot mama you see before you—is with child? Out of wedlock too. They'll never know. The baby will be born prematurely. It's about time I started playing more grown-up parts anyway. Only Mary Pickford can remain the little girl until she's seventy. I see myself as the emerging flapper of the screen. A whole new image for me. One you'll create. You did it for Lotte Lee, wherever in the fuck she is, and you can doubly do it for me."

After a certain silence again, I heard nothing else, only another slamming of the door, as she headed out, following in her mother's footsteps.

After she'd gone, Billy joined us in the library. "I assume you heard it all," he said.

"Every last word," I said. "You're wading in shit's creek."

"Without a paddle," Antonio said. "All this and Sands too. It's too much for me. I'm out of here. I don't want to get messed up in all this. It could ruin my career." He turned with a fierce look of accusation on his face. "You've murdered someone. Sands was a worthless scumbag, but you took a human life. Now you're ready to marry your own daughter and have a baby with her." He headed for the door.

Even though Billy called him back, Antonio didn't listen but yelled out to me. "Durango, are you coming with me?"

"Stay with me," Billy said.

"I've got to go," I said in protest, feeling that my heart belonged to Antonio.

Then Billy said those magic words to me: "If you stay with me, I'll make you into the biggest male film star in Hollywood. Bigger than Valentino."

*****

As I sat in his kitchen talking with him, Billy Taylor was edgy, like a man facing impending doom. "For years everything will run along fairly smoothly—for life, that is—and then almost in a twenty-four hour period everything will start to go wrong," he said. "It's like your whole life suddenly comes apart. In many ways, it began with *Vampira*. That film has really tarnished my reputation."

"I'm sorry if I contributed in any way," I said.

"What a fool I was," he said. "We don't need to sell Lotte Lee. A man in drag. I want to make a star out of Durango Jones. I think you can act. You photograph beautifully. Wallace Reid is handsome. So are a lot of other guys, including Antonio himself. Your sex appeal extends to both men and women. I don't know anybody who has met you who doesn't want to take off your trousers and inspect the goodies. I think that very special sex appeal you have will be picked up by the camera. The camera will love you just as much as it did Lotte Lee—maybe more since you'll be Durango Jones. As for your name, I wouldn't change it. Who could forget a name like Durango Jones? It'll look great on a marquee."

After all the career rejection in Hollywood that I'd faced, I was delighted to have such a boost from a respected director. Even so, as he spoke to me I had an ominous feeling he'd never carry through on his promise to make a star out of me. If anything, it seemed like mere bait to get me to stay with him. For some reason, he wanted someone in his bungalow, both Antonio and me.

He was very disappointed that Antonio had walked out on him. "I had thought he was a much more loyal friend than that," Billy said. "Perhaps he was just using me to advance his career." He leaned over the kitchen table, as his lips lightly brushed mine. "You're not here with me just seeing what you can get, now are you?" Fortunately, I didn't have to lie and answer that question. I was sitting at the kitchen table with a murderer precisely because I thought he might advance my career. Actually I wanted to be with Antonio. Even more than Antonio, I wanted to be with Rodolfo. Suddenly, from the kitchen, we heard an urgent knock on the front door.

After Peavey, Billy's black manservant, answered the door, the voice emanating from the living room was a sound I recognized at once. It was Mabel Normand.

Billy got up to greet her, warning me to stay in the kitchen. From the bar in the living room, Peavey made them both cocktails, then left for the night.

Within a few minutes, Mabel began sobbing. She sounded incoherent and heavily drugged, but she clearly was demanding the return of all of her love letters to Billy.

After the first five minutes of hysteria, Billy seemed to have a calming effect on her. She sounded more rational. Of course, from the kitchen I could only imagine the personal and unspoken interchange between these two lovers. It seemed that Billy, for whatever reason, wanted me to be a voyeur to what was taking place between Mabel and him.

"I've mailed the letters back to you," he told her, although he didn't sound convincing.

"I don't believe you," Mabel said. I agreed with Mabel, suspecting that Billy was still hanging on to the letters.

"Why do you want the love letters?" he asked. "All of a sudden?"

"You know God damn well why," she said, her voice growing angrier. "You murdered Sands. How do I know the police won't find the body and trace Sands directly to you. This whole house might be searched. If the police find those letters, I'll be implicated. Even though I didn't kill Sands, I was there. An accessory to murder. With all my other troubles, do you think I need to be tried as an accessory to a murder? Talk about the end of a career. I'm destroying my career fast enough with all these God damn drugs. I don't need to end up in jail too."

"All right," he said. "I did lie to you. I was going to tell you that my man, Peavey, mailed the letters. I was going to tell you that I gave him money for postage. Then I was going to say that Peavey probably dropped the letters in the sewer and spent the money on drink. But the truth of the matter is that I'm keeping the letters. It's my way of buying your silence if anything goes wrong about the Sands thing. I'm a sinking man right now, clutching at anything to keep myself afloat. It's better if I keep those letters and that they are never revealed to the press. I read them again only last night. They're very pornographic. It would be the end of you if they're released. As long as I own them, I'll have your cooperation. Cooperation in this context means keeping your God damn trap shut."

"You bastard!" she shouted at him. "You're blackmailing me."

"We're in this together," he said. "I have no intention of going to the gas chamber for some scumbag like Sands."

"He was your lover," she charged in bitterness.

"I do like kinky sex—it's true," he said. "Even Peavey with his falsetto voice. When I don't have anyone else, I play a few games with my manservant. Mostly S&M crap—shit like that."

"I don't know you at all," she said. "You can be with someone, make love to them, talk pillow talk with them for hours, and still not know them. All these years I've believed the mask you wear before the world. The courtly British gentleman. You're not that at all. You're a cesspool of vice and perversion. I didn't see that clearly until tonight. You took a man's life, and I think you have no guilt about it at all."

"Sands deserved to die," he said. "He was a slimy pervert. A thief. A crook. His entire life was devoted to one blackmailing scheme after another."

"So what?" she asked. "Does that give you the right to become his executioner. Since when did William Desmond Taylor assume the powers of the state?"

"Touché!" he said. "Please don't trouble your pretty head with matters such as this. Sands has been disposed of. I don't think his body will ever surface. He is history. We are living in the present, and there are more urgent matters to attend to."

I shuddered, thinking Mabel was right. Billy was much more cold-blooded than I ever realized. He was a killer. Without any proof, I suspected he had killed a man before. Maybe more than one man. During all those mysterious years he'd disappeared after deserting his wife, something deadly must have happened. Maybe up in Alaska.

As if some magic lightning had struck, I realized that there would be no future stardom for me as Durango Jones—not with William Desmond Taylor directing the show. I wanted out of here, realizing that earlier I should have followed Antonio out that door. Since Billy's bungalow backed up to a rock wall, the only way out was through the front door. I'd have to wait for Mabel to leave before making my own escape.

For all I knew, Billy was psychotic in spite of his reputation as "the nicest man in Hollywood." Nice men did not murder people, even if they were as loathsome as Sands.

"You mentioned urgent matters earlier," Mabel said. "I don't know why you demanded to see me tonight. Actually, I was coming over to see you about an urgent matter of my own."

"Our upcoming marriage?" he asked.

"More about that later," she said. "You're in deep shit, and I don't know if you'll be around long enough to be any pussy's bridegroom."

"You're going to kill me?" he asked with a slight mockery in his voice. "I'm capable of killing a man—and have before. I could even kill a woman if she double-crosses me. But in spite of all her flaws—and God knows she has many—I don't think Mabel Normand is capable of killing anyone."

"I'm not going to do the killing," she said. "But Dirty Diamond is threatening to have you killed. He's made several million running the biggest drug ring in Los Angeles. Last week when you called the police and had one of his pushers arrested on the studio lot, all hell broke loose. The police have been raiding his dope dens across the city, even the Fruitfly."

"Fuck!" Billy shouted. "Now I know I'm in for it. I did it for you. You went to that clinic and you dried out. Now you're back taking dope every day. That's why I had that pusher arrested. I didn't want the future Mrs. William Desmond Taylor to be a damn dope addict."

"Diamond is out to get you, and I think you'd better take his threat seriously," she said. "You use drugs yourself…"

He interrupted her. "Only for recreational purposes like smoking a cigarette every now and then. You're a dedicated user. I'm no dope addict."

"You've made a big mistake," she said, "and I think you'd better hire a bodyguard. Diamond is going after you. You're not safe here. Anyone could slip into this compound, with people coming and going all the time. You even answer the door yourself or leave it unlocked. You sit by your library window at night with the light on. You're clearly visible to anyone who might get out of a car around the block, walk through the courtyard, put a bullet through your head, and then casually walk away."

"Maybe you're right," he said. "Maybe

I'd better take precautions. Now you've got me really scared."

"Sorry to lay double trouble on you," she said, "but our engagement is off. I'm not going to become your wife. I don't want to belong to one man, and I know you'd never be faithful to me either. It just won't work. I could never trust you either. You threatened me with blackmail. I was with you when you killed a man. That's more than I could handle. Frankly, I'd be afraid of you. I actually fear you might kill me to hush me up. And, as I've said, I think your life is in danger."

"You're really turning this into a beautiful evening," he said. "Now I'll discuss my urgent business with you. I asked you here to call off the engagement. I am getting married whether you think I'll be alive or not. I'm marrying Mary Miles Minter. She's with child. My child. She's not the kind of intellectual companion you are, but she is good sex. She's very young, and I like that. You've been around a long time, Mabel. A very long time. At the dawn of the movies. Mary is young and fresh, and the pretty little thing adores me. I think she's going to overtake Mary Pickford at the box office as America's Sweetheart. Her movies are earning more and more every year as her popularity grows. You're in decline. I hate to say this, but your best flickers are behind you."

"May you burn in hell!" she said. The sound of her slapping his face echoed even back to the kitchen where I stood concealed behind the open door. The sound of her footsteps racing through the room and out the door was heard.

"Mabel," he called after her. "I'm escorting you to your limousine. After all, and in spite of what you say, I'm still a British gentleman."

For a paralyzing moment, I stood behind the door, reluctant to come out. I thought I heard the door open and someone come in. Perhaps Billy had returned but I couldn't be sure. Maybe Mabel had come back. Perhaps Peavey had returned as he often did if Billy needed his "services" for the night. I decided to wait until Billy came for me, telling me that it was safe to come out of hiding.

I heard someone come in through the front door as Mabel's limousine drove off. This time the sound was unmistakable. I peeked through the crack in the door, seeing that it was Billy. He was heading for his study, seemingly to answer the phone. "Antonio," he said, "Thank God you called back. I've got to see you. You've got to see me through all this."

Sucking in the air, I headed for his study to join Billy there. In the dim light of the living room, I saw a short figure in a dark overcoat moving to the door of Billy's study.

As I started to scream, I was stopped by the sound of a voice, as high as that of Peavey's himself. "You slimy bastard," the voice said. The gunman had a revolver, and one shot was fired, making a loud sound. "You'll never take her away from me!"

There was no sound from Billy in his study. The figure turned and confronted me in the hallway. I was staring eyeball to eyeball with the murderer. My life flashed before me, as I knew the next bullet was for me. The gunman pointed the revolver toward me, and I felt too paralyzed with fear to run. It was like a movie script—not real at all. Only a miracle could save me now, and that is just what happened.

I stared into a familiar face. The voice behind that face said, "We need never speak of this again." The murderer turned around and fled through the living room, leaving from the still unlocked front door.

It was only after I'd been spared from death did I realize who this mysterious figure was.

Even though disguised in men's clothing, it was the face of Charlotte Shelby.

*****

Even to this day, I find it amazing that Charlotte Shelby did not shoot me on that night of February 1, 1922. It took me years to figure this out, but I think for one moment of brilliant intuition Shelby realized that my dream of stardom was so great that I'd never go to the police and tell them I was in Billy's bungalow on the night of his murder. A potential movie career could be ruined even before it began.

When I inspected the body and saw that Billy was dead, I knew there was nothing I could do for my slain friend now. I had to leave the cottage as soon as possible. Some of the neighbors might have heard the bullet, as it was still early enough in the evening when everybody was awake.

From the phone, I could hear Antonio's voice shouting for Billy, hoping to learn what had happened. Taking out my handkerchief, I picked up the receiver from the floor and placed it back on its hook.

Impulsively I darted to the closet in Billy's bedroom, where I discovered a drag outfit I'd left behind when I was impersonating Lotte Lee. Quickly I slipped on the women's clothing and painted my mouth with a lipstick tube left in the bathroom by one of Billy's mistresses.

I figured if anyone were to be seen leaving the dead man's bungalow, I didn't want it to be Durango Jones. Better Lotte Lee than me. After all, Lotte had the ability to disappear into thin air like an invisible woman.

Dressed as Lotte, I stood over Billy's body. "Good night, sweet prince," I said to him. "We could have made magic on the screen together." With those words, I hurried from the bungalow and out into the courtyard. I feared that someone was staring at me from the house across the way but I didn't look in that direction and also didn't look back as I walked rapidly to the street and my car. I wanted to get as far from Alvarado Street as I could.

I headed for the Hollywood Hotel but before getting there, I stopped in an alleyway in a business district where no lights were on, the stores closed for the night. I removed my Lotte Lee clothing and stuffed the outfit into the garbage can before getting back into my car and heading for the hotel as Durango Jones.

Antonio and I had to talk. The cover-up had begun.

In the days and weeks ahead, in the years and the decades for that matter, the murder of William Desmond Taylor occupied even more headlines than the Fatty Arbuckle scandal.

It was Henry Peavey who discovered the body when he reported for work the next morning. Seeing Billy dead, Peavey had raced out the front door of the bungalow, running up and down the courtyard, shouting: "Murder, murder, murder. They done up and killed Mr. Taylor."

The initial police reports listed Edward Sands as the prime suspect, and a nationwide manhunt was on for Billy's former valet and secretary. Before the first hours of the investigation were under way, rumors spread through Hollywood that Mabel Normand and Mary Miles Minter were also among the suspects. Even Charlotte Shelby's name was mentioned as a possible suspect. Henry Peavey himself was also listed as a suspect, although he told the press "Mabel Normand done it."

Fortunately, before Peavey was questioned, I got in to see him before the police. I remembered how Billy had given him $500 not to implicate him in that arrest on a morals charge in the park. Earlier that morning I had withdrawn ten-thousand dollars. I met privately with Peavey. "As one homosexual male to another," I told him, "it is important that you not inform the police that Mr. Moreno and I were visiting Billy yesterday."

"I understand, kind sir," Peavey said, fingering the money. "This is a whole lot of money. It will buy a whole lot of shut-mouth. Who should I say did it?"

"Anybody," I said. "Not Antonio Moreno! Not Durango Jones!"

Peavey kept his word. Of course, there were other payments made over the years and up until his death. But Peavey never told what he actually knew about the case. He spread a lot of other stories, though. He claimed that "some mystery woman" had visited Billy before his death and before the arrival of Mabel Normand. He said that his master had asked him to stay in the kitchen during that visit and had not confided in him who the person was, even though Peavey said he could hear their muffled voices coming from the study.

There was a search for the missing letters of Mabel Normand. Somehow the knowledge that those letters existed had become known to the press. Perhaps Billy had mentioned them to friends. When the police searched Billy's bungalow, they could find no letters.

Today I can solve that mystery. Once Billy had shown me some of the letters from Mabel. He kept them neatly folded in the top of a dressing drawer in his bedroom. On the night of the murder, I had opened the drawer and removed all the letters, perhaps a total of fifty, and had taken them with me when I'd fled from the bungalow court as Lotte Lee.

One year from the date of the murder, I anonymously mailed the letters to Mabel without a cover note. She must have wondered for the rest of her life who her anonymous benefactor was. Could she possibly have thought that her benefactor was the murderer himself? Or herself as the case may be.

The real murderer, Charlotte Shelby, confronted the press, claiming, "Mary adored Taylor, as a child would her father, and is badly broken up over the tragedy. The friendship between the two was beautiful, and my daughter feels she has lost one of her dearest friends. As for those so-called love letters that have surfaced, from my Mary, they were merely the adoration of a very young teenage girl written to a man almost three times her age."

Although in seclusion and on the verge of a nervous breakdown, a statement was released by Mary Miles Minter. It differed remarkably from the statement her mother had given the press. Minter said, "Mother could never understand how I felt about Mr. Taylor. She really cannot understand just how much he meant to me. She thought, perhaps, that it was only a childish infatuation. She wanted to protect me from my own impetuosity. Finally, Mr. Taylor told me that mother was right, that in justice to me we should not be married until I had an opportunity to have more experience, to grow a little older and really be sure that I knew my own mind. He told me, after all, I was still a girl in my teens while he was a mature man."

Police found a letter from Minter pressed between the pages of one of Taylor's books in his library. In Minter's handwriting, the note said, "Dearest, I love you. I love you. I love you." There were nine little crosses and nine little kisses, plus a big cross with an exclamation point at the bottom of the letter.

That afternoon after talking to her mother, Minter "amended" her previous statement, claiming that her love for Taylor was in the sense of a young girl's love for a "big, strong, and kind man. He was brilliant, courteous, really a charming uncle," Minter said. She denied that she'd ever been engaged to him. She termed as "libel" reports that they'd had a sexual relationship.

When questioned about Minter's involvement with Billy, Peavey drew a blank, except to say that his former employer always "carried a tiny lace handkerchief—a gift from Miss Minter—and that Mr. Taylor used to take out this hanky and kiss it often."

When reporters finally located Margaret Shelby Fillmore, Charlotte Shelby's other daughter, she must have had more than her usual share of alcohol. Staring straight at the press, Margaret said, "This mean woman," meaning her mother, "would cut your heart out for a dime. Charlotte always had a gun in the house. After Taylor was murdered, I asked her where her own gun was. She claimed she'd mailed it to a distant relative in the Louisiana bayou country but that the gun had been lost en route. Charlotte didn't actually tell me she shot Taylor, but what else is a daughter to think? She hated him. She hates all men. She's a man hater—money is her god. She was scared that Taylor would take away her precious Mary and along with my sister, her millions." Shelby called Margaret's charges "ridiculous" and came up with what seemed like a perfect alibi. The veteran movie character actor and close friend of Shelby's, Carl Stockdale, came forward, claiming that he was playing cards at Shelby's apartment at the time the sound of the fatal bullet was heard.

Unlike the other cast of characters in the murder, Stockdale did not change his story until the day he died. Years later I learned from a Stockdale relative, who wanted to sell some information when I was a Hollywood gossip columnist, that a copy of a check had appeared in Stockdale's possessions. Four days after Billy Taylor's death, Stockdale, a relatively impoverished actor, had deposited $100,000 in his bank account. The source of this unexpected wealth was never investigated or revealed.

Stockdale faced the press and the grand jury, maintaining his story that he was with Charlotte all night on the date of the murder. "Find Edward Sands," he told the press later, "and you'll find who murdered William Desmond Taylor."

When Mabel finally faced the press, she denied any love affair. Her words were, "If I had been engaged to marry Mr. Taylor, I would be only too proud to acknowledge it." A reporter noted that her voice wavered and broke when she spoke of her murdered mentor. "I loved Mr. Taylor as a good comrade—a pal with whom I could discuss subjects in which we were both mutually interested."

When charges later surfaced that Billy might have been the member of an all-male cult whose members smoked opium, Mabel again faced the press. "My opinion is that Mr. Taylor was murdered for a motive of revenge, but just why someone would seek vengeance is beyond my comprehension. Never in his conversations with me had he spoken of any enmity between him and others. And I never should have suspected it, as he was the type that seemed to make everyone a devoted friend. Mr. Taylor was of irreproachable morals, a typical gentleman, who seemed incapable of stooping to things of the questionable or dishonorable sort. To me he was always a kindly adviser in my efforts to improve myself. To everyone who knew him, he was an inspiration to the nobler and loftier things of life."

Since Charlotte Shelby's other daughter, Margaret Shelby Fillmore, had been speaking defiantly to the press, it was rightly assumed that her grand jury testimony would also be damaging to her mother. It was. Reporters were gleeful.

Margaret claimed that her mother was not at home playing cards with Carl Stockdale, as both had testified. Margaret said that her mother had left the house around six o'clock expressing fear that her daughter, Mary, was about to run off and get married to William Desmond Taylor. "Not if I can help it," Margaret quoted her mother as saying.

Margaret also testified that contrary to the statement of her sister, Mary Miles Minter, that she'd been home all evening on the night of the murder, Mary had actually been gone until midnight and refused to reveal where she'd been upon her return. "I saw her come in," Margaret said. "She was in tears and rushed up to her bedroom and bolted the door behind her."

Margaret also revealed for the first time to the public that her sister wasn't the innocent, virginal girl as depicted in her many screen roles. Margaret testified that in 1916, Mary's director, James Kirkwood, had taken Mary into the woods and performed a mock marriage ceremony, declaring that he was married to Mary

Miles Minter in the eyes of God. "Sexual relations followed," Margaret claimed. "Mary became pregnant and had to have an abortion."

False leads and witnesses continued to come forth, including Billy's next door neighbor, Edna Purviance, who claimed she was out on a date that night with Thomas Meighan and didn't return home until midnight. She said she noticed a light on in Taylor's study. "That was not unusual," Purviance said. "Billy often read until the wee hours. He always burned the midnight oil."

Mabel Normand, the accessory in the Sands murder, must have been startled to read press reports of the testimony of Claire Windsor, the beautiful motion picture star. She claimed Taylor had told her, "I'm going to kill Sands if I ever lay hands on him. He's robbed me for the last time." Windsor testified that Taylor made this statement at the Ambassador Hotel.

Regrettably, she claimed that Antonio Moreno was there and had heard Billy make the threat against Sands. Antonio, according to Windsor, was accompanied by Betty Francisco, also an alleged witness to Taylor's death threat. Francisco was another pretty little blonde motion-picture star that Antonio was dating at the time, hoping to keep up his macho image before his public.

When police caught up with Francisco, she admitted to being at the Ambassador but claimed that Claire Windsor was mistaken. "I did not see Taylor that night. Nor did I hear him make any death threats. He was a kind and gentle man. I'm sure he would harm no one."

The most potentially damaging eyewitness, Mrs. Douglas MacLean, came forward. She was the winsome wife of the cinema star, Douglas MacLean. Her testimony was confused, as she claimed she'd been waken by the sound of a bullet going off. She said she'd been alone in her living room and was knitting after dinner but must have fallen into a brief catnap. "I looked out my living room window and saw a man in a dark overcoat leave from Taylor's bungalow. At least I thought it was a man. But the sinister figure didn't walk like a man. I'm a very intuitive person, and I sensed it might be a woman dressed as a man. I'm basing that entirely on the way this person walked. It was a woman's walk."

"The figure paused briefly under an arc lamp and didn't seem to know where to go at first," Mrs. MacLean said. "I felt the person was disoriented and was suffering some sort of trauma. As I said, I'm a very intuitive person. It definitely wasn't Sands. I knew Sands very well when he worked for Taylor. The figure wore a gray plaid cap. His or her neck was muffled with something—perhaps a coat collar. My husband was upstairs trying to keep warm by a little electric stove we sometimes use. It was a very chilly night—extremely cold, in fact, for Los Angeles. He might have been listening to the radio or something. He didn't hear a bullet fire."

When asked why she didn't call the police, Mrs. MacLean added, "The bungalow court faces a hill, and automobiles often climbing the grade backfire. What I heard was just such a noise."

Mrs. MacLean delivered the report of yet another sighting. "I saw this tall woman leaving Taylor's bungalow about twenty minutes later and after the first figure in the overcoat. I don't know the color of her hair because she'd placed a scarf around her head. She wore dark glasses, which seemed very unusual because it was an especially black night. The moon wasn't out. She appeared at least six feet tall and wore a trench coat. It didn't look like a trench coat a woman would wear but one Mr. Taylor would wear himself. On seeing her, I felt he'd loaned her the coat because the night was cold. I think this woman sensed that I was looking out through my living room draperies at her. She didn't seem alarmed, nervous, or startled in any way. In fact, I remember her turning back toward the living room and calling out something to Mr. Taylor, perhaps wishing him good night."

That piece of testimony Mrs. MacLean added for her own reasons. Perhaps that's how she remembered the incident. I didn't look back at all but continued on my way.

"I saw her turn into the walk between the houses and disappear," Mrs. MacLean testified. It was very dark. The walk leads to another street, where persons on that side of the court usually park their cars, I thought nothing more of it, especially since I'd seen the woman call back and bid her host good night."

I finally felt that Mrs. MacLean had exaggerated the casualness of my departure and that farewell not delivered to explain why she didn't call the police. "In fact," she said later, "I thought no more of the matter, deciding it was the backfire of a vehicle after all. It wasn't until the next morning when we heard the screams of Mr. Taylor's manservant, Peavey, that I brought up the subject at all. I remembered the man—or woman—in the overcoat followed by the taller woman in the trench coat."

As a final *adieu* to reporters waiting outside the jury room, Mrs. MacLean, accompanied by her actor husband, faced the press with this statement. "If the last woman who left Taylor's bungalow, the tall one, was a murderer, I simply cannot believe it. She acted so natural. A person committing murder would hardly act natural, would they? It is simply beyond human belief."

Each new day reporters had to come up with a different angle. On the fourth day there were reports of a pink silk lace-trimmed nightie uncovered in Taylor's bedroom. It bore the initials MMM. Billy had told me that he liked to collect women's lingerie, and even admitted that on some nights when he was alone he liked to dress in the lingerie of his conquests. Even Lotte Lee had left him some of her silk panties with her initials, LL.

Until I read of the pink nightie discovered, I was under the impression that all of the lingerie had been stolen by Sands during his last robbery in the bungalow. It didn't take the press long to figure out that the initials MMM on the silk matched those of Mary Miles Minter.

All thought of lingerie and my potential involvement in the scandal disappeared as Antonio and I attended the funeral. Some ten-thousand persons, mostly women, showed up at St. Paul's Pro-Cathedral. It was a mass of humanity, which extended far from the church doors across Olive Street and even overflowed into Pershing Square.

A squad of police officers, some of them mounted, tried to restrain the massive horde. Many stars of the industry, including the heretofore secluded Mary Miles Minter, attended. I spotted Constance Talmadge but I knew there were many other stars as well. Escorted by seven men, Mabel Normand made an appearance but she was so hatted, veiled, and furred that her features were entirely obscured.

Only one-thousand invited guests were allowed inside. Antonio and I had seats in the second row. Angry crowds outside stormed the church doors to gain admittance, and the police had to use force to hold them back. Boys were perched on lampposts to get a look, and some men climbed trees for a view. The police told the press later in the day that this was the largest gathering in the history of California for the funeral of a private citizen.

All the notables in the industry sent floral tributes, even William S. Hart. The entire front of the chancel was but a solid mass of blossoms. The largest wreath—a mountain of roses—was a gift of Mabel. Minter sent Black Prince roses, and Lila Lee, his longtime friend, sent a shower of pink roses. Tom Ince weighed in with a cross of pink roses and orchids, and Antonio and I contributed a wreath of lilies and orchids. I even spotted my one-night stand Charles Ray, at the funeral, along with Mr. And Mrs. Douglas MacLean, who lived in the bungalow across from Billy.

A British flag was draped around the open casket, and the February sun shone brightly in through the windows, even though the winds kept the day chilly. There was only a hint in the air that spring would come. A stray beam found its way through a bit of ruby-red stained glass in the chancel window. It bathed the bier in a mist of shimmering colored light.

The last person to arrive before the ceremony began was Henry Peavey, who was sobbing and supported on the arms of a white male friend. Peavey took one look at the masses of flowers, one glance at the gleaming cross on the altar, and burst into hysterics. His body shaken with grief, he threw himself on the coffin as if he wanted to reclaim the body of his dead master. Two ushers had to pull Peavey off, as tears ran unrestrained down his cheeks.

Outside we heard that the police were calling for reinforcements. The crowd was out of control, and at first there was a panic among the mourners that an unruly mob would break into the church.

As the sounds of a threatening horde could be heard outside, the organ began a slow, solemn dirge. The crowd still clamored for admittance. So much noise was made I could not hear the notes of the organ. Dean William MacCormack, standing high in the pulpit, presided at the funeral. A male quartet, their voices clear and melodious, filled the church with the sounds of, "The night is dark and I am far from home." After they'd finished MacCormack delivered a beautiful and impressive service of the Episcopal Church for the burial of the dead. After pledges of eternal life, mourners slowly marched out.

As Antonio and I filed out, we stopped briefly to take a final look at our departed friend. Although she'd collapsed in a church pew earlier, Mabel Normand had regained her composure by the time she marched pass the coffin.

A company of Scottish bagpipers in full regalia, from caps to kilts to short stockings, emerged. A bugler had been supplied by the commander of the British warship, *Calcutta*, anchored at the port of Los Angeles. These British servicemen had appeared to honor Billy's term of duty in the British army.

It was all the bluecoats could do to clear a path through the rapidly growing mob. After some battle and a lot of women fainting, the funeral cortege set off, moving slowly south on Olive Street. On each side of the hearse walked the pallbearers, many composed of Lasky studio executives.

At one point Peavey ran in front of the funeral hearse, throwing himself on the pavement near the wheels as if he wanted the limousine to run over him. The chauffeur braked in time to save Peavey's life. Police escorted Peavey away. Antonio and I in another car finally arrived at the Hollywood Cemetery, site of the burial. Cars seemed parked a mile in each direction. Someone had brought Billy's canvas-backed director's chair to be buried with him.

As the cold afternoon breeze wafted across the cemetery, the final words were said for William Desmond Taylor who became more famous in death than he was during his lifetime. After the spectators had viewed the body for a final time, three volleys were fired by a British military squad, as the bagpipes sounded their mournful refrain. Then the bugler placed his instrument to his lips and sounded "taps," the last call of the military day. The notes reverberated through the graveyard, as hundreds walked away from the cemetery in hushed silence.

Retreating with Antonio back to the Hollywood Hotel, I was stopped in the lobby by two detectives from the Los Angeles police department, the same detectives that a drunk John Gilbert had once summoned to report Lotte Lee missing.

The head detective requested a private meeting with me. Antonio excused himself, telling me he'd meet me later in the bar.

"Not so fast, Mr. Moreno," the detective said. "I like your movies very much but we want to ask you some questions too."

"We sure do," the other detective said, "I understand you were speaking on the phone with Taylor when he was shot. I also understand that you heard him make death threats against Sands at the Ambassador Hotel."

Antonio sighed as we went upstairs to my suite to be questioned by police. The one thing he dreaded, getting involved in the Taylor murder case, was about to happen.

But when we got inside the suite, the detectives put off questioning Antonio. They first had a question for me. One of the detectives reached into a gift box and pulled back tissue paper, removing a pair of silk panties with the initials LL.

"Surely these could only belong to Lotte Lee," he said, holding up the incriminating evidence before me.

"Lotte's traveling in Europe right now and has been for weeks," I lied. "I buy all her lingerie. Those are not Lotte's lingerie. I'm sure they belong to someone else. My sister was never involved intimately with Mr. Taylor."

"I know he fucked a lot of other actresses in Hollywood," one of the detectives said. "But what other actress in pictures has the initials LL?"

Without thinking, I blurted out, "Lila Lee."

*****

It was not my intention to get Lila Lee in trouble, and she was, in fact, never questioned by the police. I met with her and told her what I'd done, and she quickly forgave me, claiming that she had had only a one-night stand with William Desmond Taylor. "He begged me to give him a pair of my drawers," she said, "but I don't think I had my initials on them. Unlike Mary Miles Minter, I don't like to leave that kind of evidence when playing around. I'm more the sneaky type, like Mary Pickford."

After leaving Lila, I went to the train station to meet W.R., who had returned from the coast. He was eager to face two daunting challenges—the news direction of the William Desmond Taylor murder case and a reunion with Marion.

On those lonely miles across the plains of the American West, W.R. had decided to forgive Marion, fearing he could not live without her. He showed me a $75,000 emerald ring he'd purchased for Marion for their reunion. He said he was planning an enormous banquet for the elite of Hollywood, inviting some 160 guests, of which I'd be included.

"We've got to talk about Marion," I said, proceeding to tell him everything that had happened. On hearing of her attempted suicide, he directed his chauffeur to take us at once to the hospital clinic. His face was ashen when he confronted Dr. Brian Sheehan who immediately assured him that Marion was in good condition.

In her private hospital room, W.R. rushed to Marion's bedside and kissed her on the lips, presenting her with the ring. Before saying anything to him, she held the ring up to the light. "Sure looks like an expensive one, W.R."

"You deserve so much more," he said.

She appeared in marvelous health, not the zombie-like ghost I'd walked around her suite in the Hollywood Hotel, trying to keep her alive. She called me and planted a light kiss on each cheek. "You were there for me," she said in a soft, almost sexy voice, "and I'll always be grateful."

"And so will I," W.R. said, looking first into Marion's eyes, then at me. "But my gratitude doesn't extend to you sharing this private moment with my gal and me."

"Of course," I said, excusing myself. At the door I paused, looking back. "I must see you as soon as you're free," I said to W.R. "I've got some news to report to you that is so explosive it's meant for your ears only. I'll wait outside." With that, I was out the door, shutting it behind me.

I have always believed that I knocked an hour or two off the reunion time with Marion and W.R. As much as he wanted to make up with Marion, the news hound dog in him wanted to hear what I had to reveal as his paid informant. In less than an hour, I was waiting in the hospital room. Actually before that I'd sneaked into Brian's private office for a reunion all my own. I loved those sessions. What I found uncomfortable was when he proposed marriage to me after one of our little get-togethers. I loved Brian dearly, but after that one adventure with Rodolfo in the cottage behind Elizabeth Hutchison's house, I was not ready to settle down with anyone—that is, except with Rodolfo. But the chances of our living together in a rose-covered cottage and remaining faithful to each other appeared more remote as the days went by. Presumably he was still on the east coast visiting with Natacha Rambova. I'd heard nothing from him, and it appeared that he'd completely forgotten about me.

Meeting up with me in the corridor, presumably after he'd fucked Marion and Brian had fucked me, W.R. seemed in particularly good spirits. I suspected his impotence had been cured. I always felt that W.R. and Marion liked to stage mini-dramas with each other to keep up a little sexual tension between them. I think she deliberately flirted with other men to make him jealous. If he could count on her to be at home every night knitting, even when he had to go back east on business, W.R. might lose interest in her. He'd married Millicent, a very dependable wife and the mother of his sons. She was always there for him when her errant husband came back home. W.R. at least in my view, wanted more excitement from his mistress, Maid Marion.

W.R. ordered his chauffeur to drive us into the Hollywood Hills. Instinctively he knew I had something to tell him that went beyond mere Hollywood gossip, which titillated him. In the back of the limousine, which was soundproof, the chauffeur "sealed off" in front, W.R. and I said nothing for the first fifteen minutes. It was as if he wanted to remember every detail of his reunion with Marion before donning his newsman's hat. Finally, it was W.R. who broke the silence. "Give me some red meat, boy."

In a low voice, I confided in the Chief a limited preview of the details of the William Desmond Taylor case, including my own involvement in it and that of Antonio Moreno's. I knew W.R. would protect us. For the first twenty minutes or so, everything I told him was the truth. But from that point on, I became an accomplished liar, either editing what I told the Chief or completely falsifying what had actually happened.

As we continued our drive into the hills, I had decided which information to conceal from him and which data to distort completely. First, I had no intention of telling him that Billy Taylor had killed his former secretary, Edward Sands, and that Mabel Normand had been along for the ride. That story W.R. would have hawked around the world in headlines usually reserved for the announcement of a world war. Such a revelation would not only lead to Mabel's arrest but would involve Antonio and me. His mere involvement with Billy would destroy Antonio's career which—potentially at least—loomed big for the Twenties.

I did tell W.R. that Antonio and I had visited Billy on the day of his murder, and I reported on the conversations I had heard from Mary Miles Minter, Charlotte Shelby, and Mabel herself.

I told the Chief of Billy's plan to marry Minter and his breaking off of his secret engagement to Mabel who was becoming increasingly drug-addicted. What I left out was that Minter was pregnant and that Billy was the father. While on the subject of withholding information, I also didn't reveal that Shelby had told Billy that he was not only the father of Mary's unborn baby but her own father as well. That, I feared, was far too explosive a piece of information to give to a yellow journalist like W.R.

Like a movie scenario writer, I confided in him that I had left Billy's bungalow shortly after Antonio's departure to get my sister, Lotte, who was waiting nearby in a parked car. I claimed that I'd taken Lotte to visit Billy and had waited for her in my car parked discreetly around the block, while she'd gone inside to see Billy.

"Why did Lotte want to see Taylor?" W.R. asked.

"They had had a brief affair when he was directing her in *Vampira*," I said. "She wanted to break it off. She went there to tell him that she had fallen for another man and wanted to end their relationship completely."

W.R. settled back into his seat. "This is getting too close to home," he said. "What you're telling me is for our ears and only our ears. It must never be known that Lotte visited Taylor in his bungalow."

"You know that Doug MacLean's wife spotted a second person leaving the bungalow," I asked.

"Of course, I do, my boy," he said. "After all, I read my own newspapers. But if Lotte gets mixed up in this thing, my own name might pop up. I'm sure you know that Lotte was there breaking up with Taylor so that she could devote her life to me. I'm the man she's in love with."

"Well, then," I said in my most reassuring voice, "no one needs to bring Lotte into this thing at all."

"I have my own problems with women," he said in his squeaky voice, which was so low I could hardly hear him. "I think I'm over-committed in the female department."

"What do you mean?"

"I made Lotte the offer to become my mistress," he said. "At the time I sincerely believed I was dumping Marion. But I've had a change of heart. As you could tell from that hospital scene, Marion and I are back together again."

"That's obvious," I said, "but don't sell Lotte short. She's a lot smarter than you think. She figured there would always be some link between Marion and you. She knows she can't hold onto you exclusively."

"Do you think I've broken her heart?"

"You'll break her heart unless you agree to a compromise," I said.

He looked startled, as if not comprehending what I was saying. "I'm not following you."

"Lotte told me she'll happily settle for just a small slice of your life, even a little piece of the pie."

"She said that?" he asked, his face brightening at this flattery.

"She not only said that, but wants me to propose a way out of all this?"

"How could it work?" he asked.

"You're on the East Coast a lot," I said. "Naturally, you visit Millicent and your sons at your home there. But I understand that you no longer share Millicent's bed."

"You've got that right," he said.

"Lotte wants to continue to see you whenever you might be available," I said. "You don't take Marion to New York with you. Maybe Lotte can meet you in New York when you're not with Millicent and the boys."

"I think I'd like that," he said. "I need female companionship. I miss Marion when I'm back in New York. I'm always wondering what she's up to. I need to be with a woman."

"Why not make it Lotte?" I asked. "She's in love with you. It would make her so happy to share just a small amount of your time."

"It would mean a lot to her," he said, stating it as a fact instead of a question.

"Will you go for it?" I asked. "I've got to tell her something."

He reached for my hand. Not knowing that it was the same hand as Lotte's, he squeezed it real hard. "If Lotte is understanding about my reunion with Marion, I think she'll be understanding about all the other complications in my life."

He still held onto my hand as I looked into his eyes and told him, "She said to let you know that she's there for you any time of the day or night. She needs you. If you need her, she'll come to you right away. In fact, she even went so far as to say that there will be no other men in her life if you want her—even if it's only part-time."

"I'm flabbergasted," he said. "This is beautiful news for my ears. Of course, I can't promote Marion as a star and tout Lotte as a star too. Marion would never let me do that."

"You won't believe this, but Lotte is the only woman in the world who doesn't really want to be a movie, star," I said. "She tried that once and hated it. She wants to lead a private life. Devoted to inner peace. You know some women like to stay at home, grow flowers, work with children, stuff like that. But mainly Lotte wants to be private, lost in her inner world. Reading books, stuff like that."

"How unlike Marion," he said. "How unlike most of the women I know in my life. I'm sorry I can give so little of myself to Lotte, since I know how much she cares for me."

He settled back into the luxuriously upholstered seat of his limousine, and for a long time didn't say anything, as his chauffeur drove aimlessly through the hills. Finally, he spoke. "You're still on my payroll, aren't you?"

"I sure am," I said. "I hope you're not firing me."

"Not at all," he said. "I've been fascinated by the information you've told me today. Except you overlooked one point."

A sudden panic came over me. I feared in my lies I'd been caught. "What's that?"

"Did Lotte actually see the killer?" he asked.

"No, she was in another room," I said. "She heard a voice. It was a man's voice. She can't be sure but she suspects that Edward Sands, Taylor's former secretary, killed him."

"I think that is what happened too," he said. "I've just learned from my newsroom that the police haven't a clue as to where Sands is." Almost prophetically, the Chief added, "for all I know Sands could be dead, considering the life he's lived. Theft. Drugs. Robbery. Blackmail. Forgery. Perhaps Sands fucked over the wrong person who could have easily bumped him off. He's had so many different names his body might have been found somewhere and buried as a John Doe."

W.R. leaned forward and ordered through his speaker that his driver return him home. "I want to see Lotte in a few weeks when I go back to New York. Please make all the arrangements for me."

"That I will do," I said. "It will make her so happy. Lotte doesn't know New York at all."

"She'll be taken care of beautifully," he promised. "I have this secret apartment on Fifth Avenue. It's very luxurious. I'll install her there. Open charge accounts for her so her wardrobe can stay in fashion. Give her permission to redecorate. Stuff like that. You know how women are."

"I don't know how women are," I said. "I

don't know much about women at all."

"Oh," he said, frowning for a moment. "I forgot. You don't know what you're missing, boy. I can at least intellectually understand male-to-male bonding, but—and you must forgive my crudeness—there's nothing quite like pussy. A man can become addicted to it. But Lotte has taught me another means of sexual expression. As I get older, I think I enjoy that even more."

Back at the California home of W.R., he ushered me into his private library. "Marion wants to stay in the clinic for another two nights," he said. "I think she enjoys the rest and attention she's getting there. It's fine with me, because I have a lot of work to do." He ordered one of his servants to bring us both a glass of milk. "I want you to spend the night here. I feel a bit out of sorts. A little lonely. I'll enjoy the company."

"And I'll enjoy being with you," I said.

"Let's order us some dinner," he said, calling his servant again and placing an order for *Tafelspitz*. "That's really boiled beef," he said. I developed a liking for it in the Teutonic countries. When I was in Austria at a spa, I learned that it was the favorite dish of Franz-Josef, the Austrian emperor."

Over the boiled beef dinner with horseradish and tiny new potatoes—the rich always like baby vegetables, as Truman Capote was to observe years from now—W.R. leaned back in his chair and stared at me intently. At first I feared he'd discovered another loophole in my story about the murder of Billy Taylor.

"I understand you know this Italian actor, Valentino," he said. "At least you know him well enough to know Marion is having an affair with him even though I was told that the Dago's heart belongs to nobody except himself."

"I do too," I said. "I hope you didn't confront Marion with the Valentino indiscretion I told you about."

"Not at all," he said. "Nor do I intend to. Some information I like to hold close to my heart and not let the other party know what's going on. Take the Valentino case, for example. I want you to go to see him in New York, or wherever he is. I have a message for him."

"What's that?" I asked, a bit apprehensive. "Tell him he can see Marion at dinners, at

parties," he said. "When San Simeon is ready, I'll even invite Valentino up for a weekend. Everything will go on as usual. With one big difference." He paused a long moment before making his point. "If he ever touches Marion again in a sexual way, I'll see that he goes to the gas chamber."

"I don't understand," I said. "You mean you'll have him killed."

"No, the state will do that for me," W.R. said. "Valentino is a murderer. There is no statue of limitations on murder."

I didn't know what to say. At first it appeared to be an irresponsible accusation. W.R. detected the skepticism on my face.

"Come back into the library with me," he said, getting up from the table. Shaken, I trailed him into the library where he went to his desk and removed a red folder, which he handed to me. "Just read the first page. Everything is summarized on the first page. The other fifty pages are mere details."

Sitting down on the edge of my seat, I read the report prepared by a New York detective. It was a case I was vaguely familiar with, stemming from the day I'd confronted that New York blackmailer, Frank Stevens, who'd paid a threatening visit to the rose-covered cottage I shared with Rodolfo back when I'd first arrived in Hollywood.

Stevens had been the first to reveal to me the lurid headlines generated in New York by the de Saulles case. I knew that Rodolfo had been involved and was forced to flee from New York after Mae Murray had bailed him out of trouble with a gift of $1,000. But this was the first time I'd heard that anyone was actually accusing Rodolfo of murdering Jack de Saulles himself.

The report W.R. presented to me detailed what really happened in that notorious murder case in New York, in which Bianca de Saulles, a South American beauty, had reportedly shot her socially prominent and wealthy husband, Jack, as he was moving ahead with divorce proceedings against her. Rodolfo had been Bianca's lover at the time. The report claimed that it wasn't Bianca who had killed her husband, but Rodolfo who had fallen in love with her, even though he'd met her while still a gigolo.

"How can you be sure?" I asked.

"There is enough evidence there to convict Valentino," W.R. said. "Three or four people were aware of Bianca's scheme. Apparently her lips were used for something other than cocksucking. The little Spanish *puta* talked a lot. She took too many people into her confidence. No one will ever get to the bottom of the de Saulles case. There's enough behind the scenes crap here to write a book. But the police believed at the time they had enough evidence to bring Valentino to trial. I was in New York when the story broke, and I remember putting my men onto it. As a good newsman, I knew there was some cover-up going on. But after a few lurid headlines, I never bothered to follow up on the story because some other scandal broke that was even hotter. I dropped the de Saulles thing like a hot potato."

"You mean this case against Rodolfo could be reopened at any time?" I asked.

"It could indeed," W.R. said, "unless Rodolfo stops fucking Marion. "Mysteriously the original case against Rodolfo was dropped, and I know why. Money exchanged hands. In my view Norman Kerry is just a two-bit matinee idol out here on the coast, but he's politically well connected in New York. He is friends with the governor. Kerry, from what I've learned, had fallen in love with Valentino in New York. So I can now add Valentino to my list of homosexuals. I once said Valentino and Wallace Reid were the only known heterosexuals in Hollywood, other than myself, of course. How wrong I was."

"Let me understand this," I said. "You want me to go to New York and confront Rodolfo with this evidence. You want me to warn him that unless he drops his affair with Marion, you will personally intervene and get the case reopened."

"Exactly," he said, learning back and staring intently at me. "On second thought, I'll even make it easier for you. I'll have my men track down Valentino at the house of Natacha Rambova's parents. I'll see that he'll arrive at your new apartment on Fifth Avenue at an agreed upon time. You won't have to do anything but be there when he shows up and present him with the evidence."

Eager to see Rodolfo at any cost, I agreed to do that and immediately thought of my wardrobe. Since I didn't want to be Lotte Lee all the time, I asked W.R. if I too could use the apartment with my sister.

"Like your own home," he said. "In many ways, I feel closer to you than I do with Lotte herself. At least I see more of you, and you've been a great help to me. The abortion thing. The suicide thing. Stuff like that must never make the papers. I can keep shit like that out of my own papers, but I don't control the world's press."

After W. R shook my hand and sent me off to bed, he said he'd wake me up at eight o'clock in the morning for breakfast as he had to get to work. Sometime during the night I recalled very vividly that time in the tent at San Simeon when W.R. had come into my room and sat staring at my nude body. Although I couldn't be sure it was what was wanted and needed, I felt that when W.R. entered my room at eight o'clock I would be feigning sleep and putting on a show for him.

My instincts had been right. My eyes were closed and my dick had risen to its impressive full measure when I heard the door slowly open at eight o'clock that following morning. I must have looked like Sleeping Beauty lying there with the sheets off my nude body, my dick reaching up to the heavens. I could hear W.R. breathing beside my bed as I continued to pretend I was asleep.

A good twenty minutes must have gone by, and at that age I maintained my erection for every second. The very fact that the Great W.R. Hearst himself was sitting there eying me was a real turn-on. Maybe like Rodolfo himself, I too was a bit of an exhibitionist.

Feeling I'd played this game long enough, I slowly and sleepily opened my eyes to stare into the kindly face of W.R. "I hope you don't mind," he said, "but I've been taking a bit of advantage of you, staring at you and invading your privacy."

"Feel free," I said. "I'm your boy. I'll do anything you want."

"My requirements are very simple," he said. "I'm fascinated at seeing an erect penis. In fact, until I met you I didn't know cocks got that big when hard. I've seen men in the nude before, but never a cock fully hard, other than my own. If anything, it's disconcerting. I fear Marion will sample cocks bigger than mine. Perhaps Charlie's is bigger than mine. I'm sure that Italian stallion, Rodolfo, has a bigger one."

"Lotte told me you were just right for her," I said. "She said if you were any bigger, she'd choke."

He smiled, then chuckled softly to himself. That report from Lotte really pleased him. My hard-on was slowly deflating as we talked.

"I have a simple request to make," he said.

"Anything for the Chief."

"Please let me watch you in the bathroom," he said. "I've never viewed a man conduct his private business while getting ready for a day. Let me see you shave. Take a morning piss. Get ready. Put on your underwear. Your trousers. That's all I ask. Just see what a man normally does."

"Consider your request granted."

W.R. was true to his word. I even pissed proudly before him. There was no sexual come-in. He'd meant what he'd said. He just wanted to watch.

Arriving back at my hotel, and planning to see Charlie later in the day, I began to make plans for New York. I was very excited. It would be today's equivalent of a kid going to Disney World for the first time.

Wallace Reid had gone to New York to make a picture, and I could join him there too—that is, when I wasn't with Rodolfo.

A call came in. I went to answer hoping it might be John Gilbert, Theodore Kosloff, Tom Mix, Richard Dix, William Boyd, or possibly the newly emerged star, Ramon Novarro.

"It was a woman's voice. "This is Mary Miles Minter," she said softly as if on the verge of tears. "My mother, Charlotte, said I could trust you."

"What can I do for you?" I asked. "I love your pictures so much, I'd be honored to assist you in any way."

"We've heard through the grapevine that you are very good friends with one Dr. Brian Sheehan."

"We're kissin' cousins," I said.

"May I come over to your hotel?" she asked. "I have a pressing problem to discuss privately with you. I know you were a good friend of my darling man, Mr. Taylor. I'm sure

the kindness you showed him will be extended to me as well."

"By all means." I agreed to the meeting and put down the phone. I didn't need to guess what Mary Miles Minter wanted to discuss with me.

She wanted for me to arrange to abort the child growing within her, the seed planted by her own father, the murdered William Desmond Taylor.

*****

By the time I boarded the train for Chicago en route to New York, Brian Sheehan had signed on a new patient: Mary Miles Minter. In the wake of the murder of William Desmond Taylor, the date between Minter and me, to be arranged by Charlotte Shelby, never materialized. Now I knew it never would.

Although I relived the murder of Billy Taylor all the way to Chicago, I tried to wipe it from my mind as the train headed from Chicago to New York. Not only would I be installed in a new living arrangement, I would be seeing my two loves, both Rodolfo—pulled away from the arms of Natacha Rambova—and my darling Wally Reid, who was in New York shooting a film.

After a long and tiring journey, I at last arrived in the big city, feeling I had another town to conquer after having subdued Los Angeles.

As Durango Jones, I wandered alone in the splendor of Lotte Lee's Fifth Avenue apartment, a gift bestowed by W.R. on his second mistress, the mysterious Lotte Lee. Before that, I'd lived in the most modest of little bungalow homes in Kansas, in a tiny rose-covered cottage, and in a suite at the Hollywood Hotel, the latter far from luxurious.

Now I faced old-world style I'd never known before—genuine antiques, tapestries, crystal chandeliers, silver, paintings (all of which looked like they were by Rembrandt or by the Rembrandt school), sculpture, potted palms, and enough gold leaf to gild the dome of the Capitol.

What little I'd seen of New York on this, my second visit, was from the back of a taxicab that had taken me from the train station to this apartment. From my second look at it, New York was my kind of town. When I passed through before with Joe Godsol, I was a mere out-of-town visitor. Today I arrived as a full-time resident with one of the best addresses in town—Fifth Avenue, no less.

I was anxious to use some of those charge accounts W.R. had opened for me. Unknown to the Chief, some of the clothing I would buy would be for me, Durango, and not just Lotte Lee. From some of the suits I'd already seen on Fifth Avenue, New Yorkers dressed a hell of a lot more stylishly than did the good people of Los Angeles. In spite of my worldly experience in Los Angeles, in spite of my role as a star-fucker to some of the biggest names in Hollywood, this big city made me feel like a hick from Kansas.

In New York, I'd go to art galleries, the theater, museums, the ballet, the opera, and classical music concerts. I didn't have much else to do and that seemed like a good pursuit for me. I realized that after my beauty faded, I was going to have to learn to make conversation as I grew older. I'd already met the future King of England, also that genius, Albert Einstein. What other challenges awaited me? I fully suspected that Warren Harding would fall for me too, providing I got an invitation to the White House. W.R., if he wanted to, could invite any visitor for dinner, regardless of how distinguished.

I'd brought along some of my Lotte Lee drag but planned to dispose of it after a week's shopping along Fifth Avenue. All I had to do was walk out the door of the apartment and confront one house of fashion after another. I hadn't seen so many haute couture shops like this even in Paris.

The telephone rang and I suspected it might be W.R. calling to see if I'd arrived safety. Picking up the receiver, I was startled to find a famous New York showgal on the other end of the line. "This is Mae West, honey," she said, "and I assume you must be Lotte Lee."

After my initial hello as Durango, I quickly reverted to my Lotte Lee voice. "Miss West," I said. "I'm amazed you're calling. That you had my number and everything."

"Don't bother your pretty head about how I got it, sugar," she said. "A cockroach doesn't move across an alleyway in New York unless he gets permission from Miss West herself. I figured I'd ring you up. Give you some advice. My first advice is when you arrive in town, don't keep it a secret."

"If you're appearing somewhere, I'd like to catch your act," I said.

"From what I hear about you, I'd like to catch your act, too," she said. "Better yet, catch you in the act. My spies out on the coast tell me that every stud in Hollywood is panting for your specialty. Now you've bagged William Randolph himself. That's big game, baby. We've got to get together one night. I want you to tell me how you do it."

"I'm sure there are no secrets I possess that you haven't already mastered," I said.

She chuckled. "Forgive me, Chickadee, but Mae likes to check out the new gal in town. I steal from everybody and learn something from any source. Don't get me wrong. I'm an original. But I always keep abreast of the new act in town, and you're it, babyface."

"From what I hear, you're like no one else," I said.

"Keep that thought and stick with it," she said. "Even though I'm an original, like I said, I've been influenced by other showgals too. Take Eva Tanguay, the 'I Don't Care' gal. She's an anything-goes type of vaudevillian, and as hell knows, I'm an anything-goes kind of gal. A little flamboyance, a lot of spicy innuendo, and the stage-door Johnnies are lined up for me every night. It took a little time for me to develop my own personality. Before that, I had to suffer a lot of indignities, comparisons to such headliners as Belle Baker, Blossom Seeley, and Ethel Green. I've even learned things from that red-haired harlot, the female impersonator Bert Savoy. He was a cooch dancer before making it big. From slit skirts to fancy garters and a big wig, Bert taught me a lot. Maybe too much. Some smut peddlers claim that I myself am a female impersonator. But no man who's ever plunged into my sugar-coated hole ever said that."

For one brief moment, I feared that Mae knew I too was a female impersonator. That's why she'd brought up that subject. "What are you doing now, Miss West?" I asked.

"Call me Mae, Pleasure Woman," she said. "I'm doing everybody in town providing they've got a big bank account and a big dick. I can't waste my time on rooster meat and paupers. When I'm not out there performing and giving men along Broadway the biggest hard-ons of their careers, I'm writing a play called *The Hussy*. Don't you just love that title?"

"Sounds like it'll be a big hit," I said.

"If I'm in it, Diamond Back, it'll be a big hit, I can assure you," she said. She called to someone in the background. "Keep it at high noon, baby, Mae's on her way." Turning back into her receiver, she said to me, "Mae's got to get back to bed. There's work for me to do. Seriously now, Venus de Milo, I want to get together." She paused a minute and instructed me to write down her private phone number. "I'll take you under my wing. Introduce you to only the biggest and best in New York. You can have a very successful career with my rejects alone. When Mae's had them, I'll pass them on to you. I predict that within a year you'll collect so much ice from these johns, you'll put Greenland out of business."

"I'd love to go on the town with you," I said. "I can't think of anybody better to show me New York than Mae West herself."

"I get inspiration driving around at night," she said. "Only the other night I had my driver take me along the waterfront. I like to go and look at all the whores and the sailors just in port. I saw this one bitch who was heavily rouged and made up with enough mascara to paint every white face black in every minstrel show. She looked like she'd slept in her low-cut dress in some seedy bordello and the heels of her red shoes were wobbly. She had this white turban on her head that probably cost a buck. But perched on top of that turban were at least $500 worth of bird-of-paradise feathers. With her bum's laugh, she disappeared into the night with two stud sailors that were so hot looking I'd sell my baby daughter, if I had one, into white slavery. After I finish *The Hussy*, I'm considering using her for my inspiration for another play. I'm going to call this one *Sex*. Don't you just love that title?"

"Mae, thank you for viewing me as a possible friend—and not as competition. When I first picked up the phone, I thought you were going to tell me that New York was big enough for only one blonde."

"It's a big umbrella," Mae said. "I figure if I'm out with you and have you under my little pinkie, I can keep a better eye on what you're up to." She yelled out to someone in the background. "I'm coming," she shouted. "Soon you'll be cumming too." Back talking to me again, she whispered into the phone. "Gotta go now, sugartit. One columnist only yesterday wrote, "Of Mae West, this can be said: 'she is gross, disgusting, tiresome, utterly futile in her vulgarity, and without a single excusing feature or reason for being.' If you could see that seven and a half inches rising for me over here in the bed, that reviewer would know what Mae's reason for being is."

No sooner had I put down the receiver than the doorbell rang. I rushed to the door, knowing in my heart it was Rodolfo.

*****

In all his magnificence, the film star, Rudolph Valentino, *The Sheik* of millions of women's dreams, stood at my door, dressed like a male equivalent of Gloria Swanson, a vision in cashmere, silk, and tailored clothing. He even used a cane, although he hardly needed it—it was just for show. His shoes were shined and were as glossy as his slicked-down, raven-black hair. Suntanned as berry-brown as Douglas Fairbanks, Rodolfo somehow had managed to hide his natural male beauty behind all that finery.

When I showed him inside, he was dazzled by the apartment and asked me point blank if I'd come into some vast fortune, perhaps the legacy of a rich uncle or something.

"It belongs to my sister, Lotte Lee," I said. "I never got around to introducing the two of you before she fled Hollywood." As I said that, I recalled Lotte going down on him on his honeymoon night without Jean Acker. Rodolfo was not one to dwell too long on the good fortunes of another human being, so I quickly shifted the subject back to himself. "The press is calling you the fancy man deluxe. And from the looks of you. they've got that right."

Prancing around the apartment, taking everything in, he said, "It's easy to understand why men hate me. I'm the standard by which all women measure their legal spouses. I'm the third party on every honeymoon—the absent co-respondent in every divorce proceeding."

"Let me go on for you," I said. "Your assets? A perfect physique. The epitome of good grooming. Continental flair in your dress, poise, and movement. A intriguing Latin sheen that suggests depth and a richness of hidden resources."

"Keep that up," he said smiling at me, "and I'll make you my press agent." He continued to note the expensive objects d'art filling the apartment. "Who is her…" He paused as a sexy smirk came across his face. "How shall I put this? What rich man is Lotte's sponsor?"

"William Randolph Hearst," I said.

"How sardonic," he said. "I'm fucking Marion Davies, his mistress, and W.R. is getting some on the side from Lotte."

"You might put it that way," I said. "Sit down, please. I fear your days of fucking Marion are over."

He looked like he'd been slapped in the face, as it reddened. A vein stood out on his neck. "No one, and certainly not you, tells me who I fuck and who I don't fuck. I think that's always been understood between us."

"You went after the wrong woman this time," I said. "You're not big enough to take on W.R. He could destroy your career."

"How so?" he asked. "Writing nasty articles about me in his disgusting newspapers? His boys already do that."

"I picked up the file the Chief had given me. "Read it," I said, handing it to him, "and tell me if it's true or not. You fuck Marion and you end up in jail. Maybe the gas chamber."

He grabbed the file from me and read rapidly. The first page had summed it up clearly for him. He merely thumbed through the background information. "Norman Kerry faithfully swore to me that all these records were destroyed. How can it be? Norman lied to me."

"Norman perhaps didn't know," I said. "W.R. can dig as deep as a surgeon's scalpel."

When I looked into his face, tears were welling. I took him in my arms to offer comfort. "What am I going to do?" he asked, sobbing. "I've worked all my life to realize my dream. Just as it's about to come true, someone reaches out and snatches my hope from me."

"Is it true?" I asked. "Did you shoot Jack de Saulles?"

He didn't say anything for a long moment. "It's a long and difficult story," he said. "Those were different times. There were nights I slept in Central Park. I was homeless. Broke. Hungry. I had to get involved with people who could help me."

"Were you the one who shot de Saulles?"

"Only Bianca knows the answer to that," he said. "She said it was an intruder. The press claimed she did it. The police may never know for sure."

"Is there anybody who knows for sure, other than yourself?"

A morose look crossed his handsome face. His anger seemed to be rising. "Everybody is trying to blackmail me," he said. "From the very beginning, dating from the night de Saulles was shot. I started paying on that night, and I've paid every week of my life since then."

"I don't understand," I said. "Who is trying to blackmail you?"

"All right, I'll tell you if you haven't figured it out already," he said. "That German baron, for one. He's fallen on bad days. He used to be rich. He knows too much on me, especially the de Saulles thing. When the baron summons me to perform stud services for him, I go willingly even though I hate his guts. How do you think I feel every week going to this monster and having him coat my beautiful body with his saliva? He sucks my very manhood from him, but I have to give in to him. Every since he picked me up as a hustler he's been in love with me. He's obsessive. I think he's crazy. Instead of getting over me, he seems to want me more and more. So I've got that shit to deal with, among other things. Now this crap from Hearst."

"W.R.'s terms are a bit easier," I said. "All he wants for you to do is stay out of Marion's boudoir. That shouldn't be so difficult. You've got half the women of the world throwing themselves at you. Surely you don't need Marion. You've got Natacha Rambova."

A brooding, intense look came over his face. "You silly little fool. You have never understood my relationship with Natacha. It's not a sexual relationship. She made that clear from the beginning. It's the coming together of two artistic souls. We don't need mere sex. We have a sexual union of our minds and our spirits."

"I see, a kindred spirit. She seems more suited to the romantic fantasies of Theodore Kosloff than you. You can make commercial pictures. Natacha, the way I look at it, wants to make artistic bombs like *Salome*."

"Many artists aren't appreciated in their time," he said.

"Not Rudolph Valentino," I said. "You give the world what it wants, and the public will be at your feet."

"I'm turning over the direction of my career to Natacha," he said. "Wait until you see the latest scenario for me. I'm playing *The Young Rajah*. I'll be practically nude in the film. That's why I've been working out so much. In one scene, I am covered with pearls—nothing else."

"You're not showing that magnificent cock of yours on the screen, are you?"

"We can't go that far as you well know," he said, "but if the screen allowed nudity, I would be the first male to show a frontal nude. I'm proud of my assets. Is there a homosexual male or a woman in America who doesn't want me penetrating them?"

"I know one," I said. "Natacha Rambova."

In a sudden move, he punched me in the face, knocking me back on the sofa. I felt my nose bleeding. I raced toward the bathroom, and he trailed me there. As I wiped the blood from my face with a cold washcloth, he was on his knees, begging my forgiveness. "It was true what Jean Acker told the court. I did break in and beat her up. I have this streak of violence in me. I can't control it. Please forgive me."

After I'd cleaned my face and stopped the bleeding, I went back into the grandeur of the salon, as he followed me. "You didn't say if you murdered de Saulles or not."

"I'm not going to," he said.

"Will you keep away from Marion's boudoir?" I asked. "W.R. said you can see her at social functions. That's okay with him. But do I have your guarantee that you'll keep your hands off Marion?"

"What are you?" he asked. "The yellow journalist's God damn messenger boy?"

"You're a hustler just like me, baby," I said. "Look at this grand apartment. It doesn't matter how I got here. You've probably done a lot worse to survive. The point is we've both made it. I wanted to be a movie star just like you. That may still happen for me. Maybe I'm too much of a pretty boy for women to be attracted to me like they are to you. But I've learned that a lot of men in this world like pretty boys. At least I never had to murder someone to get what I wanted."

He went over to the liquor cabinet and poured himself a drink. "It's too late to rewrite our lives. If I'd known I was going to become Rudolph Valentino, I would have done some things differently from what I did. But, hell, thinking about that isn't going to allow me to rewrite a past I'm ashamed of. Basically, I still think of myself as a good and decent man. I did not bring corruption into my life." He downed all of the brandy in his glass in one swallow. It seemed to burn into his stomach, although his face revealed he liked this bracing fortification.

"What about us?" I asked like a lovesick fool. "Is there any 'us' any more? We never seem to talk about our own relationship?"

"I'm not a homosexual," he said, turning on me in anger. "In spite of your attempts to make me a pansy, and in spite of what the press says, I'm not your boy. You can't summon me to your bed the way the baron does."

As I stood looking at him against the backdrop of this lavishly decorated Fifth Avenue apartment, I smiled, but it was filled with a certain condescension. "Why don't you just go? The world is waiting out there to adore you. You belong to your public, your adoring fans, and mostly you belong to your kindred soul, Natacha Rambova."

"You're so jealous of her you can't stand it, admit it?"

"Maybe I was," I said. "But I'm not any more. She's welcome to you. I've fallen in love with someone else."

"Some little hustler you picked up in Central Park?" he said snidely, his face filled with utter contempt for me.

"Not at all," I said. "The man I love is called the handsomest star in Hollywood. He's one of America's biggest box-office attractions. When he appears on the screen, he makes women's hearts flutter."

"You're talking about me," he said in protest.

"For me there's another Sheik, far more exciting, sexy, and thrilling than you could ever be," I said. "He's in New York right now. Just as soon as you get out of this apartment, I'm calling him to come over."

"Who is this Greek God, the wonder of the world?" he asked.

"Wallace Reid."

Chapter Sixteen

Perhaps I was drinking too much or taking too many drugs, but the months passed before me so rapidly I can't remember exactly what I did or didn't do. Rodolfo was gone and the others drifted in and out of my life, especially William Boyd, Richard Dix, and Theodore Kosloff. Ramon had become so self-enchanted that I hardly saw him any more, and Rod La Rocque's star was rising, as was that of John Gilbert's. The constants in my life remained Charlie, W. R., Marion, and Antonio. All of us seemed bonded together if only because of our past secrets.

When I was not in New York, my handsome doctor, Brian Sheehan, remained with me, and occasionally we'd escape to San Francisco for long weekends with the bellhop, "Tom-Tom."

For reasons I don't fully understand, Wallace Reid and Tom Ince loomed in my life as dependable fixtures, especially Tom. I'd long ago stopped thinking of him as "Ince." As for Wally, he was more a fixture than dependable. As each month went by, his dependency on morphine increased.

When Wally Reid had arrived at Lotte Lee's apartment in New York, after Rodolfo had walked out, I knew then that it was the beginning of the end for Wally. Greeting him as Durango, I discovered a defeated and broken man. On the West Coast, he'd seemed to hold himself together, somehow managing to fool even the camera, in spite of the Gish sisters thinking that impossible. But back east

I'd seen Wally in a different light. Like William Desmond Taylor before his murder, Wally had seemed to come unglued. From the way he acted, he was either on the verge of a nervous breakdown or in the middle of one.

As ill as he was, Wally starred in eight feature films in 1922 alone. The heavy work schedule took an added toll on his already declining body. "When I appeared with her in *The Affairs of Anatol*," Wally said, "Gloria Swanson told me I was dancing on the edge of a precipice." Wally said that to me on the set of *Thirty Days*, a film he was making for Famous Players-Lasky.

His co-star was Wanda Hawley, who seemed more eager for her next film, *The Young Rajah*, than this one. "I can't believe I'm going to be playing opposite Rudolph Valentino," she said. "The first time I saw him in *The Four Horsemen of the Apocalypse*, I just knew he was my soulmate, even though I've yet to meet him." On the set, I chatted only briefly with Hawley, fearing she'd be just another string of leading ladies who had succumbed to Rodolfo's charms.

Throughout the entire shoot of *Thirty Days*, Wally remained depressed and morbid. "At times I feel *Thirty Days* is going to be my last film. I feel that I have only *Thirty Days* to live. I'm terrified every time I go in front of the camera that I'm going to lose control." In his dressing room, he grabbed my hand, clutching it desperately. "At long last the reviewers are catching on to my upcoming collapse." He reached for a newspaper. "Read what I've circled in red," he said. I picked up the paper. Some reviewer had written, "Reid's once diamond-like charisma is turning out to be a tarnished zircon."

As I was to learn, Wally's marriage to Dorothy was held together by a thin, frayed string of thread. The adoption of little Betty Mummert had not solidified their marriage as Wally had hoped it would. Dorothy was reduced to answering Wally's fan mail from what he described as "mushy dames."

Sometimes Wally couldn't go onto the set as he'd break into uncontrollable sobbing. I often held the best loved actor of his generation in my arms with great affection. Unlike Rodolfo, Wally wanted me to stroke his hair. The sex thing between us had dried up but still gave off a fragrance like crushed lavender. He was a shattered idealist. The only thing in life that meant the most to him, his own sense of worth, had been destroyed.

"I don't know why I've failed like this," he said one day when his latest consumption of morphine had subdued him and he could be coherent again. "Pray for me that, somewhere in the strange land into which I'm going alone, I may become at last the man I've always wanted to be."

That made me cry too, as Wally seemed acutely aware of his upcoming departure from the world. "Men who have no ideals can live with anything, even when they become disillusioned with themselves. Their sins mean nothing to them. Men who have ideals can't stand life when they become disillusioned with themselves."

His wife, Dorothy, often spent the nights with her mother, Alice Davenport, who'd acted in several Keystone films with Mabel Normand, and with Dorothy's aunt, Fanny Davenport, who'd acted on stage with William Desmond Taylor. Wally's adopted baby and his own son, Billy, was with them, but Wally bowed out of those evenings. "All they do is condemn me," he said. "They condemn but understand nothing."

Night after night after taking his morphine, he wanted to wander back into his past. "I arrived in town twenty years old. Forgive me for saying this, but I was as fine, clean, and high-minded a young American male as could be found in these forty-eight states. I was big, handsome, strong, filled with the joy of life. Little could I have known then that I'd lived two-thirds of my life."

"You speak as if you're dead," I said. "That's hardly the case with you."

"A man dies inside," he said, "before they actually cart him off to the graveyard. Dorothy was a star before me. I was assigned to her as a leading man. She'd starred opposite such stars as James Kirkwood. But she detested my screen acting. I didn't want to be an actor anyway. She told the director I was all hands and feet and knew nothing about acting. Between love scenes, we glared at each other across the set."

"But you married her," I said.

"I think what attracted her to me was my ability to ride a horse," he said. "She was quite a horsewoman herself. Some of the guys on the set didn't know about that year I'd spent in Wyoming. They fixed me up with the nastiest broncho in the stables. But I showed them, taking the corkscrews, tail spins, and sunfishes. I led that horse back to the corral sweating and conquered. I think Dorothy fell in love with me that very day."

Some nights when Dorothy wasn't home, Wally would take me into his library and play the violin for me, spending hours just playing, singing softly, and talking music, a subject I knew virtually nothing about. "You won't believe this, but Geraldine Farrar in *Carmen* let me accompany her. I'd play violin *obbligatos* whenever she sang some of her arias."

At those moments I felt Wally wanted to be a musician more than he wanted to be an actor. In fact, he wanted to be anything more than he wanted to be an actor. On occasion he'd punch a heckler in the nose when accused of getting by only on his handsome face.

Sometimes I would look at Wally and think he was like Peter Pan—he'd never grown up. My best times were the evenings he'd let me take him to the Ship Café. He'd be warmly greeted by everyone, especially the jazz orchestra. Its members would let Wally play every instrument, including the drums and the saxophone.

But after that momentary elation when I

took him back to the Hollywood Hotel, his nerves seemed stretched to the breaking point. It was like a rebellion with himself over his drug addiction. Even though still only in his early thirties, his face, one hailed as the handsomest in America, began to harden. Tiny wrinkles, not noticeable at night, were revealed in the harsh light of the California morning sun. Wallace Reid was growing old before my eyes and most definitely prematurely.

After an examination from Brian, Wally was sent to a dental clinic. Part of his pain, it was discovered, was coming from his teeth. Nine of them had to be removed, and the shock to his system and his concept of his male beauty led to an increased morphine usage. "I'm a toothless old geezer," he said. "All the world celebrates me as the male beauty of the screen. How could they know I'm going to be wearing false teeth and that I'm impotent."

Before coming back to the coast with Wally, I saw that New York had been a disaster for him. He despised the picture he was making and he hated the director, and this from a man who usually got along with everybody. Also, he had to have his hair dressed and set every day, and this enraged him. He felt there was an "unmanly quality" about acting.

In New York he saw old friends, new friends, newspaper reporters, gushing women fans, celebrities of the theater, women of all ranks, degrees of beauty, and intelligence—this parade of flesh marched against him, and he didn't seem to know how to refuse any invitation. He felt accepting invitations was expected of him. He wanted to be a good guy and do what people wanted. He was repeatedly abused and taken advantage of, especially when word spread that he was a soft touch. He ran out of money twice, and I had to lend him more, knowing he'd probably give it away and not use it for his own needs.

His nights in New York were filled with insomnia. He paced the floor of my apartment—or else Lotte's apartment—listening to music on the radio. Sometimes I'd find him wandering nude in the middle of the night. I couldn't help but notice how thin and drawn his once strapping body looked. Once he looked into my own eyes and promised he was going "on the wagon" when he got back to The Coast.

But the next day I discovered that a white mask had come across his once radiant face. His eyes looked dull and dead. Back on the coast Brian discovered that a New York doctor had given him some unknown sleeping powders to help Wally conquer what he called his "white nights." Whatever it was in those powders had made Wally worse than before.

When Adela Rogers St. Johns saw her old friend again, she told me that, "An indescribable, baffling something is surrounding Wally, and I can't understand it. It's as if some malignant fairy has transformed him with one wave of her wand into a distorted image of his former self."

All those years of working under intense lights began to destroy his vision. It was called "Klieg eye" back then. Kleig eye, which affected many stars of the era, was similar to snow blindness and was brought about by long and continued exposure of the eyes to powerful batteries of calcium lights used in the flickers. At times he complained that he couldn't see anything, and then his vision would return. Throughout the world he was known for having the most lovable and irresistible smile on the screen. Now when he smiled at me, it was only a glimmer of its former enchantment. His smile was artificial.

"I feel that an enemy from beyond has moved inside and taken possession of my body like a demon," he said one night. "This demon has blurred my vision, and numbed my mind. But mostly it has eaten into my soul. I'm going through the motions of living, but I've ceased to live any more."

Then one day he announced that he was going to race in the Indianapolis Decoration Day races. Already a licensed racing driver, Wally wanted to test out his English speed demon, the Sunbeam. He was obsessed with participating in this race, but I refused his invitation to go with him back to the Middle West. I feared that in his weakened mental and physical condition, he wanted to commit suicide on that race track, and I didn't want to see that happen.

I begged and pleaded with him not to go. "Even if you don't care what happens to your own body, think of the lives of other people, some of whom are your friends. By joining in that race, you'll be endangering their lives too."

"If I die," he said, "I'll die with my boots on."

Finally, in the middle of the night before his departure for Indianapolis, he told me he'd called it off. "I wanted one final, grand gesture. Now I won't have even that."

Wally did try to make one more picture for Lasky. It was called *Nobody's Money*, but he experienced a total hysterical breakdown on the first day of shooting. He also reported that he'd gone blind from Kleig eye. Scenes in which he wasn't scheduled to appear were shot by the supporting company who waited anxiously for his recovery. But Lasky told friends privately that "Reid will never recover." He cast the actor, Jack Holt, as the lead. Wally would never work again.

I called Brian that morning, and Wally was committed to a private sanitarium with a padded cell. At his bedside, I saw a famous man become a shell. It was as if Wally had joined forces with that demon who possessed him to bring about his own self-destruction. "It's more like a crucifixion," I told Brian, "than a slow death." I would always enter Wally's room when Dorothy had gone. I felt her recitation to Wally of all his past failures and her disappointments in him hardly helped him reclaim his soul.

One morning she couldn't make it to the sanitarium, and Wally's hope seemed to rise a bit. Flashes of his old fighting spirit came back. I had moved a phonograph into the room, and he would lie for hours listening to the great masterpieces. Sometimes he would ask me to read from the works of such poets as John Keats or Elizabeth Barrett Browning. Sometimes, he'd request one of the comedies of Shakespeare. Despite his physical suffering, he refused to allow Brian to give him more morphine, even though the doctor warned that too abrupt a withdrawal might kill him.

It was clear to me that, except for a morning or two, when his spirit flamed forth, he wasn't getting better. Each day his condition steadily worsened. Whatever ravages his body and spirit had suffered were not healing. He was on the road to death.

Almost basking in the glow of publicity, Dorothy used every opportunity she could to summon a press conference. Emerging "fresh from the bedside of my husband," she told reporters, "My husband is a sick, sick boy. I don't know if he will recover, but he has broken his habit and won his fight. He made this fight of his own free will and has won it by the strength of his own mind and will. I know that he will come back. He is fighting for his life."

In the hospital the next afternoon, Wally said to me, "Brian has told me that if I return to my old bondage, there is hope for me. He recommends a medically directed, careful, and moderate return to morphine. He said my system could not bear a sudden withdrawal from the drug."

"Then let him administer morphine in small dosages," I said. "Let him wean you from the drug gradually. It's the only way to save your life."

"I want to face death bravely and squarely," he said. "Drug free. I don't want to die with the morphine burning up the last ounces of my soul."

I kneeled beside his bed, holding his thin hands in my strong ones. There was nothing I could do but abide by his decision.

"I'll go out clean," he said. "I'd rather my body die than to go back to the thing that almost killed me. At least, I'm myself now. I believe in God. During my Hollywood years, I'd lost my belief. It's come back to me. I'm not afraid to go."

When I left the sanitarium I felt he'd signed his own death warrant. Upon my return early the next morning, another sick man lay in Wally's bed. Brian had been trying to reach me for hours but I'd been driving in the Hollywood Hills in my stagecoach. Driving and thinking.

"Wally died at four o'clock in the morning," Brian said.

*****

After burying Wally, Dorothy Davenport, the actress, became billed as "Mrs. Wallace Reid." She'd found a new role to play—that of a professional widow. Calling a press conference, she announced her intention to avenge Wally's death, although failed to make clear exactly how she planned to seek revenge on the dope smugglers who'd supplied Wally with morphine.

She drew up a list of names of Wally's friends, a group calling themselves the "Hollywood Hell-Raisers," similar somewhat to a modern-day equivalent of Leonardo DeCaprio's "posse." She referred to Wally's fun-loving guys as "Bohemians," and claimed they had led her Wally into a life of "drink, dope, and debauchery." She claimed these male friends of Wally's had turned their home into a "roadhouse," with men hanging out there every night. She had told reporters that she had to take her adopted daughter and Wally's son, Billy, and lock them up in the secluded part of the house to keep them away from the "trouble makers."

Encouraged by that little moralizing censor, Will Hays, Dorothy rushed into an antiseptic film called *Human Wreckage*, which reportedly was an exposé of the drug traffic. Overlooking the fact that she was offered "a bundle" of money to make the film, right when she badly needed the cash, she claimed she was starring in the movie to "warn the nation's youth" about the evils of taking dope and filming it in "memory of Wally." After making the film, she went on a cross-country tour to promote it. After presenting the film, she would give a lecture on drug addiction.

Wally's body was cremated so he didn't have a chance to turn over in his grave at Dorothy's attempt to exploit his fame as the newly renamed star, "Mrs. Wallace Reid." Her career as the actress Dorothy Davenport—her real name was Florence—had fizzled.

In her new incarnation as Mrs. Wallace Reid, she found that the screen fame and clout of her dead husband could not be passed on to her. She bombed and eventually disappeared from the news and the screen. I, for one, was glad to see her go.

With William Desmond Taylor and Wallace Reid only a memory for me, I turned to other pursuits—namely Antonio Moreno. He'd called to ask me to come to his home "at once." Somehow between all these deaths and other blackmailing dramas—not to mention abortions—Antonio had married a middle-aged socialite, Daisy Canfield Danziger, a wealthy divorcée with three children, all of whom later changed their last name to "Moreno" after their mother's remarriage.

Before that, Antonio had dated various women, hoping to keep up his macho image in Hollywood and to dispel rumors that he was a homosexual. I'd seen Daisy at a few parties at the Hollywood Hotel but had never spoken to her. Whenever possible, I tried to avoid the wives or girl friends of my male lovers. For me, that was a private part of their lives into which I didn't want to intrude. Since I'd first arrived in Hollywood, Daisy had been known as an investor in films.

After her marriage to Antonio, she'd moved him into a large Spanish-style hacienda which she'd called "Crestmount." In the house she'd tried to re-create Old Madrid because Antonio longed more and more for his native land. Once I gave him a ring and cufflinks made with the colors of the Spanish flag, and he'd wept at my thoughtfulness.

After his marriage, Antonio gave a press conference to declare his devotion to Daisy and her three children. But Hollywood insiders felt that the homosexual actor had married Daisy only for her money and to "keep up appearances" that he was a heterosexual. At the press conference, a reporter, Glady Halls, asked, "what with Valentino in double harness, and Richard Barthelmess, and now you, what is there left for the poor girls to hope for?" Obviously tongue-in-cheek, Antonio had said, "Ramon Novarro," knowing full well that Ramon never planned to make it with a woman, much less marry one.

Throughout his life Antonio had wanted to avoid scandal at any cost. He had claimed to me that he'd married Daisy because he feared that an investigation that probed too deeply into the private life of Billy Taylor might turn up the fact they'd been lovers for a long time. Fortunately, even though Billy was linked to homosexual circles, and news of some of his activities appeared briefly in the press, most reporters seemed to shy away from the slain director's involvement with males. They concentrated on his affairs with women, namely Mabel Normand and Mary Miles Minter. Since Antonio was actually talking on the phone with Billy at the moment he was shot, Antonio was never viewed as a suspect. Several reporters hinted, however, that Antonio knew a lot more about the Taylor murder than he was saying.

Actually Antonio knew a lot of the details leading up to Billy's murder, but did not know who fired the fatal bullet. Throughout my life I never told anyone except W.R. that I (or Lotte Lee, as I related to the Chief) had actually been an eyewitness to the murder. Antonio knew that Edward Sands had been murdered by Billy, but until the day Antonio died he never revealed that to anyone. In fact, after the confession of Billy shortly before his death, Antonio and I never spoke of that revelation. Both of us regarded it as a taboo subject.

After those serials with Pearl White and a string of lackluster roles, Antonio had a big career to protect in 1923. He'd emerged as a major new star at Paramount. It wasn't an overnight success, as he'd worked for years to get there. Billy Taylor had not only forced Antonio into a three-way with Mary Miles Minter, but had urged him to co-star with her in *The Trail of the Lonesome Pine*, one of the last films that fallen female star ever made, since Taylor's murder had destroyed her career.

When I went to visit Antonio on the set of *My American Wife*, he was feuding with its star, Gloria Swanson. "She treats me with utter contempt," he said in his still heavily Spanish accented voice. "Right in front of the entire cast, Swanson said to me in a loud voice, 'I know Paramount is trying to groom you to be the next Valentino. But you're not worthy to shine the boots of *The Sheik*. The last scene you played with me was that of an amateur.' After saying that to me, she stormed off the set and demanded that the director, Sam Wood, hire another leading man. Fortunately, Wood has convinced Swanson that I can keep the role. Apparently, the bitch has approval of her leading men. Wood told her that too much of the film has already been shot with me in it. Can you believe this shit? After the bitch tried to get me fired, I have to go back out there before the camera and make love to the cow."

"Do it," I urged him. "You're about to become one of the biggest stars in Hollywood. Don't blow your chance."

He agreed to go back on that set and face Swanson for their scenes of heavy passion, but only on one condition. "Go to the studio cafeteria," he instructed me. "Get the biggest onion you can. Bring it back here. Before kissing Swanson, I'll eat that onion raw. I only wish they had garlic like the restaurants of Spain."

The film, as much as I could gather, was another one of those Sam Wood/Swanson formula flickers called a romantic comedy. It was the story of a dashing Spanish-American, played by Antonio, of course, falling madly in love with a rich American woman as played by Swanson, naturally.

While Antonio and his onion breath assaulted Swanson before the cameras, I shared a smoked turkey sandwich with Aileen Pringle, an actress who played a supporting role in the film.

I'd heard of her, of course, and suspected that she'd been one of Rodolfo's girl friends. Or at least that was the gossip from Paul Ivano. Pringle had even caused a major jealous rage between Rodolfo and Natacha Rambova. Pringle, who was about the same size as the midget Swanson, was known throughout Los Angeles as a star-fucker and always went for the leading man in any film. I'm sure that Miss Pringle and I had shared more male bodies than Rodolfo's.

"I've been after Moreno ever since the first day he showed up here on the set, but he treats me like I don't exist," she said. "I've fucked Valentino for God's sake. But I can't seem to make it with this dime-store version of *The Sheik*. I bet he's not hung as well as Rudy anyway. I told Gloria—she and I have become dear friends—that I don't think much of Moreno. As I related to Swanson, Moreno never had an idea above the waist. And those ideas he gets below the waist aren't directed at women in spite of his so-called marriage to one."

Antonio survived the Swanson film—actually it did well at the box office unlike the dud Rodolfo made with Swanson called *Beyond the Rocks*.

On the set of his next picture, a lackluster film called *Look Your Best*, Antonio was cast opposite Colleen Moore. It was my first encounter with this rising star who, unlike Swanson, had an unpretentious demeanor.

Moore was just emerging as the bubbling flapper who would storm across the silent screens of the Twenties before the inevitable fade-out at the dawn of the Talkies in the late 1920s.

A slender brunette, she had a little girl voice. I was surprised to discover that one of her eyes was blue, the other brown. But before the invention of Technicolor, that didn't matter.

Amazingly to me, Moore wasn't particularly beautiful, as were most female stars of the time. If she'd lived, the Moore role in this film would probably have gone to Olive Thomas. Moore seemed to sense that I was appraising her lack of beauty.

"Any Plain Jane can become a flapper," she told me. "American gals who aren't great beauties identify with me. They figure if I could do it and go on to become a bigtime film star, they have a chance too. No wonder they grab me to their hearts and make me their own movie queen. After all, the average American woman can't look like Gloria Swanson or even Mary Pickford."

Although in decades to come, I would emerge as the head of one of the biggest talent agencies in Los Angeles, I must issue a dying confession. I predicted to Antonio later that night that the rising star of Colleen Moore would not make it into the heavens. He completely agreed with me.

How wrong we were.

I had failed to appreciate her piquant presence, the invigorating breath of fresh air brought to a screen that could not always survive on the heady films of those clothes cows, Swanson and Pola Negri, both of whom overdressed in every picture.

This bouncy little Peter Pan, Miss Moore, with her bobbed hair and shingled bangs, would skyrocket to the top of Hollywood stardom. She would in time become the very symbol of the sporty American woman of the Jazz Age. Soon even F. Scott Fitzgerald said of her, "I was the spark that lit up Flaming Youth. Colleen Moore was the torch. What little things we are to have caused all that trouble."

Fitzgerald was referring to the picture, *Flaming Youth*, that she would make later that year, the flicker that shot her into orbit. Moore went on to reign as the Queen of First National from 1923 to 1929. Of course, in my dire pre-diction for her career, I had not anticipated one major break for her. If you want to be a big star, it always helps to marry the head of the studio. Moore did just that, wedding John McCormick, who would become the head honcho at First National.

But it wasn't *Flaming Youth* that consumed Moore the day I met her. It certainly wasn't the picture she was making with Antonio. She was excited about appearing in *The Wall Flower* for Goldwyn. "My co-star is Richard Dix," she informed me. "I'm sure you know all about him."

I knew about him in more ways than one, but I wasn't going to confide that to Moore.

"He's a real ladies man," she said.

I didn't refute that either.

Moore wasn't the only one thinking of future films. Anxious to be done with the Swanson flicker, Antonio was filled with news of two upcoming projects. He was set to star opposite Bebe Daniels in *The Exciters*. He had also been signed to support the newly arrived Pola Negri in *The Spanish Dancer*. In the Negri film, Antonio would play the hero, of course. The villain? Wallace Beery, the discarded husband of Gloria Swanson.

Thoughts of Antonio's exciting career and my visits to him on his film sets filled my head as I drove up to the hilltop house that Daisy Canfield Danziger had purchased for him on the crown of a mountain. I never went there for sexual liaisons with Antonio, always slipping off to some private nook with him instead, most often my suite at the Hollywood Hotel. The only time I'd get invited to the hilltop manse was when Daisy and he would throw a party, sometimes with as many as one-hundred people attending.

After the Taylor murder, Antonio didn't want to be seen dining or drinking alone with either Ramon or me, preferring carefully arranged private sessions instead. Even when he invited me to a party, he always cautioned me to show up with "one of your lady friends, perhaps Lila Lee or Barbara LaMarr." The more I thought about it, the more I realized that Antonio was filmdom's first "closet queen."

That Latin lover of the screen, increasingly called "The It Man," had a special urgency in his voice when he'd called me to come to his side. I knew it wasn't for a sexual encounter, as he could easily drive down off the mountain for a roll in my queen-sized bed any time his Spanish heart desired.

In the foyer of his home, he was unshaven and appeared to have been drinking heavily. He wore only a pair of white boxer shorts.

He reached for me and took me in his arms, giving me a long, deep kiss with a penetrating tongue. "I'm not getting enough male sex," he said. "Every time I fuck Daisy, I think of you with a hard-on. Otherwise, I couldn't complete the ghastly act."

I looked around the foyer. "Obviously she's not here," I said.

"Hell, no," he said. "We had a big fight. She's gone for the weekend. Maybe forever."

"You guys have split for good?" I asked.

"We've split all right," he said, as a bitter mask of hatred formed on his face. "She's going to ruin my career. That bitch has called Louella Parsons. Daisy is going to tell Parsons everything she's found out about me." He looked at me and reached for my arm, his fingers digging in. "Even about my affair with one Kansas cowboy, Durango Jones."

*****

Although I'd bribed Louella Parsons in the Chaplin/Paul Ivano homosexual scandal, I didn't know a way for Antonio to get out of the threat from his wife, Daisy. She seemed to have all the oil money in Texas behind here, and if Lolly didn't plant items in her column about Antonio, Daisy obviously would go elsewhere.

"The only thing that will save you," I said to Antonio as we walked along his terrace, "is a reporter's fear of getting sued."

"What does that mean?" he asked, growing impatient.

"What can a reporter write?" I asked. "They can't just say you're a homosexual based on one woman's rantings. You've been in no trouble before. You've not been officially charged with anything. Exactly what does she have on you?"

"The bitch knows plenty," he said. "She's

hired someone at the Hollywood Hotel to spy on you. It's been reported to her that I've been seen leaving your suite at odd hours of the day and night. Somehow she found out what I'm up to when I go to San Francisco and screw around with that fantastic bellhop, Tom-Tom, who you put me on to. Several people have told her that Ramon Novarro and I are lovers."

"This is just circumstantial evidence," I said. "Nothing that can be proven."

"There's more," he said. "Stay out here on the terrace. To tell you the next little story, I need a whiskey. I'll bring you one too."

There was a fog in the mountains that night, and I'd almost run off the road twice getting up here. Although gloriously remote and secluded, the hacienda was also a dangerous place to reach.

Back on the terrace, Antonio spoke softly as if we could be overheard, although there was nobody for miles around. "Last night she caught me in bed with one hot stud. We were really going at it. He was plowing me in the ass like this was our last fuck on earth."

"Who is this living wonder and when do I get cut in on the fun?" I asked.

"How can you think about sex when my career is about to explode?" he asked.

"Sorry."

"He's Luis Antonio Damaso de Alonso," he said. "But he's changed it to Gilbert Roland."

I already knew of this teenage wonder, a former bullfighter and the son of a bullfighter. Only the other day Louella had carried an interview with him, predicting major stardom for this Mexican heartthrob. Like Ramon Novarro, Gilbert had been uprooted from his hometown in Mexico by the invading forces of Pancho Villa. After a move to Texas, Roland—at least according to Louella's column—had arrived in Hollywood and found screen work right away. Back in those days and for decades to come, he was extraordinarily handsome, and much of homosexual Hollywood—and the ladies too—were anxious to sample the virile charms of this newcomer, whose combination of looks and machismo seemed destined to propel him to the top.

"I told him to keep a Hispanic name," Antonio said. "Now that I've set off this Latin craze, Hispanic lovers are all the rage. Even non-Hispanics have changed their name. Take Ricardo Cortez. He's about as Mexican as Louis B. Mayer. Cortez is Jewish and Austrian. His real name is Jacob Krantz. He's just trying to cash in on this Latin Lover shit."

Hispanic name or not, Gilbert Roland was creating a buzz in Hollywood. In time he'd remake *Camille,* with him appearing in Rodolfo's part as Armand, opposite the superstar, Norma Talmadge in 1927. Gilbert even survived the debut of the talkies, although his Spanish accent reduced him to supporting roles. For reasons known only to the goddess herself, Mae West cast him as a Russian gigolo—"Warm, dark, and handsome"—in her 1933 classic, *She Done Him Wrong,* with Cary Grant.

Kids growing up in 1946 and 1947 still remember Gilbert as the Cisco Kid, a series played by many actors, including Warner Baxter, who was far too old for the role of "the kid." Before Gilbert revived the Cisco Kid, the series had ended in the early Forties when gay actor, Cesar Romero, the lover of Desi Arnaz, had appeared in the aptly titled *The Gay Caballero.*

I would follow Gilbert's career for years to come, especially during my days as a Hollywood gossip columnist. Actually I was enraptured with him for at least two decades to come. Sometimes while pursuing him, I would also encounter another potential trick, as happened to me in 1940 when I showed up on the set of *The Sea Hawk,* and met the dashing Errol Flynn, with whom I immediately fell in love. In the movie, Flynn and Roland were enemies, but in Flynn's dressing room we were a most friendly trio.

Long after the white heat of passion had dwindled to a very low flame, I continued to see Gilbert who still maintained his perfect physique and his good looks, enough so that he became known among some film reviewers as "the ageless wonder."

In 1950 I called upon him when he was playing the clandestine lover of lesbian actress Barbara Stanwyck in *The Furies.* Size queens still remember the crotch shot of Gilbert a year later when he'd starred in *The Bullfighter and the Lady.* Even though aging, his bare chest

and that ample crotch was still on display in 1959 when I showed up on the set of *The Big Circus,* with Gilbert appearing as a trapeze artist.

Lost in my wandering thoughts about Gilbert Roland, I had completely forgotten about the Bitch of Buchenwald taking dictation. She interrupted my reverie. "Get back to what happened with the sodomite spic and that oil-rich old whore he married."

On his terrace as he finished off his whiskey, Antonio told me how he met Gilbert. "He came to me to get a job, thinking I might give him a bit part in one of my films. As the first Hispanic male star, I'm a sort of role model for all the hot young Spanish-speaking studs who arrive in Hollywood. He immediately caught my attention. Or rather his basket did. Most men wear loose-fitting trousers, but he showed up in the tightest pair of trousers I'd ever seen on a man who wasn't a bullfighter. His cock and balls were clearly outlined when he sat down in a chair across from me. Needless to say we got on fabulously. When my wife Daisy and our children went back to Texas for the weekend, I invited Gilbert up here for some fun and games. We were both running around the joint stark naked and having a good time, with the radio blasting away. I didn't hear Daisy return. She came back one day early and headed right for the bedroom where I was yelling in passion. She opened the door and came in just as Gilbert's thick nine-inch uncut dick was about to blast off."

"He sounds like one hot man," I said, "but not for putting on a show for Daisy."

"When Daisy burst in on us, Gilbert pulled out of me. But it was too late. He was too far gone. That teenager yanked it out but his cum seemingly shot ten feet. It splattered Daisy's dress, and she ran screaming from the room. Gilbert put on his clothes and got the hell out, rushing off to spend the rest of the weekend with Ramon. That left me to face an enraged wife. That Daisy is one jealous cunt."

"So now Daisy has eyewitness proof that those rumors about you are true."

"Hell, yes," he said, "and where do I go from here?"

Before either of us came up with a solution, I spotted yellow car lights in the fog as a vehicle drove up that wicked, curvy drive. Looking as if prepared for almost anything, even an invading army of reporters, Antonio stood bravely on the terrace to face the invader. "It's Daisy," he said when her car came into view. "She's come back. Maybe there's hope yet."

"Do you want me to jump over the balcony and get the hell out of here?" I asked.

"She's seen your stagecoach," he said. "She must know you're here. Everybody in Hollywood knows your car."

Within minutes, Daisy confronted me on Antonio's terrace. "You're a loathsome creature," she said to me. "You've corrupted Tony. Or men like you."

"Mrs. Moreno, I am but a good friend of your husband, the way Jack and Thomas Meighan are. As you know all too well, I'm sure, Antonio is more man than most."

"Bullshit!" she said, turning with fury on Antonio. "If you're so fucking macho, why were you taking it up the ass from Gilbert Roland?"

"I'd taken drugs and become momentarily insane," he said. "Roland took advantage of me. He gave me something in a knock-out drink. When I came to, the bastard was sodomizing me."

"Things like that happen more than you think," I said, hoping to back up Antonio's lie.

Daisy looked at me, then at her husband, as if not believing a word we said. She stormed back into the living room and headed for the bar to pour herself a whiskey.

Antonio trailed her. Through the open doors leading to the terrace, I could hear everything. "Why did you come back?" he asked. "You didn't have time to go to Parsons or talk to reporters. You came back for a reason, and I want to know why."

"Why don't you ask your little pansy boy, Durango Jones, why I came back," she said looking at me.

With an invitation like that, I came forward from the terrace into the living room, although I had little desire to involve myself in this domestic chaos. "I think I know why."

"Then for God's sake, won't one of you let me in on this?" Antonio said in exasperation, also going to the bar himself for another whiskey.

"You go first, petunia," Daisy said, looking mockingly at me.

"I'm only guessing," I said, "but I think your brain started working overtime before you got to the bottom of that hill. I think you decided certain things. One, you don't want the public humiliation of being married to a homosexual. You don't want your children to suffer. You're not a pretty woman. In fact, a lot of men in this town find you repulsive. Yet you're looked up to as the wife of one of the most dashing men in films. Antonio Moreno, a man who's headed for the same stardom that Valentino has achieved. There's a lot of prestige in being married to one of the leading matinee idols of the world. As a woman, you're over the hill. If it weren't for your money, no one in Hollywood would invite you anywhere. As an oil-rich bitch and as Mrs. Antonio Moreno, you get invited to Pickfair with Doug and Mary, or out to Santa Monica with W.R. and Marion. I don't think you want to give that up. At least, Antonio wasn't fucking another woman. He was with a man. Who wouldn't like men? Even you like men."

"But men aren't supposed to like each other," she said. "I mean at least sexually."

"That's the biggest lie ever told to women," I said. "You don't know a god damn thing about homosexuality. When men get together, they fuck each other. They just don't talk about it unless they get caught. You know what a pleasure it is to get fucked by a man. Men feel the same pleasure, maybe even more intense."

"I don't know," she said on the verge of tears.

Over the next three hours, Antonio and I as a team managed to bewilder this lady from Texas who came from an environment where no one had ever mentioned the subject of homosexuality around her. She may not have believed us completely, but we fed her plenty of erroneous data to sow enough seeds of confusion to cause an overly planted garden of the brain.

When Daisy finally announced that she had a lot to think about, both Antonio and I knew the marriage was still intact, at least temporarily.

It was way past midnight when Daisy staggered to her feet. "Just for what you did with Roland, I'm going to cut you off sexually," she said to Antonio. "You're not going to get any more from me. I don't want a man fucking me who lets other men fuck him. I find that repulsive."

When she left the living room for the toilet, Antonio turned to me. "What a relief. She think she's cutting me off. At least I won't have to top the old bag any more."

Back in the living room, Daisy felt she was in a position of power. "You can go on living here," she said to Antonio, "providing you never bring another one of your boy friends here again." She looked disdainfully at me. "That goes for Durango Jones. However, Jack Pickford and Thomas Meighan are still acceptable, because no one has ever accused them of homosexuality."

"I think I'd better go," I said, getting up. "If I'm going to get my stagecoach down that dangerous hill, I'd better have nothing more to drink."

"Good night and good riddance," she said. "I don't want my Tony hanging out with the likes of you any more. Besides, you're so fucking pretty you should have been a girl instead of a man. You tell that bastard, Gilbert Roland, if he wants to fuck someone in the future, then let him fuck you."

"That is one invitation I'm bound to extend," I said to her, waving good-bye to Antonio at the door.

In spite of the Bitch of Buchenwald's objections to my jumping ahead of my story, I must reveal what happened to Daisy. She stayed married to Antonio, and he and I continued to see each other. In time I purchased a small cottage in the Hollywood Hills where I entertained gentlemen callers far from the spies who hung out at the ever-so-public Hollywood Hotel.

Antonio Moreno continued as a frequent visitor to my secret cottage. Sometimes he came with Gilbert Roland, sometimes alone, and sometimes with Ramon. The hottest nights in that cottage was when all three Hispanic studs showed up at an arranged time—Gilbert Roland, Ramon Novarro, and Antonio Moreno. I could never get enough of those Spanish sausages.

As Daisy continued to go back and forth between Hollywood and Texas, her knowledge of homosexuality grew more sophisticated over the years. She became far too hip to fall for the version of it that we presented to her in 1923.

By February of 1933, she'd had enough of Antonio and his boy friends. She announced to the press that she was separating from the actor because of "the usual minor family incompatibilities." Fortunately she didn't reveal what those incompatibilities were. In less than a week, on the night of February 23, a drunk Daisy drove up that hill to confront Antonio, arriving in a heavy fog from Mulholland Drive.

As Antonio told me later, she'd arrived in disarray, claiming that the lights on her car had failed and twice she'd nearly plummeted over the embankment. Being drunk didn't help either.

She'd come seeking a property settlement. Even though a rich woman, Daisy had demanded half of everything Antonio had plus half of his future earnings. If he didn't sign documents the next day with her lawyers, she said she was going to carry out those same threats she'd made a decade earlier. This time Antonio had been convinced she'd carry through with her threat.

After major stardom in the Twenties, Antonio's own career was going downhill in the Thirties and he was reduced to character parts. He was no longer one of the top five glamorous studs of Hollywood, so he could not use that attractive bait to a woman wanting to remain his wife. Also Daisy had tired of Hollywood and "its sissy boys," as she put it, and wanted to return to Texas to "find myself a real man, one who's not afraid to jump into a woman's pussy when confronted with one."

Later, Antonio told me, they had fought bitterly that night. "Her demands were too much" he said. "Both of us had been drinking heavily, especially her. I'm still enough of a Spanish man to refuse to let a wife talk to me the way she did. I have some pride left. At one point in our fight, things got so violent I pushed her down the steps of the terrace leading to the driveway. It was a bad fall. But she picked herself up and screamed into the night that I'd broken her arm. I stood there paralyzed, too drunk to know what to do. The bitch made for her car. I heard her starting it up. Even though it didn't have any lights and she was drunk, she headed down that God damn hill. Within minutes I heard the sound of a crash."

As I had read myself in the papers the following morning, Daisy Moreno had plunged over that embankment and had died instantly. The newspapers reported that even though the Morenos had announced a separation, that they were considering a reconciliation at the time of her untimely death. It was also reported that Antonio "collapsed" when given the news and details of Daisy's death. He vowed, "I'll never remarry. Daisy is the only woman I'll ever love."

A rich man until the day he suffered a stroke in his Beverly Hills mansion on February 15, 1967, Antonio kept his word and never remarried. As a star, his glory days were behind him when Daisy conveniently went over that hill.

But when I drove down that hill, on the night I met Daisy for the first time, Antonio's career was yet to peak. His biggest stardom lay before him in the Twenties, as long as Silents ruled the screens of the world.

The apex of his career was the 1926 *Mare Nostrum*, in which he played a restless sea captain opposite Alice Terry as a Mata Hari-like vamp. It was directed by Terry's husband, Rex Ingram, who had launched both Rodolfo and Ramon into successful careers. Antonio even went on to appear in *Beverly of Graustark*, a costume romance in 1926 with Marion Davies. He fought bitterly with Greta Garbo off the screen in her 1926 film, *The Temptress*, and hated the Swede even more than he despised another co-star, Gloria Swanson.

He is remembered today for the film, *It*, which he made with Clara Bow in 1927. Throughout the Twenties, Antonio was called the "It" man, and Clara, of course, became the "It" Girl.

As the fad of Latin lovers waned, Antonio often starred in Spanish versions of American films. Again proving what a small world Hollywood was, he frequently starred in foreign language roles that had been originally created in English by my lover, William Boyd.

Antonio's talking debut as an unhappily married judge in the 1929 *Careers* didn't ex-actly launch him spectacularly into Talkies. Over the years he was reduced to such roles as playing a gypsy in the 1936 Laurel and Hardy film, *Boehmian Girl*. Much of his time was spent in Mexico where he directed that country's first two talkies, one entitled—believe it or not—*Santa*. In Spain he ironically found himself playing an American in the 1936 film, *Maria de la O*.

Even when he landed roles in "A" films made after 1940, he wasn't the star, as exemplified by his appearance with Marlene Dietrich in *Seven Sinners*, or his appearance in 1946 in Alfred Hitchcock's *Notorious* where Antonio was one of the spies chasing Cary Grant.

Antonio was bitter at being cast as the father of another one of my lovers, Tyrone Power, in the 1946 *Captain from Castile*. By 1950 he was supporting Gary Cooper in *Dallas*, and his last American film was John Ford's *The Searchers* in 1956. Before winging off to Cuba, Antonio made one final hit. It was the 3D camp horror film shot in 1954, *The Creature from the Black Lagoon*. In it, he played a scientist leading a rescue mission in an Amazonian swamp. Antonio's last film and his swan song was the lackluster Cuban comedy, *El Señor Faron y la Cleopatra*, shot in 1958, shortly before Castro took over the country.

I cried for three days when I received a call from Hedda Hopper that Antonio Moreno was dead. By then, much of the world had forgotten him, as he spent the last two years of his life in great pain and failing health. After he told me what had happened the night Daisy died, we never spoke again about her accident. We also never discussed the death of William Desmond Taylor ever again either.

Until I got too old, I used to go every year to the grave site of Antonio to pay my respects to him and place flowers in his memory. After all, he was the first man who ever called himself my "husband."

*****

More and more Rodolfo seemed to be spinning out of control. He no longer called me. What I read about him was pure film magazine hokum. Over and over I played a record he'd made called "Pale Hands Loved Beside the Shalimar." Today it remains the only sound recording of his voice.

He also published a book of the worst love poems in the history of the English language. Called *Day Dreams,* he claimed that he wasn't the actual poet—rather it was a medium working through him. That fantasy seemed pure Natacha Rambova more than Rodolfo. For all I knew, she wrote the poems herself.

Never a good public relations person for himself, Rodolfo gave self-deprecating interviews to the press. One of his more damaging statements was, "I fear that as an actor I am growing more and more like my silly imitators," a reference perhaps to Ramon, Rod La Rocque, and even Antonio himself.

Almost in spite of himself, much of the press about Rodolfo remained glowing. I picked up a copy of *Motion Picture* and read, "George Washington may be the father of this country, and Mary Pickford may be its sweetheart. But Valentino is its lover."

Back in Hollywood after those weeks in New York State with Natacha, Rodolfo, or so I heard, had reported to work on *The Young Rajah.* From the beginning, he'd hadn't liked the script even though it was penned by his friend and mentor, June Mathis, who had helped launch him on the road to stardom with another one of her scripts, *The Four Horsemen of the Apocalypse.* At least he didn't have Natacha hovering over every scene, as she'd remained in the east. The secret source of most of my information came from William Boyd, who had been cast in the picture with Rodolfo.

From out of nowhere, Rodolfo called me one afternoon at the Hollywood Hotel. He made no mention of our last meeting in New York but claimed he wanted "to inform" me of what he was doing. "I've become a collector. Some day I'm going to open the Rudolph Valentino Museum. I'm buying antique books in many languages. I'm collecting folk costumes from every country I can. Of course, my collection of armor and firearms is growing almost daily. I'm also collecting statues. I want you to come over and have a look. He told me that he was at a rented house but had purchased a lot for $40,000 at Whitley Heights. "The

studio lent me the money. I'm ordering a Mediterranean villa built. It will help me get over my homesick feeling. It will also be a dream house for Natacha and me when the State of California finally lets us live together."

The mention of Natacha launched him into a romantic fantasy, causing nothing but a jealous rage in me. "Each day without her is a day in hell," he told me, his sentiment falling on ears that didn't want to hear that. "I thought as time goes by, I would cease to miss her. It's just the opposite. Absence has made the heart grow fonder. That heart of mine is literally breaking because of our separation. I can hardly concentrate on my work because of her."

"How charming," I said sarcastically.

"Don't be a silly little pansy," he said. "Just because Mother Nature made you incapable of appreciating a man's true devotion to his woman."

"While on the subject of women," I said, "I hear every female star in Hollywood is throwing herself at your feet."

"That's true," he said. "Even though Hearst had put a chastity belt on his darling Marion, there are zillions of others. I was at a party the other night at Pickfair. Even sweet Mary herself propositioned me. She claimed she wanted to discover what all the excitement was about. Even Nazimova tried to lure me into a three-way with Dagmar Godowsky and her. I'm sure Paul Ivano would have been delighted to take pictures of that."

"You're taking no one up on their offers?" I said, growing more jealous by the minute.

"Nobody at the moment," he said. "But I do have a solution. I called that photographer friends of yours, Rod St. Just. For special clients, as I'm sure you know, he makes a dildo. I figure I'll have a dildo made of my penis. Since every man or woman in America can't get *The Sheik* to fuck them, the dildo will have to suffice. I see it in an Art Deco style. Instead of the blatant distribution of Francis X. Bushman, I will give my dildo only to special friends like you and Ramon."

"I'd be honored to have one," I said. "Although I prefer the real thing."

"I understand that," he said. "Perhaps I have punished you long enough. I think I'll invite you over tomorrow night to deposit my seed in you. After all, you've been kind to me and you deserve the reward. Come by the set in the late afternoon."

On the set of *The Young Rajah*, I looked for William Boyd, but I soon learned that he wasn't needed in any scenes that day. Later, as I made my way to Rodolfo's dressing room, I encountered the picture's director, Philip Rosen. I had heard of him, of course, but had never met him. He seemed to know at once who I was. "Listen, Jones," he said to me, "you'd better cool your Italian boy friend down, or else he's finished in pictures."

"What's happened?"

"Every God damn thing," Rosen said. "The bastard hates everything to do with the picture. He storms off the set constantly. I hear a million times a day that Natacha Rambova doesn't want a scene shot a certain way. I'm the God damn director of the picture—not Natacha Rambova who's in New York any way."

"I'm sorry she's interfering," I said. "I know she's always urging Rodolfo to stand up for his rights. She insists he doesn't compromise his artistic standards."

"That's bullshit!" he said. "I know more about pictures than this little bigamist male whore."

In Rodolfo's dressing room, I encountered him in tears. "As the head of the studio Lasky always gets his way," he said. "He prevails in every one of our battles. The more I protest, the more the shithead blocks me. Several times I have walked off the set, refusing to face the cameras for the rest of the day. They say I'm belligerent. I'm standing up for my rights. They are to blame because of their lack of artistic vision."

"He's the boss and you've got to give in to his wishes," I said, trying to console him.

"Who's side are you on?" he demanded to know. "Natacha would never surrender this easily. I've told Lasky that in the future I'll demand script approval. I will accept films that will not only advance my career but promote the very quality of cinema itself."

"A lofty ambition," I said, hiding my true feelings about his emotional outbursts on the set. I feared he'd spun dangerously out of control. Natacha, I sensed, would eventually de-

stroy his career, with a lot of assistance from Rodolfo himself.

"Lasky is interested only in money—not art," he said.

"Name me one studio chief who's interested in anything but money," I said. "Do you think Louis B. Mayer works for charity? Samuel Goldwyn? D.W. Griffith makes pictures for money. Dear sweet Mary Pickford is a walking cash register, and Charlie Chaplin has never been known to say no to a buck."

"Lasky told me to leave the artistic details to him," Rodolfo said. "He said my job was to look sexy and wide-eyed before the camera. He also told me to show as much of my physique as the director thinks Will Hays will let me reveal. I think Lasky thinks I'm some male cootch dancer."

"You do have a beautiful body," I said.

"The world knows that," he said. "So do other studios. I'm getting really big offers. As soon as this crappy flicker is finished, I'm going to another studio to negotiate a better deal. I walked out on Metro. I can walk out on Paramount too."

"I don't think so." I said, cautioning him. "From what I understand, you've got an iron-clad contract with Lasky."

"That's for the courts to decide," he said. "They sided with me on the bigamy thing. I'm sure they'll side with me against Lasky."

At a knock on the door, Rodolfo motioned for me to answer it.

On the doorstep appeared an effete young man who announced he was Valentino's dresser. From the look in his eyes, I felt he wanted to undress Rodolfo more than dress him. At the sight of his dresser, Rodolfo stripped down to a gold lamé jock strap. The dresser then proceeded to cover parts of his almost nude body with a grotesque array of bangles, beads, and fake jewelry.

While Rodolfo "dressed," he told me that the film was a modern story about a young American, Amos Judd, at Harvard University. In reality he was the true son of the Maharajah of Dharmagar. In the film he returns to India to claim his rights from a usurper. Natacha hated the script, which came as a surprise to me when I learned that Rodolfo's character had extrasensory powers in the film. Natacha had long been interested in psychic phenomena, and she'd converted Rodolfo too. Nonetheless, they didn't like the script at all, in spite of Rodolfo's own growing interest in spiritualism. In the film he had prophetic dreams of his impending doom as *The Young Rajah* and emerges into a more exotic body in a reincarnation. That body had looked pretty good when he'd worn a form-fitting bathing suit as the young Harvard student, holding up a boat and displaying his genitals. When the picture eventually opened, and this bathing beauty shot of Rodolfo was displayed as a still, women across America stole it from theaters.

Rodolfo had urged Lasky to allow him to make the film, but Lasky had at first predicted that it would be "poison" at the box office. Eventually, it was Rodolfo himself who turned against the film, hating it, the director, and Lasky, of course.

Rodolfo's final judgment had been accurate. The film opened to modest audiences and damaging reviews—one critic calling it "a spiritual migraine." Nonetheless, Valentino fans turned out to see his bejeweled physique, especially the scene in which he reclines languidly and seductively on a swan-boat barge. That memorable scene was being shot on the day I visited the set. What movie audiences didn't know was that the scene and even the picture itself almost ended in disaster that afternoon.

On the way to the swan-boat, Rodolfo spotted a Hollywood reporter, Dick Dorgan, who wrote for *Photoplay*. Only about a month before, Dorgan had published a review in *Photoplay* that had been widely circulated throughout Hollywood. In the article, which was entitled *He Vamp*, Dorgan wrote:

I hate Valentino! I hate his oriental optics; I hate his classic nose; I hate his Roman face; I hate his smile; I hate his glistening teeth; I hate his patent leather hair; I hate his Svengali glare; I hate him because he dances too well; I hate him because he's a slicker; I hate him because

he's the great lover of the screen; I hate him because he's an embezzler of hearts; I hate him because he's too apt in the art of osculation; I hate him because he's the leading man for Gloria Swanson; I hate him because he's too good-looking.

Ever since he came galloping in with the "Four Horsemen" he has been the cause of more home cooked battle royals than they can print in the papers. The women are all dizzy over him. The men have formed a secret order (of which I am running for president and chief executioner as you may notice) to loathe, hate and despise him for obvious reasons.

What! Me jealous?—Oh, no—I just hate him.

The sight of Dorgan on the set of *The Young Rajah* caused Rodolfo to explode into a mercurial rage. "I warned Lasky that if Dorgan ever showed up on a film set of mine, I'd kill him. Apparently, Lasky didn't believe me." He turned and rushed toward his dressing room. I went to warn Philip Rosen of an impending crisis if he didn't remove the reporter from the set. When I returned, I didn't see Rodolfo. He wasn't in his dressing room, and no one knew where he was.

Suddenly, Rodolfo, still dressed in his beaded costume, emerged from between two outbuildings and was racing toward Dorgan with one of his collectible antique firearms pointed at the reporter's head. I yelled out for Rodolfo to put it down. When he didn't, I raced toward him, tackling him. As Rodolfo fell to the ground, the firearm exploded into the air, but the bullet found no human target, other than perhaps an unfortunate bird flying over.

The next few moments passed as in a blur. I remember chaos on the set, and I helped two men carry Rodolfo's body back to his dressing room. He'd collapsed and was sobbing.

In the dressing room while two men attended to Rodolfo's needs, I called Brian Sheehan to come to the set to administer a sedative to Rodolfo. The set was shut down for the day, although I heard that Lasky was rushing to confront Rodolfo. Fortunately by the time the studio chief had arrived, Brian had gotten there first. Rodolfo was sedated, and Lasky couldn't denounce him.

It was an all too painful reminder to me that this was the second time Rodolfo had tried to inflict violence or even death on a set in which he was working. Speaking privately with Brian, I said, "Things are getting a bit out of hand."

It did not help matters to have Lasky stand outside the dressing room, shouting inside to Rodolfo, who was in a coma. "You're no gaucho," Lasky yelled for all to hear. "No sheik. Not even a bullfighter. You're a rotten, double-crossing dago black-hander."

Later when Rodolfo was recovering at his home and heard what Lasky had called him, he rushed to the phone and dialed the studio chief. Lasky apparently came onto the line right away to confront his star. "You called me a God damn blackmailer," Rodolfo shouted at Lasky. The actual word Lasky had used was "black-hander." "You're nothing but a money-grubbing shithead," Rodolfo told his boss, "I happen to know you've had me shadowed by detectives from the Flynn Agency. You're hoping to catch me living in California with Natacha in violation of the law. With that knowledge, you can blackmail me into submission. Natacha is not here. Your God damn detectives are wasting their money."

Slamming down the phone before Lasky could speak, Rodolfo stormed over to his desk and tossed envelopes in all directions. "Bills, bills, nothing but bills," he shouted. "I've borrowed money from Lasky. That's why he thinks he can treat me this way and get away with it. I even borrowed that $12,000 to give to the lesbian bitch, Jean Acker. The money for my house. If that wasn't enough, an automobile dealer is suing me for nearly $3,000 in car repairs. My haberdashery bill is outrageous. There's also a bill from my jeweler. Natacha demands only the best or else she won't wear gems I give her. Lasky pays me but a pittance yet he makes millions off of me. *The Sheik* is still playing to packed houses around the world. Maybe before its run is over, *Blood and Sand* might do even better at the box office."

Over dinner that night after Rodolfo had quieted down, he told me of various séances he'd attended with Natacha. "I'm getting messages from my dear, departed mother in Castellaneta," he said. "She is urging me to return there to see my many friends and admirers, and I want to go. Natacha has even established a relationship with Meseope, an Egyptian born before the birth of Christ. The other night I was visited by Black Feather."

"You mean, the Indian chief?"

"Who else?" Rodolfo asked. "He looked down on me from Heaven that day I posed for your friend, Rod St. Just, in that Indian costume. Black Feather wants me to play himself in a movie. The film would be about the fire water the white men sold to Indians to make their brains explode."

After dinner and a brandy, Rodolfo whispered to me. "I want you to come into my bedroom. Once there I want you to worship and pay homage to my male beauty. It won't be like a lover going to bed with another lover. No Romeo and Juliet story like Natacha and I have. It will be more like that slave boy role you played in *Salome* opposite Theodore Kosloff as your Syrian captain."

Willingly and a bit eagerly, I went into his bedroom where I discovered he'd had it decorated like a set from *The Sheik*. His canopied bed looked like a tent from that film. He told me to get naked and lie on the bed. He disappeared into his dressing room. When he emerged about twenty minutes later, he was dressed as *The Sheik*. It was reality imitating art. Ever since he'd made that recording, he'd imagined himself a singer. Standing in full costume before me, he warbled the words to the current hit song of America:

I'm the Sheik of Araby.
Your heart belongs to me.
At night when you're asleep,
Into your tent I'll creep.
The stars that shine above
Will light our way to love.
You'll rule this land with me,
The Sheik of Araby.

At the end of the song, he invited me to undress him and worship every inch of his body with my lips and tongue. In the hours that followed, I passed one of the strangest nights I'd ever spent in a Hollywood bed. It wasn't *the* strangest night, but it ranked up there with the best of them.

Something happened that night that I was going to leave out of this memoir, preferring to keep a few secrets for myself because of their grotesque nature. But what the hell!

For some time Rodolfo had liked to bite into my neck when he fucked me, like some age-old male ritual, where the fucker assets his dominance over the fuckee. In the beginning this neck-biting was like mere love bites and very erotic. But as the months had gone by, the intensity and the ferocity of the bites increased until they hurt, causing me great pain and bleeding.

On the night of his rape of me in his "tent," the bites were almost vampirish. Rodolfo dug into my neck with teeth that felt razor-sharp. When I started bleeding, I thought he'd stop, especially when I'd protested. He rose up over me and slapped my face real hard, telling me to shut up. Angered by my protest, he descended on my neck even harder, drawing more blood from the wound he'd created.

It was apparent that he was holding back an approaching orgasm as long as he could to draw out his blood-drinking from my neck. When he finally erupted inside me, he continued for at least five minutes after his orgasm, sucking and drawing more blood from me. Only the sounds of his slurping and swallowing my blood filled his bedroom.

*****

Charlie's "romance," if it could be called that, with Pola Negri seemed doomed for failure from the beginning. The so-called love affair with "the king of comedy" and "the queen of tragedy" was generating almost as many headlines as the murder of William Desmond Taylor and the drug-induced death of Wallace Reid.

Charlie told reporters that he found his re-lationship with Negri "exotic," but privately he confessed to me that he was merely fucking her. As for Negri, she was using a feud with her chief rival, Gloria Swanson, and her affair with Charlie to generate mountains of free publicity to create a market for her upcoming films with Paramount.

One night after a bitter fight at Negri's house, Charlie returned to his home to tell me that he suspected she was a secret lesbian. "I think she uses men to advance her career but is not really turned on by the sex part," he said. "She seems obsessed by Gloria Swanson. I think Pola would rather go to bed with Swanson than me."

As far-fetched as that seemed to me at the time, I think Charlie intuitively was right. In the decades ahead when I became a Hollywood gossip columnist, I would see one rival female pursuing another female as in the case of Marlene Dietrich chasing after Greta Garbo or Joan Crawford lusting for Bette Davis.

Thinking I had Charlie alone for the night, I went upstairs to bathe and get ready for bed, while he stayed an hour or so in his library, fretting over his latest film, *A Woman of Paris* in which he was the director—not the star. In the film, the character of Marie St. Clair (played by Edna Purviance) from the French provinces goes from innocent country girl into a wealthy man's kept woman, an unlikely story for The Little Tramp to film.

I didn't know why he wasn't playing Napoleon or Hamlet, two characters he dreamed of portraying. Back then he still had the power to get financing for either film, should he want to, but he hesitated out of fear. When he'd first announced his intentions to film a story based on Napoleon, the dinner guests at Pickfair had laughed at him, thinking he was being funny.

I found out much later after the fact that the increasingly egomaniacal Charlie in all seriousness had told Churchill that for "my next role in pictures I want to tell the story of Jesus Christ, with me appearing as Jesus." Churchill didn't say anything for a long moment. Clearing his throat, he said, "Uh—have you—uh, cleared the rights?"

Stepping into Charlie's bedroom to turn on the light, I was anxious to deflower The Little

Tramp. Although I was getting plowed by Theodore Kosloff, William Boyd, Richard Dix, and John Gilbert, even Rodolfo himself, I also needed someone to plow into myself. Tonight was Charlie's lucky night.

When I turned on the light and to my horror, I discovered a stunningly beautiful young girl lying nude in the center of his bed. She looked Mexican, evoking the young girl, Dolores del Rio, whom Charlie had seduced, injured, and bought off for $25,000. "Who in hell are you?" I demanded to know, hoping she spoke English.

She did speak English, although accented. "I have walked all the way from Mexico to meet the great Charlie Chaplin, the world's greatest artist. I have fallen madly in love with him, and I want to give my body to him. I heard what happened to my friend, Dolores. She came to Hollywood poor and returned to Mexico rich."

"Do you want Charlie to make you rich too?" I asked.

"I want him to make me a movie star," she said. "I know he likes beautiful young girls. I want him to seduce me and take me as his mistress. In return, I want him to cast me in his movies as his leading lady."

"You still haven't told me who you are," I said.

"I'm Marina Varga, the daughter of a Mexican general," she said proudly. "I ran away from home. My father doesn't know where I am."

"I'm going to find your clothes," I said to her, "and get you out of this house and off the grounds. You'll either tell me where you put your clothes, get dressed and out the door, or else I'm calling the police."

When she rose up in bed, she had the same fierce determination that Dolores del Rio did when confronting Charlie with a blackmail demand.

"You kick me out that door," she threatened, "and it will be me who calls the police. I'll claim Charlie raped me."

The confrontation with Marina was quickly getting out of hand. I went to Charlie's chest of drawers and removed a pair of red silk pajamas belonging to him and tossed the clothing to Marina on the bed. "Get dressed. I can't stand the sight of female nudity." I headed for the door to get help.

Downstairs I found Kono and asked him to go into the library with me to tell Charlie what was going on. I knew the last thing Charlie wanted to confront was the possibility of another scandal. When learning that Marina Varga was upstairs, a panic came across Charlie's face. "I'm getting out of here. You gents handle this one for me. I'll be back tomorrow morning. In the meantime, you can reach me at the Alexandria Hotel." He stormed out the door, asking one of the Japanese members of his household to drive him to the hotel for the night.

Kono woke up two other Japanese members of Charlie's staff and together they entered Charlie's bedroom. I don't know what happened although Marina screamed one time. But when the men came downstairs, they were carrying her kicking body through the living room and out into the front driveway. She was not only wearing Charlie's pajamas, but Kono had forced her into one of Charlie's raincoats. When Kono came back, he told me the men had carried her to the street and locked the gates behind her.

That was not the end of the Marina Varga story. She was a very determined little *puta*. The next morning in her own clothes, she showed up at the door which was locked to her this time. Kono had suspected she might return and wanted to make sure the house was secured before Charlie came back. When Kono turned her away, she ran screaming down the driveway. An hour later the milk delivery truck reported that he'd seen a young girl lying in a semicomatose state near the entrance to Charlie's property.

Kono and I raced down the driveway after he'd ordered a servant to call both a hospital ambulance and the police. When the police arrived before the ambulance, they found the girl barely coherent. She claimed she'd taken poison. The ambulance pulled up at that point and rushed her to the hospital where her stomach was immediately pumped.

Regrettably the press picked up on this and ran all the wrong information, suggesting that she and Charlie were having an affair. On her release from the hospital, she told the press that Charlie had been her lover. "Even though he's an old man with gray hair," she said, "I let him make love to me because he promised to help me break into the movies."

Charlie looked like he was heading for more trouble until a friend of the Varga family recognized Marina's picture in the newspapers. Her father quickly dispensed his sister to come to Los Angeles to escort Marina back across the border. Although she'd told the *Examiner*, she was only fourteen, Marina turned out to be twenty-one years old. It was also revealed that she had a young husband waiting for her back in Mexico.

After she'd departed Los Angeles, both John Gilbert and Tom Mix reported to the press that the same girl had stalked them, hoping they would seduce her so she could blackmail them in the chance that either of those actors might help her break into films.

Later when Charlie had seen pictures of Marina in the newspapers, he was furious at me. Instead of thanking me for getting him out of a jam, he chastised me. "You didn't tell me she was that lovely. Here was the most beautiful young girl in Mexico lying nude in my bed and you let her get away before I even had a chance to fuck her." He looked at me, his face still a mask of rage. "I would have let you watch."

Within the hour, he'd forgotten all about Marina and was eager to tell me about his adventures of the previous night.

"You'll never guess who?" The budding gossip columnist in me overcame any momentary jealousy I might have.

"I met Hart Crane in the lobby of the hotel," he said. "As you know this underappreciated poet adores me and my work. He thinks *The Kid* is the greatest film ever made. Hart is the only man I've spoken to who understood the real message in *The Kid*. He told me the appeal of my movie was not just to poets or homosexuals, but to all those lost souls who feel marginalized by society. Hart said its appeal was to all those who stand outside in the bitter cold with their noses pressed against windows looking in at warm dining rooms filled with fat people eating. I think I let you read the poem, 'Chaplinesque,' that this love-sick homosexual fool wrote to me. Last night his dreams came true. He got

to go to bed with the man of his fantasy, namely Mr. Charles Chaplin of London himself."

As Charlie related the story of Crane's seduction of him, the Little Tramp took delight in telling how one of America's most talented writers had become a lovesick puppy when Charlie had walked in the door.

"I gave him some money this morning," Charlie said. "His father makes millions selling confections across the country, but he's cut Hart off without a penny. The only way he'll take his son back is if he promises never to write poetry again. There's another condition. Mr. Crane caught his son in bed with one of the old man's male employees. To come back into the Crane millions, Hart has to agree to take some brutal brainwashing treatments to cure him of his homosexuality. At least that's what the poet told me."

In the months and weeks ahead, a love letter to Charlie from Hart Crane arrived almost weekly. Even though I didn't know the exact details of that evening with Crane at the Alexandria Hotel, it must have made a lasting impression on this great American poet.

Those letters kept arriving until Crane became mired too deeply in his alcohol and dissipation. From what I'd heard, he seemed to wander the country a lost soul, feeling abandoned by the world. Taking a passenger boat from Mexico back to California, he jumped into the sea and ended his life. I will always remember Charlie's reaction to the suicide of his most beloved fan. "If a man wants to turn himself into shark bait, that is his choice." He never mentioned Hart Crane again.

Although Charlie had met Hart Crane at the Alexandria Hotel, and had had a one-night stand, somehow he had also managed to encounter another young man whom he'd invited to his home the following night. He specifically requested that I stay over and have dinner with him and his new young friend, whom he spoke of only as "George," with no last name given.

When George arrived, I was a bit stunned. He could almost be my twin, or at least an Eastern European version of myself. His good looks were marred by a nervous condition that caused him to be in perpetual motion at all times. His nervousness made other people jittery. He was like a man who was waiting for an executioner to come in the middle of the night to haul him off for a beheading. He seemed living on the edge of a dangerously high cliff and was about to be tossed off at any moment.

Nonetheless, the evening was fun as George was highly amusing. When a servant had cleared the dinner table, he yanked the cloth off and wrapped it around himself, doing a brilliant impersonation of Sarah Bernhardt with whom he claimed to have had an affair.

As the brandy flowed and the evening grew long, George spoke of his previous, rich life. It seemed that he'd been the lover of the king of Bulgaria, who bought fancy clothes and cars for him, even subsidized his going to the University of Sofia. "I was a little capitalist darling," George said. "Then one day I tossed it all aside. I left Sofia with only the clothes on my back. Gone were the jewelry. Gone was everything. I took just enough money to get me to Moscow. Arriving in Russia, I pledged to become a Red, and so I have been ever since."

From that point on, his story grew murky. It seemed that he'd emigrated to the United States and had joined the I.W.W., but more than that, he'd become a member of a dangerous cell advocating the overthrow of the United States government by violent means. Somehow his activities had led to his arrest, trial, and imprisonment for twenty years.

"I've already served two of those years at San Quentin until I got out on appeal," he said. "I'm out on bail right now. Some of my fellow Reds raised the money. Even though his name can't be used, Charlie has agreed to help me. But my lawyers told me I don't have even a slim chance of winning the appeal. I'm going back to San Quentin to serve out my term."

The thought of serving another eighteen years in a penitentiary hardly put me in the mood for sex, but Charlie was directing the show. "Gents," he said, "there's only one way to escape this gloom and doom—and that's in my bed to which each of you is now invited."

After that three-way, George disappeared, though we learned later he did lose his appeal and had to spend the prime of his life in prison for what he called "crimes against capitalism."

With George gone after a brief stint in bed, in which I penetrated both men, and with head-lines about the little Mexican girl fading, the press turned their attention once again to the Chaplin/La Negri affair.

The Polish vixen knew how to keep her name before the public. Hailed as "the essence" of café society of *Mittel-Europa*, the actress was nothing if not a bundle of lies. Always dressed in black, she learned English curse words before she'd mastered the language itself.

Throughout the years she constantly altered the date of her birth, moving it ever forward. At one point she claimed she was the daughter of Hungarian gypsies. Later it was revealed that her real name was Apolonia Chalupec, the daughter of a middle-class family of Polish Jews.

Swanson wasn't the only enemy Pola had made in Hollywood. Mary Pickford had permanently barred her from Pickfair. Charlie was still acceptable as a guest, providing he didn't bring Negri. Negri had been assigned Mary Pickford's former dressing room. The following day Negri called a press conference to denounce Pickford's taste. At the time, Pickford viewed herself as the final arbiter of style in Hollywood. America's Sweetheart had decorated the room in a Japanese style with sliding panels and furniture in a low Oriental fashion with chairs in which one sat in a lotus position. "The first time I tried to stretch out on the divan, I rolled right onto the floor," Negri told reporters.

Reporters did not view Negri's press conference with favor. One reporter for the *Examiner* wrote, "The room was good enough for our little sweetheart, Mary Pickford, but not to this German (sic) monument to temperament, La Negri. Who does she think she is? If she hates our furniture so much, why not go back to Berlin?" Perhaps the most damaging remark was found in another newspaper where a critic stated, "Miss Negri is always talking about her art. But she's not worthy to hold the candle lighting the pathway of her boy friend, Charlie Chaplin."

When I encountered her later in the evening at a small gathering at Charlie's house, Negri was fuming. She loathed being compared unfavorably to anyone, especially Charlie or Gloria Swanson. Although invited as an honored guest, she hadn't spoken to Charlie all evening. For some reason, she deigned to speak to me, whom she viewed as his lowly "secretary."

"I have no physical attraction for Charlie at all," she blatantly confessed, "even though he's insane over me. In Germany I had a great lover who I nicknamed Petronius—not his real name. He was fantastic in bed. But Charlie is effete. Maybe effeminate is the word I'm searching for. My English is not too precise. His head is too big for his small body. He has little feet, like the feet of a woman, and I can't stand that in a man. Petronius had big feet. Big everything. Charlie's most alluring physical attribute is his delicate hands. But he mars them by always holding a cigarette in them all the time. There is no electricity between us."

Then she said something that utterly stunned and embarrassed me, even though I should have been too sophisticated to embarrass at that point in my young life. "Maybe you as a homosexual find Charlie enticing in bed," she said. "I do not. He expresses passion like he's doing some vaudeville act—all waving hands and rolling eyes. My current leading man in *The Cheat*, Charles de Roche, is a real man. Chaplin calls this other Charlie a young Frog, but Chaplin is a mere upstart and low-class cockney. De Roche has breeding, aristocratic manners. De Roche owes me a big favor. I'll see that he visits you one night and fucks you. That way you'll know my taste in men if you ever become my secretary. I might take you away from Charlie. If so, I'll use you like Catherine the Great did her lady-in-waiting. There are so many men in Hollywood I want to go to bed with, but only the special ones. I don't want to waste one evening. The male secretary I plan to hire will be required to test out a man before I do. That way, I won't have to take up La Negri's time with inferior merchandise."

The offer of her present leading man was stunning, and I gladly accepted, having seen pictures of Charles de Roche in the newspapers. That was one commitment I was going to hold Negri to.

"Speaking of inferior merchandise," she said, "I understand you knew Wallace Reid. That he was a good friend, in fact."

"He was one of my very best friends," I said. "I still mourn his death. A great human being. So kind, loving, and generous to all he met."

"I was enthralled with Mr. Reid from having seen many of his films in Berlin," she said. "In fact, I was so impressed that I demanded Paramount cast him as my leading man in my first film."

"That never came about," I said, genuinely interested. "Did Wally have other commitments?"

"Fuck, no!" she said. As I've noted, Negri had learned all the English swear words. "I asked to meet him. Actually I planned to seduce him. I waited eagerly for him to arrive. When I went to the door and saw him for the first time, I almost screamed. Other than visiting a leper colony, I'd never seen such an unhealthy specimen. He virtually had the stench of death on him. His skin was yellow enough for him to pass as a Chinaman. Actually it had a green-yellow tone to it. He'd shrunken to a mere skeleton of a man. Skin-covered bones and that was about it. He could hardly talk to me. His voice was going. It was like a squeaky whisper. The thing I remember the most about him was his eyes. He'd taken so much dope that his pupils had contracted to mere pinpoints. It was like his eyes were disappearing. Real ghostly like. The eyes had shrunk so much that it looked like any day he would open his eyes and all you would be able to see were his white eyeballs. Or red eyeballs. The whites in his eyes had become red, as if they were bleeding."

It was very painful for me to hear her talk, as it brought back the desperate look on Wally's face in his final days.

"He pleaded with me," Negri said. "I can still hear his words: 'I'll take less money, give you half my salary. You can keep the other half as an agent's fee—no one will ever know. It could be a great comeback picture for me. One big money-making picture with the great Pola Negri, and Wallace Reid will be right back up there with Chaplin and Pickford where he belongs.'"

From a passing waiter, she ordered another drink. "I thanked him for coming and pleaded the excuse of an urgent appointment," she said. "I promised him we'd be in touch. Fortunately his death saved me from the embarrassment of having to turn him down."

Her callous recitation of Wally's condition made tears well in my eyes.

Negri and I had been drinking on Charlie's terrace. From out of nowhere, The Little Tramp appeared before her, ignoring me. "The title of your picture is very apt," he said to her. "*The Cheat*. Most appropriate. Rumor has it throughout Hollywood that Miss Negri has two Charlies in her life—Charles Chaplin and the inferior Charles de Roche. Sounds like 'roach' to me. How dare you carry on so blatantly with this French Frog."

"We're just good friends," Negri said defensively. "You of all people know you can't believe the shit you read in the fucking newspapers."

"All I know is that I am not escorting you tonight," Charlie said in an almost falsetto voice. "I don't want to disgrace myself in front of the major motion-picture exhibitors of America by escorting a Polish whore." With that, he was gone, the little feet that Negri had complained about doing their job of getting him off the terrace in record speed. "Let Durango escort you," he called back. "I'm sure he's not ashamed to be seen on the arm of an international prostitute."

"You fucking bastard," she shouted at him.

He stopped momentarily. "Fucking—that's something you know about. You've fucked half the men in Hollywood, and you've just arrived in town."

"I'm leaving this house for the last time," she screamed at him. "No more hysteria. No more accusing me. I won't have you camped out on my doorstep with reporters standing behind you, as you beg for me to take you back. There will be no more reconciliation. The engagement is off. The wedding is your dream—not mine. In the future, scenes such as this won't be between you and me. Only in the movies, Charlie. You'll have to go to the movies to see me in the future, the only way you'll get a look at me."

Without answering her, he turned and left.

There was a noise from the shrubbery off the terrace. Unknown to either Negri or Charlie, two reporters from the *Los Angeles Examiner* had sneaked onto the property and heard every word of the Negri/Chaplin breakup.

This made Negri all the more furious. She grabbed my arm and directed me toward the driveway and her waiting limousine. "Paramount will fire me if I don't show up in front of those exhibitors. This is my big night."

Accompanying her to the affair, I noted that she didn't even have the good manners to ask me if I would escort her. She just assumed that it was my job as Charlie's "servant" to take her.

For this banquet, the leading motion-picture exhibitors from throughout America had arrived. Paramount was making a major effort to entertain them, and, of course, had demanded that all its top stars be there. Two orchestras in white tie had been hired for the evening, and the champagne flowed. In spite of prohibition, any person could order all the bootleg whiskey he wanted to.

At the banquet hall, Negri was ushered into her dressing room, to which she invited me. A studio publicist confided in Negri that Gloria Swanson had arrived and was furious at all the press the Chaplin/La Negri affair had generated. "She's not going to be upstaged tonight," the publicist told Negri. "She's demanding to make her appearance last. She insists that she's a bigger star at Paramount than you, and her entrance will come after yours."

Negri was furious, unleashing a string of invectives only a British limey sailor knew. I had no idea who had taught her English. She absolutely insisted on being the last star to enter the room. She sent word to Swanson's dressing room that if she didn't go on before her, that Negri would not appear at all for the evening. "I'm a much bigger star than this runt," she told me. "I refuse to give in to her outrageous demands. She's yesterday—I'm here. I'm now."

When word reached studio executives that its two major female stars were digging in for the night, the chiefs ran back and forth between the two dressing rooms, trying to reach a compromise. If anything, this studio interference made Swanson and Negri more adamant.

In the banqueting hall, the motion picture exhibitors were growing impatient as the evening wore on and the drinks took effect. Finally, worried about her own career, Negri gave in. "After all, they came to see me. They were promised me. Swanson's not important."

Checking herself in the mirror before her appearance, Negri looked stunning, even if I found her beauty difficult to appreciate. She must have discovered the top designer in Hollywood, who had created a stunning gown of shimmering emerald brocade laced with gold threading. Even the leading haute couture house in Paris would have been challenged to come up with a dress to equal hers.

As Negri stood at the entrance to the banqueting hall, you could actually hear gasps of amazement. Following this moment of stunned silence, Negri was greeted with what must forever rank as her all-time greatest and most spontaneous applauding. The hysteria didn't let up for ten minutes, even as she was shown to her seat. She was placed next to Zukor himself. A waiter directed me to my name tag at one of the most obscure tables in the house, next to the kitchen. I found myself seated with a lot of young homosexual men who perhaps had also escorted stars without heterosexual dates to the function.

Also next to Zukor was an empty chair reserved for Swanson. Finally, learning that Negri had arrived in the banqueting hall, Swanson too made her dazzling entrance. I suspected that the dress of this celebrated clothes horse would outdazzle Negri.

To the stunned audience, Swanson appeared in exactly the same shimmering green brocade dress as Negri, with the same gold threading. Although this was an amazing coincidence, it was to happen several times in the decades to come among other leading actresses. The designer had apparently failed to inform either Swanson or Negri that he was selling the same gown to both of them. Later I was to learn from a fuming Negri that the designer had claimed it was an original and that no other copies would be made.

Negri's entrance had been greeted with adulation and approval. Perhaps the exhibitors had grown tired and drunk, perhaps they were furious at Swanson for making them wait for hours, but she got only scattered hand-clapping which died quickly. As she made her way to the table for her seat on the other side of Zukor, there were loud boos coming from the hall. Swanson looked nervous and ill at ease at having been completely upstaged by Negri. Before she'd even finished her appetizer, Swanson excused herself and left the room. It was clearly Negri's evening. The headlines the next day reported Negri's triumph over her arch rival.

More headlines the following day announced the reconciliation of Negri and Chaplin. From what I could learn, her bosses at Paramount had convinced Negri that marriage to Chaplin would be a great career boost for her. How could she have known that I was already the second "Mrs. Charlie Chaplin?" Going back on her previous threats, Negri decided to forgive Charlie after all and take him back into her bed, sans sexual electricity.

Before the week was out, Negri started acting as if she were already married to The Little Tramp. Charlie had purchased 60,000 acres of land on Summit Drive down the hill from Pickfair and close to the estate of Harold Lloyd. Negri arrived with reporters on the undeveloped property the day the trees were going to be planted. She personally directed the gardeners where to plant the various trees, rejecting those she found inferior.

She told the press that "Charlie and me" are going to erect a house bigger and finer, certainly "better decorated than the bungalow" occupied by Douglas Fairbanks and Mary Pickford. "When the Hollywood elite gather in the future, it will not be at Pickfair but at the mansion I share with Charlie. We will become the reigning couple of the Hollywood screen, replacing Fairbanks and Pickford, both of whom are getting a little long in the tooth, as the English horse breeders say."

Headlines were announcing the upcoming marriage of Charlie to Negri but there had been no official proclamation. One Thursday afternoon, a fuming Negri arrived at Charlie's house spoiling for a fight. "I'm very upset by these headlines, Charlie," she said. "Either announce you're going to marry me—or else. Say something."

Charlie seemed impatient with her and hardly had marriage on his mind. He was in fact planning to run off with another actress for the evening and had already booked a suite at the Alexandria Hotel. "Frankly, I think it's the lady's place to speak to the press," he said, trying to calm her.

"You are a cruel and evil man," she shouted at him, rushing from his living room. I read the next day that she'd agreed to see only one reporter from the *Examiner*, who discovered her in her living room lying prone on her sofa in grief, the place darkened with black-velvet draperies and only one big candle glowing.

"Charles Chaplin is nothing but a Casanova," she told the reporter. "I believe in mending hearts. He believes in breaking them."

None of these interviews seemed to bother Charlie in the least, as he dressed for his conquest of yet another actress. It turned out his date was with Signe Holmquist, a very minor actress and one completely forgotten today. It also turned out to be his first and only date with Holmquist.

The next morning he told Kono and me what had happened. "When I was completely naked on the bed, she went over to her luggage and pulled out a revolver. She held the gun to my head. She threatened that if I didn't swear eternal fidelity to her, she would kill me. I almost lost my iodine-coated hard-on. The evening turned out pleasantly enough, though. Holmquist is one piece of hot ass. If she shows up at the doorstep, get rid of her. After all, my pledge of eternal fidelity was forced upon me at gunpoint."

That afternoon Negri had sent yet another Charlie to call upon The Little Tramp. Charlie Hyton was the manager of Paramount Studios. He arrived filled with anger and fury. "Look what you've done to Pola," he shouted at Charlie. "She's gonna be our biggest star and you're out to destroy her."

Charlie faced the studio chief with a steely reserve. "And just what is it that I've done to Miss Negri? Other than give her a mountain of publicity and get her career launched. For that, I got a few free fucks. But just how free are those fucks? She's used me. I haven't used her."

"Paramount is prepared to invest millions in Pola," Hyton said. He was a real butterball and sweating profusely. Charlie had deliberately seated him in the hottest corner of the living room. "After all, she tells me you love her.

You do love her. Don't you?"

"I don't know what love is, my good man," he said. "I keep waiting for it to show up at my doorstep."

"You'd better marry her, Chaplin," Hyton said as if threatening him.

"And just what is Paramount going to do to The Little Tramp if I don't?" Charlie asked. "Do you think it's my job to protect Paramount's millions. What has Paramount done for me?"

"If you're not going to marry her, then don't call on her again," Hyton said, his massive blubber rising from his chair.

"Don't you think that's a decision Pola has to make, and not some fat hack Paramount sends over?"

Hyton looked as if he could strike Charlie in the face.

I had no idea what Hyton reported back to Negri. In one of those "only-in-Hollywood" occurrences, Negri went before the press the next morning and announced that she planned to wed Chaplin in a few weeks. This announcement forced Charlie to face the press himself. Otherwise, he could have no peace from reporters wherever he went. In a remarkable interview, he told the reporters, each of whom was drawing about twenty-five dollars a week, that he was "far too poor to marry Miss Negri or anyone else."

On hearing this, Negri, his jilted *inamorata*, was furious, going into a blind outrage before she too faced the press. In fact, Negri spent more time facing the press than she did in bed with Charlie. It was one hell of a public romance.

"Charlie Chaplin has destroyed my happiness," she claimed. "He has destroyed my life. Today if I would see The Little Tramp crossing the street, I would order my chauffeur to speed up and run him over. My love for him is over. He is no gentleman."

She recovered quickly from this broken romance, a habit she would demonstrate with increasing frequency in the years ahead. She appeared the following evening at the Cocoanut Grove nightclub in the Hotel Ambassador. To my surprise, her escort was none other than Bill Tilden, the famous tennis star. From my own personal knowledge, I knew that Tilden would rather be home masturbating an increasingly virile Douglas Fairbanks Jr. than escorting Negri to a night club. But back in those days even a homosexual tennis player had to keep up appearances.

When confronted by a reporter at the night club, Negri proclaimed, "Mr. Chaplin should not marry ever again. It is impossible for him to love a woman. When you spend all night staring at your own image in the mirror, it is hard to see anyone else."

Before the final Pola Negri/Chaplin affair ended, the actress called her "final press conference" on the subject. In front of reporters, she spoke not one word of truth. She falsely claimed that Charlie had called her and had begged for a reconciliation. "But I turned him down," she said. "He pleaded with me to marry me, but I cannot. I'm in love with another man, whose name I cannot reveal. Someone else has stolen my heart. Charlie is threatening suicide, but I must follow my heart."

Charlie did not call a press conference but allowed Negri to have this face-saving moment in front of reporters.

The next morning's headlines read:
POLA NEGRI JILTS CHAPLIN!

*****

One morning Charlie woke me up with a startlingly revelation. "I'm impotent," he shouted before I had fully awakened.

I rolled over in bed. "How can you be sure?" I asked. "You certainly weren't impotent last night."

"That was then and this is now," he said. "I played with myself to get hard. I was going to wake you up and demand that you go down on me. But I can't get it up."

Realizing how serious this was for him, I pulled down the covers and moved in on Charlie, plunging down, taking him in my mouth and licking, sucking, slurping with such experience that I would have given an eighty-eight year old man a hard-on. No such luck with Charlie. I tried everything but could get him to rise only an inch. "Fuck me," he ordered. "Maybe that will do it."

If Charlie didn't have an erection, I was sporting the boner of my spectacular career. I plowed into Charlie and threw him one of the greatest fucks of his life. Although I climaxed with both joy and fury, he still didn't get an erection. Sometimes he would shoot off as I plunged into his lower depths.

As we showered together, he confided in me that he'd had this problem in the past before meeting me. "There was a time when I went for three entire months without achieving an erection. No doctor could help me. There is only one person in the world who can cure me of my impotence. That's Edna Purviance."

That shocked me. Even though Edna was involved with my sometimes beau, Thomas Meighan, I always felt they had missionary style sex. As for Thomas, he might look like a masterful Victorian-style husband, but he sometimes liked to walk on the kinky side of life, as John Barrymore and I could testify. But I had always assumed that when he was with Edna, he preferred his sex straight and simple. If Edna knew how to cure Charlie's impotence, she must be some sort of sexual athlete with tricks that could have been learned only in a bordello. A fast evaluation of her was occurring in my head. As Charlie Chaplin's leading lady for years, Edna appeared somewhat Victorian to me.

Charlie ordered me to begin an all-out search for Edna when we discovered that she had not been seen at her bungalow for days, the same bungalow next door to the one occupied by William Desmond Taylor before his murder. I was almost certain Edna would come to Charlie's rescue. He was not only her boss, but he'd starred her in his most recent film, *A Woman of Paris*. He told me Edna hoped that this film would launch her into dramatic parts, because she felt her days in comedy were numbered as she was growing older.

Since Tom Ince hadn't secured any jobs as an extra for me, I had little else to do that day but drive around Los Angeles looking for Edna Purviance. The first place I headed was the home of Thomas Meighan. He had a servant who let me go upstairs to his bedroom where Thomas invited me inside. Before I could explain my mission, he pulled back the sheets. Unlike Charlie, Thomas's penis rose up like the Eiffel Tower. He certainly didn't suffer from impotence and demanded immediate relief before he would listen as to why I was here. I was only too glad to oblige.

Thomas Meighan to this day has remained one of my all-time favorites. He was like an all-day lollipop, tasting sweeter every time I plunged down on him. When I was tasting and enjoying him, I dreamed he'd marry me and take me away to live forever on some secluded island off the coast of Maine. But after the sex act, Thomas always became straight again. I felt that with him, sex with a man would forever be only a sometimes thing, no more than a harmless diversion once a month or so.

Later in his bathtub, I told him of my urgent search for Edna. "The cunt and I are through," he said. "She's a double-crossing, back alley pussy. I understood her thing with Chaplin. He uses her as a mere sexual convenience between other girl friends. But the other night I caught her in bed with that fart, Courtland S. Dines."

The name of this millionaire Denver oil broker was familiar to anyone of the time who read gossip columns in Los Angeles. His second wife had recently won a divorce settlement against him, charging him with "constant inebriety," which meant he was drunk all the time. In spite of his drinking, he managed to show up on practically every golf course in Los Angeles and dreamed of being a world champion. He was also a frequent guest at society functions and was viewed by many women in Los Angeles as a "catch." Oil millionaires in Hollywood have always found the finest doors open to them. Marion and W.R. had entertained Dines, as had Mary and Doug at Pickfair.

"Edna dumped me—rather unceremoniously I might add—for this soggy Dines creature," Thomas said. "I have no clue as to where she is."

When I left the house of Thomas Meighan that day, I just assumed I would continue to see him again. But like so many friendships of the time, our relationship just drifted off into oblivion.

As he grew older and more established as a star, his wilder days were behind him. Wherever he went, he seemed to be accompanied by his wife. Edna Purviance and I had only our memory of him, or what we saw on the screen.

Throughout the Twenties that was a lot. For Famous Players-Lasky, he starred in *The Alaskan* with Estelle Taylor and Anna May Wong, going on to make *Tongues of Flame* co-starring Bessie Love. But the Talkies signaled the end of his career as one of the dashing heartthrobs of the silent screen. In his last film, a remake of *Peck's Bad Boy* in 1934, he appeared as Jackie Cooper's father. Thomas seemed to drift off somewhere, and it wasn't until July 8, 1936 that I learned from listening to the radio that he had died in Great Neck, New York at the relatively young age of fifty-seven.

Dines lived on one of a series of luxurious bungalows at 325 North Vermont Avenue. When I arrived at his house, I discovered that the Colorado oilman was having a New Year's open house. There must have been thirty or so revelers, both men and women, wandering about drinking Dines' bootleg booze.

The word was that Mabel Normand was at the party, although I didn't see her. She was said to be drunk and drugged in Dines' bedroom in the rear.

At last Edna showed up, looking as if she'd been at another cheerful party before hitting this one. I immediately told her that Charlie wanted to see her, and the reason why. "If Charlie can't get it up, tell him to stick a coke bottle up his ass. They're selling coke bottles with Fatty Arbuckle's picture on it. That's what impotent men need."

I hardly knew the actress but she surprised me by her belligerence. She had reason to get mad. "Dines has promised to marry me," she said. "Now I hear he's carrying on with Mabel Normand. I was going to announce our engagement to the press. The other night he stood me up. I learned later he was with Mabel." She stormed off to confront Dines.

What happened next became the stuff of Hollywood legend. As we were partying up front, I heard the sound of three bullets being fired. Mabel's chauffeur, whom I'd spoken to earlier in the evening, ran back toward the bedroom in the rear, as did four or five other guests. I figured I would remain discreetly up front.

Mabel's chauffeur, Kelly, an ex-convict who went under the alias of Horace Greer or even Joe Greer, came back up front. "I shot Dines," he shouted to the party-goers. "He's dead. I'm gonna git the police."

To my amazement, Kelly was taking blame for a shooting he did not commit. I had clearly seen him in the kitchen pantry pouring himself some whiskey at the time the gunfire was heard.

Most of the party guests fled in horror after Kelly left. Some friends were in the back room with Dines, Mabel, and Edna. Deciding I'd better not join them, I too fled into the night. The last thing I needed in my life was to connect my name with another shooting. As I retreated back to Charlie's to tell him what had happened, I could not believe that Mabel was linked with another Hollywood shoot-out, so soon after the William Desmond Taylor scandal.

After the first forty-eight hours went by, it was feared that Dines was going to die, as his condition worsened. Then, as if by a miracle, he rallied on the third day, and his condition improved from then on. Within two weeks, he was attending parties. Fortunately, the bullets had gone into his lower abdomen, and neither of his lungs was pierced.

Mabel Normand—and this time Edna Purviance too—were back in the glaring headlines evocative of the William Desmond Taylor murder. Mabel's first statement to the police was a bit obvious. "I guess someone shot him, Mister." Reporters discovered that there was "an abundance of drinkables" at the party and that Dines, Mabel, and Edna were all staggering drunk at the time of the shooting.

These two motion picture stars were still drunk when taken to the police headquarters in downtown Los Angeles. Edna had arrived at the police station in her gold evening gown with matching satin slippers and even gold silk stockings, with a gold wrap. Mabel was photographed at the police station looking like a model from a Gainsborough painting in black velvet with ostrich feathers sprouting from a large black hat.

Mabel at first claimed that at the time of the shooting, she was in the bathroom putting powder on her nose. She later changed her story, remembering the incident differently. "Actually I'd stepped out onto the terrace to get some fresh air and have a cigarette." As for Edna, she claimed "faulty memory," and could not recall one single incident at the time of the shooting.

The chauffeur—the man who wasn't in the room at the time the gun was fired—had perfect memory. He accused Dines of "keeping poor Mabel so bleary-eyed that she could do nothing. I felt sorry for the kid, and I went back to that room to put a stop to it. I'm no roughneck, no cave man. From the looks of me you can see I'm no ladies man either—only one lung at that. I'm a little guy. Dines is a big oil man. Him and Mabel got into a fight. Dines picked up a bottle of Haig & Haig and was going to brain Mabel. I pulled out the gat and let the bastard have it."

The revolver, it turned out, belonged to Mabel. She told the police she'd acquired the gun in the wake of the shooting of William Desmond Taylor. She claimed that she feared for her life, thinking whoever killed Taylor might also go after her. She'd asked her chauffeur to carry the gun in case she was ever set upon.

Although Kelly had come to her rescue, Mabel denied that she was in the bedroom having a fight with Dines. For the first ten days after the shooting, she kept to her cigarette-on-the-terrace story. She distinctly recalled hearing "a sudden bang, bang, bang—I thought at first it was firecrackers, the kind I used to throw at poor Ben Turpin in the flickers."

Kelly said he meant to fire only once, but in his panic he blasted off three times. On the fourth shot the revolver jammed, a lucky break for Dines and his oil millions.

The reaction of motion picture exhibitors was immediate and hostile. The films of both Mabel Normand and Edna Purviance were banned from Ohio to Kansas. That infuriated Charlie since Edna had been his leading lady in many of his films, and the star of his latest, *A Woman of Paris*.

At the subsequent trial before Judge J. Walker Hanby, a different set of stories was heard. Edna's memory remained faulty, but Mabel recalled events with greater clarity before the judge. She did, in fact, remember being in the bedroom with both Edna and Dines. "Edna had her corset unlaced," Mabel testified, offering no explanation as to why. "When my chauffeur came into the room, I shoved

Edna into the bathroom to protect her modesty, and therefore neither Edna nor I was a witness to the actual shooting."

No reason was given for Dines' presence in the bedroom at the time—nor why Edna's modesty didn't need protection from the oilman as well. Apparently it had been all right for Dines to witness the loosened corset, but not a suitable subject for Kelly to view.

A police officer came forward. He testified that when he'd arrested Kelly, the chauffeur had told him, "I shot the bastard because he was keeping Mabel hopped up all the time on drugs. She was facing an operation for appendicitis, and needed to regain her health before the surgery."

As the days went by, it became clear what Kelly's motive was for taking the blame for the attempted murder. He was desperately in love with Mabel, and he'd stepped forward like the gallant knight he aspired to be to save the woman he loved.

At the trial, Dines himself also came forward. He was pressing no charges himself, claiming he'd blacked out at the time of the shooting and had no idea who had tried to kill him.

Bewildered and confused at this cover-up, Judge Hanby said, "There seems to be a conspiracy on the part of the witnesses to deny this court the information it needs to make a proper ruling in this case." He eventually dropped the case but threatened to prosecute Edna, Mabel, and even Dines himself for obstruction of justice. The judge never did. The case was dropped since it was obvious that everyone, including the victim himself, was lying.

But neither Edna nor Mabel got off so easily with the public. Mabel herself came in for more attack than Edna, because Mabel was still viewed as a prime suspect in the Taylor murder case. In Ohio, the film review board announced, "Miss Mabel Norman has been entirely too closely connected with disgraceful shooting affairs. None of her films will be shown in theaters in Ohio ever again." Other states followed in time.

Charlie did not want to see or be photographed with Edna until the fury had died down. But he sent me over to deliver a message to her, telling her that he did not plan to fire her.

In her bungalow Edna received me in a pink silk nightgown covered in an orchid kimono. Her blonde hair was uncombed, and she looked as if she'd been drinking heavily. Horn-rimmed dark glasses covered what appeared to be bloodshot eyes.

She was livid with rage, her anger directed at Mabel Normand. "The bitch shot Dines," she charged. "I was in love with my sweetie. Now he won't have anything to do with either Mabel or me, and I can hardly blame him after what happened. In the bedroom Mabel and I came together for a confrontation over Dines. Kelly didn't have Mabel's gat. She did. I demanded that Dines right there on the spot chose between the two of us. I asked him if he planned to dump Mabel and marry me. He looked first at Mabel and then at me, and then came to take me in his arms. He turned to Mabel and said he was through with her. He looked into my eyes and told me he was going through with his plans to marry me. Enraged and in fury, that hopped-up bitch reached into her purse and pulled out her gat and fired three bullets at Dines. It was a miracle he wasn't killed. She's God damn lucky that her lovesick chauffeur is taking the blame. But it was Mabel herself who pulled the trigger. The doped-up cow has hated me ever since I replaced her as Charlie's leading lady."

After fifteen minutes of invective against Mabel, Edna confronted me. "Is The Little Tramp going to can my ass because of this shooting and the ban on my pictures?"

"He's not," I assured her. "He sent me over here to tell you that you're still on the payroll." At that news, Edna burst into tears, and I went and sat with her on the sofa, putting my arms around her to comfort her.

The next day, before reporters, Charlie under his crinkly gray hair spoke of Edna with affection. "She's not going to lose her job with me," he said. "Everyone gets into trouble from time to time, the poor kid."

"Is she going to have the lead in your next picture?" one of the reporters asked.

Appearing a bit ruffled, Charlie hesitated. "Uh, have a cigar," he said to the reporter, offering him one. "We've been trying out a lot of people for that role. Perhaps a girl smaller than Edna would be more suitable. Someone younger. After all, Edna is appearing more matronly these days, and the role calls for a very young girl—a teenager really. You understand how types are cast. I'll need a certain type for my next picture."

In spite of what Charlie said to the press, Edna was never to appear again as his leading lady. Nonetheless, he kept her on his studio payroll as a "pensioner," as this once fabled star faded into obscurity. Occasionally she would appear in the news, including the time a jewel thief in Hawaii made off with what remained of her gems. While I was in San Francisco getting plowed by that delectable bellhop, "Tom-Tom," it was announced that Edna had been named as "that other woman" in some messy society divorce trial.

In time I heard she'd married a man named Jack Squires, an airplane pilot who worked for Pan American. For some years she lived in Rio de Janeiro with him, eventually returning to Los Angeles after he died.

Charlie always talked about plans for a comeback for Edna. At one point he considered casting her as Josephine opposite his Napoleon. That film, as mentioned before, was never made. Neither was another project he considered adapting for her—The Trojan Woman. Instead of these lofty schemes, he initially had sent Edna packing to Paris where for $10,000 she appeared in a film, L'Education du Prince. It was not a success.

Out of loyalty to Edna, Charlie did try to arrange a comeback vehicle for Edna. He'd secured the services of the German director, Josef von Sternberg, to feature Edna in a vehicle that Charlie had financed. Called either The Sea Gulls or later A Woman of the Sea, the picture actually went before the cameras in spite of von Sternberg's objections to working with Edna, who turned out to be no Marlene Dietrich.

Von Sternberg told Charlie, "Purviance is still charming, even though she hasn't worked in pictures for a number of years. She has become unbelievably timid and unable to act in even the simplest scene without difficulty. She's also drinking heavily." Nonetheless, Charlie demanded that the director complete the film with Edna. However, upon viewing it, Charlie pronounced it "unreleasable." The negative was later burned as some part of a tax write-off.

As the Twenties came to an end, and the Talkies took over, Edna lived in a modest bungalow that Charlie had purchased for her and subsisted on a monthly retainer which his payroll office sent to her, the way my check was mailed to me.

Occasionally she would have to turn to Charlie in an emergency, although the two had never seen each other since he had directed her in A Woman of Paris. When her ne'er-do-well drunken father died in 1932, Edna asked Charlie for burial expenses. She also needed money for an operation for her own perforated ulcer.

Charlie came through for her, but it wasn't until 1946 that he actually summoned her to one of his sets. He wanted her to play the part of Madame Grosnay in his film, Monsieur Verdoux. Edna and Charlie had not seen each other in twenty years. Edna arrived drinking heavily and looking more matronly than ever. She was nervous and awkward in front of the camera. Charlie told me later that she did not have the continental sophistication the part called for, and he sent her packing. When I saw her that day, she was crying but also relieved. "I just can't do it," she said. "I'm not an actress any more. Maybe I never was. When you're young you can get away with a lot before the camera."

With a heart condition and stomach ulcers marring her health, Edna retreated forever from the sound stages of Hollywood. The day she left the studio, Charlie told me, "I'm very sad. Her presence affected me with a depressing nostalgia, for she was associated with my early success—those days when everything was in the future."

In her last letter to Charlie, dated November 13, 1956, Edna expressed a "heart full of thanks" to Charlie from her bed at the Cedars of Lebanon, where she was taking cobalt X-ray treatments on her neck. "There cannot be a hell hereafter!" she wrote to Charlie.

She died at the Motion Picture Home in Woodlands Hills, California. The year was 1959 and the cause was cancer. She was sixty-three years old. Her ashes rest in the West Mausoleum of Grand View Cemetery in Glendale, California, where two other forgotten stars of the silent screen, Harry Langdon and Lafe McKee, lie with her. Today, Edna Purviance is called "Nevada's Forgotten Movie star."

With Edna faded from the picture, Charlie had found a new leading lady. Leading child would be more appropriate. At least he'd found someone to cure his impotence.

It was none other than Lita Grey, who would become his second wife and the mother of his two sons. Not surprisingly, the marriage would lead inevitably to the devorce courts—except this time, the front pages would be festooned with lurid charges of sadism, adultery, and "sexual perversion." In spite of my warnings and the warnings of his friends, Charlie moved toward Lita Grey as if wanting the international notoriety that seemed destined to come from such an ill-fated liaison.

*****

Anyone across America who attended movie theaters showing Ramon Novarro and Barbara LaMarr in *Trifling Women* faced a daunting challenge. It was difficult to follow the film's terminally weak plot when faced with two of the world's most beautiful people. Their dazzling combination virtually obscured anything actually happening on screen. All that anyone could do was look at the actors and sigh. Bisexuals of the time inevitably fantasized about having both of them in bed at the same time.

Months earlier, Samuel Goldwyn had refused to offer Ramon a contract. Goldwyn thought Ramon was "too weak and too pansy" for women to swoon over. But Goldwyn at that time was out of synch with public tastes. Several months later, launched by the Valentino invasion, exotic actors were suddenly in vogue again. After seeing *Trifling Women,* Goldwyn got the message. He knew that Rex Ingram, at rival MGM, was paying Ramon only $125 a week. In a move to steal Ramon away from Ingram and MGM, Goldwyn offered the actor a contract for $2,000 a week.

Although at first he was sorely tempted,

Ramon mulled it over for a week before saying no to Goldwyn's offer. Where MGM and Ingram were concerned, Ramon was like a loyal puppy. He told me that despite the offer from Goldwyn, he was going to stay with MGM and Ingram for far less pay. "Ingram believed in me, even when Goldwyn kept slamming the door in my face. A man has got to be loyal to something or someone in life, and I love Ingram. I'd even marry him if he didn't have that wife of his, Alice Terry, hanging on to him like a leech."

Before Ramon could be tempted by an even higher offer from Goldwyn, Ingram packed up both Ramon and his wife, Alice, and put them on a train heading south to Miami. Later, the film crew would go by boat to Cuba for location shooting. Alice Terry and Ramon Novarro were set to film their latest, *Where the Pavement Ends.*

The press hailed Ramon as Michelangelo's David with the face of an El Greco don. Ramon told me, "That goes to show you that Pickford was right. She once said my face and body don't match."

Goldwyn wasn't the only one clamoring for Ramon's services. Pickford wanted to cast him opposite her in *Rosita.* He refused, saying, "If Mary Pickford thinks my face and body don't match, how will she piece me together into a coherent whole in her damn movie?" The role of the leading man went to George Walsh. Ironically Ramon would replace Walsh in the months to come in *Ben-Hur.*

As his star rose higher in the heavens, so did the romantic spin on Ramon. He was reported in the press to be "engaged" or else "dating" various ladies about town, most of whom he hadn't even met. Metro's official biography listed him as "Spaniard," which the studio felt was easier for the American public to take than "Mexican."

When Hollywood wasn't talking about the exciting new screen stars, Ramon Novarro and Barbara LaMarr, they were buzzing with the news that my thick-dicked friend, Joe Godsol, has acquired the rights to General Lew Wallace's novel, *Ben-Hur.* Godsol as president of Goldwyn directed Goldwyn to go ahead with the film version, selecting June Mathis as the writer of the screenplay and Rex Ingram as the director.

Wavering from time to time, Godsol at one point decided to dump Ingram and offer the director's job to Erich von Stroheim, which no doubt would have inflated the budget to a billion dollars. When Goldwyn convinced Godsol that von Stroheim would bankrupt the studio, Godsol settled on Ingram once again. For the title role, Godsol told me, "Only one actor in Hollywood could play *Ben-Hur*. It needs an Italian to play an Italian. Only Valentino will do."

When I reported the news to Rodolfo, he was ecstatic. Even Natacha agreed that the role of *Ben-Hur* was in Valentino's "chart of destiny." Before leaving Hollywood, Ramon confided to me that he wanted me to intervene with Godsol and present him as the possible star of *Ben-Hur*. "It's my part," Ramon said rather petulantly. "I must do the role."

Then he was off to Florida to film the John Russell story, *The Passion Vine*, a title Ingram hated before turning it into *Where the Pavement Ends*. In the wake of Goldwyn's offer, he had upped Ramon's weekly salary to $500 a week.

In the film Ramon appeared as Motauri, a handsome young man of the islands who becomes enraptured of Matilda, a lovely missionary's daughter as played by Alice Terry. The role was about "racial discrepancies."

After telling Alice Terry he cannot marry her because he was of a different color, Ramon gives his lady love a cache of pearls and jumps to his death from a waterfall. When the studio's mogul, Marcus Loew, learned that the film ended in Ramon's suicide, he exploded. "What a miserable, shitty ending for a love story," Loew shouted. "Only homosexuals kill themselves in fiction." He ordered that Ingram reshoot the ending "and make it a happy one."

The rewrite evoked the scene in *The Sheik* where it was discovered that Valentino was not "colored," but was actually a noble Scot abandoned by his parents in the Sahara. In the new version, Ramon as Motauri turned out not to be an "islander" after all, but the lost son of a white trader. Ramon, or so the plot went, was a nutty brown from constant exposure to the sun. That left him free to marry his beloved Matilda, and Loew got his happy ending.

"Before I would marry any woman," Ramon wrote me from Florida, "I would prefer to jump over that waterfall. I liked John Russell's original version, *The Passion Vine.*"

It was in Florida that both Rex Ingram and Ramon suffered one of the great disappointments of their careers. Ramon had claimed to me that he'd practically convinced Ingram to cast him as the lead in *Ben-Hur*. But then a telegram arrived on the set one day. It was from Godsol, informing Ingram that he was off the picture. Ingram went ballistic, closing down the set. For ten days no shooting occurred as Irish-born Ingram took to his whiskey, denouncing everything and everyone about him. When his wife, Alice Terry, tried to offer him comfort, she got a black eye instead. Ramon was afraid to come around Ingram until he cooled off.

It was announced by Louella Parsons that Charles Brabin, the English director, would take charge of *Ben-Hur*. This was the Brit Theda Bara had married. Brabin immediately lobbied for Metro to give Theda Bara a leading role in the picture, promising she'd make a spectacular comeback, but the studio turned him down. "This is a story of ancient Rome," Loew had screamed to Brabin. "Not some recycled vamp shit."

Where the Pavement Ends was mere movie trivia, but audiences, mostly female, flocked to another Novarro movie, as 1,300 fan letters arrived weekly. The American movie audiences were dividing into two warring camps: the pro-Valentino fans versus the pro-Novarro fans.

Back in Hollywood, Ramon was delighted he'd remained with Metro. His salary was upped to $10,000 a week, five times what Goldwyn had offered. On signing his new five-year contract, Ramon was virtually assured the lead in *Ben-Hur*, although it had not been officially written into the agreement.

Since *Ben-Hur* was hardly ready to go before the cameras, Ingram cast Ramon as the lead in *Scaramouche*, which would turn out to be one of Ramon's biggest box office successes to date, eventually winning for him legions of new fans.

In a stroke of misfortune, shooting began on *Scaramouche* on March 17, 1923, St.

Patrick's Day. As a loyal Irishman, Ingram honored the saint by getting drunk. It was a drunk that lasted for twelve days. With all production shut down and costs mounting, Metro almost fired Ingram until he straightened himself out and launched the picture.

For Ramon's co-star in *Scaramouche*, Ingram once again cast his wife, Alice Terry, playing Aline de Kercadiou, with Lewis Stone appearing as the heavy, the Marquis de la Tour d'Azyr. Ramon, naturally, played the dashing young lawyer, actor, and duelist hero of the film. The film was budgeted at $1,150,000 dollars, one of the most expensive films ever made at that time.

Even though a movie star, Ramon remained his impulsive self. He'd long ago stopped performing at orgies but had not gotten over his reckless streak. Ever the drama queen, he preferred to go from one emotional disaster to another. If there were no immediate emergency in his life, he would create one.

As weak as that sounds, that is my only explanation for Ramon falling in love with his brother, Mariano, for whom Ramon had secured work in *Scaramouche* with his brother appearing as an extra like Ramon himself had done in his early days in Hollywood.

"Does Mariano love you back?" I asked Ramon, a bit jealous of this brotherly affection. "You had told me he wasn't a homosexual, even though he'd fooled around with you when you were kids in Mexico."

"Mariano is a homosexual and doesn't know it," Ramon said adamantly. "The other night I made him let me go down on him. He refused to take my dickie in his mouth. But I forced him to surrender his. You said he wasn't homosexual. If that's the case, why did he cum in my mouth?"

"Many men have experienced a climax in another man's mouth without being a homosexual," I protested. "If he protests at having sex with you, why force it on the kid?"

"Because I love him," Ramon said. "I want his seed. Tonight I'm going to demand that he penetrate me and take me for his bride."

"But he's your brother!" I said.

"So what?" Ramon said, looking at me with impatience and defiance. "It would be different if it were my sister. We might have a baby. But what two brothers in history ever made a baby together?"

In the face of such overwhelming logic, I retreated, although I had several talks on the set of *Scaramouche* with Mariano. "I'm not in love with Ramon," he confided to me. "Actually there is this Irish girl I'm seeing. I think I'm falling in love with her. I'm taking both English and French lessons. She's in class with me. I want to be with her at night. We're studying dramatics together. But Ramon insists I sleep in his bed. He does things to me I don't like. I do it to please him."

"Why should you?" I asked him. "Tell him you love him but only as a brother."

"You don't understand," Mariano said, as if pleading with me. "Ramon has promised to make me a movie star—even bigger than he is if that's possible. He got me a part in *The Dangerous Maid*. It starred Constance Talmadge. I know that there will be bigger roles in the future. I've even changed my name like his. I am no more Mariano Samaniego, but Mariano Novarro."

Like it did for so many other screen hopefuls, *Scaramouche* marked the end of the film career of Mariano Novarro. After a few weeks, Ramon tired of his brother and gave up on him, letting him go back to his girl friend.

Ramon returned to my bed where I proceeded to give him the kind of fuck I usually reserved for The Little Tramp. After one night with me, Ramon had seemingly gotten over Mariano. "Try as I may, I could never get him to penetrate me," Ramon said. "All I could do was go down on him. But you know what the little devil insisted upon? While I sucked and made love to his cock, he gazed at a picture of his girl friend, imagining it was his *puta* doing that to him. I've lost interest now. Besides, my brother has a dick two inches shorter than mine."

After filming *Scaramouche*, Ramon was excited about attending the opening in New York. He invited me to go with him. "If you don't go, I will be very lonely there." That I doubted, as he was one of the handsomest and biggest male stars of the screen. Many young actors in New York would want to go to bed with Ramon. Unlike the case of his brother, I fully expected these actors could also achieve penetration.

As I learned later, my prediction had come true. On the first day of his arrival in New York, Ramon had read in *The New York Times* that he was hailed as "the Barrymore of the screen." Life is nothing but coincidences and that night at a costumer's shop in Greenwich Village, Ramon encountered the real Barrymore. The two actors had never met each other before. "Barrymore reached out and shook my hand," Ramon told me later. He quoted John as saying, "So the Barrymore of the screen meets the Novarro of the stage." Apparently the two men were quite taken with each other, and they ended up drunk in John's suite later that night. "I was penetrated by the Great Lover himself," Ramon told me upon his return to Hollywood. "But I still prefer an assault from the screen's other Great Lover, Mr. Rudolph Valentino."

"Who wouldn't?" I asked in disappointment, sorry that I had turned down a possible three way with John and Ramon in New York. But "Tom-Tom," that San Francisco bellhop, had come down to Los Angeles, with five of the world's greatest male specimens, all of whom he wanted me to "audition" to see if they would be acceptable as fellow bellhops who were only too willing to perform after-duty services with the hotel's guests. With a prospect like that, even Ramon's invitation to New York dimmed.

Back in Hollywood, Marcus Loew had ordered Ingram to do a secret screen test late one night of Ramon for the role of *Ben-Hur*. For reasons known only to Loew, he didn't want anyone in Hollywood to know this test was being made.

Loew was still touting Rodolfo for the role. But when I spoke with Rodolfo the following day, I learned why Loew had ordered the secret screen test of Ramon. Rodolfo had called Loew and told him that he was turning down the part. "I can't believe that," I said in shock. "Even Natacha approves. You told me yourself it would be the greatest role of your screen life."

"It is for that very reason that I am turning it down," he said. "I cannot face the fact that if I make *Ben-Hur*, it will be all downhill for me after that. The one thing that keeps me going is that I will live to make pictures in my thirties that will be greater than those I make in my twenties. Is that so hard for you to understand? With me as the star of *Ben-Hur*, my greatness will be behind me—not in front of me."

Eventually the buzz went public. Valentino would not play *Ben-Hur*. Surprisingly, a number of other actors were announced for the part: Edmund Lowe, John Bowers, and even Ben Lyon. No list seemed to include Ramon, to his increasingly grave disappointment. Then Louella headlined Loew's choice for the role of *Ben-Hur*. To prove once again what a small town Hollywood was, the role was being tailored for Antonio Moreno.

With nothing moving forward a year later, the casting of *Ben-Hur* became a joke. *Photoplay* claimed that the movie would surely be made by 1940. The magazine even suggested that it knew who would star as *Ben-Hur*. "Jackie Coogan, the little boy of Chaplin's *The Kid*. Our sleuths in Hollywood report that Jackie spends several hours a day riding his scooter in training for the exciting chariot race."

To my knowledge, there is no copy remaining of the screen test Ramon did for *Ben-Hur* although Ingram pronounced Ramon brilliant in the part. Loew agreed, and Ramon went to bed virtually assuming that the contract for him to play in the film was being drawn up. Antonio Moreno was given the same assurance.

Ramon awoke that morning to read in the *Los Angeles Examiner* that George Walsh had been chosen to play *Ben-Hur* and would be signing the contract that week. Ironically, it was Walsh's role starring with Mary Pickford in *Rosita* that had apparently convinced Loew that Walsh could do the role. Ramon recalled painfully that it was a part that he had turned down.

After crying all morning, he invited me to go for a drive with him up the coast. I had offered to drive but he said he wanted to try out his new roadster. Five miles up the coast he floored the accelerator and forced the car to go at its peak speed. It was like he was trying to commit suicide. I screamed at him to slow down but he wouldn't. He seemed to want to take me along in his suicide. Finally, just as we were facing a dangerous curve and certain death, he slammed on the brakes, slowing the car down. When he finally brought the vehicle to a stop beside the road, he slumped over the wheel and burst into uncontrollable sobbing. "It was my part. It belonged to me."

The next day Ramon masked his acute disappointment and showed up on the set of *Thy Name Is Woman*, a film directed by Fred Niblo, which would once again team Ramon with Barbara LaMarr. Ramon had long ago replaced me in Barbara's affections, although she remained wonderfully friendly and loving toward me. Ramon was particularly nervous on the set, as it was his first major film without Ingram. Ramon was also aware of the trouble between Rodolfo and Fred Niblo when they'd made *Blood and Sand* together.

Adapted from a popular German crowd-pleaser, *The She-Devil*, first presented on the stage in Berlin, *Thy Name Is Woman* cast Ramon as a Spanish Trooper, Juan Ricardo, who makes love to Barbara, playing the wife of an elderly smuggler. Ramon's character hopes that by making love to Barbara's character, she will betray her husband and turn him in to the police.

Watching Ramon emote in one of his big scenes in the film, Barbara turned to me and said, "He'll be one of the biggest stars of all time," she said. "Bigger and greater and more enduring than Valentino. For Valentino, I predict a very short career. Three more films, maybe not even that."

Ignoring this dire prediction for Rodolfo, I turned to her and said, "but your star will rise just as high as Ramon's."

Her purple eyes assumed a faraway look. "In a couple of years, I'll be finished. I'll become one of the forgotten stars of the screen."

Even more than her appearance with Ramon, she was excited about her upcoming film. "It's *The Shooting of Dan McGrew*," she said. "Based on Robert Service's poem about the Yukon gold rush. I play the Lady known as Lou. It has a big cast. Lew Cody, Mae Busch, Eagle Eye, and the world's most beautiful child, Philippe de Lacy. Mary Pickford tried to adopt him. She offered his stepmother, Edith, a million dollars, but she turned her down. Pickford's buying flesh these days. Why doesn't she have a kid the old-fashioned way? Don't tell me that Douglas can't get it up any more. He certainly did for me."

The Hays office at first deemed the love scenes between Barbara and Ramon in *Thy Name Is Woman* too hot for general release. "The sex stuff is allowed to run wild," Hays said. But eventually, Hays was persuaded—perhaps bribed—to let the film go into general release. The public not only liked the sex scenes, and didn't faint, but made the film a wildly successful movie of 1924, even pleasing Louis B. Mayer, who surprisingly didn't find it too hot and steamy, as he often did much tamer pictures.

In spite of its merger with W.R.'s Cosmopolitan Pictures, Goldwyn Studios was experiencing financial difficulties, as was Metro itself. Metro's stupid loss of Valentino to Lasky was taking a toll on its coffers. It was Marcus Loew who suggested that Metro combine with Goldwyn. The studio would be called Metro-Goldwyn, and Louis B. Mayer would be hired to oversee the new studio, which would in time lead to Metro-Goldwyn-Mayer. Ramon seemed unaware of how these studio moguls would impact his film career and his personal life.

All he knew at the time was he had one more picture to make for Rex Ingram. It was called *The Arab*, based on the Edgar Selwyn play. Rodolfo protested that it was a shameless rip-off of *The Sheik*, and in many ways it was. In fact, many photographs shot of Ramon in the desert looked so similar to Valentino's *The Sheik* that hundreds of fans thought that Ramon in the photos was Valentino. Surprisingly, Rodolfo didn't know until I told him that Cecil B. DeMille had filmed the original version of *The Arab* in 1915, years before the release *of The Sheik*.

On the subject of shameless rip-offs, Rodolfo did not live to see one of the low points of Ramon's career when he made *She Didn't Want a Sheik* in 1937 on "poverty row" at Republic Pictures. It was later released as *The Sheik Steps Out*. He played Ahmed Ben Nesib in this dull bomb. Reviewers cited Ramon as a "one-time popular star in silent pictures." It was noted that he spoke English distinctly and "there is no reason why he should not regain some standing in films if given a part in a major production where he would be assisted by competent actors," a slap at his co-stars,

Lola Lane and Gene Lockhart.

Once again, Ingram cast his wife, Alice Terry, as the leading lady in the newest version of *The Arab,* which was scheduled for release in 1924. Ramon invited me to go with him to the deserts of Tunisia, but with all my commitments in Hollywood, including my ongoing relationship with W.R. and Charlie, I chose to remain behind, even though intrigued with the invitation.

So "Ravishing Ramon," as the press had dubbed him, set off for the desert to impersonate Valentino as an Arab sheik. When I turned down Ramon's invitation, he invited Herb Howe, the Hollywood correspondent for *Photoplay.* As I was to learn later, Ramon and Howe became lovers before the *S.S. Majestic* reached its first Mediterranean port.

Ramon remained discreet about his relationship, knowing that word of his sexual preference would doom his career. "I don't want to go the way of Mabel Normand, Fatty Arbuckle, or Wallace Reid," he told me before his departure. On the long voyage to Tunisia, Ramon entertained his fellow film cast with impersonations of John Barrymore and Charlie Chaplin. He later played a battered piano, singing "Ave Maria."

Ingram's days at Metro were coming to an end. The new head of the studio, Louis B. Mayer, demanded that rushes be shipped to him of *The Arab.* This infuriated Ingram. He was again furious to learn that Mayer "hated" the picture. Reviews were mixed. *Variety* found it the "finest sheik movie of all of them, including Valentino's version," and the *Los Angeles Examiner* reported that "Ramon Novarro is 100 degrees in the shade." Many other reviewers found the picture slow and tedious. Among its critics were Cecil B. DeMille, who had made the first version but hated the remake. He'd also predicted disaster for Valentino's *The Sheik.*

Although Ramon still badgered Louis B. Mayer to cast him in the role of *Ben-Hur,* Mayer had other plans for Ramon, rushing him into *The Red Lily,* also directed by Fred Niblo. Ramon developed an intense dislike for Niblo, although not as violent as Rodolfo's response to the director. In front of Ramon, Niblo said to some cast members. "The studio gives me a script to shoot. Instead of male heroes, I get pansies growing in my garden." The reference obviously was to Rodolfo and Ramon. So infuriated was Ramon at the director's remark, that he stormed off the set and refused to shoot for the rest of the day.

Variety found the plot of *The Red Lily* weak and hackneyed. Its female star, Enid Bennett, is little remembered today, unlike the third lead, Wallace Beery. The only thing I remembered about the film is that Ramon allowed Eduardo, his youngest brother, to portray him as a child in the film.

Still refusing to give up his dream of playing in the long-delayed *Ben-Hur,* Ramon was cast in the romantic drama, *The Midshipman,* co-starring Harriet Hammond, another forgotten name.

My lucky day came when one of my alltime favorites, William Boyd, got to play "Spud" in that movie. I had long told Ramon of William's exciting attributes, and the three of us spent many a lunch hour in Ramon's dressing room. Both of us preferred to eat William than the corned-beef sandwiches served, and William didn't seem to mind at all.

The picture opened to lackluster reviews, *Variety* finding Ramon "a good-looking undergraduate," who was "natural and convincing!"

The word reaching us from Rome was that conditions on the set of *Ben-Hur* were deteriorating rapidly. Even Mussolini had withdrawn his offer of help for the film. The dictator had found to his disgust that the Romans were getting less money in salary than the American crew imported for the job.

To our total surprise, Francis X. Bushman had been cast in the film as Messala.

"He'd better wear his Roman skirt real low," Ramon said, recalling his one sexual bout with Bushman. "Or else that thing will pop out and steal the show."

"They can always tape it up," I assured Ramon.

In 1963, *Cleopatra* with Elizabeth Taylor and Richard Burton would generate world-wide scandal and gossip. Before that, *Ben-Hur* created the most advance press of any film in history, most of it reporting on one disaster after another.

But as much as he liked to be adored and

to have me fill my every moment listening to stories of his triumphs, some of them documented in press accolades, I had other calls to make in Hollywood than the Novarro household. Beyond Ramon's limited world, major developments were unfolding.

More scandals were brewing.

*****

It was with pain and regret that I watched Rodolfo from afar launch the destruction of the very career for which he'd sacrificed so much to obtain. He was back in New York, claiming he would not return to Hollywood to make another film unless Jesse Lasky and Adolph Zukor gave in to his demands, many of which had been drawn up in a manifesto by Natacha Rambova, including the demand for script approval.

At the home of W.R. and Marion in Santa Monica, Adolph Zukor—in theory Rodolfo's boss—lamented that "millions of Americans are watching something heretofore unknown in the industry. A young actor is cutting his throat and asking the nation to be a witness to his suicide attempt."

That night as I moved through the Hearst/Davies party, the talk was often of Valentino. It seemed everybody had an opinion, often widely different from each other. The emerging flapper, Colleen Moore, told me she didn't know what all the excitement was about. "I've met Valentino," she said. "I find him dull and on the stupid side." Bebe Daniels, who ironically enough would be Valentino's next co-star when he returned to films, asked me if he were a real lady-killer. "He does not kill the ladies," I told her. "The ladies kill him."

At the very peak of his stardom, Rodolfo was not listening to anybody but Natacha. More and more I viewed her as a witch of destruction. It wasn't sex that had united the ill-fated pair. Rather it was as if Natacha had cast some demonic spell over Rodolfo.

Battling Jesse Lasky on the West Coast, Rodolfo on the East Coast called a press conference, hoping to win the public over to his side. His nattily dressed figure appeared on nearly every front page of every major newspaper in America the next day. Before New York reporters, he denounced Paramount for the "miniscule salary" he was being paid and for that studio's failure to give him publicity "commensurate with my stardom." He vowed never to return to Hollywood until Lasky addressed some of his major concerns.

While waiting for the studio executive to come to terms with him, Rodolfo announced he might go to Italy to visit his parents. A reporter from *The New York Times* reminded Rodolfo that he had claimed that both his parents were dead in previous interviews. "I'm speaking of a spiritual visit," Rodolfo countered.

Before withdrawing from the press, Rodolfo launched into an attack on Paramount's production of his films. "The photography is inferior," he charged. "The management of my career by Lasky is utterly ridiculous, almost moronic. The poor distribution of my films is appalling. The publicity generated about me, especially those movie stills sent out, makes me look like a male stripper. None of Paramount's efforts on my behalf have even begun to match my desires as an artist."

In a mercurial rage, Rodolfo had leaped up from his seat at the press conference to reveal one of the studio's darkest secrets, which at the time was not known by the general public. An assistant tried to restrain him, but Rodolfo shoved the man away. He wanted to tell the world how big Hollywood studios, especially Metro and Paramount, did business. "If Paramount makes one-hundred pictures a year, and one theater wants to show any one of them—no doubt a Valentino flicker—the poor exhibitor has to agree to exhibit all one-hundred pictures as well. You can be sure that if they're made by Paramount, at least ninety percent of them will be guaranteed stinkers. Even if a theater manager doesn't show a particular movie, he must pay Metro or Paramount for the privilege regardless. This is called in Hollywood a block-booking system. It's a disgusting practice. Extortion, really."

Even though this revelation would have been big news at the time, no major U. S. newspaper, including *Variety*, published Rodolfo's allegations. The star had been deadly accurate in skewering the practice. What they did publish was the astonishing announcement that Valentino had issued orders to his bank not to accept any more checks sent over by the Famous Players-Lasky Corporation.

The reaction to Rodolfo's press conference set off a firestorm in Hollywood, especially among Paramount executives. Overnight *The Sheik* had found himself the single most unpopular actor on the lot, and potentially the most dangerous for the film industry.

Lasky announced the next day that if Valentino wanted to resume making films, he would be welcome. "If he doesn't," Lasky said, "every legal step necessary will be invoked to keep him off the screen."

On hearing that news in New York, Natacha cancelled a planned trip to Europe "to help Rudy in his battle with the Philistines." Although they could see each other, Rodolfo was still forbidden to live with her as man and wife according to the California divorce laws of that time.

What I learned about Rodolfo came from W.R., plus bits and pieces of Hollywood gossip I heard at parties, notably from Louella Parsons, who was still taking the train back and forth between New York and Los Angeles. There were scattered and infrequent telephone calls I had with Rodolfo. Some of the details I learned much later during "pillow talk" nights in Europe when I'd been invited to accompany Natacha and him on their whirlwind European jaunt of 1923.

No doubt I would later be invited along on that European grand tour out of gratitude. Some insiders in Hollywood, especially Zukor and Lasky, wondered how Rodolfo was continuing to live in grand style, while professing to be broke. It was assumed that Natacha was supporting them, having been given money to do so from her rich parents.

Such was not the case.

Natacha was too proud to accept money from her family but she was not adverse to spending funds that came from an unrestricted loan bestowed upon them by my old buddy and partner in crime, thick-dicked Joe Godsol.

After several arguments with Godsol, I surprised even myself in getting him to agree to make a loan to the Valentinos. I didn't actually threaten Godsol with blackmail, even though

I'd shared enough of his life to know where some bodies were buried.

Natacha and Rodolfo eagerly accepted the Godsol bequest, agreeing to pay him back as soon as the feud with Zukor and Lasky was settled and when Rodolfo resumed his screen career. But by the time of his death, Rodolfo had never paid off the loan. Godsol over the years frequently reminded me of that. One day in disgust at hearing him harangue me about it, I paid back the damn loan myself. By then, I could well afford to do so.

Even though I'd secured money to help him live in exile in New York, I was still dismayed and disappointed in Rodolfo for allowing Natacha to dictate the terms of his own career. I also feared he was making a big mistake in going against a major studio. Other stars such as Clara Kimball Young had tried that and failed. Zukor again entered the fray, claiming the studio would exercise its option on Valentino's contract for another year, as it had the legal right to do. Zukor also promised Rodolfo an increase in salary, which at the time was $1,250 a week.

Zukor announced that *The Spanish Cavalier*, a vehicle slated to star Velentino, was scheduled to go before the cameras. He claimed the studio had already suffered a loss of $30,000 because of Valentino's absence, and that costs were spiraling daily. As a final revelation, Zukor let the world in on the secret that Valentino was "seriously in debt" to the studio.

Representing Rodolfo as his New York attorney, Arthur Butler Graham argued in vain to get Rodolfo out of his contract. In retrospect, some of Rodolfo's charges appeared silly when presented on a national platform. He complained that Lasky had assigned him an inferior dressing room and that Paramount would not pay for the expense of answering fans letters pouring into the studio. He also reiterated his charge that Lasky had hired detectives to follow him, hoping they would find him in bed with Natacha. "They want to blackmail me into submission to their demands," Rodolfo charged once again.

As a rather ungallant blow, he also claimed that the two women cast as his co-stars in *Blood and Sand*, Lila Lee and Nita Naldi, were "inferior stars" and not worthy of appearing opposite him in a major release film. As a parting blow, he added that Lasky had personally insulted Natacha Rambova who had presented him with brilliant artistic challenges.

In the weeks ahead, Rodolfo continued to reject any attempt at arbitration, even though his attorney, Graham, was running up expenses of $2,500 a week. Rodolfo did not have that much money to pay such a bill, especially now that his salary had been suspended at his own request.

In another blow to him, *The Young Rajah* was playing to half-empty houses around the country. Reviews, as mentioned, had been extremely poor. One critic wrote, "Instead of the spicy cocktail we expect from the great Valentino, we get a milkshake instead—this one made from sour cream."

In Hollywood, Paramount announced that it would offer Rodolfo $7,000 a week if he'd return to the fold. Rodolfo later told me he considered that a dream salary, but Natacha demanded that he not accept it until Lasky caved in to other demands such as script approval.

The weeks of suspension appeared to be taking a toll. In his infrequent calls to me, Rodolfo denounced everybody except Natacha whom he continued to place on a pedestal. He was livid with rage and threatening violence against his first wife, Jean Acker. He'd learned that she had petitioned the court to have her name changed to Jean Acker Valentino. Rodolfo's west coast attorney, W.I. Gilbert, filed an immediate challenge, claiming that Valentino was merely his stage name and therefore Acker had no right to it. Charlie had faced a similar problem with the billing of Mildred Harris Chaplin.

During all these travails, I knew Rodolfo was fucking someone—not Natacha, but someone. It was through Ramon's grapevine that I learned who was sharing Rodolfo's bed. After returning with Ramon from Tunisia where he'd made *The Arab*, Herb Howe of *Photoplay* dumped the actor. He claimed he was going to New York to pursue an "even bigger conquest than Ramon Novarro." That conquest, it turned out, was none other than Rudolph Valentino.

Even though I had created the profession of star-fucker, this vicious little faggot was scheming to follow in my footsteps as Hollywood's second star-fucker.

I made an attempt to find out all I could about Howe, since my studio work for Tom Ince as an extra saw many idle days. On a visit with "Tom-Tom," that luscious and hung bellhop in San Francisco, I went by W.R.'s newspaper offices to learn what their morgue had on Howe. Not much, I found out. He was born in either North or South Dakota, but at no known date. A source claimed he'd gone to some state university there, and that his father was a small town theater owner. Another listed his father's profession as a tradesman.

What was known was that from an early age Howe had been fascinated by motion pictures, especially its male stars. Who wasn't? In time he'd arrived in Los Angeles where he'd written publicity about the film industry and had actually authored some scenarios for one- and two-reel shorts. He attracted the attention of James Quirk, the boss over at *Photoplay*, and had been hired as a staff writer, eventually becoming the magazine's top interviewer. When Howe went to New York to see Rodolfo, he was the second major writer in Hollywood, topped only by Adela Rogers St. Johns herself.

Howe's ostensible reason for calling on Valentino was to write his autobiography, which he planned to publish in three consecutive issues of *Photoplay*. From reports reaching us in Hollywood, Ramon and I learned that Natacha had approved of Howe, finding him "an engaging and sympathetic young man and most understanding" about Rodolfo's battle with the studio bosses.

Before that autobiography was even launched, it seemed that Howe and Rodolfo had become an item. As Rodolfo poured out the story of his life to this young homosexual, it was determined that the tall tales could better be told in the privacy of Rodolfo's bedroom at a hotel, or so we heard.

Ramon and I fully expected a fictional "autobiography" from Rodolfo since the real story couldn't be told. Howe's so-called autobiography was so fanciful and fictional that it shocked even those of us who had expected major exaggeration and distortion. Instead of depicting a sanitized version of Rodolfo's early years of struggle in New York, Howe had him financed to go to America by a wealthy and aristocratic Italian family, all of whom were titled.

In his life's story, Rodolfo claimed he wasn't a draft dodger during the war but had made every effort to enlist in the Italian air force. He said he was turned down because of a visual defect in his left eye. What was left out was that Italy didn't have an air force in World War I. Since Rodolfo knew that, I just assumed that he hadn't even bothered to read Howe's proofs.

Beset with creditors and with attorneys on both coasts demanding immediate payment, Rodolfo responded by running up hundreds of dollars in bills, far more than the stipend provided by Godsol could cover. Rodolfo spent hundreds of dollars he could ill afford speaking long distance to the foremen of the construction site at his Whitley Heights home. The contractor was demanding more money. Rodolfo told the foreman if the job wasn't completed to his specifications, nobody would see a penny. Surprisingly, the contractors continued to work on the project, fearing that if they didn't they would lose all the money they had previously invested in the star's home.

To put the heat on Zukor and Lasky, Rodolfo took to the air waves, appearing at the American Radio exposition at the Grand Central Palace in New York. The broadcast was presented as "The Truth About Myself," starring Rudolph Valentino. Much of the country had never heard *The Sheik's* voice before. Instead of talking about himself, as promised, Rodolfo renewed his attack on the film industry calling it "one monstrous cannibal, devouring talent, and then spitting it out when it no longer made money." He also claimed that three-fourths of the pictures emerging from Paramount were trash and an insult to even the lowest of public intelligence. When asked if he thought the work of Rex Ingram an exception, Rodolfo didn't answer but reporters noted a chill come across his face as cold as an Arctic lake.

The January issue of *Photoplay* contained an embarrassing letter no doubt written by that cocksucker, Howe, but signed Rudolph Valentino. In the letter he claimed he was devoid of temperament. "I'm not grasping for Hollywood millions like some stars, but I seek fair pay for a day's work." He left out that he'd been offered $7,000 a week. He also confessed that he was not a great actor in the tradition of Barrymore, but felt he might improve if allowed to search for his own properties which could then be adapted for the screen. He felt it had been wrong that such inferior directors as Rex Ingram and Fred Niblo had been forced upon him. He ended the letter—or else Howe finished it for him—with a promise to the American people that he wanted to continue to be worthy of the praise and adoration heaped upon him. When confronted with the letter, Zukor exploded. He called Adela Rogers St. Johns to tell her that Valentino could go back to one of his former professions—that is, dishwasher or gigolo. When Rodolfo heard of this, he threatened to kill Zukor when he returned to Hollywood.

The *Photoplay* autobiography generated dozens of offers for the services of Valentino, even though he was forbidden by his contract to seek work as an actor. Music studios wanted him to record romantic songs, and major theaters offered him dance engagements. Some of the offers carried a $6,000-a-week salary.

"I think Rudy has lost his mind," Ramon said one morning as he showed me a story in the newspaper. In New York, Rodolfo had told a reporter that in his investigation of reincarnation he had discovered that he had lived eighteen previous lives, two of which were as famous people. He claimed that he wanted his next films to depict those lives he'd led previously. When pressed to identify the famous personages he'd been, he cited Cesare Borgio. Not only that, but he also claimed he'd lived in ancient Egypt.

"Who as?" a reporter asked. "Surely not as Cleopatra."

Rodolfo's face, it was reported, turned into an icy mask like the time he'd been queried about Rex Ingram. "Ramses," Rodolfo had revealed.

One clever public relations man, S. George Ullman, devised a scheme to short-circuit

Paramount's injunction to keep Rodolfo from working. He came up with an idea that one of his commercial clients might employ both Rodolfo and Natacha to endorse one of their products. They would, of course, dance for the public, a free performance, but would give a short speech at the end plugging the product. Ullman approached his major client, the Mineralava Beauty Clay Company, and they readily agreed to the tune of $7,000 a week, matching Zukor's office of Valentino's return to the screen.

When presented with the offer, Rodolfo accepted at once. Natacha, as was her way, objected. Rodolfo countered that he wanted to fill his stomach with spaghetti every night, but Natacha pleaded that acceptance of the offer would make him a laughing stock—a real step backward in an otherwise brilliant career. She said he could not accept this crass commercial offer which would only exploit both of them. Eventually Rodolfo's pasta argument won out, and both Rodolfo and Natacha agreed to sign up for the tour.

After the *Photoplay* publicity, Rodolfo had grown bored with the writer, Howe. This star-fucker faded into the background. Rumors circulated that he'd gone back to Hollywood to pursue Douglas Fairbanks Sr., on whom he'd also developed a crush. After Howe's departure, another young homosexual male, George S. Ullman, arrived on the scene. He even went so far as to issue a statement about his first meeting with Valentino:

Naturally, I was familiar with his pictures and thought of him as a handsome boy. I had no idea of his magnetism nor of the fine quality of his manhood. To say that I was enveloped by his personality with the first clasp of his sinewy hand and my first glance into his inscrutable eyes, is to state it mildly. I was literally engulfed, swept off my feet, which is unusual between two men. Had he been a beautiful woman and I a bachelor, it would not have been so surprising. I am not an emotional man. I have, in fact, often been referred to as coolheaded; but, in *this instance, meeting a real he-man, I found myself moved by the most powerful personality I had ever encountered in man or woman.*

The tour would be launched in Chicago where the Valentinos planned to remarry at the Blackstone Hotel. Right before the ceremony, Ullman learned that according to the laws of Illinois the couple had to wait another two weeks before the interlocutory decree in California would allow them to go ahead and wed. Ullman claimed he would search the laws of one of the "border states" that might have more lenient requirements than Illinois.

In the meantime, Natacha and Rodolfo attended the opening act of Jean Acker Valentino, appearing two blocks away as a stage act, following the debacle of her screen career.

Later, Natacha told a Chicago reporter that surely, "Miss Acker is the single worst actress who had ever tried to make it in Hollywood. She is dull and unimaginative," Rodolfo ungallantly commented that he'd been young and naïve when he'd married Acker. "What I took for brilliance was mere fluff. It wasn't until I met Natacha did I realize how much talent one woman could possess."

A few days later, on March 14, 1923, Ullman drove the Valentinos to Crown Point, Indiana, where they were quietly married in a private ceremony. Rodolfo had legally taken his second and final wife. Or was it legal? Within an hour of the wedding, a little busybody, Mrs. Edward Franklin White, deputy attorney general of Indiana, claimed that Natacha was not a resident of the county, thereby in violation of Indiana law when she married Valentino. White pronounced the wedding not legally binding. But the governor told her to go back to prosecuting cattle rustlers. He felt the Valentinos had been hounded long enough. The case was dropped.

Rodolfo later reported to me that he'd spent his wedding night with Ullman, Natacha preferring to sleep alone. "He couldn't get enough of my dick," Rodolfo claimed. "He wanted it in every hole." I noted sadly that I had gotten to fill in for the bride at Rodolfo's other weddings.

For their tour across America and Canada in 1923, Ullman had engaged a private railroad car. Natacha compared it to a set for *The Young Rajah*. Each of three staterooms had a full bath and was decorated with rugs from Persia, crystal chandeliers, mirrors trimmed in gilt, and paintings from the Flanders school. A private steward had been employed and even a personal chef. Ullman and Rodolfo would share one bedroom, Natacha another, and a third was left empty.

The train took them to Omaha but even before their arrival ice and snow were hammering the windows of the train. An unseasonable blizzard, one of the worst in that city's history, had descended. Snow piled in drifts on the streets, and all public transportation came to a standstill.

Ullman feared the opening night would be a disaster. Nonetheless, the hearty people of Omaha braved the night winds and turned up in record numbers for the premiere. The curtain went up thirty minutes late. Thunderous applause greeted Valentino as he appeared on stage looking as if he'd descended intact from the set of *The Four Horsemen of the Apocalypse*. Natacha followed to a tumultuous welcome, appearing like a porcelain figurine from Andalusia in black velvet and silk taffeta. At the end of their dance numbers, including an exotic tango, Valentino endorsed the Mineralava beauty products, and Natacha appeared to claim that the company's beauty clay was the reason for her exquisite complexion.

Wherever they went, from one Middle West Bible Belt town to another, even bastions of the Ku Klux Klan, both men and women flocked to their show. More people lined the railroad tracks to see them than they did in 1945 when the body of Franklin D. Roosevelt was shipped back to Washington after he'd died of a heart attack in Warm Springs, Georgia.

As Zukor stood by idly in Hollywood, he could not help but be aware of his errant star, the sex symbol to some fifty-million women in some 15,000 theaters across the country. Almost weekly Natacha flew into a temperamental rage, and threatened to withdraw, but Rodolfo persuaded her to keep on dancing.

They were drawing the largest show business audiences in the world.

It had been anticipated that women would flock to the shows. But an almost equal number of men showed up as well, perhaps to gaze upon Rodolfo in envy. Coming as a surprise, the Valentinos proved equally popular with children too, although no one knew Valentino's romantic image extended to grade school kids. Nonetheless, when they appeared in such cities as Wichita, Kansas, and other Midwestern towns, schools were let out for the day so the children could go and look at "The Sheik of Araby."

Sometimes demand for seats were so great riots broke out, as almost occurred in Montréal until Rodolfo cooled the audience by addressing them in both English and French.

The performance at Salt Lake City had a special meaning for Natacha since she was its native daughter. She was still known as Shaughnessy back in her hometown, and she was proud that her ancestors had been friends of Brigham Young.

Before the show, Natacha had invited Rodolfo to swim with her in The Great Salt Lake, but they hadn't noted the time. Because of heavy traffic, they were late getting to the Saltair Auditorium, where the unruly audience was practically ready to lynch Ullman. Valentino arrived in time to quiet them down, and the performance drew tumultuous applause, even in the stifling heat.

It was back to Chicago where the tour had originated. *The Chicago Tribune* up to then had generally been kind to Rodolfo, publishing such headlines as "The Sheik of Sheiks Draws Shebas in Sighful Swarms." But in the past weeks, the beauty clay people had taken out advertisements claiming that both Valentinos— not just Natacha—used their products. Finer barber shops across the country started to stock them. The beauty clay became the first major beauty product in America hoping to bridge the gender gap between men and women. The press, especially the *Tribune*, met this news with articles ridiculing Valentino. One story referred to him as a "sissy," because he not only used beauty clay at night, but was photographed wearing a wristwatch, "something no real man would do."

Enraged at this slur on his masculinity, a furious Rodolfo arrived at the editorial offices of the *Tribune*. He challenged every man in the city room "to mortal combat." He announced, "Your fists or else your weapon of choice." There were no takers that day, although a reporter noted in a story the next morning that Valentino looked weak and a nervous wreck.

To counter that charge, he appeared before the audience that night in his skin-tight gym clothing, performing different calisthenics on stage before the tango with Natacha. The audience roared its approval.

After the endorsement of the beauty clay, the Valentinos submitted to a question-and-answer period. One fat woman from down front rose to her feet to ask Natacha, "Is your husband all man?"

Without blinking an eye, Natacha replied, "Every inch of him." The audience applauded. Natacha then said, "what I mean to say was he is a man from the top of his forehead to the tip of his toes."

Rodolfo then addressed the audience. "Paramount tries to depict me as a wan, pale, and beardless youth, leisurely reclining on down sofas, supported by silken pillows and wickedly smoking sheikishly perfumed cigarettes. As you can see, though, I'm a real he-man."

Wherever he went, Rodolfo sold and autographed thousands of copies of his book of poems, *Day Dreams*. One of his poems, "Dust to Dust," was interpreted by homosexual men as an ode to male bonding. In the poem Rodolfo had written, "I take a bone—I gaze at it in wonder." The poem also praised "the shaft that held together the vehicle of Man."

Many reviewers claimed that Rodolfo's poems suggested "effeminacy." But Natacha defended him on that point, claiming they were really psychic communications actually dictated by the likes of James Whitcomb Riley, George Sand, Walt Whitman, and even Robert and Elizabeth Browning.

Knowing the tour was coming to an end, and that he would soon be facing the unemployment line, Rodolfo searched for literary properties to adapt for himself. He especially liked Rafael's Sabatini's *The Sea-Hawk,* and became so enthralled with the lead character,

a "rough-and-tumble" type of guy, that Rodolfo assumed those mannerisms in his private life. Natacha found the character repugnant and refused to dine with Rodolfo any more, although Ullman was said "to love the brutality in the man."

For their final performance in New York, the reporters and photographers were waiting, especially when Rodolfo strolled along Coney Island in skin-tight bathing trunks with two white Russian wolfhounds on a leash.

On the night of their last show, while dancing at New York's Hotel Astor, Natacha had a chance introduction to Mercedes de Acosta, a Spain-born poet and playwright. It was at curtain call, and Rodolfo quickly jerked Natacha away for an encore.

But the electricity between the Spanish beauty and Natacha was noted by Charlie Towne, the master of ceremonies, who had introduced the two women. It was obvious that Mercedes was determined to add Natacha Rambova to her list of sexual conquests which would in time include some of the most famous names of the 20th Century—Sarah Bernhardt, Eleonora Duse, Anna Pavlova, Eva le Gallienne, Isadora Duncan, Marlene Dietrich, and Greta Garbo.

Instead of returning with Ullman and Rodolfo, Natacha disappeared that night into the bowels of New York with the very talented Mercedes, who used to brag that once a woman went to bed with her, she swore off men for life.

In disgust and perhaps to spite Natacha, Rodolfo turned over all his business affairs to Ullman. Creditors had been trying to seize his bank account in New York, and he was in dire need of financial help. Before giving Ullman the nightmare job of business manager, Rodolfo revealed to him he'd had a private séance with Black Feather, and the Indian chief told him this was the right decision.

For a while Ullman was effective, reaching an agreement with Zukor and Lasky back in Hollywood. Valentino could return to Paramount for the sum of $7,500 a week, effective upon signing, although the studio had no roles for him until the fall. He could draw his salary even though he didn't have to work. He immediately decided it was time for the long-delayed grand tour of the Continent.

He called me and invited me along, claiming Natacha approved. Ullman had to stay in the States to handle his business affairs. Natacha had told Rodolfo that I would be a suitable replacement. Apparently, she hadn't forgotten that she'd lived off those loans I'd arranged through Godsol.

Eager and excited, I began to pack at once, adding to my wardrobe. My look at Europe had been severely limited when I'd gone over before with Godsol, at the time of the mysterious death of Olive Thomas. Marion filled me in on all the fun places to go, as W.R. took her to Europe every year.

Unknown to me, Rodolfo had arrived back in California to oversee construction work on the Whitley Heights home before departing for Europe. Even though I'd been invited to go along, he hadn't called me.

I was very disappointed when I'd heard he was back in town, and tried to get in touch with him but didn't know where he was staying. Ramon hadn't heard from him either, and feared Rodolfo would never speak to him again after he'd appeared in the rip-off picture, *The Arab*.

On the fourth night with still no word from Rodolfo, I grew tired of waiting at the Hollywood Hotel for him to show up. I accepted Ramon's invitation to spend the night with him.

Shortly after midnight as Ramon and I were enjoying a leisurely sixty-nine in preparation for heavier activities throughout the night, I heard a sound coming from the living room. "I think someone's breaking in," I said, rising from Ramon's cock.

"I heard something too," Ramon said, retreating under the sheet as if that would offer him any protection.

Throwing a bathrobe over my nude body, and still sporting a hard-on, I headed for the living room where a crystal wall sconce cast a dim light. "Who's there?" I shouted into the darkness, trying to sound as butch as possible. Near the French windows the moonlight outlined the figure of a man who appeared to be nude.

"It's the Sheik of Araby," came the voice at the other end of the room. "Don't turn on the lights. I've pulled off my clothes."

Ramon had recognized the voice and had come to the door to the bedroom, also completely nude.

"Rodolfo," I shouted, racing toward his arms. "You're back."

He pulled me into his nude body and gave me a kiss that made my toes tingle. Drawing back, he motioned to Ramon. "Both of you beautiful boys can enjoy my virility tonight. There's more than enough for two. That long train ride across America made me horny."

Ramon rushed over to Rodolfo for his welcome home kiss. In the living room Ramon and I took turns sampling Rodolfo's delectable tongue and fingering every inch of his body, sparing no part, regardless of how hidden. Everything seemed in proper place and working order. If anything, Rodolfo's rapidly expanding erection seemed bigger and better than ever.

"Before we retreat to the bedroom I know so well," he said, "I have a little present for my two favorite boys." He'd disrobed and his clothes were piled up around him. He reached under his jacket and removed two boxes tied with ribbons. He gave each of us one of the presents.

"This is for those lonely times," he said, "when you girls will not have the real thing to enjoy in the flesh."

In my haste, I tore open my box before Ramon. We'd been given matching gifts. "Before visiting us, Rodolfo had obviously gone a few days ago to the studio of Rod St. Just. In my hand I held Rod's divine creation—the most beautiful dildo I had ever known then or since. It was made of ebony in an Art Deco style.

The Valentino dildo remains to this day one of my treasured possessions. Since 1980 when I quit having sex with live bodies, it has been my only source of sexual pleasure.

In an act that appeared gay and fun at the time, Ramon took his dildo and slowly let it slide down his throat, enjoying every inch of it. Rodolfo and I laughed at the antic.

Regrettably and to my horror, it was the same dildo that would eventually be used by the hustler, Paul Ferguson, to choke the life out of Ramon on November 2, 1968.

Chapter Seventeen

He'd sailed to America as a poor Italian immigrant, but Rodolfo returned to the continent as a virtual God, the "king of the movies" and "the world's greatest lover." I shared his stateroom on the *Acquitania*, Natacha preferring a small cabin on another floor.

Fellow passengers were eager to snap pictures of The Sheik, and Rodolfo always appeared on deck nattily dressed, often in a forest green overcoat tied together with a snakeskin belt and sprouting a red fox fur collar. Radiograms poured in to the ship from dazzling addresses in Europe, as hostesses vied for the privilege of entertaining the tango-dancing Valentinos.

When Natacha, wearing one of the designer outfits she'd brought along in one of her twenty steamer trunks, arrived in the dining room nightly, heading for the captain's table, a silence fell over the room. She inspired awe in her fellow passengers more than Mary Pickford herself could have. The diners viewed Natacha like a film star, not just the wife of Rudolph Valentino.

As Natacha and Rodolfo were set upon by their fans, I spent many an evening in the bar talking with the actor, George Arliss, who'd made a film called *The Man Who Played God*. Ironically he is remembered today, if recalled at all, for the same film made ten years later as a Talkie and co-starring Miss Bette Davis.

Arriving late in London to check into the Carlton Hotel, after a long slow train ride from the port of Southampton, Rodolfo nonetheless faced reporters with a bright face early the fol-

lowing morning. He had predicted accurately the first question. "Mr. Valentino, do you prefer American women to British women?" Rodolfo's response? "You date American girls. You marry British women."

That had seemed to satisfy the press. Rodolfo grabbed my arm, as we headed for a limousine waiting to take us to Savile Row where he wanted to purchase a "suit for every occasion." Natacha preferred to wander alone in the museums of London, hoping to find costumes to inspire her own designs.

She told me she was going to save her more serious shopping for Paris. "I do not like the clothes British women wear. All of them make themselves up to look like horses."

Facing the formally dressed tailors of Saville Row, Rodolfo told them that the costumes in his films were ridiculous. He claimed that for his tour of the continent, he wanted to look like a well-tailored English gent, the type with a town house in Mayfair and an elegant country estate in Norfolk with a lot of dogs.

He particularly wanted a series of English boots made of the finest leather. He also told the tailors that he would need at least ten of those "divine English hats, like the Prince of Wales wears." Both tailors raised their eyebrows. Apparently, male clients on Savile Row did not refer to men's hats as divine.

Brewery magnate Richard Guinness invited all of us to his Mayfair town house, where he served Guinness, of course. To my surprise, as our meeting progressed, it became apparent that the brewer didn't exactly know who Rudolph Valentino and Natacha Rambova were. When a servant was showing them the garden, I explained as quickly as I could their backgrounds. "I see," Guinness said. "The Prince of Wales told me they were important, and his word is good enough for me."

The pianist, Artur Rubinstein, did know who they were and entertained the Valentinos with a private concert. Going backstage at a West End theater, we met the actress Gladys Cooper, starring in a play called Kiki. She listened patiently as Rodolfo complained about the crowds massing at the theater door seeking autographs. "My dear man," Cooper finally said. "They are not waiting for you but for me. I'm the star of the show. They don't know who you are."

Natacha and Rodolfo, almost with a kind of innocence, had been expecting an invitation for tea at Buckingham Palace. "After all, we are Hollywood royalty," Natacha claimed, "Rudy is the most famous actor on earth, even more so than Charlie Chaplin. Why not have us over for tea?"

No invitation came in for tea at the palace, although the Prince of Wales did invite them to have tea with him at the Ritz. His chief of protocol assured the Valentinos that this was just a casual affair and didn't carry the prestige of a royal summons. Actually it was to be arranged that the Valentinos would appear for tea at the Ritz in its palm garden, where they would casually spot the Prince of Wales who would stop by their table for a few minutes for a brief chat. There would be no formal announcement of the tea from the palace.

If he remembered me at all, and I suspected he did, I noted that I was not invited to join his Royal Highness for tea. Natacha left for the Ritz with Rodolfo, accompanied by a trio of Pekingese dogs she'd brought to Europe. When they returned from their tea, I was eager for news. "Actually the prince didn't have much to say to us," Rodolfo said. "He had seen none of my movies."

"He spent most of his time playing with my Pekingese dogs," Natacha volunteered. "The man is a complete dimwit. To think he might become the head of the British Empire one day. Amazing."

When Natacha retired to her own room, I asked Rodolfo if the prince had made a pass at him, or else eyed him seductively. "Not at all," he said. "I hear he prefers tall blond men like yourself. If you'd been invited to go with us, I think the prince would have fallen big for you. Given you a crown or something."

"He might have," I said enigmatically, having never told him that I had already met the Prince of Wales in Hollywood, thanks to Douglas Fairbanks Sr.

After midnight when Rodolfo was soundly sleeping, there was a discreet rap on the door to the suite. Putting on my robe, I answered it, discovering the general manager of the Carlton, Richard Hodges, who had welcomed us to the hotel. "I have a special favor to ask," he said rather nervously and in a whisper so low I could hardly hear him. "His Majesty is waiting in a suite on the upper floor. He has requested the pleasure of your company for a few hours. However, no one must know. Will you make yourself available?"

"In five minutes," I said without hesitation. "Time to get dressed."

After I'd changed into a black suit with a white shirt and dark tie, I opened the door to find Hodges still waiting in the hallway and still looking nervous. He escorted me to the suite of the prince. His Majesty opened the door himself, attired in a vermilion smoking jacket with a cigarette held in a holder.

"My darling boy," he said upon seeing me. "We meet again." He looked impatiently at Hodges. "That will be all for the night, my good man." He shut the door in Hodges' face.

From the very first, it'd been obvious why the prince did not invite me for tea. He took my hand and kissed its inner palm, then looked me squarely in the eyes. "You are truly the world's most beautiful boy, even more beautiful than I am." He leaned close in to me, sticking out his tongue, which I assumed he wanted sucked. After he'd had enough of that, he broke away and looked into my eyes again. "I want to lick and suck a delectable American asshole, then lick and suck some big American balls, and then lick and suck a big American cock. After that I want to get brutally penetrated like Lord Mountbatten used to do to me."

It was four o'clock in the morning before I staggered back to Rodolfo's suite, thoroughly exhausted. I couldn't recall having cummed so many times in my entire life. I'd carried out His Majesty's wishes and had upheld the tradition of virility in the American male.

The crowds were thinner as we flew into Paris arriving at Le Bourget. Rodolfo was learning that the farther south he went in Europe, the less well known he was. The same experience had happened to Chaplin who had found that his films had hardly played in Berlin.

We piled into a limousine for the Plaza Athénée. It took two other limousines to transport all of the luggage. The following morning, Natacha rushed off to the salon of Paul Poiret to try on some of his dresses and gowns called "paradoxes." He'd promised to create a series of turbans especially for her.

I went with Rodolfo to the headquarters of Voisin where he ordered a custom-made racing tourer. He even specified that the upholstery was to be in "vermilion morocco." Until the car was readied, the company lent him a deluxe Voisin touring car for his trip through Europe, figuring no doubt that he'd be photographed endlessly in the vehicle, giving them mountains of valuable publicity.

Our nights in Paris didn't go well. Natacha denounced all of Montmartre as a tourist trap. Rodolfo grandly walked out of Ciro's, telling the manager it was filled with nothing but American tourists who gaped at him like open-mouthed trout.

His only pleasure came in buying merchandise, especially clothing. At the most exclusive men's tailor in Paris, he ordered thirty shirts of silk, all made in different colors, plus two dozen pairs of pajamas. He also ordered a dozen lounge robes, preferring a deep Roman gold with black lapels, and he also wanted some smoking jackets made in vermilion and black with silver threading.

In a back room he stripped entirely nude in front of two appreciative young French tailors. He demanded that they "hand-fit" him for three dozen pairs of silk underwear, which he preferred mainly in Chinese red.

After a night at the Folies Bergère, Rodolfo almost caused an international incident. He told the press that, "When it came to showgirls, the place to see them is on Broadway at the Ziegfeld Follies, not in Paris."

Both Natacha and Rodolfo detested Deauville, where we had gone for the Grand Prix. "I loathe the crowds here," she told the press, "and I can't tolerate gambling. The patrons of Deauville think they are fashionable. They resemble women from the remotest French provinces."

Rodolfo complained about the rain and cold winds blowing in from the English Channel. He also said he found the food not fit for human consumption, "and I've dined at only the finer places. If you want good food, you must go to sunny Italy, not France."

We didn't go immediately to sunny Italy, but we did head south from Paris to the French Riviera to stay at a villa acquired by Natacha's parents. Although I volunteered, Rodolfo was eager to take the wheel of his borrowed touring car. He drove like a madman, evoking the day on the California coast where Ramon had speeded with such fury I thought he was going to kill us.

Preferring not to take the more direct route through Lyons, Rodolfo turned toward the Alps, as his driving grew more frantic. There wasn't a horse-drawn wagon or a bicycle that he didn't seem to want to run down. Long ago, Natacha had grown tired of telling him to slow down, and began yelling at him, threatening to leave him if he didn't drive better.

Outside Grenoble, as we were up on a mountain road, he continued to speed but nearly lost control of the car. Natacha screamed. I feared we were going over a cliff. At the last moment before we plunged to our deaths, Rodolfo brought the car to a stop.

Sobbing uncontrollably, he was removed from behind the wheel by both Natacha and me. He insisted on lying on the wet grass an hour to recover. "At the last minute," he said, between sobs, "Black Feather appeared before me. It was really his hands on the wheel—not mine. He saved us."

For the rest of the way toward the coast, I drove. The car was piled so high with luggage I could hardly see the road. Most of the trunks had to be left in Paris.

Arriving at the Riviera villa of the Hudnuts, Natacha's parents, Rodolfo was furious to see that it was being renovated, although suitably restored quarters had been arranged for us. The villa, at least potentially, was spectacular with great views of the sea. On the rocky coast between Antibes and Cannes, it had been built in 1860 by Queen Emily of Saxony.

The Hudnuts weren't expected until later in the month. The next morning Rodolfo complained that he didn't like living with all the hammering going on. "If I wanted to live with carpenters, I could have stayed at Whitley Heights with my own men." He was very critical of the renovations, and complained frequently that there was no boathouse. He was adamant that a little theater be constructed. On the second day, when he'd been awakened early in the morning by the sound of hammering, he said he could take it no more.

After a bitter fight with Natacha, he ordered me to drive him to the Hotel Negresco in Nice where he'd reserved a suite for us. Natacha threatened that she was going to file for divorce upon her return to America. However, two days later she called and told him that she'd forgiven him.

Eager to leave the Riviera, which had disappointed him, Rodolfo assumed control of the wheel again, heading for the Italian border. At the frontier, customs troopers tried to extort money from him. None of them knew who Valentino was. It seemed that American movies weren't shown in Italy until they were at least five years old. That way, Italian exhibitors leased the films much cheaper.

Rodolfo was unaware of this until he came to realize that the customs men were trying to take money not from Valentino, but from a man they assumed to be wealthy, since he was driving an expensive car, attired in expensive clothing, and with an expensive-looking woman in the back seat covered with expensive luggage. He was forced to bribe the men before he entered his homeland. I could tell that this was a bitter experience for him, as he expected to be welcomed as a conquering hero returning from the wars. "I left Italy unknown," he lamented, "and I return to Italy unknown."

Although Rodolfo had driven along the dangerous curves of the Riviera cornices reasonably safely, he resumed his madman driving two miles inside the frontier. Back in Italy, he seemed to become king of the road, delighting in passing horse-drawn wagons and creating clouds of dust. He sang Neapolitan love songs, and was doing just that when on the outskirts of Genoa he crashed into a telephone pole.

The borrowed car was towed away, and no one was injured, although Natacha complained that she felt he'd hurt her back. She once again announced she'd seek a divorce from Rodolfo upon their return to America.

She retreated to a private room at the hotel where several messages were waiting for Rodolfo. He was elated to learn that his brother, Alberto, was arriving at the train station shortly before midnight. Rodolfo hadn't seen Alberto in eleven years.

The pain at seeing his brother was immediately evident on Rodolfo's face. He'd expected Alberto to rush up to him and hug him, congratulating him on his international success. But his brother seemed jealous, even hostile. In a taxi on the way back to the hotel, Alberto said, "I spend most of my time denying to my friends that you are effeminate and a homosexual. I've even had guys gang up on me in Taranto just to claim they've beaten up Valentino's brother."

He told Rodolfo that few Italians had seen any of his films, although they'd seen pictures of him in the newspapers. "No virile man dresses up like you do. It's just not manly."

Over drinks in the hotel bar, Rodolfo tried to control his rage and conceal his anger toward his brother. In time he managed to do that but he never forgot nor forgave Alberto's insult to his manhood.

As we headed for Milan to see Rodolfo's sister, Maria, Natacha told me that she found Alberto personally repulsive. "He's nothing but a peasant, and he stinks too. All this talk of Rudy being of noble birth is total bullshit."

In Milan when Maria was introduced to Natacha, it was Maria who rejected her. She called her brother aside and in my presence told both of us that she viewed Natacha as "no more than a painted whore." Maria didn't want anything to do with Natacha, and was deeply offended that she wore perfume during daylight hours. "No respectable woman would do that," Maria said.

Originally Maria was to go to Siena, Florence, and Rome with us, but she bowed out, claiming she wanted to stay in Milan. Alberto also said that he couldn't go, but would take the train back to his native Taranto in the south.

The reunion of Rodolfo with his brother and sister had turned into a disaster. Upon telling Rodolfo good-bye, I heard Maria say, "For years I've been dreaming of going to California when you became rich and famous. Now that I see what fame has done to you, don't send for me. Not ever. I don't want to share a house with a prostitute."

In Siena, as I went shopping with Natacha and Rodolfo, they discovered a little alleyway off the piazza del Campo, where they were drawn to a dealer in rare paintings. Surprisingly, they purchased a painting of Anne of Cleves for three-hundred U.S. dollars which was later authenticated to be the work of Holbein. It was in a worm-eaten frame, and would command a vast fortune on today's art market. However, it was not among the inventory of Rodolfo's estate when he died. Rodolfo suspected that Natacha had taken it, and Mildred Harris later claimed she'd seen it in the bedroom of Nazimova before she sold the Garden of Alla and moved out.

At his villa in Florence, Baron Fassino, a towering figure in the Italian film world, and a close friend of the new dictator, Benito Mussolini, befriended us. He was very familiar with Rodolfo's film reputation and offered to take us to Rome to introduce us to important people in the film colony there. *Quo Vadis?*, starring Emil Jannings, was the biggest film being shot there, although there was talk that *Ben-Hur* would soon get under way.

Unlike that German baron Rodolfo knew back in Hollywood, living a life of faded glory, Baron Fassino was for real. In Florence he claimed he could arrange for Rodolfo and Natacha to meet anyone. But when tested, the baron came up short. Rodolfo had read in the newspaper that the dashing writer and adventurer, Gabrielle d'Annunzio, the lover of Italy's greatest actress at the time, Eleanora Duse, was staying at a villa in Florence. The baron claimed to be d'Annunzio's best friend. The baron claimed to be everybody's best friend, providing they were important.

Rodolfo confided that d'Annunzio was his all-time favorite hero and that he had always wanted to star as the writer in a film based on d'Annunzio's life. The baron was gone for two hours claiming he was going to d'Annunzio's villa where he would arrange for us to come over and meet this dashing figure. However, the baron arrived back at our hotel with a sad face, claiming that d'Annunzio said he was "too busy to meet with Valentino."

The pain of this latest rejection was evident on Rodolfo's face as we drove to Rome. He had surrendered the driving to me as we approached the Eternal City.

On the outskirts of Rome, Baron Fassino said he would "open the doors of the city" to us, and even held out the prospect that he could arrange a private meeting with his dear friend, Benito. The baron, it turned out, lived over Mussolini's private apartments at the Palazzo Titoni. The baron said the Italian dictator used the apartment only a place to visit privately with friends. He smiled and winked at us. "Of course, that is the place he takes his girl friend of the moment, far away from the prying eyes of his beloved wife."

The next day the baron invited us to the set of *Quo Vadis?,* where we were introduced to Emil Jannings, who in my view ranked along with Erich von Stroheim as "the man you love to hate." Speaking only German, he had asked his English-speaking wife to translate for us. A mountain of a man, Jannings had an unruly disposition and a guttural accent. He'd trained in the theater with Max Reinhardt, and was viewed as one of the biggest male stars of the Teutonic world, although still years ahead from filming his most famous movie, *The Blue Angel*, with Marlene Dietrich.

That day Jannings was denouncing everyone, especially his Italian-speaking director. He also attacked Hollywood, claiming he turned down an offer a day to make a film there. "I sent Pola Negri instead," he said. "A silly Pollack filled with lies and her own importance. That means she belongs only in America. The Americans are stupid enough to be attracted to this Warsaw cow. On a film I worked on, she told me—me, the great Emil Jannings— how to improve one of my scenes. It was all I could do to restrain myself from beating her to a pulp."

As he talked to us, he kept looking at his

watch, making me assume he was eager to get rid of us. Actually, he was impatient for the arrival of his lunch, which turned out to be a mountain of sausage. "The stupid Italians don't know how to make sausage," he said, digging into the feast. "The sausage here is the worst I've ever eaten in my life, even in the lowest German beer tavern. I hear the sausage in America is even worse." With sausage grease spilling over his lips, he said, "The Italians are peasants. America too is a primitive land. I fear going there. On the train to Hollywood, I suspect my compartment will be raided by Indians who would scalp me."

After consuming this massive lunch, including a tub of potato salad eaten in the hot Roman sun and loaded down with mayonnaise, Jannings clutched his stomach and fell over onto the floor, screaming in agony. I rushed to his aid, but Mrs. Jannings restrained me and called for the film crew's doctor, who arrived with two burly Roman assistants. Jannings lay on the floor screaming, cursing in German, and pounding his fists.

Before the attendants carried Jannings away on a stretcher, he vomited on the floor. Natacha turned away in disgust. After he was gone, Mrs. Jannings said to Rodolfo and me. "Emil gets these little attacks some times when he has had too much to eat for lunch. I keep telling him not to eat too many inferior sausages."

Three hours went by before Jannings returned to the set to play Nero. As he waited for the cameras to be set up, he passed along some confidential information to Rodolfo and me. His wife translated again. "Don't put your money in banks," he warned us. "You can't trust bankers. What is going to prevent a banker from taking your money and running away to South America? I have nearly $250,000 stashed under my pillow back in my hotel room. I brought the money with me from Germany. It's safe as long as it's with me— not in a bank."

On the set, the Italian director, through a translator, ordered Jannings to feign sleep as Nero. The director wanted the scene realistic. Jannings took him at his word. He fell asleep so soundly that it was almost impossible for the director to wake him up for his next scene.

After the shooting for the day was finished,

Jannings invited us to the only place in Rome serving sauerkraut and sausages. One would think that he'd had his fill of sausages for the day. "I vomited up the first batch," he told us in German as translated by his wife. "Now I must fill my big gut again."

When not eating greasy sausages, Jannings spoke of his love for his fatherland. To our surprise, after eighteen mugs of beer, he confided that he'd actually been born in Brooklyn of a Jewish mother and a German father. The irony of this was that in the years to come, Jannings was to make some of Nazi Germany's most notorious propaganda films including *Ohm Krüger*, in which the invention of concentration camps was blamed on the British.

Although the baron could not set up a meeting with the egomaniacal Gabrielle d'Annunzio, he was able to arrange an audience with his neighbor, Benito Mussolini, who had been in power for only a few months. The baron stressed that the meeting with the dictator would have to be private and not announced in the press. "Benito is not prudish in his personal life," the baron said. "Not at all. If he wants an amorous adventure, he takes any woman he likes. What Italian woman is going to turn down Mussolini?"

The baron explained politely that because Rodolfo and Natacha were in show business, the dictator did not want to be photographed with them. "Benito's exact words were, 'I want to meet the world's most famous Italian—other than myself, of course.' He said that he didn't want to lose support among his Catholic supporters, so he denounced night clubs, cabarets, and places like that as 'the antechambers of whorehouses.'" After taking a stand like that, the baron explained, Mussolini could never be photographed with show business people.

At the last minute the baron informed me that regrettably the invitation did not extend to me. "Benito is very busy looking after the best interests of the Italian people," the baron said. "He has time to speak only to the Valentinos, and only for a very brief moment."

At two o'clock that morning Natacha arrived back at our hotel with Rodolfo who was fuming. Rodolfo told me that after a brief ten-minute meeting, during which time Mussolini virtually ignored him, he was dismissed. The dictator claimed that he wanted to speak to Natacha privately about redesigning some costumes for an opera spectacle he wanted to stage at the Baths of Caracalla.

"Opera spectacle shit," Natacha virtually shouted. For the first time in her life, her hair was messed up and her clothing ruffled. "The moment Rudy was out the door, Mussolini attacked me like an ape. He tore apart my dress." At that point she opened her velvet jacket to expose her ripped bodice. "He felt my breasts and tried to get his dirty fingers into my pussy. I ran screaming into the hallway where Rudy and I escaped."

It proved all too much for Natacha. She'd had it with Italy, claiming she was returning to the south of France to join her parents who had arrived from New York. Rodolfo begged her to accompany us to the south of Italy where he wanted to visit his home town of Castellaneta.

"You enjoy the poverty and malaria," Natacha shouted out to him. "I'm returning to a civilized country."

Rodolfo and I headed out alone, driving toward Taranto where he wanted to pay a farewell visit to Alberto. Alberto himself warned Rodolfo to avoid Castellaneta. "It's not the same place," Alberto said. "Everybody we knew is gone. You won't like it. The town's in a bad way. I had to leave it just to survive."

Refusing to listen to Alberto, Rodolfo and I set out along dirty roads. Every time we passed a wagon we created a dust bowl. "A hero's welcome is waiting for me in Castellaneta," Rodolfo predicted to me. Before getting that welcome, we had two flat tires. Along the way we passed sadly neglected farms, many of them completely abandoned when the owners found it impossible to make a living from the inhospitable rocky terrain. Everywhere we went there was talk of raising enough money to go north to Milan, where it was reported that the streets were paved with gold.

After the arduous journey, we arrived tired, hungry, and hot. On the outskirts of town, Rodolfo honked his horn as he made his way to the main square in his new touring car. He told me he had to alert the people of the town that its most famous son had returned.

In the main square he brought the car to a halt. All of a sudden we seemed surrounded by people, gaping face after gaping face, spelling poverty. At first I thought they were going to attack us and the car. Their open mouths revealing rotten teeth begged for money. These were hungry, desperate people. In a scene from one of his earlier films, the grandly dressed Rodolfo tried to shoo the villagers away from his automobile and his luggage.

Taking off his driving goggles, he stared into the faces of hostility and suspicion. As the word spread of the arrival of some rich American, the crowd grew larger. I was afraid.

Suddenly, the mob attacked the car, but not us personally. They stole our luggage and fought over it, as the suitcases and two trunks spilled open. Rodolfo's precious wardrobe was almost ripped to shreds. All I can remember was witnessing a pair of red silk underwear waving in the air.

"Let's run for it," Rodolfo shouted at me, grabbing my arm and pulling me into a battered church that looked as if the roof were about to fall in on us. Slamming the church doors on the unruly mob, Rodolfo turned around to face a priest in a rusty cassock. The larcenous priest, with only one gold tooth in the front of his mouth, confronted Rodolfo and demanded that he turn over all his "ill-gotten gains" to the church or else God would strike us dead on the spot. Rodolfo reluctantly gave his money to the priest. Fortunately, I was able to hang on to my loot.

With the hour, with the mob still massed outside, the priest came back up front where we sat on a bench in the darkened church. With him was an Italian girl who introduced herself as Marcella. In broken English, she said she was a cousin of Rodolfo's. She claimed the two men with her were her brothers. One of the men in tattered clothes held up Rodolfo's camera. Later I learned that he'd said. "I'm taking this camera and going to Taranto to sell it. It is a black box of evil. You take pictures of a man and you steal his soul for the devil."

Marcella had brought along a dog-eared copy of *Photoplay* in which Rodolfo had dictated his biography to Howe. She read from it, translating it for her brothers. She mocked Rodolfo for claiming that he had been born to a title and that his mother had sent him to New York with "thousands of lire." After she'd done that, she turned on Rodolfo and demanded money, claiming she was living in poverty while he was enjoying all the riches of America.

Rodolfo explained that he had given all his money to the priest, but the brothers didn't believe him. One of them ripped off his jacket and claimed it for himself, as the other brother searched Rodolfo's pockets, finally removing his wrist watch. Fortunately, both of the men avoided me.

After Rodolfo's cousins had left, he waited until two o'clock in the morning when the streets were deserted. We slipped out of the church, and I took the wheel of the Voison. I fully expected the car to have been stripped, or at least the tires taken. It was intact, and amazingly, the motor started.

At its sound, eight men ran from a darkened tavern and began pelting us with rotten vegetables and garbage. Rodolfo was hit in the face with some overripe cow dung.

Two miles from the town, Rodolfo and I stopped by a little stream to wash our faces. "I'm glad Natacha did not come," he said to me. "I could not stand for her to witness my humiliation. You must never mention to anyone what happened to me back there." He looked into the darkness but no lights were coming from the town. My mother and father may be buried there, but I curse the place. I curse Castellaneta. I'm returning to America where I belong. America is my country now. For me, Italy is dead."

*****

Now locked into partnership with Douglas Fairbanks Sr. and Mary Pickford, Charlie grew to detest Pickford more every day, although keeping up appearances in public and continuing to be a guest at Pickfair where he mocked the refusal of his hosts to serve even one drop of wine to their distinguished guests.

His relationship with Pickford had always been competitive, filled with jealousy and sus-picion. He hawkeyed the gross on their mutual films, becoming furious if American's Sweetheart showed more clout at the box office than he did.

He was doubly horrified to learn that Pickford in private referred to him as a child molester. She had gone so far as to issue an edict at Pickfair that none of the four young Fairbanks nieces were to be allowed alone in a room with Charlie at any time.

One night he confronted her with the accusation. She turned bitterly on him. "But you are a child molester. You married a child—that Mildred Harris—and I hear that brat you're involved with now is about six years old, if that. You've even brought school children as your dinner dates to Pickfair. You've embarrassed me for years."

Charlie stormed out of the house that night, vowing never to set foot in Pickfair again. But he did go back in the months ahead. In spite of their personal antagonism for each other, they still had business interests through United Artists and were forced to deal with each other.

Back at home, on the night he'd fled from Pickfair, Charlie was reduced to tears by Pickford's accusation. "She does not know how I've suffered. I'm to be forgiven anything, even an interest in little girls because of what I've gone through. I was only seven years old when I had to walk my mother through the streets to the insane asylum. Street boys jeered at us and tossed stones. One rock hit my mother in the face. She arrived at the asylum bleeding." He vowed that he would do something in the future to get his revenge on Pickford.

Among his closest friends, Chaplin never called Pickford by her real name. He referred to her as "Hetty Green." At the time the real Hetty Green was one of the wealthiest women on earth. She'd schemed and connived her way into accumulating $100,000,000.

One night at Pickfair, in the early Thirties, when the other guests had departed, Pickford was in an introspective mood. Normally she wasn't known for any sense of self-understanding. "I'm like Charlie in so many ways," she said, both to Doug's astonishment and my own. "Both of us are little people in physical size. Both of us have suffered poverty and hardship. Both of us had much to overcome. With me as the little girl and Charlie as The Little Tramp, we have lived long enough to see our film characters become obsolete with changing times. Neither of us survived the shift in the public's fancy. They have new stars like Garbo to replace us with. Once we were adored by the public, but new fans have come along who do not worship the film heroes and heroines of their parents. The age of innocence is over. The Talkies didn't finish us off. We finished ourselves off by not keeping up with the public's taste." She burst into tears, and Doug told me to go home. He escorted her up the stairs to her bedroom.

Although until the end Douglas and Charlie remained friends, Charlie in time saw Pickford only at board meetings. The old warriors of the silent screen—Chaplin and Pickford—grew increasingly testy with each other. In private he called her "The Iron Butterfly," and she referred to him as "the dirty old man." At board meetings, Pickford stormed, raved, and ranted at Charlie, and he cursed her in the crudest and most vulgar of terms.

At one board meeting, with fury, he told her, "Grow up. You can't be a little girl forever. In your next movie play a hoochie-koochie dancer who takes opium, smokes old stogies, and sleeps with the marines, the army, and the navy. And while you're at it, why don't you offer each serviceman a discount if he'll do it with you a second time."

"You vile, filthy creature," Pickford shouted at him.

One day, after she referred to him publicly as a child molester, Charlie decided to get revenge. He spread a rumor through Hollywood that during her early years as the wife of Douglas Fairbanks Sr., that Charlie had been "pumping it to the bitch on the side." During a private moment of truth, he admitted to me that he'd never gone to bed with Pickford. "To me she was not one of the little girls I gravitate to. She only masqueraded as a little girl even when she was a little girl. I don't think she was ever innocent. She popped out of the womb a scheming, money-grubbing bitch."

When Pickford heard that rumor, she banned Charlie from Pickfair for the rest of her life, yet was forced to be seen with him at times in public because of mutual business interests.

With United Artists in financial trouble during the war years, the relationship between Charlie and Pickford was at its lowest point. In May of 1943, Charlie almost sued Pickford for her refusal to join with him in a mutual lawsuit against David Selznick who had swindled UA out of $300,000. When Charlie published *My Autobiography* in 1964, portraying Pickford as a miser, she announced she'd never speak to him ever again.

It was Douglas Fairbanks Jr. who visited Charlie in London in the fifties and returned home to call upon his stepmother at Pickfair. She was by then an alcoholic recluse. Young Doug claimed that The Little Tramp had mellowed toward her and might consider a personal visit. Hoisting herself up in bed, she said, "Fuck that! Chaplin always will be a son of a bitch. Don't ever mention his name again."

I fear that Doug Jr. was far too kind in telling Pickford that Charlie had mellowed toward her. At the time of my last few visits to him at Vevey, Switzerland, an aging Charlie still seemed to harbor his old bitterness toward his formaer rival. He had never forgiven her for the epic battles they'd had during the early 1940s over the future of United Artists. He was especially bitter when she'd blocked his attempt to sell out his interests for which he could have earned five-million dollars. Holding onto the same stock he did, Pickford herself would have earned seven million dollars as part of the same deal, but she decided not to sell them, pleading an "income tax problem."

Later, to both of their regrets, Charlie and Pickford were forced to liquidate their stock for far less than the five and seven million dollars they'd been initially offered. "She cost me millions," Charlie, from his base in Switzerland, would often rant. "I told her to sell when the stock was hot. But the tight-fisted bitch wanted to do it her way, and only her way, so we both ended up losing."

As reminded by that other bitch, The Bitch of Buchenwald, I had to return to the mid-Twenties.

When Charlie wasn't feuding with Pickford, he was making plans to film *Lucky Strike* about the Klondike of 1898. It was later released as *The Gold Rush*. On a Hollywood back lot, the Arctic had to be recreated with two-hundred barrels of flour and 300 tons of salt which the producers tried to pass off in the California heat as "snow."

The brat who Pickford had accused Charlie of having an affair with was none other than Lillita McMurray, actually fifteen at the time, not six years old. Charlie later confessed to me that he'd fallen for Lillita when she was twelve and had showed up at his studio in 1920 on the arm of her stern mother, Mrs. Lillian Spicer. It was love at first sight, at least on Charlie's part. He'd cast Lillita as the Angel of Temptation in a dream sequence in *The Kid.*

So taken was he with her, that he cast the little girl and her mother in his film, *The Idle Class.* But when he'd attempted to date the teenager, Mrs. Spicer claimed that her daughter could not go anywhere unchaperoned. Angered at the rebuff, Charlie did not renew either of their contracts.

Upon seeing her again three years later, Charlie noted that Lillita had become more full breasted, a bit remarkably so for a girl of fifteen. With her broad face, full cheeks, and big bones, she looked older than her actual age. He ordered a screen test of Lillita. His assistants hated the final tests, considering her the worst young actress who'd tried out for the part. Upon viewing the test himself, Charlie claimed to the entire screening room, "I plan to marry this girl. I have at last found a leading lady to replace Edna Purviance." Hired at $75 a week, Lillita became Lita Grey. He told the press she was nineteen years old and that after *The Gold Rush* was completed, he was going to cast her as Josephine opposite him playing Napoleon.

For the first two weeks of shooting, Charlie took his crew to the High Sierras. Within days Kono and I learned that Lita was seen slipping into Charlie's private quarters at night. Where was the guardian mother? Charlie had instructed his aide, Sid Grauman, to appear smitten with Mrs. Spicer and never leave her side for a minute. Once back in Los Angeles, however, Grauman showed no interest in pounding Mrs. Spicer any more. Charlie laughingly presented Grauman with a check for $500 for "stud services."

Mrs. Spicer was still set against Charlie taking Lita out on dates. But he conceived a plan to get around that. He told Mrs. Spicer that I wanted to date her daughter and that I was sixteen years old. He personally made me up and dressed me to present me to Mrs. Spicer. I could easily have passed for sixteen at the time, as I was still a young pretty boy. Tom Mix had only recently told me that during my first ten years in Hollywood, I could pass for a fourteen-year-old if the part called for it. Another Tom, Tom Ince, often got me jobs as an extra playing the role of a teenager. Mrs. Spicer found me to be a wholesome looking American youth and agreed that her daughter could go out on double dates with Charlie and me.

For his date, Charlie had selected Thelma Morgan Conversel, the twin sister of Gloria Morgan Vanderbilt, "the poor little rich girl," as dubbed by the press. Thelma had agreed to serve as a chaperone to the little teenage Lita. Charlie had secured Lita's promise not to tell her mother what actually happened on these dates.

The strikingly beautiful divorcée, Thelma, aspired to movie stardom, like so many socialites of her day. She repeated this ambition to me many times at the Santa Monica Swimming Club when Charlie was off on the beach playing with Lita. In fact, it turned out that the only reason Thelma was dating Charlie was that he had promised her movie stardom.

On these double dates, I was actually dating Thelma, as Charlie devoted all his attentions to little Lita. Thelma quickly understood that I was a homosexual, and after the first date no longer came on to me. She told me at one point that she felt particularly close to me and treated me "just like I do my sister, Gloria." Over drinks on our fifth date, she discovered that we had a lover in common. Both of us had had affairs with the Prince of Wales, although her exploits with his Majesty differed remarkably from my own. It was Thelma who would eventually introduce the Prince of Wales to his notorious future wife and almost-queen of England, Wallis Simpson.

One night on another one of our double dates, at the then fashionable Musso & Frank's restaurant, Thelma ran out of patience. She was tired of Charlie not paying any attention to her. As the weeks went by, there was also no movie contract, and Thelma in time came to realize that there would be no movie career either. She rose from her seat, got up, and walked out of the restaurant, never to return to Charlie's life.

He did not seem to miss her going, as he had another mission: to penetrate Lita. He told me that he'd first tried that in the back seat of his curtained-off limousine, but had not had success. He attempted to seduce the teenager three more times in his dressing room at the studio. "She can't take me," he said to me. "She cries that I'm hurting her. As you of all people know, I'm rather big, especially for a guy my size." Finally the following week Charlie reported success. He'd gotten Lita to enter his steam bath at his house. He'd told her to strip down and relax on a marble slab. It was there—thirty minutes later—that she'd opened her eyes to confront her thirty-five-year old pursuer and his iodine-covered dick. After seemingly endless protests from her, he'd achieved full penetration that night. Lita later told me that she found sex with Charlie extremely difficult. "I equate the pain with that of a woman giving birth to a child."

Even though pursuing Lita, Charlie still had women on the side, notably Dame Rebecca West, the British journalist and common-law wife of H. G. Wells who'd arrived in Hollywood. Charlie had told Kono and me that he'd seduced West when he'd first gone back to England with Paul Ivano.

The first night I had dinner with Dame West at Charlie's house, and we were talking privately on his terrace, I burst out with admiration of her for her first novel, *The Return of the Soldier.* She regarded me skeptically as she was bored with flattery. "Let's not talk about my writing," she said, "something you obviously know nothing about. Let's talk about Charlie's fucking habits instead. I don't know what he wants with me. I've been to bed with him twice. He was impotent in both cases. In my view Charlie can't handle a mature woman. He can only achieve orgasm with a twelve-year-old. I'm fleeing to Santa Barbara to escape his attentions."

With Dame West gone, Charlie invited Mrs. Spicer for dinner. That happened to be the week that Dr. Brian Sheehan was serving as my "husband." I believed back then in having a different husband every week. As it turned out, the handsome doctor was the perfect guest to invite. He'd been treating Charlie for his impotence.

After a lavish meal supervised by Kono, Mrs. Spicer suffered an attack. She complained of stomach cramps. Brian gave her a sedative and put her to bed in one of Charlie's guestrooms. After that, Brian and I fled for the night. The next morning I learned what had happened.

Recovering in the middle of the night, Mrs. Spicer had followed the sound of her daughter's laughter to Charlie's bedroom. Without knocking, she opened the door to discover Charlie making love to her daughter. Jumping out of the bed nude with an iodine-coated hard-on, Charlie confronted the raging mother with the explanation that he planned to marry Lita.

It turned out that Mrs. Spicer actually wanted Charlie to become her rich son-in-law. What she hadn't wanted was for Lita to surrender her virginity before the wedding.

I drove Mrs. Spicer to Brian's clinic the next day with Lita, who sat in the back seat crying. After an examination, Brian discovered that Mrs. Spicer was suffering from a blockage of her fallopian tubes and would require an operation. Quite by chance, he also examined Lita and pronounced her pregnant.

The following morning as Charlie was shooting the famous dance hall sequence in *The Gold Rush* that introduces Lita's character, she told him over lunch that she was pregnant.

He reacted in rage and bitterness, even accusing me of getting Lita pregnant. Realizing that was hardly possible, he screamed at her. "You little whore. You're trying to trick me into marrying you—just like that scheming bitch, Mildred Harris."

By that afternoon, Charlie was still fuming but not as violent as he'd been at lunch. He offered to give her $10,000 and to arrange an abortion through Brian. When Mrs. Spicer heard of this, this devout Roman Catholic staunchly refused to let Lita have an abortion.

At a meeting in his library the following night, Charlie confronted Lita and me away from Mrs. Spicer. To my astonishment, he offered me what he called "a certain sum of money" if I would marry Lita and pretend to be the father of her child. Lita screamed back at him. "Durango's a homosexual. What kind of fulfilling marriage would that be for me?" She ran screaming in tears from the library.

To escape from the increasingly strident demands of Lita and her mother, Charlie resumed his affair with Marion Davies. For some reason, Marion was punishing W.R. and didn't keep her entanglement with Charlie private. They were photographed dancing cheek-to-cheek at the popular nightclub, Montmarte.

Sometimes they would invite me to join them. When Charlie went to the toilet one night, Marion giggled at me and wanted to get confidential. "I don't know how Charlie is with you. But he'll never replace Valentino as the Great Lover. I found that Charlie likes frequent and fast intercourse with a woman, often three times a night. But he's a jump-on and jump-off kind of guy. Actually I prefer a type like Valentino who believes in taking his time."

Those pictures of Marion and Charlie were inevitably seen by Mrs. Spicer. One Sunday afternoon she'd arrived at Charlie's house with her brother, Edwin McMurray, a San Francisco lawyer. In a tense meeting, he reminded Charlie that sex with a teenager was statutory rape in California. Such a charge carried a thirty-year prison term. "If you don't agree to marry Lita—and right away because she's pregnant—I'm filing charges against you by the end of the week."

After Mrs. Spicer and her attorney brother left, Charlie sank into despair. He even threatened suicide. But by the following morning, he bowed to his inevitable fate and ordered that the film crew of *The Gold Rush* accompany him to Guaymas, Mexico. That way, he hoped to trick the press into thinking he was shooting scenes for his film there, and not getting married to another underage girl, a secret he wanted to keep from the press as long as possible. "At least until Lita gets older," he'd told me.

What the desert of Mexico had to do with *The Gold Rush* set in the Arctic was never properly explained by Jim Tully, Charlie's publicist. About five reporters were suspicious and followed Charlie's film crew south of the border.

A few days later, at four o'clock in the morning, Charlie ordered me to drive Jim Tully, Mrs. Spicer, Lita and him along a dirt-crusted rocky back road to a miserable little town called Empalme.

There in the rotting house of a justice of the peace, the marriage of the world's most famous man took place. The sun was just coming up over the mountain to burn off a heavy mist as Charlie and Lita were pronounced man and wife. I was the best man, even though I still viewed myself as "Mrs. Charlie Chaplin." A ray of sunlight penetrated through a tiny window criss-crossed with a pair of wooden bars. The shadow of its cross fell across Charlie's breast. I heard him gasp, perhaps wondering the significance of this streak of light, as he always had a sense of the dramatic.

On the way back to Guaymas, Charlie denounced both Lita and Mrs. Spicer as "bloody, money-grubbing scumbags." The next day on the train ride back to Los Angeles, he wasn't even speaking to his bride, even though it was his honeymoon. When she complained that her pregnancy was making her feel nauseous, he directed her to the back of the train, with its waist-high guard door. She told me the next day that she feared he wanted to push her over to her death. Instead he asked her, "Why don't you jump?"

The press did learn of the marriage, in spite of Charlie's attempt to keep it a secret. Not wanting her to be photographed with a pregnant belly, he announced that Lita was withdrawing from the cast of *The Gold Rush*.

To replace Lita, Charlie tested, but then rejected, a young actress named Jean Peters (no, not the one who would later marry Howard Hughes). This Jean Peters later changed her name to Carole Lombard before marrying Clark Gable. Tragically, she died in a plane crash in 1942 during a domestic tour promoting the sale of war bonds.

Having rejected the future Mrs. Clark Gable, Charlie settled on a lovely, shapely brunette, Georgia Hale. He'd seen this Chicago beauty queen in the low-budget film, *The Salvation Hunters*, directed by Josef von Sternberg before he went on to greater glory with Marlene Dietrich.

Ironically before filming the von Sternberg film, Georgia had broken into movies as an extra in a film starring Mildred Harris, whose movie career was on the wane following her divorce from Charlie. So taken was Charlie with Georgia Hale, that he ordered Jim Tully the next day "to hunt her down" and offer her Lita's part in *The Gold Rush.*

Again proving what a small town Hollywood was, Charlie learned that his best pal, Douglas Fairbanks Sr., had already discovered Georgia and was fucking her. Doug had offered her the lead opposite him in *Don Q., Son of Zorro.*

Charlie prevailed on Doug to release Georgia from the part, and Doug reluctantly agreed. The two stars, the world's biggest, arranged to fuck Georgia on alternate nights. "When I'm with Mary, you can have her," Doug said to Charlie. "When you're alone with your new wife, I'll be banging Georgia." That arrangement between the two men existed for only two weeks before another woman, an unknown actress, caught Doug's roving eye. "From now on," Charlie told Georgia, "your pussy belongs just to me." I was certain that Georgia had no intention of keeping that commitment once *The Gold Rush* was wrapped.

Occasionally when Charlie wasn't pumping Georgia, he would summon either me or Lita to his bed. He viewed his wife as a mere sexual convenience. She cried out to me that he was treating her like a common whore. "He calls me to his bed, jumps on me, then jumps off, then orders me from his bedroom," she lamented.

When Charlie Spencer Chaplin Jr. entered the world, Brian Sheehan was the attending doctor. Charlie graciously presented Brian with a check for $25,000 if he would agree to falsify the birth certificate. Brian was only too happy to oblige.

After the birth, Lita, Mrs. Spicer, and little Charlie Jr. were sent packing to a remote little cabin in the San Bernardino Mountains. When they eventually returned to Los Angeles, it was announced that Charles Jr. had been born on June 28, not May 5, his actual birth day. That way, it would appear that Charles Jr. had not been conceived out of wedlock.

Like a rabbit, those jump-on, jump-off sessions with Lita proved potent. In seemingly no time at all, after having given birth to Charles Jr., Brian discovered during an examination that Lita was pregnant again. The second baby would grow up to become Sydney Earl Chaplin.

When Charlie learned of Lita's second pregnancy, he vowed never to sleep with Lita again. He fled to New York to escape his nagging and pregnant (again) wife, and especially the obnoxious Mrs. Spicer. While he was there, *The Gold Rush* opened across the country. It would be the apex of Charlie's film career.

But before going to New York, Charlie and I accepted an invitation from Marion and W.R. The Chief was negotiating a film deal with my darling friend Tom Ince, who was my only link to the movie world with those extra jobs he provided for me. I noted he never offered me a star part, but through him I still could claim to be "in pictures."

W.R. had invited Tom to join us in a cruise with Marion and him aboard the *Oneida.*

As I boarded the yacht along with Charlie, a fierce-looking sea gull screeched at me. Was that bird trying to warn me of something?

*****

My dear, sweet sugar daddy, W.R., took care of Lotte Lee on the East Coast and Maid Marion on the West coast. He was no longer impotent. Back and forth I traveled by train from east to west, leading remarkably different lives on each coast.

In many ways, my New York life was far more glamorous than California—too much sun, too many beaches out west. In New York I dressed up as Lotte only when being seen around town with Mae West or when W.R. would stop by the New York apartment while in the city doing business and not out on Long Island with his wife, Millicent, and his sons. Otherwise, I preferred being Durango Jones, especially when I was with John Barrymore, the toast of Broadway.

Having John and Mae West for friends, with W.R. visiting on occasion, wasn't bad for a golden-haired boy from the wheat fields of Kansas.

Out on the town, Mae was always filling my head with tall tales that often turned out to be true. She even revealed to me the date of her birth, which was 1893 and not 1895 or even 1887 as had been reported in the press. She also confided that she'd toured the vaudeville circuits in 1916 as a "male impersonator." As unlikely as that seemed, she had pictures to prove it. Even then rumors on Broadway were circulating that Mae wasn't a real woman, but a man impersonating a woman like Julian Eltinge.

When I told Mae that one day when I'm old I was going to write my memoirs, she called me into her dressing room between acts. "I want you to do me a favor," she said. "As a future historian of the theater and film world, I want you to tell your readers the real truth long after I'm dead and gone." Suddenly she emerged from behind the screen fully nude. "Look me over," she ordered me. "Look at that honey pot between my legs. Remember it and write about it one day. Let the world know that Mae West is no man but a woman among women." Observing her genitals carefully, I can report in all honesty that Mae West was not a man. Not at all.

One night we met Frank Wallace in a speakeasy. Mae revealed that she'd secretly married him in 1911. I expected some muscle-bound, tall, handsome brute. Frank looked like a nervous little runt of a man, the kind depicted at the time who ran small grocery stores in some Midwestern town.

Frail and a bit timid, Frank was the son of a poor Lithuanian tailor who'd earned extra money for his family by playing the fiddle at family reunions. Frank took up the same profession for a while, abandoning the fiddle for jazz dancing which seemed to catch on big with vaudeville audiences of the day. He told me that he'd been impressed with Mae because of her "coon shouting" on stage and her petticoat-flashing, skirt-swishing dance numbers. He claimed that it was many months before Mae went to bed with him. "When she did, she came on to me like a firecracker. I thought I knew everything there was to know about sex. Mae taught me tricks none of my other girl friends had. She's one hell of a broad." In the Thirties Frank would turn up again on the vaudeville circuit, this time billing himself as "Mr. Mae West," hoping to cash in on her movie fame.

During my first months in New York John Barrymore was going through one of his periodic attempts to rehabilitate himself, even checking into a sanitarium at one point near White Plains. I'd visit him every weekend. He was always begging me to bring him liquor but I would always claim that the administration staff searched me coming in and would always confiscate the booze. The dreaded feature of each day for John was a five-mile marathon hike. When I wasn't there a trainer would ride horseback alongside John to make sure he maintained his pace. When I visited John on weekends, I would run the five miles with him. After all, I too had to keep my figure.

When John got out of the sanitarium, he started drinking and smoking heavily again. Sometimes we'd visit with his playwright friend, Ned Sheldon, who was living in New York. Sheldon no longer demanded that we perform the sex act over his face. He was in acute pain, a virtual prisoner in his bed. Almost every joint was ankylosed. He couldn't even change his position in bed without the help of his male nurse. He would remain in this dire condition for nearly a quarter of a century before succumbing to death, which must have been a merciful blessing to him.

When I encountered the lesbian writer, Mercedes de Acosta, she was still providing the sex for Natacha Rambova that Rodolfo was not. A friend of both John and Ned Sheldon, Mercedes claimed that, "Jack is the love of Ned's life. All that suffering and emotional frustration he goes through has caused Ned's illness."

When John left for England, I found New York a lonely place, even though I couldn't help but notice that John would only have sex with me when he was drunk and there were no available women around, including his wife, a woman named Michael Strange. Still I missed him when he left with Michael and their children. He was set to appear as Hamlet at the Theatre Royal on Haymarket. John rented a glamorously positioned house for himself and his family at No. 2 Cheyne Walk in Chelsea, very close to the Thames, a town house once occupied by James McNeill Whistler.

I quickly forgot about John when I learned

that Rodolfo would be filming his next picture in Astoria, Queens, and not Hollywood. Regrettably, Natacha would be with him, supervising every moment of the production.

Rodolfo had wanted to make *Captain Blood* by Rafael Sabatini for Famous Players-Lasky, but Natacha prevailed on him to appear in Booth Tarkington's novel, *Monsieur Beaucaire*, with Bebe Daniels playing Princesse Henriette to his Duc de Chartres/Beaucaire. The story was set at the time of the French Revolution.

As a means of publicizing the film even before shooting began, Rodolfo was photographed in a loincloth, Indian headdress, and bow and arrow which had nothing to do with Monsieur Beaucaire and everything to do with his still-secret longing to play Black Feather on the screen.

When Natacha read the script of Beaucaire, she demanded rewrites, including the insertion of several "beef-cake" scenes of Rodolfo half-undressed as the romantic lover. On most points Natacha was wrong. But on one point she was consistently right: Rodolfo looked better without clothes than with clothes. Finally, Natacha put her foot down and turned down the script completely, claiming Rodolfo would film it only if it was rewritten. His return to the screen was postponed as they sailed back to the French Riviera aboard the *Acquitania* to spend time with the Hudnuts at their villa. Mr. Hudnut had made the alterations to the villa that Rodolfo had demanded, and his in-laws were waiting to receive their famous son-in-law. I wasn't going along this time.

Before leaving, Rodolfo had visited me in W.R.'s apartment. I found him growing more morose and out of touch with reality. He claimed that his relationship with Natacha remained on a spiritual level, and he'd made no attempt to penetrate her after that first night.

My sexual role with Rodolfo was dipping into S&M. Anxious to please him, I went along with whatever suggestion he had in mind, including his roping me to the bed for penetrations which were violent and brutal. Forcing me to lie face down in the bed, his razor-sharp teeth bit into my neck during intercourse, drawing blood which he sucked voraciously. At first I had been repelled by this but in time the act became strangely erotic to me.

After four hours, he left the apartment to return to the suite at the Ritz-Carlton he was sharing with Natacha. I was badly bruised and felt exhausted, but I clung to Rodolfo as if I'd never see him again. He had forced me to love the pain he inflicted on me.

Before departing he opened up a jewel case and pulled out two slave bracelets, one which he gave to me and another which he put on his own wrist. "I'm already married," he said. "It can't be a wedding ring, but these bracelets will unite us. In the months ahead, our love-making will grow deeper and deeper as we explore some areas of love that much of the world considers taboo. But we'll have no taboos. Anything that two men can do together, we will do." He opened his eyes wide like he did in his films. "Including some aspects of love that you might have considered repulsive up until now."

On the *Acquitania* reporters noted the spiked platinum bracelet on Rodolfo's right wrist. It was later reported to be a slave bracelet, a present from Natacha Rambova to her now legally married husband.

Jibes about the bracelet continued in the press. Upon his return to New York, little boys chased after Rodolfo taunting him that he'd become the slave of a woman. Knowing it was not she who had given him the bracelet, Natacha begged him to take it off. He flatly refused, one of the few times he stood up to her. His explanation was that he'd introduced many styles to America, including slicked-down hair and long sideburns. Rodolfo claimed in time that men would wear bracelets, and that no one would mock them. His prediction came true. In World War II GIs began wearing bracelets, but by that time, Rodolfo was long dead and gone.

The Valentinos came back to New York after a disastrous stay on the French Riviera, where Rodolfo had lit a candle in the Hudnut Villa. The candle had blown over in the wind, causing some of the draperies to go up in flames. The fire got out of control and threatened to destroy Mrs. Hudnut's precious Gobelin tapestries and Saint Ceré needlepoint chairs, but it was put out just in time.

In Astoria, Natacha interfered in every aspect of production on the set of *Monsieur Beaucaire*, trying to take over the picture from its true director, Sidney Olcott. Olcott asked Zukor and Lasky to remove him from the film, but they insisted he stay. Thousands of fan letters were pouring in daily from all over the world. Valentino's fans, denied his screen image for two years, were anxiously awaiting the release of *Monsieur Beaucaire.*

Natacha not only berated the film crew, but attacked Rodolfo himself, denouncing his "artistic stupidity."

Every major columnist in America was writing about Valentino, including Adela Rogers St. Johns. She'd previously befriended Wallace Reid, finding him the "epitome of charm." Now she pronounced Ramon Novarro "dashingly romantic," Antonio Moreno "gay (sic) and poetic," Richard Dix "manly, brave, and daring," and Valentino "passion personified." Reading that column I felt I knew a lot more about these men than St. Johns did.

She may have found Valentino "passion personified," but her subsequent columns attacked his "small eyes, his flat nose, and large mouth—all of which fail to measure up to the standards of male beauty in this country." She also wrote that he was "an ordinary young man, with atrocious taste in clothes, and whose attributes render him devoid of physical charm."

In the midst of all the hysteria generated by Rodolfo's return to films, an ugly rumor spread across Broadway that Rodolfo was suffering from a life-threatening type of syphilis. Although this didn't appear in print, it was so widely circulated that it might as well have been headline news. The rumors persisted so strongly that Rodolfo himself began to believe he had a venereal disease. To calm him down, I asked Dr. Brian Sheehan to journey across country to examine Rodolfo, who was refusing to have any other doctor look at him for this condition. Eager to explore New York with me, Brian arrived to examine Rodolfo. After a private examination in W.R.'s Fifth Avenue apartment, he pronounced the Great Lover disease free.

When not shooting the film, Rodolfo and Natacha spent lavish sums of money they could not afford, buying fabulous antiques for their house on Whitley Heights. Rodolfo's former lover, George Ullman, now his business man-

ager, protested, but to no avail. When it seemed Rodolfo had purchased every bad portrait and every rusting suit of armor from every antique dealer in New York, he announced his intention to buy his own private airplane, a racing stable, and even a yacht. Fortunately Ullman prevailed, and these bankrupting purchases were never made. In spite of Natacha, the film eventually opened on the hottest August day anyone could remember in New York. To get into the oppressive air of the stuffy theater, long lines formed outside the Mark Strand.

Audiences came expecting to see Rodolfo dressed as the brutal, passionate lover of *The Sheik*. What they saw instead was their hero under a white wig in costly laces and embroidered satins. Not only that, but silk stockings and the tightest breeches any actor had ever worn on the screen before. Natacha had even insisted that a dressing scene be written into the film to display her husband's perfect physique. In one long sequence, Rodolfo flexes and stretches his bare torso in front of film audiences, as a retinue of mincing courtiers watch him put on his clothes. New York audiences were more willing to accept this overdressed dandy than their counterparts in small theaters across America.

As *Monsieur Beaucaire* opened on screens across the nation, men in theater after theater jeered at the screen image of Valentino. Hecklers called out to the audience that he was a sissy. Aiding in that impression was a heart-shaped beauty mark that Natacha had insisted Rodolfo wear aside his nose. In fact, she'd applied so many beauty marks to the male members of the cast that the actors looked as if they were suffering from some kind of pox.

Jesse Lasky thought Natacha had made Rodolfo look effeminate, whereas it was his brute masculinity which had thrilled women who flocked to *The Sheik*. Zukor and Lasky pondered what to do. They even considered releasing Rodolfo from his contract but finally decided to cast him in one more film to see if it would be more profitable than Beaucaire.

The return to the screen of their temperamental star with his hysterically demanding wife had proven to be a disappointment. Zukor and Lasky felt the Valentinos weren't worth the trouble and expense they caused. They also noted that Valentino's outrageous spending had caused him to go once again deeply into debt to Paramount.

I had returned to the West Coast with the Valentinos, who were eager to uncrate their antiques and objects d'art and move them into their new Whitley Heights home.

Even before calling Charlie, I telephoned W.R. who was staying at San Simeon. He invited me to come there at once. "There's a bit of trouble," he cautioned. "I can't speak about it until you get here."

Arriving at midnight at his recently finished palatial estate, I was ushered immediately to his bedchamber where he sat up looking at the moonlit ocean in the far distance. He greeted me warmly, telling me how much he'd enjoyed his times in New York with my sister. "She's all I want in a woman," he said. "I don't know why I don't permanently leave Marion."

"Is there trouble?" I asked.

"There is indeed, and only your friend, Dr. Brian Sheehan, is discreet enough to handle it."

"You mean, she's pregnant?" I asked.

"Once again," he said with a despair. "If news of this gets out, her film career is ruined. But she's stubbornly insisting on actually having the kid. I want you and Brian to go to her tomorrow and talk her into an abortion."

"I don't see any other way out of this," I said.

"Neither do I," he said. "Will you do it?"

"For you, W.R., anything," I promised.

After we'd talked for about an hour, the Chief seemed to be growing sleepy and called down for some glasses of warm milk for the both of us. After drinking the milk, I shook his hand and excused myself for the night, heading to the bedroom which had been permanently assigned to me at San Simeon.

At the door, W.R. called to me in his high-pitched, squeaky voice. "I'm feeling a little lonely tonight," he said. "Why not sleep here with me? It's the biggest bed in the castle."

W.R. undressed and put on a pair of blue silk pajamas. Since he didn't offer me pajamas, I assumed he wanted me to undress in front of him. He'd seen me naked before so I was hardly embarrassed.

In bed, he said good night and wished me pleasant dreams. Tired from the long journey

up from Los Angeles, I fell asleep at once.

Around three o'clock, I heard his voice lightly calling to me. "I'm ready, Lotte." It was almost a whisper.

Waking up dazed, I thought at first that I'd gone to bed with him while dressed as Lotte. But Lotte wouldn't be stark naked with W.R. with her bird showing.

Coming to, I whispered to him. "It's Durango, W.R. I can summon Lotte for you, but not tonight."

"I understand," he said in a calm, gentle, almost soothing voice. "If she's not here, you can do the job for her." He reached for my hand and placed it on his erect penis.

"When we're alone together in the future," he said, "it won't be necessary to wear that Lotte drag, Durango."

So the Chief knew I was a young man after all. Why should that even surprise me? W.R. was one of the most astute newspapermen in the world. How naïve I was to think I could fool him. He was hardly a homosexual, but like such actors as Tom Mix, W.R. was liberated enough not to say no to a fantastic blow-job.

I put all the love I could muster into the act. Even if I thought of Richard Dix or William Boyd when descending on W.R., I still gave him my best shot. He enjoyed it, and I felt it was an act of kindness bestowed upon a man who had shown incredible generosity toward me when I needed it.

The rule was we were never to speak of any sexual act the next morning. He didn't say that, but it was understood. To put a face on it, he told me the following morning that he was going to tell his staff and others that I had accepted a position as his personal secretary, and that was fine with me.

Tom Ince didn't give me that much film work; Charlie was busy with his women; I hardly saw some of my former beaus, including John Gilbert; and Rodolfo was cast under the spell of his Natacha, and the party and film agenda of Ramon Novarro and his best gal, Barbara LaMarr, rarely included me any more.

I did contact William Boyd on occasion, but he rarely saw me as he had a string of other involvements, all with women. I had finally come to the conclusion that actors, being actors, liked to have as many different experiences as they could, even if it were with a pretty young boy. But those experiences didn't equal a lifetime commitment. After a few rolls in the hay, they were ready, willing, and able to turn to their first love, which was pussy.

With all the showgirls in Hollywood willing to spread their legs upon request, studs such as Richard Dix and William Boyd were kept busy every night, with no time for me except maybe a sometimes thing.

My prospect of finding just one guy to settle down with grew slimmer as the months and years went by. In my heart, I didn't know if I wanted to settle down with one guy. Frankly, with so many men, such as Reginald Denny, when I'd satisfied my sexual curiosity I was ready to move on to my next adventure.

And those adventures were plentiful. For the Twenties, a whole new set of handsome young male hopefuls had arrived in Hollywood, and an entire cast of future stars was in the making. I was eager to sample all this fresh merchandise such as William Haines who was openly homosexual and didn't seem to care who knew it.

There was a young actor named Clark Gable who'd arrived on the scene and was working as an extra. I'd heard stories from Billy Haines about him, and was eager to sample Gable's wares for myself. In Gable's case, he charged men but gave it to the ladies for free. Billy had promised me an introduction if he ever got around to it. Rod La Rocque kept discovering one gorgeous hopeful after another, which he would kindly pass on to me providing he'd finished with them.

Thoughts of male seduction occupied my mind as I drove to the house of Marion Davies. In spite of her pregnancy, Marion had been drinking heavily when I arrived in Beverly Hills. I confronted a very different Marion from before. No longer the giggling, fun-loving actress I knew, this was Mother Marion instead of Maid Marion.

"I'm tired of having my kids aborted," she screeched at me. "W.R. can order some butcher to cut the living flesh from my body on command. But that's not a command I'm going to listen to. He had his sons with Millicent. He didn't have those aborted."

"But you understand the situation better than that," I said, pleading with her. "Millicent is his wife. You're his mistress. News that you are having a kid with W.R. would be a front-page scandal. It would ruin your career. All you've worked for."

"I haven't worked for a God damn film career," she said. "It was W.R. who wanted a beautiful blonde actress for a mistress. All I've ever wanted is my own personal happiness, and motherhood is what I want now. You're a homosexual and can't be expected to understand that Mother Nature intended for women to become mothers. It's in our genes. Mother Nature made women to have children. It's our basic instinct. I can feel the kid growing inside me every day, and I want it. More to the point, I'm going to give birth to it."

In the weeks ahead, Marion wavered between giving birth to her child and having it aborted. Sometimes W.R. talked her into it, only to have her turn down the idea the following morning. On one occasion Marion went so far as to have me drive her to the clinic of Brian Sheehan where she'd registered under an assumed name. But even though she'd had a complete physical from Brian, she bolted from the bed at the last minute and demanded that I return her to Beverly Hills.

She remained in seclusion, as she could not accept a film role in her condition. W.R. repeatedly called Brian urging him to visit Marion and urge the abortion upon her. As a doctor to the stars, Brian was only too willing to carry out the Chief's orders. Then one day Brian told W.R. that Marion's pregnancy was too far advanced. Because of his personal morality, he refused to perform late abortions.

"I know this will be my last chance at motherhood," Marion told me one afternoon. "I want the kid. I'm determined to have it—and that's that. I've changed my mind in the past, and I've been confused about what to do. But from this day on, and until I give birth, this is my final stand. I'm digging in my heels on this one."

Marion meant what she'd said. Utter secrecy surrounded her first and only attempt at motherhood. Disguised and registered at Brian's clinic under an assumed name, she checked in at least three weeks before the expected delivery of her child. She didn't want to risk any publicity that might be caused by an ambulance summoned to her home to take her to the hospital.

Millicent and W.R.'s sons had been installed for the summer at San Simeon, and since W.R. couldn't take Marion there he had rented a beautiful mansion for her on Bedford Drive in Beverly Hills. It was from that mansion that I drove her to Brian's clinic where she would check in and await the birth of her child.

That occasion finally arrived when W.R. had gone to San Francisco on business. Brian called me at three o'clock in the morning and asked me to come over to his clinic. "There's a surprise waiting for you," he said.

When I got there, I was surprised indeed. Marion had given birth to twins—one boy, one girl. She was resting and recovering well. "When I held those little brats in my arms, she said, "I can't believe that I almost had them aborted. My whole body shuddered at the very idea."

When W.R. heard the news, he rushed back to Los Angeles to be with Marion. Although he was adamant about keeping the birth of the twins a secret, I detected that he was proud to have fathered such healthy looking babies at his age. It made him feel virile, and I shared in his happiness. Marion vowed that she'd leave the screen to devote herself entirely to being a mother. "I don't want to be a motion-picture star any more," she told W.R. He made no protest whatsoever.

In honor of the occasion, W.R. purchased a gleaming white stucco mansion for Marion and the twins at 1700 Lexington Road in Beverly Hills. When not at San Simeon, W.R. still had his Long Island mansion and his northern California properties, but he often lived in permanently leased suites at the Palace Hotel in San Francisco or the Ambassador Hotel in Los Angeles. In New York, when not with Millicent, he stayed at that luxurious apartment on Fifth Avenue in New York.

W.R. often came to live with Marion at the Beverly Hills mansion. He'd even had a luxurious seven-room cottage built at the far corner of the property. That's where two nannies looked after the twins when there were guests in the main house. To please Marion and keep her amused, W.R. sponsored some of the most luxurious dinner parties ever given in Los Angeles. He would invite a host of film luminaries that often included Douglas Fairbanks and Mary Pickford. Tom and Nell Ince were always invited.

I was still attracted to Tom Ince and he did get me minor film jobs from time to time. But our "romance" never went beyond the stage of me giving him a blow-job as he watched a young couple in action through his peep-hole. Tom remained Hollywood's premier voyeur, and I was anxious to sample his thick inches any way I could get them, even if he were really getting off watching a couple in action when he blasted his load into my mouth. His ultimate coup was when he'd invited Doug Fairbanks and Mary Pickford for the weekend and got to watch as they'd made love to each other.

Doug and Mary were about the only couple he watched who were legally married. The other couples capturing Tom's interest through his peep-hole might be married, but not to each other.

W.R. was seeing more and more of Tom Ince as he planned to go into the film business with him. They were always talking about their upcoming merger. The Chief said he found my relationship with Tom "amusing," especially when I told him in secret about the peep-hole. That utterly fascinated him.

Louella Parsons, then working for W.R., was often a guest of Marion's at her Beverly Hills mansion. But even this eagle-eyed reporter never found out about Marion's twins. It was Hollywood's best-kept secret. But like most secrets it was just a matter of time before exposure.

Since I had been almost ditched by Barbara LaMarr who had found Ramon more fascinating than me, I became best pals with Marion. Frankly, she gave the best parties in Los Angeles, and I was eager to attend.

Charlie was a frequent visitor at these parties, comparing them to "an era of Arabian Nights." Marion at her table might seat a mincing homosexual chorus boy next to a distinguished U.S. senator, but it was all in good fun. Sometimes she'd hire a public bus and take us to Malibu Beach where she'd booked musicians. We'd build a bonfire and enjoy a midnight picnic before racing off to fish for grunions. Those were heady days, heady times, and by that very definition likely to come to an end.

One week John Barrymore arrived back in Los Angeles, and Marion invited him to spend a few days at her manse. I arranged through her to let me share John's bedroom, and I got to reacquaint myself with the Great Profile. He wasn't quite as virile as he was when I'd first met him, as his drinking had increased and made him less potent. That meant I had to work much harder to obtain a climax from him, but I eventually did the job.

On the second night of John's visit, Marion threw another dinner party, to which she'd invited Charlie and Lita Grey. She detested Charlie's new wife but included her on occasion just to keep up appearances.

Right in front of the other guests, Charlie and Lita staged a big fight, and Charlie stormed out the door. Much to my regret, John filled in as proxy husband for Charlie. He moved in on Lita and invited her to spend the night in our bedroom. I was sent packing to another guest room for the evening, as Lita claimed another one of "my men." This did nothing to endear her to me. W.R. had to return east on some urgent business I didn't fully understand. He invited me to go with him on the train, and I gladly accepted. Marion remained behind on the West Coast. After giving birth, Marion was at the peak of her blonde beauty. She'd never looked so good before or since. With W.R. out of town, and with Charlie estranged from Lita, their old affair was resumed. Neither seemed to want to keep it a secret

Newspapers called Charlie "the real Sheik of Hollywood," and he was photographed arm and arm with Marion at such major functions as the big bash hosted by screenwriter Elinor Glyn at the Hotel Biltmore. Charlie was even photographed sitting at table, holding Marion's hand and looking lovingly into her eyes.

In New York, W.R. was furious at Marion, claiming that his break with her would be permanent this time.

After the first week back in New York, the reason for W.R.'s emergency train trip across the continent became clearer. He feared some major revelation about his personal life was about to be blasted across the pages of his rival newspapers.

By then, W.R. had given up his dream of running for the presidency of the United States. Those days were behind him. However, he fiercely guarded the privacy of Millicent and of Marion. Even though W.R. and Marion were the most famous "illicit couple" in America, details of their affair were only hinted at in the press. In those times you needed a court trial or some other libel-protected public forum to reveal such private details about the life of a star. Much of America still did not know that Marion Davies was W.R.'s mistress. That was about to change.

Back at the Fifth Avenue apartment, W.R anxiously kept abreast of the trial of William J. Fallon, the most flamboyant attorney on Broadway, with clients such as Nicky Arnstein. Fallon was charged with fixing a jury that had acquitted two stock swindlers, William F. McGee and Edward Fuller, two little darlings from Tammany Hall.

At first I didn't know how this case directly involved the Chief until I learned that he'd instructed Victor Watson, his chief editor at *The New York American*, to assign an investigative reporter, the best he had on staff, to expose Fallon. That reporter, Nat Ferber, had dug deeply and had turned up overwhelming evidence that Fallon indeed had tampered with the juries.

Ferber had uncovered a former confidante of Fallon, Eddie Eidlitz, who was willing to testify against his former associate. Weighing in at 320 pounds, Eidlitz had all the evidence needed to send Fallon to prison and certainly get him disbarred. Fearing that Eidlitz might be killed or bought off before the trial, W.R. ordered that the butterball be sequestered at a hotel in Brooklyn. There Eidlitz was fed a steady diet of caviar, lobster, and some of the most expensive call girls in New York, all a present from W.R.

On hearing this, Fallon at first fled from justice but was tracked down by New York detectives. Vowing revenge on W.R., Fallon announced to the press that during the trial he would "expose the private life of William Randolph Hearst." It was to be an act of revenge for W.R.'s exposure of him during the jury-tampering case. With the promise of revelations about W.R.'s private life, reporters from non-Hearst papers flocked to cover the case.

As a skilled but slippery lawyer himself, Fallon asked each prospective juror if they knew of William Randolph Hearst or Marion Davies, identified as "the motion picture actress." Of course, the prosecution objected vehemently to the introduction of Marion into the proceedings, but the judge overruled in favor of Fallon.

Even more than Mae West, the Fallon trial was the hottest show in town. In horror at her name being brought into the case, Marion went into seclusion in Beverly Hills. In court, Fallon attacked W.R. personally, claiming that the press baron had set out to destroy him because he had copies of the birth certificates of two twins born to Marion.

The secret was out—not only out, but in blaring headlines. W.R. was grief stricken at the revelation. Of course, we knew Fallon was lying because Brian had not made out birth certificates for the twins. But somehow Fallon had bribed someone in the know in Los Angeles, and at least knew of the birth of the twins. Perhaps a spy at Brian's clinic.

To W.R.'s amazement, Fallon, who was obviously guilty on all charges, managed to persuade the jury that he was the victim, and W.R. the villain in the case. Fallon claimed that the only reason he was being hauled into court was because W.R. knew that he possessed copies of those birth certificates. Fallon was exonerated, and he was never called upon to produce copies of the birth certificates, which he would not have been able to do anyway.

On the train ride back to San Simeon, W.R. was in a morbid depression, wondering what the fallout of this revelation would do not only to him, but to Millicent and the boys and especially the career of Marion. About midway across the country, W.R. decided he would leave the movie business. He was also seriously considering breaking off with Marion because of her widely publicized affair with Charlie.

"I'm through with Hollywood, through with Marion," he said. "I'll offer a big financial settlement, and that will be that. Then she'll be free to run around with The Little Tramp or any-body else of her choice. I've had enough humiliation.

For his final showdown with both Charlie and Marion, he'd called and invited them, along with some other guests, including Tom Ince, for a pleasure cruise aboard his yacht, the *Oneida*.

*****

The *Oneida*, a 225-foot yacht, set sail on November 15, 1924 from San Pedro for what was supposed to be a rest-filled weekend cruise to celebrate the forty-third birthday of Tom Ince. Marion was aboard with her sisters, Reine and Ethel, and they had invited Elinor Glyn, the most popular screenwriter of her day. For decades to come, it was reported that Louella Parsons was aboard the *Oneida* that weekend and as a result she'd blackmailed W.R. into a lifetime position under threat of reporting what she'd seen. Parsons did not sail with us, although she later learned what happened on that cruise but went to her grave without revealing what it was.

W.R. also invited Charlie, his chief rival for Marion's affection, hoping to have time at sea to discuss the triangle that had developed among them. "If you want to have a face-to-face with Charlie?" I asked W.R., "Why invite the rest of us?"

W.R. thought for a moment. "I felt that if Charlie, Marion, and I were the only guests aboard, the tension might be unbearable. With several people invited, I thought that if, God forbid, we did have a confrontation, it would tend to be more subdued. We'd probably not shout and yell at each other, because we'd be afraid that the other passengers might hear us."

At first Charlie was reluctant to sail, but agreed to it finally, thinking if W.R. wanted to confront him, it might be better aboard the *Oneida* than in some private home. That didn't entirely make sense to me.

I asked Charlie if he wanted me to share his cabin, since he didn't plan to invite his wife, Lita, but he said he wanted to be alone when he wasn't with the other guests. He also, I suspected, preferred to keep his cabin free for whatever spontaneous pursuit might present itself during his time on board.

Before boarding, I received a call from Marion suggesting that I go by and pick up Theodore Kosloff, who had accepted her invitation. She said because of overcrowding that I would be sharing a cabin with Theodore. "From what I've seen of him dancing in those tights, that won't be a problem for you at all." I'd already told her of my involvement with Theodore and was anxious to have him in my cabin for the cruise. While in Los Angeles, he could work me only occasionally into his busy schedule. Unless he went for Glyn or one of Marion's sisters, perhaps even Marion herself, I would have him to myself.

Marion had invited both Tom Ince and his wife, Nell, to celebrate the birthday. But Nell said that one of their sons, Bill, was ill, and she'd have to remain behind to look after him.

Originally, I was to have shared Tom's cabin. He had called Marion, requesting that he bring his mistress, the actress Margaret Livingston, along on the cruise. That meant I'd been booted from Tom's cabin. Perhaps for that reason, Marion had invited Theodore to go aboard because she didn't want me to feel left out of the party.

The *Oneida* sailed for Los Angeles en route to San Diego and stopped the next morning to pick up Tom Ince at Long Beach. His date, Margaret, had boarded the previous night and was waiting for him in his cabin.

"You're out of luck this time," Tom told me. "Sorry about that, kid. But you know my first love is for pussy. I'm not cutting you off, but you'll have to wait your turn."

"My loss, Margaret's gain," I said to him. "I'll make sure to fill Nell in on all the details when I get ashore."

At first he looked startled until he realized I was joking. "You do that and you'll never work another day in pictures." He reached for his chest, as if experiencing some sort of sharp pain. "Actually Margaret isn't going to get me at my best. I've been feeling rotten for days."

I knew that Tom suffered from stomach ulcers and angina, but he refused to go to my good friend, Brian Sheehan, for treatment. I'd heard that Tom was Christian Scientist or something. Once again I brought up the subject of

his seeking treatment from Brian, but he flatly turned me down. "I believe the body can heal itself," he said. "We have to give it time." With that foolish remark, he disappeared below deck to call on Miss Livingston.

The first hours aboard after we sailed from Long Beach were rather dull. W.R. cornered Tom to discuss an upcoming merger and possible film productions they might launch jointly. Marion remained with Elinor Glyn and her sisters. After the workout I gave him the previous night, Theodore was sunbathing on deck in skimpy briefs. But why not? He had more than enough to show off.

After seeing Theodore in his briefs, Glyn told me that she'd better revise her "It" list. Instead of naming Antonio Moreno the "It Man," she felt the honor should go to Theodore. "Is that thing for real?" she asked. "I can't believe it." Long before Lana Turner and Ava Gardner, Elinor Glyn was the original size queen of Hollywood.

Charlie was alone on deck, so I went to join him. I'd never seen The Little Tramp so despondent. "She may be the mother of my children," he said, "but I want her gone."

"Why not a divorce?" I asked.

"Don't be a little fool," he said angrily. "That's exactly what I want, but at what price? Her God damn greedy family, including my mother-in-law's San Francisco brother, that shitass attorney, is demanding that I cough up one-million dollars."

"Why not a more reasonable counter offer?" I asked.

"Don't you think I've done that?" he said in despair. "She wants to bankrupt me." Charlie seemed on the verge of one of his nervous breakdowns, a frequent occurrence when he faced the prospect of losing money. "She's nothing but a Mexican tramp." He looked at me with a deadly seriousness in his eyes, making me realize that I'd never understood him at all. "If the bitch goes to the newspapers and threatens to expose me, I've warned her. I'll put out a contract for her life. It will look like an accident."

I thought he was entirely capable of that. Kono himself often spoke of Charlie's "lunatic side." Perhaps it was a gene inherited from his insane mother. Kono said that one night Charlie had pulled out his .38 revolver and aimed it at Lita's head during one of their fights. When the fight got really vicious, he threatened to kill her, then fire a bullet into the heads of each of his sons before shooting himself.

More than a comedian, Charlie was a dramatist. I felt he could actually talk himself into such an act of violence. He was forever threatening suicide. "Besides," he said, "I've fallen in love with another woman."

"Georgia Hale," I said. "Your new co-star."

"No, Merna Kennedy."

"Your woman du jour," I said. "Who will it be next week?"

As if on cue, he looked over at Marion who was dressed in a white bathing suit and talking with her sisters. "Before this cruise is over, I'm asking Marion to marry me. I want to be a father to her children."

"I think W.R. might have something to say about that," I said as a word of caution.

"Do you believe for one minute that that impotent old goat fathered those kids?" he said. "I'm the father of the twins. They even look like me. You don't think they look like Hearst, do you?"

"Not much," I said. "But they don't look like Marion either. And she's the mother." I put my hand on his arm. "If W.R. finds out what you're saying, you're dead. I can't believe you're the father."

"Just ask Marion," he said. "Go ahead, ask her." He got up and headed toward his cabin

Within the hour, when I'd cornered Marion, I related what Charlie had said to me. "I'm worried about him," I said. "I know he's brought his .38 aboard. That means he's going to threaten suicide at some point during this cruise. He always does that."

Marion didn't say anything at first but looked at me with a steely determination. "Charlie is the father of my twins. You don't think W.R. is the father, do you? Tell me you're not that dumb. W.R. will never marry me. Charlie's going to ask me to marry him after his divorce from that little cha-cha-cha child he's married to. I'm seriously considering it. I want my twins to have a proper daddy and a real name. I want to become legitimate. The next Mrs. Charlie Chaplin. I don't want to go down in film history as the mistress of some aging tycoon. What kind of reputation do you think that would be for me?"

"You know how Charlie is," I said. "How fickle."

"He's fickle because he's never been tamed by one woman," she said. "I'm that woman. Before this cruise is over, there is going to be a showdown."

"Be careful," I said.

"What the hell?" she asked. "I happen to know that W.R. is planning to leave me anyway. Personally I think he has another woman stashed away somewhere. He's getting sexual satisfaction from somewhere—not from me, I can assure you of that."

Even though I was much younger than W.R. or Charlie, I felt they were acting like children, although playing deadly adult games. Astute in matters of the arts or business, they could be frightfully immature in their love games. Charlie, I felt, would never settle down with one woman—certainly not Marion. He would always be attracted to the next teenage pubescent.

Vladimir Nabokov rather brilliantly in his 1955 novel, *Lolita*, captured Charlie's fascination with young girls. He based his character of Lolita on the real-life Lillita McMurray Grey Chaplin. Drawing inspiration from Charlie himself, *Lolita's* Humbert Humbert, with his "toothbrush mustache," suffers bouts of insanity.

Taking the long way around to San Diego, W.R. diverted his boat to Catalina Island "so the ladies could go shopping." Margaret Livingston joined Marion and her sisters, along with Elinor Glyn. Having drunk too much the previous night, Theodore asked to remain behind in our cabin to sleep it off. W.R. stayed aboard to talk privately with Charlie, but Tom Ince invited me to go along with him.

He kept complaining of stomach cramps. "I need to walk," he said. "Get my feet on solid earth. I think the boat's making me sick. Also I want to get away from Chaplin. He disgusts me."

"I thought you guys were friends," I said as we strolled along the quay.

"Not after that time I invited him to go sailing with Peggy Hopkins Joyce. Charlie couldn't tolerate it when Peggy decided to turn her attention from him to me. After only our first night together, Peggy told me I was twice the man The Little Tramp is. She found some of his actions effeminate. She was initially attracted to his celebrity, but a woman can't get fucked by celebrity. I've seen Charlie perform with women through my peephole. He doesn't know I've been watching. He hops on and off a woman like a Jack Rabbit. I'm the lover aboard that boat."

"That you are," I said. "There's none better in Hollywood."

"Coming from you, I'll take that as a compliment. After all, you've tested out all the studs in town, so you should know."

"You're the best, my man Tommy," I said.

"I should have brought you along to share my cabin rather than Margaret," he said. "She's too God damn demanding. She makes me do all the work. She wouldn't even go down on me, and you know how much I love blow-jobs. She said it was disgusting. You know what I did to the bitch. I turned around and spread the cheeks of my ass. 'Lick that,' I ordered her. She was horrified. She'd never even heard of that in her life, or so she said. She accused me of being the most disgusting pervert she's ever encountered. She's sleeping with one of Marion's sisters tonight. I'm through with Miss Livingston. If she thinks she'll work in any of my pictures, ever again, she's sadly mistaken."

In one little crafts shop, Tom purchased some silly little Mexican gifts for Nell and the kids. He asked me to join him for a drink on a nearby terrace overlooking the water. Although the morning had come on cold, the day had warmed considerably and he was perspiring heavily—much more than the weather called for. He seemed a bit feverish.

"At the ripe old age of forty-three," he said, "I'm ready for some big decisions in my life. Really big. I've decided to ask Marion to marry me after I divorce Nell."

"I find that astonishing," I said. "I had no idea you and Nell were splitting."

"She's going to file for divorce," he said. "She's stood my whoring around like a tomcat for as long as she can. She's going to take the children. As for me, I'm going to declare myself as the father of Marion's twins. I guess

you'd already figured that out. But I'm the genuine daddy of those children. It's time Marion settled down too. You can't make a career out of being a rich man's mistress."

"I'm not so sure about that," I cautioned him. "Marion and W.R. break up at least twice a year. But there's a bond there that's very solid. I wouldn't ask Marion to marry you unless W.R. is ready to dump her. You know the chief could ruin you in Hollywood."

"Don't you think I don't know that," he said. "But I happen to know that this is his last trip with Marion. At the end of the cruise, he's going to offer her some financial settlement."

"How does Charlie figure into this?" I asked, completely aware that Tom seemed to have no inkling that The Little Tramp also felt he was the father of the twins.

"The thing between Charlie and Marion ended years ago," he said. "Charlie's not much of a lover, you know. Peggy said he was often impotent when he tried to mount her. That's not all. He likes to dress up in women's clothes. Marion told me that he often put on her gowns and paraded around the room before having sex with her. What woman wants to marry a cross-dresser? Marion doesn't need to stay with an old fool like W.R. who can't get it up any more or a cross-dresser like Charlie who really would like to be with a nine-year-old. Who knows why he goes for little girls? Because he can't handle a real woman."

"There may be some truth in that," I said, "but please watch your step carefully with W.R."

"I'm not afraid of him," he said. "He's a powerful newspaper baron but his influence is on the wan in Hollywood. Frankly, his picture-making has been a bit of a failure. The Hollywood of tomorrow belongs to Louis B. Mayer—turds like that, not to W.R."

"W.R.'s just in a current slump," I said. "I wouldn't rule him out and I wouldn't try to take his mistress from him, unless he gives you the green light."

"You're not one to advise me about women," he said. "First, you're only a kid. Not only that. You're a homosexual, and you know nothing about women, other than secretly longing to be one yourself."

"I'm proud to be a man," I said. "I don't

want to be a woman. It's wrong to think that all male homosexuals want to be women. That's simply not the case."

"Suit yourself," he said, reaching into his pocket and pulling out a big white handkerchief, which he used to mop his feverish brow. "I'm not feeling so well. Let's go back to the ship. I'd ask you to visit me later in my cabin, but I'm not into sex tonight. Have you ever known Tom Ince to turn down a sexual offer?"

"I can't say I have," I said, strolling along the quay with him back to the *Oneida*.

At a dinner that night of lobster cocktail and turkey with salad, Elinor Glyn dominated the conversation, which consisted mainly of her predictions of what new male stars were headed for big stardom in Hollywood. She felt Rod La Rocque was definitely on the rise, along with William Boyd and Richard Dix. Theodore looked angry that he'd been excluded. Tom, W.R., and Charlie had little to say to each other, and Marion pointedly ignored the Chief, directing her talk to her sisters when not listening to Glyn. Margaret Livingston sat in silence at the opposite end of the table, ignoring Tom. The pleasure trip was a total dud, and everyone knew it. The women were trying to put a brave face on it, but most of the men were sulking.

Before dessert was served, Tom complained of indigestion and excused himself, requesting some bicarbonate of soda from a waiter. He asked me to go down to his cabin with him to help him settle in. Once inside he belched three times, then rushed to his sink to vomit.

"As soon as we reach San Diego," I said, "you're going ashore. I'll get in touch with my doctor friend. You've got to be cared for. Something is seriously wrong."

"I'll be all right by morning," he said, retching into the sink again.

"Can I stay here with you and look after you?" I asked.

"I think I want to be alone." Taking him at his word, I put him to bed and took down an extra blanket for him.

The dinner party ended early that night and Theodore and I retired. After sleeping all day, he whispered in my ear that he wanted to indulge in some "serious fucking of boy ass tonight." When no one was looking, he reached

over and pinched my butt. "This sea air invigorates me. You're going to get the pounding of your life."

True to his word, the next hour found me under Theodore who attacked me with a sexual violence. He liked to fuck rough, and I was up for it, kissing his neck, fondling his balls, and running my fingers up and down his back. Our cabin was next to Tom's, and once or twice we heard him retching into the sink again. The cabin on the other side of Tom was occupied by Charlie. Theodore and I were so intent in our fucking that we heard but didn't pay much attention to some argument that was seemingly coming from Charlie's cabin. We also heard a woman's voice.

Just as Theodore was blasting off in me, and I was holding on to him as if he were the world's last man, I heard a shot. It seemed to come from the direction of Tom's room. My first suspicion was that Tom had gotten Charlie's gun and had shot himself in his head. Maybe he was far sicker than I realized.

"I'm staying here in the cabin," Theodore said. "I don't want to get involved."

Putting on my robe, I rushed next door and entered Tom's unlocked cabin. He was lying on the bed with what looked like a gunshot wound to his head. I searched for the suicide gun but found no weapon.

He was breathing heavily but was still alive. I eased him back on his pillow. "I'm okay," he said. "A surface wound." He coughed and retched some more.

"We'll get into port," I said. "I'm getting a doctor whether you like it or not." Theodore had changed his mind and had put on his robe and entered the cabin to see what was wrong. I explained matters as quickly as I could before realizing that the bullet must have come from Charlie's cabin, cutting through the cardboard-like walls.

Rushing next door, I opened Charlie's cabin to discover him standing there in his underwear in front of a fully dressed Marion and W.R. Charlie's recently fired .38 revolver lay on the floor. There was a stunned silence among them. Each of them looked at me with a certain bewilderment, seemingly not knowing what to say or do next. No one claimed to have fired that shot.

"Tom has been hurt," I told them. "A bullet fired from this room went through the wall."

"Is he dead?" W.R. asked, breaking the silence.

"It appears to be a head wound," I said. "Let's get to port right away."

"I'll talk to the captain," W.R. said, leaving the room without looking at either Marion or Charlie.

"If anyone heard that gun go off, tell them that you were shooting at seagulls," I said. W.R. was known to carry a gun aboard and would occasionally fire at sea gulls for amusement, so that sounded like a believable scenario.

Marion didn't look at me but confronted Charlie when W.R. had left. "You and I are through. I'll see you at parties, at a dinner here and there, but our affair is over." She turned from him and walked out the cabin door.

"What happened?" I asked Charlie, who still seemed in a daze.

"Now is hardly the time to go into that," he said.

As the *Oneida* made its way to shore, W.R. came to call on Tom to see how he was. Tom assured the Chief that he would be all right. W.R. patted his hand and left, urging Theodore and me to look after the stricken man.

Contact had been made with shore, and Brian Sheehan was waiting there with an ambulance. Charlie had summoned Kono to pick him up. When the boat docked, Charlie was the first to leave. Fearing he might encounter reporters, he had dressed up as a woman in some of Marion's clothing and wore a blonde wig. He said nothing to me at the time.

Two of W.R.'s attendants carried Tom from the yacht and placed his body in the waiting ambulance where Brian began an immediate examination of him. "Go with him," W.R. instructed me, "and keep me informed of everything that happens." He took my arm and looked sternly in my eyes. "Say absolutely nothing, and don't go anywhere near the press. I'll handle the other passengers myself. They think Ince is sick at his stomach. No one must know of this. After it's all over, you and I must have a long talk at San Simeon."

I promised him I would say nothing. I had already told Theodore good-bye. He was to remain aboard with Glyn, Marion and her sisters. The yacht and its thirty-five crew members headed back to Wilmington, a part of the Los Angeles harbor west of the growing city of Long Beach. Other than Theodore, no one aboard, except Marion, knew of the shooting, believing the story about W.R. firing at seagulls.

In the ambulance, Brian assured me that the gunshot wound was superficial—"nothing life threatening about it." But up front in the ambulance, he said that Tom was one sick man. "I've got to examine it. There's something seriously wrong with him. He should have gone to a doctor long before this."

After stopping at a hospital at Del Mar, where the gunshot wound was treated, Brian examined Tom thoroughly, reporting to me that he was suffering from stomach ulcers—"maybe something far more serious."

In spite of his ill health, and over our protests, Tom demanded to be taken to his home. His wife, Nell, had arrived, and the sick producer was released in her custody.

The attending nurse at Del Mar later told the press that she'd learned that Tom had consumed some "bad liquor" aboard the *Oneida*. In spite of her religious teachings, Nell had seemed to recognize the seriousness of Tom's condition, and had called another doctor, Ida Glasgow, to come to the Ince mansion and look after her husband.

In the next forty-eight hours, I heard different stories of what had happened. Only Charlie, W.R. and Marion knew the truth. W. R told me that Charlie had placed the revolver at his own head in another one of his many mock suicide attempts. Not knowing if he were serious or not, both Marion and the Chief had struggled with Charlie to knock the .38 from his hand. During the ensuing struggle, or so the Chief claimed, the revolver discharged. What was not explained in that scenario was why Charlie would summon W.R. and Marion to his cabin to watch him commit suicide.

Charlie told a different story. He said that Marion had revealed to W.R. that Charlie was the real father of the twins, and that they were going to get married as soon as he divorced Lita. Seeing Charlie's .38 on the dresser, W.R. had picked it up and fired at The Little Tramp, narrowly missing him, as the bullet went through the wall into Tom's cabin.

Marion neither confirmed nor denied any of these versions, saying that everything happened so fast she wasn't sure what had transpired. "Besides, I was too drunk anyway. The whole thing's been erased from my memory."

Normally a shrewd man, W.R. ordered the Hearst organization to issue a statement to the press that Tom had taken ill while on a visit to the Hearst ranch in Northern California. The statement claimed that Tom had been invited to enjoy the ranch with his wife, Nell, and their two sons in honor of his forty-third birthday.

The statement stunned reporters. There had been too many eyewitnesses to the fact that Tom had been aboard the *Oneida*.

Until the day each of the unholy trio died, W.R., Marion, or Charlie never told what actually happened in the yacht's cabin on the night of the shooting. With Ida Glasgow as the attending doctor, Tom Ince died forty-eight hours after arriving home. Dr. Glasgow signed the death certificate, listing heart failure as the cause of death. Nell ordered that the body of her late husband be cremated "at once."

Years later Nell in a statement claimed that there had been no bullet wound in Tom's body when her husband was removed from the *Oneida*, thereby confirming that he had indeed been aboard. "His chest pains were diagnosed as angina," she said. "It all fits what we know today as a thrombosis. The end for my darling Tom came at home a week later."

What made this statement astonishing was that Tom had died within forty-eight hours of his departure from the *Oneida*. In another mysterious statement, Nell claimed that the Chief of Homicide of Los Angeles had witnessed her husband's cremation but gave no reason why he was there. The homicide chief would be a witness at a cremation only if there had been a legal examination of the body. Such an examination would have discovered the gunshot wound. The Chief of Homicide never issued any statement that he suspected foul play in the Ince death. When confronted with Nell's statement about his being present at the cremation, he said, "I'm sure the gentle lady was mistaken. I was not there, nor would I have any reason to be."

After Tom's death, I learned that W.R. had agreed to pay off the mortgages on the Ince's Château Elysée apartment building in Hollywood plus another rental property closer to downtown Los Angeles. He had also given Nell $150,000 and booked her on a three-month tour of Europe to escape nagging questions from the press.

Because rumors that W.R. had shot Tom Ince had spread throughout Los Angeles and even into the national press, the district attorney of San Diego launched an investigation a month after Ince's death. But the evidence had been buried, and all eyewitnesses issued contradictory information, the same way they did in the William Desmond Taylor murder or in the Fatty Arbuckle scandal. What happened to the .38? It remains today in my collection of Hollywood memorabilia. W.R. had told me to throw the gun overboard, but I disobeyed him, keeping it as a souvenir.

In *My Autobiography* in 1964, Charlie shed no light on the Ince shooting. In his book, Charlie denied that he was even aboard the *Oneida* at the time. In a bizarre statement, he claimed that Marion Davies, W.R., and himself visited the bedside of Ince a week after he fell ill. Charlie claimed he found his friend in good spirits and that Ince had hopes that his stomach condition would improve. "But, alas, he died two weeks later," or so Charlie said. Tom died forty-eight hours after being hauled off the *Oneida*, not in the three-week period that the autobiography claimed. What is even more amazing was that Charlie was a pallbearer at the very discreet funeral of Ince, so he was well aware of the time of the producer's death.

All Hearst loyalists, including both Louella Parsons and Adela Rogers St. Johns, rushed to the defense of the Chief. In a bizarre statement, St. Johns conceded that it was possible "for Mr. Hearst to shoot someone—maybe even in cold blood. Anybody can do that if provoked. But poison a guest at his own table in a birthday toast—NO." Up to then no one had even raised the possibility that Ince had been poisoned. Instead of helping, the St. Johns column caused new rumors that Tom had been poisoned—hence, his stomach cramps.

Before disembarking for Europe, Nell Ince faced the press and denied all rumors about her husband's death. She praised W.R. for "being such a kind and thoughtful man." To the shock of the reporters present, she then lauded the Chief's dancing skills for a full five minutes.

That scandalous sail was hardly my last trip aboard the *Oneida*. I remember standing on that very yacht, anchored at New York harbor in May of 1927, along with W.R. and Marion, to welcome home Charles Lindbergh after his solo flight across the Atlantic to Paris.

*****

It will never be known at this late date who fathered Marion's twins. Was it Charlie or the late Tom Ince? Or none of the above. It might have been W.R. himself, except The Chief didn't think so. Summoned to San Simeon, I confronted an angry man. He was furious at Charlie, at Marion, and at the rumors spread about the Ince shooting in the newspapers, and even at the twins for having been born.

"Those bastards aren't mine," he said. "Marion and I are having a showdown tonight. I don't think our relationship is going to survive this." He took my arm. "Come, let's go for a walk in the garden. We've got to talk."

I must have strolled for more than an hour with W.R. as I listened to his plan. At all cost he wanted to avoid more scandal, particularly any rumors that linked Marion and him. "She's agreed to give up the twins."

"Are you going to have them adopted?" I asked.

"Nothing like that," he said. "Too difficult. Too much paperwork and fear of exposure. I want you to handle a very important matter for me. After all, you're on my payroll."

Before lunch was served, W.R. had outlined his plan which astonished me, until I could adjust to the idea. "I'm going to bestow upon you a million dollars." Mention of that amount turned me to jelly, and I didn't think I could go on walking.

"The money will not belong entirely to you," he said. "I want you to move the brats to a house I own outside San Francisco. I want you to invest and use the money wisely to bring up those kids and put them through college. Neither of them must know where they came

from. The house where you'll take them will have a staff paid for by me. The bastards will get loving care and be brought up right and well-educated. They'll always wonder where they came from, unless you tell them."

"This is a big undertaking," I said. "Do you want me to go to San Francisco to live and bring up the kids?"

"Nothing like that," he said. "You've still got too many wild oats to sow. You can be their uncle—something like that. Just oversee everything and visit them once a month or so to make sure they're all right and have everything they need." He looked at me sternly. "You'll do it, won't you?"

"Of course, I will, providing Marion agrees."

"Why question me?" he said, his high-pitched voice filled with anger. "If I say she agrees, my word is good enough for you. I want you to go to Marion's and pack up the kids. Head out this very day with them. By tomorrow night I want you to call me to tell me they're installed in their new home and that everything is okay."

"Will I be able to see Marion before I go?" I asked, fearing that if she didn't agree with W.R.'s plan, she might bring a kidnapping charge against me.

"Marion has gone away for a few weeks," he said. "It's better that way. I have a condition attached to my request. After you call me from San Francisco to tell me that the brats got there and have been installed in their new home, I don't want you ever to mention them to me again—or to Marion, even if she begs you. Do you agree to that?"

"I guess," I said, filled with apprehension about my latest mission.

Leaving San Simeon to return to Los Angeles, I dreaded picking up the children and taking them off to an uncertain future. When I got to Marion's, a nanny had them dressed and ready for the drive north to San Francisco and their new home. I was determined to carry out my assignment, and I would try to give the children what love I could, although W.R. before I left had made it abundantly clear that I was not to pretend to be their father. I was to invent some story—in this case, that their parents had died while on a tour of Europe. When the children were old enough to understand, I was to claim to be their family's financial adviser, assigned to oversee their welfare and their upbringing.

My story of bringing up these children over the years, and what happened to the long-lost "Hearst twins," as dubbed by the newspapers, would make a memoir unto itself. Although I've not had much honor in this memoir in respecting the rights of privacy of others, I will invoke that privilege here and tell very little of what happened in honor of my long-ago commitment to W.R. who befriended me until the day he died.

The little girl grew up to be a lovely woman and had a number of lovers, but never married. She fell in love with a young sailor stationed at Pearl Harbor in 1940, but she drowned with him in a boating accident. The son grew up to be a fine but reclusive personality who rarely left the estate in San Francisco where I'd brought him as a toddler on that rainy day back in 1924. He died of complications from colon cancer but lived until 1984. The girl was always eager for stories about her parents. I had shown them a set of pictures from my own family. I presented faded photographs of Maria Jane and my own father, pretending to the children that those were their dead parents. The little girl always kept a picture of Maria Jane in her bedroom. The boy seemed less concerned where he had come from. He was much more interested in devoting his life to poetry. Like his sister, he never married. During the decades that I knew him, I never saw him take a romantic interest in anyone, male or female, although he grew up to be a rather handsome man.

He didn't resemble one of W.R.'s sons, and he certainly didn't look like Charlie or Tom Ince. I often wondered if his father was one of those grips from the studio that Marion occasionally fucked between affairs with more prominent men. Over the years I encouraged him to go out more during my visits to San Francisco, but he had no interest in meeting people, whereas his sister could not tolerate to be alone for a moment. In spite of W.R.'s instructions, I did become a father to the children. They were, in fact, the only kids I would ever have. I am so very sorry I outlived them, because I miss them so very much.

"You're crying, you old fool," the Bitch of Buchenwald shouted at me. "If there's one thing I can't stand, it's to see an ancient crone crying."

I only glared at her, wishing I had the strength to pick up something and bash her head in. My strength, it seems, is leaving my body, and I don't know how much longer I can go on dictating. The rest of my life will never be told, because I fear I won't live long enough to record it. I will just relate the final events that happened to some people dear to me, the silent screen stars, some of whom would no longer be shining in the heavens.

W.R. did not want me to remain in San Francisco after I'd installed the twins. Once they were safely settled in, their every need provided for, I returned to Los Angeles incognito. The Chief did not want me to see anyone connected with the press and suggested that I take the train at once to New York where I should remain in the Fifth Avenue apartment for a season, before returning to Los Angeles. He felt that in a few months a new scandal other than the mysterious death of Tom Ince would emerge, and all of us would be free to go on with our lives.

I was eager to return to New York because Rodolfo was there shooting *A Sainted Devil* in Astoria, Queens. But before fleeing Hollywood, I had one final date. It was with that growing boy, Douglas Fairbanks Jr.

*****

Surely there was no boy in Hollywood who'd blossomed into young manhood faster than Douglas Fairbanks, *fils*. When he was set to appear with Louise Brooks as "Neptune's Son" in *The American Venus*, he was only fifteen, although newspaper accounts of the day listed his age as eighteen. He did look much older, and his body had filled out, giving him a trim swimmer's build and devastating good looks. He was, in fact, far better looking than his old man, and Rod St. Just who had photographed both men definitely agreed.

Young Doug had been mortified when Elinor Glyn, the screenwriter who was among the passengers aboard the ill-fated cruise of the *Oneida* when Ince was shot, declared that young Doug did not have "It," in the sense that such he-vamps as Antonio Moreno did. Doug told me that Glyn had cornered him at a party at Pickfair and pronounced that she could not bestow "IT-ness" upon him because his ears stuck out too much. That didn't seem to hurt a future actor, Clark Gable.

So crushed was he by Glyn that Doug got his mother to strap back his ears at night. He took to trying to glue them back. But nothing worked. I finally convinced him that his ears were sexy, and that he definitely had "IT." Young Doug grew into manhood so fast that in only three years, at the age of eighteen, he was hired by Louis B. Mayer to play in a supporting role opposite Greta Garbo in *A Woman of Affairs*. That was its movie title. Michael Arlen's *The Green Hat* had been both a bestseller and a hit on Broadway when it was adapted for the stage.

John Gilbert was the leading man in this one. Doug was cast as the wastrel younger brother of Garbo. His character, or so the script said, was "besotted with debauchery." Hays had already banned *The Green Hat* as too "immoral" to be presented on the screen. Some cleaning up of the plot was necessary. Instead of committing suicide on his wedding night when he discovers he has syphilis, Doug was exposed as an embezzler instead.

During the filming of *A Woman of Affairs*, young Doug actually tried to seduce Garbo, who was also young. He failed. Garbo told him that, "My heart belongs only to me, and you might tell John Gilbert that too." John was having an affair with her at the time.

In 1936 Garbo told me—not for print—that she wished she had had an affair with Doug. "It was his love of me that led him into that disastrous marriage to Joan Crawford. His whole attitude toward women would have been different if I had seduced him during his formative years. Now he is doomed to wander the world a lost soul."

Even when still only fifteen, Doug looked much older. By that time he officially decided to launch the heterosexual phase of his life, as he had always threatened to do.

He was still a timid boy but had developed a crush on the New Jersey-born teenager, Betty Bronson, who had become a national sensation in late 1924 as *Peter Pan*, the first adaptation of that classic. Doug's pursuit of Betty was obviously tied in with his competition with his father. Adolph Zukor was touting Betty as "the new Mary Pickford," and it did look for a time as if the actress might become America's new sweetheart. Mary was long past the flush of youth, and many young actresses were eager to claim her crown.

Regrettably, Betty was to occupy Mary's throne for only a year. The jazz age was hot for the likes of those dancing daughters, Clara Bow and Joan Crawford, and had grown bored with Cinderella fairy tales and the whimsical roles in which Betty specialized. Paramount tried to make Betty a flapper and then a cowgirl, but nothing worked like Peter Pan. Surprisingly she was cast as the sensitive Madonna in *Ben-Hur*, but her career never took off after *Peter Pan*. She made a few talkies before retiring from the screen in 1932.

Doug was convinced that Betty was in love with him, but this pixie-like creature seemed merely to be flirting with him. He later confided in me that the extent of their romance was a kiss on the cheek from her.

Doug was going through several abortive attempts to relate to the opposite sex. Every week he seemingly developed a crush on some girl, although none as enduring as his being smitten with Betty Bronson. Far from being the raconteur and bon vivant of his later years when he was called "an American Prince of Wales," Doug was still awkward, traveling that rocky road between being a boy and a young man.

He had recently been traumatized when he'd played a key role in a lackluster film, called *The Air Mail*, starring Billie Dove and Warner Baxter. Doug developed a crush on Billie Dove. He didn't make it with Billie, but at least got to give her rough-hewn but very handsome husband, Irvin Willat, a blow-job.

To prove he was a man, Doug volunteered to do his own parachuting from an airplane at a film location outside the little desert town of Reno, Nevada. It was to be viewed as his baptism into manhood. Although determined to jump himself instead of using a stunt man, Doug chickened out at the last moment, which found him in tears on the wing of the plane. Bursting into panic, he had crawled back to his seat on the plane and the scene had to be re-shot with a stunt man. Doug felt humiliated in front of the film crew, and no doubt he felt dou-bly embarrassed because his father was known for his daredevil stunts. The director hadn't helped when he'd run up to Doug after the plane landed and told him, "You'll never replace your father. You're a cocksucker."

Sensing his insecurity and feeling he should be broken into love-making by "a real woman," I as Durango had arranged a date for young Doug with my "sister," Lotte Lee. He was thrilled at the offer, and had once told me that he suspected that his father and Lotte had had an affair a few years back. To be able to date one of his father's hot girl friends was a double pleasure and triumph for the young actor.

I had arranged for Doug to pick me up at my suite at the Hollywood Hotel, a cluster of rooms with which he was familiar having vis-ited them often to perform fellatio upon Durango himself.

Tonight was a new challenge for Doug. I had more or less suggested that Lotte had found pictures of him devastatingly handsome and that she was eager to "see you in the flesh." Up to that point, and unlike the tennis player Bill Tilden, I had never taken off the trousers of young Doug, although I'd dropped drawers for him a lot for those increasingly skilled blow-jobs.

Mary Pickford and Doug Fairbanks Sr. were somewhere over the ocean, planning a return to Los Angeles that would not be in time for one of the greatest premieres in Hollywood, the first public screening of *The Thief of Baghdad*, Doug Sr.'s latest and biggest pic-ture to date. When young Doug arrived to pick me up, I was dressed as Lotte Lee. I thought he looked older and more handsome than I'd ever seen him. He seemed enchanted by me as Lotte, and in my view I had never looked lovelier, to borrow that line that Louella Par-sons always wrote about Marion Davies even when she was growing jowls.

Grauman's Hollywood Theater had been transformed into a veritable Arabian Nights palace, filled with incense, Oriental perfumes, magnificent tapestries, rich colors, dancing girls, and throbbing Middle Eastern music.

All of the big names in Hollywood arrived, even Nazimova, pretending she was still a big star. She emerged with a new bob haircut seen above a frock of gold and coral. All in cream chiffon with orchids, the homophobic Florence Vidor arrived, as did Mr. and Mrs. Thomas Meighan, along with Mr. and Mrs. Harold Lloyd and even the Talmadge sisters, Constance and Norma. I'd heard that Mabel Normand was in the crowd but I didn't actu-ally see her. I did encounter some of my former lovers or tricks, each with his wife. That in-cluded Charles Ray (no longer thinking of Bobby Harron), Norman Kerry (who'd been dumped by Valentino), and Reginald Denny (whom Joe Godsol had once hired as a hustler for me).

The two Maes were there, Mae Busch in black and silver, and Mae Murray in some shimmering white and silver thing with a coat of delicate canary yellow. I had heard that Jack Pickford was there with his new love, Marilyn Miller, but I didn't see them in the crowd. As far as I was concerned, young Doug and I were the center of the evening. Lotte Lee was still a mysterious figure in Hollywood. Everybody had heard about her but no one had seen her on the screen. Instead of Doug Sr., the press got Doug Jr., and he seemed to relish the lime-light. I looked for Charlie Chaplin but he had staged another one of those mysterious disap-pearances.

To my discomfort, I was seated next to Mrs. Douglas MacLean, with her husband in the far seat. Mrs. MacLean looked at me a bit suspi-ciously but was exceedingly gracious. Caus-ing my distress was the fact that Mrs. MacLean had been the sole eyewitness who had seen me disguised as Lotte Lee, also incognito, leave the bungalow of William Desmond Taylor after he was shot. Through the showing of *The Thief of Baghdad*, I wondered if Mrs. MacLean might have recognized me and thought that I had killed Billy Taylor. She said nothing but looked at me several times as the film unreeled. When I turned to catch her doing that, she gave me a faint smile.

After endless photo shoots, including one from my dear friend, Rod St. Just, plus endless "congratulations to your father," Doug was ready to return to a supper at the Hollywood Hotel with me.

Over champagne (illegal at the time) he told me of his fear about his next film, *The American Venus*, starring Louise Brooks. The pageant sequences would be shot on the Boardwalk in Atlantic City. The actual star of the film was to be Esther Ralston, who was also appearing that year in *The Lucky Devil*, a popular auto-racing romance in the Wally Reid tradition. Esther, or so I heard, was moving in on my sometimes beau, Richard Dix, so I had no love for this perky little blonde. Esther and I would clash two years later when we were both making a play for the swimming star, Johnny Weissmuller, when she appeared with him in *Figures Don't Lie*. Johnny at the time was years from playing the Tarzan roles that would make him an international star.

Ironically Esther had played Wendy's mother in *Peter Pan*, starring Betty Bronson, upon whom Doug Jr. had developed that powerful crush. Esther had also appeared as the good fairy in *A Kiss for Cinderella*, also starring Betty Bronson.

The press had already determined that Louise Brooks and Esther Ralston were heading for a catfight on the film even before shooting began. Their manufactured feud was a road-show version of the jealousy between Pola Negri and Gloria Swanson. Esther already contemptuously referred to Louise as "Brooksie." Louise didn't help matters by confiding to the press that, "I'd like to put glue in Esther Ralston's hairbrush."

Word had reached young Doug that Louise had announced that she planned to seduce him before the completion of the film.

The picture—now turned to dust—became famous in America because of Louise's bathing beauty photograph, showing her in full Ziegfeld regalia. She wore a feather pompom headdress and a calf-length gown that was both backless and almost topless, except for some braided straps that had managed to cover her breasts.

Those who remember that film today, if there is anybody left in the world but me who does, recall its vivid and rather garish Technicolor scenes of the pageant at Atlantic City. Yes, Virginia, there was some Technicolor back in those so-called all black and white screen days. Louise was later to sue theatrical photographer John De Mirjian for distributing nude photographs of her snapped during the shoot of *The American Venus*.

"When I meet Louise, I don't want to be inexperienced," Doug said. "I hear she's a woman of the world." Doug told me that he was supposed to get some experience that weekend but he was so nervous at seducing his first woman that he wasn't sure he could pull it off.

In the absence of his father and stepmother, Doug was allowed to use some beach property near Laguna, opening onto a quarter mile crescent of sand lying at the foot of a small rock-strewn bluff. Nearly a dozen spacious tents, each fairly luxurious, had been erected on the site, and Doug and Mary entertained the world's elite here. I had gone there with Charlie so I was familiar with the place.

Doug had invited several of his friends down for the weekend, none of whom had much money. Freddy Anderson in particular liked to drink. When he couldn't find any bootleg booze, he drank hair tonic, sterno liquid, shaving lotion, and even shoe polish. It was a wonder he didn't die. He was bringing a girl down named Polly, who was going to spend one night with each of six boys, including Doug.

"All the other boys have told me they've screwed girls," Doug said. "I've never been with a woman before. The only blow-jobs I've ever got in my life were from Bill Tilden. Never from a woman."

I reached under the table and took his hand, squeezing it gently. "Tonight your luck is going to change. Polly is not the way for you to break in with a woman. For that purpose, you have Lotte Lee."

"You mean it?" he asked, his eyes lighting up. "You're not just flirting with me like most women."

"I mean it," I said. "I want it as much as you do." Not quite sure how I was going to pull off this deception, I headed up the stairs to my suite with Doug.

"Your brother won't be here?" he said, a

look of panic on his face.

"Durango will be here only in spirit," I said. "But he sends his fondest regards."

"Good," Doug said. "I wouldn't want him coming in in the middle of the action."

I was no longer able to resist the manly charms of young Doug. Even before my door was half shut, I patted his ass under the tails of his dinner jacket, finding the cheeks firm and globular. Up to now I hadn't touched any of his nether regions.

Locking the door behind us, I filled his mouth with my ravenous tongue. At first he was taken by surprise until I realized that he'd probably never had a tongue in his mouth before. Between our writhing bodies, my urgent fingers searched for his cock, which seemed aching to be released. Unbuttoning his trousers, I reached in and freed his dick at last. It rose to an impressive seven, almost eight inches, and fortunately stood straight and firm, not having his father's unfortunate curvature.

"You're one big boy," I whispered into his sexy ear, not caring whether it stood out or not. "Much bigger than your father's prick." Nothing I said could have inspired Doug more than a favorable comparison with his famous father. I was making it rather obvious to young Doug that I had been seduced by Doug Sr.

He curled one leg around me, nearly toppling me over, and his lips mashed into mine. It was Doug who inserted his tongue into my mouth for the sucking of its life. In my hands I rubbed his turgid cock to keep him hot and gyrating. I reached inside to fondle his ample balls. He broke from me only to remove his dinner jacket, letting it fall on the floor. I reached to feel his chest, pinching his tits through the thin cotton.

"Take off your clothes," he commanded. "I want to see everything. My first woman."

I backed away slightly. Things were getting out of hand. "We'll have to do it my way," I said. "I'm having my period. Some other time for that. Right now I want to suck you for dear life."

He looked disappointed but seemed only too willing to accept what I was offering. I backed him against my bed. When he sat down, he raised up slightly as I pulled down his trousers and underwear in one sweeping move. I gently unlaced his shoes and took off his socks, giving his feet a tongue lashing before heading north along what my lips and tongue found were the tastiest legs in Hollywood, equaled only by Johnny Weismuller's (but that's another book).

Avoiding the genitals, I used my tongue to trace patterns across his golden, sculpted chest, settling onto his nipples which were tiny but delectable. I sucked each one into my mouth, watching him squirm. There was great pleasure in my seduction of him, knowing that I was doing some things to him no one ever had before. He wouldn't be getting his first blow-job from me, but I was acquainting him with erogenous zones of his body he didn't know existed.

It must have been an hour I worked over young Doug until he was squirming and yelping in the pleasure of pain. His skin was alive to my touch, a golden boy shimmering in the dim lamplight of my suite.

I sucked each ball into my mouth one at a time. They were too large to fit in one gulp. When I'd had enough of that taste and flavor, I worked my hands to his ass. It was hard yet smooth. I pried the cheeks apart and slid my tongue into the tender crack, making small, succulent circles. He screamed in joy and dug his fingers into my shoulders, as if commanding me never to leave the spot. His whole body was writhing now, and I knew I would miss the big eruption if I didn't move quickly to swallow all of his cock in one gulp.

The moment my nose was buried in his golden pubic hairs, he erupted, the tasty load hitting against my tonsils before I withdrew slightly to better taste and savor the aroma of him. He was luscious and tender, and when I looked into his face he told me I'd been absolutely fantastic with him. I kept his cock in my mouth until it grew limp but not that limp.

"In a minute or two," he promised, breathless from exhaustion, "I want to go again. That was a mere appetizer."

It was about four o'clock in the morning before he fell into a satisfied sleep. But when he woke up at ten o'clock, Durango Jones himself was in bed, about to enter that delectable butt that I'd enjoyed with lips and tongue all night.

At first, he seemed startled and was about to ask where Lotte went, but his questions died in his throat, which let out a yell as I entered him. For the first minute or so, he begged me to pull out before changing his tune and ordering me to pump harder.

When I'd finished, Doug Jr. wanted me to return the favor. He said--and I believed him--that he'd never fucked anyone before.

I was delighted to be the first, getting to enjoy those impressive inches long before Joan Crawford and Marlene Dietrich got to sample them.

As enticing as young Doug was, I had a train to catch the next morning going via Chicago en route to New York. One Rudolph Valentino, America's most widely publicized man of the hour, was on the East Coast, and I was headed there to stake my claim.

Chapter Eighteen

Back in New York at W.R.'s Fifth Avenue apartment, I enjoyed being away from the West Coast and the lurid speculation about the death of Tom Ince. Each day some new revelation—most often wrong—appeared in the press. If you believed what reporters wrote, you would have been convinced that half of Hollywood was aboard the ill-fated *Oneida*—that is, all but Charlie Chaplin. He issued vehement denials about having been a passenger.

After having installed themselves at Whitley Heights in Hollywood, the Valentinos were back in New York at the same studios in Astoria, Queens—this time to make Rodolfo's last film, for Famous Players-Lasky before his contract expired. Now believed to be lost, *A Sainted Devil* was based on Rex Beach's *Rope's End*, published in *Cosmopolitan* in May of 1913. Nita Naldi, Rodolfo's co-star in *Blood and Sand*, was slated once again to become his leading lady.

All casting on the film had to be approved by Natacha. Jetta Goudal, the French actress under contract to Paramount, was originally cast as the vamp, Doña Florencia. Without actually saying so, Madame Goudal made her romantic "personal interest" in Valentino rather clear in front of New York reporters. She raised her eyebrows, with a smirk on her face. "I have come to America to investigate that sexual menace to the world, one Rudolph Valentino."

Why she issued such provocative statements is known only to Madame Goudal who rests in her grave. Surely she must have realized how such remarks would obviously raise the ire of Natacha Rambova, who at the time had virtual control over *A Sainted Devil*.

Events ran a predictable course. After only two days of reporting for work in Astoria, and without ever having appeared in front of the camera, Goudal was fired. She announced to the press, "I'm a victim of one woman's insane jealousy. If she can't hold onto her man and keep him in check, why should I be faulted? If Mr. Valentino finds me more alluring than his own wife, I should not be responsible for that."

Privately Goudal told me that it wasn't Rodolfo who was attracted to her, but Natacha herself. "At first I went along with her," Goudal said. "We French are understanding about sexual deviations in both women and men. But Rambova became aggressive and demanded sex from me. I refused and she reacted bitterly."

To cast and crew, it was obvious on the second day that an explosion was about to erupt between Natacha and Goudal. Even if Natacha could tolerate Goudal's sexual advances toward Rodolfo, and even if she could survive sexual rejection, she could not put up with an attack on her talents as a designer. The temperamental Goudal, in front of at least a dozen people, exploded when presented with Natacha's sketches for her vamp costumes. "These are hideous," she screeched at Natacha. "I could not possibly be seen on the screen in such atrocities. I have a reputation to protect. You have no sense of design. You are a no-talented mess from somewhere out on the Prairie. A cowgirl. A rustic. Could you imagine what a

Parisian would say of your designs? Your only talent is in marrying a lovesick fool who just happens to be one of the most famous men in the world. You don't even sleep with him. You're a lesbian. You can design clothing for men who are not real men, but you cannot design for women."

That afternoon a communiqué arrived from Famous Players that Miss Goudal "by mutual consent" had withdrawn from the role. She was replaced by Natacha's longtime friend, Dagmar Godowsky. Dagmar not only approved of Natacha's sketches, but was not one to turn down a roll in the hay with "Madam Valentino" herself.

Natacha insisted that Dagmar hold a press conference the next day, in which the actress raved about the designs of Natacha. She hoped this would balance the bad publicity Goudal had generated for her.

Joseph Henaberry was assigned as director and wisely gave in to Natacha's demands. Privately he told me that he couldn't wait for the picture to end. "I can't stand either Valentino—the one who wears the pants, Miss Natacha, or her doting slave boy, Mr. Valentino, a total fool."

Rodolfo was growing more imperious all the time. He greeted me warmly when I arrived on the set but he also wanted me to see that he'd become a star who was catered to. With a snap of Rodolfo's fingers, his valet pulled out a cigarette and lit it for him. Taking it, Rodolfo smoked only a few drags on it before dropping it to the floor. The valet crushed it out with his heel.

Natacha had dressed Rodolfo in an Argentine styled bolero, red knickerbockers, and pink silk stockings. He held up his leg for my inspection. "Natacha thinks I have great legs," he said. "She wants to showcase my legs in this film."

"You do have great legs," I assured him. "Great everything if I remember correctly."

He smiled seductively at me. "It's about time we refreshed that memory."

Rodolfo was summoned to the set where he was playing a suffering Spanish don whose wife is abducted by bandits. He told me that he was delighted to be playing a drunkard. He had demanded that the director, Henaberry,

order more such scenes for him. "I'm at my best," Rodolfo said, "when playing scenes of hopeless despair and inner turmoil where my emotions boil like a kettle. If I think of Natacha and how she makes me suffer, I can play almost any scene, providing the emotion is painful." When the film was released, *Photoplay* didn't agree with his own assessment. The film critic for the magazine wrote, "Valentino was not real in his stressed emotional moments."

A few weeks later, Rodolfo placed a stunning call to Jesse Lasky in Hollywood, demanding that the entire film be reshot. "I can play the role more virile," he said. "Henaberry has directed me like a woman. My fans expect to see a he-man on the screen, not some overdressed effeminate actor. I have been sabotaged."

Eager to get him off the phone, Lasky told Rodolfo he was pleased with the first version. There would be no reshoot. Rodolfo's contract was over. Privately at a dinner party at W.R.'s San Simeon, Lasky told the Chief that he'd gotten rid of the Valentinos, calling them "a double hernia."

Lasky immediately began to groom Jacob Krantz as Valentino's replacement. Krantz looked like a Latin lover, even though born as a Jew in Vienna. Lasky immediately came up with a new name for Krantz. From now on, he'd be billed as Ricardo Cortez.

Of all the Valentino impersonators, Cortez looked the most like Rodolfo. And he could dance! He would go on to become the leading man of Greta Garbo, Gloria Swanson, Florence Vidor, Bebe Daniels, and even the young Joan Crawford, who would also seduce him. Barbara Stanwyck, Kay Francis, Claudette Colbert, Bette Davis, and Irene Dunne were also his leading ladies. His big mistake? He married the hopelessly addicted actress, Alma Rubens, who died in 1931 at the age of thirty-four after a heroin overdose.

In theory, if Rodolfo had lived and stayed with Paramount, the roles played by Cortez opposite those legends of the screen would have gone to Rodolfo. I used to dream of Rodolfo having lived long enough to make a movie with Greta Garbo. Rodolfo cast opposite Bette Davis, however, would be much harder to conjure up.

When I became a gossip columnist in the Thirties, I was often asked, "Could Valentino have survived the Talkies?" I answered that he could have, minus his long-lashed myopic eyes and his outrageous attire. "What roles could he have played?" was another frequently asked question. "Perhaps the other man in a screwball comedy with Carole Lombard," I once wrote.

The question of, "What if Valentino had lived," even piqued interest in the President of the United States.

In 1934, I met Franklin and Eleanor Roosevelt through W.R., who had been invited to the White House, although neither man was a great admirer of the other. At one point Mr. Roosevelt asked the Valentino question. I answered, "I think he might have become the leading gangster in films, going back to his early days in silents. Not exactly Edward G. Robinson but an actor more like George Raft. Raft is nothing but a clone of Valentino. Valentino might even have starred in musicals. Did you know that he could sing? He had a strong baritone voice, a really pleasant tone. It would have recorded beautifully. In very different roles he would have been the biggest star of the Thirties."

"I'm not so sure," Mr. Roosevelt said. "If I were Louis B. Mayer, I would have cast him as a gigolo. Always a gigolo. I once asked Eleanor if she were attracted to all this sheik mess. Eleanor told me that she found Jean Arthur far more masculine and attractive an image than the Great Lover himself. So much for a woman's point of view."

After the filming of *A Sainted Devil* and the termination of Rodolfo's contract without a renewal from Famous Players, a sadness came over the Valentinos, who faced an uncertain future. Natacha made plans to head back to Hollywood. Rodolfo wanted to accompany her, but he had committed himself to two days of interviews and publicity appearance for Famous Players. He asked me to stay with him in New York. "After that, I want you to take a few days off, and go with me into the wilderness. It's way out West," he said. "A little island in a Nevada lake. A secret place. I've made all the arrangements. No one will find us there. We will run away from the world and cheat time."

There was a faraway look in his eyes. Almost intuitively I sensed that his once great career might be nearing an end. The press seemed against him, and he continued to listen to Natacha's advice, which I felt would eventually ruin him in Hollywood. He'd seriously alienated two of Hollywood's major studios—both Metro and Paramount—and his behavior on the set was growing more erratic daily.

To me, the Valentino marriage was also beginning to unravel. I felt there was madness boiling in both of them.

When I put Natacha in a taxi and took her to New York's Grand Central Station, I had no idea that this was one of the last times I'd ever see her again. I had always disliked her, and even despised the way she interfered in Rodolfo's career, but I managed to conceal my resentment and jealousy of her in order to stay in the company of Rodolfo. I pretended to be her friend and ally, but I really wasn't.

On the way to the train station, Natacha claimed she had virtually created Valentino herself. "It would have been much better if I had devoted my energies and talents to my own career rather than wasting away fighting the studios to advance his. I have presented Valentino to the world as a man to rip bodices. But the intelligent viewer got my other message. What I was actually portraying was a cutting-edge bisexual figure. I believe that bisexuality is the way the future will go. I wanted Rodolfo to be the first actor to forge ground across this new sexual frontier. In his bold partial nudity on screen, I have liberated the American male. Before I came along, directors felt the public wanted to see only women undressed. I have shown that there is an even bigger market when the male is undressed before the camera."

What Natacha said may have been true, although I noted in the next few months that one reviewer wrote that, "Valentino looks more like Nita Naldi in *A Sainted Devil* than Miss Naldi looks like herself."

For all practical purposes Natacha Rambova was fading from my life when I stood at Grand Central watching her depart on the train for Hollywood.

To piss off the Bitch of Buchenwald, who

always objects to my jumping ahead of my story, I will relate what happened between Natacha and me in the decades ahead. After the Valentino years, Natacha virtually faded from the radar screen. Most people, who remember her at all, haven't a clue as to what became of her.

Six years after the death of Rodolfo, a surprise invitation came for me in 1932 when I received a note from Natacha inviting me to the Balearic Island of Majorca off the eastern coast of Spain. Natacha claimed that she was taking over old villas and restoring them to their original condition, before renting them to tourists. She invited me to come for a visit and rent one from her. At the time I was madly in love with the young and handsome Johnny Weismuller, America's future Tarzan, and I needed a retreat for my "honeymoon" with him.

Once we arrived on the island, I was stunned when Natacha introduced herself as the Condesa de Urzáiz. She also presented her Spanish husband, a strikingly handsome Basque nobleman named Don Alvaro de Urzáiz. Slim, black-haired, and with hauntingly beautiful black eyes, he bore a slight resemblance to Rodolfo.

Descended from a noble Basque family and educated in England, he seemed miserable in his role—assigned by Natacha—as a tour guide. But Johnny and I decided to make it fun for him.

I found out later that with the fall of the Spanish monarchy, his dream of becoming a naval officer was at an end.

Johnny liked to retire early so he'd be fresh for his morning swims, and Natacha needed her beauty sleep, so I ended up night after night with Alvaro, talking sometimes until the dawn. I discovered that he was actually fucking his wife, something Rodolfo never accomplished. Unlike her days with Rodolfo, when she seemed more interested in women, Natacha had reverted back, at least temporarily, to her heterosexual life, as she had been in her days with Theodore Kosloff.

As the nights wore on in this mountaintop villa overlooking the Mediterranean, Alvaro looked sexier and sexier to me. Johnny was a daytime fucker. That left the nights free. One drunken night Alvaro confided to me that even

though he'd married a brunette, he actually preferred blondes. "I'm a blond," I reminded him.

"You're pretty as a girl," he said. "Fuck that. You're prettier than most women."

"I've also had a lot of experience satisfying hot-blooded Spaniards," I told him, remembering Antonio Moreno. Alvaro did not resist when I unbuttoned his trousers and reached in. Within three minutes, seven and a half ruddy inches emerged through his fly. In a back cottage about seventy yards from the main villa, I enjoyed Natacha's second husband—not as much as her first husband, but Alvaro ranked right up there among my top lovers. The man knew how to fuck.

He performed so admirably that I developed a passion for Basque men from that night forth. Sometimes I succeeded with future Basque conquests; at other times I came up short. My most miserable failure was when I pursued a gorgeous Basque lawyer, Jacques Bergerac, but I lost him to Ginger Rogers, sixteen years his senior when she married him on February 7, 1953. She tried to turn him into an actor, and failed at that, and I tried to turn him into a homosexual lover and I failed at that. Bergerac gave me a light kiss on the lips but informed me that, "I'm not one of the children of Oscar Wilde."

Not forgetting Johnny in the morning, I also looked forward to Alvaro in the wee hours. Before leaving Majorca, I was so smitten of him that I shelled out $5,000 to help him buy a boat to take tourists out on day sails. He agreed to pay me back but I knew he never would.

On our final night on the island, Natacha and Alvaro invited us to meet a new friend of theirs, the island's chief military officer, General Franco, who was relatively unknown at the time. Both Natacha and Alvaro were great supporters of Franco who paid almost no attention to Johnny and me during and after dinner, but spoke of his dream of returning Spain to its past glory, when it had an empire that rivaled Britain's.

Natacha became rhapsodic about the glories of the age of Ferdinand and Isabella, although Jews living in Spain at the time might have told another story. Before leaving, Franco predicted that in time he would reclaim Spain's "mystique, power, and glorious heritage." Having no interest in Spain's former glory, Johnny had fallen asleep, having drunk too much Spanish wine.

I made one more visit to Majorca to see Alvaro and Natacha. Alvaro and I resumed our fucking, an endeavor I enjoyed immensely. But I suspected that some of Alvaro's passion stemmed from his wanting me to pay the down payment on another new boat for him.

One day when Natacha had gone into the mountains, Alvaro agreed to model for some nude photographs out on the terrace, some of them with a full erection. That meant I would have nudes of both of Natacha's husbands. A series of photographs of both Rodolfo and Alvaro are part of my estate. I felt somebody had to record how they looked in the nude for future generations to enjoy.

Back in Hollywood, a few months later, I heard that Natacha was forced to flee Majorca which had erupted into a battleground for the Spanish Civil War. Alvaro stayed behind to fight with Franco's forces.

Smuggled out of Majorca by Franco, Natacha was placed on a coal freighter to Nice accompanied only by her white Pekingese dog, Bimbo. A soot-blackened Natacha arrived at her parents' Riviera villa with a "black dog," the once all-white Pekingese.

On military leave, Alvaro made only two visits to see Natacha on the Riviera. And then she never heard from him again. He had fallen for another woman in Spain.

Natacha announced to the press that no professional woman should bind herself into marriage with anyone, but should remain a free spirit. Planning to return to New York when conditions allowed, she suffered a heart attack, which marked the beginning of her physical and mental deterioration.

Back in New York she got her marriage annulled and launched a series of spiritual lectures called "The Real." In time she rejoined forces with her sometimes lover, Mercedes de Acosta, and they worked on a play together based on the Virgin Mary. Called "The Leader," it momentarily interested Lillian Gish but was never produced.

Except for a casual meeting once or twice, I never saw Natacha again until I learned she was near death in 1965 at the Lenox Hill Hospital in New York.

Because of our shared memory of Rodolfo, I went to visit her. The woman in that hospital bed bore no resemblance to the Natacha Rambova I had known. Her weight had dropped to sixty-five pounds on her sixty-eight-year old frame. Her skin hung in wrinkled loose folds around her skeleton. She looked like an ancient crone. At first she'd forgotten who I was until I reminded her.

"The nurses are trying to poison me," she claimed. "I'm unable to swallow anything." I tried to get her to eat something, but she refused. "What's the point? They'll kill me anyway?" She was being forced into shock treatments by three psychiatrists who were treating her. From one of them I learned that Natacha's condition was called "paranoid psychosis."

As she focused more and more on exactly who I was, her memory seemed to return. "You're trying to take Rudy from me," she said in a voice that sounded as if choking. "I'll fight you for him until the end. He's my husband. I won't let you have him."

"Valentino is but a shared memory for both of us," I said. "He died forty-one years ago."

"You're a liar!" she shouted at me, using what seemed to be the last of her energy before falling into a coughing spasm. I summoned a nurse.

"Get out of my room," Natacha shouted at me through her cracked voice and parched lips. "I hate you. I always did. I'll kill Rudy before I'll allow you to have him."

Those were her last words to me. I shut the hospital door, closing behind me a dream world of paranoid delusions. The hospital listed malnutrition as the cause of her illness, but insanity would be more accurate.

I never saw her again but heard she'd returned to California to die. Her ashes were scattered across a forest in northern Arizona which Natacha believed possessed "cosmic mystery."

An assistant to Louella Parsons called for my reaction to Natacha's death. I said, "It was an unhappy life. She was frustrated in both love and her career. Her talents were limitless but unfocused. She wandered in many directions, always looking for a home for her special talents but never finding one."

My memory of Natacha was rudely interrupted by the screeching voice of the Bitch of Buchenwald. "Get back to whatever you were doing to the Sheik in New York, you old fool." she shouted at me. "What happened when you returned to the hotel after putting that dyke, Rambova, on the train to Chicago without her husband?" Suppressing an instinct to strike her, I reverted back to the recitation of my memoirs:

I stood for a long moment watching Natacha's train leave, wondering what damage she'd do to Rodolfo's career when she arrived in Hollywood without him. Would she take up with Mercedes de Acosta again? Or had she found some other girl friend? Everything about Natacha was always a mystery to me.

Outside Grand Central Station, I hailed a taxi and headed back to Rodolfo, fearing I'd find him in some morbid state of mind, perhaps suicidal.

Back at his suite at the Ritz-Carlton, Rodolfo was indeed despondent. "My hopes for making her my wife have failed," he said in barely a whisper. "The marriage is over. What remains is for us to bury it. There is no more softness to her—no more femininity. She lives only for her own crazed ambitions. She talks film-making all day on the set with me and all night when we come back here. There is no home life. She finally admitted she detests even the spaghetti I like to cook at midnight for us." Rodolfo didn't seem to be aware of my presence in the room. It was as if he were having some inner monologue with himself.

"She has no concern for anything that doesn't directly affect Natacha Valentino," he said. "Even her interest in spiritualism is going. She wants to become a female Jesse Lasky and control our own studio. I no longer see her as the beautiful woman and great artist she once was. Greed and ambition have become like wrinkles across her face. She grows colder by the day."

"What did you truly expect from her?" I asked.

"A wife who would devote her entire life to my happiness, as many women in Italy do," he said. "As my mother did for my father. What I got was Natacha, who is like a man except for her body, which she does not share with me but gives freely to women. I no longer call her Babykins. That was my pet name for her but she said it was too childish and didn't fit her image. That was almost the final straw. The death of Babykins was the symbolic end of our marriage."

"Where are we going?" I asked him.

"To the wilds of Nevada," he said. "I'm going to become Black Feather and you will be my Indian brave. We will live as Black Feather lived. In that way I will find my reality again. Something I can never find in the make-believe world of Hollywood."

*****

After taking a train across most of the country, Rodolfo and I got off near a small western town that looked as if nothing had happened there since 1888.

It seemed like one of those Gold Rush towns where everybody had long ago moved on, except a few desert-hardened denizens. The place was practically deserted but a car had been arranged for us. The first night we spent in a small clapboard covered hotel that had never known a coat of paint.

In bed that night, Rodolfo told me that we'd have to drive for two days to reach the cabin where he'd made arrangements for us to stay. The cabin, he said, was owned by Wallace Beery who often retreated there with little girls. He had Charlie Chaplin's proclivities.

Rodolfo said we'd drive at night to avoid the intense heat blowing in from the nearby desert, where noon-day temperatures often registered 140° Fahrenheit. If we drove at all during daylight hours, our faces were pelted with blowing sand and hot, gusty winds.

Finally, in the early morning, we arrived at a vast blue lake where Wallace Beery's rowboat—solitary and alone—waited for us. Rodolfo and I loaded our provisions onto the boat and headed across the water, as the sun climbed higher and higher in the sky. Both of us were soaked with perspiration. Rodolfo was an expert rower, far better than me, and in forty-five minutes we arrived at the cabin.

It was only a shack with a simple three-quarter bed, but it was clean, well-organized, and neat. It had been built on a small island in the center of the lake. In the distance we could see majestic snow-capped mountains. Far removed from the glitz and glitter of Hollywood, this seemed like an idyllic retreat.

The next morning after breakfast, both of us lay nude on a rock, sunning ourselves and enjoying cool breezes blowing in from the lake. "We're going to turn as nut-brown as Doug Fairbanks if we keep this up," I said.

"Please, no mention of Hollywood," he said. "We came here to forget."

After our little sunbath, Rodolfo disappeared into the cabin and emerged dressed as Black Feather, Indian headdress and all. He wore only a loincloth and moccasins. He had brought just a loincloth and moccasins for me, too, but no headdress. "I'm the Chief," he said. "It is I who will wear the ceremonial headdress."

Before that day ended we explored every inch of the island. At one point he removed his headdress and loincloth and jumped in the water. He yelled for me to come and join him. Removing my own loincloth and moccasins, I jumped into the water too, finding it icy cold. He held out his arms to me and I swam toward him, as he enclosed me in his arms and kissed me, offering me his tongue to suck.

As I sucked on him, and planted tiny little kisses on his ears, neck, face, and eyes, I felt I'd fallen in love with him all over again. At that moment, I never wanted to see Hollywood again. I wanted the great Rudolph Valentino just for myself.

Rodolfo was like a young boy filled with the adventure and excitement of discovering the glories of nature. We fished for mountain trout and caught three. That would be our dinner. But before cooking the fish, we sat on a large boulder, watching the sun set in the west. Its dying glow cast a fiery red and gold over the wilderness.

The fish tasted better than any food I'd ever eaten, or at least I thought so at the time. But Rodolfo said he longed for spaghetti too. He put on a pot of water to boil on a wood-burning stove and made his famous tomato sauce from the provisions we had brought along with us.

The next morning he was jubilant, all his cares and woes seemingly behind him. "I am a creature of the winds and storms," he shouted. "I belong to the water, the rocks, the green trees." Like a young Nijinsky, he danced in the wind, leaping from rock to rock with the grace of a ballet dancer, his cock and balls dangling before him.

Fortunately I had taken a camera with me to record a nude Rodolfo for posterity. He especially liked posing with an erection since his cock grew incredibly large from a base that did not look that promising until it began to expand.

When we needed fresh milk and eggs, we rowed across the lake to a lumber camp. There the burly men mistook us for schoolboys on a camping holiday. None of the men in this remote part of the country attended movies, so no one recognized Rodolfo, even though his face was one of the most photographed in the world.

That night after dinner we sat on our same boulder and watched a full moon rise. The glow made the water of the lake shine like silver. In the far distance we could see the snow-capped peaks of the mountains which glistened like polished silver under the moonlight.

My sex with him on that particular night was the best we'd ever had or would ever have again. He was a far greater lover as Black Feather than as himself. I remember his taking me in the full moonlight streaming into our bedroom. He was leering down at me almost like a wolf ready for a tasty kill. I felt his heavy balls and thick cock, red and meaty, rubbing across my body as his mouth enclosed itself over mine.

His tongue went into my mouth, seemingly going deeper than it ever had before as he stretched out on top of me. He descended lower, planting tiny little kisses and nibbles over every part of my body. When he finally parted the cheeks of my ass and began to devour my rosebud, I knew what he had in mind for later.

I started eating out his armpit, enjoying the special taste of him. I buried my mouth into the sweaty pit to clean him. After moving from my ass, he bit into my nipples until I screamed in pain, but his kissing of my stomach was gentle. He grabbed my cock, licked it, and then plunged all the way down on it, slurping and sucking. After five minutes of that, he moved to his real target for the night.

He grabbed my legs and spread them apart for him. He spat in his hand and reached down. With a finger he rubbed spit up and down my ass, which had me squirming in pleasure. My breathing was growing difficult. "Slam into me hard," I shouted at him, and he obeyed.

His dickhead slowly entered my ass. Once the head was in, he plunged all at once into my guts, causing me to scream. He muffled my voice by covering my mouth with his, frenching me as he pumped madly. His strokes were long and easy at first, until he started biting into my neck, his teeth digging deeper.

When he'd first started doing this, it caused me great pain, and it still did. But it was also strangely erotic, and I began to enjoy his dominance over me. He liked the taste of my blood almost as much as he did my semen. He sucked greedily at my neck which was bruised in several places from his biting of my flesh the previous nights.

He seemed to be holding back his climax until he could drink more of my blood. I felt every bit of energy was being sucked out of me, and I was close to an explosion but he pleaded for me to hold back. When he plunged into me as deeply as he'd ever gone, I could hold back no more.

I screamed out my passion and love for him and erupted. He followed within just a few seconds, blasting away in me. He reared up but was soon back at my neck while still buried inside me. He must have lain there for at least another fifteen minutes, drinking the blood from my bleeding neck and encouraging the wound caused by his teeth marks to produce more for him.

It was the most satisfying night I'd ever spent with any man before or since.

We had to leave the next morning. I think it was the saddest day of my life. I feared we'd never return to such an idyllic setting.

On the train back to Los Angeles, Rodolfo said nothing. He instinctively knew he was heading for the West Coast and a brewing storm.

*****

By the time he arrived back in Hollywood in 1925, Rodolfo found that an independent producer, J.D. Williams, had taken over his contract with Jesse Lasky at Famous Players. The new company would be known as Ritz-Carlton Pictures, Inc. and Rodolfo and "Madam Valentino" were given the right to chose scripts and approve co-stars. Famous Players would still distribute Rodolfo's pictures. It looked like a sweet deal.

Under the *nom de plume* of Justice Layne, Natacha was preparing a script called *The Hooded Falcon*, set in Spain during the Moorish period. The projected cost of the spectacle was one-million dollars, which was a staggering sum at the time. *The Hooded Falcon* was essentially a retelling of El Cid's story, with Rodolfo starring as the hero, of course.

Upon Rodolfo's return, Natacha hardly seemed aware of him. She was totally engrossed with plans for the filming of *The Hooded Falcon.* "At last I will have achieved my dream on the screen," she said to me one day when I was calling Rodolfo and she picked up the phone. "The picture will be mine, my own creation."

Their new producer, J.D. Williams, seemed too good to be true, and eventually he was. For the moment, he authorized Rodolfo and Natacha to return to Europe, giving them a budget of $40,000 to shop for props to use in *The Hooded Falcon.*

"It will be a second honeymoon for me," Rodolfo told me at the train station where Natacha had already boarded.

"You haven't even had the first honeymoon yet," I said.

"Don't start acting like a jealous bitch," he said. "I'll still be there for you when I get back from Europe."

Once again the Valentinos crossed the country by train, boarding a ship in New York and eventually reaching Spain. Arriving there, Rodolfo sent word back to me that he'd decided to become a matador instead of an actor. Perhaps he was identifying too closely with his role as the bullfighter in *Blood and*

Sand. But within a week, he'd seemingly forgotten all about it.

In France Natacha and Rodolfo had run into Nita Naldi who'd co-starred with Rodolfo in *A Sainted Devil.* She joined them for the rest of their tour of Europe and also made arrangements to return with them to the United States aboard the *S. S. Leviathan.* I assumed that Rodolfo wasn't getting sex from Natacha, so I figured the screen vamp, Miss Naldi herself, was satisfying the Valentino libido.

After endless delays, when the Valentinos returned to the West Coast, they found themselves the toast of Hollywood. Once studio doors slammed in Rodolfo's face. Now getting him to attend a party was the dream of every hostess.

But there was trouble in paradise. June Mathis, who'd written the script for *The Four Horsemen of the Apocalypse,* had not finished revisions on Natacha's *The Hooded Falcon,* and there were also mounting production problems. Williams insisted that Rodolfo rush into a picture called *Cobra,* even though Natacha and Rodolfo found the script weak.

Rodolfo's co-star in *Cobra* was once again Nita Naldi. The director? Joseph Henaberry, who'd also directed and clashed with the Valentinos on *A Sainted Devil.* He must have really needed the money to take on such an assignment again.

"The picture will be trash," Natacha predicted, "unless I intervene to save it. But I don't like modern stories."

In *Cobra,* Rodolfo was cast as an impoverished Italian nobleman working for a New York antiques dealer. The only thing Rodolfo liked about the script was a scene calling for him to appear as a prizefighter. World champion Jack Dempsey was in Hollywood making a film, and he agreed to work out with Rodolfo, later telling the press that, "Valentino is no cream puff."

Since she couldn't move ahead with *The Hooded Falcon,* Natacha appeared on the set of *Cobra,* and almost overnight tried to become not only the director, but the set designer, the makeup artist, the costume designer, even the cameraman. She told minor members of the crew how to do their jobs. The press learned of this, and unflattering portraits of her emerged, one citing her "selfish domination" of the film. Another article claimed that her ambition was "insatiable." Natacha fired several crew members, blaming them for leaks to the press. The entire cast and crew of *Cobra* grew to despise her, although Rodolfo still seemed under her magic spell.

I visited the set frequently and talked with Rodolfo, although I rarely encountered Natacha and didn't want to, fearing she might also order me out of the studio.

Rodolfo and I had lunch several times with his co-star, Nita Naldi. Natacha was always "too busy" to join us. Miss Naldi and I never seemed to like each other. I had heard from Rodolfo that she said, "Men like Durango Jones are a bad influence on Hollywood. Pictures should be made by real men and star real men." This did not endear her to me.

The last time I ever saw this screen vamp was at a cast party on the set of *Cobra.* Natacha had sent word that she did not have time to waste on such foolishness. "You really must get a life for yourself," a drunken Naldi said, cornering me at the party. "Do something on your own. Quit hanging around Valentino like you're some lovesick puppy."

I thanked her for the advice and turned and walked away, never to see her again—not that I ever wanted to.

When the Talkies arrived, screen vamps like Nita Naldi went out of style. She found herself in the same position Theda Bara was in in 1920 when her more old-fashioned vamp character had gone out of style too. Her screen career over, Naldi married J. Searle Barclay, a multi-millionaire financier. Many screen stars found some wealthy man waiting for them when studios didn't want them any more.

I thought Naldi was fixed for life. But years later I was stunned to learn from a friend that Valentino's famous leading lady had died of a fatal heart attack in a seedy Times Square hotel. She was penniless and had been dead two days before her rotting body was discovered.

The Valentino honeymoon with the producer, Williams, came to an abrupt end. At one point Williams threatened to shut down production on *Cobra* if Natacha were not removed from the set. "If this picture is a bomb, there is only one person to blame—

Natacha Rambova," Williams shouted.

Even before Rodolfo saw the final cut of *Cobra*, and witnessed the lackluster reception it received among savvy Hollywood moguls, he too began to doubt the artistic abilities of Natacha for the first time in his life.

As filming on *Cobra* had progressed, their own relationship had grown colder. Rodolfo, I noticed, began to look at her more objectively. He told me he was going to try to divert her ambition from film-making to establishing a family with him.

When he told me that, I felt—but didn't say—"You have to fuck her first before producing *bambini*." But that seemed too obvious a remark.

"You think I'm fit only as a breeder," Natacha screeched at him. "What are you trying to turn me into? A God damn cow? You're nothing but a sleazy dago son-of-a-bitch. I hate you. I've always hated you. You don't really want children. You're seeking a son to become a mirror image of yourself."

In his way Rodolfo got even with Natacha for refusing to bear children with him. The next day he told a reporter for *The Los Angeles Examiner,* "A man may admire a woman without desiring her. He may respect the brilliance of her mind, the nobility of her character—yes, even the beauty of her face and body, yet she may not move him emotionally."

Upon reading that, Natacha burst into a violent rage and slapped Rodolfo's face. "Are you trying to tell the world I'm a lesbian?" she shouted at him.

With talk of a family hopelessly bogged down, Natacha relaunched her plans for *The Hooded Falcon.* She claimed her picture would make Rodolfo the greatest star of all time. It didn't help that she'd called its potential producer, "A vile beast—more greedy, more stupid, and more larcenous than Jesse Lasky and Adolph Zukor combined."

Like an imperial goddess, Natacha summoned Williams to Rodolfo's home at Whitley Heights. There she blamed him for the failure of *Cobra*. "Fairbanks triumphs in *The Thief of Baghdad*. You give my husband shit to film." Her attack on the producer grew so violent that he stormed out of the house,

although Rodolfo ran after him, pleading with him to come back and negotiate.

Within forty-eight hours, Williams called Rodolfo informing him that he would not film *The Hooded Falcon*. Natacha went into a deep, almost suicidal depression, then got into her car and disappeared somewhere for five days.

During that time, Rodolfo received a call from Joseph Schenck inviting him to join United Artists. Schenck had a property already set for Rodolfo. It was called *The Eagle* and based on the Alexander Pushkin novel, *Dubrovsky*. Rodolfo would play a Russian Robin Hood. The script had originally been a stage play that had co-starred Judith Anderson and Louis Calhern on Broadway.

Natacha had gone to Palm Springs to recover from the collapse of her project, *The Hooded Falcon*. Rodolfo called me at the Hollywood Hotel and asked me to go along with him in his Isotta Fraschini to United Artists, the home studio of Charlie Chaplin, D.W. Griffith, Mary Pickford, Douglas Fairbanks, and William S. Hart.

I'd never seen him so exuberant. "At last I've made it," he said. "At long last the King of Hollywood. Tomorrow belongs to me."

As I pulled his Isotta Fraschini into the studio gates, I felt his too-early pronouncement had a hollow ring.

*****

At the studio Rodolfo asked me to sit outside while he went in to meet with Schenck. The meeting lasted for two hours, and at times I heard angry shouts coming from Rodolfo but not Schenck. Finally, Rodolfo stormed from the mogul's office, demanding that I drive him back to Whitley Heights. "I'm too furious," he said. "I would smash up the car in my condition."

For the first fifteen minutes, he said nothing. "I signed the contract," he said, breaking the silence.

"You must not have liked the terms, I gather from all that shouting."

"Financially, I'm getting $10,000 a week,

the most money I've ever made," he said. "Clarence Brown will be the director of *The Eagle*, and he's one of the best in the business."

"Then what's the problem?" I asked.

"The contract is perfect in every way," he said. "But it contains a poison pill provision. Natacha is not to have anything to do with the production of the film—in fact, she's barred from the set."

"Natacha will explode when she hears that," I said.

"I fear my signing the contract will spell doom for our marriage," he said. "She'll call me Judas Iscariot."

"I'm glad you signed the contract," I said. "Let's face it. You're deeply in debt. You need the money."

"I know that," he said, impatient with me. "Schenck can blackmail me with money. I didn't tell you the good part. In addition to the $10,000 a week, I'll get forty-two percent of the net profits."

"That's fantastic." I almost shouted. "That puts you up in the Mary Pickford league."

"Wish me luck," he said, when he spotted Natacha's car in the driveway of his Whitley Heights home.

"Good luck," I said, waving good-bye as I drove back to the Hollywood Hotel for a hot date with William Boyd.

No one will ever know for sure what happened that late afternoon when Rodolfo confronted Natacha with the news of his new contract, which specifically excluded her. He never told me what happened, and Natacha never spoke of it. Apparently, though, it was one of the great husband-and-wife fights in the history of Hollywood.

In the days ahead, when I'd visit Rodolfo at Whitley Heights, Natacha was never there. When I'd ask about her whereabouts, Rodolfo would only say, "She's off driving in the Hollywood Hills."

To pacify her and in a vain attempt to salvage his mock marriage, Rodolfo agreed to put up $25,000 to finance a picture she wanted to make herself. Called *What Price Beauty?*, it satirized the cosmetics industry and the extent women will go to remain beautiful. The star would be Nita Naldi. With Natacha in charge, the film production budget snowballed into

$100,000 until Ullman, Rodolfo's business manager, was forced to put on the brakes.

In another attempt to save his marriage, Rodolfo borrowed money from Schenck to finance the construction of a princely new estate, Falcon Lair, an eighteen-room hacienda set on eight acres of rolling land. His neighbors would be Mary Pickford and Douglas Fairbanks, as well as Marion Davies, Harold Lloyd, and Thomas Meighan. Natacha wasn't impressed and vowed never to spend one night at Falcon Lair, which was later sold to the world's richest woman, Doris Duke.

After filming on *The Eagle* had begun, Natacha forbade mention of it in her presence. All she talked about was *What Price Glory?* "Years from now," she said, "movie historians will be talking about *What Price Glory?* long after *The Eagle* has turned to dust."

A few months earlier, Rodolfo had seen some pictures that Rod St. Just had taken of an aspiring young actress, Myrna Loy. I'd shown these pictures to him, and he'd become excited, thinking she might be the perfect actress as his co-star in *Cobra*. "We've got to set up a screen test for her," he said. "Natacha must meet her."

When Myrna arrived on the set of *Cobra*, she was skinny, frightened, and shaking, although Rodolfo and even Natacha tried to put her at ease. In a white turban and a golden brown brocaded dress, Natacha looked stunningly beautiful when she confronted Myrna. "I know they call me everything from Messalina to a dope fiend," Natacha said. "But I really don't eat little dancers for breakfast."

Myrna flopped in her test and the role went to Gertrude Olmstead. But Natacha remembered Myrna and called her to cast her in a small but glamorous part in *What Price Beauty?*, the starring role having gone to Nita Naldi.

Eager for news of what was happening on Natacha's set, I was happy to encounter Myrna once again. She was living in a small back room at the Hollywood Hotel.

Over drinks she recounted our first meeting on the set of *Cobra*. "I fell in love with Valentino the first moment I saw him," she said. "God, is he good looking. Like some sleek jungle creature—more panther than man."

I asked her how the shoot was going on *What Price Beauty?* "The film script is absolutely horrible," she said. "My only scene is a futuristic dream sequence in which I'm outrageously overdressed by Adrian. In Natacha's words, I'm playing 'the intellectual type of vampire without race or creed or country.' Adrian has designed this incredible red velvet pajama outfit for me. I wear a short blond wig that comes to little points on my forehead—very snaky."

After a few drinks, Myrna confided to me that Natacha was not only taking drugs and often appeared glassy eyed, even staggering on the set, but that she'd also taken a new lover—a camera technician—male for a change. "He speaks to no one on the set, and I don't even know his name," Myrna said. "He's in Natacha's dressing room whenever she's there. They arrive on the set together early in the morning and leave in the late afternoon when the shooting for the day is over. Everybody in the cast is talking about it. I think the Valentino marriage is coming to an end. I've staked him out for myself."

"Rodolfo must never know about this new beau of Natacha's." I said. "With Rodolfo's temper, he'll explode. For all I know, he'll challenge the guy to a duel."

As the evening wore down, I liked Myrna and we seemed to get along, but at the time I felt she was just another aspirant Hollywood actress, and would soon be heading back home to Montana to marry some cowpoke and settle down and raise a family. How wrong I was. In just a few years Myrna Loy would be the Reigning Queen of Hollywood, sharing a throne with Clark Gable, the king.

Although I never spoke of Natacha's involvement with her camera technician, and Rodolfo seemed unaware of it, he did tell me that she was taking drugs. "I don't know what kind of drugs or how much, but I know she's spending time with Barbara LaMarr. The last time I saw Ramon, he confided in me that Barbara is drugged out of her mind most of the time, and now she's luring Natacha there too. He said that Barbara is man crazy—actually sex crazy. In between men, she's sampling some lesbian love with Natacha."

That didn't surprise me at all. Unknown to either Rodolfo or me at the time, his ever-jealous business manager, Ullman, had hired a detective from the Burns Agency to trail Natacha. Ullman, I learned later, was hoping to get enough evidence on Natacha to break up her marriage. His secret dream was to become the president of a yet-to-be-formed Rudolph Valentino Productions, and that meant he had to eliminate Natacha.

I was at the Whitley Heights house enjoying lounging by the pool on a Saturday with Rodolfo when Ullman arrived carrying a briefcase. Right at the pool he started to present some of the detective's findings to Rodolfo, even some private photographs captured of the twosome.

Rodolfo read the material carefully, a look of disbelief coming across his face. Finally, the reports seemed compelling enough for him to accept them. "She's betrayed me," he said in a voice barely a whisper. 'It's like she's stuck a knife in my heart." Apparently, he could have affairs with women—and men too—without plunging that dagger into her heart, and he could even accept her involvement with other women. What he apparently couldn't handle was Natacha taking another man and sleeping with him, even though she consistently refused to go to bed with him after their ill-fated honeymoon night.

He got up from the chaise longue and stormed off the terrace, heading upstairs to his bedroom. Ullman trailed him, trying to pacify him. I stayed by the pool, not wanting to get involved in this triangle, fearing that I might become a victim of any possible fallout.

In about fifteen minutes Ullman came back onto the terrace, a look of panic on his face. "Rudy's gone," he said. "He took one of his guns and claims he's going to track down this cameraman and kill him. I tried to get the gun from him but he socked me in the jaw and got into his car and sped off."

"My God," I said, "he's hot-blooded enough to carry out such a threat."

"You've got to help me," he urged. "Get into your car and drive anywhere you think Rodolfo might be. You've got to stop him if you can find him. I'll get in my car and look everywhere for him too."

Hurriedly I got dressed and into my car, though thinking how foolish our mission was.

Los Angeles was a very big place to find one man, even if he were the glamorous and highly conspicuous Rudolph Valentino.

As I drove aimlessly at first, I feared if Rodolfo shot the cameraman, or even shot at him, it would become the biggest scandal in Hollywood, even dwarfing the shooting of Tom Ince. It would not only mean the end of Rodolfo's career, it might lead to his being sent off for life at San Quentin.

Having exhausted every possible site where I thought Rodolfo might go, I returned to the Hollywood Hotel where I reached Ullman at six o'clock. He had not found Rodolfo, nor had he encountered anyone who had seen him. He had seemingly disappeared. Likewise, no one knew where Natacha was.

By three o'clock that morning, when Ullman called me, I learned that Rodolfo had been found. Around one o'clock that morning, he had stormed into the Garden of Alla and had gone from room to room throwing open doors. In room eight he'd found Natacha in bed with the cameraman technician.

Fortunately, Paul Ivano and Nazimova had run after Rodolfo and had managed to grab the gun from his hand before he could fire into the bed of the lovers. Natacha had fled back to Whitley Heights, and the cameraman spent the night with Paul Ivano. Ullman was summoned and had taken Rodolfo back to Whitley Heights where he planned to confront Natacha.

About three hours later a call came in from Rodolfo. "Natacha is packing now," he said in a calm, soft voice. "She's taking the train this morning back to New York. We've agreed to a marital vacation." He seemed on the verge of tears, his words choked with emotion.

"Can I see you later in the day?" I asked.

"Not until evening," he said. "I'm taking Natacha to the station. When I come back home, I want to be alone for many hours to think things over."

Putting down the phone, I decided to spend the day at Charlie's, where not much was happening lately. The Little Tramp spent most of his time in his library and didn't want to see anyone, neither Kono nor me except on rare occasions. I felt he might be planning some big new movie, maybe his Napoleon and Josephine film.

Around two o'clock that afternoon I called Ullman from Charlie's house. He told me that there had been a mob of reporters at the station, word having leaked out that the Valentinos were separating. No member of the press had learned of the attempted shooting at Nazimova's Garden of Alla.

It was reported that Rodolfo had kissed Natacha several times and then had run along the platform, as if trying to catch up with the departing train. As the train moved out, photographs of a nattily dressed Rodolfo under a white Fedora were taken when he was shouting after Natacha to come back.

"What's the matter, Sheik?" one of the male reporters asked. "Not man enough to hold onto your own wife?" Rodolfo had slugged the reporter.

Since Charlie had still not emerged from his library, I placed a call to Rodolfo in the late afternoon. His baritone voice had become a mere whisper. "Natacha is my one true love," he said. "But she's hurt my male vanity. More than that, she's wounded the deepest part of my soul. I truly have come to believe that she is the reincarnation of Cleopatra, and I am but a mere slave in her country." Before hanging up, he agreed to meet me around nine that evening. I had wanted to come over earlier, as he sounded so despondent I feared he might be suicidal.

When I arrived at the Whitley Heights house that night, the front door was standing wide open. Anyone could have walked right in. I sensed that the door must have been just left open as someone was preparing to leave but had forgotten something and had gone back into the darkened house.

I was right. In moments a dark figure in black, like a villain in a 1916 silent film, brushed past me and headed for a battered old car parked on the street.

I caught only a fleeting glimpse on his face. He had gotten into his car and had headed down the street. It was only after he'd pulled away from the curb that I recognized the man. It was that German baron who was always stalking Rodolfo.

Slamming the door behind me, I raced into Rodolfo's bedroom where the dim light revealed him to be lying nude on top of his white sheets. He'd been bleeding around his groin. I screamed, fearing the baron had killed him.

*****

"Shut up, you little fool," Rodolfo said to me. "I'm okay. We've done this before."

"Done what before?" I asked inspecting his wound.

"The baron bled me," he said.

"He must be from the old country," I said. "This is not George Washington's day. We don't bleed people any more."

"It was for his sexual pleasure," he said.

"Who is this fucking baron?" I asked. "Some kind of vampire?" I went into his bathroom and returned with some alcohol which I spread on his groin with cotton.

When I'd finished, Rodolfo rose weakly from the bed and put on his bathrobe, taking my hand and leading me to his moonlit terrace where he sat down and inhaled deeply of the night air. "My decision is made," he said. "I will never see Natacha Rambova ever again. It is all over between us."

"You don't need her," I said. "She was bad for you. Without her restraints, your career will soar. Your artistic judgment was better than hers."

He seemed to like what he heard from me until he started to cough and clutched his stomach. He coughed violently as I stood helplessly by. I put my hands on him, offering to help. He pushed me away. "I'm okay," he said, although his voice sounded as if he were strangling.

Breaking from him, I went into the living room and attempted to place a call to Brian Sheehan for medical help, but Rodolfo forced himself up from the chair and followed me, knocking the phone from my hand. "It's bad enough that you know," he said. "I can't let a doctor know. It's always like this after I swallow the drink."

He looked so weak I directed him over to the sofa after placing the phone back on the hook. "What fucking drink? What in hell is going on?"

"I guess I owe you some explanation," he said. "You know too much already. You know that the baron holds the power of life and death over me. If he turns me in for that New York murder, I could go to the electric chair. Because of that blackmail, he can make me give in to his whims. I'm a virtual love slave to him."

"It doesn't look like love to me," I said. "How does he get his jollies? By bleeding you."

"He drinks my blood," he said. "He extracts blood from me and drinks it while it's still warm." I've done the same to you. Instead of a needle, I make you bleed with my teeth."

"I thought that was some unrestrained passion," I said. "You make all this sound like some warlock ritual."

"The ways of love are many," he said. "It's not about vampires and warlocks—none of that shit. Semen is blood. Instead of drinking semen, many people like to drink the actual blood of their beloved. It's an old sexual cult that began decades ago in Europe, and it still has its practitioners. You know nothing of these things."

"I know that hunters sometimes drink the warm blood of animals they've slain," I said. "Like a deer in the forest. They do that shit in America. But I've never heard of crap like you're talking, except from vampires."

He launched into a violent cough again, clutching his stomach which seemed to be cramping on him. Eventually he raised his face to me, slobber all over his lips and chin. I reached for my handkerchief and wiped his face clean.

"The baron carries things a little far," he said. "He talks to me endlessly about the thrill of blood-drinking. In some crazy way he got me excited about the prospect. But the idea of extracting blood by a needle and drinking it from a cup repulses me. I wanted to actually suck blood from a body, and I used you as my guinea pig. I didn't know if I'd like the taste of it or not. Until you, I had tasted only my own blood. The first time with you was wonderful. I enjoyed my dominance over you. It was complete. While I was sucking the blood right into my mouth as I was fucking you, I had the single most intense orgasm of my life. The blood from your neck dwarfs sucking the saliva from your mouth. I need more liquid from you than that—

your very blood, the essence of your life. I'm sure you'll never understand. But I could tell that after your initial horror at the idea, you came to regard it as a sexual thrill. It's the ultimate act of submission. A victim submitting to age-old dominance. Of course, I would never do this with a woman—nor a man. Only with you. The idea of drinking anyone else's blood is repugnant to me. Disgusting. But I can make you do anything I want to give me sexual pleasure."

I got up from the sofa and walked across the room. "Why are you coughing?"

"After he bleeds me, the baron makes me drink this very dark blood-red elixir. He claims it is concentrated blood from a bull. That consuming it will restore my missing blood cells and make my own blood thicker and richer than before. But for the first hour after swallowing it, I get these coughing spells and stomach cramps."

"I think there's something in the drink other than concentrated blood. Do you have any of it here?" I asked.

"A week's supply in my bathroom," he said. "The baron calls on me only once a week."

"Would you give me some so that I can have Brian's assistants examine it in their laboratory," I said. "You should know what you're consuming."

"No," he shouted at me before resuming another coughing spasm. "No one must know. Even I don't want to know what's in it."

On the sofa he burst into tears, and I went over to comfort him. I took him in my arms and held him. Feverish, he was slobbering again and appeared in deep stomach pain. I reached for my handkerchief to clean his mouth. "Run your fingers through my hair," he commanded me. I was startled since I knew he didn't like anyone to touch his hair. Gently I ran my fingers through his hair, and for the first time became acutely aware of how thin it had become. On the crown of his head were traces of the beginning of a bald spot. "I'm going bald," he cried out. "I'm losing my beautiful hair. I'll have to wear a God damn wig."

"You won't be the first actor in Hollywood—male or female—who has done that."

"I can't stand to imagine it," he said. "I think it's the baron. Maybe it's something in that drink. The baron thinks I'll look sexier if I'm bald. I'm almost afraid to brush my hair any more. It's coming out so fast. By the handful. I don't know what to do."

He pulled me to him, collapsing in my arms. "I'm going to kill myself," he said in a weak voice before drifting off into a sleep almost like a coma.

After six hours later, I woke up as the first of the morning light came into the living room. I was fully dressed. Still in his robe, Rodolfo lay on the sofa with me in a deep sleep. The ringing of the phone brought me into the reality of the day. I eased out from under him, as he groaned at being disturbed.

Making my way across the living room, I answered the phone. It was Ullman screaming that Rodolfo was late for an early morning shoot on the set of *The Eagle* where he had to appear as a dashing Cossack and masked bandit.

Somehow I managed to get Rodolfo to the set of *The Eagle* where he went inside his dressing room with a makeup artist and the head of the wardrobe department. His co-star, Vilma Banky, was dressed in period costume and was waiting on the set near a coach that was to be used on the scene. Rodolfo had asked me to go and apologize to Miss Banky for his being unavoidably late.

I approached the Hungarian actress, a stunningly beautiful blonde, and introduced myself, apologizing for Rodolfo. When she spoke to me, her limited English was fractured and so heavily accented that it would in time be called "a mixture of Budapest and Chicago."

Pictures were silent then and the public saw only her beauty on the screen. She was dubbed "the Hungarian Rhapsody," but her voice was so atrocious that when she spoke it marred her otherwise lovely features. She was satirized by the role played by Jean Hagen in MGM's *Singin' in the Rain* about the advent of the Talkies.

Banky was extremely gracious to me and assured me that she was willing to wait all day in the hot sun of California for the privilege of appearing on the screen with Rudolph Valentino. "The man's divine," she said. "Please, man, tell me something. True when he makes kiss on a woman, that woman's inside parts turn to…" She paused. "How do you say? Mush. You know…like porridge."

I smiled and answered, "When locked into an intimate embrace with this thespian, my intestines are in fully functioning order but my nether regions experience such celestial delights that it inevitably leads to a towering erection to equal the giant redwoods in Northern California." I smiled again and began to walk away.

"I will have to learn more of the English talk," she said. "Your talk is like American goulash."

Fully dressed and in character, Rodolfo strode masterfully onto the set. Defying the commands of his director, Clarence Brown, he ordered that his stand-in be removed from the saddle. Rodolfo claimed that he was not going to use a stand-in for a dangerous scene in which Vilma Banky's coach was being dragged off by runaway horses. Rodolfo's character of Vladimir Dubrovsky was to chase after the wild horses and subdue them. It was as if Rodolfo were determined to assert his manhood in front of the cast and crew.

Reluctantly Brown ordered that shooting begin. Mounting his horse, Rodolfo chased after the runaway horses. In front of the cameras, he attempted to grab the leader of the pack to bring the rest of the runaways under control. Suddenly, that horse yanked him from his saddle. I screamed as I watched Rodolfo being dragged along the rocky terrain for at least two-hundred feet.

Along with other members of the cast and crew, I rushed to Rodolfo's aid. He was coughing again. This time blood was coming up. There was a doctor in the studio standing by, and he was quickly summoned.

After helping carry Rodolfo back to his dressing room, I made a quick call to Brian Sheehan to come at once before returning to tend to Rodolfo's wounds. As I undressed him, he appeared to have severe cuts, abrasions, and bruises. Fortunately no semi-nude scenes were called for.

Although Rodolfo recovered quickly, and was able to complete *The Eagle*, he became increasingly moody and irritable. He'd moved alone into Falcon Lair, his new home, but often

wasn't there. He took to disappearing for hours at a time, driving his car aimlessly in the Hollywood Hills and up and down the California coast. He seemed shell-shocked at Natacha's departure and the end of their marriage.

He told me that, "It is important to still have a woman in my life. You are trying to turn me exclusively into a homosexual, but you will not succeed."

Sometimes he would invite his co-star, Vilma Banky, with him on his long drives. Since her English was so poor, he spoke to her in German which she knew fluently and he spoke only partially, being more skilled in French.

When I accused him of fucking Banky, he denied it. "She has confessed her true nature to me," he said. "She knows that she must marry a man to keep up her image in Hollywood, and I must be seen romantically involved with some woman to keep up my image. But in her heart Vilma likes women."

"You've found yourself another lesbian?" I said. "I'm not complaining by the way. If Banky is indeed the lesbian you say, I can be grateful for that. It eliminates some of the competition."

"I plan to divorce Natacha and take Vilma Banky as my new wife," he announced to me after the two of them had returned from a weekend from Palm Springs. He sensed the immediate protest forming on my face. "And there is absolutely nothing in the world you can do about it." He turned from me and headed for his bedroom at Falcon Lair where he shut the heavy wood and leaded-glass door behind him.

"Oh, isn't there?" I said to myself. "We'll see about that." Already an idea was forming in my head.

*****

Although I found his screen appearances unbelievably effeminate, the career of Rod La Rocque had soared. Ramon and I rarely saw him any more, because, with his success, his calendar both socially and professionally was full.

His greatest break had come with a call from Cecil B. DeMille, who in 1923 had starred Rod in *The Ten Commandments*. That was the film that made him a star, playing the brother of Richard Dix in the film.

From that time on, Rod worked for DeMille's Producers' Distribution Corporation, filming at the old Ince studio in Culver City and for Famous Players-Lasky. Jesse Lasky felt that Rod, along with Ricardo Cortez, were suitable replacements for their loss of Valentino. Americans flocked to see Rod in such films as *Code of the Sea* in 1924, *Feet of Clay*, also in 1924, and *Night Life of New York*, 1925.

A host of other films, including *Let Us Be Gay* (1930), lay before him. On the night I invited him to dinner, he was filled with excitement at playing a young Indian, *Braveheart*, his latest film. Sent East to study law, Braveheart becomes an All-America football player.

The film sounded like something I could afford to miss except for one intriguing cast member. His co-star was Jean Acker, Rodolfo's former lesbian wife. *Braveheart* is, in fact, the only known surviving film made by Acker.

In another surprise, Rod told me he was set to co-star opposite the French actress, Jetta Goudal, in *The Coming of Amos* in which he would play an Australian sheep rancher, who falls in love with an exiled Russian princess, Goudal. I recalled how Natacha had fired Goudal from the set of *A Sainted Devil*.

"It seems you're getting all of Valentino's rejects," I said, chiding Rod, although that seemed to make him angry. He never liked to be compared to Valentino.

Rod quickly returned to his favorite topic, himself. He told me of plans for an upcoming film, called *Captain Swagger* in which he would play a character who goes broke living too high and turns to crime to pay his bills. That film would have significance later in my life, as I met his co-star on the set, Sue Carol, a leading actress of her day. Sue, in time, would introduce me to her future husband, Alan Ladd, who would become one of my all-time loves, ranking up there with Tyrone Power and Errol Flynn.

"You're a Great Lover on and off the screen from what I hear," I said to Rod. "God knows what you're really up to. Carrying on affairs with Gloria Swanson and her arch rival, Miss Pola Negri—that's a bit much." The future gossip columnist already blooming inside me was eager for the real details, not what had been reported in the press.

"I find I can fuck women," he said, "if I don't think about what I'm doing. As you know, I like to be topped by men, not top a woman. Since I have such an active mind, I can imagine that it is I who is getting fucked while I'm doing the fucking." He smiled and laughed nervously. "I know that doesn't make much sense, but somehow it works for me."

In one of those only-in-Hollywood twists, Rod had been cast opposite Gloria Swanson in *A Society Scandal*. It had been successful on Broadway starring Ethel Barrymore when she wasn't fleeing from Tallulah Bankhead. To compound discomfort on the set, his rival for the Valentino mantle, Ricardo Cortez, was also cast as the third lead in the film.

"The greatest thing Gloria did for me was to tell me that I was much taller than Valentino and 'much better looking.' My first day on the set in Astoria, I had to make love to her in front of the camera. The picture, obviously, wasn't being shot in sequence. I could tell that I was turning her on."

Even though Rod was relating his affair with Swanson, his hand settled on my knee and began its upward journey, bringing back memories for me of Clifton Webb.

"Gloria invited me to her dressing room for lunch. 'My darling man,' she said to me, 'I have made love on the screen to the great matinee idols of my day. You name them— Wallace Reid, Thomas Meighan, and Rudolph Valentino himself. But I felt no attraction for them at all.'"

I said nothing to counter Rod's remark, but noted that Swanson was a liar in the case of Thomas Meighan and Valentino. She was powerfully attracted to both men, but apparently had felt no passion for the drug-addicted Wallace Reid.

"Gloria told me that I was the greatest lover she'd ever appeared on the screen with, and she didn't want the filming to end that day," Rod said. "I was very flattered. Let's face it:

Swanson is the queen of Hollywood. Before the week's shoot was over, she had fallen hopelessly in love with me. Although the prospect of making love to her night after night held no thrill for me, in one reckless moment I proposed marriage to her. We'd be the darlings of the media. With Swanson as my bride, I could get incredible publicity. If it had worked out, it would probably have made me American's biggest male box office attraction."

"That's reason enough for a marriage," I said, a bit cynically.

"Gloria became my biggest fan and press agent," he said. "She went from party to party announcing to everyone that I was physically irresistible. Not only that, she praised my brilliant mind. How many actors are praised for their genius?"

"What went sour in this romance?" I asked.

"I'm not really sure," he said. "She was all set to marry me. Gloria, as you know, stages these open houses on Sunday at her suite at the Gladstone. She invites everybody. I'm sure you've been to them. Gloria is telling everybody that I flew into a jealous rage at one of these affairs when I discovered that she'd invited mainly men. As you know, she doesn't like other women to compete with. Actually she's got it all wrong. I wasn't jealous of her. I wanted some of the men for myself. I'm going to tell you, and I've never told anybody, not even Ramon, why Gloria and I broke up. One day on the set of *A Society Scandal*, Gloria went to my dressing room thinking she'd left her purse there. Without bothering to knock, she walked in on me and discovered Ricardo Cortez pumping those mighty Jewish inches of his into the depths of my ass."

I settled back into my leather banquette. "You and Cortez? That's amazing. You two guys are big-time rivals for Valentino's throne. There's a feud between the two of you."

"Maybe that's part of the attraction," he said. "Look at Valentino and Ramon Novarro. They are actually the two biggest male rivals in Hollywood, often competing for the same roles. From what I hear, they still fuck each other."

"It's true," I said. "Hard to figure, but true. But then I hear Pola Negri is secretly in love with Gloria Swanson."

"There's something roguish about Ricardo that turns me on," Rod said. "His background in some ways is similar to Valentino's. Before becoming a star, he was a gigolo to both men and women. He's got a great body and is hung. He really knows how to fuck, so he found that being a gigolo was the easiest way to make a living. He's also been involved in a lot of shady deals. I suspect he was a smalltime crook in Chicago."

"There's one thing I don't understand about the La Rocque/Swanson/Cortez triangle," I said. "If Swanson caught Cortez fucking you, why did she start dating him after that film was shot?"

"You would have to go deep into the mind of Gloria to answer that one," he said. "She concluded from walking in on me, that I was the homosexual in the relationship—not Cortez. After all, he was doing the fucking. She felt he was the real he-man, and the one she should go after. When Gloria came into my dressing room, Ricardo pulled out of me, and she got to see him in all his full glory. I gather she was impressed. He's hung a lot longer and thicker than I am. She probably figured if Ricardo could turn on her future husband, she should give it a try too—and she did. So she dumped me and went after Ricardo."

"Only in Hollywood," I said "As for you, you went from the frying pan into the fire—Gloria Swanson to Pola Negri."

"I hustled Pola," he said. "I knew that she and Ernst Lubitsch were seeking the right kind of leading man to play Captain Alexei Czerny in *Forbidden Paradise*, and I set out to get the part for myself. I arranged to accidentally run into Pola after she'd had a day of fittings and publicity pictures. I'd heard that she had turned down twelve leading actors for the role of Alexei, including Ramon and Antonio Moreno. There was even talk of Valentino playing the part."

"Did she succumb to your manly charms all at once?" I asked.

"It took a little work," he said. "I invited her for a drive which led to a cozy little dinner at a bistro on the beach. I tried to be boyish but masculine, romantic but carefree, amusing and gay, sophisticated, debonair."

"She fell hard?" I asked.

"Not exactly," he said. "I think Pola wants

to find someone with whom she can pretend to be having a romance without the actual fucking. That's why things between Chaplin and her didn't work out. Chaplin likes to fuck. Also, get fucked, or so I hear. Pola wants the publicity but not the boudoir action. She's into women, and I really believe that."

"It sounds like the perfect formula for romance," I said. "A homosexual male and a lesbian."

"Don't knock it," he said. "I'm supposed to use Valentino as my role model. He would understand such a relationship."

"I'm sure he would."

"Things have been rough between Pola and me," he said. "She's temperamental, demanding."

"What did you expect?" I asked. "Hanging out with two of Hollywood's most tempestuous divas."

"We almost broke up over a diamond," he said. "For my birthday, Pola gave me this large diamond set in a platinum man's ring. About four nights later I was wearing it when I ran into Chaplin with Georgia Hale at the Alexandria. He recognized the gem at once. He'd given it to Pola as a loose diamond for an engagement ring. He went insane when he found out the bitch had it set and had given the stone to me. He struck me in the face. I'm over six feet tall and very athletic. I could have made mincemeat out of the shithead. But I feared we'd make the morning papers. Boiling mad, I left the room but on the set the next day I confronted Pola and told her what had happened. Instead of telling me she was sorry for not letting me know where the ring came from, she started screaming, shouting, and threatening to shut down production for the day. I was called to the set with her. I had to make love to her playing Catherine the Great. Lip readers who saw *Forbidden Paradise* must have had a ball listening to what Pola and I had to say to each other."

He told of how Pola had become so angry that day that at the end of the shoot she'd urged Lubitsch to fire him and reshoot all his scenes with another actor.

"She even refused to speak to me," he said. "I tried to visit her several times to apologize but she slammed the door in my face. One night I got a ladder and propped it against her window and invaded her bedroom. She thought it was a jewel thief because she had all her jewels at home because she needed them for her role as Catherine the Great. There was no security. When she heard me breaking in, she had a revolver and shot twice at me. Fortunately she missed. But my little daring attempt to climb into her boudoir by using a ladder won the day, and we started to speak again."

"Are you still seeing Negri?"

"We go anywhere there's press," he said, "but it's not a real romance. When I leave her off at her house at night, it's a peck on the cheek, and nothing more. But we're not making headlines like the ones generated by her affair with Chaplin. Pola wants headlines like that again. Guess who she's staked out for her next big game?"

"Douglas Fairbanks."

"Hell, no," he said. "Pickford will never give him up. Hold onto your seat: Either Ramon Novarro or Rudolph Valentino."

"It'll never happen," I predicted. Even as I said that, I wondered. It might very well happen with one of those men. If Pola Negri were indeed a lesbian, Rodolfo could very well fall into her orbit.

"The thing between Pola and me is winding down," he said. "I need to find a beautiful woman in Hollywood who will be seen with me. Maybe one I might marry. But a woman who won't make any physical demands on me."

"Do I have a girl for you," I said.

He raised his eyebrows. "What does that mean?"

"How would you like to meet the woman Valentino has proposed marriage to?" I asked. "His co-star in *The Eagle.*"

"You mean, Vilma Banky?"

"One and the same."

"Is Banky a lesbian?" he asked.

"From what I hear, the world's leading muff-diver."

"She's very beautiful," he said. "She'd look great on my arm with the photographers snapping pictures of Hollywood's new glamorous couple. I'd be game for it. It depends on her. Have you brought up the subject to her?"

"Consider it done," I said. "Don't you realize what this can do for you? You'll be known in Hollywood as the man who stole the girl of Valentino?"

"Christ," he said, his eyes lighting up. "That would make headlines. Set it up. I want to meet this Vilma Banky."

"Throughout the evening, we've done nothing but talk about your girl friends," I said. "Tell Durango who you are really fucking."

"I'm keeping him under wraps," he said. "I don't want anyone to look at him. He's the most gorgeous man on earth. He's from Montana. I call him the Montana mule. I had to practice stretching exercises before I could let him fuck me. The guy's a dreamboat. He's working as an extra on a cowboy movie right now and won't be back in town for two more days."

"Can I meet him?" I asked. "He sounds like a living fantasy."

"There's no way in hell I'm going to let Durango Jones meet my new boy friend. It's out of the question." He finished the rest of his drink and looked at me with searching eyes. "With my stud out of town, I'm horny as hell. Let's cut all the talk. Take me upstairs and fuck me hard."

*****

The ring of a phone at the Hollywood Hotel could mean anything. You never knew who was on the other end of the line. At eleven o'clock one night, when I'd been waiting for William Boyd, who had promised to fit me in between other engagements, a call came in. "This is Erich von Stroheim," the voice said. It was a voice like no other. Although I'd once kissed him on the mouth at the home of Norman Kerry, I didn't think von Stroheim remembered me. "I'm not calling you for a date," he said. "So don't get your hopes up. I'm a man strictly for the ladies. But I want you to report to work tomorrow morning on the set of *The Merry Widow*. There's a very special role in it for you. You'll be terrific in the part." He slammed down the phone without saying good night.

I was enthralled. At long last stardom had

arrived. Of course, I wouldn't be the actual male star. That role had gone to my darling John Gilbert, who had spoken of nothing but his upcoming part in this film for the past week. All Hollywood was abuzz about *The Merry Widow*. Even before the first day of shooting, the word was out that this would be the big one of the year.

Metro had cast harebrained Mae Murray as the lead in the film version of Franz Lehar's popular operetta. She was to play Sally O'Hara, of the Manhattan Follies, a *magna cum laude* graduate of the School of Hard Knocks.

Encountering me on the set the first day, Mae spoke to me only because I was a friend of Rodolfo's. Otherwise, she was not known to address extras. She was gracious, though dizzy. One had the feeling an orchestra was always playing in her head. She was in love with her part in *The Merry Widow* and told me she'd even gone to Vienna to study with the original dancing master for the operetta. "I once told you I didn't want another blond appearing in one of my pictures," she said. "But you're okay, I guess, providing von Stroheim keeps you in the background. I don't want you competing with me for a camera angle. You're too blond and too beautiful."

I had a feeling she wasn't joking. Before departing, she whispered something to me in confidence. "If only Thalberg had come up with another director. Frankly, I think Mr. von Stroheim should have stayed with his former profession—a dishwasher."

As I watched Mae glide across the set, I realized she did have cause to worry about her beauty. Actually, I was the right age to play Sally had I been a woman. Although Mae did everything she could to conceal it, she was thirty-nine years old when shooting began. Up close you could see the beginning of tiny wrinkles in her face. She had that kind of delicate porcelain skin that wrinkles prematurely. Also she was inclined to a double chin.

I'd heard that Oliver Marsh, the brother of Mae Marsh, one of Miss Murray's rivals, was testing baby spotlights encased in pink. These lights were known to cast a glow that was soft and forgiving, pouring the luminescence of youth over anyone they shone on, making aging stars of any gender look ten to fifteen years younger. Mae Murray needed this, and lots of other props too, to erase those wrinkles and make her look like the lovely young maiden she was playing in the film.

On the set I felt I was the only extra who hadn't sworn a pledge of allegiance—signed in blood—to the film's director. There was talk that von Stroheim had been a member of Franz Josef's Imperial Guard. His friend, Norman Kerry, had told me that Erich Oswald Hans Carl Marie Stroheim von Nordenwald was the son of a colonel in the Sixth Regiment of the Dragoons and that his mother had been lady-in-waiting for the empress of Austria.

As cast and crew awaited the arrival of von Stroheim, there was an electricity in the air. Everybody, it seemed, had a von Stroheim story to tell, including how he'd squandered a fortune on *Foolish Wives*, which was in production for almost a year, an unheard of amount of time back then. One extra on that film told me that von Stroheim had shot "miles of unused footage," so nobody knew what would appear in the final cut, even if he or she had a major role. Von Stroheim was known to detest stars, so there was much speculation that he was "destined" for a conflict with the temperamental Mae Murray. There were even warnings that with von Stroheim directing, the film might drag on for months and be abandoned before its completion. Since von Stroheim's monumentally long *Greed* had died at the box office, *The Merry Widow* was viewed as his comeback. In Hollywood if you lost money on one picture, your next assignment was viewed as a comeback—that is, if you ever got another assignment.

Arriving on the set, von Stroheim looked like a caricature of a Prussian militaristic egomaniac. Dressed in tall black leather boots, he marched onto the set with a riding crop under his arm. Whenever he was introduced to anyone of "rank," and not just a dress extra, he'd stand at stiff attention, his shoulders rigid. If it were a woman of some importance, he'd click his heels and reach for her hand to kiss. He oozed and smelled of leather. Under his shaved head, his face was made of granite, so no one knew what he was really thinking unless he exploded into a temper fit, which was

frequent. His monocled eye seemed to take in everything that was going on around him. He was a truly frightening creature, and I trembled at what role he wanted me to play, as I hadn't a clue.

I stood around the set all morning, not knowing what to do. I had wanted to call on John Gilbert in his dressing room, but because he wasn't needed on the set that day, he hadn't shown up.

It was almost lunchtime before von Stroheim took notice of me. He called me aside. "I should not be here," he said to me in a soft voice. "I only took this silly director's job because I don't want my family to starve. I should be in Rome getting ready to shoot *Ben-Hur*. Mayer is making a big mistake in not assigning that film to me. I would have gone after your friend, Mr. Valentino. Only he can play Ben-Hur—no one else."

He told me that he could speak only in private with me about "the special part I have in mind for you." In the meantime, I could report to the stage manager who could use me in several background shots. "Now you must go," he said, dismissing me. "Von Stroheim has to concentrate to save this silly picture."

The barracks-like dressing rooms were broken up into cubicles shared by two extras who stored their street clothes here and donned whatever costumes wardrobe assigned them. The stage manager assigned me number nine, which I was to share with another man. I was given an Australian military uniform to put on. After I stripped to my red silk underwear, a pair I'd lifted from Rodolfo, the swinging door to my cubicle opened.

A rugged-looking young man and an unlikely candidate for stardom stood before me. He looked about twenty-four, although he could have been much older. When he smiled at me, his teeth were crooked, with large gaps between them. One of his front teeth was rotting. He wore his hair parted in the middle and slicked back in the style of Valentino. His floppy ears protruded like jug handles, yet he had a tremendous raw sex appeal. "Hi," he said. "I'm Clark Gable. That's not my real name."

"Hi," I said. "I'm Durango Jones. Believe it or not, that's my real name."

"I know," he said with a smirk on his face. "I got you by default."

"What do you mean?" I asked, puzzled.

"Your reputation has preceded you," he said. "Three other of von Stroheim's extras—from the old country—didn't want to share a cubicle with you. I guess they thought you'd rape them or something. But I've been fending off pansy boys all my life, and I'm a man who can handle myself in any situation."

"Good to hear that," I said. "I'm surprised to hear that any of the extras are straight. Actually I haven't seen so many homosexuals on one set since I worked for Nazimova in the film *Salome*. Many of the same guys who worked on that film are also on this one."

"I could have guessed that," he said. "I've been eyed by at least twelve guys and propositioned once at the men's urinal. And it's only my first day on the job."

"You look like a macho man so you can expect that," I said.

"You're about to see how much a man I am." He took off his coat and hung it up before removing his white shirt. To my surprise he didn't wear an underwear top, and all men did back then. In a few years from that day, he was to remove his shirt in front of Claudette Colbert in *It Happened One Night*, revealing his nude, manly chest, and undergarment manufacturers howled in protest as sales of men's tops fell off across the country. What audiences didn't know was that Clark not only didn't wear underwear tops, he didn't wear bottoms either. Right in front of me he dropped his trousers. "You might as well take a look at my noble bird," he said. "You're going to see it sooner or later."

By then I was sitting on a bench observing the show up close, and he was clearly putting on an exhibition for me. Sad to say, Clark Gable was no Francis X. Bushman. His cock didn't match the body. The balls were generous enough but his dick was relatively small and uncut. He seemed so proud of it that I found it a bit sexy, too. Perhaps it was one of those cocks that start out unpromisingly and grow to grander and unexpected dimensions from such a small base. "Like what you see?" he asked.

"You're going to go over big in this town," I said. Like a stripteaster, he dressed in front of me, then invited me to lunch.

The kitchen had cooked sliced ham over which beef gravy was poured and served up with large batches of lumpy mashed potatoes. Clark ate like he hadn't had a meal for a day or two, and I began to suspect he hadn't. As he packed away the food, even helping me finish off my portion, he complained about the women of Hollywood. "Back in Ohio where I come from the men are supposed to take the lead in sex. Out here the rules are different. Women pursue you. I've never been to bed with a woman yet who could get enough. They wear me out!"

His face turned bitter. "My wife, Josephine Dillon, got me a small part in this God damn film," he said. "But when I went before von Stroheim, he took it away from me. The God damn Hun bastard. I wish our doughboys had blasted him off the planet during the war. When von Stroheim took one look at me, he shouted, 'We're not making a comedy about the Ozarks. Who is this American rustic? The part calls for a romantic and dashing figure of the Imperial Court of Austria, not this peasant with the rotting teeth.' That's why I'm working as an extra at $7.50 a day."

"You can learn something from every experience," I said. "Von Stroheim has a sharp eye. Maybe your teeth need work. You're a handsome guy. You could play leading parts. Everybody in Hollywood goes to the dentist and gets redesigned."

"Fuck!" he said, his anger boiling. "Don't you think I know that? I don't have any money."

"Maybe I can help," I said. "One of my best friends, Brian Sheehan, is a doctor. At his clinic there's a small dental school. They work on actors all the time. Maybe I could slip you in there for free."

He looked at me and smiled. "You little schemer. You would do that for me, wouldn't you?"

"Sure, I would."

"You sure must have liked what you saw back in that dressing room this morning," he said. "Maybe you and I should talk business. Serious business. What are you doing tonight?"

"Taking you to a steak dinner with champagne," I said.

"You're on."

Over dinner at the Hollywood Hotel Clark talked about his life and the hard times he'd known. "Silent pictures aren't for me. I'm just working as an extra until I can get on my feet. But to make it as an actor, my voice has got to be heard. That's why I'm going back to the stage as soon as I can. All the leading men I've seen out here are five feet six, and I'm referring to that soprano, John Gilbert in particular. I'm tall, big, burly, and I need big parts for me. One day all these effeminate actors will be wiped off the screen. They'll get rid of all the pansies in the script department and start writing roles rugged he-men like myself can play—not some drawing-room dandy who looks like a breeze will blow him away."

His rugged dimpled grin attracted me. He looked like the type of guy who expected dames to light his cigarette. Ever so gently I was being pulled into his orbit. The more I drank, the sexier he became. After all, not all men can have big cocks. Those who don't require loving too.

"The word is, you're the richest boy in Hollywood," he said. "Got blackmail on everybody. I hear half the big-time male stars in Hollywood send you monthly checks to keep your mouth permanently sealed." He leaned over and winked at me. "Perhaps you'll let me share in some of that good fortune. The God damn women in this town can't bring themselves around to paying for the services of a man. The men out here, especially that William Haines, aren't opposed to writing a check every now and then. I predict things are changing. In the years to come women will buy male sexual favors the way men buy sexual favors from a woman."

"I think you're right about that," I said. "In fact, I know it."

"Like I told you, I'm always getting propositioned," he said, leaning back. "Maybe I should make a proposition to you."

"I'm all ears," I said.

"No, I'm all ears," he said, laughing. "Frankly, I don't go much for sex with pansy boys, unless they are real pretty. You're prettier than most girls I've ever dated. I'll make a deal with you. You see, it's like this. I got this little lovesick show gal in trouble, and I need to arrange an abortion. If I agree to come and visit you at this hotel once or twice a week, could you give me the money to get an abortion for the poor little thing? I also need money for other things too—a car, for example. Some new clothes—some that aren't six years old—would be nice too. Maybe a little cash in my pocket to take a gal to a nightclub before I fuck her."

"You've got yourself a deal," I said.

For a moment he looked as if he might change his mind, but then seemed comfortable with the offer he'd made. "Mind you," he cautioned. "I don't do anything back to you. But you can have me right in your bed buck naked. You can only use your mouth on me. No ass-fucking. No pansy boy is ever going to fuck Clark Gable's ass."

"Can I lick it?"

"I don't get it," he said.

"I know I can't fuck it, but can I suck it?"

"Suck an asshole?" he asked in astonishment. "Never heard of that. Come to think of it, that might be fun. But I'd be having all the fun. What kind of fun would that be for you? Licking a man's asshole?"

"Don't knock it until you've tried it," I said.

"That's one thing I'll never try," he said. "So do we have a deal?" He reached to shake my hand. "A gentleman's agreement."

"You've got yourself a deal and the youngest sugar daddy in Hollywood," I said.

He got up from the table. "Excuse me, but I've got to call my wife. Tell her I won't be home for the night. I'll tell her I'm staying over with one of the extras so I don't have so far to go to report to work in the morning."

When he came back, I said, "Did she accept that?"

"It's not much of a marriage," he said. "In name only. Josephine is seventeen years my senior and mothers me. For sex I turn to other women. She is an actress herself. Teaches me acting. I'm not much of a husband. I cheat on her all the time. I've given her only two presents in my whole life—a pair of shoes so she can walk from studio to studio getting jobs for me as an actor and an alarm clock so she could get up early and iron my shirt and wash the egg off my tie. Some of the jobs she turns up for me are shit, but it keeps bread on the table.

Once she got me a job as a call boy."

"You mean a hustler?"

"Nothing like that. It was in the theater. A callboy knocks on the doors of the stars, telling them they have five minutes before going on stage. What the hell! I've been a hobo, a sawmill hand. Once I worked in a rubber factory."

As he ate and drank, I was mesmerized by his narrow, slit-eyed expression and also captivated by that wonderful smile if I could get beyond the teeth. In many ways he seemed a selfish, ambitious, and unfaithful bumpkin yet there was such a raw animal magnetism about him I couldn't wait to sample his wares. He seemed to cast a spell over me. It was magnetic.

A frown crossed his face. "Got any whiskey in the room upstairs?"

"More than you can ever drink."

"I don't know about that," he said. "That was about the best steak I ever had. Isn't it about time I fed you some meat to pay you back?"

*****

The night had been memorable and with slight variations it would be repeated for the next year or so as the young Clark Gable got his teeth fixed, a new roadster, a new wardrobe, and cash in his pocket. "Until I met you," he told me, "I'd never had more than fifty dollars in my pocket at one time."

Once he'd arrived in my suite, he'd wasted no time stripping down and plopping on the bed waiting for the action to begin. He hadn't seemed quite sure what I was going to do to him, and I'd noted a certain apprehension on his face.

I'd begun by running my fingers over the sensual softness of his skin, finding it thrilling to the touch. Almost immediately his little fuckpole had become rigidly hard. As his future wife, Carole Lombard, was to proclaim, "If Clark had one inch less, he'd be the queen—not the king—of Hollywood." Nonetheless, there was pliant suppleness to his dickhead, and I'd enjoyed holding it in my mouth for a long time as I'd tantalized him with my tongue.

With my left hand, I gently squeezed and fondled his hardened little orbs encased in a purse of fleecy skin. As I'd kept busy pumping and slurping on his elegantly sculptured cock, I gently nudged my fingers closer and closer to his rectum, which at first had caused him to pull back until he'd realized that I was merely going to tickle and tease the sensitive knot of muscles.

In the beginning Clark had remained motionless during the encounter. But to my happy surprise, I'd begun to get to him. I'd felt movement in his whole body as if he'd really begun to enjoy what I was doing to him. Pent-up feelings had been unleashed as his long legs had moved up and down my back, capturing me like his prey, his stomach heaving then relaxing, then heaving again. He'd lain on the bed writhing with pleasure as my lips and tongue had seemed to discover hidden nerve endings in him.

At first he hadn't known what to do with his hands until he'd started to feel his own chest, gliding rough fingers across the rippling muscles of his chest and abdomen.

It'd been thrilling to me to suck this young man's body as he lay completely naked and enjoying the intense pleasure I was providing for him. I'd loved the feeling of his cock gliding in and out of my mouth. It was so spongy and pliant.

I too had experienced his delirious anticipation of his own approaching orgasm, and I'd renewed the pressure on him, swallowing and plunging to the base, going up and down, up and down, until he'd screamed, erupting in my mouth.

It'd been a hot, creamy load that I'd remember for a long time. I'd marveled at the sweet flavor of his jizz. I'd sucked and sucked until I'd been convinced that I'd had the last drop. He'd given off an involuntary shudder of pleasure, before pulling out of me and collapsing on the bed.

I'd gently lulled him into a dreamy sleep by licking his asshole and tantalizing it with my delicate tongue. "Don't stop," he said. "That's the greatest sensation I've ever felt. Keep doing that all night, even when I fall asleep."

At three o'clock that morning, after some

heavy snoring, I was flattered when I'd awakened at the insertion of his hard-rock penis in my mouth for a repeat performance.

Awakening early the next morning, he was horny again and agreed to an "around the world." "Don't go above the neck," he cautioned me. "But you can have everything else."

After we'd finished and he'd shot a powerful explosion within me, he reached down and ran his fingers through my hair. "I'm ready for my bath, and you can have the honors." After bathing him and showering myself, we headed in my stagecoach to MGM to report to work on the set of *The Merry Widow*.

John Gilbert had reported to work for his first day on the shoot, and I eagerly headed toward his dressing room where he let me in at once. "I've just seen von Stroheim," he said, testing a button on his uniform as Prince Danilo. "He looked me up and down and said to me, 'you remind me of a ladies' hairdresser.' Then he stalked away in his riding boots. I could have punched him out, the bastard."

As John waited to go onto the set, von Stroheim in sweat clothes trained extras with Viennese precision, trying to make them realistic as soldiers of Monteblanco, the mythical kingdom in the film.

We settled in for a long wait before John was called to the set. "I've made it," he said. "I'm now drawing $10,000 a week, the same as Valentino. I thought stardom was what I wanted. I didn't take into account the suffering involved. That I'd have to take orders from the likes of von Stroheim. Correction. There is no one like von Stroheim."

Both von Stroheim and Irving Thalberg had objected to casting John in the role. Von Stroheim was holding out for the wooden Norman Kerry, and to John's surprise, Thalberg sided with the director, even though John had become a close friend of Thalberg's.

"It was a complete and total act of betrayal on Irving's part," John said to me. "Irving had never had sex with a woman until I started taking him on the town and introducing him to several hot-to-trot women. Until he met me, that innocent little boy didn't know that women enjoyed sex just as much as men do. Of course, Irving's got a bad heart, and eventually

his Jewish mother and Louis B. Mayer put an end to our nighttime debauchery."

John told me that the only one who'd demanded the role for him had been Mae Murray. "She saw how right I was for the part. She has approval over her leading man, and she dug in her heels and demanded Gilbert—and she prevailed over both Irving and von Stroheim."

He looked up at me through wide, hopeless eyes. "I've fallen in love with Mae," he said.

"What about Bob Leonard?" I asked. "I thought he was the love of her life."

"They're breaking up," he said. "About to get a divorce. Mae is free. Each day since she got me this big break, I send her three dozen red roses. I always enclose a note. 'Let me fall in love with you! Then I'll no longer be Bad Boy Jack.' So far, she's not given in to my sexual demands. She feels our passion should be stored up for the camera. If she doesn't come around soon, instead of American Beauties I'm going to send her a basket of hard-boiled eggs."

As I sat in John's dressing room waiting for him to be called to the set, I don't think he'd ever looked handsomer before or after. Even before the release of the film, *Photoplay* had written that, he was "much more romantic on the screen than Rudolph Valentino." That had thrilled John. Anytime any actor in Hollywood was called better than Valentino, that actor creamed in his pants.

John had gone on to marry Leatrice Joy, Cecil B. DeMille's biggest star, but the Gilberts divorced after the birth of a baby daughter. When Leatrice filed her divorce complaint, it made lurid headlines across the country and threatened to blow up John's career on the launching pad. LIQUOR IN BULK MADE LEATRICE JOY'S LIFE SAD, was a typical headline. During the divorce proceedings, Leatrice had all the public sympathy on her side. John was cast as a villain, and Mayer had gone so far as to publicly label him "a degenerate."

It had all seemed so golden on April 10, 1924 when John had been one of the first actors to sign with the newly formed Metro-Goldwyn-Mayer. The birth of his daughter on September 6, 1924 had not saved his marriage. Before coming home from the hospital, Leatrice had asked John to leave their house and move into the Los Angeles Athletic Club where I had resumed my relationship with him, calling him "Daddy Gilbert."

"I couldn't handle the marriage," he'd told me when I'd driven him to the club since he'd been drinking heavily all that afternoon. "She was the star. I was making pictures but going nowhere. Everywhere we went the public idolized her. I didn't want to spend the rest of my life being known as Mr. Leatrice Joy. Even Louis B. Mayer lets her associate with his precious daughters. He won't even let them be in the same room with me. Frankly, I was jealous of Leatrice, jealous of her career, and that is hardly the basis for a happy marriage."

Even before the final break, John had moved out once before and into a rundown Spanish hacienda on King's Road north of Sunset Boulevard. His fellow bachelor was Paul Bern, the German writer and director and one of Hollywood's leading intellectuals. I have always believed that Bern was in love with John, although one night John confided in me that Bern had confessed that he was impotent. "He's always threatening suicide," John said. "He showed me his genitals. They are those of a nine-year-old boy."

In the years to come, that didn't prevent Bern from marrying the leading blonde bombshell of the 30s, Jean Harlow. After threatening suicide for all those years, Bern completed the act in 1932, touching off one of Hollywood's major and still unexplained scandals.

Charlie lived only a block away from Gilbert and Bern, and I often used to drive The Little Tramp over there at night to sample their homemade gin and play the Ouija board. On one night in particular Charlie was doubly excited because John and Bern had invited Harry Houdini to preside at the séance. In the middle of the séance, a heavy teakwood table began to jiggle and lurch, seemingly lifting itself off the ground and slamming violently toward John who ran yelling from the house. It later turned out to be one of Houdini's many tricks but John remained convinced that it was real.

During his trial separation from Leatrice Joy, John had launched into an affair with Barbara LaMarr. I'd originally introduced him to Barbara during our three-way at Tom Ince's house, in which John had satisfied both Barbara and me. Their romance had been too volatile to last more than a few weeks. Barbara had dumped him to marry red-haired Jack Dougherty, her fifth husband. Barbara had appeared with John in *Arabian Love*, but they had not heated up the screen the way Barbara did when she'd starred opposite Ramon.

John had immediately taken up with Bebe Daniels, one of the leading screen vamps of her day. John always found it amusing to relate that on his honeymoon night with Leatrice Joy, both Barbara LaMarr and Bebe Daniels had called him to invite him to their boudoirs even though in theory he was supposed to be making love to Leatrice. "What did your wife do?" I asked.

"She told Bebe to go to hell," he said. "When Barbara called, she put the phone under the bed, turned over, and went back to sleep."

On the fourth day of the shooting of *The Merry Widow,* von Stroheim still hadn't told me what part I might play.

While I was waiting for the lunch hour, since I hadn't been assigned anything to do, an old actor came over to me and introduced himself as John Pringle. "I've got to talk to you," he said. "I noticed you visiting the dressing room of John Gilbert a lot."

"What's on your mind?" I asked, backing away, thinking that he was one of the many older homosexuals in the cast who openly lusted after the handsome young men dressed as imperial soldiers in the Austrian army. I'd already been propositioned eight times since joining the cast.

"I want you to introduce me to John," he said, calling him by his first name.

"Why should Mr. Gilbert want to meet you," I said.

"I'm his father."

"I don't believe you," I said, even though intrigued at the prospect. I willingly went with the actor to his battered old car where he produced letters from John's mother, and even a copy of the marriage certificate to Ida Adair, John's mother. "I deserted my family right after little John was born," he said. "For years I'd lost all trace of him."

"This happens a lot," I said. "Long-departed parents emerge when a son becomes a big star."

"I've been down on my luck," he said. "The jobs are few and far between."

With great reluctance, I agreed to drive Pringle that night to the Athletic Club where I had a date to meet John alone. John opened the door dressed only in his underwear. "Who in hell is this?" he demanded to know, looking with a hostile glare at Pringle.

"I'm convinced this man is your father," I said. "He's got proof."

"Hello, son," he said. "I'm John Pringle. I brought along some stuff to show you."

"Get the hell in here and out of the hallway," John said.

When John had examined Pringle's evidence, he did believe the old actor was his father. But a happy family reunion was not to be. John's face reddened with anger. "Where were you when I needed you?" he shouted at Pringle. "I believed for a long time that I was Ida's bastard son. That I didn't have a father. My childhood was miserable. I was used and exploited, all because of you. Ida once went off on a tour and left me with this couple who turned out to be pedophiles. Is that the life you wanted for your son? It is you who is the bastard."

The old actor was crying when John ordered that I remove him from his room at once. To his surprise, John encountered Pringle on the set the following day, finding that his father had been cast as one of the liveried servants standing at the doorway to the palace ballroom.

After shooting was over, John and I were having a drink in his dressing room when Pringle came and knocked on the door.

"I need to see and be with you, son," Pringle said.

"You've come into my life too late," John said. "Not when I needed you but when I became rich and famous. I'm through with you, and I don't want to see you again. I'm making arrangements with my business manager. You're to be given a monthly check from me for the rest of your life. But money is all you'll ever get from me—not love. It's too late for that now." He slammed the door in Pringle's face and never saw his father again, although he continued to support him.

At the studio the next day, I saw one of the most amazing scenes I've ever witnessed on a Hollywood set. Under von Stroheim's eagle eye, John Gilbert and Mae Murray were playing a passionate love scene. Even though von Stroheim seemed to find his two stars making love disgusting, he did not call a halt to the action, even when their passion for each other seemed to go beyond what the role had called for. Obviously John had taken Mae's advice, saving his ardor for the screen instead of off the screen.

Standing with me watching them emote was Clark Gable, the $7.50-a-day extra who would one day become King of Hollywood, dethroning John Gilbert, the actor he was watching in the love scene.

On the opposite side of the set I became aware of the penetrating eyes of Norma Shearer who was also watching the lovemaking. Norma was dating Irving Thalberg and her career looked promising. At that moment Mae Murray was the queen of MGM, but a sudden flash of intuition sent a chill up my spine. In a moment of almost psychic clarity, I sensed that this young actress, Shearer, would one day prevail as the Queen of MGM, thanks to Thalberg's help.

I looked first at Clark, then at Norma Shearer. Neither of them seemed to notice my staring at them. Each of them was too intent on watching what was going on before the camera.

Would the King of MGM, John Gilbert, and the Queen of MGM, Mae Murray, lose their crowns to the emerging Clark Gable and Norma Shearer? As unlikely as it seemed at that moment, it crossed my mind as an eerie possibility.

*****

On the set of *The Merry Widow*, the tension between its star, Mae Murray, and its director, Erich von Stroheim, grew more intense. On one hot day, as we dress extras suffocated in our military uniforms, we waited for eighteen hours for a dog to yawn!

Von Stroheim seemed intent on destroying Mae's confidence in front of the camera. At one point, he stopped shooting and yelled at her. "Madam Murray, try not to act like a cupie doll. I am ze director of zis picture. I do not vant to see your bee-stung mouth in every shot. Chase the insects away."

She fled from the set but agreed to show up the next day. Von Stroheim seemed even harsher with her. "You can not only forget those bee-stung lips. But the goo-goo eyes have got to go too. So are those Madonna-like expressions. You're not playing the Virgin Mary, but a whorish showgirl. This is not a religious picture. It is a story of sexual perversion in *Mittel Europa*." Once again Mae ran from the set but was persuaded to return after lunch.

Mae was obviously dreaming about making a romantic story about court intrigue, climaxing with the dancing scene of the lilting Merry Widow Waltz. Von Stroheim kept announcing that his aim was to strip the film of its superficial veneer and to expose European decadence, regardless of how tawdry.

In almost brutal contrast to Mae's fantasy, he wanted to depict realism on the screen. Instead of showing the luxury of the royal bedchambers, his camera narrowed in on the royal chamber pots. In one scene, he depicted the false teeth of Josephine Crowell, the actress playing the queen, resting in a drinking glass on the royal nightstand. In another scene the queen had been filmed with plasters on her face as she cut off the corns on her feet. Her ladies-in-waiting had been hired specifically because of their mustaches, which the camera cruelly revealed.

Through it all Mae seemed incapable of removing her pouty expression. The more von Stroheim yelled at her to "get rid of that cutey-cute mouth," the more determined she was to look like her lips were bee-stung. After all, it was that expression that had made her famous, and she seemed to feel she must not abandon the look at any cost.

When Mae returned to the set one hot afternoon, she seemed shocked when told of a rewritten scenario. The film's plot called for her to marry the richest man in Monteblanco, Baron Sadoja, who had an advanced case of syphilis and was forced to walk with a cane.

No longer able to have the sex he was devoted to, he had developed a foot fetish, evocative of Cecil B. DeMille. The actor, Tully Marshall, was perfectly cast as the baron, the decadent old roué. In the film the baron keeps a closet filled with the shoes of his former conquests. The implication is all too clear that he goes to the closet to masturbate. On his wedding night, he bares Mae's feet and drools and slobbers over them. Tully performed the scene with such authenticity, and with such intensity, that Mae, in genuine disgust, fainted. She was then carried off the set by three men who returned her, unconscious, to her dressing room.

When she recovered, von Stroheim stormed in to see her. "Madam Murray, we are not a bakery making cream-puff pastry!" he said. "The scene is important because of its psychological implications!" Without another word, he abruptly exited.

When Mae wasn't on the set, she learned that von Stroheim was filming degenerate parties and orgies. Oliver Marsh, the cameraman, secretly showed her some of the scenes in the film. Immediately, Mae rushed to Thalberg's office to claim that von Stroheim was shooting scenes of such debauchery that they would not get by the Hays office. Thalberg assured her what a great director von Stroheim was and urged her to return to the set and follow commands.

Throughout the filming, von Stroheim had refused to zoom in for close-ups of Mae. She virtually cried in her pleading to him, but he remained adamant. "No close-ups." Finally, when he could tolerate her whining no more, he ordered a close-up. As Mae is bending over her wounded prince, as played by John, the camera moves in on her, depicting her double chin and making her look like an old hag.

Through the cooperation of Oliver Marsh, Mae eventually became the subject of several more forgiving close-ups. Working with Marsh late at night, Mae filmed scenes behind the back of von Stroheim, although he eventually learned what she and Marsh were doing. He flipped his monocle and stormed into Thalberg's office, threatening to resign if Marsh and Mae continued to shoot scenes for the film, which he had not authorized. "I am ze director of this picture," he told Thalberg, "not some blonde floozie who announces a different bio to the press every day. Only yesterday she was claiming to have grown up an orphan on the romantic streets of Paris. Bullshit like that." Thalberg prevailed upon von Stroheim to return to the set to resume shooting.

The only actor von Stroheim was sympathetic to was the villain, Roy D'Arcy. The director seemed to want to turn D'Arcy into a caricature of himself. Soon D'Arcy was talking and acting like von Stroheim in the role of Crown Prince Mirko. Von Stroheim was spending more time with D'Arcy than any other member of the cast, teaching him how to act like the master himself. Originally, von Stroheim had wanted to play the role himself. But Mayer and Thalberg knew that if von Stroheim also appeared as an actor in the film, it would be very difficult to fire him if the need arose.

Finally, I was approached by von Stroheim who seemed to remember that he'd offered me a small part in the film. "This scene is very secret, and it will be shot at midnight. It is much too sophisticated for American audiences and will appear only in the European releases of the film."

As von Stroheim outlined his incredible plot to me, I was stunned. I was to play a pretty young blond-haired Austrian teenager who is inducted into the Imperial Army. On a long camping expedition into Hungary, eight lusty soldiers—long accustomed to having a beautiful girl whenever they wanted one—get drunk and decide to tie me up. I am to be repeatedly sodomized.

"I can do that," I said, "and make it very realistic. I've been penetrated enough so that my face can convey what it feels like."

"My dear boy," he said, "I fear you're not that good an actor. Although the actual sex won't be depicted on film, I want each of the soldiers to penetrate you. Since most of them are homosexual and have been itching to get your pants off, I had no trouble raising volunteers."

"You mean they are actually going to do it?"

"Precisely," he said, adjusting his monocle.

"That way I will achieve the realism I'm looking for."

When I saw the eight men von Stroheim had selected to play the sodomite soldiers, I agreed at once. With or without a role in the film, I would have taken each of them on. The problem was, eight of them at one time. I didn't know how I felt about that. Von Stroheim gave me two stiff drinks of Irish whiskey and then I agreed.

Before four o'clock that morning, filming had ended and von Stroheim pronounced the shot a success. I was a bit sore but satisfied. The men were good, and any of them were welcome for a repeat performance. In fact, I enjoyed that night so much that I often repeated the act in my future—notably in a bathhouse in Moscow in 1948 and later in Morocco in 1956 in a male bordello where I took on six outstanding members of His Majesty's navy.

The next day von Stroheim informed Mae that in the picture, "There will be no valtz. This is not musical comedy. It is about debauchery in the court. Ve must deal with social significance."

To Mae, there was no picture without the waltz. MGM had purchased the film rights because of the waltz. It was to be the highlight of the picture. This time Thalberg had departed for New York, and Mayer had been left in charge. Mayer wanted the waltz and threatened to fire von Stroheim if he refused to film it. Reluctantly, von Stroheim ordered the waltz to begin.

Very *décolleté*, Mae's gown was designed by the Syrian, Adrian, who would later go on to greater fame putting shoulder pads on Joan Crawford. Mae was to wear a headdress of birds of paradise. She looked stunning in her black-velvet gown as it floated up to her neck, encased in diamond strands. The orchestra struck up the music to the Merry Widow Waltz, as John and Mae swept, glided, and swirled across the floor.

They had not danced for more than one minute before von Stroheim yelled, "Cut!" To the amazement of the cast, he actually went onto the ballroom floor. At first we thought he was going to object to John's dancing, as he was not a trained dancer. To everyone's surprise, he showed Mae Murray how to execute her steps, despite the fact that she'd been a professional dancer all her life. She looked as if it were all she could do to keep from striking von Stroheim.

The filming resumed. Putting his hand against Mae's bare waist, John whirled her through the sea of dance extras who parted, leaving them dipping and swaying alone in perfect rhythm on the ballroom floor. His eyes never left hers. Perhaps for that reason, he stumbled and almost fell on top of her.

"Cut! Cut!" von Stroheim yelled again, bellowing through his megaphone. "You lousy effeminate pretender to manhood," he shouted at John in front of cast and crew. "Murray has turned you into a ballroom pansy."

Furious but saying nothing, John turned and walked off the set.

Mae could no longer contain her anger. She ran toward von Stroheim pounding her fists into his chest. "You German swine! You dirty Hun!" She too fled to her dressing room.

The extras were left standing around with nothing to do, and the cameramen remained idle. Von Stroheim sat in his director's chair, saying nothing.

Suddenly, I was shocked to see Louis B. Mayer rushing onto the set. He came up to von Stroheim. Mayer looked as if he were ready to explode. "You're fired!" he shouted at von Stroheim. Then he slapped his face and stormed back off the set. Von Stroheim rubbed his face and muttered something about bringing assault and battery charges.

John asked me to return home with him and help him pack. He'd been planning a trip to Brazil before he began shooting his next film. "I'm leaving at once," he said.

As John started to get in on the passenger side of his car, Mae ran from her dressing room crossing Washington Boulevard. Except for her headdress and diamond buckled shoes, she seemed to have forgotten she was nude. "Jack," she screamed at him. "You must come back."

At first he resisted her and tried to shake free of her. But she bit into his coat, holding the fabric firmly with her teeth. A policeman from the studio came over to her and placed his coat around her. Finally, she convinced John to go back into the studio.

On the way back to the dressing room, Mae pleaded with John. "If you run away now, you're hurting me. Without the waltz, the picture will be ruined. We have our careers to think about. This picture with the waltz will make a big star out of you. You've always wanted that."

That afternoon, with Oliver Marsh filming it, *The Merry Widow* was finished without a director.

In the end, Mae Murray prevailed and was right. Thalberg himself, returning from the East Coast, personally cut the ninety reels of film down to twelve. *The Merry Widow* went on to become one of the great hits of 1925. The music from the waltz, as originally composed by Franz Lehar are part of his 1905 operetta, *Die lustige Witwe*, swept the country.

The film is remarkable when viewed today—for one reason, John Gilbert wears a 1990s haircut. It also became notorious for charging the highest ticket prices in history, from $1.50 to $2, unheard of at the time when some laborers were making only a dollar a day.

The scenes of the soldiers and me were never presented to Thalberg. I am certain they would have ended up on the cutting-room floor. There was no way the Hays office would pass on them. Perhaps von Stroheim had taken the footage home with him. Much of the film, even without my scene, was viewed as "objectionable trash" by Thalberg.

I was heartbroken, deciding that *The Merry Widow* was going to be my last film. I was no longer going to chase elusive stardom. I decided I'd go into a different profession— that of a movie writer, a budding Louella Parsons, going from party to party, attending all of filmdom's major social events. I felt that henceforth and forever more I would observe the foibles of Hollywood and record them.

Before he left for South America, I threw a victory party for John. He'd just learned that he'd been cast by King Vidor as the star of *The Big Parade*, which would become one of the classics of the Silent Screen. Vidor had opposed casting him in the part. "I can't see a Romeo deluxe in the role," Vidor told Thalberg. "This actor must be a real soldier in the trenches with dirty fingernails." Fortunately, the director didn't get his wish. It was one of those happy accidents that occur in Hollywood—like the day when both Ronald Reagan and Ann Sheridan were not available to star in *Casablanca*.

All those years of struggle had finally paid off for John. He now had the stardom that was enjoyed by both Rodolfo and Ramon. In the months ahead his fame would be greater than that of either Chaplin or Valentino. He was filmdom's man of the hour.

John Gilbert shirts with long collars and French cuffs were all the rage, as were his signature neckties of navy blue silk with tiny white polka dots. Back in those days actors wore light blue shirts in front of the camera, which photographed as white and didn't cause the glare that real white did. Late for a party, John arrived wearing a light blue shirt, which he'd worn at the studio that day. This style was reported in the press, and suddenly men all over America started wearing light blue shirts, which had never been acceptable fashion before.

As *The Merry Widow Waltz* resounded in my head, I was taking the train to New York where I would sail to Europe, making my way to Rome where the filming of *Ben-Hur* had begun. My darling sugar daddy, W.R. himself, had given me my first major assignment as a movie writer. I was going to send back behind-the-scenes stories of what was really going on in Rome. In later years *Cleopatra*, with Elizabeth Taylor and Richard Burton, would generate almost as much press interest as MGM's *Ben-Hur*, but at the moment all roads led to Rome.

I was going to get the real story.

*****

En route to New York where I'd sail to Europe, I planned to spend time with Charlie, who had fled the West Coast to escape constant pressure from his wife, Lita, and the array of attorneys she was assembling, each of whom was making threats to bankrupt The Little Tramp.

Kono had gone east with him, having become far more than a chauffeur. He was acting more and more like Charlie's personal business manager. Kono had warned me that Charlie was "deteriorating," but I had not been prepared for his rapid descent into madness. Because of his mother's insanity, Charlie often feared that he too would become crazy.

And that is just what happened. For an amazing eighteen months, Charles Chaplin became a lunatic, although that was never reported in the press, even though journalists often interviewed him and observed first-hand his irrational behavior.

When I arrived at Charlie's hotel in New York, Kono led me into his suite. I demanded to see Charlie, but Kono said that he'd locked himself up for three days, refusing all food. "I can hear him crying. That's all he does. He sits for hours in his bedroom and moans."

"What's the matter?" I asked.

"With Charlie, I never know," he said." I've never seen him in this condition. I've seen him threatening suicide, but nothing like this before."

"Surely his concern for the divorce isn't hitting him this bad."

"He says he's out of his mind about Lita's extortion attempts, but I think it's about more than just that."

It was shortly before midnight when Charlie agreed to let me into his bedroom—that is, me and the tray of food I'd brought him. It included a bowl of chicken soup. The room was lit by a single low-wattage lamp, and I could hardly make out his features. He hadn't shaved for days. When I looked into his eyes, they were red pools. He looked drawn and despondent as if he hadn't slept for days.

When I offered him the soup, I thought he'd refuse it. But he eagerly took it and began to slurp it down. He stuffed bread into his mouth at such a rate I thought he'd choke. He didn't say anything until he'd finished all the food on his tray. He looked up at me as if pleading for more. I got up to return to the small kitchen in the suite but he called me back. "That's enough food for now," he said. "I'll eat this red apple you brought me. It's all nice and shiny."

"I'm going to Europe," I said. "An assignment for Hearst to write about the filming of *Ben-Hur*. But if you need me, I'll postpone the assignment. Apparently, it'll take ten years to make *Ben-Hur* at the rate they're going, so it'll still be there when I get to Rome."

Weakly he reached for my hand. "I want you to stay with me for a few days. I've got to get out of New York. I want to go to the beach. I need to sit and look at the ocean."

"I'll drive you down to Atlantic City first thing tomorrow morning," I said. "The sea air will be good for you."

"I'd like that," he said. "I'd also like a bath tonight. I'm very dirty and too weak to bathe myself."

I moved toward him and very slowly removed his garments. He did have a rancid odor to him. I ran him a bubble bath, then carried him in my arms into the bathroom, where I slowly immersed him into the bubbly suds. He reverted to being a kid again and in minutes was laughing and giggling, splashing water on me. Since it was a monster of a claw-footed tub, I stripped down and got into the water with him, soaping and bathing him, even washing his matted hair before rinsing both of us off. After drying Charlie and powdering him like a baby, I wrapped a large terrycloth towel around him and carried him to bed.

In bed, he whispered in my ear that he wanted me to hold him all night long. "They're after me," he said in a confidential tone. "If they come for me, you must put up a fight. I'm too weak. If you don't fend them off, they'll carry me away."

I never asked him who "they" were. These imagined ghouls seemed real to Charlie, and I wanted to offer him what comfort I could. As I cuddled with him, he took the thumb of my right hand and began to suck it voraciously. After about thirty minutes, he let up but kept it captive in his mouth where throughout the night as insecurity overcame him he sucked my thumb. For some reason known only to him, sucking on my thumb brought comfort to him and made the night easier to live through.

In Atlantic City I checked Charlie into a suite at the Broadstairs Hotel with a large verandah overlooking the beach. He was thrilled. Even though bathed and powdered, he still would not let me shave him. He might be the most famous man in the world, and one of the most photographed, but no one recognized him behind that beard, the large hat

he wore, and the dark glasses. If he'd worn a cape, he would have looked like one of those screen villains in a 1913 flicker.

Even though it was near noon, Charlie demanded breakfast on our verandah like those he used to eat in England. That took some doing, but I managed to bribe the chef into acquiring the ingredients for Charlie's menu, since the hotel didn't normally inventory blood pudding or lamb's kidneys in their larder. However, a deli ten blocks away catered to an expatriate British market and sold us the delicacies, even some kippers. I personally supervised the grilled tomatoes, which had to be coated with bacon fat before being placed under the grill.

Upstairs once more, I was delighted to see that the breakfast was a success. Charlie ate every bit of it, including all the white bread fried in bacon fat. He pronounced it the best breakfast he'd had since coming to America. "They don't know how to do breakfast over here," he told me, having taken off his hat and glasses. Since we were screened off from view, he removed all his clothes to enjoy the noon-day sun. His body was a ghostly white, and I was glad to see him soak up some of the rays of the sun. Maybe he wouldn't look as if at death's door.

While Charlie sunned, I wanted to catch up on my sleep. I was deep in sleep when he shook me awake, shouting, "I've seen a man drown. A lifeguard went to save him. But the man—he was Jewish—pulled the lifeguard under the surface of the water with him. He drowned too. You've got to call the police."

Still not quite awake, I jumped up from the bed, got dressed, and hurried downstairs to report to the manager of the hotel. He looked surprised but quickly dialed the police to report what one of his guests had seen from a veranda.

I stayed downstairs waiting with the manager. The police came by the hotel about an hour later. "Who saw this drowning?" one of the officers asked. Not wanting to reveal that Charles Chaplin was the eyewitness and a guest in Atlantic City, I volunteered that I had.

"You're mistaken," the officer said. "Maybe you had too much booze last night. There's only one lifeguard on duty, and he's still there and has seen nothing."

Embarrassed, I thanked the policemen and excused myself, heading back to the suite. On the way up the stairs, I suddenly remembered what Charlie had said. He'd claimed the drowning man who'd pulled the lifeguard into the undertow with him was Jewish. How could Charlie have known that a man so far away was Jewish? It didn't make sense. Neither did the drowning. I suspected he'd made up the whole thing.

Back in the suite, Charlie was eager for news. "You're right," I said. "You did see a drowning. The lifeguard's body washed up on shore. He's dead. They couldn't save him. But the Jew is still missing."

"I knew it," he said. "He was eaten by a shark."

Satisfied that nothing could be done, Charlie—still in the nude—came back into the living room and lay down on the sofa. "I've got to go back to Hollywood to battle that Pickford bitch over United Artists. I like Doug but I can't stand the Canadian cow. She's always lecturing me about my interest in young girls. She does not understand. I have nothing in common with the dirty old men who go to parks to look for underage pussy. I'm not a nasty old man like Pickford thinks. It is not my aim to despoil the innocence of youth. God knows, that is not my goal. I'm an artist. Like all true artists, I recognize perfect beauty when I see it. Perfect beauty can only exist in the innocence of the first bloom of a young girl. After that, it's all gone. When a woman loses her innocence, she becomes a painted face and wears a mask to cover her wicked soul. Gloria Swanson is a perfect example of that. I don't want these painted manikins in Hollywood, women like that Polish cunt, Pola Negri. To me, only a girl who's pure interests me. Lita Grey is hardly pure. I don't think she was pure when I first deflowered her. Neither was Mildred Harris. Both these women were young but already corrupted long before I got to them. I will continue my search for the perfect beauty. A little girl whose breasts are just beginning to ripen. When I slip between the legs of a young girl, I want to know that I'm truly the first, that I'm entering virgin territory where no man has ever gone before."

Before the afternoon ended, Charlie

reported two more drownings that he'd spotted from the verandah. Each time he had me go downstairs to report them to the manager. Each time I went downstairs and was gone for an hour, sipping a cold drink on the large porch in front of the hotel. I never approached the manager with any news of the other "drownings" Charlie had seen. The next morning I noticed that the newspaper reported no drownings either. I kept the paper from Charlie, even though he requested a copy to read about the drownings he'd witnessed. He had also claimed that the other two victims of the drownings he'd spotted were Jewish.

The next morning after he'd lain all night cuddling in my arms—no sex—he woke up eager to go for a swim. He said it would restore his health. He didn't want to go onto the sands, but preferred to use the hotel pool instead.

He finished one lap before pleading exhaustion. He asked me to get him some coffee from the hotel stand outside the gate. When I returned in about fifteen minutes, I didn't see him, thinking he'd gotten tired and had headed back to our suite.

I placed the coffee on a marble stand near a chaise longue, gathered up my robe, and headed back upstairs. As I stopped off by our cubicle to pick up my street clothes, I heard a strange sound coming from inside. These cubicles, or so I'd learned after a generous tip to the bellhop, were often used for quick sex even though there wasn't enough room to lie down. "They do it standing up," the bellhop said. "It's mostly homosexuals giving each other a blow-job," the bellhop told me, "but sometimes men and women go in there too."

I knocked on the door, making sure from my key that it was indeed the locker that had been assigned to Charlie and me. The door opened slowly and a little girl ran out, running through the gate toward the beach before I had a chance to get a good look at her. I couldn't tell how old she was, but she looked no more than ten.

I stepped inside our cubicle and found Charlie on his knees on the floor. "Oh, my God," I said. "let's get out of here."

"You're right," he said. "Help me up. I don't want to be recognized."

Once we'd secretly and safety returned to

the room, Charlie told me he'd given the little girl ten dollars. "She accepted my offer right away. Of course, I'm not so stupid as to attempt penetration on her. She probably couldn't take my big dick anyway. But she let me lick her little pussy. It didn't even have hairs on it. When I tried to stick my tongue into her, she giggled. I think she liked it. I wish you could find her for me and bring her here. There are so many things I've always wanted to do with a little girl that I never have. My greatest dream is to fuck a little girl in the ass. Give her stretching exercises if I have to. Even if I make her bleed, that would excite me too. Naturally, for that we'd have to go to a place way up in the woods of New York somewhere. That way no one would hear the little girl screaming. I know it would be painful for her but I'd be willing to part with a hundred dollars for the sexual pleasure it would give me."

"We'd better not," I said. "Sounds far too dangerous. You've got enough jackals in Los Angeles trying to take your money. You don't want some irate parents after you too. You might not be able to bribe them. They may want life imprisonment for you instead."

"Maybe you're right," he said before wandering back to the bedroom where he almost immediately fell into a coma like sleep, no doubt dreaming of the little girl he'd seduced—in a fashion, that is—in our cubicle.

I returned to the verandah as the sun was setting, wondering how many more scandals Charlie would avoid in his lifetime. I just knew there would be scandals. Some would never be revealed. Others would be hushed up. But many—and I sincerely believed this—would eventually make the newspapers.

The next day Charlie wanted to return to New York at once. "It's more peaceful there," he told me. "In Atlantic City, I've seen nothing but death at sea."

No longer appearing in Charlie's films, Edna Purviance was in New York en route to Paris, where she hoped to break into French cinema, having already appeared in one film there. She'd grown too old for Charlie but was still on his payroll. She'd also broken up with Thomas Meighan who hadn't called me since that last blow-job I'd performed on him. Still dependent on Charlie, Edna had gone from

mistress to pimp.

An invitation for a pre-theater dinner arrived from her, and Charlie was eager to accept, although his romantic interest in Edna had long ago dimmed. Provocatively, Edna promised Charlie that she'd introduce him to the hottest new sensation on Broadway, Louise Brooks at the Ziegfeld Follies, which was then the most popular cabaret review in the New World. True to her word, Edna saw that we arrived early at the backstage of the Follies. Within minutes she had produced the enchanting Louise Brooks, a China doll with alabaster skin and a helmet of black hair.

Louise was still only seventeen, a little old for Charlie but still enticing. After we'd met her and she had to go on stage, Charlie whispered to me, "What I like about her is that she looks like a she-boy. It's like having a boy and a girl in the same body. Very exciting." From the curtains, we watched as "Brooksie," as she was called, danced in rhinestone-studded six-inch heels to "Fine Feathers Make Fine Birds." Her headdress of emerald peacock feathers towered four and a half feet above her, almost her own height.

That night was the first time I'd seen a standup comic, W.C. Fields, who was a juggler *extraordinaire*. He also did a series of skits about a drunkard who had to cope with a nagging shrew of a wife, plus another of an obnoxious kid in a baby buggy. W.C. Fields always hated kids, and it showed.

At the show's finale, bathed in colored lights, Louise stood on a twenty-foot wooden platform with Will Rogers, who twirled his lasso for a grand finale.

As Charlie was talking with the stage manager, Edna warned me that The Little Tramp shouldn't get too smitten. "Louise has a best friend in the show. A vocalist named Peggy Fears. These gals are living together as lesbians."

Later, when I informed Charlie of this, he seemed ecstatic. "I've got to see them go at it. I'll even pay them five-hundred dollars. You go to Louise and make the offer."

"I can't," I said. "I'd die of embarrassment."

He flashed anger at me. "Listen, God damn it, and listen carefully. At any time I can cut off your paycheck. I happen to know you're stashing away all the money I'm giving you and getting rich. Do you want that cut off?"

I smiled faintly at him. "As soon as I can get to her dressing room, I'll make the pitch," I said.

"That's more like it," he said. "I'll meet you at the stage door after I've wished Edna bon voyage."

And, thus, began one of Charlie's wildest and most public affairs, even though he was still married to Lita Grey at the time. By midnight all four of us—Charlie, Louise Brooks, Peggy Fears, and myself—were sitting buck-ass naked in his hotel suite drunk on champagne. Amazingly Charlie was speaking of his mother, Hannah Hill. No longer afraid that he'd inherit her insanity, he told the girls that it was because of his mother that he'd inherited "just the proper dose of madness—just enough to give me my sense of comedy."

If Charlie had been seeking a vestal virgin, Louise Brooks' door was the wrong one to knock on. For five-hundred big ones, Louise and Peggy seemed willing to do anything, including staging a bout of lesbian love on the sofa in front of Charlie's eager eyes. The Little Tramp kept his eyes glued on the women from a perspective of about twelve inches away. I tried to look elsewhere and dream of other things, like Richard Dix, William Boyd, or Theodore Kosloff.

When the girls had climaxed, Charlie decided to entertain us with his impressions, his most brilliant being that of John Barrymore reciting the most famous soliloquy of *Hamlet* as he picked his nose. He then rushed to the bedroom and emerged in quick drag, impersonating Isadora Duncan dancing barefoot in a storm of toilet paper. His most comedic impression was left for last—that of how Lillian Gish would achieve orgasm if she ever went to bed with anyone.

After this show from one of the world's greatest talents, Charlie retired to the bedroom, and was gone for a while. Nude, Peggy rose from the sofa and headed for the bar and more champagne. Louise studied me closely as if I were under a microscope.

"I'm glad you're blond," she said after a while, "and that Charlie has dark hair—or salt and pepper at least."

Even at that early age, Louise had a provocative, challenging manner as she stared at me. "Ever since I was ten years old," she said," I've been a basket-watcher. I like really big pricks, and I'm glad to see that both you and Charlie are endowed. Actually women can get some satisfaction from most men unless they're hung like a bantam rooster. I like three things done to me, and only a big prick can truly do the job. I never waste my time with red-headed men. Their pricks are invariably small and misshapen, often bent into an unappealing form. They always have pink heads. I don't like a pink head on a man. I prefer the head to be vermilion. I plan to devote the rest of my active life to the pursuit of sex— that is, until I'm old and don't want it any more. I'll try many men and sample many different sizes and shapes of pricks, but never on a redhead."

At that point I turned to see what the cowboy-and-Indian war calls from the bedroom were all about. Bursting through the door was Charlie himself, with an iodine-coated hard-on. He began chasing Louise and Peggy around the room as the girls ran to the bedroom. I decided to remain in my armchair, listening to the radio. Charlie called back to me, "Get the hell in here. I want Peggy and Louise to go down on each other while I take turns fucking them in the ass. While I'm fucking them, I want you to plug me."

Peggy, Louise, Charlie, and I were on the town for the next two weeks, mostly showing up at East Side speakeasies where Charlie had developed a fondness for gypsy musicians newly arrived from Budapest. One night he took us to a play at the Greenwich Village Theater where I met a twenty-year-old actor named James Cagney who told me he wanted to break into movies as a song-and-dance man.

"In silents?" I asked.

"Silents won't always be silent," Cagney said. "The movies are going to talk and I'm going to be there singing my heart out."

The play was Maxwell Anderson's *Outside Looking In*, and it was about tramps, a subject dear to Charlie's heart. The cast was headed by Charles Bickford, with Blyth Daly playing the role of a fugitive who disguises herself as a boy. Although we were never sure what happened, Charlie trailed Daly to her dressing room and emerged just a few minutes later with a bleeding lip. He demanded that I rush him to the hospital right away as he was becoming hysterical and screaming he had blood poisoning. He refused to speak of what happened, but Daly had apparently rejected his proposition for sex with a fierce bite on his lip. Charlie's swollen, bloody lip did make the newspapers, with a photograph, but the actress was never identified.

The next night we saw *Cradle Snatchers*, starring Mary Boland and Edna May Oliver, with a young actor, Humphrey Bogart, in a supporting role. But most of the audience looked at Charlie, not the actors on the stage.

After all this play-going, it was back to the speakeasies. Charlie had become enraptured by this wild Hungarian violinist who had Albert Einstein-like hair. Charlie demanded that we go to hear him for four nights in a row. Charlie would sit enthralled listening to this nostalgic music of the Austro-Hungarian Empire. Later he used this memory for his variety hall act with Buster Keaton at the piano in *Limelight*.

Before leaving New York, Charlie gave one of the most shocking press conferences of his career. In fact, it was so controversial it might have destroyed him. But all the members of the press, some thirty in all, from the New York dailies seemed to protect him. Each of them presented a slightly whitewashed version of what had actually happened at the news conference.

Charlie began by announcing that he was going to film *The Suicide Club*, "or the story of my life." None of the reporters seemingly had heard of it, although there was a Robert Louis Stevenson story of the same name.

I feared Charlie had been taking drugs, as all of a sudden he launched into an ode to the beauty of ten-year-old girls, claiming "a woman is her most beautiful when she's beginning to bloom." He even went so far as to suggest that if a reporter had a young daughter at home—preferably no more than fourteen—"the great Charlie Chaplin would be the ideal man to acquaint her with the birds and bees," should that journalist bring his young offspring by Charlie's hotel suite.

Blatantly he told of his hatred of America and the capitalist system and how he planned to return to England never to visit this country ever again. Then astonishingly, he charged that Mary Pickford was attempting to sabotage United Artists because he was urging more mature parts on her, begging her to give up the little girl characterizations. Swinging widely out of control, he predicted that the marriage of his friend, Doug Fairbanks, would not last, and that Mary Pickford was actually in love with her co-star, Buddy Rogers, in *The Boy Friend*. He predicted that Pickford would divorce Doug and marry Buddy.

Actually, he was right about this. Buddy Rogers had shared my bedroom in Lawrence, Kansas, when he'd roomed temporarily with us and had indeed made Pickford the girl of his dreams. No doubt he was thinking of Pickford as I'd sucked his cock back then. It was still one of the most delectable of all I'd fellated in Hollywood.

Asked about Hollywood decadence, Charlie claimed that he'd personally seen Rudolph Valentino dress as a woman at Hollywood parties and that'd he personally seen Lillian and Dorothy Gish disappear "for hours at a time" into their dressing room with D.W. Griffith.

Fortunately, none of these accusations made the headlines, especially the charge that Charlie "personally" knew that Mabel Normand had fired the fatal shot into William Desmond Taylor and that Fatty Arbuckle was paying off a blackmailer who had all the evidence on the comedian that he'd murdered Virginia Rappé. Before we were able to get him out of the ballroom at the Ambassador, Charlie claimed that Gloria Swanson was the real mother of Wallace Reid's adopted girl.

Today Charlie's condition at that press conference might be called hypomania, a mood disorder where the patient feels grandiose, suffers irritability and insomnia, and displays erratic, often risky behavior, most often committing sexual indiscretions. Doctors examining Charlie at the time claimed he was suffering from low blood pressure and a high fever, but mostly blamed his behavior on exhaustion.

"I have decided to end it with Louise," he

told me on the morning following the press conference. He went over to his desk and wrote out a check for $2,500. "Go see her and give her this," he instructed me.

That night at the Follies, just as Louise was about to go on with her solo number, I told her that Charlie had said good-bye and wanted her to have the check. "I'll never say no to a man with a checkbook." she said, before kissing me on the cheek and dancing off into the spotlight.

I wasn't to see her again until 1929 when she was attending the premiere of *Pandora's Box* in which she played Lulu, the director (G.W. Pabst) having turned down Marlene Dietrich for the role.

For reasons known only to him, Charlie had made plans for Kono and me to accompany him to a small chalet near Lake Placid, New York. When I first heard of this, I feared he was going to abduct some little girl and take her to this remote cabin, where he'd repeatedly sodomize her to fulfill one of his long-cherished dreams.

Heading for the wild woods of New York's Adirondack Mountains, Charlie was ebullient, happy to leave the city behind him. Once we moved into our chalet in the wilderness, Charlie disappeared and was gone for three hours. He'd walked four miles and back to a little hamlet where he'd done who knows what. One of his reasons for coming here, or so he said, was to wander for hours through the woods and pastureland, hoping to restore his waning health.

Kono had been warned by the owner of the lodge that wild bears were recently seen in the area and that we were to be careful during our walks. He'd even gone so far as to lend Kono a gun in case we met up with any ferocious bears who might rush us, thinking we'd make a tasty dinner.

It was twilight, but Charlie demanded that Kono and I go with him for a walk in the woods, even though he'd been walking for most of the day. Kono warned him of the menace from the bears but Charlie wouldn't listen, calling us "sissies."

As we walked along the edge of a forest, Charlie told us that he'd heard of a serial killer in the area. "He jumps out from behind anything and plunges a knife into your heart," Charlie

said. "He's killed two people this year—one only a month ago. I'm surprised you haven't been reading about it in the papers."

"I don't understand," Kono protested to Charlie. "You want to go on this walk for your health. But at any time a bear might charge us, now this serial killer. This doesn't sound like a healthy walk to me."

Charlie laughed off our fears. "Both of you have lived in the city too long." In minutes he had returned to the subject of the serial killer. "He likes to slice open the stomachs of his victims and reach in with his hands while they're still alive. He removes their entrails which he eats in front of them. Torturers in medieval England used to do the same thing. It really freaks out a victim to see some cannibal eating his organs while the victim is still conscious."

"A thrilling prospect," I said, begging Charlie to head back to the lodge.

Charlie would hear none of that, and we walked along a ravine for another twenty minutes as the night grew darker. I feared we'd not be able to find our way back.

All of a sudden a man ran out from behind a boulder, holding a large butcher knife in his hand. He raced toward Kono with the knife held high.

An expert marksman, Kono pulled out his gun and shot the man in the heart. He fell over instantly. Kono bent over him to see if he were dead.

I stood paralyzed.

"Why in hell did you do that?" Charlie shouted at Kono. "You Japanese idiot. It was all a joke. I hired this guy in the village to scare you. He wasn't going to hurt you."

Kono rose up over the body. "How in hell did I know? He scared the hell out of me."

"What are we going to do?" I asked Charlie. "How can we explain this? A sick joke?"

"We're going to push the body down a ravine," he said. "Or stash him in one of the caves over there. Chances are his body will never be found. I talked to him in a store before hiring him. He's up here by himself trying to get some fishing in. He told me he has no family. I don't even know if anybody will file a missing person's report."

In a coma-like condition, Kono and I

dragged the slain man's body to a small cave about two-hundred yards from the boulder. Kono pulled the body into the cave, as I had no heart for the job. Kono needed his paycheck far more than I did. When the body was hidden away, Charlie turned to both of us and said, "None of us must speak of this ever again."

And we never did. Charlie had been right. No missing person's report was ever filed, and the slain man's body was never found. Both Kono and Charlie went to their graves without telling anyone what had happened, and I never spoke of it until now.

As I drove Kono and Charlie back to New York, I felt like a serial killer myself. My heart was breaking at the useless slaying of that poor man who was trying to play a nightmarish joke on us—all for Charlie's amusement. I never felt the same about Charlie after that shooting even though I could hardly blame Kono for the incident. He had been set up. Although I never viewed him as a cold-blooded killer, Charlie didn't seem to have any remorse for his own role in the incident.

After we'd returned to New York I spent a restless night in bed with Charlie, thinking of that poor slain man. Charlie slept peacefully, although I heard Kono get up several times throughout the night. Saying nothing, he was obviously suffering for his role in having shot that man out of fear.

At the train station the next morning, as Charlie headed for Chicago, I told him good-bye, not certain when I'd see him again. "Secrets," he said to me, "so many of my secrets are known to you. Life is nothing but a series of secrets, all of which we must take to our graves." He embraced me and headed for the train without looking back.

I stood on the track for a long time after the train had pulled out, thinking about all the other dark secrets we'd accumulate together over a long lifetime.

I had three more days in New York before I was to sail to France, and those days would be spent with Rudolph Valentino who was arriving in New York that afternoon for the premiere of *The Eagle*.

Chapter Nineteen

A cable from Rodolfo had caused me to wait over for another three days in New York to see him. I, too, had wanted to attend the world premiere of *The Eagle* and was delighted that he'd invited me. After that, he'd sail to England for the premiere of the film in London. I would sail on a different ship to France where he had agreed to meet me later in Paris.

I could have rearranged my schedule to sail to England but Rodolfo pointedly did not invite me, yet agreed to stay with me in New York. I wondered who would be with him on the sea journey to England. Finally, Ullman, his business manager, told me that Rodolfo was keeping his options open in case Natacha agreed at the last minute to accompany him to England.

I'd abandoned my latest conquest in Hollywood, the male hustler and aspirant actor, Clark Gable. So that he would remember me, I'd left him with two-thousand dollars, with a promise that there would be more where that came from after my return. He'd counted every bill in the stack and had looked as if he couldn't believe it. He'd fingered the money again very carefully, as if suspecting it were counterfeit.

On my final night at the Hollywood Hotel, Clark had shown me just how grateful he could be after the exchange of gratuities. "Okay," he'd said, with a sigh. "Tonight you can go above the neck. My lips, my tongue, the works. You've already had every other part of me, including some hidden crevices where I didn't know I had erotic zones. Why not the part

above the neck too? I've got a big tongue and you're going to get off on it."

How right he was. Long before Vivien Leigh playing Scarlett O'Hara got to kiss him in *Gone with the Wind* as he played Rhett Butler, and long before an array of Hollywood screen legends, notably Joan Crawford, got to enjoy a deep kiss from Gable, I drained his mouth dry.

In fact, I liked kissing him much more than I liked sucking his cock or licking his asshole. "With the lights out, I can imagine I'm in bed with a beautiful blonde girl," he told me. "Your skin is as smooth as a girl's. You smell as sweet as a girl, and when I'm kissing you in the dark, and you're sucking my tongue, it's just like a girl might do—that is, if you can find a bitch in Hollywood to suck your tongue. What I like about you pansy boys, is you'll do anything a man wants done to him. Women will go just so far. They'll let you fuck 'em—and that's that. None of this other good stuff you're teaching me."

That was not the most endearing pillow talk I'd ever heard from a lover. In the late Forties, one of my discoveries, Rock Hudson, was better at "Pillow Talk" than Clark, but from this Ohio bumpkin I took what I could get—and was grateful for it.

By the dawn's early light, I was enthralled after a night kissing and licking Clark. I'd called Brian Sheehan and arranged for Clark to get his teeth fixed while I was away in Rome.

"When you get back," Clark had told me, "I'll be showing off a new and perfect set of teeth, even if they're false and not my usual buck-toothed wonders. I'll be gorgeous. No one will ever say no to me in Hollywood ever again. Fuck Erich von Stroheim. He doesn't know talent when he sees it. Fuck the pansy actors like John Gilbert. Tomorrow's screen belongs to me. I'll go the casting couch route just like some dumb blonde showgirl but I'll get there. In just a few years, Gable himself will be directing who lies on that casting couch."

After leaving Clark to his adventures in Los Angeles, and saying good-bye to Charlie at Grand Central, I returned to the Fifth Avenue apartment to get dressed for Rodolfo. It was there I received a bon voyage call from W.R. himself. He wished me luck in my assignment to cover *Ben-Hur* but told me he would not be heading east for another month or so. He planned to stay in Beverly Hills with Marion and later go to San Francisco to look after business interests there. He'd said that he was eager to see me after my return to America where he fully expected I'd bring him up to date on all the gossip not sent to him by cable. "All the stuff not fit to print in a family newspaper," he'd told me.

After putting down the phone on W.R., I felt that the Chief and Marion had finally reconciled themselves to each other's deficiencies and had settled in for the long duration of a relationship. I certainly guessed that right. With a few bumps and grinds along the way, Marion and W.R. would stay together until death.

I would remain a fixture in their lives for the good times and the bad times, an epic journey that would make a memoir unto itself. Over the years nothing stands out in my mind more than that windy day on May 2, 1947 when I drove the Chief and Marion down the hill along the winding five-mile stretch of road that led from the castle of San Simeon to the coast.

The aging Chief, in ill health, sat in the front seat with Marion in the back. For the first lap of the road, no one said anything. W.R. was obviously trying to control his emotions, but tears were streaming down his cheeks. Sensing his acute distress, Marion leaned forward from her seat in the rear and patted his shoulder. "We'll come back, W.R.," she said in her most soothing voice. "Just you wait and see."

W.R. folded his hand over hers but said nothing. He was one smart man, and he knew what time it was. My heart broke as I saw him turn and look for a farewell view at the castle of his dreams, before he turned to face the bleak road ahead. I parked at the landing strip where a small plane was waiting to take us on the short flight to Los Angeles where W.R. would be installed in the house he'd purchased for Marion in Beverly Hills.

As the Chief had known all along, his health did not improve. It was at this same house that he died at 9:50 on the morning of August 14, 1951, as Marion slept.

Brian Sheehan woke me up at eleven that morning to tell me that W.R. had passed on. I burst into tears, realizing how much I loved this ruthless press baron who had never shown me his cruel streak but had always been gentle and kind, even when I'd done dumb things over the years to cause him distress and trouble. With both Marion and me, he was the eternally forgiving father.

Only with his passing did I realize for the first time how much I'd loved him. He would be the only father I'd ever know, and with his death something had gone out of my life forever.

Thinking that Marion might want to see her twins after W.R. had departed, I had gone to her but she refused to go to San Francisco to see them and forbade me to bring them to Beverly Hills.

It was the saddest day of my life when I drove alone to San Francisco to attend the funeral of my beloved W.R.. I felt greater pain than I did at the death of Rodolfo so many years before.

The date of August 16, 1951 is imbedded in my mind. I can still smell the flowers in the Grace Episcopal Church on Nob Hill. Knowing of my long years of loyalty to her husband, Millicent Hearst, the abandoned wife, was now in control, as I'd left Marion drinking heavily in Beverly Hills. Millicent honored me by seating me in a row reserved for distinguished guests. I took a seat sandwiched between former president Herbert Hoover and Governor Earl Warren of California, who would later become chief justice of the U.S. Supreme Court.

Even though I tried to suppress it, I was crying like a baby direly in need of a change of diapers. At one point Hoover, obviously sympathizing with my distress, leaned over and placed his arm around me to comfort me. Until that moment, I'd always thought he was the coldest and least caring man in America, considering how he'd handled the Depression before Roosevelt took office. To my surprise, Hoover had a warm and human side to him after all.

As I arrived at the Cypress Lawn Cemetery outside San Francisco, even Louis B. Mayer came up to comfort me. He had long ago learned of my devotion and loyalty to the Chief. Another cold and dark mogul, Mayer was having his own problems at the time, as he was getting booted out of MGM, a studio that still bears his name.

Standing with Millicent and her sons, I heard her ask Bill Jr. if he would read a poem, *Song of the River*, that her husband had written a decade previously. "I'm afraid I'd be too choked up," Bill said. "The words won't come out."

"I know the poem by heart," I said. "I was with the Chief when he dictated it to me. It's a lovely poem. If it would be appropriate, I'd like to read it." Without saying anything, Millicent thrust the poem into my hand.

I didn't need to read the words as I knew the poem by heart. I won't claim that it's a great poem, but it seemed fitting somehow, and I was proud to quote it in front of this distinguished crowd of people, many of whom had fought bitterly with W.R. during his lifetime but still respected him enough to show up at his funeral.

Forgive me as I indulge myself and repeat W.R.'s long-ago poem here:

*The snow melts on the mountain
And the water runs down to the spring,
And the spring in a turbulent fountain,
With a song of youth to sing,
Runs down to the riotous river,
And the river flows to the sea,
And the water again
Goes back in rain*

*To the hills where it used to be.
And I wonder if Life's deep mystery
Isn't much like the rain and the snow
Returning through all eternity
To the place it used to know.*

Back in Beverly Hills, I called on Marion to give her all the details of the funeral. She wanted to know everything, including a long and detailed description of what Millicent wore, even a report on the jewelry W.R.'s wife had selected for the funeral.

In the weeks ahead, I thought Marion would be forever married to the bottle, and in most instances that was true. That's why it came as a complete surprise when she invited me to her wedding at El Rancho Vegas Hotel in Las Vegas on October 31, 1951. W.R. had hardly turned cold in his grave.

It was to be Marion's first and only marriage. On her marriage license, Marion had listed her age as forty-five even though she was fifty-four at the time.

When I met her husband-to-be, I was stunned, as Horace Gates Brown III bore a startling resemblance to the Chief himself. He was a forty-six-year old captain in the Merchant Marine.

Marion invited me to have a drink with her as she was fitted into her wedding gown. "He's hung like Francis X. Bushman," she said, giggling. I learned that she'd met Brown only the year before when he'd been dating her sister, Rose. Brown had proposed marriage to Rose but she'd turned him down.

"If Horace is an example," Marion told me, "I'll take Rose's rejects any day."

In reference to that wedding day, I can still taste the stale turkey sandwiches, the dry coffeecake, and the good beer served for the wedding breakfast. No caviar, no champagne, even though Marion was worth a fabled fortune. For some reason she told the press in Nevada that Brown was a cousin of William Randolph Hearst. That was a total lie, of course.

The Fifties and beyond were a time of funerals, as both Marion and I watched most of the people we'd known in Hollywood pass on to be replaced by a new generation. Marion would occasionally be remembered by the old gang such as Joseph Kennedy, who'd long ago finished his affair with Gloria Swanson.

He'd been kind enough to invite Marion to the wedding of John Kennedy and Jacqueline Bouvier. Although on wobbly legs and in ill health, Marion agreed to go providing I'd fly east with her to look after her. As her drinking had intensified, Marion found it increasingly difficult to maintain her balance.

In 1956 she suffered a stroke, and three years later doctors discovered a growth in her jaw. It was diagnosed as malignant cancer. She refused surgery but agreed to cobalt treatments which made her hair fall out and discolored part of her face, turning it into a purple-blue. Although she would let me in to see her until her final days, she refused other guests, even when such notables as Clark Gable or a young Frank Sinatra showed up at her doorstep.

Her last months were spent in agony and relatively alone except for Brown who remained by her side. Sometimes. She was long ago aware that he was out most nights drinking and screwing showgirls on some of the money W.R. had left her. After eight months of marriage, she filed for divorce when he ripped out all the phones at her house because he claimed she was talking too much. He disliked all her friends, especially Mary Pickford, and often appeared drunk and unshaven until Marion felt she could no longer entertain without embarrassment. The original party-giver of Hollywood retreated to her bedroom, there to emerge only two more times.

Brown begged her not to divorce him, and in her weakened condition she agreed to take him back. But for the rest of that marriage, he remained in another part of the house, coming and going as he pleased.

A true homophobe, he disliked me intensely, and I tried to avoid him whenever I came by. If I did encounter him, he often taunted me. "Hey, fruitfly," he once called to me, "Is it true that old man Hearst used to fuck you up the ass? Or could he not get it up?" I just ignored him, heading for Marion's suite.

One drunken night I encountered him in the living room wearing nothing but a pair of white boxer shorts. "Hey, faggot," he yelled at me. "Get over here and suck on this monster dick." He reached into his fly and pulled out this gargantuan penis which he shook lewdly at me.

I retreated to the door and out into the night as he came after me. "Too big for you, pansy boy?" he shouted, standing in the open doorway as I drove off.

It was a feeble voice I heard on the other end of the phone, calling me in January of 1961. It was Marion wanting me to fly with her to Washington to attend the inauguration of John F. Kennedy. It would be her last public appearance.

Much of the press didn't recognize—or didn't care—who she was. Her movies weren't revived then, and she had become a forgotten fixture in Hollywood. When her name came up, if it did at all, most people assumed she'd died.

As her cancer and the pain grew worse, she agreed to go to Cedars of Lebanon Hospital in Los Angeles for treatment. Joseph Kennedy had flown a trio of specialists from Boston and New York to treat her. She underwent surgery for malignant osteomyelitis on her jaw on June 7, 1961.

On my first visit to her after her operation, she was happy and even cried. "It's a success," she said. "They got it. The cancer is dead. They've got it."

The glee of her pronouncement was not convincing. Two weeks after the operation she fell and broke her leg. Through that dreadful hot summer she grew worse and worse, her weight dropping. For the first time in her life she no longer made up her face. She didn't even cover her head when she saw me. She was completely bald like a caricature of Queen Elizabeth I.

When I took the still handsome but aging Brian Sheehan by to see her on September 15, 1961, he ordered her to be taken to the hospital at once. There at seven on the evening of September 22, she died.

The world's last great courtesan was laid to rest. As a pallbearer I stood between Joseph Kennedy and Bing Crosby, wondering when I too would be in the casket instead of carrying one.

But in spite of strokes and various illnesses, I seemed to go on forever as the years went by. I felt that if I kept going I would live to see everybody I knew from the old days pass on, and that is more or less what happened.

I was in New York on December 4, 1974 when television broadcasters announced the death of Millicent Hearst at her New York mansion on East 66ᵗʰ Street. Like me, Millicent had outlived all her enemies, and especially her chief nemesis, Marion Davies. Millicent even outlived two of her sons, having lost John in 1958 and then having suffered the devastating loss of her favorite son, George, in 1972.

"You've done it again," the Bitch of Buchenwald shouted at me, erasing my memories of Marion and W.R.

"You've wandered out of the time frame," she charged, her face a mask of bitterness, showing her utter contempt for my recollections. "I'll refresh your fading memory, you old goat," she said. "It's 1925 and you're at Grand Central Station in New York. You're waiting for that dago faggot, Valentino, to arrive from Chicago. He's a God damn sex pervert and vampire—possibly insane, but you're like some foolish schoolgirl still smitten with this *WOP* trash. Get back to him and get on with the story."

Too weak to oppose her, I will do just that.

*****

Disguised as an unshaven, elderly man, Rodolfo arrived at Grand Central Station. I noticed at once a severe loss of weight. He walked unsteadily. In the taxi en route to the Fifth Avenue apartment, he coughed several times and clutched his stomach. "I had some bad food on the train from Chicago," he said. I didn't believe that and urged him to check into a hospital for observation and tests. He was adamantly set against that.

Accompanied by a team of porters, who carried in his voluminous luggage, Rodolfo virtually ignored me, offering neither a hug nor a kiss. He proceeded at once to the bedroom, where he undressed before heading for his bath. When he emerged an hour later, he was stark nude and shaven. I deliberately scanned his groin area, noting several abrasions. Catching the direction of my eye, he said, "Things have been getting a little rough lately between the baron and me. For years a simple blow-job

would suffice. Now his true nature is coming out. He's demanding more and more of me. He's a deranged pervert, and he's using me like a guinea pig."

"I think he's killing you," I said. "Are you still drinking that elixir?"

"He forces me to," he said. "He demands I drink it right in his presence. I had started to throw it out."

"It's got to stop," I said. "This can't go on. Your hair is thinning. You're coughing a lot. There's something in his potion. It could be poison for all you know."

"And what do you propose I do?" he asked, irritated and impatient with me. "Spend the rest of my life in jail? I've already spent a night in jail where I was brutally sodomized."

"There are other ways," I said. "Pay him off."

"I'm so far in debt right now I'll never pay off Schenck in my lifetime."

"I have money," I said. "Let me talk to the baron. "I'll offer him a big bribe to let you alone."

"I'll see if that can be arranged, but I don't think it'll do any good."

"Let's give it a try."

He asked me to accompany him to an appointment with a well-known mystic, "the Great Dareos." Much of Hollywood had praised the ability of this crystal ball gazer, who had predicted the fortunes—much to their delight—of Joseph Schenck, Norma Talmadge, Mary Pickford, and other members of the Hollywood elite.

"C'mon, he said. "I don't want to be late for Dareos."

Dareos usually operated in Hollywood but for the moment, he had rented a suite at the Plaza Hotel. Rodolfo and I were ushered into his chambers where black-velvet draperies kept out the sunlight. In the center of the room, lit only by a meager lamp, a crystal ball awaited us. The seer ignored Rodolfo's introduction of me and demanded that we be seated at once because a vision was about to descend. "What is the question?" he asked Rodolfo.

"I have an undying love for Natacha Rambova Valentino," Rodolfo said. "What is the future of our marriage?"

Shutting his eyes tightly, Dareos threw his

head back, crinkled his forehead, then opened his eyes wide as he gazed into his crystal ball. He studied the ball for at least a minute before looking up at Rodolfo. "All is lost," he said. "Your marriage was never a marriage. Nor will it ever be in the future. You yourself are heading for disaster. A great cloud hangs over your head. You are flirting with death. In fact, at this point you'd better start running, for the Grim Reaper is on your trail and will find you sooner rather than later. There is no escaping death. As for Madam Valentino, she is fated for a longer life of bitterness and disappointment before insanity and madness will overtake her."

Rodolfo jumped up from his chair, upsetting the crystal ball, sending it crashing to the floor. "You're a liar! A fake! I don't believe a word you've said."

"The crystal never lies," Dareos shouted back at him. "You must be a man. Face the truth. You have been told the future. Don't blame me if you don't like what the future holds. I am not responsible for future events. I can only tell the victim what lies ahead."

I noted he'd strangely used the word "victim."

"You're a fraud," Rodolfo shouted at the seer. Heading for the door, he opened it and ran out into the hallway as if by doing so, he could escape Dareos' predictions.

I started to follow him until Dareos grabbed my arm holding it in almost a death grip. "That will be one-hundred dollars or you may never live to see nightfall." I reached into my wallet and handed the seer his money before fleeing from his suite.

Once he'd left the building, someone spotted Rodolfo as his natty wardrobe and white fedora had become almost a trademark. Within thirty minutes, reporters were on his trail, following him into Diamond Lil's Restaurant. Ignoring anything to do with the upcoming premiere of *The Eagle*, the press wanted to know if Natacha was going to file for a divorce. "Nothing like that," Rodolfo said. "We are the best of friends, but have differences in artistic temperament. In fact, I'll be dining with her tonight."

Natacha was staying at an apartment in New York that belonged to her aunt, Teresa Werner. Back at my Fifth Avenue apartment,

Rodolfo endlessly dialed the phone number Ullman had given him. Natacha never answered regardless of what hour Rodolfo called day or night.

Even though Natacha wasn't answering the phone, she called a press conference at Mrs. Werner's apartment. Dramatically dressed all in creamy colors from her towering turban to her high-heel shoes and silk stockings, she exuded glamour in the photographs published in the New York dailies the following morning. She announced that she was sailing for Europe to visit her parents at their villa on the French Riviera. "I don't envision a life where I sit at home baking cookies while my husband leaves for the studio at four-thirty in the morning. He gets home exhausted some time after midnight. He asks me to answer mail from lovesick females from Oshkosh to Kalamazoo. That is no life for an artist such as myself."

If I'd dreamed of a love-nest on Fifth Avenue with Rodolfo, I was sadly mistaken. The Great Lover wasn't interested in sex. He coughed violently and still refused medical attention. He spent most of the night roaming the floor, not even bothering to put on his robe. It brought back memories of Wallace Reid wandering this same apartment shortly before his death.

Rodolfo's mental condition was deteriorating, as was Charlie's. But I suspected Charlie was a greater survivor than Rodolfo, and that The Little Tramp would pull himself back from the brink. In Rodolfo's case, I feared for him. Before taking the train from California to the East Coast, he told me that he'd been drinking and driving recklessly. He'd been arrested once for speeding along Sunset Boulevard, and the story had made the newspapers.

"It wasn't the drink that made me drive like that," he told me. "I had wanted to kill myself that night."

"But you have a glorious future to look forward to," I said in protest.

"How can you say that?" he asked, turning on me in anger. "You heard what my future holds for me."

"That's bullshit," I said. "Dareos is a fake."

"He told the truth."

The press reported that Natacha was sailing

for the port of Cherbourg, where she'd take the train to join her mother at the Plaza Athénée in Paris. Her mother, Mrs. Hudnut, told the press in Paris that, "Mr. Valentino has no intention of divorcing my daughter."

On hearing that, Rodolfo the following day in New York told the press, "Mrs. Valentino cannot be my wife and have a career at the same time. For the sake of her husband, a woman must abandon her own career and devote her life to her husband's pursuits. That was the way I was raised, and I think my mother was right."

For his stay in New York, Rodolfo mostly hid out in the Fifth Avenue apartment because he attracted mobs wherever he went unless he was in disguise. When Beulah Livingstone, a publicist for United Artists working out of New York, called and invited us out, Rodolfo accepted for the both of us. She had obtained tickets to see the film, *Sunny*, starring Marilyn Miller at the New Amsterdam Theater.

At the time Miller enjoyed a wild homosexual following the way another Marilyn, Monroe, would decades from now.

Rodolfo, along with Livingstone and myself, had been seated in the movie palace for no more than five minutes when the buzz about Valentino's presence resounded through the theater. Everyone was turning in their seats or peering over the balcony for a look at the star, newly arrived from Hollywood.

Within minutes a mob began to surround him. Rodolfo rose and politely asked the crowds to depart so that the curtain could be pulled back and the film shown. No one heeded his request, even though he promised to meet in the lobby and sign autographs after the showing.

The crowds grew thicker and more unruly. I asked one of the ushers to beg the manager to call for a police escort. I feared we'd never get past the mob that had assembled inside the theater. Rodolfo took Livingstone's arm and suggested that we leave.

It was all he could do to fight his way up the aisle and into the lobby. There the mob had grown larger. This time it wasn't the typical crowd but a multitude of Marilyn Miller's homosexual fans who had descended from the balcony. I'd never seen fans this much out of

control, and I sensed they didn't want just an autograph from Rodolfo but a piece of him.

It began when one ravenous young man with long red hair removed a pair of scissors from an attaché case he was carrying and snipped off the major portion of Rodolfo's tie. That act alone set off a feeding frenzy, as some one-hundred young men surrounded Rodolfo, grabbing and tearing at his clothes for souvenirs. Many opportunists took advantage of the situation to reach and feel the size of his genitals.

With hands coming at him from all directions, Rodolfo fell to the floor. I tried to rescue him but was knocked down and kicked. Livingstone had run screaming into a Broadway alley.

The men were literally stripping every piece of clothing from Rodolfo. From what I could see, his legs and arms were bare. Soon even his underwear was ripped from his body, leaving him completely exposed before the eyes of this mob.

At the sound of police rushing into the lobby, the crowd departed. One captain took off his coat and used it to cover Rodolfo's nudity. Four men carried the injured actor up the stairs to the manager's office. I was allowed to follow behind when Rodolfo called out for me.

In the office the manager borrowed some street clothes from an usher and allowed Rodolfo to get dressed in these ill-fitting garments. A doctor arrived and quickly examined Rodolfo, reporting only minor cuts and bruises. Livingstone was reported missing, last seen running down Broadway with her gown ripped and torn.

The mob, not just the homosexuals this time, but patrons from neighboring theaters had gathered outside. The police captain told Rodolfo it would be very difficult to get him safely into a limousine. Nevertheless, the policemen cleared a path for Rodolfo, and we were ushered into the limousine. But the police could not control the mobs forming around the vehicle. "I've got an idea," Rodolfo shouted at me. From the floor he picked up three baskets of bright metal souvenir coins, which had been minted for publicity purposes for the premiere of *The Eagle*. "Throw them at the crowds," he shouted at me. I rolled down my window and began tossing the coins at the hysterical mass. The crowd scrambled for the metal coins, opening up a small river through which the chauffeur could escape before the mob formed again.

On hearing news of the attack on Rodolfo, the mayor of New York ordered heavy police guards for the premiere of *The Eagle* at the Mark Strand Theater. He called Rodolfo and said he feared a riot. At first Rodolfo wasn't going to go, but Livingstone's UA publicists would not hear of this and demanded that Rodolfo put in an appearance.

At the world premiere of *The Eagle*, it looked as if half of New York's finest were on hand to usher Rodolfo into the theater. He was accompanied by Livingstone, and I trailed along, pretending to be a publicist for UA. *The New York Times* reported the next day that the audience was in "a gay mood."

When Rodolfo appeared on the screen as a Cossack, the applause was thunderous. It was even greater after the curtain was pulled and Rodolfo appeared on the stage to thank the audience, his eyes misting.

One New York film critic wrote the next day, "At long last freed of the influence of Natacha Rambova, Mr. Valentino as the Russian Robin Hood has thrilled audiences again as he did in *The Sheik*. No longer a powder-puff, he's a real he-man in this picture, evoking the best screen roles of Douglas Fairbanks. *The Eagle* can be viewed as the comeback of Mr. Valentino."

I went with him on November 10, 1925 to the Federal Building in New York where he applied for citizenship papers. He was nattily dressed in a gray Fedora, beige and white shoes, a steel-gray suit, and a gray cravat. He gave his weight as 165 pounds, although he weighed only 150 at the time. He said he was five feet eleven and a half inches tall. He had wanted to say six feet, but the immigration official insisted on an accurate measurement. For some reason, he listed New York as his permanent address.

En route to Europe, Natacha told reporters that she was going to become a motion-picture star herself, appearing in an aptly named picture, *When Love Grows Cold*. One male reporter asked her, "Do you think a sheik makes an ideal husband?"

"How would I know?" she replied. "I've never been married to a sheik, nor do I intend to marry one. Being carried off to a tent in a desert is not my idea of a good time."

An attorney from Quebec, of all places, Benjamin H. Connor, announced that Natacha would file for a divorce in a French court upon her arrival in France. And since Rodolfo apparently wanted the divorce too, he would have to reside in France for a while to meet the requirements of French divorce laws.

On November 14, Rodolfo sailed aboard the *Leviathan* for another return to Europe. I saw him off at the pier, but there had been no intimacy between us even though we'd slept nude in the same bed in the Fifth Avenue apartment. When not coughing, he was drinking and smoking a lot.

Knowing reporters would be there at the pier to see him off, he was splendidly dressed again in green and gray, wearing a suede topcoat with an Australian opossum collar and cuffs. Before his departure, I'd given him a platinum cigarette case and lighter with a coiled cobra in honor of his previous film. To the question of whether he was still in love with Natacha, he replied. "Let us not speak of such things. A man has his pride. I will spend the rest of my life alone without the comfort of a woman."

As I told him good-bye, he said that he was going to study scripts in which he'd portray such historical figures as Cesare Borgia or Benvenuto Cellini. "The script sent by Schenck that I most adore is that of the life of Leonardo da Vinci," he said to me. "I don't know if you are aware of this, but in a previous life I was the great Leonardo."

When I saw photographs of him after his landing in Southampton, he looked much better and had put on a bit of weight after his ocean crossing. I assumed that away from the baron he was no longer taking that elixir which debilitated him.

Reports reached me that *The Eagle* had been as big a success in London as in New York, and that both women and homosexuals had avidly pursued Rodolfo, trying to strip him of his clothing. Although it wasn't reported in the press, a remarkable thing was happening. Male fans were crowding around Rodolfo and blatantly reaching out to fondle his genitals. I had never heard of that happening with any other actor.

At a château near Fontainebleau, I eagerly awaited Rodolfo's arrival in France when he'd cabled that he was taking a boat train from the English coast near Dover.

After his arrival at the Gare du Nord, where he was mobbed by hundreds of French women waiting in the bitter December cold, he was herded into a limousine and driven to Fountainebleau. His face scratched, his clothing ripped, Rodolfo appeared at the château and fell into my arms once the doors were locked. "I'm feeling better than I did in New York," he told me. "You can use me for sex since I know that's all you think about."

As he undressed for his bath, he told me of his departure from the train station. "I think three women were injured. They threw themselves in front of the wheels of the car. Some of them tried to crawl on the roof. Others clawed with bright-red fingernails at the window to my car, as if they were going to scratch me to death. Every woman in the world wants me except the woman of my dreams, my darling Natacha."

At the château I received a cable from Ramon who was in Rome for costume fittings for *Ben-Hur*. He warned that I must not bring Rodolfo to the Eternal City. "The police are receiving death threats," he'd cabled. "The young Fascists are threatening to harm him. They are urging Mussolini to have Italy boycott all his films. When word reached Rome that Rudy had applied for American citizenship, a riot broke out at newspaper offices."

Rodolfo had grown very depressed at this news from his former country. He said nothing all afternoon, but sat by the window looking at the rain fall outside on the grounds. He was learning the downside of fame. Before six o'clock that evening, he rose on wobbly legs. "I cannot go to bed with a woman ever again," he told me, "At least one I haven't known before. All over the world women have deified me. They have bestowed on me the omnipotence of a god. What if I take a woman to bed and disappoint her, as even the most masculine of men will do at times? She'd announce my failure in bed to the press or use

it as blackmail over me. I am only a man. I have my physical limitations."

That night as he cuddled close to me in bed and whispered in my ear. "The world must never know this. But since my failing health, I can no longer achieve a full erection in masturbation. I have not experienced an orgasm in a long time. I have decided to break my rule with you. Tonight and tomorrow, and then in the days following that, I want you to fuck me. If Natacha has turned me into a woman, so be it."

I was eager to enter him, and he responded with incredible passion to my penetration. As I was plowing deep within him, I noticed that he was able to achieve a full erection. When I exploded, he erupted too. He kissed me passionately, with no blood-letting on my neck. It was as if our roles were reversed, as if I had become his master, the fucker, with him as the fuckee.

Later he went into the bathroom and applied heavy lipstick to his lips and rouge to his cheeks. He put on a pair of Natacha's undergarments, which he'd brought with him from Hollywood. When he came to the bed, I looked up in total surprise.

"Tonight I want you to play the role of Rudolph Valentino, personifying me in the role of *The Sheik*," he said. "I will be Natacha. I want you to rape me violently. The more I scream in pain, the more I will be enjoying the seduction."

I thought for only a second before getting up to put on the clothing he said he'd laid out for me in the dressing room. "Your wish, my command."

From the blood-letting to the cross-dressing, Rodolfo always held a surprise for me, even if I did worry about his sanity or lack of it.

The next morning he woke in my arms, crying. "The dominance I was subjected to by Natacha has made me impotent."

"You exploded last night," I said. "I should know. I drank every drop."

"You don't understand," he said. "That was the first orgasm I've achieved lately. Sometimes I can masturbate and make myself hard but when I enter a woman I grow limp. The world's greatest screen lover and the most desirable man on the planet cannot even achieve a puny erection."

That night we were entertained lavishly by one of the wealthiest Arabs in the world, Prince Habile-Lotfallah, who was urging Rodolfo to come to Egypt where the prince would finance a production of *Antony and Cleopatra* in Cairo. "All of Egypt will be at your feet," he promised Rodolfo. "I've already cleared it with the government."

Rodolfo's eyes lit up, and he seemed eager for the project. "You do not know this, but in a previous life I was Antony."

"And I was Cleo," I said to the prince, who laughed and patted my arm.

Rodolfo, however, did not find my comment funny. You'll excuse Durango's bad humor," Rodolfo said. "He's only an American." He glared at me as if to tell me to shut up. "The truth of the matter is this: The soul of my beloved Natacha once inhabited the body of Cleopatra. As Antony and Cleopatra, Natacha and I will achieve immortality on the screen."

Later that night when Rodolfo had gone downstairs to the bar to drink more wine, I received a call from the handsome Egyptian prince. Since he'd been fondling me half the night under the table, I knew what he had in mind. When I entered his suite, it was dark. He pulled me to him and kissed me long, deep, and hard. When he let up for air, he said, "In Egypt I am known as the greatest seducer of women in the Arab world. But when I come to the more decadent west, only a blond teenage boy will do for me." As his hand went under my belt, encasing one of the cheeks of my ass, I knew how this rich Egyptian prince planned to get his pleasure for the night. Four hours later, bruised and battered, I stumbled back into the suite I shared with Rodolfo. I found him passed out and fully dressed on the living room floor. I'm sure he hadn't missed me.

Slipping into Paris secretly, Rodolfo and I arrived the following night at the Plaza Athénée where Natacha had stayed before her departure for the Riviera. There shortly before midnight a tall man in a black cloak approached us in the palm-studded lobby. From his dress, he looked like he was from Transylvania. He bore a resemblance in stature and dress to Rodolfo's German baron on the West Coast.

"Let me introduce myself, Mr. Valentino," he said. "I am the Baron Imre Lukatz. It is my intention to marry Miss Vilma Banky. I understand you have been seriously involved with my intended in Hollywood and that you've confided in friends your intention to marry her. I cannot allow that."

His male honor wounded, Rodolfo announced to him that he would marry whomever he wished.

"Then, Mr. Valentino, I will meet you at dawn in the Bois de Boulogne. You are nothing but a seducer and a pimp!"

At those words Rodolfo moved menacingly toward the baron, planning to strike him in the face. I restrained Rodolfo.

"I do not engage in street brawls with cheap Italian trash like you," the baron said. "A peasant with no manners. Gentlemen of honor such as myself settle disputes over women only with swords."

Back in our suite, I pleaded with Rodolfo not to accept the baron's challenge. "My honor has been insulted," he said. "You are but a pansy boy, and you do not know of honor among men. I will be there at dawn. I will kill Lukatz."

"But you're not in love with Vilma," I said. "And you probably never were. You just saw her a few times. She means nothing to you. Besides, I hear from the Hollywood grapevine that Vilma is dating Rod La Rocque."

"That Valentino impersonator," Rodolfo said, looking at me with contempt. He locked himself in our bedroom and wouldn't come out despite my pounding on the door. I called a United Artists official in Paris, waking him up. "Who is Baron Imre Lukatz?"

The publicist said he'd get back to me and indeed his call came into the Plaza Athénée around four o'clock that morning, only hours before the duel was scheduled.

Lukatz was no fake baron but a real one. "He's reported to be the richest man in Budapest," the publicist said. "He fell in love with Banky in Hungary but went off to military service. Apparently Banky had agreed to marry him. But once he went into the military, she took the train to Berlin where she became a star in Germany. That's when Samuel Goldwyn met her and offered her a contract to come to Hollywood. Lukatz goes around Europe raging that he can't stand to see Hollywood make a whore out of his future wife who's playing love scenes with sexual perverts like Valentino on the screen."

"Thanks for the information," I said. "Apparently Lukatz had seen Rodolfo make love to Banky in *The Eagle*, and he'd become infuriated, tracking him down in Paris for the intended duel.

At dawn at the Bois de Boulogne, I pleaded with Rodolfo for the final time. He pushed me away from him and tested his sword in the air. This did not seem like real life. It was more like a movie made by Doug Fairbanks. The vapors were rising from the cold French ground as the duelists met. Rodolfo had asked me to be his second. It was ludicrous. I knew nothing about swords. Nonetheless, to pacify him, I agreed to stand in as his second.

As the men moved toward each other, the noble baron apparently lost his nerve. He dropped his sword and bowed down in front of Rodolfo. "Mr. Valentino, I ask that you accept my apologies. I have been very wrong to confront you. I have just learned that Miss Banky is not what I thought she was. I understand from a source that my intended much prefers the company of ladies to that of gentlemen. No lesbian is worth dying for." With that, he rose from the ground and departed, never to be seen again by Rodolfo. The only casualty Rodolfo suffered from that early morning encounter was a head cold.

That night was our last together, and in some respects it was our most tender. No violence, no blood. Just gentle lovemaking and caressing. At least with me, Rodolfo was no longer impotent. He'd entered me repeatedly but also hadn't put a lock on his own ass. For the first time I felt we were both men and equal partners in our love-making.

It was sad as I said good-bye to him at the train station. I was heading south to Rome, but he was also leaving, journeying east to Berlin where he was a popular figure on the screen.

Suddenly I spotted porters carrying at least twenty trunks. I knew that much luggage could only belong to a film star. And indeed I was right. To my surprise, Mae Murray showed up on the same platform. She too was taking the train to Berlin.

Rodolfo pretended it was a coincidence that he was going to be on the same train with his former love. "We meet quite by accident," he said to Mae, bowing low and kissing her hand, although I feared that might evoke memories of von Stroheim for her.

Mae kissed me on the mouth and shared one or two fleeting memories of *The Merry Widow* before she got on the train.

He had begged me to accompany Mae and him to Berlin, but I turned him down. I actually turned down Rodolfo. Ramon Novarro occupied my thoughts these days. Earlier I'd warned Rodolfo not to go to Germany because I'd heard that young National Socialists would be waiting there to protest his arrival in Berlin. *The Four Horsemen of the Apocalypse* was still showing, and the socialists objected to that film's portrait of Prussians as brutal cowards.

While Rodolfo was getting restored to his bachelorhood, I took the train heading for Rome. The Hearst organization had arranged for me to have the most lavish compartment in my journey south. Even so, I felt lonely and wished I had someone to share my luxurious quarters with. But my thoughts were no longer with Rodolfo. All I could think about was getting to Rome and into the arms of Ben-Hur himself, one Mr. Ramon Novarro.

As the train reached a suburb of Paris, the steward knocked on my door. "Sorry to disturb you, Mr. Jones, but we have a full train and a most honored guest boarded the train late in Paris and does not have a reservation. I understand he's very important in America, and we'd like to accommodate him if we could. Since you have an extra bed, would you consider sharing your compartment with this very important person?"

Thinking it was a film star, I said I might if I could meet the man first.

"I'm sure you already know him," the steward said. "He's Mr. F. Scott Fitzgerald."

*****

Sharing the cramped compartment with me, F. Scott Fitzgerald, although drunk, was all charm and grace. It was exciting for me to talk to an American author as a change of pace from my usual diet of film stars. There was a kindness to him, a sense of gaiety, and an all-enveloping warmth, even though I sensed he was in great pain. I'd read endless Sunday supplements about Scott and his flamboyant wife, Zelda.

As we strolled to the bar on the train, Scott talked endlessly as if his voice had been silent for a long time. I was flattered that he'd heard of me and my sister, Lotte Lee. He proposed that I tell him the story of my life and that I introduce him to my sister, Lotte Lee. "I think you two would make an incredible story of two characters that exemplify the madness of the Twenties. I'm the man to make sense out of that drama."

Over several drinks Scott seemed comfortable with his passions, and he was filled with enthusiasm but also a tenderness toward life. As a writer, he was no Louella Parsons looking for the gossipy anecdote. He seemed more interested in understanding why people acted like they did instead of what they actually did.

"Each morning I awake into a world of ineffable toploftiness and promise." He actually used those words. "Every month of my life counts frantically, and every day seems a cudgel in the flight for happiness in a race against time," he said.

He told me of his latest battle against time, an attempt to spend a winter in Rome with his wife. He was eager to learn of my assignment by Hearst to record the behind-the-scenes drama going on in Ben-Hur's production. He begged me to take him around with me to the sets to meet the people responsible for the film. "Not just the stars and the director," he said, "but the people who are really making the film." I promised that I would, and, in fact, was looking forward to hanging out with the darling of Jazz Age writers. That would be another feather in my headdress, which was already top heavy and beginning to look like some ceremonial trophy collection since I'd first arrived in Hollywood.

In our compartment, Scott wasn't ashamed to parade around naked in front of me although I'd hinted several times that I was a homosexual and wouldn't be opposed to a fling with him. Amazingly, his genitals looked like a replica of those of Clark Gable's. Like Clark's pecker, I didn't think Scott could rise more than five inches even in the heat of passion.

"I saw you staring at my dick," Scott said to me one night after we'd boarded a new train at the Italian frontier. "I haven't been taking off my clothes to entice you into a sexual adventure. I'm not that way, although on a dare I did let a young guy at Princeton go down on me. I was drunk and didn't get off on the experience and haven't repeated it."

"You're not drunk now," I said. "Do you want me to try it? The second time is more fun than the first. One's too nervous then to enjoy it."

"I'm sure it would be nice, but no thank you," Scott said. "I do want you to look at my dick and give an opinion of it."

"Exactly what opinion do you want?" I asked. "If you'd let me sample it, I'd be in a much better opinion to review it."

"How would you say I measure up?" he asked. "Average?" A look of daunting pain crossed his brow. "Less than average?"

"Average," I said. That was a lie. It was less than average.

"I don't think you're telling the truth. I've seen you nude when you're getting dressed. You look like you have six inches when you're soft. I can't imagine how much more you rise when hard. I measure slightly less than five inches when I'm fully erect."

"Size doesn't count," I said, not really believing that, although I found Clark Gable terribly sexy even without a big basket.

"Zelda tells me it does," he said. "Our whole marriage is threatened."

"I don't understand," I said. "Because your dick is small."

"She was always satisfied with it before," he said. "Before meeting me, she'd had two affairs with boys from North Carolina. They were brothers. From what I gathered, they were hung pretty much like myself. When she experienced her third penis—namely mine—she just assumed all men were hung more or less the same. She wasn't as sophisticated then as she is now."

"What happened?" I asked.

"She fell in love with this French naval flyer, Edouard Josanne. I've even read what she's written about him. She's turning it into a novel. She is like a lovesick schoolgirl, writing about the muscularity of a lean, bronzed body in a starched uniform. She claims he's a sun person and that I'm a moon person."

"I gather that this French flyer, Monsieur Josanne, is hung to his knees and that Zelda now has a different opinion of male anatomy—that is, that all men are not born equal."

"You've nailed it," he said. "She claims that when I penetrate her, it is a mere tickle. That when Josanne penetrates her, he plunges into her lower depths and is deeply satisfying to her."

"Does that mean the marriage is over?" I asked.

"Not yet anyway," he said. "We're hoping that a winter in the cold city of Rome will bring us together again. We'll be away from the distractions of New York, Paris, and the Riviera. We'll just have each other to rely on. We'll survive this winter or it will be the end of us."

"Good luck," I said. Having not had sex since Rodolfo left for Berlin, I eyed Scott's genitalia once more. "My invitation is extended again," I said staring at his crotch.

"I don't think so," he said. "Some other time. Let's get dressed and get some bracing fresh air at the back of the train."

That "some other time" came shortly after midnight when we'd returned to our compartment drunk from the bar. I helped Scott out of his clothes. When I'd tossed him nude and drunk on the bed, I descended with lips and tongue between his legs. At first he tried to push me away, but I overpowered him. After a brief struggle, he accepted the inevitable, no doubt sensing my determination.

Sad to say, although I'd worked him up to a full erection twice, I never got him to erupt. He was far too drunk. But the experience hadn't been a total loss for me. Scott may not have been the greatest stud I'd ever deflowered, but he was the tastiest. I wondered if all Princeton boys from back East tasted that good, and promised myself a trip to the campus

to find out one day.

Once in Rome we said good-bye with promises to get together soon. He invited Ramon and me to join him and Zelda at the Grand Hotel for dinner the following night. I told him I'd be staying in Ramon's suite at the Excelsior.

"I hear that Novarro is a homosexual," he said. "I guess your staying with him confirms it."

"More or less," I said enigmatically.

When I called the Grand early in the evening of the following day to firm up the arrangements for dinner, I was told that Mr. and Mrs. Fitzgerald had gone to Naples for a few days. The concierge didn't know when they would return.

Forgetting about Scott for the moment, I was surprised three nights later when he called our suite at one o'clock in the morning. Ramon turned over in bed. "You deal with it," he said. "I've got to get up early in the morning."

It seemed Scott had landed in jail and needed money to bail himself out. Arriving at the foul-smelling Roman jail, I had to spend five-hundred American dollars—not lire—to get Scott released.

He appeared drunken and unshaven when released into my custody. In a taxi headed back to his hotel, he told me that he'd had an argument with a driver who had overcharged him. "One thing led to another. This policeman interfered. I slugged him and landed in jail."

In the lobby of the Grand in front of the Italian staff, Scott invited me to the bar after proclaiming he hated all Italians. "The country is a dead lane," he proclaimed over some bourbon. "Everything that needs to have been done was done and that was a long time ago. Whoever is deceived by the pseudo activity under this fascist, Mussolini, is deceived by the spasmodic last jerk of a corpse."

Within two days when I called the Grand, I learned that Scott and Zelda had left for Capri, with no forwarding address. Ten days later a letter arrived postmarked Capri. Scott was inviting me to spend a week or so with Zelda and him on the island, which he had found more to his liking than Rome.

"My new novel, *The Great Gatsby*, is about to be published," he said. "I'll send you a copy. You must read it. It's my masterpiece. At last I have done something Hemingway so far has failed to do: I have written the Great American Novel."

The water bubbling in the *Ben-Hur* stewpot prevented me from accepting the invitation of the Fitzgeralds. I was to encounter him again in the Thirties—*sans Zelda*—when both of us were living at Alla Nazimova's old "Garden of Alla," now converted into a hotel known as "The Garden of Allah." But that's another memoir.

After my second day in Rome I had fallen madly in love with someone who had been in my life for years. In Hollywood, I'd had repeated bouts of sex with this handsome guy but didn't really love him.

As the winter sun shone into our suite at the Excelsior Hotel, he woke up with his hair tousled and a little gleam in his beautiful brown eyes, which I hoped I had put there the night before. I walked toward him, my cock and balls swinging. Those eager eyes told me he needed another session with me before reporting to work at the Roman studio.

I too was eager to taste the lips and other body parts of the only man in the world I loved at that moment.

Ramon Novarro.

*****

Not since D.W. Griffith's *Intolerance* had there ever been a movie spectacle to equal *Ben-Hur*. It would go on to become one of the greatest silent pictures of all time, in spite of Hollywood's biggest error in the script. June Mathis, the original writer who'd scripted *The Four Horsemen of the Apocalypse*, had placed the film's two most memorable sequences—the battle at sea and the chariot race—in the first half of the movie, making the latter part seem dull by comparison.

If the film were ever made, with all its costly delays, the smart money in Hollywood felt General Lee Wallace's flamboyant best-seller would be a hit at the box office. "How could *Ben-Hur* lose?" was the question most often asked. Descriptions of men and women

involved in violence and eroticism filled every page. You had a Roman galley battling a pirate ship; conflicts between broad-chested warriors in armor; a chariot race, and the birth and crucifixion of Jesus Christ.

Until *Ben-Hur*, Mathis had been the most brilliant scriptwriter in Hollywood, dining out on how she personally had made a star out of Rudolph Valentino until Natacha Rambova came along to ruin his career.

My old buddy, thick-dicked Joe Godsol, had originally controlled the picture when he'd been a power at the Goldwyn Studio before the company was finally merged under the grander umbrella of Metro-Goldwyn-Mayer.

Godsol's mistake had been in believing that the judgment of Mathis was still intact. She had influenced him to cast George Walsh, the brother of the one-eyed director, Raoul Walsh, as the star. George had a grand physique, and would have been a physical match for Francis X. Bushman in their broad-shouldered armor scenes together. The only problem was, George's talent didn't match his muscular body.

Mathis had been the first woman in Hollywood to employ the casting couch. Before her, the couch was used only for women enticed there by male producers or directors. To get the part of *Ben-Hur*, George, or so everyone knew, was pumping Mathis nightly. But the romance ended when both of them were fired. Suddenly, George no longer defined the physically unappealing Mathis as a sex object.

Godsol had also listened to Mathis when she'd insisted that the alcoholic Englishman, Charles Brabin, husband of Theda Bara, be hired as the director. The footage he sent back to Hollywood, when viewed by Irving Thalberg and Louis B. Mayer, was seen as garbage. Both studio moguls ordered the footage destroyed.

Back in Rome, Mathis had lingered around the city until she'd found a lover even handsomer than George. He was an Italian named Silvio Balboni. Who knows what she promised him other than her overripe honeypot?

Whatever Mathis was holding out to Silvano Balboni must have been enticing. She would soon marry him. If I didn't have Ramon, I would have married Silvio myself. He was sexy and appealing, and with Mathis' career slipping, I figured I could entice the hustler with some sort of offer, but I was too busy to pursue that.

From the start, *Ben-Hur* became the most mismanaged film in Hollywood's history up to then. Even the trouble surrounding the making of *Cleopatra* in the 1960s, starring Burton & Taylor, was a mere party game compared to the monumental disaster looming in the Roman studios of 1925 where *Ben-Hur* was attempting to become a film.

At long last, Ramon had gotten his wish. He was to star as *Ben-Hur*, replacing George Walsh. Ramon's co-star was Francis X. Bushman whom he had not seen since we'd "serviced" Bushman's mammoth cock at his private mansion. In the ever-changing world of Hollywood, Ramon now enjoyed the same star status that Bushman once had. *Ben-Hur* represented Ramon's big chance but for Bushman the Roman epic was viewed as a virtual comeback picture for this now faded star.

Even though the events surrounding this spectacle were most often a disaster, especially the "monsoon season" beating down on Rome, my days spent in the arms of Ramon were the happiest of my life up to then. Guys like Ramon and I can know each other for years. Then, in a flash, you realize you're in love. Maybe it was all tied in with his being—for the moment at least—the biggest movie star on the planet, appearing in the greatest spectacle of all time, the notorious *Ben-Hur*.

But I think it was something different. When he'd raced to greet me as I stepped into his suite at the Excelsior Hotel, and when he'd tripped over an Oriental carpet, I caught him in my arms, falling to the floor with him. We'd rolled over each other hugging and kissing. When we'd come to a standstill, and he'd looked up at me with the world's most expressive eyes, he'd told me without saying anything that he was mine and I could do anything I wanted with him. "I exist just to give pleasure to you," he whispered in my ear. Who wouldn't love a beautiful man who whispered that to you?

Ramon was no longer the little Mexican hustler who hired out for private parties and tested out every casting couch in town hoping for some producer or director to give him a break in films. He was a full-fledged movie star, dressing and acting like one unless he was in bed with me when he became meek and submissive. In bed, the film star veneer faded away, and he became a little kid again eager to please me. He'd become the most unselfish lover I'd ever known. Everything he did was seemingly to give me pleasure. Such love and devotion only inspired me to love him back— sometimes tenderly, sometimes with brute force. He welcomed whatever maneuver I had in store for him. I never rose from Ramon's gilded bed in that suite without being totally satisfied. Before getting up, I tingled with thrills throughout my body as Ramon made love to every part of me. He neglected no zone of my body, applying equal attention to all areas before the grand finale when I topped him. That he loved most of all, completely surrendering to me.

Sometimes I'd be sitting on the terrace during the few sunny days we had between rains. Drinking my coffee, I would feel Ramon taking each of my toes and loving and sucking them tenderly. That always produced an erection on me regardless of how many times I'd pounded him the night before.

After impersonations as Lotte Lee, after servicing Hollywood straight studs with no relief for myself other than my enjoyment of them, and after my brutalizing experiences with Rodolfo and his increasing sadism, I had at last found a lover in Ramon who made me feel like a man. Almost daily in his presence I seemed to grow more masculine.

Without meaning to and without knowing better at the time, I found myself treating Ramon like my best girl instead of my male lover. The more I did that, the more he liked it. I even opened car doors for him and lit his cigarettes. As each day went by, I began to feel I owned him and grew incredibly possessive of him. He bowed to my judgment in all decisions. Whatever was proposed to him, he said he had to check with me for my approval or rejection.

Our mornings began early when we were both driven to a gym where we lifted weights to build up our muscles. I wanted to look good and to develop my body more, even though that meant I could never appear as Lotte Lee again, since as I had grown older my body had become too muscular. My teen days were over, and no one would mistake me for a girl again. I had blossomed into a lookalike for a matinee idol, watching my friends and lovers become stars, without ever appearing as that matinee idol myself. My dreams of movie stardom were at an end.

For Ramon, bodybuilding was a professional challenge. After all, he'd be practically nude in the film for many scenes, and he'd be photographed opposite Francis X. Bushman, who was known for his perfect physique and muscles. Ramon performed elaborate exercises to develop his shape chest, arms, and legs.

MGM had hired a trainer, Vittorio Anka, for Ramon, and together with my lover we ran for five miles a day while the trainer followed us in a horse-drawn buggy. Sometimes the run would be followed by us getting into a row boat, to go up and down the Tiber, building up Ramon's biceps.

Ramon had been furious the first morning he had reported to wardrobe. The department was handled by Irving Wallace, a former stage manager from New York who used to work with William S. Hart in productions of Shakespeare's plays. The old man looked skeptically at Ramon when introduced to him. "They didn't tell me MGM has cast *Ben-Hur* as a midget," Wallace said. Ramon at five feet, eight inches was sensitive about his height, especially when stacked up against that giant of a man, Francis X. I almost punched Wallace for insulting my lover but a compromise was reached. Wardrobe produced a series of footwear for Ramon to wear in the film. Now it can be told. Throughout much of the filming of *Ben-Hur*, Ramon wore high heels, which explains why you rarely see his feet in the movie. Ramon accepted the high heels but complained to Wallace about the wig he was forced to wear. "It makes me look like a bad hair version of Pola Negri."

When not on the set, Ramon enjoyed the adulation he was receiving from the public. His picture was in the dailies practically every morning. He decided to engage a horse and carriage during our entire stay in Rome. For some reason he called the horse "General Diaz," and always brought the animal rare treats to eat. Although F. Scott Fitzgerald had balked

at getting overcharged and had ended up in jail, Ramon accepted this larcenous Roman practice with grace. "I'm a movie star," he told me. "We're always overcharged," a sentiment once expressed to me by Dorothy Gish.

On the set of *Ben-Hur*, I realized I'd have to circulate since I couldn't devote every dispatch to Ramon, although he did dominate many of the articles I was producing for the Hearst organization. I had been hoping to encounter Francis X., but he was touring across Europe after being told that he wouldn't be needed for several weeks.

Ramon introduced me to his co-star in the film, May McAvoy, playing Esther. Accustomed as I was to the likes of such haughty empresses as Gloria Swanson and Mary Pickford, I found McAvoy unassuming and very petite. She stood only four feet ten, making even Swanson look like a giant compared to her. Carl Sandberg had called McAvoy a "star-eyed goddess," but I was less than impressed. Even though the critic, Edward Wagenknecht, had compared McAvoy to Italy's greatest actress, Eleanora Duse, McAvoy struck me as just another fresh-faced ingénue. McAvoy had been sent over to replace Gertrude Oldstead, Rodolfo's co-star in *Cobra*.

Once again I underestimated talent. A dedicated professional, McAvoy would go on to star in some forty films before the Talkies ended her career. This pixie-like creature, with the skin of Dresden china, an Irish-American born in New York, would found the Academy of Motion Picture Arts and Sciences in 1927.

Unlike many of the actresses I knew in Hollywood—some no more than prostitutes—McAvoy had a puritanical streak, although she did use curse words. She told me how she'd turned down repeated advances from Darryl F. Zanuck, then a rising producer at Warner Brothers. "He believes in the casting couch," McAvoy said. "I do not. Cecil B. DeMille wanted me to wear only a fig leaf in *Adam's Rib*, and I flatly refused to appear in such a disgraceful manner on the screen. I also refused to let him shoot scenes of my feet. As you can see, they are rather delicate and he practically drooled over them. Have you ever heard of anything so disgusting?"

She listened in utter fascination as I told of

Mae Murray undergoing those foot fetish scenes in *The Merry Widow*. The future Hollywood gossip columnist in me was already in full bloom.

"I've met the Pope," McAvoy said. "It was arranged through my lawyer. I even met Mussolini at the bar of the Excelsior Hotel where I'm staying with my mother. Would you believe it? The filthy dago son-of-a-bitch propositioned me as if I were a common whore. Thank God my mother rescued me from that fat pig."

"Better be careful," I warned. "He runs the country. From what I hear, he operates like a Roman emperor did. You know, types like Nero. If they saw something on the hoof who appealed to them, they commanded that person—man or woman—to their bed."

"There's no way that Mary McAvoy is going to do that," she said. "I've always been a lady and I plan to remain one even if I am a film actress."

After my interview, much of which I couldn't print back in those tamer days of journalism, I wished her well. As she walked away, I did not contemplate much future for her, especially with her strict moral upbringing. She would be cast, however, in a historic Talkie, *The Jazz Singer*, although she didn't utter a single word of dialogue.

She did, in fact, make a few Talkies for Warners, but all of them bombed. Rumors spread in Hollywood that she had a lisp and a shrill voice. McAvoy blamed the failure of her voice on the screen to faulty recordings on Vitaphone discs. Actually I remembered her voice as having a lilting tone, no lisp at all. But as long as films were silent she could be a star with her luminous blue eyes and her warm and genuine smile.

I didn't think I had to worry about her making a play for my lover, Ramon, even though, as Esther, McAvoy played the love interest, the daughter of Ben-Hur's servant.

The next day Ramon wasn't needed at the studio, and he asked me to drive him to Pompeii so he could view the ruins.

Running from his adoring Roman fans, mostly female, Ramon deliberately went unshaven and disguised to the ruins at Pompeii. But while we were ordering an espresso in a dingy café, three buses filled with overage American tourists arrived at the same spot. Ramon was immediately recognized in spite of his attempts to conceal himself. We fled with our guide into the safe precincts of the Lupanare, which was off-limits to women.

The diggers who excavated Pompeii had discovered this little villa with pornographic frescoes, some depicting various positions of intercourse between men and women and one showing Hercules with a large penis, enough meat to rival Francis X. himself.

Our guide told us that the Lupanare had been used as a setting for orgies in the heyday of Pompeii. He explained that men or women who wanted to be seduced by gladiators came here to be deflowered. "The gladiators were hired not just to kill animals in the arena, but to satisfy the libido of sex-crazed women and lusty homosexual men," the guide said.

Ramon had been turned on by the frescoes and the imagined orgies that once took place here. He bribed the guide to keep the Lupanare locked for an hour or so, and the young man gladly agreed, winking at me before he went out and shut the door.

Ramon pulled off all his clothes and invited me to follow him. He lay down on a marble slab and asked me to envision him as a vestal virgin, with me being the gladiator shipped in from one of the Hun countries in the north.

"Deflower me," Ramon pleaded with me. "Since I'm a virgin, make me bleed." When the world's major film star makes such a request, and you're a well brought up boy from Kansas, you oblige. Before I'd finished with Ramon that afternoon, I was convinced that no gladiator, either with a woman or a homosexual, had enjoyed themselves as much in the Lupanare as we had. I hadn't made Ramon bleed, as I'd become too much of a skilled seducer to do that.

Upon our return to Rome the following day, I was surprised to find a dinner invitation waiting from Baron Fassini, that influential man in the Italian film industry. I'd met him when Natacha and Rodolfo had visited Italy on their grand tour. The baron had arranged a meeting with Natacha and Rodolfo with Benito Mussolini, from which I was excluded. The premier occupied an apartment above Fassini's in the

Palazzo Titoni in the heart of Rome.

The baron paid me far more attention now that I was an official representative of the Hearst organization. But he practically drooled over Ramon. Up to then, I had no clue that the baron was homosexual. "I have spoken to Benito about the two of you," he said to us over the spectacular dinner his chef had prepared. "I've told him of how you two share a suite at the Excelsior Hotel and of how you're seen together at all the finest places in Rome."

I felt the baron could not have given a stronger signal to Mussolini that we were homosexuals. "Benito finds it amusing," the baron said. "You Americans, I mean. In fact, he's going to grant you an audience tonight in his apartment, but for only five minutes. Regrettably he has many matters of state to attend to, as he's inherited a completely chaotic Italy and must make it right again." Right in the middle of our meal, when a call came in from one of Mussolini's aides, we were ushered to his apartment, as our food grew cold on their plates.

When an aide showed us into Mussolini's library, I was shocked to see him sitting on a sofa unshaven and wearing only a pair of white boxer shorts. The aide remained behind to translate for us.

"At last I meet the noblest Roman of them all," the dictator said to Ramon, referring to the role he was playing in *Ben-Hur*. It was obvious from Mussolini's face that he'd expected a more powerfully built man. "You are handsome," he said. "Down right pretty. We need more like you in Rome. But I hear you're not Italian. My aide here informs me you're Mexican."

Ramon explained to the aide that he had been born in Mexico "but of Spanish aristocracy." Ramon was a bit defensive about his origins, but the Spanish heritage seemed to satisfy Mussolini.

"Well, if they couldn't find an Italian to play the part, I guess a Spaniard will do," Mussolini said through his translator. "But, frankly, I think the role should have gone to Valentino."

Ramon bravely handled the insult, as Mussolini focused on me. "Young man, and you're another beauty too—German, perhaps—I understand you work for the Hearst organization."

"I do indeed, sir," I responded, requesting an audience with him and hoping for an interview before I left Rome.

"Please inform your boss, William Randolph Hearst, that if his newspapers write any more lies about me and Italy, that no one from the Hearst organization will ever be allowed into this country again," Mussolini said.

"I'll do that," I said meekly.

At this point, Mussolini did a surprising thing. He raised his leg on the sofa, clearly exposing a thick uncut cock and a pair of massive balls. It was obvious that the dictator just assumed any homosexual male in his presence would be attracted to him. He seemed to want us to admire his genitalia without being obvious about it. For the first minute or so, no one said anything. Mussolini lowered his leg, even though one ball was still protruding from his underwear.

"I am very distressed to hear that you've hired Communists at your studio," he said. "On the other hand, many of your film crew are upstanding members of our party and they support the legitimate government of this country. When your Louis B. Mayer arrives in Rome, I am going to confront him about this issue. If the Communists are not fired from the picture, there may never be a movie called *Ben-Hur*." With that threat, he signaled his aide to show us to the door. Not knowing what to do, I bowed slightly in Mussolini's august presence. Following my lead, Ramon did too.

Baron Fassini was waiting for us in his apartment. "The food has grown cold," he announced to us, reaching for his wrap. "I'm taking you out on the town tonight. Champagne. The world's finest pasta. I know a place that makes saltimbocca better than any other trattoria on earth."

The baron kept his word. When I tried to bring up the subject of Mussolini later in the evening, he whispered to me. "Be careful. The night has a thousand ears."

It was dawn before the baron would let Ramon and me go back to the Excelsior. The skies of Rome were pink, as the sun was on the horizon. Poor, exhausted Ramon had to go to the studio without getting any sleep. I pleaded for mercy and asked to sleep over, promising to join him for a late lunch. I kissed him good-bye, stripped off all my clothes, and headed for bed.

At ten o'clock Ramon's manservant awoke me and said there was a distinguished visitor waiting in the living room of our suite. "Who's here?" I asked, flashing for a moment that it might be Louis B. Mayer himself, as he was due to arrive in Rome in a day or so. I'd requested an interview with Mayer from the director, Fred Niblo.

Wrapping a robe around my nude body, I went into the living room of our suite to discover George Walsh sitting there. Even though I'd never met him, I recognized him from his pictures. I had no idea why the former star of *Ben-Hur*, who had been fired, was visiting the suite of the actor who had replaced him. "I'm sorry," I said, "but Mr. Novarro is gone for the day."

"I didn't come here to see Novarro," he said, "but to talk to you. I want you to write about what Metro has done to me."

After ordering the manservant to bring us coffee, and sensing a story, I sat down, groggy as I was, across from George who was dressed expensively in a perfectly tailored Italian suit.

"I don't know if you know this, but Brabin, our former director, insisted that I take a salary cut of $400 a week. He promised me that it was well worth it for me to do so, since he said that my starring in *Ben-Hur* would make me the biggest actor in Hollywood."

"Those cheap bastards," was all I could manage to say.

"On the ship sailing to Europe, MGM secured second-class accommodations for me even though I was the star of the film," he said. "Less important people assigned to the movie were traveling in first class."

"That's certainly no way to treat a star," I said.

"At this very low pay, I had to wait four entire months in Rome before I was called to the studio for just one day of shooting," he said. "Brabin got the bright idea he could use me to do screen tests with other actors. It was Brabin's way of humiliating me."

"That's all behind you now," I said. "You can return to Hollywood and find other starring roles."

"I fear not," he said. "The word is out. I'm considered inept as an actor. *Ben-Hur* has not only cost me a lot of money and time, but word of my firing may have destroyed my career. I may be washed up."

"I don't think so," I said. "You're too much star material for that. Maybe *Ben-Hur* wasn't the right role for you. Other roles will be."

"I was perfect for the part," he said. "I would have been more effective standing up to Francis X. Bushman than poor, skinny Ramon Novarro."

"Ramon has been lifting weights and pumping iron," I said. "He's building up his body for the part."

"Are you kidding?" he said. "When filmed with Bushman, Novarro will look like a Mexican school girl. That Bushman is some specimen. I had to endure humiliation from him too. He invited me into the steam bath of his hotel. I stripped down and went into the bath first. All of a sudden Bushman barges in. Buck-assed naked. He looks me up and down, and I can't miss what he's showing. The man is not hung like a man but like some fucking donkey. He said to me, 'Now, who do you think is the greater Roman—Messala or Ben-Hur. Seems obvious to me who's won the battle before the battle begins.' I couldn't take it. If anything, in his presence, my dick shrunk even more, although the steam made him grow thicker."

"Francis does like to show off his goodies," I said.

"I haven't been comparing dick sizes since I was a little kid playing with the other boys behind the barn," he said. "With me standing there completely nude gaping at Bushman's dong, I decided to get the hell out. Bushman and I have never spoken since."

"What can I do for you?" I asked, embarrassed at this encounter.

"If you write the right kind of story about me for the Hearst people, it could jumpstart my career again. I need some good publicity after all the bad I've gotten because of *Ben-Hur*."

"I think I can file a dispatch on you if you'll give me a chance to get dressed and send down for breakfast."

After an hour of talking to George, he broke down and cried in my presence, and I realized how emotional he'd become after getting fired. "They betrayed me," he said. "Thalberg betrayed me. Mathis betrayed me. Mayer certainly betrayed me. Now even your friend Novarro has betrayed me."

"It's time for you to go back to Hollywood," I said. "There's nothing left for you in Rome."

He didn't seem ready to leave the suite. "I don't know just how to bring this up," he said. "But I, like everybody in Hollywood, has heard stories."

"You mean, about me?" I asked, raising an eyebrow.

"Yes," he said softly, looking beyond our breakfast table to the bedroom. "I haven't had much experience, and I really feel my career is on the edge." He looked at the door to the bedroom again. "I'm not sure I'll know what to do, but I'm willing to go into that room with you. If it means a feature story about me in the Hearst supplements, I'm game for it. I'm no Francis X. Bushman but June Mathis had no complaints."

I rose from the table, assuring him that I would write a sensitive story about what had happened to him. "This is not Hollywood," I said. "No casting couch."

At first he seemed relieved, but then he seemed to regret my decision. As I showed him to the door, he took my hand for a long moment and looked into my eyes. "I've heard that you have a Midas touch about you. All the men you go to bed with become big-time stars. John Gilbert. Rudolph Valentino. Richard Dix. William Boyd. Even Ramon Novarro. I thought if you took me to bed, some of that star dust might rub off on me."

"I'll call you one night when I return to Hollywood," I said, a promise I didn't plan to keep. As George left the suite, I felt he was one of the saddest sights I'd ever seen. He was like so many other actors I would meet in the future, young men who came almost to the door of stardom, only to have it slammed in their face at the last minute.

Although I never saw him again, I realized that he'd been deadly accurate in predicting the collapse of a career that had showed such promise. In time he went to work for Chadwick Pictures. That studio was on Poverty Row. If you worked there, you were going down the hill in Hollywood—not up. Chadwick signed him to a few films, all of which bombed. Eventually George ended up playing bit parts for his brother, Raoul, who was rising rapidly to become one of the biggest directors in Hollywood. George appeared in these humiliating smaller roles just to earn a living. After 1936 he seemed to vanish from the screen, and I never heard of him again.

In the lobby of the Excelsior, I picked up my mail from New York and Hollywood, which included the latest Hearst-produced newspaper supplements. I'd cabled W.R. with Mussolini's threat earlier in the day but I didn't expect that the Chief would bow to pressure from Rome. Although in the years ahead, W.R. would be accused of being too sympathetic to Hitler in his early years, he showed Mussolini no mercy in a series of anti-Fascist articles run in his newspapers, branding the dictator "a braggart, a poseur, an egomaniacal pseudo-emperor not seen in Rome since the days of Caligua."

On the set of *Ben-Hur*, I feared that Mussolini's Fascist troops would shut down the picture at any minute, since the director, Fred Niblo, would not fire any of the so-called Communists who were working as extras side by side with Mussolini's young Fascists. The political storm swirling around the production of the film seemed just another one of the many disasters looming over the shooting of this epic.

With surprise, I received a hand-delivered note from Baron Fassini at six o'clock that evening. I read the note. It said, "Benito will see you at midnight at the Palazzo Titoni. He's granted your request for an interview. But you're to tell no one of this—not even your friend, Mr. Novarro."

*****

Although Rome seemed on the other side of the world, Ramon and I were eager to read the news coming out of Hollywood. Ramon was the man of the hour. Everybody had an opinion about him, even those screen divas and rivals, Pola Negri and Gloria Swanson.

"Ramon Novarro is the greatest actor on the screen today," Negri announced at a press conference. Not letting it go at that, she also claimed that, "Novarro dwarfs the achievements of Barrymore. He is also the world's most beautiful man." Had Negri selected Ramon as her next conquest? If she had, she had an uphill battle to fight for my lover. Following her failed romances with Charlie and Rod La Rocque, Negri was obviously looking for fresh meat. Gloria Swanson weighed in the next day, claiming if their mutual studios could arrange it, she'd "love to have Mr. Novarro as my next leading man, providing Cecil B. DeMille directs, of course."

At the studio en route to Ramon's dressing room, I learned that Charles Brabin had arrived and was cleaning out his office in the wake of MGM firing him as the director and replacing him with Fred Niblo. Thinking there might be a dispatch in it for the Hearst organization, I went to his office where his door stood wide open. He was busy directing two Italian extras who were crating nearly a dozen boxes of his scripts, personal letters, and mementos. I introduced myself and he shook my hand firmly. He appeared unkempt and unshaven. He'd obviously been drinking heavily although it was early morning. We exchanged pleasantries about Theda Bara, with me telling him how much I admired his wife.

He seemed to grow impatient with that talk. "Theda's career as a vamp, or as anything, is over. It's the career of Charles Brabin that I have to worry about. After all, I'm the one bringing home the bacon these days."

He told me he'd give me an interview and that I was to print every word. "Everything about this God damn spectacle is fucked up. Just this morning I heard that labor disputes among the Italians were preventing the construction of both the Circus Maximus and the Joppa gate. Niblo is in deep shit. Frankly, I don't think any director can film this piece of trash, at least not in Italy. Maybe back in Hollywood. Rome is a three-ring circus. No one can get anything done here."

He filled me in on all the disasters he'd coped with since arriving here months ago. "For the battle at sea, I demanded 75 ships but got only 30. Mayer would budget only $200,000 but I needed much more. The rotten heaps they sent me were not seaworthy. Many sank right after their launch. The Italians at the Port Authority ordered them back to shore. After two months we tried to film the sequence again. Guess what? Those latest vessels proved even more unreliable than the first. Again, delays, delays. Mayer blames me. I'm only a director. What did he think? That I was to build the boats myself?"

Checking to see that his boxes were crated, Brabin told me before departing: "I'll give you a headline for Hearst. You can report that I'm filing a lawsuit against Metro-Goldwyn for $583,000 in damages. I'm claiming they sabotaged *Ben-Hur* by not providing me with the equipment to do a proper job. They blamed me but they were responsible." I shook Brabin's hand and wished him a safe trip home to Theda's arms.

He eventually dropped the lawsuit. I heard that Mayer gave him $33,000 under the table and promised future jobs as a director. Ironically, one of the films he would direct, *The Call of the Flesh* in 1930, starred Ramon and proved to be one of my lover's most popular Talkies.

Before leaving, Brabin had told me that June Mathis, the original screenwriter, had also been ordered to remove all her material from her office today. "MGM canned both Mathis and her lover boy, George Walsh. Walsh dumped the bitch but my cameraman, Silvano Balboni, went for the pussy. MGM has fired him too. We're all out of work."

Going over to Mathis' former office, I encountered the screenwriter with her unruly hair, sloppy dress, and face that was in dire need of some morning makeup. She was furious at her assistant for not packing her scripts properly. Looking at her, I wondered how Rodolfo had managed to get it up for her. My friend must have desperately wanted the role of Julio in *The Four Horsemen of the Apocalypse*. "Brabin wouldn't listen to me," she said. "He fucked up everything. Now I'm disgraced in Hollywood. Everything I suggested to him he refused to follow. The result was a disaster. Drinking a quart of booze before noon didn't help matters either."

She seemed bitter and asked me to censor

some of her remarks before filing my dispatch for the Hearst boys. "Men are no good. Rodolfo betrayed me. He told me he loved me, but he lied. After *The Four Horsemen*, he never went to bed with me again. I tried to help him in every way I could. I tried to make sense out of the script from that dyke, Natacha Rambova, *The Hooded Falcon*. A hood should have been permanently placed over that whole shitty film. The script should have been buried at sea."

Rifling one final time through her desk, she told me she believed that Rodolfo should have played *Ben-Hur*. "Novarro is too much of a pansy. He'll look like the bride of Francis X. Bushman instead of his male rival. I'm sorry I won't be here to see those two meet on the set. I hear that Bushman once told a friend of his that Novarro was the only pansy in Hollywood who could swallow all of that legendary big dick of his."

I'm sure Francis X. has found at least one or two others," I said.

As she surveyed her office one final time, Mathis went into her small cubicle of a bathroom and emerged with a heavy coating of lipstick. She'd slashed it across her mouth. It looked more like a bleeding cut than makeup. "I'm holding my head high walking out of this toilet in case there are photographers. It's humiliating for me. We had such high hopes for *Ben-Hur*. If it's ever made, I predict it'll be a total bomb. Just last night, I had a dream. I dreamed that Louis B. Mayer tossed me a great ball of fire. It burned against my naked chest and even set off this mop of hair of mine. But I tossed the ball of fire back at him. Even though suffering severe burns, I'm saving my soul and sanity."

She kissed me on the cheek. "Take care of Rudy," she said. "Keep him away from all the jackals—women, that is—waiting to devour him when he gets back to Hollywood. Now that Natacha has dumped him, half the women in Hollywood will be going after him." She paused and whispered something confidential to me. "Between you and me, Rudy doesn't belong in the bed of a woman. A woman's bed is alien territory to him."

Saying good-bye, she walked a few feet before an assistant informed her that photographers were indeed waiting to record her humiliating retreat from the studio. Brabin had bravely gone first and had been set upon by the paparazzi, although these vultures weren't called that back then.

As an afterthought, Mathis turned to me and said in a rather lovely voice, "Those monsters out there can see my face, and they can take pictures of it, but they can never see into my heart."

I was never to see her face or heart again. After she'd been unceremoniously ejected from Rome, the once highest paid scenarist in Hollywood arrived in California where her career nose-dived as she herself could have predicted. I heard reports that her health was also failing. Rodolfo had told me that she'd been fighting a weight problem and a heart condition since the age of nine. In January of 1927 doctors placed her on a strict diet and warned her of great danger if her blood pressure got any higher.

Attending a performance of *The Squall* at the 48th Street Theater in New York on July 26 of that year, Mathis was accompanied by her grandmother. Near the end of the final act, Mathis threw her arms around her grandmother and screamed out in the audience.

"Oh, mother, I'm dying! I'm dying!"

Ushers carried her to the alleyway outside the theater. The manager asked if there were a doctor in the house. Two physicians were attending the performance. But by the time the doctors reached the alleyway, Mathis was dead. Refusing to believe it, her grandmother continued to massage her wrists hoping to bring her back to life. "Please," she pleaded with onlookers, "make June speak to me again."

The body of June Mathis, born in 1892, lay in that sordid alleyway until one a.m. when a New York coroner arrived to take the corpse away.

When her body was shipped back to Hollywood, I went to the Strother and Dayton Mortuary on Hollywood Boulevard to pay my final respects to her. The next day I learned that her casket was placed in the same crypt which would later shelter (at least temporarily) the body of her discovery, Rudolph Valentino.

That afternoon, back in Rome, Ramon had to film one of his most difficult scenes, the plot calling for Ben-Hur to rescue Arrius. That role was played by a 75-year-old actor, Frank Currier. The director, Niblo, placed both actors in a raft in a gigantic container of water in the studio. Ramon was wearing only a skimpy loincloth in the freezing studio and the waters were icy, as the day was unseasonably cold for a winter in Rome.

One take led to another, as neither Ramon nor Currier could please the director. I feared that Ramon might come down with the flu and that the old man might suffer a heart attack if Niblo ordered more retakes. Ramon pleaded with Niblo to let a stand-in fill in for Currier, but the director refused.

As Ramon pulled Currier out of the water and onto the raft for the seventeenth time, Currier finally said, "From now on, my good man, I will portray only bankers in warm offices."

Finally, after twenty takes, Niblo wrapped up for the night, claiming he wasn't really satisfied but would go with what he had, perhaps splicing together something from all the day's shooting.

The tension between Ramon and Niblo was growing daily. "Fairbanks or even Valentino might have pulled off the shot," Niblo told Ramon. "But as Ben-Hur you looked like you needed to be the one rescued—not old man Currier."

Ramon said nothing to Niblo but turned and walked away in fury, heading for his dressing room with me trailing him. In his dressing room he tossed off his Pola Negri wig and exploded in all his Mexican fury. "I hate that son-of-a-bitch. The way I feel now, I want to walk off the picture. I don't think I can endure another day of his taunts. He mocks me in front of the crew. At one point he bellowed through his megaphone that I should stop mincing and prancing like a girl. 'Ben-Hur is a man and should be played as a man,' he shouted at me in front of the whole crew. 'Not as some drag queen.' I can't take much more of his shit."

That night Ramon became violently ill, suffering from a respiratory infection. I called the manager and ordered an ambulance to take Ramon to the nearest hospital when his fever seemed to be rising dangerously.

An hour later at the hospital, the doctor assured me that he'd done what he could for Ramon, who was now resting comfortably. His fever had gone down somewhat. "But he's in far too delicate a condition to leave the hospital," the doctor said. "His body seems severely weakened. I will keep him here for at least two more days, maybe more if I discover something wrong with him."

I knew it was my job to call Niblo early in the morning with the news that Ramon was sick and wouldn't be able to report for work. That was one call I dreaded making, until I remembered I was an accredited journalist, not a hired hand for MGM.

Back at the hotel I learned that Louis B. Mayer was set to arrive in Rome the following morning. I had already filed my request for an interview with studio publicists, and an assistant had left word that Mayer would make himself available for whatever interviews the Hearst organization wanted from him. In spite of a few differences over the years, Mayer and the Chief had remained good friends.

In the bar of the Excelsior that night, I heard rumor after rumor. The gossip was that Mayer was coming to town "to fire everybody," including both Niblo and Ramon. But the one bit of gossip I believed was that he had found a replacement for Francis X. Bushman. For years, Mayer had hated Bushman for reasons not made known. At times, he hated Bushman more than the one actor he loathed among all others in Hollywood—John Gilbert. In time Mayer would destroy the careers of both Gilbert and Bushman, but to tell how he did that would be getting ahead of my story, which I've been warned severely in these concluding pages I must not do.

By midnight I was visibly shaking, as I awaited word from Baron Fassini about my midnight interview with Il Duce. It was to be the most important journalistic assignment of my life, dwarfing any dispatches I might file about *Ben-Hur*. A personal interview with Mussolini, if provocative enough, would not only be carried by the newspapers owned by the Chief, but might appear in various forms and languages around the world. Perhaps I couldn't become a movie star, but becoming a world-class reporter didn't seem too impossible.

Baron Fassini personally came by my suite

at the Excelsior to pick me up. He ushered me into a long black limousine driven by a policeman in a uniform as ebony as the vehicle itself.

After showing me into the vestibule of Mussolini's suite, the baron directed me to wait in a gilded chair in the far corner. There, an aide would eventually summon me into Il Duce's library—the same room where Ramon and I had first met the dictator. Bowing at the waist and clicking his heels like a Prussian military officer, the baron wished me good night.

For about fifteen minutes I sat alone in the foyer waiting for my summons. Finally, an aide I'd remembered from the night before came for me. He spoke English, informing me that Mussolini was ready to receive me now, but that my interview would be limited to only thirty minutes. I checked my watch to see that it was shortly before one in the morning.

Mussolini was as informal as the night before, attired only in a pair of white boxer shorts. The aide who'd summoned me remained in the room, and an English-speaking young man sat in the far corner of the library. He rose to greet me, saying that he would translate for us.

Mussolini did not acknowledge me or greet me in any way. He went over to the large window overlooking a piazza. The room was so dimly lit I could hardly see him, and the light was so bad that I knew I'd have a hard time taking notes on his remarks.

He raised both hands into the air and started to jabber, still pointedly ignoring me. As he spoke, he allowed time for his words to be translated. "I'm a man of old-fashioned views and family values," he said. "When my daughter wanted to become a dancer, I beat her severely. No daughter of mine is going to dance and display her legs to men. Early in my life my daughter was timid and afraid. Each day I made her hold a repulsive old frog in her hand until she overcame her fear and repulsion."

He turned and looked in my direction for the first time. "What the enemies of my country, like Mr. Hearst, don't seem to realize is this: My aim is to improve the living standards of my people and make Italians better off than you Americans. One event that happened to my family was instrumental in bringing about

this realization that Italy was long overdue for social and economic change. My family lived in Milan on the Via del Castel Morrone. Our building adjoined an empty lot. My daughter used to play there. But one day she was chased away when a band of Hungarian gypsies moved in to set up camp. My little girl was knitting woolen scarves for the soldiers. We were making great sacrifices for the war effort. My wife's clothes needed mending. My own daughter was reduced to only one dress, which was worn and old. But the dresses worn by the gypsy girls were beautiful and flamboyant, made with multi-colored silks. No doubt paid for by money they'd stolen in the streets. When I saw my daughter admiring how the gypsies lived, I knew I had to do better not only for my family, but for all the families of Italy. I had to leave that apartment building. It was no place to raise a decent family. Our next-door neighbor had cut his wife to pieces and had served only three years in jail. There was a midwife across the hall from us who performed abortions. You could hear teenage girls, some no more than fourteen, screaming night and day from this hog butcher."

He turned to his desk and picked up a newspaper. He held the article up to me with rage and fury, although I could not see the print. It was obviously an article about his government written by one of W.R.'s staff writers who'd recently returned from Italy. "Do you think that robber baron, William Randolph Hearst, understands the problems of my Italy, of my people? He grows rich writing about sex and scandal and lives with some blonde mistress in a great castle in California. He is removed from the concerns of ordinary people." Suddenly, he started shouting in Italina, and the translator, not wanting to interrupt him, no longer told me what Il Duce was ranting about.

Mussolini must have gone on for fifteen minutes or so, as I perched on the edge of my seat, feeling my interview was quickly collapsing and knowing that my questions had never been asked.

Tossing the paper to the floor, Mussolini barged toward me, and at first I felt he was going to strike me in the mouth. He yanked my hair and sent me flying from my chair onto the carpeted floor. On a signal, both his aide and the translator descended on me and began ripping off my clothes, tearing at my shirt. Embarrassed, I found myself fully nude in front of the men. Mussolini dropped his white boxer shorts and stepped out of them. He was sporting a large erection.

With no preliminaries, he descended onto me, as I lay spread-eagled and face down on the floor, my legs held open by the aide. Mussolini reached between my legs and grabbed my balls, squeezing them as hard as he could. "ARRGGHHH! AHHHHT! AHHHHH! I screamed to no avail. I was in agony as he plunged into me, choking my cries of pain. Allowing not one moment to get used to him, he held me in a firm grip as his cock cut deep into me like a sword. I feared I was bleeding. Drops of his sweat fell on my back each time he raised up. It was unbearable and I felt faint. He entered me deeper, his fat knob-head plowing into me without mercy. I experienced a momentary blackout but I recovered immediately. Mussolini spat on the back of my neck. I could feel him approaching a rapid climax, and I pushed my ass back against him and squeezed as tightly as I could, feeling that the sooner I could bring an eruption from him was how soon this searing pain in my bowels would come to an end. His moans were short as he thrust his final inches into me. I could feel his pubic hairs grinding against my ass. Suddenly he grabbed my hair and started yanking and pulling on it as he jerked my face around to spit into my mouth. He exploded violently within me, his breathing and panting so heavy I feared he was going to have a stroke on top of me. The moment he erupted, he yanked out of me almost as violently as he'd entered.

He shouted at his aides before walking naked toward his bedroom. The aides yanked me from the floor and virtually tossed me back into the vestibule, throwing my clothes after me. Before I had time to dress, I was ushered out of the apartment and into the dimly lit hallway. A policeman came for me and ordered me to leave the building at once.

Shoved out onto the street, I was still buttoning my shirt as the iron gates closed behind me with a bang. I looked up and down the street, searching desperately for a taxi to take me back to the Excelsior.

As I headed up the deserted sidewalk in the dark, lightning flashed through the sky, and I expected to get fully soaked as the monsoon rains had begun again.

My dreams of scoring a journalistic coup gave way to tears as I walked up that lonely street, my body still aching from the recent assault. By the time I reached the corner I found that I was sobbing in my hurt and humiliation.

I vowed never to tell anyone, not even Ramon, what had happened to me back at that apartment. Up until now I have kept that commitment to myself.

*****

As if symbolic of what was to come, Louis B. Mayer arrived in Rome, just in time to witness one of the city's biggest thunderstorms. The clouds opened up and virtually drowned Rome, as streets were flooded. Mayer needed a boat more than a taxi to reach the Excelsior Hotel on the via Veneto. When I saw him in the lobby, he knew at once that I was working for W.R. Hearst and reporting on *Ben-Hur*. "I've got a quote for you," he said, soaking wet and looking as if he was in pain. "I was a junk man before and I know how to salvage junk. *Ben-Hur* will be saved with me here."

After checking on Ramon who was resting in the hospital for another two days, I returned to the set of *Ben-Hur*. Almost daily I was sending back a dispatch for the Hearst organization, although I could hardly write about what was really happening at the studio. Even though Mayer never liked me, he agreed to let me accompany him through a day on the set except for private meetings.

As he walked into the studio on his first morning, Mayer told me he was in great pain, that his teeth were causing him acute agony. "But I've got a job to do, and I'll do it." I urged him to go to a hospital for a thorough check-up, but he stubbornly refused in the same way Rodolfo turned down medical treatment from Brian Sheehan.

The first person to run up to Mayer was Alexander Aronson, the chief of MGM's new office in Paris. Mayer had ordered him to Rome to keep an eye on Niblo. From the start, and I'd witnessed this myself, Aronson and Niblo hated each other. Aronson disputed every call Niblo made as director and filed a daily critical and most damaging report, which was sent back to the offices of Irving Thalberg and Mayer in Hollywood.

Ignoring me, Aronson immediately pleaded with Mayer to fire Niblo and replace him with the even more famous director, King Vidor. "I've told you before, and I'll tell you again, Niblo stays on the picture," Mayer said. "Now that I'm in Rome, I'll straighten Niblo out."

After Aronson had left in defeat, Mayer turned to me. "I've fired enough people on this picture already. The only one I really want to fire is Francis X. Bushman, but I've been unable to find a replacement for him. So I'm stuck with the wife-beater and exhibitionist."

As Mayer waited for the filming to begin, he ordered that Niblo be sent for, as he'd requested a private meeting with the director. "What I have to say is not for publication so you'll need to make yourself scarce for an hour or so while I read Niblo the riot act."

Once Mayer complained that "my gums are on fire." I suggested a cognac be sent for, and he agreed to that. "Anything," he said, "to help me deal with this pain. I've experienced pain before but nothing like this."

While he waited for both Niblo and the cognac, Mayer caught me up on some of the behind-the-scenes news from Hollywood, providing I'd agree that none of it was for publication. "I plan to make a star out of Greta Garbo," he said, "providing she'll agree to quit fucking that pansy, John Gilbert."

"But I've heard the Swede was in love with her director, Mauritz Stiller."

"That slimy Stiller is letting the world think he's in love with Garbo," Mayer said. "What he's covering up is that he's a faggot. Stiller is in love with a Swedish actor named Einar Hanson. Wait until you meet Hanson. He's more beautiful than Garbo. He's such a pretty boy that I'd marry himself myself, and, as everybody knows, I'm the most heterosexual man who ever set foot in Hollywood. I always tell people there are only two bona-fide heterosexuals in all of Hollywood: Louis B.

Mayer and that rotten Samuel Goldfish. Everybody else is suspect."

A member of the production crew brought Mayer his cognac. He sipped it slowly, rubbing his jaw as his pain continued. He told me that I should interview Hanson upon my return to Hollywood. "Call my office, and I'll set it up." He laughed as if sharing a private joke. "Here's what I predict. Hanson will meet you and fall madly in love with you. Stiller is older than Hanson and quite ugly. You're known as the prettiest boy in Hollywood. You've practically turned half the town's formerly straight men into faggots, so there's no doubt that Hanson will gravitate to you, drop Stiller, and run off with you."

Even as Mayer and I spoke in Rome, Hanson was appearing opposite Garbo in *Die Freudlöse Gasse,* which had already premiered at Berlin's Mozartsaal. It would later open in London as *The Joyless Street.* By the time the film premiered in New York, its title had been changed to *The Street of Sorrow.*

"Of course, if you want Hanson you'll have some competition," Mayer said.

"You mean from Stiller?" I asked. "Or do you mean from Garbo herself?"

"No, from Pola Negri," Mayer said. "The Polish bitch is making a film with Hanson. It's called *The Woman on Trial.* I hear she's fallen madly in love with him. But she's also conducting an affair on the side with this young actor named Clark Gable, even though Gable is married to that old cow, Josephine Dillon."

I settled back in my director's chair on hearing that news. So Clark had been busy since I'd abandoned him in Hollywood. A few years back I thought Gloria Swanson was going to be my chief rival for the studs of Hollywood. Now Pola Negri seemed moving in on my turf. At least I had Ramon safely in my arms in Rome, away from her greedy pussy—not that Ramon would ever take a dive into that much-used well like Charlie Chaplin and Rod La Rocque had done previously.

To piss off the Bitch of Buchenwald, I will jump ahead of my story. Mayer was uncanny about some things, and his prediction of what would happen between Hanson and me turned out to be deadly accurate. Mayer held out such promising bait to me that I did call his office and did get to meet the strikingly handsome Hanson. After our first night together, Hanson agreed to leave Stiller, telling me the director was "rotten in bed." Hanson wanted to come and live with me, and I readily agreed. "I love all things beautiful, and you are beautiful," he told me.

Had it not been for Stiller, the few weeks I spent in the arms of Einar Hanson would have been idyllic. The director had a sexual obsession about Hanson and could not let him go, although the young Swedish actor pleaded with Stiller to quit stalking him. At least three times Garbo had to talk Stiller out of committing suicide over his loss of Hanson.

Stiller was hanging out in the lobby of the Hollywood Hotel every night waiting to see Hanson and me come into the building. The director would invariably confront the young actor, begging him to go home with him and desert me.

The tension grew so acute that Garbo called me one night and invited Hanson, Stiller, and me to dinner at her house. "This affair of the heart must be discussed in a rational way," she told me. "It is destroying Mauritz, and I love and respect him too much to see him on fire. I thought if all of us could talk about this imbroglio in a sane and rational way, it might be resolved and all of us can get on with our lives and careers."

That sounded like a reasonable approach, except for one thing—Stiller had an irrational sexual obsession about Hanson, and I didn't see how any smooth talking at any dinner, even if hosted by Garbo herself, could resolve that. Perhaps in Sweden sexual obsession and love triangles were solved over dinner, but not in America.

At Garbo's dinner, Stiller flew into a violent rage directed at both Hanson and me. He accused the young Swedish actor of "deceit, ingratitude, and betrayal."

"I made you a star," the director said to Hanson. "You owe me something." He looked at me, flashing more anger and jealousy than I'd ever seen up to then. "Einar belongs to me—not some vapid little American boy-whore who's had half the men in Hollywood."

Garbo placed her delicate hand on Stiller's and tried to calm him. "If you don't leave this house with me tonight," Stiller said to Hanson, "I will see that your career is destroyed. For all I know, you'll have to go back to Stockholm. No doubt in a few years you'll end up fat and bald like your father. Washing dishes in the kitchen of the Grand Hotel."

Hanson threw down his napkin and lashed out at Stiller. "I'm a talented actor," Hanson shouted. "Talented and beautiful on the screen. I have fans who adore me. I'm in love with Durango. To succeed in pictures, I don't have to become your property. I can make it on my own. Sure, you have given me some breaks. But does that mean I'm obligated for life to have your cold hands pawing my body? When you touch me, chills go up and down my spine. It's like being fondled by a monster from the deep."

"You bastard!" Stiller shouted at Hanson, who raced from the dining room. Wildly disturbed and seemingly mad, he headed for the front door, his dog, an Airedale, chasing after him. As I ran after him, Hanson got into his car and headed out recklessly down the coastal highway. He'd been drinking heavily, and I had wanted to drive him back to the hotel. Before pulling away, leaving me standing there, he shouted back at me, "I won't be treated like a piece of meat either by Stiller or by you."

I borrowed Garbo's car and decided to trail him even though he'd gotten much mileage on me. As I drove along the coast, I spotted flashing lights and an overturned truck. The Los Angeles police were at the scene. I screamed when I saw Hanson's car overturned along an embankment on the sandy beach. The police told me that apparently to avoid an oncoming truck and a head-on collision, Hanson had spun off the road, striking a sand bank. "We think his car turned a couple of somersaults," the policeman said.

To my horror, I discovered that Hanson was still pinned within the wreckage. His frantically barking Airedale was held on a leash nearby. Upon seeing me, the dog broke loose and ran to me, jumping up on me and licking my face as if I had the power to save his master.

I followed the ambulance in Garbo's car as he was rushed to Martin Sanitarium. There I frantically called Brian Sheehan to come over and see what could be done. Brian arrived in a panic and rushed in to examine Hanson, who was his patient. Brian came out later and told me that Hanson was going to die. "His chest is crushed. There is no hope."

I broke down in tears in Brian's arms as he offered me comfort. As I sat in a private office, Brian came in four hours later. His face was grim. "He's dead. There was no way to save him. He was only twenty-nine."

Both Stiller and Garbo attended the funeral, and I did too, in spite of the hostility between Stiller and me. "I adored the man," Garbo told me. She was dressed in black and her eyes were red from crying all night. "He was a lovely human being and deserved a long and happy life. That is, if any of us will ever find happiness." She turned and walked away.

I turned around to confront Stiller. "It's because of you that he's dead," the director charged. Not satisfied with a thousand men in Hollywood, you had to pursue the one love of my life. I loved Einar. No one will ever replace him in my heart. I'm destined for a life of loneliness, and I'll never love again. You have not only killed him, but you've hastened my own death."

I said nothing as I watched Stiller walk away to join Garbo who was getting into her car. Although Stiller's words were melodramatic, they turned out to be painfully true.

Right after the funeral I drove Hanson's dog, the Airedale, all the way north to San Francisco to the estate outside the city where the twins of Marion Davies lived. I wanted to see the children again and to bring the dog to them. Although they loved the dog and the animal brought much joy to them, the Airedale never recovered from the loss of its master. Many was the night it would bark and send up a mournful yelp to the sky. The animal would live for another four years, but all the love we could give to the dog was not enough. Only Einar Hanson himself could make that dog happy.

To quiet the protests of the Bitch of Buchenwald for racing ahead of my story, I will return to that day when I accompanied Mayer to the set of *Ben-Hur* in Rome.

Niblo had put one of his assistant directors in charge of production so he could rush over to meet with Mayer. Ignoring me, Niblo immediately launched into a series of complaints about the Italian workers employed to work on *Ben-Hur*. "The Communists and the fascists are virtually threatening to kill each other."

Mayer put up his hand as if to shut Niblo up. "I've great news for you," Mayer said to his director. "You finish this *Ben-Hur* shit, and I'll let you direct one of the biggest properties coming up for Metro. It's *The Temptress*. We're adapting it now from the Blasco-Ibáñez novel. I'm going to cast Garbo in it. I'm offering the male lead to Antonio Moreno. Lionel Barrymore's in it. He'll probably fall madly in love with Moreno and slow down production. Lionel chases anything in pants. For the important role of Manos Duros, I'm casting Roy D'Arcy. I liked his work in *The Merry Widow*. Of course, you'll have to get D'Arcy to stop acting like Erich von Stroheim. That Hun taught D'Arcy too well. I've warned him he can't be a dime-store von Stroheim in this production."

As Mayer and Niblo headed for the director's office, I wandered off, waiting for the filming of the big battle at sea later in the day.

At a tap on the shoulder, I turned around to stare into the face of Francis X. Bushman, whom I hadn't seen in years.

"You've come up in the world," he said to me. "I hear you're a very rich boy, and working for Hearst. I'm sure he pays you more than I did."

"Francis," I said. "It's great seeing you again. You look fabulous."

"Come to my dressing room with me," Bushman said. "I'm going to get dressed for my role as Messala. I'm sure that's a sight you'd like to see."

*****

As I trailed Bushman to his dressing room, I could feel the tension among the crew, some of whom glared at us. The Communists were generally supportive, but the Fascists hated the cast and production crew sent over from America. "Even though I desperately need a comeback flicker," Bushman said, "I originally told Mayer I wouldn't play Messala. To me, the script made me a filthy Roman, and up to now I've been a romantic hero in films. It was William S. Hart who convinced me that the role of Messala was the best thing in the picture. Hart played Messala on and off for years on the stage."

As Bushman turned a corner down a long row of dressing rooms, we heard a struggle going on in the dressing room of Mary McAvoy. He listened briefly at the door, then shouted, "What's going on in there?"

I heard McAvoy scream, followed by the sound of something falling over and breaking. Bushman tried the door but found it locked. With his huge frame, he rammed his body against the flimsy door, forcing it open.

I followed him into the dimly lit room. McAvoy was nude as a fully clothed man with an erect penis sticking out of his fly was forcing her down on the floor and trying to penetrate her as she struggled to escape. Bushman grabbed the man by his neck and tossed him against the wall. With a booted heel, he kicked the rapist in the groin. The man pulled himself up, clutching himself in pain, and half walked, half stumbled out the door.

I turned to McAvoy, reaching for one of her gowns, which I spread across her body. "Thanks," she said between sobs.

"I'll get a doctor," Bushman said. "I got a good look at that son-of-a-bitch. He'll go to jail for this."

Within minutes, the director, Niblo, and two of his assistants had arrived at McAvoy's dressing room. The actress was still sobbing when an ambulance was called to take her to the local hospital for an examination.

After we'd witnessed her being carried away, Bushman told me to follow him into his own dressing room. "This is all Mussolini's fault," he said, ushering me into his own dressing room and turning on the lights.

"You mean the rape?" I asked, bewildered, remembering my own rape under the brute force of the dictator.

"I don't know if you know this, but it's something you should write about," Bushman said. "Mussolini is using the film to solve Rome's labor problem. He's insisting that one out of every ten Italians hired be a disabled war veteran. Niblo has also found out that a lot of the crew forced upon us was recruited among the criminally insane. Some of the extras were let out of prison to work on this damn film. No wonder everything is so fucked up."

Even though ranting against Mussolini, Bushman started to strip. He was wearing a dark suit, white shirt, and tie. He ordered me to sit in the only chair in the small cubicle as he slowly removed each piece of his clothing. "I bet you forgot how big I really am," he said.

"That's one memory I'll never forget," I said. "After sampling half of the male stars in Hollywood, you've got them all beat."

"Even Elmo Lincoln?" he asked, a frown crossing his brow.

"By a country mile," I assured him.

He smiled at me, seemingly reassured. He stepped out of his pants and tossed them aside. He'd already removed his shoes. Clad only in his underwear, he pulled off his top. "I'll be showing a lot of flesh in the role. I've been working out to stay in shape." He ran his hands along his right leg. "I've been building up muscles in my legs too. I show a lot of flesh in this movie. I like that part of it."

"You've got a lot of flesh to show."

A smirk came across his face, as he walked over to me. "I'll let you remove the final garb," he said. I reached out and pulled down his underwear, exposing him totally. Even though it hung only inches from my face, I could not believe the size of that mammoth organ. Francis X. Bushman was no ordinary man. Even flaccid, it hung down a thick eight inches, and from experience I knew there was four more to go before it reached its full length. If male porno had existed back in those days, Bushman would have been its chief star.

Instinctively I reached out to play with it, pulling the skin back to expose the large purple knob. "You pansy boys really get off looking at it and playing with it, but many women run when they see me nude. They know they can't take it. Even though I don't get the pussy I'm after, I still get a charge seeing the stunned expressions on their faces before they flee in horror at the sight of me."

Finding such a prick irresistible, I planted tiny kisses followed by tongue lashings on it.

"Go ahead," he said. "I haven't had any pussy since I left Berlin, and I'm raring to go. Relieve me."

As I worked to polish that mighty prick, it rose and rose to an unbelievable size before my eyes. I plunged down twice on it, taking first three and then six inches, but I could not relax my throat muscles enough to swallow him to the base.

"Take off your clothes," he said. "If you can't take it one way, you'll get it another."

Lubricating himself with some cream on his dressing table, he began a slow penetration of me, inch by inch, I felt I was being split open but at no point did I back out, even bucking up and trying to open myself to take more of him.

I was in that position when there came a loud rap on the door. "Open up, Bushman," the voice shouted. "It's Mayer."

At that point Bushman had plowed eight inches into me and was in his glory, with no intention of pulling out now after he'd worked so hard for this much satisfaction. "Come back later," he called to Mayer. "I'm busy."

Even though suffering through the ninth inch, I feared that Bushman had made a big mistake. You didn't send Louis B. Mayer away from your dressing room. After Bushman told him to come back later, I feared Mayer must have left as he never called out again. As the tenth inch entered me, I thought an enraged Mayer was on his way to Niblo to have Bushman fired.

That thought perished in my mind as Bushman achieved a home run, having entered me fully. I could feel his pubic hairs against my ass. Once inside me, he began to pound. I felt I was being violated. Bushman only forty minutes previously had saved McAvoy from a rapist. But now he was the rapist and I was his victim.

After the first five minutes when I felt like bolts of lighting were being shot into me, I relaxed and enjoyed his invasion, amazed that I could take such a monster within me. Bushman was getting to me. I tried to kiss him but he turned his mouth from me, leaving a delectable ear for me to nibble on. I kissed and licked his neck and reached to jiggle his large balls as he settled in for a long ride. Even though half way through the fuck, I exploded violently because he was really getting to me

and I couldn't hold back. At that point I was so sensitive I wanted him to pull out. Instead he increased the power of his pumping. I was completely entrapped and settled in for the duration, which came after another prolonged fifteen minutes when he erupted with more violence than I had known in any man.

No longer resisting my mouth, Bushman, in the heat of his passion, bit my lips, which I opened at once to receive a deep penetration of a very large tongue. Needing something to suck on to help me forget the pain in my ass, I devoured that tongue voraciously as if it were the grandest banquet ever set before another man.

Bushman fell against me, breathing heavily. It took him a long time to pull out because I squeezed my ass muscles as tight as I could, hoping to prevent his withdrawal. The initial invasion had been painful enough. But once accustomed to him, I felt at that point I wanted him to stay in me forever. Such was not to be. When he finally withdrew, I felt a great loss, as if a part of my body had been taken from me.

Afterward, he let me wash him clean and tie on his leather pouch to hold up his genitals and keep them from falling out under the short Roman skirt he wore as Messala. "We'll do that again and again before this picture is finished," he promised. "Now that I've broken you in, I'll tell you what really turns me on. That's looking into your face and seeing the expression in your eyes as my big knob first enters you. It's just thrilling to see that stunned look of shock, surprise, and then agonizing pain."

Later on the set, I learned that Mayer had gone to Niblo to denounce Bushman. When I caught up with Mayer he said, "I'll destroy Bushman. He'll never work another day in Hollywood if I have something to say about it, and I've got a lot to say about who works in Hollywood—and who doesn't."

Niblo had postponed one of the biggest and most dramatic scenes in the movie, waiting for Mayer's arrival from America. A Roman galley was to be filmed battling a pirate boat. While waiting for the scene to be set up, Mayer told me to talk to an assistant on the film while he went away to confer with Niblo.

The man I was introduced to was William

Wyler. There was a certain irony here that I didn't know at the time. In addition to his future role as the director and lover of Bette Davis, it was Wyler who would assume the job of director in the 1959 version of *Ben-Hur*. Charlton Heston was the star. To play a joke on the homophobic Heston, one of the script's writers, Gore Vidal, wrote in a love scene between Stephen Boyd, an actor in the film, and Heston. "The joke was," Boyd told me years later, "everybody on the set but Charlton knew that it was a love scene between us. When Heston belatedly found out, he exploded in fury but was already immortalized on celluloid in his first and last homosexual love scene."

At the time I met him, I had no idea that Wyler would one day become such a towering figure in cinema. I missed my opportunity to interview him that day in Rome, but I was to have extensive interviews with him at Warners in 1937 when he was filming *Jezebel* with Bette Davis, whom he'd taken as a lover in spite of her marriage to "Ham" Nelson.

As a lover, Wyler was definitely not my type. He was short, chunky, and homely. The actor, Charles Bickford, referred to him as "the Golem," an unattractive creature in one of the German horror films of the 1920s. But Bette was smitten. I was also around to interview Wyler when he was directing the second *Ben-Hur* in the 1950s.

Within the next thirty minutes, I learned from Bushman why Wyler had been called away, as had Mayer and Niblo. Niblo's chief of production had uncovered a pile of real swords stashed under canvas on the pirate ship. The Fascists members of the crew were actually planning to use the swords for real against the anti-Fascists who were supposed to be storming their boat. Several of the Communists could have been killed during the filming if Niblo had not uncovered that plot.

In spite of that setback, the scene was ready to shoot two hours later. Mayer directed me to a platform nearby where we could view the pirate ship colliding with the slave boat. Mayer had ordered Niblo to make the scene as realistic as possible. A high-speed motorboat pulled the pirate ship into a collision with the slave boat. The ship was deliberately set on fire, but a sudden wind blew in, causing the flames to shoot dangerously out of control.

The ship appeared to be sinking. Many of the extras jumped overboard in panic. Some of them were wearing heavy armor and sank at once into the cold waters, having failed to remove their armor before taking the plunge. When they were hired, all the extras had claimed they could swim. But as they hit the water, it was obvious that some of them had lied to get the work. With or without the heavy armor, they were drowning. The ship sank into flames as some extras clung to the rudders like ants on sugar until the boat faded below the water line.

Niblo had dinghies standing by to rescue the cast in case of danger. But like those lifeboats on the *Titanic*, they were not enough to save all the men, who could be seen fighting in the water for their lives. The men flailed helplessly in the water screaming for help.

Fleeing the platform, I raced toward the water, as I was a good swimmer. Jumping into the cold waters, I managed to bring three men to shore but I feared others were gone forever.

Mayer wasn't coming to anyone's rescue except MGM's. He summoned the labor roll to be delivered to Niblo's office. There he demanded that a full report of the film's crew be made to him. Anyone missing at sea would be removed from the labor roll as if they had never worked on *Ben-Hur*. Although the exact number was suppressed, Ramon learned the next week that eight or maybe as many as ten extras had not been accounted for and were feared drowned at sea.

MGM officially announced that there had been no casualties. But many of the relatives of the dead and missing men came to the studio to protest the death of loved ones. Sometimes Niblo was able to buy them off for five-hundred dollars. All records of employment for the missing cast members were destroyed. Wyler, an assistant director, was assigned the job of supervising a "cleanup crew," which managed to gather five bodies from the water or shore. They were shipped by train to Anzio, south of Rome, where they were secretly buried in an unmarked grave, Mayer having found the caretaker of the cemetery not opposed to receiving a bribe.

Two days later Mayer was back on the set

of *Ben-Hur*, having been away suffering from acute pain. Mayer had been at the studio only two hours before he collapsed, falling onto the floor in front of the entire cast. At first I thought he'd had a heart attack. I was to learn later that he'd been rushed to the hospital where doctors had determined that all of his teeth were abscessed, his gums drastically inflamed. Although all of his teeth were removed that afternoon, the hospital staff feared that Mayer might not live. In those days many victims died from Toxemia, following tooth abscesses. That was two decades before antibiotics came in to prevent those deaths.

But Mayer survived as did the filming of *Ben-Hur*, in spite of mounting difficulties for the production of this ill-fated flick. The original budget of $750,000 now appeared to be on its way toward four million, a record-breaking figure back in those days, and so different from today when even one super-star can command twenty million per picture, in salary alone.

The chariot race, which remains the most memorable part of the film, was originally shot in Rome under the direction of William Raves Eason, whom everybody called "Breezy." He was a second-unit director whose only claim to fame up to then was as director of several low-budget Westerns along Poverty Row in Hollywood. Why Niblo wanted to turn over the most important scenes in the film to Breezy was never known. Mayer was too sick to come to the set, so the filming began.

Since arriving in Rome, both Bushman and Novarro had undergone extensive training for their roles in the chariot race. But when Ramon showed up, he looked weak and pale—no match for the more virile Bushman. I told Ramon he should have stayed in the hospital for a few more days but both Niblo and Mayer had called Ramon and warned him that his promising career as a big-time star would collapse if he didn't show up for the scene.

Standing on the sidelines watching Niblo give final directions to Ramon, Bushman said to me, "I probably should have played the role of *Ben-Hur*. The role calls for a real he-man, not a pansy boy like Novarro. He knows how to handle a big dick, but he doesn't know how to drive a carriage!"

"He's been rehearsing," I said in defense

of Ramon. "He's up to it. Only he's just recovering from the flu and he's a bit weak today."

"We'll see how weak he is," Bushman said enigmatically before being called over to talk to Niblo.

The filming began smoothly but quickly turned into a disaster. Horses were being killed at an alarming rate. No sooner was a horse killed then Breezy ordered his production crew to remove the dead animal. A stable of horses stood nearby waiting to be summoned to the arena as replacement.

A great animal lover, I was horrified, although I planned to file dispatches back to the Hearst boys in New York, not that that would do the victimized animals any good. Niblo had even arranged to peddle the dead horses to a butcher for sale to humans as meat. Sometimes a horse was only injured. In that case, the poor animal was dragged out of the arena and shot to death.

In horror I watched one of the scenes directed by Breezy. Carrying a Roman extra, a chariot rounded a dangerous curve. Suddenly the wheel of the chariot flew off, sending its driver flying nearly two dozen feet into the air. The poor wretch landed on a pile of lumber in which jagged nails were exposed. Although rushed to the hospital with internal injuries, he died there forty-eight hours later.

Bushman seemed to be deliberately and provocatively ramming his chariot into Ramon's. I protested loudly to Breezy but he claimed he had everything under control, that both actors were simply following the demands of the script.

Again to my shock, I watched helplessly as Ramon's chariot swerved dangerously into Bushman's. This time it wasn't Bushman who had crashed into Ramon's chariot. Ramon appeared to have lost control of his vehicle. I screamed, racing toward Ramon, fearing he'd been killed. Amazingly, Ramon crawled from the wreckage completely unscathed except for some bruises, none on his face. It was a miracle. One of his horses had been killed, however.

In spite of Ramon's near escape from death, an angry Bushman came over to confront him. "You certainly fucked that up, you little faggot," he said. "This is no horse and buggy ride through Central Park. You've got to wrap the reins around your little limp wrist. Jam your tiny little feet in their high heels up against the front of the chariot. Lean back straight and hold yourself like a man—not some little chorus boy in a Broadway show. You're right about one thing, though. That wig does make you look like Pola Negri."

Still shaken from his fall, Ramon seemed shocked at Bushman's remarks. I was so infuriated with Bushman that I pounded him on his chest. But he merely laughed at me and walked away, turning to look over his shoulder for one final comment. "For hitting me like that, you little fruit-fly, I'll get even with you later. You'll be the one going to the hospital the next time—not that shithead, Mayer."

That ended the chariot race filming for that day, as I retreated back to the Excelsior suite where I summoned the house doctor to give Ramon a thorough examination in case he had any internal injuries. The footage that Breezy had shot on that horrible day was deemed "garbage" when viewed by both Niblo and Mayer. Mayer ordered that no more chariot race scenes be filmed in Rome. He said a set would be built in Hollywood where the race could be reshot—"preferably with a minimum of deaths," he later told me.

The next day, though Ramon was still badly bruised, Niblo ordered Ramon to get ready for a difficult galley scene, in which he'd be depicted chained to an oar where, according to the script, he'd been for three years. Take after take didn't please Niblo. The tension between star and director was almost unbearable. Even extras who weren't involved in the scene sensed a mounting confrontation between them.

"God damn it," Niblo shouted at one point to Ramon. "If Metro had wanted to make Ben-Hur a woman, why didn't they just go ahead and cast Alice Terry in the part? Alice has more hair on her chest than you do."

To my shame, Ramon broke down and cried in front of the cast. Macho Niblo had finally gotten to him, breaking his spirit and destroying his confidence. It wasn't clear to me what Niblo had to gain by battering his star in front of everybody.

Ramon came up to Niblo. Through tears, he sobbed, "Rex Ingram should be directing the picture. He's a real director." Niblo slapped Ramon's face, sending him running toward his dressing room where I followed to offer what comfort I could.

In two hours I'd convinced Ramon to return to the set where he did not speak to Niblo, although the director shouted orders at him through his megaphone. Ramon began the scene again. But in the middle of the filming, he seemed to lose all control as he started to scream hysterically. He appeared on the verge of a nervous breakdown, and was crying incoherently. At long last, his nerves were collapsing. It'd all been too much for him. With the help of Wyler, I got Ramon to his dressing room. After thanking Wyler and ushering him out, I turned to Ramon and held him in my arms, begging him to stand up to Niblo.

But he lay there in a fetal position on his small day bed until the studio shut down at seven o'clock, the extras heading home for dinner. Niblo, we learned, had gone to Mayer's hospital room to urge the studio chief to replace Ramon with Antonio Moreno, even though the picture was nearly three-quarters shot.

When Wyler came by and knocked on our door, telling us of what Niblo was up to, Ramon rallied his forces. He spoke on the phone to someone at the Excelsior but I couldn't hear what he was saying.

Within the hour a car arrived for us, and Ramon begged me to get in the back seat with him. At first I thought we were returning to the Excelsior. But I grew alarmed when I learned that Ramon had ordered the driver to head north to the outskirts of Rome.

"I've left word with the studio that I'm too ill to report to work," he said. "We're going to the French Riviera."

"But you're the star," I protested. "This is your one big chance. Ignore Niblo's homophobic remarks. Think of your career."

"Let them fire me," he said almost fatalistically. "I'm through with this God damn picture. I prayed that I'd get the lead in it. For all I care now, Mayer can shove *Ben-Hur* up his rotten Jew ass." He reached for my hand. "Thank God you didn't become a movie star too. Stardom would destroy you too like it has done for me."

It was only when we'd arrived in San

Remo the next morning that I realized we'd left our passports at the Excelsior Hotel in Rome. Ramon made light of this problem, demanding that the driver head for the French border anyway. He looked through the car papers and produced an official-looking document in English. "These peasants don't speak English," he said. They'll think this is a passport for both of us." I didn't agree, but Ramon persisted.

At the border, the Italian guard didn't accept the car papers as passport documents and also turned down a hundred-dollar bribe from Ramon.

Ramon directed our driver to take us to the border town of Ventimiglia. There Ramon pleaded with the French consul, telling him that he was a great American movie star and was entitled to cross the border. The French bureaucrat wasn't impressed with Ramon's star status and refused his request for entry into France.

We were forced to check into a dreary little hotel in Ventimiglia. Ramon believed that once night came we could sneak across the border into France, even though it was patrolled by both French and Italian guards twenty-four hours a day.

At the hotel we learned that travelers without passports were sometimes able to rent a rowboat from a fisherman and go across the bay on a dark night. But there was danger in that too, as the border guards often shot at you.

The bellhop at our hotel told us of another way to sneak across the border. There was a rocky precipice along a narrow beach by the sea. It was the least guarded section of the border. That night we paid our driver, left our luggage in storage at the hotel and headed for the border, although I had my apprehensions. Ramon had never explained to me why it was so vital that he cross into France, and I feared he'd become unnerved working on *Ben-Hur* and no longer had sound judgment—not that he ever did, even on his finest day.

The bellhop had been right. Ramon and I sneaked around the rocks and crossed along the narrow beach into France. But after going no more than fifteen minutes, we were called to a halt by an armed French border guard. Fortunately he'd seen some of Ramon's films with Barbara LaMarr and was a fan.

Although he looked us over suspiciously, he apparently believed that we were staying at a hotel in Menton within France. From the way he eyed us, I felt he might be homosexual and was willing to help two fellow brothers out.

Ramon kissed the guard on the cheek to show his gratitude. I followed with a kiss of my own. As I moved to kiss his cheek, the guard turned his head suddenly until I was kissing his mouth. He frenched me and I loved it. After that, he turned and walked ahead, as Ramon and I made our way on foot to Menton where we checked into a hotel without luggage.

That day we went to one of the resort's best tailors and ordered clothes made for our stay on the Riviera. We also arranged for a driver with a car, and the next day we headed for Monte Carlo where we checked into the deluxe Hotel de Paris.

For four nights we stayed at the hotel, gambling at the legendary casino nearby until we'd lost all the money we'd brought with us from Rome. Wherever we went in Monte Carlo, Ramon was recognized. *Scaramouche* was a big hit in France, and Ramon was the darling of the photographers. We spent most of the day on the beach, followed by nights in the casino, followed by nights making love in our luxurious Louis XVI suite.

The next day the director, Rex Ingram, and his wife, Alice Terry, arrived, and for the first time I realized why Ramon had wanted to come to Monte Carlo. He'd suffered such a brutal destruction of his self-confidence as an actor that he felt his favorite director, Ingram, would restore some of his stature as an actor. Alice was very supportive of Ramon, too, and it was obvious they'd become very close friends, rivaling the association Ramon had with my former roommate, Barbara LaMarr.

Although he wouldn't be the director, Ingram told Ramon of an exciting new development in Hollywood. Alice would be appearing as Felicia in *The Great Goleoto*, her next film for MGM. It was all but definite that Ramon would be cast in the lead as José, with Roy D'Arcy, that Erich von Stroheim clone from *The Merry Widow*, playing Señor Galdos.

This film, later retitled *Lovers?* seemed like weak lemonade to me, and indeed turned out that way. It was dismissed by *Variety* as lacking "sustained dramatic interest," and made only $104,000 at the box office.

What Ingram held out for Ramon's future, even though neither he nor Alice would be involved in the production, was news that MGM was acquiring *The Student Prince in Old Heidelberg* and the role would be tailor-made for Ramon. Ernst Lubitsch himself, then one of the hottest directors in Hollywood, would control the picture. Irving Thalberg, the producer, was so excited about the project that he was giving the female lead to his beloved, Norma Shearer.

"Mayer's telling everybody that you're the next Valentino," Ingram told us. "He calls you his protégé. I've heard that in the rushes sent back to Hollywood, the people at MGM felt Bushman was stealing every scene from you. That he was sabotaging your real big chance. Some of the scenes of Bushman and you will be reshot, and some of Bushman's best footage will be cut from the film. MGM is doing that for you. Don't let them down."

Fortunately Ingram was so convincing that Ramon agreed to go back to Rome and face up to Fred Niblo and complete the picture, regardless of the pain and suffering it caused him. Ingram made it abundantly clear that Ramon's future as the biggest male star on the planet was worth any suffering Niblo might cause him in the next few weeks.

Back in Rome, Ramon learned that the film crew was shutting down and heading back to California, where the remaining scenes, including that ill-fated chariot race, would be completed. Ramon and I would sail away on *La France*, before the company folded its operations in Rome.

Before his departure, Ramon was invited to meet the royal family of Italy. Niblo drooled over them, especially the fur-draped queen, but did not introduce her to the cast except for Ramon. The king was more intrigued with Mary McAvoy who'd recovered from the rape that never was. Standing on the sidelines, I didn't even rate a hello from the royal entourage, my request for an interview for the Hearst organization having been unceremoniously turned down. Princess Giovanna seemed smitten with Ramon, who had protested earlier to Niblo that he was going to apply for pay as an extra, after having waited three hours in the cold for the royal entourage to arrive.

On our final night in Rome, the phone rang. It was the manager of the Excelsior. "Her Highness, the Princess Giovanna, has arrived in the lobby unexpectedly. She has been trying to reach Mr. Novarro all day but you gentlemen have been out of your suite. She is requesting a midnight supper with Mr. Novarro in a private salon we have downstairs."

When confronted with this news, Ramon went into immediate panic. "She wants to fuck me, I just know it. I hear the entire royal family is star-struck, I can't go through with it." Ramon insisted that I go downstairs and confront Princess Giovanna with the news that he had succumbed to the flu and "could not inflict my sick presence on Your Majesty tonight."

Those were the exact words I used on the English-speaking princess. Her face twisted into a bitter frown. She raised her hand and slapped my face. "Tell Mr. Novarro that slap was intended for him." With that royal pronouncement, she turned and departed from the lobby of the Excelsior with her entourage.

The next morning our trip was delayed for one day, which would make it very difficult for us to get to France in time to board *La France* before it sailed for New York.

Niblo was adamant that Ramon pose for a publicity still at the private studio of a photographer. I agreed to go with Ramon, where I encountered the Rod St. Just of the Roman paparazzi, Andrea Ciano. Amazingly, Mayer and Niblo had decided that Ramon should be photographed in the nude, with just a touch of pubic hair showing. At first I thought Andrea Ciano was lying until I confirmed the request with Aronson, who was still handling publicity for *Ben-Hur*.

"We're not going to show his cock," Aronson said, "although Niblo isn't opposed to a suggestion of pubic hair. Ramon has a great body. He'll look good in the nude. It will sell the picture. No actor's ever done this before—not even Valentino."

Since Ramon had been a nude model and was never ashamed to take off his clothes in public, he agreed to the shot, especially when Ciano borrowed heaters from a neighboring building to take the chill off the studio.

The pictures were taken, although I noted that Ciano slipped in some shots of Ramon's dick as well—no doubt for private collectors and homosexual fans of the actor.

The publicity still would eventually be released by MGM to a shocked America. Not since Rodolfo had posed in that bikini for *The Young Rajah*, had a still caused such excitement. Across America, wherever the still was posted, it was stolen by love-starved women, and perhaps a few admiring men as well.

Before departing from Rome, Ramon told Niblo the biggest lie he'd ever uttered. "You failed me as a director. I had a great dream about my participation in *Ben-Hur*. That dream, because of you, has turned into a nightmare. *Ben-Hur* will be my last film. I am through with the movies. The fame, the fortune, the adulation—none of that interests me anymore." With that startling statement he left the studio as we headed by train for Paris where we had very little time to make that boat sailing from the port of Cherbourg.

As a final disappointment, Ramon's most valuable piece of jewelry, a diamond- and ruby-studded watch, was stolen by his Roman valet, who had departed the suite hours earlier. The valet had come highly recommended, having once worked for the king. "Now I know why he's not working for the royal family anymore," Ramon said. "The shithead probably made off with the crown jewels." When I promised to buy him another watch, Ramon agreed to rush to the train station, without filing a police report.

By the time we reached Paris, we learned that a fire had burned down the Roman studio, which was really a big barn of a warehouse. That seemed to convince us that Mayer had made the right decision in returning the American crew to California, and abandoning forever the Italian crew—that is, those members who hadn't already died.

En route to America, we heard that a storm had blown down the Joppa Gate that MGM had built as one of the focal points of its set in Rome. Only the set for the Circus Maximus was left standing in Rome, but Thalberg had ordered that a duplicate be rebuilt in Hollywood.

On the ship, as it headed back to New York, Ramon refused to go into the dining room, ordering meals in our cabin. He played his guitar for hours and let his beard grow long. When I moved affectionately toward him to make love to him at night, he gently pushed me away, claiming he wasn't feeling well. I was completely baffled. Up to then he had been my willing love slave. Now he didn't seem to want to have anything to do with me.

Before we reached New York, Ramon on our final night at sea told me that he wanted to be a friend to me but not my lover. "From now on and forever more I want us to be sisters," he said. "The Rome thing was an aberration. It was wonderful while it lasted, but now my heart belongs to another person."

"Would you care to tell me who I've lost you to?" I said.

"No, it must remain a secret," he said. "You wouldn't know him at all. He's an actor but unknown."

I persisted in trying to get him to tell me who he was, but Ramon steadfastly refused.

Even before arriving back in Los Angeles, the American press was writing about *Ben-Hur*, although no one had seen the movie yet. After being idolized by journalists, the way Valentino was in his early days, negative comments about Ramon were appearing in the papers. A journalist for *Photoplay* wrote, "I can't imagine the tiny feet of Ramon Novarro, smaller than the feet of most women, fitting into the giant sandals of *Ben-Hur*."

As we arrived back on the West Coast, some one-thousand men were working day and night preparing the set for the chariot race at a site at the intersection of Venice Boulevard and Brice Road, the latter street name later changed to La Cienega Boulevard. A new Circus Maximus was being created.

In Los Angeles Ramon began acting like the imperial star he'd become, evoking memories of Rodolfo in the same situation. The first day back, he picked me up in his Lincoln coupe, claiming it had an extra gas tank so that he and his new lover could drive for miles into the California desert without fear of running out of fuel.

He drove me over to an old-fashioned mansion at 2265 West 22nd St. in the elegant

West Adams district of Los Angeles. He told me he'd paid only $15,000 for the house but would need to spend as much as $150,000 fixing it up. He showed me one wing of the house where he planned to install his own theater, although he was vague about what kind of productions he'd stage there.

Even before the filming of the chariot race, Ramon almost lost his favored position with Mayer. At the Ambassador Hotel, a reporter overheard Ramon saying to his new friend (name withheld) that, "Mr. Mayer is an uncouth little Jew with very little learning or background except how to make money."

For some reason, perhaps because he viewed Ramon as a potential money-maker for the studio, Mayer forgave him and also dismissed reports of Ramon's homosexuality. Mayer did caution the actor "to meet up with some pretty little gal and settle down in a rose-covered cottage so people will stop talking about you. Perhaps you and Barbara LaMarr can get hitched. You might satisfy her so she won't be chasing after every stud in Hollywood. I think she's gotten rid of her latest husband."

Surprisingly, UFA Studios in Neubabelsberg, Germany, was offering Ramon all sorts of big money to sail over and star in Goethe's *Faust*. Lillian Gish had agreed to co-star with him in the picture as Marguerite. But in time the deal fell through, although Ramon was delighted to learn that he was a popular and much sought-after star in Germany.

On Saturday night Ramon took me to his renovated bedroom in his new home which he'd painted a garish red and purple. There was a monumental gilded bed in the center. His lover would be arriving shortly, and I was not invited to stay. "This is where he fucks me four nights a week," Ramon said. "I'm madly in love with him. The other nights he spends with his wife."

"So this mysterious man is married," I said.

"He's married all right, just what Louis B. Mayer has in store for me but I'll never wed anyone."

At long last the second filming of the chariot race was announced. MGM had summoned its whole crew of extras, some 3,500 men and women, by five o'clock that morning so wardrobe could get them bewigged or bearded and into Roman costumes.

As I was covering the race for the Hearst papers, I invited Marion Davies to accompany me, and she was thrilled to witness what everyone viewed as a historical moment in film history. W.R. was on the East Coast, or else he would have joined us too. Charlie Chaplin turned down an invitation to go with me. But in our box sat Lillian Gish, my beloved John Gilbert, Douglas Fairbanks, and Mary Pickford. It was taking so long to set up the scene that the crowd was growing bored. Spotting Harold Lloyd, Doug called to him, and the two men staged a mock duel in front of the crowd to amuse them.

"Breezy," Niblo's assistant who had filmed the first chariot race in Rome, was nowhere to be seen on the set. Mayer had ordered Niblo to oversee some fifty cameras shooting from a 125-foot tower. Never before had so many cameras been used in one scene. Some of the cameras were placed inside mammoth statuary; others were buried in the earth to create the illusion of horse-pulled chariots racing out from the screen and over the heads of future movie-goers.

When Irving Thalberg arrived on the set, he was furious when he discovered that Niblo was employing only 3,500 extras. The production chief demanded "at least a thousand more extras."

Niblo protested that it was too late to round up so many extras. But Thalberg ordered members of the production crew to fan out into Los Angeles, dragging in extras from the streets, as they raided nearby bars, bus stops, dining rooms, and even fruit and vegetable markets. It seemed that hundreds of people were willing to sign on at the last minute in order to appear in *Ben-Hur*, which had received so much advance publicity.

The crowd of spectators was getting more and more restless. Matters weren't helped when a fog rolled in. It cleared by noon as the entire crew broke for lunch. There were lunches for only 3,000, some 1,500 short. Niblo at one point became convinced that if the extras were kept hungry, it would make the scene more realistic in their screaming for blood as in a contest between gladiators and animals.

After lunch, fifty-five actors dressed as imperial guards of the Roman Empire rode in on chariots. "Breezy," who'd directed the original chariot race in Rome, finally showed up and announced prize money for the winning chariots: $500 for the winner, $250 for second place, and $100 for third place. For that reason the drivers raced around the arena with deadly speed.

According to the script, Bushman would be in fourth position, with Ben-Hur in ninth position. The race didn't seem too exciting until one of the horses pulling the third chariot lost a shoe. The horseshoe went flying into the box of spectators, narrowly missing the delicate head of Mary Pickford who ran screaming from the bandstand, never to return. Doug later decided it was too dangerous for his Mary to watch without some sort of protective shield.

By the second race Niblo got the realism he wanted, even though it was a disaster. The wheels of a battling duo of chariots became entangled as they careened around a dangerous corner. Not knowing what was happening, two other chariot drivers rounded the same corner only to collide into the wreckage.

Even though mayhem was imminent, Niblo kept the cameras rolling, endangering a dozen men, including Bushman and Novarro. One of the extras, Henry Hathaway, ran out in front of the remaining (still undamaged) chariots and warned them of the disaster that lay just around the blind corner ahead. When Thalberg and Mayer later reviewed the scene, they decided it was so good they would keep the footage in spite of Hathaway appearing unexpectedly before the cameras. If you look at the film today, you'll see Hathaway waving down the chariots, although that was not part of the plot.

I feared mostly for Ramon. He'd barely escaped death when his chariot had overturned in Rome. Now he was racing furiously toward the wreckage of the other chariots. Perhaps because of divine intervention, Ramon escaped the clutches of death once more. His chariot just seemed to take wings and sailed over the wreckage. Driving his horses with fury, Ramon continued to head toward the finishing line as the winner of the race.

What happened to Bushman? According to the script, Messala's chariot crashed, crushing him to death. In actual fact Bushman escaped with minor wounds. Again infuriating

Mayer, Bushman claimed to the press that six horses were killed in filming his "death." Mayer angrily denied the charges, telling reporters that not one horse was either injured or killed in the chariot race.

On that final day of shooting, as I witnessed the event for the Hearst organization, Ben-Hur was a wrap. MGM's special effects men set off smoke bombs to celebrate the occasion. Pistols were fired into the air, making me wonder why so many extras were armed.

After three years with much destroyed footage, Thalberg faced two-million feet of film which had to be downsized to twelve reels before it could be brought to the screen. In time that was accomplished, and the premiere of Ben-Hur occurred on December 30, 1925 at the George M. Cohan Theater in New York.

It was the most expensive film ever made, costing $4 million, although it grossed nearly $10 million at the box office. But when Mayer's accountants tallied the final figures, their loss was more than one-million dollars, so Ben-Hur had to be rated a financial disaster for the studio. To make matters worse, Mussolini learned that in the film the Jewish Ben-Hur defeated the Roman Messala in the chariot race, although he'd been told in Rome that the opposite would occur. He immediately banned Ben-Hur from Italian cinema houses.

I did not go to cover the New York premiere of Ben-Hur, as many reporters were already in New York to do that. Instead, W.R. had wanted me to file some dispatches about Rodolfo's making The Son of the Sheik in Hollywood.

As I was dressing to go to Falcon Lair to see Rodolfo, the phone rang at my Hollywood Suite. It was Clark Gable whom I hadn't seen since I'd left for Rome I'd been very generous to him financially, and had been disappointed when I'd been unable to reach him upon my return. I had asked around for him but no one knew where he was. I suspected that he might have gotten some stage work far away from Los Angeles. When I brought this up to him, I asked what had been happening.

"I've got myself a movie star, toots," he said to me. "Don't get jealous. There are a lot of other men out here for you. But I decided to hook up with the biggest star in Hollywood.

He can do more for my career than you can. Sorry about that. I hope you're not jealous or mad at me."

"I'll get over it," I said sarcastically. "Do you mind telling me who this big-time star is? Sounds like it could only be Rudolph Valentino, Charlie Chaplin, or John Gilbert. Surely not Doug Fairbanks."

"Wrong on all counts," he said. "Clark Gable is pumping his noble tool into the delectable little rosebud of Ramon Novarro."

Chapter Twenty

Back in Hollywood, Rodolfo was in search of a new life. When he wasn't doing that, he was filming *The Son of the Sheik*, a sequel, of course, to his big hit, *The Sheik*. Under mounting debt, Rodolfo hoped this new picture would rescue him financially. He'd overspent and was hounded constantly by creditors, some of whom were filing law suits against him to collect long-overdue bills, such as for car repairs.

If *The Sheik* after the final tally had made three-million dollars, Rodolfo hoped the sequel would do even better. Rodolfo was uniquely cast as both Sheik Ahmed and also as his son and namesake. To play the elder sheik, Rodolfo would have to be made up to look much older and gray-haired. He was excited at the split-screen projections where he'd appear in the same frame as both "father" and "son."

Even though his new picture could rescue him financially, Rodolfo gave a disastrous interview to *Collier's* the day before I arrived back in Hollywood. He told reporters, "I'm no sheik. I had to pose as a sheik for five years. A lot of the perfumed ballyhooing has been my own fault. I wanted to make a lot of money, so I let the studio play me up as a lounge lizard. A soft, handsome devil whose only sin in life was to sit around and be admired by women. That's not me. At heart I'm just an Italian farmer. The only time I've been happy in my whole life was when I was homeless sleeping on a park bench in Central Park. This Great lover stuff is not for me."

Studio mogul Joseph Schenck exploded. That was the worst interview Rodolfo could give when starring in a movie entitled *The Son of the Sheik*. Ignoring the protests of his producer, Rodolfo gave yet another interview on the morning of my arrival at the train station. He said that, "If another producer comes to me with another sheik role, I'm going to murder the bastard. I'm a real actor—not some stupid sheik. I can play Hamlet or something meaningful." Then he did a surprising thing, shocking reporters present. Fortunately, journalism was self-censored in those days, and the press did not write about his concluding remarks as they were considered too controversial to print.

In front of the men—fortunately Lolly Parsons wasn't there—Rodolfo claimed he received some 6,000 fan letters a week. "All this talk about me being just a ladies' man is pure bunk," he said. "It turns out that half of my adoring fan mail is from men. Sometimes they send me nude photographs of themselves, or else they pose as characters I have portrayed in films. Most of the letters from these men are love letters. I am the first star in motion pictures who has become a sex symbol to both love-starved women and horny homosexual men. Until I started receiving all this fan mail, I didn't know so many homosexual men existed in America. On the screen, I am clearly their favorite. Let's face it: Charlie Chaplin and Doug Fairbanks aren't sexy. I have checked with other actors, and I understand they get almost no gushy fan letters from men. Half of the men who write in request a nude photograph of me." Shaking the ashes out of his pipe in front of the reporters, Rodolfo announced that after completion of the *Son of the Sheik,* "There will be no more sheiking for me."

Even before I saw Rodolfo again, stories about his love life had been told to me in New York. He'd dropped his pursuit of Vilma Banky, even though he'd almost lost his life over her in that threatened duel in the Bois de Boulogne with the Hungarian aristocrat, Baron Imre Lukatz.

Rod La Rocque had heeded my advice and had gone after Banky. Apparently, that lesbian and that homosexual man had reached an agreement to be seen in each other's company—possibly even marry one day. But what they did in private would remain their own business, as it would be for the long decades ahead when they indeed coexisted as a married couple. When I called Rod, he told me that he was escorting Banky to nightclubs and premières, but his nights were still spent in the arms of his sexy cowboy. "It's the best sex I've ever had," he said. "It's the best sex anybody has ever had." He said. He still refused to let me meet his alluring cowpoke stud.

On my first day back, I called Marion Davies to get a full report on Hollywood's newest romance—the budding love affair between Rudolph Valentino and Pola Negri. In my absence, the Polish vamp had snared my man. Marion, it seemed, had betrayed me, though she was to be forgiven, as I had never told her of my own love interest in Rodolfo. Figuring W.R. wouldn't let her have Rodolfo, she had dangled Rodolfo in front of that vixen, Negri. Marion had thrown a costume party in Beverly Hills and had brought Valentino and Negri together.

"Rudy was behaving like a sullen misogynist," Marion said, "so I decided to be matchmaker."

"What happened?" I asked.

"All I know is that neither of them would look at anybody else at the costume party once they met," Marion said.

The next week Negri told me that going to that party had led to her break with Rod La Rocque when he'd arrived at her house in street clothes—no costume. "I knew at once that he didn't want me to meet Valentino," she claimed. "He demanded that I get out of costume and stay home with him. But I refused. He threw a temper fit and stormed out, and I drove myself to the party."

At Marion's party, or so I'd heard, the guests had moved back to watch Valentino and Negri dance the popular tango, *La Comparsita.* She told Marion later that night that, "Valentino's raw sexuality reached out and captured me, binding me to him as tightly as a rope."

Although Negri came to the party alone, Rodolfo had invited Banky to go with him. No doubt Negri would rather go to bed with Banky than either Rod or Rodolfo.

Feeling frustrated that Marion had set up such an encounter, I confronted her with a bold accusation. "You know, of course, that your friend Pola is a lesbian, don't you?"

"I do," she said. "You don't possibly think I'm the naïve gal I was when I first me W.R.? Pola and I sunbathe in the nude together at my Santa Monica house. You know, girls will be girls when there are no men around."

"You mean, you've bumped pussies?" I asked.

"What gals do is no business of yours," she said. "You don't think I ask for gory details of what you guys do with each other. I don't want to hear it. My imagination will suffice. Pola called the next day, after the party. She told me, 'It was fatalism. From the moment our eyes met, I knew it was Valentino and only Valentino for me. This striking man with his Continental finesse has the power to destroy me or to take me to celestial heights. I don't know what it is going to be. When we made love after he drove me home, it was the greatest thrill of my life.'"

Later, when I saw Pola, she gave me her own version of what had happened on her first night with Rodolfo. "A heavy rain was beating against my bedroom windows. The room was illuminated from the dying embers of my fireplace. I lay in my gilded swan bed as Rodolfo descended onto me. It was an act of perfect love."

The next day, Negri crooned to the press, "I love Valentino deeply. I never knew a woman could love this much. It is my romantic Polish heart losing itself." The following day, she told another reporter: "Valentino is the perfect man. The supreme man. I am a connoisseur of men and I know that Valentino is God's greatest achievement. When God envisioned the perfect man, he came up with the Great Lover himself. When I marry him, and I will, it will last forever."

At Falcon Lair, I discovered that when Rodolfo wasn't taking Negri out to costume parties and nightclubs, he was riding his horses and furnishing his new home.

Falcon Lair, although inhabited only briefly, evolved rapidly into the new bachelor digs of Rodolfo. Unlike Whitley Heights, which he'd shared with Natacha, Falcon Lair would be occupied only by Rodolfo, except when he invited his brother and sister to stay with him. The Whitley Heights home was abandoned. After Rodolfo's death, the Whitley Heights house, originally conceived as "a temple of love" carrying a $30,000 mortgage, was put on the auction block. Although many major stars attended the auction, the house was withdrawn from the market when the highest bid turned out to be only $10,000.

When I saw Rodolfo again at his new home, I felt he had undergone some alteration of personality. For so long he'd been under the domination of Natacha. Now he was set free, but he didn't seem to know what to do with that freedom.

Instinctively he'd been drawn to the right woman, Pola Negri, Hollywood's most closeted lesbian of the time, other than Vilma Banky herself. Negri was someone to take out on the town for the benefit of photographers, but not somebody he had to sleep with.

Negri was spreading the word about town that Valentino was a superior lover in every way to "The Little Tramp," and certainly to Rod La Rocque. She had actually fucked Chaplin and La Rocque, but Rodolfo said that he'd never penetrated her. "We tried the first night," he said, "but I could not achieve an erection. She worked on me but I stayed limp all night. We finally agreed to give it up. Neither of us was interested physically in the other. Rod La Rocque doesn't know this, but Pola is spending her nights licking Vilma, or vice versa. From what I hear, that little Hungarian rhapsody has the most talented tongue in Hollywood—but only for women."

During our reunion, I was shocked to see how frequent Rodolfo's coughing spasms had increased. He confessed that he was continuing his clandestine meetings with the German baron and was taking the elixir the baron gave him. It still led to stomach cramps, which at times became so severe that production had to be shut down on *The Son of the Sheik*. Rodolfo showed me marks on his groin where the baron had drained blood from him. He was growing weaker and was losing weight. Nevertheless, he still refused to let Brian Sheehan come to Falcon Lair to examine him.

Rodolfo complained daily of his loss of hair. "It's not just thinning, but falling out," he said. "In *The Son of the Sheik*, I'm wearing a turban most of the time, so it doesn't matter. But I predict that within months I'll be sporting a toupee."

To please Negri and to delight photographers, Rodolfo accepted an invitation to a costume ball at the Biltmore Hotel. He came dressed as Gallardo, the matador he'd played in *Blood and Sand*. His date, Negri, came as the fiery gypsy she'd played in *The Spanish Dancer*. There was a certain irony to that. Originally, Famous Players had purchased a property, *Don César de Bazan*, by Vicente Blasco-Ibáñez, and had ordered the script department to fashion it into a role for Rodolfo. When he'd broken with the studio and gone on the dancing tour with Natacha, Famous Players decided to rewrite the script and turn it into a vehicle for Negri. The male lead was converted to female, with Negri appearing in her first American spectacle. It was also with a certain irony I noted that Antonio Moreno, my sometimes bedmate, was cast in *The Spanish Dancer* as the male lead. The film cost two-million dollars, a record sum back then.

At the Biltmore that night, Rodolfo as the matador and Negri as the gypsy dancer won first prize for their costumes, beating out Mary Pickford and Doug Fairbanks. She came as a little girl, Doug a swashbuckler. *Photoplay* ran a picture of Negri the next day under the caption, "Valentino's Third Wife?" She continued to give interviews about her "mad, passionate affair with Valentino."

In reality, when she called Falcon Lair the next night, Rodolfo was playing cards with some of his male cronies. When I told him his "true love" was on the phone, he said, "Get rid of the Polish bitch. What a God damn nuisance she is." Rodolfo's boss, Joseph Schenck, wanted him to continue this pretense of a Valentino/Negri affair, as the mogul felt it would increase box office grosses on *The Son of the Sheik*.

I couldn't help but notice that Rodolfo's sexual interest had waned, almost to the point of not existing. He'd abandoned his violent and often bloody love-making with me. In his bedroom at Falcon Lair, he stripped naked every night and lay on the bed, sometimes coughing, sometimes spitting up blood. On my third night back, he said, "You can have me tonight if you want me." I took him up on that offer but it was an uninspired blow-job, and he didn't get into it. Fellating this seemingly dead object wasn't a grand thrill for me. I didn't suck him off unless he specifically requested it. He seemed to want to experience an orgasm for some relief of tension instead of sexual passion. For that, I was turning elsewhere with my usual stable, which still consisted of Richard Dix, Theodore Kosloff, and William Boyd, or whatever new face appeared in town.

Pola Negri and Valentino were front-page news when they agreed to be matron of honor and best man at the wedding of Mae Murray and her hustler husband, Prince David Mdivani, who would eventually lead the blonde hare-brain to bankruptcy and ruin.

David was one of what became a Hollywood legend, the "marrying Mdivanis." Before these brothers arrived in Hollywood, they claimed to have been one of the wealthiest and most prominent royal families in the Russian province of Georgia, with enormous holdings in the Baku oil fields. All was lost during the Russian Revolution, and they set out for Hollywood to marry rich women. Alexis Mdivani would go on to marry Barbara Hutton, the second-richest woman in the world, Serge would marry the screen vamp, Pola Negri, and

the above-mentioned David would hitch himself up to Mae Murray.

On his first weekend free from shooting, Rodolfo invited me to drive up the coast with him. I was shocked at how reckless his driving had become. He was speeding so fast he seemed to want to kill both of us, a scene in the automobile eerily evocative of another experience I'd had with Ramon.

Rodolfo was heading for San Luis Obispo for the night, going eighty miles an hour. He was singing songs and enjoying a clear moonlit night. In spite of my pleading, he wouldn't slow down. At about three o'clock in the morning, a fog moved in from the coast. Still Rodolfo would not slow down, feeling if he blew his car horn loudly enough, an oncoming vehicle would get out of his way. His lead foot remained pressed hard on the gas pedal.

On the rain-slicked highway, he lost control of his big limousine, as it skidded across the road, his tires screeching. Leaping over a ditch, it bounded over the tracks of the South Pacific Railroad, destroying a crossing signal before plunging to an abrupt stop against a telegraph pole. The impact knocked him from the open car and into a gully, but I remained trapped inside.

I looked up in horror as I spotted the oncoming yellow lights of a slow-moving locomotive from Los Angeles. It just seemed to emerge from the fog. Caught in the headlights of the train, I screamed as it raced toward our wrecked car. At the last moment, the engineer slammed on the brakes, bringing the screeching train to a halt only feet from Rodolfo's car. I felt as if I was in a serial from *The Perils of Pauline*.

Pulling myself from the wreckage, I realized I wasn't injured. I ran over to where Rodolfo lay on the ground. He complained of pain in his back but, except for some abrasions, he seemed all right. His arm had been cut by flying glass.

Within minutes we were surrounded by onlookers, many disembarking from the train. Rodolfo was recognized at once by his fans. Both of us were taken to a local hospital where we were treated, the doctors finding no major injuries or broken bones.

Word reached us at the hospital that

souvenir collectors had rushed to the site of the wreckage after hearing the news about Valentino's car. The limousine had been dismantled, and within the week pieces of it were being hawked in Hollywood to curiosity seekers who wanted "a piece of Rudolph Valentino."

When he heard about the accident, Joseph Schenck of United was furious at Rodolfo for driving so dangerously during the filming of *The Son of the Sheik*. He demanded that Rodolfo stop driving until the picture was completed.

Newspapers launched an attack on Rodolfo the following day. *The Los Angeles Examiner* in an editorial wrote: "Give a swell-headed upstart an automobile and he will break his own neck or somebody else's in short order. The reckless, irresponsible Rudolph Valentino is always driving his automobiles at dangerously high speeds and is frequently in accidents. This dangerous pastime should be rudely interrupted by the strong hand of the law. Mr. Valentino should hear the slamming of a jail door."

My happiest times with Rodolfo were on weekends without automobiles. He'd purchased a yacht, the *Phoenix*, and we'd sail along the coast toward San Diego. On the boat Rodolfo would often cook in the nude, except for an apron. He made all his favorite pastas, but always refused to share the recipes with me. His food tasted wonderful.

We'd lie on the deck at night in each other's arms, looking up at the moonlight. Sometimes he'd be carefree, but at other times he'd be sad as if sensing impending doom. "I fear my world is coming to an end," he said. "All this peace and beauty will be taken from me."

He'd always take along his beloved Doberman, Kabar. The dog loved Rodolfo and followed him everywhere. If Rodolfo were happy, so was Kabar. If Rodolfo were sullen, the dog became ferocious and guarded his master. He would sometimes snap at me when I came close to Rodolfo. Once the dog attacked me in bed while I was making love to Rodolfo. He actually seemed jealous of me.

On the set of *The Son of the Sheik*, I read the script, finding it a frothy fribble of desert storms, dancing girls, violent love scenes in tents, sword fights, knife fights, gun fights, and lots of nocturnal rides and stirring chases under the desert moon or the desert sun.

Once again Vilma Banky had been cast opposite Rodolfo. Any passion that existed between Rodolfo and Banky had now ended, as she spent her time appearing in public with Rod La Rocque and her nights encased in the arms of Pola Negri. When Banky was with Negri, Rod presumably was with his mysterious cowboy.

Rodolfo had bitterly fought with Fred Niblo, who directed not only him but Ramon in *Ben-Hur*. Rodolfo always demanded that George Fitzmaurice be assigned to him as director. In *The Son of the Sheik*, Rodolfo got his wish. Fitzmaurice was the director, and he and Rodolfo were very compatible. Unlike previous Valentino films, the cast and crew worked in perfect harmony on the set, the director and Rodolfo communicating only in French.

During the shooting of this action film, Rodolfo was very weak. He saved all his energy for his appearances before the cameras, retreating otherwise to his dressing room where he rested to conserve his energy. Often shooting would have to be interrupted as Rodolfo went into another of his coughing spasms.

As the dancing girl, Yasmin, Banky played a character whose "moving hips fill men with abandon." I laughed when I read that, later telling Rodolfo, "that means Vilma gives men a hard-on. Thank God you're dressed in your baggy sheik drawers."

Although at the time, it was presented with the utmost seriousness, the film today is viewed as camp, as Rodolfo as the sheik sings to Yasmin, the dancing girl, the Kashmiri love song—"Pale Hands I Loved Beside the Shalimar."

To my surprise, Agnes Ayres, who had co-starred with Rodolfo in the original *Sheik*, was cast in its sequel in the minor role of Diana. Agnes had graciously agreed to recreate her original role in this rip-roaring story of rape and conflict in the desert. Fitzmaurice had even inserted a scene from the original film, depicting Rodolfo as the sheik carrying Ayres off on his horse, threatening her, and ordering her to, "Lie still, you little fool."

Even though Banky with her blonde tresses

seemed miscast as a dancing Arab, she was effective in close-ups with Rodolfo. Kissing, nuzzling, and nibbling at him, she murmured "sweet nothings" into his ear. Rodolfo looked more beautiful than ever in this film, even though his health was failing. The most amusing scene, for which male reporters would later write with scorn about Rodolfo, was when he kisses his way along Banky's arm, settling on one erogenous area inside the tender skin of her porcelain-skinned elbow.

Rodolfo was never sexier than when he roughly dragged Banky into his tent, accusing her of betraying him to his captors. Fitzmaurice deliberately used big candles as phallic symbols. Never had Rodolfo been so effective as a screen seducer, snorting and sneering like a great bull about to mount a cow. Tossing her about, he displays his anger as he pushes her into his bed. This is rape as romance as it had never been depicted on the screen before.

Eyes shadowed and his face coldly vengeful, Rodolfo lights a cigarette as he strips off his robe, unclasping his bejeweled belt. It appears that for one moment he is going to remove his pants and expose himself. "An eye for an eye," he tells Banky. "A hate for a hate." She clings pleadingly to his legs, at one point her delicate hand maneuvering very close to his crotch. In a mammoth close-up, Banky is photographed with dilated eyes, anticipating her rape. He grabs her and crushes his lips against her. The camera reveals a bed, as he maneuvers his captive toward it.

For the desert storm sequences, I traveled with Rodolfo and the crew to Yuma, Arizona, where the studio had rented giant wind machines to stir up the sands into blizzard-like swirls. Banky complained to me that the gritty particles were destroying her beautiful skin. Everybody hated these man-made storms except Rodolfo, who seemed to relish them, although they would often bring on another one of his coughing spasms. Somehow these artificial storms appealed to his own sense of self-destruction and hopelessness about his life.

At one point in the scenario, he mounts a horse and chases after the fleeing Yasmin as portrayed by Banky. Without warning, a seizure overcame him. I screamed as he doubled up on his horse and slumped over. It looked as if an assassin had shot him. I ran to him and helped him down from his horse, asking two extras to help me carry him to his dressing room. There he rested for the remainder of the day, even coughing up blood. I bathed his forehead with cold towels and begged him to let me take him to a doctor. He continued to refuse medical attention, claiming that if I insisted on calling a doctor, our relationship would end.

The Son of the Sheik was the most sado-erotic film ever made up to that time. In time it would develop a cult of necrophilia that flourished around the legend of the film long after Rodolfo was in his grave.

Eventually captured, Rodolfo is strung up and dangled against a wall, his silk shirt sexily ripped. His chest is exposed to the public as his torturers emerge. As he is approached for a whipping, his eyes dilate in anticipation. The ensuing scene is highly sexual as he is whipped, his biceps bulging for maximum effect. The impression that he is helpless when confronted by his captors is emphasized because of his heavy use of lip rouge and eye shadow. Savvy members of the audience just know that after his beating, the desert sadists are going to untie him, bring him down, and gangbang him *à la* Lawrence of Arabia. S&M fetishists still delight in viewing the scene today.

The Son of the Sheik had its world première at Grauman's Million Dollar Theater in Los Angeles. Looking pale, sick, tired, and grim, Rodolfo escorted Negri to the event. She was ebullient and smiling in front of the photographers. It was as if she—not Valentino—were the star of the flicker. She outdazzled him in a tight-fitting silver sheath gown, with a large pearl necklace, her jet-black hair crowned by a sparkling diamond tiara.

Caught in the dazzling glare of klieg lights, which seemed to blind Rodolfo, he told reporters, "I would rather be playing Cellini or Machiavelli instead of the role I'm appearing in tonight. Perhaps some dashing romantic hero of the Christian crusades. Why not Marco Polo?" These comments didn't seem designed to please Joseph Schenck. Much of Rodolfo's career and financial future depended on the success of the film, so I didn't understand why he wanted to degrade his role in it.

The Hollywood elite, led by Doug Fairbanks and Mary Pickford, showed up that night for the première. Mae Murray arrived in a spectacular red gown and diamonds and was escorted by her new husband, the international hustler, Prince David Mdivani. At intermission, I introduced myself to Mdivani, since I hadn't been invited to his wedding with Mae. I stood next to him at the Grauman's urinal, and saw first hand eyewitness evidence of what had attracted Mae to this fake prince. Catching me looking at him with such admiration, we exchanged introductions. He winked at me and dangled his cock a few extra times for my pleasure.

Buttoning up, he walked with me to the sinks to wash our hands. "I hear you're the richest boy in Hollywood," he said, "and quite obviously the prettiest." On the way back to our seats, he paused in the theater lobby. "Mae's not as rich as she pretends. You know she's also fourteen years older than I am—that is, she admits to fourteen. Frankly, I think she's older." He handed me his card. "I'll be waiting for your call. Mae's gone all day at the studio. I have every day free with absolutely nothing to do, and you can see from that encounter at the urinal I've got a lot to do it with."

After "The End" appeared on the screen, and the heavy velvet curtains were drawn, the first night audience broke into a roar of approval, the clapping mounting, growing into a mighty crescendo. "Speech! Speech!" came the roar from the crowd. "We want Valentino. We want Valentino." That call gave way to, "RUDY! RUDY! RUDY!"

Appearing onstage, Rodolfo made a few astonishing comments. He looked drugged and seemed to want to chastise the audience for their poor taste in appreciating such fluff as *The Son of the Sheik*. "I don't know if George Fitzmaurice and I are crazy for having made this picture in the first place, or if you, the audience, is crazy for liking it, but I appreciate the applause and your coming here tonight." He coughed briefly before disappearing from the stage. There was a long delay before the audience applauded again. After the première, Joseph Schenck gave Rodolfo three days off before he was to go on a nationwide tour to promote *The Son of the Sheik*.

The next morning Rodolfo was still asleep in his bed at Falcon Lair when a series of boxes arrived containing stills he'd requested from his pictures. He'd asked for these stills "in case someone decides to open up a Rudolph Valentino museum devoted to my memory."

"You sound like you're about to kick the bucket."

"Kick the bucket?" he asked with a raised eyebrow. "You Americans and your slang make no sense to me sometimes. Why would I want to go and kick a bucket?" He turned and headed for his bedroom.

Having nothing to do and facing a long morning, I opened the boxes, enjoying looking at the stills. The stills from *The Eagle* were the first to come into view. I'd seen the film only once and had spent all my time watching Rodolfo, playing little attention to the rest of the cast. One of the photographs caught my attention. Rodolfo was at the center of the frame. He was dressed as a Cossack with several extras, also dressed as Cossacks, in the background.

The face of one extra stunned me. Even though bearded and older, there was no mistaking who it was. It was my beloved Frank who had deflowered me in the fields of Kansas. My Montana cowpoke to whom I'd surrendered my virginity. The man who had launched me into gay sex, and the first man I'd ever loved. As I looked at his photograph, I feared I'd never gotten over him. For Frank, I would gladly abandon Rodolfo, Charlie, and even my stable of lovelies. The years had not dimmed my passion for him.

I decided to call the one man in Hollywood who might track down Frank for me, my beloved friend, the photographer, Rod St. Just.

*****

After staying at Rodolfo's Falcon Lair for three nights in a row, I arrived back at the Hollywood Hotel to pick up my messages. Since I was no longer hoping to break into pictures, I didn't expect any calls from producers. The one note that intrigued me was a message to call Clark Gable. I thought he might be at Ramon's house but the number was unfamiliar to me.

When I rang him up, a butler announced, "Miss Frederick's residence." The only Miss Frederick I knew of was the screen and stage actress Pauline Frederick.

When Clark came on the phone, he seemed glad to hear from me and asked me what I was doing for the night. "Taking you to dinner at the Hollywood Hotel," I said.

"Great!" he said. "I'll be over within the hour."

When I put down the phone, I didn't ask him why he was at Miss Frederick's residence—or why he wasn't in the arms of his "true love," Ramon Novarro. That would have been too provocative. Although I dressed and prepared myself to receive this new breed of Hollywood actor—that is, tough guy—I knew that Clark wasn't coming over to visit me because he had the hots for me. There was some other reason, perhaps financial.

Later, in my suite at the Hollywood Hotel, I was amazed at the physical transformation in Clark as we sat enjoying my bootleg bourbon. His sallow complexion was gone. Before he had an unhealthy yellow look to him. But now he appeared more robust and tanned. He flashed his new teeth at me. They were straight and gleaming white and improved his appearance remarkably. "Thanks for the teeth," he said. "It's made me a big success in Hollywood, and I'll owe you one for that."

Somehow his apelike hands looked better under the French cuffs that were held together with gold links, a gift from Ramon. I knew that because I'd purchased those gold cuff links as a gift to Ramon as Ramon and I had strolled along the via Veneto in Rome. I admired his well-tailored suit, a dark blue, thinking I had never seen him dressed so expensively.

"I'm glad you like it," he said with a smirk before winking at me. "I ordered three of them in different colors. Taking advantage of our former relationship, I sent the bill to you. You'll get it tomorrow. I'm sure you won't mind."

"I won't mind," I said, "But instead of singing for your supper, you might have to sing for those suits."

"Fair enough," he said before a waiter approached. He ordered the thickest steak on the menu cooked blood rare. Clark ate with gusto. "Forgive me for making a pig of myself," he said. "But those days of going hungry have only ended since meeting you. When I used to get various jobs in the theater up in Oregon, I never had any money. Every day my big choice was either a piece of apple pie or a bowl of hot soup. I often chose the pie. Maybe that's why my teeth rotted."

As we talked, I pointedly avoided the two big questions of the night. What was going on between Ramon and him? Was "Miss Frederick" the famous actress, Pauline Frederick, or another Miss Frederick? And, for final measure, what about his wife, Josephine Dillon? I figured Clark would reveal all when he got around to it.

In the meantime, as he enjoyed the steak and mashed potatoes with fried onions, he wanted to talk about Oregon. "I had a girl up there. I never went to bed with her, though. Would you believe it? I was a bit shy back then."

"As I can plainly see, you've gotten over that."

"I'm not shy but I'm still haunted by a lot of fears," he said. "I have a lot of insecurity about my appearance. I'm still awkward on the stage, and I'm afraid of the camera. I don't like the way I photograph."

"You photograph just fine," I said, hoping to reassure him.

"I fear I'm going to die," he announced abruptly.

"Why on earth?" I asked. "You seem like a pretty rugged specimen to me."

"My mother died of epilepsy. I think it can be passed on from mother to son." As he devoured that steak, blood dribbled from his mouth. "I still can't believe I've reached the point in life where I can order a steak whenever I want one. Up in Oregon I stole tinned cans of food from a grocery store. I had no way of heating up the food, so I'd open the tin and eat it cold. Sometimes I had to sleep on the beach and build a fire to fight off the bitter cold. I'd wrap myself in a blanket. That was stolen too. Our little theatrical troupe used to sail up and down the Columbia River performing shows at the little river towns. We always traveled on a milk boat since passage was cheaper. But those God damn boats had no cabins, so we had to sleep out on deck in the cold."

That seemed to give me a lead-in to the important questions I wanted answered. "Apparently those days are but memories. I gather you're now sharing some of the warmest and most luxurious beds in Hollywood."

"I guess you figured out where I was when you called," he said. "It's Pauline Frederick all right. I'd be with her tonight but she's talking to these producers from London about appearing on the stage in the West End."

Pauline Frederick back then was a name as famous as Sophia Loren. Divorced three times, she was a *femme fatale* even though she was forty-four years old. Rich, famous, and horny, she was a courtesan-class beauty who lived in a mansion on Sunset Boulevard. She was obviously ripe for the plucking when viewed by the hustler eyes of Clark Gable.

"I met her when I was appearing with her on the stage in San Francisco in *Madame X*," he said. "She's a bitch. But I was impressed on opening night that she got thirty-three curtain calls. As you know, she's often named as the other woman in divorce cases. She likes sex almost as much as Barbara LaMarr. I'd had Barbara several times, incidentally. Pauline always says to me, 'Live life to the ultimate,' and she tries to do that. She's left behind a string of broken hearts. One young guy committed suicide when she ditched him."

He leaned over to me and whispered. "The cunt is insatiable in bed. She wants me to be a stud hoss all night long. In bed, Pauline acts like she's never going to get laid by another man, and this is her last fuck on earth. She wants to make the most of it. I'm glad to be eating steak tonight because she's feeding me a diet of oysters. She feels they'll act like an aphrodisiac and keep me hard all night long. I hate oysters. They remind me of licking some slimy pussy, and I'm not muff-diver. I like my sex in the missionary position."

Thinking the conversation would shift to his romance with Ramon, I was surprised when he told me that he was spending much of his time with Lionel Barrymore. "You didn't know this, but Lionel is my all-time idol. He's got me a small part in his play, *The Copperhead*. I can't believe I'm working with a guy I've always idolized. For years I've been cutting my shirt collars to look like Lionel's. He thinks I look like Jack Dempsey. He says I'm even hung just like Jack Dempsey. He claims if blindfolded, and presented with my hard cock and Dempsey's hard cock, they would both be the same dick. Isn't that interesting?"

"Fascinating," I said. Having seen Jack Dempsey nude in the shower, I respected Lionel's opinion.

"When I showed up to audition for *The Copperhead*, Lionel practically drooled over me," Clark said. "I fucked up on opening night and tripped and fell into a palm tree. Lionel gave me hell backstage. Just when he was denouncing me the most and threatening to fire me, I pulled out my dick and had him on his knees in no time. There was no more talk of firing me regardless of how I fucked up on that stage."

"Pauline Frederick and Lionel Barrymore," I said. "Not bad."

"At the theater Lionel trails me around like a lovesick puppy. He even takes off my smelly socks to lick my feet and tongue my toes. I hear DeMille likes to do that too, and I know you do. I have to fuck Pauline, but Lionel is happy just to give me a blow-job. He always compliments me on my staying power. He says I can hold off longer than any man he's ever known, even his brother John. He used to be in love with his brother, and he sucked him off a lot. What Lionel doesn't know is that by the time I whip it out for him, Pauline has already drained me dry. Lionel has to work extra hard just to get a small load from me."

"I hope these two will do something for your career," I said.

"Lionel's even made a screen test for me. It was for a part in a film he wants to direct called *Never the Twain Shall Meet*. He personally dressed me in a sarong with a hibiscus behind one ear. The test bombed. Lionel told me he can't get the money to make the film. But I'll keep trying."

Clark had been right about that. He would go on from that night to other screen tests, including a famous one he made for Warner Brothers, hoping to get the lead of the tough guy in *Little Caesar*, the role eventually going to Edward G. Robinson. When Darryl F.

Zanuck saw Clark's test, he screamed, "His God damn ears are too big. The fucker looks like an ape. No woman would ever have a romantic fantasy about Clark Gable." So much for Zanuck's judgment.

"Do you ever get to see your wife, Josephine Dillon?" I asked, still avoiding talk of Ramon.

"You mean, Mrs. God?" he asked. "I try to steer clear of her whenever possible. All she does is remind me of my mistakes and tell me how to correct them. I'm getting tired of that shit. I want to be admired. Fuck her. I want every woman in America worshipping me, from the society matron to the teenage gal. That's gonna happen too." Clark, it seemed, was a better prophet than Zanuck.

Finally, when I could stand the suspense no more, I bluntly asked him. "And what about Ramon Novarro?"

"That's what I want to see you about tonight," he said. "I know that you were shacked up with Ramon in Rome. He told me he tossed you aside for me. But I want to give him back to you."

"Exactly what does that mean."

He laughed before his face broke into that familiar and somewhat smug smirk. I braced myself for the kind of notoriously racist (and homophobic) macho diatribe that Gable and many members of the Hollywood elite would, at least in 1926, drop whenever they felt like it.

"It's not working out between us," he said, "even though the little Mexican pansy has given me five-thousand dollars. I can lie back while you or Lionel gives me a blow-job. But Ramon wants to treat me like I'm his fucking homosexual husband. He wants me to fuck him and stick my tongue in his mouth. I might have gotten carried away with you once or twice, but just as a rule, I don't ever do that. First I can't stand Mexicans. They smell. To me, any man who'd fuck a Mexican would fuck a nigger."

"That's a bit harsh," I said. "Ramon hardly smells. He's the most fastidious man I've ever known. Immaculate. All he does is groom himself. He bathes twice a day. At least."

"Maybe I'm just looking for reasons to ditch him," he said. "But I can't stand making love to him like he wants. It's too faggoty for me. When I mentioned that we might be breaking up, he threatened to commit suicide. He claims he's going to leave a love note, blaming me for his suicide. It'll make all the papers. The little spic is trying to ruin my career before it even gets launched. You've got to go to him. Help him get over me. Wipe this talk of suicide from his head."

"That I will do," I said. "Ramon gets overly romantic at times. In a week he's over it and goes on to his next adventure. He won't carry a torch. But thank you for telling me this. In my way I love the little guy. I'll go to him and offer myself. If he's tired of me, I'll show up with some new prize that will be even better and more alluring than Clark Gable."

"Dream on," he said. "There ain't no man in Hollywood who's better than old Clark here. But you might find someone who'll be a meager substitute. After they've had Gable, I ruin both a man or woman for all other lovers."

I truly felt Clark exaggerated in that pronouncement. But there was something about his cocky attitude that I found intriguing until the day he died. Long after any sexual involvement with him was buried, I followed and wrote about his advancing career for years.

A pivotal moment in his career came when I visited him backstage in Chicago, where he was appearing in a play also called *Chicago* (no, not that one!). The star was Nancy Carroll who would go on to Paramount to earn $5,000 a week. Clark was pulling in $150 a week, and was proud of it.

Clark was cast as Jake, a loudmouth newspaperman, and the role would mark a defining point in his career. He appeared on stage that night with his coat collar standing up, his battered hat tilted back on his big head. He walked across the stage with the stride of a lumberman. Even when he wasn't in the main scene, he stole scenes from Carroll as he stood motionless in the background, with one arm akimbo, with that soon-to-be-famous smirk plastered across his face, his devil-may-care eyes darting about. Later he would make this bit of stage business his trademark before the camera, especially when he appeared as Rhett Butler in *Gone With the Wind*.

That night in Chicago, Clark told me, "Male reporters don't have to be slick, suave, dashing, and hand-kissing like Gilbert and Valentino. A reporter should be a rough, tough guy ready for anything, especially if it involves a woman. We don't have to walk like a gigolo, or talk like a professor at Oxford. In fact, we don't even have to stand up straight. We can be a diamond in the rough, and women will go for us all the more."

Again, Clark was a prophet, at least about his own career. He must have known what was in store for him. In his lifetime, he would appear on the screen playing reporters nine times, including his most memorable portrait, in *It Happened One Night*, where he starred opposite Claudette Colbert in roles that won Oscars for both of them.

To punish Clark for asking for more money, Louis B. Mayer had loaned the actor out for "Cohn's lousy bus picture," the script having been acquired for $5,000 by Columbia Pictures, which was known at the time as one of the Poverty Row studios. Eventually, the picture would bring glory to Hollywood mogul Harry Cohn, who, with the success of *It Happened One Night,* would go on to become a Hollywood legend of mythic dimensions, turning out such stars as Rita Hayworth and her eventual replacement, Kim Novak.

Little knowing that he'd go on to win that Oscar several months later, Clark viewed working for Cohn as "Siberian exile for hoity-toity MGM stars." In fact, Clark was so furious about having to work for Columbia that he'd shown up drunk to meet the film's director, Frank Capra, for the first time. Clark had even belched in Capra's face. The director found Clark disgusting. Capra had wanted Robert Montgomery for the role, but had been forced by Harry Cohn to settle for Clark Gable instead.

Capra hadn't fared much better when he'd taken the script to Claudette Colbert, after having had it turned down by Myrna Loy, Margaret Sullavan, Constance Bennett, and Miriam Hopkins. The film had been called *Night Bus* back then. Colbert's dog had bitten Capra in the ass, requiring hospitalization, but she agreed to take the part, providing he'd give her $50,000 and would complete the film in just a month.

It Happened One Night, as every movie buff knows, went on to become Best Picture of the Year, and Colbert and Gable were named best actress and best actor. I was there when Clark showed up on Oscar night to accept his award. He told the audience that his hat size would still be the same. Backstage he claimed to me that, "During the filming of that damn movie, I never made one pass at Colbert. The French dwarf had her head buried every night between Marlene Dietrich's legs, and had no time for me."

After the end of our dinner at the Hollywood Hotel, Clark seemed to feel he owed me a favor, not just for the suits, but for potentially rescuing his career from ruin by staving off what he feared might be an impetuous act of vengeance from Ramon. "Let's go upstairs," he said after finishing off a big slice of lemon meringue pie.

Once inside my suite, he stripped nude and stood before me, seemingly demanding that I admire and compliment his body, which I did.

At the door to my bedroom, he turned back and flashed that smirk of his which was to become famous on the screen. "This is your last night in bed with Clark Gable. I've got half the world out there, mainly women, panting for me." He reached below to fondle his "noble bird," as he called it. "You'd better make the most of it tonight, because you'll never get to taste it again. I hope you're hungry."

*****

The next day I repeatedly called Ramon but his manservant said he was gone for the day. I left several messages in case Ramon called home. Around five o'clock he called me back, saying that he was at the Whitley Heights home of Barbara LaMarr. He sounded despondent over his failure to ignite a romance with the hustler, Clark Gable, and had gone over to Barbara's home, hoping to find solace with this survivor of many a broken romance or marriage.

Ramon told me that Barbara had invited me over that evening to join them, and I eagerly accepted the invitation, setting out in my stagecoach, as thoughts of this jazz age goddess, my former roommate, filled my head.

Barbara LaMarr remains a virtual unknown today, though she's often cited in biographies of Hedy Lamarr. Louis B. Mayer, who had a long and abiding passion for Barbara, christened Hedy with Barbara's last name but with a slight alteration, LaMarr becoming Lamarr. Long before Hedy was acclaimed "the most beautiful woman of the century" and long before Mayer made her the last great superstar of his pre-war Hollywood empire, there was another most beautiful woman in the world, Barbara LaMarr herself.

I had missed her. What had started out as a beautiful friendship between us had been derailed by Ramon. He'd captured her affection when they'd appear together on the screen in such flickers as *The Prisoner of Zenda.*

Barbara was still a mystery to me. How could she marry five different husbands and still carry on so many affairs? Ramon had told me that she'd had at least forty lovers in the past two years. What were these husbands doing when Barbara was out screwing around? I'd heard that she'd dumped her fifth husband, the red-haired comedian, Jack Dougherty.

Ramon kept me posted on Barbara's romantic developments. Barbara had just broken up with her latest lover, Gilbert Roland. Having personally known the mighty inches of this heartthrob, I told Ramon that, "Barbara was one lucky girl. She should have hung onto Roland. That one can sexually satisfy anybody."

It seemed that Barbara and I had the same taste in men, and had shared several of the same conquests, notably John Gilbert. That is, we shared the same tastes in lovers, but not in husbands. Barbara was welcome to any of the men she'd married. I had no idea what had attracted her to this string of losers when she could have her pick of virtually any man in Hollywood.

"She likes women too," Ramon had told me. "She spent a long weekend with Greta Garbo but refuses to tell me what happened. You won't believe who she's fucking now. Buster Keaton."

Memories of seeing Buster Keaton unbutton his fly at a hotel urinal flashed through my mind. I would gladly concede Keaton to Barbara.

Only two days before my invitation to visit Barbara, Ramon had asked me. "Do you know who her latest conquest is?" I mean, post-Keaton?

"I can't imagine."

"Douglas Fairbanks Jr."

"She's gone from father to son. Of the two, and having known both, I would prefer Junior to Senior. Let Mary keep dear old Dad. Barbara is perfect for breaking young Doug in for other women. I predict Junior will be one of Hollywood's alltime studs. I hope he keeps his gay streak, though. I think he's ninety percent heterosexual and only ten percent homosexual."

"You should know, you lucky devil," Ramon had said.

As I headed for Barbara's driveway, I passed the lonely and deserted house in Whitley Heights where Rodolfo had lived with his bride (in name only), Natacha Rambova.

Driving the final lap to Barbara's home, I reflected on how the press had begun to look with a more skeptical eye at Barbara's allure on the screen in the wake of her having made twenty-seven films before her 30th birthday. Most critics still filed glowing commentaries on Barbara, but some recent reviews had been scathing. *The New York Times* had found her role as "the Lady Known as Lou" in *The Shooting of Dan McGrew* not to their liking, writing, "Her overdoctored lips glisten in the glare of the klieg lights, and she indulges in her usual conception of excitement by panting." Another reviewer found that her "quivering eyebrows act like untrained seals." The director of her most recent film, *The Girl from Montmartre*, was said to call out to her, "Okay, Barbara, let's now have expression number three." Barbara was said to have only five screen expressions.

Edwin Schallert, the caustic critic for *The Los Angeles Times*, decried her acting and felt that the beauty of her face was what carried her through a picture, that and "her disturbing personality." His exact words were, "She is made for lurking tragedy. One feels the beat of ravens' wings about her. Her radiance is that of moonlight in the heavy shadows of the night. Calypso she is, burning with a flame of subtle ecstasy."

To me, Barbara was always a lovely panther filled with grace and carrying a slightly silky look. In spite of her velvety softness, she possessed sharpened claws.

Ramon had told me that she almost defiantly squandered the money she earned as a bigtime movie star. "Darling," she once said to me, "money was made to circulate from pocket to pocket. One must be generous with money. Life is too short to horde it."

Until Clara Bow came along, Barbara was the ultimate Hollywood party girl, the last to leave any night club, often in dawn's early light. "If I go to bed before dawn," she once told me, "I consider the evening a failure. I must hurry and see as much of life as I can before I pass on. Sleep! Who needs it? Maybe two hours a night, if that. I can't believe Mother Nature intended for us to spend a third of our lives in a coma."

When I arrived at Barbara's, a manservant showed me into the living room where I encountered a drunken and drugged Ramon. He had been snorting cocaine from a miniature replica of a gold-plated casket resting on Barbara's grand piano.

"Help yourself," Ramon said, pointing to the cocaine. "Or if you prefer, there's opium over there." He pointed to another box on Barbara's coffee table. "There's even liquor," he said, pointing to her bar, "in case you're still old fashioned and like a whiskey now and then."

I went over and gently kissed his lips. "How are you?" I asked, taking him firmly by his arm to steady him.

"You mean do you think I'm suicidal over the breakup of that nothing thing with Gable? No way. I just threatened Gable to scare the shit out of him. It was my way of telling the hustler not to fuck with me or I could make it impossible for him in this town. I don't want any man walking out on Ramon Novarro now that I'm a star, and that goes for you too. When I'm through with a guy, I'll let him know. I can't stand it when they walk out on me. Leaving me for Lionel Barrymore and Pauline Frederick. Get serious!"

"I'm relieved to hear you're not going to commit suicide or die of a broken heart over Clark."

"I've found something better," he said, a gleeful look in his expressive brown eyes. "Younger, prettier, and with at least three inches more than Clark's stubby short one."

"Fill me in, sweetheart," I said. "Rod La Rocque keeps his new lover under lock and key, but perhaps you'll let me in on your latest."

"Darling," he said, "you know his body far better than I do. After all, you've been sleeping with him since he was two years old."

I looked startled. "You can't mean Barbara's latest, Doug Jr."

"One and the same," he said.

"But I thought he'd fallen for Barbara," I said.

"He has in a very big way," he said, "but Barbara is my sister. She's always looking out for me. In fact, she's supplied me with more of her beaus than I've ever found on my own. Barbara has told Junior that he has to satisfy me first before she'll agree to go to bed with him. Beginning last night, Junior kept his part of the bargain. He said you broke him into gay love, and he likes it, but only as a sometimes thing, providing he doesn't have to give up Barbara."

"How can I love you so?" I said to Ramon. "It seems you have to have all of my men. Not satisfied with Rodolfo, you went after Gable. Now my favorite charmer, Doug Jr., himself."

"Something like that is too good to waste," he said. "He must be shared. He's coming over tonight. Barbara wants us to keep him distracted because she's got a date with his father, and she doesn't want Junior to know. I have suggested to Doug that you and I have a three-way with him here tonight, and he's agreed. What do you say?"

"With my two favorite men on the planet, Ramon Novarro and Doug Fairbanks Jr., how can I say no?"

"You can't," he said, smiling at me, kissing me on the lips. "Besides, I was a bit hasty letting you go so soon after Rome. After Gable, I decided I'd much rather be fucked by you. You penetrate real deep and dirty like I like it. Gable, because of his physical limitations, couldn't go as far down as I need for my own sexual satisfaction."

"I understand," I said, turning around at the approach of Barbara's manservant.

"Miss LaMarr would like to see you now," he said.

Kissing Ramon again on the lips right in front of the servant, I trailed him, wondering why Barbara didn't come down and see us. Perhaps she was ill. Going up the stairs to her second floor, he led me into her bedroom. I looked around for her, but saw no one in the dimly lit chamber. The servant knocked softly on a side door. I heard Barbara call for me to come in. The man opened the door for me and stood back, ushering me inside.

In a room where candles cast forgiving lights, Barbara was nude in her enormous sunken tub, which dominated her all onyx bathroom with its solid gold fixtures. She held a little baby boy in her arms, gently washing him. "Take off your clothes, Durango, darling, and come and join us. After all, you have nothing to conceal from me after some of the things we've done."

Stripping at once, I joined Barbara and her baby in the sudsy water. "I didn't know you had a baby," I said. "A Hollywood secret, no doubt."

"It's not my own," she said, gently washing the child's left arm. "I was making a personal appearance in Dallas. At the Hope Cottage Foundling Home, I discovered this little charmer." She turned the child around for my inspection.

"He's adorable," I said. "Such expressive blue eyes. That head of blonde curls would make even Mary Pickford envious."

"He's just sixteen months old and all mine," she said, cradling him in her arms. "This is one love I need in my life now. All the attention from men—lovers or husbands—has turned to ashes in my mouth. When beauty fades, so do the men. But a child might stick with you forever. I have found men to be utter failures when it comes to love. I'm going to raise my baby to grow up to be the kind of man I've always wanted and searched for, but never found. My child—his name is Don—is going to become the man I'd want to marry myself."

Later, after our bath, Barbara put on an oriental silk robe and headed for her dressing room. She gave the baby to the servant who was told to put the infant to bed. After kissing her baby good night, she turned to me.

Up close to her, I was mesmerized by her eyes. They seemed larger than before and a bit too heavily lined. She'd always used her eyes like weapons, making conquests with them and slaying men better than any sword could. Her face was made for the close-up on screen, but I detected life draining from it.

As if sensing my concern, she said, "I've made so many pictures... I fear that each of them has taken my life's force, diminishing me somehow. I've given too much of myself on the screen. I think if I keep making pictures, there will be no life left in me. Each film has chipped away at the edge of my soul, aging me."

As she dressed in front of me for her date with Doug Sr., she said that she'd just completed work on the film, *The Girl from Montmartre*. "The director had to cut back on my schedule. Sometimes I was able to work only three hours a day because of my waning energy. Out of sheer weakness, I fainted several times on the set. In the past few months, I suddenly started to gain weight. Almost thirty pounds. To take it off, I went on this crash diet hoping to reclaim the graceful lines of my figure. But the starvation has taken a toll. My once fun-loving smile appears a bit hollow now."

"You are still the most beautiful woman on earth," I assured her.

"It's not just the diet," she said. "As you know from Ramon, I've been drinking and taking a lot of drugs. The more I take of either, the more I want. I can't stop myself. I'm also half worried out of my mind. Up to now money didn't matter. Now that I have a son, I'm thinking about money for the first time in my life. It seems I'm $75,000 in debt. I constantly overspend. I'm sure you saw that gold-colored Rolls-Royce out front. Trinkets like that cost money, as does this house with its gold fixtures."

After Barbara dressed and used makeup to cover up her dissipated look, she went downstairs where she kissed both Ramon and me goodnight after snorting a final round of cocaine. "Tell darling Doug Jr. that I had to meet with my director tonight." She paused in her foyer. "I'm sure the two of you can satisfy his libido tonight even better than I could." With that prediction, she was gone.

Barbara never kept that date with Doug Sr. Her driver told Ramon, Doug Jr., and me later that night that the screen star had collapsed in the rear of her Rolls-Royce and had to be taken to a sanitarium.

It was there that Ramon and I visited her early the next morning just as soon as visitors were allowed. We learned from her doctors that Barbara was critically ill with nephritis (inflammation of the kidneys), a condition brought on by excessive drinking and chronic drug abuse. I called Brian Sheehan, asking him to come and examine her. As Ramon and I waited in a private office, Brian came back two hours later. "She's drifted into a deep coma. I fear Sleeping Beauty will never wake up."

Ramon burst into violent sobbing, and I held him in my arms to comfort him. Brian placed both of his strong arms around us and we huddled together like a trio in mourning.

Two days later she was buried, as some 40,000 fans filed past her bier. The little chapel where she was buried had long ago run out of seats, and angry mobs formed outside, demanding entrance. Police had to battle this crowd clamoring for seats. The service was simple and straightforward, as a reader from the Christian Science Church came and conducted a brief ceremony.

I sat next to Paul Bern, John Gilbert's former roommate. Bern was said to have been in love with Barbara, and tears were falling down his cheeks. Had he too come under the spell of the "vampire?" In time, Bern would go on to love again, this time the blonde bombshell of the Thirties, Jean Harlow. He would marry Harlow before his tragic suicide, which would be followed a few years later by the premature death of the screen goddess herself.

The date of Barbara's death on January 30, 1926 is still etched on my brain. She somehow knew she'd never live to be thirty.

After the service, a mass hysteria set in. As the flower-draped casket of Barbara was placed in a long black hearse, the unruly crowd charged police lines and rushed the funeral procession. Dozens of women fainted, and the police had to rescue their bodies out of fear they would be trampled to death. Some one-hundred spectators suffered minor injuries before the hearse was allowed to proceed to the Hollywood Cemetery and Barbara's entombment.

Barbara had left behind survivors, especially her little baby, who would later be adopted by her close friend, the actress Zasu Pitts. The child would be renamed Don Gallery.

The screen vampire seemed to have cast a curse over her husbands. Her third husband was eventually sent to Folsom Prison for forgery, and her final husband, Jack Dougherty, who survived her, was found dead of carbon monoxide poisoning in a parked car in the Hollywood Hills in 1938.

After the crowds had departed, Ramon and I remained at Barbara's tomb. It was a sentimental gesture, but I took her favorite flower, an American Beauty rose, and placed it beside her tomb.

Ramon stared down sadly at it, as tears welled in his eyes. "Cut flowers bloom for just a short time."

In spite of a stray onlooker here or there, he took my hand as we strolled the paths of the cemetery, heading for the exit. As I looked around at the graves and mausoleums, I could not have known that this cemetery would soon claim another dear friend prematurely.

*****

A week after Barbara's death and my three-way with Doug Jr. and Ramon, "Ben-Hur" telephoned. "I've been thinking," he said.

"No more suicide talk?" I asked.

"Fuck that Clark Gable," he said. "If only his dick was as big as his ears. I'm a lot more interested these days in young Doug. After our three-way with him, I pursued him for a few days. But he's chasing after Norma Shearer now."

"Greta Garbo, Barbara LaMarr, and now Norma Shearer," I said. "Lotte Lee taught that boy his lessons. But Doug Jr. had better watch out for Irving Thalberg. If Irving gets wind of this, Doug might not find work in this town again in spite of his famous father."

"You've got that right," Ramon said, "but I'll let you in on some gossip now that you're a big-time Hollywood writer."

"The trouble with your gossip is I can't print it," I said.

"You can't print this either," he said. "As everybody knows, Irving has a bad heart, and there are weeks at a time when he's feeling sickly and can't satisfy Norma. She's got to get it from somebody, 'cause I hear she's insatiable. Can't get enough."

"I know what insatiable means. Insatiable is Ramon Novarro."

"No, insatiable is Durango Jones."

"Cut to the chase, boy," I said. "Give me the red meat."

"Norma is fucking Irving to become the queen of MGM."

"That's hardly news to anybody, certainly not to Louis B."

"Irving is not really her sexual cup of tea," he said. "She has a targeted interest. She's a child molester like Chaplin. Chaplin likes little girls. Norma likes little boys, the younger the better. She's mad for Doug Jr. and fucks him any chance she gets."

"Doug is very attractive and mature for his age," I said. "Any red-blooded male or hot-blooded pussy would go for that young dick." Of course, I couldn't print Ramon's latest tidbit of gossip and actually thought no more of it until two of Greta Garbo's child co-stars—years later—confirmed Ramon's spicy gossip about Shearer.

In 1927 when I knew the child actor, Philippe de Lacy, I visited him on the set of *Love,* which was the silent version of Tolstoy's *Anna Karenina.* Garbo was only twenty-two at the time, and Philippe was playing her son, Sergei. That darling, curly haired Philippe was then known as "the most beautiful boy in the world." He took me to his dressing room where he showed me some expensive jewelry Shearer had purchased for him.

"I can't believe this," I said to him. "You're a mere child."

"Just a minute," he said. "Who are you calling a child?" He then proceeded to unbutton his pants and pull out the biggest dick I'd even seen on a boy. "I'm a freak of nature."

I stared in amazement. "Most grown men, certainly Clark Gable, would love to have a dick that size. You can put it away now," I said, fearing someone would walk in on us in the dressing room and call the police.

"Norma can't get enough of it."

"You're fucking Norma Shearer, the wife of Irving Thalberg?" I asked. "You don't even come up to her waist line."

"That's fine with me," he said. "I'll get to bury my head in her tits when I'm banging her. That's not all. Greta also has the hots for me."

"But she's hot and heavy with John now," I said. My beloved John Gilbert was the male star of *Love.*

"She's tired of that pansy with his soprano voice. My voice sounds more masculine than Gilbert's. And I'm only a kid. I bet I've got him beat by a mile in the dick department, too."

"My only hope for you, boy, is that dick of yours doesn't get any bigger," I said. "Otherwise, you won't find a man or woman in Hollywood who can take it. You're the next Francis X. Bushman."

We were interrupted by a knock on the door. Going to the door, I opened it to find the cold but beautiful face of Garbo who regarded me with suspicion. She brushed past me and descended on Philippe, giving him a wet, sensual kiss. She told him she'd meet him outside, as she'd secured the makings of a picnic for them.

When Garbo had left, Philippe turned to me. "I had some pictures taken the other day by Rod St. Just. I hear he's your best friend. I even posed for some nudes for Rod, and he was amazed. He's photographed all the big hunks in Hollywood. He said no stud is accepted as a stud in Hollywood until he's satisfied Durango Jones. So I'll be calling on you one night when I can slip out of my bedroom away from my guardian, Edith."

To my total surprise, this cocky but beautiful boy paraded out the door where even the great Garbo was apparently mesmerized by him. I found myself actually fantasizing about Philippe's call. Had I become another Charlie Chaplin? If not Charlie, I was a budding Norma Shearer.

That afternoon Garbo and Philippe shot their famous scene together in *Love.* As I watched the filming, I noted that Philippe projected a Raphaelesque sensuality. With Garbo as his doting mother, he appeared to be making love to her in front of the camera. He took her hand between his and kissed her brow. She lovingly patted his cheeks. But it was the expression in their eyes that made it love. Incestuous love, that is.

Although more sophisticated audiences of today when viewing *Love* recognize that Garbo and Philippe are making love on the screen, only one reviewer at the time, a critic for the *Los Angeles Examiner*, caught the meaning of their scene. He called Philippe "an androgynous satyr."

In one of those ironies that seem to happen only in Hollywood, I was also on the set of the Talkie version in 1935. *Love* had gone back to Tolstoy's title of *Anna Karenina*, and Garbo was repeating her part, except she was now talking. Philippe's screen career and his childlike beauty had vanished, and the part of Garbo's son had gone to Freddie Bartholomew, who had captivated audiences in *David Copperfield* and would go on to win them again in his immortal *Little Lord Fauntleroy*.

When I interviewed Freddie, and in a memory that evoked Philippe, the young boy told me that he too was fucking Norma Shearer. "I'm driving the bitch crazy," he said, even though he didn't appear to have anything like Philippe's equipment. "Well, we're not exactly fucking that much," he said. "Mostly she spends all her time licking my feet and sucking my toes. Ever since I met her, I haven't had to bathe them."

Those were unpublished secrets I just told you. Of course, all of Hollywood was to learn later that Norma Shearer was fucking America's favorite adolescent, Mickey Rooney, just turned sixteen. Long before he married that North Carolina beauty, Ava Gardner, this teenage Andy Hardy was spending a good part of his MGM salary on hookers. Many of Hollywood's older leading ladies went for this precociously oversexed teenager. Chief among his movie star fan club was Norma Shearer, who according to the reports of the day couldn't get enough of young Mickey.

When not with Mickey, Norma took up with young Doug Jr. again—that is, when he wasn't with her chief rival, Joan Crawford, to whom he was married. Shearer later dumped Doug to enjoy the manly and more mature charms of James Stewart.

The only time I came into serious romantic rivalry with Shearer was over Tyrone Power. Both of us wanted this handsome hunk who knew how to please both men and women. The fight I had with Norma over Tyrone must have fine-tuned her memorable performance in *The Women*, which co-starred her rival, Lady Crawford. Long before she had to deal with Bette Davis at Warner Brothers, Joan had her nemesis, Norma Shearer, to cope with.

I don't know why learning that Norma Shearer was a child molester should surprise me. After all, she wasn't the first one in Hollywood. It was refreshing somehow to learn that she liked young meat. When I'd first arrived in Hollywood, I thought child molesters were either older men lusting after young boys, in the famous case of tennis pro, Big Bill Tilden going for young Doug, or else Charlie pursuing pubescent girls such as Dolores Del Rio and Barbara LaMarr, plus each of his first two wives. Now I realized that with Norma in the game, child molestation was an equal opportunity employer. Among lesbians of course, Nazimova led the pack of older women lusting after young girls, especially in her pursuit of Charlie's first wife, Mildred Harris.

Later, completely distracted, I spoke to Ramon on the phone that long-ago morning back in Hollywood of 1926. During that dialogue, I didn't have Norma Shearer or any of her child actors on my mind. I was obsessing about only one person, a very grown-up man named Frank. In fact, I was impatient to get Ramon off the phone, although only weeks before in Rome I thought I was madly in love with him.

"I don't want to talk about all these other people," Ramon said. "I want the Hollywood gossip in the future to be about us. I was too hasty when I ended my relationship with you. At first I thought I was in love with you because I was away in a foreign city and making a picture with a director I hated. I thought I was just turning to you in comfort. Now I know it's more than that."

"What brought about this change of heart?" I asked, still a bit bitter at how I'd been dumped.

"The other night when I was going down on young Doug, and you were fucking me, I realized it feels better from you than anyone," he said. "Even better than Rudy. I always fear with him I'll mess up his coiffure." He paused. "I want you to move out of the Hollywood Hotel and come and live with me."

I hesitated for so long that Ramon had to demand that I answer him. What I didn't tell him was that at the very moment he'd asked me, a nude William Boyd had just appeared in my living room, fresh from a night in my bed. He had his usual morning hard-on and was signaling me to come back into the bedroom.

"Let's be friends," I whispered hurriedly into the phone before hanging up on Ramon. I'd use that same line endlessly in the future on other lovers for whom my passion had faded. As a future lover, Tyrone Power, would one day say to me, "Once your curiosity is satisfied, you want to move on instead of setting up housekeeping in some rose-covered cottage."

A few minutes later I was going down on the steel-hard inches of the future Hopalong Cassidy. Even as good as it was—and it was very, very good—I wasn't thinking of this cowboy but another cowpoke. I was dreaming of my beloved Frank and what he had made me, his willing victim, do near that windmill on that deserted hill in Lawrence, Kansas.

Somewhere in the great city of Los Angeles, Frank was wandering around without the beard he'd worn as a Cossack extra in *The Eagle*. He was grown up now, and I was eager to sample him to see just how much man he'd become. Forget John Gilbert. Forget Theodore Kosloff. Forget Ramon Novarro. Yes, and dare I say it, forget even my darling Rodolfo, who wasn't always a darling to me. Ironically, there was nothing to forget about Charlie Chaplin, since I didn't really love him. He and I had developed—more or less—a business arrangement with occasional sex when he had nothing else on the hoof.

The only man I wanted in the Golden West, and a man I had to have at any cost, was Frank. He must have a last name, and I was determined to find out what it was, plus a lot more about him. I didn't know who Frank was currently bedding. Knowing him, it could be either a man or woman. Whoever it was, I was determined to get rid of the competition and put that cowboy's boots under my bed at night.

Eroticizing about Frank had inspired me to such a point that I brought William to a spectacular climax. It was one heavy load considering how much he'd spewed out the night before. I imagined it was Frank's juice I was tasting. He was my first man, and a gay guy tends to get very sentimental about "the first time."

When William had gone, I called Rod St. Just and invited myself over. With me, I brought the still from the set of *The Eagle*, showing Rodolfo in the main frame with Frank appearing as an extra in the background.

At his studio after his usual wet, sensual kiss of me, Rod studied the photograph carefully. "I know who he is."

"For God's sake, tell me," I pleaded. "How do I get in touch with him?"

"I promised his patron not to reveal a word," Rod said.

"Who is this patron?" I demanded to know.

"I can't tell you that either," he said, "but if you just happen to drop by the studio at two o'clock tomorrow afternoon, you might discover Frank, his patron, and me setting this actor up for a screen test. He wants to be the next Valentino, and he wants me to make him up as your Rudy before I shoot the screen test of him. His patron is paying for the test."

"You've got the wrong guy, I fear," I said, feeling deflated. "Frank is no Valentino. He's a guy from the Rocky Mountains. There's nothing sheiky about him."

"I agree with you, but he wants to look like Valentino in case there are any more sheik roles getting tossed about."

"You've got to tell me where I can find him," I said. "I don't think I can wait until tomorrow."

"No can do," he said. "I gave my word. His patron knows how close you and I are, and he was afraid I'd squeal. That's why he made me promise. The patron is out of his mind in love."

"I understand why," I said. "After you go to bed with Frank, he spoils you for all other guys. He was the first man to deflower me."

"C'mon," he said. "This is 1926. No one

since Victoria's day uses the word deflower anymore. Today we say he fucked you. Besides, I thought you lost your virginity to Buddy Rogers."

"Even before dear Buddy, there was a Frank. I was a virgin when I met him."

"Dear, dear, sweetcakes," he said. "A virgin, were you? I tell people you were violated while still in the womb. Your father managed to penetrate you somehow when he was fucking your mother in the ass as she was carrying you."

"You bitch! I bet you do tell people that."

Rod kissed me on the lips. "I've got to run now. Your mama's got a date with a hot new actor I've discovered. He's John Mack Brown, and I predict he's going to take Hollywood by storm. What a looker!"

At that point I'd never heard of him, but I knew Rod had a keen eye for future stars. I wouldn't meet John Mack Brown until he appeared with Joan Crawford in *Our Dancing Daughters* in 1928. The most appropriately titled film he was to ever make—and I followed him around for years and saw all his movies— was the 1942 *Ride 'Em Cowboy*.

As I left Rod's studio that day, I envisioned that my life had come full circle. I started out with Frank who had taught me what male love was all about, and I'd end up my life with Frank.

My dream exploded when I arrived the following afternoon at the studio of Rod St. Just. He was sitting up front in his living room having tea with another Rod, Rod La Rocque. I was flabbergasted to find La Rocque here. I had come hoping for a reunion with Frank.

Rod seemed surprised to see me, and a bit angry. "What in hell are you doing here?"

Inventing an excuse, I claimed I was here on a mission for Rodolfo, wanting to pick up some extra photographs of "Valentino as an Indian. In his next movie, he's going to play Black Feather. Rod's taken some great photographs of Valentino, and I need copies to show around."

"Valentino as an Indian," La Rocque said. "My God, it'll probably be a big hit. That means Moreno, Novarro, Cortez, and I will then be rushed into a series of Indian pictures. *The Sheik* repeating itself all over again."

I wanted to ask where Frank was, but didn't wish to appear obvious in front of La Rocque. For all he knew, I had never met Frank, much less been his lover. I tried to be friendly and charming with La Rocque, as much as I could be. It was painfully clear that Frank had snared himself a big-time movie actor.

I wondered how I could eliminate La Rocque from the picture and have Frank to myself. That would take some scheming, but I was determined to do it. Anything to capture Frank's heart and take him away from the clutches of La Rocque. Besides, La Rocque already had the Hungarian rhapsody, Vilma Banky. What did he need with Frank?

Not wanting to kid myself, I knew that Frank possessed something Banky didn't. Nor could La Rocque's two previous girl friends, Gloria Swanson and Pola Negri, lay claim to such an appendage either. Frank had something every woman in Hollywood wanted, and what most homosexual men dream about and never find.

As always, my faithful friend, Rod St. Just, sensing my discomfort, came to my rescue. He turned to La Rocque. "While Durango searches for those pictures of Valentino in Indian drag, I should show you some nudes I took last night of my new discovery. His name is John Mack Brown, and he's going to become the next big sensation in Hollywood. I'll take you in the back and show you the photographs. I've just printed them. Hot, hot, hot!"

Ignoring me for the moment, La Rocque seemed to be panting to look at the photographs. Consequently, I assumed that his love and devotion to Frank weren't embedded in rock.

"Better yet," Rod St. Just said. "The real John Mack Brown is upstairs in my bedroom. I'd like you to meet him." He smiled. "He sleeps in the nude with the sheet off. I hope you don't mind."

"You've got me so hot to get a look at this guy, I'd rip the sheets off of him," La Rocque said.

He motioned for La Rocque to proceed ahead of him up the stairs. Once he was outside the range of our voices, the photographer turned to me. "Frank's in back taking a shower. He had a job as an extra this morning on a sagebrush film. Would you fetch a big towel for him out of my closet over there and take it in to him? He's probably coming out of the shower right now."

With a wink, Rod disappeared, trailing the other Rod (La Rocque) up the steps and into the bedroom where this mysterious Jack Mack Brown waited to provide the visual entertainment of the afternoon. I also wanted to go and inspect Brown too, but I had bigger game to chase after.

In Rod's bathroom, I heard the sound of Frank's voice singing in the shower. With the thick towel, I waited to greet him when he pulled back the shower curtain. His voice was like a memory of my past that brought me back to the time of my innocence. I loved him for taking away that innocence. He'd launched me into life. But he'd also deserted me without a good-bye, and I was really pissed off about that, though eager to forgive him. I knew that his body must have grown, and that he might look considerably older. The same could be said for me too.

A sudden feeling of apprehension came across me. Maybe Frank liked very, very young boys, the way I used to be, and didn't go for grown men. I was fully grown now and my body much more filled out, especially after all those workouts with Ramon in Rome. I'd even become a bit muscled. Maybe Frank got off only on early teenage boys with girlish bodies. I was soon to find out, because he'd stopped singing and had turned off the water.

Frank pulled back the shower curtain. His body dripping droplets of water, he stood tall and straight, with a wisp of wet hair dangling over his bright eyes. He stood at least six feet, three inches tall—a lithe and lanky cowpoke. His Adam's apple bobbed up and down upon seeing me, but he didn't seem in the least bit startled. He gulped. Even then he was into gulping, which would become a trademark of his over the years to come.

I had deliberately kept my eyes focused above his waist, but I could no longer resist the temptation. I took in the sight of his cock. His light brown pubic hair had increased in thickness, and it crowned a massive piece of meat. If anything, Frank had grown bigger and better than ever. Even soft, he hung eight and a half thick and uncut inches over a rodeo-sized

pair of balls. His foreskin just barely covered the large head, which offered a tantalizing glimpse, like a preview of coming attractions.

A minute must have gone by before either of us said anything. He smiled at me and said, 'I've missed you, little darling."

"I've missed you too," I said. "I dream about you every night. No one, no one has ever replaced you."

"That's very flattering," he said in his monosyllabic voice with its warm drawl. "But can't you see I'm dripping wet, and you've got that big thick white towel. Why don't you put it to work?"

"Gladly," I said, falling down on my knees before him as he stepped from the shower. I started wiping him dry at his feet and worked upward along his strong legs until I reached the source of my long-ago satisfaction. His cock got a rubdown and I couldn't resist the temptation to peel back the skin and plant tiny little kisses on the purplish knob. He seemed to like that as his dick increased in girth and length, at least another two tempting inches. I dried his balls before moving upward to towel his chest and nipples. I took the unused part of the giant bath towel and wiped his face dry before toweling his beautiful hair dry too. Slowly I worked down his strong back until I reached his perfect ass, which I paid special attention to. After I'd gone inside to dry his asshole, I couldn't resist letting my tongue dart out to wet it again. He always liked that.

As I was drying the back of his legs, I heard voices coming down from the top of the stairs. "You'd better scurry out of here," Frank said. "We wouldn't want to make a big-time movie star jealous, now would we?"

I handed Frank the towel. As I started to leave, he grabbed me and held me close to his nude body, his lips enveloping mine. Instinctively I opened my mouth and was rewarded with his long, tasty tongue. It was all I could do to break from him, as Frank was rising to an utterly thrilling erection, making me wonder how I could ever take it.

"We've got some catching up to do," he told me. "For ol' times' sake."

"I'm at the Hollywood Hotel," I whispered to him. I headed down the hallway and entered Rod's kitchen where I poured myself a cup of coffee before wandering innocently into the living room where the two Rods turned and looked at me.

La Rocque was the first to speak. "I'm going to make a prediction," La Rocque said. "That Johnny boy is going to become the biggest stud actor in Hollywood. He's gorgeous from the tip of his ear lobes to his big toes, with a fat surprise waiting in the center. I think I'm in love."

"But I thought you already had somebody," I asked provocatively.

"I do," La Rocque said. "But his body is a bit skinny. The only thing not skinny about him is his fat cock. But that Johnny Mack Brown is something else. He's a perfect physical specimen. He's got a big cock too, although nothing to compare with my Montana mule."

"Size isn't everything," I said.

"Oh, isn't it?" Rod St. Just chimed in. "You gals can speak for yourself."

At this point Frank entered the room. He was fully dressed in a cowboy shirt and jeans. As if to signal his possession of this young man, La Rocque walked over to him and planted a wet kiss on Frank's lips. Then Rod La Rocque turned to me. "Durango Jones, meet my new lover, the stud hoss of the Golden West. Gary Cooper."

*****

Frank's new name would take some getting used to. Not only that, but his older, more mature, and more masculine aura thrilled me as well, although there had hardly been anything wrong or unsatisfying about the teenage Frank either. Gary Cooper was the type of guy you wanted to go ride off into the sunset with.

Putting his arm around Gary, La Rocque said. "My good man here is a flytrap to women, but no cunt in Hollywood deserves him. Gary is for connoisseurs. Only men deserve to know what he's carrying around in those tight jeans."

"I'm sure that's true," I said, as I pretended

I'd never met Gary before, and he too was pulling off that charade.

"Time is wasting," Rod St. Just said, directing all of us toward his dressing room and studio in the rear of his apartment.

Frank's new name had come from his agent, Nan Collins, who said there were too many Frank Coopers living in Los Angeles. She'd come up with the name "Gary" because she'd taken a map of the United States, closed her eyes and had blindly pointed. Her finger landed on Gary, Indiana.

Amazingly, my tall and rawboned friend, now called Gary, had insisted that he be made up to look like Valentino. I couldn't think of any two men who were as different in style and appearance as Rudolph Valentino and Gary Cooper.

A skilled makeup artist, La Rocque took a tube of lipstick and painted a cupid's bow mouth on Gary. I stood back looking on in horror. Such a mouth was more appropriate for Mae Murray, and even on her, the style had become old-fashioned, mocked by everybody, especially Erich von Stroheim. La Rocque then applied heavy eye shadow to Gary, before taking a tube of hair cream and plastering down his beautiful hair like some Valentino clone.

Gary told us that he wanted to take the finished photographs and go from studio to studio, hoping to find work as a movie actor.

Before the camera of Rod St. Just, Gary assumed a Valentino mask with half-drooping eyes. At that time Gary was stunningly beautiful in spite of his lean frame. His face was angelic. I knew that Rod St. Just didn't want to photograph him like a Valentino impersonator. Hollywood had enough of those already, including Rod La Rocque himself.

But whenever St. Just played the role of commercial photographer, his guiding philosophy was, "The John who's paying is always right." When he had finished with his photographs, St. Just invited me to the filming of a do-it-yourself screen test of Gary, for which La Rocque was paying $150.

In my stagecoach I drove them to an idle set along Poverty Row, home of low-budget pictures. The set was made available to us by a custodian after we'd slipped him ten dollars. As St. Just set up for the camera work, giving directions to Gary, La Rocque pulled me aside. "Isn't he the most gorgeous male animal on the face of the planet?"

"There's no disputing taste," I said. "That's why restaurants print menus. He's not my type, though. Too skinny."

"But that pole hanging between his legs makes you forget he's no muscle boy," La Rocque said. "The first time he fucked me I thought I was going to be split open. Just when he'd gone where no man has gone before, I found out he still had three more inches to plow into me."

"Better watch out," I warned him. "You'll develop loose stool. You won't be able to hold it back."

"You bitch," La Rocque said. "I'm glad to know you're not crazy about Gary. I don't want the competition. Everybody in Hollywood knows you've got money—God knows where you got it—and I understand you like to spend money on studs. Your thing with Clark Gable is spreading across town. I'm a bit tight with the dollar, and I don't want to spoil Gary. Putting up $150 for a screen test, maybe. Buying him a new car, forget it!"

"This is Los Angeles," I said. "A young man needs a car to go from studio to studio."

"I'm not going to buy him one—and that's that," La Rocque said. "I don't want him to think that all he has to do is shove that Montana pole of his up some gay guy's ass, and he'll grow rich overnight."

"C'mon, Rod, buy him a God damn car," I urged. "He's going to have to take those glossies from studio to studio along with this screen test. He's going to need transportation."

"No way, sugar," La Rocque said with a smirk on his face. "The only way he'll get a car is if he earns enough money to buy one for himself. Or else…"He raised a provocative eyebrow at me, the way he did in his lounge lizard movies. "Or else if you've lied about not being attracted to him and go behind my back and provide some wheels for him."

"It'll never happen," I assured La Rocque. As La Rocque went over to supervise the screen test he was paying for, I tipped the custodian of the studio another five dollars to let me go into a private office to use the telephone. I had to order a present for

someone, and I wanted total secrecy.

The street where Gary made his first screen test eerily evoked a setting from *High Noon,* which Gary would make decades from now when his inscrutable face had grown craggy and leather-like with age. A tired horse stood nearby, waiting for Gary to mount it. He mounted the horse as Rod St. Just called for "Action! Camera!"

The scenario, if it could be called that, looked dull and dreary to me, although the heavily made up Gary had never looked more beautiful, in spite of the garish cosmetics. As Rod filmed it, Gary rode the tired steed down the wide street of the town, coming to a fast stop. He dismounted by jumping off with the grace of an athlete.

He then took off his ten-gallon Stetson and wiped his brow, as he turned to face the camera, his mouth widening into a shit-eating grin. Then, as directed by Rod St. Just, Gary turned to let the camera capture his left profile and then his right profile. Full faced or in profile, all sides of Gary looked gorgeous. I wanted to eat him on the spot.

When Rod called a halt to filming, Gary came over to La Rocque and me, smiling. "If that don't do it, I don't know what will."

I feared for Gary's chances with this screen test. In those days, film companies picked their own actors for screen tests which the studios then made themselves, with a young hopeful often appearing opposite such established stars as Charles Ray, Richard Dix, or Norman Kerry.

As the sun beat down on Gary, I was enthralled to have been reunited with this lean, slouching and beautiful man from my days in Kansas. In time, of course, his beauty would fade, and he'd become ruggedly handsome, like one's fantasy of a frontiersman. Even though only twenty-four, he was at the peak of his male allure. In the bright light, his makeup appeared a bit grotesque, but back in those days of intense lighting and insensitive film, all actors were heavily made up, even rouged and lipsticked.

No one had eaten all day, so I drove the two Rods and Gary to the Ship Café where the headwaiter warmly welcomed La Rocque, dismissing the rest of us, no doubt as unknowns, even though I made frequent appearances here.

All of us were viewed as a star's entourage, circling around our butterfly, Rod La Rocque.

Over drinks, I began to understand why Gary was attracted to La Rocque, who I had always viewed as a bit effeminate. Through La Rocque, Gary hoped to break into pictures.

"My darling Vilma," La Rocque said, loud enough to be overheard at the next table, "is going to star in a movie with Ronnie Colman. It's called *The Winning of Barbara Worth*. There's a part in it that's ideal for Gary here." He reached over and patted Gary's hand, which rested on the table.

"Let's not put the horse in front of the wagon," Gary said. "I don't have the part yet, and I think the director, Henry King, doesn't think I can act."

Both Vilma and I have talked with King," La Rocque said. "I think he's more or less set on casting you. I think the picture can make a big star out of you."

King doesn't think I can pull off my one big scene," Gary said.

"What's that?" I asked, genuinely interested.

"Don't worry about it," La Rocque said. "King has a solution. In one scene Gary has to appear to have ridden through the desert for twenty-four hours. After dismounting, he has to drag his tired body up a flight of stairs at this little hotel. He knocks on the door. Colman answers it. Gary is supposed to collapse at Colman's feet. King thinks he knows how to pull this off even if Gary isn't an experienced actor. He's going to make Gary run for ten miles before filming begins. At the end of the run, he's going to throw sand dust in Gary's face, let the camera roll, and order Gary up those steps. I don't see how the scene can fail."

"We'll see," was all Gary said. "Before all this happens, I've got a new part. I'm going to appear briefly with Lightnin' the Super Dog in *Lightnin' Wins*." (At the time Super Dog was a rival of screen legend, Rin-Tin-Tin.)

"I heard you made some two reelers for that queen of the cowgirls, Marilyn Mills," Rod St. Just said.

"I did indeed," Gary said. "Pulled in fifty a week."

"How come you started acting in films?" I

asked him.

"I didn't plan it that way," Gary said. I wanted to be a cartoonist. I've had several of my cartoons published in papers in Helena. For a while, I worked as a baby photographer. I went around in the dead of winter banging on the doors of housewives, trying to convince them to let me take pictures of their little brats. A lot of women slammed the door in my face. I got used to hearing, 'Get lost, mister.' Two old bachelors, however, invited me in to get warm by their fire. I learned later they had other things on their minds. But, what the hell! A cowpoke has to do what a cowpoke has to do."

I learned that Gary had appeared in a little opus called *Tricks*. "The director said I looked like a stringbean. I played this villain. He made me wear five extra shirts so I wouldn't look so skinny. In another flick, I got to catch Tom Mix as he fell off a horse, and the next week I got to pet Rin-Tin-tin. It was my first dog picture before *Lightnin'*."

Gary told us that he'd been hanging out in Los Angeles but often weeks went by without finding work as an extra. "I heard about this park where out-of-work actors go to get picked up and taken home for the night. My first night there I was picked up by this black guy, Peavey, who took me home to his master. It was William Desmond Taylor. He promised to make me a big star, but someone shot him before he got around to that."

"Is that where you met Rod La Rocque?" I asked. "In the park?"

Gary laughed and mock-punched La Rocque. "Yes, our big-time movie star here cruises the parks to pick up handsome stud hosses like me."

"A bit dangerous," Rod St. Just said.

"I know," La Rocque said. "But I love the danger. You've got to understand this. Not only do you get to bring a guy home, but you get to experience the thrill that he might murder you at any time."

"Whatever turns you on," I said, trying not to eye Gary too much and devote an equal number of my gazes to the two Rods.

"I didn't plan to break into movies," Gary said. "One day as I was strolling along broke, I ran into Jimmy Calloway and Jimmy Galen, two boyhood friends from Montana. They told me they were making ten dollars a day just falling off horses. They said many of the so-called cowboys hired in pictures can't even ride horses. I figured I could do that, and the ten dollars a day sounded good. My first job was in a picture called *The Vanishing American*. It starred Richard Dix."

"I know him well," I said.

"With a job falling off horses, you're black and blue all the time," Gary said. "I hated to see the way studios treat horses. They deliberately trip them, usually with nearly-invisible wires stretched taut at knee level. Often a horse will break its legs right in front of the camera. After the action is over, the crew takes the injured horses away and shoots them."

As we sat there in the Ship Café on that fateful day when I'd been reunited with my beloved Frank, there was no indication that Gary Cooper was going to become a big-time Hollywood star.

At that point in time Rod La Rocque was one of the biggest stars in Hollywood, and it seemed like his star would shine forever. Gary was skinny and his biggest allure seemed to be his mammoth dick. But back before the days of XXX-rated movies, film stars weren't usually filmed full-frontal and nude. Thus, the world would be denied the chance to look at Gary's greatest asset. He'd made what appeared to be a lackluster screen test. He'd soon have glossy photographs of himself as a Valentino clone, but he was no Valentino.

Those thoughts I had back at the Ship Café came back to me again in 1941 as I was interviewing Gary and his leading lady, Barbara Stanwyck, over at Warner Brothers where they were shooting *Meet John Doe*. In one of those twists of Hollywood fate, I spent the rest of the afternoon catching up with my old friend, Rod La Rocque. No longer a star, he was appearing in a supporting role in *Meet John Doe*.

But once again, I'm forgetting my narrative. Before I completely alienate the Bitch of Buchenwald, let me return to what unfolded in the Ship Café on that memorable day back in 1926.

When La Rocque got up to go to the men's room, Gary leaned over to me to whisper something. "Can I speak frankly in front of Mr. St. Just here?" he asked.

"My lips are permanently sealed except when I open them to suck a big dick," Rod said.

"My kind of man," Gary said. "Mr. La Rocque, male movie star, is escorting Vilma Banky to a Hollywood première tonight. I'm home all alone except for his two dogs, and I've done enough dog pictures."

"What say I come for you around eight?" I asked. "Take you to dinner."

"I'd say that was an invitation I'd like to accept," he said.

"I must warn you," I said. "I've picked up a lot of tricks since I knew you."

"I have too," he said, winking and smiling at me. "You're going to be the beneficiary tonight of all the stuff I've learned since deserting you back in Kansas."

"I can't wait."

"If I didn't have Johnny Mack Brown warming my bed tonight, I'd feel like a wallflower in the presence of you two," Rod said.

"We must not let La Rocque find out," I said.

"He means nothing to me," Gary said. "After I get the role in the Barbara Worth flicker, I'm deserting him. If there's one thing I love more than sex, it's money. La Rocque is too tight for me. I'm a struggling actor. I need a patron, who's willing to open his wallet from time to time."

"Perhaps you should charge by the inch," Rod St. Just said. "There's this up-and-coming actor named Clark Gable. He charges by the inch. Of course, he'll have a hard time getting rich that way."

"Fuck!" Gary said, looking up as La Rocque was rapidly approaching our table. In a lowered voice, Gary said, "If I charged by the inch, I'd be a millionaire within the year."

*****

When I pulled up at Rod La Rocque's

driveway in a brand-new roadster, the color of butternut squash, Frank (or Gary) was already waiting outside on the patio, enjoying a cold beer. He ran over to greet me. "Hello, little darling," he said. I feared he admired the car more than he did me. It seemed so surprising that I was reunited once again with the man who had taught me to drive in the first place.

I stepped out of the car and walked over to him, finding him too busy inspecting the roadster to pay much attention to me. He was enthralled with it. "It's the color of the plains of Montana," I said. "Of course, I've never actually been to Montana."

"This is the best looking little piece of road equipment I've ever seen," he said, running his hands over the hood. "For a car like this, I might give up riding horses."

"Get behind the wheel," I said. "Let's go out toward the beach at Santa Monica on a little ride. See if you like the way it runs."

"Hot damn!" he said, racing around to the other side of the car to take charge of the wheel.

Halfway to Santa Monica, I told him the car was his. His stunned reaction almost caused him to drive off the road and into a gully caused by a recent torrential rain.

"You're a man after my own heart," he said. "I've been dying to have my own car. La Rocque won't even shell out for a Model-T piece of garbage."

"I'm no longer poor," I told him. I reached over and gently touched his wrist. "And I'm very generous."

"I'm telling La Rocque in the morning that I'm moving out," he said. "Right into your suite at the Hollywood Hotel where I know you won't make me sit home alone at night while you're taking Vilma Banky to all the galas."

"If you're in my suite at the Hollywood Hotel," I said, "I assure you I'll have no other engagements."

"Hot damn!" he said again.

At the beach we went for a long walk, making no more mention of the roadster or the sudden shift in Gary's address. As he walked along the beach, he reached for my hand, holding it in his stronger one. Except for the moonlight, it was completely dark so we were not afraid someone would see us. Right now I didn't care if Louella Parsons herself recorded our mating dance.

I felt the warmth and closeness of his body. We stopped for a few minutes looking out at the ocean, which was like a mammoth sea of red wine in the light. When I did speak to him, he answered my questions with a "yup" or a "nope," although he'd been very articulate at the Ship Café.

He turned to me, and I thought he was going to ask me something truly important. "Do you know I used to be the best hog-caller in Helena?" To prove it, he let out a high-pitched "sooie-sooie."

Later, I invited him to the remote bistro where I'd once taken John Gilbert for fun and games. Gary looked elegant tonight in a neatly tailored suit with the best looking pair of cowboy boots I'd ever seen. Artfully embroidered, they were made of the finest leather.

Noticing me looking at them, he said, "A gift from La Rocque. About the only gift he's ever given me. If you remember, I have fantastically long and narrow feet. They haven't been sucked, licked, and kissed in a very long time. La Rocque isn't attracted to feet."

He ordered a steak for dinner and told me how difficult it was to forget Montana and focus his life on Hollywood. "I still miss the ranch at Seven-Bar-Nine. It was the Cooper Ranch. Right outside Last Chance Gulch, an old gold-mining town."

"Was your hometown really called that?" I asked.

"It was later changed to Helena," he said. "People thought Helena sounded more respectable. Most of the gold was hauled away. But I used to sift out a few flakes of gold in a nearby creek. At least it kept me in licorice money."

At the bistro I felt like a man-crazed schoolgirl, as I lost myself in Gary's blue eyes, the color of an Arctic lake. He had the kind of long eyelashes that screen vamps would have died for, but, more than that, his eyes sparkled. If only the camera could capture that sparkle, perhaps he could go on to stardom after all.

After dinner as we strolled back to the parking lot, I started to get in on the passenger side, figuring that Gary would want to drive. I was startled as he approached me on my side of the roadster.

Suddenly, he slapped me. Pain shot through my nose, which started to bleed. "Let that be a lesson to you. I've heard all over Hollywood what a whore Durango Jones has become. Your whoring days are over. I won't put up with it. If I catch you with another man, I'll kill him and you too."

With that threat, he went around and took the driver's seat, ordering me to get into the car. As we drove toward the Hollywood Hotel and my bed, I was overcome with joy. He was actually jealous of me, wanting to keep me exclusively for himself. That meant he loved me and wasn't like that hardened hustler, Clark Gable.

In my suite, I could no longer resist, and I placed my hands on his crotch, feeling him harden. I unbuttoned his fly, wanting to free the cock of my dreams. Out in the open I watched it expand immediately to its full and impressive length. Unable to resist it, I kissed and nibbled at it, as I relaxed my throat muscles preparing to swallow him whole, and that was one arduous but joyful task.

With my hands on him and my lips descending, I relished the taste, texture and smell of him as I gradually swallowed that magnificent equipment. One hand held his cock firmly in position but the other hand reached inside his shorts to fondle his large balls. He was truly the Montana mule.

After about five minutes of slurping joyously, I rose from my kneeling position and removed his shirt. With my fingertips I delicately ran along the rigid length of his spine, as my tongue filled one of his ears.   My eyes fell on his chest, which was followed by my probing fingers, tracing a delicate route between his hardened nipples and his navel. Soon my tongue was exploring the trail I had created. I'd take little mats of his chest hair and gently tug at them with my teeth, which seemed to turn him on enormously.

My fingers continued their busy course as they caressed his satiny back before cupping his jutting shoulder blades. That was a tender taste treat for my lips, but it gave way to one of the longest and most drooling kisses I'd ever had in my life. Between the two of us, we must have exchanged a quart of saliva from mouth to mouth as my whole body shivered.

I lowered myself before him, taking down boxer shorts over slim hips. His cock pointed straight out, and I marveled at the size of it. His skin was alive to my touch, as I took his hand and directed him to my bed, I wanted to taste every inch of him, beginning with his toes and working my way up to his forehead, spending ample time at his asshole, balls, and cock before journeying northward. I was going around the world tonight and maybe even heading back for a repeat journey.

When I'd feasted on him for what seemed like hours, he brought the action under his control. He reared up and hoisted my legs into the air. He pried open the cheeks of my ass and slipped his hot tongue into the tender crack, circling before landing. I yelped as he plunged his long tongue deep within me. My screams of joy were too powerful to hold back.

Pulling off me, he descended on my mouth, and I could taste myself on his lips. After plunging his tongue into my mouth for a few times, he rose up again, this time inserting his cock in my mouth, which I sucked fiendishly, expecting an explosion. But he quickly pulled off, as it was obvious he had other plans.

Prying my cheeks apart this time, he inserted not tongue but his long cock. "I'm not one for lube," he said. "I like it natural."

As he entered me, I forgot about the searing pain. I'd been miraculously transported back to the fields of Kansas. I was in a dreamlike trance. Frank was back in my bed again. I didn't think I'd ever get used to the name of Gary. He pierced me with his cock, and I screamed as he plunged into my lower depths, driving unrelentingly into me, inch by sturdy inch.

He fell on me, biting my lips, which made me forget about the other pain. It worked. He distracted me enough to plunge to the final depths. The pain was replaced by the most tantalizing sensation I'd ever experienced in my body, as Gary plunged deeper and deeper into me. He'd pull out, only to thrust deep into me again and again, doing that over and over, sending shock waves through me, which I welcomed.

I began biting his naked shoulder and nibbling his ear lobes as I could no longer stand the sensation and tried desperately to retard my own explosion, as he was really getting to me.

At that moment I belonged fully to him, and he to me. I just knew we'd never leave each other again. The tears started to flow from me. Until I'd come back to Gary, I never realized how unhappy I was drifting from bed to bed. It seemed like fun at the time, but now I wanted more, a permanent commitment somehow. I didn't need a lot of men any more.

I whimpered as he plowed deeper into my ass, and the little sounds coming from my throat seemed to goad him on and on. He swerved his head to kiss and nibble my ankles suspended in the air. I ran my tongue along his sweaty neck, biting his chin.

His body shuddered as a stream of semen gushed from him and was planted deep inside me. At that very moment I exploded too, no longer able to hold back.

He must have stayed inside me a good twenty minutes before pulling out. My muscles clenched tightly around him, hoping to prevent his exit. He raised himself above me, his softening dick dangling over my face. "Here it comes," he shouted. "Ready or not." His piss blasted against my face, seeping through my lips and foaming in my hair. It seemed to go on without end.

"With all that wine I've had tonight, it should taste real good," he said to me as I was anchored under him. His piss crashed against me like a tropical storm, as I lay there gasping and spluttering under the onslaught. "I want the last of it to go in your mouth," he told me. His cock dangled only an inch from my lips, which he parted and entered, forcing me to drink him to the last drop. Completely drained, he pulled back from me, and scooted down beside me, licking my lips and sticking his tongue inside as if to taste himself. "We've got a lot of time to make up for," he whispered in my ear.

*****

Shortly after I'd moved Gary Cooper (my darling "Frank") into the Hollywood Hotel on that bright morning in 1926, the phone rang. At first I braced for the inevitable, as I fully expected it would be an enraged Rod La Rocque, accusing me of stealing his boyfriend. To my surprise, it was W.R. himself, asking me to go on the train with Rodolfo to New York for the East Coast première of *The Son of the Sheik*. W.R. had liked the dispatches I'd filed from Rome on *Ben-Hur*, and felt I could come up with some insider stuff on the Valentino cross-country tour.

Before Gary re-entered my life and before that assignment from W.R., I had been planning to go with Rodolfo to New York anyway. But after a night in Gary's arms, I was determined to call Rodolfo and tell him I couldn't accompany him on that trip. W.R.'s call changed all that. My original plan would have to be kept, even though I dreaded tearing myself from Gary so soon after our reunion. I also dreaded leaving Gary unattended in man-crazed Hollywood.

In an attempt to guarantee Gary's loyalty during my absence, I deposited five-thousand dollars in his bank account, with the suggestion that there was more to come when I got back from the East Coast. Gary was delighted and kissed me repeatedly.

One of the secrets that only a few people knew about Gary Cooper was that he adored money more than sex. The prospect of getting money could make his hard-on grow at least another two inches. To reward me, he tossed me in bed and gave me the fuck of my life. When he'd finished, he said, "Little darling, that will keep you faithful to me until you return. You're not going to find any stud in New York who can plow you like that, certainly not Rudolph Valentino who's pushing thirty. Also, from what I hear, getting bald."

In my *adieu* telephone call to Rod St. Just, I learned that I was not going to have to face an enraged Rod La Rocque after all. Only that night just gone by, he'd moved Johnny Mack Brown between the sheets so recently vacated by Gary.

"But Johnny belonged to you," I said.

"Darling, you know I'm rarely interested in a man for more than forty-eight hours," he said. "Wait until you get back from the East. Last night at the Fruitfly I discovered a guy so sensational that he's going to become the biggest thing that ever hit Hollywood. Bigger than Valentino and Novarro."

"What's his name?" I asked, intrigued at Rod's latest discovery.

"Marion Morrison," he said.

"I don't think I'd get off on a guy named Marion."

"Wait until you see him," Rod said. "He's gorgeous. Six foot four with brown hair and blue eyes. A football player at the University of Southern California. I've almost convinced him to change his name to John Wayne."

After bidding Rod goodbye and locking myself in a final embrace with Gary, I left my Montana mule at my Hollywood Hotel suite and drove to Falcon Lair where Rodolfo was impatiently waiting for me to drive him to the train station in Los Angeles.

To my horror, and I think to the horror of Rodolfo too, Pola Negri was waiting on the platform to tell him good-bye. She was surrounded by an army of photographers and reporters. With some reluctance, Rodolfo, no doubt out of embarrassment, posed with her as her prospective bridegroom. I stood behind them. "We've got to talk, Pola," he said, "before the train pulls out."

Arrangements were quickly made for Negri to come aboard the train and into Rodolfo's private compartment. I trailed with a briefcase of Rodolfo's papers and publicity instructions from Joseph Schenck.

Negri seemed aware of me for the first time. "Rudy, darling, if you wish to speak to me about matters of the heart, I insist that *that one* leave the train."

"He stays," Rodolfo said in most commanding voice.

"Very well," Negri said. "Of course, he stays. I forgot. Actors always like an audience."

"You are the most ravishing creature in Hollywood," he told her, and her face revealed that she readily agreed with this assessment. "You'll know many men. Many women too. But this crap about us getting married has got to stop. It's getting out of hand."

"Are you telling me you're not going to marry me?" she asked, pretending tears that would not fall.

"I'm too moody to marry any woman," he said. "Too mixed up. I want you to find someone else, someone more compatible. Make some arrangement with another actor, like Rod La Rocque has done with Vilma Banky."

"You can't tell me what to do," she said, responding in anger.

"It's over between us," he said, raising his voice. "No more stories of our engagements. No more publicity. I want you to see others while I'm gone. When I return, I will not be there for you."

The stunned look on her face told me he'd exploded her dream of dethroning Mary Pickford and Douglas Fairbanks as the reigning queen and king of Hollywood. She desperately wanted to be his wife in name only, because of the super status that would give her in this town. She obviously knew that marriage to Rudolph Valentino would move her to the top of the pecking order in Hollywood.

At first she looked stunned, as if she couldn't believe what she'd just heard. Surely to her, marriage to Valentino was the perfect set-up. Each could have a private agreement to pursue whomever they chose, but to the world they would look like a happily married couple, at least when a photographer was around.

Finally, Negri regained use of her voice. "You son-of-a-bitch. You Dago creep. I detest you. You're nothing but an effeminate pansy. You're not even a man. I've been made love to by some of the sexiest men in Hollywood. I have been fulfilled as a woman, but not by you. You're impotent around women. They call you the Great Lover. You're a joke of a man." She spat in his face and turned to walk out of the compartment.

I pulled out my handkerchief and wiped the spit off his face.

That earned for me a look of such contempt from Negri that I would not see such loathing again until I encountered the bitter face of the Bitch of Buchenwald. "You've got him," she said to me, "and you're welcome to him. But look at what you've got. His hair is falling out, and he's coughing up blood most of the time. So what have you got? A sick and dying man at the end of his career. A man who in a few months will be washed up in pictures, while I am just beginning my reign. Fuck both of you. I hate faggots."

I watched as Negri disembarked from the train, as photographers snapped her picture. Recovering quickly from Rodolfo's rejection, she smiled brilliantly and appeared to be a young woman radiantly in love. Pretending affection she did not feel, she stood on the platform as the train pulled out. She blew kisses toward the departing locomotive.

I read in the papers the next day what she'd called out to the train. "My darling, Rudy. My heart will stop beating until you return." It was all very romantic, and the reporters recorded every word.

One of my most vivid memories of 1926 was Pola Negri standing on that platform waving good-bye to Rodolfo, a man she'd never see alive again.

*****

On the cross-country train ride to Chicago, Rodolfo never referred to the bitter scene he'd had with Pola Negri at the Los Angeles train depot. As far as he was concerned, the fake affair with Negri no longer interested him, regardless of how much publicity it generated. His dream was to reunite with Natacha Rambova.

"When I get back to Hollywood, I'm going to launch Rudolph Valentino Productions," he vowed. "Natacha will hear of this and come back to me. She's very ambitious. I'll promise to give free reign to her artistic expressions. My new film company will be like a Venus flytrap laying a snare for a flying insect. It will win her love for me."

That seemed utterly absurd to me. Giving free rein to Natacha's ambitions in film would destroy any movie studio. Also, I didn't feel Metro or Paramount would welcome such competition. Other actors such as Clara Kimball Young and Charles Ray had been bankrupted when they'd launched their own productions.

He reached into his suitcase and pulled out a book, *The Silver Stallion*, by James Branch Cabell. On the long train ride across America, he asked me to read this medieval fantasy set in Europe. I read two chapters before discarding it. It wasn't my kind of drama at all, although it would give Rodolfo the chance to dress up in period costume, which he loved.

Before leaving Hollywood, Rodolfo had written an embarrassing article for *The New York American*, trying to explain the breakup of his relationship with Natacha. He claimed he hadn't beaten her, which came as a surprise because no one, certainly not Natacha, had ever claimed that he had struck her. That claim had come from his first wife, Jean Acker, who'd accused him of violently attacking her. Acker usually lied but in this case she'd told the truth, because Rodolfo did admit to beating her.

In the article he claimed he had not demanded that Natacha settle down in a "rose-covered cottage and make bambini for me." He said he had encouraged her to pursue her own career. "What I didn't encourage was her interference in my own film career. My marriage failed because Natacha gave up her own artistic ambitions and became too engrossed in my own film roles. She was becoming not Natacha Rambova, but a female Rodolfo Valentino."

If Rodolfo thought this article would win back the affection of Natacha, he was deadly wrong. Also, the article didn't seem to tie in with the sentiments he was expressing about Natacha artistically controlling his own future production company.

He concluded the article by saying, "Natacha subjected me to social and professional restrictions for the sake of my image. I could not allow that. I must be free to pursue my own artistic vision, which should never be based on her goals, but on my own. She must forsake her pride and admit she was wrong in trying to control me."

On the train Rodolfo was furious at *The New York American* for running the article before he'd approved its content and tone. "I told them to hold it until I was certain of my remarks, until I'd had time to reconsider them. I wrote the article in a night of bitterness at Falcon Lair. The God damn editor has betrayed me. This is just another example of how the press betrays me."

As Rodolfo slept on our first night on the train, I raised the shades in our private compartment and watched the endless miles of prairie passing before us.

Before leaving Falcon Lair, I'd stolen a capsule of the so-called elixir the German baron was forcing Rodolfo to take. I'd driven to Brian Sheehan's house and given it to him, asking him to have its contents examined in his laboratories to find out exactly what it was. By the time I reached Chicago, or at least New York, I hoped Brian would call me with the findings.

If Rodolfo thought *The New York American* had betrayed him, he hadn't read the article waiting for him in *The Chicago Tribune* upon our arrival there. Rodolfo always considered the *Chicago Tribune* his old *bête noire*, as they had panned him and his films in dozens of articles.

His arrival in Chicago was met with hundreds of screaming fans even though it was one of the worst heat waves to blanket the Middle West. As policemen fought off the crowds, Rodolfo and I went to a suite reserved for him at the Blackstone Hotel where we had only eight hours to wait before boarding yet another train for the final lap into New York.

I discovered the offending Tribune while Rodolfo showered, hoping to cool his overheated body. It was called:

PINK POWDER PUFFS

A new public ballroom was opened on the north side a few days ago, a truly handsome place and apparently well run. The pleasant impression lasts until one steps into the men's washroom and finds there on the wall a contraption of glass tubes and levers and a slot for the insertion of a coin. The glass tubes contain a fluffy pink solid, and beneath them one reads an amazing legend, which runs something like this: "Insert coin. Hold personal puff beneath the tube. Then pull the lever."

A powder vending machine! In a men's washroom! Homo Americanus!. Why didn't someone quietly drown Rudolph Guglielmo, alas Valentino, years ago?

And was the pink powder machine pulled from the wall or ignored? It was not. It was used. We personally saw two "men"— as young lady contributors to the Voice of the People are wont to describe the breed— step up, insert coin, hold kerchief beneath the spout, pull the lever, then take the pretty pink stuff and put it on their cheeks in front of the mirror.

Another member of this department, one of the most benevolent men on earth, burst raging into the office the other day because he had seen a young "man" combing his pomaded hair in the elevator. But we claim our pink powder story beats this all hollow.

It is time for a matriarchy if the male of the species allows such things to persist. Better a rule by masculine women than by effeminate men. Man began to slip, we are beginning to believe, when he discarded the straight razor for the safety pattern. We shall not be surprised when we hear that the safety razor has given way to the depilatory.

Who or what is to blame is what puzzles us. Is this degeneration into effeminacy a cognate reaction with pacifisms to the virilities and realities of the war? Are pink powder and parlor pinks in any way related? How does one reconcile masculine cosmetics, sheiks, floppy pants, and slave bracelets with a disregard for law and an aptitude for crime more in keeping with the frontier of half a century ago than a twentieth-century metropolis?

Do women like the type of "man" who pats pink powder on his face in a public washroom and arranges his coiffure in a public elevator? Do women at heart belong to the Wilsonian era of "I Didn't Raise My Boy to Be a Soldier"? What has become of the old "caveman" line?

It is a strange social phenomenon and one that is running its course not only here in America but in Europe as well. Chicago may have its powder puffs; London has its dancing men and Paris its gigolos. Down with Decatur; up with Elinor Glyn. Hollywood is the national school of masculinity. Rudy, the beautiful gardener's boy, is the prototype of the American male.

Hell's bells. Oh, sugar.

Fresh from his shower, Rodolfo emerged in a robe back into the living room of our suite. I had just finished the article and stupidly tried to conceal it from him. An intuitive person, he sensed what I was doing and walked over, demanding that I turn the Tribune over to him.

His eyes kindling with fire, he read the article as the muscles in his already gaunt face tightened. After he'd finished, he threw it down on the floor. He was livid, even balling his fists in fury. He sat down on the sofa in total devastation. "I have been insulted before the world. Tell me." He looked over at me, as tears welled in his eyes. "What does Rudolph Valentino have to do with a powder machine in a men's toilet? Why must I suffer such indignities?"

He got up from the sofa and went over to the desk in the corner. "I know how to deal with this yellow-bellied coward from the Tribune. Call a representative from the *Chicago Herald-Examiner* and ask them to come to my suite at once."

Before I could protest, he ordered me to shut up. I did as I was told, calling the newspaper's office, as Rodolfo sat in the corner drafting some response that he wouldn't let me read.

When he'd finished, he stood up. "The Tribune, I'm sure, will protect this dirty little pansy. But through my challenge in the *Herald-Examiner*, I will smoke him out."

The representative arrived from the newspaper and Rodolfo asked that his public letter be published in the morning's edition. The representative agreed and thanked Rodolfo.

After he'd gone, the tension that had been building in Rodolfo surfaced. Suddenly he clutched his stomach and doubled over in pain. I thought he was going to fall to the floor. I rushed over and braced him, practically carrying him back to the sofa. "Oh, Lord," he said. "Don't let it happen now with the whole world watching. Not now, dear Lord!!"

Easing him onto the sofa in a prone position, I begged him to let me call the house doctor. Once again he refused medical attention. The pain in his abdomen lingered, and I noted the blood seemed to have drained from his face. He had a ghostly pallor. Sex symbol or not, he looked to me like a dying man. In about fifteen minutes, he rose up. "The pain is gone," he said. "I think I was upset over the Tribune. I had a bit of gas. I'm fine now. Forget it!" His eyes looked menacingly at me, as if to signal that he would banish me from his presence if I told anybody about his pain which seemed to come more frequently since we'd left the West Coast.

"Let's go to New York," he said. "When I return to Chicago in ten days, I'll get to face the coward who libeled me. I will make him eat his words, then I'll get this big pink powder puff. In front of the reporters and photographers, I'll powder this writer's face. The world will soon learn that Rudolph Valentino is all man."

As we headed for New York, Rodolfo's challenge to the journalist was carried by newspapers all over the country, as the Associated Press had picked it up from the *Herald-Examiner*. The only paper that didn't publish it was the *Chicago Tribune*.

TO THE MAN (?) WHO WROTE THE EDITORIAL HEADED "PINK POWDER PUFFS" IN SUNDAY'S TRIBUNE:

The above-mentioned editorial is at least the second scurrilous personal attack you have made upon me, my race, and my father's name.

You slur my Italian ancestry; you cast ridicule upon my Italian name; you cast doubt upon my manhood.

I call you, in return, a contemptible coward, and to prove which of us is a better man, I challenge you to a personal test. This is not a challenge to a duel in the generally accepted sense—that would be illegal. But in Illinois, boxing is legal, so is wrestling. I, therefore, defy you to meet me in the boxing or wrestling arena to prove in typically American fashion (for I am an American citizen), which of us is more a man. I prefer this test of honor to be private, so I may give you the beating you deserve, and because I want to make it absolutely plain that this challenge is not for purposes of publicity. I am handing copies of this to the newspapers simply because I doubt that anyone so cowardly as to write about me as you have would respond to a defy (sic) unless forced by the press to do so. I do not know who you are or how big you are but this challenge stands if you are as big as Jack Dempsey.

I will meet you immediately or give you a reasonable time in which to prepare, for I assume that your muscles must be flabby and weak, judging by your cowardly mentality and that you will have to replace the vitriol in your veins for red blood—if there be a place in such a body as yours for red blood and manly muscle.

I want to make it plain that I hold no grievance against the <u>Chicago Tribune</u>, although it seems a mistake to let a cowardly writer use its valuable columns as this "man" does. My fight is personal—with the poison-pen writer of editorials that stoop to racial and personal prejudice. The <u>Tribune</u>, through Miss Mae Tinee, has treated me and my work kindly and at times very favorably. I welcome criticism of my work as an actor—but I will resent with every muscle of my body attacks upon my manhood and ancestry.

Hoping I will have an opportunity to demonstrate to you that the wrist under a slave bracelet may snap a real fist into your sagging jaw and that I may teach you respect of a man even though he happens to prefer to keep his face clean, I remain with

> *Utter contempt,*
> *Rudolph Valentino*

On the train to New York, as we sat in our private compartment, looking at the little towns we passed through, Rodolfo said to me, "I hate *The Son of the Sheik*. It's a third-rate flicker. From now on, when I get back to Hollywood, I'll appear only in first-rate films. I'm thirty-one now. I give myself another five years before

the camera. Then my male beauty will have left me. I plan to reinvent myself as a director. I predict that Rudolph Valentino Productions will dominate the film industry in the Thirties."

As I gazed upon my longtime friend, I felt his words had a hollow ring. I wasn't sure any of those films of the future would actually be made.

For the rest of the ride to New York, he sat looking out the window as if dreaming of the life he wanted to live and thinking of the life he'd actually lived. I felt that none of us, not even his beloved Natacha, had ever brought warmth to that cold heart. I'd tried to comfort him, year after year, but knew I could never break through to him. I feared I was but a mere convenience to him, to use whenever I fitted into some plan of his, but to discard the moment his attentions turned elsewhere. I couldn't help but realize that all of our conversations began and ended with him. Spectacular things had happened in my life since we'd both shared that rose-covered cottage behind Elizabeth Hutchinson's house. I'd neither told him about them, nor had he asked. Like Natacha, I feared that Rodolfo existed only for himself.

It was then that I became painfully aware that I had no place in his heart. He'd never been in love with anyone, not even Natacha. Without speaking of it to him, I decided as the train speeded toward New York, that I would end my relationship with Rodolfo after this trip. I told myself that I wasn't here because of my love for him, but I was just another journalist, a profession he loathed, and I was doing my job for the Hearst organization. What I wasn't, was a friend, and certainly not a lover.

Perhaps for nostalgic or sentimental reasons, I impulsively reached out to him one more time. He sat across from me in the compartment. I touched his hand. "We must talk," I said.

He pulled his hand from me and glared at me with more hostility than I'd ever seen in his face before. "Would you let me alone."

The rest of the ride into New York was in silence.

*****

Had I not been on assignment for the Hearst organization, I think I would have left Rodolfo in New York and returned to California and the strong arms of Gary Cooper, where I longed to be anyway. My relationship with Rodolfo was all but at an end, as he'd grown increasingly morose in private, often lashing out at all the injustices he'd received in life. He attacked virtually everyone he'd worked with in Hollywood for having exploited him. "I've made millions for them, and what do I have to show for it?" he asked me in a rage. The question wasn't meant to be answered.

This high-fevered anxiety brought on a coughing spasm, and he retreated to the bathroom where I knew he was spitting up blood. When he came out an hour later, I pleaded with him to enter a clinic both for a thorough examination and a supervised rest. He slapped my face. Stunned, I stepped back from him, rubbing my jaw. "If you say that to me one more time," he said, "so help me God I will pick up the nearest blunt object and smash it into your face. I hope I blind you."

Since the suite had two bedrooms, I retreated to the guest room, never to occupy a shared bed with Rodolfo ever again. Natacha Rambova was welcome to him.

Pink powder puff or not, New Yorkers had turned out en masse at Grand Central to welcome "the great Valentino." Policemen worked overtime to control the crowds, and it had taken a motorcycle escort—ordered by the Mayor Jimmy Walker—to get Rodolfo to the suite we shared at the Ambassador Hotel where one-hundred reporters and photographers waited to record the moment of his arrival.

So far, no writer from the *Chicago Tribune* had accepted Rodolfo's challenge for a boxing match. But after only an hour in the suite, an urgent message arrived and a challenge from Frank O'Neill, who was boxing editor for the *New York Evening Journal*. Jack Dempsey, who had once sparred with O'Neil, told the reporter that, "Valentino can really handle himself in the ring." But O'Neil

announced to the press that, "I think the champ is putting me on. I'll challenge the Great Lover to a boxing match myself. Let the world see what a pink powder puff Valentino really is."

"Another insult to my manhood," Rodolfo screeched at me. "Notify O'Neil that I'm accepting his offer. He will know firsthand the pugilistic abilities of Rudolph Valentino."

At this point I decided the best course of action was to give Rodolfo free rein. He didn't belong to me, and I had no right to exercise control over him. I would go to the boxing match only as an observer for the Hearst organization. The story was news. It seemed pointless to remind Rodolfo that he was in no physical condition to box anyone, as only minutes before he'd been spitting up blood in the bathroom.

At a gymnasium in Brooklyn, some fifteen reporters from the various newspapers were allowed in to cover the match between O'Neil and Rodolfo. In boxing trunks, Rodolfo's weight had dropped to 150 pounds, as opposed to O'Neil who weighed 200 pounds and stood two inches taller than Rodolfo.

Trying to make myself numb, I watched as Rodolfo got into the ring with this writer. I fully expected Rodolfo to be floored after the first three minutes. But surprisingly Rodolfo was very agile on his feet, almost dancing around O'Neil and striking at him with short jabs to the side of the reporter's head. Before O'Neil could slam into Rodolfo, he scored a direct punch into his opponent's face, knocking O'Neil to the floor. Rising slowly, O'Neil slammed a counter punch into Rodolfo's face, causing his nose to spurt blood. In fury, Rodolfo lunged forward toward O'Neil, punching him repeatedly as O'Neil assumed a defensive position, covering his head with his gloved hands.

In spite of his bad health, Rodolfo had worked out and was in better shape than O'Neil, who looked flabby and a bit drunk. I learned later that he'd had three beers before the boxing match, and spent most of his nights, not in a gym, but in a barroom. In poor physical condition, he obviously could take no more punching. Moving to the ropes, he dropped his gloves. "Fuck it!" he shouted to reporters. "The kid can box. He's a real man. Next time

I'll take Dempsey at his word." He called over to Rodolfo. "How about some Scotch and a juicy red steak? The treat's on me."

The next morning after Rodolfo had spent a night alone in his bedroom, he rose early but had only tea and a piece of dry toast for breakfast. He kept complaining of stomach cramps.

Reports reached the Ambassador that crowds had begun lining up at dawn in front of the Mark Strand Theater where *The Son of the Sheik* would hold its East Coast première at noon. By nine o'clock the temperature had already risen to 98° Fahrenheit, and the fans were drenched in sweat but remained in line in spite of the fierce sun beating down on them. Three women had fainted and had been carried away by the police.

Shortly before noon when Rodolfo tried to enter the theater under police guard, he was mobbed by fans. Although surrounded by policemen protecting him, he still managed to lose his tie, his cufflinks, his hat, and parts of his suit. Fortunately I had come prepared. Anticipating this, I had brought an extra wardrobe from the suite. Checking with the manager inside the theater, I ushered Rodolfo into the manager's private office where the actor washed and changed into fresh clothes. The manager suggested that it might be too dangerous for Rodolfo to go on the floor. He was advised to stand behind the curtains as the film was shown to the public for the first time in New York, and then appear on the stage at the end.

Although Rodolfo coughed slightly during the showing of the film, the music from the orchestra out front drowned out the noise. As the curtain went down, the standing-room audience responded with thunderous applause. *The Son of the Sheik*, I just knew, would be as big a hit in New York as it was in Los Angeles. The applause grew deafening as a nattily dressed Rodolfo appeared in front of the audience and spoke only a few words. He was charming and gracious. No one bothered to listen to his exact words, as everyone was too intent on seeing what he looked like. Although he'd lost weight, and I felt he looked gaunt, he seemed to pull himself together miraculously in front of the audience and revert to his older, more dynamic self.

That night he invited me to go with him to Texas Guinan's famous supper club. I'd met her briefly one time and had been captivated by her when she'd showed up early one morning at the Hollywood home of Antonio Moreno, accompanied by Pearl White. Although I felt Rodolfo should be back at the suite resting, I no longer made suggestions to him about how he was to run his life.

At the club, I was astonished to be seated at a table with Jean Acker Valentino. Unknown to me, Rodolfo had invited his first wife to join us. He asked that I be seated between them. There was an obvious chill between them, and they hardly spoke to each other after a few exchanges of pleasantries. Surely this wasn't going to be a reconciliation. There had been too much bad blood between them, too many lawsuits. When Rodolfo got up to go to the men's room, at least ten men at other tables also got up to follow him into the toilet, a problem that celebrities had back then as much as the Matt Damons and Brad Pitts of today have.

Acker turned to me. "I was shocked when Rudy invited me here. I thought he wanted to talk over things. Our getting back together is ridiculous, but I thought there would be some point to this meeting. He seems to be ignoring me completely." Her face flashed anger, as she reached for her purse. "When Mr. Valentino returns, would you inform him that I have a more pressing engagement to attend?" With that, she was gone. But right before she'd departed, she turned and said to me, "Personally, I think he's out of his mind."

When Rodolfo came back to his seat, he made absolutely no mention of Acker's disappearance. At first I thought he'd just assumed that she'd gone to the women's room. After thirty minutes had gone by and he still hadn't inquired about her whereabouts, I decided not to bring up the subject, fearing it might ignite him again. The whole purpose of his reunion with Acker made no sense.

Nonetheless, the newspaper headlines in New York the following morning carried speculation of a possible reconciliation between Rodolfo and his first wife. Despite that, it was clear to me that this dedicated lesbian had no intention of returning to Rodolfo.

The next morning it was back to Chicago for the official opening of *The Son of the Sheik* there. As of yet, no writer from the *Chicago Tribune* had stepped forward to identify himself as the author of the pink powder puff attack or to accept Rodolfo's challenge for a boxing match.

In Chicago, the première the next day of *The Son of the Sheik* was even bigger and more hysterical than it had been for the New York opening. If anything, the pink powder puff attack in the Tribune had only intensified the public's interest in Rodolfo.

Before leaving Chicago for yet another première in New York, this one in Brooklyn, Rodolfo called a news conference at which he ordered me to release an open letter to the "Pink Powder Puff Editorialist." It read:

It is evident you cannot make a coward fight any more than you can draw blood out of a turnip. The heroic silence of the writer who chose to attack me without any provocation in the Chicago Tribune leaves no doubt as to the total absence of manliness in his whole make-up.

I feel I have been vindicated because I consider his silence as a tacit retraction, and an admission which I am forced to accept even though it is not entirely to my liking.

The newspaper men and women whom it has been my privilege to know briefly are so loyal to their profession and their publications that I need hardly say how conspicuous is this exception to the newspaper profession.

Back in New York the mobs continued to surround Valentino. It was now obvious that *The Son of the Sheik* was going to make United Artists rich. It also had opened to fairly good reviews, unlike the blistering attacks that had greeted many other Valentino films such as *The Young Rajah*.

That night Rodolfo invited me to the Gus Edwards Revue at the Ritz-Carlton, where the master of ceremonies even persuaded Rodolfo to get up and dance the tango with a showgirl from the revue. The audience burst into thunderous applause, even though the dance later made Rodolfo end up backstage coughing up blood in the men's toilet.

Backstage many of the showgirls crowded around Rodolfo inviting him out for a night on the town at speakeasies. He waved good-bye to me, as he departed from the theater with at least a dozen shapely and tawdrily dressed showgirls in his entourage. Pictures would appear the next day under the caption, "A Gay Valentino on the Town."

Back at the Ambassador, I had an urgent message to call Brian Sheehan in Los Angeles. When I finally got through to him, his voice was stern. "Tell Valentino he's going to die if he doesn't seek medical attention at once."

"What's the matter?" I virtually screamed into the phone.

"I've just gotten the report about that so-called elixir you gave me. It contains tiny bits of arsenic. Although one capsule won't kill him, if taken over a period of time, the dose could be lethal. Someone, perhaps over a period of several months, has been slowly poisoning Valentino."

I thanked Brian for his help and told him I'd call him back. In the meantime, I desperately had to get to Rodolfo and tell him what I'd learned. Regardless of whether he punched me in the face or not, I was getting him to a hospital even if I would have to have him sedated and kidnapped. But he had to be checked. He could die.

As if to answer my prayer, the manager of the Ambassador Hotel called the suite, telling me, "Mr. Valentino has collapsed in the lobby. I'm having him sent upstairs at once by four of my staff members. I asked him if we could summon a doctor, and he refused."

Rodolfo was carried into the suite and placed on the sofa. I tipped the staff, shut the door, and rushed to his aid. He was complaining of stomach cramps, and also seemed feverish and asked me to bring him a cold towel from the bathroom to place on his forehead. When I came back with the towel, he had lapsed into a coma.

I checked for his pulse, finding that he was still alive. Calling the manager again, I pleaded for an ambulance. Within thirty minutes a police escort arrived with the ambulance to take Rodolfo to the Polyclinic Hospital where I announced myself as his personal business manager.

Asking for the best room in the hospital, I agreed to pay for it myself.

At 5:30 a.m., Dr. Harold Meeker, Rodolfo's new doctor, told me that an operation would have to be performed at once to save Rodolfo's life. He was diagnosed as having a gastric ulcer and acute appendicitis.

Three hours later I was admitted into Rodolfo's room where he was coming out of his sedation. He looked up at me and smiled weakly. "Am I a pink powder puff?" he asked before closing his eyes and drifting off again.

I had booked Rodolfo into the hospital's best suite, containing two bedrooms. Ironically it was the same suite where Mary Pickford almost lost her life in 1912 but was miraculously cured.

I learned that the hospital had released the news of Rodolfo's hospitalization to the media, listing his condition as "fair."

When Rodolfo revived three hours later, a nurse told me I could go in to see him but only for five minutes. Upon seeing me, he tried to sit up in bed but couldn't.

"Black Feather came to see me last night," he said. "He told me that the only place where I can convalesce the way I should is at that little shack in Nevada Lake. As soon as I'm released from here, I'm going back there, and I want you to with me. The sun there will heal me. We'll catch fish. I'll cook pasta. I'll regain my weight. I'll start life all over again. I'm finished with films. It is not my life. I'll go back to Italy and become a farmer."

He appeared weak and when my time was up I retreated into the adjoining bedroom, wondering how many days or weeks of my own life would be spent in hospitals.

Having nothing else to do but wait, I read the newspapers. Many reporters were sympathetic to Rodolfo's condition, but a few journalists filed skeptical reports, dismissing his entry into the hospital as a "mere publicity stunt" to promote his latest film, *The Son of the Sheik.*

From all over the world, telegrams were pouring into the hospital, wishing Rodolfo a speedy recovery. The switchboard was jammed with calls, and extra operators had to be employed. Vacationing in Paris, Mary Pickford and Doug Fairbanks sent a cablegram. Even Charlie Chaplin cabled from Hollywood expressing his wishes for Rodolfo's speedy recovery. Pola Negri sent a gigantic floral offering, announcing to the press that she was doing that while "prostrate with grief." She also told reporters that she fully expected Rodolfo to recover quickly and return to California where she was already going ahead with plans for their upcoming wedding.

Interrupting my reading, Dr. Meeker came into my bedroom. "Bad news," he said. "In the past hour Mr. Valentino has taken a turn for the worse. We're having to list his condition as serious again."

He told me that it would be several hours, perhaps more, before I would be allowed in to see Rodolfo again.

Feeling I was in a trap, I left the hospital and decided to go for a long walk on the streets of New York to clear my head, perhaps going over to the Fifth Avenue apartment owned by W.R. to check for mail and messages. The Chief might have been trying to get in touch with me.

As I turned the corner, I encountered a newsboy shouting and hawking papers to a crowd of people. As he held up the headline to me, I gasped when I read it.

THE SHEIK DIES.

****

It was a false headline. Some overzealous tabloid, in a rush to be the first on the streets with news of Rodolfo's death, jumped the gun. Apparently, a paid informer within the hospital had misheard a report and thought Rodolfo had died, calling the newspaper with this misinformation.

Racing back to the hospital, I demanded

to see Rodolfo at once. It was as if I believed that newspaper headline. It had such reality to it.

At his bedside, I noticed that Rodolfo's face had turned ashen. Sensing my distress, he asked me to bring him a mirror.

As his livelihood was based on his screen image, I seemed to understand that. His face was his fortune. I held the mirror up to his drawn face. "I want to see what I look like," he said in a barely audible voice. "In case I should ever play a sick and dying man on the screen."

Two hours later, I received a call from Brian Sheehan in Los Angeles. He'd arranged for a shipment of Metefhen, a mercurial antiseptic, to be sent to the clinic in New York. Invented only the year before at the University of Pennsylvania, the drug could stave off blood poisoning. Amazingly, although available in Philadelphia, there was no supply at any hospital in New York. I waited anxiously for the arrival of the drug by train, hoping it might save Rodolfo from whatever turmoil was going on inside his body.

I'd hired guards to patrol the eighth floor on which our suite lay. It was guarded day and night, as dozens of curiosity seekers had tried to gain entrance to the hospital. One middle-aged woman fan had even dressed in a nurse's uniform, hoping to slip into Rodolfo's hospital room.

Looking down into the streets from my hospital window, I could see that thousands of people had congregated outside the hospital. Even Mayor Jimmy Walker appeared in person, pleading with the crowds to go home and listen to bulletins over their radio.

By Thursday Dr. Meeker was much more optimistic. The miracle drug had arrived, and Rodolfo seemed to be responding to treatment. A hospital spokesperson claimed there would be no further medical bulletins. Rodolfo had recovered to such an extent that he personally asked me to write out a message and release it to the press:

I'm deeply touched by the messages. Some of the tributes that affected me most came from my fans—men, women and children. God bless them. I feel my recovery has been greatly advanced by the encouragement given by everyone.

Friday passed without incident as he slept most of the day. But on Saturday morning Dr. Meeker came into my room with a gloomy look on his face. "He's taken a turn for the worse. We've issued a statement to the press that his condition is serious. I fear he's entering the valley of the shadow of death."

I burst into tears as Dr. Meeker tried to comfort me. By that Sunday Rodolfo was near death. Four doctors had kept an all-night vigil at his bedside. It was decided that a blood transfusion might save him.

Major Edward Bowes ran a popular amateur talent radio program, and was a sort of Ed Sullivan of his day. That very afternoon he broadcast news of Valentino's imminent death, which set off a panic among fans across the country. In thousands of churches and homes throughout America, prayers were said for Rodolfo.

Although he'd been in a coma for most of the day, Rodolfo rallied around three o'clock Sunday afternoon. Dr. Meeker said I could visit with him for only a few minutes.

When Rodolfo opened his eyes and looked at me, he said, "Open the blind. I want to see the sunlight." It was sad for me to see that the blinds were already raised and that the sun was pouring into the hospital room.

His last words to me, at least those I could understand, were: "Black Feather has appeared in this very room. My plans have changed. He wants me to come and join him in his happy hunting crowd." After that he lapsed into a coma from which he never recovered. For the next few hours he would babble incoherently in both Italian and French.

It was ten minutes past noon on Monday, August 23, as I stood looking out of the hospital room adjoining Rodolfo's. When Dr. Meeker came into the room, I knew by the look on his face what he was going to say. "He's gone. I'm sorry. We could not save him."

I didn't cry, as I was beyond tears at that point. All the tears had dried up within me. The official report was that it was not only peritonitis, a painful inflammation of the gall bladder, but septic endocarditis, an affliction of heart tissues. The peritonitis was caused by the ulcer, the endocarditis by pleurisy.

I didn't care what the medical report said. I knew the truth. Rodolfo had been poisoned. His death certificate was filed under his legal name of Rodolfo Guglielmi. He was thirty-one years old.

Rumors spread up Broadway like a raging fire when the hospital announced that Rudolph Valentino had died. The word on the street was that he had not died of natural causes but that he'd been poisoned. Arsenic was blamed. Usually rumors following the death of a famous person are rarely true. But amazingly the public hit it right this time. It was just a coincidence but the public knew the truth.

The rumors grew so persistent that the hospital released a report that no trace of poison had been found in Valentino's body. Matters weren't helped when another doctor on the hospital staff, Eckhart Brevard, went before the press and admitted that Valentino had shown all the signs of arsenic poisoning—that is, a burning sensation in the abdomen, violent vomiting during which time he would cough up blood, a dryness of the mouth, general intestinal irritation, and a thirst so intense that water would not quench it.

Actually no autopsy was performed. I had given Dr. Meeker $15,000 not to perform one. I feared that if an autopsy were performed and traces of arsenic were found in Rodolfo's blood, the source would eventually be traced to the German baron. I feared that sordid story, if learned by the general public, would turn the adulation of the fans into revulsion. Even though Rodolfo was dead, I could at least protect his memory.

I rode in an ambulance as Rodolfo's body was transported to the Campbell Funeral Home. I had no feeling at all, only a vague numbness. I didn't even seem alive myself.

While the funeral parlor prepared the corpse, I waited in an office upstairs. There I learned of the worldwide reaction to Rodolfo's death. In Hollywood, I heard a broadcast that Pola Negri had collapsed on the set of *Hotel Imperial,* her latest film. But not before she issued this statement to the press:

My love for Valentino was the greatest love of my life; I shall never forget him. We were really engaged to be married, but the fact that we both had careers to follow accounts for the delay in our wedding plans. I loved the irresistible appeal of his charm, the wonderful enthusiasm of his mind and soul. I didn't realize how ill he was, or I would have rushed to New York sooner. He kept the seriousness of his illness from me.

Negri had also claimed that Dr. Meeker, Rodolfo's attending physician, had reported to her that the patient's final words were, "Tell Pola if she doesn't reach me in time, that she has my eternal devotion, if only from the grave." Dr. Meeker later told me he'd never spoken to Negri, which came as no surprise to me.

What I didn't know then, and know now, was that it was a symbolic time for Rodolfo to die. It was 1926, the last great year of the Silents. After that, sound would arrive, and most of the stars of the silent screen would fade away from the public consciousness, as Rodolfo himself might have done had he gone on living.

New rumors followed in the wake of Rodolfo's death. In addition to the talk of arsenic poisoning, many savvy Broadway gossips claimed that Rodolfo was actually done in by friends of the late Jack de Saulles. It was known for a fact that Rodolfo, during his early days in New York, was in love with the slain man's wife, Bianca. Even though Rodolfo fled from New York and was never charged with murder, speculation still persisted that it was Rodolfo who had fatally shot Jack, not Bianca. Knowledge of Rodolfo's involvement in the murder had led to the German baron blackmailing Rodolfo for all these years. Again, I was amazed at how these public rumors flirted so close to the truth. Of course, friends of Jack de Saulles had not actually shot Rodolfo, as speculated at the time.

As the ghouls within the funeral parlor prepared Rodolfo's body for public viewing, thousands gathered outside the funeral home waiting to get inside to view the world-famed corpse. Since I was paying for the funeral out of my personal funds, I was the first allowed in to view the body in private. I was shocked at the corpse.

His face looked ghastly and he appeared

to be a man deep into middle age. His thinning hair was slicked down in its patent-leather fashion, and eyebrows had been penciled in by a makeup man, as his real eyebrows had disappeared during his illness. His cheeks were heavily rouged, his mouth coated with a scarlet shade of lipstick. He did indeed look like the pink powder puff he was accused of being by that anonymous writer for the *Chicago Tribune*.

Looking around the room to see that I was indeed alone, I bent over the casket and gently kissed his lips. "Good night, sweet friend. Forever and ever." After that, I felt tears welling in my eyes, and I left the room without a final look. It was thirty minutes later before I noticed in a mirror that traces of his lipstick were still on my mouth.

From the French Riviera I received a cablegram from Natacha Rambova, informing me that she did not plan to come to the funeral. "Why honor an empty shell, when the spirit is gone? I'll spend every night trying to contact his wandering ghost."

Joseph Schenck at United Artists was in a panic. Up to that time, if a star died, his or her pictures were withdrawn from release. Studio bosses felt that the general public could not tolerate the sight of a dead man making love to a woman on the screen. Instinctively Schenck sensed that the time had come to break this taboo. United Artists announced that both *The Eagle* and *The Son of the Sheik* would continue in general release throughout America. Schenck was absolutely right, in establishing the new policy. Today, audiences still watch Rock Hudson make love to Doris Day on the Late Show.

A crowd of some 12,000 had gathered outside Campbell's Funeral home to view the body. Even a rainfall did not deter them. The Associated Press reported that, "Flappers in gay dresses and shabbily dressed women with shawls over their heads, and matrons attired in elegant frocks, jostled with men and boys for a place in line."

The crowd quickly turned into an unruly mob as police lines tried to hold them back. Rushing the cops, spectators surged against a large plate-glass window at the funeral parlor, crashing into it and seriously injuring twelve people who were pushed up against the jagged glass. One poor Italian woman from the tenements of New York's Lower East Side fell down and was trampled to death under the hoofs of a policeman's horse.

As the crowds poured in, the body of Rodolfo lay in a silver and bronze casket. Schenck had wisely turned down a request that Rodolfo be buried in his sheik costume. The body was formally dressed in black evening attire.

Pola Negri had sent a twelve foot by six foot pall of 4,000 scarlet roses, and I'd heard that her dressmaker had accompanied her on the train across country, desperately creating a $4,000 mourning outfit at record speed so that Negri could make a spectacular appearance at the funeral.

When I learned that hundreds of fans had gathered at Grand Central to witness the arrival of the grief-stricken Pola Negri, I knew that if anyone could upstage even Rodolfo at his funeral, it was Miss Negri herself. And I was right. At the funeral chapel, she fainted for the benefit of photographers. When some late-arriving photographers didn't capture the shot, Negri restaged her fainting spell.

Funeral services were delayed until Tuesday, August 31, 1926, when Rodolfo's brother, Alberto, arrived from Italy. He insisted that his brother's body be taken back to Italy to be buried in his native soil, but Rodolfo's friends in the movie colony intervened, demanding instead that he be buried in Hollywood.

A crowd of 7,000 had gathered for the 11 a.m. service at St. Malachy's Church. At the bier, Jean Acker collapsed in the arms of Ullman, Rodolfo's business manager, and she had to be revived by Dr. Meeker, who was also attending the funeral service. I sat between Norma and Constance Talmadge, with Mary Pickford and Doug Fairbanks on my right.

On the long train ride back to Hollywood, I stayed alone in my compartment, having no desire to be part of Negri's mourning party, staged for the benefit of reporters. She didn't want me there either, because I knew the truth—that Rodolfo had dumped her. If he'd lived, there would have been no wedding.

Rodolfo's body arrived in Chicago, and

was placed aboard the South Pacific, as I was, for the final ride back to Los Angeles. At every stop along the way, crowds gathered at the rail stations from Kansas City to El Paso, from Yuma to Colton, California. The train finally arrived in Los Angeles on Monday, September 6.

Another funeral was held the next day at the Church of the Good Shepherd in Beverly Hills where Rodolfo had been the best man at the ill-fated wedding of Mae Murray and the hustler, David Mdivani. All the big stars attended the funeral, even Charlie himself, along with W.R. and Marion. No floral tribute was as grand as that of Pola Negri, who ordered a blanket of red roses to drape over Rodolfo's casket. She was milking Rodolfo's death to the last drop for its publicity values.

Later that day I came up with a plan to upstage her, for which I earned her undying, to-the-grave hatred. I hired a private plane to drop pink, red, and white rose petals along the path of the funeral procession as it made its way to the Hollywood Memorial Park Cemetery. The pilot was Paul Whittier of the Beverly Hills Air Patrol, and he artfully scattered several clouds of petals directly in the path of the advancing funeral cortège. It was a spectacular sight.

Rodolfo was laid to rest in a crypt above that of Virginia Ruth Mathis, the mother of June Mathis, who had written the scenario for *The Four Horsemen of the Apocalypse*.

The day after the burial, another 5,000 spectators arrived to pay their respects to the sheik. In time the number per day dwindled to hundreds, then to tens, and then to nothing at all.

Except for one.

The famous "Lady in Black."

I can now reveal to you the identity of this mysterious woman. It was *moi*.

Every year on the anniversary of Rodolfo's death, I dressed up in my Lotte Lee clothes, with a heavy black veil covering my face. This was my way of paying my respects to my long-ago lover, and I kept doing this until 1968 when I became ill that year and couldn't make it. After that, I felt the tradition was spoiled, and I never appeared in the cemetery again. By that time in my life, I avoided cemeteries whenever

I could, fearing that I would be going there myself soon enough.

What became of the famous slave bracelet? On the Monday when Rodolfo died, I slipped into his hospital room and removed it from his wrist. In all the years of my life, going right up to 2000, I have never removed it, and I have made provisions in my will that I'm to be buried with the bracelet on my wrist. Sentimental perhaps, but what the hell?

The provisions of Rodolfo's will were soon made public. Jean Acker and I weren't even mentioned, but Natacha was. She was left one dollar. His estate was divided in equal shares among his siblings, Alberto and Maria. To the surprise of everyone, Teresa Warner, Natacha's aunt, was left a third of the estate. In Paris, Werner told reporters that, "I loved Rudy like a son, and he loved me." Natacha quickly moved in to claim the money left to her aunt, saying that, "It rightfully belongs to me."

In Hollywood, two weeks after Rodolfo's funeral, when I was adjusting to his death for the first time, I drove toward Los Angeles and its train depot. Once there, I was to pick up Gary Cooper. He was expected to arrive at eleven o'clock that morning, having finished three weeks of work as an extra in a western which starred Tom Mix and was shot in the desert.

As much as I tried to think of Gary, I also thought of Rodolfo. He now joined all those other friends who had passed on long before their time. That certainly included Wallace Reid and Barbara LaMarr.

I'd paid my respects to Rodolfo and would honor him for the rest of my life. But we were never lovers in the true sense of the word. He'd meant a lot to me but too many others, both male and female, had staked their claims to the sheik. Actually he'd never belonged to anyone—not even to himself.

Rodolfo belonged to the early days in Hollywood and to silent pictures itself.

Hollywood was changing, and I wanted to be a part of its new life. No longer an actor, I'd spend the years ahead recording the lives of those who became stars.

It was my own life that I wanted to pay special attention to. No longer a star-fucker, I hoped to settle down with just one man, a man

I truly loved and could devote my entire life to. That man was Frank, or Gary Cooper as he now called himself. It had not been Rodolfo that I had wanted after all but Gary.

I wished there had been no other men in my life, and that Gary had taken me with him when he'd mysteriously disappeared from Kansas and from my life on that dark day of long ago.

It would be different now that he was back in my life, giving me a second chance at the happiness I thought I'd lost forever. I would soon be in the arms of my true love, and this time I wasn't letting him escape. It wasn't Rodolfo that I wanted to share that rose-covered cottage with me. It was Gary Cooper. My relationship with Rodolfo evolved into a disaster. With Gary, the story would be different. Rodolfo never loved me. Gary did love me. I just knew we'd be faithful to each other, and that we'd live the rest of our lives together happily and in love.

Dreams do come true, even in Hollywood, the factory of dreams.

Epilogue

There's been a problem. Only a slight one. But still a tiny bit serious. After dictating the final chapter to the Bitch of Buchenwald, there was a violent argument between us. No longer able to tolerate hearing the story of my life, she'd shouted at me, "Faggots. I hate faggots. If I had my way, all of you would be sent to the gas chambers. I would drop the pellets myself and laugh as I watched you die from a safe position somewhere."

She didn't stop there but poured out such a stream of vituperation that I could stand her no more. I rose from my seat and picked up a poker from the fireplace in my library. I planned to strike her across the face, which would be the first act of violence I'd ever committed in my life. As I reached down, I fell over. Sharp pains shot through my chest. I was having a heart attack.

I must have lain there for three hours—we're not sure—before my maid, Hattie, discovered my body and called for an ambulance. The Bitch of Buchenwald had stormed out, leaving me on the floor to die. At least she'd escaped before getting her Nazi brains bashed in.

That was on November 1, 2000. I'd had a minor stroke, but I'm fine now. A little scare, nothing more. After all, I'm a centenarian. Bette Davis had once warned me, "Old age is not for sissies."

The biggest problem is that I've had a memory loss. I know that I went on from Rodolfo's death into my role as a gossip columnist, and in time I became the top theatrical agent in Hollywood. I vaguely recall the parade of young men who passed through my life: Cary Grant, Randolph Scott, Errol Flynn, Tyrone Power, Robert Taylor, Alan Ladd, Robert Mitchum, Guy Madison, Audie Murphy, Rock Hudson, Sal Mineo, Peter Lawford, Lex Barker, Johnny Weismuller, Burt Lancaster, James Dean, Montgomery Clift, Anthony Perkins. But the memory grows dim. I'm sure we had a grand time, though.

Hollywood reinvented itself many, many times during my own lifetime, and I was there to enjoy every minute of it. There were awkward moments, too, like when Lana Turner caught me in her bed with her gangster lover, the heavy hung Johnny Stompanato, but all of us have had our share of embarrassments.

Originally I had planned to stage a millennium party at the Plaza Hotel in New York to dwarf by comparison Truman Capote's famous "Black and White" masked ball in 1965.

Now I feared that in the wake of my stroke I could no longer pull off such a *fête*. I didn't feel I had the energy to fly to New York so I decided to stage a much smaller millennium party at The Blue Lagoon on Santa Monica Boulevard. The club always reminded me of a backdrop for one of those old Esther Williams movies. Only special people would be invited, namely my favorite glamour girls of yesterday. I hadn't seen any of them for years, and, as a point of curiosity, I was anxious to see how the old broads were holding up in their dotage and in their retirement. I trusted they were doing better than I was.

To replace the Bitch of Buchenwald, my agency had sent me a new secretary. I think he said his name was "Woody," or something like that. I haven't been able to remember a name for the past fifteen years. This Woody, if that is his name, looked just like the young blond actor who plays the gay teen on this new TV series, *Queer as Folk*. That title would never have been approved by Louis B. Mayer, who preferred good and wholesome family pictures.

In addition to being the cutest little thing since Brandon de Wilde (remember *Shane*?) passed on, Woody has none of the prejudices of the Bitch of Buchenwald. He told me within the first five minutes that he was gay and proud of it. He said two of his stepfathers had broken him into gay sex, and he'd loved it and had been fully enjoying it since the tender age of nine. I thought he must be one of those sexually precocious children like Doug Fairbanks Jr.

Any request I made of him, he seemed only too eager to please. He's also typing up my revisions for *Hollywood's Silent Closet*, though he frankly admitted that the only people I'd written about, whose names were familiar to him, were Chaplin and Clark Gable. Woody had watched part of *Gone with the Wind*, but found it a little boring and switched to something else on TV. He'd never seen a Chaplin movie, but had vaguely heard of him. I was astounded to learn he'd never heard of Valentino, Gary Cooper, Doug Fairbanks Sr., Mary Pickford, Tallulah Bankhead, Gloria Swanson, or even Greta Garbo.

Nonetheless, when I dictated to him my guest list for the party, he didn't blink an eye when I told him I'd like to send invitations to "just the loved ones"—Gloria Swanson (we'd since made up), Pola Negri (an uneasy truce), Bette Davis (she didn't make it in this memoir but became a long-time friend), Joan Crawford (I was with her on the nights I wasn't with Bette), Tallulah Bankhead (who launched me as Lotte Lee), Mae West (in memory of when we were two hot pussies on the town in gay New York), Marlene Dietrich (another dear friend from the Thirties), and, finally, Garbo herself. I'd also requested the presence of Alla Nazimova and Barbara LaMarr. And, for old time's sake, I wanted to have a reunion with

Theda Bara.

Woody was on the phone for most of the afternoon. At first I thought he was talking with my talent agency, and maybe he was. I feared that these popular women might have far more important things to do than attend my millennium party. But by six o'clock that evening, Woody reported back to me that my agency said it would "deliver all those old broads for my party."

At first I as a little embarrassed for them to see me in this senile state with my memory going. Only an hour before I was sitting out in my patio, enjoying the late afternoon sun, and I'd overheard Hattie, my long-time maid, telling the yard man, "Durango's not himself since his stroke. I think he's a bit touched in the head. He can't even remember my name, but always calls me Hattie. That's the only maid's name he can remember. Hattie McDaniel in *Gone with the Wind*."

The party along Santa Monica Boulevard was to begin at nine o'clock on December 31, 2000. Woody drove me there. I'd dressed carefully, since I hadn't seen these wicked gals in decades. Perhaps I applied too much lipstick and rouge, but what the hell! Rodolfo wore too much lipstick and rouge—not to mention pink powder—on the day he lay in his coffin.

Woody placed me in a comfortable chair to receive my guests. I decided not to welcome them standing up, as I was feeling a bit weak. During the past decade, I had never stayed up past nine at night.

While waiting for our distinguished guests, Woody took the chair next to me and held my withered hand. When he looked at me with that disarming smile and those incredibly blue eyes, I melted. Believe it or not, I still felt some attraction to young men. He was the prettiest boy I'd seen since Philippe de Lacy played Greta Garbo's son in *Love*.

"I've got a great idea," he said. "A wonderful way to launch the new century."

"And what might that be, you beautiful child?" I asked.

"I want to become your boy."

"My boy?" I asked in astonishment.

"Yeah, I've been thinking about it and I want you to adopt me."

"You're not after my money?" I asked.

"If you adopt me, I'll be your son, and I'm also entitled to the money. Wouldn't you say?"

"That makes some kind of sense, I guess."

"Fine, we'll go tomorrow and have the papers drawn up at your attorney's office."

"Not so fast."

At my slight protest, he reached for my hand and placed it between his crotch. "It's there and it's all for you." When I started to pull my hand away, he held it firmly in place. "There will be sex between us," he said.

"But I thought we'd be father and son. Doug Fairbanks Sr. would never have sex with his son. It's not right."

"I grew up in a house where incest was taken for granted," he said.

"You're mighty cute," I said. "But I haven't satisfied a man that way in at least fifteen years, maybe more."

"We'll work it out," he said. "How about me stripping down, straddling your chest, and masturbating right in your face? Right when I'm ready to explode, I'll stick it in your mouth and shoot off. You'll get to enjoy the fruits of the labor without the work."

"Now something like that might entice me," I said. At that moment, a waiter came up and told me that each of my invited guests had arrived.

"Every one of them?" I asked in astonishment, feeling that many of them might be so infirm they couldn't leave their bedrooms.

"Every one of them," the waiter assured me.

Woody jumped up. "I'll present them to you one at a time," he said to me.

As always, Tallulah Bankhead had pushed herself to the head of the line-up of guests. Before me stood this self-destructive, scandalous exhibitionist, a nymphomaniac, a lost child woman. "Durango, dah-ling," she said. "We've become legends in our own time—tragic legends." She laughed demonically. "And guess what? Everything they've ever said about us is true." I was amazed at how youthful she still looked. Attired in a mink coat, she seemed exactly as she appeared on the screen in Alfred Hitchcock's *Lifeboat*.

And that was in 1944.

The exotic beauty, Pola Negri, was presented to me next. This quick-tempered and strong willed Polish refugee still maintained that she loved Valentino even after all these years, although I knew she was living with a lesbian somewhere in Texas. Pola looked exactly as she did when she'd appeared in her first talking movie, *A Woman Commands* with Basil Rathbone, in 1932. "Charlie and Rudy are gone now, my dear, leaving just us on the stage. I don't know how you feel about them now, but frankly I don't think either one of them was worth messing up our mouths with."

"You're looking wonderful, Pola," I said, amazed at seeing her at the end of the century. After all, it was way back in 1922 when she was hailed as Venus, "the most beautiful woman in the world."

As Pola moved on, the woman who truly deserved the title of most beautiful woman in the world, stepped up before me—Barbara LaMarr. This startled me because I vaguely remembered attending her funeral. Or was it the funeral of Hedy Lamarr?

As I looked into Barbara's expressive eyes, they mysteriously changed in color from a deep gray to sea green. Did I detect a fleeting hint of purple? Her dusky lashes added to her beauty. But they looked fake to me. Her skin was still soft and fair, contrasting perfectly with her dark, jet-black, wavy hair. Barbara looked exactly as she did when she appeared with Ramon Novarro in *The Prisoner of Zenda* in 1922. "The fire is still raging inside me," she said. "It has never burned out. But, just between us, I fear in the next century it will burn out. But at least we lived to see another century."

Barbara faded as Theda Bara stood before me dressed exactly as she'd appeared as "the wickedest woman in the world," in the 1915 flicker, *A Fool There Was*.

"Still a vamp?" I said to her.

"Still a soulmate of the Devil," she said, laughing." But that was shit about my being born two blocks from the Sphinx. The closest I ever got to Egypt was an Egyptian cigarette."

I think I'd heard her use that line before, but it didn't matter. As we age, we tend to repeat ourselves.

The tempestuous Bette Davis appeared next, looking as she did in *Whatever Happened to Baby Jane?* in 1961. At least one of the broads wasn't holding up as well as the others. Bette let it all hang out. In a little girl's dress and in a wig of blonde curls, Bette looked grotesque.

"You became the biggest and the brightest, Bette," I said.

"Don't let Crawford hear you say that," she said, reaching for a cigarette which Woody lit for her. "I never told you what Carl Laemmle Jr. did when he first saw me. In those days he was head of Universal. He took one look at me through the open door of his father's office, then closed the door. I heard later he told his father I had as much glamour as a grape."

"Grapes are luscious things," I said, reaching for her hand and kissing it.

Bette gave way to an imperial Joan Crawford who looked as she did in *Flamingo Road* in 1949—that is, a hell of a lot better than Bette.

With her Joan Crawford fuck-me shoes and her Adrian shoulder pads, she was the supreme icon of 1940s glamour. "At first I wasn't going to show up when I heard you'd invited Davis. I mean what is Bette Davis? Take away her little gestures with the cigarette, the clipped speech, the pop eyes, the deadpan, and what have you got?"

"The important thing to remember is not that but what Joan Crawford has," I said. "No one deserves the title of movie star more than you do."

"You've got that right," she said, "and between you and me I'm coming back big in the 21st century."

Gloria Swanson stepped up next, looking exactly like Norma Desmond in *Sunset Boulevard*. God, that picture must have been shot a half century ago, if memory serves. How could she still look so glamorous after the passage of fifty years? "I remember the first day I met you." She smiled. "Let's don't tell anybody the year. You were just getting your start in Hollywood, hawking those mammoth Francis X. Bushman dildos."

"Any regrets, Gloria?" I asked.

"I've had a few," she said. "Turning down that contract with Paramount for more than a million a year and going into independent production and bankruptcy was one. There

are others."

"The most important thing is, we've survived."

"That we have, dear heart," she said, "and I'm sure we'll last for yet another century. At least."

"At least," I said.

The supreme embodiment of erotic sophistication, Marlene Dietrich, the world's last goddess, arrived next. This icon of beauty and glamour looked just as she did when she appeared on the world scene in *The Blue Angel* in 1930.

"I hear you've been sort of rewriting your own history," I said. "I mean, is it really true you never knew Greta Garbo?"

"I lied," she said. "I have decided to make every account of my own life notoriously unreliable. I have decided to throw off future biographers. Greta and I were lovers. Still are." She stepped back. "And here is Miss Garbo herself."

Standing before me was Greta Garbo, looking just as she had in her close-up in *Camille* with Robert Taylor. Although she'd made that film way back in stone-age 1937, the decades had not diminished her beauty one bit. She still possessed one of the great faces of the 20th century, even if that century were about to come to an end within the hour.

Greta Lovisa Gustafson had come a long way since she was born September 18, 1905 in that cold-water flat in a Stockholm slum. "It's been a long road," I said to her. "You've held up amazingly well. What's your secret?"

"Always be luminously evocative," she said enigmatically before giving way to Alla Nazimova.

The Thirties Camille was replaced by the Twenties Camille, a silent picture Nazimova had co-starred in with Rudolph Valentino.

"I've been applauded, lionized, and adored," she said, "then strangely forgotten. After all my accomplishments, I feel I will go down in the history books only as the godmother of Nancy Reagan." She stepped back. "I'm about to introduce you to my next guest, with whom I have only one thing in common. She and I are the only women in Hollywood who became movie stars at the age of forty."

Nazimova presented Mae West, who looked exactly like she did in *Belle of the Nineties*, made in 1934, when she'd appeared opposite that devastatingly handsome Johnny Mack Brown, who in time I would steal from the arms of Rod La Rocque. I asked her the same question I'd asked Gloria Swanson. "Any regrets?"

"Plenty," she said, "Everyone talks about my sex appeal when I should also be acclaimed as one of the great 20th-century playwrights. When you think about it, what others are there besides Eugene O'Neill, Tennessee Williams, and me?"

As the music started, and Mae departed, I turned to Woody. "Those old dames look as good as ever, all except for Bette. It's amazing what makeup can do today. But just between you and me, I feel all of them look like drag queens."

I rose to my feet for the music. Which of these legendary females would I honor with a dance? Woody asked me not to attempt to dance, but I was insistent. I told him I felt fine and wanted one final waltz. "Oh, shit," I said. "I should have invited Mae Murray. I completely forgot about her. What an appropriate way to have ended the century— me dancing with *The Merry Widow* herself."

"I don't know who Mae Murray was, but can I fill in for her?" a young brunette woman asked as she came up to me.

Woody stepped back to introduce us. "Durango, I'd like you to meet your agency's newest client. Monica Lewinsky."

This girl looked too short and a little overweight. I felt she'd never make it as a movie star, but I'd predicted Barbra Streisand would never make it either. "Have you had much experience as an actress?" I asked.

"I've had cameras on me, but I'm no actor," she said. "Your agency is shopping my story around to the studios. *The Monica Lewinsky Story.*"

"We'll have to work on that title," I said. I had no idea who this young girl was, but she seemed rather pleasant.

"It'll make a great movie," Woody chimed in." I hear Kevin Costner has been asked to play Bill Clinton."

"Your story involves Bill Clinton?" I asked,

completely dumbfounded at this point. I turned to Woody. "In a line or two, give me a quick synopsis of Monica's story."

"She was the mistress of the president, sir." he said. "A big scandal that captivated the world. Impeachment. Headlines. You must have missed it." Seemingly apologetic for me, he turned and smiled at Monica. "Mr. Jones has recently had a stroke. A memory loss, but every day he's improving."

"Mistress of the president," I said. I muddled that over for a moment as the band struck up the music from the old Alice Faye picture, *Alexander's Ragtime Band*, made back in 1938.

"Miss Lewinsky," I said, reaching for her hand, "may I have this dance?"

As Monica led me to the dance floor, she said, "We'll take it real easy—just like I used to tell the president."

Before going into the steps of the dance, an idea came to me. "Monica, please understand this as it is intended. I've read at least twenty scripts of mistresses to the presidents in my day, and some have even been filmed. One recently with Michael Douglas, Kirk's boy. Now that the 21st century is upon us, let's change your script a bit. Mistress to the president. Old hat by now. Let's get really modern. Instead of a mistress, let's make your part a young boy like Woody over there. In fact, Woody might be perfect for the role. Give the president a young boy as a lover. Never been done. Big scandal. Big headlines. A new twist on an old plot. Welcome to the millennium."

I looked into her astonished face, and put my arm around her ample waist. As weak as I was, we glided onto the ballroom floor.

As everyone from Swanson to Garbo, from Dietrich to Crawford, looked on in awe, the last dance of the 20th century had begun.